THE

SEPOY'S DAUGHTER:

A TRUE TALE OF THE INDIAN WAR.

BY

AN EYE WITNESS.

"Vain has the painter's art, the poet's muse—
The fruitless task in vain have they essay'd ;—
All art must fail, and language must refuse
To paint the charms of the young INDIAN MAID."

NAOMIE.

LONDON:

HENRY LEA, WARWICK LANE, PATERNOSTER ROW.

THE
SEPOY'S DAUGHTER.

"Vain has the painter's art, the poet's muse—
The fruitless task in vain have they essay'd; —
All art must fail, and language must refuse
To paint the charms of the young INDIAN MAID."

NAOMIE. *A Poem.*

CHAPTER I.

THE VILLIA ON THE BANKS OF THE JUMNA —OMELIA, THE SEPOY'S DAUGHTER.

BRITISH INDIA! The eastern world— that world of wealth, romance, ot novelty, and of mystery—land of all that is lovely, grand, and sublime in nature and in art; land of pleasant skies, and gorgeous land- scapes—of rich flowers, and brilliant plu- maged birds—of beautiful trees, and luxu- rious fruits—of magnificent palaces, and majestic temples—of noble rivers, and mighty cataracts. Who while reading of thee, has not felt the imagination kindle until it became lost and bewildered in the contemplation of the boundless power and resources of Great Britain; which for a century has held this mighty territory under its dominion

Alas, that foul treachery and rebellion should beset that favoured country—deluging the land with the blood of our best and most heroic sons—and that heartless miscreants, with the sanguinary malice of fiends, should hitherto have triumphed in their atrocities : in the wholesale outrage and slaughter of our own innocent country-women and children, and in the perpetration of such crimes

"As e'en make angels weep."

The hour of retribution, however, is at hand ; and terrible is the storm of vengeance which must shortly overtake those monsters disgracing the human form.

But to our tale.

The native population of India are, generally speaking, in keeping with the scenery of their country. They are picturesque in their costumes, simple in their modes of life, and imaginative. Their language is poetry itself. The heat of the climate causes them to live comparatively out of doors, and their verandahs and gardens answer to the parlours and drawing-rooms, and even the sleeping apartments of the houses, in this country. They ever have the heavens and glorious nature around them ; and in such scenes the heart should expand, and the more graceful attributes of the intellect find exercise,

The setting sun still had left a soft mingled stain of saffron and crimson on the broad waters of the river Jumna ; a refreshing coolness filled the air, and imparted a feeling of exquisite pleasure to the senses. Here might the eye wander over and revel upon scenery of the richest luxuriance. At one time a wooded promontory stretching into the water bounded the view —at another, a wide expanse of water opened before it, studded with islands, and apparently leading to regions of still greater enchantment.

The bamboo flung its long branches down with all the grace of the willow ; the noble palm tree rose in regal majesty above, and the beautiful foliage of both was relieved by the bright masses of the neem, the peupul, and a host of others—many bearing resplendent flowers of a thousand dyes. In every direction, as far as the eye could trace, (near the *ghauts,* or landing-places, built from the banks into the water), might be seen a mosque, or pagoda, or a series of small Hindoo temples : the rays of the setting sun, shining on the domes and minarets of the former, peeping through the branches of the trees, added to the general effect.

And now the shadows of night fell around, and the scene, if possible, became still more beautiful and picturesque. Innumerable lamps were lighted in the temples, the glimmering of which through the trees, had the appearance of so many small beacons. Some of the trees appeared to be illuminated, from the multitudes of fire-flies which glanced in and out, emitting a greenish, golden light, like that which would proceed from a lamp formed of emeralds. Many of these luminous insects flashed like meteors along the air, rendering the night more beautiful, even in the presence of the stars, which so thickly and so brightly studded the glittering firmament.

We must now invite the attention of the reader to one of the most handsome of the numerous fairy-like residences situated in this romantic and delightful locality. It stood only a short distance from Agra, the capital of Akbur, on the left bank of the Jumna, in the midst of charming gardens, and was elegant and tasteful in a most eminent degree. Like most eastern dwellings, the windows and doors were open night and day, and the fresh and balmy air circulated freely through all parts.

Nothing could surpass the beauty of the situation of this elegant building. The ground sloped gently to the banks of the river, of which an extensive view was there obtained. Those who have seen a gilded French bird-cage, with wings and galleries, might form some notion of this villa—especially if they should imagine the gilded cage placed down in a bed of flowers, or made the centre of a little paradise, where there was everything to charm the eye, and to captivate the senses.

The interior of this building was in perfect keeping with its external aspect. The walls were covered with the most beautiful and highly-finished paintings, and the ceilings were richly ornamented with frescos in the most exquisite taste. The columns of the verandahs were painted a pure white, and the gilded capitals gave them a chaste, yet brilliant effect. Then there were marble tesselated floors—rich draperies—splendid mirrors — magnificent furniture — costly vases, containing the choicest flowers—and everything that luxurious fancy and oriental splendour could conceive to dazzle the sight, and to excite the spectator's wonder, admiration, and delight.

Fountains played in the gardens and courts, which cooled the air. The branches of the ever-green fruit-trees bent beneath the weight of luscious fruit, and were musical with the ceaseless song of birds of every variety, of the most gorgeous plumage.

If the palace (for such it might justly be called), was not in itself sufficient to denote the wealth of the fortunate possessor, there were other circumstances that would have removed all doubts upon that subject. Numerous domestics, in handsome costumes, and turbans of white muslin, with gold and silver bands interspersed among the folds, were ready at every turn to obey the commands which might be given them, and many were the services exacted from them, which they were always attentive to perform. You could not give the slightest expression of desire which they were not prompt to obey. When the air was so sultry, hot, and oppressive, that (even to the natives and others inured to the heat of the climate), it became almost insupportable, these domestics, or slaves, would kneel before you, and exert themselves to impart relief to you with fans made of the feathers of the bird of paradise. When you wished to go abroad, they waited ready to carry you in gilded palanquins, covered with rich silken canopies. All in that beautiful villa, in fact, was luxury, repose, and elegant indolence; all around it was lovely, magnificent, and picturesque; like some beauteous scene of fabled land, such as the European, who has never been in India, can scarcely realize are upon the earth.

All this magnificence, together with the number of domestics (not forgetting that rather useful one, namely, the *Durwun*, or doorkeeper, who sits at the entrance gate, and sounds a gong upon the arrival of a visitor), were sufficient to show the wealth of the occupants of this beautiful villa. It was, in fact, the favourite residence of Mr. Arthur Melville, one of the richest and most esteemed merchants of India, whose whole hopes and affections were centered in his only daughter, the fair and amiable Flora Melville.

But there was yet another member of his family for whom Mr. Melville felt almost the affection of a father. This was a beautiful young Indian girl, (not more than seventeen), whom he had taken under his protection, (more as a companion to his daughter than a domestic), on the death of her mother, (an Englishwoman), in pity to the poverty of her father, a Sepoy, and a man of questionable character. But, of the lovely Omelia, more anon.

At the end of those charming gardens, (in the midst of which the villa stood, and which have been so minutely described), was a handsome little terrace, with gilded pallisades, and tesselated pavement, which commanded an almost uninterrupted view of the river, and the grand and romantic scenery which adorned its banks.

A noble flight of marble steps leading from this terrace, as is usual, ended in a ghaut, and near to them, on an elevated plot of ground stood a handsome Hindoo temple. The stairs were strewed from the top to the bottom with fresh flowers of the most beautiful description. Long garlands of the Indian jessamine, a large white double blossom, with a rich but heavy perfume—or of a large scarlet or yellow flower, hung over the rails, or were thrown into the water as propitiatory offerings.

And here, at the calm and tranquil hour before mentioned, leaning gracefully over the pallisades of the terrace, (her dark and brilliant eyes gazing earnestly and anxiously across the noble river, and her glossy raven tresses sporting playfully in the light evening breeze), might be seen the lovely and majestic form of the young OMELIA, THE SEPOY'S DAUGHTER.

It is indeed an arduous, if not a fruitless task, to endeavour to give any thing like an adequate description of the glowing charms of that young Indian maid. Her complexion was a bright clear olive; her features, which were formed in the most perfect mould, shewed the English blood which flowed in her veins from her mother, and were marked by intelligence, and all the courage and determination of a heroine.

The expression of her eyes, in which love and sensibility, and every womanly feeling were sweetly blended, could not be gazed upon without feelings of the greatest reverence and admiration. Her lips when slightly separated revealed teeth of shining whiteness that no pearls could rival.

The costume of Omelia, (like that of most Indian maidens, even of the humblest station in life), combined neatness and simplicity with taste and elegance. It was picturesque and characteristic in the extreme. A rich silken scarf or kerchief modestly concealed the delicate beauties of her throbbing bosom. A handsome skirt or petticoat of the most costly material descended from her waist to a little below the knees, shewing legs and ancles of the most perfect grace and symmetry, to the best advantage. Golden bracelets adorned her arms, wrists, and ancles; large gold rings with pendants of the same precious metal, decorated her ears; and a gold band set in with valuable jewels encircled her head, in the centre of which was one of the beautiful feathers of the bird of paradise. Her long taper fingers were also covered with rings of great value; in fact the appearance of Omelia, altogether, was more that of an Indian princess, than of a humble Sepoy's daughter. It was the pride of her kind benefactors, (Mr. Melville and his daughter) to see her so, and it was more in compliance with their wishes than her own desire, that she assumed so costly a dress.

And there on that handsome terrace, Omelia continued to stand, straining her eyes anxiously over the vast expanse, and her bosom heaving and throbbing as if with some powerful inward emotion.

The sun had now set, but myriads of the most brilliant stars glistened in the heavens, rendering the whole lovely scene as light and distinct as at noonday. But even amidst all this grandure of scenery on which the eyes of Omelia eagerly dwelt, the noblest feature of all was the Taj Mehal, the most splendid monument in Hindoostan, a tomb constructed at the instance of the Mogul Emperor, Shah Jehan, in commemoration of his beautiful queen, Norr Jehan—the light of the world.

This building which is erected near the City of Agra, and stands upon the north side of a large quadrangle, looking down into the clear blue stream of the river Jumna, cost 3,174,802*l*, and occupied 20,000 labourers and architects for twenty-two years!

The dazzling stars and innumerable lamps now lighted in the different little bee-hived shaped temples that adorned the banks of the river, shone brilliantly on this stupendous pile, showing its high walls of red sandstone, its magnificient gateway and beautiful mosques, with bewildering effect.

Omelia remained in the same attitude for some time, but at length an expression of sadness and disappointment overspread her beauteous features, and a deep sigh escaped her bosom.

"Oh, why comes he not?" she said, in melancholy and impatient tones. "Why does my fond and anxious heart throb in vain to meet him? Why do my straining eyes watch fruitlessly the appearance of his noble manly form; my eager ears vainly listen to catch the music of his voice? Ah! Edward, I fear your truant heart begins to wander from the poor Indian girl, who too readily, too confidently believed the fond vows of eternal love and constancy you plighted to her. But," she added, after a pause, her dark eyes flashing with a passionate and indignant expression, her features assuming a look of mingled scorn, pride, and resolution, and her bosom heaving violently, "he must not, he *dare not* trifle with Omelia's feelings thus. He has won her woman's heart—let him not despise the conquest—he hath raised her thoughts, her hopes, her wishes to bliss : let him beware, should he disappoint them and deceive her. Omelia can hate as deeply as she can love, and injustice can goad her on to revenge!"

Again she paused in the agitation of her excited feelings, and she knit her brows, and compressed her lips, in the intensity of painful thought and rising passion. But these emotions were only transient;—the dark clouds vanished from her handsome features, and were succeeded by bright and hopeful smiles, and in a voice of happy confidence, she exclaimed—

"No, no, dearest Edward, I will not, cannot doubt your faithful love;—I wrong your manly heart even by the bare supposition. Deceit or treachery ne'er for one moment could find a place within your noble, generous breast; and even if it could, and she should find you false as she believes you true, base, perfidious as guilt could make you, so fondly, so deeply is your image enshrined in Omelia's heart,—so firmly, so irrevocably is it linked with all her dearest hopes, her proudest ambition,—that her heart must break, must cease to beat, ere she could cease to love you with all the fervent, pure, and glowing passion that can only warm the fond Indian maiden's blood."

She ceased; and joy, and love, and confidence animated every feature of her beautiful countenance, and seemed to add grace and dignity to her noble and commanding figure.

Suddenly she started, as her quick ears caught the distant sounds of something on the water, and she once more strained her eager eyes across the river, in the direction from which they proceeded, while her heart throbbed with mingled feelings of hope, doubt, and expectation.

An exclamation of delight escaped her lips, and she joyfully clapped her hands at the object, which at first only indistinctly met her observation.

It was one of those beautiful and gaily-painted vessels, which ply the Indian rivers, the graceful *bholio*, somewhat resembling, though more brilliant in its decorations, the Venetian gondola. It is a pleasant sight to behold, on a fine, bright day, when there is not a speck to be seen on the clear blue sky,—these vessels, together with the frigate-like pinnace, and the handsome *budgerow*, dance upon the glittering surface of the river, or spreading their white sails to the breeze, glide merrily along. Then, too, are they strangely contrasted with the other crafts that numerously throng the river, such as boats of various dimensions, and the little *dinghee*, which looks as if the centre was formed of a hogshead, for it has all that resemblance, from the sort of awning or cabin, raised as a protection against the weather, and some of the larger kinds are rendered still more picturesque in appearance by having thatched roofs, or choppers, as they are called, a ragged sail, somewhat the colour of ochre, and by long garlands of white, yellow, and scarlet flowers, festooned from the prow.

Steadily the vessel, on which the eyes of Omelia were so attentively fixed, glided on the surface of the water from the opposite bank, in the direction of the spot on which she stood; and her heart throbbed at double its wonted pace; and she scarcely dared to breathe, as she watched its progress.

Nearer and nearer it approached, and gradually more distinct it became, until Omelia could perceive the forms of men, one of whom stood upright at the head of the vessel, in an attitude of eager impatience; and the heart of the Indian girl leaped for joy, as she was enabled to scan his person more narrowly, and could distinguish the uniform, and military cap of a British officer.

"'Tis he!—'tis he!" she joyfully exclaimed, "he comes,—and all my fearful doubts and unfounded suspicions are banished!—dear Edward, how could I ever, even for a moment, entertain a thought to your prejudice?"

With a light heart, she hastened down the steps of the terrace, and took her stand at the end of the ghaut, still more eagerly watching the approaching vessel.

Onward it came, proudly and gracefully, the favouring breeze seeming to waft it more rapidly towards the shore, on the appearance of the lovely girl, whose eyes were filled with tears—tears of joy and gratitude—as she gazed upon it.

The man standing in the boat now evidently saw and recognized her, for he waived a handkerchief in the air as if to greet her, and she answered the signal by a cry of delight and welcome, which was borne by the wind towards him.

Another minute and the vessel glided to its destination, and was moored behind the drooping branches of a beautiful bamboo-tree which grew near the ghaut; there was a hurried footstep on the shore; a rustling sound among the foliage; an exclamation of joy, and Omelia was enfolded in the arms of the beloved being she had so fondly expected.

CHAPTER II.

LOVERS' VOWS.—THREATENED DANGER—THE INTERRUPTION.—FATHER AND DAUGHTER.

The long expected lover of our heroine, and who now clasped her so rapturously to his bosom, was Lieutenant Stanley, a young Englishman, who, although not more than three-and-twenty years of age, had already seen much service. He had come out to India as a Cadet, about six years' previous to the time of which we are writing; and by his indomitable gallantry and perseverance, had quickly rose to fame and promotion.

For the lovely Omelia, Edward Stanley felt a passion as pure and ardent as it was sincere; and he was happy in the assurance that the Indian maid returned his love with equal fervour. There might have been insurmountable obstacles in the way, had young Stanley not possessed the strength of mind and the resolution to overcome them. He was connected with a noble and wealthy family. Omelia was only a poor humble Sepoy's daughter, living on the bounty of others; besides, he was fondly loved by the fair and gentle Flora Melville, whom he sincerely esteemed for her numerous virtues, but had never given any encouragement to her unfortunate passion.

The first meeting of Edward Stanley with Omelia, was on the occasion of his paying a visit to another of the houses of Mr. Melville, (who was an old friend of his father), in Delhi, and from that moment he was compelled to acknowledge his heart a captive to her superior intrinsic and personal charms.

Twice subsequently he had saved her life; once from drowning when capsized in a boat on the river, and a second time from the deadly bite of a serpent which had entwined itself around the trunk of a tree, and was about to make its fatal spring upon her.

These noble acts, if the young Englishman had not previously inspired the breast of Omelia with a warmer sentiment than that of esteem, were sufficient to kindle the passion of love in her susceptible heart, and when he revealed the secret of his dearest hopes, and solemnly declared the honour of his intentions, she candidly confessed the favorable impression he had made upon her, and they mutually vowed eternal constancy.

Although Stanley and Omelia ever used the utmost precaution when in the society of Flora Melville, her keen observation and jealous fears shortly penetrated the secret of their hearts; and although she never disclosed or even made the slightest allusion to the discovery she had made, although torturing were the feelings of disappointed hopes, and deep regret it cost her.

Thus matters stood up to the eventful period of which we are writing, which was some time previous to the outbreak of that revolt which has already been the cause of so many fearful tragedies, and which will be vividly and graphically described in the course of our tale.

"Are we alone, Omelia?" enquired the young man, in a low, cautious voice, gently withdrawing himself from her embrace, and looking eagerly and anxiously around.

Omelia answered in the affirmative.

"Are you certain, dear Omelia," said Edward, "that there is no prying eye to watch us—no eager, curious ear to listen to our conversation?"

"There is not, Edward," replied the fair Indian girl, "for Mr. Melville and his daughter are from home, and the domestics are all in the house. But why do you put those anxious questions, and look so suspiciously about you, as though you feared that——"

"Fear, Omelia?" interrupted Stanley, proudly—"'tis a word unknown to Englishmen—yet prudence, and all necessary precaution, should ever guide their actions, especially in the hour of danger."

"What mean you, dearest Edward?" eagerly interrogated Omelia; "danger, said you?"

"Aye," returned her lover — "dark treachery stalks abroad, and has already shown itself with daring front among the Sepoys stationed at Meerut."

"The Sepoys!" repeated our heroine, in a voice of extreme agitation; "and at Meerut? But my father—oh, tell me—know you anything of him?"

"Oh, how it pains me, my own loved Omelia, to have to mention anything which may cause your gentle bosom the slightest anguish. Your father has hitherto taken no active part with his mutinous comrades, who were quickly disarmed, and many of them condemned to severe punishment; but he and others are watched with suspicion, and it grieves me to be compelled to acknowledge, that in those suspicions I likewise participate."

"Alas, alas," sighed Omelia, "too well do I know the evil passions which distort his mind; his dark, his deep, designing nature. Alas! that a daughter in her regard for truth, should be compelled thus to speak of one whom it is her duty to love and revere. And you, Edward," she added —and her lovely bosom swelled with emotion — and a tear trembled in her eye; —"alas! my heart which—— leave me, Edward—fate frowns upon us—we must meet no more."

"Leave you, dear Omelia," ejaculated her lover, looking anxiously in her beautiful face, and pressing her delicate hands vehemently between his own—"alas! what have I said? What have I done, to excite this sudden feeling in your breast? You sigh —you tremble, and now you avert your looks as though you feared to meet my gaze. Dearest Omelia; fondly cherished being; you, whose fair form is ever present to my enraptured sight—even when distance separates us from each other; you, whose gentle voice, sleeping or waking, is ever in mine ears, breathing heavenly melody to my senses; you cannot—oh, you do not, doubt the fervour and sincerity of my love?"

"No, no;" returned Omelia, in a voice of the greatest emotion, "I cannot doubt the sincerity of that beloved being, who I believe to be all truth and honour. And oh, the bright, fond visions of hope and happiness that I have indulged in; it was presumptuous for one who eats alone the bread of charity to do so. You are noble, wealthy, and——leave me, I repeat, Edward Stanley; the scion of a proud and ancient English family can never become the husband of the poor humble Indian Sepoy's daughter."

"Stay, Omelia," exclaimed the young man, with increased vehemence, and detaining her as she was about to hurry away, "by heaven and all my hopes, those fond hopes which alone are centred on you, you shall not leave me thus! Cruel, cruel, girl, to think so meanly of me as to believe that the difference of our stations can prejudice the love I bear you, and which is prompted by the purest and most honourable of motives. I should loathe and despise myself could I love the simple beauteous Indian maiden but for her virtues alone. Perish rank, fortune, name, everything sooner than the passion which glows within my breast, which awakens every pulsation of my heart, that heart which now, and ever must until it cease to beat, proudly and fondly acknowledges Omelia as its mistress!"

With a burst of rapturous emotion, the lovely girl sunk upon his manly bosom, and sobs choked her utterance. But she hastily raised her head, disengaged herself from his arms, and looked anxiously towards a cluster of trees, between whose branches glimmered the lights from one of the Hindoo temples, as a noise among the shrubs and tall grass saluted her ears.

"Hark!" she said, in cautious whispering accents; "some one approaches; leave me, dear Edward, we know not what might be the consequences should we be discovered."

"Nay, dearest Omelia, you——"

"Oh, do not hesitate, for my anxious fears suggest some danger is at hand. And now I catch the shadow of an approaching form yonder. Quick! quick! if you really love me, you will instantly obey."

"We will meet again."

"Yes, yes; pray begone."

"To-morrow evening at the hour of eight, here."

"I will be punctual. Farewell."

"Adieu, sweetest," fervently ejaculated the young man, as he hastily raised her hand to his lips! "Oh, may heaven and all good angels watch over to protect and bless you."

With these words, he darted from the spot and quickly disappeared behind the bamboo-tree, near which the *bholio* awaited him, just as the approaching form of a man was more distinctly seen coming from a different direction. It was evident that his eye had caught sight of Omelia, for he hallooed to her, and quickened his pace to come up to her. Omelia needed no more to urge her to hurry away, and she ran along the Ghaut and ascended the flight of steps to the terrace, which she hastily traversed, and entered the gardens. But the man called loudly upon her to stop, in a commanding and authoritative tone of voice, and she could hear his footsteps gaining fast upon her. This added to her fears, and she quickened her speed towards the house; but she had not proceeded many paces when her foot came in contact with something on the ground; she stumbled, and must have fallen, had not her wrist at that moment been grasped fiercely by a powerful hand, at the same time a harsh, disagreeable voice exclaimed—

"Stop, girl!—has your disobedient heart become so insensible to the dictates of nature, that you fly affrighted from your *father*, as if he were some wild and savage beast of the jungle?"

Omelia started with fear and trembling at the sound of that well-known and dreaded voice, and she gazed with a feeling of terror at the forbidding features of her parent, those features which were now rendered still more repulsive in their expression from the effect of the evil passions which agitated his guilty breast. He still retained his fierce hold of the maiden's wrist, and his dark piercing eyes were fixed sternly upon her countenance, as though he would penetrate into the very secrets of her soul. Omelia shrank appalled beneath his gaze, and for a moment or two could not utter a word.

Yunadar, the father of Omelia, was a man about forty years of age, of gigantic stature, and athletic proportions. His features might have been termed handsome, were it not for the constant expression of low cunning, sarcastic bitterness, and devilry which distorted them. The whole tone of his countenance, in fact, bespoke a mind of no common order, although vitiated, and corrupted by some of the worst passions and predilections that could pollute the human breast. A black, shaggy beard, a moustache covered his chin and upper lip, and his hair hung in long black silken flakes upon his neck. Altogether he presented a striking appearance, but that of a man whose anger few would like to provoke.

His dress was that of a Sepoy of superior class, and there was that in his whole demeanour which seemed to denote him as one born to command, and enforce obedience.

"Father," at length said Omelia, in a tremulous voice; "grasp not my wrist so fiercely, nor look upon me with such eyes of wrath. I—I know you not! What brings you hither so mysteriously, and at so unseasonable an hour!"

"To whisper a secret in your ear," he replied, somewhat relaxing his hold; "and to tell you that you must with me."

"With you?"

"Aye, this night,—this very hour."

"Leave those kind friends, those benefactors to whom I owe a lasting debt of gratitude it is impossible I can ever repay? Oh, never!—never!" vehemently exclaimed Omelia.

"But you must, you shall," cried Yunadar, resolutely; "it is my will, my determination,—and you dare not disobey!"

"Oh, why would you have me abandon them?"

"They are English."

"Generous, noble minded English, and therefore do I honour and revere them."

"You must hate them, girl,—loath them as you would the savage tiger who preys upon the human race."

"Forbid it, every sacred power."

"Beware!—dare not to exasperate me. They would lure you from the faith of your forefathers, as they have already alienated your affections from me. They would make you Christian, and bring a curse upon your head, and all those who by the ties of kindred are connected with you."

"By all my hopes you wrong them,—basely, cruelly, wrong them, by such a supposition," exclaimed Omelia, her fine eyes flashing with indignation at the aspersions thrown upon the characters of her friends; "they have never sought to do so but by their own virtuous example;—their disinterested kindness and benevolence which has protected me with parental affection ever since my poor mother's death, hath won my love and gratitude; but they have never, by word or deed, tried to convert me to their way of thinking;—no, they are too just, too generous, to endeavour to coerce that liberty of conscience they demand for themselves; and had they acted otherwise, by every righteous power I swear, not all the love and reverence I bear them should have tempted the poor Sepoy's daughter to abandon that faith which, from her very inmost soul, she believes to be the only true and just one!"

Yunadar seemed confused and confounded by the energy and apparent sincerity with which Omelia gave utterance to these words, and turning his head away, and folding his arms, remained silent for a few moments, and appeared to be communing with himself. At length he turned sharply round upon her, as a sudden thought seemed to strike him, and, fixing his eyes with searching enquiry upon her countenance, in a stern voice demanded—

"What man was that I saw leave the ghaut, as I advanced?"

"Father, father," replied the poor girl, in a voice of alarm, "I pray you urge me not."

"No equivocation, girl!" cried Yunadar, in a voice of passionate impatience; "but answer me, and that quickly. Who was he I saw leave you in such haste?"

"A young English officer," answered our heroine, firmly—and mustering up all her energies for the task—"and one who merits esteem and admiration from all honourable men!"

A fearful expression passed over the dark features of the Sepoy, as Omelia thus expressed herself; and grasping her wrist more violently than before, in a voice rendered hoarse by passion, he exclaimed—

"The accursed Feringee, (Englishman) the christian dog!—and you, base, abandoned girl, to hold secret and unlawful meetings with him!"

"Begone, cruel libeller of an innocent woman!" cried Omelia, forcibly releasing herself from his hold, her fine majestic figure rising to its full height, and her black and brilliant eyes seeming to flash sparks of shame and indignation—"begone, I command; Omelia can learn to loathe and despise that man who basely and unjustly dares to suspect his daughter's honour and virtue!"

Yunadar was completely abashed and astounded; he could scarcely believe the evidence of his ears, and he gazed upon the handsome countenance of his noble-minded daughter, (as she fixed the most piercing looks of reproach and resentment upon him), with mingled feelings of astonishment and admiration.

He, however, quickly recovered himself, and once more seizing her resolutely by the arm, he cried, in a voice which shewed it was useless to attempt to oppose him—

"This way, girl, this way;—you shall not, dare not resist a father's authority!"

"Unhand me!"—said Omelia, trying to release herself;—"what would you do?"

"This way, I repeat;"—he answered sternly; "my determination is fixed (should it not be too late to accomplish my present wishes), and you are powerless to resist it!"

Thus saying, in spite of all her efforts to disengage herself from his grasp,—her tears and supplications,—he forced her back to the terrace, and descending from the ghaut, hurried her towards that part of the river's brink near which the vessel of the young lieutenant was moored while he had his interview with Omelia.

A foreboding of some approaching danger to his beloved Omelia, had caused Edward Stanley to linger for some time on the shore after they had separated, and he was half inclined to hasten to the gardens, and to watch about the villa till daylight. But all remaining quiet, and observing nothing to excite his further suspicions, he concluded that all was right, and that the man whose sudden appearance had alarmed himself and Omelia, was merely one of the domestics, who was returning to the villa, he stepped into the *bholio*, taking his former stand in it, and giving the order to the men who had accompanied him, the vessel slipped from its moorings, and gracefully glided past the bamboo-tree which grew on the bank, across the river towards the opposite shore.

It was at that moment that the revengeful Sepoy and his daughter reached the spot from which the vessel had just departed, and the fierce eye of Yunadar immediately rested upon it, and the commanding form of the young lieutenant as he stood in the boat.

"Ah!" he exclaimed, in tones of malicious exultation, "by all my hopes of vengeance, see, he is there! If my good pistol miss not its aim, he shall not escape me!"

As he thus spoke, he drew forth a pistol which he had had concealed beneath his clothes, and levelled it at Stanley, but ere he could discharge the fatal contents, with an exclamation of horror, Omelia successfully arrested his arm, and in the meantime, a fresh breeze springing up, the *bholio* glided quickly out of danger.

CHAPTER III.

THE SEQUEL OF THE ADVENTURE.

"Rash, cruel man!" cried our heroine, in a voice that would have been sufficient to shame him into forbearance, had not his stubborn, reckless heart been quite insensible to every feeling of remorse; "would you commit murder?"

"I would save your honour from destruction," replied her father, and rescue you from that terrible tempest which will shortly sweep the land, and annihilate the whole Christian population, the hatred usurpers and oppressors, who for nearly a century have held us slaves beneath their iron rule, and basely, treacherously, trampled on all our rights under the name of civilization!"

"What fearful import is there in your words? Explain the dark mystery of your ambiguous words?" demanded Omelia, with looks of anxious terror.

"Listen," said Yunadar, again grasping the shocked and trembling maiden by the wrist, and emphasising every word he uttered with terrible meaning;—"already is the spark laid to the train, and awful will be the explosion which will shortly follow, inundating the tyrant enemies of our country and religion at one fell swoop. But a few days since I beheld the stalwart limbs of many of my gallant comrades, manacled with the felon's galling fetters, and themselves doomed to a life of slavery, of brutal toil, and degradations. With burning indignation and flushing eyes, myself and many others beheld the monstrous outrage, and it but served to fan the fierce flame of vengeance which was already kindled in our breasts. That vengeance may be slow, but it is nevertheless certain."

"Forbear, be calm," expostulated Omelia, "the misguided men must have grossly committed themselves, and doubtless merited their fate."

"'Tis false!" exclaimed Yunadar; "they did but resist an unjust outrage on their faith, and they would have been base and despicable had they not done so. Know ye not, girl, that these hated English want to convert us all, and they begin by destroying our sacred customs. They have invoked the law to put down Suttees:—they have suppressed infanticide and sacrifices;—they have decreed that Hindoo widows shall marry if they choose;—they have interfered with the law of succession;—they have destroyed the thrones of the Mahommedan rulers; they would now defile our lips with the fat of unclean beasts! Shall we tamely endure these outrages? We, who are numbered by millions, shall we submit to the yoke of a mere handful of unbelievers? Hindoo tradition, and Mahommedan prophecy, though dating far back, equally fix the present time, as the epoch of the finale of foreign rule. My heart, nay, my very soul are in the righteous

No. 2.

cause, and I will not rest satisfied till I have slaked the burning thirst of my vengeance in the blood of the detested race."

As the savage Sepoy thus gave expression to his guilty feelings, his features assumed a look that was totally unlike anything human, and which made Omelia shudder to contemplate.

"Abandon those frightful designs," she remonstrated; "repent, relent, ere it is too late!"

"Never!" cried her father, with fierce determination; "I have sworn to lend my utmost aid in the destruction of those wretches we have so much cause to loathe, and no power shall urge me, no persuasion induce me to break my oath."

"Then hear me, heartless, cruel, and inexorable man," returned his daughter, firmly; "from this moment I stop the natural throbbings of my heart towards you: I discard you from my breast for ever; no more will I remember you with any other feelings than those of shame and horror: Omelia would look upon herself with disgust, could she acknowledge the cold-blooded murderer of the innocent, for her father!"

"Rash girl!" exclaimed Yunadar, furiously, "dare you thus boldly reproach and defy me? Dare you treat my authority with contempt, and beard me as a villain of the blackest dye. Oh, you have indeed been an apt pupil of the accursed; willingly, readily have you imbibed the poison from their lips; be mine the task then, to forcibly snatch you from the fearful abyss of destruction, on the very brink of which you stand. Be mine the task to recall you to reason, and bring you to repent of the dangerous course you have hitherto pursued: no more trifling, girl; resistance is vain; all is secure; there is no one near to aid you; too long have I already delayed, but nothing can now move me from my purpose. This way;—this way;—you must, you shall accompany me to the place of my destination."

"Whither would you hurry me?" said the terrified girl, struggling violently as her father endeavoured to force her away. "Spare me! mercy! oh, help! help!"

He, however, heeded not her cries, and laughed her desperate efforts to release herself to scorn. The triumph of his guilty designs seemed certain, for all chance of any assistance in that lonely spot, and such an hour, seemed to be completely hopeless, and Omelia's strength was nearly exhausted. But at that critical moment, to the relief of the poor girl, the shouts of men sounded on the air, followed by the loud report of firearms, and several shots wizzed past them, one slightly grazing the arm of Yunadur, and causing him to relax his hold of his daughter.

"Confusion!" he exclaimed; "what accursed fate hath brought this interference about? shall I at the very moment of my anticipated success, be thwarted in my designs?"

The shouts of the men were repeated, and sounded nearer; and directly afterwards, several of the domestics of the villa were seen rapidly approaching the spot from the garden. At the same moment, Yunadur, with a dreadful oath, hurled Omelia from him, and she sunk senseless to the earth; her father bounding away at the top of his speed, and managing to make his escape before the domestics could arrive at the spot.

Two or three of them hurried in the pursuit of the revengeful Sepoy, and the others raised the insensible Omelia from the earth, and conveyed her into the villa, to which Mr. Melville and his daughter had returned only a few minutes before, and were much surprised and alarmed at what had occurred.

On recovering her senses, Omelia felt much relieved on again finding herself safe in the villa, and in the presence of her benefactors; but the questions which they naturally put to her, as to the particulars of the alarming event, confused and agitated her; for if she answered them correctly, she must not only be compelled to reveal the guilt of her father, but also acknowledge the sentiments that existed between her and Edward Stanley, and their clandestine meeting. Her conscience revolted at the idea of telling an untruth, but still she could not find the resolution to relate the particulars of the facts exactly as they had occurred: and she therefore endeavoured to evade the questions that Mr. Melville and Flora put to her, as well as she was able; although she could not help thinking that the latter especially seemed to look upon her statements with doubt and suspicion.

"What could be the motive of this man, Omelia, whom you describe as wearing the dress of one of the Sepoys," said Flora, "for committing so daring an outrage, and attempting to convey you away by force from the villa? Had you any knowledge of his features?"

"Oh, yes," answered our heroine, sincerely; "alas, they were too painfully familiar to me, although it is some time since I saw them before; but I cannot reveal his name."

"'Tis strange," observed Mr. Melville; "I fear there is much more in this mysterious event than we can fathom for the present."

"Oh, yes sir," said Omelia, eagerly "there is indeed, I have too much reason to fear, and I tremble for the danger which seems to threaten you and Miss Flora, from the guilty machinations of revengeful men."

"How?" said Mr. Melville, with a look of surprise and incredulity; "what mean you, Omelia? It has ever been the study of myself and my daughter, as you know, to conciliate by acts of kindness, urbanity. and benovelence, the good opinion and esteem of all classes of the community who came within the sphere of our knowledge; and I had flattered myself with the idea that we had not an enemy in the station."

"Ah! how little, my kind benefactors, do you deserve to have the enmity of anyone," remarked Omelia; "but who are those, even among the most amiable of mankind, that shall escape deceit, jealousy, and ingratitude? Dark hints and threats escaped the man who attempted to force me away from your protection, that made me shudder to think on. The spirit of revolt, as you are probably aware, has lately exhibited itself among some of the native troops, caused by a malicious report industriously circulated, to the effect that it is the intention of the Government to compel them to become converts to Christianity, and in consequence they have secretly sworn a terrible revenge against the English, which it is supposed they only await the first favourable opportunity to carry into effect. Already the mysterious cakes, and the lotus flower (sure signs of approaching danger), have passed from hand to hand; and I fear the evil passions thus engendered, will never be satisfied until their nefarious designs are accomplished."

"Misguided men," said Mr. Melville; "they know not what they do; but I trust that they will be awakened to a full sense of the injustice and wickedness of their designs, ere they madly proceed to such extremities as must inevitably lead to their own destruction."

"Alas!" ejaculated our heroine, "when the Hindoo's evil passions are once aroused, there is no atrocity they will shrink from perpetrating in order to gratify their revenge. My mind forebodes the worst, but it is for you, my dearest friends, that my worst fears are more immediately excited, after that which I have this night heard; for much do I fear that the protection you have hitherto so kindly granted to the poor humble being before you, has aroused a feeling of hatred and suspicion against you, which may be productive of the most fatal consequences, unless the unfortunate cause be instantly removed. Oh, let me no longer remain here to endanger the peace and safety of those revered beings, whose happiness is far more precious to me than mine own existence. Suffer me to depart from hence, with your blessing and good wishes, and "depend upon it, that wherever the footsteps of the humble Indian girl may roam, and in whatsoever circumstances, she may by fate be placed, she will never cease to remember the inestimable obligations she is under to you with feelings of the most unbounded gratitude and love."

As the poor girl thus eloquently gave expression to the thoughts that so warmly glowed within her breast, she knelt respectfully at the feet of Mr. Melville and Flora, and raising a hand of each, fervently to her lips, bathed them with her tears.

"Come, come, my good Omelia," observed Mr. Melville, kindly raising her from her humble posture; "I must hear no more of these sad thoughts and forebodings;—but you must endeavour to banish them from your mind. Leave us, helpless and otherwise friendless as you are, my dear child, the idea is preposterous, and I wonder how it could ever even for a moment have occurred to you. No, Omelia, you will never I know, never return a disinterested friendship with ingratitude, and we will never cease to watch over your welfare and happiness, with the same anxious care and solicitude, as if you were our nearest and dearest relative, while you continue to deserve it."

"Generous friends," cried Omelia; and she would again have sunk on her knees at their feet, nad they not prevented her; "such unexampled and disinterested benevolence as that which you evince towards me, quite overpowers me, and I know not what to say. What return can I ever make commensurate with your goodness. May the Great Spirit watch over and bless you, and your amiable daughter, Mr. Melville, and avert any evil that may be impending o'er you."

"Thanks, dear Omelia, for your affectionate wishes," observed Flora; "for I am convinced that they spring sincerely from your heart. But come, the hour is late, and 'tis time that we sought repose."

Omelia kissed the hand of Flora in acknowledgment of her kind opinion, and, after some further conversation, they bade each other farewell, and separated for the night.

CHAPTER IV.

THE RUINS OF THE OLD MOSQUE.—THE SECRET CONFERENCE.—THE PLOT.

Curses loud and deep escaped the lips of the guilty Yunadar, as he hurried on his way to avoid pursuit and detection. He plunged into the deepest, thickest, and most intricate part of the scenery on the river's bank, and having proceeded some considerable distance, he paused in his flight to take breath, and looking back, and perceiving no one near, and not hearing the least sound which might excite suspicion, he imagined that he had eluded the vigilance of his pursuers, and was now free from every danger which had before threatened him.

The bright stars still glistened in the firmament,—the lamps continued to burn in the different temples, shedding a mellow light upon the green foliage, and all was calm and tranquil as the sleep of infancy.

But fierce was the tempest of evil and conflicting passions that raged within the Sepoy's breast, and an expression of rage and disappointment clad his dark and forbidding features, as he stood in gloomy meditation.

"So," he muttered, "for the present I have suffered my plans to be frustrated through the daring resistance of a proud and obstinate girl. She has ventured to defy me, nay, even to heap upon me her reproaches and abuse, and I had the patience and forbearance to stand tamely by and listen to them, without offering to resent them. Fool that I was to do so; however, Omelia, your triumph will be but brief. Should my colleagues be true to their appointment to meet me to-night in the ruins of the old mosque, all may yet go well, and I will have both money (of which I so much stand in need to aid me in my daring schemes), and revenge. That presumptuous Feringee, who dares to aspire to my daughter's love, must also be discovered, and dealt with according to his deserts. He may thank his lucky stars that he this night escaped me. But why do I tarry here?—let me proceed."

Casting one more keen and penetrating glance around him, to be quite certain that the coast was clear, Yunadar proceeded quickly on his way, and diverging a little to the right, and forcing himself through the thickly entangled foliage, came at last upon a more open space of ground, but which was bounded on every side by towering hills and lofty promontories; on the summit of one of which, the ruins before mentioned stood.

They had a grand and picturesque appearance even in decay, and fully showed the former extent and magnificence of the ancient building. Part of the dome still remained, together with a couple of minarets; and one portion of the edifice had almost entirely escaped the ravages of time.

Yunadar stood for a minute or two with folded arms and contemplated the ruins, and then walking towards them, climbed the promontory on which they stood, entered them with a slow and cautious step.

All within was silent, solemn, and vacated; and, as the intruder trod the interior of those sacred ruins, he could not resist a feeling of awe from stealing over him, so strange, so impressive, and so gravely striking was everything around.

Such, however, were evidently not the feelings of Yunadar, as he wandered slowly through those gloomy precincts, the hollow echo of his own footsteps upon the broken pavement, being the only sound which broke the death-like stillness of the place. His thoughts were evidently upon another subject, and a grim expression of determination, anxiety, and disappointment sat upon his stern features.

"They are not here," he muttered to himself in surly accents, "and yet 'tis some time past the hour appointed. Why are they thus tardy, when there is such important work to do. Or can they have been, and not seeing me, imagined I had failed in my resolution, and abandoned my design, and therefore again departed to execute their plot alone? I had forgotten that it is I who am behind the time agreed upon to meet, in consequence of my delay with the stubborn, obstinate Omelia. I cannot doubt their fidelity to the daring cause we have at heart, for already has it been sufficiently tested. Hark!—surely I heard sounds. There again; let me be cautious, for such business as that which at present wholly engrosses my active, anxious mind, imperatively demands it. Hist!"

He stepped quickly and silently behind a broken column in the dark shadow of the dilapidated building, and listened and watched attentively. He was certain he could hear the stealthy tread of footsteps among the ruins, but still it might not be those whom he so anxiously expected; and now the probability that it might be those who had followed in pursuit of him, for the first time occurred to him; and, as it did so, he laid one hand upon his pistol, and with the other grasped a sword which he had brought with him, fully prepared to defend himself desperately in case of any emergency that might arise.

He was not long kept in suspense, for presently a peculiar whistle sounded from a distant part of the ruins, which was repeated three times; each whistle varying in the peculiarity of its tone.

The dark features of Yunadar relaxed in their stern and sullen expression, and his eyes brightened as he listened to these sounds, and he partially ventured forth from the place of his concealment, and looked inquiringly around.

"It is the signal," he whispered, "it must be those whom I seek; but now to satisfy myself upon that point."

He applied a small silver whistle to his lips as he thus spoke, and blew a signal similar to the one he had heard; then again drew himself behind the broken column to wait the result.

Immediately afterwards, the hasty tread of footsteps upon the broken tesselated pavement, sounded more distinctly in his ears; they approached nearer, and presently the tall shadows of human forms were to be seen moving about like grim spectres in the background; and certain words in Hindoostanee were muttered in low whispering tones, but which the quick and anxious ear of Yunadar readily caught. He again, and with confidence stepped from the place of his concealment, and was immediately joined by four men, in costume, half sepoy, half civilian; but all armed ready apparently for some desperate undertaking,

"Well met," said Yunadar, "I anxiously have awaited your coming."

"'Tis you that have tarried, Yunadar," replied the foremost of the men, "we were punctual to the hour of appointment, but you were not here."

"True," coincided Yunadar, "I admit that I was rather behind my time, 'tis seldom that I fail, Allyghur; but the delay was unavoidable. I have seen and heard that which has excited my surprise and indignation."

"Ah! what mean you?" demanded Allyghur. Yunadar hurriedly related what had taken place.

"Your conduct was premature and imprudent," remarked Allyghur, "and might have proved fatal to our plot. But the young English officer, whose clandestine attentions, you say, are encouraged by your daughter, he ——"

"Curses light upon him for his presumption," interrupted Yunadar, passionately; "but for the officious hand of Omelia, who arrested me in my purpose, he would have paid for it with his life."

"And you know him not?" said Allyghur.

"I had no opportunity of observing his features," answered Yunadar.

"Then it seems that I have the advantage over you," remarked Allyghur; "I watched him this evening from the opposite side of the river, enter the bholio, which, no doubt, was destined to carry him to his secret assignation with your daughter; and I would gladly, if I could have done so with safety, have buried my knife in his heart, for he is one who is most dangerous to our cause, and who is ever on the alert to give such information to the authorities as may lead to our detection, and the frustration of our designs."

"Ah!" exclaimed Yunadar, and a dark frown overspread his contracted brow; "your words excite my curiosity; his name?"

"It is one which you must have heard before, since he has greatly distinguished himself," replied Allyghur; "it is Lieutenant Stanley."

"Stanley!" repeated Yunadar, in a hoarse voice, and at the same time his whole frame and his features exhibited the utmost excitement.

"Aye," said Allyghur; "why do you knit your brows, and frown so darkly at the mention of that name?"

"Because 'tis one that I can never hear mentioned without a bitter curse rising to my lips," answered Yunadar. "'Tis a name which is associated with a monstrous wrong inflicted against one who was as precious to this now callous heart, as the life blood which circulates throughout my veins. My only sister; pure, good, and innocent, till defiled by a treacherous villain of the name of Stanley; by him was the heart of a noble-minded woman broken; by his accursed villainy was that loving, gentle creature brought to a premature grave; and, as I gazed upon her cold corpse, and clasped it to my aching heart, (for she died, poor thing in my arms), I swore, if ever opportunity should present itself, to have a terrible revenge against her betrayer, and all who should in any way be connected with him. Oh, should this presumptuous boy prove to be related to that heartless miscreant, and to seek the ruin of my daughter, too (for honourable motives I can never believe to guide the actions of the detested Feringee); —revolting, degrading, thought; indignation fires my brain as it flashes upon it, and increases tho deadly hatred which I bear the whole accursed race."

Ungovernable rage choked the further utterance of the Sepoy, and he clenched his fist in the air, and struck his forehead passionately.

"I appreciate your feelings, Yunadar," said Allyghur; "and admire the manly, faithful spirit that urges you on to the work of retribution on the heads of our hated enemies. But the villain of whom you speak; who, and what was he?"

"A wealthy merchant, residing at Calcutta," replied Yunadar; "but he quitted India shortly after he had basely worked my poor sister's destruction, and probably is no more; for fifteen years have elapsed since that fatal occurrence took place."

"And was he a married man?"

"He was, and had at the time, two children."

"This Lieutenant Stanley might be his son, or, at any rate, some near relation," suggested Allyghur.

"Hold, Allyghur," exclaimed Yunadar; you raise maddening thoughts and anticipations in my brain, which at present I dare scarcely encourage. But this is not the time or place to discuss this business; we have other important work to do which requires our immediate attention. What's the news?"

"All goes well," answered Allyghur; "the fire of revolt is rapidly spreading; but still so secretly and cautiously that our enemies will have little suspicion of its extent and organization till it suddenly bursts upon them with the irresistible fury of the fierce monsoon, sweeping them all before it to destruction."

"'Tis well," remarked Yunadar, with a look of satisfaction; "the Sepoy's wrongs, and those of the native population of India will soon be terribly avenged; and when that day shall arrive——"

"Let no false feeling of mercy stay our hands in the glorious work of extermination, added Allyghur; not an Englishman, woman, or child, must, if possible, be allowed to escape the general slaughter."

"True; they may, and doubtless they will, call us atrocious miscreants, murderers, fiends; be it so. Is it not themselves who have set us the example? Have we not a century's wrongs, oppression, and atrocity perpetrated by their hands, to complain of?—We have, and therefore as they have sown so shall they reap. Mercy is for the merciful. Torture, suffering, horror, are the just due of the first perpetrators of crime."

"Well said, Yunadar," coincided Allyghur, "and soon shall they find the fearful realisation of those scenes of horror which we have here faintly imagined, and briefly discussed. The proud capital of the great Moguls will shortly be restored to its rightful inheritors Not long will the hated usurpers hold possession of Delhi, and little do they imagine that the city they have fortified and strengthened will contain its thousands of their sworn enemies, prepared to set them at defiance, and to deal death and destruction among their puny ranks."

"Aye," observed another of the rebels; "the work goes bravely on. Regiments that were disbanded and disarmed near Cal cutta, and at Berhampore, are rapidly making their way by different routes to Delhi, and their progress there will be the signal for increased disaffection among the native population, and of fresh revolt among the native troops. The work goes bravely on,—goes bravely on, I say."

"True," said Allyghur, "everything is proceeding as well as every lover of his country's cause can wish it. Many of our native princes are aiding the plot—both with counsel and resources; and amongst others, the adopted son of the late Peshwa, Nêna or Nâna Sahib, as he is called, is sworn to co-operate with us, even to the death."

"He is a determined man, and hath monstrous wrongs to complain of;" said Yunadar; "let the English beware of him, for he only awaits the opportunity to prove to them a scourge so terrible, that those who shall afterwards be speaking of his deeds shall not be able to do so without a shudder, or without thanking their lucky stars that they at least, with their wives and children escaped the savage ferocity of his vengeance. But come, to the more immediate business upon which we have met. We require money to assist us in the furtherance of our plans. I also demand the possession of my daughter Omelia, for through her I have schemes of self-aggrandizement to carry out, which I am resolved at all risks to accomplish. Both those objects are to be obtained at the residence of Mr. Melville, namely, money and Omelia. The hour is auspicious; there will be no difficulty in gaining access to the house, which I have duly reconnoitred. The inmates are now doubtless, all hushed in sleep, but should they become aroused, we are fully prepared for resistance, and have the means to silence them. Come, I am impatient of this delay, for it will soon be morning, and then it will be impossible to put our scheme into execution."

"We are ready," said Allyghur, "lead on, and let us all be well nerved for the task we have to perform."

Yunadar first advanced to the entrance of the ruined mosque, and looked cautiously around as far as his eyes could stretch, and finding that the coast was clear, he issued forth, beckoning his companions to follow, which they did, and the whole party of guilty men were soon threading their way towards the villa.

CHAPTER V.

THE NIGHT OF PERIL.

Omelia, on separating with her friends, with feelings greatly depressed by the stirring events of the evening, her interview with her father, and the dark hints and threats that had escaped him, retired to her chamber, but not to rest; no, painful thought banished sleep from her eyes, and she seated herself by an open oriel window, and gazed listlessly upon the fair scene before her, which seemed to have acquired fresh beauty from the serenity of the night.

The flowers had closed their graceful petals, bulbed in dew drops, but a balmy fragrance pervaded the air, such as can only be inhaled in an Oriental climate, amidst those scenes which are those of perpetual sweets, scenes such as we read of in the tales of Fairy Land.

The rich foliage of the trees was gently agitated by a refreshing breeze which came cool and invigorating to the senses: while its soft sighs among the shrubs and leaves, came sweetly on the ear like the subdued melody of song-birds when they commence to welcome the early dawn.

But as has been said before, Omelia was sad and heavy at heart, and those varied beauties which her refined taste so duly appreciated, in her present gloomy mood, had no charms for her. Melancholy presentiments and fears for the future haunted and distressed her mind, and never had she felt such a keen sense of the helplessness, loneliness, and dependence of her situation before.

In spite of the assurances of her generous benefactors, and the confidence she had in the sincerity of their regard for her, the purity of the motives that guided them in their conduct towards her, and the anxiety they felt in her happiness and welfare, her proud spirit could not disguise from itself the humiliating fact that she was merely the poor child of charity,—the pauper on their bounty,—dependent on them for everything; for home, shelter, education, clothing, even the very means of existence, and that should it please them to withdraw from her their patronage and protection, she would be one of the most wretched and friendless outcasts that ever had to struggle against the poverty and vicissitudes of life.

True, she could not doubt the sincerity of Edward Stanley's love,—the honour of his intentions;—that he would freely, gladly make her his wife, and place her in that proud position of society, which the most peerless and richest maidens might justly envy; but what claim had she, (the poor Indian girl,—the humble Sepoy's daughter, the daugher too of that man who had expressed the most deadly hatred of the English race, and whose soul she had too much reason to fear was already deeply steeped in crime), have upon the heart, the hand of that noble youth? Could she be mean enough to take advantage of such generous, such disinterested love, and consent to become the bride of one from whom she was alien in country, in religion, in every social tie, and whose friends might discard, disown him, for the rash act, look upon her with scorn and loathing, and finally heap their curses upon his head, for the disgrace which they would probably consider he had brought upon their name?

No; the proud spirit of Omelia revolted at the idea,—and she was resolved, however terrible the trial might be,—though her heart might break in the effort, and notwithstanding it would be the total annihilation of all her fondest hopes and wishes, to struggle with her feelings, and firmly to reject the hand which she could not with justice except. Besides, Edward was beloved by Flora Melville, although she had hitherto hesitated to confess the passion with which he had inspired her,—she was every way worthy of him, both by station, wealth, and womanly virtues,—and Omelia could not but consider that she was acting with injustice and ingratitude towards her, by presenting any obstacle to the promotion of her wishes.

"No Edward, dearest Edward," sighed the poor girl as she closed the window, and turned away from it;—you shall not make the sacrifice you so generously offer, the heart of Omelia must cease to beat ere it can cease to love you,—but it shall break, ere she will consent to become the bride of one of whom she might scornfully be considered only worthy to be the slave!"

All the noble and effectionate qualities of her nature shone forth in the expressive and handsome features of the young Indian girl, as she thus spoke, and no one who might at that moment have seen her, could have done otherwise than admire and acknowledge that every charm, that adorns the woman and the heroine, were in her combined.

But the struggle between love for Stanley, duty to herself, and regard for the feelings and hopes of Flora Melville, was a severe one, and Omelia, yielding to all the torturing emotions that agitated her breast, wept bitterly. She saw at once how fallacious was the sanguine anticipations of the happy future she had encouraged, and she shuddered as if upon the brink of some frightful abyss, and that inevitable fate from which no power could save her. She dreaded the following evening to arrive, when she had promised again to meet her lover; for then she must find the resolution to resign him for ever, this too probably driving him to despair, and herself to certain misery.

She remained for a short time in melancholy meditation, and then arose, and walked to the door of her chamber and listened,—as a dismal and singular foreboding of some impending danger (probably caused by the threats and observations that had escaped her father's lips), arose to her perturbed imagination. All, however, was perfectly silent in the house, in fact, it was a death-like silence, which was rather painful and ominous than otherwise.

And now, as if to add to the gloom of her thoughts, and the general languor and depression of her spirits, black clouds suddenly obscured the firmament, and the glittering stars no longer imparted their lustrous light to the romantic scenery in the midst of which the villa stood. The gentle sighing of the wind was changed to moaning sounds like that of some person in their last extremity, and a darkness unusual in that land of brightness and cheerful skies, at that season of the year, fell on all around.

Omelia was a stranger to fear, but an unaccountable and irresistible feeling of awe now came over her, and a sensation approaching to dread of being alone.

She chided herself for what she could not help, considering it a feeling of weakness, and endeavoured to conquer it, but in vain; it even gained upon her, and a cold tremor crept through her veins.

She stood near the door of her apartment in a half state of stupor, with her hands pressed upon her forehead, and seemed to be in expectation of some coming event, but which she shuddered to meet.

She was startled by the sound of what appeared to be the opening and closing of a door below, then the cautious tread of several footsteps, followed by the low and indistinct mutterings of voices.

She drew in her breath and listened more attentively,—but now all was again perfectly still, and she endeavoured to persuade herself that she must have been mistaken; but the impression had got too powerful a hold of her imagination for her to do so, and she almost feared to move. All, however, remaining quiet for a short time, she somewhat recovered herself, especially when she remembered that the domestics slept below, and that probably the noise, if such indeed it was that she had heard. proceeded, from some of them.

Notwithstanding, she felt fidgetty and uneasy, and walked again to the window and looked out, having first concealed her light behind a portion of the drapery, not wishing any of the attendants to see her, if they should happen to be about; but the darkness was now so intense that she could not see anything distinctly.

While she still lingered near the window, the same whispering sounds followed by half suppressed footsteps which seemed to proceed from the staircase at the back of the villa, saluted her ears, and this time Omelia was convinced that she could not be deceived, and strange surmises and apprehensions took possession of her bosom. What occasion had any of the domestics to be moving about the house at that time of the night? She could not believe it was them, but on the contrary, the worst suspicions arose to her imagination. She was aware that Mr. Melville generally kept a large sum of money on the premises, then there was jewellery and plate, and that might have excited the cupidity of some individuals who had become acquainted with it; or the treachery of some of the servants might have revealed it.

These and other fearful ideas passed in rapid succession across Omelia's mind, and she could not get rid of the doubts and terrors that had taken possession of her, and which were increased by the remarkable silence that reigned below. She knew not what to do, how to act; she feared not so much for herself, but she trembled for the safety of Mr. Melville and his daughter, for she could not divest her mind of the impression that some person or persons who had no business there, were moving about in the house, and should her kind benefactors happen to be wrapped in sleep, they would be unconscious of, and unprepared to meet the danger which might threaten them.

Should she raise an alarm? No, that instead of having the desired effect, might be productive of the most fatal consequences. Her brain was bewildered, and she stood irresolute, the confused noise still ringing in her ears, till, at length worked up to a pitch of the most insupportable excitement, she had just formed the resolution to endeavour to reach the chamber of Flora, which was on the same floor as her own, when a faint cry, or rather a succession of moaning sounds, and which seemed to proceed from the back of the premises, saluted her ears, and caused a trembling sensation of horror to steal through her veins, for her heart now foreboded the worst, and she clasped her hands in agony. This was followed by a violent noise as if of struggling, and a low cry for help, mingled with what appeared to be the curses and oaths of men uttered in savage voices, and,

unable any longer to endure this dreadful state of suspense, and regardless of her own safety, Omelia threw open her own room-door and rushed into the passage beyond, determined to unravel the terrible mystery at all hazards.

She could not utter a single cry; but she drew her breath short and thick, and her heart palpitated violently against her side, as she staggered on towards the chamber of Mr. Melville, from which the alarming sounds proceeded. And now a piteous shriek in a female voice, vibrated in her ears, and added to her terrors. Anxiety for those whom she so fondly revered, gave her courage, and bounding forward, the next moment she gained the door of the chamber, which was standing partially open, throwing a strong ray of light, as if proceeding from a lantern upon the passage; and at the same moment our heroine heard the plaintive voice of Flora, in piteous accents appealing to some one for mercy; followed by the scornful reply of some man in a harsh and brutal voice the tones of which were painfully familiar to her ears.

Half frantic with the agony of expectation, but scarcely giving herself time to think what she was about, Omelia threw the door hastily back on its hinges, and there a scene presented itself to her gaze which appalled and paralyzed her.

Several armed ruffians (in two of whom she recognized the faithless domestics of her benefactors, and whose presence told the treachery by which the infamous plot was carried out, and partly accounted for the silence with which the villains had been enabled to gain access to the villa), were in the room; two of them holding down the aged Mr. Melville (who was bleeding from a blow he had received on his temple), and were menacing him with instant death; while the distracted Flora was on her knees before them with clasped hands and frantic looks, supplicating them for mercy. Her hair was flying loose about her neck and shoulders, on which were several marks of violence, which she had no doubt received in her struggles to save her unfortunate parent; and altogether she presented one of the most painful pictures of agony that could well be imagined.

Several articles were lying strewed about the floor in disorder, and a plate-chest and cash-box had been forced open, at which two of the miscreants were busy securing the contents; and others were engaged in other parts of the room, ready to take the most active parts in any outrage, should their aid be required; the tall and powerful figure of one of whom (for his back was turned towards her), was fearfully familiar

to Omelia, and a sickly feeling of horror came over her.

So astonished, so bewildered was she by what she saw, that she could not move—she could scarcely breathe. The noise of the door, as she threw it back, had not startled the fellows; and, fortunately she stood in such a position, that the light did not fall upon her person, and she was concealed, for the moment, from observation. It was indeed a moment of terror. There was a fearful pause; and all the actors in the painful scene remained fixed in the same attitude.

"We have proceeded thus far," at length said one of the ruffians who held Mr. Melville (whose looks were those of anguish and despair), "and we must no longer waste time in hesitation. Now, old man—you."

"Mercy! mercy! for the love of heaven! oh, spare the life of my aged parent! exclaimed the distracted Flora, in accents sufficient to move even the most insensible heart to pity; but they had no visible effect upon the hardened wretches to whom the appeal was made.

"Quick—to business," cried the man before mentioned, turning round and advancing more into the light of the lanterns they had brought with them; "already there has been too much delay, and we have much more work to do. Fools;—why do you stand listening to the childish whinings of that noisy girl? Nay, then, since

No. 3

you fear to do so, thus do I at once stop her cries!"

With the most unspeakable horror, did the harsh tones of that voice fall upon the ear of the wildly agitated Omelia. Too well she knew them, and recognized her guilty father, (although, after he had, with his infamous associate, left the ruins of the old Mosque, taken the precaution carefully to conceal his features beneath a mask), and at the critical moment, when he was about to perpetrate the fatal deed, (Mr. Melville, having become insensible, and lying helpless from exhaustion), with a loud and frantic shriek, she darted forward, and, with the almost superhuman strength, which the desperate nature of the occasion gave her for the moment, arrested his arm; at the same time, fixing upon him a look of agony and reproach, that ought, (if his breast had not become insensible to every proper feeling), immediately to have struck him with shame, horror, and remorse.

Astonishment and confusion, however, seemed to be the principal effect it had upon him; the deadly weapon dropped from his hand, and he stood powerless before that unhappy girl, who was indeed accursed in being his daughter.

The other ruffians drew back amazed, abashed, and confounded; and poor Flora, unable to utter a word, so powerful was her emotion, clasped her hands vehemently together, and raised her eyes devoutly and fervently to heaven, mentally invoking a blessing on the head of the heroic deliverer of herself and her unfortunate parent.

"Cruel, guilty man, unnatural," cried Omelia, in a voice of mingled anguish, terror, and reproach; but before she could finish the sentence, Yunadar fiercely grasped her arm; and in a voice rendered hoarse by excitement, he exclaimed—

"Hold, rash girl! dare not to proceed further, or those you seek to protect, that instant die." Omelia uttered a faint cry of agony, averted her looks from her guilty parent, with a feeling of shame, disgust, and unutterable horror; and taking the hand of Flora, affectionately raised it to her lips, and fixed upon her a most expressive look of sympathy.

Flora Melville had never seen the father of Omelia but once, when she was first introduced to their other residence at Delhi, which was several years ago; so, that, if he had been unmasked, she doubtless would not have had the slightest recollection of his features; and she was now too much terrified and bewildered to notice what passed between him and his daughter.

"Secure the old man's daughter,—he is insensible enough, and we have no fear of his annoying us therefore," said Yunadar, after a brief pause, and addressing himself to his companions. "Now girl," he added, grasping Omelia by the arm, "you must with us."

"With you!" repeated our heroine, with a shudder of horror; oh no, no, no; spare me; in mercy, spare me!"

"Silence, and dare not to offer any useless resistance, or you know the consequences," replied her father, sternly, and pointing at the same time significantly to Mr. Melville, and his daughter. Omelia too well understood his guilty meaning; and, covering her face with her hands, sobbed aloud in the bitterness of her anguish.

In the meantime, Allyghur and the others obeyed the instructions of Yunadar, and secured Flora by a cord to one of the pillars that supported the roof, while she in vain with tears and supplications appealed to them for forbearance. This being completed, Yunadar again took the hand of his unhappy daughter; and motioning his associates to follow, he was about to force her away, when with a strong effort, she released herself from him, and, in a voice of the deepest emotion, ejaculated—

"Oh, must I then leave that peaceful, happy home that has so long sheltered me, thus?"

She rushed overpowered with anguish to Flora, throwing herself on her knees convulsively before her, clasping her hands, and raising them passionately to her lips, in a voice half choked with agony, she cried—

"Farewell; alas! too much I fear, a long farewell! dearest, best, and only friends; may the Great Spirit, lady, continue to watch over and protect from danger your honoured father and yourself: and oh, should fate ordain that we should never meet more, rest assured that the last prayer of the poor, grateful, humble object of your bounty shall be breathed in blessings springing from the inmost recesses of her heart upon your heads."

"No more of this," said Yunadar, impatiently. "This way girl, if you would not have me proceed to any greater extremity."

"Oh, mercy, I beseech you, fearful man," cried Flora, frantically, and still, in spite of the threatening looks with which the miscreants eyed her, detaining Omelia, "mercy, if not for me, at least for that poor girl, whom I love with all the fond, the fervent affection of a sister. Omelia, faithful, dear Omelia, sweet companion of mine and my aged parent's lonely hours, gentle soother of our cares and anguish, in the hours of sickness, sorrow, and tribulation, they shall not separate us thus. Oh, is there no help at hand? mercy, mercy, heaven!"

"Gag her, silence her, stop her cries!" fiercely commanded Yunadar. But there was no necessity to obey his stern orders. Flora made one last effort to detain the poor affectionate girl, to whom she was so ardently attached, than her strength was completely exhausted and overpowered by the agony of her feelings, she uttered one last piercing cry of despair, and her senses left her; while Omelia in a very little better state, was hurried from the chamber by her remorseless father, and his cruel associates in crime.

They hurried her down the stairs, and out at the door, and there, on the threshold she was horrorstruck in beholding the lifeless bodies of the *durwan* and two other domestics, who, it seems had fallen ere they could offer any resistance to the ruffians, or raise an alarm; while some of their more fortunate companions had succeeded in making their escape, among whom was the faithful Minna, Flora's favourite *Ayah*, (lady's maid) who had been in her service from a child. It was Mr. Melville's *Syces* (grooms), and a treacherous *Sircar* (a man who keeps the accounts of the establishment), who had joined the robbers and mutineers, and assisted them in the accomplishment of their diabolical schemes.

The latter villain had no sooner got outside the door, than he lighted a brand he had with him, from one of the lanterns, and was proceeding to apply it to the light fancy trellis-work near the entrance to the villa, when Omelia with a terrified shriek, as she understood at once his monstrous purposes, clung to her father, and looked up imploringly, and with tearful eyes, in his face, and in a stern voice, Yunadar demanded of the *Sircar*—

"Hold! what would you do?"

"Fire the building!" replied the atrocious miscreant, resolutely, and thus prevent all danger of detection."

The words had scarcely escaped his lips, when the report of a pistol was heard, and the *Sircar* was stretched dead on the earth.

Omelia uttered a mingled cry of astonishment and joy, while Yunadar and his companions were so completely astounded by the unexpected attack, that they were rendered powerless.

Another instant, and they were fiercely beset by several armed men (among whom were the domestics who had made their escape from the villa), and led on by a young English officer, who, having forced our heroine from Yunadar's hold, felled him to the earth with a violent blow from his pistol, and was about to plunge his sword into his body, when Omelia, with a terrified shriek, seized his arm, at the same time exclaiming—

"Mercy! mercy! take not his life, he is my father."

"Your father, dear, dear Omelia? Alas! alas!" cried the young officer, in accents of the deepest tenderness and regret; at the same time his arm fell powerless by his side.

A cry of frantic delight escaped the lips of our heroine, (for she knew his voice immediately, although she had not before had time or opportunity to recognize his features), and she sunk overpowered with her emotions on his bosom.

Scarcely could the poor girl believe the evidence of her senses. It was Edward Stanley, who, at the very critical moment, when she had given herself up for lost, had so fortunately come to her deliverance.

Yunadar fixed his eyes upon the features of the young man, which were now revealed to him by the light of the fire-brand that had fallen from the hand of the dead Sircar, and no sooner did he behold them, than he sprang to his feet with a frightful yell, and stood gazing at him as if he were thunderstruck.

"Powers of darkness!" he exclaimed; "is this a delusion, or does the base destroyer of my sister's innocence! the heartless villain who trampled on her virtue, broke the heart of the poor victim of his treachery, and brought her to a premature grave. Am I awake, or has madness seized upon my brain? Even so did I behold the miscreant Stanley, fifteen years ago. 'Tis he! his son! none other could bear his hated resemblance. Unhand her, infidel dog! pollute not my child, my daughter with your foul embrace."

"Oh, harm him not, Edward, if you would not have the curse of her who loves you, on your head," cried the distracted Omelia, laying her hand forcibly on Stanley's arm, as, in the excitement of his feelings, he was again about to raise his sword. Wretched, guilty parent, begone, fly! ere a terrible and untimely fate shall overtake you."

The desperate man felt for his pistols, but he had them not, and a fearful malediction escaped his lips on the discovery. Every moment his situation became more critical: defeat seemed certain to overtake his companions, who, however, fought with savage determination; a well directed shot wounded him, though not severely, in the arm; and foaming with rage, as he hurried from the spot, protected by Allyghur and another of his merciless associates, he shouted—

"Detested boy, the triumph this night is yours; but beware! for we shall meet again. Spirit of my much wronged sister; ill fated Niami, you yet shall not go unavenged!"

Thus saying, he plunged with the speed of the wind, behind the trees, followed by Allyghur, and vanished from the sight.

———

CHAPTER VI.

OMELIA AND HER FRIENDS.—THE HEART'S STRUGGLE.

Yunadar and his two companions were all that escaped from this brief affray, but which had it not been for the timely and fortunate arrival of Stanley and his friends might have been attended with such fatal results; the rest of the villains were either slain, or so severely wounded that all further resistance was at an end, and as the beautiful Amelia hung affectionately on her lover's bosom, her heart swelled with gratitude to him for his heroic conduct, while at the same time feelings of the most torturing description racked her breast, when she thought of her wretched and guilty parent, and the terrible future which his savage conduct, and his observations to Edward Stanley opened to her imagination. She felt a sensation of self-degradation, and gently withdrew herself from Stanley's embrace, averted her looks, abashed and humiliated, tears started to her eyes, and heart-drawn sighs escaped her bosom.

Stanley could not but dread her thoughts, and deeply did he sympathise with her in her painful and embarrassing situation, while at the same time a feeling of the most poignant anguish and regret took possession of his breast, that the fair being whom he so fondly, so passionately loved, and in whom were combined all the most noble, generous, and virtuous qualities that can give lustre to the character of woman, should be allied by all the closest ties of nature, with one so thoroughly debased as the revengeful Sepoy, Yunadar.

But could this painful discovery in the least alter the glowing, ardent sentiments he entertained towards the poor Indian girl, whose heart he knew was so truly, sincerely, fervently devoted to him? Oh, no; he would, indeed, have despised himself as one of the meanest and most ungrateful of men, could he have believed it would have that effect upon his mind. So powerful

was the hold which the innate virtues and personal charms had on his affections, that he was convinced neither time nor circumstances, whatever might betide, could banish her from his heart.

"Dearest Omelia," he said, affectionately encircling her slender waist with one arm, and pressing her slightly resisting hand to his heart, "why this emotion?— Why do you turn away from me and weep?"

"Because, Edward," she replied in a faint and faltering voice, "reason, truth, justice, self-respect, and your honour and happiness, which, oh, are far more precious to me than life, convince me that I must not, dare not longer encourage the blissful though presumptuous hopes that have hitherto animated my breast; because that I see a yawning gulf between us, Stanley, which must ever separate us; go,—go,— endeavour to banish me from your memory; or if perchance my image should still arise to your thoughts, if—if it should continue to linger round your heart, and when you offer up your prayers to the God you worship, my name should haply rise to your lips, let it be with the sentiments only of a dear friend, or such as the heart of a brother should feel towards a sister. Oh, leave me, Edward, I implore you; I shudder to think of the danger that threatens while we remain together, or give encouragement to our fatal, hopeless passion. Leave me, I say; Edward Stanley can never in safety and justice to himself bestow more than his sympathy and esteem on the unhappy Sepoy's daughter, and she is too proud to exact from him the sacrifice."

Sobs choked her further utterance, and Stanley's feelings were excited in the most painful degree.

"What do you say, Omelia?" he cried, "what rash, what cruel, and ungenerous observations were those that just escaped your lips? Cease to love you? to think of you only with the cold esteem of a friend? oh, how little can you appreciate the boundless passion which throbs my heart towards you, if you think that I could thus meanly, perfidiously turn recreant to my vows, or suffer the guilt of your misguided father to prejudice me against you. No, by Heaven, I should hate and despise myself could I become so base. But this is not the time, Omelia, to discuss this painful subject, but one with which the whole hopes and happiness of our future lives are associated. Thank Heaven, I have been enabled to rescue you from the perils and dangers that have this night threatened; but still there are those whom I know are dear to you; those friends, who—

"Ah!" interrupted Omelia, hastily, "my beloved benefactors; oh, how could I have been so thoughtless as to suffer my own sorrows to draw my anxiety from them? Let us hasten to them, dear Edward, for I tremble to think what may yet be the result of this cruel and daring outrage. Come, come."

As she spoke, she took his hand and hurried him into the villa, and they had no sooner done so and were about to ascend the stairs that led to the chamber where the ruffianly outrage had been committed, than the mournful cries of Flora smote their ears, and filled them with pain and regret, mingled with dread at what had probably taken place in the interval of delay which had occurred during their brief conversation in the garden.

They flew up the stairs, and hastily entered the apartment. There they beheld poor Flora, the very picture of agony and despair, vainly endeavouring to extricate herself from the cords that bound her to the pillar, so that she might hasten to the assistance of her unfortunate father, who was still lying in a state of insensibility on the floor, and bleeding copiously from the wound he had received on the temple.

Flora had heard the noise of the combat outside the villa, the report of the firearms, and the shouts and curses of the villains when they found themselves unexpectedly surprised and attacked by foes who were evidently more than a match for them, and her terrible suspense and fear (principally for Omelia), may be readily imagined.

On beholding Edward Stanley and our heroine enter the room, she uttered a mingled exclamation of surprise and delight; and while Omelia hastened to unfasten the cords that bound her, Stanley raised Mr. Melville from the floor, and proceeded immediateley to bind his wound and stop the further loss of blood as well as he could with his handkerchief,

On being released by Omelia, Flora sunk in her arms overpowered by her feelings, but quickly recovering herself, she flew to the assistance of her father, whom Edward was endeavouring to restore to sensibility, paused and trembled with some powerful emotion when her eyes and those of the handsome young officer met.

Omelia's keen eye marked the expression of her features and the agitation of her manner, and a pang shot through her heart as she did so, and she turned her head aside and pressed her hands upon her brow.

"Believe me, Miss Melville," said Stanley, "I deeply sympathise with you in the misfortunes that have this night occurred to you, and much regret that I did not arrive at the villa in time to prevent them."

"Dear Edward," replied Flora, in a half confused voice of trembling emotion, and evidently for the moment forgetting herself! "dearest Edward, how shall I express my feelings—that is——" she added in a faint voice suddenly recalling her thoughts, and blushing deeply, "Mr. Stanley, I feel at a loss to express my thanks to you for your preservation of—of Omelia, and—and——"

Here her voice failed her, and hiding her face in her hands in confusion, she was unable to proceed.

Every word, every expression had been narrowly watched by the keen penetrating eye of Omelia, and the throbbing of her bosom, the serious expression of her fine features, almost approaching to a frown, and the agitation of her demeanour, altogether showed too well how painfully she understood them. A feeling of jealousy shot through her heart, which she endeavoured to check, and hastily approaching the spot where Flora and Lieutenant Stanley stood, just as the latter was about to make some reply to the observations of Miss Melville, she said in rather petulent tones—

"There is no time to waste in words, Miss Melville, and Mr. Stanley must see the necessity of attending at, and to the recovery of her father."

Flora could not but remark the half angry tone in which those words were spoken by the Indian girl, also the agitation and excitement of her manner, and it increased her confusion. However, she struggled with the painful feelings that beset her breast, and faltering out some acknowledgment of the propriety of Omelia's suggestions, she requested Stanley to assist her in conveying Mr. Melville to another chamber, sent for the assistance of one of the principal domestics of the villa, who was skilled in medicines, to assist in his recovery. Omelia signifying that she would be ready to attend Flora, should her aid be required.

When they had quitted the room, and she was left to herself, Omelia, with her hand pressed upon her forehead in deep thought, stood in a fixed attitude for a minute or two, and it was evident that her passions were greatly excited by some angry and torturing feeling, and which she in vain tried to control or subdue.

"She loves him," she at length muttered to herself; "'tis evident she deeply, fondly loves him; and is he cold and insensible to the power of her charms, and the noble qualities of her mind? Have they no power to wean from me those powerful affections he has so oft professed? Men's hearts are

... as fickle and inconstant as the wind; but if I thought," she suddenly added, and her dark eyes flashed with an unnatural lustre as she spoke—"if I thought that he could dare to deceive me, to venture to meet with and to trifle with my feelings, and had merely won my love to boast of the power of his allurements, the passions that my heart, my very soul, now acknowledges for him would be changed to deadliest hate and withering scorn; and he should find that the poor Indian girl has both the spirit and the power to resent so degrading and unmanly an insult."

She paused, for the excitement of her feelings overpowered her, and she drew her breath short and quick.

"But, no, no," she at length continued, and hope and confidence once more re-animated her features, "how much I wrong the noble character of Edward Stanley by these jealous fears and suspicions. I cannot, I will no longer doubt him, for to do so would be indeed to annihilate all my hopes, and to render me the most wretched being in existence. Flora Melville loves him, I firmly believe,—fondly, truly, passionately loves him,—and, oh, how does it grieve me to be any obstacle in the way of the happiness of one whom I regard with all the affection of a sister; for well do I know how worthy she is of him. Still, dearest Edward, it is impossible for me to resign you, or to abandon those bright hopes that you have bid me cherish."

She was interrupted in the midst of this soliloquy by the sound of an approaching footstep, and hastily regaining her composure in the best way she could, she took a seat, just as Lieutenant Stanley re-entered the room.

"Dear Omelia," he said, taking her hand, and looking anxiously in her face, "I thought you seemed angry a short time since, and—"

"Lieutenant Stanley," hastily, and rather haughtily interrupted Omelia, but more with the hope of evading his questions; "Lieutenant Stanley would do well not to jump too hastily at conclusions, in judging of the motives or thoughts of Omelia by her looks, or any casual observations that may by chance escape her. But enough of this. Mr. Melville, he—"

"He has revived," answered Stanley, "and I am happy to say that he does not appear to be so seriously injured as we at first feared he was. The miscreants who caused this monstrous outrage——"

"Hold, sir," interrupted Omelia, and a frown again overspread her handsome features, "much as I abominate the character of the outrage, I cannot but remind you that my father was present, therefore I cannot sanction or recognize the strong epithet you have just made use of, as applied to him."

"Pardon me, dear Omelia," said her lover, with a look of the deepest regret; "heaven forbid that I should give utterance to a word that may offend or wound your feelings. Alas, how unfortunate it is, that your father should have become mixed up with that evil spirit of revolt and disloyalty, which I fear is too rapidly gaining strength among the native troops of India, and which may give rise to scenes of horror and bloodshed, which I shudder to think of."

"No more of this, Edward," said Omelia with an agitated look; for she fully participated in the feelings that prompted his observations; and after the strange hatred which her father had expressed for her lover, and the threats he had uttered, she could not but entertain the utmost fear for his safety. "I pray you," she continued, "let us for the present drop this painful subject. What strange infatuation can possess my father, I know not, but I trust he will yet see the madness of his conduct, and the danger as well as guilt of the designs to which he seems unfortunately to have lent himself, and which must ultimately end in the destruction of all those who take a part in the work of evil. The native troops as well as the population of India have grievous wrongs, which the Government should, and must redress, and reform; but 'tis justice they should seek, and not revenge. "But," she added earnestly, and fixing her eyes anxiously upon him, as filial affection and solicitude for the safety of that wretched parent, from whom she had scarcely ever received one act of kindness, arose in her breast; "oh, Edward, misguided, guilty though Yunadar may be, remember, he is still the father of her whom you profess to love; you will not betray him?"

Stanley paused. The question bewildered, agitated, and tortured him, and he scarcely knew what to reply.

"You hesitate," said Omelia hastily, and fixing upon him a penetrating look; "you *will* then make his guilt known, and——"

"No, no, no," interrupted Stanley, in a voice of much emotion: although it is my duty to do so. He is your father, my own dear Omelia; I cannot forget that he is the author of your being, of you who possess my heart's warmest affections, and duty must yield to love."

An expression of grateful affection animated the beautiful features of Omelia, as he uttered those words; tears started to her eyes, and she threw herself fondly in his arms, overpowered by the mingled emotions that agitated her breast.

"In the morning," said Edward, " I must leave you, Omelia. but I will endeavour to obtain leave of absence for a short time from my regiment, and I trust we shall quickly meet again."

"Oh yes, dear Edward," cried the poor girl, joyfully? my heart will fondly, anxiously anticipate the time ; and yet—" she added, and a look of melancholly usurped the place of the smiles that had just clad her features, "a fearful foreboding steals over my senses, of some approaching calamity—and—and—that——"

"Oh, Omelia," said her lover, "banish those apprehensions from your mind, and look forward to the future with bright hopes and anticipations."

"Alas !" sighed Omelia ; " fain would I do so, but it must not be. I see the black clouds gathering that will o'ershadow all our hopes and prospects, Edward, and place an insurmountable barrier between us. But whatever may be her destiny ; although she may be for ever separated from all she holds most dear on earth ; though your love may change to the deadliest hate and scorn ; even though surrounded with every horror, the heart of Omelia must e're be yours, dear Edward ; her every thought, her fondest wishes shall still cling to you in the midst of every danger ; although unknown, she will be ever by your side ; her's shall be the hand to avert the threatened evil ; her's the prayers constantly offered up for blessings on your head ; her's the voice to soothe you in the hour of sorrow and affliction, and to raise your thoughts to hopes of happiness. Good night, Edward, remember my words. I must hasten to the assistance of Miss Melville."

"Stay, stay, Omelia," exclaimed her lover ; " but a moment."

But she was gone, and Stanley stood for a minute or two, and pondered deeply, and much bewildered on the strange ambiguity of her observations.

"What torturing mystery is in her words," he soliloquised. "*Although unknown, she will be ever by your side :* what can she mean? I am lost in amazement and perplexity."

It was in vain that he racked his brain to endeavour to find a solution to this strange problem ; and the longer he reflected, the more did he become confused and bewildered. At length, tired of the fruitless task, he hastened to one of the rooms below (where he had left his companions to keep watch, in case of any other threatened danger), resolved there to await the morning, which was now approaching.

It may be necessary before we proceed further, briefly to explain the cause of the fortunate, though unexpected re-appearance of Edward Stanley at the moment of danger, and when the liberty if not the very life of her he so fondly loved, was threatened.

Notwithstanding he was anxious to reach the place of his destination, he could not get rid of the strong impression which had taken such strong hold of his mind, that some fearful danger threatened Omelia, and that apprehension was strengthened as he imagined when the bholio glided on its way, that he observed the indistinct and shadowy forms of two persons standing near the spot where he had so hastily parted with our heroine. He hesitated, undecided how to act, whether to return or not.

While he was in this state of doubt and uncertainty, the boat proceeded on its way, and had nearly reached the opposite bank of the river, when a sudden impulse brought him to a decision, and he resolved to return, and to set his doubts and apprehensions at rest by reconnoitring about the villa.

His companions, who were anxious to reach the place of their destination, ventured to remonstrate with him ; but he was determined, and accordingly the bholi was put round, and slowly (for the wind had again gone down), proceeded on its return.

It was nearly an hour before it reached the shore, and mooring it near the same spot that they had done before, and leaving it in charge of one of his companions, Stanley, accompanied by the others, landed, and proceeded first to reconnoitre about the immediate locality, before he approached the villa. He saw nothing, however, to warrant his fears, for not a human being was to be seen, and all was silent. Darkness, too, had now fallen upon the earth, and he began to think that he had acted foolishly in returning.

Some time elapsed in this manner, and Stanley remained irresolute, but while he was thus deliberating with himself, he was thus startled by the sound of voices, which were followed by hasty footsteps, which satisfied him that some persons were approaching the spot where he and his companions were standing, and he drew them aside, and retired behind the shadow of some trees that grew close by, and from whence they could obtain a view of the persons who were approaching, without being observed themselves.

They came so near that Stanley and his friends could distinctly hear what they said,

One of them spoke in terms of abuse.

and the supicions of Stanley were increased when he heard him mention the names of Mr. Melville and his daughter, coupled with something wrong which had taken place at the villa. He looked more narrowly from the place of his concealment, and by the light of the moon recognised two of the domestics of Mr. Melville (those who had succeeded in making their escape from the ruffians who had made the murderous assault upon the villa) accompanied by several armed *Ryots* (peasants, who appeared much excited, and in breathless haste.

Stanley immediately issued from his place of concealment, and making himself known to the domestics, eagerly inquired what had happened. He was soon made acquainted with the particulars of the outrage, and his alarm and agitation may readily be imagined, for he feared that the worst had befallen Omelia and her friends.

With hurried steps they proceeded towards the villa, and they had not advanced many paces, when the shrieks of Omelia reached their ears, and increased their speed. The fortunate result is known to the reader.

CHAPTER VII.

THE NARROW ESCAPE.

Foaming with rage and disappointment at the unexpected frustration of their infamous plans (the more so, as the plunder they had obtained, in the excitement and confusion of the combat they had been compelled to leave behind them), Yunadar and his two companions (all that had escaped), hurried on their way towards the ancient ruins of the Mosque, where they had before met, and which having reached, they considered themselves (for the present, at any rate), safe from pursuit or detention.

On entering the ruins (which looked more solemn and gloomy in the dusky shadows of night), Yunadar, with folded arms, and pacing to and fro with disordered steps, gave unrestrained expression to the feelings of rage which filled his guilty breast, whilst Allyghur and the other ruffian stood sullenly by, and for a few minutes did not offer to interrupt him,

"May the curses of the Hindoo pursue the hated boy, and all his race, to destruction," he exclaimed in fierce tones, and his savage features frightfully distorted by the excitement of his brutal passions;

"and that he, too, who bears the form and features of the accursed destroyer of my unfortunate sister, should be the accursed means of frustrating our designs, at the very moment when their complete accomplishment seemed certain. The thought tortures and degrades me, and fills my breast with indignation. Oh, I will not, cannot rest, until I have had a terrible revenge."

"Aye," observed Allyghur, "fear not, Yunadar, though we have this night failed in the accomplishment, the hour of vengeance (that fearful vengeance which shall sweep all our enemies, with the resistless violence of the fierce hurricane, to destruction), will not, cannot be much longer delayed. Every hour marks the secret but rapid progress of the mighty plot, and soon shall the despairing and agonized shrieks of our hundreds of victims, rend the air in vain for mercy."

"Would that the frightful storm which has been so long gathering had already burst," cried Yunadar, "that I might view with feelings of savage delight (such only as can burn within the Sepoy's revengeful breast), the general slaughter, and gloat over with mockery and exultation the dying agony of the wretches we detest. Omelia, too, my daughter, faithless to her country and the religion of her forefathers, boldly acknowledges her love for this detested boy, and sets my authority at defiance. Now could I heap my maledictions on her head, and cast her from my heart for ever!"

"Calm the fury of your rage, Yunadar," said Allyghur, "and at least be thankful that you have escaped with life, and are still reserved to witness the ultimate triumph of our cause."

"The preservation of my life loses half its value," replied Yunadar, "since I owe it to the mercy of this hated Feringhee."

"And think you that he is indeed related to the man, who you say was the base betrayer of your sister?" interrogated Allyghur.

"He bears his name and resemblance," answered Yunadar, "and the conviction flashes on my brain that he is his son. When I gazed upon his features, and the tones of his voice smote mine ears, I could scarce believe but that it was the miscreant himself who stood before me, and like the savage tiger I could have sprung upon him, and feasted my hatred and revenge in his blood."

"Be patient, and the opportunity will yet arrive. But we do but waste our time in idle words, when promptitude of action is demanded. This failure is unfortunate, inasmuch as it will prevent our return to

our regiment, and the secret working of our designs among the troops. Our characters now are known, and death we know would be our certain doom should we be taken."

"True," coincided Yunadar; "but we must be careful to avoid the danger. Our plan is now to make the best of our way towards Delhi, and to join the disbanded troops who are there fast congregating; in a short time everything will be ripe for action, Oude, Delhi, Cawnpore, Lucknow, and, in fact, the whole length and breadth of British India (as it is vauntingly called), will be prepared and eager for the glorious work; then shall the final blow be struck, and triumph is certain."

No. 4.

"Yes," said Allyghur, "failure is impossible. But come, 'tis late, there is doubtless no one now about to observe us; so let us to the bungalow."

"Lead on," returned Yunadar; "I am ready to attend you."

Allyghur and the other having first taken the precaution to look forth, and ascertained that there was no one about to observe them, quitted the ruins, Yunadar slowly following, and the three villians bending their way towards a forest close by, and in which the bungalow or thatched hut, to which Allyghur had alluded, was situated, were soon lost in the darkness of the night, and among the thickly clustering trees.

It was noon-day, and Edward Stanley still lingered at the villa, loth to leave the society of his beloved Omelia, who seemed more than usually depressed in spirits, and seemed anxious to detain him. Flora Melville, whenever she was in their company during the morning, (her father having so far revived as to be able to obtain some refreshing sleep, and to dispense with her attendance), beheld with a painful feeling which she found it impossible to conquer the affectionate attentions which the young lieutenant paid to Omelia, and the evident pleasure with which that beauteous maiden received them; and, although she endeavoured to construe that feeling into anything but one of jealousy, she saw, with bitter anguish, that the fluttering hopes and wishes she had ventured to indulge in, were crushed; and, that Stanley could never return that love which he had so ardently excited in her susceptible bosom.

Omelia, (although she concealed the fact from the observation of Flora as well as she could), read her thoughts, and a pang of sympathy and regret shot through her heart, which was as painful as it was sincere.

Evening was fast approaching, and impatient of any further delay, the friends of Stanley, who had accompanied him, urged upon him the necessity of immediately departing. But still he hesitated to leave Omelia, whose tearful eyes, and the frequent sighs that escaped her lips, showed plainly (if indeed there had been anything wanting to convince him), the deep sorrow she felt at parting. Telling the men to proceed to the boat, and to wait for him at a certain part of the river which he mentioned, and promising to follow them quickly, he prepared to take his final leave of Omelia and her friends.

Unable to conceal her emotions, Flora brought the parting between her and Edward to as speedy a conclusion as possible, and with a bursting heart, she retired from the room leaving him and Omelia to themselves.

We will pass hastily over the scene which took place between our heroine and Edward Stanley; they again and again exchanged mutual vows of constancy, Stanley assuring her that, as he expected the regiment to which he belonged would shortly be sent to Delhi, (as that ancient and magnificent capital of the Moguls was at present principally garrisoned by native troops), he would previously endeavour to obtain leave of absence, so that they might meet again.

"Enough, dear Edward," said Omelia, affectionately, and suffering him to press a chaste kiss upon her lips,—"I am satisfied and will endeavour to bear our separation with fortitude. I do not, cannot doubt your honour, but again I pray you to impress upon your memory the words I yesterday uttered to you, namely:—"Whatever may be her destiny, although she may be for ever separated from all she holds dear on earth; though your love may change to deadliest hate and scorn; even though surrounded with every horror, the heart of Omelia must ever be yours, dear Edward; her every thought, her fondest wishes shall still cling to you; in the midst of every danger, *although unknown*, she will be ever by your side: her's shall be the hand to avert the threatened evil."

"Dear Omelia," said her lover, "there is an ambiguity about those words, through which I in vain seek to penetrate, but believe me, I will ever remember them with the deepest and fondest affection. Farewell, my own beloved, and may all good spirits continue to watch over and protect you from every danger."

With one fervent embrace they separated, and Omelia, with a throbbing heart and anxious eyes, from the window, watched his receding form across the garden till it disappeared in the distance.

Sad and foreboding, Edward Stanley bent his way towards the place where he expected to find his friends waiting for him with the bholio; but, to his surprise, they were not there. He looked along the river in each direction, but could see nothing of them or the vessel, and, imagining that they might probably have moored it in some part which was concealed from his observation by the thickly foliaged trees, which bathed their luxuriant branches in the water,—and, in order to wear away the time until his arrival, had landed, he sauntered along, deeply wrapped in meditation, and especially dwelling upon the last mysterious and emphatic words that Omelia had taken such pains to impress upon his memory. He felt unusually low-spirited, to which his remembrance of the singular remarks, and savage threats of Omelia's father, served not a little to contribute. And then the reflection of the agony it must cost the sensitive mind of such a gentle and amiable being to know that she was the daughter of such a parent, a man who contemplated crimes at which humanity must shudder, tortured him even more than all. He continued to ramble on, so completely occupied with these thoughts, that he heeded not whither he was going, until running against the trunk of a tree, he looked up, and discovered, to his vexation and surprise, that he had strayed from the river's bank, and was now in the midst of a dreary forest, the darkness of which was only occasionally broken by the faint light of the moon, which at intervals peeped through the branches of the trees.

He paused, and what to do, or which way to turn in order to regain the bank of the river he was at a loss to conjecture.

Thinking that probably there might be some one strolling about the forest, who would direct him, he shouted aloud, but the echo of his own voice was the only answer he received, and he was in the same state of doubt and perplexity as before.

He could not but reproach himself for his thoughtlessness and folly, and felt keenly for the alarm which Omelia and her friends would naturally experience should the men in charge of the bholio, not finding him come according to promise, return to the villa to inquire after him.

It was useless, however, to stand thinking, regretting, and inactive, and seeing a part of the forest to the right more open than the rest; and hoping it might lead to some habitation where he might obtain the information he required, he struck into it, every now and then calling aloud, but without any favourable results, and his vexation, alarm, and bewilderment increased. Still he persevered and proceeded, especially as the way gradually became less intricate, and he was in hopes that he might reach the boundary of the forest in the direction he was taking.

At length, as he strained his eyes in trying to penetrate the dim obscurity, he fancied he beheld a faint light glimmering among the foliage at a distance, and which seemed to proceed from the window of some dwelling; and yet the idea of any person taking up their residence in such a gloomy and lonely place as this appeared to be preposterous, and he almost abandoned the thought as soon as it had risen to his imagination. Still he beheld it glimmering at intervals at a distance (although he was approaching it gradually), and he felt thoroughly convinced that he could not be mistaken. He continued to watch it narrowly, until at last it faded away from his eager vision, and all was once more buried in profound darkness.

Again he stood bewildered, and at a loss how to proceed, and he began to grow impatient and to curse his folly and imprudence in tarrying so long at the villa instead of accompanying the man at once to the bholio.

However, it was useless now wasting the time in vain regret and self-reproach, he therefore again pushed on his way as near as he could in the direction from whence the light proceeded, and he had not gone far

when it again appeard, and he *now* felt convinced that it shone from the window of some human dwelling.

Yet what description of person or persons might the occupants of that lonely habitation, situated in so wild and dreary a spot be? The present disaffection which was known to exist among a number of the Sepoys, and the uncertainty of the whereabouts of those who had been disbanded, and who, goaded on by a feeling of vengeance, were ready for the perpetration of any crime, rendered the utmost precaution necessary. Besides, this was a likely place for *Decoits* (robbers), and, although he had his sword with him, what could his single arm do, probably against numbers? The young officer, however, had faced danger too often to know fear now, and therefore hurried on, till at last he came upon a common thatched bungalow, which stood alone, and was completely overshadowed by tall trees, whose long branches intertwined above the roof. It was from the window of this habitation that the light which had attracted his attention, and guided his footsteps thither, gleamed, and he quickly but cautiously advanced towards the door, which was standing partially open, and he could hear voices within engaged in conversation, but being in the language of the country, of which he knew but very little, he could not understand it. However, it seemed to be spoken in tones of anger and excitement, and that, of course, rendered him the more doubtful and cautious.

Determined, nevertheless, to gratify his curiosity, he advanced to the window on tiptoe, and peeped in. It was a large, wretched looking room, and was evidently the residence of the poorest persons, or those of the most questionable character. At the further end of the room were seated two men, with their backs towards him, and from the position in which they were sitting, he had but an indistinct view of their persons.

They were talking very loudly, and here and there Stanley could distinguish a word which gave him no very favourable idea of their characters, but as they could not observe him, he continued to watch them narrowly, especially as his curiosity was in some measure excited.

Presently they turned suddenly round with their faces towards the window, and the light falling full upon their features, he was enabled to notice them distinctly. His surprise may be readily imagined, when he recognized in those of one of them, the father of Omelia, and in the other, Allyghur.

He could not help giving utterance to an

exclamation of astonishment on beholding them. The sound caught their ears, and starting to their feet and looking towards the window before Stanley could get away, they seemed to recognize him, and made a rush to the door.

Knowing the danger to which he was now exposed, for his sword would avail but little against firearms which the Sepoys doubtless possessed. Stanley dashed forward towards the thickest part of the forest at the top of his speed; but he had not proceeded far, when the report of pistols smote his ear, and the bullets wizzed past him, and so close, that it was only by a miracle he escaped from being hit, at the same time he heard the shouts and curses of his pursuers, and their quick footsteps among the grass, which convinced him of the imminent danger in which he was placed, and increased his speed; although, had it not been for the painful recollection that one of them was the parent of Omelia, he would not have hesitated for a moment in boldly facing them, for he had every confidence in his good sword, and the ability with which he could use it; but as it was, he made with all the speed he could for a thicket which he saw before him, hoping that he there might be able to elude the villians, but before he could reach it, they again fired at him, and he felt himself slightly wounded or grazed in the shoulder. The next moment he gained the thicket, and plunged into it, but he could hear their curses and their footsteps more distinctly, as they evidently gained upon him.

He turned, however, in another direction, and dashed on for some distance, when he was at last compelled to pause to take breath, and drew his sword and stood prepared for the worst, as it was not likely, if he were attacked, but that he would defend himself to the last. He listened, but no sounds met his ears, and he was in hopes that Yunadar and his guilty associate had at length abandoned the pursuit.

He looked anxiously around him. The moon had emerged from behind the heavy clouds that for some time had hid her silvery face, and certainly the prospect before him was anything but cheering. Nothing could be more wild and dreary, and again he cursed his folly which had placed him in so awkward and dangerous a dilemma.

He diverged a little to the left, which he thought was the likeliest to lead him into the right direction for the river's bank, and continued to hurry on for some time, till at length his further progress was stopped by a large stream of water, with lofty rocks stretching from either side, and down one of which a foaming cateract dashed with deaf-

ening sound, and adding fresh terrors to the scene.

A rudely constructed bridge formed from the trunks of trees, and with scarcely room for more than one person to pass at a time, crossed from rock to rock, one of which Stanley proceeded to ascend, and after some difficulty, (for the rock was rather steep), he succeeded in gaining the bridge, but had not advanced many paces on to it, when a couple of pistols were again discharged at him, (fortunately without effect), and he again perceived Yunadar and Allyghur toiling up the rock he had just quitted, in pursuit of him.

He hurried across the frail and dangerous bridge as quick as he could, at one time almost overbalancing himself, and fortunately gained the opposite rock, and began to descend it, before his pursuers had stepped a foot upon the bridge.

He hurried on his way beneath the shelter of the rocks, until he had reached a considerable distance, and looking back, he could not perceive anything of Yunadar or his companion, and the moon again becoming obscured behind dark clouds, it was impossible that they could observe him, so at last he thought he had fairly escaped them.

His situation was still anything but an agreeable one, the place was perfectly strange to him, and, for anything he knew, he might be wandering entirely from the right track, and at last become so entangled in a maze of difficulties that he could not extricate himself. The time, too, which had elapsed, and the apprehensions that would be entertained by his friends for his safety, all added to his dismay. He mustered up all his patience and resolution, nevertheless, and continued on his way, with a faint hope that he might yet meet with some friendly person who would direct him.

He had proceeded for some distance, when he thought he heard voices calling from a contrary direction, but, uncertain whether they might be friends or foes, he had not at present much cause for gratification.

At length the sounds approached nearer, and he could perceive lights moving about among the trees, as if from torches, and presently he was overjoyed to hear his name distinctly called, and that too in a voice which he immediately recognised as that of one of his friends, and he shouted aloud in answer, and made his way as quick as he could in the direction of the lights. In a few minutes more, emerging from behind some of the most thickly clustering trees, he came in sight of the whole party, which consisted of two of his companions who had come with him in the bholio, and several of the domestics of Mr. Melville, armed, and carrying torches.

They recognised him at the same moment, and hurrying forward, the pleasure of the meeting on both sides may be readily imagined.

Having waited for him till their patience was quite exhausted, his friends had returned to the villa, to ascertain what had detained him, and when Omelia and Mr. Melville and his daughter were informed of the fact that he had not joined his companions at the place where they had been ordered to wait for him, they became seriously alarmed for his safety, especially after what had so recently occurred at the villa, and armed domestics were immediately despatched, with the two men from the boat, in search of him.

Stanley felt keenly for the terrible state of suspense and uncertainty he knew Omelia would be in, and would gladly have returned himself to the villa, but he had already prolonged his stay far beyond the time that his leave of absence permitted, and must now make all the haste he could to rejoin his regiment. He therefore despatched the domestics as quickly as possible to the villa, to quiet the apprehensions of the inmates, and with a message to Omelia, and he and his companions hastened towards the bank of the river, from which he was informed they were distant about a mile. This they soon traversed, and Stanley having entered the bholio, was at last fairly on the way to the place of his destination.

CHAPTER VIII.

SCENE IN THE RUINS OF THE OLD MOSQUE.

For several weeks subsequent to the events recorded in the preceding chapters, nothing particular, or worthy of recording, had occurred at the villa. Mr. Melville had quite recovered from the injury he had received on the night of the outrage, and had it in contemplation to remove to his other residence in Delhi.

The aspect of affairs in different parts of the country daily became more gloomy, alarming, and threatening; and the want of proper energy, activity, and precaution on the part of the Indian Government, was most extraordinary and highly reprehensible.

The seeds of that mighty revolt, which has since resulted in such scenes of horror and savage atrocity, almost unparalleled in the records of history, were already deeply, widely sown; the angry storm clouds were rapidly gathering, threatening every hour to burst over the whole length and breadth of the land; the train was already laid; dark rumours were abroad, men began to look suspiciously at each other; circumstances took place which gave many of the rumours just alluded to the importance of facts, yet the authorities were either in a profound state of ignorance, or appeared to treat the matter with perfect contempt and indifference, and thus the mutineers were allowed every opportunity for the furtherance of their monstrous designs.

For several years it must have been apparent, even to a mere superficial observer, that the Government had lost all hold on the attachment of the Sepoys. Avarice had become their idol, the love of glory and military enterprise had ceased to act as a stimulus to zeal and discipline. The European officers, constantly withdrawn for staff and civil duties, no longer afforded the men the influence of example; war had ceased to furnish exciting employment, the pledge of allegiance had ceased to be binding.

The annexation of the kingdom of Oude to the British possessions in the year 1856, the king being deposed and sent to Calcutta, was considered a hardship and a wrong, and no doubt served to fan the flame of that rebellion which has since spread with such fearful rapidity over a vast extent of the country, and with such dreadful consequences; for the suite of the deposed nawaub, or king, some seven or eight hundred men of Oude, whom he was allowed to retain in his service, are synonymous with villains of the worst dye,—sensualists, intriguers, and who, as has been so fatally seen, were only waiting the opportunity to become murderers, or rather fiends in human shape. Then came the introduction of the Minié rifle, the cartridges for which require to be greased before they can be used. This was done with oil and wax, and a small quantity of mutton fat, to which the Hindoo has no objection. But the rumour got abroad (it is not satisfactorily known how), that the grease was composed of the fat of oxen and pigs, and thus the idea becoming prevalent among the native troops that the Government intended to Christianize them all, and the greased cartridge became the signal for revolt. In vain the European officers endeavoured to persuade them that they were labouring under a delusion; they turned a deaf ear to their assertions, their arguments, or persuasions; the fatal impression had got too strong a hold of them to be removed, and regiment after regiment refused to perform its duties, and the mutiny gradually assumed the most formidable and alarming aspect.

Such is a brief account of the origin of the Indian war, and so matters stood at that period of our tale, of which we are now writing.

Omelia watched the progress of the revolt with the most painful and fearful suspense and anxiety, and looked forward to the future events with the most dismal forebodings; for who knew better than herself what the character of her countrymen were, when their bad passions were excited, and they were goaded on to deeds of vengeance! She knew that their bloodthirsty propensities, when thus stimulated, had no limits, and that they would not hesitate to perpetrate the most hideous crimes in order to obtain the accomplishment of their wishes. Helpless women might appeal to them with all the eloquence that the Almighty has gifted his creatures with, for themselves, their husbands, and their innocent children,—it would not stay their murderous hands, or arrest them in their bloody and inhuman purpose.

Already in her affrighted imagination she saw the agonized looks of the unfortunate victims; heard their appalling shrieks; the piteous cries of their darling little ones; listened to the dying groans of the slaughtered, and heard the frightful yells and shouts of exultation uttered by their atrocious murderers; and her heart sickened at the dreadful thought, and the blood ran cold as ice throughout her veins.

And her father, too—he, it seemed, had made up his mind to act a prominent part in this dreadful tragedy; and too well was she aware that when he had formed the resolution to perform anything, be it ever so desperate or atrocious, nothing whatever could move him from his purpose; he was inexorable. How the poor girl shuddered at this thought, while feelings of shame and indignation swelled her bosom.

But Omelia's chief anxiety was for Stanley and her benefactors, (though she carefully avoided mentioning anything of her terrible fears to the latter, lest she should excite their alarm, and thus unnerve them for the dreadful trial she was confident was in store for them). She knew that when the work of destruction had commenced, not a single European, who should have the misfortune to fall into the hands of the sanguinary miscreants, would be spared from the general slaughter; and she trembled to think of the frightful fate which might too probably befal them and her lover.

"But shall I not exert myself as much as possible to avert the horrors I too fearfully forbode?" she exclaimed, and the expression of her eyes became more brilliant, her features were animated with enthusiasm, and the noble feelings that glowed within her breast, seemed to give additional dignity to her fine majestic form; "shall I stand tamely by and witness these frightful scenes of crime with passive indifference? No; even though I perish I will resist those monstrous designs to the last. It shall be seen that in the defence of the good, the virtuous, and the innocent, the humble Sepoy's daughter can become the heroine!"

Nothing could be more strikingly noble than the appearance of the beautiful Omelia as she gave utterance to these words, and all who could have seen her at that moment, must have been lost in wonder, love, and admiration. But quickly a melancholy change came over her fine features; tears were in her eyes, and frequent sighs escaped her heaving bosom. Her thoughts were fixed on Stanley, and then the form of Flora Melville seemed to interpose between them and happiness, and to scowl upon her with looks of envy, jealousy, and reproach.

Six weeks had now elapsed since her and Edward Stanley had seen each other; Omelia had heard nothing of him, and the most conflicting feelings of love, hope, doubt, and suspicion tortured her mind. Was he ill? had his regiment been drafted to some distant part of the country? or had he forgotten the solemn promise he had made her when they last parted, (namely, that he would obtain leave of absence as soon as possible, and hasten to meet her again), and repenting of his vows, after the shameful conduct of her father, had resolved to see her no more? Oh, no, she dared not encourage that fearful, that torturing th——

She ——— stood upon the garden terrace, as she thus reflected, and in the same striking and anxious attitude as she had done on the eventful evening which commenced our tale. But there was a weight of care and suspense upon her brow, which did not characterize it on that occasion.

It was a lovely morning, and the bright sun shed a flood of gold upon all around, and imparting to the magnificent scenery all the gorgeous enchantment conceived by the most fervid and exuberant imagination of fairy land. The clear, transparent river had an unusually animated appearance from the number and variety of the fancifully decorated vessels that rode gaily on its pelucid bosom, looking still more gay and picturesque in the radiant sunlight.

On the distant horizon were to be seen the stupendous mountains of the Himalaya, through the thick forests of banana-trees, where the great serpent of Hindostan was wont to secrete itself, and darting suddenly upon the unsuspecting traveller, deal him an immediate and frightful death. The Taj Mehal, that splendid edifice before spoken of, was also seen to great advantage in the golden and dazzling light of the great orb of day.

While our heroine thus stood, lost in meditation, she was startled by the sudden appearance of a *Peon*, (messenger) before her, who, after making a low obeisance, presented her with a small *chiti*, (note or letter) enclosed in a handsome envelope, and then retired to a respectful distance while she perused it, and to await her answer.

Omelia took the letter with a trembling hand, and her eyes sparkled with pleasure, and her eager heart throbbed with expectation as she gazed upon the well known characters of the superscription which were in the handwriting of her lover.

With anxious haste she opened it, and she had no sooner perused the first line than she pressed it rapturously to her lips.

This precious epistle set all the maiden's doubts and suspicions at rest, and she blushed and reproached herself to think that she had ever been so ungenerous as to entertain them. It breathed the most fervent and eloquent vows of love and constancy,—stated that he had not before been able to procure leave of absence from his regiment, that he was now at Agra, but as he felt reluctant to come to the villa, and did not wish his being in the neighbourhood to be known to Mr. Melville and his daughter, he requested that she would meet him that evening at a certain hour, which he named, in the ruins of the old Mosque, near the banks of the river.

Omelia having perused the contents of the note which removed such a burthen of care and anxiety from her mind, again and again raised it to her lips and covered it with her kisses.

"Yes, dear, faithful Stanley," she ejaculated, as she carefully refolded the letter, and placed it in her bosom; "I will indeed be at the place of appointment, and long and tedious will the hours appear to be that must intervene ere the happy time arrives."

The messenger now ventured once more to approach her, and bending low, waited Omelia's answer.

"I will not fail," was the laconic answer she returned for the peon's conveyance to Lieutenant Stanley, and he immediately disappeared.

Omelia remained a short time longer on the terrace to collect herself, so that her emotion might not attract the attention and excite the curiosity of Mr. Melville and his daughter; and she then with a light heart returned to the villa, where, after a short time passed in conversation with her friends, she made an excuse to retire to her chamber, and there she prepared herself for the joyful meeting in the evening.

At length the time for her to depart arrived, and she arose from her seat, opened the room door, and after listening on the top of the stairs for a few moments in order to ascertain whether or not there was any one about to observe her, and finding that all was still in the house, with noiseless foot steps and a palpitating heart, she descended the stairs, and issued forth into the garden.

There was no one there, and she tripped quickly across she garden, and crossing the terrace, hastened on her way to the place of appointment.

She had not been gone many minutes, when Flora Melville having something to say to her, tapped gently at her chamber door, and receiving no answer, she opened it and looked in, and was surprised and disappointed that she was not there. She was about to leave the room again, and to hasten to the garden, thinking that she might there meet her, when her eye fell upon an open letter lying on the floor, and a strong feeling of curiosity and suspicion, which she could not resist, urged her to examine the contents, but she had scarcely perused the first line, when a deathly faintness came over her, convulsive sobs escaped her bosom, and she sunk powerless in a chair, covering her face with her hands.

The reader will scarcely need to be told that it was Edward Stanley's letter to Omelia, and which she on leaving the room had accidentally dropped.

It was some minutes before poor Flora could sufficiently recover herself to again take up the letter, and it was with a heart full almost to bursting, and eyes filled with tears, that she then proceeded to read it throughout; and at the conclusion, with a burst of agony, mingled with feelings of jealousy and mortified pride, she again buried her face in her hands and sobbed bitterly.

"It is done," she sighed at last, in a voice scarcely articulate; "all hope is now at an end, and I feel the humiliation of my situation most keenly. Alas, Edward Stanley loves the poor, humble, portionless Indian girl, and despises her who would lay down her very life to win but a smile from him—her who stands in the position of Omelia's *mistress*."

A slight expression of scorn passed over the amiable features of Flora as she gave utterance to the latter word, but she quickly checked the unworthy feeling, and in a voice of the deepest melancholy and regret, she sighed—

"Cruel, cruel Edward, if you could not love me, at least I deserved not to be shunned by you as a thing of hate. And you, Omelia, surely your conduct towards me in this respect, is most ungenerous, most unkind, not to say ungrateful. I was at least worthy of your confidence. And then the impropriety of your conduct in making secret assignations with one whom you must have known had made so fond, so powerful, so indellible an impression on my heart. Oh, how torturing is all this to my mind."

She again wept bitterly, and her heart was a prey to the most poignant anguish. But after awhile she struggled with her feelings, and rising hastily from her chair, as a sudden thought seemed to strike her, and with comparative calmness of demeanour, she said,—

"But I will no longer endure this insulting scorn without at least resenting it. I will demand an explanation."

She threw the letter on the spot on which she had found it, and then with a look of mysterious meaning and determination, she hastily quitted the apartment.

In the meantime, full of hope and expectation, Omelia bent her way to the place of assignation, where she shortly arrived without meeting any one on the road, and after some slight hesitation, she entered the ruins, and looked anxiously around but did not observe any one,

The moon had risen, and shed a chaste and mellow light upon the ruins of the old mosque, and upon a portion of the river, which might be seen through an opening at the back.

All was solemnity and silence in that sacred place; and Omelia felt a sensation of awe steal over her as she gazed upon them; while at the same time she could not help giving way to a feeling of disappointment at not seeing Stanley there anxiously waiting her arrival, but for which rebuked herself immediately.

She stood for a minute or two in the middle of the ruins, and gazed around her and listened, and at length she heard the hollow echo of approaching footsteps, and with a palpitating heart, and all proper precaution, not knowing whether it might be

him whom she so anxiously awaited, or some stranger, she silently concealed herself behind one of the broken columns, till she could see who the person was.

She was not long kept in suspense; she saw the tall figure of a man advancing down the centre of the ruins, his form enveloped in a military cloak, she heard her name repeated in a tender whispering voice, and with an exclamation of joy, she rushed from the place of her concealment, as she recognized her lover.

With all the fervour of sincere love, Stanley clasped her to his throbbing bosom, and pressed his lips upon her beauteous cheek; endearments which Omelia returned with equal ardour and delight.

It is unnecessary to relate all that occurred at this interview; the mutual vows of love they exchanged with each other, and the happiness they expressed at this meeting. Time flew away unnoticed, and the interview had been prolonged to more than a couple of hours, ere they thought of separating.

"In another month, my dearest Omelia," said Stanley, "my regiment is ordered to Delhi, which at present is very inefficiently garrisoned, and as you say that Mr. Melville also has it in contemplation to remove there, I trust that we shall have frequent opportunities of seeing each other."

"And shall we not meet again till then, dear Edward?" said the fair Indian girl, with a sigh, and a look of melancholy.

"Yes, love," answered Stanley; "I shall not return to my regiment for a couple of days; so, to-morrow evening, if you will consent, I will be here at the same hour that we have met this. But I pray you keep the fact of my being in this neighbourhood a secret from Mr. Melville and his daughter. Flora I sincerely esteem for her numerous virtues; but I cannot consent to feed, by my presence, the unfortunate passion which I have too much reason to fear she entertains for me."

An exclamation of agony now startled them both, and as they looked with eager curiosity towards the spot from whence it seemed to proceed, a female form glided hastily past at the back of the ruins, and instantly disappeared.

"Ah, have we then been watched?" cried Stanley in a tone of indignation; "let me follow and demand an explanation from this insolent inquisitive."

"Stay, dear Edward, I implore you," said the agitated Omelia, detaining him; "I caught a glimpse of her features by the light of the moon, as she hurried away, and I am certain that it was poor Flora."

"Flora!" repeated Stanley, "and has

she then descended to the meanness of turning listener? I must see her, Omelia."

"No, no, not for the world, Edward, at present," returned our heroine; "poor lady, how I pity her, and to think that I should be the unhappy cause of disappointing her hopes, and inflicting this bitter anguish on her heart."

"You unjustly reproach yourself, Omelia, and——"

"Ah! no," interrupted Omelia, with a sigh, "had I never encouraged your addresses, which I should not have done, when I knew how fondly she loved you; she might in time have won your heart, and——"

"She could never have won more than my esteem, which she now possesses," re-

No. 5.

plied Stanley, "while you, my own sweet Omelia, must ever, even had you rejected my suit, must ever have owned my heart's warmest adoration."

"She is more worthy of your love than the poor, lowly Indian girl can ever hope to be, and though it might break my heart to do so, I would gladly resign my claim to you rather than see her wretched for ever."

"Generous, noble-minded girl," exclaimed . Stanley, enthusiastically, and again caressing her fondly, "what honour do those amiable sentiments reflect on you, but it must not, cannot be."

"We must part, dear Edward," replied the maiden, in an agitated voice, "to remain longer here now that we have been discovered together, might create unworthy suspicions. Farewell; to-morrow evening, even at all hazards, and in spite of whatever consequences may follow, we will meet again."

"Thanks, thanks, sweet Omelia," replied the young man, rapturously kissing her; "remember, here, and at the same hour we have met this evening. But at least let me accompany you part of the way to the villa."

"Oh, no," said our heroine, "there is no necessity for it; there is nothing whatever to fear, and I would much rather go alone. I shall be fully prepared to meet the reproaches of Flora, although they will cause me many a bitter pang of regret. Once more adieu. dear Edward, till we meet again."

"Farewell, best and dearest of women," cried Stanley, as he once more enfolded her in his arms, and embraced her fondly.

Omelia then disengaged herself from his embrace, and with a look which showed the emotions of her heart, stepped hastily from the old ruins.

CHAPTER IX.

REPROACH.—A DESPERATE RESOLVE.

What were the emotions of poor Flora Melville, as she hurried towards the villa from the ruins of the old mosque? So great indeed was the agony and excitement of her·feelings that she was frequently compelled to stop, as her trembling limbs could scarce support her. Her brain was giddy with racking thought; and her heart palpitated violently against her side, as though it were ready to burst its tenement.

If the letter which she had perused, had not convinced her of the total annihilation of her hopes, the interview she had just witnessed between the lovers, and the words she had heard from the lips of Stanley himself were more than sufficient to remove all further doubt from her distracted mind. Omelia, the poor, dependent, simple Indian girl possessed his undivided affections; Omelia reigned the supreme empress of his heart, while she (Flora), could lay claim only at most, to his esteem and friendship. Oh, how cold were those sentiments, compared with the fond hopes and wishes she had ventured to cherish. Wounded pride, a keen sense of humiliation, sorrow, regret, jealousy, despair, these were the contending passions that struggled in her breast, and tortured and bewildered her senses. For the first time since they had known each other, a feeling of animosity against Omelia, which she in vain endeavoured to conquer, took possession of her, and she resolved to load her with her reproaches, and to accuse her of hypocrisy and artifice.

But then, would not that be most ungenerous, most unjust? Yes, it would, and, when the first ebullition of her feelings had exhausted itself, she blushed to think that she should ever have entertained, even for an instant, an idea so totally unworthy of her. Well did she know the virtue, the purity of Omelia's nature, and that she would shrink disgusted and appalled from even the bare contemplation of wrong. It was her superior qualities, she was convinced, that had won the love of Edward Stanley; it was his manly merits that alone had excited reciprocal sentiments in her breast; honour, truth, and sincerity alone guided her conduct; gratitude to her (Flora), and her father had ever characterised her actions; what then, had she to blame in her; in what respect did she merit her reproaches? She tried to check the storm of angry feeling which had been fast gathering in her mind towards the innocent Indian maiden, and to submit to the disappointment of those hopes, which, knowing the love that existed between the young Englishman and Omelia, she ought never to have entertained. With fortitude and resignation she tried to do so; but the task was a difficult one, and one which Flora, at the present time found it almost impossible to accomplish.

Then she could not but accuse herself of an act of meanness in becoming the eavesdropper; and prying into their secrets. The expression of her emotions in the ruins, and which she had found it impossible to restrain, must have betrayed her; she was confident that the quick eye of Omelia had observed her as she hurried away, and how utter contemptible must she now appear in their eyes.

"Oh, Stanley," she sighed; "why did I ever behold you, since it could only be the means of engendering a passion in my breast, which you can never return, and I feel it equally impossible to conquer? Oh Omelia, much do I wrong you; sadly do I repay the sisterly affection you have ever evinced for me, but still can I not help viewing with envy the love which Edward Stanley undoubtedly bears you."

Tears gushed to her eyes, as she uttered these words, and her emotion was so great that she was compelled to pause, and lean against the trunk of a tree, till she could in some measure recover herself. But at length fearing that Omelia, on leaving Stanley might overtake her, when she was so ill-prepared to encounter her: or that her father might feel alarmed at her unexpected absence from the villa, especially after the daring outrage committed by Yunadar (although she knew not that it was he), and his base associates in crime, only a few weeks previously, she struggled against her feelings as well as she could, and, after looking round, anxious to discover whether or not she was observed by any one, she once more hastened on her way; her heart palpitating violently, and her brain distracted by the various torturing thoughts that crowded upon it.

She had got to within a short distance of the villa, when a flood of light, apparently proceeding from torches, suddenly shone from amongst the trees before her, and immediately afterwards, several of the domestics, who had doubtless been sent by her father in search of her, appeared, and evinced their satisfaction on beholding her.

And now poor Flora almost dreaded to meet her father, for in her present state of agitation it would be impossible for her to conceal the truth; for although he well knew the sentiment that glowed within her breast towards Lieutenant Stanley, and deeply regretted the freezing coldness and indifference, if not absolute disdain with which they were received by him, she feared that he would blame her for the feelings of jealousy and curiosity that had prompted her to watch their secret interview in the ruins.

However, she knew his kind and indulgent nature, and how deeply he must sympathize with her in the disappointment and destruction of all her fondest hopes, and she therefore took courage, and entering the villa, proceeded at once, though with agitated step and a beating heart, to the apartment of Mr. Melville, whom she found anxiously waiting for her, and affectionately greeted her. He was alarmed, however, by the paleness of her looks, and the agitation of her demeanour, and she, unable to restrain her feelings, after a vain effort to do so, burst into tears, and threw herself sobbing, and completely overwhelmed with grief upon his bosom.

"Flora, my dear child," said her father, with affectionate solicitude, "for Heaven's sake, what is the meaning of this? Why are you thus powerfully agitated?"

She tried to speak, but sobs checked her utterance, and mingled feelings of shame, and mortified pride, and melancholy, torturing regret, swelled her bosom. and stifled the words in her throat.

"Why do you hesitate, Flora?" hastily and anxiously demanded Mr. Melville; "come, come, my poor girl, compose yourself; you know how it pains me at any time

to see you unhappy, for you are my only joy, my comfort, my hope, in the winter of my age, and have been doubly dear to me, since it pleased the Almighty to take your beloved mother to Himself; your joys are my joys, your sorrows are also mine, and must be participated in by me. Now, my dear child, you surely cannot, will not hesitate to confide in me; tell me, what has happened to excite your feelings in this painful manner?"

"Oh, my dear father," she sobbed, and still encircling his neck with her fair arms, and weeping upon his bosom; "my heart trembles, and my tongue falters to disclose the torturing, the humiliating truth. And, you, I fear, will blame me for——"

"Blame you, Flora," hastily interrupted Mr. Melville, imprinting a fond, confiding kiss upon his beauteous daughter's cheek; "oh, no, no, no, how much you wrong me by that ungenerous supposition. Flora Melville I know can never be guilty of a single act which can call forth her father's censure."

"Beloved father," said the affectionate girl, in a voice still half stifled with the power of her struggling emotions, "oh, may kind Heaven forbid that I should ever prove myself unworthy of such loving confidence."

"You cannot,—you will not. But I beseech you not to keep me longer in suspense. Why did you leave home so abruptly and so secretly this evening? And what has caused this violent grief? Omelia, too, she is also still absent, and——"

"Name her not for the love of Heaven my father," interrupted Flora, in tones of the most poignant anguish; "she it is who is the cause of all; 'tis her who has crushed your daughter's hopes, blighted all her brightest prospects, and rendered her for ever wretched."

"Ah!" exclaimed Mr. Melville, in a voice of indignation, "and is it possible that she, the fair object of my solicitude and sympathy; that being so gentle and so loving, yet so noble and heroic, on whom, Heaven knows, I have lavished all the affection of a parent; is it possible that she can be so ungrateful as to wound the feelings of those who have so fondly cherished her, and who would willingly do anything to serve her and promote her happiness? Oh, that such cruel hypocrisy should inhabit the breast of one so lovely."

"Oh spare her, my dear father, I implore you," ejaculated Flora, "the poor girl merits not your reproaches, and 'tis I who have wronged her in speaking of her as I have done."

"What mean you, Flora? You speak

in problems. and I cannot understand you. Explain yourself."

"Grant me your indulgence," said Flora, "and I will endeavour to do so; but, alas, how painful is the task which devolves upon me."

She made a powerful effort to conquer her emotions, and, at length, in a hesitating voice, and as briefly as possible, she related the painful facts, and to which Mr. Melville listened with mingled feelings of wounded pride, sorrow, and regret.

"My poor child," he sighed, when Flora had concluded, "how sincerely do I pity you and feel for you in the disappointment of your hopes. Alas! that this unfortunate passion should ever have been created in your breast. Would to heaven that you and Stanley had never met. But does he dare to treat the daughter of Mr. Melville with cold neglect, indifference, and even contempt; to shun her presence as though she were something repulsive and unworthy of his respect. Has he become so lost to the feelings of a gentleman, so insensible to what is due to your noble worth, my child, as to insult you thus? Such conduct must not, shall not, go unresented; and Omelia, too, she has deceived us both, she has played the part of the hypocrite, with her fawning smiles and pretended affection. She has abused the kindness of those who have been everything to her since the death of her mother, and would now recklessly, wantonly throw herself into the arms of one who never can or will make her his wife."

"Hold, hold, my dear father, I implore you," said Flora, in a voice of extreme agitation, and shocked to find the painful effect which her words had caused; "oh, how much indeed you wrong the noble-minded Stanley and the amiable girl on whom he has bestowed his affections, and who——"

Before she could finish the sentence, an exclamation of indignation and grief was heard; the room door was thrown hastily open, and Omelia, in an attitude at once dignified and impressive, her features marked with a mingled expression of scorn, wounded pride, indignation, reproach, and conscious innocence, and with her full black eyes fixed sternly upon Mr. Melville and his daughter, stood before them.

"Omelia proudly, scornfully, emphatically repudiates the opprobrious observations that have been applied to her," she haughtily exclaimed, for she had overheard the words spoken rashly and thoughtlessly by her benefactor; "she boldly, fearlessly gives the lie to those who would thus meanly misrepresent her, and dare to question the virtue and integrity of her conduct,

"Omelia," said Mr. Melville, in a tremulous voice, and somewhat abashed by her words and manner.

"Enough, sir," interrupted our heroine, "you have uttered cruel observations that have gone to the heart of the poor humble creature of your bounty, and which so undeserved, so unjust, she little thought could ever have escaped your lips. I may forgive, but oh, 'tis impossible that I can ever forget them. Alas, what have I done that I should be thus scandalized and degraded?"

Overpowered by the emotions which these melancholy thoughts created, the poor girl turned away her head and wept bitterly.

The anguish of Flora was unconquerable, and while she could not but blame the undue severity and injustice of her father's observations as regarded Omelia, she reproached herself most keenly for the part she had played, and would now gladly have recalled that which had been the cause of so much misery to all concerned.

She tenderly approached our heroine (who had drawn herself aside, and with her face buried in her hands, was giving the most unrestrained indulgence to her emotions), and in a scarcely audible voice attempted to give utterance to some words of conciliation; while Mr. Melville, who found he had been too rash and ungerous in the observations he had made use of, felt the deepest regret, and, taking the hand of Omelia, was about to offer an apology, when she quickly recovered her composure and self-possession, and, with a look of dignity and offended pride, at the same time not unmingled with respect, she said—

"Hold, sir; the poor humble creature of your bounty needs not, neither will she receive an apology for that stigma on her character which nothing can atone for. She is sufficiently redressed in the consciousness of her own innocence, and the purity of her motives, and she feels herself too proud and independent (spite of her poverty), to deny her heart's affections, and the being on whom they are bestowed. She had hoped that her conduct hitherto entitled her to respect, but it seems that she laboured under a delusion, and can only express her deep regret that she so far deceived herself."

"Omelia," observed Mr. Melville; I do indeed acknowledge that I was too impetuous in the remarks I made to my daughter, unconscious of you overhearing them, and fain would I apologize and retract them."

"I seek no apology, sir," returned the Indian girl, haughtily, "neither will I accept it. Omelia will never submit to become the slave of any person's will, or to have her conduct questioned, and since it seems, she has lost your confidence, she will no longer be beholden to your *charity*. She admits that she owes yourself and Miss Flora a debt of gratitude which she fondly hopes it will yet be in her power to repay tenfold. Farewell, sir, farewell Miss Melville, and rest assured that though, when absent, the poor Indian girl, may only possess your scorn, she will never cease to remember you with those feelings of regard and reverence that is due to those who have befriended her."

"Omelia, dear Omelia," ejaculated Flora, deeply affected, and taking her hand as she was about to depart; "oh, listen to me, I implore you; it is I who alone am to blame, and deeply do I regret that I should have been the unhappy cause of wounding your feelings. Forgive me, Omelia, and pardon, my dear father for the utterance of that which he did not, could not sincerely mean."

"I forgive you, lady, I pardon your father," replied our heroine, in a voice of emotion, and tears trembling in her eyes, "but since I have lost your confidence, self-respect commands me no longer to obtrude upon you with my presence. Farewell, and may all good spirits watch over your safety and happiness."

"Hear me, Omelia, I beg of you," said Mr. Melville, but she had hastily withdrawn her hand from that of Flora, and abruptly quitted the apartment; and they stood for a minute or two abashed and confounded by the dignity and mystery of her conduct.

"Oh, my father," said Flora, at length, in a voice of the deepest emotion, "what have we said,—what have we done? Poor Omelia, oh how much do I feel we have wronged her, noble-hearted, amiable girl that she is. Why did my rash tongue reveal my thoughts, since it has been the means of leading to so painful a result as this? But her words and manner alarm me. There is some terrible meaning in them which I tremble to endeavour to penetrate. Let me hasten to her, and——"

"Stay, Flora," said her father, detaining her, "you had better not interrupt her in her present state of mind. I own that I was wrong in the hasty observations I made use of, but the morning, I have no doubt, will satisfactorily explain all. I know the good sense and generous nature of Omelia too well, to believe that she can long harbour any angry feeling. Come, my child, 'tis getting late, and we had better separate for the night. Compose your feelings, Flora, exert your woman's fortitude, and endeavour, since it seems you can never expect a return of your virtuous love from Edward Stanley, to remember him only as a friend."

Flora sighed, and a tear trembled in her eye, which she hastily and angrily dashed away, and affectionately embracing her father, retired from the room.

On the way to her own apartment, she had to pass the door of Omelia's chamber, and with a palpitating heart she paused to listen.

A light was in the room, which convinced her that Omelia had not yet retired to rest, and presently she heard her pacing the room, apparently in much agitation, and talking incoherently to herself. Then a pause ensued, which was followed by a burst of violent grief and convulsive sobs, which moved the heart of Flora to the most torturing feelings of bitter regret and sympathy. She hesitated what to do; at first she thought of knocking at the door, and seeking with her a few words of explanation and reconciliation; but she had not the courage to do so; and upon more mature consideration she thought it would be better not to interrupt her in her present excited state of mind, but to leave it till the morning, when she sincerely hoped that they would be able to meet more calm, and that this painful subject might be dispassionately disposed of satisfactorily to all parties.

Having thus decided, Flora, with a sad heart, turned away from the door, and sought her own chamber, where she threw herself in a chair, and pressing her hands upon her forehead, gave unrestrained indulgence to the feelings that tortured her breast.

Again and again she reproached herself for the part which she had acted in becoming a listener to the secrets of Omelia and Edward Stanley, and deeply did she regret the ungenerous observations made use of by her father, and which the poor girl had evidently overheard. Freely, fervently did she acknowledge the numerous virtues and noble qualities of the Indian maiden, and how little she merited the harsh terms that Mr. Melville had applied to her, and how incapable she was of the motives which he had ascribed to her, and she could fully appreciate the feelings of mortified pride and resentment which must fill the breast of Omelia.

She waited anxiously for the morrow, though she almost dreaded again to meet her beautiful and indignant rival; and she could not but entertain the most dismal forebodings of some approaching calamity, consequent upon this melancholy occurrence, but the real nature of which she was at a loss to conceive.

Yes, Omelia on her return to the villa, in passing the door of the room in which Mr. Melville and his daughter were sitting, had indeed heard the harsh and hasty remarks that had fallen from the lips of the former, and her eyes sparkled with an unusual expression, and her bosom swelled with indignation as she listened to them. The hot blood and the proud spirit of the Indian girl were excited, and unable to restrain the expression of her wounded feelings, it was at that moment that she appeared before them, as has been already described.

But now in the solitude of her own chamber, most painful were the emotions that tortured her gentle bosom, and gave rise to various conflicting thoughts of the most wild and dangerous nature. She could endure anything rather than have the virtue and integrity of her motives suspected, or, for a moment called into question; and Mr. Melville had accused her of hypocrisy and ingratitude, that had stung her to the quick, and, although she was by no means vindictive, so great was her detestation of those bad passions, and so well did she know that they could not justly be laid to her charge, that she could neither forget or forgive.

With folded arms and disordered steps she paced the room, indulging in agonising thought, and giving vent to her feelings, in the most passionate and vehement exclamations.

"They view me with suspicion," she ejaculated; "they seek to pry into the secret of my thoughts, and watch my actions with insulting scrutiny. They look upon me with scorn; would make me little better than the mere slave of their haughty will and wayward caprices, and remind me of my poverty and dependence. And shall I longer endure a life so humiliating, so degrading? No; the proud spirit of even the humble Sepoy's daughter revolts at the idea; and she could almost hate and despise herself for having so long eaten the bread of charity. She will cast aside these galling fetters; boldly rush on Fate; and at least become the mistress of her own actions,— free as the winds that sweep the mountaneous heights of Himaylaya, unshackled, uncontrolled,—independent,—free!"

A noble expression animated her features as she thus soliloquised, and in a moment her mind was made up; her determination fixed; and she had marked out for herself the line of conduct she would pursue.

"I will no longer remain a burthen on the benevolence of those whom I believed viewed me with feelings of esteem, but which I too painfully now discover to be the sad and degrading reverse," she said. "No, I will at least find courage to abandon that place I had so fondly, so fallaciously considered as my home; but where I can no longer hope to remain in peace and happiness. There are stirring scenes coming, fearful and startling events about to take place, in which Omelia must and will take an active part; and it is not fit that she should longer remain idling here. Away, then, with all mawkish feelings of sentimentality; the proud spirit of the Sepoy's daughter soars above this grovelling life of pauperism and dependence; she will become a heroine, and by her public acts, prove herself to possess true nobility of heart and spirit, although the blood of the proud aristocrat flows not within her veins. Fearlessly braving every danger; ever foremost to protect the innocent, and defeat the diabolical designs of the guilty,—she will add honours to the memory of her mother, and show herself to be not unworthy the daughter of an English woman." She paused and reflected seriously.

"But can I abandon Stanley?" she said with a sigh, and a pang of anguish shot through her heart at the thought; "can I leave him without one word at parting? Yes, it must be so; I dare not venture to keep my appointment to-morrow evening, lest the resolution I have now formed should fail me; but I will contrive some means of forwarding him a letter to the ruins of the old mosque at the time appointed for our meeting, in which I will explain all; and though it will doubtless at first cause him severe grief and anguish, he cannot but ultimately approve of my resolution, and appreciate and admire my motives. Dearest Edward, the love of Omelia will remain faithful to you, till her fond heart shall cease to beat for ever! But, unless adverse fate frown upon us our separation shall not be for long; no, your devoted Omelia, as she has promised, will be ever by your side although unknown; her woman's arm shall boldly, effectually shield you from every danger."

Her eyes sparkled, her features glowed, and her determination increased as these thoughts crowded upon her brain, and she endeavoured to compose her feelings, and to prepare herself for the hazardous task she had imposed upon herself.

"To-morrow night, then," she cried, "I quit this place most probably for ever, and commit myself to the future care of Providence; that I know will never desert me, while purity, virtue, and integrity guide my conduct."

She felt endowed with more than usual

energy and perseverance, as she thus spoke, and she was fully prepared to carry out her resolution to the very letter.

She secured the door of her room to prevent the intrusion of any one, and determined that nothing whatever should induce her to see Flora and her father again before her departure from the villa on the following evening, which must be at the time when there was no one about to observe her. She then threw herself, without undressing, on the couch, and endeavoured to court repose; but so busy were her thoughts, that it was some time ere she could do so.

Broken, feverish, and disturbed were the slumbers of Flora that night, and when sleep did close her eyelids, the most torturing visions haunted her imagination. She recollected every word, every look of Omelia in the presence of her father and herself, and she was certain that something was brooding in her mind, which she trembled to discover the nature of. Freely now would the poor girl relinquish her hopes of Stanley (though severe would be the struggles of her heart, ere she could be able to do so), to obtain the forgiveness, and once more inspire the confidence of Omelia; but knowing her character so well as she did, she feared it would be a difficult task to accomplish.

She rose from her bed at an early hour on the following morning, and leaving her chamber, descended the stairs in order to walk in the garden for an hour or so, to collect her thoughts, and compose and strengthen her feelings previous to her anticipated painful interview with Omelia. On reaching the chamber door of the latter, she paused to listen, but all was still, and therefore she concluded that Omelia had not yet risen. She entered the garden, and walking to the terrace, she endeavoured to divert her thoughts for awhile from the melancholy subject which engrossed them, in the contemplation of the charming scenery which was commanded from that delightful spot.

But Omelia had been awake, and had quitted her couch for hours, and she was busily occupied in writing her farewell letters to Mr. Melville and his daughter. But oh, a task more painful and more difficult, namely, that of explaining to, and bidding an affectionate adieu to Edward Stanley (which letter she had resolved to give to the favourite ayah, or waiting maid of Flora, for delivery unknown to her mistress, for she knew that she could safely trust her, as she had had many proofs of the girl's affection, and was convinced that she would do anything to serve her).

Her tears flowed fast as she wrote this tender epistle, which breathed a tone of affectionate fervour, which must, if possible, the more convince him, if he had entertained a doubt of the sincerity and constancy of the poor girl's love; and many was the torturing pang it cost her.

She had but just completed this trying task, when there was a gentle tap at the room door, which startled her, and she eagerly inquired who was there.

It was the ayah, and she therefore immediately admitted her. She came with a message from her mistress and Mr. Melville, to inform her that the morning repast was waiting, and that they were anxious to see her as soon as possible.

Omelia requested the girl to inform them that she felt too indisposed to attend, and that she begged not to be disturbed during the day, as her spirits were too much depressed to admit of society.

"And now, Mimi," said our heroine, taking the girl's hand, as she was about to retire from the room, and detaining her, "can I trust you?"

"Oh, yes," replied Mimi, "Missi Omely sure trust poor Mimi, who hab great lub for her, and would do anything to serve her."

"Good girl," said Omelia, kindly, "I sincerely believe you would, for many are the proofs that I have had of your attachment. But remember, that which I am about to entrust you with, must remain a profound secret from Mr. Melville and your mistress."

"Oh, yes, Missi Omely," said the girl in reply—"Mimi will nebber say a word to any one."

"Enough," returned Omelia; "I am certain I can depend upon you, and am satisfied. But in the first place, here is a little I have for you to keep for my sake, and which you must on no account show to any one till to morrow."

"Oh, tank you, missi," replied the ayah; "Missi Omely bery kind to poor Mimi."

Omelia then presented her with a very showy pair of ear-rings, with which the poor simple girl was highly delighted, and again repeated her thanks.

"Now listen to me attentively, Mimi," said our heroine, "and as you value my future esteem and friendship, and would not cause me any unhappiness, strictly, faithfully obey my instructions."

Mimi solemnly promised, and Omelia then delivered to her the letter, which she made her carefully conceal in her bosom, and enjoined her to be punctual at the hour appointed in the ruins, to place it in the hands of Lieutenant Stanley.

Mimi expressed some surprise and curiosity, but, rather proud of the commission, which had considerable importance in her estimation, she again promised faithfully to obey, and left the room.

This part being accomplished, it was a great weight off the mind of Omelia, and she again secured the door, fully determined not to see Mr. Melville or his daughter previous to her departure, but to leave the letter she had written for them on her dressing table.

Flora and her father were not surprised at the message of Omelia, though, at the same time they could not help feeling vexed and hurt.

"It is evident that her anger is aroused," said Mr. Melville, "and that she has forgotten that respect which is at least due to us."

"Do not judge too harshly of her, I pray you, father," replied Flora, "but at any rate make some indulgence for the excitement of her feelings after what took place last evening. I deeply regret that I should have been the cause of wounding the poor girl's feelings, or that jealousy and curiosity should have induced me to act as I did."

"Nay, Flora," returned her father, "you have nothing to reproach yourself with, and the natural good sense of Omelia, will, I am convinced, in her calmer moments, lead her to acquit you of all blame. We will not seek to interrupt her at present, and reflection will surely satisfy her of the folly, not to say injustice, of harbouring any angry feelings towards us."

Flora shook her head, and could not help entertaining a decidedly different opinion to that of her father. The breakfast passed over in comparative silence, and, at its conclusion, Flora excused herself to her father, and again walked forth into the garden, in order that she might give free and uninterrupted indulgence to her bewildering thoughts.

But first of all she walked round to the back part of the house, in which the chamber of Omelia was situated, and looked eagerly up at the window, with the hope of seeing her there; but she was disappointed, and, after waiting for some time to no purpose, she again slowly and dejectedly walked towards the terrace.

Here she remained for about an hour, until she could no longer restrain her anxiety, or conquer the dismal forebodings that tormented her mind; she returned to the villa, determined, if possible, to obtain an interview with Omelia, and to seek that explanation which she considered was absolutely necessary for the satisfaction of both.

She hastened up the stairs and knocked at the room-door, then she gently and kindly repeated the name of Omelia, but she received no answer, and tried the door, which finding fastened, hurt and offended at what she considered the uncalled for disrespectful and obstinate behaviour of Omelia, she retired, resolved no more to trouble herself in the matter, but to leave the angry feelings of our heroine to exhaust themselves.

The day wore tediously away, and a melancholy one it was indeed to Omelia, but whose mind never for a moment wavered in its purpose. It was sad indeed to have to leave those friends, whom, in spite of all that had taken place, she still so highly esteemed, and under such painful circumstances; but still to remain longer, and probably again to be reminded of the obligations she was under to them, and to be looked upon in future with cold indifference, if not absolute contempt, was a humiliation to which her proud and independent spirit would not suffer her patiently to submit, and she therefore could not but commend the firm resolution she had come to.

The shades of evening fell around, and the hour she had appointed to meet Stanley in the ruins, was fast approaching. Her heart throbbed violently with mingled fear and expectation. She had prepared everything for her departure, packed up the little property she possessed in money and jewellery, carefully concealed it about her person, and she now only awaited till it should become darker, and all should be quiet in the house, and no one about to observe her, to commence her flight; and while she thus reflected, and prepared herself to meet any danger which she might have to encounter, she was aroused by a low and cautious knock at the door, followed by the whispering voice of Mimi, and she immediately admitted her.

"You are punctual, Mimi," said our heroine, "are you ready to perform the errand I required you to do?"

"Oh, yes, Missi Omely," answered the girl, "Mimi be quite ready and bery willing. She do anything to 'blige Missi Omely."

"Thank you, my good girl," observed Omelia. "I know you will perform your task faithfully and cleverly, and I shall ever feel indebted to you for your kindness. Good bye, Mimi, and should it happen that we may never meet again, believe me that I shall ever remember you with feelings of respect and affection."

"Missi see Mimi when she come back from the old mosque," said the simple girl, "and she bring you such bery 'fectionate message from Massa Stanley."

"Be it so, Mimi," replied our heroine,

thinking it better not to undeceive her; " now do not delay, and should you meet with any one on the way, be careful not to reveal to them the errand you are going upon."

" Mimi be bery careful, missi," answered the girl, " an' make bery great haste indeed."

She was then about to hurry from the room, when Omelia detained her.

" Where are Mr. Melville and Miss Flora?" she inquired.

" They both gone out an hour ago to take walk, missi," replied Mimi.

" Ah, that is fortunate," said our heroine; " go, Mimi, and be sure you lose no time in hastening to the place of your destination."

Mimi again promised faithfully to obey, and left the room, and Omelia going to the window, anxiously watched her retreating form, as she hurried cautiously across the

No. 6.

garden, until it disappeared in the distance. She then sank on her knees, and after supplicating heaven for protection, she prepared herself also to take her immediate departure.

She first listened to ascertain whether or not any one was stirring in the house, and finding that all was silent, she walked to the window, and looked eagerly out across the garden; the coast was quite clear, and she quitted the house with renewed confidence.

—

CHAPTER X.

THE ADVENTURE ON THE BRIDGE OF PERIL.

With a quick step and a palpitating heart Omelia bounded across the garden, and leaving the terrace, stood for a minute or two and looked back upon the spot she had quitted with feelings of melancholy regret.

"Farewell, dear and revered scenes, in which I have passed so many happy hours," she mournfully soliloquised; "many years may elapse ere I again behold ye, even if fate permit me ever again to see you. Oh, what scenes of danger will the poor Indian girl probably have to mingle in before that time arrives, how terrible may be the change that has taken place in her circumstances. Farewell, my benefactors, Omelia will never cease to remember you with feelings of gratitude and esteem, though you may never bestow one thought of friendship on her.

Tears started to her eyes as these dismal thoughts occurred to her, but she quickly struggled with and conquered the violence of her emotions, and casting one lingering look upon the lovely scene which was now bathed in the silvery moonlight, she hastened on her way towards an adjacent forest, whose thickly clustering trees would hide her retreating form from observation.

The ruins of the old mosque were situated just on the borders of this forest, and when Omelia caught an indistinct view of them as she proceeded on her way, her heart sunk within her, and her courage failed her. She was compelled to stop, and supporting herself against the trunk of a tree, she abandoned herself to the most violent emotion.

Stanley by this time had probably received her letter, and knew of her flight, and she could picture to herself his agony and despair. And could she then go without at least one word at parting from her lips? Would he not deem her cruel and unjust? She hesitated what to do, and almost resolved to hasten to the ruins, in spite of the letter she had sent, and meet him. This idea, however, she again quickly banished, and offering up a prayer to heaven for his welfare, and invoking a blessing upon his head, she again proceeded.

Breaking through the more thickly clustering trees, she came upon a more open space, and here the scene which burst upon her view, was one of the most sublime, and wildly romantic description. Huge rocks sheltering a rapid stream, a deafening rushing cataract, with a bridge formed and constructed in the rudest manner from the trunks of trees, and which seemed to challenge the boldest heart to attempt to cross it.

But it is unnecessary further to describe this scene, as it has already been done in the escape of Edward Stanley from his revengeful pursuers of the bungalow.

Omelia viewed it with a calm and dauntless eye, and immediately commenced ascending the steep and craggy rock, which, after

some exertion, she accomplished, and stood upon the frail and tottering bridge.

It was placed at an immense height, and to look below, and to listen to the roaring cataract as it rushed with mad violence down the rocks, into the gurgling and foaming stream beneath was sufficient to turn the brain giddy, and to create a sensation of awe, not to say fear, in the breast of even the most courageous.

With cautious steps, however, Omelia proceeded, and had half accomplished her dangerous task, having gained the centre of the bridge, when she was startled by hearing a loud and commanding voice calling upon her to stop, and looking back, she beheld with some alarm the form of a man who had clambered up the steep side of the rock, and had just set his foot on the bridge in pursuit of her.

Surprised and bewildered, her usual presence of mind for the moment forsook her, and she was unable to move. The man, with a cry of exultation, bounded forward with a firm and bold step, which showed that he was no stranger to the bridge, and our heroine by the assistance of the moon recognised him in a moment It was the sepoy Allyghur, the colleague of her father, who she had every reason to fear was also close at hand.

Before she had sufficiently recovered from her astonishment to attempt to escape, the ruffian hurried towards her, and grasping her rudely by the arm, in a voice of triumph, and with a look of satisfaction, he exclaimed,

"Well met, Omelia, though most unexpectedly. I am exceedingly glad to see you, as no doubt your father will also be when I have escorted you to him."

"Unhand me, man," returned Omelia, haughtily, and trying to disengage her arm from his grasp, "such presumptuous boldness is insufferable. Unhand me, I say, and do not seek to obstruct me."

"I am sorry I cannot obey your commands, Omelia," said the fellow, with an ironical grin, "but Yunadar, I rather think, would be highly indignant if I were to suffer you to go till you have paid your respects to him. You seem to be in a great hurry, and I must confess that I did not expect to find you out at this time of night, and so far away from home. Come let us be gone. We are no great distance from the bungalow, where your father is waiting my return, but will not expect to find me with such a companion.

"Insolent!" said the indignant Omelia, fixing her brilliant piercing eyes proudly on the dark countenance of Allyghur, and still endeavouring to release herself from his hold; "let me go, or you may yet have cause to repent your boldness. Dare not to disobey, I will not be detained."

"Proud girl," replied the ruffian, determinedly, "you command in vain. You have no child to deal with in the sepoy Allyghur. In this instance I will not, at any rate, be frustrated in my designs. You must with me."

"What is your purpose?" authoritatively demanded the maiden, "what guilty design have you in contemplation?"

"To conduct you to your father who has business of the most vital importance to converse with you upon. You must attend me."

"Must," repeated our heroine, scornfully; "you forget the respect due to my sex. Omelia knows not obedience, especially to the will of one whom she despises."

"Mighty fine," he returned; "but I heed not what you say. We delay; this way—I am determined."

"Beware what you do," said Omelia, but he only laughed scornfully, and still retaining his hold on her wrist, endeavoured to force her back across the bridge. The struggle which ensued was a fearful and a dangerous one, for the least false step, and they must both have been precipitated into the rushing waters below; but Omelia remained undaunted, and desperately and determinedly resisted all the villain's efforts, and, foaming with rage, the most fearful maledictions escaped his lips.

They struggled towards the end of the bridge which our heroine wished to gain; the courage of the maiden seeming to increase with the danger of the occasion, when by a sudden movement she released herself from his hold, and bounded towards the rock —at the same moment Allyghur lost his balance and his foothold, and falling, caught desperately at the bridge, clinging to it with his hands, and his body hanging over the roaring cataract.

Omelia waited to see no more, but rushed precipitately down the rock, and when she had nearly reached the base of which she looked up, and perceived that Allyghur had just succeeded, after a most desperate effort, in regaining the bridge, where he stood, apparently quite exhausted with the remarkable exertions he had undergone.

She knew that the present was the only time to effect her escape, and avoid his vengeance, which after what had happened she was very well convinced would be excited against her; and she therefore turned from the rock, and was about to make towards the woody jungle which was at no great distance, when Allyghur aroused to recollection, and happening to cast his eyes in that direction, with a terrible oath, and a fierce shout

that rent the air, in the stillness of the night, rushed from the bridge, with the speed of the startled deer, and hurried down the rock, with the same wild rapidity, in spite of all obstructions in his way, in pursuit.

This gave wings to Omelia's feet, for she knew the desperate character of the man, and that she could not hope to do much in resistance to such a ruffian, and at that moment he discharged a pistol, which, however, she concluded was done more to alarm her and stay her progress than anything else. It had, however, the contrary effect, for she redoubled her speed, and had gained the woody jungle as soon as Allyghur had reached the foot of the rock. She plunged hastily into the thickest of it, and fancying herself, for the present, at any rate, secure, she paused for breath, and to collect herself for future action.

It was indeed a wild and savage scene in which the Indian girl now found herself, into whose gloom the moonbeams could not penetrate, and where indeed the light of day scarcely ever shone. But Omelia was inured to such scenes from childhood, and her heart was a stranger to fear. She could not, however disguise from herself the desperate nature of the course she was pursuing, and the danger with which it was fraught, but all her plans for the future were arranged, and she was determined that no want of courage or energy on her part should cause them to fail.

But oh, with what painful anxiety, with what all absorbing care and solicitude were her thoughts fixed upon her lover; how fervently, how earnestly did she mentally pray for his welfare and happiness, and that he would pardon the step she had taken, and duly appreciate her motives, although she well knew what must be the agony of his present sufferings—his disappointment, surprise, doubt, and suspicion, notwithstanding she had expressed that in the letter which she had forwarded to him by Mimi, which ought to be more than sufficient, she considered, to convince him of her unabated affection, and the purity of her thoughts and intentions.

"Dearest Stanley," she ejalulated, "oh, think not that I have abandoned you, or that this fond heart can ever cease to beat for you, and you alone. No, by all my hopes, I could sooner perish, and that, too, by one of the most frightful deaths that the malice of fiends could inflict, than prove false to one who holds my very soul in love's fond bondage. Ere long we shall meet again, though you will know me not; in the hour of danger, and also that of peace and happiness, your faithful Omelia will be constantly by your side, will listen with rapture to the sweet melody of your voice, feast her ravished senses on your manly beauties, and live alone for you, and in your presence. And you, my kind benefactors, in spite of what has recently taken place, and the feelings of prejudice you may ungenerously entertain towards me, I will not desert you—but ever remember you with the most affectionate feelings of gratitude and esteem, and do anything to serve you, even at the hazard of my life. Oh, did you but know the thoughts and wishes that at present animate the breast of the poor humble creature of your bounty, you must, you would fully appreciate and applaud the motives that guide my conduct. But the time will come, when you shall know the real character of Omelia better than you now do, till then may the great spirit watch over and protect you in the midst of every danger it may be your lot to encounter."

She felt more composed and satisfied when she had thus given expression to her thoughts and feelings, and fearful of any further delay she arose from the stump of the tree on which she had been sitting, and with a firm heart resumed her journey; though it was with cautious footsteps, and quick searching eyes that she pursued her way through the dreary wilds and mazes of the forest jungle.

CHAPTER XI.

YUNADAR AND ALLYGHUR.—A TALE OF VENGEANCE.

The rage and disappointment of the villain Allyghur, when he saw our heroine plunge into the jungle at a distance, and he knew that it would be useless to pursue her thither, may be readily imagined. He stood for a minute or two and gazed upon the spot whence her retreating form had just disappeared, with the most savage feelings, and bit his lips with rage.

"Curses light on the power which has aided her in her escape from me," he passionately exclaimed, "and that, too, when I flattered myself that I had her securely at my will, and should have been enabled to take Yunadar by surprise, and to gratify his wishes by placing his proud and obdurate daughter—upon whom so much depends for the furtherance of our designs—under his jurisdiction. To think that Allyghur should be thus defied and defeated by a girl. And what can be the meaning of her hasty flight from the villa, and the protection of her friends? It excites strange fears and suspicions in my mind, and I am confident she must have some deep designs in contempla-

tion, which I cannot penetrate. I must lose no time in making Yunader acquainted with what has occured.

After once more giving vent to his feelings of rage, in language the most coarse and brutal, the ruffian again ascended the rock, re-crossed the perilous bridge, and hastily returned on his way to meet Yunadar, whom he had left at the bungalow, where Lieutenant Stanley had so narrowly escaped them on a former occasion, as related in one of the previous chapters.

He found the father of Omelia anxiously awaiting his return, for they had decided that they should depart from the bungalow before daybreak on the following morning, to rejoin the mutineers, who were now upon the eve of commencing the guilty work, which they had so long in secret contemplated, and which they hoped would spread successfully and rapidly throughout the native troops, and ultimately the population.

"You have delayed, Allyghur," he said, in rather angry and dissatisfied tones.

"Aye," replied Allyghur, gruffly, "and methinks you will not wonder at it, when you have heard the cause. But a curse light upon the disappointment I have experienced say I."

"Ah," exclaimed Yunadar, eagerly, "to what do you allude? Why are you thus excited?"

"Your daughter—"

"What of her? Have you gained any further intelligence? Speak."

"This night she is on her flight from the villa, doubtless with some desperate purpose in view," answered Allyghur, "and—"

"Fled! fled from those friends under whose protection she has been for so many years," interrupted Yunadar, "is it possible?"

"It is true."

"How know you this?"

"But a short time since I encountered her on the bridge of the cataract; I boldly seized her, with the intention of forcing her hither, but she desperately, effectually resisted me, and I had a narrow escape of my life. She ultimately succeeded in reaching the jungle, and there eluded me."

"Gone—escaped," cried Yunadar, fiercely "I can scarcely believe the evidence of my ears. You are not mocking me, Allyghur? Quick, relate to me the particulars of this extraordinary and unexpected adventure."

Allyghur did so, in as few words as possible, and Yunadar listened to him with the utmost excitement and impatience, and when he had concluded, he paced the room for a minute or two with hasty steps, and giving vent to his rage in the most passionate oaths and exclamations.

"How little prepared to hear this, Allyghur," he observed, "and it excites my utmost amazement and disappointment. What can Omelia's strange flight portend? I am lost in wonder and perplexity."

"I can form a pretty shrewd guess as to the motives and designs of the rash and daring girl," returned Allyghur."

"Ah, what mean you?" eagerly demanded Yunadar; "what do you imagine that she has in contemplation?"

"To fly to the arms of her English lover," replied Allyghur, "and with him to concoct measures for the frustration of our designs, and the destruction of the cause which we all of us have so warmly at heart."

"She dare not do so," exclaimed Yunadar, fiercely, "unless she would invoke her father's bitterest curses, and bring destruction on her own and her hated lover's head. Already has she disgraced me by encouraging that unholy passion for the very man whom I am convinced is the son of the base destroyer of my sister. 'Twas on that very bridge, Allyghur, that fourteen years ago, my burning hopes of vengeance, although partially gratified, were ultimately doomed to disappointment."

"How so, Yunadar?"

"Listen. For months after the death of my poor sister I had sought for her betrayer in vain, my brain tortured, racked, with thoughts of fierce determination. He eluded my sight, though I knew that he was still in some part of the country, and nothing could quench the terrible fire of revenge which glowed within my breast. Daily, hourly, I fed it, and resolved that sooner or later my deadly feelings should be satiated in his blood, or I would perish in the attempt. This was the constant subject of my thoughts —waking or sleeping—and it increased in strength.

"'Twas on a night, dark as the demon thoughts that held dominion in my breast, that I was on my way home. I had to cross the bridge of the cataract on my way thither, and I had just gained the point of the rock where the bridge commences, when the libertine slowly, cautiously, and alone, appeared before my eager gaze."

"Ah, it was an excellent opportunity," observed Allyghur.

"True," coincided Yunadar, "and I hailed it with feelings of savage delight. The sight was as food to my unsated spirit of hatred. I felt the demon rise within my breast, my eyes seemed to flash fire, and every angry passion was excited to the utmost, and most ungovernable degree. He approached, and ere he could discover whom he had to cope with, my fingers were entwined round his throat, and his bloodshot eyes protruded from their sockets in ghastly and helpless agony, In vain he struggled, his tottering form was bent half o'er the tottering bridge, and the roaring voice of the torrent drowned his cries. The next moment, with a hoarse laugh of triumph, I hurled him from me over the bridge—I watched his falling form as it dashed from rock to rock into the terrific cataract. The sight was savage transport to my senses; and as I fancied that his last expiring groan fell in an indistinct murmur on my ears, I laughed aloud, and cried, 'How sweet—how sweet is vengeance.'"

Yunadar uttered the last words with terrible emphasis and expression, and any one who had seen him at that moment would not have wondered at the frightful atrocities that the Hindoo is capable of committing, when the worst passions of his nature are aroused and excited. Allyghur watched the expression of his features with feelings of satisfaction for a minute or two, and did not interrupt him; but at length he said—

"But you say that your intended victim did not perish?"

"He did not," answered Yunadar, "by some miraculous means which I could never ascertain he escaped, and a short time afterwards quitted the country, and returned to England, at least, as far as I could learn. The circumstance caused the utmost excitement at the time, and every means were adopted to endeavour to discover the perpetrator of the outrage, as it was called."

"And suspicion never lighted on you?"

"It did not. But enough of this. The extraordinary and mysterious flight of Omelia bewilders and torments me. It is evident that something particular must have occurred to urge her to so desperate and hazardous a course."

"True; and it behoves us to be on our guard, or we may be exposed to the most imminent danger before we are aware of it, or prepared to meet it."

"The girl cannot surely so easily forget that I am her father, as to betray me."

"Psha! you have taken but little pains to win her affections," said Allyghur, "and you therefore can expect but little consideration from her. Has she not already set your authority at defiance, and boldly dared to oppose your will?"

"She has," coincided Yunadar, "and my utmost indignation is aroused at the thought. But come, we must consult together what is best to be done in this emergency."

They did so, but what the result of their deliberations were we are not at present in a position to state. Let it suffice that, having been joined by several more of their colleagues, they departed from the bungalow before the break of day in the morning.

CHAPTER XII.

OMELIA AND THE SERPENT OF HINDOSTAN.

Omelia continued to journey on through the deep forest (and encountering difficulties and obstructions, which must quickly have wearied any other but an Indian foot) for about a couple of hours, and without meeting with any further adventure worthy of record. But at length feeling tired, and imagining that she was past all danger of pursuit, she stopped to rest herself.

She seated herself on a small hillock, beneath the shade of some tall trees, and the air being close and sultry, she felt an oppressive drowsiness gradually steal over her, which she could not shake off, and considering there was no danger to apprehend, she did not seek to conquer the influence, but sunk into a sound sleep.

It did not, however, long remain calm and tranquil, for soon her busy imagination, and painful visions were presented to her troubled fancy.

Once more she imagined herself supremely happy in rambling with her lover through the romantic, and magnificent scenery by which the villa was surrounded, and in listening to his tender vows of love and constancy. Then by a magical effect, common to dreams, they were suddenly transported to another and a distant part of the country, and were witnessing, all the strange and outrageous ceremonies of the festival in honour of *Doorga*, or the goddess—consort of *Siva*—which is the most splendid and expensive; as well as the most popular of all the Hindoo festivals.

During the whole of the preliminary ceremonies, which occupy several days, as well as the three days worship, business throughout the country is entirely suspended, and nothing is attended to, heard or seen, but the most unbounded festivity.

And it was in the midst of this joyous season, that Omelia, in her dream, now imagined herself, accompanied by her lover. It was the three days of worship. On those days, the houses of the rich Hindoos in Bengal, at night are brilliantly illuminated, and the doors are thrown open for the reception of visitors of every description, and Europeans are also received with all due attention and courtesy. We will pass over the ridiculous, disgusting, and extravagant ceremonies of the first day's worship, such as the ceremony of giving eyes and life to the images, performed by the officiating Brahmin; the sacrifice of numerous animals, as buffaloes, sheep, goats, &c., the offering of the flesh and blood of these animals, and

other articles to the images of the goddess, and the other deities, that are set up, and come at once to the more pleasing and rational part of the festival of the *Doorga pooja*, or the *Dusserah*, as it is called in Western India.

During the whole of the day after the *pooja* as some of the images are brought from villages at a considerable distance from the holy stream, in order to be cast in, the uproar and din are indescribable. Immense sums of money are expended on these festivals. A great deal is given in charity, and in feeding and clothing of priests and beggars, and much is also lavished in the general feasting which prevails.

Omelia thought in her dream, that herself and Stanley were witnessing the fantastic dance of a number of beautiful *Meeraseens*, the most respectable description of *Nantch girls*, or *Bayadere's*, who dance before the goddess. They gazed with delight at their picturesque figues (though somewhat encumbered with drapery) and elegant costume, which consists of a pair of gay-coloured silk trowsers, edged and embroidered with silver or gold lace, so long as only to afford occasional glimpses of the rich anklets, strung with small bells that encircle the legs. Their toes are covered with rings, and a broad, flute, silver chain is passed across the foot.

Over the trowsers, a petticoat of some rich stuff appears, containing at least twelve breadths, profusely trimmed, having broad silver or gold borders, finished with deep fringes of the same. The *coortee* or vest, is of the usual dimensions, but it is almost hidden by an immense veil, which crosses the bosom several times, hanging down in front and at the back in broad ends, either trimmed to match the petticoat, or composed of still more splendid materials, the rich tissues of Benares. The hands, arms, and neck, are covered with jewels, sometimes of great value, and the hair is braided with silver ribbons, and confined with bodkins of beautiful workmanship.

Such were the interesting objects that our heroine imagined her and her lover gazed at, amused with their curious sports, and in listening to monotonous and sonorous sounds of the *tom-tom*, and the more pleasing tones of the *veva* the principal instrument of the *Nautch* orchestra, and which is strung with seven metal wires, three steal and four brass, though the melody is generally played on one of the steal wires.

All was hilarity and gladness, but suddenly the scene was changed to one of indescribable horror. Terrific peals of thunder shook the vault of heaven followed by piercing shrieks, yells, groans, and curses, that seemed to come from a multitude of voices, men, women, and children, and which rent the air with their hideous noises. The dances, and the spectators were transformed to frightful shapes, surrounded by flames of fire, the whole atmosphere seemed to be impregnated with some deadly poison; murder, and rapine raged on every side, the streets appeared to flow with human blood, and in the horror of all that was presented to the distracted and affrighted imagination, the potent spell of sleep was broken, and Omelia awoke.

For a moment or two she was so shocked and bewildered by the latter part of her dream that she knew not where she was, and pressed her delicate hands upon her forehead to endeavour to recall her wandering recollection. She was quickly, however, aroused by a strange, hissing kind of sound, which was not altogether unfamiliar to her ears, and hastily casting her eyes in the direction from whence it proceeded, what was her horror at the appalling sight which met them.

Coiled around the large trunk of a tree which grew immediately opposite to her, and erecting its head to make a spring at her, she beheld an immense serpent.

Terror enchained every faculty, and she was riveted to the spot. She could not shriek, she could scarcely breathe, and it was fortunate that she could not, for if she had done so the monster would in an instant made the fatal spring, and then her destruction would have been inevitable.

A sudden impulse, however, aroused her, and she flew behind the trees, that spread their branches over the hillock on which she had been sleeping; and the next instant the loud report of a musket smote her ears, and, looking between the branches, she beheld the head of the serpent drooping, and a man, dressed as an Hindoo peasant engaged in the bold and dangerous task of more effectually destroying it.

This was at length accomplished, and clasping her hands, and uttering an exclamation of joy, Omelia darted forward, and threw herself gratefully at the feet of her heroic preserver.

The stranger gazed at her with no little astonishment, but apparent interest and sympathy, and, raising her from the humble position in which she had placed herself, and in terms that spoke his candour and sincerity, congratulated her warmly upon her rescue from a fearful, and which, but for his timely and fortunate arrival, would doubtless have been certain death.

"I am at a loss for words to express my thanks, gallant, and kind-hearted stranger," said our heroine; "to the preserver of my life, of however little value it may possibly be, I surely owe a debt of gratitude it is utterly out of my power to repay."

"No thanks, my good girl," replied the man kindly, "Jung Bahadom would despise himself if he were not always ready to fly to the assistance of his fellow creature (especially a woman), in the hour of need. I must, however, express my surprise at finding you alone, at such an unseasonable hour, and in so dangerous a place."

"True, my friend," returned Omelia, "you have undoubtly good reason to do so; but I cannot now, and neither is it, perhaps, necessary for me to explain further, than that having travelled some considerable distance on urgent business, and, feeling myself fatigued, I sat down to rest myself, and fell asleep."

"Enough," said Bahadom (as he had called himself), in terms of politeness far beyond his apparent humble station; "I have no wish to be impertinently inquisitive, neither is it my place to be so; you say that you have travelled far and are fatigued, and if you are not afraid to trust yourself with me, I am willing further to assist you. My bungalow is at no great distance from here, and if you think proper to accompany me there, my wife and daughter I am sure will receive you with every kindness and welcome."

The manner of the stranger was at once so frank and trust-worthy that Omelia could not for a moment doubt him. She therefore again warmly thanked him, and accepting his arm for support, for her limbs felt weak and weary. They proceeded on their way through the forest, from which in a short time they emerged, and entered upon a more open and cheerful part of the country.

The first blush of morn now appeared in the horizon, promising all the glories of an eastern day, and the heart of our heroine felt invigorated, and hope and courage animated her breast.

After about another quarter of an hour's walking, they came in sight of a comfortable-looking bungalow, which Jung Bahadom informed her was his residence, a fact which Omelia was not sorry to hear, as she really felt that she required rest, after the extraordinary fatigue and excitement she had undergone on that night of adventure.

They quickly arrived at the door, and Omelia's conductor having knocked, after a short pause, it was opened by a respectable-looking middle-aged woman, whom our heroine supposed to be the wife of Jung Bahadom, and who expressed some surprise at beholding her.

Bahadom, however, explained everything in a few words, and Nerida (which Omelia afterwards understood her name to be) then welcomed her with much affability, and she was conducted into a clean and comfortable room, where the woman having requested her to be seated, summoned her daughter, (a pretty looking girl about sixteen) to assist her in preparing refreshments. The simple repast was soon got ready, of which Omelia having partook, after some little conversation, at her request, she was conducted to a chamber at the back of the bungalow, by the girl, and returning her heartfelt thanks to providence for the protection it had so far extended to her, she gradually sunk into a sound and refreshing sleep.

And here for a time we will leave her, and return to some of the other personages of our story.

CHAPTER XIII.

THE DISAPPOINTED LOVER.—STANLEY AND FLORA MELVILLE.

It may be scarcely necessary to state that Lieutenant Stanley was punctual to the hour appointed for the meeting of himself and Omelia in the ruins of the old mosque. He could not divest his mind of certain dismal forebodings and misgivings that had taken possession of his mind, after the adventure of the previous evening, and he awaited the arrival of our heroine with the utmost anxiety.

The prying curiosity, and jealously of Flora Melville greatly annoyed him; he well knew the proud and independent spirit of Omelia, he saw how severely indignant and mortified she was at having been watched, and he was fearful that the event might be productive of the most serious and painful consequences.

There was also an ambiguity about some of the observations of Omelia, which he could not understand, and, as he now reflected on them, the uneasiness and anxiety of his mind increased.

The hour of appointment was only just past, but he became impatient, and paced backwards and forwards with disordered steps, several times going to the entrance of the ruins, and looking forth, with the hope of beholding her tall and graceful figure approaching; but it was only to return, vexed and disappointed.

"Something surely must have happened to prevent her coming," he said; "the hour is passed, and she was ever so punctual. A fearful presentiment crosses my mind, that I shall not again behold her, and—but no—I am foolish to give encouragement to any such ideas. I do Omelia injustice; she is

the very soul of truth and candour, and would scorn to trifle with my feelings; I should have more confidence in the fervour and sincerity of her love, than to entertain such erroneous thoughts to her prejudice. Some unforseen accident has alone detained her, but she will be here anon. Lie still then my fluttering heart, and let me be calm and patient."

He was interrupted in the midst of this soliloquy, by hearing the sound of a hasty approaching footstep, followed, as he thought, by the mention of his name in a low female voice, and eagerly casting his eyes towards the spot from whence it seemed to come, in the dim-light he beheld the form of a woman gliding stealthily towards him.

"Dear, dear, Omelia," he cried, not doubting for a moment that it was her; "my love, my faithful one, you are here, and I am happy."

"Massa Stanley be bery good nice gen'l'man, but he am mistaken, it be not Missi Omely," was the unexpected answer he received.

He started with astonishment at the tones of the voice, and approaching nearer, immediately recognised the unexpected visitor.

"Mimi!" he exclaimed in a tone of surprise; "how is this? Where is Omelia?"

"Missi Omely 'thome at villa, I s'pose," replied the girl, innocently, "so she send Mimi to take her place, and hab chow-chow wib massa; he, he, he!"

"This is trifling," cried Stanley impatiently, "can Omelia so little value my feelings as thus to sport with them; or are you mad, girl?"

"No, massa," returned the simple Mimi, "me no mad, massa; Missi Omely send me here wib letter for you."

"A letter!" ejaculated Stanley, in a voice of emotion, and snatching it from her hand; "what can this mean?—My heart misgives me!"

"Mimi wait while massa reads pistle," said the girl, standing aside.

The lieutenant walked hastily, and in a state of great agitation to that part of the ruins where the light of the moon penetrated more strongly, and, tearing open the letter, began to peruse the contents, but scarcely had his eye fallen upon the first two or three lines, then a deathly sickness came over him, and pressing his hand upon his forehead, in a voice of agony and despair, he cried :—

"'Tis done—my worst fears are realized —she has deceived me—gone—deserted all —oh, rash, misguided, cruel girl."

"Gone!" re-echoed Mimi, staring at him with stupified amazement; "Missi Omely gone, deceive massa—no, no, Mimi not mad

now, but Massa Stanley, missi at home—good missi."

With eager haste Stanley now read the remainder of the letter.

"Headstrong girl," he exclaimed, "to suffer the petty jealousy of Flora to have such a powerful effect on her feelings. Whither has she fled? What can be her wild intentions? My brain is bewildered. Let me again read."

He did so, as follows:—

"Dear, dear Edward, deem me not false, deceitful; self-respect, a proper spirit of independence, every principle of right that should prevail in a virtuous and honourable woman's breast, urge me to this step, which to you will probably seem rash and imprudent; but heaven knows that I am acting for the best, and, I trust, will aid me to reach

the goal of my hopes and wishes. It may be some time ere we meet again, but rest assured, my only love, that in the meanwhile the heart of Omelia will remain faithful to you; her hopes, her wishes will be all for you, her prayers be constantly offered up to the Giver of all good for your welfare and happiness."

"Poor girl," sighed Stanley, with deep emotion; "I cannot, will not doubt your love, but tremble for the dangers that may beset you in the cause that you have adopted, and what you really intend doing is to me a profound and impenetrable mystery. Surely I was more worthy of your confidence; you should have consulted me ere you proceeded to such extremities. Alas, imprudent Flora Melville, what miseries and misfortunes may your rash conduct be the cause of. But, why

No. 7

do I tarry here? It may not yet be too late to avert the evil. You say, Mimi, that you left Omelia at home, when you came on this errand?"

"Yes, massa," answered the girl, who was as much bewildered as the lieutenant, "Mimi see her standing at window when I crossed the garden; she no mean to go out, I tink."

"Let me then begone," exclaimed Stanley, hastily, "and if it be not too late, stay her in her rash purpose."

With these words, he rushed wildly from the ruins, leaving Mimi in a state of surprise and bewilderment.

"Well, I nebber," she said, "Massa Stanley must surely be bery mad, or he no talk, no act like dis. Miss Omeley gone way, leave Massa Melville, Missi Flora, and poor Mimi; oh, nebber, nebber. Oh, dis lub, he do play de bery debil; I hope him nebber trouble Mimi. Heigho! but I must go see."

Thus saying, the simple, kind-hearted Mimi quitted the ruins to return home, and puzzling her brain in endeavouring to comprehend the meaning of all this.

In the meantime, in a state of mind bordering on distraction, Lieutenant Stanley hurried on his way to the villa, his mind a prey to a variety of torturing, fears and suspicions, yet still venturing to hope that Omelia had not yet left the house. Surely she would think better, ere she took so desperate, and as it appeared to him dangerous and unnecessary a course, and abandon her intentions. To leave her home, and those friends who had been so kind to her, and to throw herself unprotected, unprovided for upon the wide world, would be surely little short of madness.

"But she must, she will re-consider this," he soliloquised, as he hastened on his way, anxiously looking forward as far as his eyes could penetrate through the obscurity of the night, in the hope of seeing her approaching form on the way to the ruins, having changed her mind; but his wishes were not realised, and still more impatient and fearful, he continued on his way, until long before he had expected it, he found himself standing upon the terrace, that favourite spot of her whom he so fondly loved, and whom he had now too much reason to fear was lost to him for ever.

Here he paused, unable to proceed further, and the most torturing thoughts crowded upon his brain, and the deepest emotions agitated his breast.

The many happy hours that he and Omelia had passed together on this delightful spot; the tender vows they had exchanged; the fond words she had uttered; the almost heavenly smiles she had beamed upon him, and which had seemed to shed a bright halo round his very existence, and to transport his soul to halcyon bliss, all rushed vividly, and with overwhelming force to his memory, and at the sad forebodings that those joys were never more fated to be renewed, he sighed deeply and beat his breast in the agony of his feelings.

He could almost imagine that he saw her graceful and fairy-like form again, standing as she was wont to do in the bright moonlight, leaning over the gilded pallisades or balcony of the terrace, anxiously, eagerly watching for his arrival when he had promised to meet her, and waving her silken kerchief in the air in affectionate delight and fondest welcome, when she beheld his graceful *bholio* lightly skimming the deep waters of the river towards the shore. Again he fancied that he encircled her form in his ardent embrace; felt her throbbing heart pressed to his, her honeyed kiss upon his lips, and heard her soft sigh of love, which came like a gentle zephyr so refreshing, so delightful to his enraptured senses. Once more he basked in the bright sunshine of her brilliant and intelligent eyes, and listened to the heaven-fraught melody of her voice, as she responded to his fervent vows of constancy. The picture which his fervid and excited imagination drew, and the dismal contrast which the present stern reality wrought, was almost too powerful and overwhelming for his reason to withstand, and sobs, which he in vain endeavoured to repress, agitated his manly breast. He pressed his hand upon his aching and burning forehead, and could scarcely restrain a tear,

For some minutes he could not attempt to move from that hallowed spot, endeared to him by so many fondly cherished associations. But at length the recollection that every moment was most precious, and the least delay was fraught with the utmost danger, aroused him from this lethargy of thought, and he hurried from the terrace into the garden, which he hastily crossed, but again paused in anguish, doubt and hesitation, when he came in sight of the villa. He dreaded to meet Flora Melville and her father, not that he dreaded their reproaches, but to Flora he felt that he must attribute all that might unfortunately have taken place, and the desperate resolution which Omelia had formed; and much as he esteemed her for her numerous virtues, he could not but now entertain a feeling bordering upon indignation towards her, and he was extremely doubtful whether or not he should be able to keep himself within the strict bounds of respect and decorum in her presence.

He gazed upon the lovely scene in which he stood, with the same feelings of melancholy transport that had occupied his mind while standing on the terrace, and it awakened in his breast the same fond recollections and associations. Every inch of that fertile spot, every plant, every tree, every shrub, had been hallowed by the presence of his beloved Omelia, and now, alas, too probably she was gone, lost to them and him for ever. The thought was maddening, and again he beat his breast in agony and despair.

Still had he not courage to enter the house.

While he thus lingered, wrapped in gloomy and painful meditation, the rustling sound of footsteps among the grass startled him, and he drew back behind the shadow of a tree which grew near the spot whereon he stood, and, with a palpitating heart, watched to observe who it was approaching.

He was not long kept in suspense, for presently he beheld two figures emerge from behind a cluster of trees into the footpath opposite to where he stood, and advance towards the door of the villa.

He immediately recognised Flora and her father, who had apparently just returned from their evening walk, and not yet being prepared to meet them, he suffered them to enter the house without observing him.

His uneasiness and anxiety increased; if Omelia had remained firm in her resolution, and had rashly quitted the house, they would now probably for the first time discover the fatal consequences of which their hasty and imprudent conduct had been the cause, and how great would be their astonishment, pain, and regret.

He trembled at the thought, but still hesitated at once to remove his terrific doubts and apprehensions.

Ten minutes more had elapsed in this manner, and still the mind of Stanley was so bewildered that he found it impossible to decide upon any course of action.

Stanley, cautiously, stealthily, as if he had some nefarious design in contemplation, walked round to the back of the house, in which he knew the apartment usually occupied by Omelia was situated. Eagerly he looked up at the windows; all was buried in profound darkness, and his fears increased.

Presently he beheld a light glimmering in the room, as if proceeding from a lamp carried by some person who had just entered. With breathless attention Stanley listened; a brief pause ensued, which was followed by an exclamation of anguish, and the light again suddenly disappeared.

The wretched Stanley clasped his forehead in agony and despair, and the terrible conviction at once came home to his mind.

"Rash, imprudent, headstrong girl, she has gone," he exclaimed, with a burst of anguish which he could not control, "she has exposed herself to dangers and horrors which I shudder to contemplate. Oh, Omelia, whatever were the feelings of indignation which the conduct of your friends have excited in your breast, I little thought that you could ever have steeled your heart to desert me thus. Alas, how suddenly are my fondest hopes and expectations blighted, and I am now indeed a wretched being. But why do I linger here?" he suddenly added, arousing himself after a brief pause, "let me at once know the worst."

He hastened from the spot on which he had been standing, with the intention of entering the house, for he could endure this state of torturing suspense no longer, but started back a few paces on hearing the front door hastily opened, and the next moment Flora Melville and her father hurried out, apparently in a state of the greatest agitation and excitement.

Stanley stepped quickly forward, and Flora on beholding him uttered a faint cry of surprise and anguish, and her father exhibited much confusion, for the wildness of the young lieutenant's looks and demeanour foreboded what was coming.

"Omelia," he hastily cried, "tell me, keep me not in suspense; she has done what she threatened to do in the letter which she forwarded to me. I see by your looks that she has—she is gone."

"'Tis too true," replied Mr. Melville, for Flora was too much overpowered by her emotions, especially when she saw the agitated and reproachful looks that Stanley fixed upon her, to speak.

"Despair," groaned Stanley, striking his forehead, "my worst, my most terrible fears are realised. Unfortunate girl, what will now become of her, alone, friendless, unprotected? And 'tis you," he added, bitterly, and addressing himself to Flora, "'tis you, who by your imprudent conduct, and unpardonable curiosity have driven her to this You have urged Omelia to that which she would otherwise never have dreamt of or contemplated. You have cast from you one who loved you as a sister, in whose breast glowed every womanly feeling of esteem and gratitude towards you and your father, you have plunged me—who fervently regarded you for your virtues, although I could not return the unfortunate passion I believe you honoured me with—in utter misery and despair, and now—now I hope you are satisfied."

With a cry of unspeakable anguish poor Flora threw herself convulsively in the arms of her father, and hid her blushing face on his shoulder.

"Lieutenant Stanley," said Mr. Melville, in a tone, and with a look of resentment, "this language, and addressed to my daughter, is most unwarrantable and uncalled for."

"Enough, sir," haugtily returned Stanley, "I have neither time, patience, or inclination now to argue the point with you. Miss Melville, no doubt, can fully appreciate the justice of my observations, and I leave you and her to discuss the disagreeable subject between yourselves. Farewell, I go in search of the unhappy Omelia, who looked to you and your daughter for sympathy and protection from insult."

"Stay, sir, I command you," exclaimed Mr. Melville, in an angry tone; but Stanley stopped not to listen to him, but darting across the garden with the speed of lightning quickly disappeared, leaving them both in a state of excitement which need not be explained.

CHAPTER XIV.

THE ATTEMPTED MURDER.—THE RESCUE.— THE MYSTERY.

For some minutes after the abrupt departure of the distracted Stanley, Flora and her father remained transfixed in the same attitude, convulsive sobs escaping the heavily surcharged bosom of the former; her brain racked almost to madness, and scalding tears chasing each other rapidly down her cheeks, on which mounted the blush of mingled shame, wounded pride, and resentment.

Mr. Melville felt the bitter and pointed observations of the young lieutenant most keenly, but though he felt himself severely rebuked, nay, even insulted, he could not but acknowledge that Stanley was a in great measure justified in saying what he had, and he could make every allowance for the powerful excitement of his feelings, after the melancholy and unexpected circumstance that had taken place, and knowing the ardent passion which existed between him and Omelia. He also inwardly admitted that they were worthy of each other, and deeply regretted that his daughter should ever have allowed those sentiments to obtain so powerful an ascendancy over her heart, that she must soon have discovered could meet with no return, or indulged in flattering hopes and fond expectations which the behaviour of Edward Stanley should have satisfied her could never be realised.

This, however, was not the time to indulge in such thoughts, when the painful circumstances demanded more prompt and energetic action; Flora was in a most deplorable condition, and almost unconscious,

so gently leading her into the house, and placing her under the care of Mimi—who had just returned, and exhibited much confusion and agitation, although, at the time, it was not noticed by Mr Melville—he gave orders to several of his male domestics to arm themselves, and to scour the country in different directions in search of the fair fugitive.

Having done this, he returned to the room where he had left Flora, and found her restored to sensibility, but still in a state of great agitation, and the simple, but kind-hearted Mimi—who had confessed everything to her respecting the letter which she had conveyed from Omelia to Lieutenant Stanley—weeping over her.

Mr. Melville dismissed the girl, and then tenderly approaching his daughter, and taking her hand, he said—

"This is a sad business, my dear child, and no one can possibly more deeply lament the circumstances than myself. But come, you must not give way to this excessive violence of grief, but endeavour to hope that although the clouds have darkened o'er us, they will soon again disperse, and all will be restored to sunshine and peace.

"Oh, my father," sighed Flora, "would to heaven that I could encourage such hopes, but in vain are my efforts to do so. Oh, I have acted wrong—very wrong towards poor Omelia, and I cannot but blush for, and despise myself, when I think of my conduct."

"Hold, Flora," said her father, "you must not thus bitterly and unjustly reproach yourself"

"Alas," ejaculated Flora, in tones of the most poignant anguish, and heartfelt regret, "I cannot do otherwise. My conduct has been mean and contemptible, and in that light Omelia must view it, or she could never have been induced to take the desperate and determined course she has done. Stanley, too, I can never forget the reproaches he has so justly heaped upon my head."

"Say not justly, Flora, they were harsh, violent, insolent, and unmerited. I can make every allowance for his excitement and disorder of mind, on the disappearance of Omelia under such extraordinary, painful, and bewildering circumstances, but he ought never to have forgotten that it was Flora Melville, the daughter of his father's bosom friend, whom he was addressing, and at least have had some consideration for her feelings, His language was most intemperate, and unbecoming a gentleman."

"Alas, my dear father," said Flora, "I feel but too keenly that he had ample cause for it. And I now feel surprised at myself to think that my jealous feelings should cause me to act as I did. Would to heaven that I could recal the past, and regain the esteem of Stanley since I can never hope to obtain his love. But oh, he views me now with contempt, if not with absolute hatred."

" Let him beware that he carry not his indignation too far," observed Mr. Melville, haughtily, " or he may find that I have the spirit to resent it. My daughter must not and shall not brook the contempt or insults of any man, no matter what his station in society. Those who may presume so far, will have cause to repent it. But come, Flora, I pray you calm your feelings; all may yet be well, and Omelia, too, even should those I have sent in search of her fail to discover her, will doubtless, ere long, see the folly of her conduct, and return to us."

" Oh, no," replied Flora, " too well do I known the proud and independent spirit of Omelia to believe that she will do so, and the letter she left behind, so bitter and re-proachful, convinces me that she will not. I shall never pardon myself for having been the cause of driving from that place which she had justly considered to be her home, one whom I loved, and must ever (though her heart may be changed towards me) as a sister."

Her tears flowed fast as she uttered these words, and her father in vain, for some time, endeavoured to console her; but at length she became somewhat more calm, and, having in vain awaited the return of those who had been sent in search of our heroine, they separated for the night

But not to rest did poor Flora retire, no, her mind was too deeply oppressed and agitated by the heavy weight of care and sorrow that burthened it, to allow her to think of sleep; and, for some time she paced her chamber with disordered steps, and gave vent to her sorrow and regret in painful but fruitless lamentations,

The observations that Stanley in the terrible excitement of his feelings had given utterance to, still seemed to ring in her ears, and every word had left a wound behind in her heart, which time even, she feared could have no power to heal. It was evident that he now viewed her with scorn, if not absolute loathing, and the object, who if she could not hope to win, to return that love she so passionately entertained for him, it would have afforded her a melancholy satisfaction to gaze upon, to listen to, to enjoy his friend-ship and esteem, she had thus, she had too much reason to fear, banished from her presence for ever.

This thought was indeed most torturing, but in vain did she endeavour to banish it; unavailing were all her efforts to tranquillise or subdue the feelings that it engendered in her breast.

" But surely," she sighed, " even wrong as I must acknowledge my conduct to have been in this unfortunate affair, I merited not such harsh and cruel observations as those he uttered towards me. Certainly I deserved more consideration and respect at his hands. I must indeed have become hateful in his eyes, or he could never have treated me thus. Omelia too, she it is too evident bears towards me the most vindictive feelings, or she could never thus have fled without deeming me worthy of a word o. explanation. Could she so easily banish from her recollection the many happy hours we have passed together; the sisterly affec-tion I have ever evinced towards her, the anxiety, the care, the solicitude I have at all times shown for her welfare? Oh, she has certainly been most ungenerous, if not un-grateful. How wretched, how truly wretched do I feel to find myself cast away as some-thing worthless and despicable, from the hearts of those dear beings whose affections I so fondly prized."

She paused, overwhelmed by grief, and the agony of her mind increased every moment instead of abating.

" What is there I would not give, what is there I would not do, could I, dare I but hope that it would be received as some atonement," she said, " and that it would mark my deep sense of sorrow and regret? Stanley, Omelia, how much do you wrong me by the low estimate you place upon my principles, my motives, and intentions."

The pang this thought caused her was most severe, and with the feeling was mingled one of mortified pride, and self humiliation, which was, if possible, even more torturing than all.

But in spite of all, her principal anxiety was for the safety of Omelia, and she racked her brain to no purpose to endeavour to fathom her intentions, for she could find no-thing whatever to enlighten her upon that subject in the letter which our heroine had left behind her. It was enshrouded in mystery altogether, merely bidding her and her father a melancholy farewell, and ex-pressing the deepest regret at the unfortunate circumstances that had rendered their separa-tion absolutely necessary. She tendered her warmest gratitude for all the many weighty obligations she was under to them, solicited their prayers and good wishes, and concluded with a hope that they might yet meet again.

What was to be gathered from all this? To what conclusion was Flora to arrive? She was at a loss to conjecture; it was a problem she found impossible to solve, and if she were allowed to judge from the observ-tions and behaviour of Lieutenant Stanley, he was left in the same state of doubt and perplexity as herself.

But whither could she go, without means or friends to afford her assistance and protection? This was a question which Flora found it utterly impossible to answer. It was not likely that she would return to her father, after what had recently taken place, and the fears she entertained of him, and Flora the longer she thus reflected, and sought to arrive at some satisfactory conclusion, became the more involved in confusion and bewilderment.

"May heaven protect her from the dangers to which she will too probably be exposed, and into which she has so rashly precipitated herself," Flora fervently exclaimed; "and may prosperity and happiness be her lot wherever fate may guide her."

She again tried to tranquillze her feelings as she thus ardently and sincerely gave utterance to her wishes, and she partially succeeded, and the night being now far advanced, she at length sought her couch, and endeavoured to obtain a short respite from her cares and anxieties in sleep.

The morning dawned, and at an early hour, being unable to rest, Flora arose, and sought the presence of her father, his voice informing her that he was already stirring.

He met her with his usual affection, but was deeply grieved to see the painful change which only a few hours had wrought in the aspect of her countenance, which was pale and careworn, as if she had been suffering under some mental anxiety for years.

He expressed himself accordingly, and endeavoured to cheer and console her, a task in which he succeeded but very indifferently.

Her first eager inquiries were respecting those who had been sent in search of Omelia, and what had been the result.

She was informed that the men had returned without being able to obtain the least tidings of her, and Flora heard the same with sincere feelings of anguish which it is quite needless to describe.

The day passed painfully and gloomily away, and without bringing any intelligence of the fair fugitive, and Mr. Melville and Flora's fears and anxiety for her safety, and perplexity as to her designs, hourly increased.

But what of Lieutenant Stanley? How shall we attempt to describe the state of his mind? That is a task in which we fear we must altogether fail.

On leaving the presence of Flora and her father in the state of excitement which has been pourtrayed, he rushed wildly, frantically on, he knew not whither, or where to direct his course; for Omelia in the affec-

tionate but melancholy letter she had sent him, had taken especial care not to throw out the slightest hint which might afford a clue to her discovery.

The anguish of Stanley was the greater, as the time he was enabled to devote to the pursuit must necessarily be limited to only a few hours, as he would be compelled to depart some time in the course of the following day to rejoin his regiment.

He had proceeded some distance without, in the confusion and bewilderment of his mind, noticing the direction he was pursuing, when he found himself compelled to pause, that he might take breath, and endeavour to collect himself.

He looked anxiously and inquiringly around him, and found that he had unconsciously taken the direction of the cataract and the bridge of peril, and a strange idea impressed itself on his mind that he was right in so doing; but for why, he could not conjecture. But alas! even if such idea should ultimately prove to be correct, what would it avail him, after the time which had elapsed since Omelia had quitted the villa? She was too probably now far beyond the reach of pursuit, and in that lonely place he was not likely to meet with any person who could give him any information which would be of the least service to him, or assist him in his search.

"Ah, no," he sighed; "vain is the task I have imposed upon myself; fruitless will be my exertions, the misguided girl has too well arranged her plans to admit of any chance of discovery being probable. She is lost, lost, I shall behold her no more, and henceforth me and happiness are strangers. Oh, Omelia, after all the tender and solemn vows and protestations you have made, how could you ever act as you this fatal night have done?"

The pangs which these reflections caused him were almost beyond endurance, and he beat his breast in despair, and for some minutes remained transfixed to the spot on which he was standing, and undecided in what way he should act.

At length aroused into action by the recollection that every moment of delay must necessarily lessen his hopes of success, he determined to cross the bridge, and proceed some distance further, with the hope of meeting with some habitation or individual to afford him information that might be useful to him.

The moon shone brightly in the heavens, showing every object clearly and distinctly as in the broad light of day, so that he had no difficulty in tracing his way, and soon arrived at the foot of the steep rock, from one point of which the bridge commenced.

He began the ascent with a faint but throbbing heart, and never did any task appear more tedious and tiresome.

At length he reached the bridge, from which indeed the view was wildly magnificent, sublimely grand, commanding as it did, from its great elevation, such a vast extent of the surrounding country.

But the mind of Stanley was too busily occupied by the painful subjects that engrossed it, to permit him now to pay any attention to that which at another time would have called forth his most enthusiastic admiration, and, with a slow and cautious step (for the danger of the position demanded it), he proceeded across the bridge, and had nearly arrived at the end, when he beheld something glittering in the moonlight at his feet, and he hastily picked it up.

It was a jewelled bracelet.

A trembling sensation came over him as he gazed upon it, and he examined it more minutely, but what were the mingled emotions that agitated his breast, on recognising in it one of the handsome and valuable bracelets which Omelia had constantly worn?

In her struggles with the villain Allyghur, as related in a previous chapter, the bracelet had been forced from her wrist, unnoticed by the treacherous sepoy, or he would most unquestionably have secured so valuable a prize.

Stanley stood transfixed with astonishment, and could scarcely remove his eyes from the bracelet. He raised it fondly to his lips, and pressed ardent kisses upon it, while his heart throbbed at double its wonted pace.

The idea then which had so strangely crossed his brain was correct; Omelia had crossed the bridge in her ill advised flight, and if he did not delay he might yet have the good fortune to overtake her, or, at least, obtain some intelligence which might furnish him with a clue to her discovery.

But a terrible thought suddenly flashed across his brain, and he stood appalled as it occurred to him. How came the bracelet where he had found it? He could not suppose that she had voluntarily thrown it there. No, it must have been forced from her by some act of violence. Had she encountered some daring robber? The wild, dreary, and unfrequented character of the place fully sanctioned the supposition, and Stanley's limbs shook with horror, and his blood seemed to turn to ice at the dreadful thoughts that engendered. She had but too probably been outraged, robbed, and finally precipitated into the roaring cataract, and thus met with a frightful and untimely death.

The thought was so horrible, yet so fearfully probable, that it almost drove his brain to madness, and he staggered to the rock, to which he clung for support, for his brain turned so giddy, and his limbs trembled so violently that he must otherwise have fallen from the fearful height.

"Oh, God," he cried with a burst of uncontrolable agony, "and can one so pure, so good, so innocent, so lovely, have met with such a terrible and revolting a fate? Oh, no, I dare not entertain the dreadful thought, or I shall go mad. Oh, Omelia, why did the rash idea ever enter your mind to incur the awful danger of this wild, this mad adventure. Kind providence in thine infinite mercy, I beseech thee grant that my terrible fears may prove to be erroneous, and, oh, protect the poor girl from every danger, and quickly restore her to these longing arms. Hope re-animates my breast," he added, after a brief pause, " I will be calm and yet look forward to the best. Something tells me that we shall shortly meet again, and I must not, will not abandon the idea. This bracelet has probably by accident become disengaged from her wrist, and I ought to hail the circumstance with a feeling of satisfaction and gratitude, since it gives me a clue to the way she has pursued. Let me no longer delay. Dearest Omelia, if fate be not opposed to me, I will yet overtake you and arrest you in your flight."

Encouraged by these hopes and ideas, he hastened forward, his eyes eagerly penetrating through the dim obscurity, anxious that his wishes might be realised, and to behold her retreating form; but in vain, although by some singular fatality he took the very direction which she had pursued. But then the time which had elapsed since she had commenced her flight was all against him.

But at length Stanley became so deeply entangled in the mazes and intricies of the jungle, that he stood bewildered, not knowing which way to go, or whither to turn. And now despair entirely overtook him, and he pressed his hand upon his forehead in mental agony and disappointment.

It was evident that fate was against him, and that all chance of his overtaking her was at an end. And then the time was so far advanced that it was impossible for him to continue the pursuit, as he must not longer delay returning to his regiment, which was to depart the day after that ensuing from its present station to Meerut which is a military station forty miles from Delhi.

"Alas," he ejaculated in the most melancholy accents, " all my fond hopes are now annihilated, and happiness can never again be mine. Omelia, whose tender and solemn vows of love and constancy I so fervently believed, has deceived me, abandoned me, left me to despair and misery, and I shall see her no more. Cruel girl to act thus towards that man in whose heart her beloved image is so deeply enshrined, and who is prepared to make any sacrifice, even that of his life, for her sake. And you, Flora Melville, have I to thank for all this—'tis you who have driven the poor girl away from that place which she had been taught to consider as her home, and perhaps plunged her in destitution. Alas, what misery has your fatal passion and ungovernable jealousy been the cause of.'.

As these dismal thoughts tortured and distracted his mind, he turned away from the spot and with a sad heart reluctantly retraced his footsteps through the jungle.

And now once more the dreadful fears and suspicions that had before beset him, on finding Omelia's bracelet, rushed upon his brain, and racked it almost te madness. In the anguish and despair of her feelings might she not have rushed upon self-destruction? Oh, no, he dared not believe that—the thought was too horrible for him to entertain it. He continued slowly on his way, a prey to mingled hopes and fears.

He was rather surprised on emerging from the dark and dreary forest into the more open space to find that it was break of day, and that was sufficient to apprize him that he had not a moment for further delay, so he increased his speed, and after more than two hours hard walking he once more reached that part of the banks of the Jumna where he had ordered a bholio to be in readiness at a certain hour to convey him across the river.

The men were punctual, and had been waiting for him for some time, so jumping into the boat, with spirits more depressed than they had ever been before, Stanley was conveyed to the place of his destination.

*   *   *   *   *

An interval of three months is now supposed to have occured, and no tidings whatever had been obtained of Omelia by those who were immediately interested in her fate.

Mr. Melville and his daughter had now quitted their beautiful villa near Agra, and were residing in the Mogul capital of Delhi, and here it way not be uninteresting to the reader to give some particulars of that celebrated place, for which we are principally indebted to the graphic pen of that able writer on everything connected with India, Mr. J. H. Stoqueler.

Delhi, the ancient capital of the Emperors of Hindostan, was, before the great mutiny, the residence of their lineal descendants. The Great Mogul, with whose effigies all card players are more or less familiar, had long been bereft of all political authority. He was a mere pensioner, but the officers of government offered him every external mark of courtesy pertaining to the regal office; and when European or native strangers reached Delhi, they were expected to call and pay their respects to his Majesty, who ordinarily invested them with a "khilut," or robe of honour.

Akbar Shah, although now a prisoner, is really a king, not merely by consent of the Honourable company, but actually created such by their letters patent.

Lord Lake found the grandfather of the present wretched old puppet an emperor in rags, powerless, eyeless, and wanting the means of sustaining existence.

The firmans of the Padshah made the general an Indian noble, the sword of the latter made the descendant of Tamberlane a Company's king, the least dignified, but the most secure of eastern dominations.

In public and private Akbar Shah received the signs of homage that were considered due to his pre-eminent station. The governor-general, when admitted to his presence, addressed him with folded hands, in the attitude of supplication. He never received letters, only "petitions," and conferred an exalted favour on the government of British India by accepting a monthly present of 80,000 rupees (£8,000).

The royal family consisted of *twelve hundred persons*, with a sure prospect of an increase every month, and how was the East India Company to support such an army of princes and princesses. But the hardship did not fall upon them, but the monarch, who was obliged to divide, and sub-divide his income, until there were princes who received only twenty-five rupees a month.

Let the honest democrats of London and Manchester try, if they can, to imagine a king's son, nephew, or cousin, however far removed, living in a state of royalty on thirteen-shillings and sixpence a week, constantly addressed as "Shad-i-Alum," the *King of the World*, and feeling it necessary for his rank's sake, on choosing a wife, to settle on her a dowry of five lakhs of rupees.

While this farce of a monarch was being kept up, the "Sulateen" continued to multiply within the royal residence, and to live on the royal bounty, their sole occupation being confined to playing on the sitar, and singing the king's verses.

In its prosperous days, Delhi was a magnificent city. It covered an area as extensive

as that of London, Westminster, and Southwark, and was remarkable for everything which could contribute to Oriental splendour.

Thus it remained till Nadir Shah's invasion. The wealth stored in its treasure-houses, the pomp maintained by its nobility, had excited the cupidity of that successful conqueror. The Persians marched into India. The Hindoos supinely waited to watch the result. Not till the close proximity of the enemy to the chief city rendered it essential that some show of defence should be made, was any step taken to impede their progress. The effort then had been too long delayed. The Hindoos were defeated, and the monarch found himself a prisoner in his own capital. Not far from the palace there is a mosque of red stone, surmounted by three golden domes. From the summit of that building Nadir Shah witnessed the massacre of the unfortunate inhabitants, a massacre which was at length brought to a close through the prayer of the defeated monarch.

According to Abul Fazel, no less than seven successive cities have stood on the ground occupied by Delhi and its ruins. It was taken in 1011, and plundered by Mahmoud Ghiznee. It was taken by the Affghans in 1193, and was the seat of the first eight sovereigns of that dynasty; in 1398 by Timour; in 1525 by Baber, who founded the Mogul dynasty. It was burnt in part by the Mahrattas, in 1736; and, three years later, it was taken and plundered by Nadir Shah, who carried off the famous Peacock throne, and an incredible amount of treasure. Shorn of much of its former glory, it now awaits its final destruction from British justice.

No. 8.

The present King of Delhi—the puppet set up by the mutineers, and hedged about with no divinity—is Akbar Shah. We have already alluded to the antecedents of this phantom potentate, but some additional particulars respecting both himself and his ancestors will no doubt be interesting.

The founder of his family bore the same name, but a very different reputation from the reigning monarch. He was the Solomon of Delhi. By his genius the empire was raised to the highest point of glory. The wealth of the family seemed inexhaustible, for on the occasion of a state marriage the bride was presented with a million in money, jewels to the amount of half a million, and a bagatelle of 150,000 a year for pin-money. Aurungzebe, grandson of the great Akbar, was another mighty monarch, who killed his three brothers and usurped the throne. Nassir-uddin, best known by being defeated by the bands of Nadir Shah, was the direct descendant of Aurungzebe. Between these two there reigned four or five kings, who were chiefly remarkable for the manner in which they killed each other. The first— Jehander Shah—was a uxorious wretch, who called himself " the King who possesses the World," and disgusted his people by his subserviency to a woman named Lalkur ; he was killed by his nephew, and his body dragged through the streets of Delhi. The nephew Ferokh-siar, likewise uxorious, had filled his harem with the most lovely women of the East ; but one night, as he dallied among them, one fair creature curled her arm around his neck, while another encircled his waist with her white arms, and other traitoresses, as if in sport, bade him close his eyes. The thoughtless king obeyed. In an instant there was a flash, a curl of white smoke, a roar of agony, and the luckless monarch strove hard to free himself from the ladies who held him ; but it was in vain. They had seared his eye-balls suddenly and remorselessly with a red-hot iron, and poor Ferokh-siar suffered that night the same torture, they say, which was inflicted on a certain Edward of England in Berkeley Castle. His cousin and successor was poisoned ; and his brother, who succeeded him, endured a like fate within a few days after his accession.

Delhi has one or two broad and handsome streets, a number of handsome private residences, and an extensive cantonment for troops. But the main attractions of the city consist in the mosques and minarets— of which we shall have occasion to speak more particularly in the course of our narrative—and other public buildings.

Trusting that this brief digression may not be considered out of place in these pages,

we will again resume the thread of our story.

Wretched and lonely did Flora Melville feel, deprived of the society of Omelia, and terrible was the anxiety which both her and her father felt at the uncertainty of the fate which had befallen her, their fears suggested the worst, and deeply did they regret the painful circumstances that had driven her from their protection.

But how shall we describe the sufferings of Edward Stanley, who, with his regiment, was now stationed at Meerut ?

The time which had elapsed without his receiving any tidings of Omelia, caused him to abandon all hope of ever beholding her again, and the agony of his feelings may be much better imagined than described. But something was about to occur which for a time, at any rate, would engage his whole attention.

The clouds that had been so long gathering, threatened to burst at Meerut. Eighty troopers had been imprisoned for refusing to perform their duty, because of the impression they had received that the cartridges were greased, and the utmost disaffection prevailed among their comrades.

Stanley watched this with suspicion and fearful foreboding, and he did not hesitate to communicate his thoughts to some of his brother officers, but they most of them treated it with indifference and incredulity.

Reflecting upon these matters, and his thoughts also still fixed upon Omelia, he had one evening wandered to a short distance without the walls of the city.

The night was fine, and deeply wrapped in gloomy meditation upon the untoward circumstances with which his fate was surrounded, he rambled on farther than he had at first intended, until, suddenly looking up he found himself in a rather lonely and unfrequented spot, though still within sight of the city.

The bracelet which he had found on the bridge of the cataract, on the eventful night of the flight of Omelia, he always carried about with him, and many were the mingled emotions that were excited in his breast, as he gazed on this relic of one whom he so sincerely and so fondly loved, though he despaired of ever beholding her again.

It would be a difficult task to describe in adequate terms, all that he had suffered, and was still suffering, since Omelia's mysterious disappearance. She was never absent from his thoughts—she was ever present to his imagination, sleeping or waking. He again beheld her arrayed in all those glowing charms, those radiant smiles, those looks of love, of gentleness, of innocence, and noble womanhood that had first captivated his heart, and held all his senses enraptured Once more he listened to the soft melody of her voice, ever so tender and so eloquent; he heard her repeat those vows of eternal love and constancy, with which she had so often delighted his ears, and rendered him the most blessed and happy of human beings; and then the thought that wayward fate had separated them, perhaps for ever, was maddening, almost beyond endurance.

Such were the reflections that now racked and tortured his brain, as he paused for awhile in his solitary ramble He took forth the treasured memento from his bosom, and as he gazed upon it, and pressed it again and again to his lips, deep sighs escaped his breast, and the most dismal forebodings haunted his mind.

"Poor girl—poor girl," he sighed, "where are you now? Whither has cruel fate guided your wandering footsteps? Alas, perhaps at this moment you are enduring the greatest miseries and privations that the imagination can depicture, and with no one near to sympathise with you, or offer you the balm of consolation. Even now you may be dying for want, and I not near to relieve you, or to receive your last sigh, to hear your last solemn vow of unalterable love, and have your dying blessing. Dreadful, torturing thought. Oh, why did the mad infatuation ever seize upon you to abandon your happy home, and those kind friends, who, in spite of their one act of imprudence and injustice towards you, in their hearts, I am convinced, really loved you so fondly?"

He was interrupted in the midst of this melancholy soliloquy, by the sound of hasty footsteps, and muttering, grumbling words, near him, and he had only just time to cast his eyes in the direction from whence they proceeded, and to draw his sword in order to be ready to defend himself from any threatened danger, when two armed sepoys, with savage and meaning looks, stood before him.

"How now?" he haughtily demanded, "what means this daring act of insubbordination? Know you not that you stand in the presence of a British officer?"

"We have shaken off the fetters of the hated Feringhee," replied one of the ruffians, in a savage and insolent tone, "we cast his authority with contempt to the winds; the clouds have burst, and the fierce tempest must now be allowed to rage in all its fury. The wronged, despised, and oppressed Hindoo will at last have a terrible retribution upon the heads of his detested and tyrant enemies."

As the villain thus spoke, he discharged the contents of a pistol at Lieut. Stanley, which fortunately missed him, notwithstanding he was within arm's length of the man.

"Traitor! miscreant!" exclaimed Stanley, as he rushed upon him, and the next moment the treacherous sepoy was stretched dead at his feet. The other villain then attacked him fiercely with a sword.

The combat was a desperate one, for although the sepoy was no match for Stanley in point of skill, he was greatly his superior in strength, and he fought with savage ferocity, parrying his thrusts with considerable dexterity.

The sword was struck from Stanley's hand, and at the same time sinking on one knee, he was entirely at the mercy of his ferocious adversary, when, at that critical moment, a pistol was discharged with unerring aim from an enclosure close by, and the sepoy was stretched bleeding and lifeless on the earth.

Before the astonished and grateful Stanley could recover from his confusion, or endeavour to ascertain who was his deliverer, his hand was raised to the lips of some one, warm tears fell upon it, and kneeling affectionately before him, he beheld the delicate and graceful form of an Hindoo youth, from whose lips fervent thanks and blessings were poured, but in accents that fell upon his senses like heavenly music, and enchained his every faculty in indescribable rapture and amazement.

He hastily raised the youth from his humble position, and gazed eagerly, and with a wildly throbbing heart, into his countenance Heavens, how he started at the sight which met his eyes! There was the light, pencilled like moustache, but every handsome feature, each fond expression of the brilliant eyes bore the loved resemblance of Omelia.

Entranced, bewildered, astonished, almost incredulous, he was rivetted to the spot, and unable to utter a word, and before he could recover himself, he beheld an officer and several men, alarmed by the report of the pistols, hastening to the spot.

Once more the heroic youth raised the hand of Stanley to his lips, and, covering it with his tears and kisses, in tones of such deep feeling that they went thrilling to the heart, exclaimed—

"Bless you—bless you, ever dearest Stanley!"

It was enough; those blessed words explained everything to the ravished senses of Stanley; it was the fond, the faithful, the heroic Omelia; she had kept her promise to be near him in the hour of danger, and it was to her courage and intrepidity he was indebted for the preservation of his life

Our heroine saw that he recognised her in her disguise, she noticed, she felt the tender emotions that agitated his breast, and at that moment the poor girl experienced a feeling of transport which it would be impossible for any language, however eloquent, properly to describe.

Stanley was about to speak, and to hastily snatch her with unbounded transport to his bosom, when the officer and soldiers hastily approaching nearer, Omelia quickly disengaged her hand, and with a fervent blessing still upon her lips, bounded from the spot, and was immediately hidden from the sight behind the enclosure whence she had emerged at the moment when Stanley's life was in such imminent peril.

CHAPTER XV.

THE TORTURES OF SUSPENSE.—THE OUTBREAK.

"Lieutenant Stanley," said the officer, "what is the meaning of all this? Have treachery and murder already so boldly shown themselves?"

"The lifeless bodies of these miscreants is my answer," returned Stanley, pointing to the bleeding and lifeless forms of the two mutinous sepoys; "but I beg of you to pursue and detain the generous and heroic preserver of my life, Captain Sommers; it is my—"

He checked himself suddenly, and then added—

"It is one whom I have a right to esteem—to love."

"Aye, it was indeed a noble act, my friend Stanley," observed Captain Sommers, "and especially in one who, from the slight glance I was enabled to obtain of him, is only a mere youth—a complete stripling. Hasten," he added, addressing himself to the sergeant of the men by whom he was accompanied, "try to overtake the stranger and bring him hither."

The men obeyed, and Stanley almost regretted that he had expressed the wish, for he well knew how anxious Omelia must be to preserve her incognito, until she had been enabled fully to carry out the designs it was evident she had in contemplation.

However, the men shortly returned without being able to discover anything of her, and they then returned to the city, Lieut. Stanley in a state of mind which may be readily imagined.

His astonishment was so great at the unexpected occurrence that he could scarcely believe the evidence of his senses, or that he was not labouring under the influence of some strange delusion. But no, he could not have been mistaken, the joyful truth was too apparent; Omelia still lived, loved, and watched over him, and a heavy weight of care and anxiety was removed from his breast, which was becoming almost too overwhelming to endure.

On reaching his quarters he hastily retired, and there when alone, abandoned himself to the various thoughts that crowded so rapidly on his mind.

To know that Omelia lived, that she had escaped the fate, which, on finding the bracelet, he feared had befallen her, was indeed a relief to his anxious mind for which he could never feel sufficiently grateful to heaven. And to feel assured that her sentiments towards him remained unchanged, inspired him with fresh hopes of future happiness, but he was at a loss to imagine what could be the motives for her present singular conduct, why she had assumed such a disguise, and by what means she contrived to exist. The principal way in which he could account for it was, by attributing it to the fears she entertained of her father, the savage and relentless Yunadar, and her anxiety to conceal herself from him, but he would have given anything did he but know the place where she had secreted herself; to again enjoy the transport of her society, and afford her that assistance which she must so much require now that she was deprived of the kind aid and protection of her former friends, Mr. Melville and his daughter.

He was interrupted in the midst of these cogitations, by the entrance of one of the corporals, with a letter which he said had been given to him by a strange Hindoo youth, with a request that he would carefully deliver it into his (Lieutenant Stanley's) hands, and that the young stranger had then immediately departed, before he could put any questions to him.

With eager haste and a palpitating heart, Stanley took the letter, and having dismissed the corporal, he gazed anxiously at the superscription. How his eyes brightened, and a burthen of suspense and care was removed from his mind, when he looked at the well-known characters. The letter was, as his heart had first assured him, from Omelia, and he pressed it rapturously to his lips.

"Dear Omelia," he said, "all my apprehensions will now doubtless be quieted; this letter will explain all that I am so anxious to know."

Hastily he opened the letter, and perused the contents, which ran as follows—

"My own, and ever dearest Edward, your Omelia still cherishes your loved image in her heart with all woman's fondest, purest affection. But you could never doubt the love of her who lives alone for you, and who has no thought, no hope, no wish, no happiness apart from you. I confide in your love and constancy. I know the noble, generous, manly heart of Edward Stanley too well to believe it capable of deceit or falsehood, and in that assurance I am happy. It is necessary that I should continue my present disguise and concealment for some time, for I have imposed upon myself a great task, which I am determined, even at the hazard of my own life, to accomplish. I know I need not urge you, dear Edward, to preserve my secret. There is a terrible storm arising, but justice will, I trust, prevail. May heaven preserve you, Edward, and trusting that the time may not be far distant when we shall be restored to each other, no more to part till death. Believe me your own fondest "OMELIA."

With what feelings of unqualified delight and satisfaction did Stanley peruse, and reperuse this affectionate epistle; and he now felt, as it were, quite another being to what he had been only a few hours before. All the torturing fears, doubts, and suspicions that had then beset and distracted his mind were now removed, and he felt inspired with the fondest hope and confidence.

"Dear Omelia," he ejaculated, at the same time pressing the letter to his lips, " oh, how could I ever doubt the truth and sincerity of that faithful heart which is a stranger to guile ? May heaven pardon me for having —in the bitterness of my anguish—done so, when you so little merited it. Heroic, noble-minded girl, may kind providence assist you in your virtuous and praiseworthy designs, and throw its shield of protection around you in the midst of all those dangers by which you will doubtless be surrounded, and grant, as your dear letter expresses, that the time may not be far distant when we shall be restored to each other, no more to be separated."

He felt so light and buoyant of heart that he could not without the greatest difficulty restrain his joy within the bounds of reason. But the dark hints which Omelia threw out of the storm which was gathering, could not fail to excite the most alarming suspicions and forebodings in his breast, and which the murderous attack made upon him that evening did but serve the more strongly to confirm.

He had, however, long foreseen this, and what had both surprised and annoyed him, and many others who coincided with his views, was the utter indifference and incredulity with which those who were placed in authority—and whose duty it was to have taken timely warning, and to have used every effort and precaution to avert, if possible, the threatened danger—treated it. Representations, coming from whatever source they might, were entirely thrown away upon them, and it would seem as if they had made up their minds to treat the matter with scorn, or as the mere vision of some disorder and excited imagination.

The awful consequences of this ignorance, or shameful neglect of duty, have been shown in the wholesale and monstrous slaughter of our countrymen, women and children.

Stanley had little sleep that night so busily were his thoughts occupied with the extraordinary adventures that had occurred to him, and in reflecting upon his remarkable, unexpected, and romantic meeting with Omelia. He pictured to himself the many vicissitudes she had encountered since their separation; the many dangers to which she was now too brobably exposed; and the more did he become lost in wonder and admiration, at the noble heroic spirit she displayed, her extraordinary magnanimity, courage and intrepidity.

"Oh, may her praiseworthy efforts be crowned with every success," he again fervently ejaculated, "and grant that providence, in its infinite mercy, may avert every evil by which she may be threatened "

He continued to invoke blessings on her head, till sleep closed his eyelids, when her form continued to haunt his imagination, and to give rise to a variety of conflicting emotions and conjectures in his bosom.

The daring and murderous assault which had been made upon Lieutenant Stanley, caused considerable excitement in the station, and for the first time the serious alarm and suspicions of those who were placed in authority were aroused, and it seemed as if they were at last awakened from the delusive dream of security in which they had indulged, to a sense of some impending danger, but of the true nature of which they were unable to form the slightest conjecture.

A strict investigation of the business, and a vigilent eye was kept upon the particular regiment to which the two ruffianly sepoys belonged, but nothing of any importance, or which was calculated to throw a light upon the subject. Everything remained involved in the same state of mystery.

But it was not long permitted to be so; another fortnight elapsed, and the aspect of affairs hourly became more gloomy. During that interval, too, Stanley had not seen or heard more of Omelia, and his mind again became a prey to the most gloomy thoughts and apprehensions. However, events were drawing to a crisis, and he had soon something to divert his immediate attention even from her whom he so fondly loved.

We will endeavour to trace the mutiny from its earliest source.

In the month of February, 1857, a sepoy of the highest caste was asked by a camp follower for the use of his *lotah*, a brass drinking vessel; and this was the uncivil reply he received—

"Lend thee my lotah? quotha. No; thy touch will defile it."

"You think very much of your caste," insidiously returned the camp follower; "but the day is come when the Feringhee will make you eat pig's fat, and cow's fat, and so convert you to Christianity. Look to your new cartridges!"

These words, no doubt uttered by a secret spy or enemy of the Indian Government, if they were meant to fan the flame of disaffection and the spirit of revolt which was already kindled, certainly had the desired effect. As has been before observed, the poison did its work; for the sepoy quietly communicated what he had heard to the native officers of his regiment, and a feeling of alarm and indignation arose which daily gathered strength, in spite of remonstrances and explanations, till at length a revolt was organised, and the 15th of May was, it is said, fixed upon as the day when a general rising and massacre was to take place.

We have spoken of the eighty troopers imprisoned at Meerut, and the consequences, and they soon became more fearful and alarming in their effects.

Worked up to a pitch of excitement, approaching to frenzy, the fellow soldiers of the imprisoned sepoys were unable to control their feelings until the hour appointed for revolt, and suddenly on the 11th of May commenced the terrible work of destruction.

On that fatal day, Stanley on returning home, to his astonishment and alarm beheld his bungalow, and those of several of the other officers in flames, while the fierce yells and execrations of the mutineers rent the air, and warned him of the danger of being discovered. He immediately hastened to the residence of the commanding officer to communicate the disastrous intelligence.

The night of that 11th of May was a terrible one; from every direction, as far as the eye could stretch, the flames kindled by the hands of the savage incendiaries ascended to the sky, and great was the consternation that prevailed. And this continued even till after daylight the following morning, a great number of officers dwellings being destroyed, and a vast quantity of property sacrificed.

This was followed by a most daring outbreak on parade—officers were shot down without mercy, and their dwellings plundered. Happily there were two or three European regiments at the stations; they were called out, and they fired upon the mutineers.

These fled to Delhi. Delhi, a town which, as we think we have before stated, is six or seven miles in extent, and walled round. It was not merely the residence of the pensioned Mogul sovereign, it was the centre of the British Government of the province. A commissioner abided here in a magnificent mansion; there were courts of law, magisterial courts, a college, churches, printing-offices, numerous handsome dwellings, rich shops, and richer factories; a military cantonment, an arsenal and park of artillery, and several police-stations.

There were besides, beautiful palaces and mosques, built by the Moslem conqueror. Not fewer than 180,000 souls were congregated within the walls of Delhi.

But to return to the outbreak on the parade.

No one had taken a more active part in the suppression of this, than Lieutenant Stanley. But the mutineers for some time maintained a most obstinate resistance.

At length, in the confusion, Stanley by some means became separated from his companions in arms, and found himself alone at some short distance from the place where the desperate outrage was taking place, and, vexed at the strange accident which had thus led him astray, he was about to hasten back to the thickest of the fray, when three fellows suddenly rushed upon him from a secret ambush, and attacked him fiercely. One of these he discharged the contents of his pistol at, and by a well directed aim, stretched him lifeless at his feet. A second he quickly despatched with his sword, but in attacking the third, his sword was struck from his hand, and he was entirely at the mercy of the villian, for he was too far from any one to obtain the least assistance.

The sepoy uttered a savage cry of exultation, and his large black eyes flashed with revenge, which deadly passion distorted his forbidding features. It was a terrible moment for Edward Stanley, and he was unfortunately rendered completely powerless to attempt to rescue himself.

The sepoy flourished the butt-end of his musket above his head, and brutal seemed to be his determination.

"Die, hated, accursed Feringhee!" he exclaimed, in a fierce voice, and the butt-end of his gun was about to descend on the head of Stanley, when at that moment a loud cry was heard, and his arm was arrested by some one behind, at the same time a dagger was buried to the hilt in his breast.

The musket fell from the sepoy's hand, he uttered an oath, and a cry of agony, and staggered from the spot.

Stanley sprang to his feet, and hastened to return his thanks to his heroic deliverer; but what was his astonishment and delight on again beholding Omelia—still disguised—standing before him, and gazing upon him with looks of the most unbounded affection.

"My Omelia—my beloved, self-sacrificing devoted Omelia," he rapturously exclaimed, rushing towards her.

"Hold, dear Edward," she returned, shrinking back; "know me not, or my life will have to pay the forfeit. You can no longer doubt the truth and constancy of Omelia. Seek not to discover my retreat, or to penetrate my actions. Farewell; we shall meet again at Delhi."

"Stay, dearest, best of women," cried Stanley, "for a moment only I beseech you."

But she was gone, and so sudden was her departure that he had not time even to notice the direction she had taken. He stood for a few moments completely lost in astonishment and bewilderment, and his bosom violently agitated with the various emotions that took possession of it.

"Mysterious girl," he cried, "powerful, noble, and heroic must indeed be the motives that can urge you to conduct such as this. but oh, how do I tremble at the thoughts of the imminent danger to which you expose yourself. Heaven only knows what will be the result of this."

The firing, which still continued at a short distance, however, warned him away, and thankful for his providential deliverance from what had appeared to be certain death, and lost in wonder, love, and admiration of Omelia, he hurried away.

CHAPTER XVI.

OMELIA.—THE SECRET RETREAT.

For a time we will now follow the fortunes of the adventurous and heroic Omelia. We shall not, however, here detain the reader by recounting all that had befallen her since her abrupt departure from the villa, and the circumstances that had induced her to assume her present extraordinary disguise. It may be as well to state though, that she had ample pecuniary means to carry out the great and noble projects she had in contemplation, and no sense of danger, personal inconvenience, or annoyance could deter her from her purpose.

Need we describe the care, the anxiety of mind that the Indian maiden had been and was still enduring? The reader, we are certain, can very well imagine it.

Sleepless had been her nights, restless her days, not a moment did she allow to escape, but which was given to the furtherance of her designs. But her thoughts were constantly fixed on Stanley, and many were the tears she shed at their unavoidable separation, and the prayers she offered up to heaven for his welfare and happiness.

Well did she know the mingled feelings of doubt, fear, and suspicion her mysterious conduct would cause him, and that thought caused her no little pain and regret.

But surely, after all the solemn vows she had uttered, and the proofs that she had endeavoured to give him of the ardent passion which she entertained for him, he could never believe her faithless. Oh, no, she could not think so meanly, so ungenerously of him, and in that assurance she endeavoured to find comfort and consolation.

She was continually on the watch for information, and she soon became acquainted with the departure of Mr. Melville and his daughter to Delhi, and of the regiment to which Stanley belonged to Meerut. From peculiar sources she had ascertained that it was at the latter place where the mutiny was likely to commence, and her plans for action were accordingly promptly arranged, and a short time found her securely secreted in the locality, with an old friend who assisted her in all her plans, and who was warmly, sincerely devoted to her service.

Many were the hours, when, confident in the security of her disguise, she wandered near the bungalow in which her beloved Stanley resided, in the fond hope of again beholding him, or, at least, with the blissful thought that she was near him, although he knew it not. Two or three times she had seen him as he entered or emerged from his dwelling, and so powerful were the emotions that the sight of him created in her breast, that it was with difficulty she could refrain from revealing herself to him.

She had been lingering near the spot on the evening of the first murderous attack on him, for a strange presentiment of threatened danger haunted her mind, and she could not rest easy or satisfied till she had seen him.

After much anxious deliberation with herself, she had written him a letter, to allay in some measure his apprehensions for her safety, and to convince him of her fidelity, and which epistle she had resolved by some means to have conveyed to him.

She was standing only a short distance from the bungalow, concealed behind a tree, from whence she could observe all that passed, without being seen herself, when the door, she perceived, was suddenly opened, and immediately afterwards Stanley issued forth, and slowly, and with a thoughtful and melancholy aspect bent his way past the spot where she was concealed.

How fondly palpitated the heart of Omelia when she beheld him, and what sincere regret did it afford her to notice the care and anguish which were depicted in his manly and expressive countenance. Her heart told her that his thoughts were fixed on her, and deeply did it respond to his emotions.

When he had got to some little distance, she slowly and cautiously followed him.

What followed has been already related, and therefore it is unnecessary to repeat it here, but the reader may form some idea of the emotions that agitated the gentle and affectionate breast of Omelia, when, after having secured the delivery of the letter she had written to her lover, she hastily bent her way on her return to the place of her concealment.

She had been the means of saving that valued life she so much prized, and the delight and gratification which that thought caused her were beyond expression. She had also revealed herself to him, he knew her secret, and that in some measure removed her own anxiety of mind, since she knew how greatly it must ameliorate the anguish and suspense of his.

From that evening she redoubled her exertions to endeavour to obtain all the secret information she could of the designs of the mutineers, and likewise to watch over the safety of Stanley.

During this time it is not to be supposed that Omelia never had any anxious thoughts regarding her guilty father. In spite of the unfeeling treatment she had ever experienced from him, and the little regard she was well convinced he had for her, she found it impossible to stifle every feeling of nature in her breast towards him, and she would have given anything could she have been the means of reclaiming him from his vicious ways, and inducing him to abandon those evil designs he had in view, and which must ultimately she firmly believed end in his own destruction.

We now come to the evening when for the second time she had succeeded in rescuing Stanley from an untimely death. Need we say that the poor girl's heart overflowed with gratitude to heaven as she hurried on her way to the place of her concealment? She felt that providence watched over and approved of her conduct, and that conviction encouraged her, and stimulated her to fresh exertions.

After walking at a rapid rate by the most unfrequented route, for above an hour, she entered the depths of a gloomy forest, where nature revelled in all its wildest phases, and darkness and horror predominated.

It was a place which few would like to venture into, even in the broad light of day;

but Omelia was a stranger to fear, and such wild and dreary scenes as the one she was now travelling through had lately become quite familiar to her.

To add, if possible, to the horrors of the scene, a storm which had been for some time gathering now burst forth with great violence, and Omelia therefore quickened her speed, in order to arrive as soon as possible at the place of her destination.

The rain came down in torrents, and the blusterous wind swept it furiously in the face of our heroine, and greatly retarded her progress.

The loud peals of thunder, and the vivid flashes of lightning, were almost incessant, in fact, nothing was wanting to complete the terrors of the scene.

With a bold heart, however, Omelia proceeded on her way, penetrating the most intricate of the forest depths, until her quick and cautious ear was startled by the sound of footsteps, and the voices of men behind her, and looking back, she saw through the darkness the forms of two or three persons in the distance.

Alone, and uncertain, of course, what the character of these men might be, Omelia could not help feeling somewhat alarmed, and she therefore drew herself cautiously aside behind a group of large trees till they had passed.

They approached, grumbling and talking in no very agreeable accents, but it was too dark for Omelia to be able to obtain any distinct view of their persons.

At last they approached so near that she could overhear nearly every word they said.

" How cursed provoking is this storm," remarked one of them, in surly tones, and whose voice Omelia thought she had heard somewhere before, " and to be overtaken by it, too, in such a place as this, where there is no chance of being enabled to obtain a shelter. However, we must push on our way, for there will be work for us to do to-morrow."

" Aye, you may well say that," replied one of his companions, the tones of whose voice were also familiar to the ears of our heroine, " we shall indeed have our work to do, and we must be prepared to meet it; so, as we cannot expect to find any human habitation in this dreary forest, we may as well brave the fury of the tempest, and push on our way with all the speed we can."

They passed close to the cluster of trees, among which Omelia was concealed, and at that moment a broad glare of lightning plainly revealed to her their persons and their features.

The feelings of Omelia may be readily imagined, when she recognised her father,

Allyghur, and two or three other mutineers. She shrunk back, and could scarcely repress a cry, but she quickly recollected herself, and crouching down, so as to avoid all possibility of being observed, they passed on, and their voices gradually died away in the distance.

"Wretched, guilty parent," cried Omelia, when they were gone, " what fresh and nefarious designs have you now in contemplation? May heaven frustrate them, and save you from that destruction into which you seem madly resolved to plunge yourself."

Filled with fresh apprehensions of some approaching danger, she now resumed her journey, anxious to reach the place of her destination, and after a weary walk of about another half hour, and when she was nearly drenched to the skin, an opening among the

No. 9.

trees, and a flash of lightning, revealed to her eager eyes the shadowy outlines of it.

Any stranger might have passed by without observing it, for who could have thought of meeting with a human habitation in such a wild and fearful place as that?

It was a pretty large, mis-shapen bungalow with a thatched roof, shutters or blinds concealed the windows, from which scarcely a ray of light, to show that the place was occupied, ever issued. Altogether it had a most cheerless and uninviting aspect.

This was the secret retreat of Omelia. The bungalow for many years had been inhabited by an old Hindoo (Kereda) and his wife, Omala, together with Miriam, their only daughter, simple, humble, but worthy people.

Kereda and his wife had known our heroine

from her childhood; from her mother they had received many acts of kindness, and for Omelia they entertained the highest esteem, and even affection.

It was to their lonely dwelling then that she had hastened immediately on her flight from the villa, knowing that from them she would be sure to meet with kindness and sympathy. They received her with every mark of affection and respect, listened to the recital of her sorrows with pity and regret, offered her all the assistance in their power, and entered freely and readily into all her plans for the future. It was at their suggestion that she assumed the disguise we have described, and which had already served so well to facilitate her designs.

These old people had a nephew, a young man of good character, a sepoy, but strongly opposed to the insurrectionary designs of most of his comrades.

This young man frequently paid a visit to his relations, and it was from him that Omelia obtained some valuable information, and the earliest intelligence of any new schemes that the mutineers might have in contemplation.

Omelia felt thankful on her arrival at the bungalow, after her adventure in the forest, and knocking upon the door the well known signal which had been agreed upon between them, it was immediately opened by old Kereda, who greeted her return with a hearty welcome, and ushered her into the room, where Omala and her daughter were anxiously awaiting her before a blazing fire, which they had prepared in consequence of the storm.

"My dear child," said the old woman, "I am so glad you have returned, for it is a terrible night, and you must be wet to the skin. You must change your clothes immediately, or you will certainly catch your death of cold. But dear me, Omelia, how alarmed you look, has anything happened?"

Kereda expressed the same anxiety as his wife, and Omelia explained the particulars of her having seen her father in the forest, and she had scarcely concluded, when there was a loud knock at the door of the bungalow.

"Who is that?" said Kereda, "it surely cannot be my nephew at this time of the night, and in such a storm."

"Now then," exclaimed a gruff voice outside, "are you going to keep us here all night waiting in the storm? Have you no feeling of hospitality in your nature?"

"Ah," ejaculated Omelia, in a low and trembling voice, "'tis them. 'Tis my father. Should he recognise me, I am lost."

The knocking at the door was repeated with more violence than before.

"Quick—quick, my child," said the old man, "retire into another room. They will probably only remain till the storm has abated or subsided."

Omelia hastily retired with the old woman and her daughter, and Kereda then opened the door and admitted Yunadar and his companions.

"You were very tardy in opening your door to travellers, old man," said Yunadar, "and on such a night as is not fit for a dog to be out in. However, here is the comfort of a sound roof and a blazing fire to make up in some measure for your short-comings. So we'll e'en intrude upon your hospitality till the storm has abated."

"You are welcome, friend Yunadar," said Kereda.

"Ah," exclaimed the former, with surprise, and starting. "Known! Who are you?— Kereda; is it possible? It is some years since we met before, and who would have thought of finding you inhabiting this dreary forest?"

"True," answered Kereda, "but the gloom of this forest agrees with my lonely habits."

"Well there is no accounting for taste to be sure," observed Yunadar. "But how is your wife, Omala, and your daughter?"

"They are both quite well, thank providence," said Kereda; "but see my wife is here to answer for herself."

Having left her daughter to keep Omelia company, Omala re-entered the room, and affected to greet Yunadar and his companions with much friendship and hospitality.

Refreshments were quickly placed before them, of which they were warmly requested to partake, and cheered by the friendly warmth of the fire, they did not seem to be in any hurry to depart, especially as the storm, although it had greatly abated, still continued with considerable violence.

"And your daughter, Yunadar—the fair Omelia, to whom myself and my wife were greatly attached in her childhood, how is she?" said Kereda.

"Name her not," replied Yunadar, in tones of wrath, "she is worthless, and I am half inclined to discard her for ever. She sets my authority at defiance, and refuses to leave those detested Feringhees, and return to my protection. They have corrupted her in her faith, and she has but too readily imbibed their pernicious principles."

"Indeed," said Kereda, with a well assumed appearance of regret; "I am sorry to hear that, for I had always entertained the highest opinion of Omelia. But let us hope that she will yet be awakened to a due sense of the folly and impropriety of her conduct."

"If she does not, be the consequences upon her own head," said Yunadar, sternly, "the rash, obstinate, headstrong girl, little does she imagine the brink of destruction she stands upon. In a few days, probably only a few hours, the spirit of anarchy, revolt, and bloodshed will have spread all over the country, and then it will be beyond my power, even had I the will, to save her from the general slaughter"

"I deeply lament the unnatural difference that exists between your daughter and yourself, friend Yunadar," said Kereda, "and hope that something will occur to avert the evils you apprehend."

"No," cried Yunadar, "'tis settled, the dye is cast, the doom is sealed, and let all those who have provoked it receive the fate they so justly merit The Hindoo's voice calls aloud for vengeance on his detested enemies, and it will be heard—it will be heard"

"May the Great Spirit prosper the righteous cause," said Kereda, emphatically.

"Aye, you speak well, friend Kereda," said Yunadar, approvingly, and not noticing the peculiar significance of the old man's observations. "Our cause is a just one; it is a bold resistance to tyranny, cruelty, usurpation, and oppression, and it must triumph. But see the tempest has at last ceased, so we must begone. We thank you for your accommodation; and should any travellers by chance stop at your bungalow, I must request you not to mention anything of our having been here, or that which we have spoken to you."

"You may depend upon my secrecy, Yunada," returned Kereda, heartily glad to get rid of his unwelcome guests so soon

He then saw them to the door of the bungalow, and watched them till their gaunt forms disappeared in the shadow of the thickly clustering trees beyond.

In what a state of trepidation, anxiety, and suspense did Omelia listen to the observations of her savage and unnatural parent; and what relief was it to her when they departed.

It was evident, from the manner in which he spoke, that he must have been made fully aware of her flight by the villain Allyghur, he had his reasons for not divulging the same to Kereda, and it was therefore clear that he could not entertain the slightest possible suspicion of the old man.

So far then Omelia had a right to consider herself safe from detection; and she was fully resolved, at every risk, to continue firm in the prosecution of her designs, which she had every confidence in being able most fully to accomplish.

Having with much gratification, heard her father and his companions depart, she returned to the room in which Kereda and his wife were seated, and thanked them both heartily for the manner in which they had acted, and the skill and precaution they had exercised, and the way in which they had succeeded in deceiving and quieting any suspicions that might have arisen in the breast of Yunadar and his companions

"Would to heaven," ejaculated our heroine, "that something would occur to induce my misguided parent to abandon his guilty purpose."

"Aye," observed Kereda, "I fear that he has resolved upon a desperate course, which he may have bitter cause to repent. For however the treacherous cause of the insurgents may for a time appear to triumph—and I shudder at the base contemplation of the horrible atrocities they will doubtless commit—they must ultimately succumb to the superior valour of British troops, and a just though terrible retribution will assuredly overtake them."

"True," coincided Omelia, "it shocks me to anticipate the frightful scenes that I have too much reason to believe will shortly be enacted; and I tremble for the safety of those whom I so fondly love; but let whatever may be the consequences to myself, I am determined that nothing whatever shall induce me to abandon those designs I have in view, and which are prompted by duty to my country and my fellow creatures, justice, and humanity"

"Noble-minded girl," said the old man, in tones of enthusiastic admiration, "may all good powers watch over and aid you in your generous and virtuous undertaking."

"Thanks, thanks," returned Omelia, "I do not fear the result; the integrity of my motives inspire me with every confidence. Dearest Stanley, I will pursue you, at any rate, and be ever near you like your own shadow."

A noble expression animated the handsome features of the Hindoo maiden, as she gave utterance to these observations, and the aged Kereda and his wife were again lost in affectionate regard and admiration for one so truly great, heroic, and self-sacrificing.

However, the time now warned to retire for the night, especially as our heroine had a design in contemplation which would compel her departure from the bungalow on the following morning.

In the meantime, Yunadar and his guilty associates, after leaving the bungalow of old Kereda, pursued their way with all the expedition they could make, and after travelling for about two hours by the most lonely, dreary, and unfrequented route, at length arrived at the place of their destination, where they met, as they had expected, a number of the mutineers from Meerut, who, knowing the sincerity and determination of the revengeful Yunadar and his companions, in the cause they had at heart, greeted them with every demonstration of welcome.

CHAPTER XVII.

THE PROGRESS OF THE MUTINY.—THE MAGA-ZINE.—A NOBLE ACT OF SELF-DEVOTION.

The mutiny spread with frightful rapidity. The fiends of vengeance had broken loose, and ravaged the unhappy country with remorseless fury, spreading terror around, and completely paralysing the faculties, and, for a time, suspending the energies of those who hitherto had been unaccustomed to fear.

And certainly nothing could possibly be more desperate and alarming than the aspect which affairs had now assumed. It was clearly discovered that the monstrous designs of the mutineers had been but too well matured and arranged, and, at the eleventh hour, the European population found themselves completely defenceless.

Regiment after regiment revolted, and those that remained apparently faithful could not but be looked upon with the utmost fear and suspicion.

Some days elapsed—terrible outrages and scenes of slaughter had taken place at Meerut and elsewhere; valuable lives among the British officers and men had been sacrificed, and women and innocent children had already fallen beneath the murderous weapons of the blood-thirsty miscreants whose horrible revenge it seemed that nothing but the extermination of the whole of the English people would satiate.

The appearance of the mutineers at one of the great gates of the city of Delhi was the signal for the rising of the regiments cantoned there. Pre-concert was established. In a moment the frightful work of devastation was begun.

The arsenal was seized—the bungalows of the officers were attacked—officers, civilians, merchants, missionaries were murdered, their houses pillaged and burnt, their wives and daughters brutally violated, their children massacred, every variety of savage cruelty was displayed, with one fell purpose of annihilating the European race.

Some few escaped in their clothes, and wandered about the country, concealing themselves until they could contrive to reach another station.

The success of the seizure of Delhi, and the proclamation of a new government in the name of the puppet king, excited the sepoys at other stations to insurrection.

Within a few days the flames of rebellion were raging at Agra, Lucknow, Allahabad, Benares, Mirzapore, Hissar, Misseerabad, Ferozepore, in fact, at every place where a regiment was located, always the same scenes —always the same frightful atrocities.

At those stations where men of nerve and foresight commanded, and where a few native troops remained faithful, the mutiny was checked at its outburst. The gibbet, the volley, and the sword had their victims; the terrible work of revenge went bravely on. But where there were no European troops nor dependable natives, the massacres, conflagrations, and spoliations were unchecked.

The red hand of the sepoy seemed determined not to be stayed until every vestige of European domination should be extinguished.

It must not be supposed, however, that the government remained inactive all this time. No; every available precaution was put in operation, and carried into effect. The European regiments were summoned from all their stations, and a large force marched towards Delhi, under the Commander-in-chief, Gen. the Hon. G. Anson, who, dying the day before he reached the town, was succeded by Sir H. Barnard. The regiments at Bombay and Madras were ordered to the Bengal frontier; messengers were despatched to bring regiments from Ceylon, the Cape of Good Hope, Mauritius, and succours were implored from England.

Regiments on their way to China, were stopped at Singapore, and their course diverted to India. The European population armed and exerted themselves everywhere. The ex-king of Oude, who, as has been before stated, resided at Calcutta, being suspected of complicity in the whole affair, his house was surrounded by a European regiment, and he himself seized, and made prisoner in Fort William.

Having thus given a few necessary particulars of the early progress of this gigantic and disastrous mutiny from the outbreak, we will once more resume the thread of our narrative at that point from which we have digressed.

Stanley's mind was now constantly in a feverish state of anxiety, and the worst and most dismal forebodings continually haunted and tortured his imagination. He read nothing but horror, misery and destruction in the future; and certainly the present ominous aspect of affairs fully sanctioned his apprehensions. How keenly did he feel for his noble countrywomen, and their helpless offspring, for, from what had already taken place, it was quite evident that the monsters would have no respect for age or sex; all who unfortunately might fall into their power would be destined to feel alike the horrors of their vengeance.

His bosom swelled with manly shame and indignation at the atrocities that had already taken place, and he invoked that just and terrible retribution upon the guilty heads of the miscreants who had inflicted them, which he was certain must sooner or later overtake them.

For his own part, Stanley would willingly have shed the last drop of his blood in the defence of that sex he so fondly loved, and whose deplorable situation, together with that of their husbands, children, and nearest and dearest relatives, so called aloud for sympathy and protection.

But the image of his beloved Omelia held the most prominent place in his thoughts. Knowing the danger to which she must be hourly, nay momentarily exposed, the risks she would have to encounter, the insults and outrages she would probably have to endure, lest she should betray herself, and he deeply lamented the circumstances that had driven her to such a desperate and dangerous course.

Should they ever meet again, which it was probable they would, he well knew that it would be useless for him to attempt to detain her, or to seek to persuade her to abandon her present designs, and to place herself in future under his honourable protection; still he resolved at least to make the trial, let the consequences be whatever they might.

He also greatly dreaded the thought of her falling into the hands of her father, whose feelings of anger were excited against her to the utmost degree, and whose desperate character would cause him to go to any extent, however monstrous and outrageous, in order to gratify his evil passions.

There was one circumstance, too, which rendered another meeting, at present, between himself and Omelia extremely doubtful and uncertain. The regiment to which he belonged was one of those that were ordered to Delhi forthwith, and surely the poor girl would not venture to follow him thither?

Anxious as Stanley was to again behold her, he almost wished that she would not do so, for he could vividly picture to himself in his imagination, the scenes of horror that were likely there to take place, and he shuddered at the thought of what might but too probably be her fate, should it be discovered by the mutineers that she was opposed to them and their diabolical designs. Her death would be certain to follow, and that, too, by the most horrible means that these refined monsters in crime could invent.

These dismal reflections cost him many painful hours.

We should probably have mentioned before that among Stanley's brother officers there was no one whom he more highly esteemed than Captain Sandford, with whom he had been acquainted for many years, they having been schoolfellows for some time, and Colonel Sandford, the parent of the young captain, having been on the most intimate terms with his (Lieutenant Stanley's) father.

Captain Sandford was about the same age as Edward, and possessed similar manly virtues, and that truly English bravery which had won for him the most honourable distinction.

Stanley had confided to this young man many of his secrets, for he knew he could depend upon his sympathy and friendship. He had made him acquainted with all the particulars of the passion which existed between him and Omelia, and what had so recently taken place, and Sandford had expressed his warmest admiration of the heroic character of the Indian girl, and took the greatest interest in her fate

It was therefore under all these circumstances, that it was with extreme regret that Stanley parted with the captain, he having been appointed to a post of some danger, namely, to take charge of a powder magazine which was situated in the suburbs of the city, and was greatly exposed to the attack of the mutineers. The number of men that could be spared him for this duty was very limited, but every confidence was placed in his skill and courage, and he himself entered upon his new appointment with the utmost avidity and hope.

The parting between Stanley and Captain Sandford was of the most friendly description, and the former could not help encouraging some painful presentiments, which he, however, prudently kept concealed within his own breast.

On the evening of the third day of the appointment of Captain Sandford, news hastily reached the station that a pretty strong body of the insurgents were on the way to the magazine, and that the situation of the gallant young officer, with his mere handful of men, was a most precarious one.

Our hero, and another officer, with a small reinforcement of troops, were therefore despatched to the assistance of Captain Sandford with as little delay as possible.

It was a very dark night, and it was difficult to distinguish objects at any distance. They had not proceeded far, however, when the loud report of fire-arms rent the air in the direction of the magazine, which convinced them that the work of destruction had began.

They therefore quickened their speed, in order to get to the relief of the beleaguered troops; but they had not proceeded far when they felt a terrific shock, like that of an earthquake: dense clouds of smoke for an instant or two filled the atmosphere, which were succeeded by volumes of sparks and burning embers, which too plainly told the dreadful tale; the explosion of the powder magazine had taken place, and Stanley and his companions had too much reason to fear the most terrible consequences.

He trembled for the fate of his friend, and feared that his most gloomy and torturing apprehensions were doomed to be realised.

They hurried on their way towards the fatal spot, and had not far advanced when they perceived a number of the enemy approaching. They immediately drew themselves up in a position to give them battle. A sharp volley took the mutineers by surprise, and threw them into confusion. They quickly fled in all directions, without having caused the least injury among the soldiers commanded by Stanley and his brother officer.

The latter with a portion of the men went in pursuit of the rebels, and Stanley, with the remainder, hastened to the spot where the magazine had stood, the most dreadful forebodings as to the fate which had befallen poor Captain Sandford, and the brave fellows under his command, haunting his mind.

On arriving at the spot, a frightful scene indeed presented itself. Scarcely a vestige of the magazine was to be seen, but numerous ghastly, blackened, and horribly mutiliated corpses met the gaze strewed about in every direction.

Stanley searched eagerly among the dead for the body of his unfortunate friend, but he was nowhere to be seen, and our hero had no doubt that he with many others had perished in the magazine, and his remains blown to some distance into the air.

A short time having been given for the smoke to disperse, Stanley and several of the soldiers were about to venture into the ruins of the magazine, when their attention and curiosity were drawn to the form of a soldier, who slowly emerged from them, and seemed to be supporting the wounded form of one of his comrades.

Stanley hastened to ascertain the facts, and his astonishment may be easily imagined when he beheld his friend, who although frightfully wounded, disfigured, and completely in a hopeless condition, still lived, though quite unconscious.

With all possible despatch the unfortunate gentleman was conveyed to the city, where everything was done to relieve him, that humanity could suggest, though from the first it was perceived that it would be without any successful results.

He died the following morning in great agony. He, however, recovered sufficiently to be able to relate some particulars of the melancholy catastrophe, by which his own heroic conduct, and noble self-devotion were made strikingly apparent.

It appeared that the little band of brave fellows under the command of Captain Sandford, in charge of the magazine, were surprised by a far superior force of the mutineers, who demanded possession of the place.

Captain Sandford, however, was not the sort of man to yield to a demand so peremptory and so insolent, and, nothing daunted, he marshalled his men, and determined to resist to the last.

The combat was desperate and sanguinary, a great number had fallen on both sides, when Captain Sandford and a few others were driven into the magazine; the awful crisis thus approaching.

"My brave fellows," said Captain Sandford, addressing himself to his companions, "the moment is a desperate one. This magazine once in the possession of the mutineers will give them a wonderful advantage, supplying them with the means to extend their atrocities. The welfare of our country and our brave comrades in arms demand a fearful sacrifice, and I for one do not hesitate to make it. There is not an instant to be lost; overpowered by numbers, our troops cannot long continue the combat. Let those who grudge their lives in their country's cause, away, and, if they would disgrace the proud name of Englishmen, seek safety in flight. This moment do I fire the magazine, rather than it should fall into the hands of our blood thirsty enemies."

A deafening shout, followed by three cheers for old England and Queen Victoria arose from the heroic men who were with Captain Sandford when he had concluded the above noble and patriotic speech, and not one offered to move from the fatal spot.

The next moment the train was fired, and the awful explosion took place, with what results has been shown.

———

CHAPTER XVIII.

AN UNEXPECTED ENCOUNTER.—OMELIA AND FLORA.

It would occupy a space in this narrative much greater than we can very well spare, were we to attempt to expiate upon all the architectural glories of the Eastern World, which are in perfect keeping with the surpassing magnificence of its scenery, a brief sketch, however, is indispensably necessary.

The grandeur of the architectural remains which still adorn every part of India, go to prove, notwithstanding the prejudices of many, that civilization among the Hindoo and Mahomedan rulers had greatly advanced from the earliest ages. The majestic temples, gorgeous palaces, and splendid tombs, still extant, though in various stages of decay, these we say which so abundantly decorate the southernmost points of the Peninsula, and so from thence to the vicinity of Delhi, go incontestibly to confirm that fact.

The Hindoo temples are the main objects of attraction in Southern India; some of them being of great height and vast extent, covering two or three acres of land, and divided into an infinite number of apartments.

It would more especially be a difficult task to do adequate justice in the confined limits of our pages, to the wonders and beauties of the cave-temples in Western India and the Deccan; the most extraordinary of which are Ellora, Ajunta, and Elephanta.

The cave-temples of Ellora—or Verrool, as it is called by the natives—are situated about a mile from the ancient Mahomedan city of Dowlatabad. In magnitude and execution they excel everything of the kind in India; and, as far as can be ascertained, they were constructed 2,500 years since, but the Brahmins assign them a much more extravagant antiquity, going even to 2,000 or 3,000 years higher than the date assigned by us, according to the scriptures, to the creation of the world.

Then there are the temples of Ajunta, not so extensive, but equally as curious as those of Ellora; the cave-temples near the Island of Bombay, on Salzette, Elephanta, &c.

Go we now to the interior of the continent, and more especially in Upper and Central India, we find the pagodas and sculptured rocks are very numerous, and illustrative of the extensive character of the mythology of the Hindoos.

At the confluence of rivers on the summit of lofty hills, at the base of prodigious rocks, in secluded places, the traveller constantly comes upon singular remains, attesting at once the vigorous conceptions and religious zeal of the statuaries.

At present our remarks must be more particularly confined to Delhi, and its immediate neighbourhood, where there are some beautiful mosques and other edifices in excellent preservation. There is the Jumma Musjeed, the Mausoleum of Hoomaioon—the scene of the late execution of the sons of the puppet King of Delhi—and Kootub Minar.

The Kootub Minar is a lofty pillar, or minaret, deriving its appellation from Kootub-o-deen—the pole star of religion—who, under the Emperor Mahomed Ghori, became a mighty general, and ultimately achieved the throne, and was the first of the Patan or Afghan sovereigns.

The circumference of this pillar measures 143 feet, and its height was formerly between 200 and 300 feet, but the upper part being struck by lightning and destroyed it now only reaches about 110 feet.

In the City of Delhi, as we have before stated, Flora Melville passed but a dull and sorry life, being without any companion suited to her tastes and habits, and her thoughts also being constantly fixed on Lieutenant Stanley and poor Omelia, who, she had too much reason to fear were lost to her for ever.

And now strange and alarming rumours reached her ears and those of her father, which created considerable uneasiness. This was some little time previous to the outbreak and massacre at Delhi, alluded to in a foregoing chapter.

Business frequently called Mr. Melville from home, and at such times, Flora tired of the dull monotony of the house, would either stroll about the city, or sometimes she would venture into the suburbs beyond the walls.

One afternoon she had—tempted by the fineness of the weather—greatly extended her usual walk, and warned by the approach of evening, she looked up from the meditations that had occupied her mind, and was surprised to find that she had wandered as far as the tomb of Hoomaioon, which is situated about six miles from Delhi.

Through masses of ruins the tomb of Hoomaioon is a noble building of granite, inlaid with marble, and in a very chaste and simple style of gothic architecture.

It is surrounded by a large garden, with terraces and fountains, all now gone to decay, The garden itself is surrounded with an embattled wall with towers or minarets, four gateways and a cloister within, all the way round.

In the centre of the square is a platform of about twenty feet high, and about two hundred feet square, supported also by cloisters, and ascended by four flights of granite steps. Above rises the tomb, also a square, with a great dome of white marble in the centre.

The apartments within are a circular room, in the centre of which lies, under a small raised slab, the unfortunate prince to whose memory the fine building is raised. In the angles are smaller apartments, where other branches of his family are interred.

It was near this magnificent monument then that Flora Melville now found herself; the moonbeams fell richly upon the noble pile, and also revealed to her distinctly in the distance the Jumma Musjeed or principal Mosque of Delhi.

This is a superb building, and in excellent

repair. It is elevated very advantageously on a small rocky eminence to at least the height of the surrounding houses. In front it has a large square court, surrounded by a cloister, open on both sides, and commanding a view of the whole city, which is entered by three gates, with a fine flight of steps to each.

In the centre is a great marble reservoir of water, with small fountains supplied by machinery from the canal. The whole court is paved with granite inlaid with marble. On its west side, and rising up another flight of steps, is the mosque itself, which is entered by three noble gothic arches, surmounted by three domes of white marble.

It has at each end a very tall minaret. The size, the solidity, and the rich materials of this magnificent building, place it nearly at the head of Mahomedan architecture now extant.

Flora gazed listlessly and indifferently at these splendid objects of attraction. At any other time they would have excited her most enthusiastic admiration; but now her mind was too busily occupied with melancholy thoughts for her to pay any attention to them beyond a cursory glance.

Finding the distance she was from home, and fearing the alarm which her father would naturally feel at her absence in the present disturbed state of the country, should he have returned before her, she proceeded to leave the spot without any further delay.

She had not got many paces, however, when she was alarmed by hearing the hasty tread of footsteps behind her, and before she could turn round to ascertain who her pursuer was, a delicate hand was laid on her arm, and a feminine voice desired her to stop.

She looked hastily on the speaker. The light of the moon only partially reached the spot on which she was standing, and the stranger with apparent caution averted his face, so that she could only have a slight and indistinct view of his features, but as far as Flora was enabled to judge from the light and delicate character of his person, and the tones of his voice, he was a mere youth, and an Hindoo. Yet she felt a strange sensation of mingled alarm and curiosity steal over her.

"Who are you, stranger?" she tremulously demanded, "and for what purpose do you seek to detain me?"

The youth hesitated for a moment, and then, in an evidently disguised voice, replied,

"There is danger at hand, lady; but trust to my guidance, and fear not; this way."

"Whither would you lead me, young man?" eagerly interrogated Flora, still endeavouring, but in vain, to get a clear view of his features; "why do you appear to take any interest in the fate of a stranger?"

"Ishmael is ever ready to aid and protect the helpless and the innocent," answered the supposed youth, with suppressed emotion.

There was something in the tones of the voice which now went to the heart of Flora, and excited her utmost curiosity and astonishment.

"Why do you so carefully conceal your features?" she anxiously inquired; "surely we have met before."

"There is no time to waste in words, lady," answered the young man, again in a disguised voice, and almost a whisper. "I would save you from threatened danger, I repeat; do not doubt me; quick, quick, this way. Hark!"

Flora now indeed imagined that she heard approaching footsteps and the murmuring of voices, and, seriously alarmed, she at once resigned herself without any further hesitation to the care of the mysterious stranger.

Turning an abrupt angle in the road upon which they had entered, the youth led Flora hastily along by a pathway which was apparently unfrequented, still concealing his features from observation as much as possible; and at length having conducted her to some distance from the spot where they had encountered each other, he paused, and said—

"You are now in safety, lady, if you do not delay. Make your way with all despatch to the city, by the path before you. Farewell, may all good spirits watch over you and protect you and your revered parent."

It would be almost impossible to describe the exquisite pathos and feeling with which those words were spoken. The emotions of Flora were excited to a most painful degree, and her heart palpitated violently. The stranger raised her hand respectfully to his lips as he spoke, and Flora then, for the first time had a distinct view of features that no disguise could possibly conceal from her penetration.

Heavens, how she started, and could scarcely believe the evidence of her senses.

"Merciful powers!" she exclaimed, "it is Omelia—dear, dear Omelia! Oh, pardon!"

The next moment they were locked fondly, fervently in each other's arms.

"Dear Flora," said our heroine at length, and gently disengaging herself from her arms, "yourself and your father did me wrong by suspecting the integrity and purity of my conduct. But 'tis past now, and forgiven. Omelia constantly remembers you in her prayers. But we must part now. If you respect my safety and happiness, mention not to any one save your father that you have seen me, or the character I have assumed. Farewell, and bless you—bless you."

"Dearest Omelia," cried Flora, " oh, surely we must not part thus."

But the poor girl only waived her hand affectionately, with a sweet smile, and in a moment she disappeared, leaving Flora Melville completely transfixed with astonishment and admiration.

"Mysterious, heroic, noble-hearted girl," exclaimed Flora, " oh, how much I wronged her by my cruel suspicions. May heaven, in its mercy, guard her from every danger, and again restore her to us."

Thus saying she hurried from the spot.

Surprised, bewildered, yet at the same time gratified to have met with the poor girl, whom she had feared she might never behold again. Flora Melville retraced her steps towards home.

Her heart felt much lighter than it had

No. 10.

done for many weeks before, and hope again sprang up in her breast, notwithstanding the present gloomy state of affairs, and the dismal forebodings to which they so naturally gave rise.

Omelia forgave the past, and harboured no vindictive feeling against her or her father. No; it was impossible for her noble, generous nature to do so; and her heart throbbed with feelings of the most sisterly love and gratitude towards her.

But Edward Stanley; he, she had too much reason to fear would view her with feelings of resentment, and would never cease to look upon her with cold indifference, if not with absolute scorn. That idea was torturing and humiliating, but she tried to stifle it in her breast, and warned by what Omelia had said to her of threatened danger, she hurried towards her home, frequently looking back to ascertain whether or not any one was watching her.

On reaching her residence, she found her father most anxiously awaiting her return, and he greeted her with much affection and satisfaction. But he quickly noticed the agitation and excitement of her looks, and eagerly inquired the cause.

In as few words as possible Flora explained to him all that had happened, and the reader may easily imagine with what unfeigned astonishment Mr. Melville listened to her.

"Noble girl," he exclaimed, "to what dangers and difficulties does she voluntarily expose herself, and for what purpose I am at a loss to imagine. Would that we could persuade her to return to our care and protection, and to forget the past."

"Oh, my dear father," returned Flora, "although nothing may induce her to relinquish her present designs, I am certain that she harbours no feeling of animosity in her bosom against us. Her words, and the sincerity of her manner, fully convince me of that; and that, on the contrary, she is ever most anxious for our welfare and happiness."

"Generous-hearted girl," said Mr. Melville, "I do believe it, and deeply do I regret that any harsh observations I might unguardedly, in the excitement of the moment, have uttered should so have wounded her feelings, and caused her to abandon us. But thank heaven, she is at present safe, though I am at a loss to unravel the mystery of her designs, or why she has assumed her present disguise."

"To further her plans, doubtless," replied Flora, "which could not be accomplished so certainly, if her sex were known. And has she not besides good cause to be in fear of her guilty parent, whose nefarious schemes, and those of his reckless colleagues, it is her object to endeavour to frustrate. Should they meet, and Yunadar detect her, I tremble to think what the consequences may be."

"True, most true," coincided her father, "such an encounter would be most unfortunate, for Yunadar is a desperate and determined man, and even the voice of nature could not move him to relent, when his evil passions were excited. Omelia has therefore acted with the greatest prudence and precaution in assuming her present disguise; and I sincerely, fervently hope and trust that providence will continue to watch over and protect her through every danger it may be her fate to have to encounter."

In this wish Flora most heartily joined, and, after some further conversation, they separated for the night.

CHAPTER XIX.

THE MUTINEERS.—OMELIA IN DANGER.

Scarcely had Omelia and Flora quitted the spot where they had met, when the forms of several men stole cautiously through the darkness towards the tomb of Hoomaioon. And having first looked carefully to the right and left, as though they feared they might be observed, they entered through the masses of ruins which conduct to this magnificent mausoleum, these men stepped stealthily, and passed on to the extensive garden by which the building is surrounded.

As has been shown the quick ear of Omelia had caught the sound of their footsteps, and their voices, and she had only just withdrawn her companion from the spot in time to avoid discovery.

It was Yunadar, Allyghur, and several more of the mutineers, who had sought the silence and secrecy of the Hoomaioon at that hour, to deliberate and consult upon the important and treacherous designs they had in contemplation.

All was profoundly silent in that sacred place, and there was no prying eye to watch them, or to penetrate their secrets.

And now the bright moon emerged from behind the clouds that, for a brief period, had obscured her silvery face, and shed a chaste and mellow light on all around. The fountains glistened in its beams, and the noble terraces, the embattled towers or minarets, and the mausoleum itself, were shown with great effect.

Yunadar, Allyghur, and their companions, advanced to the tomb itself, and on arriving there, the former applied a small silver whistle to his lips, and blew a signal, which was answered from another within the tomb, and the mutineers ascended one of the flights of granite steps that conducted to it, and entered the noble and sacred building, where several armed men were waiting to receive them, and who greeted them with rough cordiality and welcome.

"'Tis well," said Yunadar, who seemed to be looked upon as the leader and director of this part of the rebellious movement, "we are all punctual, and that is the sure stepping-stone to success."

"Aye, returned one of the men who had been waiting in the tomb, "we are all firm and true to the righteous cause we have at heart, I can safely answer for, and therefore to fail is impossible."

"True, Achmet," coincided Yunadar, "our cause is just, and it must, it shall succeed. The accursed Feringhees have yet to learn the desperate courage and determination of those whom they have for so many years tyrannised over, oppressed, and despised, and they shall be taught a bloody lesson that they can never forget."

"Vengeance is now within our grasp, and who know better than ourselves how to take advantage of the opportunity?" observed the ruffian Allyghur.

"Enough," said Yunadar, "we know and understand each other. But now at once to business. How progresses our plot Achmet?"

"As well as our most fervent wishes could expect," answered Achmet, "the revolt at Meerut, and many other places, you are doubtless aware is complete; hundreds of our comrades panting for the appointed hour, are now secretly congregated, from the various stations where they have been disbanded, in this neighbourhood, and our enemies little dream of the extensive plot that is ripening for their destruction."

"Glad news," exclaimed Yunadar, exultingly, "the realisation of the wronged sepoy's hopes is certain, and the hated usurpation of the English will soon be at an end, never more to be established in the Indian empire. But what of Nena Sahib?"

"You ought to know, Yunadar," answered Achmet, "that the Nena is the leader, and prime mover of all our designs, and that his fidelity to our cause cannot be doubted. Well has he played his part, year after year, and misled and deceived our enemies, who placed every confidence in him, and thought him one of their warmest friends. But soon will he turn the reliance which they place on his fidelity to an account it would be impossible for them to anticipate. Terrible, remorseless will be the vengeance he will wreak upon their heads, for when the tiger-hearted Nena is once aroused, the fierce tempest of his fury knows no limits."

"True," rejoined Yunadar, "we all know his courageous and resolute character, and that nothing can stem the torrent of his wrath. But the hour for us to strike the blow which shall once more make us masters of our great Mogul capital, and exterminate the hated Feringhees within its walls. When is that appointed to take place?"

"Before this week has elapsed," replied Achmet, "if adverse fate fights not against us, Delhi will be in our hands, all the Feringhees residing in it, man, woman, and child alike, slaughtered without mercy, and our work will then proceed bravely, and we may boldly set our enemies at defiance, the triumph of the Hindoo is certain."

Loud demonstrations of approbation and exultation followed this speech, which did not subside for several minutes; and then the villains proceeded to discuss more fully and explicitly their treacherous designs.

This occupied some time, when the meeting broke up, and they prepared to separate; Yunadar, Allyghur, and their comrades by the same way that they had entered the place, and Achmet and the others by a different route.

Omelia, after quitting Flora, and when she was out of sight, paused, and for a minute or two hesitated how and where to proceed. But her course was soon taken, and she retraced her steps towards the spot where they had met.

She felt gratified and relieved of some weight of anxiety, now that she had seen Flora Melvile, for whom she still entertained the warmest esteem and solicitude, and that she had, in the brief interview, been enabled to enter into some explanation of her feelings, and the motives for her conduct. She would indeed deeply have regretted had Flora or her father have been left to labour under any false impression, or to believe her to be vindictive or ungrateful, and she now thought that she had shown and said enough to convince them to the contrary, and she felt happier than she had done for some days before.

She walked slowly on, for the evening was so fine, that she quite enjoyed it, and various and interesting were the thoughts that occupied her mind.

She arrived at the embattled wall which surrounded the tomb of Hoomaioon, before she was scarcely aware of the direction she had taken, and a feeling of curiosity prompted her to enter the place, which she did, after ascending one of the four flights of steps which led to the garden.

Here she paused for a minute or two on the principal terrace, and gazed with feelings of wonder and admiration upon the picturesque and solemn scene.

She advanced to one of the entrances of the tomb, and was about to pass into the building, when the voices of men smote her ears, and arrested her in her purpose.

She drew back a few paces, somewhat alarmed, and hesitated whether or not to hasten from the spot, in case of danger; but a certain feeling of curiosity which she could not resist, prompted her to listen, and she returned to the entrance of the mausoleum, and concealing herself as well as she could, in the shade of some trees that grew near, she paid every attention, and endeavoured to catch the observations of the men within the tomb. For some moments she was unable to do this, but at length she heard sufficient to convince her of the real character of the villains, and her surprise and terror may be imagined when directly afterwards she recognised the harsh and disagreeable voice of her father. Still she was like as though she was fascinated, and could not move from the spot, and listening with breathless attention, she was now enabled to catch distinctly every word that was uttered, and she shuddered at the extent of villany that existed in her father's breast, and those of his infamous colleagues. She could have no doubt that the revolt was progressing rapidly, and that ere long some dreadful scenes of atrocity would be enacted in the capital of Delhi, and when she remembered that her beloved Stanley and those friends who were dear to her, were now there, she trembled for their safety, and yet, at present, she knew not how she could assist them, or apprize the proper authorities of the danger which threatened them.

While these torturing thoughts were still passing rapidly in her mind, she was startled by hearing that the mutineers were about to separate, and to leave the tomb, and alarmed for her safety, she hurried from the spot, and dashed precipitately down the steps, but had only just began to descend them, when she heard the shouts of the men behind her, and who had evidently caught sight of her retreating form.

Yunadar and his companions had only just issued from the entrance to the building when the former happening to cast his eyes in the direction which Omelia was pursuing, in the moonlight caught a glimpse of her receding form.

"Ah, a spy," exclaimed Yunadar, "that daring stripling, from the precipitation with which he is endeavouring to effect his escape, has evidently been listening. He is an Hindoo, but may, nevertheless, be a traitor to our cause. What-ho! rash, daring boy," he shouted aloud, "stop, and explain the meaning of your conduct, or a brace of bullets may enforce compliance."

It would be a difficult task to seek to describe the terror of Omelia, although the reader must by this time be fully aware that it was not a trifle that could daunt her, but here she had fearful odds to contend against, and the observations of her father were sufficient to terrify her beyond description; she therefore heeded not his mandates, but continued her flight.

"The boy is deaf to your commands, Yunadar," said the ruffian, Allyghur, levelling his pistol; "so here's to teach him better manners."

So saying, before Yunadar could prevent him—for he hesitated before he proceeded to the extremity which he had threatened—Allyghur discharged the contents of his pistol, it was expected with unerring aim, for the villain was seldom known to miss his mark.

The bullets whizzed close past Omelia, but did not touch her, and she continued her flight for a few paces further, when her limbs failed her, and, in spite of the consequences, she was compelled to stop.

In a few moments Yunadar and the others came up with her, and she now gave herself up for lost.

───

CHAPTER XX.

THE RESULT OF THE ADVENTURE.

"Now, boy," said Yunadar, grasping our heroine, who had averted her face, fiercely by the wrist, "speak, who are you? If your conduct is guided by no sinister motives why do you fly your countrymen in such evident alarm? No hesitation, this is no time to waste in prevarication or subterfuge; were you not listening just now outside the tomb? Answer me promptly for on that may depend your life; you have men to deal with who are desperate and determined, and who will not therefore submit to be trifled with."

Omelia trembled, but was unable to articulate a word.

"He is silent, obstinate fool," said Allyghur, sternly, "shall we submit to be treated with contempt and defiance by a mere boy?"

"Beware!" said Yunadar, fiercely, and addressing himself to Omelia, "if you are not mad, you will dare longer obstinately to resist my demands. Who are you? I repeat. What has brought you hither? and why do you thus carefully endeavour to conceal your features from scrutiny?"

Still Omelia was so greatly agitated by fear that she found it impossible to utter a syllable.

"Submit no longer to this insolence," said Allyghur, again levelling his pistol menacingly at Omelia, "force the truth from his lips."

Yunadar, with an oath, now drew our heroine hastily round, and by the light of the moon gazed sternly and eagerly into her features. Their familiarity at once struck him, and in excited tones he impatiently demanded—

"Ah, what face is this I gaze upon? Whose features are these? What means their strange resemblance? Speak, on your life I charge you, speak without any more delay, who are you? I am satisfied you are not what you would wish to appear to be."

"Spare me! Mercy father!" faltered our heroine, and. at the word, Yunadar started with amazement and incredulity.

"Ah," he exclaimed, and gazing more earnestly into the trembling girl's face. "Omelia—my daughter—away from her friends, and in this disguise; is it possible?"

"Oh, detain me not, father," she implored, tears at the same time trembling in her eyes, "I beseech you suffer me at once to depart; you know not the painful circumstances that have driven me to this disguise, and how much depends upon my safety. I will pray for you, bless you, do anything to serve you, or to snatch you from the brink of that frightful precipice on which you stand, but do not—oh, do not force me to accompany you, or suffer the wretches who accompany you, and with whom you so unfortunately associate, to insult me."

The energy of her manner, and the painful emotion which she was evidently suffering, did seem to make some impression upon her father's cold and insensible heart, for after gazing earnestly at her for a few moments, without uttering a word, he relinquished his hold, seemingly bewildered, and half unconscious what he did.

"How now, Yunadar?" demanded Allyghur, sternly, "are you mad, that you thus tamely submit to the persuasions of this bold and daring girl? Know you not that she harbours treachery in her breast, and that now she only seeks to escape in order that she may accomplish her designs? The disguise she has assumed, and her abandoning the protection of her friends, show at once the nature of her intentions. She has been listening to our conversation in the mausoleum, and death, by right, should be the reward of her daring curiosity. At any rate, she is now in our power, and she must not be permitted to escape from it. Nay, then if you are weak and irresolute, I, at least will act with decision and determination."

As the ruffian thus spoke, he was about to seize Omelia, while the other mutineers looked sullenly and threateningly on, when, mustering up all her courage, and fixing a look of bold defiance upon Allyghur and his savage companions, she drew a revolver, which she had the precaution always to carry about with her, from her bosom, and levelling it at him, and erecting herself to her full height, in a firm voice, she exclaimed—

"Back, unmanly ruffian, back! You have no timid girl to deal with, but one who has before, and will again set you at scorn and defiance. Dare to seek to detain me against my will, or advance a step to molest or pursue me, and by all my hopes, let whatever may be the consequences, I will stretch you dead at my feet."

Completely astounded by such matchless daring and heroism, Allyghur, Yunadar, and the others started back, and gazed at her with astonishment, and Omelia, taking advantage of their confusion, gradually retreated from the spot, still facing them, and levelling the revolver at Allyghur.

Having gained the outside of the wall which surrounded the garden, she quickened her pace, and hurrying towards a thicket close by, was lost to view before Allyghur and his companions had recovered from their surprise and confusion.

"Perdition!" furiously exclaimed Allyghur, "are we going to suffer ourselves to be defeated, and that by a presumptuous girl? Fool that you were, Yunadar, this is all your doing. She has obtained this night possession of some of our most important secrets, and she will not fail to reveal them to our enemies at the earliest opportunity."

"No, no," answered Yunadar, "she will not dare to do so. Yet I am ready to own that I was wrong in suffering her to escape me; quick—she cannot have got far; pursue her, but beware, Allyghur, remember she is my daughter, and I charge you on your life not to commit any act of violence against her."

Allyghur muttered something sullenly and indistinctly between his teeth, and he and his guilty companions then followed hastily in the direction which Omelia had taken. But as far as the light of the moon would allow their eyes to penetrate, they saw no traces of her, and curses, deep and bitter escaped the lips of the enraged and disappointed Allyghur.

"She has escaped, through your worse than childish weakness," he said, addressing himself sternly and reproachfully to Yunadar, "and now therefore, I trust you are satisfied."

"Hold your upbraidings, Allyghur," cried Yunadar, angrily, "for I am in no mood to brook them. This unexpected meeting with Omelia, and under such singular circumstances, surprised and bewildered me, and I scarcely knew what I did. But your apprehensions and suspicions are unfounded, consideration for my safety, will, I am convinced render her cautious, and prevent her from betraying us."

"It will be well if your surmises do not prove to be erroneous," returned Allyghur, "you place too much confidence in her, and the regard she has towards you. Her behaviour on previous occasions, ought to be sufficient to enable you to estimate the value of her filial affection, or the respect in which she holds your parental authority. She is crafty, treacherous, and designing, and there is no knowing the mischief we may have to apprehend from her. At any rate, it was sad neglect and imprudence, not to secure her person when it was in our power."

"I own it was wrong and unfortunate not to do so," coincided Yunadar, "but it cannot now be helped, so it is idle to waste a multiplicity of words in useless expressions of regret. At any rate, we know the worst, and can therefore use every timely and necessary precaution to guard against the danger, if there be indeed any to apprehend, while I do not believe there is   But come, we waste time in tarrying here, so let us at once away to the place of our destination."

Allyghur grumbled out some surly and dissatisfied reply, which Yunadar did not very distinctly hear, or if he did, heeded it not, and they then hurriedly departed from the spot, and took the way which led to the rendevous of the main body of the mutineers which they were anxious to reach by the morning.

Thankful to think that she had had so providential an escape from a situation of such imminent danger, Omelia quickened her speed, and soon got beyond the reach of pursuit.

The meeting with her misguided parent excited various emotions in her breast, and rendered her uneasy and anxious. In spite of his unnatural conduct towards her, she found it impossible to stifle every feeling of nature towards him, or to discard him entirely from her heart, and when she reflected upon the desperate nature of the lawless cause he had so recklessly espoused, and the fatal consequences it must ultimately bring upon his head, she felt the deepest regret, and apprehensions for his fate.

How to act in the present emergency she was completely at a loss, for in endeavouring to frustrate the diabolical plans she had overheard, she must necessarily place the life of her father in the greatest peril, and there was something so cruelly unnatural, in her opinion, in that idea, that her heart revolted at it with a feeling of horror.

"Misguided man," she soliloquised, as she proceeded on her way, "would to heaven that you could be awakened to a full sense of the danger, the guilt, and the enormity of the cause you are pursuing, and abandon it ere it is too late. For a time indeed, the triumph of the diabolical designs of yourself and your associates may appear complete, but a terrible retribution must assuredly sooner or later overtake you, which I tremble to contemplate. Oh, that you would repent, and render yourself again worthy of my fondest filial love. Who could feel greater pleasure in bestowing it, or more proud to acknowledge her parent, did his virtues render him worthy of it, than the humble sepoy's daughter?"

There was truth and sincerity in every word which the poor girl uttered, and the feelings that throbbed and agitated her bosom and the expression which animated her features as she spoke, plainly proved it.

Then she thought of the dark feelings of hatred and revenge which her father had evinced towards her beloved Stanley, because he happened to bear the same name as the betrayer of his sister, and the most dismal foreboding haunted her mind, and apprehensions for the consequences, should him and her lover ever again encounter each other. She earnestly prayed that providence would keep them apart, and avert those terrible evils which she had so much cause to fear."

Agitated by these reflections, she continued on her way, pondering in her mind what was best to be done, and, after a long and tedious walk, and almost worn out with fatigue, and the excitement consequent on the extraordinary events that had occured to her, she at length reached an obscured spot in the suburbs of the city of Delhi, where we will at present leave her.

CHAPTER XXI.

A MEETING AND AN INTERRUPTION.

One of the great objects in the present narrative is to blend useful information with amusement, an object we shall ever have prominently in view. Hence the following remarks, which no doubt will prove interesting to the general reader, and are necessary, previous to recording the startling events that will come more immediately under our notice.

The progress of the British in India is one of the most marvellous circumstances in the history of nations. The first British commercial intercourse with India was in 1591, when a ship from England reached India after a three years' voyage. The voyage is now made in less than double that number of weeks. When the Old Fort of Calcutta was besieged, our whole army consisted of but a few hundred British troops and a very few thousand sepoys. The company's possessions in India in 1756 were the Island of Bombay and the factories at Surat and Calicut on the West coast of Hindoostan; on the East, Masulipatam, Madras, Arcot, and Devi Cattah. In Bengal, the towns or villages of Chuttanutty (since become Calcutta) and Govindpore; lastly, a factory at Bantam in Java. The total possessions at the time the Old Fort was besieged occupied scarcely a hundred square miles of land. There was nothing that could be called territory. In this present year, 1857, the company's territories are of vast extent. They are virtually bounded by Cabul, Beloochistan, and the Arabian Sea on the West, the Bay of

Bengal on the South, the Irawaddy and the Gulph of Siam on the East, and the Himalaya mountains on the North. The provinces eastward of Calcutta embrace an area of 190,000 square miles; those in the Peninsula of Hindoostan and Island of Ceylon occupy an area of about 600,000 square miles; and from Calcutta to the confines of the Indus and the Hymalaya, the provinces spread over an area of about 690,000 square miles. The total amount of territory over which the company has now kingly authority and sway is scarcely less than a million of square miles. The present annual revenue of India (exclusively of Oude) is about £30,000,000 sterling.

Such were the state and circumstances of the Britsh in India, at the time of this monstrous revolt.

And what, after all is really the cause of the present disaffection? What has brought about the Indian rebellion? We shall endeavour to discover.

It has been suggested that the soldier's grievance lies in the fact of our assumption of the power of certain native princes. This, says a contemporary, is, in the abstract, a cause of quarrel fair enough, though, in fact, we have only used the common right of war, or taken the forfeit of broken treaties, or interfered for the common good, in support of order against anarchy and outrage, and no sooner than was necessary. But it is enough that we are not at war anywhere with the people. We are not at war with the country round Delhi, or even with the general inhabitants of Delhi. We are not at war with any country, even with Oude. The garrison of Lucknow no sooner broke through the circle of their besiegers than they found the resources of the country at their disposal. We are only at war with a definite number of regiments of idle and pampered soldiers, with certain pretenders and their armed bands, who have profited by the disturbance, or been drawn into it, and with a few, very few, mere fanatics and enthusiasts animated by a religious zeal. Thus, on the whole, there is an utter want of that common cause, that sense of justice, that nationality, or that religion, which in other instances has bonded myriads into a successful or desperate resistance to the invader or the oppressor. We have against us a disunited crowd, which has renounced its flag in sheer recklessness and wantonness. Like a silly truant, it has taken a holiday, and knows what to do with it. It is now at large, and only experiences the miseries of liberty without principle. It encounters us every now and then, but without heart, and therefore without success. It flies because it cannot stand before us; it reassembles round its flags because it has no-

where else to go to, and is waylaid and robbed by the very villagers; it returns to the war because it has nothing else to do. That, indeed, will be its course, and the natural death of the mutiny. Every sepoy fights with a halter round his neck; he knows it; yet he cannot but fight and be beaten.

Notwithstanding the alarming reports that had been spread abroad, and which recent events tended to corroborate, but a very small portion of British troops were despatched to Delhi, considering that the city was left to the mercy of so large a number of native soldiers whose fidelity could not be depended upon.

Among others was, as has before been stated, the regiment to which Stanley belonged. It was now located there in comfortable quarters.

Again must we enter into some interesting details of the history of the Mogul capital and dynasty.

The founder of the Mogul dynasty in Hindoostan was Baber, a descendant of Timur the Tartar, who, towards the close of the previous century, had opened the way for the establishment of his family on the throne of Delhi. The date of this memorable event was 1525, a year which is not altogether without its interest in European annals. Baber reigned only five years, having, after conquering Candahar, Lahore, the Punjaub, Delhi, and Behar, died in his capital in 1530.

Hoomaioon his son, succeeded to the throne, but was not long allowed to enjoy it in peace. Shere Khan, the Afghan regent of Behar, refused to give up the fortress of Chunar. A war ensued. The Great Mogul had decidedly the worst of it, and was obliged to seek refuge at the court of Persia. And again, for some years India owned an Afghan governor. But in consistency with that generous spirit of hospitality with which the Arabian Nights have made us so familiar, the fugitive king met with much practical sympathy in his house of refuge. His cause was espoused; Persian troops were placed at his disposal; and after fighting a great many battles, he was enabled to re-enter Delhi in the year 1554. He was not destined, however, to enjoy a continuance of repose. As he was supporting himself with his staff, on the marble stairs of his palace, the staff slipped, and he fell to the bottom. The accident proved fatal. He expired in a few days after, in the year 1555, the fifty-first of his age; and was succeeded in the kingdom by his son, Akbur.

Akbur was only fourteen years of age when his father died; but he had been nursed amid difficulties and dangers, and was not altogether disqualified for the office to which he was called. When Hoomaioon, with the few friends who adhered to him, first fled from India, they nearly perished in the sandy desert which lies between Ajmeer and the Indus. With the utmost difficulty, and after the loss of many lives, they arrived at Amercot, the seat of a Hindoo Rajah, about two hundred miles from Tatta, and it was here that Akbur was born. During the troubled years which followed, the life of the young prince was more than once in danger. Within an empire as yet far from settled, his chief business, as was to have been expected, consisted in the repression of insurrections and the complete establishment of his own sovereign rule; but he was not free from the characteristic instincts of his race, and we read accordingly, also of ambitious attempts made to extend the boundaries of his dominions. At the time of his death, therefore, which happened in the fifty-second year of his age, the Mogul empire was found to have received considerable enlargement. It is now divided into fifteen vice-royalties, called Subahs, each governed immediately by its own viceroy, called Subahdar. The names of the Subahs at the death of Akbur, were Allahabad, Agra, Oude, Ajmere, Guzerat, Behar, Bengal, Delhi, Cabul, Lahor, Multan, Malva, Berar, Bandesh, and Amednuggur. The reader, by examining any map of India, will be able easily to trace out for himself the boundaries of this empire. Not yet so extensive as that of the British, it was still one with which any dynasty might well have been content.

Akbur was succeeded by his only surviving son, Selim, who assumed the name of Mahomed Jehangire, or Conqueror of the World. His reign commenced October 21, 1605. One of the circumstances which had the greatest influence on the character and history of that prince was his marriage with the wife of one of his Omahs, or nobles, whom, like David of old, he removed out of his way by assassination. The story of this lady, who is known to fame by the name of Noor Mahl, has quite the air of an Arabian romance. Her father was a Tartar, who left poverty and his native country to seek his fortune in Hindoostan. While crossing the desert his wife was overtaken by the pains of labour, and gave birth to a daughter. Wanting the means of suitable conveyance, and urged on by the consideration of failing provisions, they resolved to abandon the child to its fate. They actually did leave it—and the mother held on her way as long as she kept the tree in sight under which she had placed the babe, but then her heart failed her. She could not proceed a step farther; and, having persuaded her husband to alter his purpose, the distressed pair returned to

the spot together On reaching the place, they saw with horror their infant daughter wrapped in the folds of a large snake, which appeared just on the eve of devouring her. The shriek which broke from the breast of the parents at the sight startled the creature, which dropped the child and retreated hastily to its den. A deliverance so wonderful produced a re-animating effect. The Tartar succeeded in carrying his child into India in safety—saw her, ere he died, the favourite wife of the great Mogul—and rose himself to be Prime Minister of the empire.

India appears from a very remote period, to have been exposed to incursions from the north-west—from the direction of Persia. One of the Satrapies of Darius, and that apparently the richest of them all, extended into the country, it is supposed, as far as Delhi, and included among others the provinces of Cabul and the Punjaub. Alexander, the conqueror of Darius and of Persia, did not, in his expedition into the interior, proceed so far; but his successor, Seleucus, is recorded to have gained several victories over a people living on the Ganges. With the exception, however, of the exposed districts near the Persian frontier, the inhabitants of Hindoostan may be said to have escaped the curse of foreign dominion till the year 1000, A. D., from which point we date the beginning of the Mahommedan conquests.

So early as 632, the Caliphs had become sovereigns of all the countries which were wont to own the sway of the Persian monarchy. For a time their rule was firm and vigorous, but the luxury of oriental life coming in time to produce its usual effects of feebleness and effeminancy, various military leaders holding posts on the outskirts of the empire were encouraged to assert their independence. Among the kingdoms thus formed was that of Caudahar, or Ghazna (Ghuznee). It was founded in 976, by a man who had originally been a Turkish slave, and whose son, Mahmood, was the first of the great Indian conquerors.

During a period of more than twenty years —from 1000 to 1024—this active and zealous Sultan (he was the first who claimed that title), made no fewer than twelve expeditions into the interior; overrunning Ajmeer, Lahoee, Delhi, and Cashmere; and compelling the people everywhere to acknowledge the true prophet. One instance of his zeal may be recorded :—Having, with some difficulty got possession of Sumnant, a strong castle near the city of Diee, he entered a celebrated temple, belonging to the place. Finding there a gigantic idol, he was filled with indignation at the spectacle, and with his iron mace fetched a blow at its head which struck off its nose. In vehement

trepidation the Brahmins crowded around, and offered him millions to save their god. Mahmood, however, crying that he valued the title of breaker more than that of seller of idols, gave orders to proceed with the work of destruction. At the next blow the belly of the idol burst open, and forth issued a vast treasure of diamonds, rubies, and pearls—rewarding the holy perseverance of the Sultan, and explaining at the same time the devout liberality of its defenders.

The sun was just declining behind the eastern hills, gilding the noble domes of the different mosques, and the tall minarets with its departing rays.

"All was quiet, and apparently tranquil in Delhi, there were few persons in the streets, and silence pervaded almost every house, the inmates having sought a few

No. 11.

hour's repose from the sultry heat of the weather.

Stanley left the barracks and sauntered along, with downcast eyes, and deeply wrapped in thought.

Delhi, like most of the other towns in the interior, owes its principal importance to the cantonment, which, as at Agra, Lucknow, Benares, Hyderabad, and Ajmeer, Dinapore, Cawnpore, Poona, Meerut, Bangalore, Bellary, Belgaum, and similar places, forms a considerable part of the town itself.

These cantonments are maintained by the towns which consist, for the most part of superior buugalows (villas) in compounds (enclosures), bazaars, and places of worship, those which are on the banks of the Ganges, having likewise warehouses, and handsome flights of steps.

Yet at that time, when all around was so beautiful, and glittering with dazzling effect in the sunbeams, those places seemed to be entirely deserted, and Stanley pursued his solitary ramble through the ancient Mogul city in comparative silence, and without anything to break the chain of his meditations.

These were by no means of the most cheerful or hopeful description, for altogether the circumstances that surrounded his destiny were of a sombre character, and calculated to fill his mind with anxiety and suspense.

He was too well satisfied from what had already taken place, and from his own personal observations and private information, that events were fast drawing to a crisis, and that something dreadful was about to take place, and though fear, under the most trying and perilous circumstances, was an entire stranger to his heroic and manly breast, he could not, knowing how ill-prepared the government were to meet any great and desperate emergency, but feel uneasy and apprehensive

"Land of wealth and beauty," he soliloquised; "land which the Almighty has blessed with a superabundance of its choicest gifts, and whose people, once sunk in the lowest and most degraded state of barbarism, are now beginning amply to feel the wide spread blessings of civilisation, will ye at the instigation of a few ambitious, sordid, unprincipled, and mercenary wretches cast aside the allegiance due to your benefactors, and deluge your country in blood, the blood of the innocent and defenceless, and spread desolation, horror, and despair, where all has long been happiness, prosperity, and content? Misguided people, will nothing awake ye from your dream of error, until too late? Alas, I fear not—and—" he continued, after a brief pause, and striking his forehead in anguish, "her whose safety and happiness are far more precious to me than mine own existence, dear, dear, devoted Omelia, is now a friendless wanderer, apparently without a home, or place of refuge, and will be exposed to all the horrors that, I am thoroughly convinced, will shortly break forth with irresistible fury, spreading destruction on all who come within the range of its revengeful and deadly influence. Rash, imprudent girl, oh, what madness must it have been to urge you to such a desperate course, that could induce you to abandon those friends, who, at any rate, in spite of what has recently taken place, ever proved themselves to be most anxious and solicitous for your welfare and happiness."

A deep sigh proceeding from some one near him, interrupted him in the midst of this soliloquy, and looking up hastily, his surprise, agitation, and confusion may be readily imagined, on beholding Flora Melville standing before him, and gazing upon him with an expression of intense sorrow and regret that was enough to move even a heart of the most insensible quality to sympathy.

Her face was pale, and the haggard appearance of her handsome features, showed in unmistakeable characters, the heavy weight of care her mind had long been labouring under.

On beholding the eyes of the handsome young officer (whom she still loved so truly, fondly), fixed intently upon her, a crimson blush at first suffused her cheeks, then tears, in spite of her efforts to restrain them, gushed to her eyes, and, with another deep sigh, she hastily averted her looks, covering her face with her hands.

Stanley was much moved by the emotion which the poor girl evinced, and the melancholy alteration there was in her appearance, and, approaching her respectfully, he gently took her hand, and repeated her name in accents of kindness.

She started at the sound of his voice, in tones so different to those which she had expected to hear, and looked hastily up, her eyes still filled with tears, but with mingled emotions of joy and gratitude now throbbing in her breast.

"Mr. Stanley—I—I—am happy to see you again—and hope you are well, and—" she faltered out, but was unable to finish the sentence, and, without withdrawing her hand from his, she again averted her looks, and trembled with the agitation of her feelings.

"Flora," said Stanley, in the same kind and respectful tones, "I am fully aware that I meet you under the most disadvantageous and embarrassing circumstances; but still I am most anxious to enter into an explanation upon a subject, which I fear has somewhat prejudiced yourself and your father against me. On our last interview, in the excitement of my feelings naturally caused by the painful and unexpected event that had occurred, I am afraid I made use of observations that might appear to be ungenerous, severe, and uncalled for; for having so committed myself towards those for whom I have ever felt the highest esteem and friendship, I now beg to be permitted to offer every apology, and at the same time to assure you that I have never ceased to reflect upon that part of my conduct with feelings of the deepest and most sincere regret."

"Oh, Mr Stanley," replied Flora, in a tremulous voice, but cheered and encouraged by his words, faintly smiling through her tears; "this condescension and apology is more than I or my father can have any possible right to expect from you. Certainly at the time, when we were labouring under the most torturing feelings of anguish and regret, at the rash and dangerous course which poor Omelia had thought fit to adopt, your observations on that fatal evening, did seem harsh and uncalled for. But—but—'tis past now, forgotten, forgiven, and alas! I fear that my conduct, although, heaven knows, unpremeditated, was much to be condemned, and—and—"

"No more, Miss Melville," interrupted Stanley, "I know and fully appreciate your feelings, and believe me I deeply sympathise with you. I must not venture to say more upon a subject which is so deeply painful and embarrassing to us both. The virtues of Flora Melville, must ever command my warmest regard and friendship.

"Generous, noble hearted Stanley, Flora Melville will henceforth be only too proud to be allowed to view you with a *sister's* regard," she sobbed forth; but she could say no more; her limbs trembled, and, overpowered by her emotions, she drew aside her head, and burst into tears.

Stanley, who was greatly affected, returned no immediate answer, but once more raised her hand to his lips, and kissed it respectfully

Deep blushes suffused the fair cheeks of Flora Melville, her heart faltered, her limbs trembled, and contending sensations of joy, sorrow, contentment, and regret struggled in her breast. Yet did she honour Edward Stanley, (for the manly explanation he had given, and the sentiments of esteem and friendship, he had with such evident sincerity expressed towards her) more than ever, though she was now fully aware (if she had ever dared to encourage a thought to the contrary) that esteem and friendship was all that she could expect from him.

It was a delicate moment to them both, one of mingled pain and satisfaction, of pleasure and embarrassment, and they both remained silent, although their looks fully revealed the thoughts that were passing in their minds.

They were aroused from this state of silence and inaction, by a rustling sound, as of hastily gliding footsteps, followed by a faint exclamation of surprise or anguish, immediately behind them, and turning quickly round to ascertain from whom it proceeded, they beheld standing at a short distance from them, in an attitude of astonishment, and gazing intently at them, in the dim shadow of the twilight which had now fallen around, the light form of an apparently Hindoo youth.

The heart of Flora beat violently, and so did that of Stanley, for it needed no second glance to convince them that the eyes of Omelia were fixed upon them.

"Omelia!—dear Omelia!" they simultaneously exclaimed, and they rushed towards her, but she remained fixed in the same attitude, gently waving her hand while the melancholy glances of her eyes, and the sad expression of her beauteous features, showed the painful and conflicting emotions that at that moment agitated her gentle bosom.

"My beloved Omelia," at length said Stanley, with looks of inexpressible affection, and unable any longer to control his feelings; "heroic, noble-minded girl, who with such fond devotion and anxious zeal, art ever watchful of those you love, with the care of a guardian angel, why do you thus stand and gaze silently? Oh, surely this unexpected meeting is fortunate, and, since it may bring about a reconciliation between those dear friends who never should have misunderstood each other, must be hailed by you, as well as myself and Miss Melville, with feelings of pleasure and gratification."

Omelia sighed, and a pearly tear drop was seen to tremble in her eye, which, however, she hastily dashed away, apparently ashamed of the momentary weakness she had betrayed.

Stanley hastily took her unresisting hand, which he first pressed to his lips, then to his heart, while in the tenderest, and most anxious accents of sorrow and sympathy, he ejaculated:

"You sigh, Omelia, and your looks express regret, and doubt. Oh, answer me, I implore you, why is this? What painful thoughts have taken possession of your breast?"

"Alas! alas!" sighed Flora Melville, and tears started to her eyes as she spoke, "too well do I know that I am the cause of this anguish, this doubt and suspicion, in the mind of Omelia. Would to heaven that I could lay bare the guileless thoughts that now held possession of my breast, and convince her of their purity. But my presence pains and annoys: and I would be no obstacle to the complete happiness of those whom I so warmly esteem. Lieutenant Stanley can and will corroborate my assertion, I know, that our meeting was purely accidental. But let me begone. Farewell, and may the Supreme power, in its infinite mercy and grace, watch over you, dear Omelia, and shield you from every danger, though deeply, most deeply do I regret that you cannot be persuaded to abandon this unseemly disguise, and return to those friends, who revere you as their nearest and dearest relation. God bless you.

"Stay, Miss Melville," said our heroine eagerly, and gently arresting her; "it is not thus that we must part. Some explanation is due from me to you, and I should despise myself did I for a moment hesitate to give it. Oh, how much you wrong me, lady, if you imagine that I could ever harbour one vindictive, one jealous, or suspicious feeling towards you; too well do I know the probity of your heart, and respect and honour your virtues to do so. No, 'tis no such despicable feelings which now, or ever did occupy my breast towards you; it is one of regret, of sincere and painful regret, that I should be the cause of disappointment to the hopes, which, lured by a passion it was not in your power to control or subdue, you fondly, perhaps, too sanguinely indulged in; that I should be the barrier to your happiness, by monopolising that manly heart which might otherwise be devoted to you. I feel my own unworthiness, (humble as I am) to aspire to the affections and the hand of one so far above me, and—"

She paused, for her emotions were too great to allow her to finish the sentence, and she turned aside her head and wept.

"Omelia, my own sweet Omelia!" exclaimed Stanley, violently agitated, and encircling her waist with his arm; "for the love of heaven, do not speak thus, for your words torture me, and every pang which racks your heart, is worse than agony to me. I know, you should know the generous and womanly feelings of Flora Melville too well, to believe her capable of wishing you to make any such sacrifice as that you hint at, for her sake, even if it could be productive of any favourable results to herself. Banish then such thoughts, I beseech you, from your mind; bury the past in oblivion, abandon the dangerous and mysterious designs, you have at present in contemplation, and which may be productive of consequences that I shudder to think upon, and return to the protection of those who, I am certain, will so gladly receive you, and study your future welfare and happiness, which I know they will consider as valuable as their own lives."

"Oh, yes, yes," eagerly exclaimed Flora, and she extended her hand to Omelia, which the latter pressed fervently to her lips; "it is the fondest wish, the most anxious thought of myself and my father; and surely Omelia cannot so far forget the happy past, ere those unfortunate differences arose, as to refuse to yield to our entreaties. Come Omelia, sister, I will e'en call you, I beseech you no longer hesitate; cast aside this disguise, quit the life of peril you have so rashly entered upon, let the warmth of our former friendship be only now cherished in your remembrance, and return to the arms of those who are so anxious again to receive you."

"No, no," replied Omelia, "it must not, cannot be, anxious though I am to comply with that affectionate address, and, by my

future conduct to evince the gratitude which, believe me, dear Flora, is inherent in my breast towards you and your father. Important is the great task I have freely, voluntarily imposed upon myself, and which I have sworn to accomplish or perish in the attempt. I must not, will not break my oath. Farewell, Flora, adieu dear Stanley, may the Great Power which watches all our actions, protect, love, and bless us as we desire."

She spoke these words with the most powerful emotion, and most impressive and eloquent were the looks which she fixed upon her lover and Flora Melville, who were much moved by the energy, earnestness, and pathos of her manner.

She smiled faintly, through the tears that still trembled on her eye-lashes, on Stanley, and made an effort to release her hand from his hold, but he detained her.

"Mysterious girl," he exclaimed, "how inexplicable is this conduct. Whither would you go? Where is your secret retreat? And why, oh, why should you thus recklessly, wantonly expose yourself to such numerous and fearful perils? My brain is bewildered, and I know not what to conjecture. If you really love me, you will no longer keep me in this agonising state of anxiety, uncertainty, and suspense. Nay you shall not leave me till from your lips I have received a satisfactory explanation of this extraordinary and ambiguous conduct."

"Seek not to detain me," she said; "you know not how much depends upon the prompt and certain execution of my plans; any delay might be fraught with the most incalculable danger. I have already explained all to you that it would be safe or prudent for me to do at present. Be satisfied; doubt not my constancy. Farewell, dear, dear, ever loved Stanley; Miss Melville, friend, benefactress, sister, adieu. The thoughts of Omelia will e'er be fixed upon ye both, her woman's hand will endeavour to shield ye from impending evils; her tongue will constantly invoke the blessings of heaven upon your heads."

As she gave utterance to these words the expression of her features, and the eloquence which beamed from her eyes, was beautiful in the extreme; and no one could possibly have gazed at her without entertaining sentiments of the warmest esteem and admiration towards her.

With a gentle effort, she disengaged her hand from that of Stanley, and was about to retire hastily from the spot, when Stanley, who, in spite of all that she had said, could not resist the anxiety and curiosity which prompted him, was preparing to follow her when she suddenly paused, and fixing a serious and rather reproachful look upon him, in solemn accents, she said:

"Lieutenant Stanley, if you value the sentiments I have acknowledged for you, and would not expose me to defeat and probable ruin, you will not attempt to follow me, or to discover the place of my present retreat. That, for awhile at any rate, must remain a secret; the lives of hundreds, nay, perhaps thousands, depend upon its being kept so. Remember my words, and as you value my future happiness, and your own, respect and obey them."

Having thus spoken, she tore herself away, and disappeared in the darkness, before Stanley and Flora Melville had sufficiently recovered from the surprise and confusion into which the mystery of her observations, and the determination of her manner had thrown them.

CHAPTER XXII.

THE MYSTERY STRENGTHENED.

"Shall I, can I any longer endure this suspense?" exclaimed Stanley, at length arousing himself; "no, by heaven, I will not! dear Omelia, 'tis not mere idle curiosity, but anxiety for your safety and welfare that urges me on, and, in spite of the warning you have given me, I will this night set my doubts at rest, if there be a possibility. Flora Melville adieu—excuse my abrupt departure. We shall, I trust, shortly meet again."

He awaited not her reply, but hastening in the direction which Omelia had taken, left Flora in a state of greater agitation and perplexity than ever.

"What can possibly all this tend to?" she soliloquised; "what can possibly be the result of it? The conduct of Omelia hourly becomes more impenetrable to me, I am lost in amazement and mystery."

She moved slowly away from the spot as she thus spoke, wrapped in meditation on the singular and exciting events of the evening.

Her meeting with Stanley, however, and the explanation which had taken place, had greatly relieved her mind, and she felt far more happy and content than she had done for some time before.

The further observations of Omelia, too, were also a great consolation to her, tending as they did to remove all possible doubts from her breast, as to the feelings which she entertained towards her and her father.

On arriving at home, and relating to Mr. Melville all that had taken place, his surprise may be readily imagined, but at the same time he could not but express his great satisfaction.

"I thought that Lieutenant Stanley possessed too much the soul of honour and justice," he remarked; "long to remain without offering such apology and explanation as were undoubtedly due to us. He has well and properly acquitted himself, and he has raised himself higher than ever in my estimation by doing so. To you, Flora, he has made the *amende honorable*, and, although, it is now quite certain that you can never hope for or expect a return of that warm and ardent passion he has inspired in your breast, I trust that you may find fortitude, my dear girl, to bear with the disappointment as becomes the daughter of Mr. Melville. May it please the Almighty to prolong my days to behold you the wife of one who may be equally deserving of you."

Flora sighed, but attempted no other reply, and throwing herself on her father's bosom, he embraced her affectionately.

The conduct of Omelia also greatly perplexed Mr. Melville, though he felt highly pleased and satisfied with the assurances she had made to Flora, and was ready to admit that she had fully acquitted herself of all suspicion of malice or ingratitude.

These events served them to converse about for some time, when more satisfied and contented in their minds than they had been for some time before, and encouraging the hope that the clouds that had lately lowered upon their fortunes would quickly disperse, and the sunshine of peace and happiness succeed, they retired for the night.

But a few more nights would elapse and how great and terrible would be the change of circumstances to Mr. Melville and his daughter, and most of the unfortunate persons at present residing in the doomed city of Delhi.

But we will not anticipate our tale.

In the meantime, Stanley with a palpitating heart, and filled with expectation, hurried on as well as the pale light of the moon would allow him to discern in the same direction which our heroine had pursued on so hastily leaving him and Flora, although the chance of overtaking her seemed to be but slight, as she had not taken either of the two wide and extensive streets that form the main thoroughfares in the capital of Delhi, but as well as he could observe, she had diverged abruptly to the left, and wound her way through the more narrow and intricate streets that led outside the walls.

Nevertheless he was resolved not to abandon his hopes without an effort; he therefore quickened his speed, and entered the street at the entrance to which he imagined that he had seen her disappear. It was long and winding, and offered every facility for flight, and concealment while doing so.

As has before been stated, the moon had just arisen, but the light it shed was so faint that it was impossible to distinguish objects very clearly at any distance.

Once or twice indeed, Stanley imagined that he caught a glimpse of a light, shadowy receding form, but it vanished so suddenly that he concluded he must have been mistaken. However, he pursued his way until he arrived at the end of the street, and then hastily crossing a square or open space, passed out by one of the smaller gates outside the walls.

There he paused for an instant to reflect, and now for the first time he could not but consider that he had started on a somewhat wild and hopeless errand; although he had delayed only a few moments in commencing his pursuit of Omelia, she was evidently so thoroughly acquainted with every nook and corner of the place, and inch of the ground, that she would find no difficulty in eluding him.

He had half made up his mind to abandon the pursuit, and to retrace his steps to his bungalow, when, happening to cast his eyes towards a narrow pathway, overshadowed by trees on either side, he was positive that he saw a human form glide quickly past, and which, from the dress and the stature, as far as he had time to observe, strongly resembled that of Omelia. But in an instant it was gone.

He did not wait to reflect; but quick as thought he dashed towards the spot where he had seen the form. He beheld no traces of it, but he hurried forward, his curiosity and anxiety now more than ever excited, and determined to pursue this adventure to the last.

The tall and majestic trees that grew on either side of this road or pathway rendered it a pleasant avenue, and the rays of the moon stealing in with mellow radiance betwixt the foliage, added to the pleasing effect of the scene. At the termination of this avenue the ground gradually rose, and was surmounted by huge trees that grew closely together, forming a complete forest of small extent, or wilderness of the most romantic description.

Stanley pursued his way, and had reached about the centre of the avenue, when he again caught a hasty glance of the form which had before attracted his attention, and which was making towards the thicket.

He had a distinct view of it, and was certain that he was not mistaken, that it was Omelia, and he called loudly upon her to stop, though for obvious reasons he forbore to mention her name.

Omelia, however, heeded him not; but seemed to increase her speed, and at length gained the thicket, where she again disappeared.

Stanley, however, now convinced that it was her whom he had seen, was encouraged, and dashed hastily forward in pursuit, gaining the thicket in an instant, and plunging at once into its depths.

The moon broke in a stream of light through the branches above his head, and again Stanley beheld the retreating form of his beloved Omelia, and he now appeared to be so close to her, that it seemed as if he could seize her by merely stretching forth his hand.

His heart throbbed violently with hope and expectation, and he now ventured to mention her name (though in a subdued tone of voice), for he imagined that there was no one near to overhear him.

But a moment, and Omelia turned her face towards him, and it was clearly revealed to him in the moonlight, the expression of the beauteous features of the Hindoo maiden was tender in the extreme, yet it was not unmingled with a look of gentle reproach, and she waived her hand to warn him to desist from following her footsteps, and to begone, but so eager and excited were the feelings of Stanley that he heeded her not, and bounding forward, and stretching forth his arms, he imagined to clutch her, but in a moment, and as if by magic, she seemed to fade from his sight, like some airy vision, and to sink into the earth, how, or by what means, he was at a loss even to conjecture.

Surprised, astounded, and scarcely believing the evidence of his senses, he was hastening to the exact spot whence Omelia had disappeared in so mysterious a manner, when a rustling sound was heard, and in a moment there stood before him, where she had vanished, the ancient form of a man with a venerable beard which descended to his chest, and wearing the dress of a Brahmin.

There was something particularly solemn and impressive in the expression of this aged man's features, and over whose head eighty winters seemed at least to have passed, and as his keen, penetrating, and almost unearthly looking eyes, were fixed steadily and earnestly upon the young lieutenant, the latter could not help feeling a sensation of awe almost amounting to dread stealing over him, for which he was at a loss to account.

The old man's form was attenuated, nearly bent double with age, and he supported himself on a staff,

He stood exactly on the spot where he imagined Omelia had disappeared, and as she sunk into the earth, so did he, like the magicians of old, seem to rise from it. Certainly he had neither come from the right or the left, and the only token of his approach had been a rustling sound, like the rambling of the wind among the forest leaves. And now as he stood before the young officer, in an attitude which was not only striking but picturesque, and with his small, bright, flashing eyes fixed stedfastly upon his features, he looked like some supernatural being, or such as are so often described in works of romance.

We have said that Stanley was astounded. His faculties were indeed, for the moment, almost suspended, and he stood gazing in stupified amazement for several minutes upon the singular old man, without being able to question him or even to utter a word.

Not a muscle of the stranger's countenance was disturbed, not a limb moved, all was stolid, cold, inanimate, save those bright flashing eyes, as if the figure had been sculptured from a block of stone, and placed on the spot where it stood by some invisible means, to excite the wonder and bewilderment of the beholder.

At length Stanley aroused himself; he could no longer endure this state of doubt, curiosity, and suspense, and, as he advanced a pace or two, he, in a firm voice, demanded,

"Who are you, old man, who thus appear so suddenly and mysteriously before me, and why do you stand there as if to dispute my further progress? Speak I command you."

"You command?" reiterated the old man, in a voice which seemed to come from the hollow recesses of some rocky cavern, and the expression of his countenance underwent not the slightest change; "presumptuous boy, you know not the venerable Sheikh Moolah Kootab, or you would be more choice and careful in the words you use to address him. Back, your further intrusion upon these precincts is strictly forbidden, and may be fraught with danger such as you can but little imagine."

"Am I to suffer myself to be made the dupe of some impudent imposture," returned Stanley, haughtily and impatiently; "stand aside, old man, I say, and do not attempt to obstruct me further."

"You are bold, stripling," said the singular old man, in the same tone of voice as before, "but you will soon have sufficient to put your courage to the test. Bow your head in reverence to one who is the friend of the good, the brave, and the innocent, ere I yield compliance to your wishes."

Stanley moved by the solemn impressiveness of the old man's words, did bend low his head before him. Again the rustling sound was heard; Stanley raised his head in eager curiosity—the old man was gone, and he stood alone, gazing upon the huge trees that grew around.

The astonishment and perplexity of Stanley at this extraordinary climax to the mysterious adventure were strengthened to an almost incredible degree. He looked around on the ground, and up to the very topmost branches of the trees, but nothing whatever to explain these remarkable events met his observation. He was lost in amazement and fruitless conjecture, and could scarcely believe but that he was dreaming.

All, however, was silent as the grave, save the murmuring of the wind among the branches, between which the bright face of the moon ever and anon peeped, as if she was ogling at, and enjoying the mystification and confusion of the surprised and bewildered Stanley.

Having in some measure succeeded in arousing himself, he made a strict search about the immediate spot, but could discover nothing to gratify his curiosity, or tend to the least to unravel the mystery; and deeply pondering upon all the remarkable and romantic circumstances in his mind, he turned reluctantly away, vexed and disappointed, and slowly retraced his steps by the way he had come, the lateness of the hour also warning him that it was time to return.

As he walked on his way, the various conflicting thoughts that crowded upon his busy brain may be readily imagined.

It was evident that the mysterious old man whom he had encountered in so singular a manner, was colleagued with Omelia assisting her in her plot, and that their secret retreat was somewhere in the wilderness, but how to account for their sudden disappearance he knew not, and the longer he reflected on it, the more did he become bewildered in the maze of useless conjecture.

He felt vexed, and could not but think that Omelia, however praiseworthy her intentions might be, was trying his patience somewhat too far.

He continued on his way, still ruminating on the strange and bewildering subject, without being able to arrive at any satisfactory conclusion, and at length he arrived at his bungalow, and almost immediately retired to his chamber for the night, but not to rest, for busy thought continued to rack his brain, and to banish sleep from his pillow.

CHAPTER XXIII.

THE CAVERN IN THE WILDERNESS.

Breaking in between the trees, a little to the right of the spot wherein Stanley had encountered the mysterious old man, as recorded in the previous chapter, was a bleak or large space of rising-ground, overgrown with wild shrubs and flowers of every variety of hue, such as are only to be seen in a tropical climate.

The trees clustered so thickly around this place, and their intertwining branches, so completely shaded it from the view, that a stranger might have passed by the spot a hundred times without observing it, or having the least suspicion that it was there.

Concealed artfully by a flagstone (which was easily removed) and some loose brushwood, in the side of this small promontory or hillock, was an opening, just large enough to admit of a human form. The opening widened with the descent, which was gradual, and accelerated by rude steps formed of stones and clumps of trees, partly embedded in the earth, and on alighting at the foot of which the inspector would find himself in a small square open space, with crevices above, here and there, admitting a partial ray of light, and just a breath of air.

Narrow, winding passages, of some extent, branches off to the right and left of this place, and taking the right, after traversing the passage for some distance, you would find yourself, to your utter astonishment, at the entrance to a spacious cavern, such as human hands had evidently been most industriously and ingeniously employed in rendering it to some extent, fit for habitation.

This subterranean was arched and lofty, and dimly lighted by a lamp suspended by a chain from the roof.

In a recess in one corner of this strange place, was a bed formed of rushes and leaves, and opposite was an opening which led into a smaller cavern, which contained nothing but a bed of a similar description to the one we have just mentioned.

A rudely formed table, two stools, a small globe, a few musty volumes, writing materials, cooking utensils, a musket, a couple of pistols, and an old sword, was all else contained in the cavern.

It was truly a wildly romantic place, such as we often read of in works of fiction, but which few persons had an opportunity of realising. A place fitting for the haunt of robbers, and those whose deeds would not bear the light of day, but certainly not such a one as a person would be supposed to locate himself from choice, that is unless he should be labouring under some disease of the intellect.

In another part of the principal cavern, we had forgotten to mention, was a third opening, which led into a small circular space, and in which was a deep well of pure water, a great desideratum to any one who had taken up his abode in this subterranean retreat

This then was the gloomy and unwholesome place, in which the mysterious old man whom Stanley had encountered in the wilderness, had dwelt, it was said, or supposed, for more than half a century, and it was there also that our heroine had for the present, sought and found a safe asylum.

The Sheikh, (as he was called) was indeed a most extraordinary man, and was looked upon with mingled feelings of awe, dread, and reverence by all who knew him, and there were few of the natives who resided for miles around that did not. He was supposed to possess the gift of second sight, no one dared to attempt to molest him, or to pry into his secrets; his retreat was held sacred, and was perfectly secure from intrusion.

No one knew his age, some said that he numbered more, much more than a hundred years: and the oldest persons declared that at the time when they were mere children, he inhabited the cavern in the wilderness, and appeared to be a very aged man.

Many marvellous deeds were attributed to this mysterious being, many things it was reported he had performed, which could only have been accomplished by supernatural means, but the truth of which we are not in a position to aver. Among other things it was said that he had been one who had prognosticated the downfall of British rule in India half a century previous to the turbulent period of which we are now writing, and his predictions had been looked upon with every confidence, though kept secret in the breasts of those who knew them.

Some of the most credulous and superstitious even went so far as to believe that this old man was no other than the celebrated Sheikh Saleem, whose splendid mausoleum is at Futtehpore Secree, about twenty-four miles from Agra, and of which, and the singular legend connected with it, it may not be deemed uninteresting to relate a few particulars.

The town such as it is, stands upon the back of a narrow ridge of sandstone hills, rising abruptly from the alluvial plains, to the highest, about 150 feet; and extends three miles north north-east, and south south-west.

The origin of the celebrity of the place may be thus described.

The Emperor Akbar's sons had all died in infancy, and he made a pilgrimage to the shrine of the celebrated Moin-od-deen, of Cheest, at Ajmeer. He and his family went all the way on foot, at the rate of three coss, or four miles a day, a distance of about three hundred and fifty miles.

Kunauts, or cloth walls, were ranged on each side of the road, carpets spread over it, and high towers of burnt brick erected at every stage, to mark the places where he rested.

On reaching the shrine, he made a supplication to the saint, who at night appeared to him in his sleep, and recommended him to go and entreat the intercession of a very holy old man, named Sheikh Saleem, who lived a secluded life at the top of the little range of hills at Sacree.

He went accordingly, and was assured by the old man, then ninety-six years of age, that the Empress Jodh Bace, the daughter of a Hindoo prince, would be delivered of a son, who would live to a good old age.

She was then pregnant, and remained in the vicinity of the old man's hermitage till her confinement which took place 31st of August, 1569.

The infant was called after the hermit, Mizza Saleem, and became in time Emperor of Hindoostan, under the name of Jehangeer.

No. 12.

It was to this Emperor, Jehangeer, that Sir Thomas Roe, the ambassador was sent from the English court.

Akbar in order to secure to himself, his family, and his people the advantage of the continued intercessions of so holy a man, took up his residence at Sacree, and covered the hill with magnificent buildings for himself, his courtiers, and his public establishments.

The quadrangle, which contains a mosque on the west side, and the tomb of the old hermit in the centre, is, perhaps, one of the finest in the world.

It is 575 feet square, and surrounded by a high wall, and a magnificent cloister all around within.

On the outside is a splendid gateway, at the top of a noble flight of steps, twenty-four feet high. The whole gateway is one hundred and twenty feet in height, and the same in breadth, and presents beyond the wall, five sides of an octagon, of which the front face is eighty feet wide. The arch in the centre of this space, is sixty feet high by forty wide.

The gateway is extremely grand and beautiful, composed of red sandstone, with inlaid decorations of marble, but the beholder is struck with the disproportion between the thing wanted, and the thing provided.

There seems to be something quite preposterous in forming so erroneous an entrance for a poor diminutive man to walk through, and walk he must, unless he is carried through on men's shoulders, for neither elephant, horse, nor bullock, could ascend the flight of steps.

In all these places the staircases, on the contrary, are disproportionately small. They look as if they were made for rats to crawl through, while the gateways seem as if they were made for ships to sail under.

The tomb of Sheikh Saleem, the hermit, is a very beautiful little building, in the centre of the quadrangle. It once boasted a great deal of mosaic ornament, but the Játs, when they reigned, removed it all.

But we are again wandering from the thread of our narrative, desirous as we are to give every particular relating to India, that may prove amusing and instructive to the reader.

As we have before stated, there were many ignorant and superstitious persons who believed that the old hermit who inhabited the cavern in the wilderness, was no other than this celebrated Sheikh Saleem resuscitated, and looked upon him with the most profound awe and reverence in consequence.

Many were the marvellous stories of the miracles he had at different times performed, and of the extraordinary prophecies he had uttered, that were fulfilled to the very letter; such stories might do for the weak-minded and the credulous, but we are not going to trouble the reader with them here.

Certainly he was a most extraordinary old man, and his deeds were buried in a mystery that no one could penetrate, but of his great piety no person presumed to entertain a doubt.

Here then in the cavernous retreat of this aged man, was it that Omelia had for some time sought an asylum, and from him received the greatest kindness and attention, and his ready, able, and valuable assistance in the furtherance of her designs.

The old man knew all about the revolt which was on the eve of breaking out, over almost the length and breadth of the land, with such ungovernable fury; and no one could more strongly deprecate the designs of the mutineers than he did, and he was resolved to frustrate them as far as lay in his power.

He was also thoroughly acquainted with all the particulars of Omelia's history, though by what means he had acquired his knowledge she was at a loss to conjecture. He knew well the character and intentions of Yunadar, her father, he pitied her that she was so unfortunately related, and while he was inclined to rescue Yunadar from the dangerous and desperate course upon which he had entered, if possible, he was resolved to throw around Omelia the shield of his protection.

He admired her for her noble and heroic spirit, he honoured her for her virtues and generous self-devotion.

Seated in the principal cavern—which has been minutely described—after her sudden disappearance from her lover, and which had left him in such an utter state of surprise and bewilderment, was our heroine. Her elbow was on the table, and her head rested thoughtfully on her hand. There was a mingled expression of melancholy and hope upon her features, and there was a slight glow upon her cheeks, from the excitement she had experienced in her scene with Stanley.

She arose from her seat, and paced the cavern for a few minutes with disordered steps.

"Dear Stanley," she soliloquised, "I know the suspense, uncertainty, and mystery in which you are kept must be most tediously painful to you, and likewise that you must be lost in amazement and perplexity at my conduct. But at present you must remain so, for if I were to disclose everything thus prematurely, it might frustrate all my plans, and expose you and many others to utter ruin, if not destruction. Heaven knows the purity, the integrity of my motives, and will aid me accordingly."

The sound of the old man's approaching footsteps interrupted her in the midst of these reflections, and soon afterwards he entered the cavern.

Omelia hastened to meet the venerable man, and knelt devoutly and reverently at his feet, whilst he raised his hands above her head; his lips moved, though no sound issued from them, and it seemed that he was silently but earnestly invoking a blessing.

Having concluded this, he motioned Omelia to rise, and taking a seat, she placed herself by his side.

"Thou look'st sad, child," he said in feeble accents, but those of kindness and sympathy, "the gloom of care sits heavily on thy brow, and the tear trembles in thine eye. Droop not yet. ere the storm has commenced, or thou must needs sink and perish under the first shock of the fearful tempest. Be firm, be firm."

"Doubt me not, good grandsire. as such you permit me to call you," replied Omelia. "it is not the weakness of fear that pales my cheek, and brings the tear-drop in mine eye: no, Omelia's resolution is fixed. firm, stern, and immovable, and she is fully prepared for the great and dangerous task she has imposed. and which she has sworn to accomplish or perish."

"Noble-minded. heroic girl," exclaimed the old man, "all honour to thy virtuous and patriotic sentiments. and may Heaven watch over and protect you from the numerous dangers which you will too surely have to encounter. Whence then doth thy melancholy and sorrow arise. Is it for he who hath won thine heart's affections, thine anxiety and anguish are excited?"

"Even so, my venerable friend," answered Omelia; "oh. should anything happen to him, the hopes of the poor Indian maid will be for ever blighted. and the silent grave will be her only resting-place from the cruel blasts of care and sorrow."

"Poor girl, poor girl," said the old man feelingly. and pressing her hand.

"But it is not the safety and happiness of him who by his manly virtues hath won my love. that my care and anxiety are alone excited," observed our heroine, "no, I shudder at the thought of the terrible storm of anarchy and bloodshed which too probably is gathering. and my heart bleeds in anticipation for the suffering innocent. more especially the helpless women and children. who will doubtless be exposed to the brutal outrage of the merciless wretches who will then have fiends give no bounds to their savage cruelty and blood-thirsty revenge."

"Too true, too true," coincided the hermit, "and thy father, maiden. he is one of the miscreants to whom thou hast alluded; and who is fully determined to take a most active part in the monstrous and sanguinary work."

"Alas," sighed Omelia, "wretched, misguided man that he is; but why—oh. why remind me of that too painful that degrading fact. May Heaven induce him to abandon his guilty designs. and avert the horrors that I now so fearfully anticipate."

"It will not be," returned the old man. solemnly; "it is written in the book of fate. whose pages are revealed to me. that the blood of the innocent shall deluge this fair land—that ruin and desolation shall spread around, and that death shall number among the slain, ere the full measure of their sands, that justice will overtake the perpe-

trators of the bloody crimes, and a terrible retribution shall follow."

"Oh, horrible thought." ejaculated Omelia, with a shudder. "oh. may all-merciful providence ordain that your fearful anticipations may not be realised."

"I tell thee, maiden," replied the hermit, in half angry tones, "that what I have asserted is written in the book of fate. and darest thou doubt the word of him to whom the future is clearly, distinctly revealed. as in a mirror? Look to the day after tomorrow. for then will the spark be applied to the train. and the shrieks of outraged women and the groans of the dying; the flames kindled by the hands of the fierce incendiary, and the ruin caused by their frightful ravages, will be heard and seen in the proud but ill-fated capital of Delhi."

"Horror—horror!" cried the terrified Omelia. with a shudder. and placing her hands before her eyes. as if to shut out the dreadful spectacle. which her aged companion so vividly and graphically painted in imagination.

"Aye. terrible will be that day. and those that will follow, for India." rejoined the venerable recluse: "crimes will blacken the souls of her misguided children, such as humanity must shudder to contemplate, and future ages curse, detest, and execrate. And for a time, shall the fierce tempest rage with unabated fury, and the murderers shall seem to triumph in their enormities. but then terrible will be the reverse. mighty the retribution that will overtake them; no mercy will be extended to those who ever turned a deaf ear to its pleadings and supplications; the gibbet, the bayonet, and the billowy death at the cannon's mouth. will be their doom; they will be hunted and routed in every part of this vast territory like wild beasts; their rebellious princes either stripped of all their wealth and power, and incarcerated for the remainder of their days in wretched and loathsome dungeons. or shot like dogs; all the privileges which the Hindoo previously possessed, will be denied him. India will henceforth be ruled with a rod of iron. and her rebellious, unfaithful children having madly rejected the blessings of liberty and civilisation so freely, so lavishly offered them. will in future be little better than a great nation of despised, degraded, and abject serfs."

"Oh. my venerable friend." said the trembling Omelia, "how fearful is the picture which you have drawn. My blood chills within my veins as I think of it. and my bosom swells with feelings of shame and indignation at the anticipated misery of my countrymen. but I dare not—oh. indeed I dare not place implicit reliance on the truth of your extraordinary and terrible prognos tications."

"Ah," exclaimed the old man, angrily, and grasping her wrist rather violently, while a strange expression beamed from his eyes, as he spoke, "art though so sceptical, girl? Dost thou still presume to doubt the truth of that which I have foretold? Beware, lest thou provoke the wrath of him who is disposed to be thy best earthly friend, and to aid thee in thy virtuous designs. Thou dost little know the power, the secret power of the mysterious being under whose protection thou now art, or thou wouldst be more cautious in what thou sayest. Beware, I repeat, or thou mayest have cause to regret thy incredulity."

The words of the old man, and the solemn and impressive manner in which he spoke them, alarmed Omelia, and she looked at him imploringly, and with an expression of the deepest awe, as she said—

"Oh, pardon, I beseech you, if my rash tongue has dared to give utterance to a word of doubt; I know, I feel your power but I shudder as my imagination seeks to realise the horrors you have pourtrayed; and I would fain endeavour to persude myself that providence will yet avert the dreadful calamities you have predicted."

"Girl," returned the hermit, impatiently, "I tell thee again that the doom of the treacherous Hindoo is sealed, bloodshed, merciless as it is unprovoked, must be avenged in blood, and the just though terrible retribution of an Omnipotent Power, never fails, sooner or later to overtake the guilty. Already has the work of slaughter commenced, murder in its most hideous form has been perpetrated by the mutineers at Meerut and other places, and I tell thee again that the day after to-morrow such atrocious crimes will be committed in and around Delhi, that shall make humanity shudder, and blush for the guilty and brutal character of its fellow creatures,"

"Oh, heaven forbid," fervently exclaimed our heroine, with a look of terror.

"Thou dost still seem to doubt, maiden," observed the hermit, "be it then my task to prove to thee my power, and to convince thee of the certainty of my prognostications being fulfilled. Come girl."

"Mysterious man," said Omelia, shrinking from him, "your words and manners terrify me; what is it thou wouldst do?"

"Fear not," he replied, in gentler accents, and still retaining his hold of her wrist; "I would not harm thee, maiden, or do aught that should shame and outrage thy feelings This way—this way."

Surprised, yet anxious, Omelia offered no further resistance, and the old man con-ducted her into one of the smaller caverns which has been before mentioned.

CHAPTER XXIV.

AN EXTRAORDINARY SCENE.

The cavern was small, but lofty, and at that time was buried in profound darkness, for the hermit had neglected to take the lamp from the other cavern, and when they had emerged from it, he drew a black curtain, which was suspended from the wall across the entrance of the place they were now in, and enjoining Omelia to strict silence, he left her, and retired towards the farther end of the cavern.

A death-like pause ensued, not a sound but the thick and hurried breathing of the anxious and expectant Omelia could be heard, but her keen eyes penetrating through the dark obscurity beyond the spot on which she stood, she could indistinctly observe the form of the old man busily engaged in performing some curious and mysterious antics, which he continued for a short time, when the silence was succeeded by a low, whispering, murmuring sound, like that of the subdued voice of the wind among the forest leaves, which gradually swelled to a distant roar, as if proceeding from artillery, mingled with shouts, and yells, and cries of agony.

Omelia was overwhelmed with astonishment and awe, and could scarcely believe the evidence of her senses, but she obeyed the injunctions of the hermit, and remained silent, though the state of suspense in which she was placed was almost insupportable.

At length the old man again stood by her side, she felt his hand upon her arm, and she heard him in solemn and almost unearthly tones thus address her—

"Thou dost doubt the power I possess to draw aside the curtain of futurity, girl, be it now my task to convince thee that I am no vain or idle boaster; speak not, and behold."

With trembling dread and expectation, Omelia obeyed, and the hermit again withdrew from her side and retired to the back of the cave, and, after a pause of a few seconds, his solemn voice again saluted her ears, giving utterance to the following incantation or invocation—

"Spirits of earth, and spirits of air,
Mysterious powers, hover near;
Dispel the mist, like that of night,
And the dread future bring to light.
To wondering mortal sight reveal,
The future's destiny, woe or weal.
Obey my summons—show my power,
Now black clouds gather, loom, and lower."

These mystic words had no sooner escaped the hermit's lips, than there was a renewal of the strange sounds, the distant roaring of cannon, the shouts, the yells, and the groans that Omelia had before heard, and gradually the farther end of the cave became illuminated by a pale, blue, and ghastly light, and Omelia could just distinguish a confused number of shadowy forms moving about, struggling with each other, and apparently engaged in some desperate contest.

In the back-ground was an indistinct, panoramic kind of view, which bore a striking resemblance to Delhi, and, in fact, Omelia fancied she could recognise some of the public buildings that were so familiar to her.

The spectre-like forms that the astonished Omelia gazed at gradually swelled into something like reality, and she could then perceive a bloody struggle between numbers of the mutinous sepoys—who seemed to be excited to a perfect pitch of frenzy—and the English troops, and women and children. Many were stretched bleeding, and frightfully mangled, upon the earth; infants were torn savagely from their frantic mothers' breast, and elevated in the air on the point of the bayonet, and every horrible outrage that fiends alone could imagine, was being perpetrated, and as Omelia gazed with feelings of the most indescribable astonishment on this extraordinary vision, her blood chilled with horror, every faculty was suspended, and she drew her breath short and quick.

Several of the houses appeared to be in flames, and the scene of destruction was complete.

As Omelia still looked eagerly on all that seemed to be passing before her, she imagined she beheld Stanley in the thickest of the deadly strife, and surrounded by every appalling danger, and overcome by the horror of the spectacle, she uttered a piercing shriek of terror; a noise like a loud peal of thunder reverberated through the subterranean place, the objects that had engaged her attention immediately vanished from her sight, and the cave was again enshrouded in complete darkness.

The mysterious old man once more approached her, and grasped her arm, and after what had taken place, she was completely astounded and awe-struck, and trembled with a feeling of irresistible terror at his touch.

"The spell is broken," he said, "but thou hast probably seen sufficient, girl, to convince thee of my power, and to banish thy doubts and incredulity. Come, this way."

Omelia could not answer, she was so completely bewildered and overpowered by astonishment, and the hermit led her back to the principal cavern, where she sunk on a seat, and became lost in perplexing and torturing thought, while the old man stood by with folded arms, and gazed intently upon her.

"Art thou satisfied, Omelia?" he at length demanded, "have I not shown thee enough to make thee not despise my predictions?"

"Oh, yes, yes," tremulously replied our heroine, "and my breast is filled with mingled feelings of awe, astonishment, and terror. Mysterious man, who really are you, and by what means have you acquired your mysterious power?"

"Question me not," returned the hermit, "seek not to penetrate my secrets, "it is enough for thee to know that I am thy friend, and will do anything to serve thee, and to promote thy wishes, if thou wilt not reject my kind offices. But thou must be prepared for the worst, and that quickly, for as certain as thou dost now live, will the scene which I have just revealed to thy wondering sight be enacted in reality, at the time I have stated."

"Alas," sighed Omelia, "are there no means of averting these horrors? But Lieutenant Stanley?"

"As thou didst see him in the vision," replied the hermit, "so will he be exposed to every danger, but an Omnipotent power will watch over him, and bring him through all the horrors of that eventful night unscathed."

"Oh, thank heaven," exclaimed Omelia, fervently, "but there is surely yet time to prevent the frightful events you prophecy. The authorities will pay every fitting attention to your statements and warnings, and if given timely notice will take every precaution to frustrate the designs of these rash, misguided men.'

"No," replied the hermit, "however strange it may seem to you, Omelia, "that must not be; providence has ordained it otherwise. Events must be suffered now to take their course, and time be left for justice and retribution. So it is written in the book of fate, and woe to the guilty in the dreadful outrages that are about to take place."

Omelia sighed and shuddered at the thought, and she could not but look upon the old man with increased awe and dread; for after the strange and fearful scene he had just conjured up before her eyes she could not but suppose that he was something more than mortal, and a nameless feeling of fear, not unmingled with reverence for the holiness of his character came over her in his presence.

Their conversation was, however, suddenly interrupted by a loud report of fire-arms above, followed by shouts and cries of agony, and Omelia started from her seat, and stared aghast at the old man, as she exclaimed—

"Ah," what mean those ominous and alarming sounds? Have the miscreants commenced their work of bloodshed before the time appointed? Oh, let me hasten to ascertain the cause of this uproar."

"Hold," commanded the old man seizing her arm, "caution must be used, for we know not the danger which may threaten. Follow me."

Our heroine obeyed, the hermit having placed a pistol in her hand, and concealed another himself under his garment, and he then led her cautiously from the cavern, and emerged from the secret entrance into the wilderness."

The grass was trampled under foot, the dead bodies of a sepoy and an English soldier were stretched upon the earth, near the mouth of the cavern, and from the position in which they were, it seemed that they had had a desperate death struggle, for their hands still grasped each other's throat, and their glazed eyes protruded fiercely from their sockets.

As far as the eye could penetrate through the gloom of the wilderness, there was no other object to be seen, but firing might still be heard at a distance, and the hermit, taking the arm of Omelia—whose anxiety was excited for the safety of her lover—he again conducted her back to the cavern.

CHAPTER XXV.

THE BURSTING STORM —THE MASSACRE AT DELHI.

The storm which had not only so long threatened but had rapidly gathered and burst in several of the most important stations, now had gradually spread itself to the Mogul capital, and all that the aged Sheikh had prophecied to Omelia, as related in the previous chapter, was about to be too frightfully fulfilled.

But here it is necessary to refer to events anterior to the massacre at Delhi, and which have been before slightly alluded to, and, in doing so, we shall largely quote from official documents, and private communications of undoubted authenticity, in order to render our tale strictly what it purports to be, namely, "A True Tale of the Indian War."

The disturbances quelled at Barrackpore and Berhampore, almost immediately and simultaneously re-appeared at various station in Bengal. At Agra incendiary fires signalled the coming troubles; at Sealkote, which has since re-inforced the ranks of the mutineers, inflammatory letters from the sepoys at Barrackpore were intercepted; and at Umballa conflagrations became so frequent in the lines that a reward of a thousand rupees was offered by the Chief Commissioner of the Punjab for the arrest of the incendiaries.

But it was at Lucknow that the disaffection at this time (late in April) appeared most threatening. There also, of course, the sepoys were labouring under the supposed grievance of the cartridges; and had, besides, a local or private wrong of their own. A surgeon of the 34th regiment, stationed at Lucknow, had, it seems, tasted a bottle of medicine before making it over to a sick Brahmin soldier; this was construed into a deliberate attempt to break down their caste, and the 34th accordingly revenged themselves by burning down the doctor's bungalow. The intrigues of the King of Oude may have been a more powerful incentive to such outrages; however, that is a question undecided at present. But whether from the dread of destroyed caste, or moved by the machinations of the agents of the deposed king, the sepoys held nightly meetings, and conflagrations became frequent at Lucknow as elsewhere.

Luckily, Sir Henry Lawrence, one of the Sir Charles Napier school, and perhaps the ablest man in India, was upon the spot; and he was not likely to be an idle spectator of the movement among the native troops. He applied by electric telegraph to the supreme authority at Calcutta in these few but pithy words—"I want unlimited powers—I will not abuse them;" and instantly received the required grant. He foresaw, and resolved to break down, any attempt at insurrection; nor was it long before the occasion arrived for the exercise of this resolve.

On the 3rd of May, a letter from the 7th Oude irregular infantry (formerly in the service of the ex-king) was intercepted and brought to him. This letter was addressed to the men of the 48th regiment, and its purport was as follows:—"We are ready to obey the directions of our brothers of the 48th in the matter of the cartridges, and to resist actively or passively." This letter was taken to a Brahmin sepoy of the 48th. He communicated its contents to a havildar, and the latter to a subahdar. The three consulted over it, and resolved to bring the matter to the notice of the commissioner. This was done. About the same time, the 7th irregular infantry proceeded to overt acts against their officers. Four mutineers entered the house of the adjutant, Lieutenant Mecham on the afternoon of the 3rd, and told him to prepare for death; that personally they did not dislike him, but that he was a Feringhee, and must die. Lieutenant Mecham was unarmed; they were armed to the teeth. Resistance was hopeless. He at once made up his mind to meet his fate with dignity and resolution. As the mutineers paused to listen to what he had to say, he replied—"It is true I am unarmed, and you can kill me; but that will do you no good. You will not ultimately prevail in this mutiny. Another adjutant will be appointed in my place, and you will be subjected to the same treatment you have received from me." These words, delivered with coolness, without change of countenance or the movement of a muscle, seemed to strike the mutineers. They turned and left the house, leaving their adjutant uninjured!

Tidings of these mutinous acts reached Sir Henry Lawrence on the evening of the 3rd. Without a moment's delay, he ordered out her Majesty's 32nd foot, the 13th, 48th, and 71st native infantry, the 7th cavalry, and a battery of eight guns, manned by Europeans, and proceeded at once to the lines of the mutineers, distant about seven miles. Darkness had set in before he arrived there; but so prompt had been his movements, that the 7th was completely taken by surprise. They were instantly ordered to form up in front of their lines. In the presence of a force so imposing, they had no resource but to obey. The infantry and cavalry were then formed on either side of them, the guns within grape distance in front The 7th, completely cowed, awaited their doom. They were ordered to lay down their arms: they obeyed. At this moment the artillery portfires were lighted. A sudden panic seized them, with a cry, "Do not fire! do not fire!" Mad with terror, they rushed frantically away, cowed into repentance. The ringleaders, and most of their followers, were secured that night by the native cavalry and infantry, and were confined pending trial.

Sir Henry Lawrence wisely followed up this prompt and energetic conduct. He used every effort to undeceive the credulous sepoys as to the pretences upon which their religious prejudices had been aroused, and to excite their indignation against the sanguinary treachery of the insurgent regiments. More than this, the general held forthwith a grand military "durbar" to reward the fidelity of those sepoys of the 48th regiment, who had not only resisted the temptation to mutiny, but had loyally apprised their superior officers of the attempt Everything was done to give *eclat* to the proceedings. Sir Henry himself harangued the troops in words as earnest as his deeds had ever been.

Lucknow, the centre of the revolt, was by these measures pacified for a month after the flame had broken out in a dozen places of inferior importance.

The news of this outbreak, and of the manner in which it was suppressed, seems to have aroused the governor-general to the necessity of taking vigorous measures also. His first act was to pay up and disband the mutinous 34th at Barrackpore. This was accomplished without any disturbance on the 6th of May At the same time, Lord Canning issued an order informing the army that if they still refused to trust in their officers and the government, and still allowed suspicions to take root in their minds and to grow into disaffection, insubordination, and mutiny, their punishment would be "sharp and certain."

Lucknow is one of the most populous cities in Asia—numbering 800,000 inhabitants. Its extreme length is seven miles; its extreme breadth four miles. The central part is very densely populated. The city has an imposing external appearance. Some of the more important buildings are imitations of the Greek style of architecture; others, from the Saracenic cupolas and monuments, remind one forcibly of the Kremlin at Moscow. The scenes in the streets are—or rather were, for we must now speak in the past tense— lively and picturesque in the extreme. Mounted cavaliers, clothed in cashmere stuffs elaborately ornamented with gold, and preceded by attendants carrying gold and silver sticks, swords, pipes, spears, and wands of office, passed to and fro in a continuous stream. Certain dignitaries, seated in open palanquins, richly painted and gilded, mingled in the throng; hemmed in by hookah bearers, armed attendants, and perhaps a guard of honour, mounted on camels caparisoned in red and green trappings. Others were perched aloft on the backs of elephants, seated in gracefully carved howdahs, which were in some instances of pure silver. The attendants of the more wealthy inhabitants comprised examples of the various races from all parts of India, and the aspect presented by their costumes was picturesque in the extreme.

While all this was going on at Lucknow, a storm was brewing at Meerut. Here, also, a supplemental grievance was added to that of the greased cartridges. A rumour had been spread amongst the troops that the government had plotted to take away their caste, by mixing the ground bones of bullocks with the flour sold in the market; that thus the Hindoo partaking inadvertently of the substance of the deified animal, would find himself compelled to embrace Christianity. It was in vain that General Hewitt and the commanding officers of regiments attempted to combat these ideas; it was fruitless that they pointed out to the sepoys, that during a century's occupation of India no interference with caste had ever been tried. The men were imbued with discontent, which presently exhibited itself in the usual manner by incendiarism and open disrespect to the European officers.

On the 23rd of April (we gather from official documents, and the most authentic sources) Colonel Smyth, commanding the 3rd cavalry, ordered a parade of the skirmishers of his regiment, with carbines, to show them a new way of loading without biting the cartridge, which it was thought would obviate the objection of the men to its use. He had the havildar-major and the havildar-major's orderly at his house, to show them how it was to be done; the latter fired off a carbine twice, and at night his tent was burnt down; a veterinary hospital close to the magazine was also burnt; and at night it was whispered that the men would refuse to receive the cartridges.

It was thought necessary to bring these manifestations to a test, and on the 6th of May a parade of the 3rd cavalry was ordered. The old cartridges, the same which they and their fathers had always used, were served out to them. Eighty-five men refused to take them. Once more the cardridges were offered, and again they were rejected, This being reported to General Hewitt commanding the station, the eighty-five were arrested, tried by a court-martial of native officers, and by those native officers condemned to periods of imprisonment, varying from six to ten years. The offenders were then placed under an European guard, composed of two companies of the 60th rifles, and twenty five men of the carbineers, and a general parade was ordered for the morning of the 9th. At day-break, on that morning, all the troops in the station, leaving the guards standing, paraded on the 60th rifle parade-ground; the carabineers, the 60th rifles, the 3rd light cavalry, the 11th and 20th regiments of native infantry, a light field battery, and a troop of horse artillery. The carbineers and the rifles were then ordered to load and be ready, and the horse artillery the same. This done, the mutineers were marched on to the ground; the European troops and artillery guns being so placed, that the least movement of disaffection or insurrection would have been followed by instant slaughter. The mutineers were in uniform when marched on to the ground; they were then stripped of their clothes and accoutrements; and the armourers' and smiths' departments of the horse artillery being in readiness, every man was ironed for ten years' imprisonment on the hard roads, with five exceptions, whose period of bondage was only six years.

While this was going on, the 3rd cavalry looked very much humbled—mounted, with their swords drawn and sloped, intent spectators of their comrades' punishment. The

ironing having been completed, the offenders were marched off to gaol—a building about two miles distant from the cantonment. The sepoy regiments, cowed by the preparations which had been made to quell any mutinous demonstration, moved off the parade.

Next day was Sunday; and it wore away in quiet.

The first fearful act of the tragedy was now about being perpetrated, and which we will proceed to relate.

It was the 10th of May, 1857; it was about five o'clock—church time—when, at a given signal, the 3rd light cavalry, and the 20th native infantry, rushed out of their lines, armed and furious. A detachment of the former regiment at once galloped to the gaol, which was guarded by native troops alone.

On reaching it, its gates were opened to them without resistance, and they at once liberated all the inmates, including their imprisoned comrades. A native smith was at hand to strike off their irons. These men, infuriated by their disgrace, ran with all possible speed to their lines, armed themselves, and mounted; they then rushed to the scene of action, yelling fearfully, and denouncing death to every European. Meanwhile the remaining portion of the 3rd cavalry and the 20th native infantry had proceeded to the lines of the 11th with all possible speed. Thither also the officers of that regiment, alarmed by the shouting and noise, had gone before them. They found Colonel Finnis haranguing his men, and endeavouring to keep them firm to their colours. The men were wavering when the 20th arrived. The men of this regiment, whose hands were already red with the blood of several of their own officers, seeing this hesitation and its cause, at once fired at Colonel Finnis. The first shot took effect on his horse only, but almost immediately afterwards he was shot from behind, and fell riddled with balls.

The colonel's fall was the signal for the English officers of the 11th to fly to the lines of the artillery and 6th dragoons, on the north front of the cantonment. Now riot was loosed. Whilst the 3rd light cavalry proceeded to the gaol to set their comrades free, the rest of the mutineers fired the buildings in ther own camps. Flames began to ascend in all directions from the officers' bungalows, from public buildings, mess-houses, private residences, and, in fact, every edifice or thing that came within reach of the torch and the fury of the mutineers, and of the bazaar *canaille*, who in considerable numbers joined the rising. On all sides shot up into the heavens great pinnacles of waving fire, of all hues and colours, according

to the nature of the fuel that fed them; huge volumes of smoke rolling sullenly off in the sultry night air, and the crackling and roar of the conflagration mingling with the shouts and riot of the mutineers. In this maddening scene the 3rd, with their newly-liberated comrades, and the rest of the convicts about 1,300 in number, joined. Every living thing within reach was attached at once, and the furious mob of soldiers and plunderers rushed round and round, uttering cries of revenge on the Europeans, and in the fearful carnage which ensued, neither sex nor age was spared.

Every house and building near the lines, except the hospital, had been fired; and the smoking and blazing barracks and houses, the yells of the mutineers, and the shouts and shrieks of the multitude gathered there, numbers of whom fell from the shots of the

No. 13.

mutineers, made on that dark night a scene than which one cannot be imagined more horrible. Officers galloping about, carrying orders to the European troops, were fired at, not only by the mutineers, but by the native guards placed over the public buildings for security. Ladies driving in their carraiges, gentlemen in their buggies, who had left their houses unsuspicious of evil, were assaulted, and if not murdered, treated with a brutality to which death would have been a relief. For it must be remembered that not only the sepoys, but the released gaol-birds near fifteen hundred in number—the population also, or that "vile rabble" which is always available for plunder or murder, had joined the movement, and spread terror and desolation all around them. Most of the houses in Meerut—all of those in the military lines are thatched with straw, and easily inflammable; the plan of the insurgents was to set fire to the roof, and to murder the frightened residents as they quitted the burning dwelling. Many met their deaths in this way; more, providentially, escaped: yet not one of those in the latter category owed their safety to the mercy of their assailants. In some instances outrages were perpetrated which we shall only have too many opportunities to record. These men, whom we had pampered for a century, who had always professed the utmost devotion to us, seemed suddenly converted into demons. Nor was this a solitary example; other stations were destined to witness atrocities fouler, more brutal, and more treacherous even than those of Meerut.

Passing hastily over the pursuit of the rebels on the road to Delhi, we will come at once to the events preceding and following the outbreak and massacre at the latter place.

It has been stated that at the time of the revolt, the Mogul capital was garrisoned solely by native troops; but subsequent events make such statements appear erroneous; though certainly the mere handful of British officers and men, were totally inadequate to resist the overwhelming force opposed to them.

To suit the purposes of our tale, and the better to develope the startling incidents that occurred, we have, therefore, placed Lieutenant Stanley, with the detachment to which he belonged, in Delhi.

The road from Meerut to Delhi crosses the Hindun river over a suspension bridge, fifteen miles from the latter city, but in the dry season the river is always fordable. Still the bridge would naturally be the point to which the insurgent regiments would bend their course, and the brigadier's first idea seems to have been to march to the bridge, with the 38th and 54th native infantry, and three guns of Captain de Teissier's company of native artillery, orders being given at the same time that the remainder of Captain de Teissier's company, with three guns, should escort the European ladies and non-combatants to Allyghur. The bridge would then have been destroyed, and the passage of the river contested. But, remembering the river was then fordable at various places, and that thus his position might be turned and himself compelled to contend with an enemy in flank as well as in front, the plan was abandoned. Brigadier Graves seems now to have resolved to confine himself to the immediate defence of the city and cantonments. The women and non-military residents were sent to the Flagstaff Tower, a round building situated some distance from the city, solidly built of brick, and capable of a prolonged defence. It is feared that in many instances the warning to take refuge in this fort did not reach those for whom it was intended, and by some unfortunates it was received too late.

The regiments were now paraded, the guns loaded, and the men harangued by the brigadier. His appeal to them as soldiers and subjects of a government which had ever behaved towards them with liberality and kindness, was received with enthusiastic cheering; and the brigadier, putting himself at their head, seems to have marched out of the city confident in the faithfulness of his men.

Through the Cashmere gate they marched in gallant order, and had scarcely left the walls ere a tumultuous array appeared advancing from the Hindun. In front, and in full uniform, with medals on their breasts gained in fighting for British supremacy, confidence in their manner, and fury in their gestures, galloped on about two hundred and fifty troopers of the 3rd cavalry; behind them at no great distance, and almost running in their efforts to reach the golden minarets of Delhi, appeared a vast mass of infantry, their red coats soiled with dust, and their bayonets glittering in the sun. No hesitation was visible in all that advancing mass; they came on, as if confident of the result. Now the cavalry approached nearer and nearer At this headlong pace they will soon be on the bayonets of the 54th. These latter are ordered to fire; the fate of India hangs on their reply. They do fire, but alas, into the air; not one saddle is emptied by that vain discharge. Worse still, on the approach of the cavalry, the sepoys of the 54th rushed suddenly to the side of the road, leaving their officers in the middle of it, upon whom the troopers immediately came at a gallop, and one after the other shot them down. The colonel shot two of them before he fell, but with this exception, and one said to have been shot by Mr. Fraser, none fell After butchering the officers, the troopers dismounted, and went among the sepoys of the 54th, shaking hands with them; the fraternisation was complete. The troopers were perfectly collected, they rode up to their victims at full gallop, pulled up suddenly, fired their pistols, and retreated. The countenances of the troopers wore the expression of maniacs. One was a mere youth, rushing about flourishing his sword, and displaying all the fury of a man under the influences of *bhang*. The rascals of Delhi, and the rascals of Meerut had doubtless long understood each other, or the latter would never have ventured across the Hindun.

Some of the officers of the 38th and 54th

succeeded in escaping in the direction of Meerut, whilst the sepoys fraternised; and a junction having been thus effected, the mutineers all marched back together into Delhi, destroying the bridge of boats on the Jumna as they retired.

The magazine, with its immense stores of ammunition, was situated in the very heart of the city. At the time of the outbreak, the magazine seems to have been in charge of Lieutenant Willoughby, a young artillery officer, who, with Sir T. Metcalfe and Lieutenant Forrest, was in the arsenal when news of the approach of the rebels spread through the city. Instant measures were taken to check their advance upon the arsenal. Sir T. Metcalfe went out to ascertain the extent of the movement, and never returned. Lieutenant Willoughby closed and blocked up the gates, placing two 6-pounder guns doubly loaded with grape, under sub-conductor Crow and Sergeant Stewart, so as to command the entrance. Two more 6-pounders were placed in a similar position in front of the inside of the magazine gate, protected by a row of *chevaux de frise*. For further defence, two 6-pounders were trained to command either the gate or the small bastion in its vicinity, other guns being so arranged as to increase the strength of the position generally.

These preparations had hardly been concluded when a body of mutineers appeared, and called on the defenders to open the gates. On their refusal, scaling ladders were brought up, and the rebels got on the wall and poured on to the arsenal. The guns now opened and took effect with immense precision on the ranks of the enemy. Four rounds were fired from each of the guns, Conductors Buckley and Scully distinguished themselves in serving the pieces rapidly, the mutineers being by this time some hundreds in number, increasing in force, and keeping up a quick discharge of musketry.

Lieutenant Willoughby, resolved not to allow the arsenal, with its formidable stores, to fall into the hands of the rebels, had laid a train to the magazine, to be fired at the last emergency. The decisive moment soon approached. Lieutenant Forrest being wounded in the hand and one of the conductors shot through the arm, the signal was given to fire the train, which was coolly done by Conductor Scully. The effect was terrific—the magazine blew up, the wall being blown out flat to the ground. The explosion killed upwards of a thousand of the mutineers, and enabled Lieutenants Willoughby, Forrest, and more than half the European defenders of the place, to fly together, blackened and singed, to the Lahore gate; from whence Lieutenant Forrest escaped in

safety to Meerut. Lieutenant Willoughby was less fortunate; he was killed on his way to Umballa.

The explosion, which seems to have been regarded as accidental at the Flagstaff Fort, decided the sepoys there. The company of the 38th made a rush to their arms, and took possession of two guns sent up to reinforce the defences of the forts. Brigadier Graves now saw that nothing could be effected by any further effort to retain the tower, except with the destruction of all who had sought refuge within its walls. He therefore advised every one to escape as best he could, himself remaining to the last. Conveyances were in waiting, and most of the ladies got away, the gentlemen following on horseback; and thus a safe retreat was effected towards Kurnaul for some, while others made to Meerut. But many of our countrymen and countrywomen fell into the hands of the natives, and subjected to treatment the most atrocious that ever was recorded; others only escaped as by a miracle.

Thus had the mutineers gained a most important triumph so far, and their savage exultation knew no bounds. One of their first acts on gaining the city, was to set up a king, the hoary miscreant, whose life has since with what justice or policy we cannot perceive, been spared.

At first he made a show of hesitation, he was coy, but his modesty was at length overcome, and he took at once upon himself, not only the name but the authority of a king.

He at once named certain officers of government, raised the pay of the soldiers, and the next day rode through the city, encouraging his new and precious subjects.

They (the rebels) needed little encouragement. The city was in their possession, and they at once turned their hands to plunder and murder. The bank was of course sacked, affording a rich booty to the infuriated savages, who, however, appeared to thirst more for blood than gold. Nor were they content with the mere shedding of blood. Tortures the most refined, outrages the most vile, were perpetrated upon men, women, and children alike. Men were hacked to pieces in the presence of their wives and children. Wives were stripped before their husbands' eyes, flogged naked through the city, violated there in the public streets, and then murdered. To cut off the breasts of the women was a favourite mode of dismissing them to death; and, most horrible, they were sometimes scalped—the skin being separated round the neck, and then drawn over the head of the poor creatures, who were then, blinded with blood, driven out into the blazing streets. To cut off the nose, ears and lips of these unhappy women (in addition, of course, to other the brutal usage to which they were almost invariably submitted), was merciful. As for the children, happy was the mother or father who did not live to see the cruelties practised upon them. Fearful beyond belief as it seems, they were even in some cases torn asunder by the legs, and horrors worse still were perpetrated upon their tender bodies. Commonly, their toes and fingers were hacked off *seriatim*. Or they were placed naked and bareheaded in the sun, and left without water till they died or went mad. Here is a passage from a letter written by an officer from the camp before Delhi, describing the treatment which befell those who in escaping the massacre within the walls, fell into the hands of the butchers without :—" We burnt four villages on the road and hung seven Lumberdars. One of these wretches had part of a ladies dress for his kummerbund—he had seized a lady from Delhi, stripped her, violated, and then murdered her in the most cruel manner—first cutting off her breasts. He said he was sorry he had not an opportunity of doing more than he had done. Another lady, who had hid herself under a bridge, was treated in the same manner, then hacked to pieces, and her mangled remains thrown out on the plain. We found a pair of boots, evidently those of a girl six or seven years of age, with the feet in them. They had been cut off just above the ankle. A man who witnessed the last massacre in Delhi, where he had gone as a spy, gives a horrid account of it, stating that little children were thrown up in the air and caught on the points of bayonets, or cut at as they were falling with tulwars."

Five troopers from Meerut, upon entering Delhi, proceeded to the house of an Englishman, whom they cut down at his door. They next brought out his wife, ravished her, killed her, and afterwards butchered his young children. Meanwhile other gangs were collecting the ladies they could find, ranging them in rows and shooting them, laughing at their terror, their shrieks, and their mortal struggles. Six were discovered in a single room. One, youthful and lovely, hid herself under a couch; but when the blood from the decapitated bodies of her five companions ran to her in a stream—she shrieked aloud, and so was discovered. She was dragged forth, and conducted to the palace of the phantom King of Delhi. One unhappy girl, only recently a bride, was at Delhi with her husband, an infantry officer, when the outbreak took place. The mutinous soldiers carried her before one of the braggart villains in command, who caused her to be stripped naked and wipped with bamboos until she sank senseless to the ground. She was then indecently as well as inhumanly mutilated, and

afterwards, by order of the leading ruffian, stamped to death.

Several Europeans (said to number forty-eight) were taken to the palace, or perhaps went there for protection. These were taken care of by the King of Delhi, but the troopers of the 3rd cavalry, whose thirst for European blood had not been quenched, rested not till they were all given up to them, when they murdered them one by one in cool blood. The troopers are said to have pointed to the marks of the irons on their legs before they murdered their victims, asking if they were not justified in what they were doing.

But the pen trembles, and the heart sickens at the recital of the horrible atrocities perpetrated. What, for instance, can be more truly frightful than the following.

An officer and his wife were tied to trees, their children tortured to death before them, and portions of their flesh crammed down the parent's throats; the wife was then violated before her husband, he mutilated in a way too horrible to relate, then both were burnt to death.

Two ladies, both young, and described as "very pretty," were seized at Delhi, stripped naked, tied on a cart, taken to the bazaar, and there violated. They died from the effects of the brutal treatment they received.

———

CHAPTER XXVI.

THE NIGHT OF HORROR.—THE HINDOO HEROINE.

As we wish to make our narrative as complete as possible, and, not only interesting, but valuable for future reference, the following accounts given by natives of what occurred after the irruption of the insurgents, may not be deemed out of place.

First only five troopers came into Delhi from Meerut. They first went to the house of an agent of the King of Delhi, near the Delhi gate inside the town. He came out and said that he was in the service of the king. They would not listen to him, but cut him down. They then murdered his wife and family, and told the people to plunder the house. They then went to the houses in Durya Gunj. The owner of one of them was an European. They killed him, and plundered and burnt all the houses in this suburb, and murdered all who could not escape.

By this time other troopers and infantry and townspeople joined in the work of destruction. A number of the fugitives took refuge in a building near the mosque of Aurungzebe's daughter, and began to defend it against the insurgents. They were held at bay. They left people all round, and the main body went off to the bank. There they were joined by more mutineers. They plundered and murdered wherever they found Europeans. The townspeople assisted warmly in the plunder, and the mutineers of the infantry were particularly active. The commissioner, Mr. Fraser, on hearing of the advent of the mutineers, had gone down to cut away the bridge, but was too late. On returning he met the mutineers at this place. He drove off; the mutineers followed and cut him down; but not till he had shot one of them. His escort remained passive.

The mutineers killed people on the road, but being more intent on the magazine, they went to it. After arranging matters for surrounding the place, the insurgents and mutineers proceeded to the gaol. One of the sentries shot a man, but when they said they were fighting for religion, the guard joined them, and 500 convicts were released. They then closed all the gates, and went into the fort. They paid their respects to the king; he made objections, and said he had no army; he at last consented.

It was on the second day that the miscreants went to the magazine; what there occurred has already been related.

On the third day they went to a mosque, where some Europeans had taken refuge. As they were without water &c. for several days, they called for a subahdar and five others, and asked them to take oaths that they would give them water, and take them alive to the king; he might kill them, if he liked.

On this oath the Europeans came out, the mutineers placed water before them, and said, "Lay down your arms, and then you get water." They gave up two guns, all they had.

The mutineers gave no water. They seized eleven children (among them infants) eight ladies, and eight gentlemen. They took them to the cattle sheds. One lady, who seemed more self-possessed than the rest, observed that they were not taking them to the palace; they replied that they were taking them *via* Durya Gunj. They were deliberately placed in a row and shot.

Among these unfortunate victims was a female with a child about three years old. The unfortunate mother, was a fair young thing, apparently not more than twenty, and the agony of her features, her wildly despairing eyes, as she held her little one with convulsive emotion to her throbbing bosom, might have been sufficient any one would have thought, to have moved even a fiend at heart to pity.

She wept not, but there was that expression in her looks, which spoke more, much more eloquently than tears could have done. Alas, it was all lost upon the monsters to whom she had to appeal.

"Water!" she cried; "oh, give my poor child but a drink of water, and for myself I care not, even kill me, if such is your will, but oh, give my child water!"

A laugh of derision was the only reply the wretched woman received to this, and one of the sepoys seized her child, raised it above his head, and dashed it ferociously on the ground.

The people looked on in dismay, and feared for Delhi.

The kings people took some thirty-five Europeans to the palace, on the fifty day they tried them to a tree, shot them, and burnt their bodies.

On the fifth day notice was given that if any one concealed a European, he would be destroyed. People disguised many, and sent them off, but many were killed that day, mostly by people of the city.

For two days, a kind of lull came o'er the frightful atrocities. The wretches seemed to pause to take breath ere they resumed the dreadful work of wholesale and indiscriminate slaughter.

The Durya Gunj Bazaar was turned into an encampment for the mutineers. Shops were plundered in the Chandnee Chouk and Dlereeba Bazaar. The shops were shut for five days. The king went through the city, and told the people to open the shops. At each gate there was a company of native infantry. About 9,000 mutineers were assembled. Some 4,000 or 5,000 men were raised, but they were composed principally of the rabble.

During the festival of Eed, while at prayers, there was the dust of a kafila of laden animals. An alarm arose—it was the English army, and the people all rushed helter-skelter into the city.

When the sepoys arrived in the city, they desired all the budmushes (bad characters), to plunder the houses, since they (the mutineers) would not condescend to touch the booty themselves. The troopers then murdered five gentleman and three ladies in Durreeougunge, and the remainder took shelter in the Kishungar Rajah's house. They then came to the Delhi bank, set fire to it, and killed five gentlemen; they then went up to the Kotwalee, desiring the budmushes to commence plundering, on hearing which the Kotwal absconded, and took no steps to protect the people, and even allowed the Kotwalee to be plundered. The mutineers then came to the late Colonel Skinner's house, which they did not touch, but set fire to all the houses in the vicinity of the church, killing all the gentlemen, ladies, and children therein. After this five troopers galloped to the cantonments, and on their approach all the sepoys set fire to their officers' houses, murdering all the gentlemen, ladies, and children they could find in cantonments. The remainder of the troopers proceeded to the magazine in the city. On their approach four officers were standing before the magazine gate, which they closed, and from inside fired two shots at the troopers, and then set fire to the magazine. Upwards of 1,000 men in the city were blown up with the magazine.

Two regiments from the Delhi cantonment now joined the mutineers at the Delhi Kotwalee, and commenced plundering the city in every direction.

On the 13th the mutineers attacked about thirty Europeans, who had taken shelter in the Kishungur Rajah's house, The Europeans commenced to fire, and shot thirty of the mutineers, but on their ammunition and supplies being out, the Europeans came forth. The heir-apparent now rode up to the house, and begged the mutineers would deliver them into his custody, and that he would take care of them; however, paying no attention to what he said, they put all the Europeans to death. Mr. George Skinner, his wife and children, had taken shelter in the palace; spies gave information, they were seized and put to death. Dr. Chimmun Lal, the sub-assistant surgeon, was also killed at the dispensary, and the English doctor was killed at the gaol. For three days the dead bodies were not removed, and on the fourth day the mutineers caused them all to be thrown into the river. The mutineers then asked the king either to give them two months' pay or their daily rations. The king summoned all the bankers and merchants, telling them if they did not meet the demands of the mutineers, they would all be murdered, on which they agreed to give them " doll rotee " for twenty days, adding they could not afford more. The mutineers replied, " We have determined to die; how can we eat doll rotee for the few days we have to live in this world ?" Whereupon the king ordered four annas a day. The mutineers placed two guns on each gate in the city, and brought 1,000 maunds of gunpowder from the cantonment magazine, and took possession of all the shot and shell in the city magazine. Supplies were stopped, and everything became exceedingly dear. All the neighbouring villages were up and plundering. After plundering Delhi, 200 troopers proceeded to Georgaen, and set fire to the houses, murdered the collector, and plundered the treasury, bringing away seven lacs 84,000 rupees; and with the Delhi treasury, the mutineers had in their possession 21 lacs 84,000 rupees, which was kept in the palace guarded by them and the king's troops.

Thus having given a succint account of all that took place at the outbreak in Delhi, we will now return to the principal incidents of our tale.

The sun had set upon the noble domes and lofty minarets of the mosques, temples, and other public buildings of the Mogul city, and the dark shadows of evening were fast gathering and falling upon all around. A sullen silence seemed to pervade everything and everybody, an oppressive, deathlike stillness, portentous of the approaching horrors, and yet few could conjecture the exact nature of that which they were so irresistibly in dread.

Flora Melville and her father—who for the last few days had been rather indisposed—were sitting together in one of the rooms of their residence, the windows of which overlooked one of the principal streets af Delhi. They were both unaccountably depressed in spirits, and for some time had remained silent, and gazing listlessly from the window by which they were sitting.

For some days past, Flora had been tortured by the most dismal presentiments of some approaching calamity, and it was in vain that she exerted herself to the utmost to dismiss such thoughts from her mind. They not only beset her by day, but they haunted her in her sleep at night, and conjured up the most strange and troublesome dreams to her imagination.

She thought of Stanley, and his words at their last unexpected and singular meeting; and she thought of Omelia, and the mystery of her actions, and the probable, though at present, unknown danger to which she exposed herself, and she could not help feeling the greatest anxiety on her account.

Then the declining health of her father, was a source of the utmost anxiety and uneasiness to her. He was far advanced in years, and she could not but picture to herself the dismal change that would take place in her circumstances, and the loneliness of her situation, should it please heaven to take him from her, without a relation residing near, from whom she might seek consolation, advice, and protection, and it was now that the loss of the sweet society of Omelia was felt by her more keenly than ever.

Mr. Melville—although Flora revealed them not to him—could guess the thoughts that were passing in her mind, and tried his best to banish them, but with little or no effect; in fact, his feelings assimilated with her's, and he equally as much required consolation as she did.

In this mood then, the father and daughter sat on the eventful evening we are about to endeavour to describe. As we have before stated, they had been for some time silent, and looking vacantly into the street, which was all but deserted, but a solitary passenger now and then passing through it, and there being scarcely a sound to break the dull and painful silence which reigned around. The darkness, too, increased, and that added to the general gloom and solemnity of the hour.

Suddenly, however, Flora grasped the arm of her father, and timidly directed his attention to the dark shadows of several human forms that were moving stealthily along towards the house.

They both watched them narrowly, and drew a little aside, and placed the light in such a position in the room to prevent their being observed themselves.

And now the moon which had not before appeared, emerged suddenly from behind a cloud, and revealed to them the persons of the men more distinctly, and they could discover that they wore the dress of sepoys, and that from the cautious manner in which they at times looked around them, that they were anxious not to be observed.

One of them who was somewhat in advance of the others, was a very tall and muscular-formed man, and it struck both Flora and her father most forcibly that they had seen him before.

They approached nearer the house, and, after reconnoitring in a suspicious manner about the house, the two foremost looked anxiously up at the windows, and Flora could scarcely suppress a scream, and clung more timidly to her father, when in their features she recognised two of the ruffians who had committed the daring outrage at the villa at Agra, as related in one of the early chapters.

It was Yunadar and Allyghur, who were accompanied by several of their accomplices, and evidently for no good purpose.

Mr. Melville motioned his daughter to be firm, and remain silent, and they then continued to watch the actions of the men with much curiosity and anxiety.

They seemed to walk round to the back of the building, but in a few moments returned to the same spot, and after a short consultation with each other, they moved slowly off in the same stealthy manner as they had come, and disappeared by a dark and narrow avenue.

This circumstance naturally excited their suspicions, and greatly alarmed them, particularly Flora, who remembering the horrors of that eventful night when they had so narrow an escape from the same ruffians, dreaded a similar attempt at outrage on the present occasion, and it was in vain that her father tried to quiet her apprehensions, par-

ticularly as he so strongly participated in them himself.

He, however, determined to use every necessary precaution in order to guard against any danger which might threaten, and summoning his domestics, he inquired of them whether they had seen the suspicious looking men lurking about the house.

They replied in the negative, but at the same time threw out certain ambiguous hints, which all but confirmed the dismal forebodings that haunted his own mind and that of his daughter.

Believing that he could depend upon their fidelity, he instructed them to arm themselves, and to be prepared for anything that might happen; and then dismissing them, himself and Flora again took their seats by the window, and looked anxiously along the street, at least, as far as their eyes could penetrate.

Again that solemn, death-like silence pervaded all around, and the moon having once more hid her pale face behind ponderous clouds, a darkness which was almost impenetrable prevailed.

While Mr. Melville and his daughter still sat thoughtfully by the window, and with their eyes fixed steadfastly upon the impenetrable gloom beyond, they were startled by a strange and confused noise at a distance, which was succeeded by the report of fire arms, and again they fancied they beheld human forms moving cautiously about in the darkness, and that they heard the suppressed murmur of voices upon the still air.

Flora again clung to her father, and the tremor which had seized upon her limbs, and the paleness of her looks, showed the state of alarm she was in. Mr. Melville whispered to her a word of encouragement, and they had once more resumed their anxious watch, at the same time listening to catch the slightest sound which might be stirring in the house, when there was a hasty knock at the room door, and the voice of the Ayah Mimi, who had been absent for some time from the house, on an errand, was heard outside.

On being admitted, Mimi seemed to be almost out of breath, as she afterwards informed them, with running, and her look evinced much terror.

It was with difficulty that they could elicit any explanation from the poor silly girl, who, we should probably before have informed the reader, was a native of Africa, and who had, when quite an infant, with her mother, who had been dead for some years, become the property of Mr. Melville.

"Oh, Massa," she said, "oh, Missi Flora, me run like mad all the way home, for me so *frightful*, and fear dat you be in bery much danger, and so."

"But what has alarmed you, Mimi?" anxiously, but kindly inquired her master. "Come, come, explain my good girl."

"Oh, yes, massa," answered Mimi, "me 'splain eberything 'rectly, in a minute, only gib me time. Yes, I be bery much 'larmed I 'sure you, and almost faint, 'cos me so *frightful*, as I said 'fore, for when me reach Durya Gunj, me heard shrieks, and groans, and den me saw, oh, shocking."

"What did you see, Mimi?" eagerly interrogated Flora; "pray tell us without any more delay."

"Oh, Missi Flora," returned the girl; "me scarcely know what me say, for my *mouth be in my heart* wib terror. I hid in a door-way and watch, and den me see one, two, great many, one dozen ugly sepoys, wid swords and guns, dragging poor gentleman and lady wib child in her arms, pretty dear, from house, and swearing great big oaths, bery much. De poor gentleman beg, and lady cry, and hug her baby to her breast, kneeling, and lookin' so piteously all time. Den dey shoot poor gentleman dead; and lady scream bery much, but dey only laughed, as if it was great fun, and den two of de sepoys ran their bayonets through the poor baby and its mother's bodies, and dey fall dead by side of poor gentleman."

"Oh, shocking!" exclaimed Flora, shuddering; "alas! my dear father, our worst forebodings are realised, and I tremble to think of the horrors that I fear will too quickly spread themselves throughout the land. But oh, Mimi, is it possible that you beheld these frightful crimes, without being yourself discovered?"

"Yes, Missi," replied Mimi; "though me bery much want to cry out, when me see poor lady, and pretty little picaninny killed. But me fraid to stir, and kept quite still, till de men all went into the house, to rob it, I 'spose; when I run away, and nebber stop till I got home here."

"This is indeed terrible and alarming news," observed Mr. Melville; "alas, it seems but too evident that the rumours which for some time have been afloat, were not unfounded, and there is too much reason to fear that now that the tempest which has so long threatened, has at length broken out, it will be a difficult task to endeavour to stop its fury until it has committed the most dreadful ravages among the whole of the European race."

"Alas, my father," said Flora, with a shudder; "if this unfortunate revolt should spread, what will become of the English people inhabiting this city; seeing that they are nearly left without protection, it being almost totally garrisoned by native troops?"

"Too true, my child," returned her father, "and more shame to the thoughtlessness and neglect of the authorities, after what has taken place already, and well knowing that there is no reliance to be placed in the fidelity of sepoy regiments. But be firm, Flora, and trust to the mercy and protection of Omnipotence."

"Poor Omelia," ejaculated Flora, with a look of the utmost anxiety; "alas, in the character she has assumed, and the opposition she so boldly shows to the atrocious designs of the mutineers, to what fearful dangers may she not expose herself? Lieutenant Stanley, too." A deep sigh, which she in vain tried to restrain, as the name of him who, she still, in spite of herself, so fervently loved.

"Our apprehensions are probably premature," remarked her father, though he thought very differently; "and something may occur to crush this rebellion in its infancy. At any rate, we must summon all the fortitude we can, or we shall be ill prepared to meet the dangers we may have to encounter. Retire, Mimi, and be ready to attend your mistress at a moment's notice."

Mimi, who was indeed terribly alarmed, curtseyed, and obeyed, and Flora and her father sat and discussed the dreadful story she had told, and their means of safety, in case of emergency, with varied feelings of emotion.

It was in vain that they endeavoured to conceal from themselves the fact of the real danger which threatened themselves, and the whole of the Europeans at present residing in the city, for they well knew the ferocious character of the natives, when their evil passions were once aroused, and that there were no crimes, however atrocious, which they would hesitate to commit, in order to gratify their sanguinary feelings of revenge.

They were aroused from these reflections by the repeated discharge of fire-arms, followed by loud shouts, and which seemed nearer than when they had first heard them, and looking with fearful expectation in the direction from whence they seemed to come, they beheld, to their increased alarm, fierce flames suddenly shoot up into the sky, illuminating the whole of the city, and showing but too plainly that the work of destruction had not only commenced, but was going savagely on.

The terror of Flora Melville may now be easily imagined, and that of her father, who saw that matters were fast approaching to a crisis, were scarcely

less than her own, for he saw plainly that it was now no use to attempt to disguise the critical situation in which they were placed.

The sounds so alarming increased in tumult every minute; the firing of musketry, and the brutal shouts and yells of exultation, were mingled with the frantic shrieks of women, and screams of children ; and every moment these fearful sounds (which told too plainly the dreadful work of slaughter which was going on, and which it was too well known there was at that time no power in Delhi to check), seemed to approach nearer; and the fierce flames that had doubtless been kindled by the rebels, spread more rapidly around until they lighted up the whole city, and made every object as clear and distinct as in the broad daylight,

No. 14.

And now Flora and her father could perceive numerous human forms, male and female, flying frantically in the distance, as if they were seeking some place of refuge from the blood-thirsty wretches, who inflamed with every fiendish passion, like wild beasts, were let loose upon them, carrying murder, desolation, and extermination in their train.

"Alas!" Said Mr. Melville, "will nothing restrain the fury of these misguided men?— What will be the end of this terrible outbreak?"

"Oh, my dear father," said the trembling Flora, though she tried to conceal her fears as well as she could—"I shudder to think of the atrocities that will most certainly be committed by these infuriated men, goaded on by the most deadly feelings of hatred and revenge against the English race. Would to Heaven we were once more in our native country, where my beloved mother drew her last breath."

At this sad recollection, sobs of the most poignant anguish escaped the poor girl's gentle and affectionate breast, and tears chased each other rapidly down her pale cheeks.

Her father was also deeply affected at the remembrance of that fatal bereavement which had cast a gloom over all his future prospects, and which, though so many years had elapsed since it had taken place, it was still the principal of all his sorrows.

But he endeavoured to stifle his emotions as well as he could, and drawing his daughter away from the window, he said:—

"Dear Flora, need I say how fully I appreciate your feelings, and how deeply, how painfully I participate in them? Alas! the death of your amiable and gentle mother—her who was the admired and esteemed of every one, and who shed happiness around her wherever she went—was a calamity, from the effects of which I can never possibly recover, and most painfully, most acutely do I feel assured, my poor child, that you must feel the loss of such a parent. But it was the will of Heaven, and it is not for erring mortals to question its all-wise decrees. We must try to banish such melancholy thoughts, and to look forward with hope and confidence. The storm which has so unfortunately burst over this once bright and happy land may soon pass away, and the enormities which our fears now lead us to anticipate may be mercifully averted."

"God grant that your hopes may be realized, my father," replied Flora, "but alas! I cannot but forebode the worst, and I shrink from the horrors that only a few short hours may be committed in this devoted city, with a prophetic feeling of dread which I cannot conquer."

"Nay, nay, courage, my gentle Flora," said her father, soothingly, and kissing her pale cheek affectionately; "this is not like yourself. You must not thus torture yourself, and anticipate evils that may never occur. Why do you weep thus bitterly and avert your looks, my child? Come, come, be calm, be firm, I pray you. Still you weep, and sobs of anguish escape your gentle bosom; there must be something more in this violent agitation than you have hitherto explained, or I can imagine."

"Oh, my father," replied Flora, in a voice almost choked by the violence of her emotions, and the terrible thoughts that crowded with such overwhelming rapidity upon her brain,—"in this dreadful struggle

that is now taking place, and is only in its infancy, should any thing fatal happen to you, what would become of your unhappy child, left alone and unprotected in the world, with no one to care for or love her, as she would then be?"

"The Almighty, Flora," replied Mr. Melville, solemnly,—"that all-merciful Supreme, who never forsakes the good and innocent in the hour of adversity, would, I trust, watch over and protect you in such a terrible emergency. But come, my child, again I say you must try to banish all such gloomy thoughts from your mind, and to hope for the best."

"I cannot, indeed I cannot, conquer the fears, the misgivings, and dismal presentiments that have for the last few days tortured my mind, and racked and bewildered my brain;" said Flora, with increased agitation; "at night, too, strange and awful dreams have haunted my perturbed imagination, which chill my blood, and make me shudder with horror as I recall them to my memory."

"Dreams, Flora?" said her father, "oh, surely you cannot have suffered those delusions of the slumbering senses to have made such a painful and powerful impression upon you."

"You may deride and censure my weakness," replied Flora; "but still I cannot conquer the fears those awful and prophetic visions have excited in my breast. Last night, too,—oh, dreadful recollection——"

"What, my child?" eagerly demanded her father, somewhat alarmed by the extreme agitation of her manner, and the horror depicted in her pale features; "tell me, I beseech you—explain."

"Oh, my brain becomes distracted at the remembrance of the fearful dream which last night disturbed my rest," replied Flora, "and I tremble and hesitate to repeat it to you."

"Nay, be firm, Flora, for whatever the nature of your dream might be, I am fully prepared to listen to it."

"Should it be realized," ejaculated Flora, with increased emotion; "oh God!—my heart sickens at the thought. Still will I endeavour briefly to relate the particulars of it. Methought that you and I, my dear father, were wandering alone through the deserted streets of the city, which, in the ghastly glare of the moonlight, presented fearful proofs of the atrocities that had been perpetrated, and the dreadful ravages that had been committed by the mutineers. Fresh horrors met our sight at every turn, and we found it impossible to avoid them. We had, as I imagined, abandoned our home, and alone and unprotected, were endeavouring to make our escape from the frightful and general scene of slaughter.

"Houses were burning fiercely in every direction, and the atmosphere was so hot with the terrific conflagration, that even the very ground on which we trod seemed to scorch our feet, and the air we breathed was thick and suffocating.

"Still we wandered on, as if in a maze or labyrinth, for the further we proceeded, the more remote did deliverance from the horrors and the dangers by which we were surrounded seem to be.

"Suddenly, however, in turning the corner of a bye-street, through which we had expected to make our progress with more security, we came upon a party of the miscreants, who were probably hastening from one scene of bloodshed in search of fresh victims—and, horror-struck, we fled, and endeavoured to elude them.

"But it was in vain; the wretches had observed us, and with a yell of savage exultation and vengeance, which still seems to ring in mine ears, called upon us to stop.

"As I imagined in this awful dream, fear added speed to our heels, and we hurriedly sought to retrace our steps and to avoid them.

"Another dreadful yell, mingled with fierce threats and curses, saluted our ears, the murderers quickly pursuing us,—and this was immediately followed by a discharge of fire-arms, and, with a cry of agony which I can never forget, you, my father, sunk mortally wounded in my arms. I saw your ghastly looks as, dying, you fixed them upon me;—I beheld the life blood streaming from many a frightful, gaping wound;—I felt the rude hands of the monsters upon me, as they tore me remorelessly from your arms;—I saw a dozen glittering weapons penetrate your defenceless body, and ere I could shriek for mercy, the horrible excitement of the dream broke the spell of sleep, and, convulsed in every limb, and perspiration streaming from every pore, I awoke."

Overpowered by the recollection of the fearful dream she had been so graphically describing, the voice of Flora failed her, and she sunk in the arms of her father, trembling with emotion.

CHAPTER XXVII.

THE FLIGHT.—NOBLE CONDUCT OF OMELIA. —FRESH HORRORS.

It would be wrong to say that Mr. Melville could listen with indifference to that which his daughter had thus so vividly related, and which had left so torturing and powerful an impression upon her mind.

He had, indeed, from the effects of the illness under which he had suffered for the last few days, become painfully nervous and apprehensive, and forebodings strictly in accordance with those that Flora had acknowledged had haunted his mind, and which he had in vain sought to divest himself of. The vision which she had related was therefore in every way calculated to strengthen rather than diminish those dismal and painful feelings.

He, however, knowing how necessary firmness and self-possession were, in the midst and of the dangers that threatened them, endeavoured to conceal his real thoughts and feelings from his daughter, and, after a brief pause, he said :—

"It was indeed a fearful dream, my dear child; but dismiss it from your memory. In the agitated state of mind you have been for the last few days, from the, no doubt, greatly exaggerated reports that have been circulated of the rapid spread of the revolt, it is no wonder that such frightful dreams as the one you have described should disturb your slumbers. I trust that for your sake, Flora, Providence will yet continue to watch over and preserve my life. Come, come, my child, be firm, and exert yourself to tranquillize your feelings."

Before Flora could return any answer to there observations, they were alarmed by hearing footsteps hastily ascending the stairs, which were immediately followed by a hurried knock at the room door.

Flora, whose worst apprehensions were excited, clung to her father, and looked in his face with an expression of terror.

The knock was repeated, and Mr. Melville having hastily and peremptorily demanded who was there, the door was thrown open, and Abdoo Moltah, one of the principal and confidential domestics appeared, in a state of considerable excitement.

"What alarms you, Abdoo?" eagerly demanded his master; "and what brings you here in such a hurry?—speak, quick."

"Immediate flight is the only way in which we may preserve our lives," answered Abdoo; "the whole City is one great slaughter-house. The rebels have it all their own way, and are massacreing, burning, and destroying all that comes before them. They are fast approaching in this direction."

"Oh, God," exclaimed the terrified Flora; "my prophetic fears are being realized. What, oh, what will become of us?"

"Courage, Flora," said her father, "this is not the time for useless lamentations, but one which requires the exercise of our utmost energies and self possession. How know you that which you have stated, Abdoo?"

"Anxious to ascertain all the facts I possibly could," replied the latter, "a short time since I ventured from the house into the city, from which I have but just returned; and awful were the scenes I there witnessed, at the risk of my own life. The mutineers, who are increasing in numbers every minute, were burning the bungalows, and slaughtering, without mercy, every European, man, woman, and child, they could meet with. I saw such atrocities committed that I dare not shock your ears by relating them. All those who can are flying to the Fort or the different Mosques that are not in possession of their enemies. A delicate looking native youth, has placed himself at the head of a small band of British Soldiers, (with whom is Lieutenant Stanley), to protect the women and children, and to shelter their retreat, and is performing perfect prodigies of valour. Finding that they were advancing to this part of the city, I waited to see no more, but hastened to prepare you for the worst."

"How terrible is this account," said Flora; "what is to be done?"

"We must secure what portable property we can, and then abandon the house without delay, and endeavour by the most unfrequented streets to reach some place of safety," said Mr. Melville, mustering all his fortitude and presence of mind for the trying occasion. "What do you propose, Abdoo?"

"Exactly that which you have suggested, sir," replied Abdoo; "but first of all I advise that you retire into one of the inner rooms, and remove the light from this apartment, which can be seen by those without."

"Good," agreed Mr. Melville; "are the lower doors secured?"

"They are, as well as could be expected with our limited means, and the short time we have had for preparation. But, should the mutineers attack the house, they cannot long act as any barriers against them. It is by the private door at the back of the premises that we may with greater certainty and security effect our escape."

"Fine!" coincided his master; "come, my dear Flora, subdue your terrors, and let us immediately proceed to action,—there is not a moment left for delay."

Flora did indeed combat her fears as well as she could, for the sake of her father, and the latter having dismissed Abdoo to his companions below, with strict injunctions for them to hold themselves in readiness, took the arm of his daughter, and led her from the room to an inner apartment, where, with the assistance of Mimi, (who, however,

was so violently agitated that she was of very little use), they proceeded to secure what money and articles of value that were portable that they could.

It was a terrible sacrifice to have to make, and to abandon their happy and luxurious home to the mercy of the inhuman wretches who were at that time committing such frightful enormities, but they had no alternative between that and death, and therefore to repine was perfectly useless.

They had only just completed this task, when the noise and confusion, the terrific shouts and yells in the street where their residence was situated, told them too plainly that the moment of danger had arrived, and the courage of Flora almost forsook her; but she quickly aroused herself, knowing that it was a struggle of life or death, and at that moment the faithful Abdoo entered the room armed, and ready for any emergency.

"Quick," he said; "there is not a moment to be lost; the rebels are within a short distance of the house, and you may hear their shouts and yells as they proceed with their terrible work of destruction in the street. Some of the domestics will stop to resist their entrance by the front door, till you have time to effect your escape by the back. Be firm, my honoured master; courage, Miss, and you will yet escape the villains. This way;—I will be your guide."

There was no time for hesitation; Abdoo led the way, and Mr. Melville took the arm of his daughter, and breathing a prayer to Heaven for protection, they hastily quitted the room, and, with palpitating hearts, and mingled hopes and fears, they began to descend the stairs; but they had scarcely done so, when a loud hammering against the front doors, and the shouts of numerous voices were heard, which convinced them taht the expected attack had commenced, and added to their alarm.

Abdoo hurried them on, and they had reached the bottom of the staircase, where they found three of the domestics armed, and awaiting to accompany them in their flight, when, by the loud crashing noise, and the report of fire-arms, and the clashing of swords, they found that the doors had given way, and that the mutineers were engaged in fierce and deadly combat with those who had been set to guard the principal entrances to the house.

They advanced hastily but cautiously to the back door, which opened upon a dark and narrow avenue, leading to some of the dirtiest bye-streets of the city; and having listened for a moment or two without hearing any noise outside to excite their alarm, they opened it silently, and Abdoo looked cautiously out.

"All right!" he whispered; "the coast is clear; follow, quick!"

He stepped hastily from the doorway as he thus spoke; and Mr. Melville, Flora, and the others were about to follow, when the near report of a pistol was heard, and with a loud cry of agony, poor Abdoo fell dead upon the earth, and at the same moment several armed Sepoys (among whom were Yunadar and Allyghur, the former of whom had fired the fatal shot, which killed the unfortunate Abdoo,) made their appearance, and terrified and despairing, Mr. Melville and his daughter drew back and gave themselves up for lost. The three faithful domestics, who were joined by others from the front of the house, placed themselves before them to shelter their flight.

"Why do ye pause?" demanded the villain Yunadar in a fierce voice, and addressing himself in a tone of authority to his companions; "on to the slaughter; death to the hated Feringhees!"

These words seemed to arouse all the most savage passions of the mutineers, and, with a loud yell they rushed upon the brave defenders of Mr. Melville and his daughter, and a terrific combat ensued; during the confusion of which, Flora and her father thinking it an excellent opportunity, stole cautiously into the avenue, and had proceeded but a short distance when they were observed by one of the rebels, who fired after them, and immediately a loud shriek rent the air; poor Mimi, who was closely following her master and mistress, having received the fatal shot, and falling mortally wounded.

Flora on seeing the unfortunate girl fall, her who had been her affectionate attendant from the earliest days of childhood, uttered a cry of horror; and Allyghur, who was close upon them, aimed a determined blow with his cutlass at Mr. Melville, who fortunately saw him in time to step aside and avoid it, and before the villain could repeat the murderous act, he was stretched, fearfully wounded by an unseen hand, upon the earth, and at the same moment an apparent Hindoo youth, followed by Lieutenant Stanley, and several British soldiers, rushed forward from an opening in the alley or avenue, as if by magic, taking the mutineers completely by surprise, and throwing them into the greatest confusion.

Yunadar, however, recovered his self-possession immediately, and uttering a fearful cry of vengeance was rushing upon their new assailants, followed by his savage associates, when the supposed youth darted boldly before him, and presenting a revolver at his head, in a determined voice, exclaimed :—

"Hold! cruel, guilty man, or you, even you shall die by my hand!"

At the sound of that well known voice, Yunadar dropped his weapon, and started back aghast and astounded, and Mr. Melville and his daughter were completely overwhelmed with astonishment and admiration, at such a noble and unexampled act of heroism, for they immediately recognized *Omelia!*

Yes, again had the generous-hearted, the truly noble-minded girl, fulfilled, faithfully fulfilled the promise she had made. In the midst of the greatest danger she was present to save and protect those whom she so warmly esteemed, and thus, in the most striking manner, to evince her gratitude.

The soldiers, with Stanley at their head, attacked the mutineers resolutely (Yunadar having stolen hastily from the combat on recognizing his daughter), and after a brief contest put the villains completely to the rout, and thus preserved the lives of Flora and her father, who were in gratitude about to throw themselves at the feet of Omelia, when she prevented them, and, in an impressive voice exclaimed :—

"Hold! I require not, and will not permit such an uncalled-for act of humiliation. Thank Providence who hath enabled the humble Hindoo girl to perform her duty."

"Heroic girl!" cried Stanley, fixing upon the beauteous maiden whom he so devotedly loved, a look in which the feelings of his very soul seemed to glow and express themselves; "you can receive no greater reward, I well know, than the approval of your own unsullied conscience; still, how can any one refrain from expressing their warm and enthusiastic admiration of your noble conduct? Mr. Melville, Miss Flora, I sincerely congratulate you on your present preservation from a fearful fate."

"We are overwhelmed with astonishment and gratitude, Mr. Stanley," said Mr. Melville; "Omelia, most generous and heroic of women——"

"This is no time for thanks," hastily interrupted Omelia; "the moment is a desperate one, murder and plunder hold their destructive reign in the city. In a few minutes the wretches whom we have just routed, may return, reinforced by hundreds, and frightful then would be the consequences. My task will not be complete till I have conducted you to a temporary place of safety. Lieutenant Stanley, you know my plans?"

Stanley bowed, and taking the arm of Mr. Melville, while Flora was supported by Omelia, who encouraged her by a sweet smile, they moved hurriedly from the spot.

CHAPTER XXVIII.

THE SCENE IN THE MOSQUE.

THROUGH the most unfrequented streets, yet in the immediate vicinity of the scene of destruction and slaughter, Omelia conducted them, without speaking a word, and by signs strictly enjoining them to silence, lest the least sound of their voices should betray them to their enemies, who by their shouts and the frequent discharge of musketry, mingled with cries of agony from their unhappy victims, they could hear were close at hand.

Flora had the greatest difficulty to maintain her fortitude under the trying and dreadful circumstances, and the same dismal forebodings that had so long tortured her, continued to haunt and distract her mind.

She thought of the awful fate of the poor faithful Mimi, too, with feelings of the deepest horror and regret, and many were the tears she shed to the humble creature's memory.

The presence of Omelia and Lieutenant Stanley, however, encouraged her, and she endeavoured to conquer her emotions and to bear up against the dangers by which they were surrounded, as well as they could.

With quick, but cautious footsteps, they pursued their way, lighted by the red glare of the numerous burning buildings, whose crackling timbers saluted their ears on every side, and, as they proceeded, they beheld numerous groups of men, women, and children, some half naked, flying terrified in the same direction.

Omelia was evidently well acquainted with every inch of the ground they were traversing, and no one could possibly be better qualified for a guide in the hour of danger.

Her appearance was most striking and picturesque. She wore the dress of an Hindoo of high caste, but with a perfectly military bearing. Her head was surmounted by a rich turban, beneath which only a portion of her black glossy tresses was permitted to fall gracefully down her neck and shoulders. In a silken scarf which encircled her slender waist, she carried a handsome revolver, and a gold hilted dirk, and by her side was an elegantly manufactured sabre of true Damascus steel, and which she knew how to use with a skill which would not have disgraced some of the most experienced and best disciplined soldiers.

In fact, she was the true Amazon, in every sense of the word.

Courage and determination beamed forth from her lustrous eyes, and was expressed glowingly in her handsome features, and it was impossible that any one, however insensible, could have gazed upon that beauteous and heroic girl, with any other feelings than those of the warmest love and admiration.

At length the party arrived in the open square or space of ground, at one extremity of the city, in which, surrounded by a high wall, stood a large and handsome mosque, where many of the English had sought refuge, and to which numerous others were hastening; the greater number, however, were sheltered in the Flagstaff Fort, which has been before described in a previous chapter.

Here Omelia motioned her companions to follow her, and drawing them aside into a secluded part of the square, she said :—

"Thank Heaven, I have been enabled to accomplish my task, and you are now, I trust, for the present, at any rate, in safety. May the Great Spirit watch over and protect ye; in your prayers, forget not the name of Omelia, and to implore success to her in her righteous cause. Here I must leave you. Stanley, to your future care I leave Mr. Melville and his daughter : farewell, farewell, and may Heaven bless ye !"

With these words, which were spoken with much feeling, she turned to go away, pointing significantly towards the Mosque, when Stanley detained her, and in a voice of much emotion, said—

"Stay, dearest Omelia; I beseech you; you surely will not leave us thus? Oh, how terrible will be our anxiety and suspense for your safety."

"Fear not for me," replied our heroine, "but seek not to detain me, for my time is precious, and the business I now go upon most urgent. You will find no difficulty in obtaining admission to the mosque, whither you had better go without delay; and, there, with your companions in misfortune, you can consult what is best to be done for your future safety."

"How torturing is this evil destiny," cried Stanley, in tones of anguish; "mysterious girl, oh, why should you thus continue to expose yourself to such fearful dangers? Alas! shall we ever meet again?"

"Yes, yes," hastily returned Omelia, in an agitated voice; "fear not, Providence will shield me from every harm, and I trust that the time is not far distant when we shall meet again to part no more. Once more, farewell, dear Stanley, Flora, Mr. Melville, all, farewell !"

Thus saying, she raised a hand of each to her lips, and then hurried away, and abruptly turning the corner of one of the streets by which they had come, was immediately lost to the sight, leaving them all in a state of surprise and admiration, which there is no necessity to describe.

"Kind being," said Mr. Melville; "oh, what a noble generous heart throbs within her womanly breast."

"True, most true," replied Stanley; "she is indeed perfection's self. But oh! how agonizing are the fears that continually rack and torture my breast, lest exposing herself, as she hourly does, to the horrors that now rage on every side, she should meet with some awful and untimely fate."

"May the infinite God of mercy protect and bless her!" solemnly and fervently ejaculated Flora; to which prayer they all heartily and devoutly responded, and Stanley, knowing the danger and imprudence of any further delay, then led them towards the mosque.

The gates were speedily opened to them and many other unfortunate applicants, and they shortly found themselves in the interior of the spacious building, (which had been hastily fortified, in the best manner practicable under the circumstances), and there a scene presented itself of the most extraordinary and distressing description.

The place was by this time literally thronged, and the heat was most oppressive. A buzzing, murmuring sound, with occasional lamentations and exclamations of grief and despair, and the plaintive cries of young children, ran through the place, and imparted a torturing sensation to the breast.

There were aged, grey-haired people, mourning the loss of some dear relative, or staring about them like idiots, with blood-shot eyes, and a wild and haggard expression of features.

There were many suffering excruciating anguish from wounds received; and stalwart men, cast down, powerless and desponding.

Young mothers hugged their little ones to their breasts, and looked themselves the very pictures of misery, horror, and despair.

In fact there was nothing but suffering and misery to be seen, turn your eyes in whatever direction you might; and this, probably, was but the prelude to the dreadful tortures that were in store for them; for unless some speedy relief was afforded them, the majority most undoubtedly must perish of hunger and thirst.

Nothing could possibly be more frightful than the situation of these unfortunate people.

And then the terrible tales that were told by many of them of the atrocities committed by the mutineers, and which they had been compelled to witness, were quite appalling to listen to, and were only calculated to add to the anguish and hopelessness that predominated in the breasts of the unfortunate beings.

The discharge of musketry, the falling of burning ruins, and the hideous shouts and yells of the infuriated wretches who were perpetrating these monstrous outrages, might be heard every minute, and gave them fearful warning of the critical situation in which they were placed.

Whilst some were lamenting aloud and beating their breasts in the agony of their despair; there were others who were settled down into a calm and silent melancholy; while many were engaged in prayer, and their thoughts seemed to be entirely abstracted from everything else.

Flora and her father shuddered with an indescribable sensation of horror as they gazed upon this wretched and appalling scene; but Stanley, who never for moment lost his firmness and self-possession, exerted himself to arouse them, and to calm their emotions, and in which he at last succeeded, and they contrived to obtain possession of a small space in the already crowded building, to themselves, where they endeavoured to make themselves as comfortable as could be expected under existing circumstances, though their situation was indeed miserable and deplorable enough.

The soldiers who were under the command of Stanley, had each got a small portion of food in his haversack, and the domestics of Mr. Melville (who had acted in the most praiseworthy manner throughout), had also taken the precaution, at the suggestion of the unfortunate Abdoo, to secure such provisions as in the hurry of the flight, they could, so that with frugality and economy there was sufficient to last them for a few days, and that afforded them some small degree of consolation.

Most dismally and wretchedly that night wore away; to attempt to sleep was useless; their spirits would not suffer them to talk much, and they sat the principal portion of their time, in gloomy silence, and wrapped in torturing meditation, and gazing with looks of sympathy and compassion upon the sufferings of those around them.

The thoughts of Stanley, as may be expected, were constantly fixed on Omelia, and terrible were his apprehensions for her safety. He pictured to himself the dangers she would hourly have to encounter, and he trembled with horror when he thought of the fate which too probably might befal her.

How fervently did he implore for her the protection of the Supreme, and that they might, as she had expressed the hope, shortly meet to part no more.

CHAPTER XXIX.

THE FEARFUL TRAGEDY.—THE MASSACRE IN THE MOSQUE.

THE ruffian Allyghur was severely but not mortally wounded, and after a short time he revived, and to his rage found that he had been abandoned by his villainous colleagues, and was lying on the ground faint and powerless from the loss of blood, and alone.

He hastily tore off his scarf, and bound it across the wound, (which was in the arm), to stop the further effusion of blood; and he then endeavoured to raise himself on his feet, but was unable to do that, and he sunk back exhausted by the effort, and muttering curses between his teeth.

He crawled as well as he could towards the house, with the idea of entering it, but he could proceed no further than the threshold, and propping himself up against the doorway, gazed along the now deserted street, with an expression of deadly malice.

"And must I be left here to perish?" he growled, savagely; "curses light on Yunadar and the others for deserting me thus; and tenfold curses light on the daring girl Omelia, who has been the cause of this; and yet her father is panic-stricken whenever he beholds her, instead of securing her from doing further mischief. Fool! but only let me survive this accident, and I swear that if I again encounter her, she shall not escape my most terrible vengeance."

He paused, and again looked eagerly along the street in the hope of seeing some one coming to his assistance, but he was for a time doomed to disappointment, and his fears increased, especially as he became weaker every moment, and thought that it was almost impossible he could survive without he had speedy assistance.

He listened with some degree of malicious satisfaction to the repeated firing of the musketry, and the other sounds of the deadly carnage that continually met his ears; and it inspired him with the hope, as they rapidly appeared to approach nearer, that he would shortly be relieved from his perilous and dangerous situation.

In this expectation he was not disappointed.

Yunadar and his brutal colleagues, filled with rage at their defeat, and that, too, by the daughter of the former, a delicate girl, whom it might have been expected would have fainted at the mere report of a musket; and at the escape of their intended victims, were determined to have all the revenge in their power, which was to plunder and destroy the house of Mr. Melville, and to murder all who were in any way connected with him, and whom they might chance to encounter.

Reinforcing themselves, therefore, with numbers of ruffians, brutal as themselves, they hastened to the scene of the late combat; and the satisfaction of Allyghur may be imagined when he saw them enter the street.

On they came with hideous cries of vengeance, and firing, or demolishing every English bungalow as they came along, until they at length arrived at the doomed house, when, to their no small surprise—for they imagined him to have been slain—they discovered Allyghur, who had crawled from the doorway to a spot where he thought it was not possible that he could escape their observation.

"Ah!" exclaimed Yunadar, "is it possible? Allyghur still living? This at any rate is fortunate!"

"Perdition seize ye all," said the wretch, fiercely; "is it the way to show your respect to an old and faithful comrade, even if he had been killed, to leave his body here to rot, or to be hacked to pieces by the hated Feringhees?"

"Blame us not, Allyghur," replied Yunadar; "the enemy was too much for us, and our flight was so precipitate that we had not time to remove you. It is lucky, however, that you were not killed. Are you wounded badly?"

"Yes," replied Allyghur, bitterly, "thanks to your amiable daughter who holds you in complete subjection, and of whom you stand in so much awe. But bind up my wound securely, and before you proceed to demolish the house, see if you cannot find some spirit to revive me, for I am faint with the loss of blood."

This request was complied with without, and Allyghur was then removed to a convenient spot, at a short distance, from whence he could witness the work of destruction.

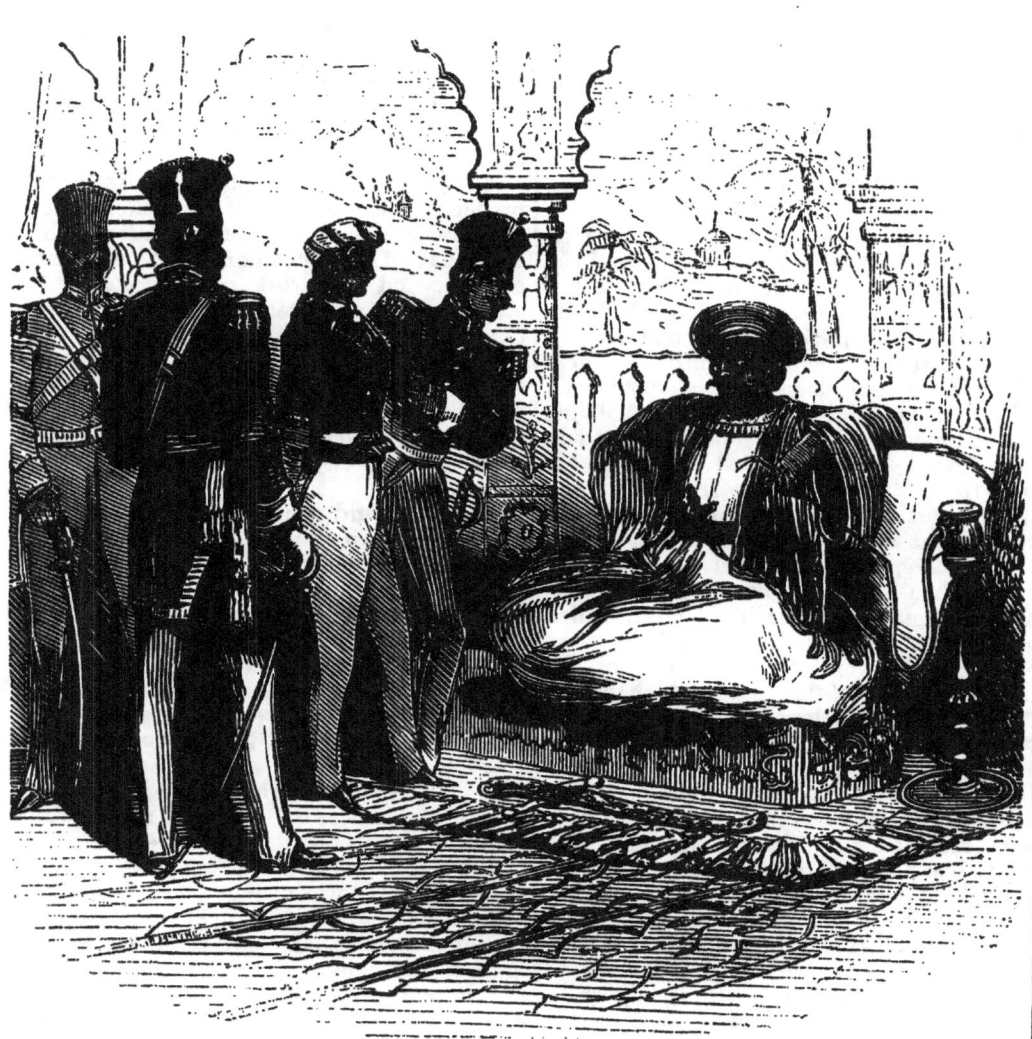

It quickly commenced, and the yells of the wretches whilst it was proceeding, were truly frightful.

They plundered the house of everything valuable, having accomplished which, they set fire to it in several places, and it was quickly enveloped in flames from the basement to the roof.

Finding the bodies of poor Mimi and the faithful Abdoo, they mutilated them frightfully, and then committed the mangled remains to the flames. After this they set up a deafening shout of triumph at the completion of their atrocious work, and while some of them removed Allyghur to a place of safety, the rest, led on by the savage and determined Yunadar, proceeded to the perpetration of fresh enormities.

We will now once more return to the unfortunate sufferers in the Mosque, whose situation was every hour becoming more fearful. Several of them had already died from sheer exhaustion, and there on the marble pavement of that splendid and sacred building lay their ghastly corpses, with their bereaved relatives and friends gazing wildly, vacantly, and silently upon them, probably counting the moments that might intervene ere the same awful fate should befal them.

It was now the second night that Flora and her father and their friends had been in this receptacle of misery, and their prospect of relief was as distant as ever.

From the different unfortunates who continued to arrive, they received the most terrible accounts of the progress of the mutiny, and the atrocities committed by

No. 15.

the rebels, and they were in hourly dread of their besieging the mosque, which, feeble as was the resistance they could offer, would be the signal for their total destruction.

Flora's fortitude now completely forsook her, and it was in vain that Stanley (who felt for the sufferings of those around him more than his own), tried his utmost to revive her, and to re-animate her with hope.

The deplorable state of her unfortunate father, too, who seemed to be sinking fast, added to her anguish and despair; and she contemplated the dreadful future with a shuddering sensation of horror, which she found it utterly impossible to conquer.

Mr. Melville struggled against the illness which bore him down, for his daughter's sake, and sought to tranquillize her feelings, and to encourage her to hope. But it was in vain that he endeavoured to conceal his real thoughts and feelings from her penetrating eye, and she was but too well convinced that he foreboded the worst.

He thought of her lonely, unprotected state, when he should be no more (if she should even escape the terrible fate which at present threatened them all), and he could not but entertain a feeling of the deepest regret that the passion which glowed so warmly in her breast could not be returned by Stanley.

The latter guessed the melancholy thoughts that were thus passing in Mr. Melville's mind, and deeply sympathized with him and Flora, and while he sought all in his power to ameliorate their grief, and to encourage them to believe that Providence would yet interpose to save them from the horrors and dangers by which they were at present surrounded, he tried to satisfy him that should anything happen to him, he (Stanley) would consider it his duty to protect Flora with a brother's anxious care, and that they might be sure that she would find a warm and affectionate friend in Omelia.

Flora and her father pressed his hand and looked up in his face with an expression of the most unbounded gratitude, as he uttered this assurance; for they were thoroughly convinced of the sincerity with which it was given and the feelings that prompted it.

But terrible indeed were the prospects of the wretched inmates of that refuge of misery, without any chance apparently of relief, and with horrors accumulating around them. Grim death in its most awful form, stared them in the face on every side; many had already sunk under their frightful sufferings, and others were fast sinking under the effects of thirst and hunger.

It was fearful to gaze upon the looks of anguish and despair which marked the pale and ghastly faces the eye encountered, turn whichever way you might, while groans, sighs, murmurings of impatient complaint and bitter lamentations resounded everywhere throughout the sacred building, and made the heart sicken, and the blood run cold.

And now the dreadful crisis fast approached, and the fate of the unfortunate beings was about to be consummated. The third day of the rebellion in the city had arrived, and the work of slaughter was still going on, and even with increased ferocity.

Numerous were the unfortunate victims, for great in numbers as the mutineers were, and well supplied with ammunition, they had it all their own way, were complete masters of the city, and set all resistance at defiance.

Nothing could restrain them in their acts of unparalleled barbarity; there was no limit to their cruelty; they indeed more resembled a legion of devils let loose, than anything bearing the human character.

Fortunate, indeed, were those who escaped, though stripped and plundered of everything they possessed, and many of those narrow escapes were truly miraculous, but which we have not time or space to relate here.

It had been a frightful day in the old mosque; death had been busy among the unhappy inmates, and many were the heart-rending scenes that had taken place.

Mr. Melville was now in a complete state of insensibility, and his final hour seemed fast approaching. He was reclining in the arms of his daughter, his head resting on her bosom, while she watched him with anxious and half-frenzied looks that told the poignant mental anguish she was at that moment enduring. She did not weep; no, her grief could not find vent in tears, but heavy sobs and sighs escaped her bosom, and spoke even more eloquently than tears could have done.

It was quite evident to the poor girl, that the earthly existence of her father was fast drawing to a close, and that she would soon be an orphan in the world; and so dismal was the prospect of the future, that she almost wished it might please Heaven to take her at the same moment that it did the author of her being.

Stanley stood by, and at times whispered words of consolation to her, which, however, fell listlessly on her ears, for the melancholy situation of her parent completely engrossed her whole attention, and her thoughts. He sincerely felt for her, and the solemn and awful trial she had to undergo, and deeply he lamented that he had not the means of rendering her any assistance under the deplorable circumstances.

It was night; night rendered doubly awful in that place of horror, and with the expectation every moment of greater terrors, if possible, overtaking them.

A death-like silence reigned throughout the building, which was only broken at intervals by some dismal groan or cry of despair. But this was not long suffered to continue; presently, loud shouts of savage voices, followed by other ominous sounds, and the discharge of fire-arms were heard without, and then the forcing of gates and doors, which told the fearful truth, namely, that the blood-thirsty miscreants were rushing upon their destruction.

And now the scene of terror in the building was truly appalling and heartrending. The shrieks of the women as they clasped their little ones frantically to their bosoms, anticipating the dreadful fate which awaited them, were frightful and piteous to hear; while the men, worn out with suffering, privation, and anxiety of mind, although many of them were armed, were in an ill state to offer even a feeble resistance; and even if they had not been, they would not have been long able to stay the work of bloodshed about to be perpetrated by their savage and merciless enemies.

Stanley and his companions, however, prepared themselves to defend the women and children to the last, and tried to encourage them to be firm and collected in the dreadful and desperate emergency.

He was about to see to the removal of Flora and her father to some place of better security in the building, when a loud shriek of the most indescribable agony from the former, startled him, and drew his more immediate attention to the cause. The awful truth was soon explained; Mr. Melville had breathed his last, and Flora held in her arms, his cold corpse, on which she gazed with a fearful expression of countenance, which showed that madness had nearly taken possession of her brain.

Stanley was deeply affected at this sad event, but there was little time for thought, for the doors in one part of the mosque had given way beneath repeated and heavy blows, and the murderers were hurrying into the place with frightful yells, and the work of slaughter had commenced with a violence, which showed the extent to which it was likely to be carried.

The shrieks, the groans of agony, the cries of children, and the curses, execrations, and shouts of vengeance and derision uttered by the miscreants, were truly appalling.

Stanley hastily sought to remove the corpse of Mr. Melville from his daughter's arms, and to take her under his immediate protection, but she clung to it tenaciously, and, with a frantic shriek, sunk insensible on the floor, with the lifeless body still clasped in her arms.

The next moment, Stanley and his companions had to defend themselves from the desperate and ferocious attack of the inhuman foes, who rushed upon men, women, and children, indiscriminately, like bloodhounds, shooting, cutting down, and bayoneting all who came in their way. It was evident that the destruction of the whole of the unhappy beings who had sought refuge in the mosque was their determination; and there was too great a certainty that, to a large extent, their monstrous designs could be accomplished.

In the confusion, some contrived to make their escape from the building, but most of them only to meet with a still more horrible fate outside; and, in fact, all the horrors and barbarities of the last three days were re-enacted on that fatal spot, and still the blood-thirsty revenge of the wretches remained unsated. Supplications for mercy only met with derision, and a still more frightful and torturing death, and the scene of horror was indeed as nearly complete as possible.

Stanley and his friends fought bravely, and many fell beneath their deadly blows; but their chances of escape were rendered extremely doubtful, surrounded as they were by overwhelming numbers, and with no chance of assistance from without.

They were quickly driven from the spot near which the unfortunate Flora Melville was lying on the cold corse of her father, still insensible, and the dreadful fate that awaited her seemed too awfully certain.

He continued to fight with the same determined valour, notwithstanding he was badly wounded, and several of his brave companions had fallen, and at length found himself with three soldiers, and two of the faithful domestics of the late Mr. Melville, outside the mosque, in the midst of a number of the mutineers and their helpless victims, whom they were putting to every horrible description of death that the minds of fiends could only conceive. There was one fearful volley which did awful execution; Stanley was again wounded, and falling to the earth, he remembered no more.

The mutineers now imagined that they had completed their inhuman work, that few of those who had sought shelter in the mosque had escaped the slaughter, and, after brutally mutilating many of the bodies of their victims, with loud shouts of exultation they retired from the scene of destruction.

———

CHAPTER XXX.

FLORA MELVILLE'S DESPAIR.—THE HERMIT'S RETREAT AGAIN.

THE moon shone brightly over one of the principal streets in the city of Delhi on the fatal night we have been describing, and all was now silent as the grave, for it seemed that the rebels had again paused for a brief period in their cruel work, and the sounds of firing had for a time ceased.

It was about two hours after the massacre in and about the neighbourhood of the mosque, and awful was the scene which that chaste, bright moon revealed.

The mangled bodies of murdered men, women, and children, lay about in every direction, and the street literally flowed with blood,

And rushing wildly among the different heaps of the slain, might have been seen a delicate female form, whose appearance told a dreadful tale of crime and suffering.

Her hair hung loose and dishevelled down her neck and shoulders; her face was as ghastly pale as those of the dead she gazed upon, and there was an unnatural wildness in the expression of her intelligent eyes, which seemed to denote that madness to a certain extent, had already taken possession of her brain.

It was the unfortunate Flora Melville. It was not until some time after the mutineers had quitted the mosque, that Flora revived, and the reader may then judge of the horror of her feelings at the frightful scene which met her bewildered and appalled sight.

She found herself lying near to one of the entrances, whither she must have been dragged, and death in its most ghastly form surrounded her. She called frantically upon the name of her father, for she could not see him, and she had no recollection of his death; then she repeated the name of Stanley, but the echo of her own voice in the spacious building was the only answer she received, and, horror struck, and distracted, she rushed over the dead, outside the building, and hurried on she knew not whither, calling frantically upon the name of her father, whom she in the bewilderment of her senses, imagined had been taken from the mosque, or had gone forth in search of her.

With frenzied haste, she wandered on, gazing with ghastly looks upon the fearful objects that met her sight at every turn; and there was no human eye to observe her, for the part of the city she was traversing seemed to be entirely deserted, and the houses were all wrapped in the most profound darkness.

What awful thoughts crowded upon the poor girl's disordered mind as she thus proceeded, looking anxiously at the pale and distorted features of the murdered victims, which seemed to gaze awfully up in her face in the light of the moon.

She had a vivid idea of the dreadful scene which had taken place in the mosque, although she had not witnessed it, she having been insensible all the time, to which circumstance she doubtless owed the preservation of her life, the murderers having probably supposed she was dead; but for the time she had lost all recollection of the death of her parent, and wondered by what accident he had been removed from her; whither he had wandered, and whether he had been fortunate enough to escape the terrible fate which had befallen so many others.

Still all seemed like some torturing and bewildering dream to her, and the more she sought to unravel it, the deeper did she become involved in mystery and perplexity.

Stanley too; oh, what had become of him? That was another question which bewildered her brain, and excited her utmost anxiety. Surely he had not willingly abandoned her to her fate, and only looked after his own safety? Oh, no, she knew his manly character too well to believe him capable of conduct such as that, and she reproached herself for having a moment suffered such an idea to enter her mind.

Still amid the ghastly dead, on that fatal night the poor girl wandered and searched, with a shuddering feeling of dread and anxious curiosity; her brain still disordered, and her recollection at fault. Suddenly, however, she paused, as a strange sensation agitated her bosom, and pressing her hands upon her forehead the whole fearful truth at once flashed upon her memory, and she uttered a groan of agony and despair which seemed to come from a broken heart.

"Almighty God!" she exclaimed, clasping her hands vehemently together, and tears of the most indescribable anguish starting to her eyes; "in mercy look down upon me and protect me, poor fatherless, friendless, wretched creature that I now am. Father! dear father, are you then taken from me, and thus the worst forebodings and apprehensions that I entertained, realized? Oh, why was I not permitted to die with you?"

Sobs, convulsive sobs for a short time choked her utterance, and she wept as though her heart would break.

"But," she exclaimed, suddenly, as a torturing idea occurred to her, "why have I abandoned the cold remains of that beloved parent, of whose protection I am now so cruelly deprived, and whose gentle and affectionate voice I shall never more listen to? Let me return to that scene of death and horror, and as I gaze upon my father's revered features, now alas, cold and inanimate, weep scalding tears of sorrow and regret, and, (since all my earthly hopes are now for ever annihilated), die! die!"

Hastily she turned to retrace her steps to the mosque, when she was startled, and somewhat alarmed on beholding a human form, (that apparently of a man), standing by, and with folded arms, watching her earnestly.

"Flora Melville," said a well known voice, in tones of solemnity, but the deepest sympathy; and with an exclamation of mingled satisfaction, astonishment, and grief, the poor girl rushed forward and threw herself sobbing convulsively on her bosom, for it was Omelia.

"Unhappy girl," said the latter, tenderly, "how sincerely do I lament your sad bereavement. Alas! death through the instrumentality of monsters, disgracing the human form, has indeed committed sad ravages, and many unfortunate beings who were but ill prepared to meet that great and awful change, have been hurried into the presence of their Maker. Surely retribution, just as it is terrible, will ere long overtake the perpetrators of these atrocities. But, Lieutenant Stanley; oh, where is he? What awful fate has befallen him? Or has he escaped the dreadful slaughter?"

"Alas, I know not," answered Flora, "my brain is distracted! oh, do not detain me, Omelia; let me hasten to return to the mosque, and searching out the cold remains of my aged parent, weep away that life which is now no longer valuable to me."

"Hold, Flora," said Omelia, laying her hand upon her arm; "terrible though this calamity is, and great and irreparable as is the loss to you, you must not be permitted thus to abandon yourself to despair and certain destruction. Your honoured father will repose in peace among the unfortunate

victims of this inhuman slaughter in the sacred building, where they now rest; and of what avail would it be for you again to rush upon those ghastly horrors. Come, Miss Melville; Providence has most mercifully and miraculously preserved your life, and you must not act in opposition to its will. This way, this way—quick, for even now danger may be nearer at hand than you expect. Come, do not hesitate, I will conduct you to a place of safety."

"Oh, I care not now whatever fate may befal me," sighed Flora, in a voice of the deepest emotion; "I am alone in the world, with no one to love me, or to sympathize with my sorrows, and what is there that I can cherish a wish to live for. Leave me to pursue my own melancholy course, dear Omelia, and suffer me at once to return to the mosque, and——"

"This is madness," interrupted Omelia, "and must not be allowed. There may be hope and consolation for you as yet, when this terrible tempest shall have subsided. Let us not delay, for I have other business to accomplish ere the night has passed away; to ascertain, if possible, the fate of Lieutenant Stanley, and see to his safety. May Heaven have preserved him from all the fearful dangers to which he has been exposed."

"Amen!" solemnly and fervently ejaculated Flora, and the anguish of her feelings increased; "but whither, mysterious girl, would you lead me?" she added, anxiously.

"To where you will be secure from all harm," replied our heroine, "and receive every kind attention and sympathy that humanity can suggest. You cannot doubt the honour and integrity of my motives, Flora."

"Oh, no," answered Flora, "Heaven forbid that I should harbour a suspicion against you; but my brain is bewildered, my heart is broken, I shall go mad; oh, my poor father, I cannot, will not live, now that you are taken from me. Let me go Omelia, the scene of horror in the old mosque is now alone in unison with my feelings."

"Nay," observed Omelia, still retaining her hold of Flora's arm, "I must not listen to what you say and propose, Miss Melville, which is opposed to all reason. Come, let us immediately quit these ghastly objects, while we can do so without obstruction."

Flora no longer offered any further resistance, for she was so overwhelmed with emotion that she scarcely knew what she did, and Omelia, after having cast a look of horror and commiseration upon the mangled remains of the unfortunate persons who had met with so cruel and untimely a fate, hurried her away from the spot, by the most unfrequented portion of the city.

Omelia's anguish of mind was almost as great as that of her companion, though she concealed it as well as she could. The most terrible fears haunted her imagination as to the fate which had befallen her lover; and it was in vain that she endeavoured to conquer those doubts and apprehensions. She was resolved, at every risk, after having conducted Flora Melville to the cavern, to venture to the mosque, and see whether she could discover any traces of him there or on the road; and it was with that determination that she hurried her afflicted companion on the way as fast as she could; but suddenly, and by accident, they came upon the street in which the late Mr. Melville and his daughter resided, and the emotions of poor Flora as she gazed upon the ruins of their once happy home, which brought more vividly to the recollection, the terrible events that had recently taken place, may be better imagined than described.

Omelia's feelings at this sad sight, were almost as powerfully excited as her unfortunate companion, and she endeavoured to hurry her from the spot; but Flora could not be persuaded to leave it so abruptly.

"Oh, God!" she exclaimed, as she gazed upon the blackened and crumbling walls; "how awful and impressive is this scene of destruction; what a fearful change have a few short hours wrought, and how terrible is the blow which has struck me and destroyed all my hopes of happiness for ever. Alas! alas! why has the hand of Heaven spared me in the midst of all these horrors? Death, surely now would be a release from miseries too torturing and overwhelming to endure."

"Calm your feelings," said Omelia, "and great as are the calamities with which it has pleased Providence to visit you, you must endeavour to bear them with fortitude and resignation."

"Oh, it is impossible," replied Flora—tears of the most poignant grief streaming down her pale and careworn cheeks;—"wretched, friendless being, as I now am, where, oh, where can I look for consolation? I shall go mad—I shall go mad."

Omelia again endeavoured to soothe her; and taking her arm, with a look of the most tender sympathy, she urged her on their way, and soon got her out of sight of the ruins.

Fortunately, they encountered no one as they proceeded; for our heroine's quick ear caught the slightest sound, and she cautiously avoided those streets where they were most likely to be observed and to meet with danger.

They at length emerged from the city, and were quickly approaching that lonely spot in which the cavern was situated, where Omelia had found so secure an asylum.

The mind of Flora was too completely absorbed by the melancholy subjects that racked it, to suffer her to pay the least attention to anything else, or she would have been curious to know to where the strange and dreary place they were now traversing conducted; but she took but little notice of the way they were pursuing, and was not aroused to recollection till they had penetrated into the very depths of the wilderness, and stood before the entrance of the cavern.

And now the curiosity and anxiety of Flora was excited, and she gazed upon the scene with no little degree of astonishment. "Whither have you led me, Omelia?" she eagerly demanded. "What wild and singular place is this?"

"Behold," answered Omelia, removing the concealment to the entrance of the cavern;—"here, in the subterranean retreat, to which this is an opening, I have in safety resided under the protection of an aged and holy man, ever since my flight from the villa at Agra; and here too will you find a secure asylum, until the horrors that now desolate the land shall have ceased. Fear not, but step cautiously."

Flora was so much surprised that she knew not how to reply; and our heroine taking her hand, they began to descend by the curious way which has been before described, into the cavern.

Flora's curiosity and interest was more than ever excited by this romantic adventure; and, for a short time, her mind was diverted from her immediate sorrows, and wholly fixed upon that which was now about to take place.

Having gained the bottom of the winding descent, Omelia still retaining her hold of her companion's hand, led her along the passage in the profound darkness and silence of the place, until they at length stopped before the entrance of the principal cavern, the lamp suspended from the roof, enabling the astonished Flora to obtain a pretty good view of the interior, and which not a little interested her.

Omelia having suffered her to gratify her curiosity in this manner for a minute or two, led her into the cavern, the hermit not being there. His voice, however, as he was engaged at his devotions, might be heard in one of the smaller caverns; and Flora felt a strange and irresistible sensation of awe stealing over her, which she had seldom before experienced.

Omelia encouraged her by a faint smile, and having motioned her to be seated, left her for a minute or two, and entered the adjoining cavern, to apprize the aged man of her return, and by whom she was accompanied.

Flora awaited in some suspense, but she was not kept so long; for our heroine re-entered the cavern, attended by the hermit, and the surprise and interest of Flora were greatly increased by the singular and venerable appearance of this mysterious being. She bent low, in reverence to the holy man, and he raised his hands above her head, and muttered some unintelligible words, seeming to invoke a blessing.

"Child of sorrow," said the Sheikh, in a voice of kindness and sympathy, and addressing himself to Flora;—"child of sorrow, welcome to this sacred retreat, the abode of virtue and innocence, and ever the place of shelter for the unfortunate and oppressed. Here thou mayest rest in safety till the dark clouds of adversity that now obscure the horizon shall happily have passed away; till misguided man shall once more be awakened to reason, justice, and humanity, and the fiends of rapine, desolation and murder shall cease to hold their fearful rule in this once happy land. May peace and consolation deign to aid thee in this the hour of thy tribulation."

The words of the hermit, and the solemn and impressive tones in which he uttered them, had a most powerful effect on the mind of Flora, who felt as if she were in the presence of some supernatural being. She knelt before him, endeavoured to speak, but a tumult of emotions of the most agonizing description rushed upon her, choked her utterance, and she burst into tears, sobbing at the same time convulsively, and as though her heart was ready to burst.

The old man again seemed to invoke a blessing on her head, an expression of benevolence at the same time passing over his venerable and striking features, which no one could gaze on without feelings of the greatest confidence, respect, and admiration.

Omelia raised the poor girl from her humble posture, whispering some gentle words of encouragement and consolation in her ear; and Flora, overpowered by her varied emotions, sunk in her arms, and burst into an uncontrollable paroxysm of sobs and tears.

"Be calm, child," said the Hermit, and learn to submit with patience, fortitude, and resignation to the decrees and dispen-

sations of that Supreme Power who guides and marks the destinies of mankind. The hand of death hath laid thy father low; and thou must feel the sad bereavement keenly, but it was His almighty will, and thou, poor weak and erring mortal as thou art, must not presume to murmur."

"Venerable man," at last with difficulty, sobbing out a reply, "your words inspire me with awe and reverence; but what, oh! what can replace the loss I have sustained in the death of such a parent? Oh! why did I not perish with him? My brain is distracted; I feel to loathe myself, and to consider life as now an insupportable burthen."

"Oh, forbear, dear Miss Melville; interposed our heroine; give not thus way to overwhelming grief and despair. Be comforted, be patient, and fear not, but happiness will again ere long dawn upon you."

"Happiness," repeated Flora, with a look of mingled anguish and regret; "oh, never again for me; never again shall I experience the radiance of its smiles. It would be madness to anticipate it, to encourage such delusive hopes. Oh, I can never survive the irreparable, the dreadful loss I have sustained. Wretched and friendless as I am, death would be a mercy to me."

She sunk on a seat unable to give utterance to another word, and, covering her face with her hands, abandoned herself to all the violence of the grief that racked her bosom.

For a few minutes the unfortunate girl was allowed to give vent to her sorrows without interruption; and Omelia drawing the hermit aside, had some conversation with him in an under tone, she then returned to Flora, and gently taking her hand, said:—

"Thank Providence, my dear Miss Melville, I have been able to conduct you here in safety, and here you are secure from every harm. Endeavour, I pray you to endeavour to conquer the violence of your anguish, and to bear your heavy afflictions with fortitude. I must now leave you."

"Leave me!" repeated Flora, with a look of anxiety.

"Aye," answered Omelia, "my departure is imperative; but fear not, I will not delay my return any longer than I can help, and in the meantime this venerable man will see to all your wants and necessities."

"Oh, whither do you go?" eagerly interrogated Flora.

"On an errand of humanity, and prompted by love, fear, and anxiety," answered our heroine; "I go in search of Lieutenant Stanley, and I cannot rest until

I have discovered him, or ascertained the fate which has befallen him."

"And may Heaven aid you in your praiseworthy errand," ejaculated Flora, sincerely, "and preserve the noble minded Stanley from the terrible dangers by which he has been surrounded. Go, go, good Omelia, God forbid that I should any longer seek to detain you."

Omelia again uttered some words of encouragement, and embraced her affectionately, then committing her to the care of the hermit, she departed from the cavern on her melancholy and hazardous expedition.

Flora saw her depart with a heavy heart, and the most dismal forebodings, and again covering her face with her hands, she resigned herself to all the anguish of her feelings, and to which the hermit suffered her to give uninterrupted indulgence.

He retired from the cavern for a minute or two, entering one of the smaller ones, and presently he returned with fruit and such other humble and simple fare as his romantic and singular retreat afforded, together with a flask containing some sober and refreshing beverage. These he placed on the little table before Flora, and in the kindest accents requested her to partake of them.

Flora, unwilling to appear obstinate or unsociable, (though her heart was too full to suffer her to feel the least inclination to eat,) thanking the aged man for his kind consideration, complied with his request, and partook slightly of the refreshments.

The hermit then seeming to think that she would probably be better if left for a time to the free indulgence of her own sorrowful reflections, or to try if she could get an hour or two's repose, conducted her into one of the other caverns, where there was a simple pallet of leaves and rushes; and after having uttered to her a few more words of advice and consolation, withdrew, and left her to herself.

Flora gazed around her, at the strange place in which she found herself, with the most unmitigated surprise and bewilderment; and she could hardly persuade herself that she was not labouring under the influence of some extraordinary dream. However, the dreadful calamity which had befallen her, and the horrors that she anticipated in the future, completely superseded every other thought, and she abandoned herself to the most absolute grief and despair. She had lost her best earthly friend, and that under circumstances so truly melancholy and deplorable, that she felt that she could never recover from the shock. Where could she seek for hope or consolation? Where again find that home and those domestic comforts of which she was now so cruelly deprived?

Her heart sickened at the reflections, and it seemed as though her senses were fast leaving her. For some time she became lost in the bewildering intensity of her anguish, then stretching her aching and exhausted limbs on the pallet, she endeavoured to find a short respite from her misery in sleep, but in vain; although she did at last sink into a kind of torpor, but yet her mind was perfectly alive to all the troubles that had befallen her, and those that, no doubt, were still in store for her.

CHAPTER XXXI.

OMELIA AND STANLEY.

WE left Stanley after the dreadful events that have been described in the preceding chapters, lying wounded and insensible not far from the mosque.

How long he had remained in that situation he had not the means of forming the least conjecture, but a slight shower of rain which happened to fall for a brief period, probably served to revive him, and although faint and exhausted, and, with some difficulty raising himself on his elbow, he gazed with a shuddering sensation of horror at the dismal scene in which he found himself, surrounded by the ghastly dead, in whose livid features he recognized many of his former friends and companions.

He had a terrible recollection of all that had taken place; of the melancholy death of Mr. Melville; of the agony and despair of his bereaved daughter, and his being forced from her side at the very critical moment when she stood so much in need of his protection; and the most dreadful apprehensions crossed his mind that she had met with the same awful and untimely fate as the other unfortunate victims of the massacre.

His wounds, which probably were not so serious as he had first feared they were, had ceased to bleed, but he felt so weak and sore, that he thought it would be impossible for him to leave the spot, (in spite of the dangers that might yet threaten him should any of the mutineers return and find him still alive), without assistance; and, when he considered the little chance there was of his obtaining that under the present

bably aggravate the danger of her position; and she therefore maintained herself with a degree of fortitude, and dignified contempt, which evinced, as her captors imagined, by a mere boy, both surprised, and to some extent, abashed them.

Enraged at her obstinacy in refusing to answer the numerous questions they put to her, they often proceeded, in the course of the journey, to acts of violence as cowardly as they were cruel, sometimes inflicting blows, and at others goading her forward at the point of the bayonet, lacerating her flesh, and causing her the most excruciating pain, but still not a sigh, not a murmur escaped the heroic girl's lips, and she maintained the same look of scorn, of irony, and utter defiance, which had marked her conduct from the beginning.

No. 19.

Hunger, fatigue, privations, threats, insults of every description, had been put in force by the savage miscreants into whose power she had so unhappily fallen, without the least effect, and they felt themselves completely defeated in their principal object, and that too, by what they supposed to be a mere strippling.

It was not so much on her own account, as that of those who were more precious to her than even her own existence. She thought of Stanley, and the probability that she might never behold him again, and her heart sunk within her, although she gave no visible signs of the emotions that agitated her breast, and distracted her brain; and she suffered the more from being thus compelled to subdue the expression of her feelings.

How torturing was that reflection. He sank back exhausted with the agony of his feelings.

Still he resolved to make a desperate effort to crawl from the spot, and to re-enter the mosque, which might afford him a shelter until Providence should in its mercy send something to his relief. After many ineffectual attempts, he again succeeded in raising himself on his elbow, and to crawl a few paces; but he was again compelled to pause, and he gazed around him with a look of agony. He was suddenly, however, startled by hearing the murmuring of the voices of men at a short distance, and directly afterwards he beheld several armed men (for he saw the shining of their bayonets in the moonlight, and could have no doubt that they were some of the straggling mutineers), approaching, and he gave himself up for lost.

Before, however, he thought that they could observe him, he crawled as cautiously as possible back to the spot he had quitted, and stretched himself on his face among the slain, so that they might imagine him also dead, and he scarcely ventured to breathe, as he heard the men coming that way, and he was convinced from the observations that accidentally met his ears, that his suspicions were correct, and that they were indeed some of the rebels.

They arrived at the spot, and paused to contemplate with feelings of savage joy the ghastly objects that strewed the ground in all directions.

"Ha!" exclaimed one of the ruffians in tones of satisfaction, "our comrades have well executed their desperate task this night, and the detested Feringhees have been made to feel the terrors of the vengeance of those men whom they had hitherto despised."

"Aye," observed one of his companions, "the work proceeds bravely; Delhi is ours, and ere long our enemies will be driven entirely from the land or exterminated. This is only a faint sample of the slaughter that will take place. But come, let us into the mosque, which is no doubt filled with the victims of the massacre, and we may yet find some stray booty which has escaped the hands of our comrades, and may be worth having."

To this proposition, the other wretches assented; and with a throbbing heart, and the greatest relief, Stanley heard them depart; and as the sound of their retreating footsteps gradually became more indistinct, he ventured once more to raise his head, and follow them anxiously with his eyes, and watched them making towards the mosque, until they were hidden from the view by some of the trees that grew near the building.

Stanley had escaped this danger, but still his situation was as dismal and hopeless a one as could well be imagined, and he saw no prospect of relief from it.

The excitement he had for this brief period undergone, and the anxiety of his thoughts were, however, too much for his exhausted strength; a deathly faintness came over him; his brain turned giddy, and he again sunk back upon the earth in a state of insensibility.

With mingled doubts and fears, and unable to dispel the gloomy forebodings that haunted her mind Omelia, on leaving Flora Melville in the cavern, hastened upon her painful errand, namely to endeavour to obtain some tidings of her lover.

The dreadful scene and the general slaughter that had taken place in the mosque, strengthened her worst apprehensions; still Flora and no doubt others, had most miraculously escaped, and surely, therefore, it was not unlikely that Providence had also extended its mercy to him.

She endeavoured to encourage this idea, but found it difficult to do so, and it was therefore with a sad and heavy heart that she bent her way (by the same unfrequented route that she had brought Flora, towards the mosque; pausing now and then to listen, and looking cautiously around her to see that she was not watched.

She had taken her usual precaution to arm herself previous to leaving the cavern, and she had already given sufficient proof that she had the courage, and knew how to defend, not only herself but others in a case of emergency; and her extraordinary acts of heroism were already known and talked of among the mutineers, though her real character and sex was only known to a few of them, or their wonder would have been more complete.

If she should happen to be taken, in spite of her being a Hindoo, and the daughter of Yunadar, she well knew that she could expect no mercy at their hands. Should she be surprised and overpowered, however, she was determined to sell her life dearly.

She had also brought with her a flask containing a powerful restorative, should she discover any person who might have survived the dreadful massacre, and stood in need of it.

It was now near the hour of midnight, and save that the bright moon ever and anon peeped forth from behind the black clouds that obscured the horizon, all was buried in the most solemn darkness, and a sullen silence pervaded the streets.

The distance from the cavern to the mosque, it has been shown, was considerable, and although she made her way as fast as possible, it was sometime before she arrived there, which she did by a way at the back of the building.

There she paused, and in spite of the firmness and courage that usually animated her, she hesitated to enter, when she pictured to herself the awful spectacle which would doubtless meet her eyes.

At length, however, she in some measure conquered that feeling, and soon found herself standing amidst all the gloom, and silence, and horror of that sacred place, where so frightful a tragedy had lately been enacted.

A deathly faint and poisonous atmosphere seemed to fill the building, and told the dreadful tale of the fearful scene of death and horror that had there taken place.

The moon now shone brightly in at the casements immediately under the dome, and Omelia, from the elevated position in which she stood, just by the entrance to the mosque, had a full view of the ghastly and mangled forms of the hapless beings who had fallen victims to the frightful vengeance of their savage foes.

The most graphic and eloquent pen could not do adequate justice to that appalling sight; and Omelia shuddered, and her heart fairly bled as she gazed upon it.

She passed among the dead with slow and solemn steps, and stooping down to examine their pale and distorted features, which told the inhuman tortures that had been inflicted upon them; and her sufferings may be imagined as she expected every moment that her eyes would encounter the ghastly countenance of her lover, who her worst fears continued to anticipate had fallen a victim to the inhuman perpetrators of the dreadful slaughter.

Firm determination, however, to banish her terrible suspense, (for even death certainly, would be far less torturing even though it brought alone despair and horror), urged her on, and anxiously she proceeded with her mournful task.

Horrors seemed to accumulate as she pursued her fearful search; but all that she had yet gazed upon were locked in the cold embrace of death, not one still lingered in its agonies, so frightfully certain had been the work of blood.

There were the mangled remains of innocent babes lying on the blood-stained bosoms of their murdered mothers; there was youth and beauty mutilated and disfigured, with upturned faces, and glaring glassy eyes, as if they were still vainly imploring mercy from their monstrous assassins;—the young, the old of both sexes were mingled together in a hideous heterogeneous mass;—which the pale moonlight as it streamed in at the windows under the dome, rendered still more awful and ghastly.

Omelia plainly proved on this occasion, the wonderful courage, the more than womanly strength of nerve she possessed, or she could never have persevered in the fearful task she had imposed upon herself; for even the stoutest heart which ever throbbed within a hero's breast, might well have shrunk appalled at so terrible a spectacle.

She recognized the features of many of those whom she had known in life among the unfortunate victims, and tears of heartfelt pity started to her eyes, while horror, disgust, and indignation swelled her bosom against the wretches she felt ashamed to call her countrymen, who had done this fiendish work.

She paused, as torturing thoughts rushed upon her mind, and racked her brain.

"And that man," she said, as a feeling of shame, of anguish, and regret shot through her heart, "that man whom I am compelled to acknowledge as the author of my being, is leagued with those monsters in human form, and but too probably hath participated largely in this dreadful slaughter of the good, the brave, the innocent and defenceless;—nay, even he who possesses all my woman's fondest love may have fallen by his inhuman hand. Dreadful thought! my heart sickens, and every feeling of nature revolts at it. Oh Yunadar, (for I dare not call you father,) guilty, misguided man,—will nothing stay you in your course of crime, and drive away the demon which hath taken possession of you?"

How agonizing were these reflections, but Omelia endeavoured to banish them from her mind, for there was no time for delay. She was surrounded by danger, and she knew not how soon she might be compelled to abandon the object she had in view. She therefore proceeded with her solemn and painful inspection.

Suddenly she paused, and a sensation of the most torturing description agitated her breast, as her eyes rested upon the corpse of one of the unfortunate beings, in whom she recognized her benefactor, the ill-fated Mr. Melville.

His features told plainly what he had suffered in his last moments, and his body had been savagely mutilated after death; and tears of the most poignant grief started to the eyes of Omelia as she gazed on the cold and disfigured remains of that aged man, to whose memory she owed so heavy a debt of gratitude; whilst her heart throbbed with the tenderest feelings of sympathy towards poor Flora Melville in her sad bereavement.

She was still gazing with feelings of the greatest sorrow on the remains of Mr. Melville, when she was startled and somewhat alarmed by hearing the voices of men near the spot by which she had entered the mosque; and, convinced that some danger threatened, she drew her pistols, and hastily retreated behind one of the massive pillars which supported the lofty dome of the building, and where she hoped she might remain concealed from observation, she awaited in breathless anxiety the result of this adventure.

She was not long kept in suspense; the voices became more distinct, and she quickly beheld several of the mutineers slowly approaching from one of the entrances towards the spot near which she was concealed, stooping down and examining the dead, evidently in search of plunder.

Disgust and indignation glowed within the breast of Omelia at the sight of these heartless wretches, and knowing as she did the revolting nature of the business which had brought them to that scene of death, but fearful of betraying herself, she scarcely ventured to breathe, but attentively watched the approach of the miscreants, and preparing herself to act with firmness and determination in case of emergency.

She looked anxiously from her place of concealment, as well as the dim light would permit, among them, to see if her guilty parent was one of the party, but he was not, and that afforded her mind some little relief.

They had now got so near that she could plainly distinguish the features of most of them; and, certainly, a more ferocious looking lot of ruffians had seldom, if ever, before met her view.

They roughly and unfeelingly turned over the different bodies, cutting the rings from their fingers, and plundering them of all the money, watches, and other articles of value which they found upon them, consigning the same to their haversacks, which they had brought with them for that purpose.

"This night's work seems likely to turn out a profitable one," observed one of them.

"Aye," replied another of the mutineers, "these Feringhees in seeking refuge here, seemed to have thought more of their money and trinkets than the necessaries of life. What a bitter mockery it seems that they should have all this property in their possession, and yet many of them perish from actual starvation."

Omelia shuddered, for she could but inwardly acknowledge the awful force and truth of these observations.

The men continued their search, frequently indulging their savage propensities by mangling the cold remains of such of the ill-fated creatures upon whom they could not find anything of value, and making use of the most brutal and disgusting remarks at the same time.

They frequently came so near the place where Omelia was concealed, that she had to use the utmost watchfulness and precaution to avoid discovery, and she awaited in doubt and anxiety the termination of this adventure.

They now came to the body of Mr. Melville, which lying beneath one of the windows, was fully revealed in the moonlight.

"'Tis the old merchant, Melville," observed one of them;—"he managed to escape here, it seems, after the attack of Yunadar and his comrades on his house."

"Aye, thanks to that treacherous Hindoo youth, who came to the rescue of this old fellow and his friends," remarked another of the rebels, "and who fought with the desperate courage of a young lion."

"And," returned the first speaker,—"if all be true that is reported, that supposed daring boy is no other than the daughter of Yunadar in disguise. You are aware that she had lived under the protection and on the charity of this old man and his daughter for years, and set the authority of her father completely at defiance."

"True," was the answer, "and should she fall into the hands of those whose cause she has so treacherously dared to oppose, there are no tortures that they will fail to inflict on her."

At that moment, in the excitement and agitation of her feelings, Omelia, accidentally dropped one of the pistols, which fell with a rattling sound on the marble pavement, and immediately attracted the attention of the mutineers.

"Ah! what noise was that?" demanded one of them.

"It seemed to proceed from behind yonder pillar," replied one of his companions," —"surely no one can be mad and daring enough to watch our actions here. Let us search,"

Omelia immediately saw the dangerous situation in which this accident had placed her, but she, as usual under similar circumstances preserved her presence of mind, and, as the men approached the place of her concealment, she silently retreated to some short distance in the shade of the building, and stretched herself on her face on the pavement. so that she was not likely to be distinguished from the rest of the unfortunate victims that strewed the place.

The murderers searched narrowly round the spot which she had just quitted and even approached close to where she was lying without apparently observing her.

"It was nothing after all," remarked one who appeared to be the leader; we suffered our imagination to lead us astray, it is not likely that any one would be foolish enough to be lurking here after what has taken place. Let us proceed with our business, which the sooner we bring to a conclusion the better, for this is no desirable place to loiter in with all those dead carcases lying about."

To this his comrades agreed, and they resumed their work of plunder, Omelia not venturing to remove from her position until they should have completed their guilty task which she awaited for with the utmost anxiety and impatience.

At length they had accomplished this apparently to their satisfaction, and they then departed from the mosque by the same way that they had entered it, much to the relief of our heroine, who, raising herself on her elbow, eagerly watched them as they retired without any danger of being observed herself.

When they were gone and she was again left alone in that solemn temple of Death she fervently returned her thanks to Providence for her preservation so far, and then, with some alarm at the delay which had taken place, she resumed her fearful search among the dead, but discovering no traces of her lover, she was filled with mingled hopes and fears, which increased in strength every minute, and as she hastily but cautiously retraced her steps from the mosque, and once more entered into the open air, where she breathed more freely.

But great was her agitation and terrible her suspense at the uncertainty of the fate which had befallen her lover, and in spite of all her efforts to subdue her fears, she could not help entertaining the most dismal forebodings and misgivings. And yet was it not possible that in the dreadful confusion which must have prevailed while the massacre was taking place, that Stanley had succeeded in making his escape, and in reaching some place of temporary safety?—she endeavoured to persuade herself that it was so; yet the mystery in which all the circumstances were enshrouded were most torturing and insupportable.

But whither could she now direct her search with any probability of success? The lateness of the hour, and the time which had elapsed since the dreadful events had taken place in the mosque, also added to her perplexity and her apprehensions. Flora and the hermit too, would also begin to be alarmed at the length of her absence from the cave, and yet she could not form the resolution to return, until her terrible doubts and suspicions were in some measure satisfied.

For a minute she paused irresolute, these thoughts pressing upon and racking her brain at the same time. Then she took the direction of the street in which she had encountered Flora, some instinctive impulse which she could not resist, seeming to urge her thither.

CHAPTER XXXII.

MOMENT OF DANGER.—THE MEETING AND THE PARTING.

GUIDED only by the pale rays of the moon, which gleamed fitfully ever and anon from behind dark and ponderous clouds, but reanimated with fresh courage and hope of success, Omelia pursued her way hastily from the mosque, cautiously looking around her as she proceeded, in case of any threatened danger; but all at present seemed secure, and a solemn calm had for a brief interval, and for an interval only, lulled the fierce and frightful tempest of men's inhuman and bloodthirsty passions.

She breathed a solemn and earnest prayer to the Power she worshipped for success, and then appeared to take fresh heart, and to hasten on her way with renewed confidence.

Again let us return to Lieutenant Stanley, for whose fate, recollecting the critical situation in which we left him, the reader will no doubt, feel much anxiety.

He continued in the same inanimate and insensible state for some time longer, yet dreamy recollections of all that had taken place, and of the imminent perils to which he was still exposed, haunted his imagination, and kept his anxiety and his anguish still awake, even in that torpid state.

He was suddenly aroused by the voice of a man, and with a sudden effort, which he might not have been expected to make in his present exhausted condition, raising himself on his elbow, gazed anxiously towards the spot from whence the voice proceeded, and had it not been that under the most desperate circumstances, he was always a stranger to fear, his utmost alarm for his safety would now undoubtedly have been excited.

Standing near him, armed to the teeth,

was the tall and muscular form of one of the mutineers, whose savage features, and the ferocious expression of whose large eyes, shewed him to be a wretch who would not hesitate to perpetrate any crime, however atrocious.

Yet the sudden restoration to life of the young lieutenant, as it appeared to be, and the ghastly expression of his features in the sickly glare of the moon, was so unexpected, that it seemed even to startle this hardened and desperate villian, and for a second or two he stood transfixed, and stared vacantly at him as if he had been a spectre.

In that moment of terrible danger, when his life seemed to hang upon a thread, Stanley's courage and presence of mind never forsook him, although he was completely powerless and at the ruffian's mercy.

Thinking to take advantage of the Sepoy's confusion, he felt for his pistol, but could not find it, and he now certainly gave himself up for lost.

"Ah!" exclaimed the man, suddenly recovering from his surprise, and advancing nearer to Stanley; "does then one of the victims of the late work of retribution still survive? 'Tis well; be mine then the satisfaction of finishing his existence. Hated Feringhee, hundreds of thy detested race have already felt the terrible vengeance of those whom they have so long oppressed, and such is the fate which now awaits thee. Prepare thyself, for thy last moments in this world have come."

He drew a pistol from his belt as he thus spoke, and was deliberately preparing to put his threats into execution, when Stanley, worked up to a pitch of desperation, at the almost certain prospect of immediate death, and, with an effort of strength which was truly miraculous and almost incredible, succeeded in raising himself on his knees, and grasping the arm of the Sepoy convulsively with both hands, exclaimed:—

"Hold! if you are not lost to every feeling of humanity; see you not that I am wounded, maimed, helpless? Surely you cannot be so utterly hardened in crime, as deliberately to take the life of one who never injured you."

"What mercy should the Hindoo show to the wretches who for so many years have usurped his native land, plundered him of his rights, and loaded his limbs with the galling fetters of slavery?" demanded the villain fiercely, and with an expression of countenance which showed how utterly useless was an appeal to him for mercy. "The knell of death hath already sounded to thine hated race, and we will not cease in our fearful vengeance till the whole are exterminated or driven from the country they have so long cursed and degraded by their presence. Oh, what proud feelings of exultation does it afford me to gaze upon the agony of thy despair. But why do I waste words on a reptile beneath my contempt? There is no hope for thee, English dog; thy fate is sealed, and be mine the hand to accomplish it—Die!"

"No, no, no; forbear! forbear!" cried Stanley, wrought up to a state bordering upon frenzy, at the thoughts of perishing by such awful means; Omelia, and all the friends so dear to him, rising to his distracted imagination at that fearful moment, and still grasping the miscreant's arm, with a frantic resolution which was quite extraordinary, "commit not a crime of such wanton cruelty and cowardice, consider my youth, and perform one act of mercy, which may go far to atone for those you have probably already perpetrated."

"Fool!" exclaimed the miscreant, "you cling to life in vain. You do but prolong your agony to no purpose. You appeal to one who only laughs your supplications to scorn. Perish, and add one more to those whose blood is doomed to satiate the Hindoo's vengeance."

He made a powerful effort to release his arm from the convulsive grasp of Stanley, that he might put his savage threat into execution, and in doing so the pistol was discharged, and for an instant he stood confused and astounded. But he quickly recovered himself, and taking a long knife from his belt with his left hand, prepared, with a dreadful oath, to plunge it in the body of Stanley, but at the moment that his arm was raised in the air to do so, he uttered a cry, or yell, that was scarcely human, and bounding slightly in the air, fell on his face, near his intended victim, mortally wounded from a frightful stab in the back.

Attracted to the spot by the report of the pistol, and the sound of voices, one heroic individual, with a throbbing heart, but determined purpose, had stole cautiously to the scene of danger, and watching the opportunity, at the very moment when the miscreant thought the completion of his inhuman purpose was certain, inflicted the deadly blow which stretched him lifeless on the earth, and rescued Stanley from a frightful and untimely fate.

There was an exclamation of mingled delight and anguish, and Stanley found himself clasped in the arms of his preserver!—

It was Omelia!—

Yes, on leaving the mosque, as has been

described, Providence had guided the footsteps of the courageous girl in the right direction, and she arrived at the spot just in time to add one more noble and intrepid act to the list of those by which she had already so remarkably distinguished herself.

How shall we describe the affecting scene which followed this extraordinary and exciting adventure?—Where find language sufficiently powerful to portray the emotions of the lovers at this unexpected and Providential meeting?—They could neither of them for a few moments give expression to their feelings in words. Tears streamed down the cheeks of the beauteous Omelia, and her heart beat at double its wonted pace, as she gazed in the pale countenance of Stanley with a look of intense affection which nothing could surpass;—and he pressed his lips fondly, rapturously to hers, and looked as though he could gaze his very soul away in love and gratitude. But the excitement of this meeting, and the great exertion he had undergone in his present weak and deplorable state, were all too much for him, and Omelia seeing the deathly faintness that was coming over him, immediately applied the restorative which she had so fortunately brought with her from the cavern, to his lips, and it speedily had the desired effect, and he so far revived as to recover the use of his speech.

"Omelia, beloved Omelia," he exclaimed, as he pressed her form still closer to his bosom, "most devoted, most heroic of women, and has kind and merciful Heaven then heard my prayers, and do we meet again?" Speak to me, dearest, for till I hear once more the Heavenly music of your voice, I can scarcely believe the evidence of my senses,—hardly dare I indulge the fond hope that you are restored to me, or that I am not labouring under some delusion of my disordered brain."

"Dear Stanley," replied the poor girl, in a voice half stifled by the power of her emotions,—"it is, it is indeed your Omelia whom you now once more clasp so fondly to your throbbing bosom, and whose swelling heart o'erflows with gratitude to Providence that she has been made the humble instrument in His hands to preserve you from the remorseless hand of the assassin. But you are wounded;—your ghastly looks excite my worst apprehensions. Alas, alas, what is to be done in this terrible emergency?"

"Be calm, be calm, my love, I beseech you," replied Stanley in a faint voice, and looking still more tenderly in her beauteous face;—"I am only weak and faint from loss of blood and long exposure; but my wounds, I trust are not dangerous. Still methinks

it would be bliss to die upon your fond and faithful bosom; to close my eyes for ever in gazing at your beloved features."

"Oh, talk not thus, dear Stanley," sighed Omelia, with increased emotion, and tears still trembling in her eyes; "for it unnerves me to hear you, and drives my brain to distraction. Oh, I could conduct you to a place of safety, but you have not strength to walk, and what can I do without assistance? Then the distance from this fatal spot is so great. My brain is bewildered, and my heart sinks with despair."

"Compose your feelings, my own Omelia," returned her lover, "for your anguish does but add to mine, and fill my breast with the most torturing apprehensions. Every moment that you delay here is fraught with danger to yourself; should any of the murderous wretches wander to this spot your valuable life would fall a certain sacrifice to their savage vengeance. Every other consideration must yield to that. Oh, away, while there is yet time and opportunity; leave me to my fate, or the care of Providence; and, oh, best, most precious and endearing of women, may heaven bless you, and bring you scatheless through this dreadful time of trouble."

"Your words torture me, Stanley," sobbed our heroine, completely overwhelmed with grief and anguish;—"oh, what do you advise? Think you so lightly of Omelia's love as to believe that she could in selfish consideration of her own safety only, leave you here to perish—abandon you to certain death? No, no, this must not, shall not be! I will not forsake you, let whatever may be the consequences."

Oh, what generous self-devotion is this!" cried the young officer, lost and bewildered in gratitude and admiration; "and how unworthy am I of it. Alas! what a cruel destiny is ours, Omelia; surely 'twould have been better had we never known each other, for you might ere this have been the happy bride of one far more deserving of you than I can ever hope to be, and never exposed to the terrible dangers by which you are now hourly surrounded."

"Cease, cease, Stanley," returned Omelia, "such observations as these are uncalled for. But why do we thus delay, when by perseverance and exertion, we may yet surmount the difficulties that now present themselves? I have brought with me fortunately, the proper remedies to apply to your wounds, and they once dressed may serve to revive you, and with my help, probably enable you to accompany me to some better place of security than this, till you can find strength sufficient to reach the place where poor Miss Melville is already in safety."

"Ah!" exclaimed Stanley joyfully; "are you then the preserver of her life also, Omelia? Extraordinary girl, how unexampled is your conduct."

"No more," said our heroine; "this is not the time to waste in useless compliments, though to receive your approval of my conduct, dear Stanley, is more, far more than a sufficient reward for all my exertions."

Stanley again affectionately kissed the check of the lovely girl, and inspired with renewed hope by her words, he submitted his wounds, which were on the head and shoulders, to her gentle and skilful treatment, and she accomplished her task in a manner which would have done credit to an experienced surgeon; and having again taken a small portion of restorative from the flask, he felt himself much revived, and at length with Omelia's assistance, he was enabled to rise to his feet, and to walk a short distance from the spot, where he had been so long exposed to the night air, the hopes of the poor girl reviving at every step he took, although it seemed almost impossible that his strength would ever permit him to proceed the distance that it was to the cavern, whither it was the anxious desire of our heroine to conduct him.

One of the principal causes of apprehension was that they might encounter some straggling party of the rebels, in which case their fate would be certain and inevitable; and these thoughts had scarcely occurred to them when they were startled by the quick and measured tread of several footsteps, and before they had time to collect themselves, and recover from their astonishment and alarm, they perceived a number of armed men approaching, having just turned an abrupt corner into the road along which Stanley and Omelia were proceeding.

Despair fell upon the heart of our heroine, still she exerted herself to the utmost to maintain her fortitude and to encourage her lover.

"All hope is at an end" said Stanley, in a voice of anguish and regret; "there is no escape for me; but Oh, God, to what a horrible fate have you exposed yourself, Omelia, in your generous devotion to me. Fly, fly, while there may yet be time; I am content since Fate so wills it, all I ask, most beloved of women, is that you will sometimes breathe a prayer to that Power you worship to the memory of that unfortunate being, to whom you are far dearer than his very existence. Quick, quick, see they approach,—but another moment's

delay, and it may be too late. Bless you, bless you, wife of my heart, and on this earth farewell for ever!"

"Never never, beloved Stanley," cried the noble girl, firmly, and throwing her arms around his neck, "I cannot, will not abandon you, and if such is the will of Heaven we will die together!"

"For mercy's sake do not thus madly persist," cried Stanley in a voice of the greatest agony, and gently endeavouring to release himself from her embrace; "you distract me;—see, the men rapidly approach, and there are no means of avoiding their observation as they come nearer,—retreat by the way we have come, and probably, in the darkness you may escape detection. For the love of Heaven do not hesitate!"

Omelia, however, was deaf to his entreaties, and still clung to him with frantic determination—her bright but now tearful eyes fixed upon his countenance with the most unspeakable agony, and her heart beating violently against his, as though it would burst its tenement.

And now the moon again burst forth from behind dark masses of clouds, and a loud shout convinced the lovers that they were observed by the men approaching. With looks of terror and despair, they gazed eagerly towards the supposed rebels, now resolved, since their fate seemed to be inevitable, to die in each other's arms,—but an exclamation of astonishment and gratitude to Heaven for its merciful interposition, escaped them, when they discovered that instead of the dreaded mutineers, those who were approaching were British soldiers belonging to the same regiment as Lieutenant Stanley, they probably being about to endeavour to make their escape from the City.

The next moment they arrived at the spot where the lovers were standing, and their astonishment and pleasure on beholding Leiutenant Stanley, who was universally esteemed, and who, they feared, had fallen a victim in the slaughter at the mosque, may be readily imagined. But their surprise on beholding his companion, whom they supposed to be a native youth, and were struck with his delicate gracefully moulded form, yet noble and dignified bearing, and the manner in which he was armed, was even still greater, and especially when they observed their attitude and the looks of affection with which they regarded each other, but seeing the weak and wounded condition of the young lieutenant, they concluded that to Omelia (or the Hindoo youth as they imagined him to be), he owed the preservation of his life.

They congratulated Stanley on his escape

from death, but expressed some anxiety at the condition in which they saw him, and informing him that they were trying to make good their retreat to a small fort some short distance outside the city, where a number of the English residents and troops who had escaped the massacre had sought refuge, and had held out hitherto against the insurgents.

They then eagerly inquired who the young native was in whose company they found him.

"This," replied Stanley, proudly and with feelings glowing with love and gratitude towards our beauteous heroine; "is my preserver, and——"

He was about to reveal the name and sex of Omelia, when a significant look from her checked him, and he added—"He is

No. 17.

a faithful and heroic youth whom I have known for some time, and to whom I am warmly attached for his amiable qualities. He was conducting me to a place of present safety, as well as my weak state would permit; but I fear that I shall be unable to proceed far without greater assistance than he can possibly afford me."

"Of course it must be our task, Lieutenant Stanley, to endeavour to see to your safety as well as our own," observed the officer who had before addressed him; "and it is most fortunate that we have met you. So far we have proceeded without being molested, and everything at present seems to favour our designs. This young man I suppose will accompany us?"

"No," replied Omelia. disguising her voice as well as she could; "Lieutenant

Stanley I hope will be secure under your protection, and I am content. My course is another way, for I have business to perform which must be attended to."

Stanley looked anxiously at Omelia, and his agitation could not escape the notice of the officer, who felt some surprise, but did not entertain the most remote suspicion of the truth; and Stanley drew her aside that they might speak together more freely.

"Oh, Omelia," he sighed, and with a look of the deepest sorrow and regret, "and must we indeed part at a time like this, and with the dreadful uncertainty if ever we may meet again? My heart sinks within me at the thought."

"Be firm, Stanley," replied Omelia, "for there is no alternative. The place whither I wished to conduct you is too far distant for you to undertake the journey without assistance, and I cannot suffer these men to accompany us. It is fortunate that we have met with them, and I trust that you now are in safety, at least that you will be ere long.

"Heaven bless you, dear Stanley, and preserve you from the dreadful fate which has already befallen so many of your unfortunate countrymen. Farewell, farewell, and oh, grant that the time is not far distant when we may meet again. Fear not but your Omelia's heart will remain faithful to the vows she hath so often and so fervently uttered."

"Cruel, cruel fate which compels us thus to separate," ejaculated Stanley, and pressing the form of the gentle and affectionate girl still more closely to his bosom;—oh, why not abandon your present dangerous life, and seek some place of shelter, where we can communicate, till these fearful times are past, and we may indissolubly unite our fates together!"

"Cease, Stanley, I implore you," said the agitated Omelia; "this is neither the time nor the place to discuss so delicate a subject, and of such vital importance to our mutual happiness. This delay is dangerous, and see the soldiers begin to grow impatient. Once more fondly, fervently adieu, and may all good spirits watch over and protect you."

Their lips met together in an ardent and affectionate kiss, unobserved by the officer or his men, and with a burst of uncontrollable emotion, Omelia tore herself from her lover's embrace, and hurried away from the spot.

She stopped anxiously when she had only got a short distance, and with tearful eyes, and a heart throbbing with emotions it is needless to describe, looked back to the spot on which Stanley and his companions still lingered. He observed her

by the aid of the moonlight, and waved his hand affectionately towards her, which she returned; and then, having first looked cautiously about to see that all was secure, she made her way towards the place of her destination with all the expedition she could, knowing the apprehensions that the hermit and Flora Melville must naturally entertain at the length of her absence, and the anxiety they would also feel to know the result of the important errand she had gone upon.

Her parting with her lover, under circumstances of such a peculiar nature, caused her much anguish of mind, and again gave rise to the most gloomy fears and forebodings that they would meet no more; and those doubts and apprehensions were no more than natural, when the awful state of the country, and the wide spread of the revolt were considered.

Deeply she regretted the circumstances that compelled them to separate; but she felt that she had her mission to perform, and she could not rest until it was fully and successfully accomplished.

With these reflections busily occupying her mind, Omelia cautiously pursued her way, almost exhausted by the remarkble exertions she had undergone for so many hours, and which had deprived her of every moment's rest, either mentally or bodily.

Danger hovered near the intrepid Hindoo maiden, and many trials were in store for her, which remain to be explained.

CHAPTER XXXIII.

THE DISAPPEARANCE OF OMELIA — EVENTS MULTIPLY—THE SIEGE OF DELHI AND ITS ATTENDANT HORRORS.

IT was not until two or three hours after the departure of Omelia from the cavern on her perilous errand, that Flora Melville awoke from her troubled sleep, in which all the terrible events of the last few days, the fearful sufferings in the mosque, the death of her father, and the massacre, were reproduced to her distracted imagination; and, raising herself from the rude pallet on which she had been reclining, she gazed with bewildered amazement at the singular place she was in, having only a dreamy recollection of where she was, and the immediate circumstances that brought her there. But the voice of the hermit, who was talking loudly and strangely to himself in the adjoining cave, recalled her to consciousness, and all the misery and hopelessness of her situation; and the terrible bereavement she had suffered, rushed at once in full force upon her brain, and pressing her hands upon her aching and burning temples, she burst into a paroxysm of sobs and tears.

The dim light emitted by the lamp, gave, if possible, a still more dismal aspect to the place, and, remembering the departure of Omelia, and anxious to ascertain whether or not she had yet returned, and what had been the result of her expedition, she timidly entered the cavern in which the hermit was, and paused for some moments to observe him, he being alone.

He was on his knees, with his back towards her, and apparently too deeply absorbed in his devotions to notice her.

He seemed much excited, frequently beat his breast, then swung his arms wildly to and fro above his head, all the time speaking rapidly and loudly in a strange language or gibberish, which sounded harshly and disagreebly upon the ears of the astonished Flora, who at the same time felt a sensation of awe irresistibly stealing over her.

She feared to interrupt him, or to make known her presence; but at length he ceased, and remained for some time solemnly silent, and in one fixed attitude, his eyes fixed vacantly up at the roof of the cavern, and his mind seemingly totally abstracted from anything but his own gloomy meditations.

Suddenly, however, he started, and rising to his feet, beheld her. There was a singular expression on his features of mingled sorrow and indignation, which struck Flora most forcibly, and filled her mind with dismal forebodings, and in a tremulous voice she eagerly enquired after Omelia; but the aged man only shook his head mournfully, and looked more sorrowful than before.

The fears of Flora increased.

"You do not speak, you do not answer, venerable man," she observed, "but your look bespeaks woe, and excite the most torturing apprehensions in my breast. Oh, tell me I beseech you, and keep me no longer in suspense, know you anything of Omelia?"

"The day now breaks in the eastern horizon," answered the hermit in slow and solemn accents, "it is some hours since she left the cavern, and still she returns not. And she will not, she will not."

"Oh torturing thoughts," exclaimed Flora, clasping her hands vehemently together, "but how know you what you have so positively asserted?"

"It is revealed to me, and I cannot doubt," replied the mysterious man, "it is revealed to me that misfortune hath overtaken the heroic maiden, and that even now she is in the hands of those whom she hath cause to fear."

"Oh God!" ejaculated Flora, with a look of agony,—"avert so terrible a calamity."

"Hush, hark," cried the hermit quickly, laying his hand on the arm of the trembling girl, and leading her towards the foot of the steps that led to the entrance to the cavern, as his ears seemed to catch some ominous sounds above.

Flora listened with breathless attention, but she could hear nothing, and was wrought up to a state of suspense that was most insupportable.

The distant report of a pistol, however, suddenly saluted her ears, and she shuddered with increased emotion and alarm which was greatly augmented, when she imagined she could hear the indistinct cries of distress in a female voice, followed by the shouts of men, as if in mockery and exultation.

She clung to the hermit, and looked fearfully in his face, but was unable to utter a word.

"My fears are realized," he said, "the savages have seized upon their hapless victim, and even now she calls in vain on them for mercy and forbearance. But be thou firm, maiden, and wait patiently here, while I go forth, and endeavour by my appearance, to awe the wretches so that they will not refuse her supplications."

"Oh, suffer me to accompany you," said the agitated Flora, "to remain here alone, and in this painful state of suspense and uncertainty, is most torturing."

"Obey my commands, girl," returned the hermit, sternly; "here thou art safe, why then rashly court danger? Detain me not, but let me at once ascertain the truth."

Flora dare not offer a word in reply to these injunctions, and with a sad heart, she watched the old man ascend the steps with an agility which seemed most extraordinary for his great age, and when he had disappeared through the opening, she sunk on her knees, and burying her face in her hands, abandoned herself to the utmost agony and despair.

The time that the hermit was absent, seemed to her an age, although it was not more than a quarter of an hour, and the various thoughts that crowded on her brain during that brief interval, were of the most agonizing and bewildering description. But at length she heard him removing the stone from the secret entrance, and eagerly rising from her knees and looking above, she beheld his venerable form, as he prepared to descend the steps that led into the cavern.

His looks were sad, and realized the worst apprehensions and forbodings of Flora, who hastened to him as he alighted in the cavern, her looks expressing all that she was so anxious yet dreaded to know.

"She is gone," said the old man, in melancholy accents, and interpreting her thoughts;—"Omelia's cries they were we heard; as my fears forboded, she has fallen into the power of the mutineers; I was in time to catch a glimpse of her form, as they forced her away, but too late to attempt to save her."

"Oh, God!" cried the distracted Flora, in a voice of the most indescribable agony; "her fate is sealed. Oh, Omelia, most heroic but unfortunate girl, terrible is the doom which too surely awaits you, and I am now alone, and entirely friendless in the world."

She could say no more; her emotions overpowered her,—the blood seemed to freeze in her veins,—her brain turned giddy,—a mist arose before her eyes, and with a deep sigh, she sunk insensible in the hermit's arms.

*   *   *   *   *   *

It is now necessary to resume our summary of the principle events that marked the progress of this terrible revolt, and in doing so we shall quote from the most reliable authorities.

Success had so far attended the sanguinary designs of the mutineers; they had rioted in human slaughter, and feasted their savage passions in the blood of numbers of their unfortunate victims, but still their thirst for vengeance increased with their triumph.

The Mogul capital was in their possession, they had established a rebel goverment, whose laws were written in blood, and created a puppet king whose decrees were those of wholesale murder;—and doubtless they imagined that with the capture of Delhi, their complete possession of India, at no very remote period, was certain. The dreadful struggle which for so many months has been going on,—the terrible reverses the miscreants have met with—the just retribution which has overtaken them, and the certain total defeat, which it is to be hoped speedily awaits them, proves how vain were their ideas, how futile all their expectations.

It was on the 30th of May, 1857, that a detachment of the European force at Meerut, (Carbineers, Rifles, and Artillery), under the command of Brigadier Wilson,

took up an advanced position at the village of Ghazee-ood-deen-nugger, where the road to Delhi crosses the little river of Hindun by a suspension bridge, some fifteen miles from the capital.

The whole force of Wilson did not amount to 1,000 of all ranks, and no sooner had he taken up his position, than the enemy appeared in great numbers, with five guns, on the further side of the stream, and an engagement immediately followed.

"My advanced pickets," reports General Wilson, "were driven in at about four o'clock in the afternoon, and I was attacked by a large force of mutineers, accompanied by heavy guns, from Delhi. I immediately sent off a company of her Majesty's 60th Royal Rifles, with another in support, to hold the iron bridge, which is the key of my position, and I detached the four guns of Major Tomb's troop, supported by a squadron of Carbineers, right along the banks of the Hindun river.

The insurgents opened upon these advanced parties with heavy guns. I ordered two more companies of the 60th to support their advance, and brought up four guns of Major Scott's battery, the Sappers, and a troop of Carabineers to protect the camp. The first few rounds from the insurgents' guns were admirably aimed, plunging through our camp; but they were ably replied to by our two 18-pounders, in position under Lieutenant Light and Major Tombs's troop, most admirably led by Lieutenant-Colonel Mackenzie, who, raking them in flank with his 6-pounders, first made their fire unsteady, and in a short time silenced these heavy guns. On remarking the unsteadiness of their fire, I ordered Lieutenant-Colonel Jones to advance his Rifles and attack. This was done in a most spirited manner. They drove the enemy from the guns; but in the act of taking possession of two heavy pieces on the causeway, close to the toll-house, Captain Andrews and four of his men were blown up by the explosion of an ammunition wagon, fired by one of the mutineers. The insurgents were now in full retreat, leaving in our hands ordnance, ammunition, and stores. They were followed for a considerable distance on the Delhi road by Lieutenant-Colonel Custance, commanding the Carbineers with the force.

The rebels gave immediate proof of the pertinacity with which they were inspired. About noon the very next day they again attacked Wilson's little force.

They took up a position extending fully a mile on the high ridge, on the opposite side of the Hindun, about a mile from the British advance picket, in front of the bridge, and commenced a fire with their guns from that long distance.

The guns of the Horse Artillery, supported by a squadron of the Carabineers, immediately moved forward to reply to the fire, and the two 18-pounders moved to the bank of the river for the same purpose. The Rifles, leaving one company in camp, went to the support of the picket at the bridge, supported by two guns and a troop of Carabineers.

The Horse Artillery found themselves exposed to a very heavy fire, which Wilson had no sooner perceived than he advanced two more guns to their support. From that time all went well; and for nearly two hours the action was one of artillery chiefly.

There was a village on the left of the toll-bar, which the Rifles gallantly cleared; and the fire of the enemy's guns slackened. Wilson ordered a general advance. The insurgents now retired, continuing their fire, however, until their masters drove them from their position and crowned the ridge, from which they beheld them in full retreat to Delhi.

To follow them was impossible—our men were so knocked up by the heat of the sun; by which, indeed many officers and men were struck down. Wilson therefore withdrew the force into camp, after having first burnt a village on the right flank, from which the insurgents had given much annoyance.

Owing to our inability to follow them in their retreat, the insurgents were enabled to carry off all their guns, which consisted of two heavy pieces and five light guns; one of their ammunition wagons only was destroyed.

The advanced guard of General Anson, the Commander-in-chief, did not approach Kurnaul till the 21st of May, the main body still remaining some days at Umballah.

When the guns arrived, or were nearing his camp, the General advanced, and had reached Kurnaul, when he was attacked by cholera, and died at that station on the 27th.

The command of the army now devolved upon Sir Henry Barnard, who, as major-general, had been at the head of the Sirhind Division.

Wilson left Ghazee-ood-Nuggur on the evening of the 3rd of June to join General Barnard, who had arrived at Alipore. His troops marched twenty-one hours without halting more than ten minutes at a time, through hill and jungle, and joined headquarters on the morning of the 6th, having made a circuit of sixty miles and upwards, " nearly the whole road too steep and rugged for a billy-goat." General Barnard now determined to push forward at once, for he had learned that preparations had been made to oppose his advance; and he knew that every hour these preparations would be increased. Alipore is distant ten miles from Delhi, and at two o'clock on the morning of the 8th, the march was commenced. Two hours after they came upon the rebels, who held a strong position at Badullee-ke-Serai. General Barnard now made the following disposition of his forces : Brigadier-General Grant, with several guns and three squadrons of Lancers, was to cross a canal, and after proceeding some distance down its banks, recross in the rear of the enemy's position as soon as he heard the action commence; the object of this manœuvre being to take the enemy in flank. The chief column was to advance along the main trunk road, while the 1st Brigade, under Brigadier-General Showers, was to act on its right, and the 2nd Brigade, under Brigadier-General Graves, on the left. The heavy guns were to remain in position on the road, the rest of the artillery to act on either side. As soon as our advanced picket met the enemy, these brigades deployed, leaving the main road clear.

The enemy soon opened a very heavy fire upon us, and, finding that our light field-pieces did not silence their battery, and that we were losing men fast, General Barnard called upon the 75th Regiment to make a dashing charge, and take the place at the point of the bayonet. This service was done with the most heroic gallantry. The 1st Europeans supported the attack, and on the 2nd Brigade coming up and threatening their right, and Brigadier General Grant showing the head of his column and guns on their left rear, the rebels abandoned the position entirely, leaving their guns on the ground. The action lasted nearly one hour, and we regret to add, cost many valuable lives. About fifty of our men were killed, among them Colonel Chester, adjutant-general of the army; but it was a gallant fight, and by it we won the advantageous position which was thenceforward occupied by our army.

The rebels, however, still made a desultory stand; and although his men were much exhusted, General Barnard determined to push on, lest a similar difficulty might be opposed to him the following day, in gaining the requisite positon before the city. The road separating, it became desirable to act in two columns—one along the main trunk road, and the other along the left through the cantonments,

To Brigadier-General Wilson, supported by Brigadier-General Showers' Brigade, was confided the conduct of the first column, which had to fight its way through gardens with high walls and other obstacles the whole way. Taking the 2nd Brigade, with Brigadier-General Graves, Barnard himself proceeded to the left. He soon found that the rebels had posted themselves strongly on a ridge overlooking the cantonments, with guns in position. General Barnard soon found himself under the range of these guns; upon which he determined on a rapid flank movement to the left, in the hope of gaining the ridge under cover of the cantonments, and taking the position in flank.

This was happily successful. The enemy hastily got their guns into position to meet the attack; while Brigadier-General Grave's brigade, consisting of the 60th Rifles and 2nd Europeans, advanced gallantly, supported by a troop of Horse Artillery, and carried the position. The rebels finding themselves taken in flank and rear, abandoned their guns; and the British had the satisfaction of sweeping the whole ridge, from the Flagstaff to Hindoo Rao's house, which had meanwhile been seized by Brigadier-General Wilson. The object of the day was effected; and the force was at once placed in position before Delhi.

Startling and exciting events followed those just related; in fact, our soldiers had no idle time of it; battle followed battle in rapid succession; fierce sorties from the enemy continually, but which were invariably repulsed. The death of General Barnard took place on the 5th of June; he, like his predecessor, dying of cholera.

On the 9th, a desperate fight took place, and the enemy were finally repulsed within the walls.

The struggle lasted from seven o'clock in the morning till nearly four in the afternoon; the great guns on the walls of the city, firing incessantly till the enemy were driven in.

"The attack was a general one," writes an officer, graphically describing this affair; "on our line of pickets, the new General Sahib, as they call him, from Bareilly, having sworn to smoke his hookah in Hindoo Rao's house in the evening. The fight was very stubborn for some time, and immense numbers of the enemy were killed. At last, after some few hours of it, the mutineers showed signs of having had enough, and a general advance was ordered on our side; at this time I was on the right, and received an order to accompany some light field guns down towards one of the gates of the city, into which the enemy were flying by thousands. I took two companies of the Guides, and was shortly joined by some more of our side, in all about 300 men. We advanced steadily down a road in front of the guns, and when within about a quarter of a mile of the city walls, the mutineers in crowds crossed the road down which we were advancing; seeing us, they gave us volleys and volleys of musketry, which took fearful effect on us, standing as we were, exposed in the middle of the road. We replied, however, to their fire with musketry, and our light field guns opened on them with grapeshot, and did good execution; having crossed the road they ran towards the city.

"We again advanced till within 150 yards of the city walls, and there found the mutineers in thousands rushing through the gate into a place of safety again. Our musketry and guns opened—they replied; three of their guns from the city walls opened upon our small force with grape shot, and with cruel effect. I shall never forget it as long as I live. The grape came with a peculiarly nasty wisking sound, in a continued pour, through and though us. I can compare it to nothing but a sleet storm, except that the sleet was uncomfortable and unusually large. We stood under this for nearly twenty minutes. How a single man escaped it is a wonder. A great number of our poor fellows were killed and wounded as also were the artillerymen and the poor horses. After the enemy had all got safely into the city we retired, still, however, under the hail of grape. At last we reached a place of safety, and never was I so glad to get my head into a sheltered spot: I never expected to come out of that fire alive. The enemy not appearing inclined to come out again, we returned to our picket about four o'clock, having been about seven hours fighting."

These combats were distinguished by many gallant personal exploits; the daring conduct of Lieutenant Hills, of the Horse Artillery, (a young man, who only four months before was a pupil in the Edinburgh Academy,) deserves particular notice. It is thus related by one of his fellow soldiers:

"I must tell you," says this gentleman, "of a noble action of Hills, of the Artillery. He was on picket with his two-horse artillery guns, when the alarm was sounded and an order sent him to advance, given under the impression that the enemy were at some distance. He was supported by a body of Carabineers, eighty, I believe, in number. He advanced about one hundred yards, while his guns were being limbered up to follow, and suddenly came on about

120 of the enemy's cavalry close on him. Disgraceful to say, the Carabineers turned and bolted. His guns being limbered up he could do nothing, but rather than fly he charged them by himself. He fired four barrels of his revolver and killed two men, throwing the empty pistol in the face of another, and knocking him off his horse. Two horsemen then charged full tilt at him, and rolled him and his horse over. He got up with no weapons, and, seeing a man on foot coming at him to cut him down, rushed at him, got inside his sword, and hit him full in the face with his fist.

"At that moment he was cut down from behind, and a second blow would have done for him, had not Tombs, his captain, the finest fellow in the service (who had been in his tent when the row began) arrived at the critical moment and shot his assailant. Hills was able to walk home, though his wound was severe, and on the road Tombs saved his life once more, by sticking another man who attacked him. If they don't both get the Victoria Cross it won't be worth having."

And here we cannot help giving one more illustration of Indian atrocities perpetrated in Delhi, before it was absolutely captured by the rebels. It is thus related.

"One day in August there arrived in our camp at Delhi, guised as an Affghan, one of the many unhappy victims of the late atrocities. The young wife of a warrant officer, gentle and fair, had taken refuge, with her three children, in the cellar of a house to which she and one of her aunts had fled for safety. On the first outburst of the mutiny, the husbands of both were absent from Delhi. Of her babes, the eldest was only four years old; and she told how patiently they lay till night, stifling their sobs in her bosom; and how, when morning came, she heard the footsteps of men in riot above and around her, and the tramp of feet on the staircase of her hiding-place. A postern-door led her out on the strand, and here she was met by two Mahometan soldiers, who stripped her of all she had. She hoped then that they would allow her to flee with her children; but she was told that she must go before the King. They dragged her back through the college garden, under the walls of the palace. Within was tumult and a scene of demoniacal orgie, from which even imagination recoils.

"A flash close enough to scorch her, a sharp blow, and she fell to the earth, holding in her arms a dying infant, pierced through by the same bullet which had ploughed its way through her own side. Faint with loss of blood she long lay there; at last, in baby tones she so well knew, she heard her little ones murmur, 'We will come and die with mamma;' and their tiny hands tenderly nursed her drooping head, as she had often before nursed theirs; but as they crept round her, a savage seized her eldest born—the little throat hardly needed so sharp and heavy a sword—one blow, and the babbling voice was hushed for ever. There was one yet left her. Uncomplainingly, she had pressed closer to the bleeding mother's bosom, whose glazing eyes were riveted on this—her last. Again the stroke descended not fatal yet. For six long hours 'Water—water!' fainter and fainter yet, till the little mutilated face was hushed at last. A moulvie had watched her, and when night closed in, and when all was quiet once more in that noisy place, he came like the good Samaritan, and poured oil on her wounds, and laid her on a bed, and carried her to his home. The women of his house tended her and fed and clothed her, as one of themselves."

"Slowly strength came again, and the stream of life flowed on, not at all bitter, for she hoped that, though her children had been taken from her, her husband might be still living; and she hopes on, and refuses to believe that she is utterly bereft. She tells of panics in the city—of the discouragement of the sepoys at their uniform ill success. At length the women of the house obtained leave on a high festival to go to a tomb and pray; and, veiled as a Moslem, she passed the gates in their company. She had been able to communicate with some of our Affghan allies, many of whom pass freely to and from the city. It was planned that at dark one of these should come to the mosque and guide her to our camp. They left it together. Twice she was nearly discovered by patrols, but in early morning they found themselves outside one of our pickets. At first she was taken for a spy, but soon overcame all difficulties, and was received by the one lady of our force—a refugee like herself."

CHAPTER XXXIV.

NENA SAHIB—THE FAIR PRISONER.

SERIOUSLY crippled, but not at all daunted by continual defeat and severe losses, the rebels remained obstinately firm to their treacherous work.

Lucknow, the capital of a deposed king, with its multitude of arms, and quarrel-loving inhabitants, was not likely to be behind-hand in the general demonstration. We have already seen, indeed, that the mutiny showed its earliest signs in this place. The chaplain, writing on May 12th, relates that bungalows were burnt more than a week before that date. He says, in a letter which gives an excellent idea of the position of affairs at Lucknow just before the outbreak :—"I told you about Dr. Well's bungalow being burnt down, and that it was supposed to be done by the sepoys in revenge for his tasting a bottle of medicine in the hospital."

"Well, a day or two after I wrote, the whole of the huts of the sepoys of the 13th Regiment were burnt, it was supposed by accident, but, from after events, that seems rather doubtful. You may imagine that huts with thatched roofs for 1,000 men made a pretty good blaze. Last Sunday week it was my turn to take the evening service at Cantonment Church. There was an unusually thin congregation. Towards the end of the prayers a servant came into church, and spoke first to Major Bird, of the 48th, and then to Mr. Dashwood, of the same regiment. They both went out, and afterwards others were called away. I began to think that some more houses had been set on fire, but of course I went on with the service. The ladies began to look very uncomfortable; one or two went out of church, one or two others crossed over the aisle to friends who were sitting on the other side.

"Altogether I had not a very attentive congregation. After service we found that the 7th Irregular Infantry, 1,000 strong, quartered at the Moosa Bagh, had mutinied, and that the 71st, 48th, 7th Cavalry, and a troop of English Artillery, with six guns, had gone to quell them. This was the cause of the officers being called out of church. The 32nd Queen's, as I afterwards found, also marched to the Moosa Bagh, and an Irregular Cavalry Regiment, so that no less than 3,500 men marched to put down the mutiny. I felt very much inclined to ride down myself to see what was going on, but as the Moosa Bagh is seven miles from our house, and as I should have left my wife all alone, I stayed where I was. I thought of what William III. said when he was told that the Bishop of Derry had been shot at the ford at the battle of Boyne, 'What took him there?' However, if so strong a force had not been sent that the mutineers were completely overawed, there might have been work for me to do.

"It was not till the 30th of May that the long-accumulated magazine of fanaticism and rebellion exploded. Every day for a week previous, the Chief Commissioner had been informed that the native regiments would certainly rise at night, and so precise was the rumour, even the hour was fixed—between eight and nine o'clock. Day by day and night after night passed over, however, without the slightest disturbance. When, therefore, the same story was repeated to Sir Henry Lawrence on Saturday, the 30th of May, he did not attach extraordinary importance to it, and merely took the ordinary precaution of doubling the sentries and enjoining vigilance on every officer.

"Nine o'clock struck, and the Chief Commissioner had begun a remark to the effect that the rumour had proved itself as unfounded as its predecessors, when shots were heard in the lines of the 71st Native Infantry. Sir Henry immediately mounted his horse, and proceeded to the encampment of the 32nd Queen's, and then moved up to the corner of the Lucknow road with two guns and a company of Europeans, to prevent the mutineers from coming down to the city. The remaining six guns remained in position at the encamping ground, guarded by Europeans.

"Bungalows now began to blaze, and the firing to become hotter, when General Handscombe was killed by a shot from the 71st lines, up to which he had ridden quite close, in the hopes that his presence and speech might have the effect of bringing the mutineers to reason. Lieutenant Grant was killed at his picket. The mutineers ran at his men, some of whom turned and fled — a shot from the mutineers then wounded poor Grant, and the subahdar of the guard concealed him under his charpoy.

"The mutineers then came up, and were told that the sahib had got away; they were not, however, to be deceived, and at last a havildar on the guard, belonging to Grant's own regiment, pointed him out to the mutineers, when he was bayoneted and brutally mutilated.

"The cantonment soon became one blaze of fire, and it was not deemed prudent to move the guns for fear of the mutineers finding their way into the city; the only means of checking them was by sending detachments of irregular cavalry through the lines. Sharp firing took place frequently between the sowars and the mutineers, without much effect, however, upon either side.

"Lieutenant Hardinge distinguished himself greatly in these skirmishes, in one of which a mutineer fired at him within a yard, and, missing him, charged him with his bayonet, which went through his wrist and entered his chest, when its further pro-

gress was stopped by a bullet from Hardinge into the stomach of his assailant, which sickened him of the contest. Lieutenant Chambers, adjutant of the 13th, had a narrow escape, and was wounded in the leg.

"This state of affairs lasted until two o'clock in the morning, when the fires began to abate, and two guns were moved up to each of the residency gates, which were guarded by a havildar's guard from the 13th and some sowars, and had escaped conflagration. At four a.m., the rebels had reached the 7th cavalry lines at Moodkeepore, which they set on fire, and then returned to cantonments, where Sir Henry had prepared to meet them.

"At length the Chief Commissioner found himself besieged by a force variously computed at from 12,000 to 20,000 men, espe-

cially strong in cavalry. His communications were cut off; provisions were becoming scarce; and though the enemy did little harm beyond this, this was death to the little garrison, and those who had taken refuge within the walls of the residency. On June 28, we hear that the insurgents were valiantly kept at bay; 'but if assistance is not rendered him, and the people who have taken refuge within its walls, amounting to several hundreds, they will all be starved out, for from the last accounts they have been obliged to feed on gram and sugar. They have next to nothing to cook it with, and no pots of any sort to cook it in. It is reported that a detachment of the 84th, the Queen's, who went over there from Cawnpore the other day, have been cut down to a man, but this has not been confirmed. There are thousands upon thousands of natives assembled there, and assistance will have to come quickly, or not an European will be saved.'

"Pressed by want of food and fuel, and reduced to the last extremity, a sortie was made on the second of June, in the direction of the enemy's camp. Their advanced guard was taken by surprise and utterly routed, after two hours' desperate fighting. A considerable quantity of provisions fell into the hands of our troops. This operation was conducted in person by Sir Henry Lawrence, at the head of 200 Europeans, chiefly her Majesty's 32nd foot; but it is said that it was made against his better judgment, and at the entreaties of some of the civilians who were with him in the fort. Returning from the scene of action flushed with success, and bearing the proceeds of their hard fight for the relief of the poor sufferers in the fort, just as our troops reached the town, the native artillery who accompanied the expedition suddenly wheeled round and opened a deadly fire from the guns on the unfortunate 32nd, and before they were able to recover themselves and face their assailants, upwards of sixty men, rank and file, were killed, and several of our best officers severely wounded—among the officers the gallant general, who was severely cut in the leg by the splinter of a shell, and died on the 4th (two days after) of lock-jaw induced by the wound."

Nena Sahib!—what deeds of horror, of unparalled atrocity, of more than fiendish conception, and merciless execution, arise to the appalled recollection at the mention of this monster's name. Yet it is of him and Cawnpore, that fearful human slaughterhouse, we must now treat.

This miscreant, whose hideous crimes have filled the civilised world with horror, was the adopted son of the late Peishwah, Bajee Rao, whom the Marquis of Hastings, after stripping of his large possessions in Western India, permitted to retain the independent rule of Bhitoor—a small state, the capital of which is situated twelve miles north of Cawnpore—and whose vast wealth Nena Sahib inherited; though the British Government, refusing to recognise him as the rightful heir, assumed the sovereignty of the territory, and at the same time discontinued the annual pension of eight lacs of rupees which had been guaranteed to the Peishwah. Both steps were justified by the tenor of the terms which Bajee Rao—with arms still in his hands, and at the head of a powerful army—accepted from Sir John Malcolm before surrendering to that general in 1817; for the treaty then made distinctly stipulated that on the Peishwah's decease no heir, except of his own body, would be recognised; and

although the Governor-general was pleased to ratify the treaty out of respect to Sir John, his lordship did not approve of the condition, which he considered much too favourable to so bitter and treacherous an enemy of the British Government as the Peishwah had proved himself to be. Bajee Rao, in selecting Dhoondoopunt as the son of his adoption, selected one who resembled himself in nature and disposition, seeing that Thornton tells us that if any additional grounds of justification were required for dethroning she Peishwah, they would be found " in the atrocious proceedings in which he had been implicated subsequently to his attack upon the British residency. His flight had been a career of crime as well as of misfortune and suffering. He had put to death two British travellers in cold blood, and committed other acts at variance with usages of even semi-civilised nations. None but himself and his coadjutors in crime, could lament his fall." His adopted successor must therefore have been a creature after his own heart. The Peishwah was *de facto* chief of the western Mahrattas, although *de jure* he was subordinate to the Sattara family, they being descendants of Sevejee, the founder of the Mahratta empire—and his adopted son, the Nena, being, according to Hindoo ideas, his legitimate successor, was consequently regarded with much reverence by the native population of the dominions over which the Peishwah ruled, and in the neighbouring country; and this circumstance, together with his great riches and large estates, have undoubtedly given him the influence of which he has recently made so bad a use.

On the death of the Peishwah, Nena Sahib strove hard, but without success, to obtain from the Indian Government a continuance to himself of the pension allowed to Bajee Rao. Failing in this, he despatched an agent to agitate his claims in England, and transmitted, it is said, to Calcutta to meet the expenses of such a mission, a single piece of Company's paper of the value of five lacs of rupees. The mission to England was of course as unsuccessful as the attempt made to influence the local government. The Indian Government may in some measure thank itself for having allowed this man to acquire the local influence he possesses. It is well known that for years back, since the death of Bajee Rao, Nenajee has kept the Begums of the Bajee, the rightful heirs to the property of the deceased chief, in close confinement in the zenanah, so that none likely to take steps relative to rescuing them from confinement or restoring them their property could obtain access to them.

A greater hypocrite, a more arch deceiver,

than Nena Sahib never existed. Dissimulative as he was cruel, he had been looked upon by all the Europeans who knew him, as a really amiable man; accomplished, generous, and fond of the society of Europeans, always appearing glad to receive them at his castle, or to accompany them on hunting excursions.

A writer in one of the weekly journals speaking of him says—

"I knew Nena Sahib intimately, and always regarded him as one of the best and most hospitable in the Upper Provinces; and certainly one of the last men to have been guilty of the atrocities laid to his charge. As is the case with many natives of India, it may have been that Nena Sahib contracted the acquaintance and friendship of the Sahibs solely in the hope that through their influence, direct and indirect, his grievances would be redressed. But the last time I saw Nena Sahib—it was in the cold weather of 1851, and he called upon me twice during my stay in Cawnpore—he never once alluded to his grievances. His conversation at that time was directed to the Oude affair.

"He was, when I saw him, about twenty-eight years of age, he looked, however, at least forty. His figure is very fat—in fact, the very expression made use of by his own moonshee, was that 'His highness was a tight man,' (tring admee).

"His face is round, his eyes very wild, brilliant, and restless; his complexion, as is the case with most native gentlemen, is scarcely darker than a dark Spaniard, and his expression on the whole is of a jovial, indeed, somewhat rollicking character."

Such is the personal description furnished us of this "unmitigated monster," whose name will be ever associated with all that is horrible and atrocious.

Well, and with matchless subtlety, did he play his hypocritical part year after year, till he at length became so trusted, that he was asked to introduce his troops into Cawnpore, to defend that place against the violence of his own countrymen. He brought them down, but no sooner had the revolt broken out, than he took away his guns and his men, joined the rebels, and assumed the command in person.

And now Nena Sahib commenced showing himself in his true character. It was now that he unveiled his treachery, and began that "reign of terror," which has filled the civilised world with horror and disgust. He marched down to Cawnpore, and commenced pounding Wheeler's entrenchment, to which he was incited by the golandazes (artillery-men) of the 3rd Oude horse battery, who, having shown signs of disaffection, were disarmed, and sent away from the entrenchment.

Early on the 6th of June, information to the effect that an attack was to be made on the garrison, having been received, every preparation was immediately made for the defence.

The rebels had secured all our magazine workpeople, classies, &c., and made them assist in putting up a few heavy guns in serviceable order. Employing Government bullocks on a service quite new to them, they brought out half a dozen guns—two of which were 18-pounders—and placing them in range, under cover of the newly-built lines of the 1st native infantry, commenced playing upon the entrenchments. The first shot was fired at about half-past ten, a.m., on the 6th. Immediately on hearing the report of the gun, a bugle sounded in our camp, "All hands to your arms!" and accordingly every person, from drummer to regimental officer, spread themselves out under the walls, or rather mounds of the entrenchment, which had been hastily built up about breast high. Here they sat nearly all day exposed to the hot winds and scorching sun of June, every moment expecting an open-handed attack from the infantry and cavalry. This the enemy, however, never attempted, though at times large bodies of armed men could be seen collected in different places. Our artillery kept up a brisk fire at this stage of the attack, and returned nearly every shot of the mutineers. In the meantime, the latter commenced setting fire to the bungalows on our (or the east) side of the canal, and brought round their guns closer up to us behind the riding-school and the walls of Compound-buildings.

On the night of the 7th of June three more guns were brought up, and their number increased daily, until on the 11th the enemy played upon the barrack with three mortars, two 24-pounders, three 18-pounders, one or two 12-pounders, about the same number of 9-pounders, and one 6 pounder. The 24-pounder guns proved very destructive, on account of their proximity to the entrenchment; shots from them brought down entire pillars of the verandahs, and went through the masonry walls of the hospital barracks.

Meanwhile the condition of the besieged was becoming deplorable. The heat was very great, and with the fright, the confinement, the want of proper food and   e, several women, as also children, die' great distress. The soldiers themse' sunstricken from exposure to the ' sometimes as many as five or si' be killed in a day. The dead people had to be thrown int the entrenchment, and th' be done at the close of could venture out in daylight, for shots and shell flew about in all directions like a hail-storm. Our entrenchment was strewn with them. We had but one available well, in the middle of the entrenchment, and the enemy kept up their fire so incessantly, that "it was as much as giving a man's life-blood to go and draw a bucket of water." While there was any water remaining in the large jars usually kept in the verandah for the soldiers' use, nobody ventured to the well; but after the second day, the demand became so great that a bheestie bag of water was with difficulty got for five rupees, and a bucket for a rupee, as most of the servants of officers and merchants had deserted, and it therefore became a matter of necessity for every person to get his own water: this was usually done during the night, when the enemy could not well direct their shots. In fact, after the first three days incessant firing the rebels made it a practice usually at about dusk to cease for about two hours, and then the crowd round the well was very great. There was no place to shelter the live cattle. All the horses were obliged to be let loose. A few sheep and goats, as well as the bullocks kept for commissariat purposes were shot, and in the course of five or six days no flesh meat was to be had; occasionally, however, a stray bullock or cow was caught near the entrenchment at night, which afforded a change of food while it lasted; otherwise, dull and chupatties were the common food of all. Several hogsheads of rum and malt liquor were burst by the enemy's cannon, but of this there was abundance, and the loss was not felt. "Altogether the distress was so great," says a survivor, "that none could offer a word of consolation to his friend, or attempt to administer to the wants of each other. I have seen the dead bodies of officers, and tenderly brought up young ladies of rank (colonels' and captains' daughters) put out here in the verandah amongst the ruins, to wait the time when the fatigue party usually went round to carry the dead to the well; for there was scarcely room to shelter the living. The buildings were so sadly riddled that every safe corner available was considered a great object."

The danger's increased, the fearful storm which had commenced so ominously, and for those in the ill-fated place, under such truly disadvantageous, and even appalling circumstances, was soon to rage with frightful violence, spreading horror and destruction around.

It is necessary that we should enter still further into the details of the most important events that proceed that atrocious act of butchery, which is unparalleled in the annals of crime, and which has stamped Nena Sahib as the greatest monster that ever cursed and disgraced society.

Soon the entrenchment was surrounded by the enemy's guns, while hordes of infantry armed with muskets took possession of the bungalows, compound walls and outbuildings nearest to the camp. They had all been burnt, but their ruins afforded excellent cover. A large body stationed themselves in the church (which was also burnt) and another posted themselves in the unfinished barracks, from which they did terrible mischief.

Captain Moore, however, of her Majesty's 32nd foot, severely wounded in one of his arms as he was, never gave himself rest, but was always foremost wherever there appeared most danger—his arm in a sling and a revolver pistol in his belt, leading and encouraging the men. This officer placed scouts with glasses on the top of one of unfinished barracks, whence every movement of the enemy could be seen; by this means our artillery were greatly assisted in the direction of their guns.

When the rebel sepoys advanced, they usually took possession of the first three of these new barracks; but whenever they attempted to advance nearer, Captain Moore would sally out with about a dozen Europeans in a storm of musket shot; and, getting under cover of the barracks, always succeeded in routing the enemy from their post. On such occasions their loss was considerable, whereas our men generally escaped unhurt. The way in which Captain Moore and his men passed from the entrenchment into the unfinished barracks was amusing even to the anxious and harassed garrison. Whenever he found the enemy too strong for the small picket placed out to protect the scouts and keep possession of the nearest barracks, he collected a number of volunteers from the entrenchment, and sent them out one at a time. As each man ventured out, scores of muskets were turned on him. Of course he set off, at a tremendous pace, over the deadly piece of "open." However, the distance was not very great, and carts, bullock-trains, &c., were placed at short distances all along the way.

On two occasions Captain Moore went, under cover of the night, with about twenty-five Europeans, and spiked the nearest guns of the enemy. But that our soldiers were so few, it would have been an easy matter, indeed to disperse the whole rebel forces. Before the face of an Englishman they were all cowards. The cavalry sometimes made a show of charging upon any little party who left the entrenchment; but whenever they advanced, a few charges of canister sent them flying. It is almost certain that if the garrison had not had so great a crowd o ladies under their charge, they might have cut their way to Allahabad; as it was, they had nothing to do but to fight like Englishmen, and die like heroes as they were.

When the enemy began to throw live shell, the difficulties of the position became almost hopeless. By this means, the officers' tents, and the barracks where the sick and wounded, the women and the children, were placed, were fired, This happened on the 13th of June. At the same moment, the assembly was sounded: it was necessary for every man to be at his post, for an attack appeared certain; and as therefore they could render no assistance, it was only with the greatest difficulty that the women and children confined in the burning barrack escaped. Forty of the invalids were burned to ashes, and the medicines were all destroyed.

The apprehensions of an attack were justified. While the hospital was burning with the poor creatures in it, and shrieking women poured into the trenches with their little ones, the enemy made several attempts to take the place. They were then about 4,000 strong; but their numbers were not yet large enough to inspire sufficient confidence to risk a hand-to-hand conflict with the Europeans. Their attacks were weak, and were successively repulsed by our artillery. Had they risked a little more, there is no doubt they would have defeated Wheeler's reduced force; but it is quite certain that this success would have been earned with frightful slaughter; the Englishmen were wrought to the last degree of hate and desperation, and their arrangements were made with a degree of coolness which would have given their warmer passions fine play. Each man had five or six muskets ready charged at his command—always standing against the wall beside him, with good swords and bayonets.

After this the same feeble attempts to take the place by storm were made daily; but our artillery continued to overawe the rebels. They then concentrated their guns upon ours, and disabled all but two.

On the 21st of June, a great mob, dressed in various costumes, were seen collecting round the entrenchment. Many of them were newly-arrived rebels. It was their intention, as was afterwards learnt from the city people, not to spare the garrison that day, even if they should all die in the attempt; to this the newly-created subahdar-major of the 1st Native Infantry had sworn. The enemy brought large bales of cotton, and placing them out, they lay under cover of the same, attempting to approach the entrenchment in that manner by pushing the bales on, at the same time keeping up a brisk fire of musketry. While this was going on

towards the S.E. side from the church compound, the three new barracks were filled with a large body, 500 men, endeavouring to drive away our picket, and take possession of the rest. These were sent back helter-skelter by Captain Moore, who advancing under cover of the several barracks, with twenty-five men, sent repeated volleys into the rebels, while a few rounds of canister from the entrenchment routed them entirely, killing about thirty-five or forty of their number. In the meantime, about a hundred of the enemy advanced under cover of the cotton bales from the church compound, in the manner above intimated, to within 150 yards of the entrenchment. This was intended as an advance force, for shortly after the insurgents in the rear gave a shout, and jumping off the compound walls, &c., advanced, led on by the subahdar-major. Almost the very first shots from our musketry killed this misguided person; and a few rounds of canister directed on the enemy at the same moment did such execution (killing and wounding about 200 men) that a general dispersion followed. At the northeast corner, however, the garrison was much annoyed, for here about 200 men of the enemy kept up a harrassing fire, which was not silenced for an hour-and-a-half.

A brave act was this day done in the British camp. One of our ammunition waggons in the north-east corner was blown up by the enemy's shot, and whilst it was blazing, the rebel batteries from the Artillery Barracks and the Tank directed all their guns towards it. Our soldiers being much exhausted with the morning's work, and almost every artilleryman being either killed or wounded, it was a difficult matter to put out the fire, which endangered the other waggons near it. However, in the midst of all this cannonading, a young officer of the 53rd Native Infantry, Lieutenant Delafosse (who escaped to Calcutta or Bombay) went up, and laying himself down under the burning wagon, pulled away from it what loose splinters, &c., he could lay hold of, all the while throwing earth upon the flames. He was soon joined by two soldiers, who brought with them a couple of buckets of water, which were dexterously thrown by the lieutenant; and, while the buckets were taken to be replenished from the drinking water of the men close by, the process of casting earth upon the flames was carried on, amidst a fearful cannonading of about six guns, all directed upon the burning wagon. Thus at last the fire was put out, and officer and men escaped unhurt.

By this time the barracks were so riddled as to afford little or no shelter. Yet the greater portion of the people preferred to remain in them than to be exposed to the heat of the sun outside, although a great many made themselves holes under the walls of the entrenchment. In these, with their wives and children, they were secure at least from the shots and shells of the enemy, though not so from the effects of the heat, and the mortality from apoplexy and sunstroke was considerable. At nights every man had to sleep out, and take the watch in his turn, and therefore nearly all the women and children also slept under the walls of the entrenchment, so that they might be near their dear ones. Here the shells kept them in perpetual dread, bursting over their heads from time to time all night long. Thus the existence of those that remained alive was spent in perpetual dread and fear, almost as terrible as death itself.

These miseries were increased by the stench from the dead bodies of horses and other animals that had been shot in the compound, and which it was impossible to remove; moreover, there was an unusually great influx of flies, of themselves distressing enough. The condition of the sick and wounded was most wretched. Many persons were anxious to get out of the entrenchment, and go into the city, thinking, from want of better information, that they would be secure there; in fact, several went out quietly in the night under this impression, and were murdered by the rebels. The general himself, indeed, had sent out several natives into the city with a promise of high rewards for any information which they could bring back; none of these spies ever returned.

Our people dreaded nothing more than the setting in of the rains; for, in the first place, the holes dug in the ground by the soldiers and others, to secure themselves and children from the effects of the sun and the shots of the enemy, would have been filled up. Secondly, the walls of the barracks, which till then afforded some little shelter, were in danger of coming down, having been well shaken in many places by the 24 and 18-pounder shots, so incessantly fired for eighteen days; and, again, the muskets would have been rendered useless, for there were a great many of them, and the men were quite unable to clean them all. These muskets, as we have said, were always kept ready loaded so that when occasion should require it, each man could use upwards of half a dozen apiece. In a word, one good shower of rain (such as generally takes place at the first fall) would have rendered the place perfectly uninhabitable and extremely insecure.

In this state of affairs, the English repeatedly requested permission to be allowed to sally out at night and take possession of the enemy's guns, or, in case of failure, die

an honourable death. Some officers urged this also, but, from a false hope of receiving a reinforcement from Lucknow, and the love of the women for their husbands, fathers, and brothers, such a course was put off from day to day. If attempted, it would without doubt have been attended with complete success, if, as we are told, the guns used to be almost entirely abandoned by the soldiery during the night, and only a few golundazes kept loading and firing them. This fact, however, was not known to the garrison at the time.

At length provisions began to fail; the water supply was reduced; the ammunition was at its lowest ebb; and from being confined 600 in number in a barrack originally designed to contain about 200, and from the number of unburied bodies which lay all around them, disease began to make havoc among the besieged. Proposals of surrender were now talked of; but ere this step was taken, a Mr. Shepherd (who survived the massacre) was sent into the town on a mission from the general.

Mr. Shepherd having lost his wife and infant daughter—the latter shot through the head—he applied to the general for permission to leave, at the same time offering to bring him all the current information that he might collect in the city. The request was granted, for the general, as we have seen, was very anxious for information. He at the same time instructed Mr. Shepherd to try and negociate with certain influential persons in the city, so as to bring about a rupture among the rebels, and cause them to desist, authorising him to offer a lac of rupees as a reward, with a handsome pension for life, to any person who would bring about such a result.

It was a bold deed, but Mr. Shepherd had all the courage and the ability to accomplish it.

He left the entrenchment in the disguise of a native cook, but fate frowned upon him at the outset. He had not got far when he was taken prisoner, and conducted to the camp of Nena Sahib, and ordered to be placed under a guard.

He was kept under custody until the 12th of July, on which date his trial took place, and he was sentenced to three years imprisonment in irons, with hard labour, from which he was released by the heroic and lamented General Havelock's troops.

And now, after this rather long, but necessary and interesting digression, we must resume the thread of our tale.

The sun's departing rays yet lingered in the eastern horizon, and a sickly air pervaded the desolate streets of Cawnpore, a tone of gloom and melancholy which too painfully told the tale of horror associated with the history of the last few days.

The roar of cannon, and the sharp discharge of musketry might be heard at intervals in the distance, and everything betokened the horrors that even at that time were being enacted.

Gradually the shades of evening fell around, and the intense gloom was only broken by the expiring flames that occasionally shot sullenly up towards the sky, from the smouldering ruins of some bungalow or other building.

Cawnpore is a place of great extent, and indeed is one of the largest cantonments in the rural districts—the scattered bungalows of the civil and military residents extending for five miles along the western bank of the Ganges, which is high and steep. The European houses are most of them large and roomy, standing in extensive compounds, and built one story high with sloping roofs, first thatched, and then covered with tiles, a roof which is found better than any other to exclude the heat of the sun, and to possess a freedom from the many accidents to which a mere thatched roof is liable. The town is shaded with neem trees of great size, and the bungalows used to be surrounded by elegant and well kept gardens, redolent with the delicious odour of violets in bloom. Close beside the beds of this humble Saxon flower might be seen the scarlet buds of the Syrian pomegranate, or the tattered plumes of the tropical banana. The residences are large, but their enormous roofs of thatch contrast oddly with verandahs supported with Ionic pillars.

There are long ranges of magnificent houses, some of which are exceedingly lofty, and surrounded by extensive court-yards; others present rich clusters of pillars in long colonades, supporting verandahs tier upon tier, while the number of fine trees which intervene, afford a most beautiful diversity of objects.

Some of the superior houses, having rather a castellated appearance, and being more secluded from view than those of Europeans may be seen half shadowed by trees, and adding considerably to the beauty and variety of the landscape.

To one of those castellated mansions, in the heart of the town, we would now direct the attention of the reader. It was there that Nena Sahib, after one of the basest acts of treachery, and cold-blooded and deliberate butcheries ever perpetrated, had fixed his head quarters.

The particulars of this fearful episode must not be omitted, although they may be fresh in the memories of many of our readers.

Mrs. Greenaway, a very aged European lady, who had been captured by the rebels was sent into the trenches with a note to the effect that all soldiers and Europeans who had nothing to do with Lord Dalhousie's government, and who would lay down their arms, should be sent safely to Allahabad.

General Wheeler gave orders to Captain Moore to act as he should consider best.

It was accordingly agreed, on the one part that all the government money, the magazine in the entrenchment, with the guns (two only of which were in serviceable order, the rest having been injured and rendered useless by the enemy's cannon), should be made over to the Nena. On the other hand the Nena undertook to provide boats, and permit every individual in the entrenchment to proceed to Allahabad unmolested. This agreement was drawn up in writing, signed, sealed, and ratified by a solemn oath by the Nena.

Never was devised a blacker scheme than that which Nena Sahib had planned. Our miserable countrymen were conducted faithfully enough to the boats—officers, men, women, and children. The men and officers were allowed to take their arms and ammunition with them, and were escorted by nearly the whole of the rebel army. It was about eight o'clock a.m. when all reached the river side—a distance of about a mile and a half. Those who embarked first pushed off from the shore; but others found it difficult to get their boats off the banks, as the rebels had placed them as high in the mud as possible. At this moment the report of three guns was heard from the Nena's camp. The mutineers suddenly levelled their muskets, guns opened from the banks, and the massacre commenced. Some of the boats were set on fire, volley upon volley was fired upon the poor fugitives, numbers of whom were killed on the spot. Others fell or leapt overboard, and attempted to escape by swimming, but were picked off by the bullets of the sepoys, who followed them on shore and even breast deep into the water. A few boats crossed over to the opposite bank, but there a regiment of native infantry (the 17th), just arrived from Azimghur, was waiting for them; and in their eagerness to slay the "Kaffias," rode their horses belly deep into the river to meet the boats, and hack our unhappy countrymen and women to pieces, as they vainly tried to make their escape. The boats were then seized upon on both banks, the river not being broad, and every man who survived was put to the sword. The women and children, most of whom were wounded, some with three or four bullet shots in them, were spared and taken to Cawnpore.

Next day, in celebration of this military success, the Nena held a review of his troops, when three salutes were fired from the heavy guns—one of twenty-one guns for the Nena, as sovereign, nineteen guns for his brother, Balla Sahib, as governor-general, and seventeen guns for Jowalla Pershaud (a Brahmin), as commander-in-chief; after which the so-called "governor-general" gave a short speech to the army, praising them for their great courage and bravery in obtaining a complete victory over the British at Cawnpore, and promising them a lac of rupees as a reward for their labours, which, however, was put off from day to day, and the army never saw a farthing of it. The Nena and his staff then returned to their tents, under the same salutes.

In the meantime some of the Nena's people followed after one or two boats, which had got adrift at the first setting off, and before the massacre. These boats, which contained a good number of officers, soldiers, and their families, were not overtaken by Nena's men, but they did not escape altogether. They were captured by the zemindar of Dowreca Kheyra, named Baboo Rambux, near Futteypore, and the fugitives, about 115, were all sent back on carts to the Nena. They arrived in his camp on the 1st of July, and on the evening of the same day all the men, about seventy-five or eighty, were killed in cold blood. One officer's lady with her child clung to her husband so that it was impossible to separate them, and they were killed together. The women and children taken on this occasion amounted to about thirty-five in number, making the total of the prisoners in the hands of Nena Sahib, about 150 in all.

The moon now sullenly broke through the ponderous masses of clouds that had before obscured her silvery face, on the evening to which we have alluded, and revealed the residence of Nena Sahib more distinctly, at the end of a long avenue of trees by which it was approached.

A small number of native troops guarded the house, from the different windows of the lower apartments of which lights were seen to issue, and the building, in fact, presented all the lively and animated appearance of the Nena's "castle" at Bithoor.

Suddenly shouts of derision and exultation were heard at a short distance, and the officer who commanded the men placed to guard the mansion of Nena Sahib, gave the necessary orders, and looked narrowly in the direction from whence the noise proceeded, in case of any threatened danger.

His curiosity was quickly gratified, and all apprehensions of danger quieted, when he beheld that the noise came from several sepoys, who were approaching along the avenue towards the house, and who seemed to be conducting, or rather forcing some person along with them.

He hastily advanced towards them, and was rather surprised on discovering the character of their prisoner, whose wrists and arms were secured by cords, and whom they were treating in the most unceremonious, and even brutal manner.

The unfortunate captive had the appearance of a handsome Hindoo youth, of slight and delicate form, but marked by more than masculine grace; and there was an expression of scorn, determination and defiance, beamed from his fine, bright, and intelligent eyes, and imparted itself to his handsome features, which shewed the dauntless and heroic spirit that glowed within his breast.

But why thus trouble ourselves to describe the prisoner? It was, as the reader has suspected, *Omelia!*

CHAPTER XXXV.

THE HINDOO HEROINE AND NENA SAHIB.

Yes, it was indeed Omelia, who on her return to the cavern, after her parting with her lover, the night of her adventures in Delhi, as described in a previous chapter, had fallen into the hands of her enemies, who not being satisfied with the answers she gave to the questions they put to her, suspected her to be a spy, and therefore they took good care that she should not escape them, and they being on their way to join the rebels at Cawnpore, resolved that she should accompany them.

Terrible were the sufferings and indignities to which she was subjected on that long and tedious journey, but by using the utmost precaution, acting with perfect firmness and self-possession, and maintaining the strictest silence, notwithstanding the taunts and threats that were held out to her, she succeeded in keeping her sex concealed.

And firm indeed was the Indian maiden's heart, under the trying circumstances to which she was now exposed, though inwardly she felt and knew the extreme danger of her position, for the strict integrity and humanity of her motives, might justly claim the protection of Providence, and in that she trusted.

Still it was hard to bear the brutal insults that were offered to her, and to which she was compelled to submit with patience, and in silence, for she well knew that any excitement, or retort in words on her part, could only lead to a betrayal of the truth, and pro-

circumstances, he almost abandoned himself to despair.

His situation was indeed a terrible one, and such as might have appalled the stoutest heart, and the young officer gave himself up to the most painful and gloomy thoughts that crowded upon him with a force which was truly overwhelming.

And in the midst of all the horrors of that fatally eventful night, what was the fate of Omelia? What had become of her during the three days that himself and his wretched companions had been in the mosque? Had she still persisted in exposing herself to all those perils that she had hitherto braved with an heroic daring which was truly marvellous and unexampled? If so, he could not but apprehend the worst! He shuddered at the thought, and

No. 16.

his fortitude under such trying circumstances, much as he tried to maintain it, nearly forsook him.

"Beloved girl," he ejaculated, "one of the noblest and most beauteous of Nature's works, could I but be assured of your safety, methinks I might be content, even though it should be the will of the Almighty that I should here perish. Oh, that I could be permitted now again to behold you, what a melancholy satisfaction would it be to me in the midst of this my terrible hour of suffering and adversity. Oh, that I could again gaze upon your lovely features, and listen to the gentle tones of your voice. But alas, alas, it cannot be. The thought is madness, and useless is it for me to encourage it: oh, Omelia, we shall never, never meet again."

Then she thought of the hermit, who had been to her so kind a friend, and she reflected on the lonely and perilous situation of the bereaved Flora Melville, and keenly she felt the agony that unfortunate girl would experience, at the mystery of her disappearance, and shuddered at the fate, which in the painful aspect of present affairs, might befal her.

Still, in spite of all, a feeling of hope buoyed her up throughout this powerful trial, and which never deserted her, and she endeavoured to look forward with the most sanguine expectations as to the final results.

Certainly the interruption to the accomplishment of the generous and heroic designs that had prompted her conduct, was most annoying and disheartening; but for her own personal safety and ultimate triumph, notwithstanding the present gloomy aspect of affairs, she entertained the utmost confidence. The discovery of her sex was what she most dreaded, and to avoid that she could not flatter herself with the hope that it was at all possible.

It was in this state of mind that the fair prisoner entered the city of Cawnpore on the evening of which we are writing, and her courage almost forsook her, when she remembered the different tales of horror respecting the late transactions there, which she had heard on the road, and ascertained from the observations of the rebels in whose custody she was, that it was their intention to take her before the notorious Nena Sahib, who was the treacherous author of many of the dreadful outrages that had been already committed, and who, in spite of his privious hypocritical and plausible conduct, she had ever looked upon with suspicion. But she conquered her feelings as well as she could, and maintained the same undaunted appearance which had characterised her throughout, much to the astonishment of the men in whose power she unfortunately was.

Mentally she invoked the protection of Heaven for her lover, and those friends so dear to her, and then prepared herself for the worst, and resigned herself to her fate, whatever it migh be.

She exhibited no material change in her demeanour, when the native officer from the house of Nena Sahib made his appearance, and he could not help looking upon her with mingled feelings of astonishment, curiosity, and admiration.

She met his keen scrutiny with calm indifference, and evinced not the least signs of fear, and the officer questioned the men in whose custody she was, narrowly about her, which they answered according.

"So young," said the officer, "and a traitor; aiding and abetting the accursed Feringhees. Who are you, boy, that thus rashly brave the vengeance of your countrymen?"

Omelia fixed upon her interrogator a look of the most supreme contempt, but returned no answer.

"Obstinate stripling," cried the enraged officer, striking our heroine on the back with the flat of his sword; "you will shortly be in the presence of one who will know how to tame this stubborn disposition."

Omelia again smiled scornfully, remained silent, and exhibited not the least signs of fear or emotion.

"Away with him," commanded the officer, "the Nena may now be seen, and he doubtless will soon find the way to break the silence of this bold young traitor."

The ruffians drove her rudely on, and in another minute they were in the outer court of the house of Nena Sahib.

The bloodhound of Cawnpore—for by no other title does he deserve to be designated—was seated in one of the lower apartments of the building in which he had fixed his temporary residence—a spacious saloon fitted up in the extreme of Oriental magnificence—and was engaged in conversation with two or three of the principal of his myrmidons, at the same time smoking his costly hookah with perfect enjoyment. His dress was of the most gorgeous description, and certainly he looked the high character of the eastern prince to perfection. His portly figure, and open, manly countenance, and expressive features, gave him a prepossing appearance, and an affable smile continually playing around his lips, which seemed to bespeak him a good humoured, and, in fact, rather a rollicking, jovial companion. Never did the features of a man more belie his character than those of Nena Sahib. It would have required a large amount of credulity to believe him capable of those hideous crimes that the mind of a fiend could alone conceive Truly, in the words of the poet, he might have said—

"I can smile,
Aye, and murder while I smile."

And doubtless even at the moment he bore the engaging and agreeable appearance we have been describing, he was with his willing instruments concocting some of those atrocious acts that have since made humanity shudder at the bare recital.

The Nena's conference with his myrmidons being at an end, he dismissed them, and was left alone, and still continuing to smoke his hookah, he appeared to drop into a deep reverie, during which the expression of his features underwent some extraordinary changes, which to a keen observer might have revealed some of the secret workings of his guilty mind.

From this he was aroused by the entrance of the native officer before mentioned, who made a most profound obeisance to him, and the Nena rather impatiently and angrily demanded the reason of his intrusion, to which the officer replied by informing him that some sepoys waited without, anxious to introduce to his presence a mysterious person, whom they had brought from some distance, and who obstinately refused to answer any questions that were put to him.

"Indeed," said Nena Sahib, with a sinister smile, "then it must be my task to endeavour to make him more communicative. Bring the prisoner hither."

The officer bowed and retired, but returned almost immediately, accompanied by two or three of the sepoys, conducting in Omelia who entered the room with a firm step and head erect, and met the stern and penetrating look of Nena Sahib with perfect indifference and composure.

He eyed the delicate form, and handsome features of the maiden, with a feeling of astonishment and admiration, which was not at all diminished by the striking firmness of her demeanour, and for a few minutes said not a word, but continued his scrutiny, Omelia evincing not the least sign of confusion or trepidation.

He then put some questions to the rebels in an under tone, which they having answered, apparently to his satisfaction, he motioned to them to retire, which they did, and Omelia was left alone with the terrible butcher of Cawnpore.

He again fixed his keen eyes steadfastly upon her, and she continued to meet his scrutiny with an expression of haughty scorn and defiance.

"So," he said at length, with his accustomed smile, "I am informed, boy, that you are of a taciturn disposition, at least it would appear so, as you have hitherto refused to answer any questions that were put to you. Perhaps my powers of persuasion may be more successful."

"You are welcome to try the experiment," replied our heroine, haughtily.

"Thus far, at any rate, I have succeeded," observed the Nena, "and you probably are aware that I am not the man to submit to be trifled with. Now, boy, who, and what are you?"

"An Hindoo, and the sworn enemy of rebels and assassins," replied Omelia, with a boldness that seemed to astonish him.

"Bold words those for a stripling and in the presence of Nena Sahib," he said; "have you no fear of the consequences of your daring and presumptuous conduct?"

"Fear," repeated our heroine, contemptuously, "no, I never understood or experienced it, especially when I had truth and justice on my side, as I have at present."

Nena Sahib frowned, and for a few moments remained silent, still gazing at her with looks of wonder and incredulity.

"Beware," he at length said, in a stern voice, "this obstinacy may cost you dear. Your name, and from whence came you?"

"It cannot concern you to know," returned Omelia, "therefore I decline to answer."

Nena Sahib again frowned, and seemed rather at a loss how to interrogate his prisoner, but though he felt mortified at being thus browed and bearded to his teeth by a mere lad, who seemed to be an object almost beneath his contempt, he could not but wonder at and admire the cool courage of his behaviour, while, as he gazed upon the delicate features and listened to the feminine tones of her voice, his amazement increased, and he felt thoroughly convinced that he had no common individual to deal with.

Omelia remained in the same attitude, and having now fully made up her mind as to the line of conduct she would pursue, she awaited with composure and perfect confidence the result of this, her first interview with the notorious Nena.

"This is a waste of time," said Nena Sahib, after a pause, "which to me, at any rate, is most valuable, I do not doubt your courage and daring, boy, for I have been informed of certain deeds you have performed, which would have done you honour in a better cause."

"A better cause!" repeated Omelia, indignantly; "can there be a better cause than that of honour, virtue, and humanity? And can that righteous cause be better served than in standing forward, as well as your abilities will permit, in the defence of the innocent victims of the atrocious wretches, whose thirst is blood, and whose pastime is the wholesale slaughter of helpless women and children? To effect this object I have lent my humble aid, and I feel a proud satisfaction in knowing that my efforts have not been altogether in vain."

"Can you be an Indian, and yet give expression to sentiments such as these you have just now spoken?" said the Nena.

"It does indeed seem strange and almost incredible," returned Omelia, sarcastically, "that in these present unhappy times of rapine and murder, that even one of the Hindoo race should possess the common feelings of humanity."

"I will not listen to such bold and insolent language as this," said the Nena, passionately. "Will you answer my questions, and inform me who you are, and why I see you thus arrayed against your countrymen?"

"I will not," said our heroine, resolutely.

"Beware how you provoke my wrath," said Nena Sahib, "for a terrible punishment never fails to follow my indignation."

"I know you, tyrant, and defy you," replied Omelia with unshaken firmness.

"Daring brat!" exclaimed the Nena, losing all guard over his temper, starting passionately to his feet, and, with his clenched fist, dealing Omelia a blow that made her stagger, and drew the blood in a copious stream from her face. Her bosom swelled with resentment and disgust; still she flinched not, and fixing upon the villain a withering look, she said:—

"Bravely done, it was a deed worthy of the miscreant Nena Sahib to strike a defenceless prisoner. Coward!"

"I will at least try whether I have not the means to tame this stubborn spirit," said the Nena, and, stamping loudly on the floor, several of his ruffianly creatures made their appearance.

"Strip yon traitor," he commanded, "and flog him near to death in my presence."

Now for the first time the courage of our heroine failed her, even the cowardly blow she had received, scarcely ruffled her cool, haughty, and defiant bearing; but her feelings revolted at the thought of the degrading punishment to which the Nena had condemned her; and more, she knew that the betrayal of her secret was now unavoidable.

Nena Sahib noticed the change in her manner, the quivering of her lips, the trembling of her limbs, and a savage look of triumph and satisfaction passed over his features, as he said:—

"So, my young hero, you begin to fear at last. That proud spirit methinks will at last be curbed. 'Tis well; I told you that Nena Sahib was not the man to be trifled with, and of that to your cost, you will now be convinced. Obey my orders," he commanded, turning to his creatures, "and spare him not."

This was indeed one of the moments of the severest trial that Omelia had ever experienced, and when she thought of the horrors that were involved in the sentence which Nena Sahib had just passed upon her, she certainly quailed beneath it. The blood gushed to her heart, her bosom swelled and heaved with shame and indignation, and resentment flashed from her eyes.

Quickly, however, she recovered her fortitude and self-possession, and re-assuming the haughty, scornful and commanding look and attitude which had characterised her at the commencement of the interview, the men whom the Nena had summoned to execute his cruel orders, were abashed, and hesitated.

"How now?" demanded the Nena sternly of his creatures; "did you not hear my orders? Why do you delay?"

The men advanced towards Omelia to seize her, and worked up to a pitch of the greatest excitement, for she knew that the moment of discovery had arrived, she exclaimed in a voice that thrilled to the heart of every one who heard it, and which completely startled Nena Sahib,

"Hold, cowards, miscreants; dare not to lay your hands upon me. Back, I say! Would you expose to degradation, and mutilate the flesh of a defenceless *woman*?"

The men staggered back awe-struck, and surprise rivetted Nena Sahib, for the moment to the spot on which he had been standing, while he fixed his dark eyes with intense curiosity and incredulity upon the handsome countenance of Omelia.

"A woman!" he repeated, "is this possible?"

"It is true," replied our heroine, calmly and firmly; "it is a woman whom you would resign to the brutal hands of these savages; I reveal the fact, but not from any expectation of mercy from one whose remorseless cruelty spares neither age or sex."

The Nena frowned slightly, but he stifled the expression of his rage, and approaching Omelia hastily, and laying his hand upon her arm, he looked into her countenance with an expression, in which astonishment, curiosity, and admiration were blended. This rude scrutiny Omelia bore with perfect firmness, and a look of the most ineffable scorn.

"Ah!" exclaimed Nena Sahib, having satisfied himself by his scrutiny; "it is indeed a woman who has thus dared to espouse the cause of the hated Europeans the enemies of her country, and to hurl defiance at the head of Nena Sahib It is a woman, and a handsome one too."

"Hold, miscreant," commanded our heroine, haughtily, and her eyes flashing with disgust and indignation; "dare not to insult my ears with your disgusting observations. You know my secret, and I am prepared to meet the brutal fate to which you will doubtless consign me. I will not condescend to supplicate for pity and forbearance to one whose breast is a stranger to every feeling of humanity."

"Be calm, girl," returned the Nena, in milder accents than he had hitherto spoken; "we must talk further on this subject when you appear in your real character; and endeavour to do so dispassionately. Conduct your prisoner to the care of two of my ayahs, whom you will instruct to array her in the habiliaments suited to her sex, then bring her again before me."

The men obeyed these orders, having first removed the cords from her wrists and arms, and Omelia walked from the presence of Nena Sahib with the same firm step that she had entered it.

CHAPTER XXXVI.

THE PRISONERS AT CAWNPORE.—OMELIA'S INTERCESSION.—THE AWFUL TRAGEDY.

Nena Sahib, who was completely astounded by this discovery, though he could not help admiring the extraordinary heroism of Omelia, awaited anxiously and impatiently for her return, but more than half an hour had elapsed before she was again introduced to his presence, and he was struck with amazement and admiration at the beauty of her appearance.

She had been stripped of her male disguise, and now appeared in the rich dress of one of the principal ladies of the Nena's harem, which became her fine figure admirably, and displayed its numerous bewitching graces to great advantage But the lovely expression of her features, and her modest, yet dignified demeanour, more completely fascinated Nena Sahib, at the same time that it awed him into respect and forbearance.

"By all my hopes," he exclaimed, " a right beauteous Hindoo woman; far better fitted for the Harem of a prince, than the dangers and horrors of war. I greet you, maiden, with becoming respect."

Omelia did not condescend to reply to this speech, only by a look of scorn and hatred; but when the Nena bent one knee to the floor, with all the courtly gallantry of the lover, and attempted to raise her hand to his lips, she withdrew it hastily, with a look of indignation and hatred, and in a commanding voice exclaimed—

"Hold, Nena Sahib, such hypocritical homage and flattery as you would fain pretend to offer me, is pollution; and sooner would I bare my breast to your dagger's blade, already deeply stained with the innocent blood of women and children, than submit to it. What is it you seek? Keep me not suspense, but at once let me know the fate to which you have doomed me, and which I will endeavour to meet with the fortitude which becomes my character."

"Truly, maiden," said the Nena, gazing at Omelia with increased wonder and admiration, " your heroism is matchless; although I have no cause to feel very highly flattered by the observations you have so freely addressed to me. Much as you have stigmatised me as a monster of the deepest dye, because I seek the destruction of the accursed oppressors and usurpers of our native land,

I am disposed to treat you with every indulgence and forbearance, if it be only to prove to you how much you wrong me by the epithets you have applied to me; but I expect candid answers to the questions I may deem it necessary to put to you, for any attempt at concealment is now perfectly useless. Once more, I ask, who are you?"

"Unfortunately," replied Omelia, " I am the daughter of one belonging to your inhuman horde of rebels, and whom I shudder to acknowlede as my parent."

"Ah, say you so?" cried Nena Sahib, with increased interest and curiosity; " you talk of rebels, girl, and yet rebel against the authority, nay, perhaps the life of your own father?"

"I acknowledge no authority which is coupled with treachery so base, and crime so monstrous," returned Omelia, firmly.

"Misguided, obstinate girl," said the Nena, angrily, " you must have been well tutored, thus to debase every feeling of duty, and principle of honour. What is the name of the parent whom you so disgrace?"

"I can gain nothing by concealing it, although it shames me to acknowledge it. That misguided parent's name, I therefore answer, is Yunadar."

"Ah !" exclaimed Nena Sahib, with a look of incredulity, " is it possible that Yunadar whom I have heard of as one of the most zealous in our righteous cause, is the father of one so fair, yet treacherous, and lost to every sentiment of filial duty? This proud spirit of disobedience, this unnatural enmity to one who should command your utmost reverence, must be broken."

Omelia again smiled scornfully as she replied—

"No earthly power shall move me from the course of integrity, virtue, and justice I have marked for myself. Ever must I continue the enemy of my father while he remains the colleague and abettor of rebels and murderers."

"Rash, daring girl," cried the Nena, sternly, " this obduracy may cost you dearly. I have not patience to listen furthur to you at present. You will now retire, and I would advise you to reflect seriously on the madness of your conduct ere we meet again, which will be in the morning."

"You have already heard the determination of Omelia, Nena Sahib," she replied, haughtily, " and neither threats or persuasions can move me from it. I trust in the protection of that Supreme Power, whose sacred lands you have so monstrously outraged; and I fear not the result."

Nena Sahib bit his lips, and frowned fearfully; then stamping loudly on the floor, the attendants reappeared, to whom he spoke a few words aside, and Omelia was then conducted from his presence to a small building attached to the house, and confined in a chamber elegantly fitted up, and left in the charge of two female attendants.

*   *   *   *   *

We must now return to the deplorable situation of the other unfortunate prisoners of Nena Sahib; and have a frightful narrative to relate

Our countrywomen, with their little ones, were taken to a small building near the assembly rooms in the city, where they remained in close custody, receiving only a small quantity of dull and chupatties daily for food for the first few days. Presently, however, a little meat, and milk for the children, was allowed; as also clean clothes were issued for those forcibly taken from the washerwomen of the station, who had them for wash, previous to the outbreak. A sweeper-woman and bheestie were also allowed.

Five of the sufferers died in bondage from want of proper care and attention. It is not easy to describe, but it may be imagined, the misery of so many helpless persons—some wounded, others sick, and all labouring under the greatest agony of heart for the loss of those dear to them, who had so recently been killed before their own eyes—cooped up night and day in a small low-roofed house with but four or six very small rooms, and that in the hottest season of the year, without beds for a whole fortnight, watched most carefully on all sides by a set of brutish rebellious sepoys. Mr. Shepherd says:—"It is reported that the lives of the poor women were spared by the Nena from bad motives, and that he appointed a wicked old hag to persuade the helpless creatures to yield to his wishes. This message, I learn, was conveyed to the women with great art, accompanied by threats and hopes; but was received with great indignation, and a firm resolution to die, or kill each other with their own teeth, if any forcible means were employed to dishonour them."

Nena Sahib had suffered a signal defeat at Futteypore, after which some reputed spies were brought before him. These were accused of being the bearers of letters supposed to have been written to distant stations by the helpless women in the prison; in this correspondence some of the Mahaguns and Baboos (gentlemen) of the city were believed to be implicated. It was therefore resolved that the said spies, together with all the women and children, as also the few gentlemen whose lives had been spared (said to have been six in number), should all be put to death, and that the Baboos of the city and every person who could read or write English should have their right hands and noses cut off. The first order was carried out immediately—*i. e.*, on the evening of the 15th of July. "The native spies were first put to the sword," says Mr. Shepherd, "and after them the gentlemen, who were brought out and shot afterwards.

It was while these atrocities were in the course of perpetration that Omelia was brought a prisoner before Nena Sahib, and after he had dismissed her from his presence, as related, enraged at the defiance with which she had treated him, and the epithets she had so boldly applied to him, he thought of a brutal plan by which he expected to intimidate her, and awe her into a proper respect for his power. This he resolved to carry into effect the following day.

On reaching the room where she was for the present to be confined, the fortitude and indifference which Omelia had evinced while in the presence of Nena Sahib, almost forsook her, and she could not but entertain some torturing apprehensions as to the fate which too probably awaited her.

But she endeavoured to conceal her feelings from the two women in whose custody she was placed, and who expressed much curiosity about her, but conducted themselves towards her with every civility and respect.

They put many questions to her which she thought it was prudent to evade in the best manner she could, and from them she elicited such particulars of the proceedings of Nena Sahib, and the awful situation of the unfortunate prisoners, as filled her breast with horror.

She slept but little that night for her mind was too busily occupied, and she had indeed every reason to apprehend the worst, being in the power of such a sanguinary miscreant as Nena Sahib. However, she determined to maintain her fortitude as well as she could, and to remain faithful to the conduct she had hitherto pursued, even let the consequences be whatever they might.

Her courage was soon destined to be put to the test.

She had just finished the morning meal, when an havildar and two sepoys entered the room, and informed her that she must accompany them immediately.

"Whither would you conduct me?" demanded Omelia, eagerly, for a dark suspicion entered her mind that Nena Sahib intended to adopt some more stringent means to intimidate her into compliance with his will.

"That you will see before long," replied the havildar; "we do but obey the commands of the Nena."

"And what if I were to refuse to accompany you?" interrogated Omelia haughtily.

"Why, then we must use violence to compel you," replied the havildar.

"And are these also the orders of your tyrant master?" asked Omelia

"They are," answered the officer.

The women who had been in attendance upon her, urged upon her the folly of resistance, and told her not to fear.

"Fear," repeated Omelia, scornfully, "I am unused to the feeling. Lead on," she added haughtily, and addressing herself to the officer, "I am prepared to attend you."

Thus saying, she motioned the men to lead the way, and was conducted by them from the room, and to her surprise and increasing anxiety to the outside of the building, where a number of the rebels were assembled to accompany her, and they eyed her with no little curiosity, and two or three offensive observations met her ears. She looked upon them, however, with thorough disdain, and was marched off in the direction of the assembly house.

And now a terrible thought flashed upon her mind, and almost shook her courage. The women who had attended her had informed her that the unfortunate women were confined in a building near the assembly rooms, and it seemed but too probable that she was about to become their companion, and if so, would share the same frightful fate to which the savage Nena Sahib had doubtless doomed them.

She mentally invoked the protection of heaven, and then became more firm and resigned to her fate whatever it might be.

In a few minutes more they arrived at the building before which she beheld Nena Sahib standing surrounded by some of his principal officers, and a number of armed mutineers, whose looks seemed to foretel some fearful approaching deed.

Omelia walked with a firm step towards the Nena, who, on beholding her, greeted her with much affected courtesy, which she returned with a proud look of scorn and defiance, and awaited the result of this adventure with more fortitude than she thought she could have acquired.

"I'm afraid I have caused you some trouble, uneasiness, and anxiety, fair Omelia, by desiring your presence here. But as you seemed to despise my power and authority yesterday, I wished to convince you what it is to become the enemy of Nena Sahib."

"I need no proof to convince me of the brutal, the ferocious character of Nena Sahib," replied our heroine, fearlessly, "his crimes have already stamped him as a miscreant of the most atrocious character."

"Beware," said Nena Sahib, with a frown, "this bold language may cost you dear. Scorn and defiance but ill become your situation."

He then spoke two or three words aside to his officers, who bowed in obedience, and then turning once more to our heroine, he said, in tones of mock politeness, but in which his irony and villany were too apparent to escape the notice of Omelia.

"I must trouble you to attend me, Omelia, I have a sight for you which will probably excite your deepest interest, and it is such a one as you doubtless never before beheld. This way, if you please."

With these words he took her arm, with affected gallantry which was truly disgusting, and led her into the house, or rather into a small open court in front of it, and there Omelia did indeed behold a scene which excited her deepest horror and sympathy.

The male prisoners had, as we have before related, already been sacrificed to the brutal vengeance of Nena Sahib, and the unfortunate women and children awaited their fate with trembling horror and suspense.

There, in the small open space, those unhappy ill-fated beings were crowded, and their emaciated forms, and pale and ghastly looks, showed the terrible sufferings to which they had been subjected, and were sufficient to excite pity in even the most insensible breast.

On beholding Nena Sahib, a murmur of horror ran through the assembled crowd of wretched beings and they seemed to anticipate that the hour of their slaughter was approaching, and Omelia now perfectly understood the brutal object for which she had been conducted there. But all her thoughts and sympathies were absorbed by the terrible situation of the poor helpless creatures before her, and she watched the expression of the Nena's features with the greatest anxiety; in that she could read the doom that speedily awaited them as clearly as if it had already taken place, and her gentle heart bled for them.

The unfortunate prisoners seemed to read her thoughts, and they fixed upon her the most piteous looks of supplication, as though her intercession was likely to have the least effect upon the brutal mind of Nena Sahib, who with folded arms stood near Omelia, and seemed to eye his intended victims with the most savage looks of satisfaction.

"You behold these wretched creatures," he said to Omelia, with a look of exultation. "Those hated Europeans. Their husbands, and the fathers of their children have already been destroyed by my orders, and these have but a brief space of time to live."

"Oh, Nena Sahib," said Omelia, with a look of horror, "cruel even as you are, you cannot surely in cold blood murder these poor helpless women and innocent children. I implore you to forbear from so fiendish a crime—on my knees I implore for them your mercy."

She sunk on her knees at the Nena's feet, as she thus spoke, and looked up in his face with an expression of the most earnest supplication, whilst a simultaneous cry of agony broke forth from the hapless beings for whom she interceded so warmly, so eloquently.

But it was all in vain, the tyrant only smiled ironically and triumphantly, as he exclaimed :—

"You must entertain a presumptous opinon of your own influence, if you imagine that you who have so boldly set me at defiance, and even dared to apply epithets to me that should have provoked my immediate vengeance, can move me from my purpose. I will show you how futile is the attempt to excite my pity or forbearance. The doom of these wretches is sealed, and this moment will I put it into execution."

"Monster!" cried our heroine, unable to restrain the expression of her feelings of disgust and horror. "Will nothing stay your cruel hand? Can you have the inhumanity thus to sacrifice those unfortunate and defenceless beings? Is not your thirst for blood already satiated?"

"No," replied the villain, with a look of exultation; "and it will not be while one hated Feringhee remains upon the Indian soil."

The wretched prisoners heard these brutal observations, and certain that the crisis of their fate had arrived, their cries of agony and despair were heartrendering to listen to.

"Oh, can you turn a deaf ear to these supplications?" said Omelia; "will nothing move you to relent? I beg of you, I humbly but earnestly entreat your mercy and forbearance."

"You plead, you sue in vain," returned the Nena, "no earthly power can rescue them from the fate to which I have doomed them. This way girl."

He rudely grasped her arm as he thus spoke, and forced her outside the court, and orders were given to the rebels to commence the dreadful work of slaughter, which it was now evident that nothing could avert, and that Nena Sahib had determined that Omelia should be a witness of the hideous and appalling scene.

The agony of her feelings may be easily imagined, and again she supplicated the Nena's forbearance, but with no greater effect than before; and soon commenced that frightful tragedy, which can never be effaced from the recollection of our indignant countrymen.

We quote from the best authorities an account of this horrible affair.

The poor females were ordered to come out, but neither threats or persuasions could induce them to do so, they laid hold of each other by dozens, and clung so close that it was impossible to separate them, or drag them out of the building. The troopers, therefore, brought muskets, and after firing a great many shots from the doors, windows, &c., rushed in with swords and bayonets. Some of the helpless creatures, in their agony, fell down at the feet of their murderers, clasped their legs, and begged of them, in the most pitiful manner, to spare their lives, but to no purpose. The fearful deed was done, most deliberately and completely, in the midst of the most dreadful shrieks and cries of the victims. There were between 140 and 150 souls, including children; and for more than two hours the monsters were occupied in completing the dreadful deed. The doors of the buildings were then locked for the night, and the murderers went to their homes. Next morning it was found, on opening the doors, that some ten or fifteen females, with a few of the children, had managed to escape from death, by falling and hiding under the murdered bodies of their fellow-prisoners, Fresh orders were therefore sent to murder them also; but the survivors, not being able to bear the idea of being cut down, rushed out into the compound, and seeing a well there, threw themselves into it without hesitation, thus putting a period to lives which it was impossible for them to save. The dead bodies of those murdered on the preceding evening were then ordered to be thrown into the same well, and Jullads were employed to drag them away like dogs.

Such was the dreadful deed, the first part of which the horror-struck Omelia was compelled to witness, and when it was complete Nena Sahib led her through the place which was literally floating with human blood, and compelled her to gaze upon the frightfully mangled remains of the unfortunate victims.

What her feelings were it is needless to describe; she could not give expression to them in words, but her looks sufficiently revealed them to the Nena, and he seemed to observe her horror with fiendish satisfaction.

She was now re-conducted to the Nena's house, where she was again placed in the custody of the two women, and there she gave unrestrained indulgence to the emotions of agony that filled her breast, and they listened to the particulars of the dreadful slaughter which she related with looks that showed their abhorrence of such atrocities, although they dared not give utterance to their feelings.

: — —

CHAPTER XXXVII.

FRESH ATROCITIES.—THE ESCAPE.

We cannot refrain from relating some of the principal and appalling events that took place about the period of which we have been writing in the previous chapter, one of which is thus related by Lieutenant Delafosse, who contrived to escape.

"A committee of officers went to the river to see that the boats were ready and serviceable; and everything being reported ready, and carriages for the wounded having arrived, we gave over our guns, &c., and marched out on the morning of the 27th of June, about seven o'clock. We got down to the river and into the boats without being molested in the least; but no sooner were we in the boats, and had laid down our muskets, and had taken off our coats to work easier at the boats, than the order was given to fire. The guns that had been hidden were run out, and opened on us immediately, while sepoys came from all directions and kept up a fire. The men jumped out of the boats, and, instead of trying to get the boats loose from their moorings, swam to the first boat they saw loose. Only three boats got safe over to the opposite side of the river, but were met there by two field pieces, guarded by a number of cavalry and infantry. Before these boats had got a mile down the stream, half our small party were either killed or wounded, and two of our boats had been swamped. We had now only one boat, crowded with wounded, and having on board

No. 20.

more than she could carry. The two guns followed us the whole of the day, the infantry firing on us the whole of that night. On the second day a gun was seen on the Cawnpore side, and opened on us at Nujuffghur— the infantry still followed us on both sides. On the morning of the third day the boat was no longer serviceable. We were aground on a sand-bank, and had not strength sufficient to move her. Directly any of us got into the water we were fired upon by thirty or forty men at a time. There was nothing left but to charge and drive them away. So fourteen of us were told to go and do what we could. Directly we got on shore the insurgents retired, but having followed them up too far, we were cut off from the river, and had to retire ourselves, as we were being surrounded. We could not make for the river, but had to go down parallel and came at the river again a mile lower down, when we saw a large force of men right in front waiting for us, and another lot on the other bank, should we attempt to cross the river. On the bank of the river, just by the force in front, was a temple. We fired a volley, and made for the temple, in which we took shelter, one man being killed and one wounded. From the door of the temple we fired on every insurgent who showed himself. Finding that they could do nothing against us while we remained inside, they heaped wood all round and set it on fire. When we could no longer remain inside, on account of the smoke and heat, we threw off the clothes we had, and each taking a musket charged through the fire. Seven of us out of twelve got into the water, but before we had gone far two poor fellows were shot. There were only five left now, and we had to swim, while the insurgents followed us along both banks, wading and firing as fast as they could. After we had gone about three miles down the stream, one of our party, an artilleryman, to rest himself, began swimming on his back, and not knowing in what direction he was swimming got on shore and was killed. When we had gone down about six miles firing on both sides ceased, and soon after we were hailed by some natives on the Oude side, who asked us to come on shore, and said they would take us to their Rajah, who was friendly to the English. We gave ourselves up, and were taken six miles inland to the Rajah, who treated us very kindly, giving us clothes and food. We stayed with him for about a month, as he would not let us leave, saying the roads were unsafe. At last he sent us off on the 29th of July to the right bank of the river to a zemindar of a village, who got us a hackery. We took our departure on the 31st of July for Allahabad, but met the detachment of the 84th regiment,

under Lieutenant Woodhouse before we had gone ten miles; and marched off with him to Cawnpore."

The enormities perpetrated by the orders of Nena Sahib were never surpassed; and some of the incidents that occurred were affecting and touching in the extreme. We will relate a few of them, and then resume our tale.

On the 10th of June, as usual, the firing commenced from the 24, 18, and 4-pounders, and one lady and one grown up young lady, and three children were coming along in a carriage from the direction of the west, and on the road some one had killed the lady's husband, but not considering it proper to kill the women and children, had allowed them to escape. However, the troopers of the 2nd cavalry caught them, and brought them into the presence of the Nena, who ordered them to be killed at once, although the lady begged the Nena to spare her life; but this disgraceful man would not in any way hearken to her, and took them all into the plain. At that time the sun was very hot, and the lady said, " The sun is very hot—take me into the shade," but no one listened. On four sides the children were catching hold of their mother's gown, and saying, " Mamma, come to the bungalow, and give me some bread and water." At length, having been tied hand to hand, and made to stand up on the plain, they were shot down by pistol bullets.

" On the 11th of June, a lady, the wife of Mukan Sahib, merchant, who had been four or five days hiding under the grass of her bungalow, came out of her bungalow at evening time, and was discovered. She was taken before the Nena, who ordered her to be killed. The head of that lady was cut off, and presented as a nazir (gift of royalty); and in the place where hundreds of Christians, and ladies and children, were killed, a crowd remained, and a Rampoori trooper, by caste a Mussulman, of the 2nd irregular cavalry, remained in the presence of the Nena, and killed these innocent ones; and whenever an order was given to slay anybody that same trooper used to slay them.

" On the 12th of June, it was reported that from the direction of the Punjab, a number of Europeans were assembled. Immediately one troop of cavalry and two companies of infantry were sent to reconnoitre, when it was found that about 136 European soldiers, and women and children, had come in three boats from some station to the east. The troopers seized them all, and took them to the Nena, who ordered that they should all be killed, and sundry Rampoori troopers of the Mussulmans of the 2nd cavalry, whom the Nena kept with him for the express purpose, killed them all. Among them was a young lady, the daughter of some general. She addressed herself much to the Nena, and said, ' No king ever committed such oppression as you have, and in no religion is there any order to kill women and children. I do not know what has happened to you. Be well assured that by this slaughter the English will not become less; whoever may remain will have an eye upon you.' But the Nena paid no attention, and showed her no mercy, and ordered that she should be killed, and that they should fill her hands with powder, and kill her by the explosion."

An ayah, or native nurse, recently in the service of a Mrs. T' Greenaway, at Cawnpore, also tells the story of the barbarities committed there, and the sufferings endured. She relates that the native infantry and cavalry regiments having mutinied, robbed the treasury, and burnt the collector's house, they proceeded to Kuleanpore, seven miles from Cawnpore, and encamped there.

"At this place the Nena Sahib met them, and said to the mutineers, ' You receive seven rupees from the British government; I will give you fourteen rupees; don't go to Delhi; stay here, and your name will be great. Kill all the English at Cawnpore first, and I will give you each a golden bracelet.' On hearing this all the mutineers agreed to the terms of the Nena. The mutineers made a subahdar of the 1st regiment general, and he again made all the havildars, and naicks captains, lieutenants, and ensigns. The Nena said, ' I will supply you all with food.'"

Under Nena Sahib's guidance, therefore, they all returned to Cawnpore, when the fighting began.

For several days after the awful tragedy which she had been compelled to witness, Omelia's situation underwent very little change, with the exception that she was spared the pain and disgust of Nena Sahib's presence, he being absent from the house, and being busily occupied in the accomplishment of his diabolical designs; and she remained in the same state of doubt and suspense as to what would be her ultimate fate, though taking all the circumstances into consideration, she could not but entertain the most gloomy apprehensions, and agonising were the thoughts that constantly racked and bewildered her brain.

She had too much reason to fear that she would never more behold her lover, or her friends, who would be so alarmed for her fate; and although she struggled hard, it was impossible that she could bear a fate so cruel with any degree of fortitude. Still she tried to hope that something would yet occur to rescue her.

The two women seemed to sympathise with her, and they continued to treat her with the greatest respect. The thought of escape frequently occurred to her, but that seemed all but hopeless, and she was almost induced to abandon it altogether. Could the two women be prevailed upon to assist her, there might yet be a chance of success; but it seemed most unlikely that they would venture to run such a risk for one who was almost a stranger to them, and she hesitated to make such a proposal to them.

She had frequently looked anxiously from the window of the room she occupied into the court-yard below, when the women happened to be for a few minutes in the adjoining apartment; and she calculated whether it might be possible, when her gaolers were in bed, and there should be no one about, to let herself down from the window in safety, and, if she were able to accomplish that, she could pass through the city in safety. Notwithstanding the apparent extravagance of the idea, and the all but certain failure of such an attempt, she could not dismiss the thought from her mind, and every hour it gained a still firmer hold on her, and she was encouraged in the hope by the continued absence of Nena Sahib, whom she sincerely prayed might fall into the hands of the British, and thus be stopped in his terrible and sanguinary career.

Two more days passed away, and still Nena Sahib returned not, and Omelia continued to indulge in the same vague ideas and hopes of escape; but she was as far off making the attempt as ever, and it did not seem as though it was likely that an opportunity to do so would be afforded her, and her uneasiness and impatience became almost insupportable. She at length determined to endeavour to put her wishes and designs into effect at all hazards; and even if she was detected, and her schemes frustrated, her situation could surely not be much worse than it was at present.

Having thus made up her mind, she matured her plans, and became more confident than ever of success, and only awaited a fitting opportunity to make the attempt, which she knew it would not do to delay any longer than possible, for when the Nena returned she had no doubt that he would make her confinement more severe, or come to a decision how at once to dispose of her, and from his savage disposition, she could not but anticipate the worst.

Still she racked her brain for some time to no purpose to endeavour to devise some stratagem which offered the least prospect of success, and there appeared to be so many obstacles in the way, that she was at times almost induced to abandon it in despair.

At length, however, providence smiled upon her, and the wished for opportunity presented itself.

One of the women who had attended upon her was withdrawn, and she was left in the sole charge of the other, who had always evinced the greatest disposition to grant her every indulgence at all compatible with the disagreeable duty she had to perform.

This woman evidently viewed her with the deepest commiseration, and that encouraged the hopes of Omelia, who determined at once to make an appeal to her, and try to induce her to assist her in her flight.

It was on the evening previous to the day which Nazimi—which was the name of the female—had informed our heroine that Nena Sahib was expected to return, that they were seated together near the window which overlooked the court-yard, and it was then that she formed the resolution of making a final appeal to the woman's humanity, and she entertained the most sanguine hopes that that appeal would not be made in vain.

They had been conversing for some time upon different subjects, and Nazimi displayed an intelligence and superiority of intellect which Omelia had not at first given her credit for.

"I am indeed surprised, my good Nazimi," remarked our heroine, at length, "to find one possessing the amiable feelings and gentle disposition of yourself attached to the service of so great a miscreant as Nena Sahib, and shut out from that society you are so well calculated to adorn."

"You flatter me, Omelia," replied her companion, with a faint smile; "but indeed the situation in which I am placed is most repulsive to my feelings, and many hours of poignant anguish does it cause me, when I reflect upon the unfortunate being I am, and the horrors that I am daily obliged to witness. But it was not always so, ah, no. Time was when I was happy; alas, that time is fled never again to return."

She sighed deeply as she uttered these words, and tears trembled in her eyes.

Omelia could not but feel an inward satisfaction, for she saw that Nazimi was in the right mood to realise her wishes, and she resolved to follow up her advantage with all the powers of persuasion.

"Do not say so, Nazimi," she said, in answer to her latter observations, "give not way to despair. But surely the circumstances must have been most unfortunate that placed you in the Nena's power, whom it is impossible that you can view with any other feelings than those of dread and aversion."

"Oh, they were indeed," returned Nazimi, "and severe indeed have been my sufferings.

I was once good and innocent, and surrounded by every happiness in the home of affectionate parents and fond brothers and sisters. I had not a wish ungratified, not a thought unanticipated, by those whose whole study and anxiety it was to contribute to my joy and welfare. Alas, the demon was at hand to break in upon my little world of bliss, to destroy my bright hopes, and ruin my prospects for ever. Oh, that terrible recollection, it curdles the life-blood in my veins and racks my brain to madness."

Emotion overcame her, and she covered her face with her hands and wept freely.

"I pray you endeavour to compose yourself, my good Nazimi," said Omelia; "and explain. Your observations interest me, and excite my warmest sympathy."

"'Tis a sad story," replied the former, "and I have not time or spirits to enter into the particulars at present. Suffice it to say that one whom I believed to be the very soul of honour, and whose insinuating manners had won my youthful heart, with flattering promises seduced me from my peaceful home and affectionate relations, and triumphed in his guilty wishes. Weak, confiding, blind, infatuated, I fell, and it was not till then that I discovered the true character of my betrayer, for he shamelessly unmasked himself, and he whom I had hitherto known only as Zharab Singh a sepoy officer, I now discovered to be no other than the adopted son of the Peishwah of Bhitoor, Nena Sahib. I trembled at the base deception which had been practised upon me, and dreaded the fate which too probably awaited me. With tears of the bitterest anguish and remorse I implored him to take pity on me, and restore me to my friends, but he only mocked at my sufferings, and scorned my supplications. I was taken to Bithoor, and there in the harem of my seducer were my shame and degradation completed.

"The villain soon tired of the unfortunate victim he had made, and treated me with every cruelty and indignity, and in his power have I remained enduring every misery ever since. Alas, when will that misery have an end?"

"Your's is indeed a sad fate," observed Omelia, "and most sincerely do I pity you. How long is it since you were unfortunately prevailed upon to abandon your home?"

"Three dreary years have elapsed since that fatal time," replied Nazimi, "years of unmitigated suffering, shame, and remorse."

"And have you never entertained the wish to return to those scenes of happy childhood?" interrogated Omelia, eagerly.

Have not I wished," repeated Nazimi fervently, clasping her hands together, and tears again trembling in her eyes, "oh, how ardently have I prayed to be once more permitted to behold that beloved home from which I have been so long estranged, those revered beings whom I so cruelly deserted, and if they still live—which fond hopes seem to whisper to me that they do—to seek their forgiveness for the past."

"Why then delay?" said Omelia, eagerly, and seizing upon the opportunity to urge her appeal, which she now saw presented itself, "what is there to prevent the success of your wishes if you form the resolution? The road to liberty is before you, and you may again be restored to those you love, and release yourself from the power of the monster Nena Sahib, if you do not reject the chance which is now offered to you. And oh, Nazimi, as I feel convined that you sincerely sympathise with me, and would regret to see me become the victim of the savage vengeance of this terrible man, who hath already exposed me to such horrors that I shudder even now to think upon; I implore you to aid me in my escape, and suffer me to accompany you."

Nazimi started and trembled, for she seemed to shrink with a feeling of dread from so bold an attempt. But Omelia continued to urge her compliance with the request she had made with all the force and eloquence in her power.

"What is it you propose?" said Nazimi, "know you not the danger with which any such attempt must be fraught in the present state of the country? Should we be detected a frightful death would be the certain fate of us both."

"Fear not," returned our heroine, "I entertain the most confident hopes of success, and am prepared to brave everything. Do not hesitate, I beseech you. Surely no fate can be worse than the one to which we are at present subjected."

Nazimi looked earnestly at Omelia for a few minutes, but returned no immediate answer, and her mind seemed to waver.

"The design is a bold one," she said at length, "and should it fail—I must alone to consider of it. Let me retire for awhile, and awaite patiently my return. Be prepared for any decision to which I may arrive."

"Do not delay, I request of you," said Omelia, "for you must be well aware of the necessity of promptitude of action. If the attempt is not made to night, it may be too late."

"Fear not," answered Nazimi, "when occasion requires it, I can act with firmness and decision."

With these words she hastily retired from the room, and took the precaution to secure the door after her.

Omelia sunk on her knees, and fervently returned her thanks to Omnipotence, for she considered that her wishes were half accomplished, and she looked forward to the return of Nazimi in a state of great suspense and expectation.

She looked anxiously from the window on to the court-yard below, which seemed to be entirely deserted, for not even a solitary individual met her observation, and an unusual silence reigned within the house, which strengthened her hopes, and she awaited the return of Nazimi with increased impatience.

The night was extremely dark and favourable to concealment, and Omelia could see nothing but the prospect of success, should Nazimi make up her mind to hazard the attempt.

Her heart palpitated violently, for she felt that it was an effort of life or death, for should they be discovered ere they got without the city their fate was certain. But she had more than on one occasion, had to encounter equal dangers and difficulties, and surmounted them, and she endeavoured to be firm, and to look with confidence as to the result on the present occasion.

Never did the time appear so long to our heroine, as the interval of Nazimi's absence, and her patience was nearly exhausted when she heard a light footstep approaching cautiously along the passage which led to the room in which she was, and directly afterwards the door was unfastened, and Nazimi reappeared, equipped as if for a journey, and the expression of her features instantly assured Omelia that she had decided in favour of her wishes.

"Good Nazimi," she said, eagerly, "quick, tell me, have you made up your mind."

"I have," answered Nazimi, "your arguments and persuasions have prevailed, we will make the attempt to escape from this den of horrors, and may kind providence crown our efforts with success."

"Oh, thanks, thanks," ejaculated our heroine, gratefully, "for this resolution. Let us but be firm and cautious, and I venture to flatter myself with the hope that our success is all but certain."

"We must not be too sanguine," returned Nazimi, "lest we should be disappointed. But there is not a moment to be lost. Everything is at present favourable to our designs; the guard have been indulging so freely in arrack, that they are most of them asleep, and the rest are quite insensible, therefore I trust that there will not be much difficulty in leaving the house unobserved. The darkness of the night is also in our favour, once beyond the city walls, by using all necessary precaution, we may probably at this hour of the night, pursue our flight in safety. This veil may serve to conceal you. Should I be fortunate enough to be instrumental in your escape from the power of such a blood-thirsty miscreant as Nena Sahib, who doubtless in his own mind has already doomed you to a frightful death, I shall indeed be happy."

Again Omelia could scarcely find words sufficiently powerful to express her thanks, but Nazimi checked her, reminding her of the dangers of delay, and placing a long veil, which she had brought with her, over her head, took her hand tremulously, and whispering her to keep strict silence and preserve strict precaution, she led her from the chamber, and they entered the passage beyond.

This they traversed as silently as possible, our heroine maintaining her confidence and fortitude, and Nazimi seeming to acquire firmness as they proceeded.

After passing through several apartments without any obstruction, they at last arrived at the open door of the guard-room, which it was necessary that they should cross in order to reach the court yard, and it was here that the danger was most imminent, for it was in that room that the mutineers who should have been on duty, were assembled, and the heavy breathing of those who slept soundly from the effects of intoxication, saluted the ears of our heroine and her companion.

They paused, and by their looks seemed to consult each other how to proceed.

There was a lamp burning in the room, and silently drawing near the door, they had a distinct view of the interior. The men, of whom there was about half a dozen, were lying in different directions about the room, and all appeared to be sleeping or in a state of insensibility. The door which opened upon the court-yard, and which was on the opposite side of the room, was standing partially open, and could they but gain that, their liberty would be half accomplished.

But in this, from the manner in which the men were disposed, there would be some danger, should any of them be disturbed. However, Omelia was the first to take courage, and whispering to Nazimi, she offered to take the lead in entering the room, if she felt any timidity in doing so.

This, however, seemed to arouse Nazimi from her temporary feeling of fear, and she immediately entered the room, as cautiously as possible, and followed closely by Omelia, who observing a dagger lying on the floor by the side of one of the men, secured it, thinking that it might be useful to defend herself in case of danger.

To gain the door, they had to pass the table on which the lamp was burning, and it was just at that spot that two or three of the men were lying in such a position, as to obstruct their passage, and it would be neces-

sary to step over them as quietly as possible, in order to avoid disturbing them.

In doing this, however, the foot of Nazimi accidentally came in contact with some weapon on the floor, and she stumbled against one of the prostrate men, and had great difficulty in preventing herself from falling upon him.

He was aroused and murmured something, at the same time stretching forth his hands, and their detection might have been certain, had not Omelia, with great presence of mind instantly extinguished the light, and seizing the arm of Nazimi hurried her noiselessly towards the door, before the man could become sensible as to the cause of his being disturbed.

Fortunately they gained the court-yard in safety, and closing the door as silently as possible, secured it on the outside as well as they could.

This was all the work of a few moments, and thus far their designs had been attended with success, and they felt renewed hope and courage. But they paused for a minute to recover themselves from the excitement into which this little incident had thrown them, and to consider how it was best to proceed, for they had yet some obstacles to surmount before they could gain the outside of the building.

They listened at the door for an instant, but all was still within the room they had just quitted, save the loud breathing of the men, which satisfied them that they were safe from any discovery by them, and they felt thankful that they had thus escaped the first danger which had threatened them.

They looked anxiously around the court-yard, as well as the darkness would permit them, but they observed nothing to alarm them, there was no one to be seen, and fortune seemed to favour them in their undertaking.

"Thank providence," ejaculated our heroine, in a low voice, "I trust we shall yet accomplish our object. Courage, Nazimi, and we shall soon be beyond the precincts of this hated building. Let us not delay a moment, but proceed. I was fully prepared to brave every danger we may yet have to encounter."

"We have a wall to scale," said Nazimi, in the same whispering tone; "for we cannot hope to be able to unfasten the heavy gates, neither would it be safe to attempt to emerge that way, as sentries are probably placed there. But there is usually a ladder standing inside the wall, which, if it is not removed, will assist us. Quick and cautious."

She took the hand of Omelia, and they stepped quickly but lightly across the yard towards the spot where Nazimi said the ladder generally stood.

They had not proceeded many paces, however, when the heavy tread of footsteps across the yard, in the direction in which they were advancing saluted their ears, and hastily they drew back into the shade in trembling anxiety and alarm, fearing that their light dresses might betray them. They contrived to conceal themselves near one of the abutments of the building which they had gained, and there awaited the result in a state of considerable doubt and trepidation.

They were not kept a minute in suspense, for immediately they saw two or three of the rebel sepoys approaching, probably to go on guard in some part of the building, and they passed so near the place where our heroine and her companion were standing that they considered it almost impossible they should not perceive them.

They, however, passed hastily on without doing so, and going towards the guard-house shortly disappeared, and Omelia and Nazimi felt happily relieved from the fears that had so strongly assailed them.

The coast was now again clear, and issuing again from the place of their concealment, they breathlessly traversed the courtyard, and passing the gates that Nazimi had mentioned, gained that portion of the wall where they fortunately beheld the ladder standing much to their relief and satisfaction.

Here they again paused to take breath, and while they did so, they again heard the heavy tread of footsteps, and the voices of men outside the wall, and their fears and misgivings were renewed.

"Assist me in placing the ladder against the wall," whispered our heroine, "and I will ascend and endeavour to ascertain the extent of the risk we have to run. We must be firm, for we have now gone too far to recede."

Nazimi silently obeyed, and the ladder having been placed against the wall, Omelia mounted it, and cautiously peeped over, and she then perceived several persons, apparently not connected with the house of Nena Sahib, passing along and engaged in conversation.

She watched them eagerly till they were hidden from her sight in the darkness, and again the danger seemed to be past, for as far as her eyes could penetrate through the obscurity, she could see nothing calculated to excite any apprehension.

"Quick, Nazimi," said Omelia, "and ascend the ladder, for all seems now secure, and the moment of liberty has arrived."

Nazimi needed no second injunction to follow these instructions, and hastily ascending the ladder, they both clambered to the top of the wall, where having stood a moment, to recover themselves from their exertions, then, with some difficulty, they drew the ladder up after them, and placed it on the other side of the wall in order to descend, and in another minute they both alighted in safety below, and had accomplished their escape from the building.

They looked timidly and anxiously around, but all was buried in silence and profound darkness, and, having hastily removed to a retired spot, they sank on their knees, and fervently returned their thanks to providence for having thus far aided them in their perilous efforts.

CHAPTER XXXVIII.

THE FUGITIVES ON THEIR FLIGHT.—FARTHER ADVENTURES.

It required all the energy and perseverence that Omelia and her companion could summon to their aid, to proceed with safety, notwithstanding they had so far succeeded in their designs, and many persons would have shrunk with fear from the anticipation of the perils they had probably yet to meet and to surmount ere they could possibly consider themselves in complete safety. But they took courage, and were determined to accomplish their purpose, or perish in the attempt, for, in the opinion of Omelia, no fate could be worse than to continue in the power and at the mercy of such a monster as Nena Sahib.

At present everything seemed to favour them, the darkness, the lateness of the hour, and the apparent desertion of the streets of the city, and if they could once get beyond that without discovery, they flattered themselves that the principal danger would be past, and they had the most sanguine hopes of their ultimate triumph over their difficulties."

Nazimi, who was thoroughly acquainted with every portion of the city, of course undertook to be the guide, and she led the way through the most bye streets towards the nearest outlet into the open country, they indulging in but little conversation, and that being conducted in whispers, though they had great difficulty in refraining from giving vent to the various feelings that agitated their breasts.

Many were the thoughts that crowded upon the brain of Omelia, as they proceeded, and various were the hopes and fears that alternately beset her. What was the fate of her lover? Did he still survive, or had he been included in the long dark catalogue of the unfortunate victims of the savage miscreants who now seemed to triumph in their barbarity? This was the principal torturing reflection that distracted her, and it was in vain that she tried to dismiss it, or to quiet the dismal apprehensions and forebodings that haunted her.

And then what had become of poor Flora Melville? Was she still safe in the cavernous retreat of the hermit, or had she sunk beneath her heavy bereavement? Even if she had not done so, how truly forlorn and deplorable must be her situation, deprived of her society, and how terrible and distracting must be her anxiety, fear, and suspense at her alarming disappearance, and under such painful and suspicious circumstances.

These thoughts passed rapidly through the mind of Omelia, but her whole attention and interest were quickly absorbed in the prosecution of the hazardous flight of herself and Nazimi, and the care and precaution that were necessary to bring it to anything like a successful issue.

Notwithstanding the lateness of the hour, and the unfrequented route which they pursued, they met several persons on the way, who, however, perceiving that they were natives, passed them without taking any particular notice of them, or apparently entertaining any suspicion of them, and this circumstance inspired them with still more confidence, and they quickened their steps, and after walking for about half an hour through gloomy streets, which showed no signs of life, and many of the houses of which were in ruins; from the guns of Nena Sahib some weeks before, they arrived at the narrow outlet which Nazimi sought, and which was not generally known.

That part of their difficult task was accomplished and they found themselves not only without the walls of the city, but on a spot so lonely and retired, that it seemed to afford every present security, while the country before them presented every means of concealment in case of necessity.

They walked to some short distance and then stopped to rest themselves, and to look back upon that city, their escape from which appeared not only miraculous, but almost more than they could persuade themselves was a fact, but when the gratifying truth forced itself upon them, their emotions may be readily conceived, and they threw themselves into each other's arms, and mingled their tears together.

"Oh, Nazimi," exclaimed Omelia, in tones that fully testified the sincerity of what she spoke, "what a vast debt of gratitude do I not owe you for the inestimable service you have rendered me, and in what way can I ever sufficiently repay it?"

"Name it not," answered Nazimi, "I have done no more than what common humanity ought to suggest, especially towards one of my own sex. Besides, have I not in assisting your escape, also effected my own from a fate, the horror and degradation of which were almost beyond human endurance?"

"True," coincided our heroine; "and nothing, I assure you, my good Nazimi, can afford me greater satisfaction than that circumstance. I sincerely hope that your troubles are now at an end, and that you will shortly be restored to that happiness from which unfortunately you have been so long estranged."

"Alas," sighed Nazimi, "I dare not encourage that flattering hope. I fear to return to my home, although so anxious, and now that the opportunity of doing so appears to present itself, for terrible must be the change which has there taken place since I deserted it. My beloved parents I am certain could never survive my loss; I may find that home desolate, my other relations either dead, or scattered I know not whither, and to whom can I then look for protection, for sympathy, or consolation?"

"Banish those dismal thoughts from your mind, Nazimi," returned Omelia, "and try to look forward with hope to the future. At any rate should your worst apprehensions be realized, as we are sisters in adversity, and companions in the flight from the terrors by which we were surrounded, we will in future share our fortunes together."

"You are good, you are virtuous, and possessed of every noble quality that can render woman estimable, Omelia," observed Nazimi, "and I fear that I but little merit your friendship. But why do we linger here, when our deliverance from danger may be still incomplete? In spite of fatigue, we must still continue our flight till we have got to some considerable distance from the city, and while the darkness of night befriends us, for should our escape be discovered in time pursuit would doubtless be immediately set on foot, and they might yet overtake us."

"True," said Omelia, "there is indeed no time to lose. Are you well acquainted with the way through the apparently intricate part of the country which is before us?"

"Yes," replied Nazimi; "the journey will be a toilsome one, and I fear it will sadly tax your strength and patience to undergo it. The nearest village where we may hope to find secure rest and shelter for the present, is at a distance of not less than three coss from here, and to reach it we must journey through a wild and dangerous part of the country, many parts of which is infested with wild beasts, that frequently afford sport to those who have the courage to hunt them."

Omelia could not help shuddering, for those were dangers indeed sufficiently alarming, but she quickly recovered her firmness and composure, and said :—

"Previous to our entering upon the execution of our design, my good Nazimi, I was well aware that it would be fraught with numerous perils, and stated that I was fully prepared to brave them, and I will not suffer my fortitude to forsake me. Fear not but that the power which has befriended us so far will continue to watch over and protect us. But is your native home, where you are so anxious to return, far distant?"

"Oh, yes," replied Nazimi, "it is far, very far from hence, on the way to Lucknow; and I almost fear that I shall never be able to accomplish so long a journey, though I have the pecuniary means to assist me in doing

so. But come, Omelia, pray let us at once proceed."

To this Omelia assented, and taking each other's arm, they resumed their journey as quickly as they could, and soon got a considerable distance from the city, striking into the most thickly entangled and intricate part, where they might easily find concealment in the event of pursuit; but although the way which Nazimi conducted was wild and gloomy enough, sufficient to daunt the courage of ordinary minds, and it was no less tedious and difficult to traverse, being thoroughly acquainted with the locality, she carefully avoided that part which she knew led to one wide, vast, and inhospitable waste, without a vestige of inhabitants or cultivation, intersected by nullahs in every direction and abounding in swamps.

No. 21.

There the jungles sprang up luxuriantly, and became the haunt of innumerable tigers, and wild animals of all descriptions. The annual inroads of sportsmen did not seem much to diminish the number of the tigers; year after year they were killed in the same spots, and it appeared that a desirable covert was no sooner vacated by the death of one than another took possession of it.

On then proceeded the fugitives in their dreary course, endeavouring to keep up their spirits as well as they could, though frequently almost overcome by the fatigue which the numerous obstacles they had to surmount caused them, and compelled them to stop to rest themselves; and the further they went the more did those obstacles seem to accumulate, and were sufficient to exhaust the patience, and to crush the hopes of even the most resolute persons, especially those of two delicate females who had already undergone so much exertion in effecting their escape from the place of their confinement and the city.

The gloom and cheerlessness of the night, or rather the morning, for it was then past midnight, was more than enough to dishearten them, for the darkness was intense, and the wind howled mournfully around, as if to mock and intimidate them on their way, and sometimes they could not help imagining that these sounds proceeded from wild beasts lurking near, and who might at any moment spring upon them, without the least possibility of their avoiding them, and, in spite of all their efforts to control them, their fears increased to an insupportable degree, and they frequently paused to listen, afraid and uncertain which way to proceed for better safety.

Thus more than an hour elapsed, and they seemed to have made but little progress, for the place they were toiling through was almost impenetrable, and every moment they appeared to become still more entangled and bewildered in its mazes, and Omelia anxiously inquired of her companion whether she was certain that they were not wandering from the direction she had intended them to take, or that they were not becoming involved in a dilemma from which it might be almost impossible to extricate themselves, to which Nazimi returned very doubtful answers, and at last candidly confessed that she was quite bewildered and uncertain, and at the same time she evinced symptoms of failing strength that added to their alarm.

Their situation was now most fearful, for notwithstanding her endeavours to disguise it, Omelia also felt nearly exhausted, and they now again stopped, and in vain tried to conjecture what it was best for them to do.

"Alas," ejaculated Nazimi, "what a terrible disappointment is this, after the success which at first seemed to attend us. The desperate nature of our design is now but too apparent, and I fear that we must yet fail fully to accomplish our wishes. Alas, what will become of us?"

"This is indeed most torturing," said our heroine, "but still we must exert ourselves to the utmost, and not give way to despair. Cannot you form any idea of the way in which we may extricate ourselves from this alarming difficulty, for to remain here in this horrible state of uncertainty may be attended with the worst consequences."

"I am bewildered and distracted, and know not how to act," answered Nazimi; "the intense darkness also increases my perplexity."

"Let us again, at any rate, proceed,' 'said Omelia, "and trust to the goodness of providence to assist us. It surely will not desert us in this fearful emergency. Courage, my friend, and companion in danger, whatever may be the result of this night's adventure, you at least are not to blame."

"I fear that you cannot much longer find strength to support this unusual and extraordinary fatigue," observed Nazimi, "and I cannot conceal the fact that I feel almost exhausted, and as if I could not possibly bear up against the difficulties that increase around us."

"We will persevere," returned Omelia, "and something may occur to release us from our present alarming and uncertain situation much sooner than we now expect. Come, let us still struggle on our dreary way, Time wears apace, and ere long it will be daylight."

They did indeed both exert themselves to the utmost, and having again supplicated the aid of Omnipotence, they once more resumed their weary and almost hopeless journey, but for some time they had the greatest dificulty in making any progress, and so far from their prospect of extricating themselves from the bewildering maze in which they had become entangled becoming brighter, it seemed to grow more gloomy and hopeless every minute, while their limbs trembled, and almost refused any longer to support them.

In spite of all her endeavours to conquer or conceal them, the most serious apprehensions assailed the breast of our heroine, and the hopes in which she had ventured to indulge on their being able to leave the city without discovery or molestation, began to fade away.

The weather, however, suddenly improved, the wind ceased to howl, and bellow among the closely intertwining branches of the giant trees that grew so thickly around, and the black clouds that had hitherto covered the sky like a funeral pall, gradually dispersed, and suffered a faint light, as day began to break, to impart something like a degree of comparative cheerfulness to the wild scenery by which the fugitives were encompassed, and had been so long bewildered.

This unexpected change somewhat re-animated the spirits of Omelia and her companion; and their hopes greatly revived as the wilds they were traversing became gradually less intricate, and they were enabled to proceed with considerable less difficulty than they had done for some time before. Still their strength continued to yield, not only to the physical exertions they had undergone, but to the great mental anxiety they had experienced, and they felt that it would be utterly impossible to proceed much farther without resting themselves. All danger of pursuit, or discovery in the place they now were, seemed to be entirely at an end, and as regarded that they endeavoured to make their minds perfectly easy.

The dull grey mists gradually yielded to the more powerful light of opening day, and the first golden tint of the rising sun appeared in the eastern horizon, and broke through the green foliage, which formed a canopy above the travellers' heads, affording a great relief to the solemn gloom in which everything had so long been enveloped. And as this agreeable change took place, they suddenly emerged into a more open space, from which, for the first time, they caught a view of the distant mountains whose lofty summits were buried in the clouds, and here Nazimi again fancied she had some knowledge of that part of the country upon which they were entering.

But at this time fatigue, and a drowsy sensation, that was quite irresistible, overpowered them both, and they felt themselves quite incapable of journeying any further until they had rested for awhile.

A fitting spot, a bed of wild flowers of every variety of hue, beneath the wide spreading branches of two gigantic tress, met their observation, and there, after having committed themselves to the care and protection of providence, they stretched their weary limbs, and soon slept as soundly as if they had been reposing on a bed of down.

Little did they dream of the fearful danger which threatened them.

CHAPTER XXXIX.

A FRIGHTFUL CATASTROPHE.

Not far from the spot where our heroine and her companion were unconsciously reposing, was a jungle skirting a meadow or wheat land, and where oxen either graze or draw the plough, but which could scarcely have been expected so near those gloomy and intricate wilds through which they had so long been travelling.

Such a place is the tiger's chief haunt. Tiger hunting is, or rather was—for it is greatly diminished now—the reader will scarcely require to be informed, one of the most favourite of the sports of India.

It would not be safe to risk the encounter of a tiger on horseback. Elephants, therefore, are put into requisition, and are trebly useful in conveying the sportsman to the field, protecting him from the tiger's charge, and assisting in the destruction of the " feline monster."

It is seldom that the tiger makes a sortie from the jungle, that he does not succeed in capturing a heifer or a young buffalo. When therefore the death of a troublesome scourge of the herds is resolved on, it is not unusual to bait the field with a cow, whose lowings at night attract the tiger. The latter sallies forth, seizes the prey, destroys it at once, and is found in the morning filled to repletion by his nocturnal repast.

The sportsmen, occupying howdahs on the backs of elephants, well armed with a couple of rifles each, which a servant keeps continually loaded, and provided with cigars, biscuits, and brandy-and-water, or pale ale, advance in line upon the tiger, and the moment he is sighted, salute him with a volley.

Death is often the immediate result, and nothing then remains to be done, but to provide the carcase with a carriage home, which is generally accomplished by throwing it over the back of an elephant, not already encumbered with a howdah.

Sometimes, however, and not unfrequently, the tiger is only wounded, or perhaps alarmed, then the combat indeed becomes desperate. With a growl and a roar, the infuriated beast springs upon the back of the elephant, and has been known by his weight to roll the latter, sportsmen and all, on to the earth; a critical situation, from whence the prostrate party are only rescued by a judiciously directed shot from a companion sportsman, who has just come up.

If the elephant on the other hand, can only sustain his weight, the tiger makes an effort to reach the tenants of the howdah. This is a dangerous position, especially for the *mahout* or driver, who is seated on the elephant's neck and has only the *hankas* or iron hook with which he urges and directs the elephant's course, wherewith to defend himself.

But if the danger of the sportsman is augmented by this charge, so also is the danger of the tiger. He has brought himself within a few feet of the deadly rifle, and it will be strange indeed if he escapes the shot directed at his *os frontis* or his chest:

Instances have been known of a tiger's tearing a sportsman off his seat, and bearing him away to the jungle, but these casualties are very rare. Ordinarily the animal falls to the repeated shots, and is carried home that his skin, well dressed, may be converted into a rug or howdah carpet, or despatched as a present to a loving friend at the Presidency or in England.

Great is the misfortune for a village when a tiger once carries off a peasant, for having once tasted of human blood, his voracity becomes enormous, and he will not be easily contented with any other description of food.

A tiger who destroys men, is called, *par excellence*, "man tiger." In the Saugor and Nerbudda teritories the natives have an idea, that after a tiger has killed one man, the rest of mankind are safe, for the spirit of the man rides upon his head and conducts him to his prey. They also believe that tigers without tails, (for such there are, victims of accident, conflict, or disease) are men, who have converted themselves into tigers, by eating of a particular root, which effects the metamorphosis at once.

Tigers that have once tasted of human blood, will establish themselves in some narrow pass, where they wait in ambush for passers by, men who carry the letter-bags, being their principal victims.

Should there be any European station at hand, the monster is soon sacrificed; but when the villagers can have no assistance of the kind, ten or twelve victims have been known to fall under the insatiable appetite of the savage, before the country has been sufficiently aroused against him to take effectual measures for his destruction.

A reward of five hundred rupees (fifty pounds) is sometimes offered by the native chief of a district, for the head of a tiger, that has become formidable to the people of a village; and a general muster of men and weapons takes place, in consequence of this stimulant to action.

Having ascertained the haunt of the tiger, where he lies in wait, to spring from the bush, which forms his cover, on the unhappy passengers who endeavour to cross the path, the whole hunt assembles, and the wilderness swarms with men; every tree is converted into a watch tower; the circle is formed, which, pressing in upon all sides, contract, until, completely hemmed in, the tiger roused in his lair, and, opposed in every direction, meets his death.

Tiger hunting is rapidly declining as a sport, under the auspices of the ploughshare. In forme times, there was no district in India more celebrated for its tiger shooting than Goruckpore, near the Nepaul frontier. Year after year parties proceeded to its apparently inexhaustible terai, and always returned with the spoils of numerous of these magnificent animals.

In the time of Sir Roger Martin, there was a well known tiger on the Nepaul frontier, who was the terror of the neighbouring villagers; man was his food, and he seemed to prey upon any inferior animal. He once attempted the enter the hut of a taroo, but the inmate received him with such a blow on the head with a jungh axe, that the tiger was glad to retreat, and carried the scar of the wound to his dying day.

By this scar he was known and recognised, and his depredations at last became so serious that Sir Roger Martin went out for the express purpose of killing him. He shot forty-eight tigers before he fell in with the one he was in search of, but the forty-ninth was "Le Balafre" himself, who fell fighting to the last, and well supported his former character for ferocity.

But to return to Omelia and her companion.

How long the former had slept, unconsciously in the very vicinity of the most terrible danger, she knew not, but she was suddenly aroused by a loud noise, which seemed to shake the neighbouring forest, and starting to her feet, she gazed eagerly and fearfully around her, anticipating the nature of the danger that threatened; but for the moment she saw nothing to warrant her alarm.

It was strange that the noise had not awoke Nazimi, but there she slept as soundly as at first.

Omelia, certain that there was something fearful to apprehend, hastily tried to arouse her, and she had scarcely succeeded in doing so, when the sound—which was the howling of some wild beast—was repeated, and Omelia casting her eyes in terror in the direction from whence it proceeded, the horror of her feelings may be readily conceived, when she beheld, coming towards them from the jungle, a large tiger; which seemed to have fixed its savage eyes upon them, and marked them for its prey.

She shrieked, but had the presence of mind —thinking that Nazimi would follow her example—to immediately ascend with all the rapidity she could one of the lofty trees, beneath the shade of whose branches they had been reposing.

But poor Nazimi seemed to be completely paralyzed, and was transfixed to the spot on which she was standing, and gazing with horror upon the ferocious monster which was now rapidly approaching to her certain destruction.

Omelia having gained the loftiest branch of the tree, was, for the present in comparative safety; but her every faculty was enchained in terror, and she could not utter a sound, which might have urged Nazimi to make a desperate effort to escape the dreadful fate which otherwise awaited her There the unfortunate woman stood, immovable as a statue.

Another moment, and a fearful shriek was heard, which told too fatally that the ferocious beast had sprang upon his prey, and that the awful fate of poor Nazimi was sealed.

The blood froze within our heroine's veins, her heart sickened, and for an instant she closed her eyes, unable to meet the appalling sight which she knew they would have to encounter, but when she did look, to her horror she beheld the unfortunate Nazimi in the tiger's jaws, which was hurrying back with its prey to the jungles, and soon disappeared.

Language must fail to describe the feelings of Omelia at this awful catastrophe. She could not speak, she could not utter the least sound, she could not move, so completely horror-struck as she was, at the frightful event; and so sudden, and unexpected had it been that she could scarcely persuade herself of its reality, or that it was not some fearful dream; and she remained for some minutes in the same distracted state of mind, and still gazing wildly towards the spot where the tiger had disappeared; but when the shocking fate of her companion was made apparent to her without a doubt, the horror and agony of her thoughts and emotions were almost beyond endurance.

CHAPTER XL.

THE DEATH STRUGGLE. — THE FATE OF YUNADAR.

The sense of her own imminent danger, while she remained there, should the savage beast return, however, soon aroused Omelia, and, first looking carefully and anxiously from the tree, to satisfy herself that all was at present safe, she descended, and alighted safely on the ground, in the midst of the horror created by the appalling occurrence,

grateful to providence for her own almost miraculous deliverance.

For a moment or two she stopped to consider what to do, and which way to proceed, and having cast one more lingering look towards the jungle, with the wild and futile hope to behold Nazimi, and to find, that by some wonderful interposition of heaven, she had been rescued from death, she hurriedly bent her way in an opposite direction, towards the distant mountains, in the forlorn hope of meeting with some village.

Nothing could now be possibly more gloomy and disheartening than the situation of Omelia stranger as she was to that wild part of the country, and deprived of the guidance and advice of Nazimi, and her courage almost forsook her, and she could scarcely help abandoning herself to complete despair.

She looked anxiously on every side, but saw nothing to encourage her hopes; an extensive tract of country was before her, but not the least signs of a human habitation, and unless she met with some speedy relief, in spite of all her efforts to bear up, she felt convinced that her strength must fail her.

And fearfully did she feel her loneliness, now that poor Nazimi was so unfortunately taken from her, and she could not help weeping bitterly at her dreadful and untimely death.

"Ill-fated woman," she soliloquised, "how my heart bleeds at the thought of your horrible fate. Had you not yielded to my supplications, and consented to become the companion of my flight, this would not have happened to you, I shudder with horror at the recollection of the frightful scene I have just witnessed, and which can never be effaced from my memory."

For a few minutes Omelia abandoned herself entirely to these melancholy reflections, and deeply, sincerely did she lament the awful circumstance which had so tragically terminated the existence of Nazimi, and deprived her of a friend and companion to whom she was so greatly indebted, and whose services she so much required, to guide her in her present perilous and uncertain way.

But knowing the danger of delay and the necessity of prompt and energetic action, she aroused herself, and once more became armed with hope and fortitude to surmount every obstacle she might have to encounter.

"Yes," she said, as she resumed her tedious and dreary journey; "I will be firm, and put my trust in that power, which knows the integrity of my motives, and which has never yet deserted me in the hour of danger. Dear Stanley, were I but convinced of your safety, I could be content. But providence will, I hope protect one so good, so noble, and so honourable, and grant that your faithful Indian maid will ere long once more be restored to your arms."

As she thus spoke she took from her bosom a minature likeness of her lover, which, at her request, he had given to her some months previously; and after gazing at it earnestly for a few minutes, and pressing it fondly again and again to her lips, she replaced it in her bosom and resumed her journey, hoping soon to reach some habitation or village where she might obtain that rest and refreshment of which she stood so much in need.

The sun was now in the meridian, and the heat was most oppressive, still, weary as she was with anxiety and excitement of mind, as well as from bodily exertion, she continued to toil on her way with that indomitable courage and perseverance which was one of her most distinguished characteristics.

After proceeding for some time, the country presented a less cheerful aspect, and her spirits revived, although she severely felt the loss she had sustained in the death of Nazimi, to whom she could communicate her thoughts, and whose generous sympathy so greatly served to dissipate her cares, and lead her on to hope.

The scenery amongst which she was now travelling was diversified, picturesque, and romantic in the extreme; and, as Omelia was a most enthusiastic admirer of the beauties of nature, the contemplation of them, where they abounded in such luxuriance, served, in a great measure, to divert her thoughts from the melancholy subjects that had before engrossed them, and to cheer her on her way.

As she farther advanced, wonder upon wonder accumulated; still directing her course towards those stupenduous mountains, soaring to the sky, and giving to the whole of the prospect, from their arrangement, and disposition by the hand of Omnipotence, the appearance of one vast, magnificent, and glorious amphitheatre; on which the sun in its golden majesty threw a flood of splendour, that made everything smile, and seem to revel in grandeur and sublimity, lifting the soul up from nature unto " Nature's God."

The farther Omelia proceeded on her adventurous journey, and the nearer she approached those majestic mountains, on either side, or to whatever point her anxious eyes were directed, fresh scenes burst upon her vision to excite her wonder and admiration. It seemed as though the whole of the beautiful in nature of the Eastern world, were concentrated in that particular locality. All that is rich in vegetation was there, the eye could not wander to any spot without encountering it in abundance.

The tropical lands are proverbially rich in vegetation. Nature has lavished upon them all her choicest gifts. The most gigantic trees, the densest forests, the broadest leaves, the largest flowers, the most luxurious creepers, luscious, fruits, nutritious vegetables, herbs of overpowering fragrance, simples of inestimable efficacy—a pharmacopeia unrivalled. These are the characteristics of the spontaneous vegetation of India.

Nowhere is there such abundance or such infinite variety. But man, not content with the free offerings of nature, or anxious to recognise and expand her fertility, has employed all the resources of art to evolve the powers of the soil, and to add to the stores of the east the useful and wholesome productions of the west, while piety has laboured to increase the indigenous offspring of the land, and commerce has demanded a multiplication of those trees which enjoy favour in countries where vegetation is comparatively scant.

It seemed that in the locality which our heroine was now traversing all the trees for which India is most celebrated, had congregated, and arranged themselves fantastically, at intervals, so as not to interfere with, or obstruct the general prospect, in order to afford the most splendid samples to the eyes of the wondering and delighted traveller.

Here was to be seen the tall, straight talipot or talpat, soaring to the height of from eighty to a hundred feet, with its large tuft of immense leaves crowning its summit; there, the peepul, growing in such abundance in all parts of India, and, as some suppose, spontaneously, and the branches of which afford so grateful a shade from the scorching heat of the sun. More wonderful still that this tree should make its appearance in that part of the country. It seemed, in some strange mood to have rambled from its favourite spots, merely to join company, and add to the effect of its noble brethren.

The peepul usually makes its appearance by the sides of the flights of stone steps leading down to *bowlies*, or large wells, above the domes of mosques, through the walls of gardens, &c.

Again, turning the eye in different directions, it met the teak, the palm, the bamboo, and the stupenduous banyan, some of which latter tree are of amazing size, as they are continually increasing, and, unlike most things in animal and vegetable life, they appear to be exempt from decay. There are some banyan trees in India which actually measure several thousand feet in circumference, and can afford shade and shelter to 8,000 persons.

Lost in wonder and delight as these objects met her enraptured sight, our heroine continued on her way, her mind experiencing for awhile, a happy respite from the gloomy and painful thoughts that had before occupied it, until she suddenly found herself within a short distance of that chain of lofty mountains to which her course had been directed, and she felt surprised that she could have travelled so far, in so short a time, and with comparatively speaking, little or no exertion.

She advanced towards an opening between two of the most gigantic of these mountains, and the prospect which there met her view, increased her wonder, and heightened her hopes of approaching some spot of human habitation, from the grove of mango trees which met her gaze immediately before her.

There is nothing for which the sylvan scenery of India is more remarkable than the groves of palm and mungo trees, planted all over the empire. A strong religious feeling influences the Hindoo in these plantations. He believes that his soul in the next world is benefitted by the blessings and grateful feelings of those of his fellow creatures who, unmolested, eat the fruit and enjoy the shade of the trees he has planted during his sojourn in this world.

The names of the great men who built the castles, palaces, and tombs at Delhi and Agra, have been almost forgotten, because no one enjoys any advantages from them, but the names of those who planted the mango groves, are still supposed to be remembered by all who eat of their fruit, sit in their shade, and drink of their water, from whatever part of the world they come.

How grateful then was the sight to Omelia in her present exhausted condition. Here for a time could she rest herself beneath the shade of the umbrageous foliage; refresh herself from the luscious fruit the branches of those graceful and friendly trees yielded in such abundance, and from the pure water of the spring, and then could she resume her journey with recruited strength and courage.

Her heart overflowed with gratitude to that Supreme power which had hitherto protected her and guided her footsteps, and, with a light heart—for it was now buoyed up with hope and confidence—she entered the grove, and having gathered some of the fruit, and slaked her thirst from the spring, by the aid of a shell which she found lying near, she sought out a convenient spot, and there, at any rate, apprehending no similar danger to that from which she had so providentially and miraculously escaped, she threw herself on the verdant turf, and yielded to the influence of fatigue, hoping afterwards to be able to proceed, and to arrive at some village where she could obtain the information she required to assist her on her uncertain journey.

Her spirits gradually became calm, and sleep almost insensibly stole upon her eyelids.

Strange dreams arose to her perturbed imagination, and many were the ideal scenes which, in her sleeping moments, she wandered through. Again she felt herself enfolded in the warm embrace of her lover, saw his eyes fondly gazing with all the earnestness of intense passion in her countenance, and listened with transport to his repeated vows of imperishable affection. Then she thought that the happy time had arrived which was to unite their fates for ever, and all around bespoke alone the future bliss which was in store for them. The very face of nature seemed adorned with its brightest smiles, beauteous flowers, as if by magic, appeared to spring up in their path, and to fill the air with their balmy and delightful fragrance, and the gentle zephyrs that wafted by, appeared to breathe blessings on their union, and to encourage them on to hope and happiness.

But suddenly the aspect of everything was fearfully changed; the sky, before so clear and transparent, became overcast with black and ponderous clouds, the thunder roared, the lightning flashed, a deluge of rain descended, the earth trembled and yawned, as if from the shock of an earthquake, and every imaginable horror reigned predominant.

Gradually, though she tried to cling to him, her lover seemed to shrink from her embrace, and his features became black and distorted. There was a loud peal of thunder more terrific than any which had preceeded it, this was immediately followed by a cry of the most excruciating agony, and Stanley sunk finally from her arms, prostrate on the earth, a blackened and disfigured corpse.

Wrought up to a pitch of indescribable horror and despair, with the shock she awoke, and gazed wildly, and in the utmost state of bewilderment around her, for the moment quite unconscious where she was.

To her astonishment, and showing the time she must have slept, it was growing quite dark, and distant objects were wrapped in deep gloom. She arose to her feet, but her brain was so distracted by her dream, that she seemed rivetted to the spot, and for several minutes was totally unable to collect herself, but when she did so, and was enabled to reflect upon all the circumstances of her singular vision, the anguish of her feelings increased, and in spite of all her efforts to conquer them the most dismal forbodings took possession of her mind.

However, she felt, notwithstanding the excitement which her remarkable dream naturally caused, much recruited in strength by the rest she had obtained, and again hoping to alight on some place where she might obtain the assistance and information she required, she resumed her solitary journey.

But the farther she proceeded, the more distant appeared the prospect of the realisation of her hopes. And now the cheerful aspect of the country was again entirely changed, and all was dreary, wild, and threatening

The weather too again became unfavourable, and the darkness of the night—which had now quite set in—was of itself sufficient to dishearten the unfortunate wanderer; still she maintained her fortitude much better than might have been expected.

Could she only have met some friendly individual who would inform her the way she was pursuing, she would have been more content; but to keep travelling on in a part of the country to which she was an entire stranger, was only involving herself still further in perplexities from which she knew not how to extricate herself.

It was, however, to waste time in hesitation or fear, and again commending herself to the care and protection of providence, she hastened on, avoiding a dense forest, and pursuing her way through the more open part of the country.

Thus then did Omelia, with the greatest patience and perseverence continue her journey for more than an hour without any prospect of that she needed presenting itself, and nothing could equal the savage features of the scenery which met her gaze on every side. Mountain steeps, and frightful precipices, yawning gulfs, and roaring cataracts, deep forests in the distance, and not one single spot which seemed to lead to hope, these were its gloomy characteristics, and certainly nothing could be more sad and disheartening.

She had just emerged from a thicket, and was making her way, almost unconsciously—for her mind was wearied and bewildered—up a lofty eminence, from the summit of which—the moon having arisen—it was likely she might obtain a more extensive view of the country, and be able the better to shape her course, when suddenly she was startled by the report of a pistol, and the voices of men in anger.

Alarmed, she drew back, and concealed herself as well as she could in the shade and awaited the issue of this adventure with some anxiety.

She was not long kept in suspense. The voices grew louder, and several angry expressions distinctly met her ears, which added not a little to her fears, but whatever the danger was she had to apprehend, she must meet it boldly, there was no alternative, for it was impossible for her to await it, the voices of the men plainly showing that they were approaching near.

Another minute, and two human beings met her sight, struggling together up the steep, near where she was standing, and who in the moonlight, she could clearly observe.

She was transfixed to the spot on which she stood, and taken completely by surprise, was rendered powerless to act either one way or the other.

The combatants (for it was evident it was a struggle for life or death) were a European officer, and the tall and muscular form of a native, and the figure of the latter was strikingly familiar to her, and increased the interest and excitement which the circumstance taking place so unexpectedly and so suddenly naturally caused her.

Grappling with each other, and giving vent to their rage in the most violent exclamations, they approached so near that Omelia thought it was impossible that she could escape detection; but still they were too much engaged in angry strife she considered, to interfere with her.

The moonlight now clearly, from the position in which she stood, revealed their features to her, and Omelia uttered a cry of astonishment not unmingled with fear, when she recognised in the Indian whom the officer was struggling with, her guilty parent.

At the sound of her voice he turned his gaze towards her, and recognised her evidently immediately, but his antagonist grasped him so violently by the throat that he could not speak, though the expression of his features sufficiently showed the wonder and agony of his feelings. But the officer seemed to take little notice of her, his mind being too much occupied with the desperate combat in which he was engaged; and they passed her, struggling up the eminence towards the summit.

She followed them with all the haste she could, and calling upon the officer in the most urgent accents to forbear, for she saw that he had the advantage of her father, who seemed almost exhausted, but he heeded her not, and she was now worked up to a pitch of agony, for they were approaching a spot which overhung a fearful abyss, and where the fate of one or both of them seemed to be inevitable.

They reached the brink; they struggled more desperately than before, and the crisis of their fate was rapidly approaching. By a powerful effort the officer, (who was a man evidently possessed of much muscular strength) succeeded in forcing Yunadar on to one knee, and in pressing his body over the verge of the precipice, but still the sepoy retained his fierce hold of his antagonist, resolved that if he must die, he should perish with him.

It was a terrible moment, and but a moment only. A shriek of terror escaped Omelia,

and she rushed towards them, with the view of interposing to save her father's life, but it was too late, at the instant they both fell together from the fearful height, and their cries of agony, as they bounded from crag to crag to the depth below, smote her ears, and struck horror to her senses.

With frantic speed she rushed to the verge of the precipice and looked anxiously and fearfully below, and the moon which then shone forth more brightly than before, revealed every object to her distinctly; and there, on a level spot of land, she beheld the unfortunate men, lying close together, and no doubt crushed and shattered to death from the immense height from which they had fallen.

For a minute or two Omelia stood completely paralysed, and every faculty suspended

in horror, while the blood seemed to freeze in her veins. But while she still gazed in fear and trembling, and her brain turned giddy, she fancied that she saw her unfortunate father move, and therefore that life was not extinct.

She looked eagerly around to ascertain whether it was possible to reach the spot where he was lying, and resolved to make the attempt though it was a hazardous one, for the ascent was steep, and could only be accomplished by the utmost care and fortitude.

Firmly but slowly the heroic girl proceeded on her perilous task, the least false step being certain to precipitate her to the bottom; but her courage never for a moment forsook her, and after immense labour, and surmounting difficulties that seemed to be impossible, she

No. 22.

at length alighted safe on terra firm, a short distance from the spot where the two unfortunate men were lying, quite breathless with the extraordinary exertion she had undergone.

She soon, however, recovered herself, and, with a palpitating heart, she hastened to the fatal spot. The officer who was frightfully mutilated, was evidently quite dead, and her father was lying inanimate, the blood streaming from his head, and evincing no signs of life.

With feelings of the greatest agony—for all the guilt of her wretched parent was forgotten in the dreadful fate which had befallen him—Omelia stooped down, raised his head upon her bosom, and gazed with the deepest anguish in his face. His features were fearfully distorted, and his eyes appeared to be closed in death. Anxiously she placed her hand upon his bosom, and she then felt his heart faintly beat, which convinced her that she had not been mistaken, when she imagined she had seen him move, but that he would ever more revive to consciousness seemed to be entirely hopeless.

Not many minutes had elapsed, however, when the hopes of Omelia were revived, for his heart throbbed more freely, and a groan escaped his lips. She pressed his head still closer to her bosom, and in the agony and anxiety of her feelings called upon his name in the wild hope that it would arouse him to sensibility, and that hope appeared likely to be realised, for he opened his eyes, and fixed them for a moment on the countenance of Omelia with an expression which she could never forget, and seemed to make an effort to speak, but without success.

"Father, unfortunate father," exclaimed our heroine, in tones of anguish which it would be almost impossible to describe, " oh, speak to me, if it be only one word. It is your daughter, Omelia, who speaks to you."

Again the wretched Yunadar opened his eyes, and fixed them for a moment or two with the most solemn earnestness upon Omelia's countenance. Once more he made a powerful but ineffectual attempt to speak, then for a moment his limbs shook and trembled convulsively, his features frightfully distorted with agony, one fearful groan escaped him, and the guilty Yunadar's earthly career was at an end.

Omelia was deeply affected, and for a time she remained with her eyes fixed upon the features of her father, stern and rigid in death, with an expression of regret, and was fixed to the spot, immovable as a statue.

Notwithstanding his savage nature, and in spite of her never having scarcely experienced one act or word of kindness from him; and although she had in the family of the late Mr Melville and his daughter been estranged from him from childhood, she could not forget that he was her parent, and all the warm and affectionate feelings of nature were excited in her gentle and sympathising breast, while the thought of the dreadful fate he had met with filled her with horror.

" Unfortunate, misguided father," she soliloquised, as she still supported his head upon her bosom, and gazed in his ghastly countenance with feelings of the deepest sorrow, " why did you persist in that course of crime which sooner or later was sure to meet with the retribution of heaven? Alas, that you should meet with so dreadful and untimely a fate, and that in the midst of all your guilt. May the Almighty power pardon you, and receive your soul."

This wish she fervently felt and expressed, and tears filled her eyes, as she stretched the stiffening corpse upon the earth, and gazed mournfully upon it for a few minutes, incapable of arousing herself from the dismal and painful thoughts and emotions that agitated her breast. All the errors of her unhappy father, all the numerous wrongs he had inflicted upon her, the heartless neglect with which he had treated her, and the sufferings to which he had at times subjected her, were forgotten by her, in the regret and anguish which she felt at present at his frightful death; and she was filled with wonder to think that providence should direct her footsteps to the fatal spot at the critical moment, and make her a witness of the appalling catastrophe.

After some time passed in this melancholy manner, and her thoughts for awhile diverted from her own danger and difficulties, she turned her gaze towards the remains of the other unfortunate man, who it seemed had met with immediate death.

His features were much disfigured, but she could perceive that he had been a handsome man, apparently about thirty years of age. She could not refuse a tear at his awful fate, although he was a stranger to her.

She was unable to account for it, but she could not resist a feeling of curiosity to know who the stranger was, and kneeling down she proceeded to search his pockets, thinking that she might possibly discover something which might afford her the desired information.

She found a well filled purse in one of his pockets, which would doubtless be of the greatest value to her in the prosecution of her tedious journey. Searching farther, she discovered a pocket-book, which on opening she found to contain several letters and papers, the former addressed to Captain

Woodford, but one of these completely rivetted her whole attention, for the superscription bore so remarkable a resemblance to the hand-writing of Stanley, that she could not but persuade herself of its identity, and the emotions that agitated her bosom as that idea occurred to her may be imagined.

She unfolded the letter with a trembling hand, and an exclamation of mingled astonishment and joy escaped her when she found that her surmises were correct. The letter was indeed from Stanley, addressed to his dear friend, Captain Woodford, and with a burst of emotion, tears gushing to her eyes, she pressed the precious epistle to her lips, and for a few moments the excitement and agitation of her feelings would not allow her to peruse the contents.

At length, however, she recovered sufficient composure to do so, and with feelings that we need not seek to describe, endeavoured to trace the well known characters of him to whom her fondest and most fervent affections were devoted, and whose present situation she was so anxious to know.

To her unspeakable delight she learnt from this letter that Stanley was safe, having succeeded with several of his comrades in escaping from Delhi, and that his wounds having been so slight that he was almost recovered from them, he had—for what reason did not appear very clear—with a detachment been ordered to the garrison of Lucknow.

This was indeed an agreeable surprise to Omelia, and at once decided her in making her way to Lucknow, with the fond hope of once more beholding her lover, and being by his side in the hour of danger.

"Yes, dearest Stanley," she exclaimed, "your faithful Omelia will, I trust, be once more restored to you. That Merciful Providence which has hitherto protected us from all the numerous perils we have had to encounter, will I trust guide her in safety to you."

Once more she pressed the letter—with heartfelt gratitude for the valuable information it contained—to her lips, and for a minute or two was so absorbed by the various thoughts that crowded upon her brain, that she could not finish the perusal of it.

At length, however, she resumed the reading of it, and with what emotions of delight and satisfaction may be imagined, when she found that her name was mentioned in terms of the greatest eulogy and affection, and that her lover expressed the utmost anxiety for her safety, and a fervent hope that heaven would ordain that they might shortly meet again, under far more happier circumstances than they had last parted.

"Bless you, noble-minded youth," Omelia exclaimed, as she refolded the letter, and placed it in her bosom; "I could never for an instant doubt your fidelity. Oh, may heaven grant that your affectionate wishes may speedily be realised. But should we indeed be restored to each other, how deep must be your feelings of anguish and regret when you learn the terrible fate of that friend whom you evidently so much esteemed, and that too in a deadly conflict with my guilty father."

That melancholy thought caused her considerable pain, and tears again rushed to her eyes, as she again fixed her gaze upon the ghastly remains of her father and the unfortunate Captain Woodford.

But she was now again aroused to the full sense of the importance of delay, and she looked anxiously around her, astonished, and somewhat dismayed, at her extraordinary situation.

She felt surprised at herself for having been able to make so perilous a descent, which might have well appalled even the most courageous person from attempting, and she was now most anxious to discover in what way she could extricate herself. To attempt to re-ascend by the way she had descended, would be madness, and could only be attended with the most fatal results.

But straining her eyes in an opposite direction to the spot on which she stood, she perceived a wide gap or opening, which she resolved to examine, in order to endeavour to ascertain whither it led.

Once more kneeling down by the cold remains of her father, and Captain Woodford, Omelia offered up a solemn prayer for the repose of their souls, and then with a sad feeling of regret she moved slowly from the spot, towards the opening which had attracted her attention, and as she approached it nearer her hopes revived, for the ground gradually rose, and she could perceive a winding pathway, formed by the hand of nature, and leading up a lofty hill to the country beyond; so that she could emerge from her present situation with comparatively but very little difficulty.

In a short time she had made the ascent, and she then found before her a much more promising and cheerful prospect than she had for some time seen.

She took heart, and commending herself to the care of the Supreme power, she proceeded on her tedious and toilsome journey.

CHAPTER XLI.

OMELIA ARRIVES IN LUCKNOW.—DESCRIPTION OF THAT CAPITAL.

Through a very picturesque and romantic

part of the country Omelia continued to travel for some time, though her progress was slow, for she felt greatly fatigued from the exertions she had undergone, and it was nothing but her indomitable courage and perseverence under the most trying difficulties that could support her.

But it was strange and disheartening that she could not yet perceive any signs of a human habitation, or meet with any person who might give her the informotion she required, and direct her in her course, and, although Omelia certainly continued to struggle on through these numerous and disheartening difficulties, her patience was almost exhausted, for she felt most deplorably the want both of rest and food, of the latter not having partaken of any for many hours.

The remembrance, too, of the awful scene she had witnessed, and the death of her father, so soon after the frightful catastrophe of the untimely end of poor Nazimi, whose loss she had such bitter cause to lament, excited in her mind the most poignant anguish, and was sufficient in itself to shake her fortitude, and destroy her energies; but she did not abandon herself to despair, for the thought of again beholding her beloved Stanley sustained her, and enabled her to conquer all those obstacles that otherwise might have been perfectly insurmountable.

"In spite of all," she said, " I will persevere, and trust in the goodness and mercy of providence yet to bear mo triumphantly through every difficulty and danger. Dear Stanley, to be again near you, and to share your fate, whatever that fate may be, what risk, what fatigue, what suffering is there that I will fear to encounter? Let me be firm, and I feel convinced that I shall yet be successful."

These thoughts seemed to reinvigorate her, and she went on with a celerity and determination which, considering the great fatigue she had already undergone, was truly surprising.

In the course of another hour her perseverence was rewarded, for on emerging from a thicket, she suddenly came in sight of a small village, consisting of about thirty bungalows, and where she had little doubt that, being a native, and having the means of remuneration fortunately in her possession she would find no difficulty in obtaining the relief and assistance she so much required.

In this she was not disappointed, for at the first bungalow she applied she was received in the most friendly manner by the humble inmates, a man and his wife, and freely offered all the accommodation and assistance it was in their power to render her.

Refreshments, coarse but ample, were placed before her without dalay, and Omelia, after long privation, made a hearty meal of the humble fare, which she relished as much as she would at another time the greatest luxuries.

The inhabitants of the buagalow were by no means curious, but they seemed anxious to afford her every information in their power, and answered all her questions with promptitude and intelligence. From them she had the satisfaction of hearing that sho was in the right direction for Lucknow, from which she was now distant not moro than a day's journey, and seeming to guess that she was opposed to the present revolt, they directed her the safest route to proceed in order to avoid the numerous hordes of mutineers that were scouring almost every part of the country. But they gave her some information that was even more particularly interesting and valuable to her, and that was that there were four Europeans, two men and their wives, at that time in one of the bungalows, having arrived in the village, much exhausted, two or three hours before, after effecting their escape from the terrible outrages at Cawnpore, and being anxious they believed to reach Lucknow, where they imagined that for the present, at any rate, they would be safe.

Omelia heard this with much pleasure, for the prospect of having companions for the remainder of the journey was a great relief to her; and her humble friends undertook to introduce her to them in the morning, as it was not likely that they would think of resuming their journey till after they had had a night's rest.

In fact the conduct of these people, who were evidently no friends to the revolt, inspired our heroine with every confidence, and after some further conversation, she was conducted by the female to a little chamber above, and where she could rest for the night.

On being left alone, Omelia, filled with gratitude at having been thus far enabled to surmount the difficulties of her weary and dangerous journey, and at the prospect of her so soon being in safety, and of probably meeting with Stanley, who had most likely arrived there long before this, fervently returned her thanks to heaven, and then without undressing, so that she might be prepared for any emergency, she retired to rest, and worn out with fatigue, and which she had met with such patient endurance, she quickly sunk into a sound sleep, which continued undisturbed till the morning.

She arose much refreshed, and fully prepared to resume her journey, and she then descended to the room below where she found the inhabitants of the bungalow awaiting her appearance, having prepared for her the best meal that their humble means would afford them to do.

But Omelia was impatient to be introduced to the strangers from Cawnpore, and the man, at her request, hastened to the bungalow in which they were, in order to make them acquainted with her wishes.

It was not long ere he returned and informed her that the fugitives were anxious to see her, and had desired him to conduct her to them without delay, as it was their intention to resume their journey in about an hour.

Omelia immediately attended the man, and was speedily introduced to the futitives, whom she found to be two English gentlemen and their wives, and their appearance sufficiently showed the sufferings to which they had been exposed.

Omelia's appearance seemed to interest them, and they received her with every courtesy and friendly feeling, which she suitably acknowledged and returned. A short time served to enter into explanations, and the fugitives were most willing that she should become their companion for the remainder of the journey, her destination being the same. One of the natives, too, on the offer of a reward, undertook to guide them to some distance on the way, avoiding those parts where danger was most to be apprehended, and thus a few minutes sufficed to make all the arrangements that were necessary, and Omelia and her companions were soon on similar terms of familiarity as if they had been acquainted for years.

Truth and candour were in every word that our heroine uttered, in the expression of her features, and in her every act, it was therefore impossible to mistrust her, but, on the contrary, to be in her company but a short time was to inspire you with confidence, and to command your respect.

Besides, Omelia thought fit to make her fellow travellers that were to be, acquainted with such portions of her history as were likely to increase that confidence and excite their spmpathy which they expressed in the warmest tones

In about an hour—they being anxious to avoid the scorching heat of the day as much as possible, and all being in readiness—Omelia having liberally remunerated the man and his wife, in whose humble bungalow she had met with so much kindness and attention, they resumed their journey with the most sanguine expectations, conducted by the native Ali Allhabab, on whose fidelity they had been assured that they might firmly rely, and they had soon got to some distance from the village, travelling with renewed vigour, and seeming to forget the great

fatigue they had already undergone, and indulging in hope, as they now so freely did.

Neither of them seemed much disposed to converse, for their minds were too much occupied by their own thoughts, and for some distance they proceeded in complete silence.

The thoughts that crowded upon the brain of our heroine were of a mingled and conflicting character; of doubt and fear, of melancholy regret, and hopeful expectation. The frightful death of her misguided parent caused her the most poignant anguish; and the remembrance of poor Nazimi's awful fate also left an impression of horror on her mind, which she found it a difficult thing to conquer or remove, but then the letter of her lover, which had by such extraordinary means fallen into her hands, and quieted her fears and anxieties in so many respects, served to raise her spirits, and inspire her with hope.

Should they be so fortunate as to meet again, what would be the joy which they must both experience? The thought reanimated her, and she continued her journey in a state of mind almost bordering upon cheerfulness, and which feeling she endeavoured to impart to her companions, and with some degree of success.

She could not help feeling, however, the greatest anxiety for her aged friend, the hermit, and particularly Flora Melville who would doubtless feel distracted at her loss, and who so much needed her society in her present lonely situation, and after the melancholy bereavement she had experienced in the death of her father.

The country through which their guide conducted them was of the most diversified character, sometimes wild and cheerless, at others rich in picturesque and romantic scenery, and in fertility of soil.

Although the guide thought it prudent to avoid them as much as possible, the travellers passed through several villages, but notwithstanding they were frequently eyed with looks of suspicion, they were not molested, Omelia and Ali always having ready satisfactory answers for any questions that might be put to them.

Many revolting objects met their sight as they proceeded, showing the savage acts that had been so mercilessly perpetrated by straggling parties of mutineers. The mutilated remains of some unfortunate victim, sometimes those of women and children, in a frightful state of decomposition, frequently met their sight, lying by the roadside, and the heart sickened as hungry vultures came flying along with a shrill cry ready to pounce upon their awful prey

At length fatigued by the excessive heat of the weather, the travellers halted for a short time to rest themselves near a small temple. They sat down under the shade of a noble peepul tree, and near which was a pool of water, and a cool breeze blowing, they felt much refreshed.

The guide at length urged the danger of delay, and after having partaken of some food, which they had brought with them, they once more proceeded on their way, Ali, on the promise of a further reward having consented to conduct them to the end of the journey, which although it had been rendered more tedious to arrive at, owing to the circuitous route they had been necessarily compelled to pursue, they were now fast approaching.

At length their further progress was suddenly stopped at one of the narrowest and shallowest parts of a river, which as there was no bridge to cross it, they would be compelled to ford.

Omelia and the guide, who were used to such difficulties, could have viewed it with comparative indifference, had it not been for the two English ladies, their companions, who naturally felt timid at such an undertaking, but there was no alternative, and Omelia and Ali after endeavouring to encourage them, led the way, fording the river instead of swimming it, as they could have done, in order to point out the depth of the water, and the gentlemen taking their wives in their arms, boldly followed, and after considerable difficulty they all succeeded in reaching the opposite side of the river in safety, though, of course much exhausted, and drenched to the skin.

Another hour's travelling brought them within sight of the place of their destination, and the hearts of all beat high with hope and expectation.

As the last glow of the setting sun was fading away in the western horizon, the travellers were standing in one of those roads without the gates, which in some places connect the residency with the city of Lucknow.

That which is called the residency is a piece of ground elevated a good deal above the rest of the city, allotted by the King of Oude, when he first put himself under British protection, some fifty years ago, to the British civil residents. It is walled round almost entirely, on one side native houses abut upon it, but on the other three sides it is tolerably clear.

Here Ali, having completed his task, after giving them some instructions, was again about to leave them, but Omelia persuaded him to accompany them into the city, as they might further need his advice as to how they should dispose of themselves for the present, and he having consented to do so, they moved along the road towards the city, the heart of Omelia throbbing high, with the various feelings that agitated it at every step they took.

Was she indeed once more near her beloved Stanley, and would kind providence in its infinite mercy once more guide them to each other's fond embrace, were the anxious questions that she mentally asked herself, and hope answered in the affirmative, and imparted a degree of consolation to her bosom after the many trials she had experienced, and which it now filled her with amazement to think she had found the fortitude to struggle against and to withstand.

Much activity seemed to prevail, and they met several persons on their way, European and native, who seemed too much occupied with their own business to take any particular notice of them.

At length, with the moon—which had now arisen—shining brightly above, and clearly revealing every object around, the travellers stood in one of the principal streets of Lucknow, and could not help gazing with feelings of admiration upon the scene which met their observation.

The city of Lucknow, the capital of the province of Oude, is a magnificent place, or rather it was as it appeared ere the glory or the shame of its ancient rule had departed from it. Many are the noble specimens of architecture that it contains, the principal of which are the tombs of the Nabob Saadut Ali, the gate of Roum (Constantinople) and the Imamburra, or cathedral; which last grand mosque, consists of two courts rising with a steep ascent, one above the other.

It contains besides the mosque, a college for instruction in Mussulman law, apartments for the religious establishment maintained there, and a noble gallery, in the midst of which, under a brilliant tabernacle of silver, cut glass and precious stones, lie buried the remains of its founder, Asuph ad Dowlah.

Noble streets there are too, containing handsome residences, and stately buildings, some of the more important of which are imitations of the Greek style of architecture, others, from the Saracenic cupolas, and monuments remind one of Moscow.

Nothing can possibly present a more lively or picturesqe appearance than the scenes which ever meet the eye in the streets of Lucknow. Mounted cavaliers, clothed in cashmere stuffs, elaborately ornamented with gold, and preceeded by attendants carrying gold and silver sticks, swords, pipes, spears, and wands of office, pass to and fro in a continuous stream. Certain dignitaries, seated in open palanquins, richly painted and gilded, mingle in the throng, many among them carrying in their hands magnificent silver hookahs, or rather gourgouris, for such is the name given to the small pipe that is deficient of flexible tube. They are hemmed in by hookah bearers, armed attendants, and perhaps a guard of honour mounted on camels, comparisoned in red and green trappings; others there are perched up aloft on the backs of elephants, seated in gracefully carved howdahs, the sides of which are in the form of a swan, and are in many instances of pure silver. The attendants of the more wealthy inhabitants comprise examples of the various races from all parts of India, and the aspect presented by their costume is picturesque in the extreme.

The following is a graphic picture, painted by the author of the "Private Life of an Eastern King."

"Strange tales I had heard in Calcutta of the peculiar features of Lucknow and its court—of the extensive menagerie maintained by the king—of his fondness for Europeans not in the Company's service—of the warlike tastes and bearing of the inhabitants of Oude, and the abundance of matchlocks, shields, spears, and swords, to be seen borne by fierce-looking fellows in the streets of Lucknow, I had heard much of all these things, and expected to be disappointed, as I had been before frequently. I was *not* disappointed, however. For once, the reality exceeded my anticipation.

"The great extent of the buildings generally called the king's palace, surprised me in the first place. It was not properly a palace, but a continuation of palaces, stretching all along the banks of the Goomty, the river on which Lucknow is built. In this, however, the royal residence in Oude but resembles what one reads of the seraglio at Constantinople, the khan's residence at Teheran and the Imperial buildings of Pekin. In all Oriental states, the palaces are not so much the abode of the sovereign only, as the centre of the government—little towns, in fact, containing extensive lines of buildings occupied by the harem and its vast number of attendants, containing courts, gardens, tanks, fountains, and squares, as well as the offices of the chief minister of state. Such was the case in Lucknow. One side of the narrow Goomty—a river not much broader than a middling-sized London street—was lined by the royal palace; the other was occupied by the *rumna*, or park, in which the menagerie was maintained. The extent of this collection of animals, and its variety, exceeded anything that I had supposed possible. Elephants in scores, tigers, rhinoceroses, antelopes, cheetahs or hunting-leopards, lynxes, Persian cats, Chinese dogs, might all be seen sunning themselves in this park,

either in their cages, or stretched listlessly on the grass, as commonly as sheep and cows in an English meadow.

"There was nothing grand or striking about the exterior of the palace—the Fureed Buksh, as it is called. Its extent was the only imposing feature about it, and struck me far more forcibly than any magnificence of architecture or loftiness of structure would have done; for I was prepared for the latter, whilst for the former feature I was not prepared

"Nor did the streets of Lucknow disappoint me. The streets around the palace have been compared to Dresden by Bishop Heber; others have declared that Lucknow resembled Moscow. I have never been in either city; but I should fancy they cannot be very like each other. The only large city that I have been in which resembles the lower part of the town, in its narrow streets, its laden camels, and its bazaars, is Grand Cairo in Egypt. Dresden, Moscow, Cairo—there is room enough here for choice; and yet in all these no counterparts will be found to many of the most striking characteristics of Lucknow.

"In the first place, with respect to the armed population, we shall find nothing similar in any of these places. The people of Moscow may wear knives about their persons, and in Cairo you may occasionally see men with arms in their hands; but in Lucknow every man goes armed. With matchlock or gun or pistol most probably, with a short bent sword, called a *tulwar*, and a shield certainly, you find every man in Lucknow pass you by. Even those engaged in the ordinary business of life have their tulwars; whilst the idlers have both pistols and shield as well, however otherwise mean their attire. The shield of buffalohide, with brass knobs for the most part, is usually thrown up upon the left shoulder; and with the fierce-looking moustaches of the Rajpoots and Patans, and the black beards of the Mussulmans, tulwar and shield together give an eminently warlike air to the swaggering figures of the self-sufficient citizens.

"The love of arms is fostered from infancy in the inhabitants of Lucknow. An arrow or a spear is the usual plaything of the boys there; small wooden models of tulwars and pistols are put into the hands of the babies, just as English nurses give their children rattles to play with.

"The streets of the town presented therefore an eminently novel aspect to me. It was as if I had found myself transported suddenly into some of the scenes of which I had read in childish histories and novels, in which all the men are heroes, and show their heroism in their gait and manners. Then there is the contrast, too, between the Hindoo and the Mussulman population, resembling each other only in the arms which they carry—in every other respect unlike. Lucknow is a city of about 300,000 inhabitants, of whom two-thirds are probably Hindoos, generally of the lower orders; the Mussulman population is somewhat aristocratic, for the court is Mussulman.

"In its present contracted dimensions, Oude is a triangular piece of country, stretching from Nepaul to the Ganges: its broader proportions skirting Nepaul upon the north, its narrow end resting upon the sacred river on the south. It slopes gradually from north-west to south-east, the only high land it contains being the strip so generously given up by the Marquis of Hastings after the Nepaulese war. This district, the Terai, is very populous—with wild beasts; and is rich—in jungle.

"Stripped as it has been of its rupees and its most valuable provinces by successive governors-general, Oude is still more populous than any of the German states in Europe, except Prussia and Austria; whilst in extent it exceeds that of Denmark; of Holland and Belgium put together; of Switzerland, Saxony, and Wirtemberg, could they be united. In Europe it would be a country superior to any of these, rivalling Bavaria or Naples in importance."

Such was the appearance of Lucknow before the outbreak of the mutiny, and many of the characteristics thus vividly described remained at the time when Omelia and her companions entered the city, and they could not but be struck—the Englishmen and their ladies especially—with the novelty of all that met their sight.

Yet in the midst of all this, they could not conceal from themselves the loneliness, embarrassment, and peculiarity of their situation, and now that they had succeeded in reaching the place of their destination in safety they were at a loss what course to adopt, and where to seek a refuge; and Ali was enabled to afford them but very little advice upon the subject, and there they stood gazing around them in a state of complete bewilderment, and without being able to come to any decision how to act.

The state of affairs in Lucknow had assumed a very serious aspect for some time past, and they grew more alarming every day and hour. The officers of the 32nd Queen's were not allowed to sleep away from the mess-house, as they formerly had been, so that they might be ready at a moment's notice. And it was feared that the native infantry and cavalry regiments were about to revolt, and then the situation of the little

garrison would be most critical. On the night before the arrival of our heroine, it had been reported by some natives that parties had been appointed in the three sepoy regiments to go round to murder all the Europeans in their beds, and set the houses on fire; and not knowing whether it was true or not, every precaution was promptly taken. A regiment of native cavalry was sent without delay, and before daylight the 32nd scarted from the city for cantonments.

The sick were taken to the residency, also the women, the residency being garrisoned by 130 men of the 32nd, and by the battery of native artillery. All the ladies, the wives of civilians likewise retired into the residency, and thus far the city might be said to be deserted.

Such was the state of excitement that prevailed in Lucknow on the evening of the arrival of Omelia and her companions, and as they sauntered through the different streets hesitating what to do, though it was necessary that they should seek some place of shelter for the night, at any rate, without delay, they met several groups of persons all hurrying in the same direction, and some of them escorted by officers and soldiers.

The heart of Omelia palpitated violently as she watched the different officers with anxious and inquiring looks; but the fond and eager hope she had ventured to encourage, and which the reader may imagine, was doomed to disappointment. Once or twice she was half resolved to make some inquiries of the officers after her lover, for she thought that if he was indeed in Lucknow, it was most likely they could give her the information she required where to find him, but still she hesitated, and remained in the same state of anxiety and suspense.

Their present unsatisfactory situation, however, the excitement that prevailed among the numerous persons they saw, all hastening in the same direction from which they had come, and the increasing lateness of the hour, at length aroused the fugitives into action, and after consulting together for a few minutes, it was resolved that they should at once make the necessary inquiries as to where they might find that shelter and accommodation of which they stood so much in need; and they had scarcely come to that determination, when an exclamation of surprise and satisfaction escaped one of the ladies, who with her husband had advanced, for the purpose before mentioned, towards a party of Europeans who were approaching, and it soon appeared that they had recognised some old acquaintances or friends from the greeting which took place.

Explanations quickly ensued, Omelia and

her other two fellow travellers were introduced by their companions to their brother and his wife, whom they had so unexpectedly, but so fortunately met, and who were on their way to a house prepared for their accommodation—in the present unsettled state of the city—in the residency, whither at once they warmly invited the fugitives to accompany them. It is almost needless to say that this was gladly accepted, and in a short time Omelia once more found herself in safety, allowed a short respite from the sufferings she had lately undergone, and, as she sincerely hoped, again near her beloved and faithful Stanley, and whom she so fervently trusted soon to behold again.

CHAPTER XLII.

MEETING OF OMELIA AND EDWARD STANLEY.

The house to which Omelia and her companions were introduced, and in which for the present they hoped to find a safe asylum, was commodious, and every way calculated to afford them the accommodation they required, and all being alike the victims of misfortunes, and exposed to the same dangers, felt for each other a mutual sympathy.

The extraordinary character, and handsome form and features of the heroic Indian maiden, however, deeply interested them all, and made them curious to become acquainted with the particulars of her history, which they imagined must be a remarkable one but of course at this early stage of their acquaintance, they could not take the liberty of questioning her upon the subject.

Her mind agitated by the various thoughts that naturally crowded upon it, fatigued also and anxious to be alone, Omelia soon after their arrival at the house, requested to be allowed to retire, and was conducted by an attendant to a handsome chamber, affording such accommodation for rest as it had not been her good fortune for some time to experience; and she could not restrain her feelings of gratitude to the Supreme for the mercy shown her.

Although weary and careworn with the great exertions she had, particularly for the last few days had to encounter, and the many vicissitudes to which she had been exposed, her mind was too busy with thought to suffer her to retire to bed immediately, and seating herself at an open window which commanded a wide range of scenery, including a large portion of the city, she gave free indulgence to her reflections and ruminations.

A cool and refreshing breeze was wafted into the chamber, by the means of the open window, affording a great relief after the excessive heat of the day, and Omelia could not but duly appreciate and enjoy the sudden and agreeable change in her circumstances.

Nothing could be finer than the night, so clear and beautiful. Myriads of stars glistened in the sky, and not a speck dimmed the effulgence of the moon, which revealed the country around for some extent, and shone brilliantly upon the cupolas and minarets of some of the principal edifices in the adjacent city. Nothing could be more tranquil than the hour. How little in keeping with the rude and violent tempest which for some time raged over some of the fairest parts of India, and was about to involve that locality in its horrors.

But that which at any other time, and under different circumstances, would have completely absorbed the attention, and excited the admiration of Omelia, was now almost unnoticed by her in the tumult of thoughts that passed so rapidly in her mind, and gave rise to such varied emotions in her breast.

She recalled to her memory all the trying and startling events that had occurred to her on her flight from Cawnpore, and that she had been able to struggle against them, and at length, after almost unheard of perils, and exposure to want, fatigue, and torturing anxiety, to reach a place of present safety, appeared to her to be little short of a miracle, and she felt that she could never be sufficiently grateful to providence, who had hitherto so mercifully sustained and preserved her through every difficulty.

Feelings of the deepest horror and commiseration agitated her breast when she thought of the dreadful fate of her father, and the kind-hearted Nazimi, to whom she was so much indebted for her escape from the power of the fearful miscreant, Nena Sahib; tears of the bitterest anguish and regret filled her eyes, and it was long ere she could sufficiently recover from the emotions which those dismal recollections excited, and turn her thoughts to any subject.

But at length her lover, and the probability of their shortly meeting again, if he should fortunately yet have arrived in Lucknow, superseded every other idea in her mind, and various were the conjectures, the sanguine hopes, the doubts and fears that harrassed and perplexed her brain upon the subject.

What would be the joyful emotions, the feelings of surprise and ecstacy that must fill the bosom of Stanley at so unexpected a meeting. What a multitude of thoughts and facts they would have to communicate to each other; what boundless happiness, yet mingled with sorrow would that meeting give rise to. The brain of Omelia became bewildered in the anticipation.

She took from her bosom Stanley's letter, which she had found in the pocket of the unfortunate Captain Woodford, and again gloated, with feelings of the most indescribable delight and affection over the beloved characters that had been traced by his hand, and with what rapture did she dwell upon that passage in which he so warmly alluded to her, and which so plainly showed the fervour and sincerity of his love, if indeed she could for a moment have doubted his truth and fidelity. She could almost imagine that he was speaking to her, and her heart throbbed with the warmest feelings of love as she pressed the letter to her lips, and thought of the many hours of unalloyed happiness they had passed together, hours which it was so uncertain whether they would ever return.

"But I will still encourage the blissful hope, dear, faithful Stanley," she ejaculated, her eyes brightening, and the colour mounting to her cheeks at the thought, "that the time will yet arrive when we shall not only meet again, but no more be separated. If I could think otherwise, what would there be to render life any longer valuable to me? Edward, Omelia's hopes and wishes are alone centered in you. It is for you alone that she continues to struggle firmly against the many vicissitudes that have marked, and which continue to mark her adverse fate; and beyond you she has no other earthly wish."

She was aroused from this interesting train of thought by hearing the sound of men's voices outside the house, to which they seemed approaching, and she started and trembled with emotion, as she could almost have sworn that she heard the name of Stanley mentioned in terms of familiarity.

But she must have been mistaken; she must surely have suffered her imagination—heated and excited by the thoughts in which she had just indulged—to deceive her; it was impossible that so fortunate a circumstance should occur at the very moment when her anxiety and expectations were aroused to the utmost pitch; and yet she could not dismiss the strange impression from her mind.

She looked eagerly from the window, and listened with breathless attention. She again heard the voices more distinctly than before, and it was evident that the men were approaching nearer.

Her heart palpitated violently with hope and expectation, and at length her curiosity was gratified, and she caught sight of the forms of four men—as near as she could distinguish, English officers—as they hastily turned an angle of the road, and approached towards the house.

They were deeply engaged in conversation, the clear bright moon favoured her observation, and she eagerly scanned their persons, but that of one of them rivetted her whole attention, and caused her heart to beat at double its wonted pace. Never had she beheld a form that in every respect so strikingly resembled the fine, manly, dignified person of her lover, but he was so situated, with his companions on either side of him, that Omelia could not have an opportunity of catching even a glimpse of his features.

Her suspense was most torturing, and as the party paused for a minute near the house she listened with more breathless attention than before, in the hope of being able to catch the tones of his voice. He, however, made no observation beyond that which was uttered in a low and almost whispering tone, and her anxiety increased to an almost insupportable degree, for the more she gazed at his form, the more forcibly did its familiarity strike her.

The officers once more proceeded on their way, but the one who had so particularly rivetted Omelia's attention, suffered his companions to get a little in advance of him, and for some reason seemed to linger, as if uncertain whether or not to proceed with them.

The next moment, as a sudden thought appeared to occur to him, he turned his face towards the house, and he was not so far away from it but that the bright moonlight would allow a distinct view of his features. And what were the feelings of Omelia when

her surmises were confirmed? It was indeed her lover Edward Stanley.

Every faculty was suspended in astonishment and delight. She tried to speak, to call upon his name, in the hope that her voice might reach his ear, and draw his attention towards the house; but so great was her agitation, that not an exclamation, not a sound could escape her lips, and before she could recover herself, Stanley had rejoined his companions, and they all disappeared in the distance.

It would be almost impossible to describe the excitement under which Omelia laboured, but delight superseded every other feeling, to know that her hopes and wishes to be restored to her lover, were almost certain of being realised, and that much sooner than her most sanguine expectations could have led her to imagine.

But suddenly she started from her seat, as a strange and rather extravagant idea flashed across her brain. If she immediately left the house, and pursued the same direction as Stanley had taken, might she not be enabled to overtake him? Hope urged her, at any rate, to make the attempt, she stopped not to think of the imprudence, if not the danger of so doing, but, fearful that even the delay of an instant might render it too late, she hastily quitted the room, and was descending the stairs as noiselessly as she could, when the door of the room in which the other inmates of the house were sitting—for they had not yet retired to rest—opened, and one of the ladies made her appearance.

She expressed the greatest surprise on seeing Omelia, and the excited state she was evidently in, and eagerly inquired what had happened to disturb her.

"Do not detain me, I pray you, madam," replied Omelia, hastily, "I am going on a most important errand, one upon which my happiness in a great measure depends. Fear not, I will shortly return."

"Consider the lateness of the hour, and the danger you may incur," observed the lady.

Our heroine, however, stopped not to make any reply, but waving her hand respectfully to the lady, she hurried down the stairs, and the next moment stood in the open air.

This had not occupied many minutes, but Omelia now for the first time saw the improbability of her being able to overtake her lover, who, no doubt, with his companions had arrived at the place of their destination.

She felt disheartened, but was still determined not to abandon her intention altogether, and without waiting a moment for any further consideration, she hastened in the same direction as Stanley and his friends had pursued; looking eagerly on every side, but without seeing anything of the beloved object of which she was in search, or, in fact, any other human being.

Still our heroine continued on her way with unabated speed, until she had got far beyond the residency, and was entering upon the city, without succeeding in the gratification of her hopes and expectations, and vexed and disappointed, she paused, seeing the uselessness of proceeding, and now wondering that she could for a moment imagine her pursuit could meet with any successful result.

She cast an anxious and lingering look towards the city, and then, with a sigh, she turned, and slowly retraced her steps, wrapped in melancholy thought.

Still she consoled herself with the hope, that now she was convinced that her lover was in the city, the time was not far distant when they would meet again; and she determined to lose no time in discovering him.

And what would be the feelings of Stanley did he but know that her on whom his most anxious thoughts were doubtless constantly fixed, was so near him? What would be his astonishment, his unfeigned delight when they again met?

These thoughts reconciled her to this temporary disappointment, and invoking a blessing upon his head, she proceeded with a lighter heart towards the house she had so imprudently quitted on such a hopeless errand, convinced that her friends would feel surprised and uneasy at her strange conduct.

She had got some distance on her return, when just as she reached a rather lonely part of the road, and the moon became hidden behind a cloud, she was startled and somewhat alarmed by hearing the sound of heavy approaching footsteps, and before she had time to collect herself, the tall figure of a man crossed her path, and observing her stopped before her, so that it was impossible for her to avoid him.

"How now," demanded the man, sternly, "who are you? and why are you wandering here at this hour of the night? Speak, I command you,"

Omelia started and trembled, for the voice smote her ears with fearful familiarity. The man, too impatient to wait for her reply, rushed towards her and rudely grasped her wrist. At the same moment the moon again emerged from behind the cloud, and its light streamed across the spot on which they were standing. Omelia with trembling eagerness fixed her eyes upon the features of the man, and her surprise and consternation may be imagined, when she beheld that it was the ruffian Allyghur, whom she had so much reason to dread.

"Ah," he exclaimed with a savage look of exultation, and grasping her wrist more fiercely, "Omelia, daring girl, to whom my hatred and revenge are so justly due, by every infernal power, this is most fortunate."

"Unhand me, villain," said our heroine, firmly, and endeavouring to release her arm from his hold; "Omelia scorns and defies your deadly malice, and will not be detained."

"Ha, ha, ha," he laughed, "these are bold words, but not likely to have the desired effect on me. It is rather unfortunate for you, girl, that you have wandered into the tiger's lair. You must with me. Come, resistance is useless. A traitress, and so great an enemy to that righteous cause in which her countrymen are struggling, it is not prudent to suffer to be at large, and she is a fit subject for punishment."

"Miscreant!" replied Omelia, in the same firm and scornful voice, and her fine eyes flashing with disgust and indignation, "you shall not triumph in your brutal and diabolical designs. I have yet the courage and determination to resist a cowardly ruffian like you. Release me, I again command, and suffer me to proceed on my way."

"Are you mad?" said Allyghur, "that you thus presume to set me at defiance? Know you not that in a moment I could stretch you dead at my feet? Exasperate me not too far, lest I—"

Before he could finish the sentence, Omelia, by a sudden effort, when the villain was off his guard, released herself from his hold, at the same time securing a pistol which he had carried in his belt, and retreating from him a few paces, she stood in an attitude of triumph and defiance, presenting the deadly weapon at his head.

Allyghur with a fearful curse, at finding himself thus so completely defeated, started back aghast, and with his at any time repulsive features distorted with rage, and his eyes glaring savagely upon the intrepid maiden, who laughed scornfully.

"Villain," she exclaimed, "you see that providence still protects me, and that the triumph is mine. I would not shed your blood, although it would be a mercy to release mankind from such a miscreant, but dare to attempt to follow me, seek again to obstruct me, and you die."

"Confusion!" cried Allyghur, in a voice of the most ungovernable rage, "shall I thus be defeated and defied by a girl? I will not be intimidated—I will not suffer you to escape."

"Nay then," said Omelia, as he rashly advanced a few steps towards her; "be your blood upon your own head, since you are thus determined to madly rush upon your fate."

She discharged the contents of the pistol

as she thus spoke, and Allyghur, with a frightful oath, staggered and fell.

Omelia waited not an instant, but precipitately hurried from the spot, grateful for her almost miraculous deliverence from the power of a villain, whose deadly malice she had so much reason to dread

Allyghur was not seriously wounded, and in a few minutes he recovered himself, and rising to his feet, whilst the most fearful maledictions escaped his lips, he hastily bound a scarf across the wound, which was in his left shoulder, and then looked eagerly in the direction by which Omelia had departed, but she was no where to be seen, and to his rage and disappointment he was fully satisfied that she had escaped him.

He stood for a few minutes in a state of the greatest excitement, giving vent to his savage feelings in the most brutal language.

"This defeat is intolerable," he exclaimed, "to think that I should hold the daring girl in my grasp, and yet suffer her to escape me. Curses light upon her, shall she ever be permitted to triumph, and to set those to whom she is so bitterly, so determinedly opposed at defiance? Why did I not at once sacrifice her to my hatred and revenge? Fool—but should I again encounter her, her fate is certain."

For a moment he again glanced eagerly along the road Omelia had taken, and then muttering curses to himself, he slowly moved away from the spot, and bent his steps towards the city.

In the meantime Omelia continued to hurry on her way to the asylum she had so imprudently quitted, and never stopped to look behind her.

She was fearful that the inmates of the house, not expecting her to return, and as it was now fast approaching midnight, would have retired to rest, in which case her situation would be one of the greatest danger, as she would have to wander about till daylight and thus deprived of that repose of which she stood so much in need.

She took courage, however, and increasing her speed, at length arrived at the house, and her hopes revived when she perceived lights in one or two of the upper rooms, which satisfied her that some of the inmates of the building had not yet retired to rest. Knocking loudly at the door, after several necessary questions being put to her, she was admitted by a female domestic, and hastily snatching a lighted lamp from her, without stopping to make use of any observation, she immediately ascended to the chamber which had been allotted to her, thankful to find herself once more in safety.

It was some time ere she could sufficiently tranquillise her feelings to reflect calmly upon the exciting events of the evening; but when she did so she could not but experience a degree of satisfaction which far superseded any other feeling.

Her fondest hopes to a certain extent had been realised; she knew that she was near her lover, she had seen him; but a few hours might elapse—for in spite of every danger she was resolved to renew her search as soon as possible—and they might meet, and in that thought she endeavoured to be happy.

Her encounter with the villain Allyghur had greatly excited her, but her providential escape filled her not only with amazement but gratitude.

No doubt her abrupt and mysterious departure from the house had created some surprise and uneasiness amongst those whom she was now inclined to consider her friends, as they were her companions in misfortune; but the explanation she had to give, she had no doubt would afford them every satisfaction, and quiet any suspicions her conduct might have created.

At length completely worn out with mental and physical exertion, she retired to bed, and soon for awhile forgot all her troubles and anxieties in sleep.

Omelia met her new found friends in the morning, and they warmly expressed their pleasure at her return, although they could not at the same time conceal their surprise at her strange conduct in leaving the house at so unseasonable an hour, knowing the danger she must incur by so doing. She briefly explained—for she knew not that there was any occasion for secrecy—and related the particulars of the events that had occurred to her; and they listened to her with great interest and attention, and when she had concluded they expressed their sympathy in her misfortunes, congratulated her on her present safety, and sincerely hoped that she would ere long receive the reward due to her heroic fortitude and patient endurance, in the gratification and happy realisation of all her wishes.

In fact, Omelia found her companions most agreeable and affable in their manners, and in their society, during the day, she found some alleviation to her cares and anxieties, and endeavoured to become calm and content.

But Stanley still continued to occupy her every thought, and she felt that it was utterly impossible for her to rest contented and happy until they had again met; and having ascertained in what portion of the city the soldiers were quartered, she resolved, at all hazards, to again go in search of him, when evening had closed in, which was the time when she thought she could do so with greater safety.

In the course of the day the most alarming reports reached them of the increasing excitement in the city, and the dangers that threatened; for the disaffection among the native troops was spreading fast, and the most terrible consequences were therefore to be apprehended, from the vast numbers that the mere handful of Europeans would have opposed to them; although every one was firmly and heroically resolved to resist to the last, that feeling not being confined to the military, but spreading itself among civilians, and equally animating the breasts of English women, of whose courage, patience, and endurance, under the most trying and dreadful circumstances, we have had so many striking examples.

Omelia thought of the horrors enacted at Delhi, Cawnpore, and elsewhere, and her heart sickened, and she could not but entertain the most gloomy apprehensions. She, however, concealed her thoughts, and endeavoured to inspire her companions with fortitude and hope.

The house, which had been the official residence of one of the government authorities, was a large one, but like every other building in the residency, was now full of the alarmed people from the city. Every available means were adopted for defence, and at present they had an abundant store of provisions and other necessaries, so that upon the whole, there was no immediate cause for apprehension.

The day wore tediously away, and Omelia anxiously and impatiently awaited the approach of evening, she having acquainted her friends with her design, from which they tried to dissuade her, but to no purpose.

At length evening came, all was quiet without, and Omelia with a palpitating heart, which beat high with expectation, and having the fervent good wishes of her friends, quitted the house, and made her way towards the city.

She had taken the precaution to arm herself with a brace of pistols in case of danger, but she apprehended none, unless she should happen unfortunately to encounter any of the murderers who had been the associates of her father and Allyghur, in which case, as they would know her, she had everything to fear. However, she did not encourage such apprehensions, and went boldly on her way, meeting several of the native inhabitants, who, as she was an Indian, did not view her with any suspicion.

Like the previous one, it was a lovely night, and the moon shone forth in all her silvery brilliancy, revealing clearly to the view a panoramic view of the city and its environs of the most picturesque and interesting description.

But Omelia's mind was too much occupied with the thoughts that engrossed it, to take much notice of that which at any other time would have excited her warmest admiration, and as she proceeded on her way, as she had been directed, towards that part of the city in which the regiment to which she believed Stanley belonged, was quartered, her hopes and expectations increased, and she felt unusually happy and confident.

"Yes, dear Stanley," she exclaimed, "I feel satisfied that the happy moment to which I have long so anxiously looked forward, is at hand, and that we shall shortly again behold each other. Blissful thought, how my heart bounds with joy as it occurs to me, and my imagination pictures to me in the most glowing colours, the fond transport of your feelings at an event you could never have ventured to anticipate. Absence does but more strongly convince me how precious you are to my heart, and well do I know that your feelings are responsive with mine own. Beloved Edward, would that the time had arrived when our fates were united, and we might never, never more be separated."

As she thus spoke, she entered one of the principal streets of the city, which was of vast extent, and contained many noble buildings, which were rendered clear and distinct, and shone conspicuous in the bright moonlight.

Here Omelia paused, for she felt a fluttering sensation at her heart which would not suffer her to proceed, and she looked eagerly along the street, and at the different persons who were passing to and fro. All was perfectly quiet, and there were not the least signs of anything going on except in its ordinary course, and nothing whatever to authorise the general alarm that prevailed. But Omelia was not to be deceived by this apparent tranquillity, she knew the crafty, deep designing character of her countrymen, and she was convinced that this calm was but the prelude to that fearful storm of passion and revenge which had already burst with such destructive fury over many parts of the country.

It was in this street, according to the information which Omelia had received, that the barracks were situated, and therefore the agitation of her feelings at that moment may be easily accounted for. But she hesitated what to do, for she had not the courage to venture boldly to them, and make her anxious inquiries, and yet if she did not, how could she expect to obtain the realisation of her hopes and wishes?

She walked slowly along, her heart still fluttering with mingled hope and fear, and her patience fast becoming exhausted. Notwithstanding this noble street was extremely long, the light of the moon enabled her to see to the farther end of it distinctly, and her attention was suddenly arrested by the form of a military man, who issued from a large building, some distance from where Omelia stood, and slowly approached.

Omelia's heart throbbed quicker than before, and she trembled with expectation, as she strained her eyes towards the stranger. The form, the noble bearing, and the step, were those of Stanley, and the nearer he came, the more convinced she was that it was he. How powerful were the emotions that agitated her bosom; but fearful that perhaps her too sanguine hopes might deceive her, or if not, not wishing to reveal herself too suddenly, she drew aside to a place where she could escape observation.

Short was the time that she was kept in suspense, the man approached nearer, her doubts were removed, it was Stanley; in the moonlight his handsome features were clearly revealed to her, unable any longer to control her feelings, she uttered an exclamation of delight, and rushing from the place where she had been concealed, she threw herself sobbing hysterically, and unable to utter his name, in his arms.

CHAPTER XLIII.

JOY AND SORROW.

It would be a difficult task indeed to describe correctly the feelings of Stanley at this totally unlooked for meeting. His astonishment almost equalled his transport, and as he strained the beauteous form of the devoted being—who had never been absent for a moment from his thoughts, since the eventful night on which they had last parted—to his throbbing heart, he could scarcely believe the evidence of his senses, or persuade himself that he was not labouring under some wild and strange delusion.

But after the first burst of her emotion was over, Omelia raised her looks with the most intense affection towards him, while the tears—tears of joy and gratitude—still trembled in her eyes, towards his face, and in the most tender accents repeated his name, and he was then convinced that his happiness was indeed a reality.

"Light of my soul, my only earthly hope," he rapturously exclaimed, as he strained her still more fervently to his heart, and pressed warm kisses on her lips and cheeks, "my own fond, faithful, dearest Omelia, and do I indeed once more gaze upon those lovely features that have ever been present to my imagination, and press your beloved form to

my throbbing bosom? Kind heaven has heard my prayers; oh, what happiness, what unspeakable happiness is this."

"Stanley, beloved Stanley," ejaculated our heroine, in accents which showed the feelings that glowed within her breast. She could say no more, her emotions overpowered her, and she again hid her face upon his bosom, and sobbed and wept without restraint.

Stanley's agitation and excitement were equal to her own, and it was some time ere they could either of them sufficiently regain their composure to speak.

He drew her gently into a remote corner of the street, near the spot on which they had met, in order to avoid the observation of any person who might be passing, and then he again found power to give expression to the feelings of transport that animated his breast in words.

"Oh, my beloved Omelia," he exclaimed, "how wonderful, how unexpected is this meeting; my happiness, my astonishment is so great, that my brain turns giddy with delight, and my heart overflows with gratitude to that All merciful providence who has so miraculously preserved you through all the fearful dangers which I am convinced you have had to encounter, and restored us to each other at a moment when I could least have hoped that such unspeakable bliss was in store for me. Speak to me, my fond one, for my very soul dwells with rapture on the melody of your voice."

"Stanley, dear Stanley," said the maiden, tears still chasing each other down her blushing cheeks, and her voice tremulous with emotion, "my feeble tongue fails to give utterance to the feelings that agitate my breast and bewilder my senses. But I again behold you. I am granted the joyful opportunity of assuring you of the fidelity of my love, that neither time nor absence can ever stale that fond passion in my breast; I still find you, dear Stanley, all that my most ardent hopes can wish, and I am more than recompensed for the troubles, the cares, the anxieties, and the many dangers it has been my lot to undergo, I am happy, Stanley, very happy."

As the poor girl thus spoke, tears rushed to her eyes, but through which shone the bright smile of joy, and she again resigned herself to the affectionate embrace of her lover, who felt the quick beating of the heart of which he reigned supreme master, while he pressed her with unbounded delight to his bosom.

But suddenly she raised her head, and a melancholy expression pervaded her features as dismal thoughts arose to her mind, and in a faint voice, she said—

"Ah, no, I am not happy, I cannot be

completely happy, when I think how soon we shall too probably have to separate, and that even this may be our last meeting."

"Nay, dearest Omelia," returned her lover, "say not so, for the thought of separation saddens the joy of meeting, and excites dismal forebodings that I would fain banish from my mind. Oh, why were our fates not united long ere this, then might you have been constantly near me, and under my protection. But your sudden appearance here, and when danger threatens, fills me with amazement; what strange fortune guided your footsteps hither?"

"My tale, alas, dear Stanley," replied our heroine, is a sad one, and I fear it will pain you to hear it. Are we safe here?"

"Yes," said Stanley, "this is a retired spot, and here we may for a time discourse in safety. Pr'ythee proceed Omelia, for I am all anxiety to know what has occurred to you since the night we parted in Delhi, and how it is I find you here, when I had thought you were far away, and with the unfortunate Flora Melville and the aged man to whom you have told me you are so much indebted."

"May the Great Spirit watch over and protect them," said Omelia, solemnly, "believe me, Edward, I did not abandon them voluntarily, but was surprised by a party of the mutineers, soon after parting with you, and forced away; and after a long and toilsome journey, during which the sufferings and indignities to which I was subjected to, I will not shock your ears by relating, I was dragged before the miscreant Nena Sahib, at Cawnpore."

"Ah, is it possible, my beloved Omelia," said Stanley, much excited, "that you have been exposed to the brutality of that most blood-thirsty of monsters? My blood freezes, and my heart shudders at the thought. But by what miracle did you effect your escape?"

"It was indeed almost miraculous," replied Omelia, "but listen, for I must be brief in relating those particulars which you no doubt are so anxious to know."

Stanley was all breathless attention and curiosity, and Omelia, after a brief pause to collect her thoughts, proceeded to relate in as few words as possible those startling events with which the reader is already acquainted, Stanley frequently compelled to interrupt her to give expression to the emotions which her melancholy but interesting narrative excited in his breast.

"Noble, heroic girl," he exclaimed, "with what matchless fortitude, perseverence, and energy have you supported trials and vicissitudes that might well have made even the stoutest heart quail at the bare conception of. Alas, that you should ever have exposed yourself to such perils and misfortunes."

"It was my fate," replied our heroine, calmly, "and my enterprising spirit would not suffer me to attempt to resist it. But let me proceed."

Stanley bowed assent, and Omelia then proceeded to relate all the perilous and extraordinary adventures she had encountered after her escape from Cawnpore; to which her lover listened with a degree of interest even far exceeding that which he had previously felt, and the terrible adventure with the tiger, and the frightful fate of poor Nazimi, called forth the expression of his deepest horror and sympathy, whilst the truly wonderful escape of Omelia filled his breast with feelings of the warmest gratitude.

But when Omelia came to the death struggle between her father and Captain Woodford, and the awful fate of both of them, and moreover related the extraordinary discovery of his (Stanley's) letter on the person of the unfortunate captain, and produced the same, which she had ever since carried in her bosom, his amazement exceeded all bounds, and he could not help giving unrestrained expression to his feelings, and his deep regret at the untimely death of his friend.

"Poor Woodford," he observed, "he was a noble-minded, gallant fellow, and a warm, enthusiastic, and sincere friend. We had been on terms of the greatest intimacy for many years, and many a scene of danger on the battle-field have we braved together. Unfortunate Woodford, that you should meet with such a fate. And your father, too, Omelia, what must have been your feelings of horror and anguish when you made the fearful discovery."

"My heart trembles, and I shudder with fear when I recal that dreadful moment to my memory," said Omelia, and tears at the same time starting to her eyes; "wretched, misguided parent, with all your faults I cannot restrain those feelings of nature that rise within my breast, and pity and regret mingle with my sorrow at the remembrance of your awful fate, and in the midst of your mad career of crime and bloodshed."

Stanley again fondly embraced her, and with words of the deepest and warmest affection, endeavoured to soothe the poignancy of her anguish.

"Dear Omelia," he ejaculated, "how can I express the boundless transport of my feelings at this moment, my overflowing gratitude to heaven for your preservation and restoration to my arms. Never for a moment has your beloved form and features been absent from my anxious thoughts. They have followed me like mine own shadow, in my waking moments, and through every scene, they have ever been present to my

imagination in the hours of slumber. I have fancied I heard the soft melody of your voice in the murmuring breeze, and saw your beauteous face smiling sweetly and hopefully upon me from the clear, star lighted sky; and it has calmed the tumult of my feelings, excited by care, doubt, and anxiety, and encouraged me in the hour of danger. Beloved Omelia, mistress of my soul's purest, warmest affections, must we indeed ever part again?"

"Alas, it must be so," sighed Omelia, "and that immediately. Heaven only knows when we may meet again, dear Stanley, but rest assured that whatever may be her fate, wherever she may be, or whatever trials she may still have to encounter, your Omelia's affections shall ever remain the same, your beloved form must ever remain deeply

enshrined in her heart till that heart shall for ever cease to beat."

"Think you, my Omelia," said Stanley, as he pressed her more fondly to his bosom, "think you that I can doubt your constancy? oh, I should indeed be unworthy of your love could I do so. But shall our present bliss be only transient, fading as a dream? I cannot, dare not part with you, even though I know that you are now so near me, for dismal forebodings, in spite of all my efforts to subdue them, seem to tell me that some fresh danger is about to arise, which for a long time may separate us, if not for ever. Would to heaven, I say again, that you were my wife, that I might claim to have you constantly under my protection.

The eyes of Omelia, that sparkled through her tears, showed how warmly her heart responded to his feelings, and she hid her blushing cheeks on his bosom.

"We must no longer remain together, dear Stanley," she said, "the growing lateness of the hour warns us to separate. But oh, the happiness of this meeting, and to know that you still live, are near me, and still remain faithful to those fond vows you have so often pledged to me, imparts the most blissful feeling of hope to my throbbing heart, and removes a weight of care and anxiety from my breast which was almost insupportable. We shall meet again, Edward, but a few hours' shall elapse when I sincerely trust that our present happiness will be renewed."

"Yes," said her lover, with renewed hope, "I will, I must cherish that fond idea. And there is every probability in its being speedily realised. Dangers accumulate around us in the city, and our small force will doubtless shortly be compelled to evacuate it, and to retire to the residency, where our presence is so necessary for protection against our enemies. Even with our limited numbers, having for the present an ample supply of provisions and ammunition, with the skill and courage of the gallant Ingliss, the brave officers and men under his command, and the well-known patience, fortitude, and endurance of our fair countrywomen, under the most fearful and trying circumstances, the garrison may be able to hold out for some months, or till fortunately relieved. Courage, then, my dearest Omelia, for even before the sun shall set to-morrow, your faithful Stanley may be by your side again, there to remain until yourself and companions in misfortune are happily placed beyond the reach of danger."

An expression of hope and joy irradiated the beauteous features of Omelia, as she listened to the observations of her lover, and having again embraced each other affectionately, they prepared to separate.

"Farewell, dear Stanley," said our heroine, in accents that told most eloquently the fervour and sincerity of her love, "for a brief period, I trust, farewell. Oh, may all the hopes and wishes we both so warmly cherish be realised, and may that Almighty power which knows our hearts, reward our faithful love."

"Heavenly words," cried the enraptured Stanley, once more pressing an ardent kiss upon her willing lips, "sweet innocent, oh, I could dwell upon your gentle voice for ever, and gaze my very soul away upon those lovely features. But I cannot possibly leave you till I see you in safety in your place of refuge."

"I do not apprehend any danger, for all seems now secure," said Omelia, "and your absence from your quarters may excite surprise and displeasure."

"Fear not for me, my love," replied Stanley, "I can easily account for my absence, and your safety is paramount over every other consideration. Come, then, let us no longer delay."

Omelia offered no farther objection, and they quitted the spot, and in conversation, and with emotions, such as it is needless to describe, made their way towards the residency, without meeting with anything to excite their fears or suspicion.

And there, having arrived in sight of the house in which Omelia at present found an asylum, her and her lover, with many vows of eternal constancy, and blessings upon each other's heads, parted, and Stanley anxiously watched her beloved form until, waving her hand to him in farewell, she was admitted into the house.

Omelia in the present state of her mind, after her affectionate interview with her lover, would willingly at once have sought her chamber, in order that alone she might have given free indulgence to the various thoughts that crowded upon her imagination, but she could not avoid her friends—who anxious for her safety, feeling, as they now did, as great an interest in her fate, as if they had been acquainted for years—were sitting up for her, and expressed their pleasure at her return.

After partaking of refreshments, and passing a short time in conversation with them, she was about to retire, when they were all startled and alarmed by hearing the sharp and loud discharge of fire-arms, apparently in that part of the city immediately contiguous to the residency; volley after volley being repeated in rapid succession, and which plainly showed that some conflict of a determined description had taken place between the soldiery and the mutineers, and the heart of Omelia sickened when she thought of Stanley, who it was most likely was in the midst of the danger, and the utmost consternation prevailed amongst the numerous persons in the house, which was increased as the firing became more fierce and frequent, mingled with the loud shouts of the combatants, seeming to approach nearer every minute, and they could see from the windows the reflection of flames, rising evidently from burning buildings in different directions.

Omelia's feelings were excited to the highest pitch, she clasped her hands in agony together, not from any feeling of personal fear, for to that she was ever a stranger, and it was with difficulty she was prevented from rushing from the place, and boldly, but rashly exposing herself to all the dangers of the deadly strife which was evidently going on.

Some minutes of terrible anxiety and suspense succeeded, the cause of alarm increasing in violence, when an officer and several men entered the house, and informing the inmates that a fierce engagement was at that time taking place between the European troops, who had been stationed in the city, and a large number of the mutineers, near the residency, they could no longer remain there in safety, and that by the orders of Colonel Inglis, they had come to conduct them immediately to the garrison.

The greatest confusion, bustle and activity now prevailed, and every one hastily prepared themselves to depart.

Omelia had formed in a moment a wild and desperate resolution, and her mind once made up, as has been shown on many occasions, nothing whatever could move her from her purpose.

She had still the loaded pistols about her with which she had taken the precaution to arm herself, previous to her departure in search of her lover, and she determined at all hazards to venture to the scene of conflict.

The idea was little short of madness, but she could not resist it, and on leaving the house in the company of the other inmates, in order to proceed to the garrison, she loitered behind, and watching her opportunity, hurried off with courage and determination towards the scene of danger.

As she proceeded, all the terrors of the deadly combat were made apparent to her, in the sound of the firing, the yells and shouts of the combatants, the lurid reflection of flames, and the dense clouds of smoke from numerous conflagrations coupled with the rumbling noise of falling ruins, and it was evident that an outbreak of the most serious and alarming description had taken place.

But still this entrepid girl hurried on, totally regardless, in the anxiety of her feelings, of the fearful consequences that were almost certain to follow so daring and rash a venture. But one thought urged her, and that was her lover, and the wish of sharing with him in those dangers in the midst of which she had no doubt he at present was. The improbability of her encountering him among the numbers and in the confusion of the combat, never for a moment occurred to her. For a time her reason seemed almost to have forsaken her in the excitement of her feelings, but such a thing as fear was entirely a stranger to her breast.

A few minutes more, after turning an abrupt angle in the road, Omelia came immediately in sight of the fierce strife, and a fearful and exciting scene it was, the work of slaughter being maintained with equal determination on both sides, and numbers of the dead and dying already strewing the ground in every direction.

The rebels were in considerable force, but the superior skill and indomitable bravery of their opponents, left very little doubt as to the ultimate result, the mutineers already beginning to give way, and the English soldiers following them up with a dash and daring which could scarcely fail to lead to their speedy discomfiture and defeat, but not until there had been a frightful slaughter on both sides.

Omelia had succeded in placing herself in such a position as to be out of immediate danger, and where she could obtain an almost uninterrupted view of the fearful scene that was being enacted, and it was with a palpitating heart, and many dismal fears and forebodings that the heroic girl watched the progress of the bloody strife, and many were the fervent prayers she uttered for the safety of him whose life was even more precious to her than her very existence.

A loud cheer from the English troops suddenly rent the air, the enemy had given way, and presently Omelia saw them, in great confusion, flying in all directions.

Her excitement and anxiety were now at the highest pitch, for the scene of confusion, horror, and bloodshed that prevailed in the general rout which had taken place among the enemy, even exceeded that of the more determined combat.

Great slaughter took place among the retreating mutineers, for the troops, wrought up to a pitch of revenge for the monstrous outrages that had been perpetrated by the miscreants, gave them no quarter, showed them no mercy, but shot down or bayoneted all who came in their way; but many of them found the courage to make another stand and to renew the combat, which they did with a brute-like valour, or rather ferocity, caused by desperation, although it stood but little chance when opposed to the cool courage and determination of even the small number of their gallant opponents.

Still, although the best which she had the opportunity of selecting under the circumstances, the position in which Omelia stood was one of considerable danger. Straggling parties of combatants frequently approached to within a few yards of her, shots whizzed past her, some of which she escaped by a mere miracle, and yet to have ventured to move from the spot, to attempt to change her situation, would only have been to involve herself in still greater danger, or even to meet with certain and instant death.

But nothing could daunt the courage of

that heroic girl, in fact she thought not of danger, her lover alone occupied her mind, and the certainty that he was one who was engaged in the sanguinary strife, and the probability that he had fallen completely superseded every other idea, and kept her in a continual state of anxiety and suspense.

Once indeed she was observed by a savage looking sepoy, in whose forbidding features —rendered more repulsive by the excitement of the strife—she immediately recognised those of one of the principal associates of her late father, and he seeming also to know her in a moment; with a fierce yell of vengeance, he rushed towards her, sword in hand, evidently with the intention of sacrificing her on the spot, but ere he could have the opportunity of accomplishing his deadly purpose, with that cool intrepidity which ever characterised her conduct, Omelia discharged the contents of the pistol, with which she had so fortunately armed herself, at his head, and with a frightful cry of agony the unhappy wretch fell dead before her.

She then, with the same coolness and deliberation, reloaded the pistol, in order that she might be prepared for any other danger which might threaten her, and resumed her anxious watching.

The combat, however, was not yet at an end, in fact it had now assumed even a more desperate and doubtful aspect. Reinforced by large numbers of native troops from the city and suburbs, the retreating mutineers had in some measure re-organised themselves, and resumed the fierce strife under every advantage, the soldiers in their turn being compelled to make a retreat—which they did fighting resolutely at the same time—towards the garrison, in which they could only hope now to maintain themselves, or to make anything like a formidable resistance.

Omelia's anxieties increased, and the most dismal forebodings distracted her mind, one of the principal and most torturing of which was, that her lover had fallen, and that they had that fatal night beheld each other for the last time. With eager eyes she watched through the smoke, every English officer, whom she could observe, as they approached nearer the place of her concealment, with the desperate hope that she might recognise her beloved Stanley; but no one at all resembling him met her observation, and her anguish of mind increased every moment, and which the exciting and fearful scene did not serve at all to diminish.

She saw officers and men now falling fast before the overwhelming numbers of their savage foes, and the battle had assumed the most alarming form, for unless they could make good their retreat—which they would have the greatest difficulty in doing as the rebels pressed on them so hard—their total annihilation seemed to be inevitable.

Shouts and yells of triumph and of vengeance from the mutineers now rent the air, and mingling with the groans of the wounded and the dying added to the horrors of the appalling scene.

In every part of the city too, in which any Europeans had not had an opportunity of retreating, still remained, the work of destruction and inhuman slaughter was frightfully proceeding; houses were blazing and falling in every direction, men, women, and children were dragged forth into the open air, barbarously murdered, and their mangled bodies then cast into the flames. Monster's in human form were seen rushing exultingly about with poor innocent children writhing on the points of their bayonets, while the wretched parents were subjected to such tortures as only the minds of fiends could possibly conceive.

While these dreadful outrages were being committed, and the miscreants absolutely revelled and luxuriated in human bloodshed, Omelia, who from her position, fortunately had no chance of witnessing them, could yet, as she imagined, at intervals between the firing and the confusion of the other noises, hear the shrieks and groans of the unfortunate victims, and terrible were the feelings that it excited in her breast. But still the probable fate of her lover was uppermost in her thoughts, and her fears were strengthened when she saw the advantage which the rebels had now obtained, and the number of European officers and soldiers who were falling before the superior force that was opposed to them.

It was evident that this outbreak had been well organised and matured, and fatal and horrible were the results. Omelia's heart bled as she thought of them, and she was half disposed several times to rush into the midst of the deadly strife, and by lending her humble aid, alike expose herself to all those dangers by which so many others were surrounded. A strange and extravagant idea haunted her imagination that providence would guide her to her lover, and preposterous even as it was, it every moment gained strength in her mind, until she found it impossible any longer to resist it. Nothing could shake the courage of the noble-minded and heroic Hindoo maiden, and there was no danger, however appalling, which had any terror for her.

More than an hour had now elapsed since Omelia had taken up her hazardous position, and watched with trembling anxiety the horrors that were being enacted before her, and still an irresistible spell appeared to fascinate and rivet her to the spot, and her anxiety for her lover to absorb every other feeling.

And now she heard the loud report of cannon from the garrison, which made it appear that an attack on that was also taking place, by which the retreat of the soldiers might be cut off, unless they could fight their way through the beseigers, which, from their diminished numbers, might be rendered difficult, if not absolutely impossible

"I can endure this suspense no longer," at last said Omelia; "I must, I will brave everything with the hope of once more beholding you, dear, noble Stanley; and oh, if you should have fallen in the deadly strife, let me also perish on your cold corse, for life would then become a hateful burthen to me."

Boldly she grasped her pistol, and with rapid steps and features animated with hope and expectation, she fearlessly rushed from the place where she had hitherto been concealed, towards the troops that were retiring to the garrison, hotly engaged with the mutineers as they endeavoured to make good their retreat; no fear or misgiving could daunt her, no danger be suffered to retard or impede the intrepid girl's progress. Carnage and horror reigned on every side of her, but she shrunk not from it. The shots fell thick and fast around, yet into the midst of the hottest of the strife she hurried, actually startling and electrifying everybody who beheld her by the singularity of her appearance and the boldness of her demeanour, and in consequence of her being a native, no one could have any idea of what were her real intentions, and offered not to molest her.

With the wild and disordered look of some wretched maniac, she rushed in among the combatants, seeming to set the death which threatened her from every side at defiance, and to be specially protected by some merciful and invisible power.

Indeed such was the extraordinary sensation her appearance had created, that no one offered to obstruct her, but all suffered her to pass them, on her strange errand, unharmed.

Perhaps the mutineers viewed her with some superstitious kind of awe, however, whatever might be the nature of the feeling, it was a fortunate one for Omelia, for it seemed to place a shield of protection before her, and to aid her in her designs.

Eager were the looks she cast around her at the combatants, and often at the ghastly faces of the dead and dying, that so thickly strewed the ground, but without encountering the features of Stanley. Many were the miraculous escapes she had, and at last she found herself in one of the main streets of the city, and apart from the spot where the strife was raging most fiercely and the dan-

ger was the greatest. Here she paused to recover herself, and to collect her thoughts; and when she viewed the frightful scene through which she had passed, she was astounded at her own achievement, and could scarce believe the evidence of her senses.

Still her hopes had not been realised, her uncertainty and suspense remained the same, and she could not rest until they were in some measure removed.

"Dear Stanley," she exclaimed, "even though I perish in the attempt, I must, I will continue to pursue the search. What danger is there that your Omelia would shrink from encountering for your sake? And yet, how wild and hopeless is this search? Whither can I now direct my footsteps?"

She was interrupted by the noise of a struggle and the clashing of swords in a small bye street, that opened almost on the immediate spot where she was standing, and grasping her pistol firmly, she drew a little aside into the shade, fully prepared to meet this fresh adventure, whatever the nature of it might be.

She was not long kept in suspense, for the combatants emerged from the street, fiercely engaged, and, although she could perceive they were a tall and powerful sepoy and an English officer, the darkness was too great to enable her to observe them more narrowly. Her heart palpitated violently, and strange thoughts and presentiments came over her, which increased to an almost insurmountable pitch every instant.

Fighting desperately they approached so near to the spot from whence she was watching them, that she was enabled to observe their persons more distinctly, and that of the English officer more particularly, but just at the moment when its familiarity struk her most forcibly, the sword was struck out of his hand by the heavy blows of his antagonist, he sinking on his knee with the violence of the shock, and the officer was thus left at the mercy of the sepoy—for it seemed that he had no other weapon of defence—who, with a cry of exultation was about to seize his advantage by thrusting his sword in the defenceless man's body, when Omelia, with unerring aim, fired and the Indian fell mortally wounded to the earth

The officer turned hastily to ascertain who was his deliverer, and Omelia was hastening towards him, when a shot from some unseen enemy took effect in her side, and with a faint exclamation, the poor girl staggered, and sunk senseless in the arms of her lover.

Yes, it was indeed Edward Stanley, whom the heroic maiden had so providentially rescued, and who had probably sacrificed her own life in doing so, and with the wild frenzy of despair he strained her bleeding form to his heart, and called in agony on her name. But he had not a moment given him for the expression of his feelings. He saw the man who had probably committed the fatal deed, approaching him stealthily, and seeing at once the desperate situation of himself and the unfortunate Omelia, he hastily regained his sword, and aroused to perfect fury, he stood upon his defence, and avoiding the shot which the sepoy aimed at him, while he supported the inanimate form of Omelia in one arm, with a desperate blow he cut the fellow to the earth, and then stood transfixed to the spot, with a bewildered and agonised brain, and gazed first upon the pale face of his insensible burthen, and then wildly around him.

The moment was one of the greatest horror that Stanley had ever experienced, and it was in vain that he tried to control the poignant and insupportable anguish of his feelings.

"Omelia—beloved Omelia!" he exclaimed, with a burst of emotion which no language could properly describe, "speak to me—for the love of heaven speak to me if only for an instant to remove the horrible fears that beset my mind, and to convince me that you are still alive. No, she cannot speak; her eyes are closed, she breathes but faintly, and the blood flows fast from the fatal wound. And here there are no means of rendering her that immediate assistance she so much needs. Omelia, devoted, heroic girl, must you thus perish? I shall go distracted. Oh, God, what a terrible calamity is this."

Again he strained her to his bosom, and kissing her frantically, endeavoured to recal her to life. But even in the expression of these feelings he was not long allowed to indulge; loud shouts rent the air, followed by repeated volleys, and the next instant a number of the combatants fiercely engaged rushed towards the place where the distracted Stanley, still supporting the inanimate form of the senseless Omelia in his arms, was standing, and before he had time to defend himself or to protect her whose life was more precious to him than his own, he received a blow on the head from the butt-end of a musket, which felled him senseless to the earth, and Omelia sunk prostrate by his side.

CHAPTER XLIV.

THE FATE OF OMELIA—FRESH TROUBLES.

The mutineers were, after a sanguinary struggle, driven back with great loss, and the troops, who had acted so bravely, made their way in safety to the fortress, the inmates of which were in a state of great alarm, as they had expected every moment the appearance of their inhuman and remorseless enemies.

Thither also the insensible Lieutenant Stanley, together with several more wounded officers and men, was conveyed, but Omelia was left behind on the spot where she had fallen, and left to her fate.

On being restored to sensibility, and finding himself lying in bed in one of the rooms of the garrison, Stanley at first had but a vague recollection of what had happened; but suddenly it all rushed upon his memory with horrible force, and for some time the excitement of his feelings—especially when he could obtain no information respecting Omelia, and he had every reason to believe that she had perished—assumed the most alarming aspect, his senses wandered, he raved wildly, and it was found impossible to control or soothe him.

At length he did become somewhat more calm, and then the melancholy manner in which he bemoaned the fate of Omelia, and gave utterance to the despair and agony of his feelings, were piteous to listen to.

"Unfortunate girl," he sighed, "by what strange fatality were your footsteps guided to that spot, in such a moment of terrible danger? Why were you induced to run so fearful a risk, when you might still have been here safe from every harm? We shall meet no more; doubtless you have fallen into the hands of the inhuman foe, and the consequences of which are too fearfully certain. Oh, God! that one so lovely, so good, so innocent, should meet with so dreadful and untimely a fate. This calamity is too much for me. I shall go mad."

He beat his breast as he thus spoke, and abandoned himself to all the violence of his grief, which acting upon the injury he had received, and which was severe, threw him into a high state of fever, and produced other dangerous symptoms.

The whole of that fatal and eventful night he remained in the same state and his ultimate recovery seemed to be extremely doubtful. At times he was quite delirious, and then the mournful lamentations to which he gave utterance excited the deepest sympathy in the minds of all who heard him.

"Cruel, cruel, fate," he would sigh in his calmer and more reasonable moments, "thus remorselessly to deprive me of that one fair and gentle being who was all that I most prized on earth. Alas, how fatally are those fond hopes and visions of happiness in which I had ventured to indulge, destroyed, annihilated at one fell swoop. There is nothing now left me for which I wish to cling to life. The future is all misery and dark despair."

Thus Stanley continued for some days, and then his recovery to anything like health was painfully slow and tedious.

But what was the fate of Omelia?

How long, from the loss of blood, she had remained insensible, she had no means of ascertaining, but on reviving it was broad daylight, and the sun was streaming in at the window of a chamber in which she found herself, lying upon a mattress, and attended by two Indian women of rather forbidding features and unprepossessing appearance altogether.

Her wound had been carefully dressed, and although extremely weak and faint, she felt perfectly free from pain.

At first her brain was too much bewildered for her to arrange her thoughts in anything like order, or to recal what had happened to her memory, but the voices of the two women—who were engaged in conversation in under tones, and seated on the opposite side of the room—aroused her from forgetfulness, and as the recollection of her extraordinary meeting with Stanley, and under circumstances of such danger, recurred to her memory, she could not help giving utterance to a cry of agony, of which the women seemed to take no notice, but still continued their conversation.

The character of the room in which she was, and the appearance of the women convinced her that she was not in the house which she had so imprudently left on the fatal night of the outbreak, and a feeling of terror and foreboding stole over her which she could not resist or conquer.

The room was large, but mean and dirty, and badly furnished, and there was something about its aspect altogether which gave it a prison-like appearance.

With difficulty Omelia raised herself on her elbow in the bed, and gazed around the place with eager curiosity, and the women probably for the first time noticing that she had revived, approached, and one of them in a coarse and unfeeling tone inquired what she wanted, adding that she thought if she were wise she would remain quiet.

"What place is this?" she anxiously demanded, "where am I?—who are you? Oh, tell me, am I with friends or foes?"

"You are with those who were your father's friends," answered one of the women, "and but for your conduct, so unworthy of the country which gave you birth, they should be your's also."

"Ah," cried Omelia, in a voice of despair, "am I then known, discovered, and in the power of the rebels? Then indeed am I lost. Oh, terrible misfortune."

She pressed her hand upon her forehead, and could not refrain from tears.

"But you will not harm me," she exclaimed, eagerly, after a pause, "you will not seek to detain me?"

"Hark ye," returned the woman, "and let the brief explanations I am about to give you suffice for the present. In searching for their wounded comrades, you were found by a party of those whom you have ventured to call rebels, and being recognised as the treacherous daughter of Yunadar, and finding that you still lived, you was conveyed to this bungalow, which is situated without the city walls, and is well guarded since you have been brought here."

"And what is it intended to do with me?" interrogated our heroine, with a look of alarm.

"That question I am not prepared to answer," said the woman, "but you may depend upon it that one who has proved herself so dangerous a character, and a traitress to our righteous cause, will be well taken care of."

"Alas, alas," sighed Omelia, "I see at once my hopeless and desperate situation. But have you no feeling of pity for one of your own sex?"

"No," answered the woman, sternly, "not for one who is the enemy of her country and the friend of the hated Feringhee. Your deeds are well known to those who now hold you in their power, and you will have to answer for them to one whom you should have cause to dread."

"Then there is no hope," said Omelia, and her heart seemed to sink within her. But suddenly her courage revived, and fixing a proud and haughty look upon the woman she before addressed, she observed—

"I see that you are destitute of every feeling of humanity, that you exult in my misfortune, and therefore it would be a waste of words and a degradation on my part, were I to condescend to appeal to you. There is one above who knows the rectitude and justice of my motives, and who will, I trust, continue to protect me from the deadly malice of my enemies. Omelia, the Indian maid, who has boldly faced the greatest danger, and risked her life to save that of others, is not to be so easily intimidated; she will not faiter now."

"These are bold words," replied the woman, "but they are lost upon me. I will leave you to discuss that matter with my husband, whom probably you may recollect as the particular friend of your father—Allyghur."

"Allyghur!" repeated Omelia, in astonishment, "is it possible that I am in the power of that heartless miscreant? Then indeed I have everything to dread. But still I will be firm, and hold him at defiance."

"You will probably change your tone, young woman, before long," remarked the woman who had not before addressed her; "but come, Zoa," she added, speaking to her companion, "let us retire for awhile, as our *friend* here can probably dispense with our society."

"Aye," returned Zoa; "there is all that is necessary for you in your present state," she continued, pointing to a small table which had been placed near the bed, "but I would advise you to endeavour to cool your temper, and obtain some sleep if you can."

Our heroine fixed a scornful look upon her, but returned no answer, and the two women quitted the room, and she was left to the indulgence of her own thoughts.

The torturing nature of these may be readily imagined, and in spite of all her efforts to the contrary, she could not but abandon herself to feelings of the most painful apprehension, if not absolute despair.

In the power of such a villain as Allyghur, whom she had on several occasions given cause for feelings of revenge, she had everything to dread, and certainly she could expect no pity or mercy from him, therefore nothing could be more terrible than the prospect before her, and she shuddered at the contemplation of it.

But there was one agonising thought which completely superseded every other, and racked and distracted her brain. And that was the fate which had befallen Stanley, for it seemed but too probable that he had been sacrificed to the savage vengeance of the rebels, and all thoughts of her own situation were completely lost in that terrible idea.

Never had she felt so truly wretched as she did at that moment, a feeling of uncontrollable horror pervaded her senses, scalding tears gushed from her eyes, and she beat her breast in all the intensity of mental anguish.

"The only one bright link which held me to life, and hope, and happiness is severed," she mournfully ejaculated; "that noble youth whom I prized above all earthly beings is—I feel too forcibly the terrible conviction —no more, and now it matters but little what becomes of me. Oh, Stanley, alas, why did we ever know each other, and learn to love so fondly, passionately, and fervently, since fate has ordained that we should thus be separated?"

Her tears flowed faster than before, as she thus gave utterance to the violent emotions that agitated her, and convulsive sobs escaped her bosom. All the horrors of the night, and the fearful circumstances under which she had met her lover, recurred to her recollection, and confirmed her worst apprehen-

sions. She tried to hope that by some miracle Stanley had escaped, and was now in safety, but in vain; and the more she endeavoured to do so, the greater became her anguish and despair.

For some time she continued thus, but at length as a sudden thought occurred to her, she aroused herself, and exerting all her strength, she arose from the bed, and with a feeble step, walked across the room to the window, which she found was too strongly secured to render any attempt to open it effectual.

The window looked upon a tastefully arranged garden of considerable extent, and in which she beheld several of the sepoys seated, or loitering about at their ease, drinking, smoking, and apparently enjoying themselves freely, and it therefore seemed that the bungalow, or mansion—for it was a building of some consequence—was used as a kind of barracks or rendevous by a portion of the mutineers, and thus all hope of escape —if she had entertained the idea—was at an end, and she had everything to fear from the brutality of cowardly ruffians, who were capable of any atrocity, and were entirely insensible to every feeling of shame.

The house and gardens were surrounded by a high stone wall, beyond which appeared the distant mountains, soaring to the clouds, and this was the limited prospect which was afforded to Omelia from the dreary room in which she was confined, but which was now rendered a little more cheerful by the bright noonday sun.

She again became lost in gloomy meditation. She had hoped that the villain Allyghur had fallen by her hand, when she last encountered him, and that she had thus got rid of one of her most inveterate enemies for ever, but now that she found he still lived, and that he held her in his power, she could not but expect that he would wreak his deadly vengeance on her head; and she therefore endeavoured to prepare herself to meet with fortitude and resignation the terrible fate which seemed too probably in store for her, and which, unless by some merciful interposition of providence, it appeared it was impossible to avoid.

She sat for some time wrapped in these reflections—having managed to dress herself —and she then walked to the door, which she tried, but found it fastened, so that it was evident she was in every sense of the word a prisoner.

She then knelt down and solemnly invoked the mercy and protection of the Supreme, and prayed that her beloved Stanley might be still alive, and implored of heaven to continue to preserve him, and shower its blessings upon his head, even

though it might be their fate never to meet again.

She felt more composed after this, and awaited patiently and with becoming fortitude the result of the day.

More than an hour passed away in this dreary manner, Omelia continuing at the window, with her eyes fixed admiringly upon the garden, and the beautiful variegated flowers it contained, and which in some measure served to divert her thoughts from the dismal and painful subjects that had before engrossed them. She wondered that the woman called Zoa—who had stated herself to be the wife of Allyghur—or her companion, did not return, though from the vulgarity and unkindness of their behaviour, and the manner in which they had seemed to exult in her misfortune, she had no reason

to court their society. Her chief, though melancholy consolation, was in re-perusing again and again Stanley's letter, which she had found in the pocket of the ill fated Captain Woodford, and which she had ever since carried in her bosom, and how varied and torturing were the emotions that agitated her as she did so. She could almost imagine as she traced the beloved lines—although every word that the epistle contained was indelibly stamped upon her memory—that she could hear the voice of her lover repeat them, and that idea made her dwell upon them with still greater fondness and melancholy delight.

At length she was aroused from this busy train of thought by the sound of footsteps ascending the stairs that led to the room in which she was confined, and hastily replacing

No. 25.

the letter in her bosom, she summoned to her aid all the fortitude she could, to meet whatever was now about to take place.

The door was quickly opened, and Zoa entered, and evincing some surprise on beholding that Omelia had arisen, she beckoned to some one outside, and the next moment the dreaded Allyghur made his appearance.

He stood for two or three minutes near the door, and fixed his eyes upon the countenance of his intended victim with a savage expression of malicious triumph, which, however, Omelia met firmly, and returned with a look of scorn and hatred.

"Leave the room, Zoa," he said at length to his wife, "my business is with the girl alone."

Zoa obeyed, and the ruffian then approached our heroine nearer, and folding his arms again gazed upon her for a few moments with the same looks of exultation and revenge, without speaking. Omelia, however evinced not the least fear or agitation, and the firmness of her demeanour evidently disappointed him, and took him by surprise.

"So," at length he said, in tones of bitter sarcasm, "the daring female champion of the enemies of her country, the heroine, the amazon, is at last stopped in her career, and finds herself in the power of him whose life she had sought on more than one occasion; what mercy do you expect at his hands?"

"I neither expect nor condescend to ask for any from a villain whom I know to be utterly insensible to every feeling of humanity and shame," replied Omelia, firmly, "I place my reliance on the protection of that power whose laws you have so monstrously outraged, and defy the utmost that your most deadly malice can inflict. Omelia, conscious of the justice and integrity of her own conduct, and the motives that have ever guided it, entertains no fear of your threats."

"Indeed," returned Allyghur, "but methinks you will be inclined to change your tone when I put your boasted courage to the test? What if I should inflict bodily tortures upon you, so terrible, that even all those that so many of our detested enemies have suffered might appear insignificant to them?"

"I scorn them," replied Omelia, with the same unshaken firmness.

"You pride yourself upon your virtue and innocence," continued the miscreant, "what if you were despoiled of that, and made a thing of shame, hateful to yourself, and despised and loathed by even the most despicable of your own sex?"

What feelings of horror and disgust swelled the bosom of the indignant girl at those brutal, those monstrous observations. But while the burning blush of outraged mo-

desty glowed on her cheeks, and the deepest resentment flashed from her eyes, in a voice that even abashed the villain who thus dared to insult her, she replied—

"Miscreant!—shameless wretch! whose guilty mind can conceive and devise that which none but monsters of the deepest dye could imagine; still will I scorn and defy your brutal threats, you dare not put them into execution. The terrible wrath of heaven would descend upon your head in the atrocious attempt, and crush you."

"Ha, ha, ha," he laughed scornfully, "I mock and despise the power on which you profess to depend; what then should deter me from my purpose, knowing that any resistance on your part, if I were so resolved, would be perfectly useless? But that task will probably devolve upon another, whose name, in spite of your affected courage, you must tremble to hear, and whose power you must dread. Dare you defy Nena Sahib?"

"Nena Sahib!" repeated Omelia, with a look of terror which she could not conceal.

"Aye," replied Allyghur, "your looks convince me, in spite of your boasted courage, how much you shudder at the mention of one so terrible to his enemies, so implacable in his hatred and his vengeance. Hark ye, it is no secret to me, as you are doubtless aware, that you have already been in the Nena's power, from which you have but recently escaped. No doubt he would well reward those who should be the means of restoring you to him. That task shall be mine, and no doubt you can shrewdly guess the fate which you may expect at his hands, and in the certainty of that, my revenge will be fully gratified. Ah, you tremble—'tis well, my triumph is doubly complete, for I have changed to abject fear the daring courage you pretended to feel."

Omelia's heart did indeed fail her, and she shuddered with horror at the threat which Allyghur had uttered, and which she was satisfied he would fulfill, and the thought of being again placed in the power and at the mercy of the monster Nena Sahib, and the fate which would then inevitably await her, was almost too terrible for contemplation.

"Allyghur," she said, in a subdued tone, and with a look of remonstrance and supplication, "cruel and heartless as I know you to be, and deadly as is the hatred you bear me, I cannot, dare not believe that you will put your terrible thought into execution. You will not consign me once more to the power of that most fearful of miscreants, the atrocious Nena Sahib. I implore you to have some consideration and pity for my youth and sex. Surely I have not deserved from you such brutal vengeance. Whatever

I have done towards you, was but in self-defence, and——"

"You appeal to me in vain," savagely interrupted Allyghur, "I have no pity, no forbearance to show towards the presumptuous girl who has made herself the associate and partizan of those whom every truly patriotic Indian seek to extirminate; why should I show any mercy to her who has shed my blood? 'Tis mine now to triumph."

"Allyghur," said the maiden, wrought up to a most painful pitch of excitement by the dread of the horrible and revolting fate with which the villain had threatened her, "you will not surely remain thus inexorable. As you hope for mercy from that Almighty power whom you have so grossly offended, and whose avenging wrath even now threatens to descend upon your guilty head, you will pause ere you commit a crime so hideous that it must consign your soul to perdition. Rather this moment plunge your dagger in my heart than consign me to a fate more horrible than even the most torturing death could possibly be."

"Ah," cried the ruffian, his features frightfully distorted with his brutal passions, "so then I have fairly triumphed o'er the proud and obstinate spirit which lately laughed my threats to scorn, and the haughty sepoy's daughter, her who dared to despise and trample on her father's authority, and to oppose him in all his designs, deigns to sue to me for pity. Oh, what self-humiliation is there, and what satisfaction does it afford me. Grant you death; no, that would indeed be too great a mercy, lingering torture, and the greatest degradation which can possibly befal a human being, can alone satiate the hatred and the vengeance I owe you. Already have I despatched intelligence of your capture to the Nena, and before many hours have elapsed you will be on your way to his palace at Bithoor

"Then may the curses of the Great Spirit, as assuredly they will, pursue you," exclaimed our heroine, mustering up all her fortitude, and re-assuming all her former dignified and defiant demeanour; "I will sue to you no more. Begone, miscreant, leave me; Omelia has still the courage to laugh your utmost malice to scorn."

"Ha, ha, ha," again laughed Allyghur triumphantly and contemptuously, as he moved towards the door, "bold words, bold words these, but the time will quickly arrive when we shall be better enabled to judge of their importance. I leave you to the pleasure and gratification of your own reflections."

As he thus spoke, fixing upon Omelia a look of the most repulsive and malicious description, he quitted the room, and the unfortunate girl, overwhelmed with the power of the various emotions that agitated her breast, and almost maddened her brain, sunk back in her chair, and almost fainted away.

CHAPTER XLV.

THE DEPARTURE.—THE DARK OMEN OF THE FUTURE.

The fortitude with which Omelia had hitherto supported herself under the most trying and distressing circumstances, now, for the time being, at any rate, entirely forsook her, at the thought of her return to the power of the sanguinary Nena Sahib, and the dreadful fate which consequently, in all probability awaited her, and she gave way to a violent paroxysm of grief which for some time she could not even attempt to subdue.

The threats which Allyghur had held out to her, she was well convinced he would not fail to carry into execution to the fullest extent, and she could encourage no hope, could see no prospect whatever, of being able to avoid the horrors they involved. Such were the terrors that the bare anticipation of that fate created in her mind that she was worked up to a pitch bordering upon frenzy, and had she possessed the means, she might have been hurried into an act of self-destruction, rather than been exposed to the danger of encountering it.

For some time so bewildered was her brain, that she could not arrange her thoughts into anything like order, or give expression to the acute anguish of her feelings in words. Hysterical sobs escaped her bosom, her eyes were fixed on vacancy, and she clasped her hands vehemently together in all the intense and insupportable agony of despair.

And thus, for more than an hour, she remained transfixed, speechless, inanimate as a statue, and every faculty suspended in horror, in her chair, and no one came to interrupt her. But at length she started wildly from her seat, as if awakened from some frightful dream, and pressing her hands upon her burning temples, she exclaimed, in a voice in which all the most poignant anguish of her feelings was powerfully expressed—

"Powers of mercy! what have I done that I should be doomed to such a revolting fate as this? Surely you will not forsake me, knowing the integrity and purity of my motives, will not forsake me in this the time of my greatest need and danger, and suffer the guilty to triumph in their diabolical, their monstrous designs. Rather let me die, than be destined to that from which my soul recoils in unspeakable disgust, and the bare anticipation of which freezes the blood in my veins with horror. But no, it cannot be, I dare not, will not believe that heaven will so far abandon me as to leave me to such a doom. Oh, Stanley, beloved, noble Stanley, if you have indeed escaped the fate which I have too much reason to fear has befallen you, and are still living, your fondest, your most anxious thoughts, I know are fixed on me, and what, oh, what would be the agony, the horror, the despair of your feelings, could you but be aware of the dreadful situation of her to whom your noble heart, your very soul is so ardently devoted, at this moment? Look down with pity upon me All Gracious Powers, and avert the horrors that are impending o'er my head."

In a delirium of indescribable agony, the poor girl sunk upon her knees as she sobbed forth the last words, and even the most hardened, the most callous-hearted person who could have seen her at that moment, and marked the thorough misery, and hopelessness that were expressed in every lineament of her beauteous features, and thrilled through every vein, must have been moved to pity.

The intensity of the thoughts that crowded upon her, was almost too much for human nature to support, she staggered to her feet, a mist seemed to gather before her eyes, a deathly faintness came over her, and appeared to chain every faculty, her brain turned giddy, and she sunk upon the bed in a state of utter unconsciousness.

From this, after remaining in it for a considerable time, she was aroused by the entrance of Zoa, on beholding whom, and the recollection of all that Allyghur had said to her and threatened her with rushed upon her brain, she started up in the bed, and gazing at her for a few moments with mingled looks of anguish and supplication, she said—

"Save me, save me—in mercy save me from the dreadful fate with which that terrible man whom you call your husband has threatened me. Surely, if your heart is not altogether invulnerable to pity, if every spark of humanity is not altogether extinguished in your breast, you cannot turn a deaf ear to the supplications, the earnest prayers of a poor friendless and helpless girl who is standing on the brink of ruin. Nay turn not away from me with looks of scorn, and feelings of indifference. I never injured you, and surely then cannot be unworthy of your sympathy. If you are indeed a woman and possessed of woman's gentlest feelings and attributes, I shall not, cannot plead to you in vain. Oh, hear me, in mercy hear me, and interpose to rescue me from that which presents more horrors to my affrighted imagination than even the most lingering death of torture.

Overwhelmed with the violent tempest of her feelings, Omelia, whose fortitude and self-possession had never on any occasion so entirely deserted her, could say no more, but again clasping her hands vehemently and convulsively together, she burst into a paroxysm of sobs and tears, and it seemed as if reason, for the time being, had almost forsook its seat.

Zoa so far from being moved to compassion, seemed to view the grief and misery of the unfortunate girl with the most perfect indifference, or even satisfaction, and while a satirical smile was on her harsh and repulsive features, she said—

"Is this the firmness and thorough contempt with which you stated you were prepared to meet whatever fate with which you might be threatened, and to hurl defiance at Allyghur? I thought that it would but require an interview with him to cause you to alter your tone."

"Oh, forbear thus to taunt and mock me," said Omelia, in vain endeavouring to tranquillise her feelings, and to regain her wonted confidence, "you surely cannot close your heart against me?"

"You only waste your time, girl, in thus appealing to me," replied the brutal woman, "I have no power to serve you, even if I had the will. Allyghur is not the man to be moved from any purpose upon which he has fixed his mind. You have by your own conduct provoked and braved his wrath, and you must take the consequences."

Omelia fixed upon her one look of mingled disgust, shame and reproach—which Zoa met with the same frigid scorn and indifference—and then uttering a groan of anguish, which she could not restrain, and covering her face with her hands, she relapsed into silence and abandoned herself to all the misery of her feelings.

But at length ashamed of the weakness which she imagined she had betrayed so unnatural to her real character, and seeing how completely useless it was to try to move to anything like feelings of pity, one who was evidently a stranger to every sense of humanity or womanly quality, she aroused herself, and assuming all the resolution she had generally at her command, she determined to meet the worst with composure and firmness, and she felt the greatest relief when Zoa—after having in vain tried to persuade her to partake of some refreshment and again dressed her wound, which was very slight, and caused her but little pain—again retired from the room, and she was once more left to the solitude of her own melancholy reflections, the nature of which must be too apparent to the reader to need any description from us.

Still at times a ray of hope would dawn upon her mind that something would yet occur to avert that which she so much dreaded, and to thwart the base and malicious designs of the villain Allyghur, and in that hope she endeavoured to be firm, and await the issue with patience and resignation.

The day passed away tediously, but without anything more particular occurring, Allyghur did not again obtrude himself upon her, and Zoa only visited her once more for a few minutes in the evening, in order to see to her necessities for the night, when Omelia, to whom her presence had now become thoroughly disgusting, refrained from entering into any conversation with her.

It was very little repose that Omelia could obtain that night, and when she did, the busy thoughts that had occupied her mind during the day, conjured up wild visions to her disordered imagination, rendered those of sleep even more painful and harrassing than her waking moments.

She arose the following morning sad and melancholy, and was soon afterwards joined by Zoa, who seemed to be in a more agreeable mood than usual, and even condescended to enter freely into conversation, and to profess some degree of kindness and sympathy for the fair prisoner, expressing her regret that she was so soon about to lose the society of Omelia, but this was spoken in a tone of sarcasm that could not be mistaken by our heroine, and she treated it with the contempt it deserved.

Omelia was not to be deceived by the plausible manners of Zoa, on that occasion, and she took good care to show her that she was not so. Her observations were few and pointed, and delivered in a tone of haughtiness, yet becoming dignity, which no doubt was extremely mortifying to the woman, treating her as it was with scorn and evident abhorrence, and, after a short time, Omelia having been induced to partake of some refreshment, she quitted the room.

Before she went, however, she unfastened the window, and raised it slightly, letting in the fresh morning breeze, and the fragrance of numerous beauteous flowers from the garden.

This was indeed a great boon to Omelia, and she felt grateful for it. She took her seat by the window, and inhaled the pure air with a feeling of delight, and watched the rising sun as it burst forth in all its majesty in the eastern horizon, its bright beams imparting fresh beauty to the face of nature, and glittering amidst the waters of the several fountains that sported in the garden.

Bright visions of the past stole upon her memory, and caused her mingled pleasure and pain. She thought of the earlier days of her childhood, when she first came under the protection of the late amiable and benevolent Mr. Melville, and she could not but shed a tear of heartfelt gratitude to his memory. Then she recalled to her remembrance the many happy hours that her and Flora had passed together in the beautiful residence, and in rambling amongst the lovely and romantic scenery at Agra, she thought of the truly sisterly affection that fair and gentle being had ever evinced towards her, and her anxiety for the fate which had probably befallen her since their separation, and so soon after her melancholy bereavement, increased, and she breathed a fervent prayer for her safety and welfare.

But the thoughts that haunted her imagination and racked her brain more than all were the circumstances of the early love of Stanley and herself. Their joyous meetings, their mutual vows of affection, his noble sentiments, his solemn promises, (one of which he had never broken) all were treasured in her memory with the fondest delight, and now they rushed upon her with tenfold force, bringing with them feelings of pleasure, yet of anguish.

"Happy days," she sighed, "gone, alas, I fear, for ever; oh, how can I recall ye to my memory, and contrast them with the gloomy present without feelings of the most poignant anguish and regret? Oh, would that I were again the happy child I was, wandering hand-in-hand with poor Flora, among those lovely scenes that must ever be endeared to my recollection, and treasured in the deepest recess of my heart, or climbing the lofty hills or mountains in sportive play, while our joyous laugh, would make the air (balmy with the breath of flowers) resound again. And then when childhood ripened into youth, and fresh hopes and prospects dawned upon my glowing imagination, painting the future in the most vivid and flattering colours, you, dear Stanley came to add fresh energy to my ambition, and happiness to my heart. Oh, the bliss, yet sorrow of that recollection, how it throbs through every vein, and rushing to my brain bewilders my senses. Alas, since cruel fate seems to be opposed to our union, and we are now separated I fear, alas, for ever, better, much better would it have been if we had never met, never had know each other. Oh, Edward, I cannot think of you without a bursting heart, for something seems to whisper to me that you are now no more, and if so the sooner the poor, lonely, wretched Omelia is permitted to join you in a better world, the better will it be for her miseries."

She pressed her hands upon her forehead, and her tears flowed fast, while convulsive sobs heaved and agitated her bosom.

It was some minutes ere she could at all regain her tranquillity; but she was aroused by the voices of men in the garden, engaged in noisy conversation, which was followed by loud and vulgar laughter, and looking in the direction it proceeded from, she beheld two men emerging from behind a group of tall trees at the farther end of the garden, and in the person of one of whom she immediately recognised the villain Allyghur.

She could not help shuddering as she gazed upon the villain who had held out to her such atrocious threats, and which she had not the slightest doubt he would fulfill, but still she could not avert her eyes from him.

Allyghur seemed to be highly amused with the subject that himself and his companion were discussing, for he frequently laughed heartily; and there was that in his very laughter which could scarcely fail to excite disgust, and to create a foreboding of evil.

He stopped underneath the window, and before Omelia had time to withdraw herself from it, he nudged the arm of his companion, and they both looked up towards the window.

Seeing our heroine there, Allyghur bowed with mock gallantry and politeness, and she could observe the sardonic and sarcastic smile with which he accompanied his affected courtesy.

With a feeling of the utmost disgust, at the same time she could not help a sensation of dread stealing over her, Omelia hastily closed the window and retired from it to another part of the room, and throwing herself upon a chair, she abandoned herself to the disagreeable reflections to which this simple circumstance gave rise.

In these she was, however, not long permitted to indulge without interruption, for she heard footsteps on the stairs, and before she had time to collect herself, the room door was unceremoniously opened, and Allyghur again stood before her, with the sarcastic look of triumph and undisguised malice with which he had before met her. Omelia, who quickly recovered her usual firmness, returned it with one of contempt and defiance, and then calmly awaited to hear what the villain had to say to her.

"So," he at length observed, "you were enjoying the beauties of the gardens from the window of this elegant apartment, fair Omelia. They are very charming, are they not? but still insignificant in comparison with the pleasures that no doubt are in store for you at the palace of that truly amiable man, Nena Sahib."

"Villain," returned the maiden boldly, and fixing upon him a withering look, "think not to wound or mortify me by your unmanly irony, for it does but excite my contempt, and increase my detestation. I am prepared for all that your malice can invent to annoy me. I still put my trust in that power which has hitherto proted me through so many dangers and difficulties, and which, I feel convinced, will not desert me now."

"What matchless heroism this would be," said Allyghur, with the same look of villany, "if it were only real. But I am not to be so easily deceived, Omelia, and in spite of the scorn and bravado you assume, I can read your thoughts, and perceive the terror that agitates your breast. And certainly you have ample cause to feel it; the Nena is never unmindful of those who have offended him, and evaded his power and authority. No doubt you can imagine the reception you are likely to meet with on your restoration to him."

"I will brave it all," replied Omelia; "firm in virtue, what cause have I to fear?"

"Your tone was very different when you so pathetically appealed to me yesterday," said Allyghur, ironically; "the change is truly marvellous, but cannot deceive me. Your pretended courage will soon be put to the test. I now come to inform you that I have made all the necessary arrangements for your long journey, and to morrow I have fixed upon for your departure, accompanied by myself. Probably among the adherents of the Nena you will meet your father, who—"

"My father," interrupted Omelia, with a shudder of horror, as the recollection of his dreadful and untimely death flashed across her brain; "alas! wretched, guilty, misguided parent, terribly have you paid the penalty of your crimes. May heaven pardon you."

"What mean you girl?" demanded Allyghur, with a look of astonishment and eager curiosity.

"You start, you tremble," replied Omelia, "and well you may, in anticipation of the fatal truth. He who was plunged still deeper into crime by the incitement of yourself and your atrocious associates, has met the fate which should have been your's—he is no more."

She covered her face with her hands for a moment, and could not refrain from tears, to the memory of that guilty parent from whom she had never experienced one word or act of affection.

"No more," repeated Allyghur, with increased astonishment, and a look of incredulity; "Yunadar dead—'tis impossible!"

"'Tis true."

"How know you this?"

"With mine own eyes I witnessed his frightful death," replied Omelia, again shuddering at the recollection; "alas, that they should ever have to encounter so dreadful a sight."

Allyghur looked at her narrowly and suspiciously for a moment, seeming still to doubt the truth of her assertion; then folding his arms, he paced the room to and fro for a short time, wrapped in thought.

Suddenly turning to our heroine, and fixing upon her a stern and penetrating look, he said—

"I read at once the fatal truth, girl, you are a murderess—your father perished by your hands."

Omelia started appalled at the dreadful and unnatural thought, but she quickly recovered herself, and with a look of resentment and conscious innocence, she said—

"Base libeller, to dare to utter such a monstrous accusation, to harbour such a monstrous thought. Begone! the sight of one who can believe me capable of so hideous a crime, disgusts and appals me. Leave me, I say—I command!"

"You command, ha, ha, ha," he laughed, scornfully; "however, your apparent indignation will not alter my opinion. I again accuse the amiable, the virtuous, the gentle Omelia of the murder of her own father, from motives of revenge, and as the friend of the enemies of her country. That crime you will have to answer for, and no doubt you will meet the fate which you deserve. I shall have the pleasure of seeing that fate accomplished."

Omelia stared at him aghast, for in spite of all her endeavours she could not conceal her horror at an accusation so frightful, so unnatural, and so unexpected.

"Your looks condemn you and confirm your guilt," said Allyghur; "but that point the Nena will have to decide. You will find him a most impartial judge, and nothing can be more summary than his justice. I leave you to your own pleasant reflections. Remember, to-morrow you leave this place to commence a journey which may be far more tedious than pleasant."

As he thus spoke he stalked from the room, leaving our heroine in a state of agitation and excitement which, for some time, she found it impossible to conquer. To be charged with a crime so truly hideous as the assassination of her own parent, was so horrible in itself, that her blood seemed to freeze in her veins at the thought, and even the consciousness of her own innocence, could not for awhile remove the impression or subdue her emotions.

"The heartless monster, to dare thus foully to asperse my character," she ejaculated, "and to accuse me of a crime at which humanity must shudder, and of which if I were guilty, would stamp me as one of the most atrocious wretches that ever disgraced or polluted society. But why should I heed anything that falls from the lips of such a miscreant, who will say or do anything which may gratify his cowardly feelings of revenge? It is worse than weakness to give way to this emotion; Heaven knows my innocence, and in spite of all that malice can do to prevent it will, I doubt not, make it apparent to the world."

With these thoughts she endeavoured to console herself, and to regain her composure; but it was some time ere she could succeed in doing so.

But at length other thoughts, equally painful, banished the subject from her mind, and she sat brooding over them in melancholy silence until her brain became almost distracted.

She could not contemplate her journey on her return to that fearful place, from which she had with so much peril escaped, and the prospect of so soon again becoming the prisoner of the blood-thirsty monster, Nena Sahib, with any other feelings than those of the utmost dread, and her very soul shrank appalled, when she recollected the horrible atrocities that had been inflicted upon so many unfortunate persons, and imagined what her own fate might be.

"Oh, Stanley, dear Stanley," she exclaimed, "would to God that I had died in your arms on that fatal night on which we were separated, perhaps never to meet again. It would have been merciful, and saved me those tenfold horrors and sufferings that now too certainly seem to await me. Heaven—kind heaven interpose to save me, I implore, or I am lost for ever."

She clasped her hands together and raised her hands devoutly and imploringly towards heaven as she thus spoke, and after a few minutes spent in prayer, her spirits revived, and her wonted fortitude in a great measure was restored to her.

"Away with these dismal, these torturing thoughts," she ejaculated, "it is cowardice to give way to apprehensions that may never be realised; I will be firm, and put my trust in that Almighty power whose protection I have just invoked."

She again seated herself at the window and endeavoured to divert her thoughts from these gloomy subjects in the contemplation of the picturesque and interesting scene before her, which now appeared to double effect beneath the bright and genial rays of the sun which was now in its meridian; though there was a beautiful and refreshing breeze, which greatly counteracted the heat that otherwise would have been very oppressive; and the fountains were even cooling to look upon.

Thus the time wore away, and Omelia by great exertion and perseverence became more reconciled, and determined to await the circumstances she would probably have to undergo with patience.

She received no farther interruption during the day, except when Zoa entered the room to bring her provisions, and then the observations that were exchanged with each other were as brief as possible.

Omelia did not retire to rest until a late hour, and then it was some time before she could compose herself to sleep, for her thoughts were fixed on the morrow, and the events it might probably produce, and she could not look forward to it without considerable anxiety and uneasiness.

She arose almost before daylight the following morning, and dressed herself, and she had not long done so, when the room door was opened, and Zoa entered with the morning repast.

"So you have arisen," she said, "that is well, for in a very short time your departure will take place, and if what Allyghur has told me be true, and you are indeed a murderess, why—"

"Hold woman," interrupted Omelia, with a look of indignation and disgust, " dare not to repeat the monstrous scandal, the atrocious falsehood with which the wretch whom you call your husband shocked my ears yesterday. Are you or he not satisfied with the brutal wrongs that you have already inflicted on me, and those to which I am probably about to be exposed, but that you must thus endeavour to add to the bitter anguish of my mind, by accusing me of a crime of which you have not the slightest cause to suspect me guilty, and from the bare idea of which my soul recoils with horror? Shame on you, I can scarcely believe you to be one of my own sex, when I hear the monstrous observations you seem to take delight in uttering."

"Indeed," said the woman, with a malicious look, "no doubt you can play the hypocrite to perfection, though it will be well for you if you can convince him, to whose power you are about to be consigned, of your innocence. I wish you a pleasant journey, but would advise you to take some refreshment before you commence it, for it may be some time before you will again have the opportunity of doing so."

Omelia did not condescend to return any answer to this, and she turned from the coarse provisions that Zoa offered her with a look of disgust, and resuming her seat, awaited the arrival of the time fixed upon for her departure with all the patience and

composure she could muster, Zoa still remaining in the room without addressing any further observation to her.

She had not to wait long, for the door was presently again opened, and Allyghur, equipped for the journey, entered the room, and approaching her attempted to take her hand, which, however, she hastily withdrew with disgust and resentment.

"The time has now come," he said, "our escort awaits outside, and all is in readiness, so there need not be any delay."

"I am ready, villain," said Omelia, disdainfully, and rising from her seat, "think not that I fear the utmost that your malice can prompt you to. I put my trust in that power which will not fail to protect me from all the dangers with which you threaten me."

"We shall see the value of those assertions before long, no doubt," returned Allyghur, "but come, we waste time."

Omelia, with an air of calm dignity, motinoed him to lead the way, which he did, and quitting the room they descended the stairs.

After passing through several well furnished apartments, Allyghur opened a door, which led into a small court, and here Omelia beheld a detachment of mounted troops, who seemed to eye her with much curiosity when she made her appearance, and she could hear many opprobious observations and jeers from several of them, which, however, she listened to with well merited contempt.

After exchanging a few words with his wife aside, Allyghur took Omelia's hand, assisted her on to one of the horses, and mounting another himself by her side, he gave the word of command, and the whole cortege passed through the open gates, and entering upon a lonely road to the right of the building—near which there was no other —they started off at a pretty brisk pace towards the wildest part of the country, our heroine maintaining her seat well, although she had only on two or three occasions mounted a horse before.

***

CHAPTER XLVI.

THE EVENTFUL JOURNEY.

Omelia now completely resigned herself to her fate, and though her thoughts were naturally, under the trying circumstances in which she was placed, of the most gloomy and painful nature, she did not entirely abandon herself to despair, something, she ventured to think, might yet occur, when the least expected, to rescue her from the fate

which seemed to be impending over her, and that hope she endeavoured to encourage all in her power.

One of the principal chances of rescue was in the mutineers on the way being met by any detachment of European troops, and their defeat, but that hope almost vanished when she considered the probability in the event of such a circumstance taking place, that the villain Allyghur would not hesitate to immediately sacrifice her life sooner than that she should fall into the hands of friends. However, she maintained her fortitude much better than might have been expected, placed in the alarming and critical situation that she was.

Allyghur much to the relief of his fair prisoner, maintained the strictest silence for some time, so that she was left to the un-

interrupted indulgence of her own thoughts, and without having her ears insulted by his brutal observations.

The grey mists of early dawn had hardly yet disappeared, and the weather was cheerless with lowering clouds hanging upon the sky, threatening a storm at no remote period of the day. They travelled also through the most dreary part of the country, which was not at all calculated to raise Omelia's spirits, but she kept a better heart than might have been expected.

After riding at a brisk rate for more than an hour, they reached the chain of lofty mountains which Omelia had seen from the window of the room in which she had been confined, and passing between them they entered upon a still wilder tract of country, if possible, than that which they had pro-

No. 26.

viously travelled through, with a road, if such it might be called, that was almost impassable, with a jungle on either side, and a dense forest in the distance.

The storm which had threatened, passed over for a time, and the sun just making a feeble appearance behind the clouds, imparted a little more light and cheerfulness to the scene.

And thus they continued to travel without anything particular occurring for some time, until they arrived at the gloomy forest, into the depths of which they penetrated, although that was a task of considerable difficulty, and the men were frequently compelled to dismount and lead their horses over the many obstructions, and through the deeply entangled intricacies of the place.

On these occasions, Omelia was supported by the arm of Allyghur—who still remained silent—for she could not have proceeded without, and even then it was a task of great labour and fatigue, and being still weak from the effects of her wound, she suffered much, but without complaining, for she well knew that had she done so she would only have met with insult instead of sympathy.

At length, after they had been thus wearily journeying for three or four hours, and the men of whom Allyghur had assumed the command, began to murmur and grumble among themselves; he ordered a halt in a convenient spot, and such provisions as they had brought with them in their haversacks were shared out, a portion being offered to Omelia, together with some arrack, the former of which, not having broken her fast for many hours, she was reluctantly compelled to accept.

After this coarse meal, having rested for a short time, they resumed their journey, gradually breaking into a more open part of the forest, although still as dreary and as tedious to travel through as could well be imagined.

They continued much in the same way till late in the afternoon, Allyghur still maintaining his taciturnity unbroken, much to the surprise but no less satisfaction of our heroine.

The forest seemed almost interminable, and the gloom which pervaded it was sufficient to fill the mind of our heroine with the most dismal thoughts if she had even had no other cause to disturb her. But the calmness and fortitude with which she behaved surprised Allyghur and the other rebels.

The storm which had threatened in the morning now commenced, and bid fair to become most violent. The thunder which at first only grumbled at intervals, at a distance, by degrees swelled into deafening peals in rapid succession, echoing through the forest depths, with more than the noise of a whole park of artillery, the lightning flashed and blazed frightfully, splitting huge trees, or levelling them with the ground like so many twigs, and the rain came down so violently that it was almost impossible for anything human to stand against it.

And now the situation of poor Omelia was indeed most deplorable, and for the first time her courage failed her. She was worn out with fatigue, and drenched to the skin, and it seemed almost impossible that she could proceed much farther.

She looked imploringly at Allyghur, but he, as might have been expected, evinced no sympathy for her, and his whole anxiety was for himself and his companions, who were growling and swearing amongst themselves in the most unmeasured terms, looking savagely at our poor shivering heroine as though she were the cause of the severity of the weather.

"I can proceed no farther," at length she said, in a faint voice, and completely exhausted, "it is impossible for me to continue to travel through such a tempest as this in my exhausted condition, though I have not till now murmured or complained; here then you must leave me to perish, and surely a fate so terrible as that must satiate your vengeance."

"Bah!" replied the brutal ruffian, Allyghur, "what cause have you to grumble any more than us? Are we not equally exposed to the fury of the tempest? You must arouse yourself; as for leaving you here to die, it would not answer my purpose, and you must think me mad to do so."

"Cruel man, if man indeed I may call you," cried our heroine, "alas, what then will become of me?"

"It's no use standing grumbling here," replied Allyghur, "for that will not mend the matter. Come, I will assist you to mount before me on my horse, and then I can support you."

"For heaven's sake, is there no hope of shelter?" interrogated Omelia in an agony of despair.

"Yes," answered Allyghur, "on the borders of this forest, which we must be fast approaching, there is a village where we can get all that we require. So let us push on through every difficulty, for that is the only way to extricate ourselves. Now, men, to horse again, we can ride the rest of the way without obstruction."

The men obeyed surlily, and muttering to themselves, and Allyghur having, as he had said, assisted Omelia on to the back of his horse, he mounted behind her, encircled her exhausted form with one arm, and they then made their way through the forest with all the speed they could.

The tempest still continued to rage with unabated violence, in fact there seemed no prospect of its subsiding for some time to come, danger spread around, the lightning doing its frightful work; the earth seemed to tremble at every roar of the thunder, the rain rushed down in overwhelming torrents, and nothing could possibly surpass the horrors of the scene.

Omelia was in such a wretched state, that she felt as if she could not possibly survive much longer, and it was with difficulty that she could retain her senses.

At length, however, towards evening, and after being exposed to the violence of the storm for more than an hour, they emerged from the forest, entering upon a somewhat less lonely scene, and the village of which Allyghur had spoken of, consisting of a few bungalows of the humblest description, then appeared in sight, a welcome sight indeed to all under the circumstances.

Here Allyghur and his companions immediately demanded food and shelter, which was readily granted by the villagers, Allyghur with Omelia, and two of the men taking possession of the largest, and the rest betaking themselves to the other bungalows.

As soon as Omelia was borne into the house her strength entirely failed her, and she became insensible.

The bungalow was occupied by a couple of native women, apparently mother and daughter, and they expressed their sympathy for the deplorable situation of the poor girl in the warmest terms to which the savage Allyghur replied with an oath, and commanded them to see to her relief at once, whilst he and his two comrades seating themselves before a blazing fire to dry themselves, at the same time warming their insides with a plentiful supply of arrack.

The women needed no second order to induce them to comply, and Omelia, was conveyed to a pretty comfortable chamber above, and being undressed was placed in a warm bed, and attended to carefully.

In a short time, by the humane exertions of the two females, Omelia showed signs of returning life, and was soon sufficiently recovered to recollect all that happened, and where she was, and struck by the kindness of the women, she returned her thanks most warmly.

Allyghur and his two companions had taken up their quarters for the night in the room below, and the women resolved to remain with Omelia, putting themselves to every inconvenience for the accommodation of their unexpected guests.

The storm continued throughout the night, and in spite of her fatigue, kept our heroine a long time waking, during which, finding the females intelligent, she communicated to them some of the particulars of her history, and her present melancholy situation and fearful prospects, and they expressed their deep sympathy in terms which convinced her of their sincerity, deeply regretting that it was not in their power to render her any assistance that might enable her to escape from the power of the merciless villains who held her captive.

Omelia again thanked them, and although she could not but anticipate the future with the utmost dread and the most dismal forebodings, she endeavoured to prepare herself to meet her fate, whatever it might be, with fortitude and resignation.

At length sleep closed her eyelids, and she awoke not till the morning, feeling much refreshed by the repose she had obtained.

The storm had entirely ceased, and the sun was already shining brightly, and giving every token of a fine day. Omelia arose, and having partaken of a suitable repast which had been prepared for her, she received a summons from Allyghur to attend him immediately.

With a sad heart, yet concealing her real feelings as well as she could, Omelia, accompanied by the females, descended to the room below, where she found Allyghur ready to resume the journey, his comrades being already mounted on their horses, and waiting outside the bungalow.

It was not without feelings of the deepest melancholy and regret that Omelia quitted the bungalow, and resumed the tedious journey, but she concealed them as well as she could, and assumed an air of composure to which she was really a stranger.

Allyghur received her with the same looks of triumph and malicious satisfaction with which he had at first met her, and having assisted her to mount, he took his place behind her on the same horse, and they departed in silence.

The way they now pursued was much more cheerful and easy for travelling than that of the preceding day, and Omelia's dismal thoughts were frequently diverted for a time from the melancholy subjects that engrossed them in the contemplation of the romantic scenery which burst upon her view.

The fineness of the weather, too, which presented such a remarkable contrast to that which they had before experienced, tended to raise Omelia's spirits, and by degrees she became perfectly calm, and again encouraged the hope that providence would yet interpose to rescue her from the fate with which she was threatened.

They stopped two or three times during the day at convenient places to rest and refresh themselves, Allyghur still maintaining the same silence towards her that he had done from the commencement of the journey much to the relief of his fair prisoner, and at night they were travelling through a wildly romantic part of the country, the moon shining brightly above, and revealing surrounding and distant objects as clearly as in the broad daylight.

Omelia who felt fatigued with the many hours that they had been travelling, now ventured to inquire when their journey was likely to terminate, or whether they were to stop again at any village for the night.

"You must be patient," said Allyghur, "our journey will be at an end some time to-morrow, no doubt, so it is my intention to make to-night for the nearest village, which I believe is about a coss and a half from this place."

Omelia returned no answer to this speech, which was addressed to her by Allyghur in milder tones than he was accustomed to use, and they continued on their way with unabated speed.

Suddenly, however, Allyghur checked his horse, and drawing the attention of one of his principal comrades who was riding by his side, pointed in the direction they were going, and Omelia eagerly following his eyes imagined she beheld the dark shadows of horsemen in the distance, but a dark cloud at that moment obscuring the moon, prevented her from ascertaining whether or not her surmises were correct.

The looks of Allyghur and his companion, however, showed that they were alarmed, and all but confirmed her suspicions, and a strong hope of rescue for the first time sprang up in her breast, and which gathered strength every instant.

She continued to gaze in the same direction, and again fancied that she beheld the horsemen approaching, but the intervening trees prevented her seeing distinctly, but she felt satisfied by the behaviour of Allyghur, and the anxiety he evinced, that she was not mistaken.

"This looks suspicious," observed Allyghur, aside to the man to whom he had before spoken, but in tones sufficiently loud for Omelia to overhear what he said; "we must be on our guard, for any sudden surprise from a force larger than her own might cost us dear. Ride cautiously forward and reconnoitre."

"Their is no necessity for that," replied the man, "for the sound of their horses' hoofs may be plainly heard as they come this way, and see, they now appear distinctly in the moonlight, and there cannot be the least doubt but that they must observe us. They are English cavalry."

"Kind heaven be thanked," fervently ejaculated our heroine, as she gazed towards the approaching soldiers, who did not seem to outnumber the mutineers, "I may yet be saved."

"Do not flatter yourself with any such delusive hope," returned the villain Allyghur with a malicious look, "for should the tide of fortune turn against us, you, at any rate, shall not live to fall into the hands of our enemies."

"Monster," cried Omelia, with a shudder, and thoroughly convinced that he would put his inhuman threat into execution, despair again fell upon her heart.

"You may call me what you please," returned Allyghur, "I heed it not. What I have promised I will perform, you may depend upon it. Ah, see they are close upon us. Prepare yourselves, my lads, for we shall have a smart contest, no doubt, though I trust that we shall prove more than a match for them. Now, Omelia, the crisis of your fate is probably at hand."

She trembled, but endeavoured to become firm, though the situation in which she was placed was a most fearful and critical one. Allyghur drew his sword, and encircling her waist with his arm more fiercely, he awaited the conflict that must immediately ensue.

There was a loud shout from the soldiers as they galloped forward to the strife, followed by the discharge of pistols on both sides, and the next moment the rebels and the soldiers were fiercely engaged together in a hand-to-hand combat, which was maintained for some time with equal courage and determination on both sides.

The soldiers were under the command of a gallant young officer, whose whole object seemed to be the rescue of Omelia, whose looks told briefly but distintly the story of her wrongs, and the terrible situation in which she was placed, and he quickly and boldly engaged with the miscreant Allyghur, who, however, with the rest of the rebels, fought with a bravery and resolution which was worthy of a better cause, and for some time the issue of the deadly combat seemed to be extremely doubtful.

Omelia struggled to release herself, and to throw herself from the horse's back in amongst the soldiers, but in vain, and the fierce looks of Allyghur, and the dreadful oaths that escaped his lips, convinced her that should he find that he and his comrades were likely to be defeated, he would not fail to put his threat into execution.

Many times she was placed in the most imminent danger, and narrowly escaped the blows which the young officer aimed at his antagonist, and the former being wounded by Allyghur, and bleeding copiously, it seemed but too probable that in spite of his skill and bravery, he must shortly yield.

Indeed the advantage now appeared to be all on the side of the mutineers, several of the soldiers being placed *hors de combat*, though their courage never gave way, and that of the mutineers seemed to increase with their success.

One fatal blow on the head from the powerful and determined Allyghur, now struck the unfortunate officer from his horse, and Omelia uttered a cry of horror as she saw him fall, and all chance of her deliverence now seemed to be entirely at an end.

The death of their gallant officer now evidently disheartened his men, although they still struggled desperately for a few minutes, but many of their comrades having also fallen in the sanguinary combat, all hope of triumph was completely at an end, and they therefore took to flight, the mutineers pursuing them to some distance, and suffering but very few of them to escape.

Allyghur, however, remained behind with Omelia, who was so completely overpowered by the excitement of the fearful scene, and the dreadful fate which had attended the brave young officer who had so nobly struggled for her deliverence, that her senses almost left her.

Allyghur assisted her off the horse, and she sunk on her knees by the side of the corpse of the young man in an agony of grief, disappointment, and despair.

Allyghur cast a hasty glance at the ghastly face of his unfortunate victim, and then, with a look of fiendish triumph, said—

"The fool has paid dearly for his daring; the striplling though he fought bravely was no match for the sepoy Allyghur. Thus perish every hated Feringhee."

"Inhuman wretch," returned our heroine, with a look of the most indescribable disgust and horror; "you do well to exult o'er the cruel work of your hands; but a terrible retribution, depend on it, will yet overtake you."

"At any rate the hope of deliverence that you had so fondly entertained is, as I predicted it would be, annihilated," said Allyghur, "and the fate to which I have destined you is certain. To-morrow will again see you in the presence of Nena Sahib."

Omelia sighed and wrung her hands in anguish, for it was impossible that she could any longer conceal the emotions that the contemplation of that fearful fate caused her. Allyghur noticed her feelings and read her thoughts, and his looks sufficiently expressed his brutal satisfaction.

Those who had gone in pursuit of the de-feated soldiers now returned to the spot, and Allyghur having replaced Omelia on the horse, and remounted himself, they resumed their long, eventful journey, hurrying on as fast as they could to reach the village of which Allyghur had spoken, and where it seemed they expected to find another party of rebels.

Again the fortitude of Omelia failed her, for such a rapid succession of exciting events and the long fatigue to which she had been exposed, and that which was doubtless yet to follow, before she could reach the end of the journey were almost too much for human nature patiently to endure. And then the fate which she could not but anticipate would befall her at the hands of the notorious and atrocious Nena Sahib, doubly excited to revenge as he would probably be at her former escape, and that of the unfortunate Nazimi, made her tremble, and abandon herself to utter despair.

At length, after riding for about another hour, through a lonely part of the country —the moon, however, emerging from behind the clouds at intervals, and lighting up the scene—they came in sight of the village, which was of considerable extent, and where they were quickly given to understand that a part of one of the mutinous regiments, having arrived there on the day before, on their way to join Nena Sahib at Bithoor or Cawnpore, had taken up their quarters in a range of large buildings that had once been used for the government offices, and which were situated at the farther end of the village.

Thither Allyghur and his companions resolved to go, and they were received with every demonstration of welcome, the appearance of Omelia exciting much vulgar curiosity and interest.

Surrounded by such a set of heartless ruffians, who were capable of committing any crime, and who eyed her with looks that made her shudder, Omella in spite of her efforts to conquer it could not but entertain a feeling of the utmost fear, and she even looked forward to the time of resuming the journey with anxiety and impatience.

She earnestly requested Allyghur to allow her to remain in one of the bungalows, and under the care of her own sex, for the night, but to this he would not listen, and seemed to take a malicious pleasure in observing the anguish of her mind.

After having been subjected to the rude remarks of the rebels for a short time, she was conducted to a small room at the back of one of the buildings, which contained no other article of furniture than a small mattress, on which she was to sleep, the door was fastened upon her, and she was left in darkness, and to her own dismal reflections for the night.

Unable any longer to restrain her feelings now that she was alone, she burst into a violent paroxysm of tears and sobs, and for some time, she could not find the least degree of consolation. All hope was now entirely banished from her mind, and the horrors of the fate which awaited her, became more apparent every moment, and continued to haunt her imagination until her brain was almost distracted.

It was indeed wonderful how she had found strength sufficient to support such a succession of terrible and trying events with the fortitude that she hitherto had, but she had been sustained by a feeling of confidence in the interposition of providence to rescue her from the terrors and dangers to which she was exposed, but confidence continual disappointment had now almost completely destroyed, and she could not but anticipate the worst.

Tired even as she was, the situation in which she was, and placed at the mercy of ruffians of the most brutal description, would not suffer her to sleep much, and she continued for the greater part of the night seated on the mattress, and giving way to all the gloomy thoughts which the circumstances gave rise to, or in offering up her fervent prayers to heaven for its merciful interposition.

But amidst all her troubles, and in the apprehension of those that were yet in store for her, Stanley was never for a moment scarcely absent from her thoughts, and it was in vain that she tried to believe that by some providential means he had been saved from that fate she had too much reason to fear he had met with on that fatal night when she had fallen into the hands of the villain Allyghur.

The next morning Omelia felt so weak and ill that it seemed almost impossible that she could travel any further for the present, but the brutal Allyghur would listen to no solicitations for delay, and as it was evident that she could not travel in the same way that she had previously done, a dawk or palanquin—a certain if not rapid means of conveyance in India—was procured, in which she could rest herself with comparative ease, it being furnished in the usual manner, with a well-stuffed mattress, covered with silk or Morocco leather, supported by pillows.

On this mattress the traveller, lying at his length, ensconced in the palanquin, is borne upon the shoulders of four natives, who are accompanied by four or eight others to relieve them at brief intervals, is carried up the country at the ordinary rate of three miles an hour. In the front of him, at the upper end of the interior of the palanquin, are a shelf and a drawer, and nettings containing books, a telescope, writing materials, biscuits, and a bottle of weak brandy-and-water. And thus by this mode of travelling in India you may pass over many miles delightfully enough.

You stop where you please, and at intervals arranged by yourself you halt at a bungalow, or small building on the ground floor, which the government has constructed for the accommodation of travellers in a country where no roadside inn affords shelter to the wayfarer. Here an active servant prepares you a breakfast, or a simple dinner of curried fowl, while a mussachee will procure you the means of having a refreshing bath, in a room appropriated to such purposes.

Such was the way in which our heroine was permitted to perform the remainder of the long and tedious journey, although without most of the comforts we have enumerated, and it enabled her to recover in a great measure from her fatigue, and to prepare herself to meet with firmness and composure all the future circumstances of her untoward destiny.

The remainder of the journey was accomplished without anything particular occurring, and towards the evening they arrived within sight of the place of their destination.

Here for the present we must leave Omelia.

CHAPTER XLVII.

FLORA MELVILLE AND THE HERMIT.

The reader will no doubt feel curious to know what has become of Flora Melville, whom we left in a state of the greatest agony of mind, in the hermit's cavern, on the fatal and eventful night when Omelia fell into the power of the rebels who conveyed her for the first time to that most atrocious of miscreant's, Nena Sahib.

The loss of that noble-minded and heroic girl, who was as dear to her heart as if she were her own sister, and so soon after the melancholy and irremediable bereavement she had sustained in the death of her father, was one which was calculated to make a powerful and lasting impression upon her, especially when she so much needed the support of her advice and consolation, and in the present state of the country, and when Omelia was well known to have made herself so prominent in opposing the designs of the mutineers, now that they had got possession of her person there was no doubt that they would not fail to wreak their vengeance on her head, and Flora shuddered with horror when she thought of the barbarities that were hourly being perpetrated, and the fate which might be inflicted on her.

Coupled with this fear and anxiety was the uncertain fate of Edward Stanley, of whom, as the reader is aware, Omelia had gone in search, for that hopeless passion which she had ventured to encourage for him, notwithstanding all her endeavours to stifle it, still lingered in her heart, and she felt convinced that it must continue to do so even to the latest hour of her existence.

And what was now to come of her, deprived of her father, and left entirely friendless and unprotected in the world? To remain under the protection of the aged recluse and a burden to him on whom she had no claim was repugnant to her feelings, and yet whither could she go? where seek an asylum? These thoughts were sufficient to distract her brain, and during the remainder of that night she continued in a most deplorable and inconsolable state, lamenting the cruelty of her fate, and regretting that she had been suffered to survive the death of her beloved parent.

Truly her situation was a most painful and delicate one, and the venerable hermit, who deeply sympathised with her, did all he could to abate the anguish of her mind, and to tranquillise her feelings. His regret at the loss of Omelia, to whom he had become as affectionately attached as if she had been allied to him by blood, was fully as great as Flora's, but fearful of adding to her misery and grief he concealed it as much as possible, and assumed all his usual calm and unruffled demeanour.

"Give not way to this violence of emotion, girl," he said, "but put thy trust in that unseen and Almighty power which ordains everything for the best, and whose will weak mortals must not presume to question or to murmur at. Here in these caverns, far hid from the prying eye of man, and whose precincts have ever been held sacred, you may find a safe retreat, and I will protect you from every danger, until the fierce tempest of men's brutal and guilty passions shall have passed over, and peace shall again be restored to this unhappy country. Be calm then I say—be calm."

"Calm," repeated Flora, looking wildly in the face of the aged man, and her anguish rather increasing than abating, "oh, how can I be so, with such an accumulation of horrors upon my mind? What hope of peace is there for a poor friendless being like me? Oh, why did not the same moment that closed my poor father's eyes in death also terminate my wretched existence? And now, too, when I so much needed her gentle consolation and advice, to be deprived of that poor girl who was so dear, so precious to my heart, and to be left in this terrible state of fear and suspense as to the fate which may befall her. My brain is distracted; I shall go mad; let me go forth, and at once end those sorrows that are too great for human endurance in death."

"Forbear," cried the hermit, solemnly, and seizing her wrist, "forbear to give way to those sinful thoughts, but bow in submission to the decrees of providence. Omelia may and will no doubt be exposed to great suffering and danger, nay, even narrowly escape a frightful death, all this do I foresee, it is revealed to my mind's eye as clearly as if it were reflected to my sight in a mirror; but she will yet surmount all, triumph over every difficulty, and ultimately be restored to that happiness and prosperity to which her numerous virtues entitle her."

The old man uttered these prophetic words with an earnestness and solemn impressiveness of manner which struck Flora most forcibly, and filled her with surprise and a feeling of awe which she could not resist, and she looked at him steadfastly for a minute or two without being able to utter a word. She had heard many of the strange stories that had been told of him, and of the marvellous powers that had been attributed to him, and she could not but look upon him with a feeling somewhat bordering upon superstitious dread.

"Your words are strange, old man," she said at length, "and you speak in a tone of confidence, as if you could penetrate into the secrets of futurity, and you were certain that your predictions would be realised."

"Those who know me well," answered the hermit, "presume not to doubt the power I possess. But enough, girl, bear in mind that which I have uttered, and rest assured that all which I have stated will be fulfilled. Abandon not yourself to useless grief and lamentation, but be firm."

As the old man thus spoke he raised his hands above her head, as if invoking a benediction, and then slowly retired into one of the inner caverns, motioning her to remain where she was, and she could hear him for some time muttering strange and unintelligible words to himself, after which he sunk into a profound silence, which for several minutes remained unbroken, and at length he returned to the cave in which he had left Flora, and his appearance was, if possible, still more singular and impressive than it had been before.

In spite of all the exertions of the hermit, however, to tranquillise her feelings, the agony of the unfortunate Flora Melville increased, and so great did it at last become, and such were the terrible thoughts that racked her brain, that at length her reason temporarily sunk beneath their influence, and for a few days after the disappearance of Omelia, her situation was most alarming and melancholy, and she occupied the whole care and attention of the hermit, who watched over her with all the anxiety and tenderness that humanity could suggest.

At length her senses returned, but she was reduced to a condition from which it seemed likely that she would not quickly if ever recover, and so weak that she could with difficulty leave the humble pallet on which she reposed in this singular and subterranean retreat.

Often did the old man—whose store of knowledge seemed almost inexhaustible, and who related historical facts that had occurred nearly a century previous, with the same preciseness, and in the same terms of authority as if he had been living at the time, and was a personal observer of that which he was now recording—seek to chase the poor girl's melancholy, and to divert her thoughts, by some interesting anecdotes and narratives, and occasionally he would even wander into the romantic regions of fiction, in which he was as happy as in the more instructive and learned subjects.

For a brief period these efforts of the hermit would have the desired effect, and Flora in listening to him, which she ever did with the deepest interest, found a temporary respite from the more poignant sorrows that afflicted her mind, and which tended in a great measure towards her recovery to composure, if not entirely to health and spirits.

In fact nothing could be greater or more unremitting than the kindness and attention of the good old man, he seemed to make it his constant study to ameliorate Flora's sufferings, and to soothe her to resignation, and her heart could not but overflow with gratitude and veneration towards one to whom she was so much indebted for shelter and protection in this the time of her greatest need, and who acted from such purely disinterested and benevolent motives.

Thus a week passed away, and nothing more could be heard of Omelia, although the hermit frequently went forth in the vain hope of obtaining some information of her, at such times strictly enjoining Flora, not to venture from the cavern, and although the violence of her grief had somewhat abated, a deep melancholy settled itself upon her mind, which it was evident that time and circumstances could alone serve to dissipate.

It was evening, and all was silent in the cavernous abode of the hermit, and the fair object of his care and solicitude. For a considerable time Flora and her aged companion had been engaged in conversation, but suddenly painful thoughts seemed to rush upon the poor girl's mind, and sighing deeply while the tears trembled in her eyes, she relapsed into silence.

The hermit sat and watched her for some time without interrupting her, and with looks of the deepest sympathy, but at length he said—

"The dark clouds again hang upon thy brow, maiden, and sorrow lies deep at thine heart. Fain would I endeavour to chase it, and to impart peace and consolation to your mind."

"Alas," sighed Flora, "they can never, I fear, again be mine."

"Say not so, child," remarked the hermit, "but endeavour to struggle with your emotions, and to encourage the bright sunlight of hope. When the mind is oppressed with grief, there is nothing which at times serves more to relieve it than the recital of some interesting narrative, which, however great may be our troubles, there are others who have suffered even more than ourselves, and which should teach us patience and resignation."

"True, most true, father," said Flora; "fain would I hear you relate some pleasing tale to pass away the weary hours, for I am indeed sad at heart."

"Listen then to a tale of the American Indians, and to the loves of the brave Pootanama and the lovely Azemi," said the ancient man. "Many, many years have passed away since the events I am now about to record took place, but they are still treasured in the memory, and have often been listened to with feelings of interest and melancholy pleasure."

Flora again expressed her willingness to hear the story, and the hermit after pausing for a minute or two as if to collect his thoughts, thus commenced:

* THE HERMIT'S TALE

What Indian youth could surpass the young Pootanama for bravery and nobleness of spirit; and what maiden's could equal the beauty of the gentle Azemi? They were the admiration and the envy of all who knew them.

Pootanama was the son of a mighty chief. He looked on his tribe with such a fiery glance, that they called him the eagle of the Mohawks. His eyes never blinked in the sunbeam, and he leaped along the chase like

---

* It is right to state that this tale is altered and adapted to the present work, from a beautiful production published many years ago.

the untiring falls of the Niagara. Even when a little boy his tiny arrow would hit the frisking squirrel in the ear, and bring down the humming bird on her rapid wing.

"Pootanama was the pride and joy of his father's heart. He longed to toss him high in his sinewy arms, and shout—

"'Look, eagle-eye, look, and see the hunting grounds of the Mohawks! Pootanama will be their chief. The winds will tell his brave deeds. When men speak of him they will not speak loud; but as if the great spirit had breathed in thunder.'

"Such was the prophecy of the chief, and it was fulfilled.

"When Pootanama became a man, the fame of his beauty and carriage reached the tribes of Illinois; and even the distant Osage showed his white teeth with delight

when he heard the wild deeds of the Mohawk Eagle. Yet was his spirit frank, chivalrous, and kind. When the white men came to buy land, he met them with an open palm, and spread his buffalo for the traveller. The old chiefs loved the bold youth, and offered the hands of their daughters in marriage. The eyes of the young Indian girls sparkled when he looked on them; but he treated them all with the stern indifference of the warrior, until he saw Azemi raise her long dark eye-lash. Then his heart melted beneath the beaming glance of beauty.

"Azemi was the fairest of the Oneida's. The young men of her tribe called her Sunny-eye. She was smaller than her nation usually are, and her slight graceful figure was so elastic in its motions, that the long grass would rise up and shake off its dew-drops after her pretty mocassins had pressed it. Many a famous chief had sought her love, but when they brought the choicest furs, she would smile disdainfully, and say—

"'Azemi's foot is warm. Has not her father an arrow?'

"While they offered her food according to the Indian custom, her answer was—

"'Azemi has not seen all the warriors. She will eat with the bravest.'

"The hunters told the young eagle that Sunny-eye of Oneida was beautiful as the bright birds in the hunting land beyond the sky, but her heart was proud, and she said that the great chiefs were not good enough to dress venison for her.

"When Pootanama listened to these accounts, his lip would curl slightly as he threw back his fur-edged mantle, and placing his firm, springy-foot forward, so that the beads and shells of his rich mocassin seemed to vibrate at the very sound of his war-song. If there was vanity in the act, there was likewise becoming pride.

"Azemi heard of his haughty smile, and resolved in her own heart, that no Oneida should sit beside her till she had seen the chieftain of the Mohawks.

"Before many moons had passed away, he sought her father's wigwam, to carry delicate furs, and shining shells to the young coquette of the wilderness. She did not raise her bright melting eye to his when he came near her, but when he said, 'Will the sunny-eye look upon the gift of a Mohawk; his barbed arow is swift, his foot never turned from a foe,' the colour of her brown cheek was glowing as an autumnal twilight, her voice was like the troubled note of the wren as she answered—

"'The furs of Poontanama are soft and warm to the foot of Azemi. She will weave the shells in the wampum-belt of the Mohawk Eagle.'

"The exulting lover sat by her side, and offered her venison and parched corn. She raised her timid eye as she tasted the food; and then the young eagle knew that sunny-eye would be his wife.

"There was feasting and dancing and the marriage song rang merrily in Mohawk cabins when Azemi came among them. Pootanama loved her as his own heart's blood. He delighted to bring her the fattest deers in the forest, and load her with the ribbons and beads of the English. The prophets of the people liked it not that the strangers grew so numerous in the land. But the young chief laughed them to scorn, and said, 'The land is very big. The mountain eagle could not fly over it for many days. Surely the wigwams of the English will never cover it.'

"Yet when he held his son in his arms, as his father had done before him, he sighed to hear the strokes of the axe levelling the old trees of his forests.

"One day he left his home before the grey mists of the morning had gone from the hills, to seek food for his wife and child. The polar star was bright in the heavens ere he returned, yet his hands were empty. The white man's gun had scared the beasts of the forest, and the arrow of the Indian was sharpened in vain.

"Pootanama entered his wigwam with a cloudy brow. He did not look at Azemi, he did not speak to her boy; but silent and sullen he sat leaning on the head of his arrow. The muscles of his face betrayed the struggle within his soul.

"Azemi approached fearfully, and laid her little hand upon his brawny shoulders, as she said—

"'Why is the eagle's eye on the earth? What has Azemi done that her child dare not look in the face of his father?'

"Slowly the warrior turned his gaze upon her, and answered—

"'The eagle has taken a snake to his nest; how can his young sleep in it?'

"The Indian boy all unconscious of the forebodings which stirred his father's spirit, moved to his side and peeped up in his face with a mingled expression of love and fear.

"The heart of Pootanama was full even to bursting. His hand trembled as he placed it in the sleek black hair of his son.

"'The Great Spirit bless thee—the Great Spirit bless thee, and give thee back the hunting grounds of the Mohawk,' he exclaimed. Then folding him for an instant in an almost crushing embrace, he gave him to his mother, and darted from the wigwam.

"Two hours he remained in the open air, but the clear breath of heaven brought no relief to his noble suffering soul."

CHAPTER XLVIII.

THE HERMIT'S TALE CONCLUDED.

At this part of the aged narrator's highly characteristic tale, with which Flora felt so deeply interested, he was interrupted by a strange noise above at the secret entrance to the cavern, in which the confused murmur of human voices, as if in altercation were clearly distinguishable, and Flora, with a look of alarm, started from her seat, and clung timidly to the hermit.

"What sounds are those?" she said, "danger threatens. Oh, should any of the miscreants have discovered this retreat, and—"

"Hush, fear not," interrupted the hermit, "we are safe here; and now all is again quiet. The persons, whoever they were, have doubtless quitted the spot. There is no danger to apprehend."

With this assurance Flora endeavoured to be satisfied, but it was some minutes after this event, simple as it was, ere she could entirely regain her composure. The old man then, at her request, resumed and concluded his tale in the following words :—

"Once more Pootanama returned to his hut, and then his countenance, though severe, was composed. He spoke to Azemi with more kindness than the savage usually addressed the wife of his youth, but his looks told her that she must not ask the grief which had put a woman's heart in the breast of the Mohawk Eagle.

"The next day when the young chieftain went on a hunting expedition, he was accosted by a rough, square-built farmer.

"'Pootanama,' he said, 'your squaw has been stripping a dozen of my trees, and I don't like it over much.'

"It was a moment when an Indian could ill brook a white man's insolence.

"'Listen, buffalo-head,' he shouted, and as he spoke he seized the shaggy head of the unconscious offender, and eyed him with the concentrated venom of an ambushed rattlesnake; 'listen to the chief of the Mohawks. These broad lands are all his own. When the white man first left his cursed footprints in the forest, the Great Bear looked down upon the big tribes of Iroquois and Abanaquis. Had the red man struck you then, your tribes would have been as dry grass to the lightning. Go; shall the sunny-eye of Oneida ask the pale-face for a basket?'

"He breathed out a quick and convulsive laugh, and his white teeth shone through his parted lips, as he shook the farmer from him with the strength and fury of a raging panther.

"After that his path was unmolested, for no one dared to awaken his wrath; but a smile never again visited the dark brow of the degraded Indian chief. The wild beasts had fled far from the settlements, so that he would hunt for days and days without success.

"At last his boy sickened and died of a fever he had caught among the English. They buried him beneath a spreading oak on the banks of the Mohawk, and heaped stones upon his grave without a tear.

"The young mother did not weep, but her heart had received its death-wound; the fever had seized her, and she grew paler and paler every day. One morning Pootanama returned with some delicate food he had been seeking for her. He asked her to eat, speaking in a tone of subdued tenderness; but she answered not. The foot which was wont to bound forward to meet him was motionless and cold. He raised the blanket which partly concealed her face, and saw that the sunny-eye was closed in death. One hand was pressed hard against her heart, as if her last moments had been painful; the other grasped the beads which the young eagle had given her in the happy days of courtship.

"One heart-rending shriek was wrung from his agonised bosom—he tossed his arms wildly above his head—and threw himself by the side of her he had loved so fondly, deeply, and passionately as ever a white man loved.

"For hours he watched the corpse in silence; then he arose and carried it from the wigwam. He dug a grave by the side of his lost boy—laid the head of Azemi towards the rising sun—heaped the earth upon it, and covered it with stones according to the custom of his people.

"The next day a tree, which Azemi had often said was just as old as their boy, was placed near the mother and child. A wild vine was struggling amongst the loose stones, and Pootanama carefully twined it around the tree.

"One long, one lingering look at the graves of his kindred, and the eagle of the Mohawks bade farewell to the land of his fathers.

"For many a returning summer a lone Indian was seen standing at the sacred spot I have mentioned; but just thirty years after the death of Azemi, he was noticed for the last time. Age had not dimmed the fire of his eye, but an expression of deep melancholy had settled on his wrinkled brow. It was Pootanama, he who had once been the eagle of the Mohawks.

"He came to die beneath the broad oak which shadowed the grave of his wife. Alas! the white man's axe had been there. The tree he had planted was dead, and the vine which had leaped so vigorously from branch to branch, now yellow and withering, was falling to the ground.

"A deep groan burst from the breast of Pootanama; he broke his bow-string, snapped his arrows, threw them on the grave of Azemi, and departed for ever.

"None ever knew where Pootanama laid his dying head."

Thus the hermit concluded his pathetic tale, and Flora could not help shedding a tear of sympathy at the mournful incidents it described. The character of the little episode, and the language in which her venerable friend had related it, had rivetted her attention and diverted her thoughts for the time from her own sorrows; but they quickly returned to them, and she sat for several minutes buried in profound silence, brooding dismally upon the past, and with equally gloomy forebodings anticipating the future, the hermit again suffering her to indulge in her reflections without interruption.

But this silence was at length broken by a noise similar to that which had before disturbed them, and which again appeared to proceed from a spot immediately near the secret entrance to the cavern, and which sounded like the trampling of several feet, mingled with the voices of men and women.

Flora once more evinced considerable alarm, and clung to the old man, who, however, maintained his usual composure, and by his looks endeavoured to reassure her.

"There is nothing to create any alarm," he said, "the sounds doubtless only proceed from some travellers passing over these caverns, on their way through the wilderness; and now all is again still, and they have probably proceeded on their journey."

"It may appear a weakness on my part," returned Flora, "but I cannot conquer the apprehensions that beset me."

"'Tis folly, child," remonstrated the old man, "what have you to fear? But remain here for a few minutes, and I will endeavour to remove all your doubts and fears, by going forth to ascertain the truth. Do not venture to follow me."

Flora was about to offer some objection to this, but the old man having peremptorily motioned her to silence, ascended the rude steps that led to the mouth of the cavern or caverns, she anxiously watching his departure with a strange presentiment of some approaching evil on her mind, for which she was hardly able to account. She felt that she would much rather that she had been permitted to accompany him, and she almost dreaded to be left alone in this strange place; but remembering the hermit's injunctions, she tried to wait his return with patience and fortitude.

Again she thought she heard the same confused noise that had smote her ears before, though at a greater distance, and more than once she almost imagined that cries of distress rent the air, though she endeavoured to persuade herself that it could only be her timid and disordered fancy that had deceived her.

She was, however, unable to rest where she was, and ascended the steps, half resolved, even in spite of what the old man had said, to follow him. But she paused on the steps just below the entrance which the hermit had carefully closed after him, and listened with breathless attention to catch the least sound of alarm which might happen to reach her ear.

At first, however, all was perfectly silent, save the wind, which had arisen, and was murmuring among the foliage of the trees above, and the fears of Flora began to evaporate, she blaming herself for having ever entertained them, when the report of firearms at a short distance revived them with redoubled force; and on the same being repeated, her alarm became decided. She was satisfied that something serious was taking place, and her apprehensions for the safety of her venerable friend and guardian were not only of the most intense description, but seemed to be too well founded.

She held her breath and continued to listen with trembling anxiety, which was increased by the hermit's continued absence, and one more report of the discharge of firearms.

"I can endure this suspense no longer," she said; "let whatever may be the consequences, I must endeavour to leave the cavern, and to ascertain the situation of the aged man. Why did my fears urge him thus to expose himself to that danger which I shudder to think upon? Heaven protect him, and give me strength to accomplish my design."

She had, however, a much more difficult task to perform, in her present delicate state of health, than she had calculated upon, and some minutes elapsed before she could remove the stone and brushwood which concealed the entrance, but she at length succeeded in doing so, and cautiously emerged into the open air, and stooping down in the shadow of the rising ground before the entrance to the cavern, the better to conceal herself from immediate observation, she looked timidly around her, to see that the coast was clear.

Although the evening was somewhat advanced it was yet sufficiently light to distinguish objects for some short distance, and as nothing to excite her fears met her observation as far as her eyes could penetrate, and all was again silent, she took courage, and proceeded in the way which she imagined the hermit had most likely to have taken, in the confusion of thoughts forgetting to close and conceal the entrance to the cavern.

CHAPTER XLIX.

A TRAGICAL EVENT.

For some short distance Flora timidly advanced into the wilderness, but meeting with no obstruction, or anything to excite her suspicions or alarm, she took courage, and proceeded more boldly, her fears and anxiety for the old man's safety, however, increasing at every step.

She now also remembered that she had left the entrance to the caverns open, and chiding herself for thoughtlessness, and apprehensive of the consequences, she hesitated what to do, whether to proceed or return. Resolved, however, to accomplish her wishes, if possible, and banish her suspense, since she had ventured so far, she decided on the former, and once more advanced on her way.

At length, however, she came upon a spot which gave evident signs of a desperate struggle having recently taken place. The grass was trampled under foot, marks of blood were visible here and there, in one place was a sword and a military cap, and in another part of a woman's dress, which seemed to have been forcibly torn from her.

Flora shuddered and breathed short and quick, while again her fears almost prevailed, and turning slowly from the spot she was about to retrace her steps to the cavern, trusting that the hermit, seeing the danger to which he was exposed might have returned there by another way, when she was suddenly arrested in her purpose by a deep groan, the sound of which transfixed her to the spot with horror, and she stared eagerly in the direction from whence it came, which seemed to be from behind a cluster of trees a short distance before her.

Again and again the groans were repeated, and at length humanity superseding every other feeling in the breast of Flora, she proceeded in her search.

Every step that she took confirmed her worse surmises of some dreadful event having taken place, and at length to crown her horror, she came upon the ghastly corpses of men, a sepoy and an European, whose hands yet grasped the weapons with which they had defended themselves, and whose gaping wounds, and frightfully distorted features, shewed the desperate nature of the deadly combat in which they had been engaged.

Recent events had almost inured Flora to such terrible spectacles, but still she could not subdue her feelings on the present awful occasion, which were increased, when on proceeding two or three steps further, the mangled remains of two men, a woman, and a child (which, in death, she still clasped to her cold breast) met her appalled gaze, and were proofs too startling of the dreadful tragedy that had occurred.

She stood aghast, and as she continued to look upon the ghastly remains of those unfortunate persons, her heart sickened, every limb trembled, and her courage almost forsook her.

It was from one or more of these slaughtered victims that the groans which she had heard, doubtless proceeded, and having thus satisfied herself Flora would have returned, had it not been for the doubts and fears which she still entertained for the safety of her aged friend; and those fears were strengthened on her again hearing a dismal groan, as if from some person in their dying agony, and which proceeded from a spot close by, but apart from the awful objects that met her present observation.

With the greatest anxiety, but still with an intrepidity and resolution, for which she had not before given herself credit, she was about to hasten forward, to ascertain who the unfortunate sufferer was, when, on the groan being repeated, and looking more anxiously through the fast gathering darkness, her eyes encountered the white dress of what appeared to be a human being, crawling with difficulty on his hands and knees towards her.

She uttered a cry of the greatest anguish and terror, as the fatal truth flashed instantaneously upon her brain, and rushing towards him, sunk on her knees, and clasped the venerable man to whose kindness she was so much indebted, and who was bleeding from a wound on the forehead, in her arms.

He fixed one earnest look upon her, made a fruitless effort to speak, then pointing to a leather flask, containing some powerful restorative which we always carried about with him, the poor old man uttered a deep sigh, and faint and exhausted, his head sunk upon her bosom.

How Flora obtained such fortitude and self-possession under such appalling circumstances, it is impossible to say; but she lost not an instant in attending to the desperate and deplorable case of the venerable man. Hastily but carefully and tenderly she bound a scarf across his wound, and then applied some of the liquid to his lips, and supporting him on her knees in her arms, with his head reclining on her bosom, she gave free vent to the intense agony of her feelings, imploring the Almighty to look mercifully down, and to assist her humane efforts on such a terrible, and trying occasion.

What would she not have given were they in the cavern, where she might the better see to his recovery, but although the distance was not great, it seemed utterly impossible, in his helpless state, that she could ever find strength to conduct him there; and all the horrors of the circumstance, and the fate which seemed inevitably to await him, rushed with overwhelming force upon her brain, distracting her senses, and leaving her completely at a loss what to do.

"Unfortunate man," she sighed, tears of anguish and compassion trembling in her eyes, and her breast heaving with the powerful emotions that agitated it; "that you should live to this patriarchal age to perish thus. Alas! why did you thus rashly venture upon so dangerous a task?"

A sigh from the aged sufferer, who seemed to cling with wonderful tenacity to life, startled her, and again applying a small portion of the liquid to his lips, she endeavoured by every tender and affectionate means in her power to recall him to his senses. She bathed his temples with some of the same restorative, and after the lapse of a few minutes, he so far revived as to be able to open his eyes, and gently raising his head from her bosom to gaze earnestly, and with a mingled expression of sorrow and gratitude in the pale and anxious countenance of Flora.

"All merciful providence, I thank thee," she fervently ejaculated; "his life may yet be preserved. Oh, give me strength, I beseech thee, to support him to the cavern, where I may more properly attend to his wants."

The unfortunate old man again fixed an expressive look upon her, and which convinced her that he understood what she said; and after a pause, during which he made two or three ineffectual attempts to speak, in a faint and almost inarticulate voice he ejaculated:

"Thanks, thanks, gentle maiden for—for these thy kind attentions. The will of Fate be done, the fatal blow is struck, the old man's long earthly career is now almost run, and I bow my head in submission to the Great Spirit. But—but I must not die here. No—no, in that lonely retreat which hath for so many years sheltered me, must I breathe my last. There must my remains rest."

"Alas! alas!" sighed Flora, "would to God that I could find strength to support you there, but that seems to be impossible. Oh, what is to be done in this terrible emergency?"

For a minute or two the ancient hermit could not speak, but he looked gratefully in her face, and with an expression which seemed meant to encourage and invigorate her, and then a faint smile overspread his venerable features, as, with a strength almost incredible and superhuman, placing his hands upon her shoulders, with her assistance, he arose upon his feet, and in a voice whose tones, considering his hopeless condition, completely astonished her, he said:—

"The Great Spirit has heard my prayer, I feel imbued with more than mortal strength; poor child, it is an arduous task for thee, in thy delicate state, but heaven will assist thee. Give me thy support, and I may yet be able to reach the cavern ere I die."

It was indeed a severe trial for poor Flora, but providence seemed to empower her with more than natural fortitude to meet it, and supporting the form of the old man with her arms, while he exerted himself in the most extraordinary manner, she slowly led him fatal spot.

Frequently were they compelled to pause to rest themselves, and sometimes the courage of Flora nearly failed her, and that of the sufferer seemed also sinking, but with an extraordinary effort they soon were sufficiently able to recover themselves to proceed, though their progress, as may naturally be supposed, was tediously slow and difficult, and oh, how agonising were the thoughts of Flora, as almost fainting, she persevered in the accomplishment of her arduous task.

At length they reached the entrance to the cavern, to descend into which was more difficult even than what they had already surmounted, and here the hermit sunk once more upon the earth exhausted, and Flora, with feelings of anguish and despair, which it is needless to attempt to describe, again knelt by his side, supporting his head upon her bosom, and watching the ghastly changes in his countenance, so fearfully betokening the rapid approach of death, with anxiety and grief, which were almost overwhelming.

It was indeed a heart-rending and solemnly impressive sight to watch that venerable man in his dying moments. Yet was his features calm, and expressive of resignation and future hope; and with his hands crossed devoutly on his breast—for he still seemed to retain his senses—he appeared to be breathing a prayer to Heaven.

Flora, as well as she could, wiped away the blood which had streamed from his wound, down his face, and bathed his long grey beard, and again adopted all the means that she had in her power to revive him, and her humane exertions were at last rewarded with partial success. He again, with her assistance, arose upon his feet, and leaning on her shoulder they entered the opening, and commenced the descent into the cavern, which, with much difficulty, and with great pain to the old man, they at last accomplished.

Here the unfortunate sufferer, sinking upon his humble pallet, seemed quite exhausted, and it was quite evident that he could not long survive.

With all speed Flora applied such remedies as she found in the cavern, and to which the hermit directed her as well as his melancholy condition would enable him to do; and then kneeling down, and his head resting on her throbbing and agitated bosom, she awaited the awful event in a state of mind that may be easily imagined.

There was a death-like silence of several minutes, during which the breathing of the aged man became more difficult, and his pale and venerable countenance, though perfectly calm, showed in characters too strong to be mistaken the rapid approach of death; and the anguish and despair of poor Flora—who could not look forward to such a catastrophe without feelings of the greatest horror—became insupportable.

The dying man was perfectly conscious, and seemed to understand and appreciate the feelings of Flora, for a faint smile overspread his pale features, evidently meant to thank and console her, and he pressed the hand which held his vehemently. Several times he attempted to speak, but in vain, and Flora's emotion was so great that it was some minutes before she could give utterance to a syllable.

"Unfortunate old man," she at length ejaculated, fixing upon him a look of the utmost compassion; "and must you, whom I had began to look upon as my only earthly friend, be thus suddenly taken from me, leaving me to all the horrors of misery and despair? Oh, how my heart bleeds for you."

Again the hermit made an effort to speak, and after much exertion, in a faint and solemn voice he said—

"Murmur not, girl, at the will of Heaven. It sees fit to summon me after my long earthly pilgrimage, and I hail the change which in a few minute must take place, with pleasure and impatience. Yet do I feel for thy lonely and wretched situation, poor child. May God give you fortitude to support, and strength to surmount the many troubles you may have to contend with. Ah, that pang! it warns me that the final moment is at hand, and—"

His breath failed him, and unable to finish the sentence, his head again drooped upon Flora's bosom.

"All gracious powers!" she cried, and her looks sufficiently spoke the state of her feelings; "how agonising is this. Will nothing stay the remorseless hand of death? I shall go mad!"

The hermit once more raised his head, and with a look of mild reproach, with some difficulty, and in faltering accents, said—

"Forbear, girl, cease this unavailing grief and be firm, be calm, be resigned. I fear not to die, for Heaven knows the purity, the integrity, and virtue that have marked my conduct, and guided all my actions during my long life. The moment is coming—the gates of Heaven open to receive my soul—and my spirit wings its flight to eternity. Quick, girl, for my breath grows weak, and darkness closes before mine eyes—I—I—oh, God!"

These were his last words. There was something more that he evidently wanted to to say, some dying instructions that he wished to give her, and she listened with breathless attention; but it was all in vain, one faint sigh only escaped his lips, then a heavenly expression passed over his aged features—his eyes gradually closed—his head sunk back on her bosom—and the distracted Flora held in her arms a corpse.

For some minutes Flora Melville's brain was so confused and distracted by this awful event that she was almost in a state of utter unconsciousness, and continued to hold the corpse of the poor old man in her arms, and to gaze wildly and vacantly in his ghastly face, without being able to utter a word.

Every faculty was for the time suspended, and she was pale and inanimate as a statue.

But at length she was aroused to a full consciousness of the fatal truth, as though awakened from some frightful dream, and in a frantic voice she exclaimed—

"What means this awful silence? He does not sleep, and yet his eyes are closed and he speaks not. His heart has ceased to beat—his face is cold—his features are fixed and rigid: the fearful truth flashes upon my maddened brain! God of Heaven! he's dead—he's dead!—and I am alone in the world!"

The corpse of the old man sunk from her arms on the humble pallet as she thus spoke, and with a wild shriek of agony and despair, she sunk senseless by the side of the cold remains.

CHAPTER L.

THE CELEBRATION OF THE MOHURRUM.—NENA SAHIB AND OMELIA ONCE MORE MEET.

It was the fourth day of the annual celebration of the Mohurrum, and notwithstanding the awful events that had recently taken place, and which were still exciting the whole country, that most remarkable of all Indian public ceremonies lost none of the usual spirit which characterises it on the present occasion.

It was on the evening of this day that Omelia once more a prisoner, and with all the horrors of the fiendish malice and revenge of the miscreant Nena Sahib before her, arrived at the end of that long, tedious, and painful journey which has been so minutely described in the previous chapters.

The annual celebration of the Mohurrum in all large Mahomedan communities of the Sheah sect, though strictly speaking, a fast of the most mournful description, is accompanied by so much pomp and splendour, that strangers are at some loss to distinguish it from festivals of pure rejoicing.

The Sheahs, who are settled in Hindostan, are in some degree obnoxious to the charge of introducing rites and ceremonies, almost bordering upon idolatry, in their devotion to the memory of the Imaum's Hossein and Houssein.

Imbibing a love of show from long domestication with a people passionately attached to pageantry and spectacle, they have departed from the plainness and simplicity of their ancestors, and in the decorations of the *tazees* (mimic tombs) and the processions that accompany them to the place of sepulture, display their reverential regard for Ali and his sons in a manner which would be esteemed scandalous if thus accompanied in Persia and Arabia, where the grief of the Sheah is more quietly and soberly manifested.

Several processions take place during the celebration of the Mohurrum. At Lucknow, on the fifth day, the banners are carried to a celebrated shrine or *durgah* in the neighbourhood, to be consecrated, it being supposed that the standard of Hossein, miraculously pointed out to a devout believer, is deposited at this place. The veneration in which this sacred relic is held, nearly equaling that which in some places in Europe, is displayed towards pieces of the true cross, affords another proof of the corruption of the Mahomedan religion by the Sheah sect.

The gifts deposited at the *durgah*, consisting of money, clothes, and other valuable articles, become the property of the officiating priest, who is expected to disburse the greater portion in charity.

All the Moslem inhabitants in Lucknow are anxious to consecrate the banners employed at the Mohurrum, by having them touched by the sacred relic, and, for this purpose they are conveyed to the shrine with as much pomp and ceremony as the circumstances of the proprietors will admit.

A rich man sends his banners upon elephants, surrounded by an armed guard, and accompanied by bands of music. The arms and accoutrements, representing those worn by Hossein, are carried in some of these processions, and one of the most important features is Dhull Dhull, the horse slain with his master in the fatal field of Kurbelah; his trappings are dyed with blood, and arrows are seen sticking in his sides.

Multitudes of people form these processions, which frequently stop while the Moollahs recite the often-told but never tiring story, or the tragic scene is enacted by young men expert at broadsword exercises, and, as Hossein is surrounded and beaten down, muskets are fired off, and shouts and beat-

ings of the breast, attest the sincerity with which his followers bewail his untimely end.

On the seventh night of the Mohurrum, the marriage of Hossein's daughter with her cousin, a faithful partizan of the house of Ali, is celebrated with much pomp and show. The procession of the marriage of the unfortunate Cossim and his ill-fated bride is distinguished by trays bearing the wedding presents, and covered palanquins, supposed to convey the lady and her attendants; the animals employed in the cavalcade, with the exception of the favoured Dhull Dhull, are left outside the walls; but the trays containing sweetmeats, &c., a model of the tomb of Cossim, and the palanquins of the bride, are brought into the interior, and committed to the care of the keepers of the sanctuary until the last day, when they make a part of the final procession to the place of interment.

The most extraordinary feature, however, in the commemoration of the deaths of Hossein and Housein, is the participation of the Hindoos, who are frequently seen to vie with the disciples of Ali in their demonstrations of grief for the slaughter of his two martyred sons, and in the splendour of the pageant displayed at the anniversary of their fate. A very large proportion of Hindoos go into mourning during the ten days of the Mohurrum, clothing themselves in green graments, and assuming the guise of fakeers.

The complaisance of the Hindoos is returned with interest at the Hooly, the Indian Saturnalia, in which the disciples of the prophet mingle with the heartiest good will, apparently too much delighted with the general license and frolic revelries of that strange carnival, to be withheld from joining it by horror of its heathen origin. The ceremonials observed at the celebration of the Mohurrum are not confined to processions out of doors; persons of wealth and respectability having an Imaum-barrah constructed in the interior of their own dwellings. This is usually a square building, containing a hall and other apartments, in which the mourning assemblages during the period of the festival are congregated. It is decorated for the time with all the splendour which the owners can afford. The *tazee* is placed upon the side facing Mecca, under a canopy of velvet or tissue richly embroidered; and near it there is a pulpit very handsomely constructed of silver, ivory, ebony, or carved wood, having a flight of stairs covered with an expensive carpeting of broad cloth, velvet, or cloth of gold.

The *tazee* is lighted up by numerous wax candles; and near it are placed offerings of fruit and flowers presented by pious ladies to do honour to the memory of the Imaums.

The remainder of the hall is fitted up with

considerable splendour, furnished with mirrors, which reflect the light from numerous lustres, lamps, and girandoles. Poorer persons are content with less glittering ornaments; and in all, an assemblage is held twice a day, that in the evening being the most imposing and attractive The guests are seated round the apartment; the centre of which is occupied by a group of hired mourners, consisting of six or eight persons.

These men are usually of large stature, and of considerabla muscular strength. They are very scantily clothed in a drapery of green cloth, their breasts and heads being perfectly uncovered. A moollah, or priest, selected on acconnt of his superior elocution, ascends the pulpit, and proceeds to the recital of a portion of a poem in the Persian language, which contains a detailed account of

No. 28.

the persecution and tragic fate of the Imaums. The composition is said to be very pure; and its effect upon the auditory is prodigious.

After some well wrought passage, describing the sufferings of the unhappy princes, the reader pauses, and immediately the mourners on the ground commence violently beating their breasts, and shouting " Hossein, Hossein !" until at length they sink exhausted on the ground amid the piercing cries and lamentations of the spectators. A part of each day's service consists in a chant in the Hindostanee language, in which the whole assembly join, and the Sheahs end it by standing up and cursing the usurping Caliphs by name, devoting the memory of each offending individual to universal execration. The Socunees hold these solemn assemblies; but their grief at the cruel sufferings of so many estimable members of the prophet's family does not assume so theatrical a character. Attired in the deepest mourning they evince the most profound sorrow; and it is persons of this persuasion who manifest the greatest indignation when there is any risk of their processions being crossed by the heathen revelries of the Hindoos.

The pomps and ceremonies which precede it are nothing to the grandeur reserved for the display on the last day of the Mohurrum, when the *tazees* are borne to the place of interment. This pageant represents the military cavalcade of the battle of Kurbelah, together with the funeral procession of the young princes, and the wedding retinue of the bride and bridegroom divorced by death upon their nuptial day. The banners are carried in advance, the poles being usually surmounted by a crest, composed of an extended hand, which is emblematical of the five holy personages of the prophet's family and a symbol particularly designating the Sheah sect. Many make a declaration of their religious principles by holding up the hand; the Soonee displays three fingers only, while the Sheah extends the whole five. The horse of Prince Hossein and his camp equipage appear furnished with all the attributes of sovereignty; some of the *tazees* of which there is a great variety, are accompanied by a platform, on which three effigies are placed—the ass Borak, the animal selected by Mahomed to bear him off his ride to heaven, and two houris. The tomb of Cossim, the husband of Hossein's daughter, is honoured by being carried under a canopy; the bridal trays, palanquins, and other paraphernalia, accompany it, and the whole is profusely garlanded with flowers.

These processions, followed by thousands of people, take the field at break of day; but there are so many pauses for the reading of the poem dedicated to this portion of the history of the events of Kurbelah, and such numerous rehearsals of Hossein's dying scene, that it is night before the commencement of the interment. Devout Mussulmans walk, on these occasions, with their heads and their feet bare, beating their breast and tearing their hair, and throwing ashes over their persons with all the vehemence of the most frantic grief; but many content themselves with a less inconvenient display of sorrow, leaving to hired mourners the task of inciting and inflaming the multitude by their lamentations and bewailments.

The zeal and turbulence of the affliction of Ali's followers are particularly offensive to the Soonees, who professing to look upon Hossein and Houssein as holy and unfortunate members of the prophet's family, and to regret the circumstances which led to their untimely end, are shocked by the almost idolatrous frenzy displayed by their less orthodox brethren; and the expression of this feeling often leads to serious disturbances which break out on the burial of the *tazees*. Private quarrels between the sects are frequently reserved for adjustment to this period, when, under pretext of religious zeal, each party makes an assault upon his enemy without exposing the real ground of his enmity. In a few places which border the Ganges or Jumna, the *tazees* are thrown into the river; but generally there is a large piece of ground set apart for the purpose of the burial.

It is rather a curious spectacle to see the tombs themselves consigned to the earth, with the same ceremonies which would attend the inhumation of the bodies of deceased persons; the *tazees* are stripped of their ornaments, and when little is left but bamboo frames, they are deposited in pits. This ceremony usually takes place by torchlight, the red glare of innumerable flambeaux adding to the wild and picturesque effect of the scene.

We have said that such were the curious and remarkable ceremonies being performed with all their original spirit at the time of our heroine's arrival at Bithoor, where for the present that most refined of monsters, Nena Sahib, had taken up his quarters, at his old castle, or palace as it might more properly be designated.

But, if religious devotion had at any time found a place in his savage breast, on those that ought to be solemn occasions, it certainly did not at the time of which we are writing.

In a spacious pavilion, fitted up in the most elaborate style of eastern splendour, and lighted by innumerable lamps, which gave a dazzling effect to the profusion of gilt fancy work, and rich drapery that decorated the place, the Nena was seated, surrounded by some of his principal officers and attendants, and apparently bent to enjoy himself to his heart's content.

A bland smile was on his features, for "he could smile, ay, and murder while he smiled," and he frequently laughed heartily, probably at some joke uttered by his companions on some particular act of atrocity which had been perpetrated during the day by his orders.

At length, apparently growing tired of this, Nena Sahib motioned to one of his attendants, who seemed to understand him, and struck a gong at the further end of the pavilion.

Immediately the strange and barbarous music—if such it can be called—of the Nautch orchestra was heard, the rich crimson curtains at the back of the pavilion were drawn aside, revealing the beautiful gardens and numerous fountains, like the interior of the building, brilliantly illuminated, and a troop of the *kunchunee*—that class of Nautch, or dancing girls, who only perform for the amusement of the male sex, and in every respect are at their command—tripped into the splendid apartment, and having made their obeisance to the Nena and his friends, commenced their strange evolutions and songs, accompanied by guitars and very small kettle drums.

These girls were probably some of the most beautiful of that description of performers, and their dresses were of the richest character, and their persons decorated with a profusion of jewellery.

The passionate fondness of the natives for the Nautch, has in it something extraordinary. Many Europeans also were formerly so expressively devoted to it, as to excite the special ridicule of a distinguished satirist in the following lines—

"Shrilly she shrieked, and high above
The music of her fiddles three,
Rose the romantic strain of love,
Cheta, chota, natch-lee!

   *   *   *   *

And then she danced! for so they call,
Jingling her anklets while advancing,
With many a horrid squeal and squall,
With twirling hands and sudden kicks,
Her charms of person much enhancing;
People may patronise such tricks,
But shouldn't, surely, call it dancing."

For some time these females continued their fantastic performance much to the amusement of the Nena and his friends, and when tired of that entertainment another was immediately ready to supply its place.

But the festivities were suddenly interrupted by a loud noise outside the pavilion, followed by the agonised shrieks of a female, and Nena Sahib rising hastily from his seat, angrily demanded the cause. Before any of his attendants could answer that question, a woman with frantic looks, dress disordered, and bearing an infant in her arms, rushed wildly through the gardens to the pavilion, followed by several savage-looking men, in the midst of whom was an English officer whom they were goading on at the point of their swords and bayonets, and answering his appeals for mercy with frightful yells and shouts.

The unfortunate woman, who was young and handsome, had evidently already received the most brutal treatment, and was bleeding from two or three wounds about her neck and bosom, but she hugged her infant convulsively to her breast at the same time she cast the most anxious and agonised looks

towards her husband, for such the officer was.

"How now? What is the meaning of this?" hastily and peremptorily demanded Nena Sahib; "why am I thus rudely interrupted and disturbed?"

"Oh, mercy—save me, save my husband and innocent child," almost shrieked the poor woman, in the intense agony of her despair, and throwing herself at the feet of the Nena.

Her husband knelt not, his demeanour was firm and manly, but he appealed to Nena Sahib by a look which was sufficient to move any but the most callous and brutal heart to pity.

The Nena, however, as is well known, was not likely to be actuated by any other feelings than those of malice and exultation, and after having gazed at them for a moment or two with a look of scorn and derision, he said—

"Nena Sahib has no pity for the detested enemies of his country; he has sworn to rest not till he has seen the annihilation or extermination of the whole of your accursed race. You crave for mercy, woman; this is my answer."

With these words, which were received with shouts of applause from his savage myrmidons, the inhuman miscreant deliberately discharged the contents of a pistol at the head of the officer, who fell dead at the feet of his wife, who with a wild shriek enough to appal the ear was about to throw herself upon his bleeding corpse, when at a sign from the Nena, she was savagely dragged by the infuriated sepoys to her feet, in spite of her shrieks for mercy and the cries of her helpless infant.

"I leave the woman and her brat at your disposal," said Nena Sahib, addressing himself to the men; "you need no farther instructions from me. Away with them to death, and see that we receive no farther interruption to our festivities."

These orders were obeyed with brutal alacrity, the wretched woman with heartless violence was dragged by the hair of her head across the garden, and for several minutes her cries rent the air. All was then silent—the fate of the mother and child were sealed.

The body of the unfortunate officer was removed, and the Nena then with as much cool indifference, as if nothing of any consequence had taken place, ordered the girls to resume their dance, and seated amongst his friends seemed to enjoy himself greatly.

This cold-blooded and atrocious act, notwithstanding the many authenticated particulars recorded of the crimes of that most refined of monster's Nena Sahib, may appear incredible to the reader, and to have originated only in the imagination of the author of the present tale. It is, however, unfortunately, no fiction, although out of respect to the feelings of the surviving relatives of the unfortunate victims their names are concealed.

In fact, the horrible crimes committed by this miscreant and the other rebels, so far exceed in refinement of barbarity anything before recorded in ancient or modern history, that it is not at all remarkable there should be found many persons to disbelieve them, or, that other individuals, even in the face of the most positive proof, should have the temerity to deny that they ever occurred.

With un-English advocates of sepoy atrocity, we have no other feelings, however, but those of shame, abhorrenc, and contempt.

To our tale.

The Nautch girls having again concluded their fantastic performance, Nena Sahib suffered not the amusement of himself and friends to relax the least in spirit, other entertainments of an equally enlivening character, following each other in rapid succession, but which were in anything but keeping with the virtual celebration of the Mohurrum, and it seemed as if the Nena was fully determined to give no limits to his festivity and enjoyment.

The evening was beautiful, and the chaste moon shed her beams upon a scene of eastern splendour and romantic beauty, which might well have excited the enthusiastic admiration of even the most dull and insensible, under different circumstances, and could the mind have been divested of the thoughts to which the horrors that had lately been enacted, and were still being perpetrated, naturally gave rise.

The gardens upon which the pavilion, where Nena Sahib and his associates in crime were assembled, opened, were of vast extent, and art and ingenuity seemed to have exhausted themselves in their arrangement. Rich parterres of the most lovely flowers bloomed on every side, and the air which was cool and refreshing, was redolent of their fragrance.

Stately trees, too, reared their heads aloft, here and there, their luxuriantly foliaged and wide spreading branches, affording a delightful shelter from the heat of the noonday sun, which was enhanced by the cooling effect of the waters of the various fountains.

At length, however, the sports were once more interrupted by the entrance of a domestic, who in reply to the hasty and impatient interrogatory of the Nena as to his business, said—

"A man who calls himself Allyghur, and who states that he is not unknown to your highness, has just arrived hither, atttended by numerous others, and requests the honour of an audience."

"Allyghur," muttered Nena Sahib to himself, "ah, I know him well; he has already done our cause some service, and is worthy of trust and confidence. Show him in," he commanded aloud, and the attendant immediately departed to obey the order.

"You will be pleased to retire for awhile, my friends," observed the Nena, with all his customary politeness, and addressing himself to his guests, "my interview with this man must be private."

The guests bowed and obeyed, and immediately afterwards Allyghur—who evinced all the humility of the most abject slave before the Nena—was ushered into his presence.

The Nena eyed him with a scrutinizing look for a minute or two, from which Allyghur did not shrink, and then demanded, hastily—

"How now, Allyghur, whence come you?"

"From Lucknow, your highness," was the reply.

"What news from there?"

"The small force under the command of Colonel Inglis, together with all the English who were in the city, have betaken themselves to the residency," replied Allyghur, "and if they have a plentiful supply of ammunition and provisions, which it is said the late Sir Henry Lawrence had the precaution and foresight to secure, they may be able to hold out for some time to come."

"Humph," ejaculated the Nena, with a sardonic expression of features, "we shall see—we shall see. But I should marvel much, if with the overwhelming force that will be brought against them, they should be able to escape the fate which has already befallen so many of their countrymen and women, and which I hope will attend all of their accursed race, who pollute our country with their presence."

"It will not be the fault of the patriotic Nena Sahib," said the servile villain Allyghur, if those righteous wishes are not realised."

Nena Sahib smiled, and evidently received this as a flattering compliment.

"Now, Allyghur," he said, after a pause, "what business brings you hither?"

"That which I trust will afford your highness satisfaction," replied Allyghur; "I bring you a female prisoner, and one who is not unknown to you."

"Ah," exclaimed the Nena, with a look of curiosity, "who is the female of whom you speak?"

"Behold," answered Allyghur, moving towards the entrance to the pavilion from the gardens, and motioning to those who out of sight were awaiting there.

Immediately our heroine, whose features were perfectly calm, and whose carriage was firm and dignified, was conducted from the gardens into the presence of the dreaded and brutal Nena, who started, and could not help giving utterance to an exclamation of astonishment on beholding her.

"This is indeed an agreeable surprise, Allyghur," he observed, "and I shall not be unmindful of your services. Retire for awhile, I must speak to this daring girl alone."

Allyghur bowed and obeyed, and the Nena then folding his arms across his broad chest, stood and gazed at his unfortunate prisoner with a sarcastic look of triumph, which—without shrinking in the least, or evincing the remotest signs of fear, though painful indeed were her inward emotions—she returned with one of the most ineffable contempt.

"So then," he at last exclaimed in ironical tones, I have the honour and the pleasure of beholding the amazon champion of the enemies of her country once more. It is a pity that fortune who once favoured your escape from my power should now have deserted you, and that the wild bird, so eccentric and ambitious in its flights, should thus be caged again. However, I welcome you, Omelia, and will not fail to do full justice to your merits."

Omelia smiled scornfully, remained fixed and firm and resolute in her attitude, but did not condescend to return any answer.

Nena Sahib could not but admire her for her heroic courage, and he continued to gaze at her for a few minutes without making use of any observation.

"You are silent," he said, at length, "have you no answer to return to my observations?"

"None but one of the bitterest scorn, miscreant," replied Omelia, with unflinching firmness; for she had prepared herself for the worst, and was resolved to meet her fate undauntedly, whatever that fate might be.

A fearful frown lowered upon the brow of the Nena, at the epithet she so fearlessly applied to him, and he grasped her wrist fiercely, as he said—

"Ah!—dare you, girl? Know you to whom you thus venture to address yourself?"

"Yes," resolutely returned our heroine, "to the rebel, Nena Sahib, the wholesale murderer of innocent women and children."

"You seem to forget that you are now again in my power, and that one word from me would consign you to an instant and terrible death," he said.

"I know it," replied Omelia, "and yet you see I do not tremble, nor does my heart quail before you, How is this? I will tell you. It is because my motives are pure and just; I am firm in the consciousness of rectitude and virtue, and I feel confident in the protection of that Supreme power, whose laws you and your infamous colleagues have so monstrously outraged, and whose terrible retribution yet awaits you."

"Ha, ha, ha!" laughed Nena Sahib, scornfully, "your bold predictions amuse me; I can but afford to smile at visionary ideas of a mad-brained girl."

"You may affect to scorn my words, Nena Sahib," said the intrepid maiden, solemnly, and fixing her fine expressive eyes earnestly on his countenance, "but nevertheless, as sure as that we now stand in each other's presence, they will be verified. For a time this savage rebellion may triumph in its most sanguinary features, but the terrible day of retribution will arrive, then woe to you and the misguided wretches who have perpetrated crimes that make humanity shudder. England will muster her armed hosts of heroes—for how oft has every British soldier proved himself to be a hero —carrying extermination to their brutal enemies wherever they may encounter them. Mercy to the murderers of helpless women and children would be a crime, and you can expect it not. Again I say the dreadful day of retribution will arrive. The blood of the innocent will not go unavenged."

The manner in which Omelia uttered these words, and the energetic expression of her handsome features at the time, could not fail to make some impression even upon the most stubborn and insensible being, and Nena Sahib, although he tried to conceal it, quailed for the moment under their influence.

But he quickly recovered himself, and in a tone of bitterness, not unmingled with scorn, said—

"And these are the sentiments of an Hindoo maiden; 'tis thus she dares to speak of her countrymen, and to sympathise with the detested enemies of her native land—those robbers and usurpers who for a century have held the people of India in in bondage, ruled them with a rod of iron, trampled on their religion, dethroned her princes, and plundered them of their dearest rights. Have not treaties been disregarded; the most solemn promises been broken, and faith, right, and justice scattered to the winds? Have I not bitterly experienced the wrongs, the shameless destruction of every principle of honour and justice, in my own person? They execrate my name, and hold me up as a monster of iniquity, be it so;—but who have made me what they represent me to be?—they, and they alone. They alone are responsible for all my present actions. They have plundered me of all that I possessed—that I inherited from the illustrious prince who adopted me—and by turning a deaf ear to my just claims, and in shamelessly rejecting them, aroused those dormant passions that will not be subdued until they have had an ample and bloody vengeance."

The Nena was terribly excited as he thus gave utterance to his feelings, and Omelia could not gaze upon him without a shudder of horror; although at the same time she was compelled to acknowledge to herself that there was some slight show of truth in many of the observations he made use of.

Nena Sahib paced the apartment to and fro with disordered steps, and it was some minutes ere he could regain his composure. At length he turned to Omelia and said—

"But I degrade myself by talking thus to the wretched girl whom I hold in my power, and who has dared to raise her feeble arm and voice in defence of the enemies of the country which gave her birth. Your fate is in my hands, the only way by which you can hope to escape the horrors I may inflict upon you is by renouncing your present mad sentiments, and divulging all you know of the movements and designs of the enemy. These are lenient terms, and if you are wise, you will not fail to appreciate my clemency, and to comply with them."

"Never!" exclaimed our heroine, firmly, and her indignation fully revealing itself in the expression of her features, "I should hate and despise myself could I be intimidated by threats into a compliance with anything so utterly repugnant to my feelings. Do with me as you please, I am fully prepared to brave everything that your brutal and cowardly malice can inflict."

"Indeed?" said the Nena, "we shall see. Your vaunted courage will be fully put to the test, rest assured. I will give you time to consider, and our present interview is now at an end."

Omelia shrunk not, nor wavered in her determination, but replying only to his observations with a look of contempt, awaited that which was about to follow with fortitude and resignation.

Nena Sahib then summoned one of his officers into his presence, and commanded him to bid Allyghur to return to the Pavilion.

This order was quickly obeyed and Allyghur and some of the mutineers who had accompanied Omelia on her long and tedious journey, quickly re-appeared.

There was a savage expression of malice and exultation in the looks of the villain, as he fixed them on Omelia, but she met them with perfect indifference.

"I again thank you, Allyghur, for the zeal you have displayed," said Nena Sahib; "you will now convey your prisoner to a place whither this officer will guide you, and to-morrow I will see you again."

Allyghur bowed, and the Nena then having drawn the officer aside, and given him some instructions in an under tone, Omelia was delivered to the custody of Allyghur, and conducted from the Pavilion, her fortitude never forsaking her even for an instant.

The guests were now resummoned, and the entertainments were resumed, as though nothing of an important nature had happened, and continued with unabated spirit till a late hour.

CHAPTER LI.

THE SUFFERINGS OF OMELIA.—HER THREATENED FATE.

Notwithstanding the violent and brutal passions of the Nena preponderate over every other feeling, it has never been denied that he has some few redeeming qualities, and therefore in spite of the indignation which her observations and the epithets she had applied to him, excited in his guilty breast, he could not but admire the noble heroism of Omelia's character, and that made him hesitate in what manner he should ultimately dispose of her.

Strange, too, that such a monster, who could ruthlessly order the slaughter of innocent women, and exult in their dying agony, should not be insensible to the tender passion, but such is the fact, as asserted by those who know him well, and have had the opportunity of analysing many of the peculiar features of his character, and so it was that the transcendent beauty of Omelia, had made some impression upon him, but her proud and haughty demeanour awed him into forbearance, and restrained that guilty desire, which might otherwise have exposed his helpless victim to the most brutal violence.

Guided by the officer, with whom he continued in conversation, Allyghur conducted his prisoner from the palace, or "castle"—as it was usually called—of the Nena, and although the villain frequently glanced at her with looks that showed the unmanly feelings of exultation that filled his breast, he never spoke to her.

Omelia felt relieved, notwithstanding her precarious and dangerous situation, now that she was released from the hated presence of Nena Sahib, but in spite of the fortitude she had displayed, her mind was disturbed by the most torturing doubts, thoughts, and apprehensions, for certainly nothing could scarcely be more dismal than the prospects before her, and knowing the savage and relentless character of the Nena, and how completely she was in his power, she certainly had a right to encourage the most fearful anticipations, especially after the manner in which she had set him at defiance.

Such were the melancholy reflections that occupied the mind of Omelia as she was being conducted to the place in which she was to be now confined, but still she concealed her real emotions, and maintained all that fortitude of demeanour which had hitherto characterised her.

After crossing a small court, and passing along a narrow passage, they came upon a range of prison-like looking buildings, and these, too, were in the immediate contiguity of the Nena's splendid residence.

Nothing could be more gloomy than the appearance of these buildings, and their blackened stone walls seemed to frown despair upon our unfortunate heroine, who, however, kept up her courage as well as she could.

She had no doubt that one of these buildings was destined to be her future prison, and that conjecture was quickly confirmed, for the officer, who had performed the office of guide to Allyghur, unlocked a strong iron-barred door in one of these miserable-looking dens, and which seemed to communicate with the whole range, and ordering the sepoys, the companions of Allyghur, to remain outside, he motioned the latter to follow him with his prisoner, and then led the way into a long passage, which seemed to run along the whole series of cells—for such they undoubtedly were—and was dimly lighted by a lamp suspended from the roof.

The man stopped before a low door, which was immediately opposite this lamp, and removing the heavy bolts, threw the door back upon its hinges, and then addressing himself to Allyghur, said—

"This is the place in which the Nena has ordered that the prisoner shall be confined. I will leave you now, but will return in a few minutes."

With these words he left them, and disappeared under an archway on the right, at the farther extremity of the passage.

Allyghur, with a malicious look, motioned Omelia to enter the dungeon, which she did, with a firm step, and haughty demeanour, and he followed, without closing the door, so that the light from the lamp might reveal all the gloomy and disgusting features of the place.

The atmosphere of the place came sickly, unwholesome, and oppressive to the senses.

Omelia cast an anxious and melancholy look around, and she could not help inwardly shuddering at the loathsome aspect of the dungeon in which she was to be confined, probably for an indefinite period.

It was limited to the smallest possible space that it was likely any person could at all exist in. The blackened and mouldy walls were dripping with unwholesome moisture, the ground was covered with filth, apparently the accumulation of years, and the only light which was admitted, when the door was closed, excluding that emitted by the lamp before mentioned, was through a narrow crevice in the wall.

On one side of this awful place was an iron chair, fixed by a strong staple to the wall, with a ring attached to the other end; and on the damp earth beneath was a heap of straw, which no doubt had formed the only resting place for many an unfortunate prisoner, and by the side of which stood a small earthen pitcher, which still contained a portion of filthy water.

All that the eye rested upon in this frightful living tomb, brought vividly to the imagination the revolting scenes of cruelty that had but too probably been enacted in this place, even for years before the present rebellion; and it was impossible that Omelia could contemplate the disgusting scene, and anticipate the horrors that seemed inevitably in store for her, without a feeling of dread.

In spite of her efforts to disguise them from the villain, Allyghur appeared to penetrate the thoughts and emotions that agitated her bosom, and he exulted with all the malice of a fiend.

"This, then, for the present," he observed, with a satirical grin, "is the accommodation which the truly amiable and gallant Nena Sahib, provides for you, Omelia. I congratulate you on the cheerfulness of your prospects."

"Heartless wretch," returned our indignant and disgusted heroine, "your brutal taunts fall harmlessly on mine ears. I am fully prepared to meet and brave all that deadly malice can inflict on me, and to meet whatever fate may be in store for me, confident that there is a power above that will not suffer my wrongs to go unavenged."

"Indeed," sneered the cowardly ruffian; "you boast much of your courage, but I am inclined to think that a few days residence in this not very delightful place, and especially with such sumptuous fare as will doubtless be supplied to you, will cause you to alter your tone. It is a pity that your noble and heroic aspirations should be thus nipped in the bud."

The bosom of Omelia swelled, and her

bright eyes flashed with resentment, but she returned no answer, and met the triumphant glances of the villain with that firmness and contempt which had characterised her behaviour throughout.

The officer now returned with some provisions of the coarsest possible kind, and another pitcher, containing brackish water, which he substituted for the other, and then having exchanged some words with Allyghur in an under tone, without another observation to Omelia they quitted the dungeon, barring and bolting the door after them, and the poor girl was left in that frightful place, where it seemed scarcely possible for any human being to exist even for the most brief period, in a state of utter darkness, with the exception of the faint and scarcely perceptible ray of light which stole through the crevice in the wall before mentioned.

For a few moments her mind was too much bewildered to enable her to view it as anything more than some frightful dream, and she stood transfixed to the spot, with her eyes glaring wildly and vacantly upon the door, and her hands clasped vehemently together.

But too soon the whole horrid truth flashed upon her brain, and that unexampled fortitude which had supported her hitherto now entirely forsook her, and with an exclamation of agony she sunk senseless and inanimate upon the damp and mouldering straw which was to form her only bed.

To what a state of anguish did she recover, to find herself immured in this loathsome place, with no prospect of relief, and with nothing to commune with save her own torturing thoughts; surely it was a refinement of cruelty such as the mind of a demon could alone conceive.

It appeared utterly impossible that she could long survive in such a dreadful situation, and the awful doom which awaited her might be considered inevitable. Already she seemed to feel the chill of death benumbing her limbs, and a leaden weight pressed upon her fevered brain which threatened to hurry her to madness.

Terror usurped every faculty, despair held prisoner her heart, and unable any longer to control her feelings, the poor girl pressed her hands convulsively on her burning forehead, and burst into a violent paroxysm of sobs and tears.

And thus dismally passed the first hour or two of Omelia's incarceration. The awful silence, too, which prevailed, like that of the tomb, was sufficient to add to the horror which pervaded her distracted mind, and even opposed to every superstitious feeling as she naturally was, she could not but give way, in some measure, to its influence, placed in the dreadful situation in which she was.

And now all the awful atrocities she had herself witnessed, and of which she had heard, recurred to her memory with tenfold force, and she pictured to herself the tortures she might expect to be inflicted upon her by such a monster as Nena Sahib, and to which the present was probably but a prelude.

Then she thought of Stanley, and her heart sickened, and her agony was increased tenfold.

"But after all the hardships I have endured," she soliloquised, "and the many dangers I have escaped, shall I be suffered to perish thus? Shall the monster who holds me in his power, be for ever permitted to triumph in his enormities, and to set every law of nature, justice, and humanity at defiance? I cannot, I will not believe it. No, even horrible as are the circumstances in which I am placed—in fact, too horrible almost for contemplation—I will not yet abandon myself to entire despair. Providence in its mercy will, I trust, interpose to save me. Stanley, too, dear, noble-minded Stanley, if you are indeed still living, oh, may kind heaven watch over your future safety, even though it may never be our fate to meet again.

Again her tears flowed fast as these melancholy reflections occurred to her, and for some time her mind was completely absorbed in grief.

She felt a burning thirst parching her throat, but notwithstanding she turned away with disgust from the filthy water contained in the pitcher, and for the moment felt as if she could sooner perish than drink it.

She got close under the crevice in the wall in order to inhale the scanty portion of fresh air that it admitted, but still nothing could counteract the stifling effects of the pestiferous atmosphere of the place, and a deathly sickness came over her, and a stupifying sensation stole upon her senses, which she could with difficulty resist. The silence remained unbroken, and the gloom seemed if possible to increase.

Omelia cast a timid look towards the chain fixed to the wall, and she pictured to her imagination in the most fearful colours the many unfortunate victims like herself, who probably had been incarcerated in this frightful place, and the dreadful sufferings to which they had been subjected; nay, to such a wild pitch was her disordered imagination wrought, that she could almost fancy she heard their dying groans of agony, and saw their ghastly features as they writhed convulsively in their last struggles.

Every moment the thirst of poor Omelia

became more intolerable, and unable to endure it any longer, but scarcely knowing what she did, she seized the jug, and raising it to her lips, drank of its nauseous contents.

This caused a re-action; the blood seemed to rush cold as ice through her veins, while a burning fever was upon her brain. All strength forsook her limbs, for the time being her faculties appeared to be suspended, and she sunk back powerless on the straw which formed her wretched bed.

CHAPTER LII.

THE DEATH DOOM.

It must now have been long past midnight,

and awful indeed was the stillness that reigned around, not even broken by the slightest murmuring of the wind.

And there was no pitying eye to view with compassion the misery of the hapless Omelia, no soothing voice to offer her the balm of consolation, as she reclined helplessly on her pallet of straw surrounded by all the horrors of that frightful dungeon.

A kind of stupor had fallen upon her senses, yet was she partially conscious, and her distracted mind was keenly awake to the terrors of her situation.

And in this wretched state she continued throughout the night, and till a feeble ray of sunlight struggled in at the small aperture in the wall of her dungeon. Care, anxiety, and imprisonment had even in the few hours that she had been confined already done their baneful work, and so altered was her appearance that the change seemed almost incredible.

Nevertheless, with that indomitable energy and perseverance which never for any length of time forsook her, even under the most trying circumstances, she struggled against her sufferings, and so far succeeded as to gain a degree of comparative composure. She put her trust in a Supreme power, and her apprehensions of that which might be yet in store for her, were deprived of half their terrors. Yet, heaven knows, considering all the alarming circumstances of her melancholy case there was but little room for hope.

And thus slowly, tediously, drearily the day wore away with the beauteous prisoner, the only visitor she had being a man—who she supposed to be her appointed gaoler—to bring her a fresh supply of coarse provisions, though she had scarcely touched those with which she had been provided before, and he made use of no observations, and as his looks were forbidding, she did not venture to put any questions to him, anticipating as she did some insulting answer.

Again night approached, although it was almost perpetual night in that fearful place, and still the same unbroken silence reigned around, and added, if possible, to the gloom and melancholy of our heroine's feelings; but still upon the whole she bore her misfortunes with a patience and resignation that was truly surprising.

That night, worn out with fatigue both of body and mind, Omelia did obtain a few hours sleep, notwithstanding the wretchedness of her situation, and when she awoke she felt considerably refreshed, and animated with fresh confidence and resolution.

"Even great as are the dangers that surround me," she exclaimed, "terrible as is the fate with which I am threatened, I will not yet despair. There is a power above which can avert all the evils I have too much reason to apprehend, and I will not fear. I will be firm; resist boldly all the designs of my cruel oppressor, and look forward with every hope to the result. Something tells me that I who have fearlessly risked so much in the cause of humanity, am not destined to meet with the fate to which the blood-stained monster, Nena Sahib, would probably consign me, and I will yet treat his threats with scorn, and hold him at defiance."

These thoughts inspired her with fresh spirits and renewed courage, and she awaited the events of this, the second day of her incarceration, with somewhat more composure than might have been expected under the painful and terrible circumstances.

As well as she could judge, it was about midday, when she was suddenly aroused from a deep and melancholy reverie into which she had fallen, by hearing the bolts of her dungeon door being withdrawn, and she started to her feet and awaited impatiently to see who the intruder was, in an instant foreboding some approaching evil, although she could not but consider that to know the worst at once would be much better than to be kept in such a terrible state of uncertainty and suspense.

The door was quickly thrown back upon its hinges, and the ruffian Allyghur stalked into the dungeon, with an expression of countenance which plainly showed the guilty thoughts that were passing in his mind.

Omelia quickly regained her self-possession, and while Allyghur seemed to gaze upon the change in her appearance, and the misery by which she was surrounded, with feelings of the most brutal satisfaction, she returned his looks with those of contempt and abhorrence, and without waiting for him to address her, in haughty tones she demanded—

"Now, ruffian, what evil business brings you hither? What fresh work of guilt have you in the eagerness of your malice and revenge against a defenceless woman undertaken to perform?"

"You affect a boldness and indifference as to your fate, girl," replied Allyghur, "which you do not feel. You cannot deceive me; haughty and contemptuous though your tone and demeanour are, your quivering lips, and the restless expression of your eyes, betray the agony of your mind, and the fears that even at this moment shake your soul. 'Tis well, this obstinate spirit will at last be broken, and the proud Hindoo maiden, who has dared to act in concert with the hated enemies of her country, will yet be humbled with the dust."

"Liar!" exclaimed Omelia, in a voice, and with a look of determination, that somewhat startled and astonished Allyghur; "villany is powerless to intimidate me, tortures are unavailing to crush Omelia's spirit or to move her from those principles which are sanctioned by virtue and justice, and the dictates of her own heart. But I waste words and degrade myself by deigning even to reply to your brutal observations. You come hither to mock me, and to triumph o'er the fate to which you have been the principal cause of consigning me. But I defy your utmost malice, and that of the atrocious criminal whose ready tool you are. Begone, villain, and leave me to the gloom of this wretched dungeon, and my own thoughts."

"Weak fool," returned Allyghur, "so abject and so powerless, and yet to presume to command. "'Tis your's to obey. This way, the Nena, your friend, demands your attendance."

Omelia could not help inwardly shuddering, as a fearful foreboding crossed her mind, but she concealed it as well as she could from the observation of Allyghur, who seized her rudely by the arm, and hurried her from the dungeon into the passage, where two or three other sepoys were waiting, and she was conducted again to the princely residence of Nena Sahib, on the way endeavouring to collect herself, and to be prepared for whatever might await her.

Nena Sahib was seated in the pavilion, attended by some of his most confidential followers, to whom he was giving instructions on matters of importance, when the arrival of Allyghur with his prisoner was announced, and that was the signal for the breaking up of the conference, and the individuals having retired, Omelia was ushered into the Nena's presence, and having regained her wonted composure, from which she was not the least disturbed by the scrutinizing look which he fixed upon her.

He motioned Allyghur to retire, and Omelia was once more left alone in the presence of the miscreant whom she had so much reason to dread, but before whom she again stood with the most unflinching firmness.

Nena Sahib did not offer to rise from his seat, but for several minutes continued to fix his keen and penetrating eyes upon her countenance, and to watch narrowly the expression of her features, evidently endeavouring to read the thoughts that were passing in her mind.

"Come hither, girl," at length he said, in a commanding tone, yet with that bland and hypocritical smile in which he usually clothed his intelligent and good-humoured features.

Omelia obeyed, still without evincing any signs of fear or other emotion, and again Nena Sahib gazed earnestly upon her handsome countenance, the almost matchless beauty of which seemed to strike him more forcibly than ever, while he could not but admire the calm dignity of her demeanour under circumstances that were sufficient to daunt the firmest spirit.

But whatever the thoughts of Nena Sahib were, he took good care to conceal them from the observation of his prisoner, and at length said—

"Now girl, I trust that calm reflection in the solitude of the not very agreeable apartment to which I consigned you, has brought you to your senses, and destroyed the rebellious and dangerous spirit which has hitherto characterised you."

Omelia looked disdainfully upon him, but remained silent, and a dark frown lowered upon his brow, and an expression of anger passed over his features.

"You do not answer," he said, in a stern voice, at the same time hastily rising from his seat, and grasping her wrist; "beware; this obstinacy may cost you dear."

"I expect no mercy from one to whom the feeling is a stranger," returned our heroine, boldly; "it is not by acts of cruelty such as Nena Sahib can alone inflict on his unfortunate and helpless victims, that the obstinate spirit of Omelia, as you are pleased to call it, can be crushed. It does but strengthen her in her virtuous resolutions, and increase her abhorrence for the miscreants who can be guilty of outrages that make humanity shudder."

"Rash girl," he exclaimed, passionately, and again grasping her wrist, "are you mad? Know you him to whom you thus address yourself?"

"Yes," answered Omelia, erecting her fine, graceful, and majestic form to its full height, and her eyes flashing forth an expression of shame and indignation that seemed even to awe Nena Sahib, "yes, it is to Nena Sahib that I speak—he who bears the form of man, but whose acts are those of a fiend."

The Nena relinquished his hold of Omelia, and starting back a few paces, stood and gazed at her apparently astounded.

Nothing could be more commandingly striking than the attitude in which the Indian heroine stood at that moment. Never did she look more beautiful.

Nena Sahib was lost in amazement and admiration, and the rage which her withering observations had excited in his breast, was in an instant subdued. Again that tender feeling which it has been before stated was one of the strange ingredients of his otherwise savage nature, asserted its influence, and for the moment superseded every feeling of resentment or revenge, and after a pause, during which he never removed his eyes from her, in a softened voice, and in a tone of regret, he said—

"What exquisite beauty; and what a pity that a mind so endowed should be led astray by false notions of right and wrong. Hark you, Omelia, could I but persuade you to abandon your present ideas, and to swear fidelity to that righteous cause, the cause of your long oppressed country, and which it is your duty to do, I could not only forgive the past, but place you in a position that would secure you fortune, ay, and honour."

"To become the friend and adherent of Nena Sahib," replied Omelia, "must be to abandon honour and every noble feeling; to become a thing of scorn and loathing. I reject your offer with the disgust and indignation it merits."

The pride of the Nena was wounded by the boldness of her words, but he stifled his feelings, and the guilty thoughts which the beauty of the Indian girl had excited in his breast, shone forth in the expression of his eyes and features.

Omelia watched him narrowly, and in a moment her quick eye penetrated to the base and revolting truth, and every feeling of virtuous resentment, shame, and offended modesty, was excited in her breast; at the same time her powerless and dangerous situation, burst with irresistible force upon her mind, and almost overpowered her.

She looked anxiously around the place, with the vain hope of escape should any violence be offered her, and in a moment her eye fell upon a pistol, which by some fortunate accident had been placed on a richly carved and gilded table, which stood near her, and a desperate thought immediately flashed across her brain, which she resolved as a last resource to put into execution, and for that purpose, without attracting the particular attention of Nena Sahib, she gradually drew nearer the table until the deadly weapon was within her reach.

"Your bold words, Omelia," he said, after a pause, "shall not excite my wrath, for your beauty has raised other passions in my breast, which I fain would gratify. You understand me."

"Shameless villain!" cried Omelia, unperceived by the Nena, putting her hand behind her, and securing the pistol, "too well I do; and have not language sufficiently strong to express my disgust, indignation, and hatred."

"Beware," he said, as he approached her nearer, "you are powerless to resist my wishes, and it would be madness to attempt to do so. I can enforce that for which I condescend to sue."

"Villain!" exclaimed the intrepid girl, at the same time levelling the pistol at his head; "be this my determined answer. I can boldly meet death rather than dishonour, degradation, but dare to advance a step towards me, or attempt to pollute me with your unhallowed touch, and even the weak arm of a woman shall rid the world of a monster who has become the scourge of his fellow creatures!"

Nena Sahib for the moment was paralyzed with astonishment and confusion, but he quickly recovered himself, and with an exclamation of ungovernable rage, and the rapidity of a tiger springing upon his prey, he rushed upon her, and arrested her arm, but not until she had discharged the pistol, and Allyghur and several others, who had overheard the latter observations of Omelia, rushing in, the former received the contents of the deadly weapon in his breast, and with a frightful yell, fell dead in the arms of one of his companions.

Surprise and consternation enchained the faculties of Nena Sahib and his myrmidons for the instant, but Omelia stood firm, calm, and perfectly collected, and gazed with a look of satisfaction upon the corpse of the wretch to whose villany she was indebted for the horrors of her present situation.

The Nena, however, soon recovered himself, and in a fearful voice, turning to Omelia, he said—

"Rash, obstinate, desperate girl, you have sealed and hastened your doom. Take her hence to her dungeon, in another hour she dies!"

CHAPTER LIII.

THE MOMENT OF EXECUTION.

It was a fearful decision, and the manner and tone in which the remorseless Nena delivered it, showed his cruel determination. The bold resistance of Omelia to his revolting advances upon her honour—her virtue; her dignified and scornful demeanour, and the last act, had aroused all his worst passions, and vengeance now alone predominated in his guilty breast

But terrible even as was her situation, and with the all but certainty of speedy death before her, Omelia trembled not, for she felt a happy confidence in the merciful interposition of providence, and could therefore look upon the awful doom to which the miscreant had consigned her with the most perfect indifference.

She cast one look of exultation at the ghastly corpse of the wretch who through her hands had met with so just and terrible a retribution for his crimes, and then turning a look of the most haughty scorn and defiance upon Nena Sahib, she walked with a firm step from the pavilion, guarded by the creatures of the rebel chief to whose custody he had committed her.

Nena Sahib motioned the attendants to remove the body of Allyghur, which being done, and he left alone for a few minutes, with folded arms and a contracted brow, he paced the apartment with disordered steps, and in a state of the greatest excitement.

"Yes," he muttered to himself, "she shall die; the bold, presumptuous girl, who dares to beard the lion in his den, and laugh his threats to scorn. The weakness, which by the force of her charms for the moment infatuated me, is past, and revenge has entirely superseded the feeling. She shall die—yes, in another hour she shall die."

With that cruel determination the Nena quitted the pavilion to give instructions for the execution of his innocent and unfortunate victim.

In the meantime, Omelia had been reconducted to her loathsome dungeon, and there left alone to prepare herself, in the brief period that was allotted her, for the awful change she was doomed to undergo.

And now, it must be admitted, that much of the heroic fortitude which had hitherto sustained her, forsook her, and she was compelled to yield to those feelings of dread that must naturally be excited in the stoutest breast at the prospect of a violent death, and that in all the springtide of youth, and with sunny hopes not yet extinguished. She sunk upon her knees, clasping her hands together, and raising her eyes towards heaven engaged in mental prayer, although her brain at the same time was so much bewildered, that she could not arrange her thoughts into anything like reasoning order.

At length, however, she aroused herself, and all her wonted courage and confidence returned. She arose to her feet, and firmness and resignation marked her whole demeanour.

"Why should I fear death?" she ejaculated; "heaven knows the purity and rectitude of the motives that have ever guided my conduct, and I have nothing to regret or reproach myself with. If it be the will of the Almighty power that I should die the death to which this incarnate fiend has doomed me, I submit without a murmur, and will meet my fate with the same fortitude which I trust has ever hitherto characterised me. Heaven bless you, dearest Stanley, if you be still living, and give you strength to support the anguish which I know will lacerate your manly heart, should you ever learn the particulars of your Omelia's untimely fate, of her whose love and constancy nothing could ever destroy."

She could not control the power of her emotions as the latter thoughts occurred to her, grief choked her further utterance, and tears chased each other down her cheeks.

She took from her bosom the letter of her lover to the ill-fated Captain Woodford, which she always carried about her, and with melancholy delight re-perused, as she had a right to imagine, for the last time, the precious contents, pressing it to her lips again and again.

Still she was perfectly resigned, and awaited the appointed time with becoming firmness.

The brief hour had nearly elapsed, and all the preparations for the execution, or rather the murder of the unfortunate girl were completed.

The scene selected for this bloody tragedy was the garden attached to the palace, and there a body of the Nena's soldiers were drawn up, his "butcher," or executioner, standing grimly by, with all the ghastly instruments of torture, the wretch seeming to await impatiently the arrival of his helpless victim.

Nena Sahib was on the spot to superintend the inhuman work, and was pacing to and fro with hasty steps, deeply wrapped in thought.

"So young, so beautiful," he muttered to himself, partly wavering in his brutal purpose, "'tis hard that she should thus perish. But away with these thoughts, the daring conduct she has pursued, and the scorn and opprobrium she has heaped upon me, have provoked and justified her fate, and I will not suffer any weakness or indecision on my part to rescue her from it. She shall die, yet shall her death be not one of torture. Away," he said peremptorily, addressing himself to the executioner, "I shall not require your services."

The fellow looked disappointed, and skulked slowly and reluctantly away, and Nena Sahib, turning to one of his havildar's who was standing by, said—

"Bring hither the condemned prisoner."

The officer and two sepoys departed to obey this order, and a brief interval of suspense and expectation succeeded, the Nena giving some instructions to the officer in command of the soldiers present, from which it appeared that he had decided that Omelia should be shot.

A slight murmur among the men intimated the approach of the unfortunate victim, and soon she appeared, walking with a firm step, and a perfectly calm and undaunted expression of countenance, and stood before the Nena in an attitude which showed the utter scorn in which she held him, and the heroic fortitude with which she was prepared to meet the awful fate to which he had consigned her.

He gazed at her for a few moments in silence, unable to suppress the feelings of admiration which the firmness of her demeanour under such appalling circumstances excited, and again half relenting, but he quickly recovered his wonted sternness and inflexibility, and addressing himself to her, said—

"The fatal moment has arrived, girl—grim death awaits you; do you not tremble at its approach?"

"It is for such blood-stained wretches as Nena Sahib to tremble at the approach of death," replied Omelia, boldly; "my con-

science is free from crime, virtue and rectitude have prompted all my actions, and I
fear not. Proceed to put your murderous
designs into execution, I am prepared."

"It may not yet be too late to move me
to mercy," said Nena Sahib, "if you will
abandon your rash principles, and be guided
by the future line of conduct I shall mark
out for you."

"Never," replied the intrepid maiden, resolutely, "I disdainfully reject mercy at your
hands and on such terms. Death is preferable to such a life of shame and degradation."

"Take then your choice, obstinate fool,"
he exclaimed, "one minute more and you
will be in eternity."

By the Nena's orders, the poor girl was
immediately seized, and bound to a tree opposite the soldiers who had to carry the
monstrous sentence into effect, and even in
that awful moment, when all hope seemed
to be at an end, Omelia trembled not, and a
smile of defiance animated her features.

She mentally offered up a prayer to heaven, and then prepared to meet her doom.

"Once more I ask you, will you retract
and live?" demanded Nena Sahib.

"No," was the laconic and determined
answer, delivered in a firm and unhesitating
voice.

"Then die!" exclaimed the Nena; "soldiers, make ready, present—"

He hesitated to utter the last fatal word,
for the looks of the heroic girl again shook
his resolution, and ere he could recover himself, one of his principal attendants arrived
hastily on the spot, and placed a sealed
packet in his hands.

He opened it, and the contents of the first
letter seemed to excite him greatly, and, turning quickly to the officer, he said—

"Stay the execution for the present, and
re-conduct the prisoner to her dungeon."

Omelia heard this repite without in the
least altering her demeanour, or exhibiting
any signs of emotion, and being unbound
from the tree, she was once more conducted
to her dreary dungeon; the Nena re-entering
the pavilion, apparently much disturbed by
the nature of the contents of the packet,
which had so fortunately been delivered to
him at the critical moment when the fate of
Omelia seemed to be inevitable.

Once more secured in her dungeon Omelia
was left to herself, and there, unable any
longer to restrain her feelings, she sunk on
her knees, and poured forth her gratitude to
heaven for her miraculous preservation.

CHAPTER LIV.

AN UNEXPECTED FRIEND.—ANOTHER ESCAPE.

This sudden and unexpected deliverance
from an untimely death, when every vestige
of hope had entirely vanished from her
mind, was almost too much for the poor girl,
and it was some time ere she could regain
her composure. Indeed her escape was so
miraculous that she could hardly believe the
evidence of her senses, and it seemed as if
she had only just awakened from some fearful dream. But she could not long remain
unconvinced that it was no delusion of the
senses, and again her heart overflowed with
gratitude, and the hope that something
would shortly occur to release her altogether
from the power of the savage, Nena Sahib,
revived in her breast.

"All merciful Providence, I thank you,"
she ejaculated, "you have not yet deserted
me, and terrible even as my present situation
is, I will remain firm and confident. Dear
Stanley, it is for your sake, and with the
fond hope that we may be permitted to meet
again, that I wish to live; and Heaven will
not turn a deaf ear to my prayers."

These thoughts reassured her, and she became comparatively tranquil.

In this manner she remained for some
time without interruption, when her dungeon
door was unfastened, and she started to her
feet as the terrible thought rushed upon her
brain, that she was again about to be led
forth to execution.

The door was opened, and a man entered
and placed before her some provisions, at
the same time looking earnestly at her, and
seeming half inclined to speak.

It was not the same man who had before
attended upon her, and, as well as she could
observe his features in the dim light of the
dungeon, they struck her most forcibly as
being familiar to her, though where she had
seen him before she could not at the moment
recall to her memory.

So strong was this impression on her mind,
and so greatly was it increased by the looks
of compassion with which the man appeared
to eye her, that she was about to address
him, when there was a noise as if of some
person approaching along the passage, and
the man placing his finger significantly on
his lips as if to enjoin her to silence, abruptly
quitted the dungeon, securing the door after
him.

This circumstance caused much speculation in the mind of Omelia, and fresh hopes
were excited in her breast. It was evident
to her that the man had looked upon her
with commisseration, and the longer she re-

her, and dwelt upon his features as earnestly as she now, convinced did she become that he was not unknown to her, though who he was or where it was likely she might have seen him before, she could not remember.

She continued for some time to rack her brain to no purpose, but at length it suddenly flashed upon her recollection. It was Mirza Duleep, formerly one of the most faithful domestics of the late Mr. Melville, and who had ever shown her the most marked respect and attachment.

This was indeed a fortunate discovery, and it brought with it the most flattering hopes; for she could not entertain the least doubt of Mirza's friendship and sympathy; and now therefore the prospect of escaping from the power of the inhuman Nena Sahib was most cheering.

By what means Mirza had fallen into his present situation she could not conjecture; but she was confident that it was not of his own free will, for she knew his character too well to believe that he would ever willingly become the partizan of such wretches, or join in the perpetration of such atrocious crimes as those of which they had been guilty.

She imagined she could at once read his design, it was she believed her deliverance, terrible though the risk would be, and the better to enable him to accomplish that object, he had probably by some clever scheme got himself appointed to his present situation.

Such were the thoughts, the hopes, and wishes that Omelia now indulged in, and she fondly trusted that her sanguine expectations would not be disappointed.

She waited anxiously throughout the remainder of that eventful day, with the hope of again seeing Mirza; but he did not revisit her, and she became impatient and restless, and began to think that the hopes she had ventured to encourage were premature, and after all might prove to be fallacious.

But no, she could not doubt the goodness of Mirza's intentions, although the opportunity had not yet been afforded him of explaining them to her; his looks satisfied her of the truth of this conjecture, and she therefore endeavoured to wait patiently till the following day, when he was almost certain to visit her to bring her the usual supply of provisions.

Still every moment of delay was torturing to her, and fraught with danger, for it was not at all unlikely that Nena Sahib would yet speedily carry his inhuman determination into effect, and while she remained in his power the prospect of death must be constantly before her.

These thoughts kept her waking nearly the whole of the night; and many were the fervent prayers she uttered, that the hopes that excited in her breast might be destined to be realised.

The following morning came at last, and the anxiety and impatience, the mingled hopes and fears of Omelia every moment increased.

Hour after hour wore tediously away, and still no one came near her, and her spirits began to droop. But at length she heard the bolts of her dungeon door withdrawn, and her heart beat high with expectation. Not an instant was she kept in suspense—Mirza again entered the cell, and closed the door cautiously after him.

"Mirza, good Mirza!" eagerly ejaculated our heroine, and laying her hand on his arm, at the same time looking imploringly in his face.

"Ah!" he said, "you do then remember me? But speak low, for even these walls may have ears. At present I am unsuspected."

"Ah, you do then sympathise with me," said Omelia, again looking eagerly in his face, "you are my friend?"

"Can you doubt me?" replied Mirza, with a look which showed his sincerity. "I am resolved to aid you to escape from those fiends in human form, even at the risk of my life."

"Oh, thanks, thanks, noble-hearted man," said Omelia, tears of gratitude gushing to her eyes.

"Hush, speak lower," said Mirza, in a whisper. "I have not time to explain more now, for should I remain here longer some suspicion might be excited. At midnight be prepared to see me again, and then if everything should favour my design, I will not fail to put it into execution. Be firm. Be confident, and success, I trust, is certain."

Omelia was again about to express her thanks, but Mirza by a significant look enjoined her to silence, and pressing her hand warmly, in token of his fidelity, he quitted the dungeon, leaving behind him some provisions of a much more delicate description than those with which she had been previously supplied since her confinement.

It would be impossible to describe the varied emotions that now agitated the bosom of our heroine, but those of hope and gratitude predominated over every other, and she again poured forth her thanks to heaven for having thus mercifully interposed to save her from the fate which seemed to be so certainly impending o'er her head.

She could not, however, conceal from herself the boldness of the design, and the apparently almost insupportable difficulties and dangers by which it was surrounded, but she had no doubt that Mirza had well matured his plans, and she placed every reliance on him, besides it was better to run every risk than to remain in her present awful situation, and she therefore looked forward to the appointed time with impatience.

The hours passed slowly away, but at length, as well as she was enabled to conjecture, the time approached, and she listened at the door with breathless anxiety to catch the least sound of approaching footsteps. But all remained silent, and Omelia was still kept in a state of the most painful suspense, sometimes fearing that something had occurred to prevent Mirza from keeping his promise, or that he had otherwise changed his mind, and left her to disappointment, but the latter idea she quickly rejected, and reproached herself for having for a moment entertained it.

Some farther time elapsed, and still Mirza came not, and now indeed the most serious apprehensions beset her mind, and she could not control the anxiety of her feelings. She paced the gloomy cell in a state of the greatest agitation, and never had its horrors appeared so great, so appalling as on that momentous occasion.

Surely Mirza could not after all have deceived her? Oh, no, she could not believe him capable of conduct so base as that, and surely it would be the refinement of cruelty thus wantonly to sport with her feelings; to raise hopes which he never meant to realise.

Omelia again tried to calm the agitation of her feelings, and to wait patiently the issue of this night's adventures. She still listened with breathless attention at the door, and after the lapse of a few more minutes, a confused shuffling noise, as if two persons engaged in a violent struggle in the passage beyond met her ears.

This was soon followed by a deep groan, and then the falling of something heavy upon the ground, and again for a moment all was silent.

Omelia trembled; it was a moment of terrible suspense and anxiety to her, and torturing were the fears and conjectures that passed rapidly in her mind.

But her doubt and anxiety were quickly removed, for the dungeon door was unfastened and thrown back upon its hinges, and Mirza, armed with a sabre and pistols, with a poinard in his hand, reeking with blood, and looking much excited, stood before her.

She could not repress a faint cry of terror at the wildness of his appearance, and a feeling of doubt and suspicion arose in her breast, which Mirza, by a faint and rather ghastly sort of smile endeavoured to dismiss.

He then gently placed his hand on Omelia's arm, and led her a few steps into the passage, and there, by the light of the lamp, to her horror she beheld stretched lifeless on the ground the sentry weltering in his blood.

Mirza led her back into the dungeon, and partially closing the door, in a low voice, said—

"It was a fearful deed, but I could not avoid it in order to accomplish my object. However, the poor wretch has probably only met with the fate he deserved. I stole upon him unawares, and did not give him much chance to offer any resistance. Place every confidence in my fidelity, be firm, and all will be well. Are you ready?"

Omelia in a tremulous voice—for it was impossible that she could help being slightly agitated in such a critical and important moment—and replied in the affirmative, at the same time anxiously inquiring the course Mirza was about to pursue

"I pray you ask no questions at present." he replied, "but leave everything to my prudence and discretion."

Omelia nodded assent, and Mirza then lowered the lamp in the passage, and lighted a small dark lantern he had brought with him.

"Now then, lady," he whispered, "courage, this way."

He immediately led her from the dungeon on uttering these words, and locked and bolted the door, then conducted her with noiseless steps along the passage, and stopped before a low door at the farther extremity, which he unlocked from a bunch of keys he had with him, and holding the lantern above his head in order to accelerate his view, Omelia beheld a winding flight of stone steps that probably led to some dungeons below.

Again some doubts and misgivings entered the mind of Omelia, but Mirza encouraged her by a look, and then taking her hand conducted her carefully down the steps on reaching the bottom of which she found herself in a long dark passage, on either side were several heavily barred doors, which she had no doubt opened into dungeons similar to the one in which she had been confined, and probably possessing still more awful features, if possible.

This subterranean passage was of great extent, and having reached the termination of it, Mirza led the way under a low archway on the right, and after descending a few broken steps, they found themselves in another long passage similar to the one that they had just traversed, with the exception that there did not seem to be any dungeons beyond its blackened walls.

This passage like the other seemed almost

interminable, but at length they reached the end of it, and Mirza, placing the lantern on the ground, with some difficulty unlocked an iron door, and after crossing a kind of arched vault, and turning an abrupt angle, Omelia found that they were standing in the open air, and apparently at some distance from the city

She was going to express her surprise and thanks to Mirza, but he silenced her by a significant look, and taking her hand he hurried her along towards a chain of hills at a short distance, having first looked cautiously round to see that all was safe and the coast was clear, and every step they took which led them further from the residence of the dreaded Nena Sahib, the heart of Omelia grew lighter, and her hopes expanded.

No. 30.

CHAPTER LV.

THE FLIGHT CONTINUED.

The night, or rather morning, for it was now long past midnight, was very dark, and that was all in favour of the fugitives, and our heroine every moment became more confident, especially when as far as her eyes could penetrate through the darkness, she could not discover any signs of a human being, till approaching nearer the hills, a shrill whistle was heard, which Mirza answered by another, and immediately afterwards Omelia beheld a man mounted on horseback, and leading another, issue from a narrow road between the hills, and approach them.

"Be not alarmed," said Mirza, "you have nothing to fear; this is a friend, and one who is to be the companion of our flight; the time is propitious, success has so far attended us, and it will not, I trust, abandon us now."

The man, who was a native, and had a prepossessing countenance, now came up to them, and he and Mirza greeted each other in the most friendly manner.

"You are punctual, Murad," said Mirza; "did you meet with anything to excite your suspicion on the way hither?"

Murad replied in the negative.

"'Tis well," said Mirza; "then we must make no delay; a sharp ride of three or four hours will place us beyond the reach of pursuit. Now, lady, let me assist you to mount."

Omelia, whose fears were now completely banished, did so, and Mirza then taking his place behind her, they dashed at full speed along the road between the hills, and had soon got to some considerable distance from the scene of the late danger.

The feelings of gratitude that now filled the bosom of our heroine were almost too great for utterance, and the further they proceeded, and without meeting with any obstruction, the more did those feelings increase, and the looks which she fixed upon her deliverer spoke more eloquently than the most powerful language could possibly have done.

They proceeded, however, for some time in silence, when the road, if such it could be called, becoming very bad, they somewhat slackened their speed, and Omelia then could not restrain the expression of her feelings any longer, but in the warmest manner thanked Mirza for the great risk he had run to serve her, and at the same time regretted that it was not in her power to reward him as he deserved.

"Hold, Omelia," said Mirza, in reply, "those observations are uncalled for, I need no expressions of thanks, or any reward for having done no more than my duty as a man towards an innocent and helpless woman, whose life was threatened, and would no doubt ere long have been sacrificed by one of the most brutal and atrocious miscreants that ever existed as a scourge to society. I esteem you, Omelia, from a long knowledge of the numerous virtues you possess, and I am also under many obligations to you, which I incurred while in the service of the excellent Mr. Melville."

"The generosity and nobleness of your character, Mirza, cannot but elicit my most enthusiastic admiration," remarked our heroine; "but I am lost in astonishment at the singular circumstances under which we again met, after not having seen each other for so long a period, and at that critical time when I am bound to confess I almost abandoned myself to complete despair? By what strange accident did I find you in the service of the monster Nena Sahib, for I cannot believe that you would willingly have joined him in his rebellious cause?"

"Most true," answered Mirza, "you do me no more than justice by that supposition, for no one can more strongly deprecate or hold in greater abhorrence the inhuman conduct of the Nena than myself. But this is not the time for explanation; though if it will afford you any gratification, I will do so on some future occasion."

Omelia again thanked him, and then inquired whither they were going?

"To an obscure village some distance from hence, and where myself and the worthy Murad here have many friends," replied Mirza, "there, disguised, you may remain in perfect safety till you have decided upon your future course."

"I feel that I am much indebted to the kindness of your friend Murad," said Omelia, "and I beg to return him my acknowledgements for it."

"Don't mention it, lady, I pray," returned Murad, "I am only too proud to have it in my power to render you any service."

"I am so confused and astonished by all that has taken place in the last few hours," said Omelia, "that I can hardly persuade myself of its reality. What will be the rage of Nena Sahib, on discovering my escape?"

"It will probably be some hours before he does that," observed Mirza, "and by that time we shall, I trust, be far beyond the reach of pursuit, and out of danger."

They had now entered upon a less difficult road, and again goaded their horses into full speed; and in this manner they proceeded for more than another hour, when daylight began to break upon the scene, and the aspect of the country through which they were journeying became much more pleasing and cheerful than that they had previously been traversing.

"We are approaching the place of our destination," said Mirza, "and shall soon be in safety. Fortune has hitherto smiled upon us."

"Thank heaven," ejaculated Omelia, fervently; "oh, indeed I cannot again help the warm expression of my gratitude to you, my kind friends, and it is no more than your just due, and I should despise myself if I thought I could be unmindful of it, for do I not to you owe the preservation of my life?"

"And the more thankful should we feel, Omelia," replied Mirza, "that providence has made us the humble instruments, in its hands, of performing so worthy an act. We have yet to use all necessary prudence and precaution though in order to ensure security."

"Most true," coincided our heroine, "and I will be guided entirely by you, good Mirza."

"'Tis well," remarked the latter, "and you may depend upon it that you will have no cause to regret the confidence you are pleased to place in me."

"I believe it, Mirza," replied Omelia, "my previous knowledge of your sincere and generous character, and your noble and disinterested conduct on the present occasion—a conduct which involves so much personal risk—are more than sufficient to convince me that in you I have a sincere and ardent friend."

"You have, Omelia," returned Mirza, fervently, "and with that assurance, I beseech you, let all further thanks or compliments cease."

It was impossible for our heroine to help admiring the delicate, modest, yet manly feelings that prompted these observations, and she complied with Mirza's request; feeling at the same time comparatively light of heart, and hopeful, even under all the dangers and difficulties it might yet be her lot to have to encounter, and in spite of the dismal forebodings that would obtrude themselves upon her mind, when she thought of her beloved Stanley, the painful circumstances under which they had been separated and the probability that they would never again behold each other.

And scarcely less was her anxiety for the aged hermit to whose kindness she owed such a heavy debt of gratitude, and to the unfortunate Flora Melville, who since her melancholy bereavement, so much more than ever needed her society, sympathy, advice, and consolation.

The sun broke forth in all its radiant glory, while at the same time there was a refreshing breeze which rendered the atmosphere cool and pleasant, and was every way calculated to exhilarate the spirits however depressed.

At that early hour, all things in vegetation rose fresh and beautiful from the dews of night, courting, as it were, the bright smiles of the sunbeams, and the air was impregnated with balmy fragrance.

The fugitives proceeded on their journey with somewhat slackened speed, for they had now got far beyond pursuit, and had no immediate danger to apprehend.

The picturesque diversity of scenery amongst which they travelled, served in a great measure to divert for a time the thoughts of Omelia from the melancholy subjects that had previously engrossed them, and she gazed with feelings of the most unbounded and enthusiastic admiration upon the varied beauties of nature so strikingly and impressively developed in her native land.

For a time they journeyed through forest scenery of the most romantic description, where grew the huge banian, its long branches spreading far around, peacocks glittering in the sun upon the lower boughs, and troops of monkeys grinning and chattering above. Here was to be seen the fantastic, crooked sissoo, disdaining, like its companions, to tower up with a straight stem, there the invaluable cocoa-nut tree, from which nearly all the wants of the Hindoo can be supplied;* the peepul, the teak, the talipot, in fact almost every description of tree natural to the different parts of India were to be met with there, exciting wonder, from the singular variety, as well as admiration.

And now the scene was once more changed, and they found themselves amidst mountains and rocky eminences, interspersed with ravines and dells; and they had not proceeded far when they were startled by the report of fire-arms, and Omelia looked at her companions with some alarm, and Mirza and Murad at first seemed to feel some anxiety, and checked their horses. But their fears were quickly dissipated by the appearance of several men making their way towards an adjacent ravine, and whose actions plainly showed that their object was sport, not mischief, in fact, the manly and interesting sport of the bear-hunt, some few particulars of which may not here be considered out of place.

The number of sportsmen is never less than three, for it is no easy task to pursue bears over rugged ground with any chance of success. These are also supplied with about a dozen beaters, to roll down rocks into the glen, and start the game.

The sportsmen having assembled at the ravine by the break of day, two of them take the hither brink of the ravine, while the third accompanies the beaters along the further verge, inciting them to shout, and cast down rocks into the gulf below. If the bear happens to be outside his den, he is generally aroused by this disturbance, and

---

* This is an indisputable fact, regarding the value of the Cocoa-nut tree. The Hindoo can build his home entirely of it. The walls and doors are made of cadjans—the leaves plaited—the roof is covered with the same, the beams, rafters, &c., are made of the trunk. The builder needs no nails, as he can use the coir rope made from the outside husk. If he wants a spout, he hollows the trunk, split in two. It also supplies him with spoons, laddles, and cups, pans and drinking vessels, hookah-bowls, lamps, and water-buckets; the refuse of the kernel, after the oil is extracted, serves for food for cows and pigs; the milk from the kernel is used in his food. In short, if a man has a few cocoa-nut trees in his garden he will never starve.

will be seen either at the very bottom, or making his way along the side of the precipice, by paths where the human head would whirl with giddiness, and the human foot find no security.

No time is to be lost in firing, as the bear having so decidedly the advantage in the race over ground for which nature and experience have particularly fitted him, the space between him and his pursuers increases every moment. If not struck, he will seldom turn, and there is little prospect of coming up with him, because the sportsman has every now and then to make a long detour to avoid broken ground.)

The bear is struck when near his pursuers, and then comes one of the most exciting points of the sport. He turns upon them, and coolness is now the great essential on the part of the sportsmen, not to throw away their fire until he approach so near as to give them the choice of the wound they shall inflict.

The sportsmen drop on one knee in taking aim, to bring them more nearly on a level with the bear, and thus preventing the advance of the animal from materially altering the line of fire. Nearer and nearer Bruin approaches, grumbling and growling with rage, at the same time most anxious to get his enemies within his ardent embrace. Whizz, bang! a roar of agony, and poor Bruin falls, having received his death blow. But even now he must be approached with caution, although he appears dead or dying. The native servant of an officer was scalped and killed outright by a single blow from the paw of a wounded bear, which he approached under the idea that it was defunct.

Such is one of the wild sports of India, and one in which Omelia—who could use the musket or the rifle with the most extraordinary skill for a female—had often taken a part, and the present circumstance, therefore, recalled to her memory some of the happiest days of her life; when her breast was a stranger to care, and she could look forward to the future with the brightest hopes and fondest anticipations.

She watched the sportsmen anxiously on their way, and felt as if she could find even then a temporary respite from care in the contemplation of the animating scene of the hunt, but Mirza suggested that although they might have nothing at present to fear from them, still it would be prudent to avoid being observed by them, as it might be attended with some ultimate danger, and afford a clue to them should there be any pursuit; they therefore drew back beneath the shade of some trees until the sporting party had disappeared, when they once more resumed their journey.

The distance seemed much greater to Omelia—who now began to feel fatigued—than she had been led to expect from what Mirza had said, and she now eagerly inquired of him whether they had much further to travel ere they should arrive at the place of their destination.

" I do not wonder at your anxiety to know, Omelia," replied Mirza, " for after the extraordinary fatigue and excitement you have undergone, you must greatly require rest and refreshment, and I cannot but express my warm admiration of the patience and courage with which you have acted. I rather miscalculated upon the distance, in consequence of my forgetting that I have been compelled to take a more circuitous route in order the better to avoid the danger of detection. But we have now but a very inconsiderable distance to go, and shall therefore soon arrive at the end of the tedious journey."

Omelia expressed her satisfaction, and they continued their journey with renewed hopes and spirits; meeting with very few persons on the road, who took little notice of them, and who were mostly natives going upon their ordinary business.

At length the appearance of everything betokened their near approach to the village which Mirza had stated to be the place of their destination; and in a few minutes more Omelia caught sight of one of the bungalows between the trees, by which it appeared the village was completely encompassed.

"Thanks to providence," said Mirza, "I have been enabled to accomplish my task, and you are now in safety, Omelia."

The heart of the latter swelled with gratitude, and she pressed the hand of Mirza warmly, whilst her looks sufficiently testified the feelings she entertained towards him.

"Oh, Mirza," she said, "how can I ever repay you for this noble act of humanity? But for you, even ere this I might have become the victim of the monster Nena Sahib's most deadly vengeance."

"True, lady," answered Mirza, "and it was the certainty of that which made me resolve, even at the hazard of my own life, to frustrate the tyrant in his brutal designs. That I have succeeded is a source of gratification to me which I cannot describe, and the consciousness of having performed my duty, is more than an ample reward."

"I will say no more, Mirza," returned our heroine; "you know how fully I appreciate the inestimable service you and the good Murad here have rendered me, and I need not farther express my thanks."

Mirza bowed, and then addressing himself to Murad, said—

"It would be prudent, I think, that you should first enter the village, while myself and Omelia wait here, to see that all is safe, and apprise our particular friends of my arrival, and under what circumstances."

"True," answered Murad, "it is as well to use every precaution, although we have no reason to apprehend any danger. I will return in a few minutes."

He then left them, and Mirza having dismounted, and assisted Omelia to alight, conducted her a little aside, among the trees, to await the return of Murad.

"In the bungalow to which I am about to take you, Omelia," observed Mirza, "is one whom I think you will be glad to recognise, and who I am certain will welcome you with every feeling of pleasure and satisfaction."

"Ah, say you so, good Mirza," said Omelia, with a look of surprise and eager curiosity; "to whom do you allude?"

"Some four years ago," answered Mirza, "a poor friendless girl, flying from a brutal and abandoned master who sought the destruction of her virtue, sunk worn out with fatigue, hunger, and anguish of mind, in a lonely spot not far from the residence of Mr. Melville. She must have perished, for she had not strength to proceed farther, and even if she had, she knew not where to seek for assistance. But the Great Power had not forsaken the poor girl in her adversity. A gentle, sympathising being came to her relief in the terrible hour of her need, who conducted her to a place where she received all the kindness and attention that humanity could suggest. Need I remind you, Omelia, that the gentle being to whom I allude was yourself?"

"Ah," exclaimed our heroine, eagerly, "and the poor girl to whom I was so fortunately permitted to perform that simple act of humanity and duty was Naomie."

"True," replied Mirza, with visible emotion, "and whom I afterwards discovered in a most miraculous manner to be my own sister, who was stolen from her home in childhood."

"Yes, yes," observed Omelia, "I well remember the circumstance of your extraordinary discovery. Pardon me, Mirza, that in the confusion of my thoughts I forgot to inquire after her to whom I was so warmly attached. Tell me, I pray you, does she still live, and—"

"Listen, Omelia," he interrupted, "and I will briefly explain that in which you are pleased to evince so deep an interest. You are aware of the circumstances that compelled me to leave the service of Mr. Melville, to whom, and his amiable daughter, I am under such a weight of obligation. Naomie could not bear the thought of being separated from a brother whom she had so lately discovered, and although she deeply regretted leaving your society, Omelia, who

had ever treated her with sisterly regard, and that of those generous benefactors who had behaved to her with such unexampled kindness, she insisted upon accompanying me, and I could not but yield to her wishes and solicitations. What afterwards occurred to us, there is not time now to relate. Naomie remained under my immediate protection until she married one who I am happy to say has proved himself every way worthy of her, and—but hark, I hear voices; Murad returns, prepare yourself, Omelia, for what I have no doubt will be an agreeable surprise."

CHAPTER LVI.

THE RAGE AND DISAPPOINTMENT OF NENA SAHIB.

Before Omelia had time to return any answer to the observations of Mirza, approaching footsteps were heard amongst the grass, and the next instant Murad appeared, accompanied by the tall and graceful form of a native female. There was an exclamation of delight, which was responded to by our heroine, and Naomie—for it was that affectionate and grateful being of whom Mirza had been speaking—and they threw themselves into each other's arms.

Naomie was a beautiful young woman of about the same age as Omelia, with a fine intellectual countenance, and bright expressive eyes, while her form was grace and symetry itself. She was a being, in fact, whom it was impossible to look upon without feelings of the deepest interest and the warmest admiration; and her intrinsic qualities fully corresponded with the charms of her person.

It was indeed a surprise of the most agreeable kind to both our heroine and Naomie, and it was several minutes before they could sufficiently recover themselves from their emotions to speak, while Mirza and Murad stood by and watched the affectionate meeting of the two friends, without offering to interrupt them.

"Dear Omelia"—"Dear Naomi," at length they mutually uttered, and then they again embraced each other with all the affection of sisters.

And indeed as such they had ever regarded each other, and it was a source of most heartfelt regret to them both when they were compelled to part. But to meet again under such circumstances, and so unexpectedly, was so extraordinary, that it would have been wonderful indeed if their feelings had not been wrought up to the highest pitch.

At length, however, their emotions found

vent in words, and they then exchanged mutual congratulations of the warmest and most sincere description.

"Dear Naomie," ejaculated our heroine, "I am so astonished and bewildered at this unlooked for and joyful event that I know not what to say to you, in what terms adequately to express my feelings. But oh, Mirza, why did you on your journey delay to inform me the joy which was in store for me?"

"Pardon me, Omelia, if I did so," replied Mirza, "but it was only with the wish of rendering your gratification at the end of our journey the more complete. I have another surprise for you. Allow me to introduce to you the husband of my sister Naomie in the person of our friend, and the companion of our flight, Murad."

Omelia was again taken by surprise, but expressed her congratulations to Murad in the most respectful manner.

"But why do we loiter here," observed Naomie, "when Omelia must so much require rest and refreshment after her weary journey? Come, there is no one about the village whose curiosity might be annoying, so let us immediately to my humble dwelling. Come, dear Omelia."

She took the hand of our heroine as she spoke, with a look of the most unbounded pleasure, and led her from the spot, Mirza and Murad following, while Omelia was so surprised and bewildered by the extraordinary events, that she could hardly believe in their reality.

The village contained several bungalows, some of which were of a superior description, and one of the latter, detached from the rest, was the dwelling of Naomie and her husband. The comfort and neatness of its interior corresponded with its outward appearance.

Provisions were immediately placed on the table by Naomie, and of which Omelia and her companions, standing so much in need after the many hours they had been without, having partaken heartily, our heroine, who could no longer bear up against the great fatigue and excitement she had undergone, excused herself to her friends, and requesting to be allowed to retire to rest for an hour or two, she was conducted to a little chamber above by Naomie, who, having again affectionately embraced her, refrained from all further conversation for the present, and retired from the room.

But, notwithstanding her fatigue, it was some time ere the agitation and excitement of Omelia's feelings, caused by the remarkable events that the last few hours had produced, would allow her to obtain that rest of which she stood in so much need; and the longer she reflected upon all the circum-

stances that had occurred to her, and the many marvellous and narrow escapes she had experienced, the more did she become lost in amazement, whilst her heart overflowed with gratitude to that Almighty Power which had so mercifully protected her through every adversity and danger which had hitherto befallen her.

She pictured to herself the rage and astonishment of Nena Sahib when he should have discovered her escape, which he had doubtless done ere this, and she could never be sufficiently thankful to Mirza and Murad for the humane and generous feelings that had prompted them to expose themselves to such imminent dangers, in order to rescue her from the fate which otherwise had assuredly awaited her.

The extraordinary and unexpected meeting with Naomie, whom she had ever so warmly regarded, afforded her the most indescribable pleasure, and inspired her with every confidence, and having besought the protection of heaven for Stanley, and prayed that they might shortly be restored to each other, she at last composed herself to sleep.

And now having seen our heroine in safety, and under the protection of friends on whose fidelity she could so firmly reply, for a time we will again leave her.

The letter which Nena Sahib had received at the critical moment when he was about to sacrifice the life of Omelia to his savage vengeance, was of the utmost importance, and required his immediate attention.

After some time spent in deliberation, having given particular instructions to one of his officers regarding our heroine—upon whose fate, through this fortunate intervention, he was now undecided—he mounted his horse, and attended by some of the principal officers of his staff, rode from the city in great haste, evidently urged by business of the most vital importance.

And now occurred an incident (it is a fact, although the real name of the officer is concealed) which it may not be uninteresting to the reader to relate, as it will show the strange incongruities and contradictory passions of which the nature of this man is composed.

Continuing to ride at the same brisk rate, he and his companions had soon got to some distance from the city, when the report of a pistol suddenly startled their ears, and turning round the foot of a hill, from the back of which the report which they had heard proceeded, they came upon a scene which immediately arrested their attention.

With one arm encircling the waist of a delicate-looking female—probably his wife—a young English officer, of manly and soldierly person, was engaged in a desperate sword combat with two sepoys, and seemed resolved to sell his own life, and that of the fair being he protected, dearly. Another sepoy lay dead upon the earth, having doubtless fallen by the pistol, the report of which Nena Sahib had heard.

"Hold," cried the Nena, at the top of his voice, at the moment when the sepoys having struck the sword from the gallant young officer's hand, and seized the terrified and shrieking female, were about to bury their weapons in his body.

The tones of the Nena's voice were evidently familiar to the rebels, and looking towards him, and immediately recognising him they desisted from their murderous and cowardly intention, and the officer having regained his sword, and once more seized the female, stood boldly on his defence, but anxiously awaited the approach of Nena Sahib, whom he also appeared to know, and who quickly rode up to the spot.

He looked earnestly at the officer and his wife for a moment, and a feeling of pity, which it is too well known is almost a stranger to his savage breast, suddenly came over him.

Turning sternly to the men, who seemed awed in his presence, he demanded—

"How is this?—three sepoys no match for a single Feringhee? Are ye a sample of the brave fellows I have to depend upon? If so, I fear our cause is all but hopeless, in spite of our vast superiority of numbers. How now, young man, who are you?"

"Captain Ashton of her Majesty's lancers," answered the young man firmly, but at the same time respectfully; "and you are Nena Sahib."

"True," said the Nena in that tone, and with that look of affability he knew so well how to assume; "you seem to be a gallant fellow. 'Tis a pity you are an Englishman."

"I glory in the name," was the resolute reply.

"And yet," coolly returned the Nena, "you have little cause at this moment to value it much, seeing that, being an Englishman, I am your inveterate foe, and that your life is forfeited. Is this female your wife?"

"It is," answered the captain, "and we have not yet been married a twelvemonth. She is far, far more precious to me than my own existence; I entreat you then, if my life be forfeited as you say, to forbear to shed the blood of this poor innocent being who will shortly become a mother.

"For the love of mercy, to which your breast is surely not entirely a stranger, oh, spare my unfortunate husband," implored the fair young creature, sinking on her knees, with clasped hands, tearful eyes, and distracted looks.

"Rise, woman," commanded the Nena, "Nena Sahib requires no such homage.

"Why should I show more mercy to your husband than to any other European?"

"Because you owe me a debt of gratitude," replied Captain Ashton, "which the critical situation of myself and my wife alone induces me to remind you of."

"Humph," ejaculated the Nena, with a smile of incredulity, "Nena Sahib owe a debt of gratitude to the detested Feringhee, whose country has plundered him of his rights? Explain yourself, and that quickly, I command."

"One evening, three years ago, whilst you were walking alone in a dreary spot near your palace," replied Captain Ashton, "a cowardly attempt on your life was made by three or four of your treacherous attendants, with what motive I know not. Two English officers happened to be passing the spot, and hastened to your rescue, notwithstanding the disparity of numbers; one of them arrested the arm of the ruffian at the moment when it was raised to strike the fatal blow—you at the time being without the means of defence —at the same time plunging his sword in the miscreant's heart. He and his companion then attacked the others with a resolution which speedily put them to flight. Do you remember the circumstance?"

"I do; what then?" demanded the Nena.

"I am that officer who saved you from death," answered Captain Ashton.

"What proof have you of that?" interrogated Nena Sahib, eyeing the officer narrowly who, however, shrank not from his gaze; "I have no recollection of your person, and I am not bound to take your bare word."

"In token of your gratitude for the service which the officers had rendered you, you presented each of them with a valuable ring," replied Captain Ashton.

"True."

"Behold, I wear one of those rings," said the captain, at the same time exhibiting it to the Nena, "doubtless you will be enabled to identify it."

The Nena glanced at the ring, and immediately said—

"Enough, I am satisfied. You shall find, Captain Ashton, that, heartless monster as your countrymen presume Nena Sahib to be, gratitude is not yet extinct in his breast, when any circumstance, any service he may have formerly received, at the hands of those who are his enemies, demand it. The noble act of which you have spoken has saved the lives of yourself and your wife."

"Oh, thanks, thanks, for this act of mercy and humanity," exclaimed the lady, with a burst of emotion.

"No more," commanded Nena Sahib, impatiently and peremptorily, "I require not thanks, but that you will do me justice by a fair representation of this fact to your countrymen." He then added, in a more gentle tone, and with a look which assured them of his sincerity, "I will not fail to ensure you being conducted in safety to the nearest station of your people at the earliest opportunity."

Then addressing himself to one of the officer's of his staff, he said :—

"Conduct Captain Ashton and his lady to my palace, there to await my return, and see that every necessary respect and attention are paid to them."

The captain and his wife seemed astonished at this act of clemency on the part of that man, whose very name at that time, excited horror and disgust in every English breast, they were about again to return their acknowledgements, when the Nena motioned them to silence, and delivering them into the care of the officer, he stopped for a minute or two to see them conducted from the spot towards the city, then he and his companions once more urged their horses into full speed, and pursued their journey.

The authenticity of this anecdote, although not generally known, and we believe now for the first time recorded, may be relied on, although—as has been before stated—for obvious reasons, the real name of the officer, and of the regiment to which he belonged, have been concealed, and it will be admitted that it strikingly illustrates one of the most remarkable traits in the Nena's character, although it is not related for the purpose of extenuating in the slightest degree the frightful atrocity of his conduct.

At a late hour of the night the Nena returned to his palace, and he immediately retired to his sleeping apartment, where he threw himself upon an ottoman, and became for some time lost in a deep reverie.

At length he started once more to his feet, and traversed the room with hasty and disordered steps, muttering incoherent sentences to himself, and evidently in a state of much excitement.

"This defeat has frustrated one of my finest stratagetic movements," he at length said aloud, there being no one at hand to overhear him—he was alluding to one of those brilliant victories achieved by the lamented General Havelock, and his mere handful of heroes, on his memorable march to Cawnpore—"and given an immense advantage to the plans of the enemy, and which I may find it difficult to counteract. The craven dogs to fly before an enemy, whom their numbers alone should have overwhelmed. It proves beyond a doubt the truth of that which has so often been asserted of the vast superiority of the courage and fighting qualities of the Feringhee, over the native troops, notwithstanding the almost equal discipline of the latter. That Have-

lock is a general of whom England may indeed be justly proud. Every battle with him, is a victory. Brave man, much even as I have cause to dread you, I could not hear of your death without a feeling of regret, or paying due honour to the memory of so great an hero. If fate should unfortunately ordain that India should still be preserved to England, she may thank Havelock as its principal saviour."

In this strain he continued to soliloquise for some time, and his excitement seemed rather to increase than abate. But at length he hastily threw himself on his couch, and gradually sunk to sleep.

––––––

CHAPTER LVII.

THE DREAM OF NENA SAHIB.—THE DISCOVERY OF OMELIA'S ESCAPE.

But the slumbers of Nena Sahib, were not of that tranquil and refreshing description that bless the pillows of good and innocent. The excitement of his waking moments pursued him in his sleep, and conjured up visions of the most torturing description to his disordered imagination.

At one time he fancied himself in the midst of victory, the British troops flying before him in dismay, like chaff before the wind, whilst heaps of their dead and dying strewed the scene of his triumph in all directions. With his legions he pursued the flying enemy through rivers of blood, and every moment, he imagined that they added to the hideous slaughter, till there was but a remnant of them left to escape.

His triumph was complete; India was free, and to him, to him alone was it due. And now the victor's reward was in the homage and ovations of the people. He was treated with regal splendour; all India was in gratitude at his feet, and countless multitudes of voices shouted and sung their praises. He fancied himself riding in a chariot of gold drawn by a hundred of elephants, and the whole of the Indian princes, of whom he was now the imperial master, following in his train. The country was one blaze of light, and nothing but rejoicing was to be heard around.

Quickly, however, the scene was again changed, and once more he found himself in the midst of all the horrors of the battlefield. But this time victory was against him, and his troops were mowed down by the cannon of the enemy, cut up by the sword, or pierced by the deadly bayonet in thousands, until he found himself left with only an intrepid few

The hour of retribution had arrived, and

awful indeed was it, and all his courage entirely forsook him, whilst conscience seemed to thunder in his ears, "Cawnpore! Delhi! Lucknow! Vengeance!" and the ghastly phantoms of the slaughtered rose in a host before his appalled sight, and mocked his agony.

And now once more was the scene changed, and he found himself in the midst of thousands of the English, caged like some wild beast, and suspended over a slow fire, while all around, as far as his eyes could trace, lofty gibbets met his sight, from which hung the bodies of his wretched and bloodthirsty adherents.

Frightful were his agonies, he cried for mercy, but his shrieks were answered alone with loud yells and shouts, and bitter execrations, again the fearful words, "Cawn-

No. 31.

pore! Delhi! Lucknow!" were thundered in his ears, and the ghastly phantoms of his murdered victims again stood before his eyes.

The horrors conjured up by his frenzied imagination were too much, the spell of sleep was broken, and Nena Sahib started from his couch with a cry of terror, gazing around him with a wild look of bewilderment, for a moment or two not being able to persuade himself that it was only a dream.

Large drops of perspiration stood upon the forehead of the guilty man, and he trembled in every limb. No one who might have had an opportunity of seeing him at that moment, and of noticing the abject terror that convulsed him, and suspended all his faculties, could have believed that that was the desperate, the determined, and inhuman monster whose frightful crimes for months past had filled all the civilised world with horror.

But he quickly recovered himself, and assumed all his wonted looks and demeanour.

"Bah!" he muttered to himself, as he again paced the room to and fro with disordered steps, "shall I suffer a mere vision of the heated and disordered imagination to agitate me thus? I will not, for certain I am that the latter part will never be realised, though my sanguine hopes of ultimate success, lead me to believe in the fulfilment of the former. Nena Sahib is not the man to be frightened at dreams or shadows"

He walked from the room after he had indulged in this soliloquy, and entered the gardens of the palace, as it was now broad daylight, and the air was refreshing, and his thoughts now wandered to Omelia, while again his resolution wavered as to the way in which he should dispose of her, while a feeling more than akin to pity took possession of his breast.

"She is very beautiful, she is good and heroic," he soliloquised, "and I hesitate to put my threats into execution. Could I but win her to my purpose, for I would fain do so rather than enforce it, I should be gratified. I will once more try what persuasion can accomplish."

As Nena Sahib uttered these words, he walked from the garden, with the intention for the first time since her incarceration, of visiting Omelia in her dungeon, but he had not proceeded far on the way when he was met by one of his attendants coming in great haste towards the palace, and whose looks evinced much consternation, which seemed to be increased when he beheld the Nena.

"How now?" hastily demanded the latter, "why do you hurry, and what alarms you?"

"The prisoner," gasped forth the man, unable to finish the sentence.

"What of her?"

"She has escaped."

"Escaped?"

"Yes."

"It is impossible."

"'Tis true," answered the man, "at least I have too much reason to suspect so, although the door of her dungeon is still secured on the outside, for the sentry lies stretched lifeless at his post."

"Ah," exclaimed Nena Sahib, with an oath, "then the man who was newly appointed her gaoler on the illness of the previous one has betrayed me. The accursed dog. Hasten and procure the keys, and then return to me at the prison."

The man obeyed, and the Nena, foaming with rage at this unexpected occurrence, and uttering execrations, went towards the prison.

On arriving there the dead body of the unfortunate sentinel in the passage upon which the range of dungeons opened fully confirmed the statement of the man, and Nena Sahib gave vent to a burst of passion which he could not control.

He called loudly at the door of the miserable cell in which Omelia had been confined, but no answer being returned, it was quite evident that his worst suspicions were correct, and his rage increased.

"To be thus again defeated in my purpose by this obstinate, daring girl," he said, "who seems to set me at defiance, is most humiliating. Fool that I was to spare her life yesterday when she was brought forth for execution, I should then have rid myself of one, who although a woman, may yet prove to me a dangerous enemy. But it may not yet be too late to pursue her, and should she again fall into my power her doom is sealed, and she shall learn by the most terrible and lingering deaths what it is to arouse the vengeance of Nena Sahib."

As he thus gave expression to his exasperated feelings, his looks showed how fully he was determined to carry his brutal threats into execution, should the opportunity be afforded him.

The man now rejoined him, and hastily taking the key from his hand Nena Sahib hastily applied it to the lock, having first withdrawn the bolts, threw the door back on its hinges and entered the dungeon, and there the confirmation of his worst suspicions drew from him another volley of frightful excecrations, and hastily returning to the palace, he summoned some of his principal officers, and ascertaining, beyond the least shadow of a doubt, that Mirza was the companion of Omelia's flight, he ordered an immediate pursuit of the fugitives in every direction, but with how little success has been already shown.

But to be thus baffled and defeated by a mere girl was a mortification to the proud spirit of the tyrant Nena which he could ill endure, and it was some time ere he could subdue the feelings of rage and disappointment which it excited.

"Oh, that I had her and the vile caitiff who has planned and effected her escape, again in my clutches," he exclaimed; "there are no tortures that I could consider too horrible to inflict upon them. But they have eluded my vigilance, and are doubtless now far beyond the power of my vengeance, and that thought does but add to my mortification. Curses light upon them I say."

He frowned fearfully and bit his lips as he gave utterance to these words, and continued to pace the room for some time in the most disordered manner, his attendants, who so well knew every phase of his character, faring to approach him while he was in that mood.

Several days elapsed without any clue being obtained to Omelia and her deliverer, and the search was abandoned as hopeless, especially as the pressing and more important business of Nena Sahib, demanded his whole attention, and banished Omelia from his thoughts.

CHAPTER LVIII.

THE PERILS OF FLORA MELVILLE.

Poor, lonely, bereaved, and wretched Flora Melville upon whom the remorseless hand of adversity had fallen so heavily, what was now her situation? Be it our task to discover.

In a wildly romantic part of the country some miles from Delhi, on a lofty eminence, from which might be commanded a panoramic view of the most picturesque, extensive, and diversified description, which whether seen glistening in the flashing rays of the sun, or reposing beneath the soft mellow light of the moon and countless myriads of twinkling stars, had a grand and sublime effect,

"Raising the soul from nature
Up to Nature's God,"

stood an old fort, which for some years had been abandoned, and had partly fallen into decay, although there was a sufficient portion of it that was perfectly habitable, and might for a time, afford shelter to a number of persons. Through its walls appeared the branches of the delicate and beautiful peepul trees, the vital power of whose roots as we think we have somewhere before stated, are such that when they have once penetrated deeply into a building, they will send out their branches again, cut them off as often as you may, and carry on their internal attack with undiminished vigour. "No wonder," says Colonel Sleeman, "that superstition should have consecrated this tree, delicate and beautiful as it is, to the gods. The palace, the castle, the temple, and the tomb —all those works which man is most proud to raise, to spread, and to perpetuate his name—crumble to dust beneath her withering grasp. She rises triumphant over them all in her lofty beauty, bearing high in air, amidst light green foliage, fragments of the wreck she has made, to show the nothingness of man's efforts." In the very rudest state of society, among the woods and hills of India, the people have some deity whose power they dread, and whose name they invoke when much is supposed to depend upon the truth of what one man is about to declare. The peepul tree being everywhere sacred to the gods, who are supposed to delight to sit among its leaves and listen to the music of their rustling, the deponent takes one of these leaves in his hand, and invokes the god who sits above him, to crush him, or those dear to him, as he crushes the leaf in his hand, if he speaks anything but the truth: he then plucks and crushes the leaf, and states what he has to say. The large cotton tree is, among the wild tribes of India, the favourite seat of gods still more terrible, because their superintendance is confined exclusively to the neighbourhood, and having their attention less occupied, they can venture to make a more minute scrutiny into the conduct of the people immediately around them. The peepul is occupied (according to the Hindoos) by one or other of the Hindoo triad, the gods of creation, preservation, and destruction, who have the affairs of the universe to look after, but the cotton and other trees are occupied by some minor deities, who are vested with a local superintendance over the affairs of a district, or perhaps, a single village.

But we are digressing.

The old fort then was an interesting building, and might yet afford a welcome retreat in the hour of danger, to those who might have occasion to seek its shelter.

In an extensive and pleasant valley not far from this building, was a village, occupied by peaceful and industrious natives, and at present remote from those horrors that were being perpetrated in so many other parts of the country.

In the fort, about a dozen persons, men, women, and children, worn out with fatigue and suffering, had for the last few days sought refuge, until such time as they could recruit their strength, and find means to seek some European station.

They were kindly attended to by the inhabitants of the village, who supplied them with provisions and other necessaries, and furnished them from time to time with such information as they thought might be of value to them, and which had come to their knowledge.

It was on a beautiful, clear, moonlight evening, that a female form might have been seen approaching the foot of the lofty eminence upon which the old fort stood.

Her step was hurried, and terror seemed to urge her on, her soft glossy tresses floating in the night breeze, and her dress in many places torn and disordered probably by the brambles and brushwood through which she had been compelled to force her way.

She was an English woman young, and beautiful, but with looks wild and terror-stricken, and which bespoke the disorder of the brain.

But why should we thus minutely describe one with whom we have already made the reader familiar, for it was Flora Melville.

But melancholy indeed was the appearance of that poor girl, and it was impossible for any one who might at that time have beheld her, to help being moved by feelings of the deepest compassion.

Her cheeks were ghastly pale as those of a corpse, her lips livid, her handsome features distorted with agony, and there was a wild, vacant glance in the expression of her eyes, which showed too plainly, that, for the present, at any rate, reason had abandoned its seat.

On she rushed madly, still shaping her course towards the old fort, but ever and anon she would stop and listen, and look back as though she feared pursuit. Then she resumed her flight, and arriving at the foot of the eminence, ascended it with frantic speed, gained one of the entrances of the fort, but there exhausted nature could no more, and with a faint cry, she sank powerless and insensible on the earth.

Fortunately at that particular time, two of the villagers ascended the eminence to the fort with a fresh supply of provisions for those who had there sought refuge, and they beheld with feelings of surprise and pity the unfortunate girl.

At first they feared she was dead, so inanimate was her form and so ghastly pale her features, but raising her from the ground they found that her heart had not ceased to beat, and that she still breathed.

They gave the usual signal which had been agreed upon between them and the inmates of the fort, and immediately the door was cautiously opened, and Flora was conveyed into the building.

The fugitives being like one family party, usually assembled together for society in one apartment, and they were so on the present occasion, and when Flora was brought in, and they beheld her deplorable condition, they were all moved by compassion, and anxious to render every assistance that might tend to her recovery, but for some time she gave no signs of returning life.

While they were thus occupied, an elderly gentleman, and a young man who from the likeness he bore, was evidently his son, and who had been in some other part of the fort, entered the room, and quickly ascertaining the cause of the excitement which prevailed among their companions in misfortune, hastened to observe the unfortunate object of sympathy, they no sooner beheld her features than an exclamation of astonishment and emotion escaped them both, which excited the curiosity of their friends.

"Alas! alas! poor girl," exclaimed the elder gentleman, in a tone of the deepest sympathy; "it is poor Flora Melville—my niece."

"Oh, agony!" cried the young man, with a burst of grief which he could not restrain, taking her cold hand, and raising it to his lips, "so long since we have met before, and then to see her thus. For heaven's sake exert yourselves for her recovery, for she is every way worthy of your care and sympathy."

"I can make every allowance for your emotion, Alfred," observed his father; "but control your feelings, be calm, be calm."

The young man made no reply, but it was evident by his looks that the advice of his father was lost upon him, and he continued to gaze upon Flora with looks of anguish and anxiety that showed plainly the thoughts which were passing in his mind.

Mr. Meadows the brother-in-law of the late Mr. Melville, was like that gentleman, a wealthy merchant, who had been for two years, with his son, residing in another part of India to that where Mr. Melville dwelt, and although they regularly corresponded, they had not seen each other during that period.

Business of importance, however, called Mr. Meadows to Agra, where he saw the ruins only of his brother-in-law's former beautiful residence—minutely described in the first chapter of our tale—and he had too much reason to fear that both Mr. Melville and his daughter had fallen the victims of some terrible outrage. However, making every possible inquiry of the persons in the neighbourhood, he ascertained that Mr. Melville with his daughter and gone to his place of business in the city of Delhi.

Notwithstanding the disturbed state of the Mogul capital at that time, and the terrible storm which treatened ere long to burst over it, Mr. Meadows whose anxiety was great to behold his relations, determined with his son, to repair to the city.

They arrived there the day after that terrible slaughter in the old mosque, and beholding the ruins of Mr. Melville's house they could now entertain no further doubt as to the actual fate of that unfortunate gentleman.

They were now placed in a most perilous situation in the city, the insurrection spreading hourly, and they had good reason to regret having ventured there, and were only too anxious to be able to effect their escape from it.

But the anguish of Alfred Meadows was most intense, at the supposed fate of Flora Melville and her father, the cause of which will be more fully and satisfactorily explained presently.

It is not necessary to detail all that befel Mr. Meadows and his son, until they ultimately, with much difficulty, effected their escape from the city, in the company of the other persons who had sought refuge in the fort.

Alfred Meadows was a handsome young man, highly accomplished—every care having been bestowed on his education—and most amiable manners. He had passed many of his earlier years in the almost constant society of his fair cousin, and almost unconsciously had suffered her to take so powerful a hold on his heart, that nothing he felt could ever eradicate the passion from his breast.

But his fond hopes and wishes were doomed to disappointment. Flora esteemed him, warmly esteemed him for his manly virtues, but she candidly acknowledged to him, when he confessed his love, that no warmer sentiments towards him could ever find a place in her breast, and when the time arrived that they were compelled to separate for an indefinite period, the parting was a most painful one to them both.

This will account for the extraordinary emotion displayed by Alfred Meadows on beholding again that beloved being whom he had thought was no more.

CHAPTER LIX.

MORE EXPLANATIONS.—THE DELIRIUM OF FLORA MELVILLE

But it is necessary to relate what had occurred to Flora, after the death of the venerable hermit, and prior to the events just recorded.

We left her in the cavern in a state of insensibility lying by the side of the corpse of the poor old man, who, after living to so patriarchial an age, had met with so tragical an end.

It was some time ere she recovered to consciousness, and then she found herself in complete darkness, and her brain was so bewildered that she had but a vague and dreamy recollection of what had taken place.

She, however, arose, intending to endeavour to find the lamp, but in walking to the place where it was usually deposited, her feet came in contact with the corpse of the aged man, over which she fell, and then for the first time became fully aware of the awful calamity that had taken place, and of her dreadful situation.

She uttered a cry of horror, shrinking from the corpse, and trembling in every limb, she then with difficulty gathered herself to her feet, and staggering to a seat, fell into a state of stupefaction.

This continued for some time, and when she did revive to some degree of sensibility

the horror and agony of her feelings may be imagined but cannot be properly described.

Fearful was the silence that reigned in that subterranean retreat, only broken by the hollow murmuring of the wind, which might be heard above as it swept through the dreary wilderness in which the cavern was situated.

The blood of Flora seemed frozen to ice, and for the time being every faculty was suspended, and she remained inanimate as a statue.

Involved as she was in the solemn darkness of that dismal place, and with the stillness which reigned around, it seemed as though she were entombed alive, and so powerful was the fearful impression that for some minutes she could not divest her mind of it.

But at length she aroused herself sufficiently to find and light the lamp, and then she gazed appalled at the stiffened form, and pale features of the venerable hermit, calm and placid in death, and clasping her hands together in agony, sunk upon her knees, and offered up a prayer to heaven to help her in her terrible emergency, and for the peace of the poor old man's soul.

For more than a couple of hours she continued in the same attitude, gazing wildly and vacantly at the old man's ghastly corpse, and the perfect picture of despair. Surely nothing could be more horrible than her destiny. Deprived of every friend she had in the world, and without the means of support, what was to become of her?

The trial was too severe for human nature to endure with any degree of fortitude, and she felt her senses gradually leaving her. She fixed her gaze so long and so intently upon the livid features of the corpse, that she became, as it were rivetted and spell-bound in horror.

Her disordered imagination was at work, again she gazed, and as she did so, she could almost fancy that the old man's eyes were fixed upon her in death, and that his lips moved as if to address her. The delusion was too great, and with a wild and frantic shriek, which rung hollowly through the caverns, she again fell prostrate on the earth in a state of utter insensibility, in which she remained for the rest of that fearful and eventful night.

When she again recovered, it was as if from some frightful dream, a sudden impulse seized her, and starting to her feet, and fixing one more earnest look upon the pale face of the dead, with fevered, maddened brain, and scarcely knowing what she did, she staggered from the spot, and scrambling up the steps, emerged from the cavern, and rushed frantically through the wilderness, impelled by terror.

The grey mists of early morn were upon the dreary scene, and the air was remarkably cold and damp for the climate, and particularly at that season of the year. But the mind of poor Flora was too much agonised and distracted to suffer her to take any heed of the weather, and she hurried on at the top of her speed, like some wretched lunatic escaped from confinement, and without any settled purpose, or knowing whither she was going. Her sole thought, her only object seemed to be to escape from the gloom and horror of the cavern, and the dangers to which she might expose herself never for a moment occurred to her.

Still pursuing her strange flight with unabated speed, she arrived at the spot where the fatal affray had taken place, and where lay the bodies of the slain. It was a ghastly a fearful sight, and Flora gazed appalled, and trembled in every limb.

While she thus stood, transfixed to the spot, she was startled by hearing the voices of men, and aroused to a sense of threatened danger, at that lonely hour and in such a place, she hastily cast her eyes in the direction from which the sounds that had alarmed her proceeded, she beheld two or three armed men—sepoys—who had evidently observed her, at some short distance, but rapidly approaching the spot on which she stood.

All the dreadful outrages of which she had heard, and many of which she had witnessed, immediately rushed upon her memory, and aroused her into action. With frantic speed she darted away, making for the thickest part of the wilderness, where she might elude them, and conceal herself till the danger was past. But the men pursued her, shouting aloud for her to stop, and although she did not venture to look back, she could hear by the sound of their voices that they were gaining upon her.

This added to her speed, and onward she rushed, in a state of terror which may readily be conceived, but which was greatly increased when one of the miscreants discharged the contents of a gun after her, the shots whizzing past her, and which cowardly and brutal act plainly showed their guilty intentions.

She almost gave herself up for lost, but still providence gave her strength sufficient to continue the flight, and plunging into the thickest part of the wilderness, she now ventured to look back, and could see nothing of the men, and not hearing their voices, she began to hope that they had abandoned the pursuit.

Still that idea did not induce her to abate her speed, notwithstanding she panted for breath and was almost exhausted.

She took her way through the most intricate mazes, suffering in her terror no obstacle to impede her progress, but at length she was compelled to stop and take breath, and to endeavour to recover herself, let the consequences be whatever they might.

But she had now penetrated to the very depths of the forest, all was silent and lonely, and for the present, at any rate, it seemed that she was out of danger.

She sunk exhausted on the earth, and the nature of her feelings and the terrible thoughts that rushed with overwhelming force upon her distracted brain, were almost too powerful for endurance.

What could she do? whither could she direct her footsteps in this terrible hour of adversity? She saw nothing but death before her, and she abandoned herself to complete despair.

She could not weep, but she beat her breast in the intensity of her agony, and the most piteous groans and lamentations escaped her lips.

And thus she remained for some time without being able to move from the spot. But at length she exerted herself, and once more, with a sad heart, proceeded on her uncertain way.

Throughout the whole of that day she continued her dreary wandering, in a state of mind which it is useless to attempt to describe, and resting at intervals.

The part of the country through which the poor girl travelled, was of the wildest and most cheerless description, and she met not a person on the way, or saw any signs of a human habitation.

And now when night set in, the prospect before her became still more dreary to her disordered imagination, although there was a bright moon.

It was wonderful how she could find strength to proceed on her way, but still she wandered on, although her weary limbs trembled beneath her, and many miles during the day must she have travelled.

At length, however, she suddenly came upon the ruins of a temple, which were lonely and deserted, and, having first listened cautiously, she entered the sacred place, which she found capable of affording her a much better shelter than from its external appearance she could have anticipated.

Having first fervently invoked the protection of heaven, she stretched her aching and weary limbs on the cold, bare pavement of the temple, and endeavoured to compose herself to sleep.

Sleep was just about to come to the poor wanderer's relief, when she was startled by a sound which smote her breast with horror, and almost paralysed her.

It was the hideous roar of some wild beast in search of prey, and it appeared to be at no great distance.

It would be impossible to pourtray her feelings; the reader may imagine her terror, especially as her exhausted state rendered flight so difficult, but to remain where she was, was certain death, as the ferocious animal seemed to be making his way thither.

The roaring of the wild beast again and again reached her ears, and seemed to approach nearer. The thought of meeting with so frightful a fate gave her strength, and at once aroused her into action. There was not a moment to be lost, and mentally committing herself to the care of providence she quitted the temple, and fled precipitately.

She cast one hurried timid glance around, but as far as the light of the moon would allow her eyes to penetrate, she could see nothing whatever of the object of her terror, and to her affrighted imagination he seemed almost behind her.

On, on flew the terrified girl, over rugged ground which under any other circumstances she could scarcely have traversed, and at length the roaring of the savage beast gradually died away in the distance, and at length subsided altogether.

But notwithstanding it was quite evident that Flora had fairly outstripped the animal, and that she had nothing more to fear, so great was her terror and excitement, at the same time that madness seemed to have seized upon her brain, that she continued her flight with unabated speed, seeming to set exhaustion at defiance.

At length the fort met her sight, and with frantic haste she made towards it, and bounded up the steep and rocky eminence with perfect ease. What followed has already been related.

At length the praiseworthy exertions of the females were rewarded, and poor Flora gave signs of reviving.

Alfred and his father watched her recovery with the greatest anxiety, especially the former, and at length a deep sigh which escaped from her bosom gave notice of returning consciousness, and the young man who had been watching her with the greatest sympathy seized her hand, and raising it passionately to his lips, uttered her name in a tone which told the nature of the feelings that occupied him.

Flora seemed to start as if from some dream, and gazed vacantly upon the persons present, then in accents that went to the heart of Alfred, and filled his breast with melancholy and despair, she exclaimed—

"Stanley, dear Stanley, then you do love the poor lonely bereaved one. They said 'twas the beauteous Indian maiden, Omelia, to whom you had plighted your troth, and that you despised the love of Flora Melville, who could not live without possessing your heart's pure and ardent affections, but 'twas false; you have not deserted the poor girl who now has no other hope but in you. Joy, joy! Stanley, beloved Stanley, I am your's till death."

With these wild expressions, she sunk in the arms of the agitated Alfred, almost again in a state of unconsciousness.

"Alas, poor girl," ejaculated the young man, in a voice of the deepest emotion, "long suffering has at length done its fearful work, and her senses wander. Dear Flora, oh, that I—"

"Ah," exclaimed Flora, suddenly arousing herself as he gave utterance to these words, and staring at him with an expression bordering upon terror, if not absolute disgust, "that voice. 'Tis not he—'tis not that beloved being who constantly haunts my thoughts, and holds such firm possession of my heart's warmest affections. Away, you are but a mockery, whom I cannot look upon with any other feelings than those of repugnance."

She withdrew herself from the embrace of Alfred as she thus spoke, and the looks she fixed upon him chilled his heart, and added to the almost insupportable anguish of mind he at that time experienced.

Flora, dear, unfortunate Flora," he cried, "oh, how bitterly it tortures me to meet with you thus. Do you not know me? 'Tis your cousin, whose heart bleeds for you, and whom you ever esteemed, although unfortunately you could not return that passion he has so often acknowledged for you. Oh, speak to me, Flora, but one word of kindness and friendship, and I will endeavour to be content.

Flora fixed upon the young man a look of stupified amazement, for a minute, as though she was endeavouring to recall her scattered senses, and to recognise him, then with an idiotic laugh, she cried—

"False, false, false! you are not he, you are not Stanley, although as such you seek to impose yourself on me, and wherefore? Ha, ha, ha! I'll tell you. It is because you see that remorseless fate, cruel suffering have accomplished their work upon my poor afflicted mind, and that reason has fled its seat. All, all are gone, I have no one left to love me now, I am the lonely one upon the world's wide desert; the outcast, the thing of scorn, yet can I laugh at the mockery of mankind, and look upon them with proud indifference and contempt. Ha, ha, ha!"

She sunk back in the arms of the females who had been so kindly and so anxiously tending to her recovery, and again became insensible to all that was passing around her.

It was too painfully evident that reason had for the present, at any rate, vacated its seat, and the feelings of Alfred and his father at the deplorable situation of that unfortunate relative whom they had thus met under such extraordinary and melancholy circumstances, may be better imagined than described.

"Alas," said the young man, who could not, in spite of all his efforts to do so, restrain his emotions. "how torturing is this. It distracts my brain, and racks my heart to behold one so truly good and virtuous thus. Heaven help her, for I fear without its merciful interposition, her senses have fled for ever."

"Calm your feelings, Alfred," said his father, "and even sad and dismal as her fate at present appears to be, endeavour to hope for the best. Poor girl, it is indeed painful to behold her thus, but she has, I am convinced, the warmest sympathy of all our companions in misfortune here, and I trust that their kind exertions for her recovery will be shortly crowned with success, and that the present malady under which she now unfortunately labours, will be but temporary. Come, let us retire for awhile, and leave her to the care of the ladies, who, I am satisfied will do all for the poor sufferer that humanity and benevolence can possibly dictate. Come Alfred."

Alfred returned no answer to this, but having fixed one more look of affection and melancholy regret upon the pale features of Flora, and entreated the females who were attending upon her to give him immediate notice should any unfavourable change take place, with his father he quitted the room.

But torturing were the emotions that agitated the breast of the young man, and it was in vain that his parent, who well knew the unfortunate passion which he entertained for Flora Melville, tried to calm and console him.

The words which Flora had spoken in the wild delirium of her brain, and which too fully proved the utter hopelessness of his love, and that her affections were fixed upon another, had penetrated to his heart, and even the faint expectations that he had yet ventured to cherish, that the time might come when she would return his passion, if not with the same fervour as that he entertained for her, at least with equal sincerity, were completely banished.

His father reasoned with him upon the painful subject, and endeavoured to persuade him to try and conquer a passion which had so little prospect of ever being gratified, and which could only be a source of pain and embarrassment to both himself and Flora; but all his arguments were in vain, and he ultimately, seeing that his presence to him, in the present state of his mind, was only an annoyance, he retired from the room and left him to his own thoughts.

For some minutes Alfred paced the room with disordered steps, and gave full vent to his anguish and regret in the most melancholy expressions.

"She loves another it is evident, fondly loves another, and it is little short of madness for me to presume longer to encourage a passion which can hope for no return from the beauteous being who has inspired it in my breast," he soliloquised, as he struck his forehead with his clenched fist in the intensity of his emotion. "But yet is her dear form so firmly rivetted in my heart's warmest affections that nothing whatever can remove it. Oh, Flora, why did heaven form you so to captivate, and to enslave and infatuate my senses? How do I envy my rival, and yet I dare not reproach her for having placed her affections upon one who is doubtless every way worthy of her."

"But," he continued after a moment's reflection, "the observations that escaped the poor girl's lips, convince me that the object of her passion returns it not, and therefore how doubly great must be her suffering, her mortification, and disappointment. Stanley, surely I have some recollection of that name. Let me think. Yes, it must be so, 'tis the gallant young officer Edward Stanley, whom I met on one occasion, and whom I have every cause to respect. Fortunate man to gain the heart of one so lovely and so truly amiable. But he deserves it. And yet he love her not. No, the words of Flora convince me that he does not, but that to the beauteous Hindoo maiden the gentle, yet noble-minded Omelia his affections are devoted, and that probably, if such were his honourable intentions, and I cannot think otherwise, upon her he has already bestowed his hand. Let me not then entirely despair, should Flora yet recover, and reason be restored to her, I may ultimately win that affection, without which life can possess for me but few charms."

These hopes revived his spirits, and he endeavoured to give every encouragement to them, and to become more calm and patient.

Flora remained in much the same condition during the night, and when she did somewhat revive so as to be able to speak, the observations that fell from her lips plainly showed that her senses still wandered.

Under the kind care of those friends among whom accident had thrown her, we will for the present leave her, and resume the adventures of Omelia, whom we left in safety in the bungalow with Mirza, Murud, and his wife Naomie.

———

CHAPTER LX.

MIRZA'S NARRATIVE.

Omelia had been now two days in the bungalow of Murad and his wife, and she had completely recovered from the effects of her imprisonment at Bithoor, and the fatigue of the long journey she had had to undergo in her escape; and in the society of such warm-hearted friends, who exerted themselves to the utmost to contribute to her comfort, she soon regained her customary spirits, and endeavoured to arrange her plans for the future; for to remain long in her present situation, she considered would not be prudent, neither would it meet her views.

The persons who resided in the village, as

has been before stated, were humble and peaceful natives, who were well disposed towards Omelia, especially as she was the friend of Mirza and Murad, who were great favourites among them, and to whom they were at all times ready to render any service in their power.

One day when Omelia had been entering more fully into the particulars of her adventures, up to the time when she was so fortunately and so mercifully rescued from the power of the miscreant Neua Sahib by Mirza, the latter after a few minutes reflection, said—

"Your's has been an eventful life, Omelia, but there are others whose misfortunes and trials have been far more severe, though by patience and fortitude, and the merciful interposition of heaven they were able to surmount them. If you have no objection, and will not consider me tedious, I will corroborate that assertion by relating the sorrows and misfortunes of the parents of myself and Naomie, which probably may interest you."

Omelia expressed her willingness to listen to the narrative, and Mirza, after a brief pause in order to refresh his memory, thus commenced

THE TALE

"Many years have elapsed since the remarkable events which I am about to record took place, and the two principal actors in the drama have long since been no more. I will tell the eventful story as well as my memory will allow me in the precise words in which my parents often related it to me.

"The maternal parent of my mother was an Englishwoman, so that the latter in complexion was scarcely darker than that of an European, she was considered very beautiful, and I have every reason to believe, as well as I can remember—for she died when I and Naomie were very young—that she was so, or had been in her more youthful days, and before she had experienced the severe trials it was her lot to undergo.

"But great as were her personal charms, they were far surpassed by the virtues and graces of her mind. Dear mother, so gentle, so kind, so affectionate, can I ever cease to revere your memory, while one spark of manhood remains within my breast, or till my heart ceases to throb responsively to the feelings of filial love and gratitude?"

Tears trembled in the eyes of Naomie at this affectionate allusion to a mother to whom she had been so fondly attached; and it was some minutes ere he could sufficiently conquer his emotions to proceed.

"Pardon me Omelia, for this slight digression," he at length said, "but it was a tribute due to the memory of a parent so truly good and virtuous.

"The name of my mother was Onani, and her and my father were cousins, by my father's side. They had been brought up together from childhood, and had been destined by their parents for each other; and their affectionate regard, and the similarity of their tastes and dispositions at an early age, showed how judicious was this resolution.

"I will pass over the days of their childhood, which were those of the most boundless and uninterrupted happiness. Their love strengthened with their years, and at length the bright dreams and hopes they had so long cherished were realised, and they were united.

"I was the first fruit of their mutual love.

"The island of Majorca, is surrounded by the vast expanse of the waters of the Mediterranean, far, far away from this our native land, and why I should here allude to it may surprise you, but I will shortly show you the necessity of my doing so.

"This island gave birth to a band of navigators, endowed with valour equal to the most intrepid warriors the world could produce.

"Perfectly free from restraint, and trained to all the dangers of the seas, they bore a like share of the toil in fitting out the vessel manned by themselves, for the purpose of trading to the several shores that offered an opening for their commercial speculations.

"What strange accident, or spirit of enterprise it was, that led my father to this island, and to join the navigators of whom I have just spoken, I cannot undertake to say, but while I was still a mere infant he did so, my mother accompanying him.

"Little did they dream of the fearful trials that awaited them.

"It was on one of their expeditions that their little bark, after a severe and merciless contest, was overpowered by an Algerine of immensely superior crew, who carried them as slaves into the Bay of Tunis.

"Here for a period of seven years, seven long and weary years they remained in slavery, under the cruel sway of the reigning Dey, the arrogant Abdallah.

"You, Omelia, whose heart throbs so tenderly, and with feelings of the warmest sympathy for the misfortunes of your fellow creatures, may imagine what my unfortunate parent suffered during that long period.

"Thus humbled, torn from his home, his friends, his beloved wife and little one, the manly form of the fettered Mirza—for I bear my father's name—fast wasted away.

"The few of his companions saved from the slaughter, had paid the debt of nature, and my father alone survived, the solitary wreck of his once daring crew.

"'Oh, my country, bright sunny land of India, from which in an evil hour my rash footsteps wandered,' he would exclaim, straining his eyes across the dusky waters that rippled in the Bay of Tunis, 'my wife, my child, when shall the degraded Mirza again review the haven of your fostering smiles? When, my beloved Onani, shall nature's throb unite to your's this poor, this lacerated heart? When, my sweet boy, my prattling Mirza, shall your infantine lips caress those of your miserable parent? God of my country, oh, be not deaf to the voice of pity, give me once more liberty, or close the career of a being wretched as myself.'

"Having offered up this fervent prayer, my wretched parent would measure his weary length on the pallet of his dungeon.

"I will not tire your patience, Omelia," continued Mirza, "by recounting all the sufferings that my poor father had to endure during the many years of his captivity, but come at once to important particulars.

"The night was far gone, and my father had sought to refresh his aching limbs, when the silver beams of the moon lighted to his cell the pirate Ali, the confidant of the Algerine governor.

"'Mirza,' he ejaculated, his voice scarcely beyond a whisper, 'Mirza, I say, awake! the sentinels are hushed on their posts; for the sake of friendship I come to warn you of the intended purpose of my master, the great Abdallah, who this night has decreed to you a task, which at once gives you liberty or death. Remember, Mirza, the resolutions of Abdallah never admit of delay or disappointment; therefore have I stolen thus clandestinely to bid you prepare yourself to acquiesce in his propositions, be their tenor what they may. Trifle not, then, if the wish of liberty is not dormant within you, but confirm yourself his favoured slave.'

"My father listened sullenly, and eyed Ali with a look of suspicion as he thus spoke, and after a moment's pause he gloomily said—

"'It may be so, and for this caution receive my thanks.'

"'I need no thanks, Indian,' roughly interrupted Ali. 'Attend to my counsels and fear not, or death will be your only refuge. Adieu.'

"The nocturnal visitor hastily departed, and it was not long before Abdallah, preceded by two slaves, each bearing a flambeau, entered the damp retreat.

"'Mirza,' said one of the slaves, 'attend to the commands of the all-powerful Abdallah,' and he advanced to disturb the recumbent position of my father.

"'To that Abdallah,' firmly he said, 'time and suffering have alone taught me to yield, I wait his pleasure.'

"'Listen then, slave, and be wise,' sternly exclaimed the Algerine Dey; 'the patience with which you have so long borne the mandates of my will, has not passed idly observed. I have condescended to look with pity on your lingering fate. It is to be hoped that the captive Mirza will not with impunity spurn at the price by which he may at once regain his liberty.'

"My father bowed submission.

"'I promised in the dark hour of my adversity to repay the act of bravery by which your sturdy arms rescued me from a watery grave, and bore me with life to these my shores—'

"'A virtuous act needs no prelude,' tauntingly interrupted my father, 'what is the purport of Abdallah' visit?'

"'You are precipitate, Mirza,' said the tyrant, sternly, 'beware, lest you spoil my good intent. Know then, that within the walls of my harem lives a female beauteous as the heavens. She is one of your country but fair as an European.'

"The heart of my father throbbed violently in his breast, and an unaccountable emotion shook his limbs.

"'It is not the nature of Abdallah,' continued the Dey, 'to sigh for baubles so trivial as women, but this model of perfection so haunts my imagination that at once my soul, stern and relentless as our prophet moulded it, is softened into love But mark me, Mirza, I have offered her my heart, to dedicate my life to her pleasures, to nourish her in my bosom, to love no other woman but her, a splendour not all the splendour of Barbary could otherwise hope to obtain. She has dared to reject my suit, and since I cannot touch her heart, I must force her to my will. You, Mirza, being her countryman, may have power to soothe her to my purposes, this completed, rest assured your chains are loosened, and you may speedily return to your native land. Think of this, slave, and do not falter from the attempt of crowning by one deed your own wishes, and those of Abdallah. But beware, deceive me not,' he continued in a stern voice, 'or by my hopes of our prophet's pardon, the sharpest tortures the rack can inflict await you.'

"The various feelings that at that moment agitated my father's breast you may imagine—his mind pictured a thousand happy scenes; to once more embrace his lovely Onani what could he not have undertaken? though his soul loathed the task he was to stoop to for the gratification of his most inveterate enemy. Still what would not affection dare, to share the smiles of her that binds your soul to existence.

"He hesitated, and the Dey became impatient.

"'Now, slave,' he demanded, 'what is your determination?'

"'The slave Mirza,' replied my father, with forced humility, 'accedes to your desires.'

"''Tis well,' said Abdallah, 'you have decided wisely.'

"He then commanded one of his slaves to remove my father's chains, which was done, and Abdallah, commanding the former to follow, retraced his steps to the grand chamber.

"I will not seek to pourtray my father's emotions when he was left to the uninterrupted indulgence of his own thoughts, for you can far better, I am convinced, conjecture them.

"He awaited with the utmost anxiety the

arrival of the succeeding night, which was appointed for his visit to the harem. Armed with a dagger, and bearing a small lamp, he ascended the staircase which led to the apartments of Abdallah's intended victim.

"The soft rays of Cynthia brightened the chamber, by whose light my father cautiously approached

"The figure of a female, partly veiled, reclining on a supurb couch, canopied with pale blue drapery, that hung in folds around her downy pillow, met his gaze.

"The cherub form of a child had carelessly twined its little arms on the bosom of its parent, who 'slept the sleep of sweetened innocence.'

"The aching heart of Mirza was nearly bursting at the hallowed picture. He thought of his Onani, of his child, and he shrunk with aversion from the task he had undertaken.

"But the hour is getting late, and I had better defer the finish of my tale, which seems to interest you, Omelia, till tomorrow."

Our heroine expressed her anxiety to hear the conclusion of the simple but interesting narrative, but, as it was time to retire to rest, she could not object to Mirza's proposition, and after some further observations, they separated for the night

CHAPTER LXI.

CONTINUATION OF MIRZA'S TALE.—THE DISCOVERY.

The following morning, at the urgent request of Omelia, Mirza resumed his story in the following words—

"For a few minutes my father stood and gazed transfixed on this beauteous object.

"The moon reflected full upon the shaded features of the female.

"'She seems very lovely,' exclaimed my father, mentally, 'yes, beauteous as heaven's first born. Oh, spotless innocence, how can I betray you to the heartless libertinism of a wretch like Abdallah?'

"Still did he continue to gaze upon her, till breaking the silence he softly ejaculated,

"'And shall I, by villainous artifices, betray her to the wishes of a rapacious tyrant? Alas, what will be her sufferings when left to Abdallah's brutal passions? Grief soon must end her days, her unhappy days, and her child, her smiling boy, when he calls on his mother, that mother whose dying breath alone respires with curses on the base betrayer! I—I that betrayer. Oh, no, it cannot be.'

"Again he paused, and looked sorrowfully on the sleeping fair one, whilst every feeling of pity and compassion moved his manly heart.

"'Liberty,' he soliloquised, 'you are indeed most sweet, yet, after the sacrifice of a virtuous woman, can I repose in peace? Can I press to my heart my wife and child, and forget how I regained them? Oh, never.'

"My father uttered these last words emphatically, and they awoke the sleeper; she looked around the apartment in suspense, but her sighs alone broke its silence.

"My father concealed himself behind the arras of a magnificent recess.

"She arose from the couch, and lifting her eyes towards heaven, in a voice of melodious and sylph-like expression, thus ejaculated—

"'All merciful powers that deign to look with unerring goodness upon the most humble of your creatures, protect, oh, protect the hapless being who now petitions you. By the morning's declining day has the tyrant Abdallah sworn to make me the victim of his brutal passion, or to the raging deep shall the life of my innocent boy be sacrificed. But, oh, kind providence, prevent this threat from being carried into execution, and save myself and my boy from so horrible a doom. Oh, forsake us not, Almighty Power, rather suffer one grave to hold us in that unfathomable ocean, where the body of my husband is immured, and then, my husband, heaven will award your toils by indissolubly reuniting you to your own Onani.'

"'Onani!' re-echoed the voice of my father, as he rushed from the place of his concealment, 'sweet air-drawn vision, say, repeat that name, and let me cherish the illusive thought that alone has the power to bless me still.'

"'Mercy—mercy!' shrieked Onani—for it was indeed my mother, who, together with myself, had fallen into the power of the fierce Abdallah—'who could repeat a name so loved?'

"'I—I, your husband, your own Mirza!' wildly exclaimed my father, and in an instant they were locked in each other's arms."

Mirza was here compelled to pause for a minute or two in his narative, for his emotions overpowered him, and those of Naomie and Omelia were equal to his own.

"My poor parents," said Naomie, while tears trembled in her eyes, "terrible indeed were your sufferings; but this fond, this unexpected meeting doubtless repaid you for those sorrows you had endured with such exemplary patience and fortitude."

"Most true," coincided Omelia, "but pray proceed, good Mirza; the tale excites my warmest sympathy and interest."

Mirza complied, as follows—

"Thus they continued till my my mother thus broke the short entrancement—-

"'All merciful powers, you have heard my prayers—he is here!—he lives! the breath of life from him warms my veins. My love, my Mirza, close, closer to these long widowed arms, see, see your Onani has lived to bless your existence.'

"Again they embraced, and for a few minutes their senses were lost in transport.

"But how soon were they aroused to terror. The stern voice of Abdallah filled the apartment.

"'Holy providence!' frantically cried my mother, 'shall the demon still haunt me? Mirza, we have met only to be doomed to an eternal separation—we indeed must part.'

"'Never, Onani, till the heart of your husband is torn from it's tenement,' replied my father, still holding her fair form convulsively to his bosom

"Casting his eyes wildly around, he beheld the Dey, whose ferocious look betrayed the workings of a heart swelling with resentment.

"Ardently clasping the form of Onani, my father courageously exclaimed—

"'Now, tyrant, use me as you will; I am the husband of that Onani, whom you would by depravity have annihilated.'

"'What say you, dog?' furiously cried Abdallah, his eyes flashing with the most diabolical rage, 'the slave Mirza the protector of Onani? Psha! babbling fool! What, have the charms of her I permitted you to gaze on maddened your intellects? Poor senseless worm. You her protector?—ha, ha, ha!—such a protector could the foot of Abdallah crush for ever.'

"'This then to let out your blasphemous soul, and prove the determination of Mirza,' replied my father, in a voice harrowed up by phrenzy and revenge, aiming at the same moment a blow, which the gigantic strength of Abdallah arrested, at the same instant wresting the poniard from his enfeebled grasp.

"Clutching the emaciated form of my mother, the Dey was about to plunge the weapon in her husband's breast, but for the recruited powers of Onani, who rushed forward, and fixed herself on his uplifted arm.

"With a look of savage disappointment, Abdallah withdrew his hold, and retreated precipitately to a small balcony, from which he led the tall figure of one of his slaves, whom he commanded to tear the prisoners asunder.

"'Saib,' he commanded, 'call forth my guards; bid them take away this presumptuous fool, this slave Mirza, to the dungeon beneath the fortress, whence no mortal ever returned to picture its horrors; bear him hence, I say.'

"The attendant of the fierce Abdallah moved not his erect posture; his eye fixed on my poor mother, who clasped with ardent embrace her threatened husband.

"'Did'st thou not hear me, Saib?' demanded the Dey.

"'Ay,' replied the other, firmly, 'and with disgust at your tyranny. No, Abdallah, my heart revolts at this persecution of an innocent man. Never shall it be said that I lifted a hand for his destruction.'

"Dumb be the voice that tells me so, cowardly ingrate!' Beware, Saib, of my vengeance, rouse not my wrath, or this gleaming sabre may uproot the heart that equals not in abhorrence that of Abdallah's. Kindness indeed to slaves who would destroy us in return; oh, no, they are our rights, beasts of burden, or baubles for our pastime. As such, Saib, treat them.'

"'If you entertain the thoughts that Saib will adhere to such tenets you wrong him,' replied the latter, 'and for your threats, mighty Dey, I heed them not; as the winds they are harmless,' he calmly added, while Abdallah frantically bit his lips as Saib thus concluded his sentence.

"'Know, proud Dey, the soul of a Christian is embodied in Saib—a Christian was his parent, and though nurtured in your domains, the sentiment of filial duty sleeps not so secure but the voice of calamity may awaken it.'

"'Peace, driveller,' cried the Dey, passionately, 'or your words shall parch your lips. The ears of Abdallah must not be disgraced by such degenerate sophistry; so leave me, recreant, lest my sight should blast you.'

"'Ha, ha, ha,' laughed Saib, scornfully, 'ribaldry which I scoff at.'

"'A truce then to that ribaldry, as you term it, and receive the reward of a traitor.'

"And ere my astonished father could interpose, the poniard of Abdallah was sheathed in the heart's blood of Saib.

"Saib fell, but not unavenged; for closing with the Algerine he levelled him with the earth, and with the dagger which still smoked with his own blood, he terminated the existence of the tyrant Abdallah.

"My father stood no longer to witness the dismal scene, but breathing a prayer for the soul of the dauntless Saib, he hurried his wife and myself, who had beheld in terror the tragical event, to the beach, where he unmoored a small boat that floated near to it, and steered in safety from the Bay of Tunis.

"In the course of the following day they were fortunately picked up by and kindly received on board an English ship, which was bound to Calcutta, and in due time, after an absence of so many years, my parents once more trod their native land, which they resolved never to leave again"

Thus Mirza concluded his romantic and interesting narrative, which had been listened to with the most profound attention, and most powerfully were the sympathies of Naomie excited for the misfortunes her parents had undergone, and which she had never before heard so minutely described; and in those feelings Omelia also most warmly participated.

"Truly the trials of your parents were severe," she observed, "and their restoration to each other after the lapse of so many years, and their escape were indeed most providential. Your narrative bears all the character of romance."

"True, Omelia," answered Mirza, "but I have not in the least exaggerated, but given it word for word, or at least, as well as I can remember, as my father related it to me. If it has served to amuse you, and to divert your thoughts for a time from more painful subjects, I am satisfied.

Omelia thanked him.

"But," she remarked, after a moment's reflection, "there are one or two circumstances connected with your story, Mirza, which I think you have not sufficiently explained. Namely, in the first place, by what means your mother and yourself fell into the power of the tyrant Abdallah?"

"Into that circumstance I never took the pains to inquire," said Mirza, "therefore I am unable to inform you."

"And your sister Naomie?"

"She was not born till after these events took place," replied Mirza, "so you see that I am many years her senior."

The conversation then dropped, and the rest of the day was passed by the friends in the most agreeable manner, under all the circumstances, Naomie, her husband and brother doing all that they possibly could to contribute to the comfort of our heroine.

The society of Naomie, whose amiable disposition entirely assimilated with her own was a source of much pleasure to her, and served to beguile many weary hours that would otherwise have been insufferably tedious.

Yet did Omelia feel anxious and restless, for she had been hitherto unable to come to any satisfactory determination as to her future plans, and delay was a sad trial to her patience.

Her chief anxiety, however, was for her lover, whose fate it seemed impossible for her to ascertain, though, in spite of all her efforts to the contrary, she could not but forebode the worst, and deeply did she regret the circumstance which had last separated them, and at such a critical moment.

Should Stanley be still living, how torturing must be his suspense at the uncertainty of what had become of her.

"Noble-hearted, beloved Stanley," she cried, in a voice of the deepest emotion, "and shall we indeed never be permitted to meet again? No more allowed to indulge those bright hopes and visions that floated so vividly before our too glowing imaginations? Alas, have I not reason to entertain the worst apprehensions?"

She sighed deeply as these painful and melancholy thoughts occurred to her, and in vain endeavoured to find some degree of consolation.

Flora Melville too, and the aged man to whom she was so much indebted, were the objects of her anxiety, and she felt keenly for the misfortunes and melancholy bereavement of the former, now that she was left friendless and destitute in the world.

Anxious, however, as Omelia was once more to be able to join those friends, who must have given her up for lost, the present dangerous and excited state of that part of the country through which she wished to proceed, rendered travelling impossible with any degree of safety; and the accounts which daily reached the village were most alarming. The rebellion—for no other word was applicable to it—still continued to spread, and notwithstanding the gallant exertions and brilliant achievements of a Havelock, Outram, O'Neill, and many other distinguished heroes, it seemed to make but little impression on the rebels, and British rule in India appeared rapidly drawing to a close.

It were almost idle to attribute the origin of the rebellion mainly to the greased cartridges, although that ill-advised business had no doubt a considerable share in it; the annexation of Oude there cannot be a doubt (and it was the opinion of Mr. Layard, and other eminent men whose assertions were worthy of the utmost confidence) was the primary cause, to that we have to attribute all the fearful events that have followed.

Up to the period of which we are writing, how fearfully had the work of destruction proceeded; the whole of central India had then been placed at the mercy of sixty thousand rebellious soldiers. Towns, stations, cantonments, comprising palaces, churches, colleges, arsenals, courts of law, treasuries, banks, dwellings, barracks, shops, &c., &c., had been utterly destroyed, after undergoing a rigid and remorseless pillage.

Entire libraries and valuable records had been committed to the flames. Society had been ruthlessly rent asunder, the most frightful barbarities perpetrated with relentless cruelty, the relations of subject to sovereignty totally annihilated. For many hundreds of miles the authority of the British government was at least in abeyance, not a foot of land could be regarded as constituting our possessions which was not held by Eupean troops, aided by a mere handful of foreigners.

But we fear we are growing tedious, and should not have alluded to this subject but for the purposes of our tale.

Although from the secluded situation of the village, and the friendly disposition of its inhabitants, there was no immediate danger to apprehend, Omelia never ventured from the bungalow till after the shadows of night had fallen upon the earth, and then she was always accompanied by Murad and Mirza, who treated her with the utmost respect, and most anxiously watched over her safety.

Beyond the clustering trees, and lofty hills by which the village was enclosed, the scenery which burst upon the sight on a clear moonlight night was very picturesque and beautiful, and being on the way from Cawnpore towards Agra, Meerut, Kurnaul, Simla, from thence through Delhi, Jypore, to Mhow in Malwa, and the banks of the Nerbudda, it presented many objects of interest and architectural beauty to the eye of the spectator, especially when viewed from the summit of some lofty hill.

As has been repeatedly stated, India abounds with monumental remains, and when all that England has accomplished in the architectural way shall have crumbled into dust, the majestic works raised three or four centuries ago by Hindoos and Mussulmans will survive to attest the sublimity of their conceptions, and the magnificence of their expenditure.

Numerous specimens of architecture, and a most diversified prospect, as we have before stated, could be obtained from any of the hills beyond the village in which our heroine at present sought refuge, and it was no wonder then, enthusiastic admirer as she was of everything beautiful in nature and art, that she so delighted to contemplate them, and thus to divert her thoughts from the melancholy subjects that would otherwise have engrossed them.

There at a short distance might be seen a handsome town, the rich variety of whose mosques, palaces, houses, and other edifices, interspersed with trees, gave to the whole the character of a city built in the midst of an immense garden.

Thus would Omelia occupy her mind for some time in the cool of the evening, and derive consolation and amusement from it, and had Stanley been near her, and away from those dangers by which she had too much reason to fear that he was at present surrounded, even if he was still living, of which she was sometimes induced to entertain a doubt, she could have been comparatively happy.

But this short respite from danger was about to be interrupted in a most alarming manner, and which we will proceed to relate in the ensuing chapter.

———

CHAPTER LXII

A FEARFUL SITUATION.—HEROIC CONDUCT OF OMELIA AND NAOMIE.

More than a week had now elapsed since the arrival of Omelia in the village, and such was the dangerous state of the country and the fearful account of the outrages committed which daily reached their ears, that to venture to pursue her journey to the cavern in the wilderness, which Omelia was so anxious to do, and where she hoped yet to find the old man and Flora Melville in safety, would have been little short of madness, and likely to be attended with the most fatal consequences.

She seldom, however, missed an evening taking her customary walk, accompanied by her friends, but on the eventful evening which we are about to write, she was only attended by Naomie, Mirza and Murad having been compelled to leave home at an early hour in the morning on business of a private nature.

Omelia had been more than usually depressed in spirits during the day, and dismal misgivings racked her brain, foreboding of some approaching danger, from which neither the fineness of the weather—for it was a beautiful night—nor the efforts of Naomie, could succeed in arrousing her.

She gazed listlessly on the lovely prospect before her, now bathed in the silvery moonlight, and it failed entirely to excite those feelings of pleasure and admiration in her breast which it was wont to do.

"What can be the meaning of the strange and painful thoughts which beset my mind?" she said, "I cannot banish them, yet am completely at a loss how to account for them."

"Endeavour to arouse yourself then, dear Omelia," said her affectionate companion, "for I trust sincerely that there is nothing to fear."

"I cannot," answered Omelia, "try all that I may. I feel an irresistible presentiment of some approaching danger, but of the nature of which I cannot form the slightest conjecture.

"Surely this is a weakness which you ought not to give way to."

"You may call it so, if you will, but I cannot conquer it, and it seems to grow upon me every moment. I wish your husband and your brother were not absent."

"They probably will be back shortly,"

said Naomie, "for they will be anxious to rejoin us as soon as possible. I trust no harm has befallen them, your fears and forebodings make me feel anxious and uneasy."

A sudden and ominous change now took place in the weather, and the moon became overcast by black and threatening clouds, the wind also having arisen, and murmuring in fitful and hollow gusts around.

"We shall have a storm presently," said Naomie; "let us return home."

To this Omelia silently assented, and they retraced their steps quickly from the spot towards the village, and entered the bungalow in no very agreeable state of mind.

The threatened storm commenced, and seemed likely to rage with violence, and this only served to add to the depression of their spirits"

"I cannot banish the dismal feelings that obtrude themselves on my mind," observed Omelia, after a few minutes occupied in meditation. I am certain that there is some danger impending. I wish that Mirza and Murad would return."

"I had hoped they would have done so ere this," returned Naomie, whose looks betrayed equal anxiety and uneasiness to that which our heroine experienced. "I cannot think what has detained them."

They again relapsed into silence, but awaited the return of Mirza and Murad with the utmost suspense.

The storm now raged fiercely, and there was every sign of its being a fearful night and they became still more impatient for the return of Mirza and Murad.

And thus passed half an hour away, without any change taking place, and their fears and forebodings increased rather than abated.

"It is a fearful night," observed Omelia, "and that has doubtless caused the delay of your brother and your husband. It is impossible that they could continue their journey in such a storm."

"True," coincided Naomie; "and I wish it would abate."

"It is not likely to do so to-night," returned our heroine, "and we may therefore make up our minds to their continued absence."

"Oh, no, I cannot think that," replied Naomie; "they will rather brave the fury of the storm, than delay their return to night, knowing the anxiety and suspense we shall experience."

"Hark!" interrupted Omelia hastily; "what sound was that?"

"I heard nothing but the voice of the tempest," answered Naomie; "what now alarms you?"

"Between the pauses of the thunder," said Omelia, "I could almost swear that I heard the sound of the distant discharge of fire arms."

"You were mistaken."

"No, I am positive I was not. 'Tis there again. You must have heard that, and be convinced that it was not the thunder,"

"True," returned Naomie; "there could be no mistaking that, it was certainly the report of fire-arms, but let us not unnecessarily alarm ourselves. Our neighbours are doubtless all in their dwellings, and will be ready to assist us should any danger threaten."

The heavy and hasty tramping of horses' feet approaching, was now heard, and the fears and suspicions of Omelia and her companion being now more than ever aroused, they opened the door of the bungalow, and looked out through the storm.

They could not refrain from giving utterance to an exclamation of astonishment and pleasure on beholding the long expected Mirza and Murad, galloping at the top of their horses' speed towards the bungalow, and it was evident that they were urged by some causes of alarm, which the agitation of their looks fully confirmed, on their approaching nearer.

They immediately dismounted and entered the house, and Omelia, and Naomie could not disguise their terror, when they perceived that the left arm of Murad was bound round with a scarf which was stained with blood.

"For mercy's sake what has happened?" interrogated our heroine, anxiously, "you are wounded, Murad?"

"But slightly," he replied; "danger threatens, a party of the mutinous sepoy's are approaching the village, doubtless with the intention of plunder."

"Ah! then," exclaimed Omelia, "my forebodings are realised. What is to be done?"

"Do not give way to fear," said Mirza; "for everything depends upon coolness, prudence and promptitude of action. Not an instant is to be lost, the villagers must be forewarned of the approach of the enemy so that they may be prepared to offer a determined resistance, which I doubt not will be attended with success, as the number of the mutineers is not great. We were suddenly surprised by them on our way hither, and being known by their leader to be opposed to the revolt, they endeavoured to take us prisoners. We, however, fought our way through them, Murad being slightly wounded as you see—and although the shots flew thickly around us, we managed most providentially to escape and to outstrip them."

"Thank heaven for that," ejaculated Naomie, fervently.

"But in a few minutes they will probably be here," said Murad, "goaded on by feelings of revenge, and the hope of plunder,

so we must immediately to business. There is no lack of arms and ammunition in the village, so that we have not much occasion to fear the result. Now, Naomie, and Omelia you must be firm, and fear not. Keep yourselves confined in the house, and we will defend you to the last."

"Omelia understands not the meaning of the word fear, when danger threatens, and the cause to defend is just," replied our heroine proudly, and her features glowed, and her eyes flashed with the amazonian heroism that ever animated her breast, and imparted itself to her actions; "she has never yet shrunk from facing death in its most frightful form, even woman though she is, nor will she do so now, confident of the protection of that Almighty power she never invoked in vain. Give me the means, and

you will find that I know how to defend myself."

"And I," said Naomie, resolutely, "do not tremble to render my aid in this deadly struggle. It will be my pride to emulate the courage of Omelia."

Mirza and Murad were lost in surprise and admiration; but there was no time for further delay in conversation, and they hurriedly departed to apprize the villagers of the approaching danger.

"Now, Naomie," said Omelia, when they were gone, "let us be prepared to show your husband and brother that we have made no empty boast of our courage. Here are pistols and muskets, and we must convince the enemy that we know how to use them when the occasion demands."

Naomie agreed to this, and the intrepid

women having armed themselves awaited the result with anxiety and impatience, but at the same time with firmness and confidence.

It was all the work of a few minutes, the villagers were quickly gathered together, and being informed of the impending danger, immediately armed themselves, and prepared to offer a resolute resistance.

Mirza and Murad now returned to the bungalow, and informed our heroine and her companion that they had resolved to go forth and endeavour to prevent the entrance of the enemy into the village.

"Keep yourselves confined to the house, as I said before, and no harm will befall you," observed Mirza.

"And why should we shrink from that danger which you so boldly go forth to meet and to resist?" demanded Omelia. "Naomie and myself will accompany you, and whatever the peril, we at least will share it."

"Heroic woman," said Mirza, "how greatly do I admire and honour your character, but to comply with your wishes would not only be cowardice on our parts, but at the same time little short of madness, and—"

He was interrupted by loud shouts proceeding from the farther end of the village, and which were immediately followed by rapid discharges of musketry.

"Ah," exclaimed Mirza, "the enemy is upon us—they have attacked the village. Quick, Murad, our immediate aid is required."

Motioning Omelia and Naomie to firmness and confidence, Mirza and Murad hurried from the house to join their comrades, who were now hotly engaged with the murderous sepoys, and the fighting was most obstinate and desperate on both sides, the villagers being led on and commanded by Mirza and Murad, who were possessed of great bravery and skill of arms.

It was a scene of the greatest excitement, and the terrors of it were added to by the fury of the contending elements—for the storm continued with unabated violence—the thunder at intervals completely drowning the voice of the rapid volleys, and the shouts, the yells, the execrations, and cries of anguish of the combatants.

The mutineers were little prepared for such a determined resistance from a mere handful of peaceable villagers, and they were somewhat disheartened by it; but nevertheless they continued the combat with unabated vigour, and for some time with apparent advantage, although several of their comrades had fallen, and the courage and resolution of their antagonists remained undaunted.

And now the rebels succeeded in firing one of the bungalows, which burnt fiercely and added to the awful effect of the scene, but being detached from the other houses, the conflagration was not likely to spread.

Omelia and her companion remained for some minutes confined to the house in a state of the greatest suspense and excitement, and listened to the fierce din of the deadly combat with much anxiety. But at length the patience of Omelia was exhausted, and her heroic spirit was aroused to the utmost degree.

"I can no longer tarry here," she exclaimed, "whilst those whom I have so much reason to regard as my best friends are running every risk in my defence. Come, Naomie, follow me; we will at least be participators in the danger."

Naomie returned no answer, but her looks sufficiently showed how fully she agreed to and approved of what Omelia proposed, she hastily followed her example by providing herself with a couple of pistols, and they were then about to quit the bungalow, and venture into the midst of the strife—rash and imprudent as such a course undoubtedly was—when the shouts of the combatants were approaching nearer, and they turned back, and ascending to a room above from which they could command a view of the whole scene without being exposed to any immediate danger, they looked cautiously from the window, and beheld that the rebels had at length given way, and were being driven from the village, all the time, however, continuing to fight desperately.

A shriek from Naomie somewhat startled our heroine, notwithstanding she had observed the course of her agitation and alarm almost at the same instant.

Mirza and Murad, who had been engaged in a desperate and deadly combat with two of the enemy, were struck to the earth, and the ruffians were about to terminate their existence, when Omelia with the quickness of thought seized a rifle belonging to Murad, which happened to be in the room, and levelling it at the antagonist of Mirza, with unerring aim, shot him dead; at the same instant that Naomie discharged one of her pistols at the villain who held the life of her husband at his mercy with equal success.

Mirza and Murad instantly regained their feet, and once more joined resolutely in the combat, and a loud shout of enthusiastic admiration arose from the villagers who had beheld the noble and heroic act of Omelia and Naomie.

Several shots, however, were fired into the room by the mutineers, to avenge the death of their comrads, which our heroine and Naomie fortunately escaped, and having seen that all was now in favour of the villagers, who were driving the enemy before them in all directions. they retir d for safety to the back of the bungalow, to await the return of the victors, and where they gave free vent to the feelings that animated their breasts.

"Thank heaven," exclaimed Naomie. "present danger is at an end, and that the villains have been defeated in their designs."

"True," coincided Omelia, "but still there is much to apprehend. This affair, and the defeat of the rebels, will doubtless bring down speedy vengeance upon the villagers; and I shudder to think what may be the consequences. Hark, the firing has not yet ceased, and the mutineers seem still to offer a daring and obstinate resistance."

"It is useless," returned Naomie, "many of their comrades have fallen, and if the rest contrive to escape from their pursuers they may consider themselves fortunate. The firing grows fainter and less frequent, and new it has ceased altogether."

The villagers with Mirza and Murad at their head, continued to pursue the small remnant of the defeated sepoys from the village with irresistible determination, and did not suffer one of them to escape to tell the tale. They then returned to the village to exult at their victory, and anxiously Mirza and Murad hastened to the bungalow where our heroine and her companion were eagerly waiting to receive them.

The two friends could not find words sufficient to express to Omelia and Naomie their admiration and gratitude for their unexampled heroism of conduct, and to congratulate them on the defeat of their enemies, to which latter feeling those noble-minded women most cordially responded, and all parties then endeavoured to compose themselves after the extraordinary events of the night, and the great danger and excitement to which they had been exposed.

CHAPTER LXIII.

FRESH CHANGES AND MORE PERILS.

The village had suffered no serious damage from this sudden and unexpected attack, with the exception of the bungalow which the mutineers had fired, and which was entirely destroyed, and the triumph was of course from the total annihilation of the enemy, considered complete.

The storm had ceased with the combat, and the weather had again become promising. The dead were removed, and the wounded—which was chiefly among the villagers, only a few of their number being slain—were attended to promptly, and then assembled together to congratulate each other on their success, and to arrange plans for their future defence, in the event of their being again attacked.

Murad and Mirza left the bungalow to join their gallant friends in their deliberations and demonstrations, and Omelia and Naomie, who were also anxious to express to the villagers their thanks for the brave conduct they had displayed, requested to accompany them, which was complied with.

All signs of the recent fearful storm had entirely disappeared, and the moon had again emerged in all her chaste splendour, and was shining brightly upon the scene of the late strife, and the distant prospect which was clearly revealed in her silvery beams.

The whole of the villagers with their families were assembled before their dwellings, and there was much congratulation on all sides.

Omelia and Naomie were received with every cordial demonstration of pleasure and admiration, and the uncommon fortitude, heroism, and presence of mind they had displayed, met with the most unqualified approbation.

Omelia especially excited the most lively interest, while her fine expressive countenance, handsome and commanding figure, sweetness of manners, and nobleness, yet gentleness of bearing, at once created surprise, admiration and respect.

The deepest sympathy was expressed in her fate, and every one evinced a desire to serve her to the best of their ability.

Omelia warmly expressed her acknowledgements for their good feelings towards her, and herself and her friends then returned to the bungalow, the villagers retired to their dwellings, and everything re-assumed the same calm and quiet aspect, as if nothing of a serious nature had happened.

Omelia, however, notwithstanding the success which had attended her friends, could not but feel the most serious alarm at the events of the night, and she did not attempt to conceal her feelings and apprehensions from Mirza and Murad.

"I'm afraid it will not be safe for me to remain here much longer," she observed; "Nena Sahib may hear of the place of my concealment by some means or other, and such is the deadly hatred and feelings of revenge with which I am satisfied he must now view me, convinced as he is that I am one of his most inveterate enemies, that he will leave no means untried to get me again in his power, in which event my fate is certain."

"Quiet those apprehensions, Omelia," replied Mirza, "and let not the exciting events of this evening alarm you. I need not, I am certain, assure you of the fidelity of our friends in the village, after the conduct they have this night displayed. Not one of them would betry you, and by what other means, therefore, can he become aware of the place of your retreat? Besides the Nena is at present too much occupied with more important business to trouble himself about you."

"But I cannot rest," said Omelia, and a tear trembled in her eye as she spoke, "till I have ascertained the fate of those beloved beings who are so precious to my heart, and from whom I have so long been separated. Dearest Stanley, unfortunate Flora Melville, oh, how anxiously are my thoughts ever fixed on ye, never can I know peace or happiness till I once behold ye."

"I do not wonder at your uneasiness, and impatience to know what has become of those friends whom you regard with such warm, such fervent esteem," remarked Mirza, "but you must consider the almost insurmountable difficulties that are placed in the way of the gratification of your wishes, and that it would be folly for you at present to rush headlong into danger, without the least prospect of a favourable result. Be patient, Omelia, and I trust that yet all the fond hopes you now entertain will be realised."

"Oh, how vainly you talk to me of patience," returned our heroine; "with all those torturing doubts and fears upon my mind. The time that we have been separated the circumstances under which we parted, and the terrible events that have occurred since then, all serve to strengthen my apprehensions, and to increase my dismal forebodings."

"Providence will, I trust, protect them from the harm which you fear has befallen them, and shortly again restore them to you?" observed Naomie.

Omelia shook her head.

"Oh, would that I could think so," she said; "I might then learn to be content, and to wait with patience and confidence, but, alas, I cannot do so. I am tired of remaining inactive, and would rather even be exposed to all the horrors of this fearful revolution than continue so. The City of Delhi is now surrounded with British troops, and its speedy fall is all but certain, the garrison at Lucknow still hold out bravely, heroically, in the residency, and the gallant, the invincible Havelock is marching to their relief. Could I succeed in reaching either of those places, I might obtain some intelligence of Stanley, and should receive protection. At any rate, could I but reach the aged hermit's rocky retreat in the wilderness, my anxiety respecting poor Flora would be relieved, and I should be in safety. I must endeavour to find my way thither."

"Pardon me, Omelia," returned Mirza, "but I cannot help saying that such an idea is little short of madness. Every road is beset by danger which increases daily, and the fate that you would meet with is all but certain."

"With the least chance of obtaining my desires, I am ready to brave it," answered our heroine; "besides, as a native, what cause have I to fear? Those who met me could have no suspicion of my real character or intentions."

"Be not too sure of that, Omelia; your heroic conduct on many occasions, has rendered your name famous among the rebels, and there are few that would not detect the noble-hearted Indian maiden, the daughter of the late misguided Yunadar."

Omelia sighed at the remembrance of her guilty parent's awful fate, and she returned no immediate answer to Mirza's last observations.

"Good Mirza," she as length said, in her gentlest accents; "I owe you an immense debt of gratitude, one that I am afraid it will never be in my power adequately to repay. You have already encountered sufficient, and run too many risks for my sake, and heaven forbid that I should be the means of exposing you to any fresh dangers. I ask but your prayers and good wishes, and will proceed on my tedious and adventurous journey alone."

"Impossible!" said Mirza, "think you I will ever permit that? No, I should despise myself if I could thus recklessly abandon one whom I so much esteem, leave her without protection, or the means of existence, perhaps to perish for want on the road. Since you are determined, much as I disapprove of it, I know it is useless to attempt to dissuade you from it. However, let me beg you to wait patiently for a few days, until I have hit upon some safe plan for your secret departure—for I do not think it would be prudent to let it be known, even to them—and then I will accompany you, together with Murad."

"Generous friend," exclaimed Omelia, warmly, "I know not in what language to express my thanks. I do accept your kind offers."

"Alas!" said Naomie, "and must I then so shortly lose your beloved society, dear Omelia. I had hoped that I should have continued to enjoy your society, till happier days should once more have dawned upon us."

"It grieves me, dear Naomie," replied our heroine, "that we should be compelled to do so, but I trust that the time is not far distant when we shall meet again. Believe me I shall ever entertain a lively and grateful sense of your's and your husband's kindness."

Some more compliments passed between the friends, and, after some further conversation, the subject dropped, and they separated for the night.

Omelia continued for some time awake, and to give indulgence to busy thought, which the startling events of the evening, served not a little to contribute to create.

She became more and more anxious to leave the village, and to proceed on her journey, with the hope that she might be able to gain some intelligence of those so dear to her, and to learn, in spite of the imminent dangers by which they had been surrounded, that they still lived, and were in safety.

"Oh, Stanley," she cried, and her bosom heaved with the purest, the fondest emotion as she repeated his name; "could I but be assured that you still live, and have escaped the fiendish cruelties that have been inflicted on so many of your unfortunate fellow creatures, what a terrible weight of care and dread would it remove from my mind. And you my poor afflicted friend, dear, kind-hearted Flora, now left alone in the world without a protector or the means of support, how does my heart bleed for you, and how glad should I be to be restored to you, that I might endeavour to impart consolation to your lacerated breast. Heaven grant my wishes and I shall be comparatively happy."

These thoughts imparted some comfort to her, and she shortly afterwards composed herself to sleep.

Three more days elapsed without anything occurring to disturb them, or to excite any apprehensions in their breasts.

The village was quickly restored to tranquillity after the late alarming affray, and no one had any cause to fear that anything unfavourable would result from it, as the total destruction of the ruffians who had attacked them, would cause it to remain a profound secret.

But Omelia's impatience to depart on her journey, suffered no abatement, and she frequently questioned Mirza on the subject and inquired whether he was trying to form any plan for the gratification of her wishes, to which he replied in the affirmative.

"I must still desire you to wait patiently, and to leave everything to me, Omelia," he said, "and you will have no cause to regret your confidence. The utmost precaution is necessary, as you must be aware, to enable us to proceed with any chance of safety and success."

"Most true," coincided Omelia, "and I know I can depend upon you, good Mirza, but still you must make every allowance for my anxiety, as every moment of delay appears an age."

"I will lose no time," remarked Mirza, "and no doubt in a day or two the opportunity you so much desire will present itself.

In the meantime, you will make all the necessary preparation."

"I will do so," replied our heroine, "and I must again return my acknowledgements for the troble you put yourself to, and the deep interest you take in my fate."

"I require no thanks, Omelia, and I need not again assure you that there is nothing I would not do to serve you."

The conversation here dropped, and Omelia felt animated with renewed hope, which she trusted would not end in disappointment.

There was only one cause of regret which our heroine experienced at the prospect of leaving the village, and that was her separation from Naomie, whom she had learned to look upon almost with the regard of a sister, and that feeling the latter warmly reciprocated, and would willingly have accompanied her had circumstances permitted her to do so.

The following day after the above conversation had taken place, Mirza, having been absent from home since the morning, suddenly entered the bungalow, where Naomie and Omelia were seated in conversation, and his looks showed that he had something particular to communicate, and the heart of our heroine palpitated with curiosity and expectation.

"At length, Omelia," he observed, "the opportunity which you so much desire, presents itself; and I have made secure arrangements—which I have no doubt you will approve of—for your secret departure from the village, at daybreak in the morning."

"Oh, thanks, thanks," said Omelia, joyfully.

"To-morrow morning?" repeated Naomie, with a look of melancholy regret, "so soon?"

"Believe me, dear Naomie," observed our heroine, affectionately, "there is no one who more sincerely laments the necessity of the separation than myself, but I trust that it will not be for long. Tell me, good Mirza, for you are well aware how anxious I am to know, what are the arrangements you have made?"

"Listen," he answered; "to-morrow morning at an early hour, some friends of mine, although in far superiour circumstances to myself, and in whom I can place every confidence, proceed on a journey of some distance, travelling on the back of an elephant, which they have hired for the occasion. They will pass by the end of the village, before any of the inhabitants are stirring, and will proceed some distance on the route it is necessary for us to pursue. Knowing that I could trust them implicitly, I ventured to entrust to them the particulars of your history, Omelia, and your wishes. Having heard of your noble and heroic conduct, they deeply sympathise with you, and

262   THE SEPOY'S DAUGHTER.

readily offered to enter into any plans, and
to render you all the assistance in their
power."

"Oh, Mirza," said our heroine, "this is
indeed kind of you, and seems to offer all
the opportunity and security that I could
desire. Pray proceed."

"Seated in the howdah, in the midst of
the travellers, and accompanied by myself
and Murad, you will be concealed from
observation," continued Mirza, "and will
have nothing to fear. In this manner you
will be conveyed on your journey as far as
our friends have to proceed on your way,
where on leaving them, I will make all the
arrangements that may seem most advisable
for the safe prosecution of the remainder of
your journey. Do you approve of my plan,
Omelia?"

"How can I do otherwise?" answered
our heroine; "you say that you can depend
upon the fidelity of your friends, Mirza, and
therefore do I entertain every hope of success.
Fortune appears to smile upon me, but deeply
do I regret that it is not my power to reward
you for your unexampled exertions to serve
me."

"Reward!" repeated Mirza, with a look
of offended pride, and in a tone of mild reproach; "surely Omelia cannot do me the
injustice to suppose that mercenary motives
guide my conduct towards those whom I
wish to serve, especially one whom I so
warmly esteem as yourself. I should hate
and despise myself if it were so. The only
reward I seek, is the approval of my own
conscience."

"Pardon me, Mirza," said Omelia, "if in
the warmth and gratitude of my feelings, I
express myself wrong. I need not assure
you, that it was the farthest from my
thoughts to utter anything that might offend
you."

"Enough," returned Mirza, "I can
sincerely believe you, and need no apology.
To-morrow morning then, as soon as daylight appears in the horizon you will be ready
to depart?"

Omelia replied in the affirmative.

"And yet," she added, after a moment's
reflection, and looking affectionately at
Naomie, who had not spoken a word during
the time that her brother had been explaining the plan of our heroine's departure from
the village, though the deep melancholy expression of her features plainly showed the
melancholy thoughts that were passing in
her mind, "it grieves me sincerely to have
to part from your amiable sister, from whom
I have ever experienced such affectionate
kindness and esteem, and I should only be
too happy did circumstances permit her to
accompany me. Dear Naomie, I know you
will not fail sometimes to bestow a kindly

thought on the wandering Omelia, when she
is far away."

"Oh, no, Omelia," replied Naomie,
fervently, "I can never cease to remember
you with the warmest feelings of regard, and
to pray for your welfare and happiness."

"Happiness!" sighed our heroine, "that
can never again be mine, till I am restored
to my beloved Stanley, and should he have
perished, which sometimes my foreboding
fears predict that he has, life will henceforth
become an insupportable burthen, of which
I care not how soon I am relieved."

"Encourage not such gloomy thoughts,
Omelia," said Mirza, "but live in hopes of
the future, and I trust that they will not be
disappointed."

"I will endeavour to do so," said our
heroine, "and in those hopes seek consolation for the troubles I have hitherto had to
endure, and fortitude to meet those that
may yet be in store for me."

Murad now rejoined them, and after some
further conversation, Omelia and Naomie
retired to another apartment that they might
the more freely communicate their thoughts
to each other.

We need not say with what mingled feelings of hope and fear our heroine looked
forward to her departure in the morning, for
although the assurances of Mirza, regarding
his friends, were calculated to inspire her
with every confidence, she could not but feel
a certain timidity at being placed among
persons who were entire strangers to her.

Business connected with the journey of
the following day, called Mirza and Murad
again away from home in the course of the
afternoon, and as they did not return at the
time expected in the evening, the weather
too, being remarkably fine, Omelia and
Naomie for the last time together, took their
favourite ramble to the hills to enjoy once
more the beauties of the magnificent prospect
commanded therefrom, revealed with such
effect in the broad moonlight, and beneath
the bright rays of the countless myriads of
twinkling stars that glittered in the firmament.

They had passed some time in contemplating the lovely scene, and engaged in conversation, and were about to retrace their steps
towards home, when they were startled and
alarmed by observing the shadow of a human
form upon the ground, although they had
heard no footstep, and turning hastily round
their surprise and terror may be imagined
when they beheld the tall and muscular
figure of a man, dressed as a sepoy, standing
behind them, and who had evidently from
his fixed attitude been listening for some
time to their conversation.

Naomie could not help giving utterance to
a cry of alarm, and they were both about to

hurry from the spot, when the man grasped the wrist of Omelia roughly, and arrested her in the purpose, at the same time exclaiming :—

"Stop, girl, you and I must have a word or two before we part."

The voice of the man struck our heroine as being strangely and painfully familiar to her, but she mustered up all her courage, and indignantly demanded :—

"Who are you, man? and why do you thus insolently address me, and seek to detain me?"

"This meeting is quite as unexpected as it is fortunate," replied the man; "do you not know me, Omelia?"

At the mention of her name, and again in those familiar tones, Omelia started with astonishment, and by the light of the moon examined his features more minutely. That astonishment was increased, to which was added a feeling of alarm, when in the savage and repulsive countenance of the man, she recognised one of the most brutal of the colleagues of her late father and the villain Allyghur, and whose eyes were fixed with an expression of deadly malice full upon her face.

"Ah!" she exclaimed, "villain, I do know you now. You are the friend and associate in crime of the miscreant Allyghur—who has paid the penalty of his guilt—and consequently my mortal foe. But though I am well acquainted with your bloodthirsty character, and that feelings of hatred and revenge excite your guilty mind against me, think not to intimidate me, or that I will tremble in your presence. Unhand me, ruffian, I command, and suffer me to proceed on my way, or you may have cause to repent your insolence and daring!"

"Ha! ha! ha!" laughed the scoundrel, scornfully, "fool! so you think to play the heroine with me, as you have hitherto done with others. Beware! this is a lonely spot, there is no one at hand to render you any assistance, and you see that I am aroused. You understand me?"

Naomie once more uttered an exclamation of terror, and, scarcely knowing what she did, was about to fly from the spot, with the vain hope of being able to obtain some assistance, when the ruffian hastily drew a pistol from his belt, and presenting it at her, exclaimed, in a voice, which showed that he was fully prepared to put his inhuman threat into execution :—

"Hold, woman! dare but to utter one more cry, or to move from the spot, and your life shall instantly pay the forfeit of your daring!"

Naomie shuddered with horror and despair, and did not dare to attempt to disobey, and the villain still retaining his fierce hold

of the wrist of Omelia, and turning upon her a look of exultation, said :—

"I repeat, proud Omelia, you who are the acknowledged friend of your country's bitterest enemies, the accursed Feringhees; you who set a father's authority at defiance, and would not have hesitated to consign him to death; I repeat, I say, that this is a fortunate and unexpected meeting—though I have long anxiously wished for, and sought for it—and I will not neglect, believe me, to take advantage of it. Nay, frown not, nor fix upon me those looks of scorn, for I heed them not."

"Villain! daring cowardly villain!" cried our heroine, in a tone of unflinching firmness, though she could not help feeling some degree of alarm at his threats, knowing his desperate character; "what is your guilty purpose with me?"

"Hark ye, Omelia," he replied, at the same time fixing upon her beauteous countenance a peculiar look which excited her utmost disgust, "I will be candid with you. Though the conduct which you have hitherto pursued makes you my foe, and should excite my most deadly and implacable hatred and revenge, your charms have inspired a different passion in my breast, which I would fain gratify, and which—"

"Heartless, shameless monster!" interrupted the disgusted and indignant maiden, her eyes flashing with resentment; "is every spark of manhood extinguished within your guilty breast? Release your hold, I again command, and begone, and no longer pollute and insult my ears, with so odious and brutal a confession."

"Nay," said the ruffian, "think not to intimidated me from my purpose by your looks of scorn and detestation. This way, you must with me. Woman," he added, speaking to Naomie in a stern and determined tone, "dare not move from the spot where you now stand, or to raise any alarm, though there is no one near to hear you. Now, Omelia."

He endeavoured to force her away as he spoke towards a more gloomy and retired spot, near the foot of the hill, and his eyes fully expressed his monstrous thoughts and designs, but our heroine made a violent, and resolute resistance, and in doing so, the pistol with which the miscreant had menaced the life of Naomie, fell from his hand, at the same moment, Omelia, by a sudden exertion of strength, released herself from his hold, and stooping hastily down, she got possession of the pistol, which laying one hand on the arm of the trembling Naomie, she presented at his head, at the same time exclaiming in a resolute voice :—

"Cowardly, unmanly ruffian! providence has not deserted me, it is my turn to triumph now. Move you from the spot whereon you stand, or attempt to follow or molest myself and my friend, and take the consequences with which I now threaten you."

A frightful oath escaped the lips of the man, and he made a slight movement to approach her, but she again raised the pistol, and cried—

"Scorn not my threats, unless you would rush upon certain and instant death, for I am determined."

"Curses light upon this accident," cried the infuriated ruffian; "but you will not dare to—"

"I dare do anything in the defence of honour, and to punish the miscreant who would brutally seek to outrage it," boldly returned our heroine, and still laying one hand on the arm of Naomie, they slowly retreated down the hill, the ruffian being afraid to follow, but standing transfixed to the spot in confusion and dismay.

They gained the bottom of the hill, and looking up, found that the man had disappeared. Fervently returning their thanks to providence for their miraculous deliverance, they then hastily retraced their steps to the village.

They had not proceeded far on their way, when they were hurriedly met by Mirza and Murad, who having returned home, and finding Omelia and Naomie absent, became alarmed, and immediately started forth in search of them.

Seeing the pistol in Omelia's hand, and noticing the agitation of her manner and looks, as also those of Naomie, they eagerly inquired what had happened, which our heroine related in as few words as she could.

"Is it possible?" exclaimed the astonished Mirza; "the scoundrel! how wonderful and how fortunate was your escape, Omelia, and all owing to your own intrepidity. But 'tis a pity you did not inflict that punishment upon the brutal ruffian which he so justly merited. But come, let us return home, where we may the better discuss this strange and alarming adventure."

Omelia and Naomie made use of no observation, but complied, although the former could not but feel greatly excited and somewhat alarmed at what had taken place, and in which feelings Naomie also warmly participated.

On their arrival at the bungalow, Omelia in answer to the anxious inquiries of Mirza and Murad, entered into further particulars of the adventure, and the threats and observation of the ruffian, which excited their utmost disgust and indignation.

"The villain," remarked Mirza, "would that myself and Murad had happened to have arrived at the spot at the critical moment, he should not have escaped so easily.

However, I cannot sufficiently admire your courage and presence of mind, Omelia, which completely defeated the designs of the cowardly miscreant."

"True," returned Omelia, "and most grateful am I to providence that enabled me to do so. But I fear that he will be goaded on by feelings of revenge, and that, should he become aware of my having been concealed here, and have any of his guilty associates lurking in the neighbourhood, you may have to suffer for it, or that during your absence from home some harm may befall Naomie."

"Nay, Omelia," said Mirza, "do not thus unnecessarily alarm yourself; it seems to me that it was mere accident which caused yourself and the fellow to meet, but should your fears that he has associates at hand prove to be correct, and he should with them attempt any outrage, during my absence from home, Naomie will be safe under the protection of the brave villagers, who will not fail to defeat any villainous designs that they may have in contemplation.

"Heaven grant that they may do so," said our heroine fervently, "but I sincerely wish that this circumstance had not taken place, as it will make me uncomfortable and apprehensive for Naomie on my journey."

"Fear not, dear Omelia," remarked Naomie, assuming all the calmness and confidence she could, "providence will, I trust, protect me from every threatened danger, and as my brother has justly observed, I know I can depend upon the fidelity of our friends the villagers, in case of any emergency. The observations of the ruffian towards you, I confess alarmed me, but as he is probably alone, he will doubtless not think it prudent to persist in his villanous designs, especially when he finds that you are no longer in the village, if indeed he should be aware that you have here been concealed."

"But he may make the circumstance known," said Omelia, "and bring down the vengeance of the rebels upon the peaceful inhabitants at some future period."

"Let not that thought disturb you," returned Mirza, "for knowing the danger which may threaten, they will be upon their guard. But come, Omelia, the hour grows late, and it is necessary that you should be stirring at the earliest time in the morning, it is fit that you should at once retire to rest."

To this our heroine agreed, and they at once separated for the night.

Naomie, who looked forward with the most painful feelings of regret to the few short hours that must elapse ere they must be separated for an indefinite period, if indeed they should be ever destined to meet again, at the desire of Omelia—who did not feel disposed to retire to bed just yet—accom-

panied her to her chamber, so that they might for a short time interchange their thoughts with each other, and take that farewell, which they would have such a limited time to do in the morning; and they continued in affectionate conversation with each other for more than an hour.

In spite of all the arguments which had been used, both by Mirza and Murad, our heroine could not but continue to entertain the apprehension that some harm would ensue from the adventure of the evening, and she regretted that herself and Naomie had not remained in the bungalow during the absence of Mirza and Murad, instead of being so imprudent as to take their customary walk.

Naomie concealed her own fears and forebodings, which were equal to those of Omelia, as well as she could, and endeavoured to reassure the latter, and to dismiss her apprehensions, and at length after joining their prayers together for mutual happiness and prosperity, and the merciful interposition of the Supreme, in the event of any threatened danger, they separated for the night.

But still Omelia did not feel inclined to retire to rest, but sitting by the open window —for the night was close and sultry—became lost in the multitude of conflicting thoughts that crowded upon her busy brain.

A large tree grew immediately before the window, and the light breeze that was stirring scarcely disturbed the foliage. All was still around; nothing could be more calm and tranquil than the hour, and the moon shone as brightly, and the stars glittered as radiantly in the clear firmament, as ever.

No. 34.

A feeling of gentle melancholy stole over the senses of Omelia, and all the strange and varied events of the past rushed vividly upon her memory, imparting mingled joy and sorrow, whilst she anticipated the future that was in store for her with sanguine hope, not, however, unalloyed with doubt and fear.

Fondly and principally did her thoughts wander to her beloved Stanley, and mentally and fervently she prayed to heaven that he still lived, and that her footsteps might be guided to him.

She was aroused from these meditations by a rustling sound, something like the hurried tread of footsteps, and quickly casting her eyes below, she was almost convinced that she beheld the shadow of a human form, glide like a ghost past the tree, and disappear in the darkness.

She felt alarmed, but immediately chided herself for her weakness, as if even she had not been deceived by her imagination, surely there was nothing remarkable in the circumstance, as it was probable that it was only one of the villagers returning to his dwelling.

She, however, could not entirely dismiss her fears, and she strained her eyes as far as she could in the direction which she believed the supposed form to have taken, but without beholding any object that was calculated to excite her curiosity or suspicion; the coast was perfectly clear, and trying to persuade herself that she must have been mistaken, and knowing also that it was necessary to endeavour to snatch a few hours repose, in order to prepare herself for the journey in the morning, she closed the window, securing it at the same time, and then threw herself on the bed, but without undressing, and without extinguishing the light.

She was just dropping off into a gentle slumber, when she was aroused by a noise at the window, as if caused by some person attempting to force it open, and raising herself hastily on her elbow, and casting her eyes towards it, an involuntary exclamation of astonishment and alarm escaped her, for she distinctly saw the face of a man, between the branches of the tree, glaring in the chamber, and full upon her.

But in a moment it was gone, and Omelia starting to the back of the room, notwithstanding her wonted courage and presence of mind, became transfixed with amazement and terror.

This time she was certain that she had not been mistaken, and from the brief sight which had been permitted her, she was almost convinced that the features were those of the ruffian who had so alarmed herself and Naomie in the evening.

It was several minutes before she could sufficiently recover herself from her confusion, to decide how to act under such strange, suspicious, and alarming circumstances, but at length she again ventured to walk to the window, and without unfastening it, in case of any threatened danger, to look as far as she could beyond it.

No object met her sight, and the utmost silence reigned around.

Still, in spite of all her efforts, she could not dismiss her apprehensions of some approaching danger, and she feared to remain alone.

She opened the room door, and listening, she heard the voices of Mirza and Murad below in conversation, and was therefore convinced that they had not retired to rest.

She resolved to seek their presence, to inform them of what had taken place, and to put them on their guard, in case of any sudden surprise, and taking the lamp in her hand, she descended the stairs, and knocked at the door of the room in which they were sitting.

It was opened by Naomie, who evinced no little surprise at beholding her, and observing the agitation of her manner, which was shared in by Mirza and Murad, who eagerly inquired what had occurred to alarm her.

Our heroine briefly informed them, and their astonishment may be readily imagined.

"This extraordinary circumstance is indeed most alarming and suspicious," said Mirza, " but are you certain that you did not suffer your imagination to deceive you, Omelia?"

"Oh, no, it was impossible that I could do so," she answered, "I had not extinguished the light, as I have before observed, so that I had a clear and distinct view of the face of the man, as he looked eagerly into the room, but it vanished immediately on my giving utterance to the exclamation of astonishment which such a strange appearance, and at such an hour of the night, naturally elicited."

"And think you," interrogated Murad, " that you should know the features of the man—if such indeed they were—again?"

"Oh, yes," replied Omelia, "they are present to my imagination at this moment, and I can never forget them. They were I am convinced those of the ruffian who so outraged my feelings this evening."

"The villain!" exclaimed Mirza, " what could have been his design?"

"I shudder to think."

"At any rate, should he make any attempt which I do not think is likely, since you discovered him, Omelia, since we are now put upon our guard, we shall be prepared to counteract it. Quiet your fears, and retire with Naomie to her chamber; myself and Murad will remain up to keep watch."

Omelia returned her thanks, and her and Naomie retired to the chamber of the latter, leaving her husband and brother, well armed, to guard the bungalow.

Omelia, to the anxious inquiries of Naomie, positively delared that it was no dream which had thus alarmed her, and also her firm conviction that it was the man whom they had met in the evening, and the latter could not doubt her, and expressed her belief that it had been his design to enter the chamber, but his plans were fortunately frustrated, and it was not likely that he would repeat the attempt.

Omelia appeared to coincide with this opinion, but she was far from satisfied, and could not but entertain strong fears that some unpleasant and dangerous consequences either to herself or her friends would follow this adventure.

Naomie and her companion continued to converse upon this perplexing subject for some time longer before they retired to bed, and listened attentively to catch the slightest sound which might be calculated to excite suspicion; for Omelia could not rest satisfied —notwithstanding she had agreed to the opinion of Naomie—that the ruffian would so readily abandon his design, whatever it might be; and she feared that he had colleagues at hand, or he would not have ventured on so daring an enterprise.

But all remained perfectly quiet, and dismissing their apprehensions, Omelia and Naomie sought their couch.

At an early hour in the morning they were aroused by Mirza knocking at their chamber door, and informing Omelia that it was almost time to depart; and having hastily dressed themselves, they entered the room where Mirza and Murad were sitting.

And now came the trying moment of parting between the two amiable friends, Omelia and Naomie, and a most affectionate one it was, for the similarity of their dispositions, and associating as they did in ideas, had formed a sisterly attachment between them.

"We shall meet again, dear Naomie," said our heroine, as she affectionately embraced her, "I am convinced that we shall meet again, and under far happier circumstances."

"Heaven grant that your predictions may be verified, dear Omelia," replied Naomie, "and I will endeavour to believe that they will. May the great spirit watch over and protect you, and prosper you on your journey, and in the accomplishment of your fondest wishes. Adieu, my best of friends."

"Farewell," cried Omelia, emphatically, and returning her affectionate kiss, "farewell, and believe that I will never cease to remember you in my prayers."

They once more embraced, and all then being in readiness, our heroine was conducted from the house by Mirza and Murad, they having first ascertained that there was no one about in the village.

Naomie stood at the door and watched them anxiously till they disappeared in the distance, and she then re-entered her dwelling with a sad heart.

It was scarcely yet daylight, but the weather was particularly fine. Omelia and her friends soon emerged from the village, and had not proceeded far, when they beheld the expected party approaching, borne by the elephant, and accompanied by attendants.

It consisted of three natives of the better order, and one English gentleman, who, however, kept himself studiously out of sight, seated behind his companions in the howdah.

Omelia was received by her new friends and companions with every mark of kindness and respect, and Mirza and Murad were about to assist her into the howdah, when she uttered an exclamation of terror as the report of a pistol was heard, and the bullet was so near reaching its deadly aim, that it passed through a portion of her dress without in the least injuring her.

With a burst of indignation, Mirza and the others looked in the direction from whence the pistol was discharged, in order to discover the cowardly assassin, and beheld a man retreating hastily in the distance, and who as well as our heroine and Mirza could distinguish ere he disappeared, they believed it to be the same ruffian who had before molested her.

It would, however, have been useless to attempt to pursue him, if there had even been time, therefore congratulating Omelia —who evinced her usual firmness and presence of mind—on her providential escape, Mirza and Murad assisted her into the howdah, the journey was commenced, the spirits of our heroine becoming more exhilarated by the conversation of her friends the farther they proceeded, and her mind diverted and charmed by the beautiful scenery through which they travelled, and which met her gaze on every side.

After journeying for some miles the friends of Mirza being compelled to pursue another route, our heroine and her two companions separated from them with regret, and had to proceed on foot, but Mirza informed her it would not be far, when they would arrive at a large village or town, where they would be sure to be received with every hospitality and friendship, the more especially as it was the annual Mahomedan festival of the *Buckra Eade*.

This festival which is confined to the followers of Mahomed, and, as stated above, is called the *Buckra Eade*, or goat sacrifice. Claiming to be descendants of Abraham,

through his son Ishmael, whom they avor to
have been chosen for the offering to the
Almighty, and not Isaac, they celebrate the
event. It is commemorated by the sacrifice
of particular animals: camels, sheep, goats,
kids, or lambs, according to each persons
means; this is supposed to answer a double
purpose, not only honouring the memory of
Abraham and Ishmael, but the sacrifices
assisting in a time of great need.

It is supposed that the entrance to Paradise is guarded by a bridge made of a scythe,
or some instrument equally sharp, and
affording as unstable a footing. The followers of the prophet are required to skate
or swim over this passage, and it will be
attended with more or less difficulty, according to the degree of favour they have obtained in the sight of heaven.

The truly pious will be wafted over in
safety, but the undeserving must struggle
many times, and be often cut down in the
attempt, before they can attain the opposite
side. In this extremity, it is imagined that
the same number and kind of animals,
which being clean, and esteemed fitting for
sacrifice, they have offered up at the celebration of the *Buckra Eade* will be in waiting
to convey them in safety along the perilous
passage of the bridge.

Under this belief, the richer classes of
Mahomedans supply their poorer brethren
with goats and sheep for the sacrifice, a
work of charity, incited by the purest motives,
and to which, if not possessing all the efficacy ascribed to it, at least furnishes the
poor man's home with an ample and a welcome feast; for though poverty compels the
lower classes of Mussulmans to imitate the
Hindoos in the frugality of a vegetable meal
they never refuse meat when it is procurable.

Under these favourable circumstances,
therefore, the travellers as they had anticipated found no difficulty in procuring accommodation till the following day, and
everything that they required; and after
partaking of necessary refreshment, Omelia
separated from her two kind friends—they
undertaking to procure some means of conveyance on the following morning—and retired to rest.

Her hopes were now revived, and she
began to feel every confidence in the future
for something seemed to assure her that
Stanley still lived, and that they would ere
long again be restored to each other.

CHAPTER LXIV.

FLORA MELVILLE'S MADNESS AND ATTEMPTED SUICIDE.

The unfortunate Flora Melville still remained with her friends in misfortune in
the old fort, in the same deplorable situation
in which we left her in a previous chapter,
and was watched with all the care and attention that the circumstances would admit,
still the most serious results were too reasonably to be apprehended.

Reason had indeed for a time completely
abandoned its seat, and in her delirium the
melancholy observations and lamentations
she gave utterance to were enough to move
even the most insensible heart to pity.

Her late father, Stanley, and Omelia were
alternately the subjects of her wild ravings,
while at other times she would subside into
a gloomy silence, with occasional sobs and
tears, which were, if possible, even more
piteous to listen to than her most violent
outbursts of insanity.

With what feelings of anguish, sorrow,
and regret did young Meadows and his
father, particularly the former, behold the
poor girl's sufferings, and how dismal were
their forebodings.

Notwithstanding more hopeless than ever
was the young man's passion for his fair
cousin, he felt it daily hourly increase, and
he looked forward to the probable fatal results of her malady with a feeling of dread
which he could not conquer, for then he felt
assured that all his hopes of future happiness would be destroyed for ever.

His father was well aware of the sentiments he could not help encouraging for
Flora, sentiments that had never found any
responsive feeling in her breast, and he
could not but deeply regret the fatal consequences that were likely to befal him through
that unfortunate passion. But he endeavoured to arouse him from his gloom and
melancholy, and to inspire him with the
best hopes he could, but with very little if
any success.

"Poor girl," he would observe, "I fear
that long suffering has obtained too strong a
hold upon her intellect and delicate constitution ever to be removed; and can I witness her misery, view the wreck of one so
good and lovely, and to whom my heart is so
fondly devoted, without emotions of the
deepest anguish and despair? It is impossible, and the more I endeavour to stifle my
feelings, and regain firmness and consolation.
the more powerful does my anguish become.
May heaven look down upon her with mercy,
and realise those hopes I would fain but
dare not entertain."

"To those wishes, I need not say that I most heartily respond," replied his father, "and no one can more deeply regret the unfortunate circumstances that have led to the poor girl's present malady; still it was most fortunate that providence guided her footsteps here, or she must certainly have perished, and that, too, in the most frightful manner."

"Most true," coincided his son, "and I shudder to think what that fate would have been. Would that she might recover, and that I could at least excite similar sentiments in her breast, to those that glow within mine own; but alas, I fear that that can never be; consequently I can never again look forward to happiness."

"Be firm, be patient," said Mr. Meadows, and all may yet turn out much better than you now anticipate."

"Would that your words might prove prophetic," returned the young man; "but alas, I dare not indulge in ideas that there is too much reason to fear will prove delusive. Oh, Flora, could you but in your moments of reason, should that indeed ever again be restored to you, know the real ardour, virtue and integrity of that affection which animates my breast towards you, and the bitter anguish which rends my heart to think that my passion can hope to meet with no return, surely you would pity me."

"Nay, Alfred," said his father, remonstratively, "surely this is a weakness quite unworthy of your manly nature. You possess, I'm sure, your fair and unfortunate cousin's warmest esteem, but blame her not if her heart cannot feel any more tender sentiment towards you. Rather struggle against your fatal passion, and endeavour to stifle it in your breast."

"Oh, my father," replied Alfred, impatiently, "how easy is it to advise, but I feel the impossibility of the task you would impose upon me."

"Poor girl," remarked Mr. Meadows, "does she not deserve your warmest sympathy, for unfortunately she loves one with all the strength, the unconquerable strength of woman's purest and most fervent passion, who returns it not."

"Ah, Edward Stanley," ejaculated the young man, in accents of the deepest sorrow and regret, "oh, how I envy him the possession of that heart to which he is so cold and indifferent."

"Edward Stanley is a noble-hearted young man," said Mr. Meadows, "generous as he is brave and honourable, and I wonder not that he should have made so favourable, so powerful an impression upon a heart so susceptible as Flora's. But no blame whatever can attach to him, for although at all times treating her with every respect and friendship, he has never given any encouragement to her passion. He loves the beautiful Indian maiden, Omelia, who returns his love with the greatest fervour, and whose virtues render her every way deserving of him. Edward Stanley, I repeat, is a noble young man, and worthy your warmest admiration, emulation, and esteem, Alfred."

"True, most true," coincided the latter, "he is all that you have described him to be, and I honour him for it; yet, in spite of myself, I cannot help envying him the place he holds in my cousin's heart."

"Beware, Alfred," said his father, seriously, "give not way to such thoughts and feelings as these, for you know the fatal consequences they might insidiously produce. Again, I say, you must endeavour to conquer your love, since it is entirely hopeless; and should Flora be restored to convalescence—which I yet hope and trust that she may—you must never more repeat those sentiments that you know to be so painful to her, especially when, Heaven knows, she has so much to grieve and distract her mind already."

Alfred returned no answer to this, for although he well knew the justice and wisdom of his father's advice and admonition, he too keenly felt the difficulty, the almost insurmountable difficulty, of complying with it.

The subject dropped.

And with increasing anguish and feelings of despair, did Alfred Meadows watch almost hourly the progress of his hapless cousin's fatal malady, and anxiously but vainly look for some favourable change; and with what agony, what heartrending agony did he listen to the wild, the wandering, and melancholy observations that escaped her lips, and the frequent allusions, which in the paroxysm of her insanity, she made to Edward Stanley, whom she sometimes seemed to fancy was present, and that he returned her love.

This tortured him more than all, and often was he compelled to rush abruptly from the room, in order to conceal the intensity of his anguish, and to give vent to his excited feelings alone.

Sometimes after he had been watching her with earnest emotion and most heartfelt sympathy, and trying to awaken her dormant reason, she would suddenly appear to recognise him, and shrinking from him with a look of repugnance, as though he were her greatest enemy, she would load him with reproaches for persisting in his fatal passion when he knew that she had no heart to give him in return.

These paroxysms, however, were only of brief duration, and she would then burst into tears, and in the most piteous accents implore his forgiveness, and that he would cease to remember her with any other feelings than those of respect and sympathy.

To attempt to pourtray the feelings of Alfred Meadows on such dismal and painful occasions as these would be a fruitless task, and he would again be compelled to rush into solitude, that he might give unrestrained indulgence to his emotions.

To add to his grief, the situation of himself and his unfortunate companions threatened to become alarming; the persons dwelling in the neighbourhood of the fort, who had hitherto so generously sympathised with them, and supplied their wants as far as was in their power, feared that ere long they would be compelled to discontinue their assistance as their humble means were daily becoming more limited.

This prospect was indeed most disheartening, but the more so as it was feared that the place of their retreat was becoming known, and that the worst consequences might be anticipated to themselves and to those who had acted in so friendly a manner towards them.

This caused them all, but especially Alfred Meadows and his father, the most gloomy apprehensions, for in the present frightful state of the country, every part being beset by hordes of bloodthirsty miscreants, who every day became more cruel and determined in the hideous work of extermination, what was to become of them? Whither could they go—how escape the fate which had befallen so many of their unfortunate countrymen and countrywomen? And then, how was it possible to remove poor Flora Melville in her present deplorable and helpless condition?

There was no alternative left but for them to remain and fortify themselves in the best manner they could in the old fort to the last extremity.

And in this manner matters remained for several days longer, they being often placed in the most painful difficulties.

Flora's malady, however, fortunately assumed a milder form, and there were times that she was perfectly rational; but the melancholy which the terrible afflictions to which she had lately been subjected had caused to take possession of her mind, it was too much to be feared could never be eradicated.

It was in such brief intervals as these that the poor girl fully recognised her cousin, and seemed to appreciate the sedulous attentions of himself and his father; but did he ever venture to allude in the most remote manner to his unfortunate passion, a most fearful change would in a moment come over her, and she would relapse into her wildest paroxysms, which it was difficult to calm.

One day Alfred Meadows sought her presence in the little room, where she was usually accustomed to sit in her more calm moments, and where it was considered most prudent to leave her alone

He was surprised to find that she was not there, and as no one had seen her for some time, he became alarmed, and immediately proceeded to search for her in every part of the building which was accessible, but to no purpose, and his surprise and apprehension increased.

Within the walls of the old fort—that were very lofty—was a garden, which had formerly been arranged and kept in order with great care and taste, and even now, in the wild luxuriance of its wreck, presented something pleasing and refreshing to the sight.

It was to this place, then, that poor Flora had rambled, in one of her most painful moods, on the day in question. Wild indeed was the expression of her pale but handsome features, alarming her gestures and demeanour, and to render it still more so, she carried an old rusty dagger in her hand, which she had accidentally found in one of the rooms, but which she played with in a listless manner.

Her eyes wandered vacantly for some time around the place, then she stooped, and with much apparent delight—for her wild but merry laugh rang upon the air—gathered several of the wild flowers that there grew in profusion, and seating herself upon a bank, and gazing at them and playing with them like a child for a few minutes, she suddenly, in a voice of the most touching plaintiveness, broke forth into the following portion of a simple song, which she had been accustomed to sing in happier days,

"Sweet pretty flowers, fair blooming flowers,
　I've gather'd from their parent stem;
From valley green, from shady bowers,
　To form a fragrant diadem.
　　　　　　Sweet pretty flowers.

"And they shall deck fair maidens' brow,
　And blossom in her silken hair;
Or nestle in her breast of snow,
　For sunlight midst the snow is there.
　　　　　　Sweet pretty flowers."

Again the poor girl's strange mad laugh rang around, and she continued to play with the flowers with childish simplicity.

It was at this moment that Alfred Meadows arrived at the spot, the wild tones of her voice having reached his ears, but fearful of too much exciting her if he suddenly presented himself before her, he paused behind, to observe her for a few moments without being seen by her.

His agitation, while he did so, may be imagined, and the wild mirth she evinced was even more torturing to him, if possible, than the moments of her most violent paroxysms.

But at length after having picked the leaves and petals from the flowers she had gathered, and cast them angrily away, she suddenly started from the bank on which she had been sitting, and in a voice most painfully changed she cried:—

"No, no, they are false to me, they die and wither at my touch, like all things dear to me, and leave me alone to weep and bewail their loss. 'Twas even so my aged father did, at the time when I most needed his love and protection, 'twas so that Stanley left me to loneliness and scorn. There is no real affection or gratitude in the world. All, all, hate and despise me, why then should I remain here? Why do I not hasten where the flowers bloom for ever, and all is sunlight?"

"Oh, God!" sighed Alfred; "what heart-rending, what insupportable agony is this!"

Silently, cautiously he approached nearer to her, for he saw that she had advanced towards a deep well, and the attitude she had assumed, and the excitement under which she laboured, aroused his fears and suspicions.

For a moment or two she stood and gazed intently down the well, he saw that she clutched something resolutely in her hand, but what it was he could not distinguish. He continued to advance with the same cautious step till he stood close behind her, and he then beheld to his alarm, that what she held in her hand was the rusty dagger before mentioned.

The next moment with a frantic laugh, she raised her arm in the air, and was about to plunge the deadly weapon in her bosom, when her cousin, with an exclamation of horror, grasped her wrist, and prevented the fatal deed.

"Flora, dear Flora," he cried, "oh, what in the wild frenzy of your wandering senses would you do? Nay, look not so upon me, for it racks my heart to behold it. Do you not know me?"

"Ha! ha!" laughed the poor girl, "know you? Yes, for he who would rob the noble Stanley of that fond heart which he alone possess; but you shall not tempt me to be false to him, although he loves another, and can never be mine. Away! away! leave me.'

As she thus spoke she endeavoured to break from him, but in a state of mind too agonising for utterance, he continued to hold her, and after struggling for a minute or two, and rending the air with her frantic shrieks and ravings, unable longer to resist the power of her excited feelings she fainted in his arms.

For a short time the wretched young man stood transfixed to the spot, supporting his fair insensible burthen in his arms, and gazing on her with looks of the most unmitigated sorrow and despair.

"Lovely but unfortunate girl," he sighed, and in a voice half choked with the violence of his emotions; "oh when will these dreadful, these cruel sufferings have an end? Heaven be merciful to her, and assist her in the midst of trials certainly too great for human nature to endure."

He ventured to press a fervent kiss upon the poor girl's pale lips, and then raising her in his arms, carried her into the fort, and having seen her placed under the kind and sympathising care of two of his female friends and companions in misfortune, he hastened from the room to give vent to the anguish of his thoughts and feelings alone.

He threw himself on a seat and buried his face in his hands, and for sometime completely abandoned himself to the wild and torturing emotions that distracted his brain.

Then he hastily arose, and paced the room in which he was with hurried and agitated steps, giving utterance at the same time to the most dismal lamentations and observations of heartfelt sorrow and regret. Seldom, if ever, had his mind been in such a state of excitement before, but how truly thankful did he feel to providence for making him the instrument of saving her from the awful and untimely fate which she was in her madness about to rush upon.

How every word that she had uttered had penetrated to his heart, and if he had indeed ventured to indulge in hope before, how terribly did those words now confirm his despair, even though they were spoken in all the frenzy of madness.

How sadly he dwelt upon her allusions to Stanley, which so plainly showed, notwithstanding that he returned not her passion, that his image was so firmly fixed in his heart that neither time nor circumstances could remove it.

"Madman that I must be," he soliloquised, "ever to aspire to the heart of one so lovely, so good, and innocent, and of whom I am so unworthy. I deserve to be punished for my presumption, and have no right to complain. But can I ever stifle the passion which glows within my breast towards her, and consumes me? No, no, it is impossible. Even though the encouragement of that fatal passion should bring me to a premature death, it must hold its empire in my heart till that heart shall cease to beat for ever."

He was interrupted in the midst of these gloomy meditations by the entrance of his father, who had heard of the fearful attempt which his unfortunate niece had made upon her life, and came to inquire into the melancholy particulars.

Alfred related them in as few words as

possible, and of course Mr. Meadows was not at all surprised at the agitation his son evinced, although he tried all he could to calm it, and congratulated him upon his having so opportunely and providentially arrived at the critical moment to prevent so dreadful a catastrophe.

"Poor child of sorrow," feelingly observed Mr. Meadows, "her life has indeed been a chequered one, and the sad bereavement she has so recently experienced, coupled with the numerous other afflictions that have befallen her, together with the disappointment of her hopes, in the rejection of her love—from the most pure and honourable motives—by Edward Stanley, have been almost too much for her delicate nature to struggle against. But keep up your spirits, Alfred, for notwithstanding her present alarming symptoms, and the unpleasant and dangerous circumstances in which she as well as all of us are placed, I do trust, that with care and attention she will yet be restored to convalesence."

Alfred shook his head mournfully and despairingly, and then replied in a voice which fully showed the anguish of his feelings.

"Ah, no, my dear father, those hopes, I have too much reason to fear are far too sanguine, and can never be realized. Her unfortunate malady has now reached a degree of violence which is most alarming, if not entirely hopeless, and long mental and bodily suffering have made such sad inroads upon a constitution at any time extremely delicate, that her recovery must be considered almost as a matter of impossibility."

"Much depends upon yourself," observed his father, "and the precaution you use, in being careful in future not to make any allusion to your unfortunate passion."

"Alas, alas." sighed the young man, "how hard is the task you set me."

"It is your imperative duty, and, if you really love Flora Melville, and are anxious for her recovery, you will not shrink from it. But arouse yourself, Alfred, I say again, and depend upon it at some future period you will meet with one whom you can love as well, and who may be as worthy of you as your fair and amiable cousin."

"Ah, no," returned Alfred, "that is quite impossible, I can never bestow my heart's most fervent affections upon any other woman than Flora Melville, and thus are all the bright hopes I have so long ventured to cherish, now completely annihilated, and I care little what becomes of me."

He could not restrain his emotions as he uttered these melancholy words, but he averted his looks in order to conceal the expression of them.

His father again expostulated with him, and endeavoured to banish such gloomy and torturing thoughts from his mind, but finding that all his attempts were useless, he abandoned them, and, after a few more observations, they separated, and young Meadows, with a sad heart, after having made the necessary inquiries after the suffering object of his anxiety, once more sought the solitude of his own thoughts, away from his companions.

CHAPTER LXV.

SUFFERINGS OF THE FUGITIVES IN THE OLD FORT.—THE NIGHT ATTACK.—THE FIRE.—FEARFUL SCENE.

Poor Flora Melville remained in the same melancholy and dangerous state for several days, and no one anticipated for a moment her ultimate recovery.

However, contrary to all expectations, and much to the surprise and gratification of all, her malady suddenly took a most favourable turn, her reason entirely resumed its seat, and although necessarily weak from long illness, she was shortly enabled to sit up, and to talk rationally to those about her.

Need it be said what feelings of gratitude and melancholy delight Alfred Meadows experienced at this unexpected event? He felt his hopes revive in some degree, though he prudently checked them, and tried to act with as much calmness and self-possession as possible, which were so indispensably necessary under the circumstances.

He requested an interview with Flora that he might congratulate her on the happy change which had taken place in her health, and with which she complied, but prudently, though delicately suggested that it should be in the presence of his father.

She received them both with the greatest respect, but a slight blush suffused her cheeks on Alfred addressing her, and he could not without much difficulty control or conceal his emotions, embarrasment, and confusion.

Mr. Meadows and his son were as much surprised as gratified at the extraordinary change which so short a time had wrought in her appearance. She was perfectly calm, too, in her demeanour, and appeared quite resigned to her fate, and all the dismal circumstances by which she was surrounded; more especially as she had now the consolation and protection of her uncle and cousin, whom she had never expected to see again, particularly at the very time when she so much stood in need of their assistance and advice.

They entered most feelingly into conversation, talking of past events and future prospects, which were gloomy enough, but

they endeavoured to reconcile Flora, and to inspire her with hope; but every allusion to the unfortunate passion of Alfred Meadows was most carefully avoided, and he was too much gratified at the remarkable change in her health, not to stifle his real feelings, and to be anxious not to say anything, or even to hint anything by look or word, which might cause her pain.

Flora thanked her cousin in the most delicate manner she could for the recent service he had rendered her, meaning of course, the prevented act of suicide, but he fearing to touch upon such dangerous ground, evaded the subject as well as he could, and broached another of a less painful nature as quickly as possible.

Alfred felt much relieved after this interview, and endeavoured to look forward with

better spirits and much more confidence than he had previously been enabled to do, especially as Flora continued to improve, and there was every prospect that, unless she unfortunately suffered a relapse, she would be restored to comparative convalescence, although it was not at all likely that she could ever banish from her mind entirely the gloom and anguish which the recent melancholy events had naturally created.

But all these sanguine hopes were again suddenly dissipated, not by any relapse suffered by Flora, but from the misery of the circumstances that rapidly grew upon them all.

The provisions in the fort were nearly exhausted, and their kind friends, the natives in the neighbourhood, informed them with the deepest regret that they could supply them with no more; so that the most terrible prospect it is possible to imagine opened itself before their eyes, and in what manner to help themselves, or to escape from the danger which threatened them, they were totally at a loss to form the least conjecture.

It was astonishing to observe, considering her recent illness, the fortitude, the patience, and resignation which Flora Melville displayed under these desperate and alarming circumstances. She never once uttered a murmur of complaint, but, on the contrary, tried all in her power to raise the hopes and spirits of her companions, when they were the most depressed.

But the misery of their fate hourly grew upon them, their provisions became more and more scanty, so that they were compelled to share them out in the smallest portions among them, and unless providence should mercifully send them relief, nothing but starvation stared them in the face.

The agony of Alfred Meadows, as might have been expected, was most intense, but it was more, much more for his father and Flora than himself. Fervently, sincerely he prayed to heaven to avert the frightful dangers that threatened them; but so inevitable did they appear to be, that, in spite of all his efforts, his heart almost sunk within him in despair.

The terrible moment long looked forward to at length arrived; the last portion of food was consumed, and to add to their misery and regret, their former friends discontinued visiting them, so that they had not even the means of receiving their advice, added to which they were not without their apprehensions and suspicions of treachery, in the event of which their fate was certain.

And here, in this awfully critical moment, when death in its most ghastly and appalling form presented itself vividly, palpably to the apprehension, the fortitude, the true heroism of woman, under difficulties of the most trying nature, were never more strongly exemplified; Flora Melville, notwithstanding the fearful illness, from which she had only partially recovered, being a bright example.

Even on the second day of their privation, when the squalid looks, and ghastly features of all showed the characters unmistakable, the terrible suffering that hunger was inflicting, and the consequent dreadful anxiety of mind that accompanied it, not a murmur, not an impatient observation was to be heard, but silent and mutual sympathy—far more expressive—prevailed.

True, the men looked sullenly, sternly—if we may so use the terms—upon their gentle companions in adversity, but no squash, no bad feeling originated those looks—no, it was mainly sympathy with those they loved, and the torturing reflection that they had not the power to relieve them from their sufferings.

The mother pressed her little one to her milkless breast, and with feelings of agony such as fond mothers alone can experience, under similar circumstances, consoled and hallowed it with her tears and caresses.

But that mother murmured not. No, she with true piety, resigned herself and those she loved, to the will of the Supreme, with the full confidence that, in His infinite mercy, He would not desert them in the hour of their need.

Water they had a plentiful supply of from the well in the garden, which has been before mentioned, and that served in some measure to revive them, and to counteract the awful effects that the total want of food inevitably produced.

Truly solemn was the deathlike silence which pervaded that desolate refuge of misery. But the vacantly glaring eyes, and pale, and even livid features, told the heart-rending tale, much more truthfully, far more graphically, than the most bitter lamentations or eloquent language could possibly have done, and must have made the most powerful impression upon any one who had had the painful opportunity of witnessing it.

And with all this hideous amount of physical suffering and endurance, they had to struggle against the too well-grounded apprehensions of treachery, which might at any moment expose them to a fate, perhaps more merciful, because more speedy, but still too revolting for contemplation.

And what was the anguish of Alfred Meadows and his father, during this horrible trial? Not for themselves, but for their unfortunate companions in misery, especially that fair and amiable being, who, to the former of whom, was far more precious than his own existence. Any language would be preposterously feeble and inadequate properly to pourtray it.

The heart of Alfred Meadows, it need scarcely be said, was ready to burst as he watched the pale looks, but patient endurance of Flora, and knew that he had no power to afford her the least relief, and that any attempt at consolation would appear like insult or bitter mockery. Never could he possibly have more forcibly evinced the sincerity of his love, or Flora more fully appreciated it, or deeply regretted that her heart could not respond to the passion.

And the gentle looks, the melancholy tender expression of her eye, and the warm pressure of the hand, sufficiently told those feelings, and imparted some degree of consolation to the young man, even in the midst of his anguish and despair.

Seated by her side, she permitted his arm to fondly encircle her slender waist, reclined her head upon his shoulder, and even at times faintly, but tenderly smiling, and whispering a word of hope and assurance.

Even in this dreadful hour of adversity, as we have before said, these were the most happy moments that Alfred Meadows had for some time experienced, and gloomy as was the prospect before them, a ray of hope and confidence flashed upon his mind.

The night of the second day of actual privation, came on, dark and threatening as the frightful fate which glared upon them, that eventful night set in, and found the unfortunate inmates of the old fort still silent, uncomplaining, patient, resigned but with looks that painfully revealed the triumph of the vulture which was consuming them, and foreboded the quick approach of the time when they must succumb to his voracity.

Two or three were so much exhausted that they lay prostrate, and almost inanimate, and poor Flora Melville, in spite of all her endeavours, could bear up no longer, but reclined listlessly, and almost insensible in her lover's arms.

Now indeed was the moment of trial, the time when it required all the energies of human nature to battle against the terrible amount of difficulties by which they were surrounded, and every instant seemed to render the possibility of surmounting those difficulties yet more apparent.

They looked gloomily at each other, foreboding the speedy approach of the fate which providence alone could avert, but the mind of every one was too much bewildered to offer any suggestion or advice.

Indeed, what had they in their power either to suggest or advise that was at all practicable? It would have been madness for them to abandon their present place of refuge, without any prospect of another asylum or assistance, and at the risk of falling into the hands of the remorseless and blood-thirsty enemy, and there was then no alternative for them, but to remain where they were, and to put their trust alone in the merciful interposition of heaven to save them.

We have said that the night had set in in unison with the gloomy thoughts and feelings of the unhappy inmates of the old fort, and it continued its threatening aspect until the thunder murmuring in the distance, and fitful and mournful gusts of wind sweeping round the building, indicated an approaching storm. But the minds of every one were too busily occupied with their own dismal thoughts and forebodings, to suffer them to take much heed of the battling elements, and thus they continued for more than an hour.

Suddenly, however, they were all startled and alarmed from the deep lethargy of despair into which they had almost fallen, by loud shouts from without, and Alfred Meadows and one or two others hastened to a window, or rather loop-hole, from which they could command an extensive view, and to their utter consternation, they beheld several armed men, dashing up the hill on which the old fort stood, and led by one of those very natives, whom they had considered to be their best friends.

Thus were their fear and suspicions too fatally confirmed, and the almost certainty of their fate made apparent.

But weak and exhausted with hunger and long endurance of suffering as they were, the men were in a moment aroused into action, and seizing such arms as they happened to have in their possession, prepared to defend themselves and their fair companions to the last.

And now the fortitude and self-possession of woman, under the most trying circumstances, was again displayed in a most striking and extraordinary manner, all of them, with the exception of poor Flora—whose strength was completely exhausted, and whose faculties were entirely suspended—rushing to their feet, seizing upon guns and other weapons, and showing a determination to act with the same firmness and intrepidity as the men.

A scene of great excitement ensued.

The shouts from the enemy without increased, and presently they were heard battering at the gates, and endeavouring to force their way into the fortress. Still the courage and self-possession of the starving beleagured inmates never for an instant forsook them, and they were fully resolved that, if they must perish, they would at least sell their lives dearly.

The room in which they were all assembled at that critical moment was situated in a round tower of the fortress, and in a most commanding position both for attack and defence, but it had one great advantage for the purposes of the latter, namely, as it possessed several windows and loop holes, from which the defenders might fire upon the enemy without any danger of a return, and at those different appertures, both men and women, such as possessed fire-arms—there fortunately being a plentiful supply of fire-arms—planted themselves, ready to commence operations at the first opportunity which presented itself.

While the destruction of the gate was proceeding, others of the enemy, more impatient for the work of bloodshed, were attempting to scale the walls, lofty as they were, but at length the gates yielded, and the whole of the marauders rushed into the garden or court, with such frightful shouts and yells as only such miscreants could give utterance to, and received an unexpected volley from the brave defenders from their lofty position, which killed two, and wounded several others, showing them that they might depend upon meeting with a determined resistance, and that their triumph in their bloody work would not be accomplished so easily as they had probably anticipated.

Still they perished dauntlessly, and having got within the walls, they made a desperate attempt to force their way into the fortress itself, the inmates continuing to fire upon them all the time.

While this was going on, the storm increased, the lightning competing with the thunder in fury, and the rain absolutely descending in torrents; thus adding to the frightfulness and excitement of the scene.

All the time, Flora Melville, who had with difficulty crawled near the spot where her cousin and his father were standing, remained in a half-stupified state, uttering not a word of complaint, fear, or otherwise.

The door which opened upon the tower was soon forced open, but before the marauders could enter, a fearful explosion—from what cause it was impossible to imagine—was heard, part of the round tower fell, with a lumbering and deafening noise, and flames burst forth, which, carried by the wind, threatened quickly to ascend to the room in which the unfortunate persons were, and to spread to other portions of the building. Their situation was now truly fearful, for death either by fire or the enemy seemed to be inevitable, and they were completely at a loss what to do.

But there was no time for reflection or hesitation, for rapidly the flames spread, and it seemed that the total destruction of the tower, and that in an inconceivable short space of time, was certain.

Their previous presence of mind, and determined courage, under these appalling circumstances, almost entirely forsook them, and a scene of the utmost confusion ensued. The men stood for a minute or two completely paralysed, and the women, unable any longer to restrain their feelings, shrieked aloud, and one of them, in her frenzy, before any one could attempt to prevent her, precipitated herself from one of the open windows, leaping from that fearful height to certain and immediate death.

The yells of fiendish exultation that now burst forth from the wretches below—who considered that the total destruction of the unfortunate beings was certain—were indeed frightful, and they watched the progress of the flames with laughter and derision.

But at length aroused to desperation, and thinking that it would be better to risk their lives by an encounter with the enemy than to perish in the flames, they rushed to make their escape if possible from the burning tower.

Alfred seized the now senseless form of Flora in his arms, and shielding her as well as he could from the flames, rushed down the burning staircase, followed by his companions in misfortune.

With the utmost difficulty they reached the open air, and then had to encounter the bloodthirsty miscreants, who rushed upon them with shrieks of vengeance and triumph, and sought at once to accomplish their destruction.

CHAPTER LXVI.

THE RESULT.—THE SURPRISE.

A desperate hand to hand combat now ensued, the rebels thinking to overwhelm their brave antagonists by the force of numbers, and the latter making such an obstinate and gallant resistance that rendered the issue extremely doubtful.

Alfred Meadows still supported the inanimate form of his beauteous cousin on one arm, and fought resolutely, dealing destruction around him, and endeavouring to force his way, with his senseless burthen down the hill.

And now every portion of the tower was in flames, and its ruins were falling in all directions.

The combat continued with unabated resolution on both sides, and still the result remained as doubtful as ever. Several of the rebels were slain or wounded—the treacherous native among the former, by a well directed blow from the sword of young Meadows—while the Europeans, although most of them were more or less seriously wounded, had but one slain.

The combat was now no longer doubtful, the sepoys, evidently taken by surprise at the daring and unflinching bravery of their antagonist, on whose destruction they had doubtless calculated, gradually began to give way, and at length fled in all directions in complete confusion.

But scarcely had they cleared the hill, retreating in all directions, whilst some of the late inmates of the fort, followed in pursuit, when loud shouts were heard proceeding from the borders of the neighbouring forest, and immediately a small detachment of British troops made their appearance, much to the consternation of the retreating miscreants, who now saw that their total annihilation was inevitable.

Alfred Meadows as well as his friends hailed this welcome sight with the most grateful feelings of pleasure, and, the rebels having been quickly disposed of, the officers of the troop which had so fortunately arrived at that critical time, and who had probably been attracted by the reflection of the flames to the spot, came forward to congratulate them on their escape, but no sooner had Alfred Meadows appeared conducting Flora Melville—who was now restored to consciousness—than an exclamation of astonishment and delight burst from some one amidst the throng, and immediately a female form rushed forward and threw herself in the arms of Flora, whose feelings were too powerful for utterance, at which the reader will not marvel when we inform them that it was Omelia!

CHAPTER LXVII.

THE MEETING OF FRIENDS.—CONGRATULATIONS.

Any attempt to describe the feelings of our heroine and Flora Melville at this extraordinary and unexpected meeting, would be completely idle, and we will therefore not occupy the time of the reader by doing so, any more than to say that, for several moments they remained in each other's embrace, and wept tears of joy and gratitude which it was impossible to restrain, but without being able to utter a single word.

The astonishment and delight of Alfred Meadows and his father, at this providential reunion it need scarcely be said was equal to that of Omelia and Flora, but they stood respectfully by and suffered them to give unrestrained indulgence to their emotions, without offering to interrupt them.

In the meantime while this scene was going on, the work of destruction was proceeding in the fort, without any attempt being made to extinguish the conflagration.

But the fire had now exhausted itself, having laid the tower—to which it was fortunately entirely confined—in smouldering ruins.

"Dear suffering Flora," at length Omelia exclaimed in accents of the most unbounded affection and sympathy, "oh, heaven be thanked that after so long a separation we meet again."

"Omelia! my own affectionate Omelia!" replied Flora, in a voice almost stifled by the power of her emotions, and gazing mournfully, but with unspeakable satisfaction through her tears upon the beautiful young Indian heroine, "friend, sister, kind providence has then heard my fervent, my constant prayers, while reason held its sway o'er my brain, you still live, and are restored to my anxious bosom. Almighty God you are indeed most merciful!"

She could say no more, and the looks of Omelia sufficiently told the feelings that agitated her. Again they fondly embraced, and sighed and wept upon each other's bosom, every one present being much affected at the meeting.

But at length they partially recovered themselves, and Alfred Meadows and his father—who were well known to Omelia—then introduced themselves, and the most warm and friendly greetings took place on both sides.

Mirza and Murad now presented themselves, and Flora Melville felt not a little surprised and gratified at meeting with them, knowing as she did, that they entertained the utmost respect for her, and sympathy in her misfortunes.

But it was necessary that some little time should now be given to the consideration of what was best to be done, under the present extraordinary circumstances, and they therefore, accompanied by the officers, entered that part of the old fort which the flames had fortunately not reached, the soldiers disposing of themselves in the best manner they could to await farther orders.

The first consideration, however, was to see to the immediate relief of the necessities of those who had suffered so much for the last few days from privation; and fortunately there was an ample supply of provisions in the soldiers' haversacks, which were shared out with care to all those who stood immediately and so much in need of them.

But it was some time ere our heroine and Flora could regain sufficient composure to converse calmy upon the extraordinary events of the past, and with their friends discuss and arrange their plans for the future, and when in answer to her anxious inquiries, Omelia was informed of the melancholy death of the good old hermit, to whose generous friendship and kindness, at the time she stood so much in need of them, she was so greatly indebted, it is needless to say how sincere and fervent were her sorrow and regret.

"Poor old man," she ejaculated, "it was indeed a sad fate for one so aged and so deserving of every reverence to meet with, may the great Father of all receive his spirit. But alas, my dear friend, how terrible must have been your sufferings."

"True, true," sighed Flora, "they have indeed been most severe, and I dare not trust myself now to speak of them. At some future time I will endeavour to enter into that explanation, which in your affection for me you are no doubt, so anxious to receive. You too, Omelia, to what troubles and dangers you must, I fear have been exposed since that fatal night which separated us. Heaven again be thanked for your preservation."

"Yes," answered Omelia, "I have had

much to encounter many apparently, insurmountable difficulties to overcome. But I have met with friends, and none more true and generous than Mirza and Murad. It was by their means I was rescued from death when doomed to it by the monster Nena Sahib."

Flora looked her thanks to Mirza and Murad, but made use of no observation, and Omelia continued:—

"But let us not at present dwell upon these melancholy subjects, dear Flora, but be grateful to that Supreme power that has watched over us in the midst of all our troubles, and restored us to each other, and I trust that it may be long ere we may again be separated. Could I be convinced that Edward Stanley still exists, and is in safety, methinks that I could learn to be comparatively content."

At the mention of the name of that being whom she was still, in spite of all her efforts to conquer the fatal passion, so fondly attached, Flora Melville blushed, then became ghastly pale, and Alfred Meadows, who had sat and listened to the conversation between the two friends with the deepest interest and attention, quickly noticed her extreme agitation, and knowing too well the source from which it sprang, felt the most poignant anguish and regret, and saw at once how utterly hopeless was the ardent affection he entertained for her.

But he averted his looks, anxious to conceal the expression of his emotions from observation.

Omelia's keen eye, however, quickly, noticed the emotion she had caused by her allusion to Stanley, and she deeply regretted it, the more especially as it was too painfully evident that Flora had not yet been able to conquer the unfortunate passion which had taken possession of her heart. She pitied her, and immediately changed the delicate subject.

Being late, it was now necessary to make some arrangements for the night, and this being accomplished, and accommodating themselves as well as they could, the soldiers and officers in the lower part of the fort, our heroine and Flora parted from their friends, and retired to a small apartment which had been hastily fitted up in the best manner that their scanty means would permit for their temporary use.

The startling events of the night however, kept them for some time longer in conversation, and when their extraordinary nature is taken into consideration, it will not be wondered that the two friends should be much excited.

Omelia listened to Flora's account of the sufferings of herself and her companions for the last few days from want, then the night attack on the fort, and the horrors of the conflagration, with the most profound attention and sympathy, and she could never enough admire the intrepid and heroic fortitude with which they had endured their troubles, and the noble courage with which Alfred Meadows had behaved throughout, especially in rescuing his fair cousin at the risk of his own life from the flames.

Omelia was well aware of the sentiments that young Meadows entertained for Flora, and that they met with no responsive feeling from her, and she deeply regretted it, for she was fully satisfied of the excellent intrinsic qualities of Alfred, and that he was every way worthy of her.

She would fain have endeavoured to persuade her to try and conquer the repugnance she had for his suit, and to give him room to hope that he might yet succeed in making a favourable impression on her heart, but she feared to touch upon so delicate and painful a subject at present, and she had too much reason to believe how fruitless would be the task, and what torturing recollections it might awaken in her breast.

Again and again they congratulated each other on their restoration, and that too at a time so unexpected, and when they so much needed each other's advice and consolation.

"Oh, Omelia," observed Flora, "need I tell you what was the anguish and anxiety of that aged man and myself on the fatal night of your disappearance, for under all the circumstances, we had too much reason to fear that something dreadful had befallen you?"

"Most true, dear Flora," replied her companion; "and believe me my agony was equal to your own, for I had every cause to apprehend that we should never meet again. Thank God, those fears, have not been realised, and I trust the day is not far distant when our troubles shall be at an end, and we shall again be restored to happiness."

Flora shook her head mournfully.

"Alas, no," she sighed, "I can never, never more know what real happiness is. My poor father no more, he used to look upon me with even more than a parent's indulgence and affection, and whose wise counsel and advice, I so much now require, my prospects are indeed dark and gloomy."

"Your bereavement, Flora," returned Omelia in her most gentle and sympathising accents, "is a most melancholy one. But you must endeavour to submit to it with patience, fortitude, and resignation, and still hope on. Have not the trials it has been my lot to endure as severe as those you have experienced?"

"Yes," coincided Flora, in wondering tones, "but," she quickly added, with an expressive look, and the utmost emotion "you have still those left whom you love, and who return your passion, while I—"

She suddenly checked herself, and unable to finish the sentence, she pressed her hands upon her forehead and burst into tears.

"Poor Flora," said Omelia soothingly, and gently pressing her hand between her's, "too well do I know the feelings that occupy and torture your mind, and from my very heart I pity you. But try and banish such gloomy ideas, since it is the will of fate that your wishes shall not be gratified. Alas! Edward Stanley may no longer live to—"

"Cease Omelia," interrupted the blushing damsel, with increased emotion, "for heaven's sake cease to dwell upon a subject so torturing to us both. Oh, why did my wayward tongue ever reveal the fatal secret of my breast? What presumption was it on my part, pardon me, Omelia, I do you a cruel wrong by encouraging such thoughts as these, and deserve alone your scorn."

"Say not so, Flora," replied Omelia, "for it pains me to hear you. I know the truth and virtue of your nature, and cannot believe you capable of harbouring one improper thought. But you have also one who loves you, sincerely, passionately, I am convinced; one who would willingly lay down his life to win your smiles, and who is good and honourable, and every way worthy of you. Your cousin Alfred, who—"

"Oh, name him not, dear Omelia," she again implored, and tears trembled in her eyes as she spoke, "Alfred is all and more that you have represented him, and he has my warmest esteem, but never, never can he possess my heart."

"Poor Alfred," ejaculated Omelia, "how sincerely then do I pity him, for well do I know that he will never experience true happiness without you. But no more on this painful topic, it is late, and so we had better endeavour to get an hour or two's repose, after the fatigue and excitement we have undergone."

To this Flora assented, and having returned thanks to heaven for the favourable issue of the events of the night, so alarming and startling in themselves, they sought the rude pallet which had been hastily prepared for them on the floor of the apartment.

Flora, quite overcome with fatigue, soon fell off to sleep, but Omelia's busy thoughts, and the extraordinary circumstance which had restored her to that fair being whom she so much esteemed, and whom she was doubtful whether she should ever behold again.

But still more firmly and anxiously did Edward Stanley occupy her thoughts, and many were the hopes and fears she entertained for the fate which had befallen him, and the probability that they would ever be restored to each other, but she dared not

abandon the idea that he still lived, and the fond hope often whispered itself to her that they would not much longer be separated.

It is necessary that we should give some particulars of the journey of Omelia and her friends, and the circumstance which placed them under the protection of the troops, and led to the fortunate discovery we have just related.

We have stated the friendly and hospitable manner in which the travellers had been received by the inhabitants of the place on the occasion of the celebration of the festival described, in a previous chapter, and of the easy mode of travelling procured for Omelia on the following day, and pursuing a route with which Mirza and the others were well acquainted, and which was not supposed to be infested by any of the insurgents, they proceeded in comparative safety, Omelia's hopes and spirits reviving the farther they advanced on the way, and in which frame of mind Mirza and Murad took good care to encourage her.

We have before described the mode of travelling in India by the *dawk* or palanquin, and Omelia felt herself perfectly easy, though she would have been much better pleased had it been more expeditious, as she was most anxious and impatient to reach the end of her journey—which as we have before said, was the hermit's cavern in the wilderness—as soon as possible.

During that day they travelled on without any incident occurring worthy of being recorded, halting at intervals at a bungalow or small building on the ground floor, used as a place of refreshment for travellers. Here those who wish it can always have an active servant to prepare them a breakfast, or a simple dinner of curried fowl, and they may remain if they like a whole day at the bungalow for the small charge of one rupee, of course, paying extra for the meals, a mere trifle.

At night they stopped for rest at some place with which either Mirza or his friend Murad were well acquainted, and resumed their journey at daybreak in the morning.

But at length the journey became tedious and weary, they not being able to procure the same accommodation for Omelia as before, and their means becoming limited, they were compelled to pursue their way on foot, and by the most dreary and unfrequented routes, supporting the delicate frame of the Indian maiden over the rugged ground, and encouraging her as well as they could.

But although she began to feel somewhat impatient and uneasy, she never complained, and only expressed regret that they should be put to so much trouble and inconvenience on her account.

The third day of their journey had now

arrived, and Omelia, notwithstanding the courage with which she had hitherto sustained herself, and resisted fatigue, now began to feel her strength failing her, especially as the lonely way they travelled in order to avoid observation, offered them no place of rest or refreshment, and was fraught with considerable danger from the number of wild beast that were known to infest that part of the country.

To add these miseries and difficulties, the weather became dark and lowering, and threatened to become extremely tempestuous and Omelia felt herself getting weaker and weaker every minute, and could not help becoming somewhat alarmed.

She eagerly inquired of Mirza, when they were compelled to pause for a short time to rest themselves, whether they had much further to go.

"No, Omelia," he answered, " this day will probably bring us to the end of our journrey, and if you can only bear up for an hour or two we shall arrive at a place where we can procure rest and refreshment."

"Thank providence for that," remarked Omelia, "for although you know that it is not a little that will daunt me, I have had so much exertion and excitement of late, that it is almost too much for my strength to support."

"Very true," replied Mirza, "and I need not say how much I admire the heroic fortitude with which you have hitherto borne the severe trials to which you have been put. In order to avoid the danger of encountering any of the straggling mutineers, from whom we need expect no mercy should they happen to know us, or to have any suspicion, as you must be aware, I have been compelled to take the most tedious and circuitous route, which has taken us considerably out of our way, but we have hitherto, been most fortunate, in not having encountered any danger or met with any obstruction."

With this Omelia agreed, and they then once more resumed their journey.

The road became less difficult for travelling, and at the prospect of speedily accomplishing the tedious task, Omelia felt her spirits revive.

At length, as Mirza had promised, after walking for an hour or so, they arrived at two or three straggling bungalows, in any of which he knew that they could procure anything they required in safety, and after having rested themselves for a short time, proceed on their way.

They soon found themselves seated in one of these bungalows, and with all their wants supplied.

And now as Omelia approached so near the place of her destination, her heart beat high with hope and expectation. and her anxiety to meet again poor Flora Melville and the venerable hermit, who she knew must have felt her mysterious disappearance so severly, increased.

But the hope of being able to hear something of her beloved Stanley, to find that he was in safety, and probably to be ere long restored to his fond embrace, was paramount in her mind, and the longer she encouraged it, the more sanguine that hope became.

Having sufficiently rested themselves, and as the day was advancing, they left the bungalow, and travelled with recruited strength, and now as they advanced on their way, every spot and object became more familiar to Omelia, and she was convinced that she was but approaching scenes with which she was well acquainted, and to which she had been accustomed.

However, they continued to proceed till night set in, and all became strange, wild, and dreary again, and Mirza and Murad admitted that they found they had mistaken the way, and were at some loss how to extricate themselves.

This was vexatious, the more so as the storm which had long been gathering now commenced in earnest, and they had not the slightest means of shelter, or the prospect of procuring any in that part of the country.

Omelia could not but feel uneasy and disappointed, but she did not complain, although her companion felt for her, and deeply regretted their mistake, which of course was caused by accident, and not from any neglect on their parts, and they were now at a loss how to remedy it.

"It is truly unfortunate," remarked Mirza, " and I know not how to apologise to you for my error, but it is no use wasting time in useless regrets and complaints, the only thing is for us to try and get out of the dilemma in the best manner, and as soon as we can."

"Have you no idea where we are?" eagerly inquired our heroine.

"It is so dark," replied Murza, "save when the lightning flashes at intervals, that I have not an opportunity of forming the least idea, still I am inclined to think and hope that, from the distance we have travelled and the route we have hitherto taken, that we cannot be far from the Old Hill fort, near Agra, which has been long deserted, and where we could find shelter which we seek, and of which we stand so much in need."

Omelia expressed a wish that Mirza's conjectures might prove to be correct, but they still stood at a loss how to proceed, whilst the lightning blazed around and the thunder reverberated loudly through the dreary wild, and what rendered it still more dangerous and fearful, was that hitherto there had been no rain.

They looked around them for a few moments with a feeling fast approaching to that of despair, and then forcing their way through a thicket, Mirza led the way, as well as his imagination would permit him, Omelia supporting herself upon the arm of Murad, and exerting herself to meet the disagreable circumstances with all the coolness and fortitude she could.

This was, however, no very easy task to accomplish, and their situation seemed every moment to become more hopeless and bewildering.

A flash of lightning more vivid than any which had preceded, it followed by a terrific crash, now elicited an exclamation of alarm from Omelia, and on recovering themselves from the shock, they discovered that the lightning had struck one of the largest trees

near our heroine, splitting its huge trunk from the top to the bottom, and it seemed to have been only by a most extraordinary miracle that she had escaped with her life.

The danger of their situation was now made the more apparent, and Omelia could not help feeling some degree of alarm, although she tried to conceal it in the best manner she was able.

They again hesitated what to do, and both Mirza and Murad, with regret, of which there was no reason to doubt the sincerity, were compelled to acknowledge themselves to be in as great a state of uncertainty and bewilderment as ever.

And now the rain which had so long been sullenly lingering in the black and heavy clouds, came down violently, so that the light dresses of the travellers, particularly

No. 36.

that of Omelia, were quickly wet through, and that, of course greatly added to their misery.

They deeply regretted that they had not remained at the bungalow; but it was no use doing so, they had become involved in a dilemma, and all that they could do was to endeavour to extricate themselves from it in the best manner they could.

There were no signs of the storm abating, and their situation every moment became more disagreeable and annoying.

"This is certainly most provoking." observed Mirza, "and I cannot conceive how I could make such a blunder, so well acquainted as I am with every inch of the route I had proposed taking. Yet, as well as the darkness will allow me to penetrate, I cannot help thinking that this place is not altogether unfamiliar to me."

"True," returned Murad, "and I am of your opinion, Mirza, namely, that we cannot be far distant from the old Hill Fort."

As these observations were passing between them, they had entered upon a spot less entangled by the branches of the thickly clustering trees, and no sooner had they done so than they were somewhat startled by the sudden reflection of lurid light in the sky, followed by ascending smoke and flames, evidently proceeding from some fierce conflagration just broken out, and at no great distance; and soon the outlines of the burning building, standing on a lofty eminence, were clearly revealed to them, and Mirza and Murad exclaimed together—

"Ah, it is the old Hill Fort; we are therefore right in our conjectures."

"It has doubtless been struck by the lightning," observed Omelia, looking anxiously towards the burning pile, "it is most unfortunate, for all chance of our obtaining shelter there is at an end."

"Do not despair, Omelia," returned Mirza, "for we may yet find all we seek. Not far from the fort is a small village, which I had forgot, and the inhabitants of which we may I believe safely trust—come, let us push on our way. See the fire seems to be confined to one part of the building, or rather buildings, and the destruction of that is inevitable."

The flames did indeed appear to spread rapidly, and the sight, from the elevated position of the fort, and the wildly romantic scenery around, reflected the broad glare of the light, had an awful, but at the same time most impressive effect.

"What is that?" exclaimed Mirza, with a look of doubt and alarm, as between a pause in the thunder, a sound, resembling the heavy tread of numerous approaching feet from the right, suddenly smote their ears.

"A number of persons is coming this way," replied Murad, "and the regular measured tread is evidently that of the military. We must be cautious, for we know not whether they are friends or foes. Let us draw aside for a moment behind the shelter of those trees and watch."

Quickly and cautiously they did so, and awaited impatiently the arrival of the strangers. They were not long kept in suspense—the men came on, busily talking together, and our heroine and her companions had soon the satisfaction to discover from their language that they were European soldiers, and thus all their doubts and apprehensions were at once at an end, and the next moment they made their appearance led on by their officers, and making rapidly towards the scene of the conflagration.

Omelia and her friends immediately presented themselves, and were received by the officers with some surprise, but every mark of respect, and a brief explanation having been entered into, from which it appeared that the detachment were on their way to join the forces at the nearest station, the three travellers pleased at finding themselves so unexpectedly under such efficient protection, proceeded with them towards the burning fort, from the direction of which the rapid discharge of fire-arms was now heard, and which convinced them that some unfortunate persons had sought refuge there, and were probably at present occupied in defending themselves from an attack of a portion of the enemy, so that not a moment was to be lost in rendering them every assistance.

They soon arrived at the scene of action, and what followed has been already related.

CHAPTER LXVIII.

FURTHER INCIDENTS.

Notwithstanding the lateness of the hour at which they had retired, and the great need in which they stood of rest, Omelia and Flora quitted their humble pallet by break of day the morning following the exciting events recorded, and hastened to join Mr. Meadows and his son, and Mirza and Murad, in order that they might consult together what was best to be done in their present situation, for it was necessary that some prompt measures should be adopted, as it would not be safe for them after the serious affray which had taken place, for them to remain much longer in the fort, and the soldiers being compelled to resume their march with as little delay as possible, could afford them no other protection than such as they would receive by accompanying them. Besides the want of provisions which they must again experience—and the villagers who had before befriended them should have the means, and be induced again to supply their wants—would render the old fort no longer tenable.

Several of the unfortunate persons gladly availed themselves of the offer of the officers, to attend them on their march, but there were two or three others who felt too weak and exhausted from that they had already suffered to allow them to travel, and dismal as was the idea, they were compelled to remain where they were until they might obtain relief, and to leave their fate in the hands of providence.

Among the latter was Flora Melville, who, in spite of all her efforts to resist them, felt the effects of the fearful events of the previous night so severely, that she was almost reduced to the same deplorable condition from which she had only recently revived.

If there was anything which could have given her strength and fortitude, it would have been her fortunate and unexpected restoration to the gentle and affectionate Omelia, and the soothing influence of her advice and sympathy, but she felt herself unable to bear up against her illness, and she regretted it the more in consequence of the care and anxiety it would cause, and the trouble and inconvenience to which it would put those whom she so much esteemed.

A great part of that day was passed in the discussion of this important business, before they could come to any satisfactory arrangement or conclusion; but as it was impossible to remove Flora Melville, and two or three of her female companions in misfortune till the necessary means of doing so were procured, and as it was not likely that Omelia, or any of the friends of the former, could think of abandoning her, it was finally agreed that the officers who with the men under their command were compelled to depart on the following morning at the latest, should send them such assistance with all possible despatch, as they so much required, and in the meantime a small number of the soldiers were to be left behind to guard them in the event of threatened danger.

It was the wish of Mr. Meadows and his son, accompanied by their fair relative, to endeavour to reach the vicinity of Lucknow, where, in a quiet, romantic, and yet retired spot, the former had a handsome mansion, and which he had reason to hope that, if his own servants were not unfaithful, remained uninjured, especially as it would be protected in a measure by the brave troops of General Havelock, on their way to make the first attempt to relieve the garrison, which still held out with a courage and determination which has obtained for it a glorious and imperishable place in the pages of history.

At the mention of that place in which she had met with such startling adventures, and where she could not help indulging the fond hope at times, that Stanley still survived, notwithstanding the painful circumstances under which she had been snatched from him, so soon after their meeting near the residency, Omelia's heart throbbed with the various mingled emotions that agitated her breast, and in spite of the numerous dangers she had encountered, the many hairbreadth escapes she had had, and the tedious journey she had so recently performed, she could not but feel an anxious wish to accompany Alfred and his father, the more especially as she would be near Flora Melville, who so much needed her society, and whom she loved with all the affection of a sister.

Alfred Meadows, although he was most thankful to heaven that he had been enabled to render Flora such essential service, and to save her from the dreadful fate which had recently threatened her, could not but feel the deepest anguish and regret, at the circumstance which would prevent her from leaving the fort, where they might yet be exposed to so much danger and suffering; but what tortured him, if possible, even still more, was the thought that, under any circumstances he could never hope for a return of that passion he so warmly entertained for her.

The day wore away without anything particular occurring—persons having been despatched to various parts of the neighbourhood to endeavour to ascertain whether any danger of a surprise was to be apprehended—and, as all appeared secure, the confidence of all parties was in a great measure restored, and our heroine and Flora retired to the same room they had occupied on the previous night at an early hour.

Poor Flora was very ill and low-spirited, and Omelia was in a very ill-condition to offer her advice and consolation, although she exerted herself to the utmost to do so.

"Alas," sighed the poor girl, "how can I be otherwise than truly unhappy, wretched, when I contemplate the misery of my own destiny, and consider the burthen I am to others, the trouble, the anxiety, and inconvenience I cause them? You, for instance, dear Omelia, was it not the imprudence of my conduct, which first drove you from the paternal roof of my late lamented father, and plunged you into dangers and difficulties, which only one of your noble and heroic spirit could have surmounted. Even now I could almost regret that we have again been restored to each other since it may be the means of exposing you to fresh care and anxiety. Leave me, dear Omelia, abandon me to my fate, for I feel myself unworthy of your sympathy and solicitude."

"For heaven's sake talk not thus, Flora," remonstrated our heroine, "for it grieves me to hear you do so. You do both your self and me an injustice by entertaining such gloomy and torturing ideas as those to which you have just given utterance. Abandon you in your present deplorable state, and when you so much need the aid and support of my advice and consolation, never, you must indeed think meanly of Omelia if you think her capable of conduct so cruel and unjust. No, dearest Flora, I should both hate and despise myself if I thought I could. Thanks to providence, I have both the strength and energy to endure with patience and submission any vicissitudes that it may be my lot to have to encounter, and I will not shrink from the faithful performance of my duty to one whom I so sincerely esteem, and to whom I, as the poor humble sepoy's daughter, the child of your late revered father's bounty, and that of yourself, am so much indebted. I will remain with you, under every circumstance, till it shall please heaven to restore you to convalesence, and once more place you in safety."

"Generous, noble-hearted Omelia," ejaculated Flora, fervently, raising the hand of the beauteous Indian maid to her lips, and tears of love and gratitude trembling in her eyes; "oh, how can I ever sufficiently repay such unexampled kindness as this? I—"

"Enough, Flora," interrupted Omelia, "it is sufficient for me that you know my heart, and can fully appreciate the feelings that prompt it."

"I do, indeed I do, and honour and revere them."

"Let then sweet hope cheer you on, and rest assured that your wishes will ultimately be realised. Under the care, and watchful love of such friends as your amiable cousin and his father, they cannot fail to be so."

At this allusion to Alfred Meadows, Flora blushed deeply, sighed, trembled, and evinced other signs of the greatest emotion.

"Oh, Omelia," she at length replied, in a faltering voice, "believe me, no one can better appreciate and honour the manly qualities and virtues of my cousin than myself, but—"

"I know what you would say, dear Flora," interrupted our heroine, with a look of sympathy, and in a voice of kindness, "you regard Alfred Meadows as a friend and relation, but cannot entertain for him any warmer sentiment, which, believe me, I sincerely and deeply regret, for he loves you ardently, and is I am convinced, every way worthy of you."

"Oh, true, most true," coincided Flora, tears starting to her eyes, "Alfred Meadows

is all and more than you have represented him, Omelia, and deserves the love of a far more worthier being than myself. But I pray you to drop a subject so painful and embarrassing. May you shortly be restored to that noble being from whom you have been too long separated, and be happy in a continuance of his love."

Sobs choked her further utterance, and she averted her looks from those of Omelia, who was not less affected than herself.

A silence of some minutes ensued, when Omelia said :—

"Come, Flora, let us endeavour to banish from our minds thoughts so torturing to both of us, and to resign ourselves to the will of fate. Heaven forbid that I should say a word to you that might cause you pain, for indeed I have your welfare and happiness as dear to my heart as if you were my own sister."

"I know it, indeed, I know it, dear Omelia," returned Flora; "and I need not say, I am sure, how warmly and sincerely I return that feeling. If by word or deed I have ever wronged you, oh, how deeply do I regret it."

"You never have, Flora," answered our heroine, "and you do yourself a great injustice if you imagine that you have. But try to tranquillise your feelings, and depend upon it, gloomy as your prospects appear to be at present, the dark clouds will pass away and all will yet be well."

Flora promised that she would endeavour to follow her amiable friend's advice, and thus the conversation dropped, and they endeavoured to compose themselves to sleep, in which they at last happily succeeded.

At an early hour the following morning, the officers, and the principal portion of the men under their command, quitted the fort, having on the previous night, compelled the inhabitants of the village, to supply the unfortunate inmates with such provisions and other necessaries as they might have the means of doing, and which, regretting what had happened, they promised faithfully to do to the best of their humble ability.

Flora Melville continued too ill to leave the chamber during the day, and Omelia remained almost constantly in attendance upon her, soothing her into tranquillity by her gentle sympathy and advice, and endeavouring to inspire her with the brightest hopes for the future, which somewhat ameliorated the anguish of her sufferings, and tended more than anything else towards her ultimate recovery.

Alfred Meadows and his father visited her during the day, and added their efforts to those of our heroine to afford her every consolation, and to raise her expectations for the future.

The mingled feelings that agitated the breast of the former, as he watched the pale face of his beauteous cousin, may be imagined, but fearful of paining or embarrassing her, he concealed them as well as possible, and sedulously avoided making any observation in allusion to his own unfortunate passion, although he felt that passion hourly, momentarily increase in strength, and knew that neither time nor circumstances could possibly subdue it.

This day passed over without anything taking place to disturb them, the embers in the ruins of the old tower had died out, that portion of the fort which the fugitives now occupied, had been made as comfortable as circumstances would permit, by those who were able, their former friends, the villager's, had visited them, assuring them of their willingness to assist them all that was in their power, and they therefore calmly and patiently settled themselves down to await the relief which had been promised them by the officers, and which they had no doubt they would fulfill.

The next day Mirza and Murad sought an interview with our heroine, and expressed their regret that they should be compelled to leave her, and return to Naomie, for whose safety, after what had happened at the time of their departure on their journey, they were most anxious, but at the same time they sincerely trusted that they left her in the society of those on whose friendship she might depend, and that they might shortly meet again under far happier and different circumstances-

Omelia could not but feel extremely sorry to be compelled to separate from two friends to whom she was so largely indebted, and expressed herself accordingly, at the same time most cordially thanking them for the great services they had rendered her, and regretting her inability to reward them as she wished, and as they deserved.

"Name it not, Omelia," returned Mirza, with a slight look of offended pride ; "thanks to providence, neither myself or Murad are in circumstances to require any pecuniary reward, and even if we were we should despise ourselves if we accepted it from one whom we so highly esteem."

"Pardon me, my good friend," said our heroine, " if inadvertantly I have said anything offensive to you, which I need scarcely tell you was the farthest from my thoughts. But I could not appear so ungrateful as not to express my full sense of your kindness, and of the imminent risks you have run to serve me. Farewell, pray convey to the amiable Naomie the assurance of my best love and wishes for her welfare, and the sincere hope that ere long we may be permitted to meet again."

Mirza and his companion promised to do so, and a short time afterwards, took their departure from the old fort, much to the regret of everyone.

CHAPTER LXIX.

ANOTHER SURPRISE.—FOND HOPES REALISED.

Three more days elapsed without any material change taking place in the situation of the inmates of the fort, or any further danger threatening them.

The natives in the adjacent village, to whom they had at first been so much indebted, were faithful to the promises they recently made to them, and brought them an ample supply of provisions daily, so that they were in no danger of suffering in that respect, and those of the fugitives who had been so much reduced from long suffering and anxiety of mind, were rapidly regaining strength and spirits, so that the prospect brightened on every side.

Flora Melville, too, contrary to the most sanguine expectations of her dearest friends, and thanks to the tender care and exertions of Omelia, was so far recovered, both in health and spirits, as to be able not only to leave her chamber, but to join with some degree of cheerfulness in the conversation of her companions in the fort.

We need scarcely say, what an infinite source of gratification this was to them all, but more especially to Alfred Meadows, who felt himself greatly relieved from a weight of care and anxiety which was becoming almost too painful to endure.

He was never so happy as when in her society, and she seemed to feel less embarrassment in his presence, and to try to convince him, how deeply she held him in her esteem, and how anxious she was for his happiness and welfare.

We have before described the beautiful scenery which surrounded the lofty eminence of the old fort, and a delightful view of which might be commanded from almost every part, and much of the time of our heroine and Flora Melville was now occupied in that enjoyment, which they obtained from the windows of one of the loftiest apartments, and which served in a great measure to divert their thoughts from them melancholy subjects that might otherwise have engrossed them.

They were often joined by Alfred Meadows and his father, and in whose eloquent remarks upon the beauties of nature as they then met their eye, they could not but feel the greatest pleasure.

It is true that Omelia could not but feel

her present situation as tedious and monotonous, and she was anxious again to mingle in these active and exciting scenes, to which she had lately been so much accustomed; but greater than all was her anxiety to be able to ascertain the fate of Edward Stanley, and, if possible, to behold him again.

That thought was the dearest to her heart, and it constantly occupied it, while hope led her to believe that her fond wishes would be realised.

It was on one of the finest evenings that the departing rays of the setting sun had ever shone upon even in an eastern sky, that Omelia, Flora, and Alfred Meadows, were seated near the windows of the apartment to which we have before alluded, engaged in conversation, and in admiring the beauties of the wide spread and diversified prospect before them, and which at that calm and tranquil hour, was seen in all its grandeur and sublimity of effect.

As the bright monarch of the day departed in a heavenly flood of purple, gold, and every variety of tint that could enter into the imagination of the most accomplished painter a cool, refreshing breeze arose, that came with balmy influence to the senses, and added to the pleasure and zest of the delightful prospect over which the enraptured eye eagerly wandered.

The spirits of Omelia had been more than usually animated during the day, and she endeavoured to impart the same feeling to her companions, in which she greatly succeeded.

A presentiment of some approaching happiness—for which she was at a loss to account—continued to hold possession of her mind, and seldom had she felt more buoyant and hopeful.

The sun went down, twilight gradually ceased to be, and the bright face of luna burst forth in the midst of fleecy clouds—and accompanied by a countless host of glittering stars, each of which seemed to impart a ray of happiness to the heart of care and sorrow.

The spirits of Omelia and her companions continued to rise with the beauty of the hour, and they expatiated upon all that met their observation with the most enthusiastic feelings of admiration.

But suddenly their attention was arrested by the forms of several persons, in the distance, and who appeared to be, but slowly and as if worn out with fatigue, approaching the hill upon which the fort stood, and the curiosity and anxiety of our heroine and her companions were greatly excited.

As well as they could distinguish from the distance at which they were from the strangers, the party seemed to be composed of men and women, but whether natives or otherwise, they had no means at present of ascertaining

Once or twice they seemed to pause, as if to rest themselves before they could proceed, but when they did so, they still made their way in the direction of the fort, of which they had probably long obtained a view in the bright clear moonlight.

As they advanced nearer, they were enabled to snatch a better view of their persons, and they then discovered, so far as they could see from their costumes at least, that they were Europeans, and, in consequence their interest and curiosity were the more excited.

"They are probably unfortunate fugitives, like ourselves, flying from the cowardly and blood-thirsty foe," observed Alfred Meadows, "and seeing this old fort, they doubtless hope here to find a temporary refuge. They appear, from the slowness of their pace weary with travelling, and but too likely want."

"True, most true," replied Flora, in a voice of pity, "unfortunate creatures, and my heart bleeds for the horrible sufferings these remorseless wretches are daily, hourly inflicting. Oh, when will these frightful succession of tragedies be brought to a termination?"

"Ah! when indeed?" said Omelia, "I shudder at the thought, at the same time my bosom swells with shame and indignation to think that my countrymen should be the perpetrators of such fiendish atrocities. I know not how it is, but I feel a strange, and more than usual emotion at the appearance of these persons."

"See," remarked young Meadows, "they have arrived near the foot of the hill, and gaze with anxious eyes up at the fort. Our suspicions are confirmed, they are indeed Europeans. The men wear the tattered uniform of English officers, and the forms and features of the females—as well as we can distinguish them at this distance—cannot be mistaken."

Omelia returned no answer to this, for her whole attention was immovably fixed upon the figure of one of the male strangers, who stood a little in advance of his companions, and she trembled with a strange and unaccountable emotion.

They now began slowly to ascend the hill, and from the difficulty of the progress they made, it was quite evident that they were almost exhausted with fatigue.

"They have made up their minds to seek an asylum in the fort," said Alfred; "come, let us hasten to receive them, and to ascertain who and what they are. You look agitated and tremble, Omelia, how is this?"

"I know not," answered our heroine, in a faltering voice, "but I cannot resist the feeling that comes over me, and I am anxious, yet almost dread to meet those unfortunate persons."

Alfred made no reply, but taking her arm and that of Flora, he conducted them from the room, and down the stairs to the lower part of the building.

The strangers had already been admitted, and a piteous group they formed, enough to excite the deepest sympathy in any one who saw them.

But the eyes of our heroine wandered to him who had so completely rivetted her attention outside the fort, and at the same moment his gaze became fixed upon her. Gracious powers! was it a dream? was it some wild delusion of the wandering and distracted senses? No, it was impossible that either of them could be mistaken; a mutual and almost frantic exclamation escaped their lips—they rushed to each other's arms, and Omelia fainted on the bosom of her long lost lover!

CHAPTER LXX.

MOMENTS OF TRANSPORT.

What an affecting and exciting scene was that which followed. The pen must pause as it attempts to pourtray it. Flora who had recognised Edward Stanley at the same moment as Omelia, overpowered by the various emotions that rushed tumultuously upon her brain, also uttered a faint cry, and sunk insensible in the arms of her cousin, whilst he and every one present, stood completely paralyzed with amazement, perplexity and utmost incredulity.

But what a melancholy change had anxiety, and long suffering wrought in the handsome form and features of Edward Stanley. He looked not like the same being—he was but a phantom of his former self. His face was pale and ghastly, his eyes sunken and lustreless, and his form bent and fearfully emaciated, showing the fearful ravages which sorrow had made upon his once robust frame and constitution.

Again and again he hugged the lovely form of that beauteous being to whom his whole soul was devoted to his throbbing heart, whilst convulsive sobs had only the power to escape his lips.

And thus all parties for a few minutes were transfixed to the spot on which they were standing, their faculties for the time being completely suspended, and unable to give utterance to a syllable.

But the agony of Alfred Meadows was, if possible, more intense than that of any other person. He saw before him that man

to whom the heart of Flora was so fondly yet hopelessly devoted, that heart, which if she had never beheld him, he might probably now have been the happy possessor of, and, in spite of his manly and generous nature, for the moment he could not help a feeling of repugnance and jealousy entering his breast.

At length the mingled feelings of transport and astonishment that agitated the breast of Edward Stanley were suffered to find vent in words, and after repeatedly pressing the most ardent kisses of affection upon his adored Omelia's lips and cheeks, in a voice tremulous with emotion, he cried—

"Omelia, beloved, angelic being, light of my soul, and beacon to all my hopes and wishes, and are you again restored to these longing arms and throbbing bosom? Do I once more gaze upon those dear features which during our long separation have never for a moment been absent from my imagination? Kind, merciful heaven, you have heard my constant, my most fervent prayers; 'oh, bliss transcendant, joy unutterable!'"

Once more he pressed her with half delicious ecstacy to his bosom, and seemed to be quite unconscious of the presence of any one but himself and Omelia.

Alfred Meadows could not speak, he could not endure the trying scene; but as Flora still remained insensible, and the bewildered Stanley had not yet noticed or recognised them, he hastily but silently bore her from the room, the other persons having retired before, and the faithful lovers were left to themselves.

Edward Stanley having held the form of the insensible Omelia in his arms for some minutes longer, whilst he gazed with unspeakable rapture upon those gentle features which, even in his most sanguine moments of hope, he had never expected to behold again, gently placed her in a seat, and hanging tenderly over her, watched her recovery with an anxiety and impatience which no language, however powerful, can properly describe.

Scarcely could he yet persuade himself that he was not labouring under the delusion of some too happy dream, and he felt his brain so bewildered, and his mind so distracted with the strange and conflicting thoughts and emotions that held dominion over it, that he could scarcely contain or control himself.

He looked round the room, and finding that there was no one present but himself and Omelia, he became still more lost in perplexity.

Once more he pressed warm kisses upon her lips, which seemed to arouse her, for she revived suddenly, and opening her eyes fixed them full upon him, and frantically calling upon his name, threw herself sobbing convulsively on his bosom, and almost again relapsed into a state of insensibility.

We must pass as briefly as possible over the affecting scene which followed.

"Omelia," exclaimed her lover, still enfolding her in his arms, and looking into her face with a tenderness and intensity of expression which was sufficient to penetrate to her very soul, "it is your Edward, your own, your faithful, and adoring Edward, who now speaks to you, and holds you to his enraptured and palpitating heart. Oh, let me again hear the music of your gentle voice—that ever charmed and soothed me in the moments of my greatest sadness—to assure me that this unspeakable bliss is not delusion."

"Edward, dear Edward," ejaculated the maiden, in a voice of the most exquisite and touching tenderness, and her eyes swimming with tears of love and transport, "you still live; I feel your fond heart throb responsively to mine; I hear your lips pronounce the dear assurance of your unshaken constancy, and I am happy."

She hid her beauteous face upon his bosom, and for some minutes they were neither of them able to give utterance to another word.

Omelia was the first to recover herself sufficiently to speak, and looking at Stanley's pale and careworn features and emaciated form, with an expression of the most mournful regret, she sighed—

"Alas, dear Stanley, what a melancholy change has come over you since last we met. Sorrow and suffering have indeed fearfully done their insidious and cruel work, and it racks my heart to see it."

"Nay, beloved Omelia," he replied, faintly smiling, "torture not your gentle bosom, I beseech you, in your anxiety for me; 'tis true that my sufferings both of body and mind have been most severe, but you are now restored to my anxious arms, sweetest, and that at the very moment when least expected, and I am more, far more than amply rewarded for all that it has been my fate to have to undergo."

"What tender words are these, dear Edward, which you have just now spoken," said Omelia, "but," she added hastily, as if suddenly recollecting herself, "thoughtless that I am, why do I detain you here, when your looks too fearfully tell how much your wants require immediate attention. Come, dear Edward."

She smiled affectionately upon him, and he encircling her slender waist with his arm, suffered her to conduct him from the room.

*   *   *   *   *

For a time we will leave the lovers to themselves, and relate the incidents that had occurred to Stanley during his separation from Omelia.

In order to do this, we must once more shift the ever varied scene of our eventful narrative to Lucknow and its vicinity.

We would describe the world famed Kaiserbagh, and we cannot better do so than in the matchless language of Mr. Russel, the "Times" special correspondent, in his graphic account of the fall of Lucknow.

At the date of my despatch (says the writer), we had then attacked the Imaumbarrah or Imambarra with such vigour that the enemy, dismayed by the stern onslaught, by the fire of our artillery, and by the lesson they had received at the storm of the begum's palace, abandoned their position, and flying in disorder into the Kaiserbagh, so entirely disheartened the garrison, already decimated by the bombardment, that they gave up the key of their position almost without a struggle. Every one was on the spot as speedily as possible. The air was still heavy with gunpowder; bullets were whistling around from the desperate men shut up in the works, and from the enemy in the inner line of defences. Our men were just crashing through the rooms of the palaces, which were yet filled with the evidence of barbaric magnificence and splendour, and the cries of the dying were not yet stilled when we entered. The Kaiserbagh cannot be described.

The place is a series of palaces, kiosks, mosques, all of fanciful Oriental architecture —some light and graceful, others merely fantastic and curious, connected generally by long corridors arched and open in front, or by extensive wings, which enclose the courts and gardens contained within the outer walls. In every room throughout the endless series there was a profusion of mirrors in ponderous gilt frames. A universal gilding of cornices, furniture, and everything that would bear the process seemed the prevailing taste in the royal court. From every ceiling hung glass chandeliers of every age, form, colour, and design. As to the furniture in many instances it looked like collections from the lumber-rooms of all the old palaces in Europe—Louis Quatorze clocks and cabinets, Renaissance mirrors and chairs, buhl-worked ebony chests, marqueterie tables, solid lumpy old German state chairs, gilt all over; but these were relieved by the richest carpets, by sumptuous divans, by cushions covered with golden embroidery, by rich screens of Cashmere shawls, and by table-covers ponderous with pearls and gold.

In some of the rooms there were a few good pictures, said to be by Sir Joshua Reynolds, Lawrence, Zoffany, and Beechey, but I did not see any traces of Sir Joshua on the walls

when I entered, and there was only one picture which looked at all like a Lawrence. There were numerous portraits of the present and former Kings of Oude, and oil copies of the portraits of Governors-general, of Wellington, Nelson, George IV., and Bonaparte, many Chinese drawings, French crayons, and English engravings of all sorts, even those from "Williamson's Wild Sports of the East," an old and almost forgotten book on tiger hunting, in gorgeous frames, but the hand of the spoiler was heavy among them all. Those hung out of the reach of the musket stock and bayonet were scarcely safe from a bullet or the leg of a table. Down came chandeliers in a tinkling, clattering rain of glass—crash! crash! crash! door and window, and mirror and pendule. Sikh and soldier were revelling in destruction and

delirious with plunder and mischief. Those who could not get in at once to carry on the work searched the corridors, battered off the noses, legs, and arms of the statues in the gardens, or, diving into cellars, either made their fortunes by the discovery of unsuspected treasure, or lost their lives at the hands of concealed fanatics. There was no time to guard against indiscriminate plunder inasmuch as it never was expected that the Kaiserbagh and all its treasures would have fallen that day into our hands. It was stormed at once, but it could scarcely be said that any great resistance was offered by the enemy.

A lovely moonlight flooded the Kaiserbagh on the night of which we are writing, gleaming resplendently on its mosques and temples, its kiosks, its magnificent palaces, and its minarets; and imparting a chaste mellow grandeur to that which from its gorgeousness is almost too dazzling to the sight, in the golden beams of the sun.

There was a stillness and repose in all around, which was in perfect keeping with the serenity of the hour; the air was refreshing, and rendered still more cool and pleasant by the waters of the playful fountains that are there to be found in abundance, in fact, all around, above and below, was strictly in accordance and under the influence of the tranquil and genial season, and was well calculated to soothe the breast oppressed with care, and lead the desponding mind once more to hope.

It was at this hour, and in the road leading to the begum's palace, and so on to the Imammbarrah, might have been seen the tall and graceful figure of a man, standing with his arms folded across his chest, supporting himself with his back leaning against the trunk of a tree which grew by the roadside, and apparently deeply wrapped in thought.

His eye wandered vacantly over the magnificent scene before him, but his mind at that moment seemed to be insensible to its beauties, and not to soar beyond the region of his own gloomy meditations.

There was a marked expression of care and anxiety upon his manly brow, and his handsome features were pale, almost to ghastliness, showing not only the effects of recent illness, but also of some secret grief, which bore him down, and seemed likely ere long to bring him to a premature grave.

He was clad in the undress uniform of an English officer, but it is a waste of time to describe him further when we inform the reader what he has already guessed, namely, that it was Edward Stanley.

But what had brought him to that particular spot—where danger lurked on every side—and at that hour, whether it was accident or design, must be explained hereafter; it is quite sufficient for our present purpose to state that he was there, and within sight —as has been observed—of the gorgeous palace of that amiable lady who rivalled that female fiend, the Ranée of Jahnsi, in the atrocities perpetrated upon our countrymen, women, and children.

Yes, painful indeed was the change that the short period of two or three months had wrought in the face and person of the brave and noble-minded Edward Stanley, but his heart had undergone no change; no, that still throbbed with every manly and generous feeling towards his fellow creatures, and with the most fond and passionate ardour for that beloved being, from whom he had been separated under such trying circumstances, and whom he despaired of ever beholding again.

Yet within the last few days he had accidentally caught a brief sight of a beauteous being who so strongly resembled Omelia—at least from the slight glance that he had been enabled to obtain of her—that in spite of the improbability, he could almost imagine it was her own dear self, who like a guardian angel, watched over him, braving every danger, and anxiously seeking the opportunity to rejoin him, and lead him to safety and happiness.

It was near the spot on which he was at present standing, wrapped in gloomy meditation—as we have described him—that he had on one or two previous occasions, by accident, and which, as has been before observed, must be explained on some future occasion, seen the same lovely Indian maid, appearing like some bright vision before him, but for an instant, to dazzle and bewilder his senses, and raise his hopes and expectations, and then to vanish as suddenly as she had presented herself to his wondering and enraptured sight, and leave him to perplexing conjecture, and torturing anxiety.

It was with the faint hope of again beholding her, of addressing her, and having his doubts removed, that he had by the most ingenious stratagem, and at imminent risk, ventured thither; and for some time had he been waiting without any prospect of his hopes and wishes being gratified; and still so great was his anxiety, that his patience was not yet exhausted.

"But what madness is this," he ejaculated, "and what pains do I take to torture myself with idle conjectures and delusive hopes. It is impossible that this can be her to whom my very soul is devoted; and it is only my heated and disordered brain which has conjured up the resemblance to my imagination. Alas, Omelia, dearest, best of beings, fate, cruel and remorseless fate, has it surely sealed our doom, and we shall never behold each other again. Dreadful thought! what unutterable anguish does it inflict upon me, and yet I cannot banish it, in spite of all my efforts, it haunts me constantly, like some grim phantom, driving peace from my distracted mind, even if it should seek to shed its genial influence upon it."

He cast one anxious look around, and then resuming his former attitude, once more relapsed into silence and melancholy thought.

CHAPTER LXXI.

A STRANGE CONFESSION.

Still brighter became the moonlight, still more lovely the appearance of the sky with its floating clouds of silver, and myriads of

-tars: and still more grand became the works of nature and of man, as they glittered in the flood of glory shed upon them.

For a moment Stanley was aroused from thought, and gazed with rapture and enthusiastic admiration upon the lovely scene in the midst of which he stood.

His eyes wandered towards the splendid palace of the begum in the distance, and as they did so, he suddenly uttered an exclamation of pleasure and satisfaction at the object which rivetted his attention, and which was approaching him from the direction of the palace.

It was a female form of the most exquisite beauty, a young native woman, graceful in person, handsome in features, and fascinating in demeanour.

She did not appear to be more than eighteen years of age, and there was something in her whole personal appearance which so strongly resembled Omelia that they might very well have been taken for two sisters.

It was the lovely being whom Stanley had so frequently beheld before, who had so greatly excited his curiosity, and whom with the hope of again beholding he had ventured —in spite of the danger of so doing—to the present spot.

He could not help giving utterance to an exclamation of mingled surprise and satisfaction, and moving from the attitude in which he had been so long fixed, hastened towards her, resolved at length to address the beauteous being who had excited so strange and deep an interest in his breast.

But on beholding him approach—which she could distinctly do in the clear moonlight, she suddenly stopped, and seemed to hesitate what to do, not that she seemed by any means to wish to avoid him.

Edward Stanley, however, continued to advance towards her, and when he had got to within a few paces of her he suddenly stopped, more than ever struck by her surpassing beauty, while she herself did not appear to have the least power to move from the spot on which she was standing, but at the same time she exhibited the greatest confusion and retiring modesty of demeanour.

She was dressed with the greatest taste, and altogether a more interesting being could scarcely be imagined.

But if Stanley was charmed with the personal appearance of this young stranger, her great likeness to his beloved Omelia, and which had on one or two occasions that he had seen her before, almost induced him to believe that it really was her, astonished and bewildered him more than all; while the conviction at the same time that it was really not her, was a source of the most painful disappointment to him.

He advanced nearer still to her, with looks of admiration but the utmost respect, and the stranger did not attempt to avoid him, although she seemed rather embarrassed, and to await the result of this meeting with trembling anxiety.

At length Stanley, who could no longer restrain his curiosity, gently ventured to take her hand, which she did not try to withdraw, and, in a voice which showed the nature of his feelings, and the thoughts that were passing in his mind, he thus addressed her—

"Oh, tell me, I implore you, beauteous resemblance to one so warmly, so fondly cherished in my heart of hearts, you who have so often blessed my enraptured sight before, but to disappear and to leave me in still greater doubt and perplexity, tell me, I again beseech you, who and what are you that have created emotions in my mind for which I am myself almost at a loss to account?"

The young stranger seemed to become more embarrassed than before, and trembled excessively, but she still suffered him to retain his hold of her hand, and did not appear to be offended with the observations he had made use of.

At length she ventured to look up in his face, and there was an expression in her fine bright eyes, so exquisitely tender and so full of meaning, that it was impossible for Stanley to behold it without the greatest agitation.

She spoke, and there was a soft melody in the tones of her voice, which thrilled to the heart, and rivetted the ear in attention and admiration.

"The perhaps too presumptuous Miriami would not appear bold and forward, or be willingly guilty by word or deed of anything which might create a wrong impression, and—"

"Those looks, that voice!" interrupted Stanley, looking at her with increased astonishment, "so like my Omelia, that I could almost imagine that she stood before me. Gracious powers, what marvellous coincidence is this?"

The young Indian—Miriami, as she had called herself—exhibited the utmost agitation as Stanley thus spoke; she sighed, half averted her looks, as though fearful of encountering the penetrating gaze of Stanley, and then in a faint and tremulous voice, she said—

"The noble-minded, heroic girl, the beauteous and amiable Omelia, who loves you, Lieutenant Stanley, and possesses and deserves your heart in return, is not unknown to me, but we are in no manner related, and—"

"Ah," interrupted Stanley, with the most

unaffected and unqualified surprise and almost incredulity, "how is this? what strange mystery is this? You know me and Omelia, you bear her beauteous resemblance and yet I never remember to have spoken to you before."

"True, most true," replied Miriami, in still more faltering accents, "and yet, how have I longed and prayed for the opportunity to do so."

"Your words astonish and bewilder me, Miriami, for such you have told me is your name," said Stanley; for heaven's sake keep me not in suspense, but explain the meaning of your ambiguous words."

"Oh, I dare not," sighed Miriami, and again partially averting her looks, in order to conceal the agitation of her features from the observation of Stanley, "I must not, dare not, for you would hate and despise me if I did so, although the Great Spirit knows that there is no danger I would shrink from encountering to serve you, and to win one word of approbation from your lips."

She could say no more, for the violence of her emotions choked her utterance, tears trembled in her eyes, and her bosom heaved with the feelings which at that moment agitated it in so extraordinary a manner.

Stanley again took her hand, which trembled in his, and he could scarcely believe the evidence of his senses, so remarkable were all the circumstances of this adventure.

"How perplexing, how torturing is this," he ejaculated at length, "once more I implore you to explain the meaning of your words? How do you know me? how have you become acquainted with my name? and why do you seem to be so anxious for my welfare and happiness?"

Miriami hesitated for a moment or two, and evidently was violently struggling with her feelings. But at last, in a voice scarcely audible, and trembling in every limb, she thus replied to his observations—

"Because, Edward Stanley—and, alas, how bold and presumptuous you must think me for the acknowledgement—because I have suffered your image to take possession of my heart. I—I love you—weak, unjust, imprudent, daring as I am, I encourage a passion for him who can never return my love, and upon whom another has every claim."

She could say no more, and had it not been for the support of Stanley's arm she must have fallen to the earth.

But what were the mingled feelings of surprise, pity, embarrassment, and incredulity that agitated the breast of Edward Stanley at this strange and unexpected confession from one who was a stranger to him, to whom he had never even before spoken, but who so much resembled his beloved

Omelia that he could almost imagine it was her who was addressing him? He was completely lost in wonder and confusion of thought.

And then how similar was this hopeless passion to that which poor Flora Melville entertained for him. The coincidence was most painfully striking, and it appeared as if it was his fate to excite sentiments in the breasts of others which he could not return, and to have to blight the hopes and destroy the peace of those whom he would fain be the means of rendering happy.

So astounded was he by the confession of the poor girl, and so deeply did he sympathise with her, that he was at a loss for some time what answer to return, what to say to assure her of his regret, and his wish to convince her of his respect and to spare her feelings.

Miriami trembled and continued to avert her looks, and it was evident that she felt surprised and abashed at herself for her conduct which might seem to be so bold and indelicate.

"My poor girl," said Stanley, at length, in accents that showed the sincerity of that which he uttered, "how does it pain me to think that I should be the unwilling cause of one moment's disappointment or anguish to her who, although a stranger to me, I am convinced is so worthy of every respect and happiness."

"Pardon me, oh, pardon my bold, my rash, and wayward tongue for having ventured to give utterance to such a confession, Mr. Stanley," faltered Miriami, "but the fatal secret is revealed, and though you may despise me for it, I have relieved my breast of a heavy load that was almost too much for me to bear, and I will endeavour to be content."

"Despise you, Miriami," replied Stanley, with a look of compassion, "oh, what injustice you unknowingly do me, if you suppose that I can ever entertain such a feeling towards one who I am convinced so little merits it. What could ever have warmed your heart towards me thus?"

"Alas," returned Miriami, "I know not; it must have been some instinctive power, some strange infatuation, which I am at a loss to understand, but cannot resist. For months I have watched you, secretly watched you from place to place, but never before now had an opportunity to reveal my thoughts, or the courage to do so. But 'tis done now, I ask your forgiveness, and will never again annoy or pain you. Omelia lives, you will be restored to each other, and may you be happy, though Miriami can little hope to be so."

Tears gushed once more to her eyes as she spoke these words, and her voice failed her.

The generous-hearted Stanley could not help feeling deeply affected.

"Nay, my poor girl," he said, "do not talk in this melancholy and desponding manner. Unacquainted though I am at present with you, I am satisfied that you are possessed of virtues that will meet with their due reward. But you tell me that my Omelia still lives. Blessed assurance! with what fond hopes—yet doubts and fears—does it inspire me. But how know you this; oh, tell me, I beg of you?"

"I saw her on her escape from the power of the monster Nena Sahib," answered Miriami, "she was then under the care and protection of those in whom she might safely rely, and no doubt at present is in a place of safety."

"Thanks, thanks, for this information, good Miriami," exclaimed Stanley, gratefully, "oh, what a weight of care and anxiety has it removed from my mind. But you, my poor girl—for there is a certain mystery about you which I cannot penetrate—who are you? who are your friends? To whom do you belong, and—"

"Alas," interrupted Miriami, in melancholy accents, "I am humble and friendless, and but few gleams of happiness have ever shone upon my pathway of life. Circumstances over which I have no control, at present detain me in yonder palace, in the service of the hated begum, to whose flinty breast mercy, or indeed any other feeling of humanity, is a stranger. But the time is not far distant, I hope, when I may be able to escape from it. In the meanwhile, Mr. Stanley, I warn you, and your companions in misfortune, against the danger that threatens you. Should it fortunately be in my power to render you any assistance to escape, oh, what happiness will it afford Miriami to be able to do so."

"Kind, generous girl," returned Stanley, quite overwhelmed by her observations, and the feeling in which she spoke them, "how can I express my acknowledgments for that which I had so little right to expect."

"Enough, enough," said Miriami, hastily, "pardon, I pray you pardon me for that I have said, and instantly quit this spot, even beautiful as it is, for you know not the danger which may lurk unseen. Already have I acted most wrong and imprudently to detain you so long. Farewell, Mr. Stanley, and may all good powers watch over your safety."

"Farewell, Miriami," replied Stanley, "my best wishes shall be with you, rest assured, wherever you may be. But shall we not meet again?"

"I trust to providence that we shall," she answered, fervently, "and under far happier circumstances; once more farewell."

She smiled sweetly and affectionately, but still with a melancholy expression, as she spoke, and then hurried away with a light step, and had soon got some distance from the scene of the extraordinary meeting, leaving Stanley with mingled feelings of surprise, admiration, and regret.

CHAPTER LXXII.

MORE TROUBLES.—MIRIAMI AGAIN.

Edward Stanley watched the lovely and mysterious girl till distance hid her light and graceful form from his view, and then, notwithstanding the warning she had given him, and the prudence and necessity of which he was fully aware, so great was the confusion and agitation of his feelings at the extraordinary adventure, that he remained for a few minutes on the same spot, buried in reflection. In fact, there was something so remarkable about it altogether that he could scarcely believe in its reality.

The lateness of the hour, however, and the idea of the danger he might have to encounter on his way back to his companions, at length aroused him, and moving hastily from the spot, having first looked cautiously round to see that no one was watching him, he hurried on his way, surprised at himself, and half blaming himself for his folly and imprudence in having made so bold a venture, merely to gratify his curiosity. However, as we have before stated, he had been urged to this by the strong resemblance which Miriami bore to Omelia, and the impression which at one time rested on his mind that it was indeed the latter.

In that he had been disappointed, but still he could believe the assurances of Miriami, namely, that Omelia was still living, and in safety, and the heavy weight of care and anxiety which that thought removed from his breast, and the bright hopes that it revived, may be readily imagined by the reader.

"Yes, she still lives, the fond, the beloved being upon whom all my thoughts and wishes are fixed, still lives," he exclaimed, as he proceeded on his way, "kind providence has preserved her to me, I am convinced, and we shall yet be restored to each other, and that thought, in spite of all the troubles and dangers by which I am surrounded, makes me feel comparatively happy. Dear Omelia, with what unspeakable feelings of joy and expectation do I anticipate that blissful moment, and something seems to assure me that I shall not be disappointed. Even now your thoughts, dear girl, are fixed on me, and your prayers ascend to heaven for my safety. Poor Miriami, how strange that she too, like Flora Melville—but under such far more extraordinary circumstances—should have suffered such sentiments towards me to have taken possession of her, to encourage a passion for me to whom she was entirely unknown, and who never till this evening spoke to her. She is very beautiful, and no doubt good and virtuous. May she be happy."

He walked on at a quicker speed than before when he thus soliloquised, for he remembered the warning Miriami had given him, and he well knew the folly as well as danger there would be in neglecting it, and although, as the reader must be fully aware, by what has been related of him in the course of our narrative, he was not a man given to idle fear, even in the midst of the most imminent perils, he could not help giving way to a dismal foreboding of some fresh approaching trouble, which had suddenly beset him.

Still as he proceeded, as fast as he could, ever and anon looking back to see that he was not watched by any one, the beauteous but mysterious Miriami, and the words she had uttered, the confession she had so candidly but so modestly made, and every circumstance connected with this singular adventure, continued to occupy his thoughts, and the longer he reflected, the greater became his wonder, admiration, yet sincere regret.

"Poor Miriami," he said, in tones of the deepest sincerity and manly feeling, "how warmly do I sympathise with you in your unfortunate passion; and how gladly would I do anything in my power to stifle it in your breast, and to destroy the cankerworm which I fear it must too surely create, especially in one so susceptible as I am convinced you are. Your virtues, I am certain, entitle you to my esteem, my confidence, and regard as a brother, but any more tender sentiment it is impossible for me to feel towards you. Strange indeed does your destiny appear to be, fraught with sorrow, and every care, anxiety, and disappointment. And what a strange fate is mine, thus constantly being the unwilling cause of trouble to those whom I must esteem, and whose welfare and happiness I would gladly, if possible, contribute to. Miriami, amiable Miriami, so young and lovely, yet, I fear, so old in sorrow, better, far better would it have been for you had you never beheld me."

These reflections caused him feelings of the most painful description, and he would fain have endeavoured to banish them, but all his efforts were useless.

Thus deeply wrapped in thought, he had taken but little notice of the way he was proceeding, but suddenly aroused to a full sense of his carelessness, and the danger to which he was thus unnecessarily exposing himself, he looked around him, and then discovered, to his alarm and vexation, that he had unconsciously wandered out of his road, and was in a part that was quite unknown to him, but evidently quite remote from the place to which he wished to go.

He paused, and became completely bewildered how to act, in what way to extricate himself from the dilemma in which he had thus placed himself, and he now at once saw the folly and imprudence of which he had been guilty in venturing forth from the place in which himself and companions were in present safety, at all events

The moon was still shining brightly, and revealed everything to him distinctly, but that only served to show him still more clearly his embarrassing situation, and the difficulty in which his thoughtlessness had placed him, without in the least assisting or directing him how to extricate himself.

The Inammbarrah, and the Kaiserbagh, were entirely lost in the distance, and that served to perplex him the more, as, if he could have seen them, they would probably from their well known situation, have enabled him to shape his course in the right direction, as it was he was quite at a loss which way to turn, or how to act for the best.

"How unfortunate is this," he muttered to himself, "and how rash and foolish I have been, in thus venturing upon so wild and dangerous an errand. But it was for your sake, dear Omelia, and with the hope of beholding you that I did so, and surely the imprudence therefore of my conduct is, in some measure, excusable."

He now saw more forcibly than ever the importance of the warning which Miriami had given him, and the danger in which he had placed himself by allowing her so long to detain him. But it was useless for him to remain where he was, giving expression to vain regret, and he therefore once more proceeded, leaving it to chance to direct him right.

The farther, however, he went, the more did he appear to become involved in difficulty, the greater his doubt and bewilderment, and the more powerful, in consequence, his apprehensions.

Again he was compelled to pause, in order to consider in what manner to act, but without being able to come to any satisfactory conclusion, and his vexation and perplexity increased.

He was suddenly aroused, while he was thus standing on a secluded spot, overgrown with tall and thickly clustering trees, by hearing sounds that were well calculated to add to his alarm.

The sounds proceeded from the voices of men, who were evidently at no great distance off, and coming in the direction of the spot where he was standing, and he could distinguish from the language in which they spoke —which was of the coarsest and most ribald description, that they were those whom it would be prudent for him to try to avoid; in fact that they were enemies, and that, too, of the most reckless and brutal character.

To strengthen that opinion, and to warn him still more of the danger to which he was exposed, while he still listened, he heard the piteous accents of a female, seemingly appealing to the men for mercy and forbearance, and to which they only replied by savage and exulting language, and brutal and derisive laughter.

Stanley now felt his anxiety to render any assistance in his power to one, or perhaps more of his unfortunate countrywomen, thus exposed to the brutality of ruffians capable of perpetrating any outrage, however cruel, almost superseded his regard for his own safety; he drew his sword—which he happened to have with him—and stood for a moment hesitating how to act, but the idea of the great odds he might have to contend against, and the almost certainty of his falling a victim to his own courage and humanity, without benefitting those whom he desired to serve, decided him.

The voices sounded nearer, and convinced him that there was not a moment to be lost, but yet they were so close upon him that he knew not how he could possibly avoid them, but by concealing himself till they had passed, and again the voice of the hapless female, as she appealed to them for pity, caused him to hesitate, and excited all his manly sympathies.

There was no time for reflection, however, another instant and they must be upon him, and then his destruction would doubtless be inevitable, so drawing back behind a cluster of entangling trees to the left of the spot on which he had been standing, and from whence he could notice all that passed, without, as he hoped, being himself observed, he held his sword firmly, standing ready for self-defence in case of need, and awaited calmly but anxiously the the result of this adventure.

He had not to wait long, the party he expected appeared, and passed so near where he was concealed, that he almost feared to breathe lest he should betray himself.

It consisted, as he had feared, of about a dozen of the rebels, well armed, and three unfortunate Englishwomen, who looked the very pictures of anguish and despair, with torn and disordered clothes, dishevelled hair, and naked feet, and whom the heartless miscreants were driving before them amidst shouts of derision, and with every cruel indignity that their savage natures could suggest.

The heart of Stanley bled for these poor helpless creatures, whose fate in the hands of such monsters seemed certain, and his bosom swelled with indignation against the cowardly villains, while his regret and anguish were rendered still more intense to know that he, as only one individual, was quite powerless to render them the least assistance.

The wretches stopped a short distance from the place where Stanley was concealed, and, in spite of their shrieks, their tears, and piteous supplications for mercy, commenced a series of monstrous outrages upon their unfortunate victims, which filled the breast of Stanley with disgust, indignation, and horror to witness.

At length to such an extreme did they carry their atrocious conduct, that Stanley could no longer restrain his feelings within the bounds of prudence, and uttering an exclamation of shame and resentment, scarcely knowing what he did, he rashly started from the place of his concealment, and stood before them, sword in hand, and in an attitude which looked as though he was prepared and determined to oppose at the certain sacrifice of his own life, such unequal numbers.

The hapless females shrieked with mingled feelings of hope and despair on seeing him, and even the rebels seemed struck by the boldness and daring of his conduct, and for a moment stood and stared at him with amazement, and without offering to interfere with him. But they quickly recovered themselves, and with a loud yell of revenge such as savages could alone give utterance to, they rushed upon him, and before he had time to defend himself, if he had been desperate enough to do so, he was disarmed, struck with every cruelty and indignity, and his arms being pinioned with a cord, he, like the women, found himself completely in the power and at the mercy of those who were utter strangers to humanity.

He had expected nothing less than a frightful death upon the spot, and as it was his fate appeared to be certain, but he concealed his thoughts and feelings and conducted himself with a bold and manly bearing, under such fearful circumstances, as became an English officer and gentleman.

The poor woman looked at him an expression of pity and despair, and the eloquent expression of his features fully showed how deeply he commiserated with them, and how comparatively indifferent he was to his own fate.

"So," said one of the miscreants, who appeared to be the leader of the party, " your boldness and impetuosity have cost you dear, Ferringhee. If you had had only the wisdom and prudence to have remained where you was, and not venture to make a fool of yourself, you might have escaped detection, as it is, much against your will, no doubt, accompany us, and I dare say you can form a pretty good guess as to the fate which awaits you.

Stanley made no other reply to this brutal speech, than by a look of contempt, and the women and himself were then conducted from the spot, in the direction of the Imaumbarrah, as well as he could imagine, being subjected to every cowardly insult on the way.

But, in spite of his firm and calm demeanour, Stanley could not but feel most painfully his present dangerous and almost hopeless situation, and bitterly, more bitterly than ever did he regret the folly and imprudence which had induced him to run the risk he had done to gratify his curiosity.

He anticipated the fate which too probably awaited him, with feelings of anguish and despair, not so much on his own account as that of Omelia, who should she never more behold him, and hear of his untimely end, would, he was convinced, from the ardour of the love she bore him, be driven to a state of the most abject despair, and never more know what happiness was.

Besides there was something so awful in being thus barbarously and prematurely cut off by savages, in the spring tide of life, instead of dying with those we love near us, or a soldier's death upon the battle-field, that his heart recoiled with horror at the thought of it, and it required the exercise of all his energies to maintain his fortitude.

He recalled to his memory all the many hours that himself and Omelia had formerly passed together, before this terrible rebellion this reign of terror, had brought sorrow and calamity, he dwelt with a feeling of melancholy transport upon the early days of love, when all was bright above and below, and nothing seemed to threaten the ultimate completion of their happiness, he remembered their joyous meetings, their delightful rambles beneath the bright moonbeams, the twinkling stars, and amid all the varied beauties of nature's works again he listened in fond imagination to the sweet and mutual vows of love and constancy exchanged between them with all fervour and sincerity, and the prospect which now opened before his eyes, the almost utter hopelessness of the renewal of those days of halcyon bliss, became not only dismal and appalling, but actually insupportable.

Oh, what would he not have given if that which he too reasonably apprehended and anticipated, was to be his untimely fate, could he have been permitted to see, to speak once more to his adored Omelia, if only for a few brief minutes prior to his death, that he might enfold her to his heart, press his last farewell upon her lips, again assure her of his undying love, and receive her parting blessing?

This, he imagined would have reconciled him to death, but all possibility of that was at an end, and that rendered the agony of his mind the more severe.

The observations, the taunts, and mockery of the rebels, which were of the most brutal kind, did not divert his thoughts from this painful subject, yet were his best sympathies drawn in the most lovely manner towards the poor suffering women who were his fellow prisoners, and whose looks showed sufficiently, although they uttered not a word, the agony both of mind and body they were enduring.

They appeared to have been brought by the wretches in whose custody they were, from some distance, and to have suffered every privation as well as insult, for they were almost sinking with fatigue, while their feet, which, as has been before stated, were bare, were cut and bleeding from the rugged roads over which the miscreants had purposely brought them.

The events we have been recording, had necessarily occupied several hours, midnight was long since past, the moon had gone down, the dull gray mists gradually disappeared, and by the time that the rebels and their unhappy prisoners approached the Imaumbarrah, day began to dawn, and showed them the different buildings on their way more distinctly.

After proceeding some distance, they stopped before the door of a gloomy prison-looking house, which Stanley could quickly understand was to be the place of their present confinement, and the leader of the rebels was about to knock for admittance, when the attention of all was arrested by an exclamation of astonishment and emotion in a female voice near them, and Stanley immediately directing his gaze towards the spot from whence it proceeded, to his no little surprise and agitation, beheld standing on an elevated piece of ground at no great distance from the palace of the begum, and gazing earnestly upon them, the beautiful Miriami.

For an instant, and an instant only, she remained in the same attitude, looking with a pitying and melancholy expression upon Stanley, then waving her hand to him significantly, she hastily turned away and immediately vanished out of sight.

The men seemed to take very little notice of this circumstance, but Stanley, as may be expected, was very much agitated, although

he concealed his thoughts and feelings from observation as well as he could.

The door of the building was at last opened, and Stanley and his companions were thrust unceremoniously in, the rebels following immediately and closing the door after them.

They entered a dark and narrow winding passage, and no sooner had they done so than dismal moans and lamentations, as if from persons in the last extremity of suffering, smote their ears, and gave them terrible warning of that which they had to expect in that apparently frightful place.

In spite of his efforts to subdue his emotion, and to maintain his usual fortitude, the heart of Edward Stanley sickened as he listened to these doleful sounds, while the wretched women groaned aloud, and ex-

hibited other symptoms of intense fear and insupportable anguish, which only met with the exultation and derision of the brutal miscreants in whose power and at whose mercy they were.

They were conducted, or rather driven and goaded like cattle, along the passage by the leader of the party and another sepoy, the rest remaining behind; and at length they stopped before a small but strongly barred door, from which issued the melancholy and heart-rending sounds they had before heard, and which now fell with terrible intensity of effect upon their ears.

The door was unlocked, unbarred, and unbolted, and the next moment the prisoners stood in the presence of their fellow victims and companions in misery.

No. 38.

CHAPTER LXXIII.

A CHAPTER OF SUFFERING.

What a frightful scene of misery and refined cruelty was presented to the gaze.

It was a small dungeon-like room, with damp and blackened walls, unboarded, or unpaved floors, where there was an accumulation of filth, and only one small aperture high in the wall, to admit air and light.

The noisome, fœtid atmosphere of this horrible receptacle of human misery, was overpowering, and it was wonderful that anything but rats and other vermin could live in it for many hours.

Added to this, imagine the burning sun of a tropical climate—with an average of ninty-nine deg. in the shade, at certain seasons of the year—streaming in at that narrow aperture, and the reader may form a pretty correct idea of what the combined horrors of this hideous living tomb must have been.

But the frightful picture which we are endeavouring to draw is not yet half complete.

Within that confined space, at the time of the arrival of Stanley and his companions, no less than a dozen of our unfortunate countrymen, women, and innocent children, who had fallen into the hands of the enemy, had been incarcerated by the orders of that atrocious she devil, the Begum—of whom so much has been written latterly—for more than a week, with nothing to subsist upon but a small portion of the most loathsome food, and enduring horrors, than which immediate death, if even in the most revolting form would have been mercy.

And now to these hapless creatures, already having scarcely room to move or to breathe were to be added Edward Stanley and his helpless fellow victims

The heart of humanity must shudder at the bare contemplation of this ghastly picture, but unfortunately it is neither a solitary or exaggerated one, as may be proved by the most unquestionable authority.

Stanley himself with all his natural courage, was completely horror-struck, and shrunk back, while the prisoners on beholding him and the other captives, uttered a simultaneous cry of despair, and their squalid livid features assumed a still more ghastly aspect than before.

The men who had led them to this dreadful place of confinement seemed at first to exult over and to enjoy the horror they evinced, and contemplated them in silence, but with a most malicious and fiendish expression on their dark features, but they now seemed to grow impatient, and the one who appeared to be the leader turning to Stanley said—

"Now, then my gallant Feringhee you have inspected your new lodging, and that of these wretches long enough. Whether you approve of the many comforts it presents I neither know nor care; so in with you, and enjoy yourself."

"Heartless miscreant," exclaimed Stanley, firmly, and with a look of disgust and scorn, "you consign me and those poor women to a frightful death I know, still will I not condescend to appeal for mercy to a wretch like you, satisfied that a terrible retribution will most assuredly overtake yourself and your cowardly and infamous associates in crime."

The ruffian returned no answer to this, but his large dark eyes flashed with indignation, and his repulsive features were more than ever distorted with rage, while clenching his powerful fist—for he was a muscular man—he struck Stanley a heavy blow, which knocked him down stunned, among the poor creatures in the dungeon, and thrusting the poor women with brutal violence after him, closed the door, locking, bolting, and barring it, he and his companion left them to their misery.

It was several minutes before Stanley recovered his senses completely from the effect of the cowardly ruffian's blow, and when he did, how truly frightful, how appalling was the situation in which he found himself. It was more than sufficient to daunt the boldest spirit, and the pen almost shrinks from the task of describing its horrors.

Here were now no less than fifteen unfortunate human beings confined within the narrow limits of that fearful dungeon, and it seemed to be a matter of utter impossibility that death could long delay putting a period to their sufferings.

They were so closely huddled together, and the heat was so intolerable, coupled with the filthy and poisonous atmosphere of the place, that they could scarcely breathe, and two or three—among whom were the hapless females who had been the fellow captives of Stanley—had sunk on the damp and filthy earth, and seemed to be fast dying.

Stanley gathered himself up as well as he could, and gazed with feelings of pity—forgetting his own misfortunes at the time—upon the miserable beings in the midst of whom he found himself, and he shuddered with horror as he gazed upon their ghastly features, their sunken, bloodshot eyes, and listened to their low moaning sounds of agony.

But not a word did he dare to offer them of hope or consolation, which must have sounded like a bitter mockery, and they all appeared to have been long past the power of consolation.

But other and more torturing thoughts

crowded upon his fevered imagination, and drove him almost to madness. The form and features of his beloved Omelia presented themselves to him, looking as lovely as they were wont to do, and when he reflected upon what his awful doom was likely to be, and that he should never behold her again, he lost all patience and resignation, and was driven almost to a state of distraction.

But in the midst of this wild tempest of torturing and conflicting thoughts, he remembered the gentle Miriami, and all that she had said to him, and the look she gave him on entering the prison, and the promise she had made him to render him a service if she should ever have the opportunity, did impart to him a slight and transient ray of hope, and afforded him a brief period of consolation.

But how was 't likely that Miriami with all her professions, and her will in unison with the same, could have the power to assist him in his present dreadful situation? The idea appeared to him to be preposterous, and he therefore almost immediately banished it from his thoughts as soon as he had formed it.

She had stated that she was a humble, friendless girl, the mere slave of the begum, and therefore her influence, her interposition could effect nothing, and he saw not the least prospect of his deliverance, unless providence should so ordain it.

Yet did he feel grateful to poor Miriami for the good will she bore him, and he felt confident that her deepest sympathy with him in his misfortunes, and the dreadful fate which seemed inevitably to threaten him.

Every moment he felt the horrors of the place becoming more oppressive and insupportable—the heat was intolerable, his throat was parched with a burning thirst, and yet the water with which they were supplied was of that filthy description, that on putting one of the pitchers to his lips which contained it, he turned away from it in disgust, and was compelled to endure his agony for the present.

He had contrived with difficulty to withdraw himself to one corner of the dungeon, a little apart from the rest of his wretched companions, and that afforded him some trifling relief; still he felt so faint and overpowered that he could with difficulty support himself, and he thought it impossible that either he or any other human being could long survive in such a dreadful state of suffering, and the most gloomy thoughts and fearful forebodings haunted and distracted his mind.

And there he sat on the damp earth, crouched down in the corner of that fearful dungeon, and watching the ghastly faces and half idiotic looks of the wretched beings before him, until a kind of stupor—it could not be called sleep—gradually stole over his senses, and for a brief period his misfortunes and the terrors to which he was now exposed were lost in forgetfulness.

And how solemn, how awful was the silence—broken only at intervals by sobs and groans, or the plaintive cry of poor little suffering children—which reigned in that dreadful place. It was even more painful, if possible, than to witness the pale cheeks, distorted, haggard features, and emaciated forms of the sufferers.

It was more than a couple of hours before Stanley aroused himself from his lethargy, and then he started as if from some frightful dream, and glared wildly and vacantly upon the awful spectacle before him, scarcely conscious of where he was, or what had happened, or whether the ghastly objects that his eyes rested upon were the creatures of his own disordered imagination or reality.

But his own suff'rings quickly awakened him to a full sense of the dreadful truth, and he could not help giving utterance to a groan of anguish, which was mournfully responded to by many of his wretched fellow prisoners.

He felt so faint and languid that it seemed as if all his physical strength had entirely deserted him, and he could scarcely support himself.

The morning must have been far advanced, for it was some hours since Stanley and the females had been brought to the dungeon, but nobody had visited them, and it seemed as if it was the intention to starve them to death, if the frightful horrors of the place did not kill them.

The most terrible thoughts continued to haunt and agitate the mind of Stanley, and at times he worked himself up to such a state of excitement that he was almost in a state of frenzy, and not knowing what he said or did, cursed himself and the whole of his poor helpless companions in misfortune.

Unable to endure the intolerable thirst which had been upon him for hours any longer, he took a hearty drink of the nauseous water, which only seemed to make him worse, and for some time his senses wandered, and he continued to rave like a maniac.

But at length he became more calm, and endeavoured to meet his cruel fate with fortitude and resignation. Still painful were his reflections, and he looked in vain for something which might afford him hope and consolation.

"And has it indeed come to this," he mournfully muttered to himself, "shall this be the dreadful fate of Edward Stanley, whose prospects in life were once so brilliant, and whom such a proud field of glory was laid before? Must I perish by the foul hands of the worst of assassins, when my death should have been upon the battle field? No, it cannot be. Every feeling revolts against the thought. Let me then endeavour to dismiss it from my mind, and still to look forward with hope to happiness. This is but a trial of my fortitude, and patient submission to the will of providence, and I must learn to endure it as becomes a man."

"Happiness," he repeated, after a pause of reflection, "ah, can I ever hope that that will be mine, if my beloved Omelia lives not, and it be not my fate to be restored to her, no more to part? It is impossible, for she is my only hope of ultimate bliss, yet in spite of all my efforts, do the most dismal fears and forebodings continue to haunt my mind that those fond hopes will never be realised, and 'tis that which makes me wretched."

He sighed deeply as he spoke, and then relapsed into silence, and gloomy and torturing meditation, in which state he continued for more than another hour.

But at length he was aroused by an exclamation of agony and horror proceeding from the further end of the dungeon, and finding that it was uttered by one of the females who had been his unfortunate companions to the prison, his anxiety and commiseration were excited, and mustering up all the strength that he could, even weak and exhausted as he was, he crawled to the spot where the wretched woman was kneeling, he found her gazing with stupified horror upon the face of a corpse, the remains of another of his ill-fated companions.

It was that poor woman's only sister. Worn out by the cruelties that had previously been inflicted upon her, and the horrible sufferings experienced in that fearful dungeon, nature had yielded, and death mercifully terminated her sorrows.

Stanley was deeply affected, but the words of consolation he would fain have offered to the afflicted and bereaved sister, were not permitted to pass his lips, while the other unfortunate beings looked on with a sort of stupified and stolid indifference, or if not so, with a feeling of regret that they like her, were not yet released from their sufferings, and permitted to sleep for ever in peace.

And there in all the pale livery of death lay the corpse of that hapless being, that young gentle thing—who when in life, and ere the devastating hand of sorrow and adversity had made its cruel ravages upon her, had been so fair, so beautiful—with the pale and ghastly face of her sister looking vacantly and tearlessly down upon her, and with throbbing heart, which threatened every moment to burst its tenement, gasping, panting, mentally praying that she might quickly join her in eternity.

It was a sad, a mournful, a heart-rending sight, one that few, however cold and insensible their nature, could not behold unmoved, and Stanley, the more especially in his present state of mind, could not dare trust himself to continue to look upon. He therefore gently took the hand of the broken-hearted sister, raised it to his lips, gave her one look of heartfelt sympathy, the manly tear trembling in his eye—for we repeat that his overwhelming emotions would not permit him to speak—then slowly, and with tottering limbs returned to the spot in that ghastly abode of death, from which he had with motives of the purest christian charity, and the greatest difficulty come, and sinking down upon the cold earth, again abandoned himself to the horror and agony of his own thoughts, the nature of which it would be entirely useless for us to attempt further to describe.

The same solemn and painful silence—only broken at intervals by sobs, and sighs, and groans of mental and bodily suffering—continued to pervade that wretched living charnel house, while death with grim visage hovered around, and awaiting impatiently but mercifully his next victim.

At length Stanley was aroused from the deep lethargy of thought into which he had fallen, by hearing the door being unfastened—but the other wretched inmates of the dungeon stirred not, changed not the expression of their corpse-like features, at sounds which they knew would bring them no relief—and soon afterwards the savage gaoler entered the place, bringing with him a fresh supply of the coarse provisions.

He cast one exulting look around upon this frightful scene of squalid misery, and observing the corpse of the ill fated female for an instant, he thrust it brutally aside with his foot—it being in his way—and having deposited the food where he wished to place it, he returned to the door, and looking from it, beckoned to some one outside, and another man entering the dungeon he whispered some words to him, pointing to the cold remains, and after they had both indulged their fiend like feelings in a laugh, they proceeded to remove the body.

And now occurred a scene such as those who witnessed it—if any of them be still living — could never by any possibility forget.

No sooner had the wretches laid their murderous hands upon the corpse in order to raise it, than the sister, who had before appeared so powerless and inanimate, with a frantic shriek, which reverberated awfully through the dungeon, arousing even the rest of the prisoners into consciousness, rushed forward from the spot which she had previously occupied, and clinging to the cold remains, endeavoured to prevent the men from carrying their intentions into effect.

She struggled with them fiercely, desperately, all the time continuing her fearful shrieks, but at length, with a terrible oath, the inhuman ruffians struck her to the earth and bearing the corpse from the dungeon, with looks of savage exultation, closed and secured the door after them.

With what nameless feelings of horror, disgust, and indignation, Edward Stanley had beheld this dreadful and revolting scene it would take a most eloquent pen to describe. The blood rushed scalding hot through his veins, every limb was convulsed with the power of his emotions, and his manly bosom heaved and swelled with shame. Had he but the strength to do so, he could have rushed upon the monsters and dragged them beneath his feet, but he was powerless, and could only continue to gaze with increased and increasing horror, without being able to follow the dictates of his own will, and to interpose to save the poor bereaved creature from their brutal violence.

But now when the villains had departed with their lifeless burthen, and he saw the poor sister stretched inanimate on the earth, he partially recovered himself, and gathering together all his strength, he once more slowly moved towards the spot where the woman lay, in order that he might endeavour to ascertain the extent of her injuries, although he could render her no assistance.

She was lying on her face, he stooped down and placed his hand upon her bosom, he could not feel the slightest palpitation of her heart, and the awful truth in an instant flashed upon his conviction.

With the greatest difficulty he raised her in his arms, and her head fell powerless on his shoulder. With fearful eagerness and expectation he gazed in her pale face, and then at once his suspicions were confirmed.

The heart of the poor women had burst its bounds, accelerated by the violence of the savage men, and her spirit had fled to join that of her sister!

For a minute or two Stanley continued to hold the lifeless body in his arms, and his heart bled with manly sympathy, while he did not try to restrain a tear—an honour to him—then gently replacing her cold remains upon the earth, he murmured a brief prayer to heaven for the repose of her soul and that of her sister, and again retired with a sad and heavy heart to his former situation.

Slowly, tediously, solemnly, the hours wore away, without any prospect of relief, indeed Stanley, by dint of great mental exertion had almost learned to resign himself to his fate, whatever that fate might be, night closed in, with all its gloom and horror—doubly awful in that frightful place—and thus passed the first day of the gallant young officers confinement.

CHAPTER LXXIV.

LINGERING MISERY.—MIRIAMI.—HOPE.

Two more days and nights have elapsed, and still no hope of succour, no prospect of deliverance from sufferings too horrible to dwell upon—save by the hand of death—to the unfortunate prisoners.

And death had mercifully done its work in that brief space of time, for the number of the unhappy victims was reduced from fifteen to nine, thus affording them some melancholy relief indeed, so far as regarded the overcrowded state of the dungeon.

And Edward Stanley, how had he battled with terrible adversity, and supported himself with fortitude and patience during that time?

Better, far better than might have been expected.

He had again fortified himself with hope, notwithstanding the tearfully disheartening circumstances in which he was placed, and that enabled him to surmount many difficulties to which others were forced to succumb.

Omelia and Miriami by turns occupied his thoughts, and various were the reflections they gave rise to in his mind. Now that he was separated from the former, and with such little prospect of their ever beholding each other again, his love for her seemed hourly, momentarily to increase, and the more did he become convinced in his own mind—if indeed he had ever for a moment entertained a doubt—of her fidelity.

That idea was sufficient of itself to arouse him from the lowest depths of despair, and to encourage him to fresh exertions to struggle against the many horrors by which he was surrounded, and ultimately to come off triumphant.

"Yes, dearest girl," he would soliloquise, as the thoughts passed through his mind, "for your sake, I will brave every danger, every calamity with which it may please heaven to visit me, in the confidence of your love and constancy, I will still unmurmuring, boldly suffer on, in the firm conviction that an all-merciful and all-wise providence will never desert me, while I continue patiently to do so, but will at last banish my fears, remove my cares, my sorrows, and anxieties, and realise all my fondest, my dearest cherished hopes and wishes. I will be firm, I will not abandon myself to despair, for something tells me, assures me that, after I have passed through this ordeal, every happiness is in store for me, in possessing the hand, as well as the heart of my beloved and faithful Omelia."

His eyes would brighten, and his countenance glow, with joyful animation as these thoughts occurred to him, and his present sufferings and those with which he was still threatened, would appear to sink into comparative insignificance.

And then when he thought of the gentle Miriami, her affectionate observations, and the sincerity with which she had uttered them, also that she was aware what had befallen him, and the place where he was confined, it did not fail to strengthen his hopes, and to lessen the severity of his troubles.

In fact, the extraordinary resemblance of Miriami to Omelia, and the similarity of their manners, often led him to the strange conclusion that she was especially sent by providence to cheer him in his gloom, to remind him of her so fondly loved, to test the fidelity of his heart, and finding it faithful, to lead him again to hope and happiness.

But every hour more terrible became the situation of the prisoners, and it was wonderful how any of them could survive it. Hunger was working its deadly, its awful effects, and threatened soon to complete its dreadful task.

Many of them from long fasting and agony of mind, had become too ill, and too much exhausted to receive the coarse food supplied them, hungry though they were, and consequently, being deprived of all support, their fate was certain.

Two of the children and one more adult were swept away, and thus, in the short space of four days, out of fifteen persons that that dungeon had contained, six now only survived.

The bodies had been removed from the horrible place of confinement with every brutal insult and degradation, and stripped and mutilated, were thrown into the open air by the roadside, there to rot and decay.

But it was astonishing, as we have said before, that Stanley during all this time, when so many were perishing around him, should retain comparative health in spite of all his sufferings, but the same may be easily explained.

Notwithstanding that he had at first turned away with disgust from the coarse food, and his stomach had rejected it, he, knowing what the consequences must be if he followed the example of his fellow prisoners, persisted, and partaking only of the best of it, and that sparingly, it kept up his stamina sufficiently to enable him to combat successfully

with the terrible hardships that he had to undergo.

But at length something was about to occur, once more to impart a ray of hope to young Lieutenant Stanley and his fellow prisoners.

On the fifth day of their confinement, and when every hope of deliverance had vanished, the door of the dungeon was suddenly opened, and a stranger entered, bringing with him some provisions in a basket of a delicate kind, and a bottle or two of some reviving drinks suited to the peculiar and critical situation of the sufferers at present.

He was a young Indian of handsome person, and benevolent countenance, and his whole appearance was such as to excite the deepest interest and to encourage hope.

He closed the door cautiously after him when he had entered, and then after standing a moment and surveying the unfortunate beings with looks of compassion, he advanced towards them, and commenced sharing out the refreshing viands without speaking a word.

He then approached Stanley, who had risen on his entrance, and was gazing at him with a look of surprise.

His curiosity and anxiety excited to the utmost degree, Stanley was about to address him, when the young man put his finger to his lips, thus enjoining him to silence, and having placed a note in the astonished Stanley's hand, he made a respectful obeisance, and retiring hastily from him, abruptly quitted the dungeon securing the door the same as it had been before.

So great was the wonder of Stanley at this strange adventure, that he was for a minute or two completely lost in bewilderment, and could scarcely believe the evidence of his senses.

He looked at the superscription on the note, and his amazement increased. It was written in an elegant female hand, and addressed to him, in perfect English.

It must be from Miriami, there was no other female who could thus address him, and his heart palpitated and his hopes revived.

With a trembling hand he unfolded the note. It was indeed from Miriami, and continued only these brief words:—

"Miriami has not forgotten her promise, she has vowed to save you, and she will do so, even at the hazard of her life. Despair not, Mr. Stanley, for yourself and your companions to-morrow night shall be at liberty and shortly safe beyond the reach of pursuit. The young man who bears this is a friend, and you may trust him. Prepare yourself and your fellow unfortunates to see me and Abdal Moorsha to-morrow, at midnight. Destroy this after perusing it."

It requires no lengthy description from us to pourtray the feelings of Stanley after perusing this epistle, which he did two or three times. Suffice it to say that his heart overflowed with gratitude towards the beauteous and amiable Miriami, for this unexampled act, and he fervently invoked of Heaven a thousand blessings on her head.

"Generous-hearted, lovely girl," he enthusiastically exclaimed, "how nobly do your acts prove the sincerity of your words, and shew in such a dazzling light the brilliant virtues that adorn your mind, and shed a lustre around you. May every happiness that can attend us on earth be your lot through life, that is my sincere, my fervent prayer, and heaven grant that it may not be in vain. Oh, would that two kindred souls like your's and my Omelia's might meet together. What a bright source of happiness would it be to you both. You should be sister's in love alike, as you are in form, in features, and in mind."

He was completely carried away by the feelings excited by this happy and natural thought, and for a few minutes he could not recover himself; but when he did, he walked to his fellow prisoners, and read to their astonished ears the contents of the note.

How sudden and extraordinary was the effect it produced. It was like awakening the dead to life; they seemed to be all convinced of the sincerity of Miriami's promises —fresh hope and energy reanimated them in an instant, and sinking on their knees, with tears and sobs of gratitude, they returned thanks to the Almighty for the prospect of deliverance from their horrible captivity, at the same time beseeching his blessing and protection for the lovely maiden who was thus willing to run such fearful risks to serve her fellow creatures.

Groans and sobs of poignant anguish and bitter despair were heard no more in that den of horror, but all was hope, gratitude, and expectation.

Stanley allowed them sufficient time to calm their emotions, and then congratulating them on the prospect before them, advised them how to use the caution which was necessary for the successful accomplishment of that upon which all their hopes were now so fondly fixed.

This advice they all promised to follow, and to be guided by him and Miriami alone in everything.

They then partook sparingly of the provisions that Abdal Moorsha had brought them, and that portion which was left was then concealed, so as to prevent discovery, and they then conversed freely upon the coming event, arranged their plans and prayed to heaven for a successful result.

It was impossible to recognise in those now hopeful beings, the same wretched, suffering despairing creatures that they were a short time before, and in those feelings Stanley could not help but warmly participate.

But when he thought of the great danger which Miriami must have to incur in her generous endeavours to rescue them from the power of their savage enemies, he could not but more sensibly feel the enormous weight of gratitude they would be under to her, and to feel still more anxious for her safety.

She was indeed a most mysterious girl, and although he would have despised himself could he for a moment have harboured one doubt of her truth and sincerity, he was bound to confess that he could not unravel her.

By what means had she contrived, in spite of apparently insurmountable difficulties, to gain for her colleague in the plot admission to the dungeon, and communication with himself, and how did she propose to carry out her designs to a successful issue? He was at a loss to conjecture and must leave it to time and circumstances to explain, although it was quite certain that she possessed more power and ingenuity than she had hitherto given herself credit for.

He was lost in wonder and admiration of conduct so noble and so disinterested, and after taking care, according to her instructions, to destroy the note he had received from her, he entered freely into conversation with his fellow prisoners on the subject, all being anxious to render full praise and gratitud to the noble-minded Indian maiden.

They awaited impatiently for the following eventful night, so big with fate, though all were fully prepared to act with calmness, firmness, and decision.

Their conversation was at length interrupted by hearing the dungeon-door again being unlocked and unbolted, and they immediately—not knowing who it might be that was about to visit them—assumed, as well as they could their late miserable appearance, in order that no suspicion might be excited.

They were not kept long in suspense, for the next instant the door was thrown back upon its hinges, and their original gaoler entered, to bring them a fresh supply of provisions, and probably to see whether any more had fallen victims to the horrible atrocites inflicted on them.

He stood for a minute or two and looked at each one narrowly, but not appearing to perceive any change, he placed the food on the ground before them, without observing that that which had been previously brought, remained untouched, he again quitted the dungeon much to the relief of them all.

Two hours elapsed since the visit of this ruffian, and most of the inmates of the dungeon, in fact, all, with the exception of Stanley—whose mind was too busily occupied—were endeavouring to compose themselves to sleep, when they once more heard some one cautiously unfastening the door, and, again in doubt as to who it might be, they resumed their old attitude, but quickly changed it, and looked joyfully and thankfully upon him, when they saw that it was him whom they had so much reason to believe to be their friend, namely, Abdal Moorsha.

He had again brought with him a basket of a much larger size than the other, which he placed in a dark corner of the dungeon, directing their attention to it.

The poor prisoners could no longer restrain themselves, and gathering round Abdal, were about to give expression to their feelings, but he hastily prevented them, and by a significant look enjoined them to silence.

Of course, they immediately obeyed, and he then having once more placed a note, or rather a slip of paper in the hand of Stanley, who received it in silence, but with a look of the most profound respect, Abdal quietly and cautiously retired from the dungeon.

Stanley placed himself immediately under the aperture through which the moon was shining, in order to assist his vision, and then read the following lines :—

"All goes well. I entertain no doubt of success, if yourself and your companions only endeavour to gather all your strength and energy—which must have suffered so much from the recent atrocities inflicted—for the important occasion. I send a few necessary articles for the females. For the present, adieu. Remember, to-morrow at midnight." "MIRIAMI."

This note, as he had done the other, Stanley read to his companions, afterwards destroying it, and the generous and considerate conduct of Miriami, again elicited their warmest praise and admiration, and strengthened their confidence in the success of their design, all looking forward to the arrival of the following, eventful night, with the most indescribable anxiety.

Soon after this they sought repose with calmer feelings than they had long before experienced.

CHAPTER LXXV.

THE EVENTFUL NIGHT.

What a day of anxiety and impatience, of mingled doubts, and hopes, and fears, was the day succeeding the one we have been describing in the previous chapter, it became at last absolutely painful. Not that they doubted—for they would not have done so for the world—the integrity and fidelity of Miriami, for what could she have to gain by doing so, helpless, destitute, and miserable as they were? but that some accident might occur to betray them, to frustrate their plans, and thus to expose Miriami and themselves to a dreadful and certain fate, which they could not think upon without shuddering.

Stanley, however, entertained no such apprehensions, his expectations were most sanguine, and he endeavoured to inspire his companions with the same confidence, and in which he at last succeeded much better than, under all the circumstances, might have been anticipated.

In the course of the day they were visited by the ruffian gaoler, as usual, but as they again played their parts to perfection while he was present, he had no cause for suspicion or they for alarm, notwithstanding they felt much relieved when he departed, trusting that it was the last time they should behold him.

As night approached, of course, the anxiety of them all increased, and they listened with breathless attention to catch every sound which might greet their ears, but all remained profoundly silent, and they immediately set about preparing themselves for the important and critical moment whenever it might arrive.

This task was very soon accomplished, for they had very few preparations to make, the ladies made good use of the articles sent by the kind consideration of Miriami, namely, such as shoes—for they were most of them barefooted—light scarves, and veils, &c., for travelling, and many little trifling articles of comfort for those who had children, and thus so far as that went, everything was completed and in readiness.

Whilst waiting the arrival of the appointed hour, Stanley still busied himself with thoughts and conjectures as to what fresh adventures were likely to be in store for him but he endeavoured to make up his mind to meet with fortitude what ever might happen to him, whether good or evil, but to strongly indulge in hope for the former, and in which he trusted that he should not be disappointed.

There was one thing which caused him much speculation, and that was as to the course which Miriami would resolve to pursue. Surely she would not think of returning to the palace, after she had released them, and seen them part of their way in safety, for it was impossible that she and Abdal Moorsha could escape detection, and then their fate would be certain.

Besides, Miriami had declared to him on their interview, how great was her anxiety to escape from the service of the begum, and that she would lose no opportunity to do so, and after that assertion—candid and truthful as he believed her to be—it was not at all likely that she would break her word, more especially under such critical and dangerous circumstances as those in which she was placed.

He therefore concluded that it was most probable she had resolved to accompany them in their flight, an event which he could not but look forward to with the deepest interest.

Gradually, but remarkably sluggishly to the imaginations of the prisoners, the time stole on, and midnight at last approached.

As it did so all was excitement and ex-

pectation among the other prisoners, but Stanley was perfectly calm and collected, and he endeavoured all that he could to persuade them to become the same, as on that the success or failure of their designs much depended.

They took his advice, owning the justice of it, and mustered up all their firmness, self-possession, and resolution, for the important task they had to perform, and which if they failed in, their lives they very well knew, would all be forfeited to the blood-thirsty vengeance of the monsters from whose unparalleled cruelties they sought to escape.

They sunk on their knees and supplicated the mercy and protection of heaven in that they were about to undertake, after which they felt more calm and confident, and awaited the approach of the moment without any more emotion or excitement than was perfectly natural for persons placed in their situation, and under all the circumstances.

Again they listened attentively to catch the least sound, but all remained quite still, and it seemed as if they had nothing to fear from any person being about to observe them.

Stanley now looked at his watch, by the light of the moon whose beams still streamed brightly in at the aperture, and found that it wanted only five minutes to the hour of midnight; and now indeed all hearts palpitated violently with expectation, and they listened for the sound of the welcome and expected footsteps, with bated breath.

The long expected, and anxiously looked for moment came at last, and precisely to the time stated in the note of Miriami, they heard the cautious tread of footsteps along the passage leading to the dungeon, and a feeling of mingled hope, and doubt, and fear came over the captives, which they found it utterly impossible to resist.

They drew back, and awaited the disappointment or realisation of their hopes and wishes. But it was only for an instant that they had to endure this suspense. They heard the bolts being cautiously withdrawn, then the massive key turned in the lock, the door flew open, and they could with difficulty suppress an exclamation of joy and gratitude when Miriami and Abdal, equipped for travelling, entered the dungeon.

Stanley eagerly, and with looks that fully expressed his feelings, advanced towards them, and taking the hand of Miriami—who at that moment he could not help thinking with the gentle and amiable expression of her features, and the encouraging smile that beamed, as it were, from her sparkling eyes, looked more like his beloved Omelia than ever—raised it with the most profound respect to his lips, as he said:

"Kind, generous-hearted Miriami, in what language can I convey to you and your companion the thanks of myself and those of my fellow prisoners, I—"

"No more," interrupted the beauteous girl, in low but silvery tones, "no more, Mr. Stanley, I pray you, you and our unfortunate friends, I am convinced, fully appreciate the motives that prompt me to this, and place every reliance in the sincerity of my intentions, and I am satisfied. But this is not the time for further explanation; the moment is propitious; thank providence everything at present favours our designs, and we must not therefore delay. Come then, my friends, for such I will call you, follow me and Abdal, but silently and cautiously."

A murmur of gratitude ran through the group of unfortunate beings, and they then with eager but cautious footsteps, followed Miriami and her companion from that frightful dungeon, in which they had suffered so much, and which they had feared would form their tomb, into the passage beyond.

All was buried in solemn darkness, and not a sound was to be heard, save that of their own light footsteps as they proceeded, keeping as close to their conductors as possible, and they soon came to the end of the passage, and the door having been left ajar by Miriami and Abdal on their entrance—the former having first looked cautiously out to see that there was no one near to observe them—they emerged once more into the fresh air of heaven.

We will not seek to describe their emotions, but their conductors did not give them time for the expression of them, but motioning them to follow as quickly as they could, led the way from the gloomy prison, where so many hapless beings had met with a frightful and lingering death.

The night was dark save from the stars that twinkled so brightly in the firmament, and all was favourable to the escape, no signs of a human being appearing, and all being quite silent, and impelled by hope, and the sweet smiles of encouragement that Miriami ever and anon beamed upon them, they proceeded with freer and quicker footsteps than could have been expected, after the dreadful sufferings they had endured so recently, and the hopeless state of exhaustion to which they had been reduced.

The young Indians conducted their unfortunate charge by the most lonely way, to avoid the probability of encountering any one, and the quick eye of Miriami, and that of the young Abdal Moorsha, was ever on the alert to watch for any threatened danger.

We should have mentioned that Miriami, like Abdal, was armed with a brace of pistols in a leathern belt around her waist, together with a small dagger, and altogether she so admirably looked the amazon, that she even still more forcibly reminded Stanley of Omelia, as she appeared to him on their first meeting after her flight from the residence of the late Mr. Melville, and that called up such fond and bright remembrances, that he was more prepared than ever to love her "as the sister" of her who held supreme dominion in his heart.

Abdal had also brought with him a sword and pistols for Stanley, and thus the fugitives presented something like a formidable array for self defence, in the event of their being surprised and attacked by anything like equal numbers.

Proceeding in this quiet but still speedy manner, they had in a short time—a much shorter time than could have been anticipated under all the circumstances, left the prison and its neighbourhood a considerable way behind them, and having so far met with no obstruction, they all breathed again, and every heart overflowed with feelings of unbounded gratitude towards their generous, noble-minded, and heroic deliverers, which they could no longer refrain from expressing in language warm and enthusiastic as it was sincere, Stanley, from the peculiar nature of his relations with Miriami, being the most eloquent and fervent among them.

The eyes of the lovely maiden filled with tears, and her bosom swelled with the most indescribable emotions, as she listened to him, and it was not till after the lapse of a minute or two that she was enabled to make a reply, but at length she said, in a voice, every tone of which thrilled to his heart, and enshrined her more deeply in his affections—

"Stanley, *dear brother*—for such at least Miriami *must* be permitted to *call* you, and as such to *love* you—oh, how can I properly, adequately express in words the joy of my heart at being thus far enabled to serve you, how speak the fervent hopes so fondly cherished of being able to accomplish all my wishes by placing you in safety, and the arms of that gentle being, that noble minded girl whom I know you so truly and so justly love? It is my ardent prayer, it is my soul's ambition, the beacon light which shows and directs my only way to earthly happiness. And you will appreciate the truth, the purity of my thoughts, my motives, I know, dear *brother*, and in the full sincerity of your heart, grant the poor Indian girl, who would freely, willingly live your slave, all that you can *honourably* bestow, or that she can *virtuously* aspire to."

Convulsive sobs choked her further utterance, and so great was the agitation which shook her frame that she must have fallen to the earth, had it not been for the willing arms of Stanley that were extended to receive her.

But what were the feelings that were excited in his breast, by the simple, eloquent, and touching words to which she had just given utterance? We must fail if we attempt to pourtray them.

There was truth, there was fervour, there was purity, there was holy love in every word, in every expression of her beauteous features, and cold must have been the heart that could remain unmoved by them, base the wretch who could have dared to misconstrue them, or to harbour one guilty thought to her prejudice.

He continued to hold her lovely but trembling form in his arms—he could not, he dared not to resign it—she had appealed in irresistible language to the best feelings of his nature, she had appealed to his heart, and that heart responded, honestly, honourably responded to the appeal as he pressed her to it, and gazed with rapture, admiration, and affection upon her; but for a few minutes to endeavour to utter a word in reply he found to be impossible.

"By heaven," he at last exclaimed, "it is my own fond Omelia that speaks through your voice, and bids me, commands me to call you *her sister, my sister*. As such I am henceforth prepared to consider you, dear Miriami, as such to honour you—*love* you."

"Blessed words," cried the poor girl, with a burst of the most overpowering emotion; "I am permitted to call him *brother*, and I am happy—happy."

—

CHAPTER LXXVI.

THE DEATH OF MIRIAMI.—THE SECRET.

Overpowered by her emotions, and yielding entirely to the dictates of her heart, the poor girl sunk in the arms of Stanley, who impressed by the tender eloquence of her words, could not but deeply sympathise with her, and feel as greatly affected as herself.

It was several minutes ere either of them could recover themselves sufficiently to speak, and Stanley still continued to hold her lovely form in his arms, and press her to his bosom, while Miriami raised her bright and languishing eyes towards his countenance with a look which it would be difficult to depicture, and burst into tears.

"Dear Miriami," at length said Stanley, in the most gentle accents, and looking affectionately in her face, "dear Miriami, for such I may now be allowed to call you, I cannot adequately describe the emotions that now agitate my breast towards you. But why do you weep?"

"They are tears of joy, dear brother," replied the beauteous girl, "oh, how supremely happy have you made the humble Miriami, who is prepared to live and die for you. You will not turn me from you, Stanley? Say, shall not our fates and that of Omelia—to whom providence will, I am convinced, guide our footsteps—be henceforth linked together?"

"Yes, yes," eagerly replied Stanley, "indissolubly so, dear girl. Again I say that I am prepared to bestow upon you all a brother's affection, and Omelia will I am certain only be too happy to call you sister."

"Omelia—sister," repeated Miriami, in confused and hesitating accents, while a strange expression passed over her handsome features which did not escape the observation of Stanley, but which he was at a loss to understand; "sister, that name, so dear, and to which I—oh, Stanley, I have deceived you, Omelia is—stay, stay, my rash impetuous tongue—not now, not now."

"What mean you, Miriami?" said Stanley, whose curiosity was now more than ever excited by the ambiguity of her manner, "why do you exhibit such emotion at the mention of Omelia's name? And even now you look so like her, that I could almost persuade myself that it was her dear form I held in my arms, and fondly pressed to my bosom. Oh, unravel this strange mystery, I implore you, tell me how is this."

"Oh, urge me not, Lieutenant Stanley," she replied, in a faint and tremulous voice, and looking earnestly in his face with the utmost affection, "I do confess that I carry a secret in my breast, which I must not at present divulge; but rest assured that the time will come—and probably it is not far distant—when you shall know all, and till then, I pray you, rest patiently and contented."

Stanley could not but look upon her with increased amazement.

"Strange girl," he observed, "how remarkable and inexplicable are the feelings which your words excite in my breast, and the longer I gaze upon you the more bewildered do I become."

Miriami faintly smiled through her tears, but returned no answer.

The other fugitives had respectfully drawn themselves aside while this conversation was going on, but they marked the emotion which Stanley and the mysterious Miriami both evinced with the deepest interest.

"But why do we thus delay?" said Miriami, at length, "why do we thus waste moments so precious? We must proceed on our way as fast as we can, before the light of day breaks in upon us.'

"Whither do you intend us to steer our course?" eagerly interrogated Stanley.

"Leave everything to me," she replied, "and all will, I trust, go well. One thing rather bewilders and troubles me."

"And what is that, dear Miriami?"

"It is a small river which we cannot avoid, and which I am at a loss how we can cross, as it is too deep I fear for us to attempt to ford it."

"That is indeed most unfortunate and perplexing," said Stanley, "but still we must not permit ourselves to give way to despair. Providence will, I trust, aid us in our designs. Come, dear Miriami, come my friends, let us proceed with firmness and confidence."

They did so, Miriami leaning at times upon the arm of Stanley, and looking affectionately in his face, and at others walking a little in advance of the travellers, and looking cautiously about her to endeavour to ascertain whether or not any danger threatened.

The night was fine, and the moon's light now guided them on their way, and thus they continued to journey on for about a couple of hours, unmindful of fatigue, so grateful were they to escape from the accumulated and unmitigated horrors to which they had so recently been subjected.

At length they came in sight of the river which Miriami had mentioned, and stood upon the bank.

Here their further journey appeared to be brought to an abrupt termination, for there was no bridge by which to cross it, and, although it was narrow, yet, as Miriami had intimated, it was too deep for them to venture to ford.

They consulted with each other what was best to be done in this dilemma, but neither of them was prepared to offer any advice which appeared at all practicable.

"Let us proceed a little along the bank," suggested Abdal, "and who knows but something may yet present itself to assist us?"

This suggestion was adopted, and after proceeding for some distance, their surprise and gratitude may be imagined, when they beheld a boat moored alongside the bank, and in which some unfortunate person or persons like themselves had probably crossed from the opposite side of the river.

Having returned thanks to the Almighty for this unexpected and providential aid, the fugitives entered the boat, and were soon making their way to the other side of the river, where they landed in safety.

And now day began to dawn, but they had got such a distance on their journey that they considered themselves beyond the reach of immediate danger, and their spirits revived.

Stanley, who was naturally anxious, again inquired of Miriami whither she proposed going, and when she informed him that it was her wish to make her way towards Agra, where she hoped to find friends, he could not help remarking on the length of the journey, and the difficulty of their being able to accomplish it, without money or the means of obtaining provisions.

"Fear not, Mr. Stanley," remarked Abdal, "myself and Miriami are not so poor as you may imagine, we have in our possession money sufficient for all that may be required on the journey, and doubtless we shall not fail to meet with some friendly natives who will not refuse to render us all the assistance in their power."

"Yes," said Miriami, with a smile of satisfaction, "Abdal has spoken the truth, and therefore, dear Stanley, our prospects are far from being as bad as you have probably anticipated.

"Oh, thanks, thanks," said the grateful Stanley, "but you must now be tired, as well as our friends here, considering the distance we have already travelled, and under such peculiar and extraordinary circumstances. Know you of any place where we may for a short time rest in security?"

"Yes," replied Miriami, "as well as my recollection serves me, a short distance on this side of the river there are several bungalows inhabited by those who might be disposed to act friendly towards us, and there we may obtain all that we can require."

Stanley expressed his satisfaction at this, and Miriami—who now seemed to be most happy and light of heart—again leaning on his arm for support, they again proceeded on their way.

By the time the first bright beams of the morning's sun had gilded the eastern horizon, the travellers, in better spirits than they had been for some time before, came in sight of the dwellings mentioned by Miriami, and before which two or three of their occupants were standing, and who exhibited no surprise at seeing the fugitives, whom, however, they seemed to view with kindness and compassion, and that afforded them much encouragement.

Miriami advanced to one of the men and females, to whom—judging from their appearance that she might trust them—she ventured to address herself, and briefly stating the circumstances in which they were placed, and what they required, requested to know if they could accommodate them.

To this, these humble, but kind-hearted people immediately replied in the affirmative, and the whole of the weary party soon found themselves seated in a comfortable bungalow, and with everything placed before them that their necessities required, and with every attention being paid to them that kindness could suggest.

Accommodated in two of the bungalows, and free from every apprehension of danger, our travellers made up their minds—as they so much needed rest previous to resuming the arduous task which they had to perform —to remain there for that day and night, and they had no doubt that they should be able to re commence their journey with renewed vigour at an early hour the following morning.

They did so, and the next day continued on their way with perseverance and confidence, but without meeting with any incidents of sufficient importance to be recorded in these pages.

And yet there were times when the beauteous Miriami seemed to be greatly depressed in spirits, and lost in gloomy and torturing thoughts, from which Stanley and Abdal in vain sought to arouse her. Tears would start to her fine expressive eyes, and sighs escape her bosom, and which seemed to indicate that some fearful foreboding of approaching calamity racked her brain, and which she found it impossible to conquer.

The third day of their tedious journey was frightfully hot, indeed one of the hottest ever experienced in India even.

And here, in order to show the terrible hardships to which the fugitives were exposed, and as it is also our wish to make our work as instructive as amusing, it may not be considered out of place if we say a few words upon the climate of India, which we shall take the liberty of doing by quoting from the great experience of that eminent writer Mr. J. H. Stockqueler.

"How about the climate?" is a question which very naturally suggests itself to all persons purposing to take up their abode in India. Any advantages in the shape of pecuniary gain and social position which India may confer are dearly purchased at the expense of health; indeed, these advantages cannot be reaped at all if there is not some measure of certainty, or some reasonable chance, that the climate will be found suited to the constitutions of those who may proceed to either of the Presidencies.

Of course, in so vast a continent, varied in its physical features, and embracing twenty degrees of latitude, there must necessarily be a great diversity of climate. The air of the hills is purer and cooler than that of the plains; the presence of jungle and swamp is more pernicious than their absence; excessive aridity is as injurious as superabundant moisture. In India we find all the topographical peculiarities which induce contrariety of effect; and each Presidency is more or less affected by its difference of geographical position.

The situation of Bengal is low and level: in some parts remarkable for dry and sandy —in others for moist and clayey—soil. For eight months in the year, that is, from November to June, scarcely a drop of rain falls, excepting in the shape of an occasional storm, which lays the dust and cools the heated atmosphere. On the other hand, from July to October inclusive, a dry day is a rarity. Rain either falls for many days together, or for certain portions of each day, swelling the rivers and the tanks and diffusing universal humidity. To enable the reader to judge of the degree of heat, without reference to qualifying circumstances, it will suffice to state that the lowest range of the thermometer in January is 52 deg. early in the morning, and its highest 65 deg. in the afternoon. This is mild and pleasant enough. At no period of the year does the thermometer fall below 52 deg. After January it gradually begins to ascend, reaching in the evening of February 75 deg.; in the afternoon of March 82 deg. In April the mercury runs up to 90 deg. in the shade and 110 deg. in the sun. In May it ranges in the shade from 85 deg. in the morning to 98 deg. in the afternoon, rising to 140 deg. if exposed to the sun. June finds it still on the ascent. It is frequently 99 deg. in the shade at noon; but the rains begin to fall in the middle of the month, and the air becomes cooler as we advance towards July. The thermometer, in the latter month, falls to 80 deg. and 89 deg. It preserves the same range in August. In September it falls to 78 deg. in the morning, going up to 85 deg. in the afternoon. In October it seldom reaches a higher range than 80 deg. in the afternoon, whence it declines in November to 75 deg., and in December to 65 deg. in the afternoon.

The seasons at Bombay correspond with those of Calcutta. The thermometer takes much the same range as in Bengal; and although, in the hottest months, the casual advantage of a thunder-storm is never obtained, the sea breezes which set in towards the middle of the day essentially mitigate the heat of the atmosphere. Early in June the S.W. monsoon commences, the rains fall in rich abundance, and the air becomes cool and agreeable.

The Madras seasons and temperature differ from those of the other Presidencies. January and February are the coldest months in the year. The thermometer ranges from 75 deg. to 78 deg. Rain falls in slight showers continually, leaving a deposit of fractions of an inch. From March to June the range is between 73 deg. and 87 deg. In July the rains commence, and the thermometer then falls to 84 deg. It retains that position with very little deviation through August, and about four inches of rain fall. In September the thermometer falls to 83 deg., and the rain increases. In October the clouds begin to assume a more dense appearance than heretofore; the thermometer declines to an average of 81 deg., and the rainy season fairly commences, just as it has terminated at the other Presidencies. During November the rains fall heavily—not less than fourteen inches being deposited. The thermometer falls to 75 in December, and the rains abate.

Of course every scheme that human ingenuity can devise to mitigate the discomfort of heat is resorted to. The punkah is continually kept swinging over the head of the European; the window-blinds of the houses are closed to exclude as much light as may be consistent with convenience; matting of fragrant grass is placed at doors and windows, and continually watered; and every possible attention is paid by the prudent to clothing and to diet. From November to March woolen clothes may be worn with advantage: during the rest of the year everybody is clad in white cotton. No one ventures into the sun without parasols of a broad and shady form, or in palanquins roofed with tuskas.

Nevertheless the European constitution is exposed to the attacks of many diseases. Fevers, dysentery, affections of the liver, cholera, morbus, and rheumatism, are common; and there are numerous minor disorders, the effect of climate acting upon a slight or an excessively robust system, which few can escape. These latter consist of a troublesome cutaneous eruption called prickly heat, boils, and ulcers. Boils grow to a large size, are excessively painful and disturbing, and the lancet is often necessary to the relief of the patient. Constipation is also a common complaint, needing exercise and stimulating medicines.

Yet it does not follow that all persons should be assailed by the diseases of India. Very many individuals go through life in all parts of the empire, with perhaps only a single attack of one or two of the greater complaints—and not a few will pass thirty years in India unscathed. The writer of these pages was singularly favoured. During a residence of twenty-one years—one half the time at Bombay—the other half at Calcutta—he never had a single day's illness.

And if sickness should overtake the dwellers in any one of the Presidencies, baffling the skill of the practitioner, great facilities exist for resorting to the sanatory hills in the vicinity of each town. The resident of Calcutta can find relief by proceeding to the Darjeling mountain—one of the Sinchul range—where he finds a climate as temperate as that of his own native land. The place is reached by very easy stages in three or four days, and from the burning plain the invalid finds himself transported 7,200 feet above the level of the sea in a temperature of 55 deg. From Madras the Neilgherry hills are reached with ease in a week, and at Ootacumund, the principal station, or settlement, the finest climate in the world is found, and convalescence rapidly achieved. Bombay boasts its Mahabuleshwar hills, which are less than seventy miles distant, and easily accessible by boat or palanquin. Here the mean annual temperature is at 66 deg., and beautiful scenery, added to healthful breezes, gives life to the valetudinarian.

Perhaps the best proof after all that can be given of the healthiness of the climate of India is to be found in the great prosperity of the life-assurance offices. Their losses are rare, for it has been demonstrated by actuaries, who have recently given much attention to the subject, that the annual decrement of European life in India does not exceed the mortality in England by more than ¾ per cent.

As has been before stated the third day of the journey of our travellers was one of the most intense heat usually experienced in tropical climates, and they had to traverse an extensive plain, with nothing to shelter them from the sun's burning rays, so that the reader may imagine the terrible sufferings those who had already experienced so many were now compelled to endure.

It was almost too severe a trial, but they bore up against it with much more fortitude than might have been expected, although the torture of the thirst was almost intolerable.

Stanley felt it most oppressive, but he bore it manfully, and did not utter a word of complaint; but his unfortunate companions —the women and children especially—were almost exhausted, and it seemed impossible that they could hold out much longer.

Miriami, although she tried to conceal it, and to exercise all her fortitude, notwithstanding that she was a native, and in every way consequently inured to the climate, appeared to suffer more than the rest, and had it not been for the support of Stanley and Abdal, she must frequently have fallen overpowered to the earth, and unable to proceed farther.

We need not say with what deep sympathy and anxiety Stanley watched the poor girl, and how sincerely he regretted that he was unable to render her any relief or assistance.

She read his thoughts, and her looks sufficiently testified her gratitude, while she again struggled to conquer her feelings.

"Alas, Miriami," said Stanley, "how does it grieve me to see you thus, and to have it not in my power to afford you any relief. You are suffering greatly from this burning heat, although you seek to conceal it, and to bear up with the courage of an heroine, and here on this interminable plain there is another to afford you even a temporary shelter. May heaven help you."

"Torture not yourself for my sake, dear Stanley," she replied in a faint voice, "for I shall be better soon, I trust. The heat I own is more intense than I ever before remember it to have been, and it has taken an extraordinary effect upon me, while there is a strange sensation in my head which till now I have not before experienced. But— but, I am very foolish to trouble you with my whims and fancies; I shall be better soon, as I said before."

She tried to smile as she thus spoke, but she could not, and it was plain to be seen that her sufferings increased every moment, and it seemed certain that she would not be able to proceed much farther.

Stanley became seriously alarmed, and could not help giving expression to his feelings.

"My poor girl," he observed, "you have undertaken a task which I fear you have not strength sufficient to accomplish, great as is your generous will to do so. How deeply do I regret that you should be exposed to these sufferings, and that in your humane wish to serve those who had no claim upon you."

"Oh, say not so, Stanley," said the young Indian maiden, with a look of the most fervent affection, "no claim on me; oh, who can have a greater claim on the sympathy and humanity of the humble Miriami, than those whom cruelty and oppression have made their unoffending victims. Oh, that I might be permitted to realise my heart's fondest wishes, to see you happy, Stanley, in the arms of that faithful being, from whose thoughts I am so well convinced you have never been absent for an instant. But in spite of all my efforts I feel my strength gradually failing me—my limbs almost refuse to perform their office, and exhausted nature will at last I fear be compelled to succumb. And now a fearful foreboding of some approaching calamity rushes upon my brain. What can this mean? Oh, what is it that shakes my soul with terror?"

As Miriami thus with difficulty spoke, a wonderful and alarming change came o'er the expression of her handsome features— her eyes swam in tears—her limbs trembled —all strength of action seemed immediately to forsake her, and with a deep sigh she sunk powerless in the arms of the deeply affected and alarmed Stanley.

"Beauteous Miriami, kind, gentlest of human beings," he ejaculated, in a voice of the greatest emotion, "it can be no common —no ordinary feeling which can effect you thus. Oh, look up, speak to me, I beseech you, and remove the terrible doubts and fears that have taken possession of my breast."

The poor girl moved slightly in his arms, a sigh escaped her bosom, and opening her eyes, and fixing them upon Stanley for an instant, made an effort to speak, but could not, and then sunk back again on his bosom powerless and apparently insensible.

The agitation of Stanley now amounted to perfect agony, for he had but too much reason to apprehend the most awful and fatal consequences, and all hope of procuring any assistance in that wild and desert place was quite futile.

The other unfortunate beings were also in a most deplorable condition, and seemed as if they would be compelled to yield to the insupportable intensity of the weather before long.

More fiercely hot became the rays of the

sun, streaming down upon the unhappy fugitives and making the ground beneath their feet like one immense sheet of fire.

To continue their journey for a short time, and until they might in some degree have recovered themselves was utterly impossible, and they looked at each other with woe-begone countenances and expressions of the deepest and most irresistible despair; still their sympathies for poor Miriami were excited over their own sufferings, those of Abdal Moorsha, who hung over her as she was supported in the arms of Stanley, with all the anxiety of the most affectionate brother.

And in those moments of anguish and suspense, the extraordinary resemblance in form and features of Miriami to Omelia struck Stanley more forcibly than ever, and he found it impossible to remove his eyes from her.

"Alas," ejaculated Abdal, in the most melancholy and pathetic accents, "sweet, gentle Miriami, too much do I fear that this is but the prelude to the most fatal consequence. It is impossible that even with her unexampled fortitude she can long bear up against such terrible sufferings as those. Oh, but for a draught of water to moisten her lips."

The sun streamed down with increased heat, and an exclamation from Miriami, together with the agonised distortion of her features, and the strange and peculiar expression of her eyes startled and alarmed them all, and the fatal truth was too soon made apparent.

"My worst fears are realised," said Abdal, with a look of the most profound emotion, "'tis the fatal sun-stroke which has sealed her doom. She is dying. Oh, Miriami, gentlest, and best of women, what a terrible blow is this."

His manly heart swelled with the anguish of his feelings, and kneeling down he took the hand of the poor sufferer in his, and raising it respectfully to his lips, endeavoured to recal her to life.

But the feelings of Stanley at this awful occurrence, and in a place where not the least assistance could be obtained, were, if possible, even more overpowering than those of Abdal Moorsha, and he could not control them.

"Unfortunate girl," he sighed, "and must you indeed perish thus awfully and prematurely, in the springtide of your youth and beauty. Must death claim one who bid so fair to be a blessing to her fellow creatures, shedding peace and happiness wherever her footsteps approached? How sad, how torturing the thought. It seemed to be cruel and unjust. But soft, she breathes again, she revives. Heaven in its infinite mercy will spare her yet."

Miriami did indeed show some signs of returning life; she sighed, and presently afterwards she again opened her eyes, the lustre of which were dimmed, and fixed them with such an intensity of feeling upon Stanley and Abdal Moorsha—who was still kneeling by her side—such as no language however eloquent, could properly describe.

The other unfortunate beings gathered round, and watched the result of this painful and affecting event with the greatest anxiety and suspense.

"Miriami, dear Miriami," said Stanley, in a voice half choked with the power of his emotions, "oh, how can I describe the poignant anguish that rends my heart at this unforseen and dreadful calamity? But, oh, if you have the power, I implore you to speak to me, to let me once more hear the sweet tones of your voice, so much, so forcibly reminding me of my beloved Omelia, say that you are better, and that all who now stand around you, and so deeply sympathise with you, may revive again to hope.."

Still more touching and affectionate was the look which Miriami fixed upon Edward Stanley while he was thus giving expression to his feelings, and she again endeavoured to speak, but for a few moments her voice failed her. But at length, in low tone, she said—

"The will of the Great Spirit be done; I submit without a murmur, I feel that the end of my brief earthly career approaches; I am dying, but to die in your arms, dear Stanley, and with your looks fixed with affectionate sympathy upon me, oh, that is indeed bliss most indescribable, sweet consolation for the many sorrows it has been my lot to have to endure. You will not despise the memory of Miriami, who with her dying breath again assures you of the unbounded love she bears you, when she is no more?"

"Oh, do not talk thus, dear Miriami," said Stanley, manly tears, unrestrained starting to his eyes as with difficulty he spoke, "for every word thrills to my heart, and racks it to distraction. You must not perish thus, no, no, the Almighty will not surely permit it."

"Flatter not yourself with hopes that are fallacious, Stanley," returned Miriami, in the same faint but sweet accents, and with a look of resignation, "for I feel assured beyond all doubt that my final hour is come, and that life is fast closing around me. But oh, it is better that I should die in my innocence than live probably to stray from the paths of virtue into those of sin. You hold me to your heart, beloved Stanley, I feel that heart beat responsive to mine, and I am happy. Oh, this is indeed a bright foretaste of heaven."

She paused for breath, and a sweet smile overspread her features, which showed the heavenly joy that filled her soul.

Stanley and his companions could not speak, but they watched the dying girl with the most intense anxiety, their sobs of heartfelt anguish being the only sounds that broke upon the silence.

At length Miriami again revived sufficiently for a few moments to speak, and she then said, in the same touching tones as before—

"I could have wished to live that I might again behold Omelia, and impart to her with mine own lips a secret which has long been confined to my own breast and that alone of my dear cousin, Abdal. But Omnipotence has ordained that it should be otherwise, and I must not, will not complain. And

now, Stanley, I solemnly commit that sacred charge to you, beseeching that you will faithfully obey my dying injunctions."

"Oh, name them, my poor Miriami," said Stanley, fervently, "and I solemnly vow to obey them to the best of my abilities, whatever they may be."

"Oh, thanks, thanks," gratefully ejaculated Miriami, "that sweet assurance gladdens me in my last moments, and lights my soul on its way to eternity. Pardon me, dear Stanley, if in one respect I have deceived you in regard to my connection with Omelia, but I did it for the best My breath grows short, my eyes are becoming dim, and I feel that there is not an instant to be lost. Raise my head, and support me while I endeavour to perform the task I wish."

Stanley did as he was desired, and then

awaited that which she had to communicate with the greatest suspense and impatience.

Miriami placed her hand in her bosom and drew forth a sealed packet, which she placed in the hands of the astonished Stanley, with these words—

"To your care, beloved Stanley, I now commit this packet, with strict injunctions that you shall carefully and faithfully follow these my dying instructions regarding it. This contains the important secret to which I have already alluded, and will explain all that may have appeared mysterious to you in my conduct. But I charge you do not break the seal of this packet, or seek to pry into its contents till providence shall happily have restored you and Omelia to each other, and then peruse the contents to her. Do you promise, Edward Stanley?"

"Solemnly, sincerely I do," he replied.

"Enough," said Miriami, with a look of satisfaction, "that task is accomplished, and I can die happy. And the moment has arrived; eternity opens upon my sight, and all earthly things fade away. Stanley—Abdal, your hands—I cannot see you now—bless you, bless you both—bless, oh, heaven bless Omelia, and receive my spirit. The poor Indian girl's race is run; Father, I come, I come—"

Her eyes closed, her lips ceased to move, not the slightest emotion convulsed her frame, not a sigh escaped her, but calmly, peacefully the gentle spirit of the beauteous Miriami fled to its Maker.

CHAPTER LXXVII.

THE JOURNEY CONTINUED.

Yes, there resting in the arms of Edward Stanley was the corpse of that young Indian maiden, who but a short time before was living in all the pride of beauty, love and innocence, whose deeds won for her the esteem and admiration of all who knew her, whose heart had ever responded to the call of suffering humanity, and whose gentle voice never failed in its tender melody to impart sweet consolation and hope to the afflicted.

It was a sad sight, and for some minutes a solemn silence pervaded all the unhappy fugitives, who knew not how soon a similar fate awaited them, and they could only stand in trembling awe, and gaze with looks of sincere and poignant sorrow.

But calm and placid were those lovely features in the sleep of death, and a sweet and heavenly smile seemed to play around her lips, and to betoken the bliss of eternity.

The susceptible heart of the manly Stanley was full to bursting, and that of Abdal Moorsha fully shared in the grief and anguish of his feelings.

At length, gently Stanley laid the corpse of the poor girl upon the earth, and he and his companions in misfortune kneeling around it, solemnly and fervently offered up a prayer to the Most High for the repose of her spirit, and which prayer was alone disturbed by the heartfelt sobs of the women and children.

Thus several minutes elapsed, and none of them attempted to move from the spot on which they were kneeling, or to make use of any observation.

And now suddenly a refreshing breeze sprang up, and the excessive heat of the sun was abated, which was a great relief to them all, although their sufferings were still very great, and the burning thirst that was upon them was intolerable.

They were at length aroused into more immediate action; in what manner were they to dispose of the cold remains of poor Miriami? It was impossible for them to carry them with them, with the hope of obtaining for them proper and direct interment, and they could not think of leaving them there exposed to the rude gaze of any passing traveller, and to rot in the sun.

It was quickly decided; Abdal and Stanley removed the valuable rings she wore from her fingers, and then commenced digging as well as they could, with their swords, a humble grave upon the exact spot where she had breathed her last, which, after the lapse of some time, and with considerable labour they managed to accomplish. The body was then wrapped in the large white scarf of one of the females, deposited in its last resting place amid the sobs and tears of all present, the earth gently placed upon it, a mound being raised above it, covered with green grass turf, and all once more knelt around the hallowed spot, and offered up their solemn prayers to heaven.

It was a touching and impressive sight, and all who witnessed it could never banish it from their memory.

That melancholy task performed, and the fugitives having given full vent to their grief, it became necessary that they should endeavour to resume their tedious and weary journey, in the hope of being able at last to get beyond the plain, and to obtain some relief in this the terrible hour of their need.

But in their present enfeebled condition how arduous was that task, and they almost shrunk with terror from attempting it.

But it was imperative for them to exercise all their energies and arouse themselves into action, for every moment of delay was fraught with fresh danger.

Therefore fixing a last farewell look upon the grave of poor Miriami, and paying the honest tribute of their tears to her memory, they turned from the spot, and supporting themselves as well as they could on each other's arms, they slowly moved on their way.

Sad indeed were the hearts of them all as they proceeded, and gloomy and torturing were the thoughts to which the awful and untimely death of the amiable and beauteous Miriami gave rise.

Stanley and Abdal were more especially affected, and it was some time ere they could find spirits sufficient to talk to each other. To the former so sudden and wholly unexpected was the calamity, that even now he could scarcely persuade himself that it was anything more than some fearful dream, and he could almost fancy that he still saw the bright smiles of the beauteous Indian girl beaming upon him, and heard the mellifluous tones of her voice as she had affectionately addressed him.

Every word that she had uttered was stamped upon his memory in characters that nothing whatever could eradicate, and the more he thought of them, the greater were his interest and curiosity excited.

What could be the extraordinary and important secret contained in the packet she had so carefully delivered into his hands? He was all anxiety and impatience to know, but was unable to form anything which appeared like a reasonable conjecture.

He would have questioned Abdal Moorsha upon the subject, for he was satisfied that he was well acquainted with all the particulars, but he remembered the solemn injunctions of Miriami in her dying moments, and he therefore carefully refrained from doing so.

"Poor Miriami, generous hearted, noble minded girl," he at length observed, with a deep sigh, and looks that fully showed the intensity of his grief; " that she should meet with so untimely a fate, be snatched so suddenly from among us, at the time when our hearts were o'erflowing with gratitude for the unexampled, the inestimable services she had rendered us. Heaven pardon me for the observation, but it is almost enough to make us in the distraction of our grief murmur and complain of the dispensations of providence."

"Ah," remarked Abdal in the same melancholy accents; "she was indeed most good, most lovely in mind and person, and her death has proved a shock to me from which it will be a long time ere I can possibly recover. Oh, had you known all her glowing virtues, Mr. Stanley, as well as I did, even more great must have been your admiration of her, more violent your grief at her loss."

"Oh, believe me, Abdal," replied Stanley, "brief as was the period that we were acquainted with each other, no one could more duly appreciate the surpassing virtues of Miriami than myself, no one can more deeply deplore her loss than myself. May heaven rest her soul in peace. And if I have understood rightly, Abdal, you and this lovely being were related to each other."

"Yes," answered Abdal, " we were cousins, and mutual was the regard that ever existed between us. But I dare not trust myself further upon that melancholy subject at present, Mr. Stanley."

Stanley bowed assent to this, for he also felt too melancholy to discourse upon so painful a topic, and he relapsed into silence, abandoning himself to the most gloomy reflection.

Slowly the fugitives proceeded on their way, and it was wonderful, considering all that had taken place, the distance they had already travelled, and the great fatigue and exertion they had undergone, how they were enabled at all to support themselves, but the merciful eye of providence watched over them, and sustained them throughout difficulties, which other circumstances would probably have compelled them to sink under.

At length, but not until the evening was approaching, they emerged from the plain, and then found themselves approaching the mountains, from which a cool and refreshing breeze was wafted, but as yet no signs of a human habitation met their view.

They had not proceeded far, however, in the direction of the mountains, when they suddenly came upon a spring of pure water, which was indeed most welcome to them, and amply slaking their thirst they felt much refreshed, and journeying on a short distance further, and arriving at a convenient spot, they seated themselves on the grass not far from the mountains, resolved for a time to rest themselves, and to consult with each other what was best to be done, and how they should now proceed.

They could have fallen to sleep, but they resisted that as well as they could, fearing that they might be exposed to danger by so doing.

And now Stanley not feeling inclined for conversation, gave himself up to all the melancholy reflections which the recent exciting events naturally gave rise to in his mind. Again he recalled to his memory every word that poor Miriami had uttered, and the longer he reflected upon the sterling and unostentatious virtues that adorned her mind, the more was he lost in wonder and admiration, and the greater was his regret at her sudden and melancholy end.

Then the strange secret which the packet was said to contain, again occupied his thoughts, but the more he endeavoured to form a conjecture as to the nature of that secret, the more did he become involved in doubt and perplexity.

Again and again he pondered o'er her extraordinary likeness to Omelia, and when he remembered the allusions she had made too, and the ambiguous hints she had thrown out respecting that, beloved being, strange thoughts, and surmises, and suspicions entered his mind for which he was at a loss exactly to understand, but found it impossible to dismiss.

But the critical situation of himself and his companions, worn out as they were with hunger and fatigue, and the necessity of their endeavouring to find some place of shelter and accommodation for the night, aroused him from these reflections, and having briefly consulted with Abdal, they resumed their weary journey, wending their way towards the mountains, beyond which they hoped to meet with that which they so anxiously longed for, and of which they stood so much in need.

A cool and pleasant evening—as we think has been before stated—had succeeded the excessive and overpowering heat of the day, and greatly refreshed by the rest they had taken, and the allaying of the parching thirst which had been upon them, the travellers were enabled to proceed with renewed courage and vigour, and had nearly gained the mountains, making towards a convenient mountain-pass, which by the aid of the moonlight had been revealed to them, when they were startled and somewhat alarmed by hearing the voices of men, and the quick tread of numerous feet, approaching from an opposite direction to that which they were going, but still towards the mountains.

They drew back behind the shadow of some gigantic trees that grew near, and from whence they could watch all that passed without any fear of being observed themselves.

They had not to wait long in suspense, for presently numerous armed rebels, attended by elephants, camels, &c., loaded with baggage and ammunition, made their appearance, laughing and talking noisily, many of them being apparently in a complete state of intoxication.

They soon reached the mountains, and winding their way along the pass were quickly hidden from the view.

Stanley and Abdal then cautiously followed, and having watched the direction they took after leaving the mountains, and suffered them to get to a convenient distance, they beckoned to their companions, who quickly rejoined them, and they all then took their way along the pass, watching cautiously, and listening attentively—in case of any sudden surprise—as they proceeded, and found themselves in a short time, in present safety, beyond the lofty mountains.

CHAPTER LXXVIII.

THE FUGITIVES COMPLETE THEIR JOURNEY.

The scenery amidst which the weary but persevering travellers now found themselves was of a much more cheerful character than that they had previously experienced, and they therefore proceded with renewed courage and hope, trusting that providence would at length guide their footsteps to some friendly place of shelter, where they might obtain that rest for a few hours, which they so urgently required.

They also found an abundance of wild fruit growing about, which was a great relief to them, satisfying in a great measure the gnawing cravings of hunger they had for some time experienced, and thus recruiting their strength for the remainder of the distance that they might that night have to travel.

The aspect of the country even improved as they proceeded, though they met with no person on their way who might probably direct them where they might procure that which they so anxiosly sought, and they were compelled to leave their success or non-success to chance.

In this manner they journeyed on for about an hour, when breaking from among the clustering trees, and coming into a more open space, they suddenly came in sight of a small village, which drew from them an exclamation of satisfaction and gratitude.

Stanley and Abdal knowing the necessity of using the utmost precaution, and willing to run every risk themselves, rather than endanger the safety of their companions, desired them to wait behind for awhile till they went forward to the village to make the necessary inquiries, and to endeavour to ascertain whether or not they might trust the natives, and calculate upon receiving the requisite friendship and hospitality.

It was not long before they returned with a most favourable account of the reception they had met with, the villagers having offered them every accommodation in their power, and that with an apparent candour and sincerity that inspired them with every confidence.

The whole party then proceeded to the village, and were received in a manner which fully corroborated the statement of Stanley and Abdal, and elicited their most warmest thanks.

Their most urgent necessities were immediately seen to, in the most kind and considerate manner, and after having partaken of such humble but wholesome refreshment as their friends could afford, and for which Abdal was prepared to make every pecuniary remuneration, they bade each other adieu, and were shown to a comfortable place of rest for the night.

But Stanley on finding himself alone, notwithstanding the extraordinary and unusual fatigue he had undergone for so many hours, was too busily occupied with painful thoughts to suffer him immediately to retire to rest, and he sat pondering in his mind all the exciting and melancholy circumstances of that eventful day, totally regardless of the lapse of time.

It was to no purpose that he might even for a brief period, seek to banish the remembrance of the fate of Miriami, and the awful and truly impressive circumstances under which it had taken place, and the longer he dwelt upon these, the more acute became his anguish.

"Unfortunate girl," Stanley soliloquised, "never, never can I cease to cherish and revere your memory, or refuse a manly tear for your untimely fate. Your numerous and brilliant virtues must be for evermore enshrined in my heart, coupled with a feeling of sincere regret that mankind should be deprived of the blessing, the happiness of your society, in the bright morn of youth, and innocence, and beauty. Oh, how happy would my Omelia have been to have known you, to cultivate your friendship, and to call you sister! Sister! there is something in that name which excites an extraordinary and indescribable sensation in my breast, and kindles a feeling which I am at a loss to understand, but cannot conquer. But the mysterious packet which the poor girl delivered into my hands, she said would explain all, and till such time as I am permitted to break the seal, and peruse the contents, I must endeavour to wait with patience."

He took the packet from his pocket as he spoke, and after gazing at it for a few minutes, with a melancholy look, and heaving a deep sigh, he pressed it fervently to his lips, and solemnly invoked a blessing to the memory of the unfortunate writer.

At last, worn out with thoughts such as those we have but imperfectly described, Stanley retired to rest, and quickly sunk into a sound sleep from which he did not awaken till an early hour in the morning.

Hearing the inmates of the bungalow stirring, he immediately hastened to the room in which they were—much refreshed and invigorated by the few hour rest he had obtained—and there found his fellow travellers already assembled, and the morning repast prepared previous to their resuming the journey, which it was resolved to do with as little delay as was necessary.

They congratulated each other upon the favourable change which a few hours repose and the kind treatment they had received from the hospitable Indians had wrought in them, and Abdal having duly rewarded them, and all returned their warmest thanks, after the villagers had given them some valuable advice and instructions as to the way they should go in order to avoid the rebels staggling about the different parts of the country in the perpetration of their monstrous outrages, Stanley, Abdal, and their companions took their departure, and resumed that long and perilous journey, which had already occupied them several weary days, and had been attended with so many exciting and painful events.

They proceeded according to the directions of the villagers, which they found to have been prompted by an honest and friendly spirit, for they met with nothing to excite their alarm or suspicions, while the part of the country through which they travelled presented the most favourable and agreeable aspect, and none of those difficulties which they before had to encounter.

The temperature of the atmosphere was much more genial than it had been the previous day, and they could therefore travel without experiencing that excessive fatigue which they had before suffered.

During the day Stanley and Abdal conversed freely upon all that had hitherto taken place, and their prospects for the future, and they were never tired of speaking of the virtues of the late beauteous Miriami, and bewailing the melancholy fate which had befallen her.

"Poor girl," observed Abdal, in tones of the utmost tenderness and affection; "the loss of her, she who was the innocent companion of my childhood, and ever the warmest friend in more mature years, is one that neither time nor circumstances can ever replace. Oh, Mr. Stanley, had you had the happiness of knowing that beauteous girl as long and as intimately as myself, you could more properly appreciate my feelings at her untimely death, than you probably now do."

"Nay, Abdal," returned Stanley with a look of mild reproach, "you do me an injustice if you can suppose me insensible to the awful calamity which has taken place, or that I do not mourn the death of the lovely Miriami, with all fervour and sincerity of heart. The numerous virtues which were her's have made an impression on me, which time can never efface, besides I owe her an enormous debt of gratitude, for the great service she rendered us must ever endear her memory to me."

"I do believe you, Lieutenant Stanley," said Abdal, and cordially pressing his hand; "I do sincerely believe you, and pardon me if, in the agitation of my feelings I unintentionally said anything which was calculated to offend you."

"Enough," said Stanley, returning the pressure of his hand, "I understand you, Abdal, and honour you for your feelings. I trust that our friendship commenced under such remarkable and peculiar circumstances, may long continue."

"Most heartily do I hope so, sir," replied Abdal, "that is if, when you know me better, you should consider me worthy of it."

"I cannot doubt it," remarked Stanley, "the man whom the amiable Miriami honoured with her warmest esteem, cannot possibly be unworthy the friendship of any one. Besides, your present generous, noble, and disinterested conduct towards those in misfortune, sufficiently proves how justly you are entitled to every friendship and regard."

Abdal Moorsha bowed his acknowledgements for the flattering compliments that Edward Stanley had been pleased to bestow upon him, and the conversation upon that subject dropped.

Stanley then questioned him more minutely as to the place of their destination, and the further time that it was likely to occupy in completing the journey.

Abdal in reply to the first question stated as he and the late Miriami had done before, namely, that the place where he proposed going to, and where he had friends, was not far distant from Agra.

With this Stanley was perfectly satisfied for the neighbourhood of Agra was endeared to him by many fond associations in his early love for Omelia, as related at the commencement of our tale, and he could not divest his mind of a strange presentiment, which for some days past had taken possession of it, that it was there that they would meet again.

There was one thing, however, which caused him some fears and misgivings, and that was the distance which Abdal informed him they had yet to travel, and the time it would occupy in doing it, for he could not but doubt the ability of his companions to accomplish it, after all the difficulties they had already had to encounter, but Abdal endeavoured to encourage him by informing him that they had now a much more favourable part of the country to travel through, and that he had still sufficient money left to procure them every necessary on the road.

With this Stanley tried to be satisfied—at least he was so, as far as regarded himself —and he then turned his attention to his fellow travellers, whose confidence he endeavoured to inspire by every means in his power, and succeeded beyond even his most sanguine expectations.

That day was one of the least fatiguing they had yet experienced; they met with several bungalows on their way, where they stopped to rest and refresh themselves, and at night they received every accommodation from some friendly natives, so that they were enabled to continue their journey on the following day recruited in strength and spirits, and to make more progress towards the place of their destination than they had previously been enabled to do.

But we fear we should become tedious were we to enter into any further particulars of the long and weary journey of the fugitives. Suffice it to say, that after enduring many hardships and being reduced to the last extremity, on the eventful evening which has been particularised in a previous chapter, they found themselves scarcely able to drag their weary limbs after them, in sight of the old hill fort where Omelia, Flora Melville, Alfread Meadows, and his father, and the others, at present found refuge, and having given an account of the joyous and unexpected meeting, we will return to that part of our narrative from which we have so long digressed to relate the adventures of Edward Stanley since the time that he had been separated from his beloved Omelia.

CHAPTER LXXIX.

THE SEALED PACKET.—THE SECRET REVEALED.

After Omelia, in a state of transport which we find it impossible properly to describe, had conducted her equally delighted lover from the room in which their first interview after their long estrangement from each other had taken place, she led him to the apartment in which his fellow travellers were assembled, to whom he introduced her, particularly Abdal Moorsha, and the wants of them all being immediately attended to, as they required rest with as little delay as possible, after the most affectionate parting, they separated for the night.

But Omelia continued for some time longer in conversation with Flora, her cousin, and his father on the joyful occurrence, and various and powerful were the emotions that agitated their breasts.

Flora Melville felt a melancholy pleasure on again beholding Edward Stanley which she scarcely knew how to describe to herself, and Alfred experienced a sensation of uneasiness, doubt, and embarrassment—particularly as he had remarked with pain and regret, the extraordinary expression of his fair cousin's countenance, on again beholding that man to whom she had so unfortunately resigned her heart—which he could not conquer or control.

It was not, however, till our heroine was alone in her chamber that she ventured to give free indulgence to the unbounded and tumultuous feelings of surprise, of joy, and gratitude that overflowed her heart, agitated her bosom, and bewildered her senses. She could scarcely believe in the reality of the event, it seemed indeed more like some bright, delusive vision, too delightful to last, and it was long ere she could thoroughly persuade herself to the contrary, but at length when she was convinced of the truth, a flood of tears relieved her overjoyed heart, and throwing herself on her knees, she poured forth her soul in thanks to that Almighty power who had thus far extended His infinite mercies to her, in suffering her dearest cherished hopes and wishes to be realised.

It was sometime ere she could sufficiently recover herself to collect and arrange her thoughts, but when she did, in a voice of exquisite feeling, while the tears still glistened in her eyes she said :—

"Joy, joy, joy! Stanley, beloved Stanley is restored to these longing arms, my prayers have not be offered up to the throne of mercy in vain, the fondest wishes of my heart are gratified, and my tongue is far too weak to speak my boundless sense of gratitude. Oh, what are all the manifold sufferings of body and mind it has been my lot to have to endure, when I am thus rewarded by such indescribable happiness? Oh, Stanley, dearest Stanley, may it be the will of the same beneficent power which has thus again brought us together that we shall never more be separated. And yet do I dread to hear the tale of your sufferings, so painfully depicted in the melancholy change which time has wrought in your appearance, but I am consoled by the blissful thought that your heart, at least, has undergone no change, that that is faithful, and that there your own fond Omelia must ever reign the sole and happy mistress!"

Such were the delightful thoughts that continued to occupy the mind of Omelia till she retired to rest, and which pursued her in her dreams, and she awaited impatiently for the arrival of the morning, when she should behold her lover again.

And in what language shall we attempt to pourtray the feelings of Edward Stanley, when, like Omelia, he was left alone in the solitude of the chamber, appropriated to his use, and which had been hastily fitted up for his reception in the best manner that the limited means of the inmates of the old fort would permit? So powerful were they, in fact, that for a few minutes he could scarce contain himself within the bounds of reason.

"How wonderful are the ways of providence," he ejaculated, "that have guided my footsteps hither, conducted me to the goal of happiness, after having to endure miseries, sufferings, and disappointments, that might have broken many a stouter, firmer spirit. I can scarcely believe the evidence of my senses. And oh, how miraculously have the presentiments I ventured to encourage been confirmed. Oh, Miriami, poor, ill-fated girl, surely your bright and gentle spirit has been hovering about me, and, with the assistance of heaven, brought about this blissful result."

He paused, and still continued to reflect with wonder, admiration, and almost incredulity upon the extraordinary manner in which all these important events had been brought about, and the strange manner in which the predictions of Miriami, as to his restoration to Omelia had been fulfilled, and the longer he reflected the greater became his amazement.

"Poor Miriami," he ejaculated, "dear gentle, and most affectionate of human beings, oh, that it had been the will of All-merciful heaven that you should have lived what a bright halo of happiness would you have shed around us, how fondly would my own sweet Omelia have been prepared to love you. How great must be her grief when I relate to her the sad particulars of your untimely and lamented death, after enumerating your transcendent virtues, and the service you rendered to myself, and my companions in misfortune, who must have perished in that fearful, loathsome dungeon, had not your noble, generous heart prompted you to run so great a risk to save us. And in doing so, did you not sacrifice your own precious life? Alas, that it should be so."

The emotions caused by these painful thoughts, overpowered him, and he was again compelled to pause to give indulgence to them in silence.

"But the secret contained in the mysterious packet," he at length said; "oh, what can it be? Now that the time has arrived when it is permitted to be revealed to me, I almost tremble to discover it. Yet something seems to assure me that it is one of the utmost importance to myself and Omelia, and that it will bring both joy and sorrow to us both. Let me be calm, for to-morrow the mystery must be unravelled, my own impatience and anxiety, and obedience to the dying injunctions of Miriami, will admit of no further delay."

Having thus reflected and formed this resolution, he endeavoured to compose his feelings, and stretching himself on the rude pallet which had been formed for him of different articles of wearing apparel, spread upon the floor, he at last sought that repose of which exhausted nature stood so much in need.

Remarkable and perplexing were the dreams that haunted his imagination, and in which the late Miriami and Omelia bore the most conspicuous parts; and when he awoke he endeavoured to recollect them, and to interpret them, but he only became still further involved in bewilderment and uncertainty.

The early morning's sun was streaming full in at the windows of the room, and he had not risen many minutes, when there was a knock at the door, and the voice of Abdal Moorsha requested to know whether he might be admitted.

Anxious to see him, that he might communicate his thoughts to him and receive his friendly advice, Stanley immediately opened the door, and the young Indian and himself greeted each other in the same cordial and friendly manner as if they had been intimately acquainted for years.

After mutual inquiries as to how they had slept, Abdal said—

"I was anxious to see you alone, Lieutenant Stanley, that I might have some conversation with you on this extraordinary adventure, and also to congratulate you on the truly happy and miraculous manner in which the realisation of your hopes and wishes has been accomplished, and your restoration to Omelia effected."

"Oh, Abdal," replied Stanley, in a voice of emotion, and grasping his hand, "and to you and the late Miriami am I not entirely indebted for this happy consummation? I know not, indeed I know not how to express my feelings. I am again restored to my beloved Omelia, I find her heart still faithful to me, and my happiness is complete, I am more than amply rewarded for all the sufferings it has been my fate to experience."

"Omelia," observed Abdal, "is indeed most beautiful and amiable—the lovely counterpart of the late lamented Miriami in every particular. While I gazed upon her, I could almost imagine that my poor cousin was recalled to life, and again stood before me."

"Ah, Abdal, it is that extraordinary resemblance which continues to surprise and bewilder me," said Stanley, "you of course, I am convinced, know the particulars, oh, tell me then what strange and impenetrable mystery is this, which fills my mind with thoughts and surmises that I dare not trust myself with?"

"The packet delivered to you by Miriami will explain everything," answered Abdal, "my lips are not permitted to reveal the important secret. Prepare yourself and Omelia, Mr. Stanley, for a surprise, a joyful yet melancholy surprise, I have no doubt, of a most extraordinary nature. If you feel yourself sufficiently composed to do so, I would not have you delay the gratification of your curiosity and anxiety over to-day."

"True," said Stanley, "I will act as you suggest, good Abdal, and I feel all impatience to do so."

"'Tis well," observed Abdal, "but remember, Mr. Stanley, that at present, to no other ears than those of Omelia must the secret be divulged."

"That injunction shall carefully be attended to," answered Stanley.

"When you have perused the contents of the packet," added Abdal, "you will probably be anxious to consult me on the subject; and I need scarcely say that you may command me at any time."

Lieutenant Stanley thanked him most cordially, and they then hastened to join Omelia at the morning frugal meal, in one of the best rooms of the fort, from the windows of which might be obtained an extensive view of the surrounding country, and where her, Flora Melville, and Alfred Meadows, and his father were waiting to receive him.

We need not describe the feelings of delight and unbounded affection with which the faithful lovers met each other, and the fond congratulations and observations they exchanged with each other. They were at a loss for words adequately to express their transport, but their looks spoke far more than any language could possibly have done.

The joy of his unexpected meeting with his beloved Omelia, and the few hours rest he had obtained, had already worked a wonderful change in the appearance of Stanley, which Omelia could not behold without feelings of the most unbounded gratification and delight.

Flora Melville, Mr. Meadows, and his son, could not but join Omelia in their warm congratulations to Stanley on his restoration, but the former did so with a diffidence, and the latter with a look and manner of embarrassment, which showed the unpleasant emotions that agitated their breasts, though Stanley was too busily occupied with our heroine to take any notice of them.

Abdal Moorsha was also received with the most marked respect, and Stanley having anxiously inquired after his fellow travellers, and ascertained that they had benefitted greatly by their night's rest, and were then receiving every attention from the other inmates of the fort that their necessities required, the happy party freely entered into conversation of the most cheerful and delightful description.

At length Stanley being anxious privately

to communicate his thoughts to Omelia, and to accomplish the extraordinary and important task entrusted to him by poor Miriami in her dying moments, excused himself to their friends, and then requested our heroine to accompany him to another apartment, as he had something to say to and explain to her, which must be listened to by her ear alone.

Omelia looked at him with some degree of surprise and anxiety, but complied with avidity, and they instantly retired to another room, where for a minute or two they could not help again giving vent to the feelings of transport which animated their breasts.

At length becoming more calm, they seated themselves by each other's side, and Stanley encircling the slender waist of Omelia affectionately with his arm, after a brief pause said,

No. 41.

"Dearest Omelia, I have that to communicate to you, which I know will excite your utmost astonishment, interest, and sympathy, but I must request you to listen to me patiently, and with as much composure as you can."

"Pray proceed, dear Edward," replied Omelia, "for the solemnity of your manner, and the ambiguity of your observations, render me the more anxious to hear your explanation."

"I will do so, Omelia," said Stanley, "and that in as few words as the subject will permit me to do; but first it will be necessary for me to give you some account of that which has befallen me during the time of our separation."

"Oh, yes," returned our heroine, eagerly "and need I assure you, my own dear

Stanley, of the deep interest with which I shall listen to you?"

A pause of a few minutes ensued, and then, Stanley having sufficiently collected his thoughts, and prepared himself for the recital, commenced and continued the narrative of his adventures to the conclusion, as they have already been related to the reader.

Need we say with what profound emotion and attention Omelia listened to the interesting, but at the same time melancholy tale what strange and overpowering feelings agitated her breast as her lover proceeded, and more especially in every point and passage of that narrative which referred to the ill-fated Miriami?"

Surprise, regret, love, and admiration alternately held predominance in her breast, and she was frequently compelled to interrupt Stanley in the course of his recital to give expression to her feelings.

But when he had concluded the full ebullition of her emotions she allowed to take place, and after a flood of tears which she could not, and Stanley did not attempt to restrain, she said, in a tone of voice which showed the sincerity which dictated her words—

"Oh, Edward, how can I fully express the mingled emotions that have done, during your extraordinary and affecting narrative, and do now agitate my breast? I am lost, bewildered in wonder, heartfelt sympathy and regret. My own sufferings sink into insignificance at the contemplation of those you have had to encounter, and so manfully endured. But the ill-fated Miriami, the bare repetition of whose name seems to thrill to my heart, and to command its most ardent love, in what terms, how can I speak of her? in what language convey my admiration? I know not that I have, or if so, where I have seen the lovely, the amiable being you have so eloquently described, but she is present to my mind's eye now, as vividly as if in life, and I am prepared to treasure her in my memory, in my heart, as my sister."

"Sister!" repeated Stanley, almost overcome by his emotions, "blessed word, it was the sacred name by which she desired to call you, Omelia, by which, almost with her last breath, she begged to be remembered to you. Oh, that it had been the will of heaven that Miriami should have lived, and that you should have met together, how fondly, I know, from the similarity of your dispositions, the equality of your virtues, would you, must you have loved each other."

"Oh, yes," responded Omelia, her eyes at the same time filling with tears at the remembrance of the beauteous being of whom she spoke, "you do but justly appreciate my thoughts and feelings, Edward, for well

am I convinced, as I have before observed, that the gentle Miriami as, you have portrayed her to my rapt imagination, was worthy of all a sister's love. But the secret: my heart palpitates with an indescribable sensation till I know it, and you say it is permitted to be revealed to me?"

"Oh, yes, dear Omelia," replied her lover, "and you may believe me when I say that I am equally as anxious as you can possibly be to hear it. It is contained in this packet, and, as the good Abdal Moorsha, the cousin of that amiable being whose death we so deeply lament, observed to me, we must prepare ourselves for a surprise which will cause us both mingled feelings of joy and sorrow."

With these words Stanley took the important packet from his pocket, and looked at it with an expression of sorrow and veneration, while the heart of Omelia palpitated violently with expectation.

"Look, read dear Omelia," he observed, "what the superscription says."

Omelia eagerly took the packet in her hands and read the superscription as follows—

"To those whom Miriami so truly loves. Not to be opened till in the presence of the ever dearest Omelia."

"Beloved Miriami," ejaculated our heroine, with a burst of feeling which she could not, and did not seek to restrain, "in those few words I read at once your character, and the emotions, the principles that guided and prompted your heart. Here, Edward, into your hands I return the packet, the moment has arrived, the injunctions of the departed, of her whose soul is now in heaven, must be obeyed; you are in the presence of Omelia, and the secret we are both so anxious to know may be divulged."

Stanley took the packet, and with a trembling hand, for he could scarcely understand the strange and irresistible feelings that came over him at the moment, he broke the seal, and the first thing that presented itself to his sight, was the miniature likeness of a lovely European female, so life-like, that the bright expressive eyes seemed fixed affectionately upon him, and the ruby lips appeared parting as if about to address him.

An exclamation of admiration and delight escaped him, and he continued to gaze on the miniature completely fascinated, and unable to remove his eyes from so charming a sight.

Omelia watched his emotions with similar feelings, but her curiosity was excited to the utmost degree, and unable any longer to restrain it, she said—

"Dear Stanley, how your looks and the extraordinary emotions you exhibit agitate me. For heaven's sake what is it you are looking at so earnestly? I implore you, dear Edward, to keep me not longer in suspense."

"Look, look, dearest Omelia," replied her lover, placing the miniature in her hand, "and share with me in rapture and admiration, as I know you must."

Omelia took the miniature, but no sooner had she fixed her eyes upon the lovely features it represented, than an exclamation of astonishment and unbounded transport escaped her lips, and her whole frame became violently agitated.

"Gracious powers!" she exclaimed, "can I believe the evidence of my senses, or is it only some bright vision created to delude and bewilder them? No, no, those gentle features, this radiant, loving smile, those mildly beaming eyes, speak the blissful truth to my throbbing grateful heart, this is the dear resemblance of my sainted mother!"

With a burst of emotion such as it would be difficult to find language sufficiently to describe, she sunk in the arms of the astonished Stanley, as she spoke these words, and he continued to gaze at her, and the packet which he held in his hand alternately, and unable for a few minutes to give utterance to a syllable.

Then he eagerly snatched the miniature from the trembling hand of the almost insensible Omelia, and as he once more fixed his earnest gaze upon it, he exclaimed—

"Your mother, did you say, beloved Omelia? Yes, yes, I see the dear resemblance to yourself and Miriami in those beauteous features; oh, blind, stupified that I must have been not at once to have recognised it. Now indeed does my heart foretel the wonderful, the joyful, yet melancholy truth this packet doubtless reveals. And here is a small slip of paper addressed to you, Omelia, may I be permitted to read it to you?"

"Oh, yes, yes," answered our heroine, eagerly, but in a tremulous voice, and looking up anxiously, "read, read, dear Stanley, for I am all impatience to hear the marvellous secret, which I am convinced that paper reveals, but mine eyes are too dimmed with tears to suffer me to read it myself."

Stanley paused for a moment to collect himself for the brief but important task, and then in a clear and emphatic voice he read the following extraordinary lines—

"Dear Omelia, a stranger to you personally, but whose heart throbs in kindred feeling with your own, now by the command of heaven, and the holy ties of nature that link us together, ventures to address you, and to reveal a truth which the All-righteous God will confirm

"Look on the revered features pourtrayed in the miniature, they must, they will be known to you, and sacred to your heart; that miniature faintly represents the features of your mother, and that of your hitherto unknown, but ever affectionate *sister,*
"MIRIAMI."

CHAPTER LXXX.

THE VOICE OF NATURE.—THE SISTERS.

An exclamation, such as lips could only utter when the heart is bursting with the most powerful and holy feelings, escaped Omelia on hearing this wonderful, this astounding disclosure, and she immediately fainted in the arms of her equally astonished and agitated lover, who was completely paralyzed by the remarkable discovery, but which his heart had for a long time foreboded.

The packet fell from his hand, but he still held the important paper, and looked at it with wondering eyes, and read it again and again before he could convince himself that his senses were not deceiving him.

No, it was no delusion, the voice of the dead spoke the solemn truth, and he could not, dared not doubt.

But, oh, who can describe or even imagine the various thoughts and feelings that agitated his manly breast at the moment, and while he pressed the beauteous form of the beloved Omelia to his heart?

The extraordinary likeness between Omelia and the late lovely Miriami was fully and satisfactorily explained, the long hidden secret was revealed, the mystery unravelled, and surprise increased the longer that he reflected.

Omelia quickly revived, and a flood of tears having relieved her overcharged heart, in a voice of the most melancholy tenderness, she ejaculated—

"Sister, sister! dear, revered name, can I believe the evidence of my senses? Am I indeed so blessed, and yet so forlorn and wretched? Oh, yes, my heart's fond pulsations, the still voice of nature proclaims the sacred truth. But what strange and mysterious fate could have so long withheld that knowledge from you? What motive could poor Miriami have had in concealing it? I am lost in astonishment and perplexity and know not how to express myself."

"Oh, Stanley," said Omelia, "need I say how sincerely I participate in your feelings, when I assure you that my parents—for what reason it is impossible for me to imagine—never so much as hinted that I had such a relation in existence, and therefore it is not likely that any suspicion of the fact should have entered my mind."

"It is most extraordinary and inexplicable," observed Stanley, "but doubtless Miriami, in these papers, has explained everything in the most satisfactory manner. Let me see what is written on the ouside of the packet."

He looked at it, and read the following line—

"*The History of the Wanderer, Miriami.*"

"Yes," said Stanley, "this history—a sad one I fear—will no doubt unravel everything —relate every particular that we are so anxious to know. Shall I commence reading it, Omelia?"

"Oh, no, not now," she replied in an agitated voice, "I dare not trust myself to listen to it in my present state of mind. To-morrow, dear Edward, not now."

"Be it so, Omelia," said Stanley, whose excitement at the extraordinary discovery was not less than her own, but who, notwithstanding the great curiosity he felt to be made acquainted with the remarkable particulars which the manuscripts no doubt revealed, did not feel himself at present—especially when he had so much to say to his beloved Omelia on other subjects so dear to them—sufficiently collected to peruse them; "but we must prepare ourselves to hear that, I anticipate, which will not only excite our deepest astonishment and interest, but which may also appear so marvellous as to become almost incredulous. Still am I thoroughly convinced that the hand—now cold in death—which penned those lines, could never be guided by an untruth."

"Never, never," returned our heroine, vehemently, "my heart which throbs so fondly, so reverently towards her memory and that of the dear sainted being who bore us both—as the voice of nature assures me —tells me, convinces me that it could not. Poor, unfortunate Miriami, never can my scalding tears cease to flow whenever I think of you, and what, oh, what can ever banish you from my memory? Cruel fate that did not suffer us to meet, that we might have reciprocated each other's love, and lived together in all that pure, that holy, that unbounded affection that the children of such a mother alone can feel."

"True, dear Omelia," said Stanley, "most deeply is it to be regretted that providence did not permit you to do so, for never were two gentle beings more truly formed to love each other, and to be worthy of each other's love. But probably heaven ordained it for the best, and severe as is the trial, we must not murmur at its will."

Omelia gazed once more earnestly at the superscription on the manuscript, and read the solemn and remarkable lines that have been already quoted, while tears filled her eyes, and deep and heart-drawn sighs escaped her breast, then resigning it again to the keeping of Stanley, who deposited it in his pocket, then with looks of affection and melancholy delight which it would be difficult to find language to describe, but which the most sacred grief and filial affection alone could dictate, she once more turned her whole attention to the miniature likeness of her mother, in the contemplation of which for several minutes she was completely absorbed, her lover not venturing to interrupt her, but drawing aside, that she might give unrestrained indulgence to her thoughts and feelings.

"Revered parent," she soliloquised, in a voice rendered tremulous by the power of her emotions, "oh, what tender, what unspeakable thoughts, recollections, and feelings of useless regret, yet delight, does the bare contemplation of those beloved those amiable features excite within my throbbing bosom. I could almost imagine that you smiled upon me with that sweet maternal affection you were wont to do, and that your dear lips were parting to invoke heaven's choicest blessings upon the head of her who, until now, believed herself to be your only child. Beloved mother, oh, may your bright spirit, and that of her, who I am now convinced—previous to perusing the proofs— was indeed my sister, continue to look down upon me, to watch over me, and to guide me how to act, that I may never deviate or stray from those paths of rectitude and virtue that can alone do honour to your memories."

Again and again she pressed the miniature to her lips, and then consigned it carefully to her bosom, nearest her heart, where she had devoutly resolved that it should evermore remain.

Edward Stanley was deeply affected, and for some time stood by in silence, and contemplated the beauteous being who held supreme possession of his heart, with mingled feelings of sympathy, love, regret and admiration; but at length advancing towards her, and gently encircling her slender waist with his arm, while at the same time he ventured to imprint a fervent kiss upon her willing lips, he said, in tones of the utmost tenderness—

"My own sweet Omelia, with what melancholy feelings of pleasure and admiration have I dwelt upon every word which has just escaped your lips, and need I say how fondly my heart responds to all that you have so feelingly, so truthfully, so vehemently, and so devoutly expressed? My heart, if possible, throbs with redoubled love, nay, adoration towards you, and I feel more forcibly than ever how truly I am blessed by heaven in possessing such a maiden's love, and that after our long separation from each other, and encountering so many sorrows, dangers, and difficulties. we should thus—and that, too, in such a miraculous manner, that at times I can scarcely persuade myself it is not some bright delusive dream—be suffered to meet again, and to breathe those vows of pure affection, which our hearts assure us are so sincere."

Omelia looked in his face with an expression of such unbounded love as no language could do adequatee justice to in description. as she thus in her most gentle accents replied,

"Dear, faithful Edward, with what emotions of transport, and gratitude, and admiration do I listen to every beloved word which falls from your lips, and which I know so well are prompted by the pure dictates of that heart which beats for the humble, yet devoted Omelia alone. Oh, how I have longed, have prayed for this blissful moment to arrive; and it was alone the bright fond hope that my wishes would be realised, that heaven in its infinite mercy would listen to and grant my prayers, that sustained me through trials and sufferings, under which I must probably otherwise have sunk."

"Ah, dear Omelia," said Stanley, "it was the fear, the conviction of that you would have to undergo, and that your valued life would be sacrificed in the struggle, that kept my mind in a continual state of anxiety, suspense, and torture. Still there were times when the gentle voice of hope would whisper sweet words of consolation to me, and I fondly and confidently trusted to the mercy of the Supreme for the gratification of my wishes. But you have but yet hinted, beloved Omelia, at the various circumstances that befell you during the time of our separation, and if it will not tax your strength and feelings too much to relate them, need I say how anxious I am to be made acquainted with the particulars?"

"Yes, Edward," replied our heroine, "you are indeed correct in supposing the adventures it has been my lot to meet with during our separation to have been of the most exciting and extraordinary description, and fraught with dangers from which many would have shrunk appalled. But thanks to providence I have been enabled to surmount them all, and now that I am once more restored to your arms, dearest Stanley, I can learn to look back upon them without any poignant feelings of sorrow and regret. Allow me but a few minutes to collect my thoughts, and then, in as few words as I can, so that I may not become tedious, I will comply with your wishes, and relate such particulars as those with which you are not yet acquainted."

To this Stanley, of course, assented, and after a brief pause, Omelia proceeded to relate all those remarkable events that had occurred to her, the numerous perils it had been her lot to have to encounter, and the many hair-breadth escapes she had met with

—with which the reader is already fully acquainted, and to which, it need scarcely be added, Stanley listened with mingled feelings of wonder, admiration, pity, and indignation, and when she had concluded, embraced her affectionately, and in a voice which showed the sincerity of his observations, said—

"Oh, what can I say, my beloved Omelia, after listening to your interesting and extraordinary narrative, how express my astonishment and admiration at the unexampled the heroic fortitude with which you supported the many heavy trials to which you were so cruelly and unjustly subjected; how sufficiently evince my gratitude to heaven for having preserved your precious life throughout so many dangers, and permitted us to meet again? My heart o'erflows with indescribable joy, and I am more than amply rewarded for the many troubles I have experienced. Oh, that it might be the will of fate that we should never, never part again."

"That, dear Edward," returned Omelia, fixing upon him a look of innocent love, "need I assure you, is also my sincere and fervent prayer? And although circumstances may for a time once more separate us, I trust that it will not be for long, and that all our fondest hopes and wishes may be ultimately realised, and our fates be indissolubly united."

Stanley again enfolded her rapturously in his arms, and imprinted soft kisses on her lips and cheeks, and then after some further conversation of the same tender description, and having finally fixed the following day for the perusal of the manuscript, the lovers hastened to rejoin their friends, whom they had no doubt would feel anxious for their return to their society.

CHAPTER LXXXI.

MIRIAMI'S TALE.

Flora and Alfred Meadows and his father had indeed felt most dull and uncomfortable at the long absence of Omelia and her lover from their company, and impatiently awaited their return, therefore we need scarcely say that they greeted them on re-entering the room with feelings of the most unfeigned pleasure, and so well had our heroine and Stanley conquered their emotions at the strange and important discovery they had made, and were enabled to conceal the real emotions that occupied their minds, that their friends were unable to perceive anything unusual about them.

Our heroine, however, required the solitude of her own thoughts, and after some little time passed in the company of her lover and their friends, she made an excuse to retire

Abdal Moorsha, who had also been present, frequently by the significant looks he fixed upon Stanley, showed his anxiety to speak with him, and the latter understanding the subject upon which he wished to address him perfectly well, immediately on separating from the others followed him into the garden of the fort.

"You know the secret," observed Abdal, when they were alone, "I can see it by your looks. Is it not so, Lieutenant Stanley?"

"True, most true," replied Stanley, "and I confess that I am completely astounded, notwithstanding I was somewhat prepared for such a discovery, in consequence of the remarkable likeness between poor Miriami and Omelia, and the extraordinary hints which the former had thrown out."

"But Omelia," eagerly inquired Abdal, "how did she receive the discovery?"

"You may judge of her feelings, Abdal," answered Stanley, "much better than I can describe them. How deeply is it to be regretted that two such sisters were not destined to meet together, and to live to love each other with that warmth of affection which only two such hearts could feel and cherish."

"True," coincided Abdal, "and believe me that I lament it as deeply as yourself, Mr. Stanley. But the manuscripts—have you perused them?"

Stanley replied in the negative, and stated the reason for his not doing so, with which Abdal expressed his satisfaction.

"Is the packet still in your possession?" he interrogated.

"It is," replied Stanley, "and to-morrow, if Omelia should feel disposed to listen to it, which she will no doubt be most anxious to do, I will peruse it to her."

"Good," said Abdal, "but in the interim I would wish you not to read it yourself, as that I consider would not be strictly in accordance with the instructions and injunctions of poor Miriami in her dying moments."

"True," said Stanley, "I will not fail to follow your advice, good Abdal."

"I am fully prepared to vouch for the truth of every word which those papers contain," remarked Abdal.

"Oh, I doubt it not," returned Stanley, "for whom who knew her, could presume to doubt the veracity of the amiable but unfortunate Miriami?"

"Prepare yourself for astonishment and the deepest interest on the perusal of that extraordinary narrative," said Abdal. "Alas, hapless girl, how many weary and tedious hours did those important documents cost her in the writing of them; but she worked at them with avidity and assiduity, in the fond assurance that they would one day be placed in the hands of that beloved being for whom they were intended. That time has providentially now arrived, and I am satisfied."

"Yes," observed Stanley. "I can fully appreciate your feelings, Abdal; but is it not strange that Miriami should have deferred so long in revealing so important a secret, especially personally to her to whom it was of the utmost interest?"

"I agree with you that it does," replied Abdal, "but no doubt Miriami had her reasons, which I dare say will be fully explained in the manuscripts."

After some further conversation, they re-entered the fort, and rejoined their companions.

When our heroine found herself alone, she gave free indulgence to the various thoughts that busily occupied her mind, and which the remarkable events, so recently related, had naturally excited, and the longer she reflected upon them the greater became her emotions, and the more her astonishment increased. So extraordinary indeed were all the circumstances that had taken place that she was half inclined to treat them with incredulity.

Again she took the miniature likeness of her mother from her bosom, and with tearful eyes and a heaving bosom she dwelt upon the beauteous and beloved features with feelings of unbounded transport and reverence it would be difficult for even the most eloquent pen properly to describe.

Then her whole thoughts were alone devoted to Miriami, and the secret which she had revealed, and the more she reflected on it the deeper she became involved in astonishment and perplexity.

From the glowing description which Stanley had given of her, she was enabled to form a pretty vivid picture in imagination of what the poor girl really was; and how ardently as a sister she would have been prepared to love her, had it pleased heaven that she should have lived, and they should have met together; and she could not but deeply lament that she should have been so suddenly and so unexpectedly snatched away, and her tears flowed freely to her memory.

She awaited anxiously the perusal of the manuscript—although she could not find sufficient composure to listen to it to-day—for there were many remarkable circumstances, and ambiguities, which she was eager to know, and which it would probably unravel.

There was one circumstance in particular, which caused her much bewildering conjecture without being able to come to any satisfactory conclusion, and that was the motive which could have caused her mother to abandon her own offspring—as it appeared she had done—and never to inform her (Omelia) or even to hint at such a thing, that she had one so nearly related to her, and whom it was her duty to love living, and that fact seemed to become even more surrounded by mystery the more she reflected on it.

Could it be possible that Miriami was the child of shame? Oh, no, Omelia dared not to cast so foul an aspersion on the unblemished character of her beloved mother by entertaining such a suspicion; but above all this was a circumstance which she wanted to have fully explained, and which made her anxious to know the contents of the manuscript.

"Oh, what a strange and deeply interesting narrative do I anticipate having to listen to" she soliloquised, "how anxiously my heart throbs with vain conjecture and expectation. Poor Miriami—for so I must and will now call you—oh, that it had pleased the Great Spirit, the Father of all, that you should have lived to relate the no doubt wondrous tale yourself, with what mingled feelings of joy and sorrow should I doubtless have listened to you, while that sisterly affection which it would have been my duty to have felt towards you, must have increased with every word you uttered. Still, although it was my fate not to see you, and to hear the sweet words of reciprocal affection from your lips, though far, far away your cold remains rest in a humble grave, and that grave it may happily never be my lot to behold, that I might kneel upon it, and weep tears of pure sisterly love to your memory, still in my heart shall that dear memory be most fondly cherished, till the time arrives when I shall be summoned to join you and our blessed mother in eternity."

Her tears flowed fast as these melancholy thoughts occurred to her, and she knelt down and offered her prayers to the Supreme—prayers that were prompted by every virtuous and holy feeling.

And such were the thoughts and feelings that haunted her throughout the day, and pursued her in her dreams.

Similar also had been the reflections of Stanley when alone, and he awaited with as much, or even greater impatience and anxiety as Omelia, the arrival of the following day, when the strange facts no doubt contained in the manuscript would be revealed to them, and that curiosity which it was so natural should be excited in their breasts would be gratified.

And yet how much more must it have contributed to the happiness of Omelia and himself had that beauteous being Miriami, been permitted to live and to have been constantly with them; what a bright halo of love would the poor Indian girl have shed around her, and what sweet consolation in the midst of any troubles they might have to encounter, would the two lovely sisters have derived from each other's society and holy affection.

This thought made him, if possible, more deeply lament than ever the untimely death of Miriami, and that it had not been the will of the Almighty that her and Omelia had not known each other before.

Still the joy of his restoration to his beloved Omelia, completely superseded every other feeling in the breast of Edward Stanley, and he could not but forebode from it the happiness, which, after all their trials awaited them in the future.

At length the morning came, and Stanley and Omelia, together with their friends, met each other in the same spirit of cordiality and welcome that had hitherto marked them, and the greeting of the lovers was all that the feelings of their hearts could dictate.

The looks of our heroine showed anxiety yet composure, and Stanley who well understood her thoughts, for his own were in unison with them, took the earliest opportunity of retiring from the room with her, in order that they might accomplish their important task without further delay or interruption.

"Dearest Omelia," said Stanley, "need I tell you how eagerly I have waited for this moment, a feeling which no doubt has also agitated your breast? I trust that you are now sufficiently composed to suffer me to proceed with the perusal of poor Miriami's important narrative."

"Oh, yes, dear Edward," replied Omelia, eagerly, "pray commence the manuscript without any further delay, for I am now all impatience to hear it, so that the mystery which to me at present is so bewildering and impenetrable, may, as I trust it will be, unravelled."

Stanley waited to hear no more, but taking the packet from his pocket, after a short pause—Omelia seated by his side, and listening with breathless attention to every word that fell from his lips—commenced reading the contents.

THE MANUSCRIPT.

As we believe has been before stated, the important documents, or records of facts, were written in an elegant female hand, purely English in diction, and which showed at once—if indeed there had been anything else that Stanley required than what he had experienced of the late Miriami, during the short time they had been acquainted to convince him—the accomplished mind of the youthful and beauteous writer, and as he proceeded, the truth was so apparent in every word, in every line, in every sentence, that even if our heroine and her lover had felt so disposed before, they could no longer doubt the authority of the extraordinary circumstances that were so simply yet forcibly recorded, and their attention and interest were consequently the more powerfully excited.

The manuscript commenced in the following words—

"Beloved sister, should this narrative ever be destined to meet your eye, which I trust to heaven it will, rest assured, should you feel disposed to doubt the truth of that which it states, that they are the words of your mother, my mother—whose soul is now in the realms of eternal bliss—communicated to me by her, in the last solemn interview I had with her, previous to her death, and when I was indeed but a very little child, but which at the time stamped themselves indelibly on my memory, and from which in more mature years, I thus committed to paper.

"Treasure them, respect them, believe them, though the hand that now pens them at the time that you peruse them may be cold in death, for I repeat that they are the words of your mother, speaking through me, and addressing you, my sister."

"I will, by all my soul's future hopes, I will," solemnly and fervently ejaculated Omelia, tears glistening in her eyes, and her handsome features animated with an expression that could only have its origin in the most holy and virtuous feelings, "for these introductory lines appeal to my feelings in the powerful, the irresistible voice of nature, and I dare not disobey its solemn injunctions. Dear mother, snatched from me when I was so young, what strange and probably painful history of your wrongs, your misfortunes, and your sufferings am I about to listen to? I almost tremble to think."

"Compose yourself, Omelia," enjoined her lover, "and endeavour to listen with calmness and patience to that which I am about to read."

"I will, dear Edward, I will indeed try to do so," answered Omelia, "pardon this interruption, and pray proceed."

Stanley did so accordingly in the following words—

"Oh, my sister, what a strange, what a chequered, and life of trouble has been mine—few rays of sunshine have ever gleamed across my path, nearly one perpetual gloom has pervaded my fate, and the fair flowers that bloom to gladden the days of youth and innocence, have had but little fragrance to bestow upon the hapless Miriami.

"It has been my untoward fate to know nothing but sorrow, even from the earliest days of childhood, although heaven knows how earnestly, how incessantly I have tried to merit at least a portion of those blessings which many of my fellow creatures so abundantly enjoy.

"I oft'times think that I have no business in this world, and that it would have been a mercy had I never been born, or it had pleased that Almighty Being to whose great will we must all submit that I should have died in infancy, and ere I could have known what sorrow was.

"But still I will not murmur or complain, but endeavour to bear my gloomy destiny with all the fortitude, patience, and resignation I can, and which I feel it is my duty to do.

"But pardon these preliminary observations, and let me not become tedious.

"My earliest recollection of myself finds me a little playful child probably about four years of age, residing with two middle-aged people—whom, of course, at that time I looked up to as my parents—in a miserable bungalow, situated in an obscure village, not far from the banks of the Ganges.

"I say that I looked up to these people as my parents, but even at that early age it was more with a feeling of dread, if not absolute terror and repugnance, for they were stern, harsh and repulsive in their manners, and treated me at all times with the greatest unkindness, rejecting my childish endearments, checking me in my innocent gambols, seldom permitting me to mingle with or play with other children, and not unfrequently beating me cruelly, as it would appear from mere brutality of disposition, and not for any error which I might thoughtlessly have committed.

"Thus it will be seen that the sorrows of Miriami—for by that name I was called—commenced in the very infancy of life, that joyous time when, to most children, all is sunshine and happiness.

"I have said that I was naturally of a playful disposition, but this unnatural treatment soon subdued and ultimately crushed that healthful temperament, and I became a poor melancholy, reflective little thing, devoid of all that elasticity—if I may so term it—of spirit, which belongs to children of the tender age I was then.

"When alone, and out of the sight of those I called my parents, I would frequently weep bitterly, for I thought about the green hills and the pretty flowers, and could not but think it hard, very hard that I was not permitted, like those who would gladly have been my little playfellows, to sport and frolic among them, and enjoy their many sweets.

"I never knew those persons by any other names than Ali Kishna—my supposed father and Buddah, his wife.

"They did not appear to be poor, or to want for anything, although they resided in so miserable a dwelling, and followed no employment. But although they fared well, and indeed sumptuously at times, the food they gave me was of the coarsest quality, and that too so small in quantity that it was barely sufficient to sustain life.

"Yet with all this sorry treatment, I throve in health, as if to shame and reproach them for their unnatural conduct; happy, however, I no longer was.

"Sometimes, but at long intervals, the bungalow was visited by a tall, and he might be called a handsome man, had it not been for the stern and repulsive aspect of his countenance, which I could never look upon without trembling.

"But I need not attempt to describe him

No. 42.

more minutely, dear Omelia, when I inform you that he was Yunadar, your father."

Our heroine shuddered, and she was so overpowered by the emotions that the mention of that parents name, from whom she scarcely ever remembered to have experienced one act of kindness, that Stanley was compelled to pause, and it was several minutes before he could resume the perusal of the manuscript.

___

CHAPTER LXXXII.

MIRIAMI'S TALE CONTINUED.

At length Omelia having recovered herself, requested Stanley to proceed, which he did to the following effect—

"Whenever Yunadar came to the bungalow—which I always looked upon with a feeling bordering upon terror—I was harshly driven from the room, and he would remain in conversation with Ali and Buddah for sometimes hours; but what they conversed upon I had no opportunity of knowing, and, in fact, felt no interest in, although always after Yunadar had taken his departure, my treatment was more cruel than before, and both Ali and his wife would frequently beat me with the most brutal severity, for what I know not.

"Heaven pardon me if, in my childish ignorance, I was wrong, but I could not at times help thinking that these people were indirectly endeavouring to murder me at the instigation of Yunadar."

"Great Spirit of mercy," exclaimed the horrorstruck Omelia, "is it possible, can it be possible that that fearful idea could have been correct? And yet, how terribly probable does it not appear to be? Too well do I remember the cruel, the savage temper of my guilty parent, not to feel convinced—and it is with heartfelt sorrow I say it—was capable of even a crime so monstrous as that thus indicated. Poor Miriami; unfortunate sister, already at the outset of your melancholy narrative, too painfully do I perceive how cruel, how unmerited was your fate."

"Alas," said Stanley, compassionately, "'tis too true, and most deeply do I feel for her, and deplore the terrible sufferings which even at so tender an age she was evidently doomed to undergo. May heaven rest her soul in peace and reward her for all that it was her sad fate to experience in this world."

To this wish our heroine most fervently responded, and Stanley then resumed—

"But I now come to a brighter, and far more important part of my tale, and even as I now dwell upon it my heart throbs with wild emotion, scalding tears of mingled joy and sorrow chase each other down my cheeks, and every fond, generous, and virtuous feeling of my nature seems to rise and glow within my breast with redoubled vigour.

"Dear remembrance, with what strange, what sad yet joyful circumstances are you associated. I am anxious, yet do I almost dread to relate them.

"I could not have been more than six years of age, when an English lady—for so she was in appearance—visited our bungalow, and although she was evidently well known to Ali and his wife, they received her but with anything like warmth or cordiality, but on the contrary, seemed to think her visit far more free than welcome and agreeable.

"But after exchanging a few words with Ali and Buddah, in a low tone, she fixed her whole attention on me, gazing at me for a moment or two with a melancholy yet intensely affectionate expression of countenance, which it is utterly impossible that I can ever forget, then, while tears gushed to her eyes, snatching me up in her arms, and covering my face with her kisses.

"Great Spirit of heaven! how my childish heart warmed in an instant towards her. What indescribable transport yet awe and reverence I felt in the presence of that beauteous, that gentle being. Those were the first affectionate caresses I ever remembered to have received, and I could have fallen on my knees and worshipped her for them; while tears streamed from mine eyes, and I sobbed as though my young heart would break.

"It was nature, all-powerful nature that dictated the feeling, for, Omelia, her of whom I speak was *our mother*."

Omelia clasped her hands vehemently together, and raised her eyes, which were filled with tears, devoutly towards heaven, as if in earnest supplication, when Stanley came to this affecting passage, and he could not but feel an emotion similar and almost as powerful as her own.

It was several minutes ere either of them could recover themselves sufficiently to speak, but at length Omelia, in a voice tremulous with the agitation of her feelings, said—

"Dear sainted mother, you whose heart ever throbbed affectionately towards all your fellow creatures, even those who had proved themselves to be your most inveterate enemies, with what indescribable feelings does my bosom swell almost to bursting at the bare mention of that revered, that sacred name. Look down, I humbly beseech you from that world of light and glory which you now inhabit, upon your poor child, and continue, through the mercy of the Supreme, to protect and guide her in the way that she should go."

Stanley sincerely joined in this solemn invocation, and again proceeded with the narrative, which now began to hold a tenfold interest in their breasts.

"Need I describe to you, my sister, the personal and intrinsic beauty of our beloved mother? Oh, no, I will not attempt to do so, for her image must be enshrined in your heart, and far more powerful, more eloquent pens than mine must fail to do adequate justice to the subject.

"But it was not till some time afterwards that I knew our parent in that sacred character, though every proper feeling of my young heart prompted me so to look upon her, even at this, our first meeting.

"She spoke but little on this occasion, but when she did it was to invoke the blessings of heaven upon my head, in such silvery, such pathetic tones, that they vibrated and thrilled to my very heart. And then she continued to nurse me, to hug me to her throbbing bosom—as though she were fearful that I might be snatched from her fond endearments—and bathe my cheeks with her tears.

"And while this affecting scene was going on, Ali and his wife stood at the further end of the room, gazing sullenly at us, and occasionally muttering some observations to each other, in a low tone, which could not be understood.

"At length the melancholy moment arrived, when my newly found and mysterious friend was compelled to tear herself away, and terrible was the struggle that she had with her feelings ere she could do so; while I looked up in her beauteous face with an expression I dare not attempt to describe, and cried and sobbed as though my heart would break.

"Again and again she hugged me to her, as though she were unable to part from me, and wept, and kissed me with maternal fondness; but at length with one vehement, one fervent 'God bless you, dear child,' in a voice half choked with emotion, she released me from her arms, and, after a few observations with Ali and his wife, which were inaudible to me, she hurried from the bungalow, without venturing to look again towards me.

"With a half-frantic outcry, I hastened to the door with the intention of following her, and imploring her to stop, but Ali seized me fiercely by the arm, and thrusting me with brutal violence towards the room-door opposite, in more than his usual savage tones, commanded me to depart to the wretched place in which I slept, a mandate, which you may be sure, trembling with fear, as I always was when in the presence of himself, and his no less hateful wife, I was not at all unwilling to obey.

"There I threw myself on my knees, and for some time became completely lost in the bewilderment and agitation of my new thoughts and feelings.

"The adventure was so strange, and so mysterious to me that it was impossible for me to penetrate it, and the longer I reflected on it, the more did my heart warm towards the gentle and amiable stranger.

"Who could she be, that she should appear to take so great, so extraordinary an interest in me? This was a question which I was unable to answer, by even the most remote conjecture, and I was therefore compelled to abandon it in despair.

"Then in the sincerity of my heart, and all the innocence and simplicity of my childish age, I attempted to pray, invoking blessings on the head of her, who I now could not help looking upon as the only earthly friend I had, and praying that the time would be short ere I might be permitted to behold her again.

"She was not suffered to be absent from my thoughts even for an instant. I still beheld her sorrowful, her affectionate, her almost heavenly looks, as they had been fixed upon me, the moisture of her tears still seemed to be upon my cheeks, the warmth of her kisses were on my lips, and the tender music of her voice still vibrated thrillingly in mine ears.

"I retired to my humble bed, but the form of that revered being followed me in my slumbers, her amiable features smiling benignantly upon me, and her lips seeming to part, as if in the act of invoking blessings upon my head.

"From that moment the form and features of that beloved being whom I afterwards discovered to be my mother, were ever present to my imagination, and never did I retire to rest, or leave my lowly mattress without offering up my simple, childish, but fervent prayer to heaven for her.

"Time, however, rolled drearily and tediously on, and she came not again, although I anxiously daily and hourly looked for her.

The treatment which I received from the brutal Ali and his wife, was, if possible, still more severe and frequent, after the visit of the fair stranger, than ever, and I dared not in any way to mention or allude to her, for fear of the consequences, though they held out the most terrible threats to me, if I should venture to make any complaint of their conduct to the 'lady,' should she come to the bungalow again.

"And thus was I doomed to the most torturing anxiety and suspense for some months longer, before I again saw the constant and beloved subject of my thoughts, and I had began to fear that I should never more behold her, and my heart sickened with despair and disappointment.

"But providence was good; once more she came at last, and I thought that she looked more beautiful and amiable than ever.

"And oh, the transport of my heart at this second meeting, how can I describe it? I could not conceal my emotions, even in the hated presence—for I had long since looked upon those who pretended to be my parents, but whom I was convinced were not so, with terror and aversion—of Ali and his wife, but with a cry of unspeakable delight, immediately on her entering the room, was once more pressed to her loving, throbbing bosom.

"The lady—for as yet that was the only name by which I knew her—having somewhat recovered from her first emotions, assumed a more firm and commanding demeanour towards Ali and Budrah than she had done on her former visit, and desired them to leave the room for a short time, as she wished to be alone with ' the poor dear child for a few minutes,' and they very reluctantly obeyed, fixing upon her a sinister and significant look as they did so.

What an interview was this; it can never be effaced from my memory while existence lasts. It was then that the dark curtain of mystery was for the first time withdrawn from before mine eyes, and the first, but transient ray of hapiness permitted to dawn upon me."

CHAPTER LXXXIII.

THE VISION.

Stanley hastily dropped the manuscript at this most interesting part of the affecting narrative, for a faint cry from Omelia alarmed him, and looking anxiously and quickly towards her, he was still more surprised and agitated on beholding her ghastly pale, and in a fainting condition.

"Dear Omelia he exclaimed, "what is the meaning of this? For heaven's sake what is the matter with you?"

"Do not alarm yourself, dear Edward," she replied, with difficulty, "it is only a faint and sickly sensation which has suddenly come over me, probably from the excessive heat of the weather, or the excitement caused by the perusal of the manuscript. But I trust I shall soon be better, and—"

She could not finish the sentence, for her strength failed her, and she fainted in the arms of her lover.

Much alarmed, Stanley bethought himself for a moment, and then raising her in his arms—having first returned the manuscript to his pocket—he bore her to the room in which he knew that Flora Melville, her cousin and his father were seated, and who was as much shocked as himself on beholding her, and eagerly inquired what had happened.

Stanley replied that he could not account for Omelia's sudden illness in any other way than by the heat of the weather, and Flora immediately set about adopting every means for her recovery, Stanley and the others watching anxiously and impatiently the result.

In a short time Omelia revived, and to the anxious questions of her lover she replied, that she felt it was nothing serious, but only a faint and nervous sensation, from which an hour or two's quiet would probably recover her, and for that purpose she begged to be permitted to retire to her chamber.

This, of course, was immediately granted, and she was accompanied thither by Flora Melville, who suspecting that it was something more than the heat of the weather which had caused her illness, ventured to question her more closely, but without being able to elicit anything more from her.

After a short time passed in conversation, our heroine feeling, as she said, much better, expressed a wish to be alone, as she intended to lie down, to see whether she could not obtain an hour or two's rest.

Flora, therefore, immediately withdrew.

The reader will hardly need to be informed that it was the excitement caused by poor Miriami's interesting narrative, the feeling and affecting allusions to her mother, and the melancholy reminiscences it awakened in her mind, that had been the immediate cause of Omelia's sudden indisposition, and now that she was alone, she abandoned herself to the various and conflicting thoughts to which they naturally had given rise.

She regretted that there should be another delay in the perusal of the manuscript, for she was most anxious to hear it to the end; but the feeling and impressive manner in which Miriami had writen her little pathetic history of facts, was so overpowering, and required so much reflection as it progressed, that Omelia felt incompetent to the task in any hurried space of time.

In every line of that remarkable record, the noble mind, the generous heart, and virtuous sentiments of the writer shone conspicuously, while the tender yet melancholy tone, and the sorrows of the poor young thing who was now at rest, were sufficient to move even the most insensible heart to pity.

How deeply did Omelia deplore that Miriami should have been brought to so untimely an end, and that they had not been destined to meet; how fondly would she have been prepared to love so amiable, so gentle a being as a sister.

And then the faithful description which Miriami had given of the personal appearance and character of her mother—so faithful indeed, that as well as she could remember that beloved being in childhood, Omelia could almost imagine that she at present stood before her—convinced her that there was truth in everything she stated, and added a tenfold interest to the narrative.

In such reflections as these Omelia continued for some time to indulge, not feeling disposed to rejoin her friends in the present state of her mind; but at length the heat of the weather overpowered her, and feeling fatigued and inclined for sleep, she stretched her limbs upon a sofa which the room happened to contain, and slumber soon afterwards descended upon her eyelids.

The thoughts that had crowded upon her brain in her waking moments followed her in her sleep, and conjured up visions to her imagination of the most extraordinary description, one of which in particular was so appropriate to the present nature of her feelings, and the circumstances that had originated them, that it made the most powerful impression upon her mind, and it was long ere she was likely to be able to efface it from her memory.

She imagined that it was one of those delightful evenings so often experienced in tropical climates, after the excessive heat of the day has subsided, and a cool refreshing breeze is wafted from the mountains and expansive rivers that stretch their course in various directions. The sky was almost as bright and clear as that of Italy at noonday, the broad bright face of the moon, and the countless myriad of stars rendering the boundless arch of heaven still more beautiful.

Strangely diversified and picturesque was the scenery which she fancied she was rambling amidst. Sometimes she wandered through forest glades, whose lofty trees seemed soaring to the skies, and whose emerald foliage danced and whistled in the breeze, and glittered in the moonbeams.

Anon she strolled near the banks of a silvery stream, and in whose clear waters the lights from numerous temples were reflected. The light from innumerable fireflies also added greatly to the effect of the charming scene.

Another change, and she bent her delighted footsteps through beautiful gardens that seemed interminable, and where the loveliest flowers bloomed in every direction, breathing rich perfume on the air, which was quite overpowering. Whichever way the eye was directed, graceful fountains in full play met the sight, and added to the coolness of the atmosphere which came so grateful to the senses.

On, on she rambled, more enraptured at every step she took, and charmed by the seraphic strains of heavenly music which seemed to float upon the air, and held the senses captive.

She wandered on till she reached a mound of earth, beneath the wide-spreading branches of a majestic tree, and where the choicest flowers of every variety of hue and fragrance bloomed in abundance.

Upon this delightful spot, from which she could command an extensive and uninterrupted view of the splendid scene, she imagined she reclined herself, her senses still charmed by the heavenly music which had led her footsteps thither. Innumerable birds, she fancied, made the air resound again with their mellifluous notes, and completed by their harmony the enchantment of the scene.

Gradually, Omelia thought in her dream, she was lulled to sleep, but still she was sensibly alive to all the beauties of the scene, and the same sweet music that had delighted her in her waking moments.

Suddenly a mist seemed to float before her eyes, and a presentiment of something remarkable about to happen appeared to take possession of her mind.

Gradually the mist dispersed, and in its place appeared a bright celestial light, so dazzling that the eyes could scarcely bear to gaze at it.

More sweet, more overpowering became the heavenly music, and while Omelia, as she supposed in her dream, continued to gaze in rapt amazement at the bright halo, which by degrees expanded, a shadowy form, in the midst of it, rose slowly from the earth, and becoming every instant more distinct, revealed the lovely figure and features of a young Indian girl, so closely resembling herself in every respect, that it might have been said to be her own counterpart.

Omelia's eyes became rivetted on this beautiful vision, and she could not remove them. It smiled upon her, and seemed to beckon her to come to her, but she felt, as it were, spell-bound, and could not stir.

Suddenly a voice of melting sweetness, which she knew to be that of her mother, sounded in her ears with impressive solemnity, and these were the words which she heard it utter—

"Daughter, thy mother's voice calls upon thee from the grave, and bids thee kneel in reverence to the spirit of thy sainted sister, Miriami."

Omelia felt an instinctive impulse to act in obedience to this solemn mandate, which she could not resist. She did kneel before the lovely phantom of Miriami, and clasping her hands together, bent low her head in reverence.

Again that holy strain of melody, so solemn, so sublime that it lifted the soul to heaven; so plaintive that it might melt the most insensible being to tears.

It floated melodiously on the air, and all things seemed to smile, to dance, to revel in the sacred harmony.

With a feeling of awe, yet of unspeakable pleasure, Omelia imagined that she at length once more ventured to raise her head, and to gaze upon the phantom of Miriami. And oh, how lovely, how heavenly was the expression of those features upon which she looked.

They smiled upon her; the arms were outstretched towards her, as if to embrace her, then raised above her head in signification of a blessing.

And while Omelia still gazed, the form and features of the phantom gradually became more and more indistinct, until they faded away altogether; the music ceased, the celestial light disappeared, the mist again arose, all was dim obscurity, the bright vision had vanished, and Omelia awoke.

She rubbed her eyes, she looked vacantly around the room; was it then only a dream? It was so like reality that she could scarcely persuade herself to the contrary. Her brain for the moment was bewildered.

But when she was enabled to convince herself that it was indeed but a vision, an indescribable feeling of awe, yet joy, and not unmingled with sorrow took possession of her. She had been permitted to gaze upon the bright spirit of that sister whom in life she had never known; she had heard her mother's voice from the tomb proclaiming the fact that Miriami *was* her sister, and she felt a sensation of happiness and satisfaction, which she had never experienced before.

Throwing herself on her knees, she poured forth her feelings in a solemn prayer to heaven. Then she arose, and after a few minutes reflection, having sufficiently composed herself, and feeling in better spirits than she had done for some time before, she quitted the room in order to rejoin Stanley and her friends, who she had no doubt would feel anxious to know whether she had recovered from her late indisposition.

Stanley, Flora and the others, were all most agreeably surprised to observe the favourable change which a few short hours had wrought in the appearance and spirits of our heroine, and warmly congratulated her, no one, as may be imagined, more cordially than her lover.

After passing a short time in the company of Flora Melville, Alfred Meadows, and his father, Stanley and Omelia retired together, for they were anxious to communicate their thoughts to each other, especially our heroine, who could not rest until she had related to Stanley the particulars of her remarkable dream.

"I have seen her, dear Edward, I have seen her, gazed upon her lovely features, and received her smiles and blessings," she exclaimed joyfully, when her and her lover were alone.

Stanley looked and felt astonished.

"What mean you, Omelia?" he eagerly interrogated, "seen her, to whom do you allude?"

"To my sister—to Miriami," she replied.

"Dear Omelia, this—"

"Nay, Edward," she interrupted, with a sweet smile, "think not that my senses wander; 'twas but a dream, but oh, so bright a dream, that I would it should often occur to me again, that I might gaze upon the lovely spirit of that dear sister, whom I was ne'er destined to know, but whose dear memory I now so fondly revere."

"Oh, my beloved Omelia," said Stanley, "how thankful I am that this bright vision should have appeared to your imagination, since it has thus imparted such happiness to you. But I pray you relate it to me, that I may share with you in the wonder, the pleasure and admiration which it seems to have afforded you."

Omelia paused for a minute or two to collect herself, and she then proceeded to gratify her lover's anxious curiosity, and he heard her with silent attention, and dwelt upon every particular with the deepest interest.

"It was indeed a solemn but delightful vision, my own dearest Omelia," he observed, when she had concluded, "and I wonder not at the interest it has excited in your breast. Poor Miriami, your sister, depend upon it, now from those bright realms of glory to which her gentle spirit has fled, looks down upon you with blessings, which she uttered so fervently in her dying moments."

"I know it, I feel it," exclaimed Omelia, emphatically, and her fine eyes sparkled, and every feature seemed to glow with fresh animation as she spoke, "and in the midst of my deep sorrow for the loss of that dear sister whom I was so well prepared to love, I am happy, for I am convinced that she is happy with my blessed mother in heaven."

"True, most true," said Stanley, "but now that you have recovered from your late indisposition, Omelia, and as the hour is not late, shall I resume the perusal of the manuscript?"

"You may believe me, dear Edward," replied our heroine, "and especially after listening to the deeply interesting portion of the recital which you have read already, how anxious I am to hear the remainder, but after what has occurred, I do not feel myself in a fit state of mind to do so to-day. To-morrow then, till to-morrow only, let us defer the gratification of our curiosity, and the elucidation of the mystery."

To this Stanley readily assented, for he himself did not feel altogether disposed to continue the perusal of the manuscript that day, notwithstanding he was most impatient to become acquainted with the whole of the remarkable facts which it recorded, and they soon afterwards rejoined their friends for the remainder of the evening.

CHAPTER LXXXIV.

THE MANUSCRIPT RESUMED.

The next day, Stanley and Omelia being alone, the former resumed the perusal of the late Miriami's remarkable and interesting narrative in the following words—

"How shall I, how can I describe the strange, the unutterable, the overwhelming feelings that agitated my young breast, when I found myself for the first time alone with that revered being for whom my heart throbbed with all humility, love, and admiration? Vain would be the task were I to attempt to do so.

"I wept for joy, yet trembled with expectation.

"As for the lady, for such I must continue to call her till the fitting time arrives, exhibited, if possible, still greater emotion than myself, placing both her hands upon my head, and gazing into my face with an intensity of feeling, such as is still fresh and vivid in my memory, and can never be forgotten by me. But she spoke not a word, though a deep sigh would frequently escape her bosom, and which evidently came from the deepest recesses of her heart.

"But at length she suddenly withdrew from me, and going to the door by which Ali and his wife had quitted the room, she gently opened it, and looked out to see that they were not there to listen to what she was about to say, and having apparently satisfied herself that they were not near, she closed it again, and hastily returning to me, she snatched me up in her arms, pressed me to her bosom, and gave way to a violent paroxysm of uncontrollable emotion, in which I freely joined, for my heart had long been full to bursting.

"This lasted for several minutes, and sobs, sighs, and tears alone escaped us both. But at length recovering herself, and gently releasing me from her loved embrace, she looked at me earnestly for a moment, and then said in a voice of tender sweetness which still seems to vibrate in mine ears—

"'Do you love me, Miriami?'

"Oh, what a question to put to the poor trembling, panting child who could have adored, have worshipped her as some celestial being.

"For a moment my feelings would not allow me to reply, but at length while tears gushed to mine eyes and almost blinded me, and emotion almost choked my utterance, I said—

"'Love you, sweet gentle lady, oh, that I could speak the love I bear you. But I am only a poor simple little child, and know not what I ought to say. Miriami sees you when you are not here, sees you in her thoughts, sees you in her dreams, prays to you when she prays as a good spirit from heaven.'

"How a poor ignorant little child like me, who had been so totally neglected by those who called themselves my parents, and had never been taught right from wrong, could ever have given utterance to language such as that I have just described, it has often

since I will rack my brain to conjecture; but I must have been inspired, and it was nature's voice that must have been speaking with the sense and eloquence of maturity from the lips of infancy, and for the time I felt myself like some other being, and possessed of thoughts which I could not understand.

"The gentle, the beloved being to whom the words were addressed seemed to be completely overwhelmed with astonishment, and emotion, her bosom heaved, her eyes swam in tears, and every limb was violently agitated.

"It was some time ere she could speak, and I waited once more to hear the sweet tones of her voice with panting breath, and in trembling expectation.

"At length again convulsively enfolding me in her arms, she fervently ejaculated—

"'Sweet, beauteous child of sorrow, of cruel destiny, poor little outcast on the world's wide and cheerless desert, with only one to love you as fondly, still more fondly than her own life's blood, and she so powerless to befriend you, to protect you as it is her duty, and her ardent will, to cherish you to guide you through those paths of virtue you so young have entered upon, oh, with what indescribable feelings does my poor bursting heart throb as I strain you to it. All-merciful powers, will this unparalleled suffering never have an end?'

"Sobs choked her further utterance, and her tears flowed unrestrained, while I could only look up in her beauteous countenance with earnest sorrow, and weep the same.

"'But tell me, sweetest,' she said at last more calmly, and struggling with her feelings, 'why do you love me, when you know me not?'

"My young heart immediately prompted the answer, and without any hesitation I said—

"'Because you are good, sweet lady, and something tells me, though they—I could not call those people who had ever treated me so cruelly by the sacred name of parents—never told me, that I should love all that is good, and you are good, lady, and say kind words to me, and kiss me, and cry over me, oh, so like a dear mother, that I cannot help loving you as one, and should feel so happy if I might call you so.'

"What extraordinary emotions shook her frame, and seemed to thrill through every vein, as I thus spoke. The colour forsook her cheeks and returned again rapidly, her lips trembled, and the words that she wished to utter seemed struggling to suffocation in her throat.

"'Great God of heaven!' she at last exclaimed, and once more clasping me convulsively to her bosom, 'can poor, suffering human nature longer endure this? Can my lips longer refuse to reveal the secret which every feeling of love and duty prompt me to disclose? Miriami, my own sweet cherub, Miriami, it is your mother, your own fond mother who now holds you to her breaking heart!'

"I sunk senseless in the beloved arms that entwined my tender form so fondly, my mother.

"The recollection of that moment overpowers me, and bewilders my senses. For awhile I must drop the pen, for my trembling hand refuses its office."

There the manuscript was stained and blotted in several places as though by the tears of the unfortunate writer.

Stanley dropped the papers, for he was completely overcome by his emotions and unable to proceed.

Omelia was so deeply affected by the truly pathetic nature of the narrative, and the touching manner in which the unfortunate writer related it, also with her immediate association with the beloved characters and events so graphically and so eloquently described, that her faculties for the time seemed to be suspended, and the power of expressing her feelings was denied her.

A silence of some time ensued, and the lovers sat and gazed at each other with looks that spoke as eloquently, if not more so, the emotions that agitated their breasts, than words could possibly have done.

"Beloved mother, dearest sister," at length sighed Omelia, while the tears trembled in her eyes, "oh, how my heart bleeds at the dismal recital of your mutual sorrows, it would seem almost too great for human nature to endure. Oh, why were two such amiable beings ordained to meet so cruel a fate?"

"True, dear Omelia," replied Stanley, "it does indeed appear most severe and unjust, but we must not arraign the wisdom and mercy of the Supreme. Let us hope that they are now both reaping the reward for their sufferings in this world in heaven."

"Oh, yes," returned Omelia, "my heart convinces me that they are. Would to heaven that I had been made acquainted with these melancholy facts before."

"Nay, Omelia," remarked her lover, "'tis useless and sinful to regret it, and perhaps it is better as it is, and may have saved you a deal of anguish and anxiety of mind."

"But I should then have known that I had one living whom it was my duty, and whom I could also so fondly have loved," returned our heroine, "and what a sweet consolation would that have been to myself and poor Miriami. What a many cares, anxieties, and troubles it might have saved us both, and the untimely death which my sister met with might providentially have been averted. Alas, I now feel the melancholy, the severe, and irreparable loss I have sustained, more keenly than ever."

"I know, dear Omelia," said her lover, "that I need not assure you how fully I appreciate your affectionate feelings, which are so natural, and do honour to your head and heart, but I pray you endeavour to compose yourself, and to conquer all fruitless regrets, since it was clearly the will of heaven that you and your unfortunate sister should never meet together on this earth. But was it not marvellous the manner in which Miriami and I encountered each other?"

"True," coincided Omelia, "and it is the recollection of the affectionate regard which she evinced towards you, and the inestimable services she so generously rendered you, and the imminent risks she run in doing so, that endears her memory still more to my heart."

"Ah," sighed Stanley, "to her I am indebted for the preservation of my life, poor generous-hearted, and noble-minded girl, and she sacrificed her own in saving mine. It is a melancholy reflection. May heaven reward her as she deserves now that she is no more."

To this wish it need hardly be said how fervently our heroine responded, and as she recalled to her memory the dying scene of her beauteous but unfortunate sister, as it had been so pathetically described to her by her lover, all the tenderest feelings of her nature were excited, and she wept bitterly, Stanley not attempting to interrupt her as he sincerely hoped and trusted that it would be the means of relief to her overcharged bosom.

It required some time for them to compose themselves, but at length they succeeded in doing so, and Stanley then took up the manuscript, and went on to read it.

CHAPTER LXXXV.

MORE ASTOUNDING REVELATIONS.

"After the lapse of some days, for I found it utterly impossible for me to collect myself sufficiently for the task before, I again resume the pen, and am compelled to record painful facts that will rend your heart, dear Omelia, should these papers ever meet your eyes, to read them.

"What torturing feelings rack my breast while I relate them I will not attempt to describe.

"Yes, the all important secret was revealed, and I had at length discovered the real beloved being who had brought me into the

world although I still remained in ignorance as to the cause of my being so strangely and so cruelly discarded from her affectionate bosom, or at least deprived of her fostering care and protection.

"How long I had remained in the senseless state in which I have described myself to have fallen into our mother's arms, Omelia, of course I have no means of forming even the slightest conjecture, but I was suddenly aroused to consciousness by loud shrieks, and being torn from my mother's affectionate embrace, and oh, what a scene of agony then met my distracted sight. I shudder to describe it.

"Our unfortunate parent, Omelia, was struggling in the arms of Yunadar—yes, Yunadar, your guilty father, pardon the words, but I cannot help them—and another

man, shrieking frantically, and bleeding from a wound inflicted on her arm, while I was being fiercely held by the savage Ali, who with his wife were looking on with a brutal expression of exultation.

"I shrieked aloud and called upon the name of my mother, who reiterated my cries, and then in piteous accents implored them not to tear her from her child.

"But dreadful oaths, and bitter mockery were the only answers she received to her supplications, and in spite of her struggles, they forced her from the bungalow, and I heard her mournful cries till they died away in the distance.

"I then, child as I was, in the madness of my grief, attempted to tear myself from the hold of Ali, but a violent blow which the inhuman monster dealt me soon rendered me senseless, and I remembered no more till I found myself lying in a damp and gloomy vault, which, for some nefarious object doubtless, had been formed some years before beneath the bungalow."

Here again Omelia and Stanley were so deeply affected that they were compelled to pause to give expression to their feelings of horror and disgust, and it was some time ere they could control their emotions sufficiently to suffer them to proceed with the melancholy and exciting tale.

"I rubbed my eyes" the manuscript went on to say, "and looked around me, not knowing where I was, and at first supposing that I was under the influence of some frightful dream, but when the dreadful truth flashed upon my childish brain, I started madly to my feet, and rushed from side to side of the horrible place in which I was thus mercilessly incarcerated, screaming frantically for help.

"For some minutes there was no answer to my cries, and I had thrown myself upon the damp earth in an indescribable agony of terror and despair, when the door of the vault or dungeon was unbolted, and the villain Ali entered with a lighted lamp in his hand.

"I shrunk from and trembled with horror at the sight of him; but in a moment afterwards I turned towards him, and in piteous accents, which from so young a child might have been thought enough to move even the most callous heart, I implored him to restore me to my poor mother.

"'Cursed brat,' he replied in a hoarse voice, grasping my tender arm fiercely, and fixing his large black eyes upon me with a fearful look, 'dare not to repeat that name —you will behold her no more.'

"One appalling shriek escaped me on hearing this terrible announcement, and I again became insensible.

"I must doubtless have remained in a half unconscious state for several days, but on recovering I found myself lying on a filthy mattress, in a strange place, and before I had the power to utter any cry of alarm, the room-door was thrown open, and Ali and his wife entered, and on beholding me upright on the mattress—from which I could not stir—and staring aghast, they laughed derisively, and seemed to enjoy my surprise and consternation amazingly.

"I could only clasp my hands together with agony, but I had not the power to utter a word, and before I had recovered myself sufficiently to do so, Ali advanced, and roughly laying hold of my arm, with an oath pulled me on to the floor, and then looked at me with a fearful expression for a minute or two which made me think it was his intention to murder me.

"'So, accursed brat,' he at length exclaimed in his usual savage tones, 'you still live to be hated and be tortured. I scorn to take the trouble to murder anything so insignificant, or you would have been rotting in the earth long ago. Besides, I have not yet received any instructions to do so, or I dare say I should not have hesitated to obey them. Why don't you die, and thus escape the misery that awaits you?'

"Can I properly describe the horror of my feelings at this monstrous speech? It is impossible for me to do so. But at length wound up to a pitch of the most insupportable agony, I threw myself upon my knees before the brutal miscreant, and, with streaming eyes, and in a voice half choked with emotion, I implored him to take pity on a poor little child who could never by any possibility have done him harm, and to restore some to that unfortunate being who had claimed me for her offspring.

"His eyes glared still more frightfully and fiercely as I uttered this appeal, and feelings of the most deadly rage seemed to agitate his breast.

"'Ah,' he exclaimed, 'there it is, the wretched woman who gave you being, by disclosing that secret which she had sworn never to divulge, has sealed her own doom, and that of your's also. Consider her no more, for you will never behold her again.'

"I wrung my hands in utter despair, and Ali having ordered his wife to bring me a scanty supply of coarse food, which she did, they both quitted the room, locking the door after them, and left me to my misery.

"I staggered again to the mattress and sunk upon it in a state of mind which you may conceive, but I find myself totally inadequate to pourtray. But my brain was so completely bewildered, and I was altogether so terrified, that I had no power to arrange my thoughts in anything like reasoning order.

"And in this deplorable condition I for some time remained.

"But when all the real horrors of my present situation, and from the terrible threats of the heartless villain, Ali—who from woful past experience I too well knew was fully capable of carrying any act of atrocity which he promised into execution— those I had to anticipate in the future, were presented to my sight as vividly and as clearly as if they had been reflected in a mirror, my young heart sickened, and I shrunk appalled at the contemplation.

"In what a strange and terrible mystery was my fate involved, and by what possible means could I, child as I was, penetrate it, or even form the slightest conjecture? Why was I thus, in the infancy of life, helpless innocent as I was, looked upon as a thing of hatred, viewed with feelings of the most savage malice, cruelly torn from every kindred tie, and selected as the victim, the hapless victim of the most brutal, the most unexampled persecution? It was a fearful problem, and the brain became bewildered in the useless attempt to solve it.

"And then that gentle, that kind, that revered being who had claimed me as her child, and whom my heart had long before instinctively acknowledged for my mother, how came about her frightful destiny? Why was she thus compelled to cast me from the shelter of her fostering bosom, and forbidden to approach me, or to own me as her own beloved offspring?

"Mystery upon mystery, conjecture distracted by conjecture, it was impossible to penetrate the solemn darkness.

"And oh, what agony filled my breast when I recalled to my memory the dreadful scene I have already related, and pictured to myself the awful fate, which, after she had been forced away from the dwelling of Ali iy Yunadar and his savage companions, had too probably befallen her?

"Still could I fancy I beheld her as she struggled with her relentless foes, I saw the blood streaming from the gaping wound which had been inflicted on her—as I afterwards learned by her own guilty husband, Yunadar—I saw her wild and distracted looks, I heard her call upon my name, her piteous cries for mercy, and I still fancied that I beheld her last look of despair and agony as they forced her from my sight, alas, I had too much reason to fear for ever!

"The picture was far too dreadful for contemplation, and my senses reeled beneath the stunning and maddening effect.

"At length I found some relief in a copious flood of tears, and then once more sinking on my knees, as well as I could, I prayed to heaven for mercy and protection for my mother and myself in the midst of the apparently insurmountable dangers and difficulties by which we were surrounded.

"Night came, and I was left in complete darkness, save the faint light admitted into this miserable room by a small window, and my situation was rendered, if possible, still more wretched and lonely.

"I almost feared to retire to rest, lest in my slumbers the murderer's knife should be raised against my life, and that fear, after what the cruel Ali had said, did not appear to be unfounded.

"The moon rose, and its beams faintly streaming in at the window before mentioned, somewhat relieved the intensity of the darkness.

"The window was placed rather high, but by standing on the top of an old stool, which was almost the only article of furniture the room contained, I might contrive to reach it and look through it, and thinking that this might serve in some measure to divert my thoughts for a time from the gloomy subjects that at present engrossed them, and afford some temporary and partial relief to the loneliness of my situation, I mounted the stool, and by the assistance of the moon, gazed on the situation in which my new habitation was placed.

"Cheerless and dreary enough it was, and by no means calculated to afford me any satisfaction or to enliven my spirits.

"Before me stretched a wild tract of country, with no signs of a human dwelling, as far as the eye could penetrate. To the right were craggy steeps, soaring above a river, with a mighty cataract falling from an immense height, and whose dashing and roaring, although at a considerable distance, I could distinctly hear.

"On the right was a dark, and, to judge from the thickly clustering and gigantic trees, and the underwood, almost impenetrable forest, the mere aspect of which was sufficient to excite the most gloomy thoughts and apprehensions.

"Such was the prospect which met my observation, and not the least signs of anything human could I see to relieve the dreariness of the scene.

"The bungalow in which I was now confined, as far as I could observe, stood alone in this rude and dismal part of the country.

"But strange as it may appear, poor, helpless child as I was, a complete stranger to the world, without one being that I knew and from whom I could seek assistance or protection, or would take compassion on my misery, as I continued to gaze for some time longer on this dreary scene, the idea of making my escape from the cruel wretches who had from the earliest days of my recollection, held me in their power and at their mercy, and wandering I knew not whither—anywhere, so long as I could escape the present horrors by which I was surrounded—suddenly flashed upon my brain, and awakened, as it were new thoughts and feelings.

"Wild and impracticable as this idea was, I could not banish it, and the longer I dwelt upon it, the more it seemed to urge itself upon my consideration.

"Surely, I thought, nothing could possibly be worse than the cruel fate to which I was at present subjected, to my young and inexperienced imagination, it seemed impossible that human nature could be so bad, that I should despair of meeting with some one who would take pity on a poor, friendless, and destitute child, but allow it to perish, and even if such should be the dreadful case, and I was doomed to die at that early age, it appeared to me far preferable to the

lingering and fearful fate I was now enduring.

"But there was one thought, one hope
which urged me on to the desperate attempt
much more than all, and that was the hope
that the all-powerful instinct of nature, directed by the mercy of providence, might
guide my wandering footsteps to my mother!

"There was heavenly transport in the
thought, even if we were fated to meet only
to die in each other's arms, and my heart
leaped as it occurred to me.

"Oh, what bliss unspeakable it would be
to gaze once more upon that angelic countenance, to bask in the mellowed radiance of
her eyes, to listen to the heavenly melody of
her voice, to be enfolded in her loving arms,
to nestle my childish head in her throbbing,
maternal bosom, and to feel the honeyed dew
of her affectionate kisses on my cheeks!

"The picture that my imagination thus
drew was almost too powerful for my feeble
senses to withstand, and my brain turned
giddy as I contemplated it.

"All improbable, and even preposterous
as the idea was, such was the influence it
had immediately on its suggestion obtained
over me, that I could not banish it from my
mind, and some inscrutable, some instinctive
power, seemed to strengthen me in my resolution to adopt it.

"I looked once more upon the dreary scene
before me, and then tried the window, and
to my great surprise and satisfaction, I discovered that it was not fastened. This encouraged me in my design, for it seemed as
though providence smiled upon and favoured
it.

"Not that night, however, was I prepared
to make the hazardous and desperate attempt
for it would have been madness, in my present weak state, and without further reflection to do so.

"I quitted the window, for the lateness of
the hour warned me to do so, and having
implored the Supreme to direct me in the
way to act, and to avert any evils that might
threaten me, feeling weary, I once more
sought my wretched mattress, and endeavoured to find a temporary respite to my
sorrows in sleep.

"But the wild idea which had so strangely
taken possession of me, and now occupied all
my thoughts, kept me for some time awake,
and when sleep descended at last upon my
eyelids, it pursued me in my dreams."

CHAPTER LXXXVI.

MIRIAM ATTEMPTS TO ESCAPE.—THE RESULT.

Stanley now, at the suggestion of our

heroine, paused for a brief period in the
perusal of the manuscript, in order that they
might properly discuss and digest that which
he had already read, and having done so, he
thus continued:

"The following morning arrived, and
found me somewhat recruited in strength
and spirits, after the few hours rest I had
obtained.

"But I was in the same state of mind, as
regarded the attempt to escape, as on the
previous night, and my resolution was, in
fact, strengthened.

"In my dreams I had imagined that the
beloved form of my unfortunate mother had
appeared to me, and smiling affectionately
upon me stretched forth her arms for me to
come to her.

"This I interpreted as a good omen of the
success of my designs, and I determined that
very night, at all hazards, to make the attempt to carry them into effect.

"But I am fearful that my narrative has
already run to a much greater length than I
at first anticipated, and that I may become
tedious. I will therefore be as brief as
possible in the remaining important facts
which I have to disclose.

"Ali visited me again in the course of the
day, and I received a repetition of his unmanly taunts and abuse, and of similar
threats to those which he had held out to me
on the previous day.

"But I bore with it meekly, and without
murmuring, for I feared to answer him,
knowing the consequences that would be
sure to follow, and with the sanguine hope
that a few short hours would with the blessing of providence, release me from his
cruelty.

"The day passed slowly away, and I
waited impatiently for the arrival of night
when all would be still around, and there
might be no one to interrupt or observe me.

"As the hours waned away, my heart
throbbed with mingled hopes, and doubts,
and fears, as to the result of my designs, but
still my resolution wavered not, for my
mother's voice seemed to urge me on and to
encourage me.

"Through the window I eagerly watched
the last golden rays of the sun as it sunk in
the western horizon, then the dusky shades
of evening, and at last succeeded by the
sombre gloom of night.

"And now my heart beat quick, and every
nerve was violently agitated by the excitement of my feelings.

"The magnitude of the design which I
was about to attempt to accomplish rushed
with full force upon my imagination, I could
conceive, in spite of my youth and in-
experience, the immensity of the dangers and
difficulties I must necessarily have to en-

counter in such an undertaking, but so terrible was the fate from which I sought to release myself, that I never for a moment hesitated, but, on the contrary, my determination became firmer every moment.

"The room in which I was confined was at the back of the bungalow, and, as I imagined, some little distance from that occupied by my cruel persecutors, so that the chances of accomplishing my object, and that, too, without observation, were all in my favour.

"I waited for some time longer, and listened attentively to catch the slightest sound, which might give me any cause for apprehensions, and caution me for a while to forbear. But all being profoundly silent, my confidence was strengthened, and I at once resolved to make the desperate attempt.

"Previous, however, to doing so, I knelt down, and earnestly commended myself to the care and protection of the Great Spirit of all good.

"I arose from my knees, fortified with a courage and energy truly wonderful for my age, and mounting the stool, with some difficulty, but as noiselessly as possible, I raised the window, and looked out cautiously.

"There was a bright moon shining at the time, and by its light I was enabled to see objects distinctly for a considerable distance, but could perceive nothing whatever to excite my alarm or suspicions.

"I then examined the distance of the window from the ground, and found it was so inconsiderable, that I could reach the latter with perfect ease and in safety.

"I once more looked cautiously and narrowly around, but the coast being clear and all remaining still, I considered there was no necessity for any further delay, and accordingly forced my small body through the open window, and alighted easily on the ground.

"I paused for a moment or two to collect myself. The task, so far, had been accomplished with so little difficulty, that I could hardly believe in its reality, and my joy, on finding myself away from my miserable place of confinement, and, for the present, at any rate, at liberty, was so great, that I could scarcely contain myself.

"But I did not delay long, but ran from the hated bungalow with all the speed that my young limbs, and the important object which I had in view could impel me, towards the forest, which notwithstanding its gloomy and forbidding aspect, I chose for the present, as I thought it would afford me concealment, in case my escape should be discovered sooner than I apprehended, and I should be pursued.

"But as I continued my flight with unabated speed, I frequently looked cautiously and half fearfully behind me, to see that no one was following me.

"It was a clear, moonlight night, as I have intimated before, and I could therefore still see the bungalow distinctly, but saw nothing whatever to excite my alarm, and my courage and confidence therefore increased.

"At length, however, from the speed at which I had proceeded, and the naturally great excitement of my feelings, I was compelled for a few moments to pause and to take breath.

"The forest, which was still some distance off, looked black and discouraging enough, and as I gazed towards it, I thought of the many frightful tales I had heard Ali at times relate of the wild beasts that I believe inhabited such places.

"Still I would not suffer myself to be intimidated, and having rested myself sufficiently, I proceeded boldly on my way.

"And thus I hastened on till I had arrived within a few yards of the forest, and my heart now felt elate and buoyant with hope.

"But that was not destined to continue long, for all my resolute designs were doomed to be most fearfully frustrated, and that at the very moment, too, when I flattered myself their success was all but certain.

"Alas, what a life of constant sorrow, care, anxiety, transient hope, and cruel disappointment has been mine.

"As I have stated before, I had got to within a few yards of the gloomy place of my destination, when to my horror and surprise the form of a man suddenly emerged from it, and in a moment I recognised the terrible being from whose power, so cruelly exercised, I had fondly but delusively hoped I had released myself."

"Poor Miriami," said Omelia, at this interesting part of the melancholy tale, "unfortunate child, what a cruel disappointment was this, and I shudder to think of that which would be certain to follow."

"Yes," remarked Stanley, "her's was indeed a severe and unfortunate destiny, and it is truly wonderful how a child so young could long survive troubles and persecutions from which even many persons of mature age, and of every strength of nerve, and power of endurance, might well have shrunk appalled to contemplate. But let us see the result of this adventure, as related in her own simple but forcible language."

"Omelia nodded assent, and Stanley proceeded—

"Language must fail to do adequate justice to the horror of my feelings at this moment. My very blood seemed frozen to ice in my veins, my faculties were suspended, and I was completely paralysed to the spot with terror and despair. Thus were all the wild hopes I had so freely indulged in at once annihilated, and that I had precipitated my fate seemed equally certain.

"But I was not allowed many moments for reflection. The miscreant Ali immediately beheld me, and with a savage cry, which sounded in my affrighted ears like a death knell, he rushed towards me, and grasped my arm with a ferocity which made me shriek with pain, and such was the terrible excitement of his brutal passions at the moment, that he could not utter a word.

"Never shall I forget the frightful and unnatural expression of his repulsive features, as he fixed his eyes, blood-shot, and protruding from their sockets, with rage upon me. They were hideously distorted, and my heart sunk within me at the contemplation, for in those looks I fancied that I could read my doom.

"'Hated whelp,' he at length exclaimed, in a hoarse voice, every tone of which struck horror to my soul; 'daring insect, whom in a moment my hand could crush, and so you thought to escape me? Oh, by every infernal power I swear you shall suffer dearly for this.'

"I had not the power to return any answer to this, or to make a useless appeal to him for mercy, and the monster, inhumanly grasping me by the hair of my head, dragged me from the spot in the direction of the bungalow, while my frantic cries of terror and agony rent the air, but of which he took no further heed only to give utterance to the most frightful oaths and threats.

"All the horrors of a most frightful death, such as a heartless and bloodthirsty villain like Ali could alone be capable of inflicting, arose to my terrified imagination, and I have often since wondered that I did not immediately die of fear, or at least that I could retain my senses.

"But fate had reserved me for still greater sufferings.

"Still grasping me by the hair, the brutal ruffian hurried me along until we had nearly reached the bungalow, when Buddah, whom my piteous cries had probably alarmed, appeared at the door, and seeing me and her husband, with looks equally as savage as those which distorted his features, she hastened to meet us.

"'The brat out of her place of confinement,' she said, in tones which convinced me, even if I had had any doubts upon the subject, that I need expect no mercy from her, 'how is this, Ali?'

"'Why, I should imagine you can guess,' he replied surlily, 'and have no occasion to put such a question to me. The daring girl has had the hardihood to endeavour to escape from our clutches, and it was fortunate that I happened to encounter her when I did, or it is not unlikely that she might have accomplished her object. We shall know how to reward her, however, I fancy for the trouble she has taken. In with you,' he added, hurling me into the room like a dog, and with such violence that I sank nearly senseless on the floor.

"Again he dragged me by the hair to my feet, and followed by his wife, hurried me to the miserable room in which I had been confined, where the open window showed the manner in which I had made my temporary escape, if any doubt could have been entertained on the subject, and Ali cursed his own folly and negligence in not having properly secured it.

"'Now,' said the villain as he released my hair from his hold, and looked at me with an expression of the most demoniacal malice, 'now, what think you is the punishment you deserve for this daring act of disobedience?'

"I thought that my last moments were come, and I trembled violently, and almost feared to look him in the face, thinking that I should read my terrible doom there. But wrought up to a pitch of frenzy and despair I sunk upon my knees before the hard-hearted man, and with vehemently clasped hands, and while the tears flowed rapidly down my cheeks, I said, in a voice half stifled by sobs—

"'Oh, Ali, if your heart still possesses one feeling of pity, I pray you to act mercifully towards a poor friendless child, who, driven to despair by anguish and suffering, did indeed seek to escape, and to cast herself on the world. Think of my tender age, and that it is impossible I could ever have harmed any human being, and spare me.'

"Once more, I say, that it must have been some Omnipotent power, and the terrible excitement of my feelings, that enabled a child like I then was to make this appeal, and in such forcible language.

But it had no other effect upon the heartless Ali than to excite his scorn and brutal derision.

"He laughed exulting at my agony, as he thus replied—

"'Young idiot, and think you then to move me to pity by your tears and supplications? Bah! you might as well appeal to a rock of adamant as to me. You will soon see the extent of the mercy I will grant you. Prepare her, Buddah, against my return. You understand me?'

"Buddah grinned horribly, and nodded a reply to the miscreant's question, and he hastily quitted the room.

"It certainly would have been a mercy to me at that moment if I had lost my senses, that I might have become unconscious to the horrors and atrocities that were about to be inflicted on me. But distracted, and dreading the worst from the observations of

Ali, and the expression of his frightful countenance on quitting the room. I turned to Buddah, and with all the eloquence of despair, implored her to intercede for me with her husband, but she only laughed at me, and to my horror and shame, commenced stripping me, which, in spite of my frantic cries she proceeded with, until she had completed the brutal task, and I was completely naked.

"Ali now re-entered the room, bringing with him a thick strap, and I then at once saw what was the terrible infliction to which he had doomed me.

"I dare scarcely trust myself to detail minutely the horrors that now followed, the dreadful sufferings I had to undergo.

"Surely no poor child could ever have been subjected to such unparalleled brutalities before, and I only wonder that I did not expire under the barbarous infliction.

"Having secured me by cords, which he had also brought with him, to a rude pillar that supported the roof of the bungalow, Ali immediately commenced flogging me in the most monstrous manner on various parts of the body, with the strap, and my loud shrieks of agony, as I writhed under the terrible infliction, and the blood streamed from almost every lash, which seemed but to increase the monster's ferocity, while his wife stood by and looked on, seeming absolutely to enjoy the inhuman torture that I was suffering.

"But at length, nature could endure no more, and it was a mercy to me that I became quite insensible."

Stanley for the present could proceed no further with the heart-rending recital, for his feelings completely overpowered him.

We need not add that Omelia was, if possible even more deeply affected than himself. They looked at each other for a minute or two with an expression of the most indescribable horror, and then after having exchanged a few observations with each other on the painful subject, they deferred the conclusion of the manuscript, which they found to be of much greater length than they had at first anticipated, to the following day, and then returned to their companions in misfortune.

CHAPTER LXXXVII.

AN UNEXPECTED MEETING.

On retiring to rest, and when she had to sleep, the dreadful sufferings which poor Miriami had experienced—as particularly recorded in the preceding chapter—were presented to the imagination of Omelia in the most painful dreams, and on awakening it was sometime ere she could remove the painful impression they had naturally made from her mind.

After the scanty morning meal—for the supply of food to the unfortunate inmates of the fort, by the friendly villagers, was again becoming extremely limited, and they daily looked in vain for the arrival of that assistance which had been promised them, to reach the nearest military station.—Omelia and Stanley again withdrew themselves from the society of their companions, and the latter, after a brief pause went on with the perusal of the manuscript, from the affecting passage at which he had left off on the previous day.

"How long I had remained in this state of insensibility, it is impossible for me to say, probably some considerable time, and had I never again revived to consciousness it would have been a mercy to me, for how many, and what terrible sufferings it would have saved me, but it was the will of that Almighty Power to whom we must all submit, that it should be otherwise, and in spite of the monstrous and unparalleled treatment I had received, and the bare recollection of which makes me shudder with horror, I still most miraculously lived.

"On recovering my senses, I found myself stretched, in the same state of nudity as when the horrible torture was inflicted, on my miserable mattress, with old Buddah seated on the stool by the side, and watching me with stern and malicious looks.

"My poor body was frightfully lacerated, by the brutal blows which the monster Ali had inflicted on me, and I was suffering the most excruciating pain.

"My wounds had been somewhat carefully dressed and attended to by Buddah, as I afterwards learned, for she was an excellent judge of herbs, and of their proper application in such cases, but still so serious were the injuries I had sustained that my ultimate recovery seemed to be extremely doubtful.

Buddah said nothing to me on my restoration to sensibility, and I was in far too much bodily pain and mental anguish to attempt to address myself to her, especially when I well knew that I could expect no sympathy from her, but that she would rather exult at my suffering.

"She, however, had the humanity to offer me a soothing cordial which served greatly to revive me, and then after covering me with a coarse rug, she quitted the room, and for a time left me to all the horrors of reflection, and the bodily anguish I was so acutely suffering.

"What the nature of those reflections were, I need scarcely describe, but it was wonderful how the weak intellect of a mere child could withstand them, or that I could bear my unexampled sorrows and sufferings, with the patience and resignation that I certainly did.

"I now saw too palpably the madness of the wild design which I had attempted to accomplish, and the utter futility of all my hopes to escape from the clutches of the barbarous wretches who so cruelly persecuted me, but by death, and there was no alternative therefore, left me, but to resign myself to my fate, which I endeavoured to do with all the fortitude I could call to my aid.

"I was left to myself for about an hour, when I was again disgusted and horrified by the presence of the inhuman Ali and his wife.

"The villain approached the mattress on which I, his innocent and helpless victim was laying, with the same savage expression of features which ever characterised them, but I shrunk from the sight of him, and shuddered with the same feelings of terror as if my eyes had encountered some frightful and unearthly object, and I trembled in anticipation of the moment when the villain should address me.

"He remained, however, for some time silent, and appeared to contemplate me, and the bodily suffering I was evidently enduring, and which it was totally impossible for me to conceal, with looks of the most brutal satisfaction.

"'So girl,' he at length said, in his usual savage tones, 'you have not died after the punishment I so justly inflicted on you for presuming to set my authority at defiance, and for daring to attempt to escape from my power. Perhaps it's as well that you have not. You ought to feel thankful to me that I saved you from becoming a mouthful to some wild beast Well, I trust the castigation you have received will teach you better conduct for the future.'

"With what unutterable disgust and horror did every word which the heartless scoundrel uttered, fill me. It was some time ere I could find strength or resolution enough to reply, but at length in accents that must have moved any other heart to pity than the stoney one which he possessed, I said :—

"'Oh, Ali, and can you thus triumph over the cruelties you have thus inflicted upon a poor friendless child, who should command your pity and protection, not your malice and revenge? Oh, would indeed that I had died, rather than live to have to suffer the fresh horrors that you no doubt have in store for me.'

"'That which you may yet have to endure, girl,' he unfeelingly replied, 'will depend in a great measure upon yourself. But mark me, any resistance to or murmuring at my will from a wretched brat like yourself will but serve to ensure my vengeance. Come Buddah.'

"And thus saying, with a fierce look which was evidently meant to assure me that he would not fail to carry his brutal threats into effect, he and his wife retired from the room, bolting the door after them—though there was not the least necessity for their doing so, in the utterly helpless state that I was—and I was again left to the solitude and agony of my own thoughts.

"And thus did I lie in the same wretched condition for several weeks, and it was thought that I should never again be completely restored to health, and indeed, such was my unexampled misery, that I hourly prayed for death to release me from my sufferings.

"But my mother principally occupied my thoughts during this long and painful period, and I entertained the most dismal apprehensions as to the fate which had but too probably befallen her. But I never even for a moment flattered myself with the hope that I should behold her again.

"But I am afraid that I shall tire your patience, let me, therefore, hasten to the conclusion of my narrative as quickly as possible.

"At length I so far recovered that I was able to leave my mattress, and to sit up in the miserable place of my confinement.

Ali and his wife, too, somewhat relaxed in the severity of their treatment; they supplied me with better provisions, and such as were more suited to the delicate state of my health, and rendered the room in which I was confined more comfortable, and when they addressed me it was with far less harshness and brutality than they had been accustomed to do.

"But this favourable change in the conduct of my persecutors towards me, inspired me with but little hope, for I could see no prospect of ever being released from the life of misery I had so cruelly experienced, even from the earliest period of my existence that I could recal to my memory, and surely death would be far preferable to a fate so lingering and so torturing.

"Months, more than twelve months rolled on, and still there was no change in my condition, still was I fettered to the same monotonous and dreary life, still doomed to linger on in the same deplorable state of wretchedness and despair.

"I was now, as near as I can imagine, from what I was afterwards informed, about nine years of age, but sorrow and constant torturing reflection had so matured my mind that I possessed all the grave demeanour, and capacity of intellect of a woman even old enough to be my mother.

"I was indeed a poor, grave, careworn, melancholy little thing, yet with spirits—had they not been crushed—as naturally

happy and buoyant as any other child of my age.

"Surely the desolating hand of care and sorrow was never felt more cruelly or unjustly by one so young and innocent.

"But a change, a wonderful change was about to take place in my circumstances, and the light of hope at length to be permitted to dawn upon the hapless child of sorrow.

"Ali was seized with a serious illness, which from the first it was evident would prove fatal.

"He continued to linger for a long time, and his sufferings were of the most violent and excruciating description, a just punishment for the monstrous cruelties he had inflicted on me and others.

"And it was then, when trembling at the

No. 44.

certain approach of death, and all the crimes he had so wantonly and recklessly committed during a long career of infamy, were presented in hideous array before his memory, that all the horrors of remorse and the terrible reproaches of conscience goaded on to the madness of despair the wretched guilty man, and his frantic ravings were at times quite frightful to listen to.

"But in his calmer moments he seemed anxious to make all the atonement, for the innumerable wrongs he had done to others, in his power.

"I was released from the gloomy room in which I had hitherto been confined, dressed in better clothes than I had ever been accustomed to wear, fed in the most delicate manner, spoken to by Buddah in tones so different to those which I had always before heard from her, that I could scarcely persuade myself that she was the same brutal and repulsive woman, at the bare sight of whom I had always trembled with feelings of dread, disgust and horror; I was even permitted to walk forth alone occasionally, to a short distance from the bungalow, and in short, so marvellous was the change in the treatment I now received, that my brain was bewildered, and I could with difficulty believe the evidence of my senses.

"And now after my many years of patient endurance—even child as I was—were I about to receive that reward at last which I believed myself to deserve? I could not help encouraging the hope that it was so, and my soul rose in gratitude to the merciful and Almighty Dispenser of all good.

"Ali died, and I believe truly penitent. His death-bed scene was a painful one; but I will pass that hastily over. He earnestly implored my forgiveness, strictly, solemnly enjoined his wife to treat me kindly for the future, and in every respect the same as if I were her own child, then after a few minutes delirious raving, which it was quite frightful to hear, the guilty man breathed his last

"Now then it was that I hoped the long hidden secret of my birth, and the reason of my being so cruelly and unnaturally banished from the protection of my unfortunate mother would be revealed to me; but in this I was doomed to be disappointed, and the torturing mystery to remain for some time longer unravelled.

"Buddah assured me that she dared not disclose the important facts I was so anxious to know to me, as she was bound by a fearful oath, the same as her late husband had been, to keep them secret, and that if she broke that oath, it would lend to the inevitable and immediate destruction of myself and her.

"This, however, she did venture to inform me for my satisfaction, namely, that the lady whom I had seen on two occasions was indeed my mother, but Yunadar was not my father. She also told me that my revered mother was still living, and that it was not at all improbable that, sooner or later, I might behold her again, and that she would place no obstacles in the way of our meeting though she would run great risks in not doing so.

"Oh, what happy feelings of hope and consolation did those assurances impart to me. But I will not attempt to describe them, for I am certain that whoever reads this manuscript, and pays careful attention to all the painful incidents that it records, will be able duly to appreciate them.

"Some weeks after the death of Ali, we were visited by the sister of Buddah, also a widow, but in comfortable circumstances, and the very opposite to her sister in natural disposition; but she felt for Buddah, notwithstanding that proper affection which the former had so long neglected to return.

"This good woman, for such she certainly proved herself to be, seemed to view me with feelings of the deepest compassion, and to take the greatest interest in me, and her subsequent behaviour to me, convinced me how right I was in the estimate I had formed of her character.

"Yielding to the earnest and benevolent desire of her sister, Buddah consented to abandon the wretched bungalow which we at present inhabited, and to go and reside with her, she having no family, and having sufficient to keep us in comfort.

"We quickly departed from that hated place in which I had suffered so much, and, after a journey which occupied more than a day, arrived at the dwelling of Buddah's sister, which was a comfortable and even handsome bungalow, situated in a pleasant and romantic part of the country; and which indeed appeared to me, after the miserable places in which I had hitherto dwelt, or rather been imprisoned, a perfect little palace, and my spirits began to feel something of their natural elasticity, and I could not but fondly hope that brighter, far brighter days than those that I had yet experienced, were in store for me.

"Nothing could possibly exceed the attention and kindness which I received from this my first benefactress, the sister of Buddah, and never, oh, never can I cease to remember it with feelings of the deepest gratitude.

"She was an intelligent woman, and had received a liberal education from the English family with whom she had lived as a domestic in her more youthful days, and that had been cultivated by perseverance, study, and experience.

"To her I am indebted for the knowledge and learning I possess, and without which it would have been impossible for me to have penned this melancholy history of facts, so important to you, my dear Omelia, and to others. May every blessing, and all due honour attend her memory.

"Daily, hourly, she exerted herself to the utmost to instruct me, and apt scholar as I cannot help saying I was, I listened to her with delight and avidity, and in the course of a few short months, I had so wonderfully improved under her careful tuition that I could scarcely credit the fact myself.

"And thus twelve months of the only happiness I had ever experienced elapsed, and I had so greatly improved both in personal appearance, in health, in spirits, and intrinsic qualities, that it would have been scarcely possible for those who had seen me in the days of my greatest misery now to recognise me. There was only one thing that I really wanted—and for which my soul panted—to render me completely happy and content.

"Need I say that that was to behold my beloved mother again? to be once more enclosed in her fond embrace; to be pressed to her throbbing and affectionate bosom, and to receive a blessing from her lips.

"And that happiness was in store for me much sooner than I had dared to anticipate, but, alas, it was followed by events which I cannot recal to my memory without feelings of the deepest sorrow, anguish and regret.

"How often did I offer up my prayers to heaven for blessings on the head of my honoured, my beloved parent, and that we might be suffered to meet. Daily, hourly I did so, and hope often whispered to me that my prayers would not be offered up in vain,

"But to the all important fact.

"It was on as bright and beautiful a day as ever gladdened the hearts of the Almighty's creatures, that I was rambling alone, a short distance from the bungalow, among the romantic scenery in the neighbourhood, as I frequently did, deeply wrapped in those thoughts that constantly engrossed my mind, but at the same time gratefully enjoying the refreshing beauty of the weather, when my kind benefactress who had been absent from home some hours, suddenly appeared, and hastened to meet me, which she did in the most affectionate manner.

"But I could see in an instant from the expression of her features, and the agitation of her manner, that something had occurred to excite her, and I ventured eagerly to ask her what it was.

"'Dear Miriami,' she replied, 'I cannot now wait to explain. I was hastening home to fetch you, be not alarmed, my child, but you must instantly with me, and prepare yourself for a surprise.'

"Her words agitated me, and my heart throbbed violently with mingled feelings of hope, fear, doubt, and expectation.

"I looked tremblingly, and inquiringly up in her face, but with a faint smile of encouragement she took my hand, and led me from the spot.

"After walking for some short distance, during which time I felt greatly agitated, speculating and wondering within myself how this adventure would end, we came to the ruins of an old temple, situated on a romantic spot, and which I had often selected as the scene of my meditations.

"Here my conductress suddenly stopped, and addressing me, said—

"'I must leave you now, Miriami, to enter the temple alone, but I shall be close at hand should you require my presence. Be firm, and be happy.'

"There was a mystery in her words which I could not understand, but before I could question her further, she hastily quitted me and became lost to my sight in the midst of a cluster of trees that grew not far from the spot.

"My heart now palpitated at double its wonted pace, for I was satisfied that something of the most vital importance was about to happen to me, and I was anxious yet almost fearful of entering the ruins, and when I did so it was with a trembling step.

"Gracious powers! what a surprise indeed there awaited me. I cannot even now after so many years have elapsed forget it, or the feelings that I experienced on the occasion.

"Kneeling down, apparently engaged in prayer, was a female form, attired in white, and with her back turned towards me.

"I could not move a step further at the moment, so great was the agitation of my feelings, and the presentiments that crossed my mind

"But I was not kept in suspense; the female arose from her knees, she turned towards me, and with a frantic cry of unspeakable, uncontrollable joy I rushed to the dear arms that were open to receive me, and was pressed to the throbbing bosom of my mother!

CHAPTER LXXXVIII.

MIRIAMI'S TALE CONTINUED.

"For some minutes I remained locked in the affectionate embrace of my beloved parent, sobbing and weeping, but we were both of us so overpowered by our violent emotions that we were unable to give utterance to a word.

"Yes it was indeed that dear mother who had scarcely ever been absent from my thoughts even for a moment, but whom I had feared that I should never behold again. But oh, how melancholy was the change that had taken place in her personal appearance. Long mental and bodily suffering of the most unprecedented description was most painfully marked upon her revered features, and told the terrible tale much more powerfully than any language however eloquent could possibly have done. Dimmed was the lustre of those eyes which still were fixed upon me with such intensity of mingled affection, sorrow, and anxiety, that I find it difficult, nay, utterly impossible for me properly to describe.

"How wasted, too, was that once lovely and graceful form which her enfeebled limbs seemed now scarce able to sustain; in fact, since the last time that we had met, ten years seemed to be added to her age, and it was but too evident that her earthly career was rapidly drawing to a close.

"For some time longer my mother continued to strain me to her bosom, bathing my cheeks with her scalding tears, while convulsive sobs stifled the words to which she was so anxious to give utterance; and I need scarcely say that the power of my emotion equalled if it did not exceed even that of her own.

"Still the anguish of my feelings at the melancholy change which was wrought in her appearance, was mingled with one of the most unspeakable delight to think that heaven had permitted us to meet again, and that at length most probably the long hidden secret of my birth would be explained, tho impenetrable mystery which had enshrouded my fate would be unravelled, and all the many doubts and fears that had so naturally beset and bewildered my young mind would be removed.

"'My child, my sweetest, poor little one of cruel destiny,' she at length exclaimed, still holding me in her arms, and in tones, and with an expression of countenance I cannot describe, but which can never be banished from my memory to the latest moment of my existence, 'oh, with what mingled feelings of joy and sorrow does your mother, your own unfortunate mother, forbidden to acknowledge you, again press you to that fond heart, which, alas, too well I know ere long must cease to beat. With what nameless feelings do I gaze upon those innocent features that at once so solemnly and so touchingly appeal to my maternal breast, and yet seem unconsciously to reproach me for that cruel desertion of you even in the tenderest years of your infancy, but which heaven knows that I had no power to prevent. Speak to me, Miriami, my own darling offspring, poor child of sorrow, let your wretched, heart-broken mother once more hear—and probably for the last time—the beloved tones of your voice, and tell me whether or not your heart, prompted by the dictates of nature, acknowledges me for that unhappy parent whom I have stated myself to be.'

"What were my feelings while I listened to those dear words, every one of which seemed to thrill through my veins; how could I reply? For a minute or two my emotions rendered me totally incapable of doing so, whilst the tears that gushed to my eyes nearly blinded me.

"But at length I gently withdrew myself from her embrace, and throwing myself on my knees before her, with hands clasped vehemently together, while I looked up in her pale face with an intensity of feeling which I must leave to your imagination, dear Omelia, I ejaculated—

"'Mother, mother! oh, that blessed word so new to my ears, how can the poor simple child, Miriami, describe the thoughts the feelings that agitate her, while she listens to it, and uttered by the lips of that adored being who came to her in the midst of her gloom and sorrow like an angel of light? Of that revered being who from the first moment that heaven permitted her to behold her, has never been absent from Miriami's thoughts, has been the constant subject of her childish prayers, Oh, yes, my heart does indeed assure me, that however unworthy I may be of such a blessing, you are my mother, and thus do I kneel in all humility and reverence before you, and implore your blessing. Mother, mother!'

"I could say no more, but the look I fixed upon her was sufficient, more than sufficient to prove the sincerity of my words.

"My mother seemed astounded to hear such language escape the lips of one so young, so inexperienced, and who had been so cruelly neglected, and for a minute or two she gazed at me with looks of the greatest astonishment, with a heaving bosom, and did not utter a syllable.

"But at length in a wild paroxysm of mingled emotions, she raised me from the earth, and again enfolding me in her arms, we sobbed and wept for some time together.

"'My child, sweet and innocent daughter of affliction,' she cried at last, 'oh, what a terrible trial is this—more especially when she too surely feels convinced that this is the last time on this earth that we must ever meet again—to your distracted mother's breaking heart, and to know that she has no power to assist you, or to lessen the miseries of your fate. Alas, how great, how fearful are the risks that I have ran to accomplish this task, in order that I might at least reveal to you the fatal the dismal truth, and give you my farewell blessing. The result may even yet be the sacrifice of my life, but can I regret that, when that life has so long been to me an insupportable burthen?'

"I shuddered with horror as I listened to these fearful observations, and it was with difficulty, and that not till after a pause, that I could make any reply.

"'Beloved, but unfortunate mother,' I at last said, 'oh, what can be the meaning of those mysterious and fearful words to which I have just been listening? Who is it that you thus seem to dread, and who could be cruel enough to seek to tear you from your child?'

"She cast her eyes anxiously around the place for a moment or two, as though she almost expected to behold the object of her terrors, and then, in a tremulous voice, she said, in answer to my question—

"'That terrible being, Miriami, who so

cruelly forced me from you in the dwelling of that heartless man, the brutal Ali—he, Yunadar, my husband.'

"'And—and,' I said, in a faltering voice, and with a shudder, 'my father.'

"'No, no, my child,' my mother replied, hastily and fervently, 'heaven forbid that he should be your parent, although, alas, he is the father of another sweet innocent offspring of mine, the little Omelia, your sister, but whom I have too much reason to fear it will never be your fate to behold.'

"Nothing could exceed my astonishment on hearing this, and I looked up anxiously in her face for an explanation.

"'Sister—sister!' I repeated, in accents of bewilderment, and almost incredulity, 'what strange feeling is it that overpowers me at the mention of that sacred name? Oh, can I indeed be so doubly—yet under such gloomy circumstances—blessed as to have one whom I can call sister.'

"''Tis true, Miriami,' answered our dear mother, Omelia, with a sigh, 'Yunadar, my second husband, and the father of Omelia. But short as is the time that I am allowed to stay with you, my poor child, and although it breaks my heart to think of it, this is our last earthly meeting, I must seize the opportunity to briefly relate to you those melancholy facts you are so anxious to hear, and which it may be so necessary for you to know.'

"'Our last earthly meeting, my beloved mother,' I gasped forth in trembling accents, and looking in her pale and sorrowful face with the most unspeakable agony, 'oh, say not so, repeat not those fearful words which make me shudder to think of.'

"'Be calm, Miriami,' she replied, again embracing me, and wiping the tears from my eyes, 'I feel that it is the will of heaven that it shall be so, and I must not murmur. And yet to part from you, my unfortunate child, from you, who have ever till lately been estranged from me, is torture the most indescribable to my soul. But listen to me, and let that which I am about to relate to you be impressed upon your memory, and guide your future conduct through life. It is a painful task that I have imposed upon myself, but it must be accomplished, and I hope that heaven will give me power to do so, and without being interrupted.'

"I did not attempt to make any reply to this, but the solemnity of her words and manner struck me with a sensation of awe, and I awaited in a state of anxiety which I need not describe, for her to commence the important narrative.

"Before doing so, however, my mother walked cautiously to the entrance of the ruins, and looked out cautiously to see that there was no one at hand from whom any danger might be apprehended, and who might listen to that which she was about to relate.

"Finding that there was nothing to sanction her doubts and suspicions she returned, and seating herself on a portion of the fallen ruins, I knelt before her, with my hands locked in hers, and looking up affectionately and anxiously in her face, greedily, and with breathless attention, devoured every word that fell from her lips.

"Notwithstanding the years that have passed away since that important event, and the many troubles and vicissitudes it has been my hard lot to have to encounter, every particular as that beloved being related it is as fresh in my memory as if I had listened to them but yesterday.

"But the length to which I have already proceeded will but allow me to give the substance of our dear mother's affecting narrative, Omelia, without adhering, as I would wish, to her language, and which was to the following effect."

CHAPTER LXXXIX.

A MOTHER'S SUFFERINGS.

Stanley again found it necessary to pause in the perusal of the manuscript, in order to give Omelia some little time to prepare herself for the startling disclosures to which they were no doubt about to listen; and our heroine could not help again giving full expression to the feelings which the remarkable and interesting events which the lengthy but by no means tedious papers had recorded, naturally excited.

"Oh, my unfortunate mother," she observed, "how little did I ever imagine—notwithstanding the cruel treatment which you ever received from my guilty father—the extent of the troubles it was your hard fate to have to undergo. How can I ever sufficiently admire the unexampled fortitude and resignation with which you must have endured them."

"True, dearest Omelia," coincided her lover, "most true; and I cannot but wonder and regret that such an amiable and lovely being as your unfortunate mother evidently was, should have ever been sacrificed to such a man as Yunadar, whom I cannot but almost blush to call your father."

"Alas, that it should be so," sighed Omelia, "it was surely a strange and monstrous fatality that could bring two individuals so widely opposed in minds and dispositions to each other together. But guilty as I knew my father to be, I could never have suspected him to be so completely callous to every feeling of humanity, as what the manuscript has already revealed. May heaven pardon him, for indeed he has much to answer for."

"But is it not strange, Omelia," said Stanley, "that your mother should never even have hinted to you during her lifetime, any of the important facts that Miriami has related?"

"I was, as you have often heard me say," replied our heroine, "very young when my poor mother died, and she doubtless did not think me capable of understanding matters of such grave importance; besides, dread of my misguided father, and the fear of prejudicing my young mind against him, probably withheld her."

"It is only reasonable to suppose that," remarked Stanley, "but do you remember the circumstances under which the death of your mother took place?"

"I was always led to believe that it was consumption," answered Omelia, "but I have often since suspected that it was the ill-treatment of my father which had hastened her dissolution, and what poor Miriami has already related confirms those suspicions. But proceed with the manuscript, dear Edward, for I am now anxious to know the extraordinary particulars of my much wronged mother's history."

Stanley complied, and thus the manuscript went on to say—

"Although, my dear sister, you doubtless are aware of the fact, it may be as well here to repeat what our mother stated at the commencement of her tale of sorrow, namely, that she was the only daughter of a once wealthy East India merchant, but whom severe losses had reduced to comparative poverty.

"He had been a widower for several years, and his daughter, the gentle and beauteous Rose Harcourt—our mother—was the only solace to him in misfortune and his declining years, and doubtless her numerous virtues prompted her to exert herself to the utmost to deserve the unbounded affection which he lavished upon her.

"And thus time flew by, and Rose Harcourt—for by her maiden name I will now call our parent—was just ripening into womanhood, when accident introduced her father and herself to an Indian gentleman, one Kerah Bardah Singh.

"He was a young man of good property, highly accomplished, of the most prepossessing address and manners, and handsome person and features, and between him and our mother a mutual affection of the most sincere and fervent description soon sprung up, and which met with the entire sanction of Mr. Harcourt, who entertained the highest opinion of Kerah, so that in due time the lovers were united—Kerah having embraced the Christian religion—and there seemed to be nothing which was likely to throw a blight upon the happiness of their future prospects.

"Their happiness was increased by the birth of myself, but, alas, it was not fated to last long.

"I should have mentioned that there had been residing with my father for some time previous to his marriage, a cousin whom he highly esteemed, and who had ever appeared to return his friendship with the same sincerity and warmth of feeling.

"This individual was Yunadar, your misguided father, Omelia, and you will, I know, pardon me if in relating the sorrows and wrongs of our mother and myself, I should appear to write of him anything unnecessarily severe; but, alas, they are painful undeniable facts that I shall alone have to deal with, and of that, to your cost, you are too well aware.

"Yunadar at that time—of course, I am merely repeating your mother's words—was, like his cousin, Kerah, young and brave, and of most insinuating manners, and he succeeded in gaining our mother's warmest esteem and friendship, but unfortunately, beneath all this specious cloak lurked a guilty mind, which only awaited the fitting opportunity to gratify its lawless passions, and to show itself in its true colours, in its natural deformity.

"Under the protection of my father, too, was also living an orphan boy, not more than four years of age. This was my cousin Abdal, with whom I did not become acquainted for many years afterwards.

"May heaven bless him, for his unremitting kindness since we have been restored to each other I am indeed most largely indebted.

"Abdal is the son of my father's only sister, who died soon after her husband, leaving her infant under the protection of her brother, who had ever behaved to her with the greatest affection; and well and faithfully did my father perform his duty to the poor child, who also found in our mother, it is needless to add, the tender care and solicitude of a parent.

"The first misfortune which our mother experienced was in the death of her truly excellent father, Mr. Harcourt, who only survived little more than twelve months after her marriage, and died deeply regretted by all who had the pleasure and honour of his acquaintance.

"It was some time ere that daughter who had so fondly loved him, and upon whom from her earliest days of childhood, he had ever lavished with the most affectionate regard, could find the least consolation for the melancholy and irreparable bereavement she had thus sustained. But at length her own Christian resolution, and the soothing voice of her husband prevailed, and she learnt to bear her loss with patience and resignation.

"But, alas, another, and, if possible, still greater calamity was shortly in store for her, her husband was taken seriously ill, and symptoms soon showed themselves that were calculated to excite the greatest apprehensions as to a fatal result.

"No doubt it would be a fruitless task for any one who had witnessed them, to attempt to describe the agony and despair of our mother on this occasion, and we therefore, my dear sister, can only be expected to picture them in our own imagination. But oh, how terrible must her sufferings have been at the prospect of losing, so shortly after the death of her father, a husband whose existence was even far more precious to her than her own, and without whom life—if it had not been for the sake of her infant child—must become almost an insupportable burden.

"And my father, too, although he could otherwise look upon his approaching dissolution with the calmness and resignation of one whose conscience reproached him not, could not but regret that he was so soon to be snatched from a beloved wife and child who so much needed his protection, and for that reason his fervant prayers were hourly offered up to heaven that it might be its all merciful will to preserve his life, so those whom he loved might not be cast as it were upon the wide and desert world, with no one to care for them, or protect and succour them in the hour of need.

"No one was more assiduous in his attentions on this melancholy occasion, or evinced greater sorrow and anxiety than Yunadar, and that more than ever won for him the esteem of our amiable and afflicted mother, and my poor father evinced his boundless gratitude for the same in every possible way.

"But little could they suspect the dark thoughts which at that very time were passing in the mind of Yunadar, the plot of villany he was even then concocting.

"Once more, Omelia, I must solicit your forgiveness for the strong language, which in the excitement of my feelings I am compelled to make use of in reference to your misguided father, but, alas, it is too well justified by his own subsequent conduct.

"But let me pass over this dismal portion of our unfortunate mother's disastrous history as quickly as possible.

"The disease of my father completely baffled the utmost skill of the physicians, and in less than a month from the time of his first attack, he breathed his last in the arms of our distracted mother, and after solemnly commending her to the future protection of his cousin Yunadar, whom he had amply provided for in his will, and which injunctions, Yunadar with equal solemnity

and apparent sincerity promised faithfully to obey.

"To pourtray the heart-rending grief of the young widow would defy the power of the most graphic and eloquent pen, and no one seemed more deeply to sympathise with her and to mourn the loss of the noble-hearted Kerah, than Yunadar.

"But for some time, as may be expected, our poor mother remained perfectly inconsolable, she was confined to her bed, delirium seized upon her senses, and for several weeks her recovery was entirely despaired of.

"During this melancholy period, no one could possibly be more unremitting in his attentions, Omelia, than your guilty father, and he appeared to feel the sufferings of the unfortunate invalid most acutely.

"But youth, and a naturally strong constitution triumphed o'er the disorder of our parent, and at length she was sufficiently restored to be considered out of danger, although, of course, after what she had had to undergo, and that which she but too probably had yet to experience, it must be a long time before she could have been expected to be restored to complete convalescence.

CHAPTER XC

THE MANUSCRIPT CONCLUDED.

"On opening the will of my late father, it was discovered to the infinite surprise and emotion of our mother, that he solemnly enjoined her, at the expiration of a sufficient time to mark the respect due to his memory, to bestow her hand on his cousin Yunadar, who he said was every way worthy of her, and was convinced would do his duty by her as an affectionate husband, and a fond father to their dear little Miriami.

"Need I say with what astonishment, not unmingled with the deepest regret, our mother read those extraordinary injunctions, and which, however repugnant they might and must be to her feelings, with the remembrance of that husband whom she had loved beyond all earthly beings, she dared not disobey.

"'Tis true that, as I have stated before, our mother had ever admired the apparent manly virtues of Yunadar, and viewed him with the greatest esteem, nay, she could regard him as a brother, but to look upon him in the character of a husband, her heart at first completely revolted from the idea of, and many were the hours of poignant anguish and regret that the reflection cost her.

"Yunadar for some time refrained from pressing his suit, and when he at length did so, it was with the utmost apparent respect and kind consideration for the feelings of our mother.

"He assured her that from the first moment he had beheld her she had made a most powerful impression upon his heart, such as it was not easy, if at all possible, to eradicate, but that respect for his cousin, and the most profound reverence for her had caused him to endeavour to stifle the unfortunate passion in his breast; but now that he discovered that it was the wish of the late Kerah that he should become her lawful protector, he ventured to make known to her his sentiments, with the flattering hope that in time they would meet with some return from her, although, of course, he could not expect that she could ever bestow upon him the same ardent affection that she had felt for the excellent husband she had lost.

"How our unfortunate parent was enabled to reply to this I will not attempt to describe, but you need not wonder, Omelia, that the gentle and respectful manner that Yunadar urged his suit, made a most favourable impression upon her, and she could not—so plausible was his conduct, and such was the mask of hypocrisy he was enabled so well to assume—for a moment entertain a doubt of the sincerity of his words, and Yunadar, no doubt, saw at once that his triumph was certain; in fact, how could it be otherwise, when it was the dying wish, nay the command of the late deluded Kerah.

"From that moment Yunadar redoubled his attentions to his intended victim, and to myself; and he seemed alone to be happy when in our mother's presence, and to anticipate her every wish, and by degrees she became more reconciled to her fate, although at times she could not but suffer some dismal forebodings and misgivings to cross her mind.

"In fact, not to become unnecessarily tedious, at the end of a little more than twelve months after the death of her husband our mother became a second time a wife, by bestowing her hand on Yunadar, the triumph of whose guilty hopes and wishes might now be considered complete.

"Fatal hour, how terrible were the consequences that followed; alas, how little could any one have anticipated them, and even now my hand trembles to record them, and my pen almost refuses to perform its office.

"For some months after their union, Yunadar's conduct towards his beauteous and amiable wife was all that could be wished, and his love for her and myself seemed daily to increase. He appeared constantly to study how he could best contribute to the happiness of our mother, and to replace by every means in his power the loss she had sustained in the death of her first husband, and it was therefore that her heart gradually warmed towards him, and she began to feel contented, if not supremely happy.

"From that delusive dream, however, she was too soon destined to be awakened.

"In due time, my dear sister Omelia, you were born, and for a time Yunadar's happiness seemed to increase and he lavished upon his wife, and yourself and me the greatest tenderness. But oh, how fearful was the change that quickly came over him.

"He became morose and sullen, absenting himself from home, also, for days together, and replying to the gentle reproaches of his wife, always impatiently, but not unfrequently with even cruel severity, and turning with scorn and indifference from her tears and remonstrances.

"But what was more distressing to our mother was that marked dislike he now openly displayed towards me, mere infant though I then was; spurning my innocent caresses as though I were something loathsome to him, and frequently applying epithets to me that showed the hatred he bore towards me, and which were disgusting to listen to.

"To the little Abdal, too, Yunadar's hatred was equally extended, and it was quite evident that we were the obstructions in the way of the completion of his inhuman designs, which he was determined to remove.

The first practical proof which he gave of that determination was to convey Abdal from home altogether, no one knew whither, although he stated that he had placed him in charge of those that would take all the care of him that such a friendless brat deserved, but that he had been troubled with him too long.

"The shock given to our unfortunate mother's feelings by this cruel circumstance, and which more than ever revealed her guilty husband in his true brutal character, and unveiled his diabolical designs, was almost too overpowering for her to withstand. She could now only view him with feelings of horror and hatred, for the terrible idea took possession of her mind that, notwithstanding what Yunadar had said, poor little Abdal had been murdered, and it seemed but too fearfully evident that it was his savage determination to get rid of all that was related to the deceased Kerah, and who, for what reason she could not imagine, had become hateful in his sight, and she shuddered when she thought of the fate which was but too probably in store for myself and her, for towards you, Omelia, he did not at that time evince the same feelings of abhorrence.

"How bitterly did she reproach him for his inhuman conduct, and the manner in which he had so infamously abused the con-

dence of her late noble-minded husband, and the sacred trust which he had committed to his charge. But this only served to exasperate Yunadar the more, and, after a torrent of the most savage abuse—oh, how can I record the revolting fact?—he struck her—our beloved, our amiable and gentle mother, Omelia—a blow which felled her senseless."

At this part of the manuscript—the intense and thrilling interest of which seemed to increase the farther it proceeded—Omelia's feelings compelled her to interrupt Stanley, in order that she might give expression to those sentiments of disgust against the atrocious conduct of her guilty father, and of sympathy for her unfortunate mother in her unparalleled sufferings, which she found it impossible to restrain, and in which it is

quite unnecessary to add her lover fully anticipated.

"Oh, Almighty Powers!" exclaimed our heroine, her whole frame agitated in the most violent and painful manner, and the expression of her features, at the same time, fully corresponding with the feelings to which she so warmly, so vehemently gave utterance, "how torturing, how truly heart-rending is it to listen to atrocities such as these, committed against a mother so every way undeserving of them. My heart bleeds to think of them, while my bosom swells with feelings of honest indignation against the base perpetrator of them, which it is utterly impossible for me to describe. Father I dare not, cannot call that being who could thus so monstrously outrage every feeling of nature and humanity. What demon could

No. 45.

have taken possession of his breast, and urged him on to the perpetration of crimes so revolting, that the bare contemplation of them must make even the most insensible shudder?"

"The reflection is indeed a most melancholy one," remarked Stanley, "and I am lost in wonder and almost incredulity. It seems impossible that any one bearing the human form could thus frightfully have committed himself, especially when the object of his barbarity was his own wife, whom he had solemnly vowed to love, protect, and cherish, and who could never by any possible means have given him cause for conduct worthy only of a savage. But pardon me, dear Omelia, if in the excitement of my feelings I am urged thus to speak of him who was the author of your being."

"Alas," returned Omelia, tears at the same time trembling in her eyes, "that it should be so. But from this moment I must discard him from my breast, and cease to remember him as my father. Oh, that cruel fate should ever have linked him to one so good, so gentle, so loving, and so truly virtuous, as I so well know my mother to have been."

Stanley returned no answer to these observations, but his looks sufficiently testified how fully and fervently he reciprocated those sentiments to which Omelia had given utterance.

It was some time before either of them could sufficiently regain their composure to resume a narrative which recorded such revolting, remarkable, and startling facts, but at length having done so, Stanley thus proceeded with his painful task—

"A nameless feeling of horror pervades me, as I know it must do you, my dear sister, when you peruse this, and my pen almost refuses to perform its office.

"Alas, that I should have to record such atrocities committed by your own parent against our unfortunate, unoffending mother, but they are the facts, and however repugnant to my feelings, and torturing to you to hear, they must be related.

"But this was but a mere prelude to the horrible sufferings which it was the hard lot of our unfortunate mother to have to experience.

"From that moment Yunadar made no attempt to conceal the real guilty and brutal motives that stimulated his conduct, and his cruelty towards his helpless victims—our mother and myself—every day increased.

"My mother was shortly confined within her own room with her children, scantily fed upon the coarsest of food, and forbidden all communication with any person. If she dared to offer a murmur of complaint, it only served to aggravate the rigorous cruelty

of her treatment, and to draw forth the most dreadful threats of Yunadar, which she knew too well he had both the power and the will to carry into execution, and to appeal to him for mercy and forbearance was equally a fruitless task.

"He never spoke to me, poor little helpless child as I was, but with the vilest epithets, and he openly cursed and reproached the memory of my father, that man who while living he had professed to regard as a brother, and whose confidence and warmest esteem he had so unfortunately and fatally insinuated himself into, at the same time that he must evidently have entertained for him feelings of the most deadly malice, and coveted his wealth, the possession of which was the sole object he had in view in seeking the hand of our mother.

"Towards yourself, Omelia, it is true he sometimes evinced less brutal feelings, but it was quite evident that the real affection of a parent was an entire stranger to his flinty and insensible breast."

"Alas," sighed our heroine, once more interrupting her lover, "how terribly have I had to experience the truth of that statement; and how much am I indebted to the late Mr. and Mrs. Melville, who took pity on my helpless state, after the death of my poor mother, took me under their protection, and even treated me with the affection of parents."

"And may heaven bless their memory for having done so," observed Stanley, "oh, how I shudder to think, my Omelia, what might have been your terrible fate had you not met with such benevolent friends. But suffer me to hasten to the conclusion of this extraordinary and mournful history, which has already gone to so great and unexpected a length, and which has now become almost too painful for perusal."

Omelia nodded assent, and Stanley once more resumed his task.

"It would be but a tedious waste of time to attempt to describe what were the sufferings of our mother, thus doomed to a fate almost more horrible than that which ever before fell to the lot of human being, but we may, we must imagine them, and how agonising must be the reflections that they must ever give rise to in our minds.

"But I cannot trust myself to dwell longer upon this painful subject.

"It was indeed wonderful the fortitude with which our mother bore these unexampled cruelties, but it was the thought of her infant children, and the fate which would but too probably befall them, should she sink under the horrors to which she was subjected, which doubtless sustained her, and rendered her capable of struggling against that, from the bare contemplation of which under any other circumstances, she probably would have shrunk with terror.

"But there were, if possible, still more dreadful trials in store for her.

"It was the hour of midnight, and our poor mother, worn out with fatigue and anguish of mind, had fallen to sleep upon her wretched pallet, in the dreary room, or dungeon—for it had more the appearance of one—in which she was confined, with yourself, Omelia, and me clasped to her fond and aching bosom.

"But soon she was awakened by our cries, and starting up with terror, and a dismal foreboding of that which had already taken place and was about to follow, she beheld Yunadar standing in the room, at the foot of the mattress, holding me, screaming in his arms, and his features distorted by the most savage and unnatural passions.

"With a frantic cry our mother started from the mattress, seeming to read the diabolical intentions of her inhuman husband in the expression of his countenance, and throwing herself on her knees before him, in delirious accents implored his mercy, and not to deprive her of her innocent child.

"He laughed aloud in derision of her agony, and tears, and supplications, and was about to hurry from the room with me, when driven to a pitch of frenzy our mother clung to him, and while she endeavoured to tear me from his arms, in which he held me with the most brutal ferocity, she made the place resound again with her piteous cries.

"'My child, my child!' she frantically exclaimed, 'inhuman man give me back my innocent child! Cruel even as your are, you surely cannot deprive that hapless mother, whom your barbarity has already rendered so indescribably wretched of her offspring.'

"'Fool!' he answered, 'think you that this display can excite any other feeling in me than one of contempt? You now behold your brat, the hated child of him, whom in my heart I ever loathed and despised, for the last time. Content yourself with the one I leave you, and thank me for the mercy I show towards this, by, instead of sacrificing its worthless life, consigning it to the future care of those who will henceforth be known alone as its parents. The treatment it will receive from them will depend entirely upon your own conduct, I repeat that you will see it no more.'

"'No, no, no!' she again wildly shrieked, and still frantically clinging to him, 'it is impossible that you, even you, can contemplate so hideous a deed. All merciful heaven will prevent it, and not suffer the poor broken-hearted mother to be deprived of her innocent offspring! Spirit of my beloved Kerah, oh, I beseech you to avert so horrible a crime!'

"'Rash, obstinate fool!' Yunadar fiercely exclaimed, 'you must be aware that any opposition to my will is quite useless, that any appeal to me for mercy and forbearance is equally vain.'

"'Monster!' cried our wretched mother, wrought up to a perfect pitch of madness and despair; 'you shall not tear my tender infant from my fostering breast, and leave it to the mercy of those who, following your inhuman instructions will take a savage delight in torturing it. Even death would be far less terrible than such a fate. Nay, you shall not triumph in your fiendish designs, I will cling to you while I have life, but you shall not deprive me of my child!'

"Her struggles now became desperate, but of course they were completely ineffectual, and only served the more to exasperate the cruel Yunadar, who nothing could move from his savage determination. But at length completely exhausted, and overpowered by her maddening emotions, she relaxed her hold of her husband, who pushed her brutally from him, and she sunk on the floor in a state of insensibility.

"From that state of unconsciousness it would probably have been a mercy if she had never more revived, but when she did do so, to what a dreadful certainty was she awakened. The lamp on the table gave a glimmering light, which only served to make the utter misery of her situation the more distinct. You, Omelia was sleeping calmly in unconscious innocence, but Yunadar with myself was gone, and the whole fatal truth rushed at once upon our wretched mother's distracted brain.

"With a frantic shriek she rushed to the door, and, in her frenzy, attempted to force it open, but it was to well secured for her to be able to do so, and throwing herself in utter despair upon the floor, her senses again left her.

"She remembered no more for above a week, for during that time she remained in a complete state of unconsciousness of what was passing around her, although the agony of her sufferings ever remained the same.

"Weeks passed away, and what she endured—knowing then as she did, that I was too surely torn from her, and doubtless for ever—may be better imagined than described.

"But when Yunadar again dared to present himself before her, which he shortly did, how terrible was the scene that took place. How piteous were her supplications to him for mercy, for him to restore me to her, and to drive her forth with her children upon the wide and cheerless world, since it was quite evident that they had all become so hateful to him, and she promised him faithfully, solemnly, that they should sooner perish than they would trouble him again.

"But Yunadar remained inexorable, was deaf to all her supplications, and only mocked at, and seemed to take a fiendish delight in her sufferings, and thus was she left to all the horrors of despair.

"Can it be wondered at that such a dreadful trial as this should, for a time, deprive our unfortunate mother of reason? What brain could possibly withstand so frightful a shock?

"For months she remained in a state of insanity, and it is only due to Yunadar to state that during that period he relaxed in his cruelty towards her—as she was afterwards informed by those whom she could believe—and employed proper persons to take every care of her and you, my sister, but at the same time, with strict injunctions to see to her security.

"It may be asked why Yunadar was permitted to commit all these atrocities—for which no punishment could have been too severe—with impunity. But at that time Yunadar was rich with the wealth which had belonged to my lamented father while living, he had great influence with those high in authority, and had every means of concealing his crimes from mortal eye, or even if they should be discovered, of escaping the consequences.

"I will pass hastily over the years of suffering our mother had to undergo, after I had been so cruelly taken from her, and rather than which death would have been a mercy. But still improbable as it was, she could not but encouraged the idea that she would see me again, and it was that hope, and the careless, and innocent prattle of yourself, dear Omelia, that alone sustained her.

"At length Ali having visited Yunadar, it was in a conversation which she overheard between them, that she had the unspeakable gratification to discover that I really still lived, and where I then was.

"Oh, what a relief was this to her deeply lacerated heart, and how fervently did she return her thanks to heaven for it.

"From that moment all her thoughts were occupied in endeavouring to find the means of beholding me and again pressing me to her bosom before she died.

"By the connivance of one of the females who attended her, during the temporary absence of Yunadar from home, she was enabled to accomplish her fond and anxious desire, but it was with a solemn promise that she would return, and the better to ensure the fulfilment of that promise, she consented to leave you, Omelia, behind.

"What subsequently occurred I have already related, and thus having given you the melancholy history of our ill-fated mother, as she disclosed it to me, I will come to the concluding startling events that followed this our last meeting.

"Having finished her sad recital, and allowed ourselves both time to recover ourselves from the excited feelings which it naturally caused, my mother, fixing upon me a melancholy look of affection and torturing regret, which spoke volumes, and went immediately to my heart, addressing me, said—

"'And now my own adored child—child of sorrow and cruel destiny, my own sweet Miriami, you have heard all the painful particulars of your mother's history, at least as far as time and circumstances will permit her to relate them. You will treasure them in your memory. You must, you will, for they are connected with your very existence, and should fate ordain that you and your sister Omelia should meet at some future period, repeat it to her, and may you be happy in each other's love.'

"I could not attempt to make any reply, I could only kneel before her in devotion and veneration, and look up in her pale face with all that intensity of affection and sorrow, which my feelings prompted, but I could not utter a word.

"She then suspended the miniature likeness of herself, which I enclose in this packet, from my neck, and having with heartdrawn sobs and tears invoked heaven's blessings on my head, after a pause, during which she was convulsively struggling with her feelings, she said—

"'And now, my beloved Miriami, upon this earth we must part for ever. Oh, what words for a broken-hearted mother to have to say to a child so dear to her, but it must be so, and I have no control over the cruel destiny that pursues me. I must leave you, and return to the custody of my tyrant, for should he return and find me absent, he would not hesitate to sacrifice the innocent Omelia, your sister, to his vengeance. The kind-hearted woman in whom you have already found so sincere a friend, will continue to protect you, and—'"

At this important and interesting passage, much to the surprise and disappointment of Omelia and Stanley, the manuscript abruptly ended, and left them in a state of mystery as to what followed at this painful interview between Miriami and her mother, which it was completely useless for them to attempt to unravel; and for some time they were lost in amazement, pity, sorrow, and indignation at the extraordinary and startling incidents which the narrative revealed, and were compelled to give free vent to their feelings before they could regain their composure.

———

CHAPTER XCI.

ABDAL MOORSHA'S EXPLANATION.

"What could have caused Miriami to have thus abruptly broken off?" said Omelia, "she leaves us in a state of almost as great a mystery as we were at the beginning. I shudder as I picture to myself the sufferings of my poor mother after what we have already read, but that we can now never hope to have explained."

"It is to be regretted," said Stanley, "but now do I bethink me how the conclusion of the narrative may be supplied. Abdal desired to see us after the perusal of the manuscript, that he might furnish us with any additional information we might require."

"Ah," said Omelia, "that is fortunate, for doubtless Abdal can fully explain that which we wish to know."

"I will seek him immediately, Omelia," said Stanley, and he quitted the room for that purpose.

While he was gone, Omelia reflected upon all the extraordinary circumstances of her mother and Miriami's history, and the longer she did so the more was her astonishment excited, and her feelings of sympathy and regret aroused.

Stanley quickly returned to the room, accompanied by Abdal, whom Omelia greeted with every mark of esteem, and he returned with the utmost respect, and he then prepared to give the explanation required.

"It was sudden illness," he observed, "which caused my unfortunate cousin to bring the manuscript to such an abrupt and unsatisfactory conclusion; and she never afterwards had an opportunity of resuming it. But I am acquainted with all the particulars, and I was desired by Miriami to explain them to you, after you had perused what she had written. These are the facts:

"Before your unfortunate mother, Omelia, could finish her affecting speech, and while poor Miriami hung upon her every word with rapt attention and emotion, they were both startled and alarmed by the loud and frantic shrieks of a woman, which they had no doubt proceeded from the kind woman who had proved so great a friend to Miriami, and while they stared at each other aghast, and were unable to move from the spot, to try to avoid the danger which too evidently threatened, Yunadar, followed by several others entered the place.

"I am afraid that I must fail to give anything like an adequate description of the scene which followed, and I wish I could give it in the same eloquent and affecting language that Miriami related it to me.

"Terrified at the sight of Yunadar, and the ferocious looking men by whom he was accompanied, Miriami uttered the most piteous and piercing cries, and clung to her unhappy parent who held her convulsively to her bosom.

"But Yunadar savagely, and with a dreadful oath, struck her a violent blow which immediately felled her to the earth in a state of insensibility, at the same time grasping Miriami by the arm with that degree of ferocity that made her cry with the pain, and fixing upon her a look which made her shudder with horror, for in it she imagined that she could read the fate which awaited her and her mother.

"In a state of the utmost distraction she called upon that unfortunate parent's name, and implored the mercy of Yunadar. But as well might her supplications have been made to the forest trees as to that cruel, callous hearted man.

"I pray you pardon me, Omelia, for speaking thus of your father, but unfortunately the truth compels me to do so."

"Alas," replied our heroine, "I am too painfully convinced of that, and my bosom swells with shame and indignation while I think of Yunadar's inhuman conduct towards my poor mother and Miriami, and I blush to call him by the name of father. But I beg you to proceed, good Abdal."

The latter immediately complied with this request in the following words—

"Miriami was immediately by the orders of Yunadar dragged away by two of the men, after they had received some secret instructions from him, and that was, as her mother had too truly stated the last time that she was ever permitted to behold her, for in little more than a month after this event, your unfortunate parent, Omelia, as myself and Miriami were informed, died of a broken heart, and from the long brutal treatment which she had received from her unnatural husband."

"Oh, yes," remarked Omelia, with much emotion, and tears trembling in her eyes, "young though I was at the time, well do I remember that melancholy event, and the bitter anguish it caused me. I also recollect the stern indifference with which my guilty father watched her in her dying moments, and the ghastly looks of terror and reproach which she fixed upon him. Never, never can I banish it from my memory, and that dismal and painful scene is presented as vividly to my imagination, as if it had only occurred yesterday. I also recollect that she seemed to wish to reveal something to me, but was prevented from doing so by the presence of my father. But pardon this interruption, Abdal."

Abdal bowed and then proceeded with his tale in the following words—

"How terrible were the sufferings of poor little Miriami, on being thus savagely torn from her mother, I need not seek to describe as you can imagine it much better, and her agony and horror were increased on her beholding a short distance from the ruins, stretched upon the earth apparently lifeless, and weltering in her blood, her unfortunate benefactress, who had thus doubtless fallen a victim to the vengeance of Yunadar.

"This more than all convinced her of the dreadful fate which no doubt awaited herself and her mother, and she made the air resound again with her cries, and implored the men to take pity on her, and restore her to her parents. But they only mocked at her anguish, and continued to drag her along in the same savage manner till they arrived at the bungalow where she had long resided, and where horses were waiting at the door.

"They did not stop to enter the house, but mounting their horses, and placing Miriami (who was now insensible) before one of them, they started away towards the most gloomy and unfrequented part of the country at the top of their speed.

"I may as well mention here, that the arrival of Yunadar and his companions at the bungalow at the very time when the interview between your mother and Miriami was taking place, Omelia, was quite accidental, and not by design, and their suspicions being excited by finding no one in the place, they made inquiries of the neighbours, who gave them sufficient information to direct them to the fatal spot.

"But to return to Miriami and the villains who were conveying her away, as it would then have appeared to certain destruction.

"On recovering her senses, she found that it was quite dark, and that she must consequently have been in that state for sometime.

"The speed at which they had dashed along on leaving the bungalow, remained unabated, and the part of the country through which they were travelling was of the wildest possible description, and together with the gloom of the night, and the dreadful thoughts that crowded upon her brain, and which were increased by the fierce and threatening looks of the men, was more than sufficient to strike terror into the breast of any one especially a mere child like the ill fated Miriami, and she almost feared to look at the ruffians, but to venture to speak to them, or to supplicate them to take pity on her, and to inform her whither they were conveying her, or for what terrible purpose she dared not. In fact it would be a fruitless task to seek to pourtray the feelings of the little sufferer in that dreadful hour of trial.

"But her anguish at the thought of the shocking fate which had too probably befallen her mother, and the certainty that she had seen her for the last time, far exceeded that which her fears for herself created in her breast, and she was completely distracted, and it was truly wonderful that she did not immediately sink under the influence of her torturing feelings.

"The gloom and wilderness of the scenery, through which they were travelling, increased the further they proceeded, and at length they entered upon an almost impenetrable forest the very aspect of which was more than sufficient to strike terror into the breast of the spectator, and fill the mind with dismal forebodings of that which was but too likely to be about to take place.

"In short, so powerful was the effect which the aspect of all around, and the apprehensions that naturally distracted the poor girl's brain, had upon her, that her senses again left her.

"How long she had remained in that condition she had no means of ascertaining, but to what fresh horror was she awakened.

"She found herself alone in one of the wildest parts of the forest, lying upon the ground, and where she had no doubt been left to perish by the cruel orders of Yunadar.

"Judge of the feelings of your helpless and unfortunate sister, Omelia, at that moment, for it is impossible to describe them."

"Ill-fated girl," said our heroine, the tears trembling in her eyes, and her looks sufficiently testifying the sincerity of what she uttered; "how my very heart bleeds to think of them. What a terrible situation it was for one so young to be placed in. It would almost have been a mercy to her, if she had never again awakened to consciousness, for what manifold and unparalleled sufferings it might have saved her."

"Most true," replied Abdal, "but it was the will of heaven that it should be otherwise, and the greatest wonder is that she did not immediately die of terror."

"She started to her feet with a cry of horror, and gazed around her, as well as her eyes could penetrate through the utter darkness of the frightful place, but not the least signs of a human being or habitation met her sight, and she renewed her cries, and wrung her hands in despair.

"What to do she knew not; it seemed as though she might wander through that fearful place for ever, without the least chance of meeting with any relief; and nothing but an awful death either of starvation or by wild beasts, which no doubt infested the forest, presented itself to her imagination.

"But at length, half mad with the agony and horror of her feelings, she rushed from the spot as fast as her feeble limbs would permit her, she knew not whither.

"Horrors seemed to accumulate around her the farther she proceeded, and the darkness appeared every moment to become the more intense. The wind arose and howled through every avenue and among the foliage in the most tempestuous manner. Not so much as a star deigned to twinkle in the black sky, and even if it had its faint light could not have penetrated the darkness of that wild and frightful place.

"In fact, everything seemed to frown despair upon the poor girl, and mock her anguish.

"At length, completely heart-sick with the terror of her feelings, and fancying even additional horrors to those that actually surrounded her, she was again compelled to pause, for at present, uncertain into what danger her footsteps might lead her, she was afraid to proceed farther.

"And while the tears chased each other down her cheeks, and convulsive sobs almost choked her utterance, she knelt down, and in language of simple earnestness which might well have moved the heart of the most insensible person to pity to have heard her, she besought the mercy and protection of the Supreme for herself and mother.

"Small as it was, this did afford her some relief, and after a short time she again resumed her weary way, with the wild hope of meeting with some human habitation, where she might find shelter, and meet with friendly advice and assistance, though it was not likely that she would do so in the midst of that savage and dreary forest.

"Still louder howled the blast, and the further she went the more did the unfortunate Miriami become involved in the intricacies of the place, and the more frightful became her situation.

"She felt a gnawing sensation of hunger upon her, which was most torturing, for it was many hours since she had tasted food, and it was fearfully uncertain when if ever she would do so again.

"It was impossible for Yunadar to have devised a more diabolical design to gratify his cowardly and deadly vengeance, and the bare thought of it is enough to make the stoutest heart shudder."

"Cruel, misguided, guilty father," interrupted Omelia, "if I dare still to call you by that sacred name, how terrible are the crimes for which you have got to answer to outraged heaven. Unfortunate sister, poor, innocent, friendless Miriami, what a dreadful fate was that which pursued you; how marvellous that one so young should be able to find the strength and fortitude to bear up against it. Oh, may your bright spirit now be receiving its due reward in the realms of eternity."

To this wish Abdal and Stanley both fervently responded, and the former then proceeded.

CHAPTER XCII.

MIRIAMI'S FURTHER SUFFERINGS.

"And now to add to the misery of the little wanderer," continued Abdal, "the sullen murmuring of the thunder in the distance, and the occasional flashes of lightning which darted across the sky, proclaimed a gathering storm, and she could not contemplate its approach, in such a frightful place, and all alone as she was, without feelings of the greatest terror.

"Again she paused, and sobbed and groaned as if her heart would break, and wrung her hands in the utter agony of her insupportable despair, but no prospect of any relief appeared, and worn out with mental and bodily fatigue as she then was, it was quite impossible that she could proceed much farther, but must lie her down and perish.

"The storm quickly commenced, and fearful indeed was it in its violence. The war of the angry elements grew fiercer every instant, and was truly frightful and appalling at such an hour and in such a place.

"Poor Miriami trembled with terror, and made the air resound with her cries, in the intervals between the pauses of the thunder which, however, were very brief.

"She was almost afraid to proceed, for the lightning as it darted its fury among the giant trees, seemed to threaten death at every step. It was then that she more deeply regretted than before that she had ever again been restored to consciousness after the villains employed by Yunadar had abandoned her, and she could not but consider it the refinement of cruelty that they did not immediately deprive her of life, rather than consign her to a fate so horrible, so truly hideous as that to which she was now exposed.

"It rained in torrents, but from that she was almost entirely sheltered by the thick foliage of the trees which formed a canopy above her head.

"And thus through the gloom and the terror of the scene, the poor girl continued slowly and with difficulty to wander for some distance further without the least signs of any relief appearing. But at length her weary limbs could support her no longer, and she sunk on the damp earth completely exhausted, and with no other alternative but to endeavour to resign herself to her dreadful fate, which seemed to be inevitable.

"The tempest was now at its height, and

nothing could be more appalling than its violence, especially to the terrified imagination of so young a child, and one who had at her early age such unparalleled experience in the school of adversity. Her brain could endure it no longer, she cast one fearful glance around her, and then with a frantic cry of agony and despair, her senses in mercy left her, and for a time she became unconscious of the misery of her situation, or that which but too probably was yet in store for her.

"A shuddering sensation of benumbing coldness at length aroused her, and hastily raising her aching head, gazed vacantly around, lost in bewilderment and terror.

"During the time that she had slept—if sleep indeed it could be properly called—all that had happened from the fatal interruption of the interview between herself and her unfortunate mother, was re-enacted in her imagination.

"It was now daylight, and the storm had entirely ceased, still the misery of the unfortunate girl's situation was melancholy and terrible indeed, and the prospect before her was quite as hopeless as before, and she could scarcely muster sufficient fortitude to resume her dreary way, especially with all the horrors of a lingering death of starvation unless she met with speedy relief, staring her in the face.

"But luckily the latter fear was soon destined to be greatly diminished, for on wandering some distance farther she discovered an abundance of wild fruit, of which she greedily partook, and which not only appeased the cravings of her appetite, but seemed to her imagination one of the greatest luxuries which she had ever met with.

"And oh, how agonising were her reflections as she proceeded, more with regard to the but too probable fate which had befallen her unfortunate mother, and that kind friend the poor woman, her benefactress, to whom she was so much indebted, and who she had every reason to believe had fallen by the murderous hand of Yunadar or his myrmidons.

"These thoughts were indeed so overpowering, that it is no wonder they almost drove her to madness.

"Still she persevered through every disheartening difficulty, and continued her weary wanderings in the forest's intricacies, but seeming to be as far off relief as ever.

"At length the aspect of all around her appeared somewhat less wild and cheerless, and she emerged from the thickest part of the forest, into a more open space, and entered upon something like a beaten track, she pursued, with the faint hope that it might at last lead her to some part of the country where she was more likely to meet with the assistance of which she stood so much in need, for she could not believe so badly of all her fellow creatures as to think that no one would take pity on her deplorable and destitute situation, and leave her to her fate.

"The country became even more cheerful as she advanced, and her spirits greatly revived.

"Another hour's walking brought her to an outlet of the forest, and the landscape which then met her eye, smiling beneath the golden beams of the sun, which was then shining brightly, was of the most picturesque and romantic description, and such as led her to hope that before long she would at last arrive at some village or human dwelling, where her necessities would be administered to, she therefore increased her speed, reanimated with fresh fortitude and confidence.

"The scenery was enclosed, in the background by lofty mountains, towards which she made her away, trusting that beyond them she might behold the gratification of her wishes accomplished.

"Not much farther, however had she advanced on her way, when suddenly there appeared in sight, in the distance, a party of horsemen, who were coming leisurely towards her, and her heart beat high with hope and expectation.

"So sanguine was the poor girl, that she could not encourage the idea of the possibility of their being enemies, and she hastened towards them, clapping her hands and shouting aloud, though she knew not whether they could yet observe her.

"As they came nearer, and she could examine them more narrowly, she could observe that they were a mixture of natives and Europeans, and as far as she was enabled to judge from their appearance they formed a hunting party, making their way in all probability, to the wilds she had just quitted, in order to enjoy their sport.

"They at length evidently saw her, and quickened their speed to come up with her, while she paused to await them, and to prepare herself for either the gratification or the disappointment of her hopes.

"She was not kept long in suspense, they came up to her, and evinced the utmost astonishment at beholding one so young, and so interesting, alone, and at such an early hour of the morning.

"But Miriami imagined that she could perceive them viewing her with even greater pity than curiosity, and she took courage, and sinking on her knees, she implored them with tears in her eyes, to take compassion on a poor friendless child, and to direct her to some place where she might find that benevolent assistance she so much required.

"This simple appeal evidently had the desired effect, and the foremost of the party, dismounting from his horse advanced kindly towards her, and raised her tenderly from her suppliant posture, at the same time fixing upon her a look of the deepest sympathy.

"He was an English gentleman. Having encouraged her to take heart, he anxiously inquired who she was, and how she had come into the situation in which he had found her.

"Miriami briefly but correctly informed him, and he appeared more amazed than ever, but at the same time thoroughly convinced of the truth of her extraordinary statement.

"'Unfortunate child,' he remarked compassionately, 'can it be possible that there are such wretches, such heartless wretches in the world as those whom you have described? It is fortunate, however, that providence guided your footsteps this way, for you have met with those who will not, rest assured, turn a deaf ear to your supplications, but will treat you with every humanity and consideration.'

"Oh, what a relief was this assurance to Miriami—what blessed words were they to her ears, and overpowered by feelings of the most unbounded gratitude, she again threw herself on her knees, and poured forth her thanks in language as simple as it was sincere.

"But the gentleman again raised her, and motioning to one of the natives, who seemed to be a domestic, he desired him to return with the poor child, and to see that everything was done for her that her remarkable case and necessities required.

No. 46.

" 'You will soon find, my dear,' the gentleman remarked, 'that you have fallen into the hands of friends, who will readily do all that they can for you in your destitute condition, or that humanity can suggest. It may probably be evening before you will see me again, but in the meantime make yourself quite content.'

"Miriami was too much bewildered to know how to reply but the gentleman smiled affably upon her, and then motioning again to the native, he took her in his arms, and mounting his horse, placing her before him he gallopped off with great speed towards the distant mountains, and soon left the party far behind.

"The mingled feelings that agitated the breast of poor Miriami may be imagined; but before I proceed to relate what further befel her, it may be as well to state that the house to which she was now being conveyed was, by a most fortunate and singular circumstance, the very one in which I had found an asylum since the time when Yunadar had consigned me to a similar fate as that to which he had so cruelly condemned her, and the English gentleman (Mr. Raymond) before mentioned was the same who so kindly befriended and protected me.

" Passing at length beyond the mountains, the Indian with his innocent charge dashed on at the same speed through a romantic part of the country towards a distant village, and at one end of which the handsome and commodious dwelling of Mr. Raymond and his wife was situated; and the farther they proceeded the more did the hopes and confidence of Miriami gain strength, though neither her or her companion exchanged a word with each other.

"In due time they entered the village, and soon afterwards stopped before the mansion, at which poor Miriami gazed with mingled feelings of surprise and pleasure.

"Having been admitted by one of the domestics, Abdallah—the native Indian who had conveyed her—conducted Miriami into a room on the ground floor, which overlooked the spacious and tastefully arranged gardens that were attached to the house, where he kindly desired her to wait a few minutes, while he went to apprise the amiable Mrs. Raymond—from whom I received the affection of a mother—of her arrival and to deliver to her the instructions of her husband.

"When Miriami found herself alone, she gave full vent to the tempest of mingled feelings that agitated her breast, and bewildered her senses.

"So extraordinary was the circumstance, and so wonderful the change—from comparative death to renewed life, from abject misery and despair, to sanguine hope and expectation—that she could scarcely believe in its reality, hardly could she persuade herself that she was not under the influence of some marvellous and delusive dream.

"Tears started to her eyes, and she was almost overwhelmed by the powerful excitement of her feelings, but gratitude superseded every other emotion in her breast, and sinking on her knees, as well as her sobs would permit her to do, she poured forth her thanks to heaven, and implored its future protection.

"I was with my benefactress, Mrs. Raymond, on the entrance of Abdallah, and I need not describe the astonishment of that excellent woman and myself as we listened while he briefly related the particulars of the extraordinary adventure, and delivered the message of his master.

" As for myself, I felt more than usually agitated, and a presentiment of what was about to take place. The circumstances under which the unfortunate child was discovered were so similar to my own, and the description of her so closely corresponded with what I imagined my little cousin Miriami, if she still lived, now to be, that my heart palpitated with hope and expectation, and I could not conceal my feelings of impatience and anxiety to behold her.

"Mrs. Raymond took me by the hand, and we both immediately repaired to the room in which the poor little fugitive was.

"Her back was towards us, and we entered the room so cautiously that she did not hear us, but continued for a minute or two to gaze upon the garden, which seemed to excite her wonder and admiration, Mrs. Raymond looking at her with the deepest interest, but not offering to disturb her.

"There was something about the poor girl's personal appearance which immediately enlisted my sympathy, while I felt my anxiety and curiosity increase every instant.

"At length Miriami turned round, and perceiving us in the room, exhibited the most indescribable emotion, in which I fully participated on beholding her lovely and innocent features, which, notwithstanding the time which had elapsed since my removal from the residence of Yunadar were perfectly familiar to me, and my heart acknowledged who she was, even before her lips could reveal it.

"Mrs. Raymond was much struck with the appearance of the little unfortunate, and kindly approached her, extending her hand towards her with a sweet and encouraging smile; but Miriami immediately sunk on her knees before her, and with clasped hands and streaming eyes, looked up in her face with a nameless expression which I can never forget, but could not utter a word.

"Mrs. Raymond was deeply affected, and with every gentleness of manner, she said—

"'Compose yourself, my poor child, for rest assured that you are now with friends who will fully sympathise with you in your misfortunes, and do everything to alleviate your grief, and shield you from the malice and persecution of your cruel enemies. Your name, my dear?'

"'They call me, Miriami, lady,' she replied in a sweet but timid voice.

"No sooner did I hear her pronounce the name, than with an exclamation of surprise and delight, much to the astonishment of Mrs. Raymond, I rushed towards her, and enfolded her in my arms, whilst the most convulsive sobs escaped my bosom and completely choked my utterance.

"My forebodings were realised, there could no longer be any doubt of it, and the emotions which at that moment agitated and excited me I need not attempt to pourtray.

"Miriami seemed too much confused and astonished to speak, and could only gaze at me with looks of the utmost bewilderment and curiosity.

"'For heaven's sake, what is the meaning of this, Abdal?' demanded Mrs. Raymond, but no sooner had Miriami heard the name by which she had called me, than she recognised me, and with a cry of the most unbounded astonishment she sunk nearly insensible in my arms.

"I shall not seek to describe minutely the scene which followed between myself and my unfortunate cousin, but feelings of delight and gratitude to the Supreme for our mutual preservation and restoration to each other at a time so unexpected, quite superseded every other in our breasts, and we could not but weep upon each other's bosom, whilst my excellent benefactress stood by and watched us with feelings of surprise, sympathy, and the deepest interest.

"'I am at a loss, Abdal,' at length said Mrs. Raymond, ' to understand the cause of the extraordinary excitement exhibited by yourself and the poor child on beholding each other. It would indeed appear that you are no strangers.'

"'Strangers, madam,' I repeated, still retaining my hold of the willing hand of Miriami, and looking with the most affectionate solicitude in her beauteous countenance, 'ah, no, we are indeed too well known to each other by the similarity of the fate which has pursued us, but never did I expect that providence would permit us to meet again. Oh, my revered benefactress, how great your astonishment will be when I inform you that this is my young companion in misfortune, my poor little cousin Miriami.'

"You may indeed imagine, my friends," continued Abdal, "how great the astonishment of Mrs. Raymond was on receiving this information, sympathy for the unfortu-

nate little sufferer, the hapless child of cruel destiny, filled her compassionate breast, and tears trembled in her eyes, and showed plainly the feelings that agitated her as she snatched poor Miriami to her bosom almost with the same affection as if she had been her own offspring, and in accents of tenderness that showed the sincerity of her sympathy, said—

"'Poor helpless child of sorrow, innocent victim of unexampled cruelty, and has it been the will of heaven to release you from your terrible fate, and to conduct you to those who will gladly protect you from future danger, and endeavour to reward you for the unmerited sufferings you have already undergone? Be happy, be contented now, my child, if you can, for you are now with those who will bestow upon you all that affectionate care and attention that humanity dictates, and that your deplorable condition demands.'"

"Excellent woman," said our heroine, unable longer to restrain the warm expression of her feelings, "unknown as you were to me, my heart overflows with gratitude towards you for the humanity thus shown to my unfortunate sister in this, the terrible hour of her need. May heaven reward you as you merit."

"Yes, Omelia," remarked Abdal, fervently, "most sincerely do I respond to that wish, and kind heaven has not failed to do so both to her and her husband, depend upon it, for the manifold virtues they possessed, and the generous manner in which they exercised them towards Miriami and myself. But suffer me to proceed, for I have but little more to add in conclusion."

Omelia and Stanley expressed their anxiety for him to do so, and Abdal having again collected his thoughts went on as follows—

"Miriami was several minutes before she could speak a word in reply to the observations of my benefactress, but her looks and her tears sufficiently testified the feelings of gratitude that swelled her bosom, and she would have again sunk upon her knees before Mrs. Raymond had she not prevented her, and with looks of encouragement and the most unbounded compassion observed—

"'Enough, my dear child, your sorrows have every claim upon my pity and assistance, and I should despise myself could I for a moment withhold them. Oh, what a heartless miscreant must that be who could treat with brutality one so young and helpless, and who could never have offended him.'

"'Ah, gentle lady,' sighed Miriami, and the tears chased each other rapidly down her cheeks, "I have indeed had to suffer that which it makes me shudder to think upon.

and I have often thought it would have been a mercy if I had never been born, or that it had pleased heaven to take me in my infancy, and ere I knew what sorrow was. But they have torn me from my poor mother, and it is the idea of the dreadful fate which but too probably has befallen her that tortures me more than all. Oh, surely, it was most cruel not to suffer me to die upon her bosom. Mother, beloved mother, shall I never be permitted to behold you again? Ah, no, I dare not, must not encourage such a thought, and Miriami, can never, never possibly know happiness.'

"Convulsive sobs choked her further utterance, and it was in vain that the amiable Mrs Raymond and myself endeavoured to console her.

"But the melancholy condition of the poor girl, after what she had had to undergo, demanded immediate attention, and my benefactress and myself having once more embraced her and sought to reassure her and to calm her feelings, conducted her to a room where refreshments, of which she stood so much in need, were prepared for her, but of which she could only partake but sparingly.

"As you may expect, I had soon after I came under the friendly care and protection of Mr. and Mrs. Raymond, related to them all the particulars of the early history of myself and Miriami; but many were the anxious thoughts that I had bestowed upon her, and how eager was I to learn the fate which had befallen her, although that to which Yunadar had consigned me, and the hatred with which he had ever seemed to view her, were quite sufficient to make me apprehend the worst.

"Anxious, however, as myself and Mrs. Raymond were to learn all that had happened to her, and the circumstances that had brought her into the situation in which she had been found by the humane Mr. Raymond and his friends, we considered that she was in too exhausted and agitated a state to gratify our curiosity for the present, and after some short time, during which I again and again expressed my gratitude to heaven for her preservation, and congratulated her on our being restored to each other in so miraculous, providential, and unexpected a manner, feelings in which it is unnecessary for me to say that Miriami most warmly participated, she was conducted by Mrs. Raymond to a chamber, where she was permitted to seek that rest which she so much required.

"Mr. Raymond shortly afterwards returned home and made the most anxious inquiries after the young stranger whom he had so fortunately discovered, when she must probably either have perished of hunger or become the prey of wild beasts. His surprise on learning who the poor child was, you may form a pretty correct idea of, and his gratification at having been able to save her from the fate with which she had been threatened, was greatly increased.

"But I am afraid I am becoming tedious. Miriami was not disturbed during that day and night, Mrs. Raymond having visited her frequently to see that she did not require anything, and leaving a servant in the chamber to watch her during the night.

"The next morning early, Mrs. Raymond anxious to know how she had rested, and to conduct her to the presence of her husband, visited her chamber, and found that she had already risen, and was looking much better in health and even spirits than could have been expected, and that benevolent lady felt if possible even more deeply interested in her appearance than before, and all her warmest sympathies were aroused for the poor little unfortunate who had thus, like myself, been thrown upon her humane care and protection.

"Again did the grateful Miriami, in her simple heartless style, pour forth her thanks, and Mrs. Raymond having encouraged her by words of the utmost kindness, and given her sufficient time to collect herself, conducted her from the chamber to the room in which Mr. Raymond and myself were waiting anxiously to receive her, and in which the morning repast had been prepared.

"I need scarcely say that Miriami met with a most affectionate reception from my excellent benefactor, Mr. Raymond, whose susceptible and manly heart could not but be moved to feelings of the deepest commiseration towards one so young and so interesting, and who had been already exposed to sufferings and cruelties that were not only almost unparalleled, but incredible.

"And Miriami was so deeply affected by the kindness which was thus lavished upon her by strangers, and those upon whom she could have no possible claim than that of common humanity, that her feelings nearly overpowered her, and she could only evince her gratitude by sobs and tears.

"After a time, however, by the exertions of Mr. and Mrs. Raymond and myself, she did become more composed and confident, and then complied with the request so urgently but feelingly made, to relate such melancholy and extraordinary particulars as those with which you are acquainted, and Mrs. Raymond and myself were moved to tears while we listened to her, and Mr. Raymond's bosom swelled with mingled emotions of sorrow, pity, and indignation.

"Again he earnestly expressed the gratification he felt at having been the fortunate means of rescuing her from the cruel fate to which Yunadar had consigned her, and, together with his wife, endeavoured to assure Miriami of his future protection and kindest consideration, for which the poor girl could not find language sufficiently powerful to return her thanks.

"And well did Mr. and Mrs. Raymond fulfil their promise, and lavished upon Miriami the same affectionate attention as if she had been their own child, meeting with the only reward they sought, namely, in the consciousness of having done their duty, and in the sweetness of her disposition, and the love and reverence she ever evinced towards them.

"And companions as we had been in adversity, it is unnecessary to state how ardently myself and Miriami were attached to each other, and what a pleasure we took in each other's society, feeling unhappy unless we were together.

"But it was impossible for your poor sister, Omelia, to rest until she had learned the fate of your unfortunate mother and yourself, and that Mr. Raymond lost no time in ascertaining.

"The death of that hapless parent from whom she had, from the earliest days of childhood, been separated, was a severe shock to Miriami, and it was a considerable time ere she could sufficiently conquer the violence of her grief so as to admit of that consolation which our benefactor and benefactress so earnestly endeavoured to impart to her, and that sorrow and regret was increased by the uncertainty whether yourself and her would ever be permitted to meet, for she loved you with all the ardent affection of a sister.

"But time, and the parental attentions which she received from Mr. and Mrs. Raymond, served in a great measure to ameliorate her grief, and she became comparatively happy.

"That feeling was greatly strengthened when she heard that you had been taken under the protection of Mr. and Mrs. Melville, Omelia, and that you had thus escaped from the stern and unnatural treatment of your father.

"In this manner five years passed away and they were years of the greatest happiness that Miriami had ever experienced. Mr. and Mrs. Raymond being unremitting in their affectionate attentions to us both, and leaving no means untried to render us content. Every care was taken of our education, and it was thus that Miriami became that accomplished being which you, Mr. Stanley knew her to have been.

"But that happiness was at length destined to be destroyed. Misfortune overtook those excellent persons to whom myself and Miriami were so largely indebted; several

failures in mercantile houses greatly impaired their property, and the fatal result of a lawsuit in which Mr. Raymond had unfortunately become involved, reduced them at last to comparative poverty; their establishment became almost immediately broken up, although there were one or two faithful domestics, who had resided with them for years, who could not be persuaded to leave in their adversity, and all hope of their ever being able to recover themselves appeared too likely to be at an end.

"How painful this melancholy change in the circumstances of those whom we had so much cause to revere was to myself and Miriami I need not attempt to describe, the more especially as we felt ourselves to be a burthen to them which they could ill afford to support.

"Mr. Raymond endeavoured to bear up against the misfortunes that had thus overtaken him with that manly fortitude which was so characteristic of him, but his health gradually sunk under them, and it soon became but too painfully evident that medical skill must fail ever to restore him to convalescence.

"With what torturing and increasing anxiety did Mrs. Raymond and Miriami watch by him during his illness—the latter with all the affection of the fondest daughter—and with what feelings of heart-rending sorrow and regret did we all look forward to that fatal moment which must deprive us of one of the best of earthly friends.

"It came at last; the soul of the excellent Mr. Raymond departed to heaven, and left his lady myself and Miriami quite inconsolable at the melancholy bereavement.

"We foresaw from the first what the result of this would be, for we were certain from the devoted attachment these kind people bore towards each other, that she could not long survive his loss, and those fears and forebodings were too fatally realised, for only two months had elapsed since his death when she was seized with a serious fit of illness which compelled her to take to her bed, and from the first her physician expressed very little, if any hope of her ultimate recovery.

"The poor lady bore her painful illness with the greatest patience and resignation, the only regret she expressed at the approach of death being that she was compelled to leave us to the mercy of the world, and unprovided for.

"Miriami was too much overwhelmed at the prospect of the second loss we were about to sustain to be able to control her grief, and the poignant anguish of mind which she suffered was truly melancholy to witness.

"Mrs. Raymond in vain, almost with her

latest breath sought to impart consolation to her, she could not listen to it, even from her revered lips with any degree of patience, and every moment her anguish and despair became the greater.

"The fatal moment arrived; and calm as an infant, after having invoked the choicest blessings of heaven upon the heads of poor Miriami and myself, Mrs. Raymond resigned her spirit into the hands of her Maker, and rejoined that of her husband in eternity.

"So great was the shock your sister had sustained, Omelia, in this our second irreparable loss, that she was completely distracted, and for several days she remained almost in a state of unconsciousness, and, in fact, I might say that I was scarcely less affected than herself.

"We were now left quite friendless, if not destitute, for the house of our late benefactress was taken possession of by a distant relation of the deceased, who soon showed by his behaviour that our presence would be no longer agreeable there, and with sad hearts, therefore, we quitted the place where we had enjoyed so many of the happiest hours of our lives, and for a time retired to the bungalow of an acquaintance, who had kindly offered us the use of it, and for the present we enjoyed all the limited comforts which the poor man's house could afford.

"But, of course, this could not long continue, and wandering to some short distance from that place where we had for so many years found an hospitable asylum, we obtained a situation in the humble capacity of servants, in the family of a lady and gentleman who had been on intimate terms with the late Mr. and Mrs. Raymond, and where we remained for some time.

It would only be a useless waste of time to enumerate the different menial situations we held, and the many difficulties and vicissitudes we had to encounter, for we shared our fate together like brother and sister, and I watched over the safety of Miriami with a jealous eye, and did all I could to contribute to her welfare if I could not to her happiness.

"We frequently received intelligence of you, Omelia, and Miriami, who so closely resembled you in features and manners had a longing desire to see you and to speak to you, but the fear of meeting with Yunadar—who she knew was lurking about in different parts of the country—and that he might recognise her prevented her, although I need not assure you that she continued to the last moment of her existence to entertain for you all the warmest affection of a sister."

"Poor Miriami," observed our heroine, and tears of sincere sorrow and regret trembled in her eyes as she spoke, "how well can

I appreciate the warmth of the sentiments you entertained towards me, although unfortunately we were never destined to meet. But she had seen Lieutenant Stanley on several occasions, had she not, my good Abdal?"

"Yes," replied the latter, "and before the poor girl knew the sentiments that existed between him and you, Omelia, she loved him, and in vain tried to banish his image from her memory. It was that unfortunate passion which induced her to watch for him on various occasions, and at length when she had an opportunity of speaking to him, unable to control her feelings within the bounds of prudence, she confessed those sentiments she had no reason to hope could ever meet with any return. You must recollect that memorable evening, Lieutenant Stanley?"

"Oh, yes," replied Stanley, with deep emotion, "every word that the unfortunate and ill-fated Miriami then uttered is stamped upon my memory in characters that nothing can ever eradicate. Dear Omelia, I know that you will believe the love which your sister had so strangely and unhappily imbibed for me, sprang from the purest and most unselfish of motives, and when she found that her fatal passion could meet with no return from me, but that you alone possessed my heart, she exerted herself to the utmost to stifle it in her breast, although I much fear that it was a severe trial to her feelings to do so."

"Oh," returned Omelia, "although I never beheld her only in imagination in my dreams, I cannot for a moment doubt the honour and purity of my sister, and never can I cease to remember her with the most ardent affection."

"And she deserved it all," said Abdal; and had it been the will of providence that she should have lived, and that you had met, how happy would you have been together. But regret is useless, and we must not murmur at the decree of fate."

To this our heroine and her lover assented, and the subject for the present dropped.

CHAPTER XCIV.

THE DUEL.—FATAL CONSEQUENCES.

Thus had Abdal arrived at the conclusion of the somewhat lengthy details and explanations which Omelia and Stanley had required after the perusal of the interesting narrative contained in the manuscript of the late Miriami, and which gave rise to a variety of feelings in their breasts, the principle, of course, of which were those of the most heartfelt sympathy and regret for the unprecedented sufferings of Miriami and her mother, and of the utmost indignation against the brutal Yunadar for the cruelties and wrongs he had inflicted on those whom he should have protected.

"Alas," sighed Omelia, who felt an unconquerable repugnance to calling him parent, "what demon could have possessed him to urge him to act so cruel, so heartless, and revolting a part towards those who should have been dear to him, and whom it was his duty to protect from harm, even at the hazard of his own life? I shudder with horror and feelings of disgust which I cannot control, when I think of the many years of horror that my beloved mother and poor helpless sister had to endure. Misguided, guilty father, how many are the crimes, so revolting to human nature, that you have got to answer for."

"Most true," coincided Stanley, with a look of regret, "and when I recall to my memory all that we have read, and which our good friend Abdal here has related, I can scarcely bring my mind to believe that one who evidently possessed so savage a disposition, and whose breast was a stranger to every feeling of humanity, could have been so closely allied to you in blood, my dear Omelia. But you must endeavour to banish him from your memory, for to think of him is only to revive feelings of the most torturing description."

"Alas, that it should be so," replied Omelia, "but there is no denying the painful fact. Heaven rest your souls in peace, my dearest mother and sister, and reward you with that everlasting happiness which the patience and resignation with which you endured your manifold earthly sufferings entitle you to."

Tears gushed to her eyes as she uttered this solemn prayer, in which Stanley and Abdal fervently joined, and she clasped her hands vehemently together, and raised her eyes above, becoming wrapped in the deepest emotion which neither of her companions offered to interrupt.

After some further conversation upon the same melancholy topics, having regained their composure, Stanley thinking that it might serve to divert the thoughts of Omelia, which had become most painful and oppressive, proposed that they should join the society of their friends, to which she agreed, and accompanied by Abdal—whose company had now become most valuable to them—they repaired to the room in which the other fugitives generally congregated, and where they found Mr. Meadows and several of them seated, and discussing the stirring events of the day, and the probability of their being able shortly to leave the old

fort—where they suffered many inconveniences and privations, and were exposed to considerable danger—and to reach some place of safety.

Alfred Meadows and Flora Melville were not present when they entered the room, but in a short time they made their appearance, and Omelia and her lover could not help noticing that both of them looked unusually excited, particularly Alfred Meadows, who having thrown himself in a most unceremonious manner on a seat apart from Flora, and nearly opposite to where Stanley was sitting, cast frequent glances at the latter of anything but an agreeable or friendly description, but of which the young officer took but little notice, although they were not unobserved by Flora Melville, who seemed most painfully to understand the meaning of such strange conduct.

At length Alfred Meadows, whose strange conduct towards Stanley continued for some considerable time, apparently unable to control himself any longer, arose from his seat and in the most abrupt manner quitted the room, without saying a word even to Flora Melville; but the poor girl's eyes followed him with a strange expression of emotion as he departed.

Mr. Meadows was far to busily engaged in conversation to notice the singular conduct of his son; but poor Flora continued to become more and more agitated, until she at length in a faint and tremulous voice excused herself to her friends, and evidently with a heavy heart also retired from the room.

Omelia thought she could guess the cause of Flora's agitation, and she could not but feel both pain and regret, not only for her sake but that of Alfred Meadows her cousin, was was a worthy young man, and she (Omelia) saw that he loved her fervently and sincerely, but in spite of all Flora's efforts to conceal it, it was too evident that she had been unable yet to conquer the unfortunate passion which Stanley had excited in her breast, and the consequence was that Alfred had hitherto been unable to obtain more than her esteem, and that created the most painful feelings and drove him at times to absolute despair.

Omelia suspected that the young man had that day again been pressing his suit, with the usual unfavourable result, and that consequently was the cause of the excitement he had exhibited, but as has been before stated, she did not like the angry looks which he had fixed upon Lieutenant Stanley, which seemed to show that he had permitted some unreasonable and groundless feeling of jealousy to take possession of his mind, which she could not but consider was totally unworthy of him and insulting to Stanley. However, she hinted nothing of her suspicions to Stanley, and feeling rather indisposed from head-ache, she shortly afterwards bade him and their friends good evening, and retired to her room, that she might endeavour to learn from her friend the reason of the emotion which her and her cousin had displayed.

Stanley remained with the persons in the room some time longer, engaged on various topics of conversation, but which beginning to flag, and to become dull and tedious, he also quitted the room, but as it was yet early in the evening, he did not feel inclined to retire to the apartment in which himself and two or three of his companions slept, he strolled to the gardens that surrounded the old Fort, and which had now an agreeable appearance, it having been the amusement of two or three of the fugitives for some time past, to arrange them with considerable taste, so that they formed a pleasant source of recreation in the dull monotony of their confinement.

The day had been remarkably hot, but the evening was cool and refreshing, and there was a full bright moon, to shed its lustre upon all around.

Stanley continued for some time to stroll about the gardens, enjoying the refreshing breeze which was wafted from the adjacent mountains, at the same time deeply wrapped in meditation upon the extraordinary events recorded in the manuscript, and that which Abdal had recorded, and which had more the character of romance than of stern reality.

He had reached a small arbour situated on one of the most pleasant spots of the garden, and was about to enter, when the voice of a man whose tones were familiar to him, and who appeared to be soliloquising in no very agreeable strain, struck his ears, and arrested him in his purpose.

Stanley was by no means curious to pry into the secrets of others, but still there was something which seemed to urge him to it, and he could not resist the temptation on this occasion.

He approached the arbour nearer, but placed himself in such a position that he might distinctly overhear all that was said, while he could not possibly be seen by the speaker, even if he should leave the place suddenly.

He had scarcely done so when he heard his own name pronounced in a tone of anger and disrespect, and that, of course, excited his curiosity more than all.

He listened attentively, and presently heard the followingly words uttered in tones that showed the excitement under which the speaker laboured.

"Yes, 'tis clear she loves him, she has boldly confessed that she does, and therefore do I loathe him, for it is he who hath annihilated all my brightest, fondest hopes, and his presence here drives me to madness and despair. And it is evident that he gives encouragement to her love, in spite of his affectation to the contrary, or she would never persist in fostering a passion which could meet with no return. And shall I be weak fool enough to endure this, and to be looked upon with scorn by both? By heaven I will not. My feelings rise indignant at the idea, and I should hate and despise myself if I thus tamely submitted to be looked upon and treated as a thing unworthy even of contempt."

The speaker paused, and the curiosity of Edward Stanley was more than ever excited, for he was all but certain that it was the voice of Alfred Meadows he was listening to, and he had a strong suspicion that he was the person to whom he alluded as having created feelings of jealousy so groundless within his breast. That which shortly afterwards followed, convinced him that he was not mistaken in his conjectures, and pained him considerably.

Again the person in the arbour soliloquised, and Stanley listened with the deepest attention, for he now began to suspect that he was justified in doing so.

"I will endure it no longer," said the speaker, vehemently, "every manly feeling of pride and self respect revolt at the idea, and let whatever may be the consequences, I am determined to have an explanation. Lieutenant Stanley, 'tis you that are—whether wantonly or not I know not—destroying my peace of mind and blighting my prospects, and I cannot rest until I have had satisfaction, I will not allow you to triumph in my misery."

Stanley thus finding his suspicions confirmed, and feeling indignant at the idea of his honour and fidelity to his beloved Omelia being called into question, could not patiently endure more, but darting from the place of his concealment at the same moment that Alfred Meadows quitted the arbour, they confronted each other with looks in which surprise, reproach, and indignation were mingled.

"Alfred Meadows," said Stanley, trying to speak as calmly, but at the same time as much to the purpose as possible, "you have presumed to couple my name with that which is untrue and dishonourable, at the same time that it is highly discreditable, mean, and uncharitable in one who claims the title of and whom I have hitherto looked upon as a gentleman, to do so, and therefore it is I who have an undoubted right to demand an explanation."

"So," returned Alfred Meadows, in a tone of resentment and bitter sarcasm, "you, Lieutenant Stanley, no doubt prompted by the consciousness of guilt, have, it seems, descended to the meanness of turning listener, and of prying into the secrets of others. 'Tis well—'tis well."

"Beware, Mr. Meadows," returned Stanley, mortified and indignant at the tones in which Alfred Meadows spoke, and the ungenerous and unjustifiable observations he made use of; "beware what you say; Edward Stanley is not the man to brook unmerited reproach or insolence. We now, at any rate, meet each other face to face, and I peremptorily demand, sir, of what it is you accuse me?"

"You have heard," replied Alfred, "since you acknowledge that you have been lis-

No. 47.

tening; but since you are bold enough to demand it, I accuse you of acting the part of an hypocrite and deceiver, by encouraging the love of Flora Melville, and, in spite of your solemn vows to the too confiding Omelia, endeavouring by the most insidious means to rob me of that which is far more precious to me than mine own existence. These are my accusations, and deny them if you can."

"I do deny them," exclaimed the enraged Stanley, his fine manly countenance flushed with the feelings of resentment that agitated his breast; "most emphatically, most scornfully, and indignantly, I deny them; they are as unfounded, as false, as you are unjust and uncharitable to give utterance to them. I cannot but deeply regret the fatal sentiments which Flora Melville (whom I sincerely esteem) acknowledged that she had unfortunately imbibed for me, but never by word or thought, I swear, have I sought to encourage them. I hold possession of the beauteous Omelia's heart, and heaven can bear me witness how faithfully, how ardently, how sincerely I return the passion with which she deigns to honor me. But enough of this, Alfred Meadows. I would fain dispossess your mind of the dangerous and torturing delusions under which it now labors; I am not inclined to quarrel with you, I am even disposed to make every allowance for the feelings under the influence of which you at the present act; but dismiss them, arouse yourself, become again a man, awaken to reason, and let us be friends."

The calm and persuasive tones in which Stanley spoke the latter observations, only served to exasperate the rash and misguided Alfred Meadows the more, and in a voice in which scorn, and rage, and sarcasm were blended, he replied:—

"Friends!—friends with that man whom I now loathe and despise, and who is the author of all my misery,—never. The friendship of Lieutenant Stanley would be worse than degradation."

"Beware," returned Stanley, feeling himself incapable of much longer bearing these unjust remarks, which he knew himself so well not to deserve;—"you seem to forget, sir, that I wear a sword." And at the same time he put his hand on the hilt of it significantly.

"And many a coward wears the same, but fears to use it," retorted Alfred, passionately.

The bosom of the gallant young officer (of he who had already so highly distinguished himself in many a hard-fought battle), swelled with indignation at this gross and unmerited insult, and he could no longer control his feelings.

"Coward in your teeth, vile calumniator," he exclaimed, partly drawing his sword from the scabbard; but that you are unarmed, and I scorn to take any cowardly advantage of you, I would have instant satisfaction for that word, which no one before ever dared to apply to me. But another time, if you would maintain the name of a man and a gentleman, I demand, I insist that you recal it, with every apology, or take the consequences."

"Another time," repeated Alfred Meadows, resolutely,—"no, now; I will not, I do not recal the word, and am prepared to defend it. Wait here, sir, till I have procured the means, and we will at once settle our differences."

"Be it so, sir," said Stanley, haughtily, and with a look of the utmost defiance; "I shall await your return with impatience."

Alfred Meadows fixed upon him a look of scorn and the most deadly malice, but did not deign a reply, and, hastening from the spot, he entered the fort.

During his absence, Stanley paced to and fro in a state of great excitement. This event so totally unlooked for, and so unprovoked on his part, caused him the deepest pain and regret, the more so when he thought of the anguish Omelia and Flora Melville would experience when they should come to hear of it, especially if any fatal consequences should unfortunately result from the duel which was about to take place, and which it seemed could not be avoided.

He respected Alfred Meadows sincerely, and therefore the more deeply lamented the difference that had arisen between them and the unfortunate delusion under which he laboured; but the language he had applied to him, and which he had persisted in, must either be withdrawn or resented; and let the quarrel terminate in whatever way it might, he had every reason to apprehend consequences of the most unpleasant description.

"Rash man," he said, "how unfortunate it is that he should have suffered his excited feelings to get the better of his reason, and thus to torture himself without any just cause."

He was aroused from this soliloquy by hearing the sound of footsteps, and he then beheld Alfred Meadows hastily approaching the spot, now armed with a sword with which he had provided himself, and his face still flushed, and his features distorted with rage.

He advanced towards Stanley, (who met him with a firm demeanour, but at the same time with a look of regret and remonstrance), and standing before him in an attitude of defiance, said,—

"You see, Lieutenant Stanley, I am true to my word; I hope I have not detained you long; so now with your permission, gallant sir, if you have got your courage to the sticking point, we will at once settle this little business."

"Alfred Meadows," replied Stanley, calmly, "notwithstanding all that you have said to me, I bear you too much respect not to wish to remonstrate with you on the folly, injustice, and impetuosity of your conduct. Surely you cannot know what you say or do at the present moment, when you have suffered your feelings to become unnecessarily excited, or you could never act in a manner so outrageous. Reflect, reflect, ere you proceed to extremities which you may afterwards have cause to repent. Have you no respect for the feelings of her you profess to love? Come, man, arouse yourself;—withdraw the obnoxious observations you have so unjustly made use of towards me, and here is my hand offered in all the spirit of friendship that I have ever felt towards you."

"Never," said the obstinate young man, disdainfully; "I scorn to take the hand of the man who has ruined my prospects of happiness for ever. I do not, I will not recal a word that I have uttered, but, on the contrary, I repeat them, and that more emphatically than before."

"Madman," said Stanley, passionately, "you seem bent to rush upon destruction. But again I will expostulate with you, and——"

"Hold!" interrupted young Meadows, impatiently, "I want none of your expostulations, sir. Think you, that I am such a very thing as to be thus idly trifled with, or is it fear that keeps your sword in its sheath, and urges you to a compromise which every coward seeks?"

"Fear!—coward!" repeated Stanley, now excited to the utmost pitch of resentment; "by all my hopes this is too much. Draw, sir, and prove yourself, if you can, not to be the craven-hearted dastard you have represented me to be."

The rash but high-spirited young man, needed no second challenge; following the example of his gallant antagonist, his sword flew quickly out of its scabbard, and in an instant the combat commenced with much skill and bravery on both sides, (young Meadows being an excellent swordsman,) and so it continued for several minutes, without either of them gaining any marked advantage over the other.

If advantage indeed there was, it must be confessed that it was on the side of Lieutenant Stanley, who from his cool and collected manner, was enabled to parry the thrusts, and avoid the blows of his impetuous and excited antagonist, until he had almost exhausted himself, and he (Stanley) might then be said to have him completely at his mercy; but he seemed not to avail himself of the chance.

For a moment both combatants paused as if by mutual consent, and Stanley addressing himself to young Meadows, said,—

"This unseemly duel, I cannot help thinking, has proceeded quite far enough. Again I assure you, Mr. Meadows, that I bear you no ill will, no angry feeling, and deeply regret that this misunderstanding should have occurred between us. Tender me a similar apology for the words you have uttered, the aspersions you have un-

justly cast on my character, and all will be ended in a manner which must be satisfactory to us both."

"Once more I tell you that all you can say to me to dissuade me from continuing the combat, will have no effect," replied Alfred, in the most contemptuous and obdurate manner; "come on, sir; it is not I who will first yield, unless death should compel me to do so."

"Then since you are deaf to the voice of reason or persuasion," said Stanley, "you must e'en take the consequence of your obstinacy."

The combat was now resumed with the same determined skill and bravery that it had commenced; and so it continued for some time longer, when a thrust from the sword of Stanley wounded Alfred Meadows severely in the fleshy part of the left arm, and had the former thought proper to follow up the advantage he had obtained he might immediately have placed his antagonist *hors de combat*, for the shock caused him for the moment to drop his sword arm, thus leaving himself entirely exposed to every danger.

But again Stanley refused to avail himself of the opportunity which was presented, and while he allowed Meadows to bind a handkerchief round the wound, in order to stop as much as possible the effusion of blood, he again endeavoured, by every argument he could make use of, to persuade him to come to an amicable arrangement.

It was all, however, to no purpose; Alfred Meadows still remained foolishly obstinate, and seemed determined to rush upon his own fate, for it was now evident that he stood little or no chance against the superior skill of his antagonist.

It was with the greatest reluctance that Stanley renewed the combat, but he was compelled against his will, and when he did so he merely parried the thrusts of Alfred Meadows, and attempted to disarm him, thinking that then at least he would be forced to yield without any further injury being done.

With no such manly and generous feeling, however, did young Meadows fight, but redoubled his efforts to inflict some mortal injury on him whom he considered to be his greatest foe, smarting as he did under the severe wound he had received.

The part of the garden where the duel was taking place was where no one could see or hear them from the fort, so that they were not likely to be interrupted. It had lasted now for nearly half an hour, and there seemed to be little more likelihood of its being brought to a termination than at the beginning.

But suddenly the foot of Stanley accidentally slipped, and his sword falling from his hand, goaded on by passion, which completely, at the moment, overpowered every proper feeling, Alfred Meadows was about to take a cowardly advantage,—when, at the instant, a loud shriek rent the air, and before Alfred could draw back his arm and arrest himself in his desperate and deadly purpose, Flora Melville rushed frantically in between him and Stanley, and receiving the sword of the former in her side, sank bleeding and senseless on the earth; Omelia, who had followed her from the fort, arriving on the spot at the fatal moment.

CHAPTER XCV.

THE RESULT.—THE DESPAIR AND MADNESS OF ALFRED MEADOWS.

HORRORSTRUCK at the frightful catastrophe, the sword fell from the palsied hand of the wretched Alfred Meadows, and he stared aghast at the bleeding and inanimate form of that unfortunate girl to whom he was so truly and so fondly attached, but who it was now to be feared he had brought to a shocking and untimely end.

Stanley was equally as appalled, and gazed in stupified horror and amazement, almost fearing to trust the evidence of his senses, and without being able to render the least assistance.

Omelia stood for a second or two, and looked on with a feeling of awe and anguish, but at length she raised poor Flora, (who gave no signs of life,) from the earth, and attempted to staunch the wound she had received, and which was bleeding copiously.

"Rash man," she said, in tones of the most melancholy regret, and the deepest reproach, addressing herself to Alfred Meadows, "what have you done? Oh, Stanley, could you not have avoided this?"

"Alas! alas!" sighed Stanley, "Heaven knows how earnestly I endeavoured to do so, and cursed, cruel Fate ordained it otherwise, and I am filled with horror at the frightful result. Oh, Meadows, obstinate, wretched man, why did you not yield to my persuasions and advice?"

The distracted Alfred Meadows groaned deeply and struck his forehead with his clenched fists, but was unable to utter a word.

But Omelia amidst all the anguish and horror that naturally filled her breast at the dreadful calamity which had befallen her unfortunate friend, did not lose her presence of mind; she knew that there was not a moment to be lost, in seeing to the wound which poor Flora had received, and she therefore aroused her lover, and urged him to assist her in removing the unfortunate sufferer without delay to the fort.

Stanley looked at the poor girl (who seemed completely lifeless), with feelings of the deepest sorrow, and then, without waiting to make use of any observation, he immediately complied with the request of Omelia, and between them they carried Flora with all the expedition they could to the fort, leaving Alfred Meadows on the fatal spot where the duel and the terrible catastrophe had occurred, with his face buried in his hands, and apparently in a state of utter unconsciousness as to all that was passing around him.

It was several minutes ere the wretched man moved from this fixed attitude, or was aware that Stanley and Omelia were gone with the unfortunate victim of his mad impetuosity and obstinacy; but he suddenly started as if from some frightful dream, and looked with horror around him, the whole dreadful truth at once rushing upon his memory. And then when he saw that there was no one there but himself, and his eyes marked the blood which had flowed from the wound of the ill-fated Flora, he uttered a cry that rent the air, and must have appalled the senses of all who heard it, and again covered his face with his hands whilst his limbs trembled convulsively, and madness was upon his brain.

Again he started as if from a fearful dream, and looking around him with frenzied eyes, in a voice hoarse with the unsupportable agony and excitement of his feelings, he exclaimed, :—

"Monster that I am, what hideous crime has my guilty hand perpetrated? The voices of fiends seem roaring and exulting in mine ears, and proclaim me murderer! The cowardly, the inhuman murderer of one of the fairest and gentlest of human beings!—Heartless miscreant, what fate is there too terrible to fall upon your guilty head? Where is the retribution too awful for your monstrous crime? The fierce thunderbolts of Heaven should descend and annihilate me; lightnings should blast me; but oh! there is no atonement I can make for the innocent blood which I have this night shed. Flora,—Flora,—where are you? Dare I again behold you, when it will be to gaze upon your mangled corpse? I shall go mad!—I shall go mad!—Open, earth, and hide me from all mortal sight!"

Again he groaned in all the frightful

agony of his soul, and beat his breast and tore his hair in the frenzy of his feelings; then as his eye fell upon the sword which had inflicted the fatal wound, and which was still reeking with the blood of the unfortunate Flora, a sudden and fearful thought appeared to strike him, and he snatched it hastily from the earth, and for a moment or two gazed at it with an expression of horror which it would be impossible to describe.

"Accursed, murderous weapon," he exclaimed, "it was you, directed by my guilty hand, which struck the fatal blow, and spilt the life's blood of one of the best of human beings. Oh, hideous deed!—and shall I, the perpetrator of it, dare to live now that it is committed, and the curses and execrations of all mankind must pursue me for it, and hunt me to destruction? No, no, no, even though perdition await me, thus, thus, will I perish!"

He was about in the dreadful agony of his remorse to put his threat into execution, when the deadly weapon was snatched from his hand, and his arms were grasped by some person or persons behind him, and looking round, he perceived Abdal and two more men, who had come from the fort in search of him, and to prevent him from doing himself any harm, as soon as they heard of the dreadful catastrophe, and had only just arrived in time to prevent the unhappy man from adding to the horrors of the awful tragedy by committing the act of self destruction.

For a moment or two he stared at those who held him appalled, as though he feared that they were the officers of justice come to apprehend him for the fatal deed he had committed; then in the frenzy of his feelings, he struggled to extricate himself from them, at the same time exclaiming:—

"Off! off! release me! it is I who have done the monstrous deed, it is I who am the brutal murderer of all that was good and innocent; but though there is no punishment too severe for the frightful crime, I must not, dare not die upon a public scaffold, amidst the execrations of a gaping crowd. Release me, I say, and suffer me, if I must die, and meet that dread eternity I now fear to enter, to perish by my own hands!"

"Unfortunate man," said Abdal, "be calm, and do not thus add to the sufferings of those who are already too deeply afflicted by the awful calamity which has taken place. Come, come, you must accompany us to the fort."

"No, no," cried Alfred, with a look of terror, "I dare not enter there, where every one will curse and call me murderer.

Oh, why do you seek to torture me thus? Why do you try to arrest me in my purpose?"

Abdal again remonstrated with the wretched man, and tried to calm him, but it was all in vain, so violent was the shock that his system had undergone through the dreadful occurrence, that his senses reeled and tottered on their throne, and all who saw him, while they must have condemned the rash infatuation (if we may so term it), which had placed him in such a terrible dilemma, could not at the same time help deeply sympathizing with him.

It need scarcely be added that the kind hearted Abdal Moorsha was one of that number.

He and his companions tried to remove the unfortunate man from the fatal spot as gently as possible, but he became more violent as every circumstance connected with the catastrophe rushed more forcibly upon his memory, and struggled to release himself, at the same time raving wildly.

"You shall not drag me hence," he again cried, "though I deserve to be incarcerated in the most frightful dungeon that the imagination of fiends could conceive, and loaded with the heaviest and most galling fetters of the vilest criminal. For am I not one? Did there ever live a greater miscreant, a more heartless monster than myself? Oh, no, no, no; it is impossible. I have shed the blood of the most beautiful and innocent of God's creatures, and therefore do I deserve to die, but I cannot, will not do so by the hands of the executioner. Let me perish here, and by my own hand let my death be accomplished. Oh, Flora, poor murdered Flora!"

"Again, Mr. Meadows," said Abdal, in the kindest and most persuasive accents, "I request you not to give way to this violent emotion, terrible though I admit, as is the circumstance that excites it. Even now it may not be so bad as your affrighted imagination pictures it, and notwithstanding the injury she has received, the unfortunate Miss Melville may yet survive to forgive you, and make you happy."

"Liar! deceiver!" fiercely exclaimed young Meadows, and all the madman was in the expression of his features as he spoke; "you mock me;—you deride my misery and despair. She is dead,—dead,—and I am her murderer! Off—off, I say, you shall no longer keep me from my fate!"

His struggles became so great that, being a powerful young man, it was not without the greatest difficulty that Abdal and his companions could hold him; but at last overpowered and completely exhausted by the violence of his exertions and emotion, he uttered a wild delirious laugh which was re-echoed far around, and sunk senseless and inanimate in the arms of Abdal Moorsha.

" Poor young man," said Abdal, compassionately, " I sincerely pity him, and lament the rash folly which hurried him into so dreadful a position. I fear that his reason will never be able to withstand the horrors of remorse. But come, my friends, while he is in this state of insensibility, and unable to offer any resistance,—let us remove him to the fort."

They did so, and the unfortunate Alfred Meadows was quickly conveyed to an apartment in the fort, where every proper attention was paid towards his recovery.

CHAPTER XCVI.

A TRYING SCENE.

IN the meantime the ill-fated Flora Melville had been conveyed by Stanley and Omelia to the fort, where the greatest consternation and excitement prevailed on the dreadful occurrence being made known to the inmates; for Flora was highly esteemed for her numerous unassuming virtues and gentle manners by every one.

She was immediately conveyed to bed and attended upon by Omelia, and the medical gentleman who happened to be one of the inmates of the fort, and who having examined and dressed the wound, expressed his melancholy opinion that it must prove mortal (some of the most vital parts having been severely injured) though death might not ensue immediately.

We need not attempt to describe the poignant anguish of our heroine's feelings on this announcement. She could not have felt more keenly had Flora been her sister, for they had been companions from the earliest days of childhood, and had ever felt the warmest attachment for each other; and after all the misfortunes she had met with, to meet with such a dreadful and untimely fate, and that from the hands of her own cousin, was truly melancholy and heartrending to think of. ·

" Poor Flora," she sighed, as she hung over her, and watched her pale countenance with the most anxious solicitude, " what would I not give had this dreadful occurrence never taken place, and to see you restored to health and happiness? But that you should thus perish in all the bloom of youth and beauty; and that too by the hand of him who I am certain loved her both fondly and sincerely, is almost too shocking for reflection. Alas! Alfred Meadows, unhappy young man, you have done that in your moment's of unfounded jealousy and excited feelings, which (although unpremeditated and purely accidental) must continue to haunt your conscience till your dying hour. Oh, why did not heaven avert the fatal meeting between you and Stanley?"

This thought added to her anguish, although she was satisfied that her lover was in no way to blame, and that no one could more sincerely lament the shocking event than himself.

And she was correct, for Stanley, (notwithstanding he had nothing whatever to accuse himself of, he having done all in his power, as has been shown, to calm the feelings of Alfred Meadows, and to prevent the unfortunate duel from taking place), was completely distracted, and it was some time before he could at all succeed in tranquilizing his feelings, especially after he had heard the unfavourable opinion expressed by the medical gentleman, as to the recovery of the unfortunate girl.

But how shall we portray the feelings of poor old Mr. Meadows, when the terrible news was imparted to him? His senses almost forsook him, and it was some time ere those about him could succeed in restoring him to anything like a degree of tranquillity.

He loved his son with a father's affection, and had bestowed every care on his education, and the effort to inculcate those principles of honour and virtue which he himself possessed, and hitherto he had every reason to be proud of him, and to feel happy in thinking that he had a son who would never disgrace his grey hairs, but now to find him in so awful a position, and to think of the fate of the amiable and gentle Flora Melville, (whom he also loved with the same affection as if she had been his own daughter, and by which name he had hoped soon to have had the happiness to call her, notwithstanding her unfortunate and hopeless passion for Edward Stanley,) was far too dreadful for contemplation, and the poor old gentleman almost sunk under the shock.

" Wretched boy," he exclaimed, " into what a frightful situation has his headstrong folly and impetuosity and obstinacy plunged him; and how can he ever forgive himself for that which he has done, although not wilfully? The blood, the innocent blood of his unfortunate cousin, is upon his conscience, and nothing whatever can banish the horrid truth from his memory. Maddening thought!—my brain whirls round as it rushes upon it, and my blood freezes in my veins with horror! Alas! alas!—the poor old man will soon be fatherless and alone in the world."

The power of his emotions choked his further utterance, and sinking in a chair, and covering his face with his hands, he gave vent to the overwhelming agony of his grief in a paroxysm of sobs and tears, which deeply affected the persons present, although they did not venture to interrupt him in the indulgence of his grief, which they hoped might afford him some relief.

In this manner several minutes passed away, and the poor old gentleman seemed to be so completely absorbed in grief and the terrible reflections that racked his brain, as to be quite unconscious that there was any one present; but suddenly he started from his seat, as a painful thought occurred to him, and in a hoarse voice and with a look of terror, he demanded :—

"But where is he? Where is the wretched boy? Has he been abandoned to that fate which in the frenzy of his feelings, he would most assuredly inflict upon himself, if not prevented. For Heaven's sake I beseech you, my friends, to relieve an aged parent's terrible anxiety, and inform him what is the fate of his unfortunate son."

He was informed that his son had fortunately been arrested while in the act of committing suicide, and removed with every care to the fort.

This information was given by Abdal, who was one of the parties now present, he having just entered the room for that purpose.

"Oh God, I thank thee for this!" exclaimed Mr. Meadows, clasping his hands vehemently together; "thou hast not yet deprived me of all that can render life worth preserving. My poor boy!—but I must see him, not one moment can I rest without beholding him, and endeavouring to impart consolation to him in this, the terrible hour of affliction."

Abdal would fain have dissuaded him from the pain of visiting his unfortunate son for the present, and till he had in some measure calmed his feelings; but Mr. Meadows would not listen to his advice, and he was therefore conducted to the room to which Alfred had been conveyed.

On his arrival at the fort, Alfred Meadows had been removed without delay to a chamber in a state of insensibility, and the surgeon having first seen to poor Flora Melville, immediately attended upon him, and dressed the wound in the arm which he had received from the sword of Edward Stanley, and which, although severe, he pronounced to be by no means dangerous, although in the present naturally excited state of his feelings there was much to be apprehended.

It was some time before he was restored to consciousness, and then, after staring wildly around him for a moment or two, and noticing the sorrowful looks of those present,—the whole dreadful truth seemed to rush with overwhelming force upon his memory, and with a groan of indescribable agony, he relapsed into a state of insensibility.

It was while he was in this state, that his unhappy father entered the room, and hurrying to the humble mattress on which his son was reclining, he gazed on his pallid, distorted features, which only a brief hour or so had served to change in so remarkable and melancholy a manner, with a bursting heart, and for a few minutes he could only give vent to the agony of his feelings in convulsive sobs and tears.

Yes, the poor old man (and all honour to him for so doing,) wept like a very infant.

No one offered to interrupt the sacredness of that grief, but all were moved to feelings of the deepest and most heart-felt sympathy.

At length the old man spoke, and it was in a voice which showed the intensity of the anguish, the almost unsupportable agony which racked his soul, that he did so.

"My poor boy, my noble-hearted boy," he sobbed forth, with clasped hands, and swelling bosom, every muscle of his frame and features showing the profound emotions that so violently agitated him, "and do I indeed see you thus? Oh, that I had died ere I could have been the distracted witness of such a harrowing spectacle. Alfred, dear Alfred, awake from this lethargy, I beseech you, and hear from the lips of your wretched father, not reproaches, but the assurance that he at least, can sympathize with you in your misfortunes, Alfred, my son, my only one, the prop of my declining years, the one bright ray of sunshine, upon the gloom of my existence, you will not die and leave me here to weep and wail, a lonely wretched old man, like some solitary plant upon the desert wild. Oh, no, Almighty God forbid that it should be so; or if it be Thy will, that he should perish in the spring-tide of youth, oh, grant in Thine infinite mercy, that I, his aged parent, should perish with him."

A violent paroxysm of grief followed these melancholy and impressive observations, and Mr. Meadows threw himself by the side of his son in the distraction of his feelings, and embracing him, endeavoured to recal him to his senses by every means in his power.

Abdal and the other persons present with difficulty raised him, and sought by every means in their power to pacify him, but for some time in vain,—and the doctor, (who was in the room,) would gladly have been able to persuade him to retire, for he feared that should the young man be restored to sensibility, in his present state, the excitement would be too much for him, and might be attended with the most dangerous consequences.

But the old man at length became more calm, and throwing himself on his knees by the side of the mattress on which his son was reclining, for some minutes he was engaged in silent but earnest prayer.

Suddenly he was aroused from this, for a deep groan escaped the lips of his son, and immediately afterwards he opened his eyes, and raising himself by an effort on his elbow, stared vacantly around the room, without apparently being able to distinguish any particular object.

"Ah! he still lives!" exclaimed Mr. Meadows, throwing himself into the arms of his son, and straining to him his bosom before any one could interfere to endeavour to prevent him;—"my son, my poor unfortunate boy, oh, look up, speak to me, I beseech you, 'tis your father, your distracted father, who thus holds you in his arms, and comes alone to commiserate and to seek to console you in this dreadful hour of trouble."

Alfred in a moment recognised his unhappy parent's voice, and fixed upon him a look of horror, such as no language can properly describe, but which plainly shewed that the madness of despair was upon his brain, as he exclaimed:—

"Father!—parent!—no, no, I have no parent now;—all must hate me, discard me, for I am a murderer!—Off, off, old man; come not near me, for my touch is contamination. Do you not see that my hands yet reek with human blood,—the blood of the innocent, of one whose soul was pure as virgin snow, and whose every thought was holy. Away, away, lest I stain thy grey hairs, and bring down the curses of heaven upon thee, the same as upon my guilty head! Oh, I am a wretch unworthy to live, and yet, oh, how unfit to die."

Thus saying, the unfortunate young man disengaged himself from the embrace of his father, and sunk back on the mattress completely exhausted, whilst large drops of perspiration stood upon his temples.

For a few minutes the distracted Mr. Meadows continued to gaze at him with clasped hands, and looks of agony and despair; but without being able to utter a word, and he suffered himself, being almost in a state of unconsciousness, to be withdrawn from the side of the mattress to another part of the room, and for a short time all remained hushed in profound silence, the persons present being too deeply shocked by what they had just seen and heard to say a word, and the unhappy patient having once more closed his eyes, and seeming to be entirely lost to everything around.

But at length Mr. Meadows suddenly started from his stupor (if so it might be called), and tearing himself away from those who had held him in another part of the room, again hastily approached the place where his suffering son was reclining, and once more throwing himself in a distracted manner by his side, in tones of anguish that thrilled through the veins of every person present, exclaimed:—

"Once more awake from your death-like slumber, my son, and speak to your aged parent in those words of affection and filial reverence you were wont to utter. Who dares to call you murderer?—They are liars!—base and reckless liars!—Your soul was too pure, too manly, too noble, ever to be guilty of crime. My son! my son! it is your father calls upon you, and you must, you will answer him. Nay, I will cling to you till you do, and may the curses of Heaven light upon those who dares to separate us, or any longer to calumniate your spotless name!"

Thus saying, the poor old man, whose mind had evidently become disorderd like that of his son, by the intensity of his mental anguish, was again about to startle the suffering young man from his present lethargic state, and to enfold him in his mad embrace, when Abdal and his companions forcibly interposed to prevent him, and the doctor, seeing that persuasion or remonstrance were useless, was compelled to resort to more determined measures, and observed:—

"Indeed, Mr. Meadows, under the melancholy and dangerous circumstances in which your son is placed, I cannot any longer permit this, if I am to be allowed to see to his recovery; I can and do make every allowance for your feelings, but you must endeavour to control them, for I need scarcely say that, in his present condition, the least excitement might be attended with the most dangerous, nay, fatal consequences. I beg you to retire, with the assurance that everything that humanity can suggest shall be done for the unfortunate young man."

"Heaven bless you, my dear sir," replied Mr. Meadows, awakened to reason, by the sensible and friendly observations of the medical gentleman, and warmly pressing his hand while he spoke, "may Heaven bless you, sir, I repeat for those kind words;

for the tone in which they were spoken convince me of their sincerity, and have imparted a ray of comfort to me in the midst of my heavy affliction, for they assure me that my poor boy has those who can sympathise with him, even under the peculiar circumstances in which he is placed. Pardon me that I have given vent to a parent's feelings on so trying an occasion, and I will instantly comply with your request, satisfied that everything will be done towards his recovery.

Having made use of these observations, the poor old man once more quietly approached his son—who was lying in the same state of unconsciousness—and for a minute or two stood and gazed upon his pale and hagard features, with a look of the most intense affection and melancholy regret,

No. 48.

sighed deeply, murmured a brief prayer for his speedy recovery, and then suffered himself to be re-conducted from the room.

Shortly after his departure it was noticed a most favourable change had come over the features of Alfred Meadows, they appearing comparatively composed, and free from that expression of agony which had before characterised them. He also breathed more freely, and the doctor and every one present were surprised at so very extraordinary and sudden a change, and augured from it the best and most unexpected results.

In a few minutes afterwards he was once more restored to consciousness, and looking around him, and observing the persons present, whom he recognised, he calmly, but at the same time anxiously inquired what had happened, and why he found himself in his present situation, but seeming in a moment to recollect himself, and before any one could reply to him, he exhibited much emotion, but not of a violent description, and even tears trembled in his eyes as the whole melancholy truth seemed to rush upon his memory.

At length perfectly rational he inquired after Flora, and being informed that she lived and there was no immediate danger, he clasped his hands vehemently together, raised his eyes towards heaven, and his whole demeanour, and every expression of his features showed the grateful feelings that throbbed within his breast, and the relief that it was to his mind.

"Almighty God!" he exclaimed devoutly and fervently, "for this I thank thee, and implore thy forgiveness for the misery that my rash, my mad conduct has caused. Oh, that I could recal the dreadful past, and be again free from the heavy blame which now attaches to me. What demon could have urged me on? But I must have been mad, or I should have listened to Lieutenant Stanley's generous advice, and then this dreadful calamity would never have occurred. Flora, dear Flora, ill-fated girl, may heaven in its infinite mercy watch over you, and quickly restore you to health, and, as I hope, to future happiness, though, I fear, I may never be able to contribute to it."

Abdal and the doctor glad to see him in this vein, encouraged him in it by every word of consolation they could find, and they succeeded in their praiseworthy efforts, for by degrees he became perfectly calm, and shortly afterwards sunk into a tranquil sleep from which he did not awake for some time; so leaving a person to watch him, Abdal and the doctor retired from the room, the latter returning to the chamber of the unfortunate Flora Melville.

CHAPTER XCVII.

THE SICK CHAMBER.

Whilst the scene which we have just described was being enacted, and Stanley and the whole of the inmates of the old fort were wrapped in the deepest gloom through the unfortunate and melancholy events which the last few hours had produced—Stanley, as may be expected, being more particularly excited and affected than any of the rest—the gentle Omelia continued to watch by the side of the still insensible, and all but lifeless Flora Melville with an anxiety of mind and heartfelt sorrow, which it would be useless to attempt to describe.

She was thoroughly convinced from the nature of the injuries which the unfortunate sufferer had received, that she could not possibly recover, in fact, the doctor had assured her to that effect, and she felt her approaching and untimely end to be almost as great an affliction and bereavement as if she had been her own sister.

In fact, Omelia and Flora had ever behaved with the affection of sisters towards each other, and had it not been for the hopeless passion which the latter unfortunately formed for Edward Stanley as soon as she beheld him, and which she could not conquer—notwithstanding that she was convinced she could never make any impression on his heart, which was so sincerely devoted to Omelia—there probably would have been no interruption to their happiness, and certainly this terrible calamity, under such circumstances could not have occurred.

But to think that the noble-minded Stanley should have been the innocent, the indirect cause of the catastrophe, pained her more than all, and she knew well how keenly he must feel, how great must be the anguish of mind which he must be enduring.

Omelia could not, also, but feel the greatest sympathy for the wretched Alfred Meadows, whose impetuous nature, and ill-founded jealousy had produced such awful consequences, and for which it was quite certain he could never forgive himself, or know real happiness again.

During the time that the doctor was absent in attendance upon Alfred Meadows, Omelia was left alone with her unfortunate friend—who, although she certainly seemed to breathe with less difficulty, still exhibited no signs of returning life—and had every opportunity to give free indulgence to the gloomy and torturing thoughts which the circumstances naturally gave rise to in her mind, and the principal emotions that agitated her, we need scarcely say, were those of the deepest sorrow and regret.

"Poor Flora," she sighed, as she gazed upon the pale countenance of the unfortunate sufferer, once so fresh and lovely in the bloom of youth; "your's is indeed a sad fate, and it makes my heart bleed to think of it, for you have been friend, benefactress, sister, all to me, and to lose you now, so soon after the death of poor Miriami—whom it was my melancholy fate never to behold, or to know till heaven had recalled her to itself—renders the calamity doubly torturing to me, and still more insupportable. Oh, my beloved friend, never more shall I hear your jocund laugh, as it was wont merrily to ring out in those halcyon days when sorrow was unknown to us, and all was bright sunshine and uninterrupted happiness. No more shall we wander through those rich and lovely scenes of my native land, as we were wont to do, luxuriating in the various beauties and glories of Nature's most wonderous works that met our enraptured gaze at every turn, and which called forth all our most enthusiastic admiration. Poor ill-fated Flora, when can I ever cease to mourn your loss? When can I forget your numerous virtues, where shall I ever again find so true, so generous, so warm-hearted a friend?"

Omelia's tears—which she could not restrain—now flowed faster than ever, as these dismal and painful thoughts occurred to her, and she could find no room for hope or consolation.

She knelt down, and imprinted an affectionate kiss upon the pale lips of the insensible girl, then fervently she offered up her prayers for her to heaven.

She feared that Flora would never more awake to consciousness, a circumstance which she should the more deeply regret, as she would be deprived of the melancholy satisfaction of receiving her dying words, and hearing her utter her forgiveness to the wretched and distracted Alfred Meadows, for whose deplorable situation she (Omelia) felt most keenly.

She was at length interrupted in her gloomy and painful reflections by a gentle knock at the room-door, and on opening it she was surprised yet gratified on beholding Stanley, who had been unable to rest longer without personally inquiring after the condition of poor Flora, and beholding Omelia, who he feared might entertain some mistaken idea as to the cause of the fatal duel between himself and Alfred Meadows.

The meeting of the lovers, under such painful circumstances was of the most affecting description, and Omelia could not but notice with sorrow the melancholy change which anxiety of mind, since the fatal catastrophe had taken place, had wrought in him.

She led him, in silence, towards the mattress on which Flora was lying, and he gazed at the poor girl with looks of the deepest emotion, for he could read in the ghastly expression of her pale features that her speedy death was inevitable.

"Alas, poor Flora, unfortunate girl," he sighed, "with what poignant feelings of anguish do I lament your awful and unmerited fate, and the circumstances that led to it. Oh, Omelia, much I fear that you will blame and reproach me for the share which I had unhappily had in producing the calamity; but heaven knows how little I am to blame for that which has so unfortunately taken place, and how earnestly I endeavoured to calm the feelings, and dissipate the mistaken ideas and suspicions of the too hasty and passionate Alfred Meadows. He heaped upon me every insult, he called me coward, and refusing to withdraw the offensive and unmerited epithet, I had no other alternative but to resent it, or admit myself to be the truth. But who could dream of the dreadful consequences that were about to follow? My heart bleeds when I think of it, and while I gaze upon the pale and melancholy features of this ill-fated girl, whose virtues entitle her to every earthly happiness. Oh, Omelia, can you, do you blame me for that which has happened? It would indeed drive me to madness and despair if I thought you could."

"Oh, no, dear Edward," replied Omelia, with a look of mingled sorrow and affection, "I should indeed both hate and despise myself, if I thought that I could do you that monstrous injustice as to attribute to you the slightest blame. You cannot, I am certain, believe me capable of doing so, for I should be totally unworthy of your love—which I value above all earthly blessings—if I could."

"Bless you, my own dear Omelia," cried Stanley, rapturously, and embracing her, "bless you for those words of fond assurance, for they have removed a weight of care and anxiety from my mind which had become almost insupportable."

"It is lamentable to think of the dreadful consequences of Alfred Meadows' unfounded jealous and suspicious feelings," said our heroine; "alas, how bitterly must he evermore reproach himself."

"True, Omelia," coincided her lover, "and I cannot but deeply commiserate with him in the sufferings which he must experience. As far as regards myself, most sincerely do I forgive him for the injustice which he did me, and the opprobrious epithets he heaped upon my head. May poor Flora revive to forgive him also."

"Heaven grant that she may," said Omelia, fervently, and at the same time fixing a sad look of despair upon the insensible Flora, "how grateful should I feel for it, and oh, how much more so for her ultimate recovery; but of that, alas, I fear there is not the remotest room for hope. Indeed Dr. Mansfield has, from the first, expressed the worst apprehensions, and it is therefore better to prepare ourselves for an event which seems to be inevitable."

"True, dear Omelia," coincided Stanley, "but is it not most melancholy and painful to think that one so young, so beautiful, and so amiable should meet with this shocking and untimely end?"

"Alas," sighed our heroine, "it is so, and I am sure I need not tell you, dear Edward, with what feelings of anguish I anticipate that awful event. Would that providence might avert that calamity we so much dread, and which appears but too likely shortly to take place."

Stanley most heartily responded to that wish, and was about to return some reply, when he was prevented from doing so by the re-entrance of Dr. Mansfield, after leaving Alfred Meadows and his afflicted father, of whose condition, at the earnest request of Omelia and Stanley, he fully informed them, and they both expressed their sincere sorrow.

Stanley having again asked Mr. Mansfield's opinion of poor Flora Melville, and urged him to use his utmost skill, with the limited means at his command, for her recovery, quitted the room, and Omelia and the doctor were again left to endeavour by every means in their power to restore poor Flora to sensibility."

CHAPTER XCVIII.

THE LAST MOMENTS OF FLORA MELVILLE.

Flora underwent little or no change for some hours, and Omelia—although she was often urged by Dr. Mansfield to retire and seek that rest of which she stood so much in need, after the great exertions she had undergone—continued unremitting in her attentions, and watched by the couch of her unfortunate friend with the greatest solicitude, and in much suspense.

At length there was a slight convulsive movement about the frame of the sufferer observable, and a faint sigh escaped her lips, which sufficiently announced her return to consciousness, and Omelia awaited what was likely to follow with the utmost impatience, while Dr. Mansfield paid every attention to his fair patient.

In a few minutes she sufficiently recovered to open her eyes, and fixing them upon Omelia, whom she appeared to recognise, she attempted to speak, but could not, and again sunk back on her pillow, quite exhausted even by that slight exertion.

Omelia took her hand in her's, and looking with the most affectionate sympathy in her pale face, in low and gentle accents, said—

"Dear Flora, do you not know me? It is Omelia, the companion of your childhood, the object of your benevolence who is so highly indebted to you, and whose heart is now racked with sorrow at this terrible calamity, and the terrible sufferings to which you are now subjected. Oh, how can I describe to you what I feel, my dearest friend, my more than sister? May heaven in its infinite mercy look down upon you, and restore you to health and happiness."

Flora looked at her steadfastly for a moment or two, then shook her head mournfully, and tears trembled in her eyes. But still she could not speak, though she pressed the hand of Omelia warmly, and her looks testified how gratefully sensible she was of her sympathy and the kind attentions she paid her.

A pause of several minutes ensued—Dr. Mansfield having expressed an opinion to our heroine that it would be imprudent to address too many observations to his unfortunate patient in her present condition, and which might only serve to excite her; but they continued to gaze at each other with looks of melancholy affection, and the expression of their features spoke much more than words could have done.

Dr. Mansfield administered a draught to Flora, which seemed to revive her, and Omelia, even at the least favourable change, could not help encouraging a degree of hope.

Flora at length seemed to revive, and again exerted herself to the utmost, and contrary to the advice and wishes of Dr. Mansfield, after two or three powerful efforts she was enabled to give utterance to the following words, in a faint and almost inaudible voice—

"Dearest Omelia, this is kind, most kind, and I cannot find words to express the feelings that throb at my heart—that heart which will soon cease to beat for ever, and—"

She was unable to finish the sentence, for the power of her emotions choked her utterance, and both Omelia and the worthy Dr. Mansfield—who was a man of the most amiable disposition and susceptibility of feelings—were deeply affected by the impressive solemnity of her manner.

"For the love of heaven, my dear and unfortunate friend, do not, I beseech you, talk in that melancholy and desponding strain," said our heroine, still looking in her face with the utmost tenderness and solicitude, "your valuable life will, I trust and pray most fervently, most sincerely, yet be spared, and—"

"No, no," impatiently interrupted the poor suffering girl, "seek not to flatter me with such vain and delusive hopes, for they cannot deceive me; heaven ordains it otherwise, and I gladly yield to its decree. My final hour is fast approaching, but—but—I fear not death—I wish not to live, since were I to do so, I and happiness must be henceforth strangers. My weary soul looks anxiously forward to the grave as the only place of rest. But oh, Omelia, how dare I ask for your forgiveness for the wrong that I have done you?"

"Wrong, Flora?" repeated Omelia, "oh, what wrong, even by word, by act, or thought, have I ever experienced from you?"

"You have, you have," hastily returned Flora, and her excitement increased to a most painful degree every moment; "oh, how I blush to think of the cruel injustice I have done you in presuming to encourage a guilty passion for him to whom your affections are devoted, and who loves you so fondly and so faithfully in return. May heaven pardon me for so doing, and for the anguish my presumptuous passion must have caused you. But 'tis over now, and the wretched Flora Melville will soon cease to be a misery to herself and to those who at the same time she has ever loved with the fondest affection. Bless you, Omelia, may you and—and Stanley be happy in each other's love long after the silent grave has closed over my cold remains."

She now became so violently agitated by the excitement of her feelings, that she sunk back completely powerless, and gasped for breath, and Omelia and Dr. Mansfield were seriously alarmed, and saw the danger of continuing the conversation for the present.

The worthy doctor having administered a soothing medicine to her, she became more composed, but attempted not to speak, and, after a short time, she gradually sunk off into a calm slumber, which they were glad to see, as they hoped it would do her good, and also as it showed that she suffered but comparatively little pain from her wound.

In the meantime, Lieutenant Stanley, after leaving the chamber of Flora, sought the presence of Mr. Meadows and his unfortunate son, whom he was anxious to see that they might enter into an explanation, and effect a reconciliation.

Stanley felt deeply for the painful situation of the wretched young man, and wished not only to convince him that there was no vindictive feeling on his part, but to impart to him all the consolation under the deplorable circumstances that was in his power.

Mr. Meadows received the young officer with every respect, for he held him in the highest possible esteem, being no stranger to his generous, noble, manly qualities, but at the same time, as might naturally be expected, he could not help experiencing a torturing feeling on beholding him, which was fully expressed in his countenance, but on Stanley warmly pressing his hand, and evincing other signs of his earnest sympathy the poor old gentleman became more composed.

Alfred Meadows was reclining on his mattress—immersed in all those agonising thoughts to which the melancholy situation in which he was placed naturally gave rise—on the unexpected entrance of Stanley, but on seeing him, an expression of the utmost agony passed over his pale features, and uttering a deep groan, he averted his looks, while the convulsive emotion which agitated his whole frame, showed the torturing feelings of regret and self-reproach he was at that time suffering.

"Mr. Meadows," said Stanley, after a pause, "you will probably be able to understand and appreciate the motives that have prompted me to visit you and your son on this unfortunate occasion. They are to express to you both my earnest desire that no feeling of animosity should exist, and, at the same time to assure you that no one can more deeply lament the unforeseen catastrophe which has taken place than myself, or, without attaching blame to any one, regret the unfortunate circumstances that have accidentally been the cause of it."

"Mr. Stanley," replied Mr. Meadows, in a voice of great emotion, "the feelings by which I am convinced you are actuated do honour alike to your head and your heart, and I thank you, most fervently thank you for them. It is a terrible occurrence, and I shudder to think of the fearful consequences that will be sure to follow. My poor headstrong boy, he—"

He could not finish the sentence, for his feelings overpowered him, and Stanley again took his hand, and endeavoured to reassure and compose him.

Alfred Meadows was evidently suffering the most insupportable mental agony, and he groaned repeatedly.

Stanley approached him nearer, and after looking at him for a moment with the greatest commisseration, in a voice which showed the sincerity of every word he uttered, he said—

"Alfred Meadows, I come not here to exult in the anguish I know you must experience, but to offer you the hand of friendship, and to beseech you to forgive me if I have ever done anything to injure you, or to wound your feelings, the same as I forgive you."

The wretched young man turned upon him a mingled look of surprise, shame, and emotion, then covering his face with his hands, he again groaned repeatedly.

Stanley awaited his recovery from this paroxysm of grief ere he again ventured to speak, but it suddenly subsided, and looking up, he extended his hand towards Stanley, saying—

"Generous, noble-hearted Stanley, dare a guilty wretch like myself, whose accursed feelings of jealousy towards you have been the cause of this dreadful calamity, offer you his hand, and solicit your forgiveness? Oh, no, I cannot venture to do so, for I feel that I am unworthy of anything but your disgust and abhorrence. Oh, would to heaven that I had fallen in the combat which my unbridled passions provoked."

"It was unfortunate," said Stanley, in calm accents, "but still do I sincerely pardon you, and trust that all may not turn out so bad as we are now compelled to anticipate."

"Oh, seek not, Stanley," said Alfred, with a look in which all the agony and despair of his mind were depicted, "to flatter me with false and delusive hopes, which reason too thoroughly convinces me can never be realised. Poor Flora, villain that I am, am I not her murderer?"

"You reproach yourself too severely, Mr. Meadows," said Stanley, "fearful though the catastrophe is, and deeply as we must all lament it, it was entirely accidental, and there was no actual blame attached to you."

"Oh, forbear," groaned Alfred, "attempt not to extenuate my conduct, which is only worthy of the utmost abhorrence I feel myself a guilty wretch, with the blood of the innocent upon my hands, and I deserve the severest punishment that heaven or man can inflict. Oh, it was most cruel to prevent that fate which I sought to rush upon. Flora, Flora, poor murdered girl, your dying curses must and will be on my head"

"My unfortunate son," said Mr. Meadows, whose emotion we need not attempt to describe, "I beseech you to endeavour to calm your feelings, and to encourage hope and consolation."

"Hope—consolation," repeated Alfred, with a mournful look, "oh, there is none for a villain like me; I deserve no pity, no rest from the upbraidings of a guilty conscience. To bid me be calm, and to encourage hope and consolation is a bitter mockery to me, and does but serve to make the heinousness of my guilt the more apparent. The ignominious death of a felon is alone my due."

His anguish of mind again became most intense, and for some minutes he was unable to give utterance to a word, whilst his father and Stanley stood by and did not offer to interrupt him in the indulgence of his grief, though, seeing the sincerity of his remorse, they could not but feel for the unhappy young man the deepest commiseration.

At length he did become somewhat more composed, and ventured to inquire after Flora. Stanley gave as favourable an account of her as he could, but Alfred shook his head mournfully and incredulously as he said—

"Seek not to deceive me, Mr. Stanley, for I feel convinced that the wound my rash hand inflicted must prove mortal. Oh, how horrible is the thought. I am surely one of the most atrocious of miscreants that ever existed. Even now methinks I see the once bright eyes of my unfortunate victim fixed reproachfully upon me, and hear her curses ringing in mine ears. Would that I were dead, and yet, oh, how unfit am I to die."

He struck his forehead in the agony of his feelings, and again groaned heavily, but at length, after much exertion, Stanley and Mr. Meadows did succeed in abating the violence of his emotion, and the former, after some further conversation, withdrew.

To return to the chamber of Flora.

She suddenly started from the deep sleep which had so long enwrapped her senses, but so far from having the desired effect, and which Omelia and Dr. Mansfield had anticipated it would the symptoms she betrayed were of that violent nature to excite their utmost alarm.

"It is coming," she ejaculated, in accents that were quite pitiable to hear, "grim death is coming, but I hail his approach with pleasure, for life has long been a curse to me, and every hour that I might live would but serve to increase my misery. Weep not for me, dear Omelia, but rather thank heaven which is about to release me from my sufferings."

"Oh, I cannot bear to hear you talk thus, my unfortunate friend," said our heroine, with all that emotion which she might be expected to experience in such a trying moment, for the looks of Flora showed but too plainly that her end was indeed fast approaching; "heaven will, I trust, yet restore you, and you will live for many years to experience all that happiness which your transcendant virtues so richly merit."

"No, no," returned Flora, impatiently, "it must not, cannot be, already I feel the hand of death upon me, and if you wish me happiness you will rather pray to heaven for my speedy dissolution. Oh, would that I had perished at the same time as my unfortunate father, what a world of misery would it have saved me. Omelia, when I am no more you will not refuse a tear to my memory?"

Omelia was so deeply affected by the melancholy and pathetic tones in which she spoke these words, that she knew not what to answer, and for some minutes she remained silent, and watching the poor girl, who seemed to be rapidly sinking, with anxious fear.

Dr. Mansfield also evinced by his looks his worst apprehensions, and Omelia therefore endeavoured to prepare herself for that sad event which now seemed to be inevitable.

That, however, was a most difficult task to accomplish, and Omelia tried for some time in vain to tranquillize her feelings.

During this interval Flora seemed to be engaged in silent but fervent prayer, but suddenly as a fearful change came over her, and the ghastliness of death overspread her features, and every limb was convulsed, she exclaimed—

"Father—father! your child, your Flora is coming; gladly her spirit hastens to join you in eternity; open then your arms to receive me. Omelia—Omelia, where are you?

My sight grows dim, but the light of heaven breaks in upon my soul, and I long to take my flight to those realms of bliss, whither, I trust, that I am going."

" Oh, my dear Flora," said the affectionate Omelia, "and must we indeed part? Oh, would that heaven would avert that calamity I cannot contemplate without feelings of the utmost dread."

"Again I tell you," said Flora with impatient earnestness, "that I wish not to live. Life is now a burthen to me which I can no longer bear; and the sooner I am rid of it the better. A few minutes more, and all I feel will be over, but oh, I am happy, happier, far happier now than I have ever been before. May heaven bless you, Omelia, and the noble-minded Stanley when I am no more, and may you both be enabled to bury my faults in oblivion."

She took the hand of our heroine, and raised it to her lips as she thus impressively spoke, and Omelia could only answer with her sobs and tears, whilst Dr. Mansfield, who could do no more to restore her, for she was past all human skill, stood by and watched the approach of death with feelings of the most sincere sorrow, for, as we before stated, he was a most kind-hearted and amiable man, and indeed poor Flora by her gentle and unassuming manners had endeared herself to every one, and the terrible event that had befallen her cast a gloom upon all the inmates of the old fort, which she could not resist.

Suddenly she again aroused herself, and in an eager voice she exclaimed—

"But the unfortunate Alfred Meadows, oh, where is he? How great, how terrible must be his anguish at that which he has been the innocent, the accidental cause of. Oh, let me see him before I die, that I may assure him of my forgiveness, and invoke for him that future happiness which he so well deserves."

"Pardon me, Miss Melville," observed the worthy Mr. Mansfield, "but I fear that such an interview would be too much for both yourself and Mr. Meadows under the present melancholy circumstances. The least excitement might probably be attended by the most fatal consequences."

"I fear them not, for I know too well that nothing whatever can retard my fate, and that my moments are numbered," said Flora; "I cannot die happy if my request be not complied with. Oh, had I returned the love which he so fondly felt for me, this event would never have happened, and I might have lived to experience every happiness. But heaven's will be done; I will not murmur or complain. Omelia, I implore you to request Alfred Meadows to see me ere I die, or it will be too late."

" If it will afford you any satisfaction and consolation, my dear girl," said our heroine, " I will do so, and may heaven give you strength to bear a meeting which must be so painful to yourself and Alfred."

The poor girl looked her thanks, and our heroine, leaving her for a few minutes in the care of Dr. Mansfield, quitted the room in order to make Alfred Meadows acquainted with her wishes, and also to inform Stanley of the near approach of her death, and to desire him also to accompany her, that he might be a witness to her last moments.

The reader may imagine the feelings that agitated the breast of Alfred Meadows on receiving the unexpected message from the unfortunate Flora, and it was some time ere he could sufficiently collect himself to make use of any observation, or to give adequate expression to his feelings.

" Dear Flora," he said at last, and manly tears, which he found it impossible to restrain, trembled in his eyes as he spoke, "ill-fated victim of my impetuous passions, and can you indeed forgive me, I that have brought you, in the midst of youth and beauty, to an untimely end? Oh, it is more, much more than a wretched guilty being like myself deserves. Your dying curses should much rather be heaped upon my head, and you should view me with disgust and horror. I cannot, dare not see you, for madness must surely seize upon my brain in your presence, and in witnessing your sufferings."

" Be firm, Mr. Meadows," said Omelia, " and meet our unfortunate friend, who is so shortly to be taken from us, with the fortitude, calmness, and resignation which the solemn occasion demands. Come, there is not a moment to lose."

Alfred Meadows did struggle with his feelings to prepare himself for the melancholy task, and Stanley having entered the room and joined his arguments and persuasions to those of Omelia, he became more composed, and with a palpitating heart and trembling footsteps he accompanied them to the chamber of the dying girl.

The silence of the grave pervaded the room on their entrance, for Flora had sunk off into a kind of stupor, and Dr. Mansfield was standing by anxiously watching, while his looks plainly showed that he had given up all expectation or hope of her recovery, and looked forward to her death as fast approaching.

It is impossible for us properly to describe the feelings of the unfortunate Alfred Meadows as he tremblingly advanced to the place where the poor ill-fated girl was lying, and with what inexpressible feelings of agony he gazed upon her pale features, that, although they were perfectly calm, bore all the symptoms of approaching death. He clasped his hands together, groaned deeply and frequently, and was quite unable to control his grief within the bounds of reason.

It is almost needless to say that Omelia and Stanley were nearly as deeply affected, and they could not but await the interview between Flora and her unhappy lover with the most painful anxiety, for they had too much reason to fear that the excitement caused by it would be too much for her, and that it might be the means of hastening her death.

They endeavoured to calm the violent emotions of Alfred Meadows, in which they partly succeeded, though he knelt down by the side of the bed, and offered up a silent but fervent prayer to heaven.

Flora quickly was aroused from the stupor we have described her senses to have been wrapped in, and breathing a sigh, which was responded to by the persons present, she opened her eyes and fixing them upon Alfred, her features underwent a change, in the expression of which sorrow, regret, and pity were blended, and which he could not behold without the greatest feelings of agony and despair. But he could not speak, and for the moment it seemed as if the whole of his faculties were suspended.

Flora extended her thin pale hand towards him, which he dared not take, and after a brief struggle she faintly said, whilst every word which fell from her lips could not fail to make the most painful and lasting impression upon those who listened to her—

"Alfred, my moments are numbered; already the darkness of death is gathering around me, and although it was your hand which accidentally inflicted the fatal blow, I could not close my eyes for ever on the world without assuring you of my forgiveness. I regarded your virtues with the highest esteem, but my heart refused to love you, which I deeply lament as it has been the cause of so much misery to you. When I am no more, may you meet with one more worthy of your love than myself, and who can return your passion with fervour and sincerity."

"Oh, much-wronged, ill-fated girl," replied Alfred, in a voice half choked with emotion, "oh, can I, the cause of this terrible calamity, dare to gaze upon you in such an awful moment as this, and listen to words like those you have just now given utterance to, and which should be replaced by curses? What can I say? what can I offer in extenuation of my conduct? I feel myself to be a guilty wretch whom all should hate and despise, and henceforth life must become an insupportable burthen to me, and never, never can I cease to reproach myself, never can I again know a moment's peace or happiness. Flora, dear, innocent Flora, and must you indeed meet with so premature and terrible a fate as this, and I the author of all? Oh, would to heaven that we had never met. Flora, Flora, I shall go mad."

"Cease, cease," said the dying girl, with a look of resignation, "cease these useless self-reproaches, or to murmur at the will of the Almighty, in whose presence I shall shortly be. I wish not to live; no, life has long had no charms for me, and I look anxiously forward to death, as a joyful release from all my cares and sorrows. When my cold remains repose in the silent grave, try to forget that ever such a being existed as Flora Melville, and may you experience all that happiness and prosperity to which your manly virtues entitle you."

"Forget you, Flora," said the distracted young man, and his looks showed more plainly than before the intensity of his anguish, whilst the gentle-hearted and afflicted Omelia could not restrain her tears, but wept bitterly, "oh, is it possible that I can ever banish from my memory that fair being whom I have ever so fondly, so sincerely loved, and whom I have been the guilty cause of bringing to so untimely an end? Oh, how terrible will be the feelings of remorse with which that sad remembrance must be associated."

Flora looked at him for a moment with an expression of the most poignant anguish, and the deepest sympathy, but the exertion she had undergone was too much for her, and she could not utter a word. She again extended her hand to Alfred, which he tremblingly took in his, and raising it to his lips covered it with his kisses, while his bosom swelled with the power of his emotions, and he felt as though his heart would break.

It was a torturing, a most solemn and impressive scene, and it was impossible for those who witnessed it ever to forget it.

At length, after another effort, poor Flora found sufficient strength to speak again, and fixing her eyes—now every instant becoming more dim—upon our heroine and Stanley, in low but clear accents she said—

"Dear Omelia, noble-minded Stanley, in these my dying moments I would invoke heaven's choicest blessings on your heads, and implore you to forgive my errors. May you both be happy in each other's love."

For a moment or two Omelia and her lover were too much overpowered by their feelings to speak a word, but they knelt down by the side of Alfred, and the poor girl raising her hands above their heads, breathed a brief but ardent prayer to the Supreme in accordance with her words.

"Oh, my best, my dearest earthly friend," at length sobbed Omelia, as if her heart was breaking "and must we indeed part? Will

nothing stay the cruel hand of relentless death? What dreadful agony is this to have to endure."

"It comes, it comes," said Flora, in a voice the tones of which thrilled to the hearts of her afflicted listeners, "the final moment approaches, and my eager soul is about to wing its way to the realms of eternity. Already does the light of heaven break upon my enraptured sight, and I feel happy, oh, how happy, for hope and confidence cheer my passage to the grave, and I wish no longer to linger in this dreary world. Alfred—Stanley," she added, taking a hand of each and joining them, "forget, I beseech you, all that has passed between you, and henceforth be friends, be brothers. Omelia, one fond embrace, it is the last, and may you live to—"

She had not strength to finish the sentence, but sunk back on the pillow, and it was now too painfully evident that in a very short time she would be no more.

With breathless anxiety they all awaited that dreaded moment, and the agonising excitement of Alfred Meadows' feelings in particular were almost beyond endurance. Mr. Mansfield motioned them to be calm, but it was impossible that they could be so, and the silence which would otherwise have prevailed in that chamber of death, was broken at intervals by their sobs.

Again the poor girl partially revived, and then while a sweet and heavenly smile irradiated her features, in a calm voice she ejaculated—

"Father of heaven, I am ready, into thy hands I commit my spirit—I come—I come!

No. 49.

Almighty God!—bless, oh, bless them all, and take my eager spirit to Thyself."

These were the last words she was heard to utter, though for two or three minutes her lips moved as if in prayer, and her eyes were raised devoutly towards heaven.

Suddenly the expression of her countenance again changed, and nothing could be more calm and beautiful than it at that time appeared. For a moment or two she fixed her eyes affectionately on her sorrowing friends, then while a faint sigh escaped her lips, with scarcely a pang they closed for ever in death.

CHAPTER XCIX.

THE DEPARTURE FROM THE OLD FORT.

So silent had been the departure of that gentle spirit, that for two or three minutes they could scarcely persuade themselves that she was no more.

But too soon the solemn truth flashed upon them, and the wretched Alfred burst into a violent paroxysm of grief and lamentation which it was utterly impossible to restrain, and as he knelt down, and with clasped hands gazed distractedly on the pale features of that gentle and amiable being whom he had so fondly loved, his excitement became so great that Dr. Mansfield expressed his alarm at the consequences, and endeavoured to persuade him, but to no purpose, to retire.

"Flora, my own loved Flora," he raved madly, "oh, speak to me, I implore you, but one word. This fearful silence, and those ghastly looks shake my very soul with terror. What awful meaning is there in this? Flora, speak to the wretched guilty being who thus on his knees implores you, or madness will surely seize upon his brain."

"Alas," cried Omelia, in a tone of agony which may be better imagined than described, "she will never speak more, no more will her gentle voice gladden the hearts of those who loved her, never more will the soft radiance of those beauteous smiles charm their sight, and rivet their soul in admiration. Flora, unfortunate, beloved Flora, my more than sister, she is dead!"

"Dead—dead!" repeated Alfred, with a look of horror and incredulity; "no, no, recal that dreadful word; she does but sleep—and yet how pale, how lifeless are her features, and how still and inanimate her form. Great God of heaven! can it be?—Dead! and 'tis I that have killed her. Oh, monster—monster that I am!"

He covered his face with his hands, and the sobs and groans of anguish that escaped his bosom were quite piteous to hear."

"I would advise you, Mr. Meadows," said Dr. Mansfield, "to retire from this dismal and painful scene, and seek to compose yourself, for the most dangerous consequences may follow if you give way to this violent excitement. And you, Miss Omelia, had much better leave the room with Lieutenant Stanley and try to tranquillise your feelings."

"True," coincided Stanley, who, in fact, was almost as deeply affected; "come, Omelia, let us away, and seek consolation in the assurance that the spirit of poor Flora Melville—whose virtues ever shone conspicuous—is now in heaven. Mr. Meadows, you will see the necessity of following the excellent advice of Dr. Mansfield."

"Ah, no," groaned Alfred, with a look of distraction, "I cannot, will not leave her, I cannot cease to gaze upon those features, so beauteous in life, and still so lovely in death. Dead!—oh, no, I cannot persuade myself that she is so: surely I must be labouring under the wild influence of some hideous dream. Let it not be said that I am guilty of a crime so atrocious."

Again he groaned, and his whole frame was frightfully convulsed by violent emotion.

The grief of Omelia was unabated, and she continued to gaze upon the ghastly face of the corpse with looks of the most heart-rending description, and for a short time was quite deaf to all the expostulations of Dr. Mansfield and her lover, and took no heed of their advice.

And yet so tranquil had been the last moments of poor Flora, that it was sufficient to afford them that melancholy consolation of which they all stood so much in need.

"Alas," sighed Omelia, after some minutes spent in dismal and torturing reflection, "how little could any of us dream of such a dreadful calamity as this but two or three days ago? Poor Flora, your's was indeed a cruel fate, and yet how worthy were you of every happiness."

"Yes, yes," hastily exclaimed Alfred, suddenly aroused from the deep lethargy, into which, in the intensity of his grief and despair, he had for the last few minutes fallen, "terrible was the fate which pursued her, and fearful and untimely was her end. And it is I, heartless villain that I am, who have been the cause of all, and what punishment is there severe enough for me? Oh, I should be looked upon with disgust and horror, or shunned with fear and hatred by all my fellow creatures."

His agony became almost insupportable, and it seemed as though distraction had seized upon his brain.

"Mr. Meadows," remonstrated Stanley, who could not but deeply sympathise with him, "why do you thus give way to this violent excitement? You reproach yourself too severely; and poor Flora forgave you, which should afford you every consolation under the trying circumstances. You cannot have forgotten her dying words."

"Forget them," returned Alfred, in the same melancholy and desponding accents, "ah, no, it is impossible that I can do so, but alas, what can ever efface from my recollection the fate she has met with, and that it was at my hands she received it? That thought drives me to madness, and it is in vain that I may seek to tranquillise my feelings—I shall never again know peace or happiness. Oh, Flora, would to heaven that I too were dead, for now that you are no more, the world must become insupportably hateful to me."

And thus the unfortunate young man continued for some time longer to lament, and Omelia and Stanley fully participated in his grief, and could find but few words or arguments to seek to afford him consolation.

At length, however, Alfred Meadows was induced to retire, although it was indeed with a sad heart that he did so, and Omelia and her lover remained for some time longer in the chamber of death, and gazing with the most unqualified sorrow upon the corpse of that unfortunate being whom living they could not but view with the most affectionate esteem, and whose memory they must ever revere.

Our heroine recalled to her memory all the many happy hours that they had passed together in the innocent days of childhood, and before care or sorrow were known to either of them, and when she contrasted them with the recent events, and the many troubles that had attended them both, but especially Flora, she could not but give way to feelings of the most poignant anguish and regret.

It was not until she had again and again kissed the cold pale lips of the corpse, and wept bitterly over it, that she could be persuaded by Stanley and Dr. Mansfield to retire from the room, and then she did so very reluctantly.

The melancholy death of Flora Melville, which had not been expected to take place so soon, cast a gloom upon all the inmates of the old fort, by whom she had been held in the highest esteem for her numerous amiable qualities, but as has been already shown no one felt it more keenly than Alfred Meadows, who, in spite of the forgiveness which Flora had so solemnly uttered in her dying moments, could not cease to reproach himself most severely as the cause, for if he had not been hurried by his impetuous passions and jealous feelings into the duel with Stanley, the dreadful catastrophe would never have taken place, and Flora would still have been living, perhaps in time to re-turn the love he bore her, and to be the means of showering upon him every earthly happiness. But now all his hopes were annihilated, and he could only look forward to future misery and despair.

His father sought his presence immediately on his leaving the chamber of death, and imparted to him all the consolation he could on the melancholy occasion, but it was with very little effect that he did so, and at times the grief of his wretched and unfortunate son was so excessive that it almost amounted to madness, and he was afraid to leave him for a moment, lest he should again be tempted to seek to lay violent hands on himself.

After some time passed in melancholy conversation with Stanley, who tried his utmost, but to little or no purpose, to alleviate the violence of her grief, Omelia could not be dissuaded from again visiting the room in which the cold remains of Flora Melville were lying, and there she remained for hours watching by the corpse of her friend, and giving free vent to her tears, and the sorrowful lamentations that escaped her lips must have moved even the most insensible heart to pity to listen to.

Two days were suffered to elapse after the death of the poor girl, before her remains were committed to their final resting-place, which was in a humble grave dug beneath the wide-spreading branches of an ancient and stately tree in the garden of the old fort, and near the fatal spot where the shocking catastrophe had taken place, and the whole of the inmates of the building were present on the melancholy occasion, to pay the last sad tribute to the memory of one who in life had been so highly and deservedly esteemed by all who knew her.

The dismal task was accomplished, several beautiful flowers were planted over the grave by the hands of the affectionate Omelia and the distracted Alfred Meadows, and slowly the funeral party re-entered the fort, deeply impressed with the solemnity of all that had taken place.

For some days after the funeral Alfred was in a most deplorable state of mind, and would admit of no consolation, in fact it was but too evident that his sorrow had become too deep rooted ever to be removed, and his intellect was at times so much affected, that he required to be constantly watched to prevent the fatal consequences which there was every reason to apprehend.

He daily visited the grave of Flora, and there in bemoaning her sad fate, and praying fervently to heaven for the repose of her soul, he would pass many dreary hours, no one venturing to interrupt him in the sacredness of his grief.

Many tedious weeks had now been passed

by the unfortunate fugitives in the old fort, and their situation was every day becoming more gloomy and irksome. They were miserably supplied with the coarsest provisions, and that, too, most grudgingly by the villagers, who seemed to have grown tired of the burthen; and there were many circumstances in their conduct of late which were calculated to excite suspicion, and to give them reason to apprehend some act of treachery which might end in the destruction of them all.

A consultation was therefore at length held among them, at which it was resolved to abandon the old fort, and again trusting themselves to providence, endeavour to gain some station or other place of safety.

No one was more anxious for this than Omelia, whose active mind again sought employment in the more important events of the day, and who had determined to follow the future fortunes of her lover, let whatever might be the consequences.

Night was the time fixed on for their departure, and they resolved that it should take place unknown to the persons in the village, and as any longer delay was considered unnecessary, the following night was the time appointed for the departure, and Agra was the place they purposed endeavouring to make for.

The night came, and every preparation having been duly made, and the coast having been ascertained to be clear, the departure commenced, Stanley and Omelia—both of them being armed—having first bade a final visit to the grave of Flora, being the first to issue from the fort, followed by Abdal, Alfred Meadows—whose grief had settled into a deep melancholy, from which nothing could arouse him—his father, and the others, in all amounting to several individuals, men, women and children, and most of whose looks showed too plainly what they had suffered from care and privation.

They had chosen a time for their departure when none of the villagers in the neighbourhood of the fort were likely to be about, for they had every reason to suspect—as has been before stated—that they contemplated some act of treachery towards them, and they saw nothing to excite their apprehensions, journeying as they did, too, by the most secluded route, and using the utmost caution.

They had money amongst them sufficient to procure them assistance from any of the friendly natives, whom they might meet with on the way, for some time to come, which on their suspicions being excited they had taken care to conceal from the villagers, so that in that respect they had nothing to fear, their principal anxiety being for the women and children, who they were fearful, in their pre-

sent weak state, might sink under the fatigue of the tedious journey. However, they mustered all the fortitude they could, and proceeding at a moderately rapid rate at first, they soon lost sight of the old Hill Fort, which had so long offered them a place of refuge, in the distance.

CHAPTER C.

THE SURPRISE.—A DESPERATE SITUATION.

The time which had elapsed since our travellers had been immured in the old fort had been one full of remarkable and startling events. The rebels, who had met with such numerous and decided defeats from the great Havelock, Sir James Outram, and other heroes, remained undaunted, continuing the desperate and bloody struggle with an obstinacy and determination which it seemed that nothing could destroy, and it was evident that many more valuable lives must be sacrificed and the utmost of skill and bravery effectively employed before the rebellion could be subdued.

Havelock was on his final march to relieve Lucknow, which still nobly held out. Nena Sahib continued his atrocities to an extent unheard of in the annals of crime. Sir Colin Campbell was on his way from England to take the chief command, our officers and men daily, hourly performed prodigies of valour, and all was excitement, anxiety, and suspense, it being the opinion of many persons who were in a position to judge, that matters were fast approaching a crisis. How far unfortunately they were out in their calculations subsequent events have proved.

Nor can it be denied that, as we have before stated in the course of our narrative, India had much to complain of, many things to incite the natives to rebellion, through gross mismanagement and aggression on the part of the company, much to redress, much to be atoned for, and these of many years standing, as the history of the country will be sufficient to show.

But to return to our travellers.

On the route they had chosen to pursue, several determined engagements had taken place, the British sometimes suffering defeat as well as the enemy, although not of such frequent occurrence, and being occasioned mostly by surprise, overwhelming superiority of numbers, or from want of a sufficient knowledge of the country, and not owing to any lack of courage on the part of our men, or the want of skill in the officers under whose command they ever fought so bravely.

One of those sad reverses had taken place not any considerable distance from the fort, two or three days before the fugitives quitted it, in which the British were driven to make so precipitate a retreat that they were compelled to leave their wounded behind them to the mercy of the bloodthirsty miscreants with whom they had been so fiercely engaged, and of the dreadful slaughter which on that occasion had taken place, as our travellers proceeded, they discovered the most fearful and revolting traces, the mutilated corpses of the unfortunate victims being left to rot in the open air, and the whole presenting a still more ghastly and appalling appearance in the pale and sickly light of the moon.

They shuddered at the sight, although the gentle, yet heroic Omelia and her gallant lover being more inured to such scenes than most of their companions, although experiencing all the same feelings of humanity, and sympathy for the fate of so many unfortunate beings, exhibited considerable more firmness, and sought to dissipate the fears such horrors were naturally calculated to excite.

"The terrible day of retribution will yet arrive," observed our heroine, and the bloodthirsty miscreants—whom I blush and shudder to call my countrymen—will receive the reward due to their enormous crimes."

"True, dear Omelia," said Stanley, "there is a just and Almighty Power above that will not fail to inflict a fearful punishment on the perpetrators of atrocities unparalleled in the history of the world. But alas, how many hundred may have to suffer ere that time arrives?"

"I tremble to think," returned Omelia, "oh, India, bright land of my birth, when will thy fertile soil cease to be deluged with the blood of the innocent? When will weak and helpless women and children no longer call upon thy misguided sons for mercy in vain?"

An expression of the deepest sorrow and regret overspread her handsome features as she gave utterance to these observations, and her whole appearance was impressively beautiful and striking.

Armed by a brace of silver-mounted pistols, and a dagger in the richly studded and embroidered belt that encircled her slender waist, and walking at the side of her lover, with an air at once commanding, graceful, and dignified, all the amazon showed forth in her appearance, imparting a double lustre to her fine bright eyes, and exciting the admiration, nay even the reverence of her companions, who could not but look upon her as a superior being, and felt themselves honoured in her friendship and sympathy.

And how proud did Edward Stanley feel of the noble-minded girl, how happy to possess the love of so beauteous a being, that love which spoke so forcibly, so eloquently, so sincerely in the glances of her fine expressive eyes that ever beamed so fondly upon him, and how grateful did he feel to heaven for restoring her to him, and that, too, at a time when he had began to despair of ever beholding her again.

Yet, although he could only be happy when she was in his presence, and he could listen to the soft melody of her voice, every tone of which breathed affection, he deeply regretted that she should be exposed to so many dangers and vicissitudes for his sake, notwithstanding nothing could more forcibly prove the fervour and sincerity of her passion.

"Oh, my beloved Omelia," he observed, as they proceeded arm-in-arm together, slightly a-head of their companions, "when will the time come, when the horrors that now beset this unhappy country having ceased, we may calmly indulge the virtuous passion which now animates our breasts; and no longer any obstacle presenting itself to the union of our fates, I may hope to call you mine? Would to heaven that that blessed time had arrived upon which all my hopes of earthly happiness are fixed, and that you no longer should thus expose yourself to those dangers which few could bear with the heroic fortitude that you have done."

She looked in his face with the fondest emotion and affection, as she replied—

"Omelia sees no danger, knows no fear, while by your side, dear Edward, and she is blessed in the assurance of possessing your constant love. To be near you, to hear you speak, to know that you so fondly reciprocate the sentiments that glow within and animate her breast, there is nothing which the humble Indian maiden is not prepared to brave, while sweet hope guides on to those bright days of mutual happiness which she feels convinced are in store for us."

And those fond hopes, beloved Omelia, will be fully realised," returned Stanley, joyfully, warmly pressing her hand to his heart, and returning her looks of affection, "heaven, I am satisfied, whatever may be the troubles we are yet destined to undergo, will not permit them to be disappointed, and in those hopes are centred all my happiness."

"And yet," sighed our heroine, and tears filled her eyes as she spoke, "there are thoughts that will obtrude themselves upon me, and cast a cloud of sorrow and regret upon that happiness, that supreme unmingled happiness I should otherwise experience. My ill-fated sister, the gentle, suffering Miriami, and that dear friend, poor Flora, whom we have so recently lost, oh, had they been spared to share our happiness, that happiness which we at least so fondly anticipate, and which their virtues so richly merited, then, Edward, we should indeed have had no wish ungratified; but, alas, now—"

She could not finish the sentence, for her emotions choked her utterance, and Stanley who was also as deeply affected as herself was about to make some reply to her melancholy observations, when he was prevented from doing so by Abdal, who approached to consult with and advise them how it would be best for them to proceed through a part of the country with which he was much better acquainted than themselves.

"Of course," he remarked, "it is our principal object to avoid those districts as much as possible that are more or less disaffected, at the same time to endeavour to reach some British station, or other place of safety as quick as we can; and that I have every reason to believe we can do by pursuing our present course, notwithstanding the aspect of the country is not very prepossessing. The women and children I am afraid will not be able to endure—after what they have already suffered—the fatigue of any lengthened journey."

To this Stanley and Omelia assented, and they and their companions agreed to place themselves entirely under his guidance, and they resumed their journey with renewed hope and confidence.

The aspect of the country was certainly as Abdal had described it, rather uncouth, but at the same time possessing many wildly romantic and diversified features, characteristics by which Indian scenery is ever distinguished. There was much to admire, even to enthusiasm, much to create wonder, and alternately to excite terror, and the travellers proceeded on their tedious way indulging in the various reflections that those scenes, and their own peculiar circumstances engendered.

The weather was in their favour, and the night was remarkably fine, the air cool and refreshing, and the bright face of the moon, and her companion stars peeping in between the foliage of the majestic trees, and shedding a soft mellow light around.

It was night, as before stated, ere the fugitives thought it prudent to commence their journey from the fort, and having been travelling for some time, partly through a wild forest track, it was now getting very late, and as they felt fatigued, some friendly habitation where they could obtain rest and refreshment would have been no unwelcome sight, but that they could not very well expect to meet with, and it was therefore agreed as soon as they could find a convenient spot that they should halt for the night, more particularly to rest the women and children, while the men took it by turns to watch in case of any threatened danger.

They had scarcely come to this resolution when they emerged from the uncouth and somewhat cheerless place they had been traversing, and entered upon a tract of country presenting such a remarkable contrast—so beautiful and romantic, that they were lost in wonder and admiration, and by the light of the moon, whose beams were now completely unobstructed, they were gratified at beholding at no great distance the outlines of a large building, which seemed to be embosomed amid clustering trees, whose leafy branches seemed to sparkle in the chaste light of the lamp of heaven.

"Ah," exclaimed Abdal, in tones of satisfaction, as he gazed towards the building, "I am now fully aware of the part of the country we are traversing. Yonder building is the old mosque, celebrated in Indian history, situated many miles from Agra. It has been deserted for more than a quarter of a century, and is partly in ruins. There then we can safely rest for the night, and what is more, we may obtain from the various trees that grow around it so luxuriantly some of the most delicious fruits that India produces."

This was indeed most agreeable information to the weary travellers, and quickening their speed, they soon arrived at the noble ruins of the ancient mosque, rising in the midst of trees yielding almost every variety of fruit—of course in a wild state—natural to a tropical climate.

And writing of Indian fruit, it may not be amiss here to mention that, Nature, as if in anticipation of the total abstinence of millions of Hindoos from the use of animal food, has been wonderfully liberal of her supply of vegetable diet. No part of the world is so fruitful of those products which are at once nutricious and agreeable. Every fruit and every vegetable known to mild and even cold regions, is produced on the hills or the plains of India; and in addition to these, vast varieties, peculiar to the tropics, grow in luxurious abundance.

The fertile soil of India yields mangoes, pine-apples, plantains, pomegranates, pumplenoses, jacks, custard-apples, leechees, guavas, melons, oranges, lemons, limes, grapes, soursops, almonds, gooseberries, strawberries, tamarinds, plums, figs, dates, citrons, loquats, potatoes, cabbages, cucumbers, yams, brinjalls, peas, beans, artichokes, salads, &c., and many of the trees bearing the above mentioned fruits grew around the mosque, and in its immediate neighbourhood in singular beauty, giving a charm to the spot, especially when seen at that calm and tranquil hour, glittering in the moonlight, which could not fail to excite both wonder and admiration.

Leading the way through a grove of mango trees—which afford by their dense, dark shade, the most grateful shelter from "the traveller's enemy" the sun—Abdal conducted them to the mosque, so grand and solemn in its ruins, and upon whose lofty dome a broad flood of silvery moonlight was streaming, and Omelia, Stanley, and their companions paused for a few minutes before the once magnificent pile lost in admiration.

The solemn silence which reigned around was scarcely broken at intervals by the softly murmuring wind among the foliage, and everything spoke of safety, and invited to rest.

Abdal led the way to one of the entrances to the ancient place, and the fugitives willingly followed, being quite weary with the distance they had travelled, and anxious to obtain rest, and on entering the building they were struck with the grandeur of its architecture which even surpassed that of its exterior, the light of the moon streaming in at the different apertures, rendering everything upon which the wondering and admiring eye fell perfectly distinct.

A most convenient spot having been selected in the least ruinous part of the building, the gentlemen spread their coats and cloaks upon the broken tesselated pavement for the accommodation of the females and children, the former disposing of themselves in the best manner they could, and Abdal and Stanley having mutually agreed to keep watch by turns.

Worn out with fatigue, sleep soon descended upon their eyelids, and nothing occurred to disturb them, they continued to enjoy that rest which was so refreshing, till the sun had arisen in the morning.

They then partook of some of the provisions which they had brought with them from the fort, together with a portion of fruit gathered from the different trees surrounding the old mosque, after which they felt their strength and spirits greatly recruited, and began to prepare for the resumption of their journey.

The sun, however, had risen to such an oppressive heat, that, after a brief consultation among themselves, it was considered advisable to remain where they were till the cooler part of the day, when, after such a lengthened rest, they might pursue their journey without much inconvenience, and probably to greater advantage.

After a time passed among their companions in conversation on past events and their probable future prospects, Stanley, Omelia, and Abdal, walked forth a short distance from the mosque, in order to enjoy the beautiful scenery by which it was surrounded, and they were surprised and delighted at the extensive and magnificent prospect which was revealed to them on every side as far as their eyes could penetrate, but no signs of a human dwelling met their gaze, and Abdal remarked that, as far he could recollect of that part of the country, they had yet some distance to travel before they would come to any town or village, where they might venture to stop.

Beneath the shade of the trees, or in the old ruins of the mosque, the fugitives continued till the approach of the evening, when the sun having sunk to rest, and a cool and refreshing breeze sprung up, they once more resumed their journey, Abdal as before acting in the capacity of guide.

Nothing particular occurred to them for some time, and until night had set in, and they pursued their way with every confidence not having any reason to apprehend danger, but at length they entered upon a less cheerful part of the country, notwithstanding that in some respects it was picturesque enough, and they had not proceeded far when they were startled and alarmed by hearing confused sounds, like the trampling of several feet, and the muttering of voices—the voices of men—near them, and before they had time to recover themselves, or to think what was best to be done to avoid any danger which might threaten, several armed men—sepoys—appeared from behind a hill before them in the moonlight, and at so short a distance that it was impossible to help encountering them, and the terror and dismay of the females—except Omelia, who with her usual undaunted spirit in the face of the most imminent danger even, was fully prepared for everything—may be imagined.

Stanley, Abdal, and their other male companions drew their swords, and prepared to offer a determined resistance, and our heroine taking the pistols from her belt, placed herself by the side of her lover, with a look of resolution, and in the attitude of a heroine.

"There is nothing left for us but to fight boldly," observed Stanley, "and to put our trust in providence as to the result. But, oh, dear Omelia, how does it torture and distract me to think that in your noble and generous devotion to me, you should be again exposed to such imminent peril."

"Fear not for me, dear Edward," replied the heroic maiden, "I am prepared for all that may happen, while you are by my side. We will live or die together. Courage, my friends, and great as is their superiority of numbers, with the assistance of the Almighty power above, we shall yet triumph over our enemies."

There was no time for further words, the enemy had at first seemed astounded at the determined attitude which the unfortunate fugitives had assumed, and paused as if scarcely able to believe the evidence of their senses, but quickly recovering themselves, and uttering a frightful yell which resounded far around, they rushed fiercely to the attack with sword and musket, several of them firing a murderous volley, which stretched the elder Mr. Meadows and one of the unfortunate females lifeless on the earth, at the same time Omelia discharging one of her pistols, by a well directed aim mortally wounded one of the rebels who appeared to be the leader of the party, and then with all the courage of a second Joan of Arc, having placed herself in an advantageous position, she was prepared to resist to the last, and to sell her life dearly.

The desperate scene which followed baffles description, the contest was frightful in the extreme, the small number of the fugitives having to contend against such fearful odds, that to escape total destruction seemed to be impossible.

The yells and oaths of the sepoys, worked up to a perfect fury by the unexpected resistance, and at seeing two or three of their comrades fall, were terrific, and the shrieks of the affrighted women, and the piteous cries of the poor children rent the air.

Stanley had become separated from Omelia, already his sword had dealt destruction among the desperate foe, and he was now engaged in combat with two of them, by whom he would probably have perished had not Abdal fought his way to his assistance.

The unfortunate Alfred Meadows from the commencement of the combat, had fought recklessly, and had even seemed to rush madly on death. Poor fellow, if that were indeed his object, it was too soon accomplished, he received the sword of one of the rebels in his body, and sunk lifeless by the side of his aged father.

And such, so soon after the melancholy death of poor Flora Melvile, was the untimely fate of Alfred Meadows.

The situation of the fugitives was now a most desperate one indeed, for their party was so reduced in numbers, and most of those who had not yet fallen being more or less severely wounded—among the latter, Stanley—the result of the deadly combat appeared no longer doubtful.

The women and children were in a most deplorable state of agony and despair, for they well knew what they had to expect at the hands of the inhuman wretches, should their protectors be defeated, which it was now but too evident they must.

But the sepoys had hitherto been too hotly engaged with their brave antagonists to pay any attention to the unfortunate women and helpless children, against whom they reserved their brutality for a more fitting opportunity, which seemed but too likely soon to present itself.

The rebels had suffered severely, several of their villainous comrades having fallen,

which only served to enrage them the more, and still the bloody combat continued with unabated fury on both sides.

But in the midst of all the danger and the horrors by which he was surrounded, Stanley's most anxious fears were for his beloved Omelia, whom he had missed from his side in the confusion of the combat, and the most dreadful apprehensions beseiged his mind as to the but too probable fate which had befallen her, and drove him nearly frantic.

But suddenly the rich tones of her voice shouting defiance to the remorseless foe saluted his ears, and at that moment having slain his adversary, he desperately fought his way towards the spot from whence he had heard her, and the sight which he then beheld at once filled his breast with feelings of wonder, awe, and admiration.

Two of the villains had the heroic girl already slain by stabbing them to the heart with her poinard, and having secured the undischarged rifle of one of them, she was in the act of shooting a third miscreant who had come to attack her.

He endeavoured to reach her, calling frantically upon her name, but before he could do so, he again had to defend himself from the ferocious attacks of those who rushed upon him, and Omelia was again hidden from his sight in the smoke, and among the contending parties.

Suddenly loud shouts rent the air, the hasty trampling of horses was heard, and a detachment of British dragoons were seen galloping towards the scene of the sanguinary conflict, just as Stanley received a sabre wound on the head which sent him bleeding and insensible on the earth.

The sepoys were thrown into dismay, and fled in all directions, the soldiers pursuing them, and suffering but few to escape. They then returned to the scene of the combat to look after the wounded and the survivors, and thus terminated this startling and terrible event.

CHAPTER CI.

MORE SUFFERINGS FOR OMELIA.

But what had become of Omelia?

She had been separated some short distance from the other combatants, while engaged with one of the ruffians, and was felled to the earth by a violent blow from the butt-end of a musket, which rendered her insensible and apparently dead.

How long she had remained in that condition we are unable to state, but on her recovering her senses, she found herself lying in a small hollow into which she had fallen

on receiving the blow, with the bright moon shining above her and the twinkling stars looking down upon her, but no one near, and all signs of the late desperate combat having ceased.

With difficulty she arose to her feet, and looked with bewildered amazement and terror around her, having at first but a vague and dreamy recollection of what had taken place, and her head feeling giddy from the effects of the blow she had received.

But too soon the whole dreadful truth flashed upon her memory with overwhelming force, and horrorstruck at the idea of the terrible fate which had befallen Stanley and his unfortunate companions, she rushed wildly towards the scene of the late combat, calling frantically upon his name. The echoes of her own voice alone replied to her,

for all was now wrapped in solemn and profound silence, and it was evident that the deadly strife was over, and how it had terminated the distracted maiden could not entertain the slightest doubt.

She clasped her hands together in all the agony of despair, and still rushed madly on, the most piteous cries and lamentations escaping her lips, and making the air resound again.

And now she reached the fatal spot, and fearful was the scene which there presented itself; the dead lay weltering in their blood in all directions, and never had the bright moon shed her silvery light upon a more ghastly spectacle.

With the wild look of a maniac, Omelia rushed from side to side, still calling upon the name of her lover and examining the faces of the dead, expecting to find him among them.

She beheld the cold pale corses of the unfortunate Alfred Meadows and his father, she recognised several others that she knew, and who had been her companions in misfortune, but that beloved being whom she sought was alas, no where to be seen, there was no one to inform her what had become of him, and she beat her breast, and tore her hair in the phrenzy of her despair and anguish.

For some moments she stood transfixed to the spot in a state of stupified horror, and unconscious to all around her, but at length again reviving to painful sensibility, in a voice whose tones must have thrilled to the hearts of all who could have heard it, she exclaimed—

"Edward, beloved Edward, oh, where are you? What cruel fate has befallen you, and left me to all the horrors of despair and madness? Again are we separated, and this time I have too much reason to fear for ever. Edward, 'tis your Omelia who calls upon you and implores you to return to her. No, no, he hears me not, I shall never behold him more; the monsters have torn him far away, and even now too probably are exulting in the horrible, the fiendish tortures they are inflicting on him. That thought is agony too great for human being to endure. I shall go mad."

The poor distracted maiden pressed her hands upon her burning forehead, and convulsive sobs and groans escaped her overcharged bosom, but she could not shed a tear.

One more she started with the horror, the intense horror of the feelings that rushed so tumultuously upon her and almost overwhelmed her, and resumed her fruitless and fearful search among the dead, then as she became more thoroughly convinced that Stanley had disappeared, the full extent of her misery was made frightfully apparent to her, her anguish amounted to a pitch that was beyond all control within the bounds of reason.

"Cruel, accursed fate," she cried, "what have I done that you should thus relentlessly pursue me? If it was thus your will to deprive me of all I loved and cherished most on earth, why did you ever again suffer me to revive to life and consciousness? All now is gone, perished, and the wretched, heart-broken Omelia is left alone, alone in the wide and desert world. Edward—dear Edward, this is indeed the climax to all my miseries; I cannot live without you."

She rushed to some distance from the fatal spot, regardless whither, and calling wildly on his name, then she returned as a dreadful thought flashed upon her maddened brain, and standing for a moment or two before the ghastly corpse of one of the sepoys, contemplated it with looks of horror and fearful meaning.

Another moment, and she snatched a poinard from his belt, and clenching it firmly in her hand, in desperate accents she exclaimed—

"Why should I hesitate? Every hope is annihilated, life could only now become a torturing, an insupportable burthen to me, this friendly weapon will rid me of it, and thus I—"

She did not finish the sentence, but raised the dagger in her hand determinedly, as she spoke, and whilst a fearful expression agitated and distorted her beauteous features, she was about to plunge it in her bossom, when some inscrutable power seemed to interpose mercifully to save her from the perpetration of so rash and guilty a deed, her faculties were suspended, the dagger fell from her nerveless hand, and with a dismal groan which reverberated far around, she sunk insensible on the blood-stained earth, amidst the ghastly and mangled remains of the dead.

It seemed as though she would never more revive—and perhaps it would have been a mercy to her if she had not—for the night had passed away, the grey mists of early dawn had dispersed, and the first golden beams of the sun began to illumine the eastern horizon ere she again opened her eyes to consciousness, and gazed around her with vacant looks, as if she was still suffering under the delusion of some frightful dream.

But when the dreadful reality was made apparent to her senses, and she again gazed upon the ghastly faces of the dead, a burst of the wildest emotion escaped her, and her whole frame was agitated and convulsed in the most fearful manner.

For a few moments she stood transfixed to the fatal spot; then pressing her clenched fists upon her forehead, with the wild and piercing shriek of a maniac she hurried away—dashing precipitately over the rough and uneven ground, unconscious whither she went.

The sun was now high in the heavens, and the heat became intolerable; but nothing heeded Omelia in the present distracted state of her mind. Horror, phrenzy, and despair appeared to enchain all her faculties, and every other feeling was absorbed in that of the dreadful uncertainty of and anxiety for the fate which had befallen her lover.

It seemed but too probable that Stanley, who certainly had not perished on the blood-stained spot she had just quitted, had fallen into the hands of the remorseless and savage foe, and if such unfortunately should be the case the tortures that the bloodthirsty miscreants would not fail to inflict on him, were far too frightful for contemplation.

The horrid picture arose so vividly to the imagination of our heroine that her heart sickened, the blood ran cold in her veins, her limbs trembled convulsively, her brain turned giddy, and she was once more compelled to pause in her wild and uncertain flight, in order to endeavour to recover herself, and as she did so her heart palpitated so violently that it seemed as though it was ready to burst from its tenement every instant.

In all the trials and vicissitudes it had been the lot of Omelia to encounter, never had her fortitude so completely forsook her, never had she felt such poignant anguish absolute despair as she did on that fearful occasion, and the longer she reflected upon all the startling circumstances that had taken place, and the utter misery and loneliness of her situation, the more did her anguish and despair increase.

We have before stated that the sun was at its height, and that the heat was so excessive that it was almost insupportable, and even those most inured to the climate could not help feeling it most severely.

Omelia threw herself beneath the branches of a banian tree which happened to grow near, and completely abandoned herself to all the agony of those terrible thoughts and feelings which it has before been attempted to describe.

Deprived as she was of her lover, and in utter despair of ever again being restored to him, she was quite indifferent as to what befell her, what became of her, and indeed she considered that death would be a happy relief to her from her sufferings.

"Cruel fate has conspired against me, at every time that my hopes and prospects appear to be the brightest," she soliloquised, in the most mournful accents, something occurs to destroy them, and to sink me into the lowest depths of misery and despair, and to mock and torture me. Real happiness I feel but too surely is never destined to be my lot, and therefore why should I continue to live, when all that could render life tolerable is torn from me, and I am left a lonely wretched wanderer in the desert world? Why did I not perish in the fatal and deadly strife, or, at any rate, why were I not permitted to share the fate of that noble-hearted and beloved being whatever it may be? Oh, Stanley, if you be still living, how terrible I know must be your suffering, how great and insupportable your anxiety for me. I shudder at the thought, and my heart sinks within me. May the Great Spirit in his infinite mercy, watch over and protect him from those horrors which I have but too much reason to apprehend"

Again Omelia wrung her hands, and groaned in the intense agony of her feelings, and she turned her eyes in every direction, undecided what to do or whither to go, and perfectly indifferent as to either.

There was an extensive tract of country before her, and the scenery which on every side met her gaze was of the most diversified description, and at times when the eye wandered over the vast expanse which was spread before it, the beauty and variety of the landscape could not be surpassed in any part of the favoured land of India.

At any other time she would have revelled with delight in the contemplation of that lovely scene, but as it was, her eyes wandered vacantly over it, and she was perfectly indifferent to everything but the misery of her feelings, and the torturing anguish of her thoughts.

For some time Omelia remained in the same state, when suddenly aroused by a faint ray of hope which flashed upon her brain, having first on her knees implored the guidance and protection of providence, she proceeded on her weary journey, although she was quite at a loss what direction to take, with the chance of finding relief, or the hope of avoiding any danger which might threaten.

But long the unfortunate maiden travelled on without meeting with anything which was at all calculated to realise her wishes, until anxiety of mind, and exhausted nature could endure no more, and she again sunk down in the midst of a cluster of trees that spread their friendly and thickly foliaged branches across the road she had been pursuing, and overpowered not only by her own mental sufferings, but the intense heat of the sun, she fell into a kind of stupor, which could scarcely be called sleep, for she was partially conscious of her lonely situation, and keenly alive to the recollection of the exciting events that had so recently occurred.

But after a short time she was aroused even from this lethargy, if so we may call it, by the sound of the rolling wheels of some vehicle, which was approaching, and looking cautiously, and at the same time anxiously from among the trees, she perceived a buggy (a sort of hooded cab, accompanied by several syces, or grooms, who not only groom and feed the horses, but either take their places behind a carriage, or run by its side, or by the side of the equestrian who may be paying visits, and require his horse to be occasionally held) coming at a moderate rate in the direction of the spot on which she was standing.

Excited by the hope of relief, for she felt so completely worn out with fatigue, and the sufferings to which she had been exposed, that she could not have proceeded much further, and without stopping to ask herself whether the persons approaching were friends or enemies, Omelia emerged from the place in which she would probably have remained concealed from observation, and rushed hastily towards the approaching vehicle; but ere she could proceed many paces, a strange sensation came over her, her brain turned giddy, her limbs failed her, and with a faint cry she sunk upon the earth in a state of insensibility.

The syces, and the persons who occupied the buggy, had perceived her immediately, and drove towards the spot where she was lying.

These travellers consisted of two ladies and two gentlemen, evidently Europeans, and whose sympathies were warmly excited on beholding the helpless and deplorable state of the unfortunate being before them, and they immediately alighted to examine her more narrowly, and to see what assistance they could render her.

The extreme beauty of the young Indian maiden immediately struck them with admiration, and the peculiar circumstances under which they had discovered her, also created their astonishment and curiosity.

"Poor girl," said one of the ladies in the most gentle accents, " I fear that she has been exposed to some terrible misfortune, to judge from her appearance. She is very lovely.

"True," coincided the gentleman who had been seated by her side, and who was, in fact, her husband, "true she is most beautiful, and were it not that she is a native, I should feel inclined to think that, from her appearance, she was one of the unfortunate victims of the atrocious miscreants who are at present deluging the country with innocent blood. She has fainted, probably from fatigue and long privation, and it is fortunate that we came this way on our return home, or she might have died from the want of timely assistance. Poor girl—poor girl. If the expression of her features do but speak the truth, her's is indeed a sad history."

The words were spoken in tones of the deepest compassion, and to which the looks of the gentleman's companions showed they sincerely responded.

"But come," added the gentleman, after a brief pause, "this is but a waste of time, and there is not a moment to be lost in hastening to our residence, where proper means may be adopted for the recovery of this young stranger. Place her in the vehicle, and we will then proceed on our way without any more delay."

To this neither of the ladies nor the other gentleman raised any objection, and the men in attendance proceeded to do as their master desired, and were about to lift Omelia into the buggy, when an exclamation of astonishment from one of them, accompanied by a singular and malicious expression of countenance, attracted the attention and excited the curiosity of the gentleman before mentioned, and who was his master.

He was a tall, powerfully-built Indian, with forbidding features, and large black eyes, which sometimes were fixed upon you with a peculiar and sinister expression which excited anything but a pleasant sensation, and conveyed a meaning that few could properly understand, yet every one would look upon with suspicion if not with dread.

"How now, Kotah?" demanded his master, eagerly, "what meant the exclamation you just now made use of, and the look which you fixed upon this poor girl? Have you any knowledge of her?"

"I—I, sir," returned Kotah, evidently confused, and seeking to evade the question, "certainly not; it is not likely—how should I know her?"

The gentleman looked at him narrowly and suspiciously for a moment, and then observed—

"Your answer does not satisfy me, Kotah, I observed the strange emotion you exhibited on beholding her features, and it struck me at the time that you recognised them, if so, you surely can have no objection to inform us who she is, and what you know of her."

"You are mistaken, sir," returned Kotah, "the girl is a stranger to me, I never remember to have seen her before, though her remarkable likeness to a deceased sister of mine certainly struck me at the moment, and was the cause of the agitation I exhibited."

His master again looked narrowly at him for a moment, but said no more, and our heroine being lifted into the buggy, and attended to with the greatest kindness and solicitude, especially by the ladies, but still remaining in a state of unconsciousness, it was driven off in the direction they wished to go.

In a few minutes afterwards Omelia revived, and opening her eyes looked with astonishment and bewilderment at those under whose care she found herself, and eagerly inquired the meaning of it, and whither they were conveying her.

"Be not alarmed, my poor girl," replied one of the ladies, in kind and gentle accents, and at the same time looking compassionately upon her, "for you are with friends, and those who can sincerely sympathise with you in any misfortunes that may have befallen you."

"Ah," exclaimed Omelia, in a voice of the greatest emotion, and clasping her hands vehemently together, " I remember all now; all the terrible events of the last few hours rush upon my memory with overwhelming force, and rack my brain to madness. The inhuman wretches have deprived the poor Indian girl of all that she loved or valued on earth, and why did they suffer her to live? It would have been a mercy had they killed me, since all the hopes and prospects to which I so fondly clung are destroyed. Oh, Stanley, dear Stanley, we shall never more behold each other, and that thought alone is sufficient to drive me to madness."

These words were uttered with such melancholy emphasis, that showed the intensity of her anguish, and aroused the deepest sympathies of those who heard her, and covering her face with her hands she burst forth into a most violent paroxysm of grief, and again became almost unconscious to everything, save the dreadful thoughts that agitated and distracted her mind, and from which her companions did not attempt to arouse her, waiting patiently a fitting opportunity for an explanation, their curiosity being more than ever excited.

It may here be as well to inform the reader that the persons under whose care and protection Omelia had now so strangely and so fortunately fallen, were English people. Mr. Sinclair and his wife, and a brother and sister, who had hitherto escaped the horrors and enormities that had already taken place, and which were daily and hourly increasing in the most frightful manner, although they were wealthy, and were well known throughout the country, and their amiable qualities had gained them the esteem of all who had become acquainted with them.

They resided in a handsome house, in a quiet, beautiful and retired spot, at some distance from Agra, but not far from the place where they had discovered Omelia. The business which had called them forth on that occasion it may be unnecessary here to explain, suffice it to say that after travelling at a moderate pace for about half an hour, during which time Omelia was too violently agitated and engaged in her own gloomy thoughts to enter into conversation, and her companions did not think proper to disturb her, the buggy arrived at the place of its destination

CHAPTER CII.

OMELIA'S NEW ASYLUM.—FRESH DANGER.

The house which formed the residence of Mr. and Mrs. Sinclair, and their brother and sister, was one of two stories, and one which might be considered to be on a grand scale. It contained no less than twenty rooms, with broad verandahs, bathing-rooms, and out-offices, and stood in the midst of a beautiful and extensive garden, laid out with exquisite taste, containing flowers of every hue and fragrance, majestic trees, the deep cool shade of whose widely-spreading and intertwining branches was most inviting, and handsome fountains in different directions which gave a still more pleasing effect to the scene.

Reader, before we proceed farther with our tale, let us inquire whether you have any knowledge of European life in India? If not a brief description here may prove useful and interesting.

* "The order, the routine, so to speak, of European life in India, is unavoidably uniform and monotonous. People rise very early—before the dawn of day—for dawn and twilight are of brief duration in India; and when the sun is once "up," we begin to experience his influence. An hour's exercise —either on horseback or afoot—is supposed to be necessary to insure the healthy action of the liver.

"Returning home, a bath, which literally consists in having jars of water poured over the body, is taken, the newspaper is read, and everybody proceeds to business of some kind or other, while ladies, defying the sun, sally forth in their carriages to pay visits and make purchases.

"From ten in the morning until five in the evening everybody is at work.

"A bath and a change of dress precede the evening ride or drive. Everywhere there are strands, courses, beaches, where the denizens congregate to gossip or listen to the music of military bands. Night closes in and the gay groups separate to return home and dine.

"This is a sketch of every day English life, but of course it is varied by the seasons and the ordinary usages of society. There is much interchange of dinner-giving; balls are frequent at private houses and military messes. Billiards and cards furnish excitement to great numbers; a few persons cultivate music, and now and then an amateur play, a discharge of fireworks, at the expense of some rich native, a regatta, or a *nautch* (native dance), enliven society. The races are also a great source of amusement, for most people having access to the race-course during the 'trials' and training of the horses, become cognizant of their powers, and interested in their success. There is little or no trickery on the Indian turf, and the actual races, which last for a fortnight, the running taking place on alternate days, bring together all classes of society bent upon amusement. The horses which come to the post, are Arabs, country breds, and the produce of the Cape of Good Hope.

"Jaunts to places of interest—old temples, manufactories, curious ruins, picturesque localities, where the scramble and make-shift

* "India."—By J. H. Stocqueler.

of a pic-nic impart excitement to the scene, are by no means unusual, and those who are fond of yachting find ample entertainment when the weather is fine and settled.

"Yet, after all, the principal amusement of the English exile, his solace when all other things fail, is to be found in literature, of which, happily, there is never an insufficient supply. The local dress teems with publications.

"The life of an English lady in India is one of perfect leisure. No household cares occupy her thoughts or kill her time.

"The *khansumah* and the *ayah* between them assume all the duties which in England pertain to the mistress of a household, and she has little left her to do beyond reading the stock of a circulating library, and doing a little knitting and crochet work. If she be an equestrian, and is so circumstanced as to have horses kept for her, the early mornings and late evenings may be consumed in out-of-door exercise—if she is musical, or cultivates the fine arts, a part of the day may be pleasantly employed in illustrating the scenery of the country, and the costumes and habits of the people. If piously or charitably inclined, or disposed to activity in the absence of ennobling motives, the numerous ladies' committees of the branches of the bible societies, or associations for the promotion of education among the Christian poor or native females, open a scope to her philanthropy. Should she happily be a mother of children, the *baba logue*, or little people, as the olive branches are called in India, engage much of her care, and mitigate the solitude of her position, while her husband is engaged in his official duties."

We have deemed it the more necessary to give this sketch of European life in India, because it will explain many things that will occur in the course of our tale which might otherwise be unintelligible to the reader.

It may be added that the expense of "life" at one of the presidencies depends upon the circumstances and position of the individual. A man may live on £200 a year, or 170 rupees per mensem, and he may also spend without difficulty £10,000 a year.

Mr. and Mrs Sinclair, although they resided in a retired part of the country, kept up their establishment on the most expensive scale. The apartments were all furnished in the most elegant and costly manner, and could not fail to elicit the admiration of every person of taste who saw them.

Then they had all the numerous servants, regardless of expense, which are considered necessary in any establishment on a grand scale.

There was the *khansumah*, or butler, two or three *khetmugars*, who also attend at table, clean the plate, &c., a *valet* of the khetmut-gar class, who takes care of the linen and clothes of his master, and looks after his toilet; a cook and a deputy, a *sirdar* and bearers, whose duty is to prepare the bath, polish boots and shoes, &c., a *musalchee*, who acts the part of a scullian, a *bheestie*, or water-carrier, a *mihtur*, or sweeper, who does all the dirty work of the house, a *dhobee*, or washer*man*, there are no washerwomen in Indo-European establishments; a *durzee*, or tailor: a *durwan*, or door-keeper, an *abdar*, or "keeper of the water," a watchman, several syces, or grooms, a *peon*, or belted messenger, an *ayah*, or lady's maid, *migturanee*, or female sweeper, a *sircar*, who keeps the accounts of the establishment, *dooreahs*, or dog-boys, where persons keep dogs, *chowkeydars*, or private constables, who patrol the grounds during the night, *manjies* and *dandies*, where a boat is kept, *coolies* to carry burdens, *hookah burdars*, or prepares of the hookah, &c. &c."

Such is the rather expensive and extensive domestic establishment of a European of wealth and position in India, and such was that of Mr. and Mrs. Sinclair, whom we have thus introduced to the reader, and we will now, therefore, resume the thread of our narrative.

The stopping of the buggy on arriving at the house of Mr. and Mrs. Sinclair, aroused Omelia from the lethargy of dismal thought into which she had fallen, and she looked with surprise at the handsome building before her, and the strangers with whom she found herself, while in spite of the anguish of her mind, the novelty and beauty of all that met her sight, especially as it was then seen to advantage in the golden rays of the sun could not but excite in her breast feelings of admiration.

The looks of sympathy and kindness which her newly found friends bestowed upon her went deep to her heart, and remembering the forlorn situation in which she had been left after the dreadful and sanguinary affray which had separated her from her lover, probably for ever, and the fate which might have befallen her, little although she now valued life, her breast overflowed with gratitude, and throwing herself on her knees before Mr. and Mrs. Sinclair, she endeavoured to pour forth her thanks, but sobs and tears choked her utterance, and she could only express the powerful emotions that agitated her breast by the looks which she fixed upon them, and which those amiable people could well understand and appreciate.

Mrs. Sinclair, who was a fine handsome woman, in the prime of life, and with a countenance beaming with intelligence and every kindly feeling, gently raised her, and pressing her hand warmly within her's, she said—

"Pray be calm, my poor girl, and rest assured, as I have before told you, that you are with friends who can sympathise with you in your misfortunes, and will do all they can to assist you, which your appearance, or we are much deceived, convinces us you so fairly merit."

"Gentle lady," replied our heroine, in accents of such plaintive sweetness that they immediately went to the heart, and convinced those that listened to her that sincerity dwelt upon every word to which she gave utterance, "oh, these are indeed words of kindness from the lips of a stranger that the humble Indian girl Omelia, little expected to hear, and indeed she knows not where to find words to express her gratitude, valueless however as life is now to her. May the Great Spirit above watch over and bless you and your's for your sympathy towards one who at present, heaven knows, stands so much in need of it."

"Omelia," repeated Mrs. Sinclair, looking at our heroine still more earnestly and inquiringly, "surely I have heard that name before?"

"Yes, my love," replied her husband, and at the same time he looked with anxious curiosity and the deepest interest upon the expressive features of Omelia, "that name is indeed familiar to our ears, since that deplorable revolt which has spread such frightful ravages throughout the country, for 'tis one that is associated with all that is noble and heroic in woman. Surely," he added, addressing himself to our heroine, "you must be the beauteous and intrepid being of whom I speak?"

"There is little praise due, kind sir," replied our heroine, in the most modest and unassuming manner, "there is little praise due, I repeat, to those who perform no more than their duty towards heaven and their fellow-creatures. Disclaiming then, the eulogy you so generously and flatteringly bestow, I do acknowledge myself to be that once happy but now wretched girl of whom you have just spoken."

"Heroic, noble-minded Omelia," cried Mr. Sinclair, in a tone of pleasure and admiration, "I felt convinced you were no other, I could have sworn so, for your looks and manners assured me. Friend of humanity, bright honour and example to your sex, thrice welcome I say to all that I, my wife, and friends can do to serve you."

Omelia was about to reply, when a low muttering and disagreeable voice close to her prevented her, and looking hastily round, she beheld the dark eyes of a repulsive looking Indian—whose features it struck her most forcibly she had frequently seen before —fixed maliciously upon her, and she could not help shuddering as she did so; but in a

moment he withdrew his gaze, without having been observed by Mrs. Sinclair or her husband, who happened at the time to be engaged in giving some instructions to one or two of their other servants, and immediately disappeared, the eyes of Omelia scrutinizingly following him as he went, and feeling more and more convinced that she was not mistaken, but that she had seen him somewhere and often before, and that, too, under circumstances of the most unfavourable description.

It was the man Kotah, who has been already introduced to the reader, and of whom more anon.

"Mr. Sinclair and his lady, now turning to Omelia, noticed her agitation, and eagerly inquired the cause, but she not liking to explain at that time, endeavoured to evade the question, and they naturally attributing it to fatigue and anxiety of mind, again smiled kindly and encouragingly upon her, and the latter then taking her hand in the most friendly manner, conducted her across the garden—the beauty of which, even in the midst of her sorrows, excited her most enthusiastic admiration and delight—through a grove of mango trees to the house, which they entered.

Kotah—in whose mind something of a guilty nature was evidently brooding— watched them enter the building, from a short and convenient distance, where he could not be observed, and as he again fixed his piercing eyes upon the lovely form and features of Omelia, with a look of eager scrutiny, his brow lowered more than before, he bit his lips, and raising his clenched fist in the air, muttered a fearful oath between his teeth, and then walked slowly, and towards a more secluded part of the garden, where, with his arms folded across his broad chest, he remained for some time buried in the most gloomy and guilty thoughts, and pacing to and fro with disordered footsteps.

"The opportunity I have so long panted for," he soliloquised, while a still more repulsive and malicious expression distorted his forbidding features, "the opportunity I have so long eagerly panted for, at length presents itself, and I will not fail to avail myself of it. 'Tis her, the hated daughter of Yanadar, she against whom my feelings of revenge are so powerfully excited, and till I have gratified which, I have sworn never to rest satisfied. Proud beauty, did you but know the deadly enemy who is so near you, methinks you should have cause to tremble. Allyghur, my former friend, my more than brother, your death shall yet be most terribly avenged."

Thus saying the villain—for such his words unquestionably proclaimed him to be —stalked from the spot on which he had been standing and entered the house by a back way.

As Omelia was conducted by her new found friends through the various apartments to the sitting-room, the taste and elegance displayed in the manner in which they were furnished—and which, as well as the numerous servants that formed the domestic establishment, showed the wealth of the proprietors—in spite of the dismal thoughts that occupied her mind, excited her warmest admiration, and to which she could not help occasionally giving expression.

But at length they arrived in the sitting-room, which even surpassed all the others in the costliness and beauty of its furniture, and there Mrs. Sinclair having in the most friendly and familiar manner conducted her to a seat, again addressed to her words of the utmost kindness, requested that she would make herself quite at home, and to endeavour to tranquillise her feelings as well as under the present circumstances she could possibly do.

Omelia tried to return her acknowledgements for such unprecedented kindness from those who were complete strangers to her, her heart, however, was too full to enable her to do so, though her looks spoke more than even the language to which she wished to give utterance could have done, and Mrs. Sinclair and her husband—who as we have before said were deeply interested in her—were perfectly satisfied, and exerted themselves by every means in their power to convince her that they were so, desiring her to defer all explanation to some future occasion, and till she found herself in a more fitting condition to do so.

An excellent repast was quickly put upon the table, of which Omelia was invited to partake, which she did, though sparingly for her mind was too wretched, and the thoughts that continued to distract her brain were of too painful a description to suffer her to eat, and Mrs. Sinclair feeling for her exhausted and dejected condition, suggested that she should retire to rest of which she evidently stood so much in need, and hoping that the same would serve to tranquillise her feelings in a great measure.

For this Omelia felt most grateful, for she was indeed anxious for a time to be left to the indulgence of her own thoughts, and the Ayah being summoned, she raised the hands of Mr. and Mrs. Sinclair respectfully to her lips, and having in simple, but at the same time impressive terms thanked them for their kindness and consideration, was conducted by the servant from the room to a commodious and well fitted-up chamber at the back of the house, and from the windows of which was commanded a fine view of the gardens in which the building was situated,

and the extensive and romantic surrounding scenery.

Here after offering her further services, which Omelia declined, the ayah quitted the room and left her to those mournful thoughts and feelings of which the reader will be able to form a pretty correct idea.

What an extraordinary change had only a few short hours wrought in her circumstances and how terrible and fatal were the events that had taken place. She scarcely dared venture to reflect upon them, yet the longer she continued to do so, the more powerful and insupportable became her anguish and despair.

But where was her beloved Stanley? what was the fate which had befallen him? Such were the principal and more torturing questions that suggested themselves, and to which she trembled for a reply, but the most fearful conclusion was the only one she could arrive at, and in vain she endeavoured to look for hope and consolation. Several times had they been restored to each other, after a long separation, in a most miraculous manner, but now she could not but too much fear that they would meet no more.

The fact of her not having been able to discover anything of him among those who had fallen in the sanguinary combat, rather increased her fears and anguish, for at the time of the arrival of the English dragoons being insensible, and consequently not aware of it, she apprehended that Stanley had been taken prisoner by the sepoys, in which case his fate would undoubtedly be far more dreadful than if he had fallen in the deadly conflict, and could not think of it, without the most shuddering sensations of horror.

"Oh, heaven!" she exclaimed, clasping her hands together, and looking the very picture of despair, "how terrible, how insupportable is this state of suspense, and when shall I ever again find anything to relieve me, or to remove the heavy weight of care from my mind which now oppresses it? Alas! never, never more, I fear: the fate of him I so fondly, so devotedly loved is sealed, and mine must be so also; oh, why was it not ordained that we should both perish together? Look down with mercy upon me kind heaven, and if it be your will that myself and Stanley should never again meet upon this earth, suffer me no longer to live in misery far too great for human nature to endure. Why, oh, why indeed, am I now preserved?"

Her tears flowed fast as she thus mournfully soliloquised, and for some time she completely abandoned herself to the poignant and overwhelming anguish of her feelings, for there was nothing to which she could look for hope or consolation.

And thus, indulging in such painful

thoughts as those which have just been described, she continued for some time, and thought not of seeking that rest to obtain which she had been requested to retire, although she so much required it.

While she still sat, wrapped in thought, she was aroused by hearing a fine manly voice singing a song, in a style that was sufficient to prove him to be a most accomplished musician, and in spite of the melancholy feelings that engrossed her mind, she could not but listen with attention and some degree of interest.

The song seemed to proceed from the sitting-room where she had left Mrs. Sinclair, her husband, and their friends, and it was probably one of the gentlemen who was singing it; but the emotion of Omelia may be imagined when she recognised in the air that

of a favourite ballad, which she had frequently heard Stanley sing, and on listening attentively, and which she now did with breathless interest, she discovered that the words of the song were the same.

They were as follows—

When the heart's oppress'd with anguish,
  And vainly friends seek to beguile;
There's a charm awakens gladness,
  That charm is woman's sunny smile.
Like a light from heaven beaming,
  Breaking through dark clouds that lower,
And man, beneath its radiant beaming,
  Owns dear woman's magic power.
    Fond woman's magic power,
    Loved woman's magic power,
Man, 'neath woman's bright smiles beaming,
  Owns her ever magic power,

Though no flowers his pathway blossom,
  But all is sterile, dark, and drear;
He may find one gentle bosom
  Throb to sooth his anxious care.
And his heart though cold by nature,
Warms and melts from that one hour;
  And as he views each lovely feature,
  Yields to woman's magic power.
    Dear woman's magic power,
    Fair woman's magic power,
And as he views each lovely feature,
  He yields to woman's magic power.

Who'd such fetters break assunder?
  From such bondage who'd be free?
But in homage, love, and wonder,
  Gladly bend the suppliant knee.
'Tis a spell, there's no resisting,
  A mighty spell 'neath which we cower;
A fairy thraldom man exists in,
  Dear woman's ever magic power.
    Fond woman's magic power,
    Dear woman's magic power,
It is a thraldom man exists in,
  Lovely woman's magic power.

The voice ceased, but Omelia still continued to listen, fearful of losing a note, or one word of that song with which she was so familiar, and which was so fondly treasured in her memory. But what mingled feelings of pain and pleasure did it awaken on that occasion, and when she was so little prepared to hear it? Every word thrilled to her heart with indescribable effect, and she could not resist her tears.

"Surely," she sighed in the distraction of her thoughts, "this must have been done to torture me, and to mock my misery? Oh, Edward, never again shall I hear your voice sing the words of that well known song with which you have so often charmed me—and yet could I fancy that they are still ringing in mine ears, and that I gazed upon your beloved features as they were wont so affectionately to look while you gave utterance to them. But it is all a delusion; death hath silenced your voice for ever, and there is madness in the thought. Oh, Stanley, would that your faithful Omelia reposed with you in your silent grave."

Her tears flowed afresh as she thus spoke, and the agony of mind which she experienced was too painful for description.

But suddenly she arose from her seat, dashed away her tears, and the expression of her features and her whole demeanour underwent a most remarkable change, as strange thoughts and feelings seemed to take possession of her.

"But no," she exclaimed, in a firm voice, "let me not abandon myself to this weakness of despair, but let Omelia, the Indian maid, the humble sepoy's daughter, proud and resolute in her own integrity of spirit, and the purity of her motives, once more arouse, and be herself again. The noble mission which she feels she has to perform, is not yet accomplished, nor can she die until it is. Dear Stanley, if indeed you have perished by the hands of the cowardly, the inhuman and accursed foe, let me live to avenge your death in the blood of your murderers, and the brutal murderers of my own unfortunate sex, and their helpless, innocent children. And here do I swear to cast aside all womanly fear, and to boldly brave every danger I may have to encounter to achieve that object. Omelia scorns to stand tamely by, whilst duty to the laws of humanity and justice call upon her, though a woman, to lend her feeble aid in hurling retribution upon the heads of the atrocious miscreants who thus feast and revel in the blood of their fellow creatures."

As the heroic girl gave utterance to these words, determination animated her handsome features, glowed in her countenance, and flushed brightly from her beautiful expressive eyes. Her graceful form seemed to dilate itself, and her bosom swelled and heaved with the noble feelings that now agitated it, and aroused all the energies of her nature.

The true portrait of the amazon was there, and few persons could have gazed at her at that moment without feelings of admiration almost amounting to awe.

For several minutes she stood in the same commanding and striking attitude, and as she did so her courage and determination seemed to increase, but at length she knelt down, and supplicated in the most fervent and devout terms the mercy and protection of the Supreme, then rising, with a calm look of confidence and resignation, she seated herself by the open window, and while wrapped in meditation, her eyes wandered over the beautiful and extensive prospect which was revealed to them by the light of the moon, which had now arisen in all its chaste splendour.

She felt grateful for the kindness with which Mr. Sinclair and his wife had already treated her, and she could never be sufficiently thankful to providence for having placed her in such friendly hands, at the time when she was surrounded by so many dangers, and so much needed sympathy and assistance.

She remained at the window, buried in thought, yet charmed and delighted with the beauties of nature, as seen in that calm and tranquil hour, but at length feeling tired and inclined for sleep, after again committing herself to the care and protection of the Almighty, she retired to rest.

———

CHAPTER CIII.

A NOCTURNAL ADVENTURE.

A refreshing night's repose blessed the pillow of Omelia, and she awoke the following morning in much better spirits than she had been the day before.

Visions of the most hopeful and cheering description had attended her in her slumbers, and which had the most beneficial effect upon her spirits, and she left her couch inspired with fresh hope and courage.

It was early, only just dawn of day, but the ayah who had conducted her to the chamber, shortly made her appearance, to see whether Omelia would require her services to assist her to dress, and informing her that Mr. and Mrs. Sinclair were already awaiting her at breakfast, and anxious to know how she had rested during the night.

The ayah, or ladies maid, was an intelligent young Indian woman of prepossessing appearance and manners, and she had won upon the favour and good opinion of our heroine from the first moment she had seen her, for she saw plainly that she sympathised with her, and she felt grateful for it.

Having completed her toilette, Omelia was conducted by the ayah to the breakfasting-room, where she found Mr. and Mrs. Sinclair and the brother of the former and his lady, and was received by them with the same kindness and friendship as if they had been intimately acquainted for years.

She was overwhelmed with gratitude and before they could offer to prevent her, she sunk on her knees before them, and poured forth her thanks as her feelings prompted.

They were all much touched by the fervour and sincerity of her manner, and Mrs. Sinclair raising her, and smiling kindly upon her, said :—

"My poor girl, why will you give way to this excess of feeling, so humiliating to yourself and which we do not require, having done no more than that which it behoves every one to do towards their fellow creatures."

"Oh, madam," returned our heroine, "I must indeed loathe and despise myself, could I for a moment refrain from expressing to you and your generous-hearted husband, my unbounded gratitude for the kindness which I, a poor, unknown and humble girl, have already experienced from you. May that almighty power which watches over the actions of all mankind, reward you, and never suffer me to forget the obligation, the heavy obligation I am under to you."

Mr. and Mrs. Sinclair were much affected by the simplicity and sincerity of her manner, and after anxiously inquiring how she had rested, and expressed their gratification on being informed, Omelia, encouraged by the friendly manners of her amiable host and hostess, took her place at the breakfast table, and that meal passed over in the most agreeable manner, our heroine already beginning to feel herself quite at home.

Mr. and Mrs. Sinclair then requested her, if she could sufficiently control her emotions to do so, to explain the circumstances which had placed her in the melancholy situation in which they had found her, and with which she immediately complied, and proceeded to relate those more important particulars with which the reader is already acquainted, and which alternately excited the wonder, admiration, and sympathy of those who listened to her.

When she had concluded, Mr. Sinclair, took her hand, and pressing it with all the warmth and sincerity of friendship in his, said :—

"Noble-minded, heroic girl, what an extraordinary and eventful life has been yours, and whilst I sincerely commiserate the sorrows and misfortunes it has been your lot to have to encounter, I cannot but express my unqualified admiration—and I am sure that Mrs. Sinclair entertains the same sentiments—of the unexampled fortitude with which you have endured them, and performed deeds of heroism, that shed a lustre on your character which nothing in the character of woman can ever outshine. May you be rewarded by all that happiness and prosperity which you so richly merit."

"Generous sir," replied Omelia, in a voice of much emotion, and tears trembling in her eyes as she spoke, "oh, where shall I find adequate language to express to you my sense of the flattering compliments you have been pleased to bestow upon me? But alas! how can I ever know happiness while the fate of the unfortunate Edward Stanley remains involved in mystery? Should he have fallen into the hands of those blood-thirsty sepoys, the terrible doom that awaits him, and which has but too probably already overtaken him, is certain, and can you wonder that the thoughts almost drives me to distraction?"

"Still Omelia," remarked Mrs. Sinclair, "you must not abandon yourself entirely to despair, sad and gloomy even as are your prospects, but endeavour to hope that your lover is still in existence, which I sincerely trust he is, and that providence may, ere long, again restore you to each other."

Omelia sighed, and shook her head mournfully.

"I thank you most sincerely madam," she said, "for your generous sympathy, and most willingly would I think as you have suggested, but, alas, under all the painful circumstances, I cannot do so. But," she added, as a feeling of determination came over her, and her looks showed the thoughts and feelings that were passing in her mind, "think not that Omelia will alone tamely resign herself to unavailing grief, and droop in despair, when there are other things to call her energies into action. No, I have pledged myself to die in aiding to avenge the death of him I loved, and the innocent blood that has been shed by those monsters in human form, rather than remain inactive, aye, and I will keep my oath, and as I do so may the Great Spirit aid me!"

It would be almost impossible properly to describe the beautiful, the noble, and heroic expression which animated the features of the Indian girl, and gave majesty to her form as she thus spoke, and as Mr. and Mrs. Sinclair gazed on her they became completely fascinated, and lost in wonder and admiration.

"Heroic girl," said Mr. Sinclair, "how well do I appreciate the noble feelings which glow within your breast, and prompt your actions, and providence will not fail to smile, depend upon it, on the efforts of one, who is so worthy of its favours. Be firm, be patient, and I trust that you will yet meet with your reward in being restored to the man who possesses your heart, and with him partake of every happiness that two fond and faithful hearts can experience."

Again Omelia returned her thanks for the kind feelings which Mr. Sinclair and his amiable lady expressed towards her, and the conversation then became of a more general description, and in which the intellectual qualities of our heroine shone forth to great advantage, and frequently elicited the most warm and sincere eulogy of her friends.

The day passed agreeably away, and Omelia at an early hour in the evening retired to her chamber.

When alone, however, her spirits again drooped, and the most torturing thoughts, and dismal forebodings beset her mind. In spite of the kindness of these excellent people under whose care and protection she had accidentally fallen, she felt that it would be impossible for her to remain contented beneath their hospitable roof, while she was still left in torturing uncertainty as to the fate which had befallen Stanley, and she could not but consider that she was to blame for delaying even an hour in her endeavours to ascertain it.

But how was she to accomplish that task? Whither could she direct her course, how prosecute her inquiries? She felt completely lost and bewildered, and the anguish and anxiety of her mind every moment increased, the more so as the difficulties that would not fail to present themselves in her way, and the almost utter hopelessness of success became the more apparent.

"Alas!" she sighed, "how sad, how dreary is the prospect now before me. I am left alone in the world, for all those who were most dear to my heart are taken from me, Stanley, Flora, all, all, and can happiness ever again be mine? Oh, it would be madness for me to entertain such an idea even for a moment, there is nothing left for me but misery and despair. Oh, Stanley, dearest Stanley, if it were the will of fate that we should thus be doomed to suffer, why, oh why did we ever meet?"

Again her tears flowed fast as these melancholy reflections occurred to her, and it was some time before she could at all compose her feelings.

She remained undecided how to act.

As she had done on the previous evening, she seated herself by the open window, which admitted the cool and refreshing breeze, thinking for a time to divert her thoughts from the melancholy subjects that engrossed them in the contemplation of the beautiful scene before her.

The evening was remarkably fine, and the bright moon, attended by myriads of stars shone forth in the cloudless sky, and imparted a sweet and cheerful aspect to the fair face of nature.

The house stood upon an eminence, so that from any of its windows an extensive view of the surrounding country, with all its picturesque and diversified features was commanded, and the eye could never grow tired of gazing at the various beauties, that on every side were presented to it.

But although Omelia gazed, and that too with apparent wonder and admiration, she was almost unconscious of what she saw, so completely did painful thoughts occupy her mind, and more gloomy and abstracted she became every moment.

Time wore on, but still she continued at the window, and thought not of retiring to rest, but suddenly she beheld the long shadow of a human form on the earth, in the moonlight, and looking more narrowly she beheld the tall figure of a man approaching along the avenue before her, and though she knew not why, she could not help watching him with some curiosity and anxiety.

He advanced slowly, but at length stood only a short distance from the house, and immediately opposite the window at which Omelia was seated, and folding his arms across his chest, raised his head, so that by the light of the moon, she could have a distinct view of his features, and an unpleasant sensation almost amounting to fear came over her when she recognised the man who had so particularly attracted her attention the first day of her arrival at the house, and whom she felt certain she had seen several times before, but where she could not call to mind.

That impression became stronger as she now gazed earnestly at him, and scrutinised minutely his forbidding countenance, and she racked her brain to no purpose to try to recollect who he was, and under what circumstances they had met, as she felt certain they had, often times before, while Kotah—for it was he—remained fixed in the same attitude, and gazed earnestly up at the window at which she was seated, with threatening and malicious looks, and it was evident that some guilty thoughts were passing in his mind.

Omelia felt somewhat alarmed, though she knew not why she should be so, and yet she found it impossible to remove her eyes from him, the more especially as she was at a loss to conjecture what motive he could have in watching in that particular spot so narrowly, and it was quite evident that he observed her.

Suddenly the recollection flashed upon her, and she remembered him as the relation of the villain Allyghur—who had justly though accidentally fallen by her hand—and one of the most savage of her guilty father's colleagues.

This discovery excited the most unpleasant feelings in her breast, for knowing the guilty character of the man, and the hatred he bore towards her—for he had once dared to make the boldest and most insolent advances towards her, encouraged by her father, and on her scornful rejection had vowed revenge—she could not but look upon him with dread, especially when she knew him to be the inmate of the same house with her, and that he would thus have an opportunity to put any guilty design which he might have in contemplation into effect.

At length, however. Kotah having fixed upon her a strange and menacing look, which expressed quite as much as words could have done, withdrew from the spot, and turning hastily round an angle of the building, disappeared, and Omelia, uneasy and foreboding, closed the window, and removing from it, became lost in the numerous perplexing and painful thoughts which this discovery gave rise to in her mind.

She saw at once the danger by which she was threatened, and that she must at once leave the house, and those who had already been so kind to her, and with whom she could otherwise have remained in safety until she could have arranged her plans for the future, in order to avoid it, and we need not state the pain and regret it caused her to be compelled to do so.

She also felt alarmed for the safety of Mr. and Mrs. Sinclair, for she felt convinced that the villain Kotah could only have entered their service with some dark and sinister motive, satisfied as she was that he was still connected with the rebels.

They could not possibly have any suspicion of his real character, and so great was her anxiety on their account, that she would immediately have informed them of the discovery she had made, and thus warned them of the danger by which they were threatened, had she not imagined that they had retired to rest, however, she determined not to defer doing so later than the morning, when she might at the same time consult with them what course it might be best for them to adopt under the circumstances.

For some time longer she continued wrapped in painful thoughts, but at length feeling weary, and all being silent in the house, she threw herself on the couch without undressing, and quickly sunk off to sleep.

But her slumbers were disturbed by painful dreams, in which all the startling events that had recently taken place, were re-enacted in her imagination, and at length she awoke with a shuddering sensation of unaccountable fear upon her, and at the very moment to her astonishment and alarm, she beheld the room door—which she had forgotten to fasten—slowly and cautiously opened, and the dark features of the villain Kotah peering into the room towards the couch on which she was lying, and the fiendish expression of his countenance plainly revealed the atrocious errand he had come upon, the more fearfully so, as he stepping silently into the room Omelia perceived that he held a dagger in his hand.

Few persons could have witnessed such a sight as this without evincing the greatest terror, and raising an alarm, but Omelia lost not her presence of mind, and became more firm and determined as the desperate and critical nature of her situation became the more apparent. She moved not a limb, she scarcely dared to breathe, but cautiously she watched the ruffian as he approached the table on which she had left the lamp burning on going to rest, and having taken which he advanced on tip-toe to the bed, where she lay perfectly still and inanimate, and feigned to be sound asleep.

It was a terrible moment, and it was wonderful that Omelia could find the nerve to meet it with such cool intrepidity. But as we have said before, her presence of mind, and natural courage in the time of the greatest danger, never for a moment forsook her, and she prepared herself to make the desperate effort on which her life or death depended.

Kotah stooped down, and listened to her breathing for a moment, then having passed the lamp two or three times across her eyes, in a low voice he muttered to himself—

"'Tis well; she sleeps soundly, little dreaming, I dare say, the fate that awaits her. She shall wake no more. "And yet,' he added, after a pause, "'tis a monstrous deed to destroy one so lovely. Psha! away with such weak thoughts, or they might unnerve my hand; 'tis but one blow, and the deed is accomplished and my revenge gratified. Thus then let her die, thus perish Omelia, the sepoy's daughter."

As the miscreant thus spoke, he raised the dagger to strike the fatal blow, but ere his hand could descend, Omelia started up in the bed, and grasping his arm with more than woman's strength, so took the ruffian by surprise, that the deadly weapon fell nervously from his hand, the intrepid girl seized it in a moment, and plunging it into his side inflicted a frightful wound, from which the blood streamed copiously.

"Powers of darkness, I am slain," cried the villain, with a fearful look, as he staggered from the spot towards the door, "but to be thus defeated by a woman; oh, curses, eternal curses light upon you for this!"

Pressing his hand upon the wound in order to stop the effusion of blood as well as he could, the guilty wretch staggered from the room, and Omelia having heard him with difficulty descend the stairs, fell upon her knees, and fervently poured forth her thanks to heaven for her extraordinary preservation from the awful death that was intended her.

CHAPTER CIV.

A FEARFUL TRAGEDY.

Hardly venturing to believe in the reality of the extraordinary and startling event that had taken place, and the intrepidity of her own conduct, Omelia, who had heard the outer door close, went to the window, and then beheld Kotah staggering from the house across the garden, bleeding profusely and appearing ready to sink every moment, and she then felt satisfied that there was no farther danger, and she therefore did not think it necessary to alarm the inmates of the house, but to wait till the morning before she informed them of what had taken place.

She was too much excited, however, to think of again retiring to rest, and again seating herself by the window, she abandoned herself to the thoughts which this exciting adventure, and her extraordinary and providential escape from the awful and untimely death that was intended her, naturally occasioned.

She felt astonished at her own courage

and presence of mind, and she could hardly persuade herself that she had not been labouring under the delusion of some fearful dream, but the blood stains on the floor quickly convinced her of the startling fact, and she could never be sufficiently grateful for her truly miraculous preservation.

That the wound she had inflicted on the miscreant Kotah would prove mortal she had very little doubt, and thus had she fortunately been enabled to rid herself of one of her most dangerous enemies, and that too at the very moment when he had imagined the accomplishment of his atrocious design certain.

She awaited the arrival of morning with some impatience, but continued to watch from the window that she might be prepared should any fresh danger threaten. But nothing occurred to alarm her or excite her suspicions, and she became more confident.

At length daylight dawned in the eastern horizon, and shortly afterwards she heard the persons in the house stirring, and having succeeded in composing herself after the extraordinary night of adventure and excitement she had experienced, she quitted the chamber, and made her way to the room in which she expected to find Mr. Sinclair and his lady.

They expressed their surprise at seeing her so early, and noticing the agitation of her manner they eagerly inquired the cause. Omelia proceeded to inform them, and their astonishment as she did so may be readily imagined.

"Good God!" exclaimed Mrs. Sinclair, when Omelia had concluded, "can this be possible? Surely, Omelia, your disordered imagination, under the influence of sleep, must have deceived you in some strange dream."

"Ah, no," replied our heroine, "it was no dream, and I have sufficient proof that it was not. This dagger, still wet with the villain's blood, will convince you."

She then produced the deadly weapon with which Kotah had intended to accomplish his monstrous design, and Mr. and Mrs Sinclair's astonishment increased, for they could no longer doubt the truth of that which Omelia had related.

"The miscreant," said Mr. Sinclair, "to think that I should unknowingly harbour him. But I had lately began to suspect him, and kept a strict watch on his conduct. But where can I find language sufficiently powerful to express my admiration of your unexampled and courageous conduct, Omelia, by which you preserved your own life and probably that of many others."

"It was the merciful interposition of providence that enabled me to do so," replied our heroine, "and I can never be sufficiently grateful for it. But it is necessary that we should endeavour to ascertain whether the wounded man still lives and has been able to leave the place, although I think it is scarcely possible."

"We will examine the garden and see if we can discover any traces of him," said Mr. Sinclair, "for should he live, he must be secured in order to prevent him from doing any further mischief."

To this Mrs. Sinclair and Omelia agreed, and having summoned two or three of his servants Mr. Sinclair, accompanied by his wife and our heroine, immediately quitted the house, and entering the garden, proceeded in their search, in the direction which Omelia pointed out, as the one which the wounded man had taken, though she had no occasion to do so, as it could plainly be traced by the marks of blood upon the earth.

These they had followed for some short distance across the garden, when a low moaning sound, as if proceeding from some person in great agony, smote their ears.

"Ah," exclaimed Mr. Sinclair, "those sounds doubtless proceed from the villain we seek; he still lives."

The groans were repeated, and hastening in the direction from whence they came, which was from among a cluster of trees that grew at the further end of the garden, they beheld the wounded wretch weltering in his blood upon the ground, writhing in agony, and evidently dying.

The expression of his countenance was truly awful, for his savage features were frightfully distorted, and every quivering muscle showed the dreadful agony he was enduring.

The sound of their footsteps as they approached aroused him, and with some difficulty he raised his head, and fixed his eyes, now glazed and filmy with the approach of death, upon them, especially Omelia, with an expression which was truly appalling to behold, then he clenched his teeth and groaned again in the intense agony of his mental and bodily feelings.

In spite of his monstrous character, Omelia could not thus behold him in all the horror of his last moments without feeling for him some degree of pity, and even Mr. Sinclair and his wife shuddered, for nothing could be more truly fearful than his appearance at that moment.

"Wretched, guilty man," said Mr. Sinclair, "a just though terrible retribution has overtaken you in the midst of your crimes. It is evident that you have but a few moments to live, let then those be passed in penitence."

A still more frightful expression of rage bitter mockery, and deadly vengeance passed over the features of the dying man, as Mr. Sinclair gave utterance to these words, and after several convulsive and ineffectual efforts he said, in a voice, the awful tones of which made all who heard him shudder.

"Penitence—bah! the cant of fools, the cant of the hated Feringhee; Kotah scorns it, and breathes his dying malediction upon the head of the accursed girl by whose hand his life-blood flows. But beware all of ye, for hear me while I swear that my death will not go unavenged. Curse ye—curse ye all!"

He fixed a terrible look upon them as he gave utterance to these words, and shook his clenched fist with fiendish malice, then his body writhed again with agony, one more fearful lengthened groan escaped him. It was his last—his head fell back upon the earth, and the guilty wretch had ceased to exist.

Omelia and her companions gazed at the ghastly corpse for a few minutes with a feeling of awe which they could not resist, then Mr. Sinclair having given the necessary instructions to his servants to remove it, and to see to its interment without delay, they returned to the house, deeply impressed with the awful scene they had witnessed.

"The poor wretch has paid the penalty of his crimes," remarked Mr. Sinclair, "and we have nothing more to fear from his guilty machinations."

"True," replied Mrs. Sinclair, "and I can never cease to congratulate Omelia on her narrow escape from the dagger of the murderer, which was entirely owing to her own courage and remarkable presence of mind. The hatred which the villain bore towards her must have been most inveterate."

"It was," said our heroine, "and I will explain the cause of it."

She did so, and Mr. Sinclair and his lady listened to her with the deepest interest and attention, and again congratulated her on her miraculous escape, which Omelia duly acknowledged.

"But," observed Mrs. Sinclair, after a few moments reflection, "the dying threats which Kotah held out to us, have made a painful impression upon me, and filled my mind with strange apprehensions of some secret danger, which I cannot conquer."

"Heed them not," returned her husband, "for I do not consider them worthy of a second of serious thought."

"Pardon me, sir," remarked Omelia, "but I fear they require more serious consideration than you seem to imagine, and I fully participate in the fears expressed by Mrs. Sinclair. These are times in which no European is safe an hour; the death of Kotah will probably soon become known to the rebels, and the manner in which he was connected with them may raise such a feeling of revenge among them, that might prove dangerous to yourself and your family. I would have you be on your guard, for you may have secret enemies even among your own servants."

"I thank you for your advice Omelia," said Mr. Sinclair, "although I really cannot share in the presentiments of yourself and my wife. Providence has hitherto protected us, and I sincerely trust that it will continue to do so."

Omelia heartily responded to that wish, although she felt far from satisfied or easy upon the subject, and she could not banish the dying words of Kotah from her memory.

The startling adventure of the previous night, and the death of Kotah, served them to converse upon for some time, and caused no little excitement among the domestics, many of whom Omelia could not help viewing with some degree of suspicion, although Mr. Sinclair and his wife appeared to place every confidence in them.

In the course of the day her new friends questioned our heroine as to her future plans, at the same time expressing the deepest interest in her welfare, and requesting that she would make their house her home.

"Oh," said Omelia, with honest fervour, "I am certain my dear friends—for such I may now take the liberty of calling you—you will believe me when I assure you how sensible I am of this kindness, towards me a complete stranger, but indeed I cannot avail myself of it. It is impossible for me to remain here, with the terrible uncertainty on my mind as to the fate of Edward Stanley. Could I but learn that, even though it should be all that my worst fears have suggested, I might learn to resign myself to it, but this state of suspense is worse, far worse, more torturing than the most terrible certainty."

"True," coincided Mr. Sinclair, "and I can properly appreciate your feelings, though I trust that your fears may yet turn out to be erroneous. But what course do you mean to adopt?"

"My mind is made up to one, and one only," answered our heroine, "and that is to endeavour to discover what has become of Lieutenant Stanley, for which purpose it will be necessary for me to take again to the wanderer's life, and to expose myself to many dangers, but I fear them not, should I discover that he has indeed fallen by the hands of these savage sepoys, my future life shall be devoted to one object, namely to avenge his death in the blood of the monsters, who now spread misery and desolation wherever they approach."

"It is a bold and romantic idea, and one fraught with the most imminent danger," observed Mr. Sinclair, "and I would fain endeavour to persuade you to abandon it."

Omelia shook her head mournfully.

"Ah, no!" she said, "my determination is fixed, and I should consider myself unfaithful to the vows I have so often uttered could I do as you advise, sir. Besides I cannot help at times encouraging the hope that I might be successful, and should I be so, oh, how amply should I be rewarded for all the care and anxiety it may cause me, or the troubles or the dangers to which I may be exposed."

"Heroic girl," said Mr. Sinclair, "how much do I admire the noble and dauntless spirit that guides you in all your actions, and no one—short even as our acquaintance has been—can be more anxious for your future happiness than myself. But if you are determined to adopt the course you have described, I must request that at least you will not leave us for some days, till you have quite recovered yourself from the severe trials you have lately experienced.

This request was seconded by Mrs. Sinclair, in the most persuasive manner, and Omelia could not but yield, although it was very reluctantly that she did so, for every hour seemed an age that she delayed commencing her wild and adventurous expedition.

That day passed tediously away, for neither Omelia or her friends could get rid of the excitement which the daring attempt of the villain Kotah, and his subsequent death had caused them, and our heroine on taking leave of Mr. and Mrs. Sinclair for the night, and retiring to her chamber, felt a heavy depression of spirits which she found it impossible to conquer.

A sensation of terror came over her when she looked around the room, and at times she could almost imagine that the tall form of the miscreant Kotah stood before her, and that she beheld his dark and savage features scowling upon her with that fiendish expression of malice, which was so appalling to contemplate.

Sometimes, to such a pitch of terror was she excited that she almost trembled to be alone, and regretted that she had declined the proposition which Mrs. Sinclair had made her, namely, that the ayah, who had been appointed to attend upon her, should sleep with her; but she chided herself for giving way to what she could not but consider almost childish weakness, and endeavoured to arouse herself out of it though it was with but little success.

With the hope of being able to divert her thoughts to other subjects, she walked to the window, but the night was dark and gloomy, and anything but calculated to cheer her spirits, and she sat wrapped in the most melancholy meditation for some time, and without being able to make up her mind to retire to rest.

The most fearful forebodings of she scarcely knew what, continued to haunt and torture her, and she was often worked up to such a state of dread that she was half inclined to return to the room in which she had left Mr. and Mrs. Sinclair, fearing that something had happened to them, but the thought that she might excite ridicule if not censure by so doing, prevented her, and she returned to her seat, and endeavoured to conquer the strange feelings that had come over her, but to no purpose.

And now her thoughts wandered to Stanley, and most agonising were the feelings that came over her, when she reflected upon all the melancholy and painful circumstances that had again separated them, this time, she feared, and with too much reason, for ever.

"Oh, it would be madness, worse than madness," she soliloquised, "to encourage the hope that he still lives, or that we shall ever meet again. Alas, no, terrible has doubtless been the fate he has met with at the hands of the merciless wretches who had him in their power, and I now feel that life is not only hateful to me but insupportable. Oh, why was I not permitted to perish with him? Dear Stanley, I cannot survive your loss; my heart must surely break, and death put a period to the existence of the poor Indian girl whose every wish, whose every hope, whose every happiness was centered in you."

Scalding tears chased each other down her cheeks as she gave utterance to these words, and convulsive sobs agitated her bosom. She remained for some minutes silent, and seemed completely lost to everything but the utter and unconquerable misery of her own feelings.

Suddenly she started, for she could almost imagine that she heard a low moaning sound, as if from some person in pain, and which seemed to proceed from the room below in which she had left Mr. and Mrs. Sinclair, and who she believed had not yet retired to rest, and she walked to the door, and opening it, listened attentively, but all was perfectly silent, and she returned into the room.

"How foolish I am," she said, "to thus unnecessarily alarm myself. I must have been mistaken, and the sound I heard could only have been the sighing of the wind. Yet it so strongly resembled a human voice that I can hardly persuade myself to the contrary. Psha! how weak I am to-night. I am ashamed of myself, and must not give way to it."

She resumed her seat, and endeavoured to rally her spirits, but with little or no effect, and thus she remained for some time longer, and almost feared to move or to look around her.

At length, forming a resolution to banish these dismal and painful feelings, and to retire to rest, she arose and locked the door, and then without extinguishing the light or stopping to undress herself, she stretched her limbs upon the bed, and endeavoured to compose herself to sleep.

Still the same feeling of doubt and uneasiness pursued her imagination, and rendered her sleep disturbed. Every now and then, half sleeping, half waking, strange and confused noises seemed to buzz and murmur in her ears, and at times she could almost have sworn that she heard half stifled cries of agony, followed by the voices of several men.

But in spite of all this, she endeavoured to persuade herself that she must have been mistaken, and again sunk off to sleep, but only experienced dreams of the most painful and fearful nature.

How long she had continued in this state it matters not, but the loud sound of fire-arms, proceeding from below, awoke her, and now thoroughly convinced that the fears and misgivings she had previously entertained were not without foundation, and that some danger threatened, she sprang from the bed, and was at first so bewildered and alarmed that she knew not how to act, or what to do for the best.

She ventured to silently open the room door, and stepping on to the landing, she listened with breathless attention and anxiety, and was too soon painfully convinced that the worst apprehensions she had entertained were being realised, and that some terrible work of slaughter was at that time taking place, for groans and cries of agony, mingled with the clashing of swords, the trampling of

many feet, and the shouts of mens' voices in deadly malice, and exultation, distinctly met her ears, and left no further room for doubt upon her mind, and her agitation and excitement at such a moment of terrible danger may be imagined.

She was completely at a loss what to do, how to escape, and defend herself, for she was rendered completely powerless, and her fate seemed to be inevitable.

The noise—which proceeded from two or three of the rooms below—increased, and ever and anon a piercing shriek in a female voice, followed by coarse oaths, and triumphant and scornful laughter, too plainly told the frightful tragedy that was taking place, and Omelia even partly forgot her own dangerous situation in her fears for Mr. and Mrs. Sinclair and their relations.

Distracted, and scarcely conscious as to what she did, our heroine returned to her chamber, and looked around in the wild hope of discovering either some means of defending herself or effecting her escape, but it was all in vain, nothing of the kind presented itself, and for a minute or two she stood bewildered, and wrung her hands in the utter misery and excitement of her feelings.

Then she rushed to the window as the thought occurred to her that she might probably by that means be able to make her escape by descending into the garden, but there her hopes were doomed to be sadly disappointed, for she beheld the garden half filled with armed men, among whom were several of the male domestics of Mr. Sinclair, thus clearly showing the base act of treachery which had goaded them on, and realising the dying threats of the villain Kotah.

The object of the wretches was evidently plunder as well as revenge, for the ground was strewed with every description of valuable article, and numerous others were every moment being added to the ill-gotten booty, whilst demoniacal shouts of triumph and revenge rent the air.

Transfixed to the spot, Omelia gazed in wild despair at all that was taking place, and giving herself up entirely as lost, for to avoid the fate which at present threatened her, seemed to be utterly impossible, and the terrible feelings that agitated her breast may be far better imagined than we can possibly describe them.

But after all the dangers she had so fearlessly encountered and surmounted, to perish thus was almost too fearful, too agonising to contemplate, and for the time being all her wonted courage, energy, and presence of mind entirely forsook her, and her faculties, in fact, seemed to be suspended.

But fearful shrieks, accompanied by oaths, laughter, and threats, at length aroused her, and drew her attention to the place from which they proceeded, her horror and expectation being wrought up to the highest and most insupportable pitch.

Not an instant was she kept in suspense, and dreadful indeed were her worst fears realised.

Pierced and goaded by the swords and bayonets of the savage monsters, and the blood streaming from many a gaping wound, the brother of Mr. Sinclair and his unfortunate wife—who was a very beautiful woman—both half naked, and exhibiting many other frightful signs of the brutal outrages that had been committed against them, were driven from the house into the garden, there to meet with the horrible fate which the remorseless and sanguinary wretches had resolved to inflict upon them.

The hair of the hapless lady was flying loose and dishevelled about her neck and shoulders, and the expression of horror, agony and despair that was exhibited in her pale and ghastly countenance was truly frightful to look upon.

The appearance of her husband was not less appalling than that of his wife, but he was silent, though every shriek that escaped her, as some fresh cruelty, which only the malice of fiends could conceive, was inflicted on her, seemed to have a maddening effect upon him, and to pierce him to the heart.

In vain the wretched, ill-fated woman clasped her hands vehemently together, and with looks of anguish which might have moved even the most flinty heart to pity, sued for mercy, such heart-rending appeals were only met by the most brutal mockery, and some fresh act of cruelty and indignity, and the more that she and her husband seemed to suffer, the greater became the exultation of the atrocious miscreants, to whom pity was an entire stranger.

Omelia gazed appalled, for she anticipated from that which she witnessed, the fate that awaited herself, and which there were not the slightest means for her to avoid. And awful indeed was the scene that she was doomed to witness.

The unfortunate victims were each bound to a tree, and the dreadful work of mutilation commenced and was proceeded with with a refinement of cruelty which it would be sickening and almost impossible to describe, while the shrieks of the hapless sufferers rent the air, and were answered only by the taunts and shouts of their tormentors.

After this had lasted several minutes, and the unfortunate gentleman and his wife were so mutilated and disfigured that they scarcely bore any resemblance to human beings, the husband was first murdered in the most barbarous manner before the appalled eyes of his wife, who was then literally hacked to pieces by the swords and knives of the monsters, who then hurried to the perpetration of fresh atrocities.

Omelia moved away from the window, unable to witness more; the blood chilled in her veins, and madness and despair seized upon her brain, for it was impossible to think of the dreadful doom which awaited her, and from which there appeared at present no possible means of her escaping, with any other feelings than those of the most intense horror.

The dreadful confusion and noise inside and outside the house, continued unabated, and still our heroine remained fixed as a statue to the spot and completely bewildered, terrified, and powerless to act.

And now another appalling shriek smote her ears, and directly afterwards Omelia heard footsteps ascending the stairs to the chamber in which she was, and anticipating the worst, that the murderers were seeking her out, and her doom was at hand, the most insupportable and indescribable feeling of horror came over her, and convulsed her limbs.

Hastily she rushed to the room door, and secured it in the best manner she could, and the next moment she heard some one attempting to open it, and it then to her affrighted imagination seemed that there were only a few minutes between her and eternity.

Again she looked for an instant towards the window, half resolved to throw herself from it, and rather to meet with an immediate death than one of lingering torture; but a voice outside the door startled her, and partly removed the terrors that had taken such powerful hold on her senses.

It was that of Onada, the ayah.

"Pray open the door, Omelia," she said, in an agitated voice; "it is I, Onada. Quick—quick, on your life."

Our heroine waited to hear no more, but opening the door the ayah, with looks wild and disordered, and bleeding from a wound that she had received, staggered into the room, and grasping the wrist of Omelia, fixed upon her a look in which horror, disgust and pity were blended, while the latter was too much agitated to speak or to put any questions to her.

"Oh, Omelia," at length the ayah ejaculated, in a voice, and with an expression of features that showed the dreadful state of excitement to which her feelings were wrought, "what a night of horror is this, how frightful is the scene I have just witnessed. We have been betrayed by several of the servants, who were the friends of Kotah, a number of the bloodthirsty sepoys hold possession of the house, and already a most inhuman slaughter has taken place; poor Mr. Sinclair and his lady."

"Ah, what of them?" eagerly interrogated our heroine, "I tremble to put the question"

"They are both no more," answered Onada, "they were most brutally murdered before my eyes; oh, when I think of it the blood freezes in my veins, and it is impossible, should I be permitted to live, that I can ever banish it from my recollection."

"Are there no means of escape?" eagerly demanded Omelia.

"Alas, no," answered the ayah, "the wretches have surrounded the house, and it would be madness to attempt to force our way through them."

"Oh what then is to be done?"

"The only chance we have of saving our lives," replied the ayah, "is by endeavouring to conceal ourselves until the murderers have quitted the house."

"Know you of any place where we can do so?" asked our heroine.

"Yes," said Onada, "follow me, quick, for another instant probably and the miscreants will be here."

Omelia nodded assent, but said not a word, and Onada, having opened the door, and listened a moment, then beckoning to the former to follow, she led the way along a winding gallery on which the chamber and several other rooms opened, and passing into a remote corner at the farther end, stopped at the foot of a ladder, and holding the lamp which she had brought with her above her head, Omelia perceived a trap door, which opened on to the roof.

"The villains may probably not think of this," observed Onada, "and if so, we may yet be able to escape from their murderous hands. From the roof, too, we can see all that passes outside, and watch our opportunity to quit the house without danger. Come—there is not a moment to be lost."

She quickly ascended the ladder as she spoke, our heroine following, the trap being unfastened, they emerged on to the roof, without difficulty, securing the trap-door after them.

CHAPTER CV.

THE FEARFUL SITUATION.—THE RESULT OF THE ADVENTURE.

They had scarcely got on to the roof, when they could plainly hear the voices of the ruffians as they ascended the stairs towards the chamber they had just quitted, and where they no doubt expected to find Omelia, and they trembled with the greatest suspense to hear whether they would prosecute their search further, but to their great relief they did not, and they heard them retrace their steps down the stairs, uttering exclamations of rage and disappointment.

Stretching themselves at length upon the roof—which was a flat one—to escape observation, they watched eagerly the proceedings of the sepoys in the gardens below.

The scene was one of the greatest and most painful excitement. The wretches it seemed had completed the work of slaughter, and the horribly mutilated bodies of several of their unfortunate victims, whom they had brought from the house strewed the ground in different directions, many of the murderers exulting over the inhuman work of their hands, while others were busily occupied in removing every portable article of value, and triumphing in the rich booty they had obtained.

Omelia felt her heart sicken, and she was filled with the most torturing feelings of horror and regret, when she thought of the dreadful fate which had befallen so many innocent persons, particularly those from whom she had received so many acts of kindness, namely, Mr. and Mrs. Sinclair.

"At present," observed Onada, "we are safe here; "the villains have evidently no suspicion that we are here, but doubtless imagine that we have by some means or other contrived to escape from the house."

"Would that they would retire," said Omelia, "for our situation is still a most critical one, while they remain here. Ah, what mean those shouts?"

Terrific yells and shouts were heard, and the next moment a number of sepoys rushed from the house, several of them bearing lighted torches, and all exhibiting the utmost excitement.

Presently dense clouds of smoke were seen to rise from some of the lower rooms, and being quickly followed by a crackling sound, and a lurid reflection showed too plainly what had taken place, and completed the horrors of that dreadful night's work.

"The inhuman monsters, not contented with the innocent blood they have so remorselessly shed, have fired the house," said Onada, "and the only alternative that is left to us, is either to resign ourselves into their hands or perish in the flames."

"The latter death," returned Omelia, "even frightful as it is, would be preferable to the fate to which these fiends in human form would consign us. Still we must not abandon ourselves entirely to despair, but trust to the infinite mercy of providence, who surely will not fail to interpose to save us."

"Alas," remarked Onada, "our situation is a most awful and desperate one; the flames spread rapidly, and must soon reach the place where we stand. Oh, how terrible is it to perish by such a horrible fate as this."

"Be firm," said our heroine, "and we shall yet be saved."

But although Omelia maintained her fortitude and presence of mind in the most remarkable manner, she could not conceal from herself the frightful danger by which they were surrounded, and the very faint hopes there were of their being able to escape from it, especially as the villains remained near, and exulted in the monstrous work of their hands.

The flames spread rapidly from room to room, and carried by the wind, which at the time blew briskly, threatened soon to reach the roof, and the smoke was almost suffocating.

"It is madness to remain here," said our heroine, "without at least making an effort to save ourselves. Could we reach the lower part of the house, we might surely, in the confusion which at present prevails among the miscreants make our escape by a back way, and once beyond the premises, we could conceal ourselves till, having witnessed the completion of the work of destruction, they shall have taken their departure."

"Alas," replied Onada, "I fear 'tis quite hopeless: I see no other prospect but a frightful death before us. But at any rate, desperate even though it is, we will at least make the attempt."

"Lead the way then," said our heroine, "you are better acquainted with the premises than I am, and I will follow."

The flames had now reached to a fearful height, and the heat was most intense. Our heroine and Onada stood upright on the roof and cast an anxious look below, and as they did so they were distinctly seen by the wretches whom they had so much cause to dread, and who set up a frightful yell of demoniacal exultation on recognising them, and immediately the contents of several rifles were discharged at them, but fortunately without having the effect which the villains desired.

The same instant Omelia and her companion disappeared in the midst of the smoke, and the sepoys probably thinking that the shots had taken effect, rent the air with their shouts of triumph, and watched the terrible work of destruction with the greatest satisfaction.

In the meantime, Onada and our heroine had made their way from the roof, and descending the ladder, the former took the direction which led to a back staircase, and which she was in hopes that the destructive element had not yet reached, but the thick volumes of suffocating smoke which met them as they proceeded, soon convinced them to the contrary, and they were almost overpowered.

They reached the staircase by which they had hoped they would be able to escape with much difficulty, but here their farther progress in that direction was stopped, for they found it in flames from the top to the bottom, and as all escape appeared impossible, the shocking fate which awaited them was made too awfully apparent.

Scarcely knowing what she did, and almost blinded and suffocated with the smoke, Omelia endeavoured to retrace her steps to the chamber which she had occupied—thinking that if it was not too late, and the flames had not obtained too great an ascendancy in that part of the building they might make their escape by the window—and called upon Onada to follow her, but no answer being returned, she looked anxiously back, but missed the poor girl, and, with a feeling of horror which it is useless to seek to describe, she concluded that she had fallen, overcome by the smoke, and that she must consequently perish in the flames, and her own fate also appeared to be almost certain, although she determined to make a desperate effort to avert it.

Scarcely knowing whither she went, she struggled on through dense clouds of smoke, and the crackling and roaring of the angry flames, and amid the noise of falling ruins, but she found that it was utterly impossible to reach the chamber, and wound up to a complete pitch of desperation, she tried to regain the ladder which led to the roof of the building, although with what chance or prospect of escape that way she knew not, for by that time nearly the whole of the house was completely enveloped in flames.

Never had Omelia, in all the narrow escapes from death which she had experienced during her eventful career, been placed in so awful and dangerous a situation as she was at present, and had she not been possessed of the most extraordinary nerve she could not have struggled against it so resolutely.

But she struggled on with a determination not to perish without at least using every exertion that it is possible for human nature to do under the most appalling circumstances to save her life, and at length she found herself at the foot of the ladder, and the next instant standing once more on the roof of the building, which the flames had now partly reached.

She looked down into the garden through the smoke and beheld that the coast was quite clear, the sepoys having entirely disappeared. But what was to become of her? there on the roof of the burning building, without any one to offer to render her the least assistance, even if it had been in their power, all possibility of her escaping from the dreadful fate which threatened her seemed to be at an end.

She wrung her hands in despair, and for a

few moments stood bewildered, not knowing what to do. But suddenly she remembered having seen a tall tree, which grew near one side of the building, which the flames had scarcely yet touched, and some of the highest branches of which completely overhung that portion of the roof, and as the thought struck her that by that means she might probably be able to descend to the garden in safety, she uttered an exclamation of renewed hope and made her way towards it.

She could reach one of the branches without much difficulty, and having again looked below, to see that there was no one watching her, although it was not likely that there should be so, and having committed herself to the care of providence, she with some exertion caught hold of one portion of the branch with a firm grasp of both hands, and swinging herself off the roof, and for a few seconds, till she could get foothold on one of the lower boughs, she hung suspended in the air, and at a sufficient height from the ground, that if the branch had broken with the weight of her body, and she had fallen, her death would have been all but certain; but as it was she descended without much difficulty, and alighted safely on terra firma. There, almost overpowered with her emotions, at such a miraculous escape, she sunk on her knees, and fervently poured forth her feelings of gratitude to a Supreme Power.

Having somewhat recovered herself, she moved from the spot, and had scarcely done so, when the roof of the burning building fell in with with a terrific crash, and clouds of smoke, sparks, and flames shot up into the sky, and spread for some distance around, imparting a grand but awful aspect to the scene, which no one could contemplate without feelings of the deepest emotion and excitement.

Omelia cast one fearful look towards the still burning ruins, thought of the shocking fate of Mr. and Mrs. Sinclair and their brother and sister—not forgetting poor Onada—with feelings of the deepest horror and anguish, and then slowly and sadly bent her way from the awful scene of destruction, having first secured a sword, which she found lying upon the ground, and which she placed in her belt by her side, determined to use it with her usual intrepidity, should she have occasion to do so.

—

CHAPTER CVI.

THE ADVENTURES OF OMELIA.

It must now have been near midnight, and all around was hushed in profound silence, save the wind, which blew in fitful gusts, murmuring rather dismally among the foliage, but coming pleasant to the senses of poor Omelia after the intense heat and suffocating atmosphere to which she had just been exposed.

With a brain bewildered, and a sad and foreboding heart—for still more terrible, if possible, were the circumstances in which she was now placed—she crossed the garden and walked to some short distance from the scene of the late dreadful events, without knowing whither to go or what course to take, but at length she paused for a few minutes to collect her thoughts, and to look around her.

The red glare of the reflection from the conflagration still lighted up the sky, and clouds of mingled smoke and sparks ascended from the ruins of that elegant and hospitable dwelling in which Omelia had lately found a friendly shelter, but those amiable beings who had owned it were no more, and so sudden and so dreadful was the fate which in a few short hours had overtaken them, that it seemed more like some fearful dream than an actual occurrence.

As these reflections stole over her mind the anguish of Omelia was almost too great for utterance, and she could not resist the tears that gushed to her eyes in fervent sympathy and regret to the memory of those who for their excellent qualities of head and heart she had been so well prepared to honour and esteem.

She shuddered with horror at the recollection of the frightful tragedy, and sincerely did she invoke the curses of heaven on the heads of the inhuman wretches, who could be guilty of, and delight in the perpetration of such enormities, and she blushed to think that they were her own countrymen.

"Oh, when will those atrocities cease to disgrace my native land, and fill the world with shame and unmitigated horror?" she soliloquised; "when will the miscreants be aroused from their dream of crime, and cease to revel in the innocent blood of their fellow-creatures? But justice must and will at last assert its power, and most assuredly terrible will be the retribution that will overtake them. Alas, this is another addition to the misery of the fate which pursues me, and seems to mock my sufferings. And it seems my fate to bring misery and destruction to all who have the misfortune in any way to become connected with me. I am a curse to my fellow creatures, and therefore would it be a mercy if I were no more. And should I perish, deprived of all that I loved and cherished in life, who then will there be to drop the tear of pity to the memory, and to pray for the repose of the soul of the humble Omelia? Oh, heaven, what a poor friendless outcast wretch I am."

Her tears flowed still faster as these melancholy expressions escaped her lips, and her bosom swelled and heaved with the power of her emotions.

Never had she so keenly felt the loneliness and misery of her situation, and the longer she reflected upon all the dismal circumstances by which she was surrounded, the more did she abandon herself to despair. In fact, in whichever way she directed her thoughts not the least ray of hope appeared to gladden her; nothing whatever to relieve the insupportable horrors of her fate.

"But oh, what have I done," she sighed, "that I should be thus constantly doomed to suffer? Surely no conduct of mine can have merited so cruel a destiny as that I have experienced."

She paused, but still continued to meditate mournfully, and the solemnity of the hour, and the profound silence that pervaded everything did but serve to increase the gloom and anguish of her thoughts and feelings.

The spot on which she stood, was an elevated plot of ground, and which commanded an uninterrupted view of the country on a clear day or night, for miles around, abounding in scenery of the most beautiful and picturesque description, intermingled with all that is wild and romantic in nature. But at that time glowing beneath the lurid reflection from the fire, it had a remarkable but awful effect, and Omelia could not gaze upon it without experiencing the deepest emotion, and the longer she gazed, so far from abating, her misery and regret increased.

It was indeed painful to contemplate the now smouldering ruins of that dwelling which but so short a time since was so remarkable for elegance and taste in all its details, and the inmates of which enjoyed all that peace, and happiness, and prosperity to which their numerous virtues so justly entitled them. Terrible was the scene of destruction and desolation, and Omelia shuddered as she viewed it, and her heart sickened as she thought of the dreadful crimes such wretches were hourly committing, and of which this atrocious outrage was so appalling a sample.

Again she invoked the heaviest maledictions of offended heaven upon the guilty heads of the assassins, and then became quite lost in the agonising thoughts that held supreme possession of her breast.

The cruel fates seemed to have conspired against her, and she racked her brain to no purpose to endeavour to devise the means of extricating herself from the numerous and apparently insurmountable difficulties by which she was surrounded, and the more she tried to do so, the greater became her perplexity.

Deprived of every friend, destitute, homeless, alone in the world, what would become of her? To whom could she look for sympathy and assistance, how could she exist? Indeed of what value to her was existence? And when she considered the utter hopelessness of her condition, and anticipated the miseries and sufferings that were but too probably yet in store for her, she could not but even envy the fate—horrible though it was—of Mr. and Mrs. Sinclair, and the other unfortunate victims, for all their troubles in this world, at any rate, were now at an end; and to such a pitch of excitement was she wrought by this thought, that, in the distraction of her feelings, she was almost driven to lay violent hands on herself.

But at length the necessity of adopting some course or other, which might help to relieve her from her present difficulties, aroused her from the train of melancholy thoughts that had for some time engrossed her mind, and casting her eyes dismally around, with a heavy heart she slowly moved from the spot, totally regardless of the way she took, for all seemed alike to her, and the fortitude for which she was usually distinguished under difficulties of the most trying description, having almost forsaken her.

Nothing could possibly be more deplorable or disheartening than the condition in which the unfortunate wanderer now found herself, and it was no wonder that she should abandon herself to the most dismal forebodings and apprehensions. She had, she was well aware, to travel many dreary miles before she could reach some military station, which was her only chance of receiving assistance and protection, and how she was to exist on the road—unless it should be her good fortune to meet with some charitable persons, who could sympathise with her—she knew not, and that reflection was sufficient to make her shrink appalled from the task she had to undergo, and to destroy that energy which she had hitherto exhibited on so many extraordinary and trying occasions.

She now felt the melancholy death of poor Onada more severely, for she might have acted as a guide on the tedious journey, and, at any rate, would have formed a most agreeable companion, and have served in some measure to alleviate if she could not have entirely dissipated the troubles and anxieties that beset her mind.

But even all the startling and dreadful events that had so recently taken place, and the torturing reflections to which they naturally gave rise, could not banish from her thoughts the unfortunate Edward Stanley, and in vain did she seek to encourage the smallest gleam of hope that he still survived, or that they would ever meet again. The circumstances under which they were separated, it seemed to her would render it next to madness to entertain any such idea, and which could only end in the most bitter disappointment.

The vows of affection they had so often exchanged with one another, were as fresh and vivid in her memory at that moment as if they had been but just uttered, and when she thought of the manly and faithful heart which had throbbed for her alone, but which had doubtless now ceased to beat for ever, the agony of her grief exceeded all bounds, and it was in vain that she endeavoured to find the least degree of consolation.

Yet amidst all her grief she felt that she could never rest until she should have been enabled to ascertain the fate which had befallen him; and it was that idea which made her cling to life, and to exert herself to the utmost, in spite of all the troubles and vicissitudes she might have to encounter, to accomplish her wishes.

To add to the misery and depression of her spirits, the night was particularly gloomy and cheerless for the season of the year, and everything upon which her eye rested seemed to wear an aspect in accordance with the weather, and was calculated to make even those who had no trouble on their mind wretched. The bright moon never once deigned to peep from behind the black masses of clouds that obscured it, and not a single star was to be seen, whilst the wind which had before, as has been stated, only blown in fitful gusts, had now risen to a complete hurricane, sweeping everything before it, and rendering the night even still more wretched than it would otherwise have been.

Omelia, however, took but little heed of it, and walked slowly on wrapped in gloomy meditation, until she found herself when least aware of it, near the entrance to a jungle, which she had wished to avoid, as there were many dangers to apprehend, which she was not prepared to encounter.

While she still stood hesitating which way to proceed, in the pauses of the wind, she plainly heard footsteps, and the voices of men speaking in her own language proceeding from the jungle.

As they evidently approached nearer, she could distinctly catch some of the words they uttered, and the allusions they made to "the accursed Feringhee," and several other allusions, convinced her that they were enemies, and alarmed at the danger which she had so accidentally and unfortunately fallen into, she fled in a contrary direction, but had not proceeded far when two or three commanding voices called upon her to stop, and hastily looking back, she was terrified on beholding several armed sepoys issuing from the jungle, and making towards her.

This only served to increase her speed, and she hurried on with all the precipitation that a full sense of the danger with which she was threatened would enable her to do, but she had not proceeded far, when several shots were fired after her, but fortunately missed her, although they passed so near her person that it seemed to be quite by a miracle that she escaped.

Again the villains, with fearful oaths and threats, called aloud on her to stop, and again she increased her speed—the more so as she could hear that they were in hot pursuit of her—and at times their hasty footsteps sounded so distinctly in her ears, that she feared they were gaining fast upon her, and that she must fall into their hands, for it seemed almost impossible, after what she had that night undergone, for her to find strength to outstrip them.

However, the more imminent the danger, the greater the necessity for exertion, and Omelia continued to hurry on her flight with a speed which she had never thought she could accomplish, and again a volley was fired after her, from which she received no injury, but which showed the desperate character of the miscreants, and what she might expect from them if she should happen to fall into their power.

From the desire they seemed to have to capture her, and the determination with which they followed up the pursuit, she was half disposed to think that they were some of the men who had done the work of destruction at the house of the ill-fated Mr. and Mrs. Sinclair, and that they had recognised her, and that thought only rendered her the more apprehensive of falling into their power.

She proceeded with unabated speed, until she suddenly came upon the banks of a river, where from their loud shouts of exultation, the sepoys seemed to think that her capture was certain, and they rushed forward with the greatest precipitation to secure her.

Like most Indian females, however, Omelia was an excellent swimmer, and seeing that her liberty, probably her life depended upon that moment, she did not hesitate, but plunged at once into the river, she fortunately being at the narrowest part of it, and swam with all her might towards the opposite side.

She looked back once and saw two or three of the sepoys standing on the bank she had just quitted, and several more in the distance approaching; but on reaching the opposite shore, which she did after much exertion, they had disappeared, and it seemed, therefore, that not feeling disposed to ford the river, they had abandoned the pursuit, and once more, for the present, at any rate, the intrepid girl was in safety.

She proceeded a short distance from the river, when quite exhausted with the fatigue

E. WHYMPER. Sc.

which she had already undergone, and feeling a deathly faintness come over her, which she could not resist, she sunk upon the earth in a state of insensibility.

————

CHAPTER CVII.

SUFFERINGS AND PRIVATIONS.

In this state of exhaustion and unconsciousness Omelia must have remained some time, for when she again revived, the sun had risen, and was already high in the heavens, and the face of nature was clothed in its most cheerful and genial smiles, presenting a remarkable contrast to the gloom of the preceding night, that night so full of

No. 53.

fearful adventure to our heroine. It was with much difficulty she arose to her feet, for her clothes which had been saturated from her immersion in the water, had dried upon her in the scorching rays of the sun, and her limbs felt cramped and stiff, while a burning thirst was upon her, and her brain was bewildered and feverish.

She pressed her hands upon her temples, and gazed vacantly about her, not knowing where she was, and for the moment having no clear recollection of what had happened.

The prospect before her, notwithstanding it was gilded by the bright beams of the morning sun, was anything but cheerful, and as far as Omelia could tax her memory, she had no recollection of ever having been in that part of the country before, nor could she form the least idea where she was, or in what direction to proceed with the greatest chance of obtaining that relief of which she stood so much in need.

But at length all the fearful events that had taken place on the previous night flashed upon her memory with the most overwhelming force, and a cold shuddering crept through her veins as it did so, and her natural courage almost abandoned her, when the terrible situation in which she was placed was presented to her imagination in all its darkest colours.

Such thoughts as those which at that moment beset her, were sufficient to drive her to despair, and she felt that it would require all her strength and energy of mind to enable her to bear up against them.

Every horrid feature of the bloody tragedy at the house of the late Mr. and Mrs Sinclair, recurred to her, and again she could imagine that she heard the fiendish shouts and yells of the assassins as they proceeded with their frightful work, and inflicted such inhuman and lingering tortures upon their fellow creatures. Again the fierce flames from the burning building seemed to shoot up around her, death in all its most ghastly terrors seemed to meet her at every turn, and her own escape was so truly wonderful, that it seemed almost impossible.

But from this dismal train of thought she was awakened to the necessity of present and determined action, but the numerous difficulties that presented themselves before her were so great, that she almost shrunk from encountering them, and, in fact, her fortitude had never before been put to so severe a trial, and it seemed as though she must inevitably sink under it, unless she met with some timely relief and assistance.

Exerting herself to the utmost, she moved from the spot, but her limbs trembled, and she had not proceeded to any considerable distance, which occupied her some time in accomplishing, when her strength failed her, her brain turned giddy, and she again sunk powerless upon the parched earth, now burning with the scorching heat of the sun, and totally unable for the present, at any rate, to make the least exertion.

The heat of the sun was intense, and the thirst that was upon Omelia was intolerable, and had the most maddening influence upon her brain, and it being many hours since she had partaken of food, and then but sparingly she also began to feel the gnawings of hunger, so that every horror seemed to accumulate upon her, and she felt a sickly sensation as if of approaching death, such as she had never before experienced.

And in that painfully trying moment, when the termination of her earthly career to her disordered imagination seemed to be rapidly approaching, all the circumstances of her eventful life, particularly the spirit-stirring incidents of the last few months, passed vividly before her mind's eye, as in a panorama, and various and conflicting were the thoughts and feelings that they engendered, exciting pleasure, grief, regret and wonder by turns.

The earlier days of childhood, passed but sadly until taken under the protection of the late Mr. Melville and his wife, and till cheered by the society of the gentle Flora, whose sad fate could never be effaced from her memory; her first meeting with Edward Stanley, and the mutual sentiments of affection that had immediately sprung up between them, the hopes, the doubts, the fears, the trials, vicissitudes, the disappointments they had experienced; the various tests the fidelity and sincerity of their love had been put to, and yet passed through the ordeal triumphantly; the many fearful dangers by which they had so often been surrounded, since the present revolt, and the hair-breadth escapes they had had, all that had occurred to them up to their last fatal separation, arose to her memory, and so powerful was the impression caused by the review of facts so important, and of such vital interest to every feeling of her nature, that her brain became bewildered in the retrospection, and the whole appeared so extraordinary that it surpassed in imagination the wildest conceptions of the novelist, or the delusions of the strangest dream.

"But all is over now," she mournfully soliloquised, "the delusive dream is past; bright hopes so vainly yet so fondly cherished have fled for ever; cloud and sunshine have alternated, expectations have been raised in all their most flattering colours never to be realised, and now the stern, the fearful reality appears, and all is absorbed in gloomy, dark despair, and all the horrors of cruel destiny rush upon me with overwhelming force, and drive me to distraction. For what have I lived, but to be a source of misery to myself and others? And now I find myself alone, abandoned in the wide world like some solitary plant upon a dreary desert, left to the agony of my own maddening thoughts, without one human being to sympathise with me or to care for me. Heaven be merciful to me, and suffer me no longer to linger out a life of misery which has become insupportable."

Again she paused, overcome by her emotions, and her tears flowed fast and unrestrained, but which, however, afforded her some relief.

But the longer she thought of them, the more gloomy and hopeless did their prospects appear to be. Reduced to want, weary with travel, and in a part of the country which was quite unknown to her, and where she could scarcely hope to find any one to relieve her, especially in the present disturbed and dangerous state of affairs, she could see no chance of escaping a horrible death from hunger, and her heart sunk within her at the bare contemplation of such a fate, notwithstanding that life had now become of such little value to her.

"Heaven help me, in this the most dreadful hour of my trial," she ejaculated, in a voice which showed the anguish of mind she was enduring, "oh, why was I reserved for such a fate as that which my mind now pictures, and which I have so much reason to anticipate? Oh, would that I had perished on that fatal night which separated me from Stanley, what a world of misery would it not have saved me?"

She once more supplicated the mercy and protection of the Supreme, and then endeavoured to regain her fortitude, so that she might yet exert herself to proceed on her dreary journey, with the faint hope of meeting with some assistance.

Once more she cast her eyes anxiously around her, and at some distance it appeared to be more sheltered from the rays of the sun, which had now become more intense and overpowering, by shady trees, which grew in abundance about; and that part Omelia was anxious to reach, as she would there, at any rate, be in the shade, which under her present circumstances, would afford her some important relief.

With some difficulty she again arose to her feet, and struggled on a few paces, when she was compelled to pause to rest herself, for her enfeebled limbs could scarcely support her, and there was nothing to raise her depressed spirits, or encourage her to proceed.

Suddenly, however, a strange feeling of hope came over her, and she seemed to possess renewed strength, her footsteps became more firm, her heart appeared lighter, and she walked on with fresh fortitude and resolution.

She had not proceeded far when her eyes were gratified with the sight of a spring, which at that time, and coming upon it so unexpectedly, was far more welcome to her than the greatest treasure she could have received.

The well, or spring, was overshadowed by the wide-spreading branches of two tall and gigantic trees, and near it was a shell, forming an excellent drinking cup, for the thirsty traveller to help himself.

Eager to quench the burning and intolerable thirst that was upon her, Omelia filled the shell, and was about to raise it to her lips, when a fearful thought flashed upon her brain, and it fell from her hands.

She remembered the reports that had been so widely circulated, and generally believed, namely, that many of the public wells had been poisoned by the rebels, and by that means many unfortunate persons had perished; and she hesitated whether or not to run the risk.

"But I can no longer endure this dreadful torture, this intolerable thirst that is upon me," she said; "the pangs of death cannot be worse."

In a moment she refilled the shell, and without any more hesitation raised it to her lips, and hastily quaffed the contents.

Oh, what could be more delicious to the poor girl than that draught? How great was the relief that it instantaneously afforded her. Again and again she drank off the sweet cooling and refreshing water—far more beautiful and grateful, under the circumstances than the choicest wine—and it seemed immediately to re invigorate her, and to inspire her with fresh life.

She sunk on her knees, and having returned her heartfelt thanks to heaven, she resumed her journey with that renewed strength and confidence which even surprised herself.

And thus she continued until she arrived at the spot before alluded to, where the tall trees growing on either side of a narrow road, which their richly clothed branches completely overshadowed, resembled closely one of those pleasant walks to be found in an English park, and afforded a welcome shelter to the weary traveller.

Omelia proceeded a short distance along this shady avenue, when feeling again fatigued, she resolved to rest herself till the more intense heat of the day had subsided, and she could pursue her way with less difficulty and inconvenience.

Having selected a convenient spot, which was a flower-covered mound of earth, beneath one of the largest of the trees, she reclined herself upon it, and endeavoured to obtain that tranquillity, patience, and resignation of which she stood so much in need; but for some time the painful and bewildering thoughts that occupied her, prevented her from doing so, and she felt anxious, doubtful, and uneasy.

At length, however, an irresistible feeling of drowsiness came over her, and having first looked anxiously about to see that there was no immediate danger to apprehend, she resigned herself to that repose which gradually stole upon her, and steeped her senses in temporary forgetfulness of her sorrows.

She was suddenly aroused by an exclamation, and some one shaking her by the shoulder, and looking up, with astonishment and alarm, she beheld the tall figure of a man—whose features were partly concealed from her in shade, from the position in which he stood—standing before her, and apparently much excited at seeing her.

"Gracious powers!" exclaimed the man in a voice of emotion, and every tone of which was familiar to our heroine, and thrilled to her heart; "is it possible that I am so fortunate as to behold you again, and under such extraordinary circumstances. Omelia, unfortunate maiden, whom providence has so miraculously preserved, do you not recollect me?"

Startled by the tones of his voice, and the familiarity with which he pronounced her name, Omelia raised herself on her feet, and gazed anxiously in his countenance; she uttered an exclamation as she did so, and her astonishment and satisfaction may be easily conjectured, when she recognised the features of Abdal.

CHAPTER CVIII.

ABDAL AND OMELIA.

The mingled feelings that agitated the breast of Omelia at this unexpected but welcome meeting, may be imagined, and for a moment or two she was unable to give utterance to them in words, and Abdal was scarcely less excited than herself.

"Oh, Abdal, kind friend," she at length said, "for such I know full well I am permitted to call you, how providential is this meeting, but yet under what melancholy circumstances does it take place. Edward Stanley, my own dear Stanley, tell me, I beseech you, know you anything of him?"

"You are faint and weary, Omelia," replied Abdal, "and require rest and refreshment, and it is fortunate that I can assist you to both. Come we must defer conversation upon subjects so interesting and important to us both till a more fitting opportunity."

"Oh, I pray you, Abdal," said our heroine, with much emotion, to keep me not in suspense. Tell me, if you know, what has become of Lieutenant Stanley? Whether he still lives?"

"Alas, Omelia," answered Abdal, in a voice and with a look of melancholy regret, "I know not, though I trust that he was rescued on the fatal night of the sanguinary engagement with the sepoys, by the dragoons who came up at the critical moment, as I was afterwards informed, and put the miscreants to the rout."

"Ah, can he indeed have been so providentially saved?" ejaculated Omelia, "but I dare not encourage so flattering a hope, which too much reason have I to fear can only end in disappointment. But how did you escape, Abdal?"

"That must I explain hereafter," returned the latter, "come, Omelia, let us not delay, but suffer me at once to conduct you to where you can obtain that assistance of which you stand so much in need. How fortunate it is that I have met you, and that I have the power to relieve you in your present difficulties."

Omelia looked at him with increased astonishment, anxiety, and curiosity.

"Whither would you lead me?" she interrogated, "your sudden and unexpected appearance at a time when I thought myself left entirely alone in the world, has taken me so by surprise that I can scarcely believe the evidence of my senses."

"I wonder not at it," said Abdal, "and my astonishment and gratification; I need scarcely inform you, is equal to your own. Alas, your looks too plainly tell me what you have suffered, but thank heaven that has guided my footsteps to you, and will enable me I trust to protect you from further danger, and to restore you to happiness."

"Happiness, repeated Omelia, with a deep sigh, "alas, that can never again be mine, unless Stanley lives, and it should please providence that we might meet again."

"Despair not, Omelia," said Abdal, "and depend upon it that providence will yet realize your wishes, and that too much sooner than you anticipate. Let us begone.

Omelia said no more, although her anxiety was aroused to the greatest pitch, and taking the proffered arm of Abdal, he conducted her along the avenue, and turning to the right on arriving at the end of it, made his way towards an enclosed spot at a short distance, and where the trees grew thickly.

Breaking in between these, they suddenly came in sight of a few straggling bungalows of a superior description to those usually inhabited by the poorer natives, and leading Omelia forward he stopped at the door of one standing apart from the rest, and which bore an appearance of comfort that was most inviting, especially to one placed in the peculiar circumstances of our heroine.

"This place is inhabited by those to whom I am much indebted," said Abdal, "and who I am convinced will receive you with every kindness. But it is necessary that before I introduce you to them, I should enter into a brief explanation with them. Wait here then a minute or two while I do so, and I will quickly return."

Omelia nodded ascent, and Abdal entered the bungalow.

While he was gone she could not but reflect with astonishment and gratification upon the singularity of this adventure, and the longer she did so, the more bewildered did she become, and she endeavoured to anticipate that which was about to happen to her.

Abdal, as he had promised did not keep

her waiting long, but re-appearing beckoned her to approach, which she did, and he then conducted her into the bungalow, where he introduced her to a middle-aged native man and woman, of respectable and kindly appearance, and who received her with the utmost cordiality and respect, and immediately set about affording her that accommodation which she so much required, at the same time assuring her of the sympathy they felt in her misfortunes, and of their willingness to afford her all the assistance in their power.

Omelia warmly returned her thanks for this disinterested feeling of friendship towards one who was a complete stranger to them, but they heard her with evident impatience, and again assured her that they required no acknowledgements for anything they might do, and that they only felt too happy to think that they were able to serve her.

Refreshments of a light and delicate kind suited for the occasion, and the condition she was in, were quickly placed before her, of which she was invited heartily to partake, and the man and his wife then left the room.

"I can fully appreciate your anxious feelings, Omelia," remarked Abdal, when they were alone, "and I will therefore at once proceed to relate to you such particulars regarding what has befallen myself as may probably prove not uninteresting to you."

"I had missed Lieutenant Stanley for a minute or two, in the confusion of the combat, and was about to go in search of him and yourself, who I feared might be exposed to some imminent danger, when I received a blow on my head from the butt-end of a musket from some person behind, which felled me senseless to the earth, and I remembered no more for some time, for when I was again awakened to consciousness it was just the break of day, and all around was wrapped in the most profound silence.

"I raised myself on my elbow, and cast my eyes anxiously over the scene of the late sanguinary conflict, and appalling indeed was the sight, mutilated corpses, weltering in blood, meeting my gaze at every turn, giving fearful evidence of the terrible slaughter which had taken place, and that I had myself escaped creating my utmost surprise.

"With some difficulty I staggered to my feet, and then eagerly I examined the ghastly countenances of the dead, fearing to see amongst the number those friends whom I so highly esteemed, but in vain was my search for Stanley and yourself, and I was left in mingled doubt and fear, and useless conjecture as to what had become of you, although I had but too much reason to fear that you had been taken prisoners by the sepoys, and in which case I knew too well

the terrible fate which the inhuman wretches would not fail to inflict upon you.

"These thoughts, I need scarcely say, filled me with the greatest grief which almost overpowered me, and I lost all thoughts of the misery of my own situation, in the anxiety I felt about the fate which had befallen you.

"I repeated my search for some distance to where the combat had extended, but only to meet with the same disappointment, and I abandoned all hope of being able to ascertain what had become of you.

One thing, however, astonished me greatly and that was the number of sepoys that were slain, but more than all was the discovery of the bodies of two English soldiers.

"This satisfied me that some assistance had arrived previous to the termination of the combat, and revived my hopes that yourself and Stanley had been rescued, and removed to some place of safety.

"I felt considerable pain from the blow I had received, and for some time stupified and bewildered how to act, throwing myself again upon the earth, and abandoning myself to all those painful thoughts which crowded so rapidly upon me, and which the misery and loneliness of my situation, and the dismal prospect before me naturally engendered.

"At length, however, I aroused myself as well as I could, and mustering up all my courage, I proceeded as well as my strength would permit me from the spot, though I knew not what direction to take which was likely to lead me to some place where I might find temporary shelter and assistance.

"The whole of that day I continued to wonder, without meeting with anything to gratify my wishes, and it seemed the farther I proceeded the more distant did my prospects of relief become.

"Heart sick and despairing, I also had to suffer all the tortures of hunger and thirst, and ready to sink from the effects of them.

"Night came on, dark and gloomy as the thoughts that crowded upon my mind, and still no signs of a human being or habitation had I seen, and nothing could be more wild and cheerless than the aspect of the country through which I was travelling.

"But I felt so completely worn out with fatigue that I knew it would be impossible for me to proceed much farther until I had rested myself, and this I determined to do as soon as I could find out a convenient spot.

"After walking, with much difficulty some little distance further, I accidently alighted upon a large excavation—forming a perfect cavern—in the side of a steep hill, and having first carefully ascertained that it did not form the lurking-place of some wild animal, I entered it, and throwing my weary limbs upon the earth, endeavoured to resign myself to sleep.

"Such was the state of my mind, however, that it was sometime ere I could accomplish this, and when I did so the most painful and bewildering dreams haunted my imagination.

"I was suddenly awakened by the roaring sound of some wild beast, and crawling cautiously to the entrance of the cavern, and looking out I beheld to my horror, by the light of the moon—which had now broken from behind the clouds that had so long obscured it—a large tiger approaching in the direction of where I was, and so short was distance which separated us, that it seemed almost an utter impossibility for me to escape it.

"I nearly gave myself up for lost, but there was not a moment for delay, and crawling out of the cavern therefore on my hands and knees, I endeavoured to work my way round to the back of the hill, where I might make good my retreat ere the dreaded enemy should have seen me.

"But the keen eyes and scent of the tiger, it would seem had quickly discovered me, for with a roar which made the place resound again, he bounded forward, and I having instantly gained my feet, fled with a speed that terror could only have enabled me to do, making my way to the back of the hill, and the tiger pursuing me, and gaining upon me every instant.

"This certainly was one of the most perilous adventure of my life, and I must acknowledge that at the prospect of so frightful a death and which it seemed impossible for me, unless by a complete miracle to escape, my courage almost forsook me, especially as I had nothing but my sword to defend myself with.

"I, however, hurried on in the direction of a forest, though with what better chance of escaping there I knew not, and still the tiger pursued me, and seemed determined not to abandon his intended prey.

"I plunged into the thickest of the forest, and although I could still hear his roar, it was more faint than before, and satisfied me that I must at least somewhat have distanced him, if not I must resign myself to my fate, dreadful though it would be, for I was too much fatigued to render it possible for me to proceed much further.

"Again the voice of the tiger sounded nearer, and every hope of escape now seemed to be at an end. Mustering up all my energies, however, I determined to make another desperate effort, and rushed on with renewed speed for some distance further, but finding that the savage beast was once more gaining fast upon me, and I had no other means of avoiding him, I exerted all my remaining strength, and hastily climbed to the topmost branches of one of the tallest trees, and where I knew it would be impossible for the tiger to follow me.

"I had scarcely done so, when the fierce beast again appeared in sight, coming in the direction I had taken, and even passing the tree, and I was glad to see him hurry on till he was lost to view in the darkness beyond.

"For several minutes, however, I hesitated to descend from the tree, and while I was still so doing, I was startled by the loud report of fire-arms, which was quickly repeated, and was immediately followed by the deafening roar of the tiger, who was doubtless attacked by some armed travellers who had accidentally encountered him and would no doubt succeed in destroying him.

"There was another report of fire-arms, then all was silent, satisfying me that the savage beast was no more, and I then descended from the tree, and proceeded in the direction from which I had heard the firing, with the hope of at last meeting with those who could assist me, and who would be willing to do so, and I had not advanced far, when the tramping sound of horses smote mine ears, and directly afterwards three mounted Indians, with their rifles slung at their backs appeared in sight, and entertaining no suspicions from their appearance, I hastened towards them resolved to appeal to them for assistance under the difficulties in which I was placed.

"They stopped their horses on beholding me, and seemed surprised, but I immediately addressed them, requesting them to direct me if they could to some place where I might find shelter for a time, and other assistance of which I stood so much in need.

"They put several questions to me which I answered, as it seemed satisfactorily, and my appearance evidently excited their pity, for they immediately offered me all the assistance in their power, informing me that they were on their way to a village which was situated a few miles distant across the forest whither I might accompany them and receive that assistance I required, and for which I most warmly returned my thanks.

"One of them then opened a canvass bag which he had also slung at his back, from which he took some biscuits, and a flask containing arack, which he gave me, and I eagerly partook of, and felt much refreshed and reinvigorated afterwards.

"I then mounted a horse behind one of them, and we proceeded on our journey, in a different direction through the forest to that which I had been pursuing.

———

CHAPTER CIX.

ABDAL CONCLUDES HIS ADVENTURES.

"I am afraid," said Abdal, "that I shall tire your patience, so will be as brief in conclusion as possible.

"The strangers put several questions to me, which I answered cautiously, but at the same time in a manner which seemed to satisfy them, and in due time we arrived at the village, where I was received into the bungalow of one of the men, and treated with every kindness and hospitality by him and his wife; but still I felt anxious and uneasy about the fate which had too probably befallen yourself, Omelia, and Mr. Stanley, and could not rest satisfied until I had taken some means to ascertain it.

"One circumstance, however, I learnt which somewhat revived my hopes, and that was, that on the morning after the deadly conflict with the rebels who surprised and attacked our little party after our retreat from the old fort, a small detachment of troops had passed through the village having with them two or three wounded persons, one of whom was a young officer, the description of whom strongly corresponded with that of Lieutenant Stanley."

"Ah," ejaculated Omelia, eagerly, and a feeling of hope for an instant springing up in her bosom and irradiating her features, "could it indeed be he? How my heart throbs at the bare idea, and fain would I flatter myself with the fond hope that it was so, and that my beloved Stanley was rescued from the hands of the merciless sepoys, and still lives. But, alas, brief is the period that hope can exist, I dare not encourage it; even if he did not fall into the hands of those miscreants, he was I fear too sadly wounded to recover, and therefore what alleviation can I find to the bitter anguish that affects my mind?"

"Be calm, Omelia, and give not way entirely to to despair," said Abdal, "for I cannot entirely banish from my mind the idea that your lover yet survives, and that you are destined, and that too before long, to meet again."

"Oh, heaven grant that your wishes may be realised," fervently exclaimed our heroine, "I should then indeed feel myself sufficiently rewarded for all that I have suffered, and be one of the happiest of human beings. But whither were the soldiers of whom you speak going, Abdal?"

"That," replied the latter, "I was unable to ascertain. They only remained in the village till they had seen to the wounds of one whom they had under their charge, and procured the means of conveying them to the place of their destination, which would doubtless be the nearest military station."

"How torturing is this suspense and uncertainty," said Omelia, "when will those torturing doubts be removed? But proceed, good Abdal."

"I have not much more to relate," he observed, "and I must do so in as few words as possible, for you must be exhausted with the fatigue you have had to undergo for so many hours, and need repose.

"I remained in the village but a couple of days, and being anxious to pursue my journey to the nearest station, with the hope that I might there prosecute my inquiries with success, and obtain some clue to you and Stanley, having received some useful instructions and advice from those who had been so kind to me, and other assistance to help me in my way, I resumed my journey, and in due time arrived here, on the evening of a fearful storm, form which I sought shelter in this bungalow, and to my no small surprise and gratification, discovered in the persons of those who inhabit it, two former friends, whom it had been in my power to serve upon two or three occasions.

"I have been here three days, and to-morrow it was my intention to resume my journey, but little did I expect to have met with you, Omelia, under such extraordinary circumstances, and need I say how thankful I am that providence has permitted me to do so, and that at a time when you were placed in so critical a situation, and might have been exposed to such imminent danger?"

Thus Abdal concluded his simple narrative, and Omelia expressed her satisfaction, and they again congratulated each other on their fortunate and unexpected meeting, at the very time when they both stood so much in need of the counsel and advice of each other.

Omelia now related the particulars of what had happened to her since the night that had separated them, and with which the reader is already acquainted, and to which Abdal listened to with much interest.

He could not but express his admiration of her conduct throughout, at the same time he most deeply sympathised with her in the misfortunes to which she had been so undeservedly exposed, and which were more than sufficient to try the patience and fortitude of the firmest individual.

"But I trust, Omelia," he observed, "that you will meet with your due reward, by being ere long restored to that happiness and peace of mind from which you have been so long estranged."

"Alas," sighed our heroine, "never can I hope to be so unless fate ordains that Stanley is still in existence, and we may meet again. Fond hope, still must I endeavour to cherish it in my bosom, for it is that alone which can now render life endurable to me."

"Continue to encourage it, Omelia," returned Abdal, "and something convinces me that you will not be disappointed. The fate of your lover must be ascertained by some means or other, and I need not assure you how readily I will afford you all the assistance in my power, that may lead towards the accomplishment of your wishes."

"Oh, thanks, thanks, good Abdal," said our heroine, with a look of gratitude, "well do I know the manly and generous feelings that prompt you, and that I may depend upon your friendship. But what course do you propose? for I am all impatience till we proceed to the performance of the important task we have allotted to ourselves."

"As soon as you feel yourself in a condition to travel," answered Abdal, "for after the extraordinary fatigue you have undergone for some time past, and the anxiety of mind you have endured, I propose that we should depart to the nearest military station, which I find is some few miles distant from hence, and where we may probably hear some intelligence of the regiment to which Mr. Stanley belongs, and to which he would no doubt return should he not have fallen into the hands of the rebels. The brave General Havelock, to whose little band of heroes your lover was at one time, you know attached, is from the last accounts I have heard, again on his march to endeavour to relieve Lucknow, and no one, I am sure, would be more anxious to fight under his command, than your gallant lover.

"True, true," coincided Omelia, hope and enthusiasm animated her beauteous features at the idea, "and oh, what strange, what powerful feelings glow within my breast at the thought, while I feel endowed with more than woman's strength and courage. My mind is fortified for the task, and in endeavouring to discover the fate of him to whom my whole soul is devotedly, and in avenging his death, should he have perished by the hands of these blood-thirsty miscreants, I will prove myself a heroine, or perish in the attempt. But I cannot brook delay, every moment that intervenes between myself and the accomplishment of my designs will appear an age, let then to-morrow witness our departure, Abdal, and may heaven speed us on our expedition, if you find Omelia shrink for a moment from the task she has undertaken, or murmur at any obstacles she may have to encounter, visit her with that contempt she will then alone merit."

The form of the maiden seemed to dilate itself as she thus spoke, and the expression which the ardour of her feelings imparted to her features, could not be looked upon by even the most insensible, without the warmest admiration.

Abdal looked upon her as a superiour being, and could not help even experiencing a feeling almost approaching to awe in her presence.

"Noble minded girl," he exclaimed, "how can I sufficiently express my feelings of admiration at the observations you have just now given utterance to, and the heroic spirit which dictated them. But we will talk further upon this important subject to-morrow, let me again suggest to you the propriety of your now seeking that rest you so much require."

To this Omelia, who now certainly felt exhausted, after the fatigue and excitement she had been exposed to, assented, and having bid Abdal good night, she was conducted by the mistress of the bungalow to a comfortable chamber, where she was left to herself.

Her thoughts were now busy, as the different events of the last few days occured to her memory, and mingled feelings of hope, doubt, and expectation of the future agitated her mind.

Her meeting with Abdal, however, on whose friendship and assistance she knew she could rely, afforded her the greatest satisfaction, and she felt impatient for the time for them to depart on their important errand to arrive.

"Dear Edward," she exclaimed, "I must, will not delay, for something seems now to assure me that my efforts will not be in vain, but that ere long we shall meet again, and that those bright hopes and wishes we have so long and so fondly cherished will at length be accomplished. Blissful thought, I dare not, cannot banish it, for it is now the only one that inspires me with fortitude, and urges me on to perseverence."

Such were the reflections in which she indulged for some time previous to her retiring to rest, and when she did so, dreams of the most varied and perplexing description haunted her busy imagination, calculated alternately to excite hope, then doubt, and fear.

She arose at an early hour the following morning, much refreshed, and hearing the persons in the house moving about, she rejoined them below, where she found Abdal already waiting to receive her, which he did with even more than his usual warmth of feeling.

We will pass over what occurred during that day, which was employed by Omelia and Abdal in arranging their future plans, and they finally made up their minds to depart on their adventurous expedition the following morning, our heroine consenting to be guided alone by the advice of Abdal.

The next day they commenced their journey

accordingly, filled with sanguine hopes as to the result, and here for the present we will leave them, and relate such particulars as are all important to the interest of our tale.

CHAPTER CX.

DEEDS OF HEROISM.

Several weeks are now supposed to have elapsed, and the excitement of the events of the war every hour increased, the principal anxiety being for the brave little garrison of Lucknow, who still nobly held out against the overwhelming force of the enemy who had so long beseiged them with a courage and determination—under sufferings of the

No. 54.

most painful description—unparalleled in the history of war.

The hero Havelock had made his first advance to the relief of Lucknow (for it is necessary here again to refer to facts that had taken place some time previous) and failing to accomplish his object from the want of sufficient troops, more especially cavalry, after the determined and desperate battle on the plain of Subador, close to the spot on which our heroic garrison had so long defended themselves, he was compelled to withdraw, and with this action his first brilliant campaign for the relief of Lucknow might be said to have terminated.

And a gallant and remarkable victory was this action, which cannot be better described than in the words of the hero himself as conveyed in a field force order issued next morning.

"The Brigadier-general commanding, congratulates the troops on the result of their exertions in the combat of yesterday. The enemy were driven with the loss of 250 killed and wounded, from one of the strongest positions in India, which they obdurately defended. They were the flower of the mutinous soldiery, flushed with the successful defection at Saugor and Fyzabad. Yet they stood only one short hour before a handful of the soldiers of the state, whose ranks had been thinned by sickness and the sword."

"Strictly speaking, perhaps," says "The Mutiny of the Bengal Army," "Havelock's first campaign was concluded on the day on which he re-crossed the Ganges.

"In this great effort he had fought five pitched battles against an enemy vastly superior in numbers; he had been compelled to leave open his communications, to carry with him sick and wounded, to dare the rays of a scorching, often a deadly sun, to march without tents, to carry with him every article of supply.

"With these difficulties to encounter he had advanced three times, and three times had struck so great a terror into the enemy that his retreat had invariably been unmolested."

In the month of September following, General Outram arrived at Allahabad with the reinforcements destined for the relief of Lucknow, they were small, but the exigency was most urgent, and Havelock made preparations to advance when they should arrive. But the inadequacy of his force was his great cause for apprehension.

On the 15th, the 5th fusileers, part of the 90th light infantry, and some companies of the 78th, came into Cawnpore, and the next day brought General Outram.

At this period no little sensation was caused among the troops by the reports of the remarkable and heroic exploits of a handsome Indian girl, bearing all the appearance of an amazon, frequently engaging sword in hand in the deadly strife, always on the side of the English, and performing such deeds of bravery, that filled all who witnessed them with wonder and admiration, nor had any attempt been made to check her in her daring conduct.

She frequently made her appearance when least expected, boldly placing herself at the head of the troops, sword in hand, and cheering and urging them on to the combat in a manner that could not fail to excite their wonder and enthusiasm.

She was invariably accompanied by a young Hindoo man of commanding form and handsome features, and whose heroic conduct excited no less surprise than that of his beauteous companion.

The reader will scarcely need to be informed that these extraordinary persons were Omelia and Abdal, and many were the strange and romantic acts which had happened to them since the day that they had started from the village on their important journey, but of these more anon.

On the 19th of September—to resume our narrative of Havelock's re-advance to the relief of Lucknow—he crossed the Ganges. This was an arduous affair, for the river then in flood was running rapidly, and there were heavy guns, elephants, camels, ammunition waggons, and commisariat stores, as well as long trains of armed men, doolies for the wounded, and troops of burden-bearing coolies to be got over, at length it was effected, and the march began.

"On the previous night," says the Rev. W. Brock in his excellent biographical sketch of Sir Henry Havelock, "most of the troops had been marched down to the river's bank to await the advance of the morrow. As they moved along, the regimental colours carried in their dark cloth covering, rose up now and again from the forest of glistening bayonets, 'like yew trees in a garden.'

"The moon struggled through the rain which had been falling all the day, and threw a dim light over the river, looming mournfully on the blackened ruin where the brave old soldier Sir H. Wheeler and his devoted garrison had closed their last days on earth.

"After some skirmishing by the river's banks had cleared away the enemy, the army advanced by the most fatiguing marches, for the Ganges having acquired its extreme height, had overflowed its banks for several miles on the Oude side.

"As Havelock advanced, the rebels rapidly retreated, and then of him and his force nothing was heard for some days.

"Since the day that the tail of our army left," wrote a correspondent of Hurkaru, "no vestige of news has reached us. They ploughed a way through the tide of rebellion that overflows Oude, but the waves closed again, and we have no means of hearing from them, or of communicating with them.

"Yesterday a hundred men who had been sent to keep the Lucknow road open, were cut up by the rebels almost to a man, and our cossids have returned with no news."

Again we quote from the work of the Rev. Mr. Brock.

"It was Saturday afternoon, and the labour of crossing the guns had been very severe, and the army were halted for the night among the sand hills on the edge of the river, now about two miles from its ordinary course.

"The next was the day of rest, and except that the volunteer company went out to reconnoitre, the army were permitted to repose. Many great battles have been fought on that

 by; but General Havelock in his own practice avoided fighting on the Sabbath whenever he could.

"He had seen nothing in this case to depart from his usual rule, and he probably
gained much by its observance. He knew
that many of his men had already advanced
from Allyhabad to Cawnpore and he wanted
them to move still more rapidly to Lucknow.
He had more heavy guns to bring over, and
the delay permitted him to bring up more
baggage.

"Although, therefore, the enemy was entrenched in force, two miles from his position, and had fired on the volunteer cavalry,
he permitted them to remain unmolested.

"The weather changed again that afternoon. The hot sun was hidden and shroud-
ed in the thick veils of clouds, and the rain
fell in torrents upon the almost unsheltered
army.

"Through the entire night it came down
in sheets, and the soldiers' miserable bivouac
was turned into an immense puddle. Men
slept, however, and slept soundly, until called
upon by the bugle with the dawn of Monday
morning.

"Shortly after daybreak the column was
again in motion. They had not advanced
more than a mile before the artillery of the
foe opened upon them. Major Eyre's battery
was ordered to the front, and answered the
fire. General Havelock had, however, no
intention of walking his men straight up to
the batteries which his opponents had taken
days, and perhaps weeks to prepare and
strengthen. He ordered the artillery, protected by the 5th, to throw shot and shell
among them for a time, until he moved
through the swamps a strong force on their
right.

"The close practice of the guns with him,
soon began to tell fearfully upon the rebels,
while the ponderous shells cast among their
numerous cavalry with the precision of rifle
practice, carried confusion into their ranks

"The enemy detached a horse battery to
attack Havelock's flank. They were out-
manœuvred, however, and long ere it had
reached its intended position, Captain Maude
was seen spurring in hot haste across the
road, at the head of his horse artillery.

"Round after round was rapidly exchanged, and in less than a quarter of an hour the
guns of the enemy were silenced.

"By this time the infantry had turned
their right and this completed their defeat.
Their guns were horsed rapidly, and their
positions quickly abandoned. Two of their
guns were left for our infantry. They did
not wait to receive the bayonets which were
closing fast with them, but as they fled they
encountered a new foe.

"Sir James Outram, heading the volun-

teer cavalry turned their flight into a rout,
capturing two more guns, and leaving 120 of
the enemy sabred on the plain.

"The battle of Nungarwar caused little
loss to General Havelock's army, but it was
attended by serious results to his enemy,
who fought no more till they reached the
Alum Bagh.

"The rebels had made admirable arrangements to receive General Havelock had he
advanced in the direction they expected him
to take. He would have had to storm a
breastwork so formidable that it had to be
levelled before his baggage waggons and
guns could pass. He selected another path,
and for that departure from the high road
the enemy were not prepared.

"The battle over, the march followed, a
long and dreary march in a deluge. The
rain had poured incessantly upon a country
already turned into a lake, and in many
places, as the army moved on, the water assumed great depth.

"Passing Unao, the scene of former conflicts, through Bassurat Gunge—all abandoned by the enemy in their flight—Havelock's army marched that day twenty miles
in an Indian flood after gaining a decisive
victory.

"Towards evening they reached an abandoned village, cheerless and dirty, but still
capable of affording the shelter which all
required, and here they passed the night.

"Early in the morning of the 22nd the
army resumed its march, the rain still falling
heavily. Many of the coolies who had been
engaged to assist in the conveyance of the
baggage and the wounded, deserted during
the night, for they dreaded the approach of
Lucknow. But there was no time to wait to
supply their loss. Precious lives were hourly
sacrificed in that beleaguered station, and to
its inmates every day was an age. Onward
Havelock and his noble army pressed, wet,
and often weary, but sustained by the hope
of effecting the object of their march.

"The day's advance was an incessant
struggle through fields turned into morasses
and swamps, by the continual rain, with
heavy guns and lumbering waggons, delayed
by some accident or some new obstruction
almost at every turn.

"After a toilsome march of fourteen miles
through a lane of mud, the force reached
another deserted village, and in its empty
houses they found a shelter for another com-
fortless night.

"The artillery booming around the residency of Lucknow were now heard, and a
royal salute from the heavy garrison fired in
the hope that their friends in danger might
hear the report, and comprehend its purpose.

"The 23rd opened with little change in
the dull leaden sky. Noon had passed, and

they had not yet reached Lucknow, while their cavalry, then in advance, had brought them no intelligence of the enemy. At length at two o'clock they were seen slowly falling back. This excited apprehension. and immediately afterwards, as the force advanced, the rebel army was discovered in great force, their right drawn up behind a chain of hillocks, and their left resting upon the enclosure of the Alum Bagh.

"Havelock now perceived that he was not to enter Lucknow without a severe struggle. A single glance convinced him that the flower of the enemy was before him, and that here the first passage to the Residency must be fought.

He made his dispositions with that alacrity and precision which had so often been the means of baffling his foes, and, although his troops had marched with very little interval for seven hours, no time was lost in attempting to clear the road to Lucknow.

"The mutineers had selected their position with a view of neutralising Havelock's habits of turning the lines of his opponents, of which they had obtained experience in frequent and disastrous engagements.

"The trunk road passed through deep and wide morasses, which, at that season, ran close up to its edges, and were altogether impassable.

"Immediately where the morasses ceased, and firmer footing could be obtained, and on a rising ground, the rebel army were massed in strong battalions of infantry, with many guns, and cavalry on the centre, the left, and the right.

"The only available means of attack was by this road, and upon it the enemy conveyed the fire of their artillery. Havelock's guns replied with some effect; but he instantly saw that his men were too closely grouped. His infantry, therefore were pushed forward rapidly on his old plan; and, although a hurricane of round shot and shell were ploughing through their ranks, and thinning their sections, they never faltered.

"At length his left enveloped the enemy's right; and charging through the soft ground, where the men sank deep at every step, they drove the foe before them, capturing one village after another, and seizing five guns.

"While the enemy's right was thus crushed and driven from the field, his centre was exposed to the effective artillery fire from Havelock's batteries; and as the battle now pressed upon his left, that wing and the centre at length broke up and fled, Sir James Outram at the head of his handful of cavalry bravely pursuing the enemy, regardless of the odds, till after a tedious but never dubious fight, the battle of the Alum Bagh was won."

Need we again refer to the heroic defence of the garrison of Lucknow? few indeed are the parallels it has in history. "With batteries that had not only been hastily constructed, but were surrounded by lofty buildings which afforded a safe shelter to at least 8,000 malignant and well trained marksmen, who thirsted like tigers for their prey; with many large guns playing on them; with scarcely indifferent food, with sickness in its worst and most distressing forms; undergoing all the vicissitudes of heat, cold, and rain; harassed by false alarms that broke in most cruelly every night, upon the brief interval of repose which the seige permitted, for all were needed to labour in the mines, and every one did so; with artillerymen so few that the gunners had to speed from one battery to another wherever the fire was the hottest, the maintenance of the position seemed impossible, yet with all these difficulties within the Residency, this illustrious band of not 500 men held its own against at least 50,000, without yielding a foot of ground, or conceding to the enemy a single success.

"Such was the condition of the garrison, when the firing of the artillery at the Alum Bagh, on the 23rd, was plainly heard by them, and announced the arrival of the army of relief at the entrance to the city."

Our space will not allow us to enter into all the details of that which subsequently took place, neither do we wish to detain the reader too long from the main thread of our tale, but we cannot pass over entirely the fierce struggle of the 25th, which was the most fearful they had yet encountered; for the City of Lucknow, with its narrow, tortuous streets, still lay between the beleaguered garrison and the army of relief at Alum Bagh; and this labyrinth must be penetrated.

Desperate indeed, and fearful were the difficulties they had to encounter, the fire from the heavy guns of the enemy as they resolutely advanced, raked the road with a murderous fire of grape, canister, and round shot, ploughing up the ground, and tearing up trees, and everything that came in its way, while the sepoy sharp-shooters, who filled the jungle through which the road to the town passes, galled the troops as they approached and passed with an incessant fire of musketry. These stirring events we can only briefly refer to, but at length after a march of some hours the brave army reached the king's palace, or Kaiser-Bagh.

Again let us quote from the work of the Rev. Mr. Brock.

"It was long past noon when the column reached a place of temporary shelter under the walls of the Furred Buksh. The troops were sorely exhausted. For six weary hours they had struggled in deadly fight with a fierce enemy, and all the while under a scorching sun. Faint and worn out they endeavoured to snatch a brief respite from the double foe.

"Darkness was coming on, and they were still some distance from the beleaguered garrison, who had all the time listened with intense interest to the firing at the Kaiser Bagh. To both the generals it was a moment of deep anxiety. Many considerations favoured the occupation of the Mooter Mahul for the night, postponing to the break of day the march to the Residency. Their troops were utterly exhausted with their many hours' fight, and with the heat; they had many wounded, the transport of the heavy guns and baggage waggons would greatly retard the progress of the troops in the line of fire they had yet to pass through. On the other hand the enemy might congregate in the night in such overwhelming masses, and so completely invest their temporary position that when the morning came they might find themselves so hemmed in as to be threatened with extermination. Besides the garrison were known to be in great extremity; any hour might be its ruin. The swarming hordes of Lucknow, said to be 50,000 strong, ferocious as tigers about to lose their prey, might that night concentrate their fury upon the garrison, and with the relieving army at its doors, the massacre of Cawnpore with all its horrors, might be repeated.

* * * * *

The generals after much consideration, determined to push on their way, and placing themselves at the head of the highlanders and Sikhs, they dashed on to the Residency.

"No words can picture that march of fire and death. Broad deep trenches had been cut across the road, furnished with every kind of obstruction. Every inch of the way was covered point blank with unseen marksmen; at every turn, heavy artillery belched forth its fiery storm of grape and canister. Above, below, everywhere, crowds of human tigers glared from house-top and loop-holed casement upon the intrepid band; while as they rounded the corner which opened upon the squares of the palace, they had to encounter from many thousand rifles an iron hurricane of destruction and death.

"As the brave 78th were passing through an archway, 'which literally streamed with fire,' a bullet struck General Neil on the head, and he fell to rise no more. The men enraged, fired a volley against the wall, in vain the hope that some stray bullet might enter the loop-holes, and avenge their brave leader's death.

"Recalled to their duty by Havelock's word, they marched on, leaving the dying and the dead behind them at every step. It was now dark, but the road was lighted up by the incessant fire of shot and shell, and the furious play of musketry. One obstacle after another was conquered, and the way at last was clear. The gate of the Residency was before them, and with a cheer which only British soldiers know how to give, the vanguard of Havelock's 'Column of Relief' entered in, bringing to the beleaguered garrison safety at least, if not deliverence."

———

CHAPTER CXI.

OMELIA AND ABDAL.

Sir Colin Campbell was on his march for the final relief of Lucknow, for Havelock and Outram were now with the garrison surrounded by the enemy. This was in the month of November, and it may well be imagined the anxiety with which his progress was watched.

It was night, and the bright moon shed a rich flood of silvery light upon the scene to which we now wish to call the attention of the reader.

It was one at once both awful and imposing, for it was one where but a day before a desperate and sanguinary engagement had taken place, and fearful were the traces it had left behind in the number of the slain, which strewed the earth in every direction.

And now in the distance, and approaching the spot, might be seen a couple of human forms, that of a man and woman, both armed to defend themselves from any danger which they might have to encounter.

They appeared almost worn out with fatigue, but still they persevered, and continued on their way, although they were only enabled to do so slowly, and after a little time they arrived at the place we have mentioned, where they paused, and their looks and behaviour showed their great anxiety and emotion.

The reader will doubtless have guessed that the persons here mentioned were Omelia and Abdal, who after encountering many perils and dangers, in the vain and romantic endeavour to ascertain the fate of Stanley, were now following in the route of Sir Colin Campbell, having heard that the regiment to which the young Lieutenant belonged, formed part of the force now proceeding to the relief of Lucknow, and a faint hope entering Omelia's mind that by the merciful interposition of providence Stanley might have been rescued from the fate which she apprehended, and that they would be permitted to meet again.

In Abdal she had found an excellent friend

and guide, and they had shared every danger and difficulty together. And most extraordinary had been the exploits of our heroine, as we have before stated, and numerous and startling had been the advantages she had met with, the hardships she had undergone; but although her mingled hopes and fears, and troubles and disappointments kept her in a continual state of excitement, there was very little change in her personal appearance. Her handsome features were still animated with every noble and generous feeling, and the same intellectual expression glowed in her countenance and beamed from her eyes.

And now they arrived at the place which had formed the scene of the late fearful struggle to which we have alluded, and which as usual had ended in the total defeat and flight of the rebels, leaving behind them a number of slain, while the loss of the British troops was comparatively trifling.

The sight which here presented itself to Omelia, although no novelty to her, was one sufficiently appalling, and such as she could not gaze upon without feelings of the greatest anguish, for again the probable fate of Stanley rushed upon her brain, and notwithstanding all her endeavours to do so, she could not stifle the feelings that agitated her breast. Abdal read her thoughts, and he could not but participate in her feelings as his eyes glanced over the ghastly forms that strewed the earth around, and presented so fearful a spectacle.

"Death has again performed its awful work," remarked our heroine, "and many a brave man, many a noble spirit has been doubtless summoned to eternity. How terrible is it to gaze upon this scene of bloodshed and destruction. Alas, when will these horrors cease, and peace once more bless this ill-fated land?"

"It is a sad thought, Omelia," replied Abdal, "and one that cannot but excite the most painful feelings. But come, let us proceed, for we know not the danger to which we thus expose ourselves, and must continue to do till we reach some place of safety, or find ourselves again among the English troops, some of whom, if we lose no time, we may probably overtake."

"I cannot leave this awful scene," said Omelia, "till I have gazed more narrowly upon the ghastly objects which strew the earth, for ever do I fear to behold the corpse of the unfortunate Stanley, whom I cannot but believe that I shall behold again, even though it be under the most dreadful and hopeless circumstances. Come, let us examine the pale and livid features of the dead, and remove if possible the terrible doubts and fears that haunt my mind."

Abdal would have been glad to be able to dissuade her from this melancholy task, but he knew it would be useless to do so, and he therefore accompanied her on the dismal search, as she solemnly proceeded to examine the pale features of the corpse of every Englishman who had fallen in that deadly strife.

Slowly she bent her way among the ranks of the slain, stooping down ever and anon the better to accelerate her view, and her heart palpitating violently with the almost insupportable and torturing feelings that agitated it, and which increased every moment.

Every ghastly countenance that she gazed upon, distorted with the agonies of death, seemed with their glassy eyes to look up at her with despair, and to mock her anguish, but all were strangers to her, the wild idea and fear that she should amongst them find the cold remains of him from whom she had been so long separated, not being realised.

"He is not here," she sighed, turning a melancholy look upon her companion, "and oh, what feeling of madness can it be that still urges me to this fruitless search, and keeps me in a continual state of anxiety and suspense? Oh, Stanley, too surely has your fate long ere this been decided, and I shall never be able to learn it, though I have too much reason to believe that you are no more, and therefore since all the fond hopes I cherished are thus annihilated, why should I continue to live to be thus a misery to myself and to all with whom I may become connected?"

"Banish these sad and torturing thoughts, Omelia," said Abdal, "and let us at once quit this awful scene, which cannot but serve to increase the anguish of your mind."

Omelia returned no answer, but still lingered on the spot, and seemed loth to quit it, and yet to experience feelings of the greatest fear and misery while she remained. Abdal, however, at length gently took her arm, and led her away, she being so engrossed by the painful thoughts that constantly haunted her as to be almost unconscious what she did.

But both herself and Abdal were almost exhausted, for they had walked many weary miles that day, and they had not partaken of any food since the morning, and great were the exertions they had undergone for several days previously, Omelia, however, remaining firm in the wild and extravagant resolution she had formed not to rest till she should be restored to him to whom her very soul was devoted, or she had ascertained the fate which had befallen him; and many were the hopes and fears she constantly gave way to, though the latter more frequently prevailed.

The moon had now become hid behind dark clouds, and the scene became dreary and cheerless, the more especially as they had entered upon a wild and apparently uninhabited part of the country, and to which they were both of them entire strangers

"My strength begins to fail me," said Omelia, in a melancholy voice, "and I fear that I shall not be able to proceed much farther. Alas, what a life of constant fatigue and anxiety both of body and mind is that to which I am destined. When will there be an end to it?"

"Struggle with your feelings, and keep up your spirits as well as you can, Omelia," said Abdal, "and I trust that something may ere long take place to realise those hopes and wishes to which you must still endeavour to cling. Could we but meet with some place where we might obtain rest and shelter for the night, we should be enabled to resume our journey with renewed strength and courage in the morning."

"True," coincided Omelia, "but what chance is there of meeting with any friendly shelter in such a wild and lonely place as this? My heart sickens at the thought."

"Our prospects are certainly gloomy enough," returned her companion, "but still let us persevere, and we may yet be able to surmount the difficulties by which we are at present surrounded. Could we only meet with any of the troops on their way to join Sir Colin Campbell, who is now on his march to Lucknow, we should, no doubt, receive protection, and our dangers would be at an end, though at present we scarcely know what we may have to apprehend, as numerous hordes are prowling about the country in all directions."

He had scarcely given utterance to these words, when the report of fire-arms at no great distance smote their ears, followed by appalling shrieks, and surprised and terrified as they could not help being at such a circumstance, and the danger which seemed to threaten them, they were rivetted to the spot, and for the moment all their presence of mind forsook them.

The shrieks still continued, and sounded nearer, and aroused at length into a full sense of their danger, they concealed themselves as well as they could among the brushwood, which fortunately grew thick near the spot on which they were standing, and they had scarcely had time to do so, when two females and a gentleman, all of them in a wild and disordered state, and apparently wounded, rushed frantically past, followed by several rebels from whom they were hopelessly endeavouring to escape, but to whom it was too evident they must shortly become the victims.

The alarm of Omelia and Abdal may now be imagined, and they scarcely dared to breathe, lest they should betray themselves to the dreaded enemy, although the darkness of the night—for the moon was still obscured —and the place in which they had concealed themselves was all in their favour.

The fate of the unfortunate beings, however, was sealed: again the report of fire-arms, followed by piercing shrieks and cries of agony, rent the air, and all was then silent, the miscreants no doubt having completed their bloody and inhuman work

Still, however, Omelia and her companion remained in their place of concealment, and scarcely knew what to do, for the still greater danger that might threaten them if they ventured to proceed further for the present was apparent, and they remained where they were for a few minutes longer, to see whether the rebels would return. They came not, and looking around and perceiving nothing of them, they ventured to leave their hiding place, though it was with the utmost caution that they did so, and moved in a different direction to that which they had before been pursuing, fear giving them new strength, and imparting speed to their feet. They had soon got to some distance from the spot where this event had taken place, and found themselves in the midst of a scene more wild and gloomy, if possible, than that which they had hitherto been traversing.

They were approaching a dark stream of water, near which huge rocks were piled upon each other, and down the sides of which a foaming and roaring cataract dashed.

This stream was crossed by a narrow, crazy-looking bridge extending from rock to rock, and which it would require some strength of nerve to venture to cross, for it seemed scarcely able to afford foothold, or of bearing the weight of a human being, and to Omelia and Abdal in their present exhausted state it presented difficulties that appeared to be almost insurmountable.

There was, however, no time for hesitation, so Abdal having spoken to our heroine some words of encouragement took her hand, and began to assist her in ascending the rock to the bridge, which was a task of the utmost difficulty.

But after some labour they succeeded in reaching the bridge, which was raised at such a height in the air that it almost turned the brain giddy to contemplate it, and Abdal still retaining his hold of his beauteous companion's hand, commenced leading her across to the opposite side of the stream.

The cataract roared and foamed beneath them, and but the least fear or hesitation, one false step, they must have been precipitated below, and to meet with certain death.

Omelia at first shuddered but she took courage as she proceeded, although the frail bridge seemed to totter beneath their weight, and at length they reached the other end, and carefully and slowly descending the rock they alighted on terra firma in safety.

The moon now again showed her bright face from behind the clouds that had for some time obscured it, and they were able to see everything before them distinctly for some distance, and beheld nothing to excite their alarm or suspicion.

Having paused for a minute or two to take breath and to rest themselves, they resumed their journey with renewed courage, our heroine still leaning on the arm of Abdal for support, but endeavouring to struggle against fatigue as well as she could.

Still nothing could be more cheerless and disheartening than the prospect before them, for it was impossible that they could proceed much farther without rest, and there seemed to be not the least chance of their meeting with any place of shelter, or that assistance which their wants so much required.

They paused, and consulted with each other what was best to be done, but so bewildering was their situation, and every moment their difficulties seemed so to accumulate that they were unable to come to any satisfactory decision.

They pursued their way in gloomy silence for some distance farther, when entering upon a more secluded part of the country, enclosed by a range of lofty hills, they beheld before them, to their no small surprise, an encampment, and as far as they were enabled to discover, it was one of British troops, but uncertain as to the fact, they hesitated at first whether to venture to proceed.

While they thus stood they were suddenly surprised by the picquet, and were immediately taken into custody, their appearance under such singular circumstances, and at that hour of the night, of course, naturally exciting suspicion.

———

CHAPTER CXII.

THE SEQUEL OF THE ADVENTURE.

It was one of the columns then on its way to Lucknow to join Sir Colin Campbell, that was encamped for the night in that part of the country to which Abdal and our heroine had been accidentally led, and to the tent of the general they were immediately conducted, and who received them with no little surprise and curiosity, the personal appearance of the handsome young Indian maiden in particular exciting his deepest interest, and for a minute or two he gazed at her earnestly and without saying a word, while Omelia met his searching glances with becoming modesty, but still with firmness and confidence.

"Now, stranger," said the general, addressing himself to Abdal, "who are you? and what brings you and your companion here under such singular circumstances?"

"'Twas accident alone, sir," answered Abdal, "and I trust a fortunate one, for we have travelled far, and much need assistance. We are no spies, or secret enemies, and therefore I hope that we have nothing to fear."

"Of that I must have satisfactory proof," remarked the general; "your name, young man?"

"Abdal Moorsha," was the reply; "it is one that I have never yet disgraced, and therefore I do not hesitate to acknowledge it."

The general again looked at him narrowly for a moment or two, and then observed—

"You seem candid and sincere, young man, and I am disposed to believe you. And this female, is she your wife?"

"No, sir," answered Abdal, "but she is one whom I regard with the same feeling as if she were mine own sister."

"Your name, young woman?" inquired the general, with an anxious look, and unable to conceal the admiration with which her handsome form and features, and her retiring modesty inspired him.

"Omelia, sir," she answered, in respectful accents, "and though humble, and now almost friendless, still possessing the deepest sympathy with the cause of the English, and the utmost horror and abhorrence for the atrocities perpetrated by my misguided and inhuman countrymen."

The general looked at the lovely Hindoo maid—whose appearance at that time was even more than usually prepossessing—with still greater astonishment, and the earnest tones in which she spoke, the observations she made use of, and the intelligence that beamed so eloquently from her fine dark eyes, and imparted additional animation to her features, could not but convince him of her sincerity, and likewise assure him that it was no common individual that stood before him.

He spoke a few words to an officer who was in attendance upon him in an under tone, and Abdal was then requested to retire, which he did with much reluctance, and greatly to the embarrassment of our heroine, who, however, still maintained her firm and respectful demeanour.

"The observations you have just uttered, young woman, were those of true patriotism and heroism," said the gallant general, "and there is something in your looks and manners that inspires my confidence, but still it is strange that one of your sex and so young should thus voluntarily expose herself to such imminent dangers and sufferings as you must have done. Have you no relations, no friends, save the one who accompanies you?"

"Alas, sir," replied Omelia, with a sigh, "I have none, death I fear has deprived me of all that was most dear to me on earth."

"And what could induce you to expose yourself to such fearful risks and perils, as must have threatened you every moment?" inquired the general, anxiously.

Omelia averted her looks at this question, and hesitated previous to returning an answer. Indeed the subject was one of so delicate a nature, that her confusion and timidity were not to be wondered at. And yet the thought that probably she might gain some intelligence of Stanley emboldened her, and at length she replied in accents that rivetted the attention of the general and excited his deepest sympathy.

"It was, sir, in the hope that perchance I might be able to discover whether one whom I love far dearer than my own existence still lives, or the fate which has befallen him, that urged me to brave every danger I might have to encounter, and to endeavour to surmount every obstacle which might be thrown in the way of the accomplishment of my object. Should that beloved being be indeed no more, life to the wretched Omelia would no longer be endurable; but let me at least perish in lending my feeble aid towards the defeat of those inhuman wretches who have spread such horror and desolation around. I will not rest satisfied till I have assisted, as far as my humble power will allow me, in avenging the murder of those of my own sex and their innocent offspring."

As our heroine gave utterance to these words, her graceful and majestic form seemed to dilate itself, her bosom swelled with the

No. 55.

power of her emotions, and her eyes sparkled with even more than their wonted brilliancy, and altogether she appeared at that moment as a being of a superior order, and which few could gaze upon without feelings of the greatest wonder and most enthusiastic admiration.

The general looked at her for a few minutes in silence, for he was unable to find words to give expression to the feelings her words and manners had excited. He, however, resumed his seat, and extending his hand to Omelia, which she raised respectfully to her lips, he said—

"My poor girl, I have listened to you with the deepest interest, and must again express myself in terms of the warmest eulogy of the noble and heroic sentiments you have uttered, and which are the more extraordinary, and to be admired, coming as they do from one of your gentle sex, and so youthful. I must become better acquainted with your history before we part. But this loved individual about whose fate you profess so great an anxiety; he is your countryman, I presume?"

Omelia hesitated for a moment, and then replied timidly that he was a young English officer.

"Ah," exclaimed the general in amazement; "but," he added, after a pause, "I do not wonder that one so young and beautiful should capture even the most cold and insensible heart. And loved he you in return?"

Our heroine cast her eyes modestly to the ground and her heart palpitated violently, but at the same time she replied in the affirmative, and tears chased each other down her cheeks as she did so.

"His name?" interrogated the general.

Omelia again hesitated, but at last answered in a faint voice—

"Lieutenant Stanley."

"A brave youth," said the general, warmly, "a gallant youth, one who has been often favourably noticed by Sir James Outram, under whose command he served I knew him well and his father before him."

How Omelia's heart throbbed and her eyes glistened at hearing the character of her lover thus highly but deservedly eulogised; and again unable to control the expression of her feelings, she bent one knee respectfully to the earth, and bowed her head in reverence before him, while in an anxious voice she inquired—

"Oh, tell me, sir, I beseech you, know you whether he of whom I speak, still lives?"

"I regret," he replied, "I sincerely regret, my poor girl, that I cannot inform you. If he does, he probably is with the troops of the brave Generals Outram and Havelock in Lucknow, and to the final relief of whom and the garrison, His Excellency the Commander-in-Chief—whom I am on the way to join—is now going."

Omelia clasped her hands together, and raised her eyes devoutly towards heaven, as she expressed a fervent hope that the ideas of the general might be realised.

"But alas, honoured sir," she at length said, fixing upon the veteran hero a persuasive look, "I fear that the request which I am about to presume to make is too bold and extravagant to be granted."

"Name it," said the general, "and fear not if it is in my power that I will fail to meet your wishes."

"I would be permitted, with my esteemed friend Abdal, to accompany you," replied our heroine, "and there is no hardship that I would hesitate to encounter to accomplish my wishes."

The general hesitated and reflected.

"It is indeed an extraordinary request," he at last said, "and one which I know not whether I should be justified in complying with. Besides, it is fraught with dangers such as I fear to expose you to."

"Oh, name them not, noble sir," replied the heroic damsel, fervently, "name them not, I implore you. I have made a solemn vow, which nothing can induce me to break, never to rest, and to brave every peril, till I have accomplished the one great object I have so much at heart, and even death itself in its most appalling form can present no terrors to me in the furtherance of that design."

"You are a true heroine, Omelia," observed the general, again unable to restrain the expression of his admiration, "and stranger even as you are to me, it would afford me the highest gratification to see your fond hopes realised, that Lieutenant Stanley may be found not only to survive, but that you may meet him again. I comply with your request, and will afford you my best protection and assistance in the furtherance of your wishes."

It was utterly impossible for our heroine to find words to express her feelings of gratitude to the gallant general for his kindness and condescension; but her looks, and the tears she so abundantly shed, spoke much more than language, however powerful could convey, and made every impression upon the mind of the general, who raising her from her humble and suppliant posture, said—

"Enough, my poor girl, there is no time for further conversation, there is but a short time left for repose, for we must be on the march again by the earliest dawn of day. This gentleman (alluding to the officer who had been in attendance during the interview but had drawn himself respectfully aside) will conduct you to where you will find some of your own sex, and refreshment and rest, which you doubtless much require."

Omelia again returned her acknowledgements in the warmest manner, and then with a palpitating heart, and feelings such as it would be difficult to describe, but which the reader will probably be able easily to imagine, she followed the officer from the general's tent.

In the meantime the immediate necessities of Abdal had been attended to, and he sought that brief repose of which he stood so much in need, though as may naturally be expected, he was most anxious to learn the result of the interview between the general and our heroine.

The tent to which Omelia was conducted, was occupied by two or three English females and a native woman, by whom she was received with much respect and no little curiosity; but they forebore to put any questions to her, and following the instructions they had received, they supplied her with such provisions as they could, and of which she partook but sparingly, as her heart was too full to permit her to eat.

She then stretched her weary limbs upon the earth, and endeavoured to compose herself to sleep. But busy thoughts kept her for some time—notwithstanding her fatigue—waking, and she pondered seriously upon the extraordinary and exciting events of the past, and anticipated with mingled hopes and fears those that were likely to follow.

And when sleep descended upon her eyelids, strange and varied were the visions that were conjured up to her imagination, and the form of her lover was presented constantly to her eyes in positions and under circumstances that were calculated to excite alternate hopes and fears in her breast.

At times she beheld him stretched upon the awful battle-field, bleeding, and in the agonies of death; she saw his ghastly features distorted by pain, and heard him in mournful accents call upon her name, and invoke the blessings of heaven upon her head. Then again she beheld him, in the hands of the savage and remorseless foe, and awaiting the dreadful doom, which they in their bloodthirsty and cowardly feelings of revenge were about to inflict upon him. She noticed with agony his looks of despair, and yet the manly struggle with his feelings to meet his fate with becoming fortitude.

Once more the situation and the scene were changed, and now all was happiness and sunshine instead of horror and the darkness of despair. She was walking with her lover 'neath bright clear skies, and through lovely and romantic scenes, where no traces of war and bloodshed could be seen, but all was peace and tranquillity. Smiles were on their features, joy was in their hearts, and love was on their lips. Everything around them, all upon which their eyes rested, even the very air they breathed was redolent of content and happiness, and the distant prospect presented still far brighter scenes than those they now wandered among.

From such a blissful scene as this, it were indeed a pity that our heroine should e'er awake to the tortures of stern reality; but she was suddenly aroused by the bugle's sound, and starting up in confusion, she found that all was activity and excitement, the troops making every necessary and hasty preparation to resume their march, and very shortly after all was in motion; previous to which, however, Omelia was again honoured by a brief interview with the general, who having spoken some encouraging and complimentary words to her, and given instructions that she should be accommodated as well as possible in one of the baggage waggons, Abdal—who was waiting to receive her—being placed near her among the coolies according to his own desire, left her, and the march towards the Alum Bagh, where the junction with the Commander-in-Chief was expected to take place was pursued with celerity.

CHAPTER CXIII.

THE MARCH AND ITS DIFFICULTIES.

The day had only just broke above the hills when the troops quitted the place where they had been encamped for the night, and although the morning broke promisingly, the weather soon afterwards assumed a most unfavourable aspect, and their way lay through a tract of country which was extremely uncouth in appearance and presented many obstacles.

In many parts of the road deep entrenchments had been cut by the enemy that rendered it nearly impassable, and as well as greatly retarding the progress of the march made it doubly tedious and wearisome.

But nothing could daunt the courage of the men who were in excellent spirits, and were anxious to join the force of Sir Colin Campbell, and to advance at once to the relief and capture of Lucknow, and to hurl that terrible and certain retribution on the foe, which their unparalleled enormities so richly merited.

And as they proceeded, so did the hopes of our heroine revive, and the novelty of her situation afforded her mind relief and amusement. She thought not of the dangers they might probably have to encounter, all her hopes were fixed upon her meeting with Stanley, for something seemed to whisper to her and assure her that he still lived, and that it would be their fate to be restored to each other, much sooner than she now dared to anticipate.

She recalled to her memory the dreams that had haunted her imagination on the previous night, and they served, at least the last of them, to strengthen her hopes and ideas which she could not help but encourage.

And should it indeed be the will of providence that such happiness might be in store for her, what would be the feelings of herself and Stanley on again meeting, after so long and torturing a separation, and when they had given themselves up as lost to each other? The widest stretch of the imagination could scarcely conceive them, and her brain actually became bewildered on reflecting upon them.

And if Stanley did indeed still survive, had the sentiments he had so often and so fervently avowed for her undergone no change? Did he still cherish her image in his heart with the same warmth of feeling which he had ever professed to do? Could she doubt him? It was impossible that she could do so, and she reproached herself for having even for a moment encouraged the thought.

"Ah, no, my beloved Stanley," she soliloquised, "never, never can I believe you capable of such base hypocrisy and deceit. I must be most ungenerous and unworthy of your love could I do so. Well am I convinced that you would loathe and despise yourself could you be capable of sporting with the feelings of that poor girl whose whole soul was ever most fondly devoted to you, and who would have been willing at any time to have sacrificed her life to serve you, to promote your welfare. Heaven pardon me for suffering anything approaching to a doubt of your truth and honour to enter my mind, and grant that mutual happiness may be our ultimate reward for our love and constancy, and the many trials and vicissitudes we have had to encounter, and which we have both borne with such exemplary patience and fortitude."

Again her hopes strengthened as these thoughts occurred to her, and she felt more sanguine and light of heart than she had done before for many a day, and she could never be sufficiently grateful for the accident which had guided herself and the faithful Abdal to the place where the troops had been encamped, and the friendly and generous spirit in which the gallant general had received them, strangers as they were to him, and humble as were their positions in life.

Abdal remained near her during the whole of the march, and he frequently engaged in conversation with her, encouraging her hopes

and endeavouring to relieve the tediousness and weariness of the journey by every means in his power.

And a dreary march indeed was that, which although diversified at intervals in the character of the scenery, presented but few favourable aspects, and as they proceeded fresh obstacles arose in their way sufficient to tire anything but the most indomitable patience and perseverance.

Sometimes their way led through an almost impenetrable forest, where the guns and the baggage waggons could not proceed without the greatest difficulty, and which often appeared almost insurmountable; at others over a plain covered with thick jungle and sugar canes, which reached high above the heads of the men, and where a passage was frequently compelled to be cut; then they had to toil through difficult mountain passes, and along rugged roads, which they could only traverse very slowly, and that not without the most infinite labour, which must soon have exhausted any other than British soldiers, but still the spirits of the brave fellows never for a moment drooped, and in fact it seemed that no hardship was too great for them to meet and to struggle through, and that nothing whatever could have the power to daunt their courage and determination.

And now the rain fell heavily, and added to the miseries they had to contend with, but they bore it all with the same firmness, and exhibited no signs of discontent.

Thus the weary march continued throughout the day, with few intermissions, when the men were allowed to halt for a short time, only on again proceeding to have to encounter fresh hardships, and at length night closed in, remarkably dark and gloomy, and shortly afterwards arriving at a deserted village, where it was resolved that the troops should take up their quarters for a few hours they being much harrassed with the extraordinary fatigue they had undergone, and requiring rest, but as there was the least time possible for delay, and the general was most anxious to push on his way, it was resolved to resume the march at an early hour in the morning.

Omelia and Abdal after some brief conversation separated for the night, the former being accommodated in one of the deserted dwellings with several other females, amongst whom she had already excited the deepest interest, and curiosity, and who looked upon her with the greatest respect.

Notwithstanding the fatigues of the day which she had so courageously endured, it was some time ere our heroine felt inclined for sleep, but abandoned herself to those thoughts the circumstances in which she was placed naturally gave rise to.

At length, however, she fell asleep, and slept soundly, but from which herself and her companions were shortly aroused by the noise and bustle which prevailed amongst the troops, and the cause of which was soon made known to them.

A small party of the men, under the command of an efficient officer, who had been sent forward towards the evening to reconnoitre, had suddenly returned in great haste, to inform the general that they had seen the enemy in considerable force advancing no doubt with the intention of taking the English by surprise, and of preventing the junction of this column with Sir Colin Campbell.

No time was therefore to be lost, the general acted with promptitude, and made every immediate preparation to receive the enemy warmly. The position held by the troops in the village was favourable, and the issue of the battle, notwithstanding the fatigue they had undergone could be very little doubted, and they were all in the best of spirits, and eager for the contest.

Omelia felt anxious to take an active part in the strife—for it was impossible to restrain the heroic spirit which ever glowed within her breast, and which had already stimulated her to so many daring acts, to the surprise and admiration of all who had witnessed them—but she knew well that it would be useless for her to solicit anything apparently so extravagant or permission to do so; and she therefore forebore to do so, although she was fully determined not to permit any opportunity to escape her of gratifying her wishes.

Abdal quickly sought her presence, and expressed the greatest anxiety on her account but the intrepid girl endeavoured to quiet his apprehensions, and seemed to look forward to the deadly combat which was so shortly about to take place with the utmost impatience and expectation.

"Fear not for me, Abdal," she remarked, "for Omelia, as you know, never yet shrunk from danger, trusting as she does in the mercy of the Almighty Power which has never yet failed to protect her, and the spirit which always goads her on to throw aside the weakness of woman in her wish to contribute her humble aid to hurl destruction on the miscreants who had so savagely outraged all the feelings of humanity in their thirst for blood. I feel as though I had a mission to perform, and there is no risk that I will hesitate to incur in order to fulfil it."

"Noble-minded girl," exclaimed Abdal, "what matchless heroism and self devotion do you ever display on the most trying occasions, and which must surely ere long meet with their due reward in the gratification of all your hopes and wishes."

"Alas," returned Omelia, "I have too much reason to fear, after all, the many disappointments it has been my lot to experience, that can never be. But one thing I enjoin you, Abdal, and I feel assured that your friendship towards me will prompt you to comply with my wishes and solicitations."

"Name them, Omelia," he said, "and you may be certain that there is nothing you may desire me to do to serve you, that I will refuse to do, should it be in my power."

"I know it, I am convinced of it, Abdal," said our heroine, "and I need not express my gratitude for the feelings of friendship you have ever so generously evinced towards me. Should anything serious happen to me in this struggle with the remorseless foe, and you should be saved, will you promise me to exert yourself to the utmost to discover whether my beloved Stanley still lives, and assure him of the unshaken constancy of Omelia's sentiments towards him, even up to the last moment, and that her earnest prayers were ever offered up to heaven for his welfare and happiness?"

"Oh, need you ask me?" replied Abdal, whose looks sufficiently testified to his sincerity; "I swear to do so, and you know you may depend upon me; but banish the dismal forebodings and misgivings you seem to have suffered to take possession of you, for I cannot help still encouraging the hope, and I would wish you to do the same, that not only is Mr. Stanley living, but that the time is not far distant when you will be again restored to each other.

"Oh, thank you for that wish, Abdal," observed our heroine, "and which I would fain fondly and sincerely hope may be realised. But hark! those sounds give warning of the commencement of the deadly strife, and my anxiety to mingle in the exciting scene increases."

"It would be rash and imprudent to do so, Omelia," returned Abdal, "why should you thus expose yourself to danger? I request you to remain where you are till, at any rate, there may be a necessity for removing from it. I will return to you as soon as I can, and in the meantime may providence protect you."

Omelia made no reply—though her mind was made up, and nothing whatever, as has been frequently shown, could move her from her purpose, when once she had formed a resolution—but extended her hand towards him, which he raised respectfully to his lips, and then hastened to join the combatants.

The roar of the cannon, volley after volley in rapid succession, and loud shouts that rent the air from the combatants, showed that the battle had indeed commenced in real earnest, and Omelia, whose feelings as may be expected were wrought up to the highest pitch of excitement, could not resist them, but watching her opportunity, and having first commended herself to the care and protection of providence, quitted the place unobserved, and with the utmost intrepidity made her way to the scene of danger.

And the scene was certainly one of the most desperate and exciting description. The enemy were in great force, their numbers far exceeding those of the English, and apparently forming some of the flower of the rebel army, and notwithstanding the destructive fire poured forth upon them by the guns of the former which occupied an excellent position at the entrance to the village, they pressed forward with fierce determination, and seemed resolved to maintain the combat to the last.

The British, also, under the cover of their guns, advanced boldly to meet them, until they had obtained a sufficiently advanced position to get a flanking fire on the enemy's line, which seemed to paralyse them for a moment, and to throw them into some confusion, but they quickly recovered themselves and renewed the combat with increased energy and determination, the fire which was kept up on both sides being fearful, and the dead and dying quickly strewing the earth in all directions.

And in the midst of all this dreadful scene of carnage, Omelia fearlessly mingled; where the danger was greatest there was she to be seen, fighting sword and pistol in hand, with all the heroism of the bravest of our soldiers, and exciting them to still more daring deeds by the force of her example, and at the same time creating feelings of the greatest wonder in the minds of all who beheld her.

The shots flew around her in perfect showers, but still she escaped uninjured, and seemed indeed to possess a charmed life.

It was indeed a most extraordinary and exciting sight to behold that young and beauteous Indian maiden thus fearlessly exposing herself to all the horrors of the deadly strife, and fighting with a skill and bravery which could scarcely be surpassed by even the most courageous and experienced of the soldiers and officers then engaged, her appearance seeming to create quite a panic amongst a portion of the rebels who doubtless could hardly look upon her as anything else than a supernatural being.

The battle still continued with unabated courage and determination, but still the advantage—notwithstanding the superiority of the rebel force, as regarded numbers—was on the side of the English, from the commencement, and of the ultimate issue of the battle from the first there could be very little doubt.

Suddenly, however, our heroine, to her dismay, found herself hemmed in and surrounded by the enemy, and her fate appeared to be inevitable. A dozen rifles were immediately presented at her, and her death must have instantly followed, but at that critical moment a loud and authoritative voice was heard commanding them to forbear, and one of the rebel leaders who seemed to possess great influence over them, and who was a remarkably fine looking man rode in amongst them, and in an instant the deadly weapons were lowered, and Omelia was rescued from death but to find herself a prisoner.

"Hold," replied the rebel chief, "the life of this daring and extraordinary girl must at least be spared until we have learned something more about her. Secure the prisoner, and bear her from hence to await my farther orders."

Our heroine, notwithstanding the danger of her situation, and that she had every reason to fear the worst, did not suffer her fortitude to forsake her, but fixing upon him a look of scorn and defiance, she said—

"You have made a bold capture of a woman, forsooth, and I cannot but congratulate you on it. But still the spirit of Omelia will remain undaunted."

"Bold words these," said the chief, "for one whose life is now in the hands of those whom she affects to despise. But we shall see how long this boasted courage will continue. Away with her to the rear."

The words had scarcely escaped his lips, when one of the ammunition waggons at no great distance from the spot where they were standing, exploded with a terrific noise, throwing the rebels into alarm and confusion and at the same time, a portion of the English soldiers making a dashing charge on the right of the enemy, threw them into a panic, and they turned and fled, and Omelia found herself, to her no small wonder, once more at liberty.

The victory was complete, and the enemy being pursued were dreadfully slaughtered, and leaving their guns, baggage and ammunition in the hands of the victors.

Omelia was conducted into the presence of the general, who could not refrain from eulogising the remarkable intrepidity of her conduct in the warmest manner, while at the same time he expressed his disapprobation of her exposing herself to such risks and so unnecessarily.

"It would appear," he observed, "that you have become completely reckless of your own life, since you thus voluntarily expose it."

"Ah, sir," replied the damsel, "life has now indeed but few charms for me, since it has been the will of providence to separate me from him who possessed all my heart's warmest affections, and I have but too much reason to fear that we shall never behold each other again."

"I sympathise with you, my poor girl," returned the general, in a tone of sincerity which could not be mistaken, "and I trust that your melancholy misgivings may not be realised; but that accident may restore you to each other when you the least expect it. But return to the house in which with the other females you were quartered for the night; there are yet two or three hours for rest, previous to our resuming the march, and of that, especially after the exertions you have lately undergone, you must stand so much in need."

"But my companion," said Omelia anxiously, "the good Abdal, to whom I am already so much indebted, he took an active part in this late sanguinary battle; is he safe?"

"He was not unwatched by me," replied the general, "and voluntary as it was on his part, I could not but admire him for his conduct; he distinguished himself bravely, and I have every reason to believe that he escaped uninjured.'

"He is here, sir," said an officer, who had at that moment entered the presence of the general, accompanied by the object of inquiry, and Omelia could not restrain the expression of her feelings of satisfaction and delight at beholding him in safety, while Abdal evinced the same pleasure on seeing her, as he had naturally entertained the most serious apprehensions for her safety knowing the imminent dangers to which she had so boldly exposed herself.

The general having condescended to congratulate him, and eulogise him for the brave part he had acted in the late battle, Abdal conducted Omelia to the house in which the other females had collected as before, and after congratulating each other on their escape they separated.

By break of day, the wounded having been collected, the march was resumed, and continued with all possible expedition, the general being anxious to meet the Commander-in-Chief at the time appointed.

CHAPTER CXIV.

THE RELIEF OF LUCKNOW.—THE LOVERS.

We will now return to the Residency where since the arrival of the gallant Havelock and his brave colleague Sir James Outram, the utmost excitement had prevailed, and the garrison who had so nobly defended themselves, and resisted the overwhelming force by which they were surrounded with such indomitable courage and determination, had felt considerable relief, after all the doubts, the hopes, and disappointments they had been fated to encounter, but still the difficulties, the dangers, and horrors they had yet to endure and surmount were of the most fearful description, and sufficiently disheartening.

It would be impossible, however, to overrate the immense help which the arrival of Havelock and his gallant band of warriors had afforded the besieged, by the great accession of strength which it brought them. They were now rendered independent of the native troops, upon whose fidelity their very existence had for weeks depended, as will be seen from the observations of Lieutenant Jones, who says:—

"Our real danger consisted in the probable determination of the natives still with us to abandon us soon—the fearful exhaustion that would consequently have ensued—the necessity of abandoning our outposts—the losses by musketry and mining which would have followed. Opposition to an assault would, with our then diminished numbers, have been next to impossible, and thus most assuredly does the Lucknow garrison owe its lives to the timely arrival of Generals Outram and Havelock, and their brave troops."

But not an hour's respite scarcely were they allowed from the enemy, who kept up an incessant fire which did great destruction, and every day increasing their difficulties, and their powder growing short, they look d forward to the arrival of Sir Colin Campbell to their final relief with the utmost impatience and anxiety.

This anxiety was at length relieved, for about the 12th of November, it was ascertained that the Commander-in-Chief was advancing from Cawnpore, and on the morning of the 15th his march to Lucknow with the relieving army of five thousand men was the welcome intelligence telegraphed, and every heart beat high with hope and expectation, while his progress was watched with the deepest interest.

It is necessary that we should relate in as few words as possible, from the limited space allowed us in our tale, the particulars of the march of Sir Colin Campbell to the final relief of the so long beleaguered garrison, until the day that struck the decisive blow, and released, so many from that long captivity in which they had experienced so many sufferings and privations, sufferings, in fact, unparalleled in the history of similar events.

Innumerable were the difficulties the brave commander had to meet with as he proceeded on his march, with all the expedition he could, but the veteran hero surmounted them with all that skill and bravery for which he is so pre-eminently distinguished, driving the enemy in confusion before him, gaining victory after victory, securing position after position, and every hour making the distance between him and the city less, and ensuring that success which he afterwards so nobly accomplished.

The foe was entrenched in great force as he made his way, in a series of strongly fortified buildings, but braving every danger, and conquering every obstacle that presented itself, no matter however formidable, he continued his march on the Sikunder Bagh, which is a strong square building surrounded by a wall of solid masonry, and presenting every means for defence and resistance.

Terrible was indeed the resistance which the Commander-in-Chief and his brave army here encountered, the enemy being in great numbers, and they also holding possession of a village on the opposite side of the road. But the struggle though severe lasted no great length of time, our brave soldiers suffering not the overwhelming numbers of the enemy or the strength of their position to daunt them, but sweeping all before them with the rifle, the sword, and the bayonet, and driving the rebels across the plain in the utmost state of terror and confusion, they leaving heaps of their dead and wounded behind them on the ensanguined ground where the dreadful conflict took place.

And while this was proceeding, the struggle at the Sikunder Bagh was terrific, for there the guns of the artillery had for some time been battering the walls with little or no effect. But when at last a breach was effected, the charge that followed was one of the most gallant, or rather heroic, ever recorded in the annals of war.

And now the gallant Highlanders, and the no less daring and invincible Sikhs, with shouts that made the air resound again, and might be heard even above the mighty roar of the cannon which belched forth their fury on the devoted place, rushed to the wall and through the breach, encountering the rebels with irresistible bravery, and dealing death and destruction around them, for the miscreants, the blood-stained monsters of Cawnpore, and the other scenes of their atrocities had no means of escape but must meet the awful fate which was in store for them. Truly the terrible hour of retribution had arrived, and nothing could check the wrath of our soldiers in dealing it.

"What passed within that house of horrors," we once more quote from the work of the Rev. Mr. Brock, "none who survive care to tell. Every now and then a plumed bonnet and a tartan plaid were laid upon the grass outside the blood stained entrance. Beneath them lay a stalwart form whose eye will never more gladden the northern cottage

from which the dead man came. Hour after hour passed in that awful struggle. As we read of the storming of Sikunder Bagh, it may seem as if it had been the work of a single hour. It was the work of several hours. Anxious men stood this crater outside, wondering how the battle sped, and when it would be won.

"But the volcano within the thick walls still raged like a fiery furnace, and life was its costly fuel. Gradually the sphere of action widened as the different parts of the building were carried and allowed the entrance of fresh men, but not more than four hundred soldiers of our army were at any moment inside, and once in, there was no egress. The mutineers, whose numbers were at first overwhelming, struggled hard for life against the avenging column. At last the struggle closed, the work of death was done, the Sikunder Bagh no more intercepted their march of mercy, and as they looked on the piles of dead, men were constrained to say, ' Here surely is retribution for Cawnpore.'

Thus the invincible army under the command of his excellency, Sir Colin Campbell to victory, the first days operations had been brought to a close, success the most triumphant having crowned every operation.

In the meantime, the progress of Sir Colin having been most anxiously watched by the garrison, every preparation was made to assist him as soon as he should reach near enough, and that was done by the explosion of mines with good effect, and at last when the bugles sounded the advance, the enthusiasm which animated the breasts of all reached its highest pitch, and the signal was received with the most deafening cheers by the troops, and all awaited the result of the arduous and bloody struggle which was so fast approaching, with feelings such as even most powerful language might well fail to give an adequate idea of.

"Their cheers," writes the lamented Sir Henry Havelock, in his last despatch, "echoed through the courts of the palace, responsive to the bugle sound, and on they rushed to assured victory. The enemy could no where withstand them. In a few minutes the whole of the buildings were in our possession, and have since been armed with cannon, and steadily held against all attack."

The following day brought the hard earned struggle in the cause of humanity and the terrible punishment of the rebel miscreants to a close. The building called the Mess-house was heavily cannonaded by Captain Peel. At about 3 P. M., it was stormed without much risk, and was carried immediately with a rush.

"The troops," continues Sir Colin Campbell's despatch, from which we obtain the

above particulars, then pressed forward with great vigour and lined the wall separating the Mess-house from the Motee Mahal, which consists of a wide enclosure and many buildings. The enemy here made a last stand, which was overcome after an hour, openings having been broken in the wall, through which the troops poured with a body of sappers, and accomplished our communications with the Residency.

"I had the inexpressible satisfaction, shortly afterwards of greeting Sir James Outram, and Sir Henry Havelock, who came out to meet me ere the action was at an end.

"The relief of the beseiged garrison had been accomplished."

The victorious troops had entered the Residency, and amidst the yet booming sound of the cannon, and the fire of the

musketry, might be heard the glad shouts from many a brave heart which had long beat high with mingled hope, and fear, and expectaiton, many a once bright eye was dimmed with tears of gratitude for deliverence from sufferings that seemed too great for human nature to endure, yet had they been sustained by delicate women and children for months with a fortitude and heroism that have seldom been equalled, but certainly never surpassed.

It was night, the moon had just arisen and shed its pale light over a scene, which might well defy and baffle description even by the most powerful pen, rendered at once so ghastly and impressive by the deadly work of destruction that had long been carried on in that devoted place. In whatever direction the eye was turned, the awful effects of that work of destruction were to be observed, in huge heaps of the ruins of fallen buildings and walls that had been battered down by the incessant fire from the cannon of the beseigers, and it seemed indeed miraculous that any one could have survived in that locality of death and horror.

About this hour, and when it might have been thought unsafe for any one to venture abroad, the forms of a native man and female might have been seen stealthily wending their way past that series of palaces, in continuation of the Residency stretching along the banks of the Goomtee, and which up to the time of the arrival of Sir Colin Campbell had been occupied by the relieving column under the command of Sir Henry Havelock and Sir James Outram.

It was something more than mere curiosity which seemed to have called those persons forth, for in their countenances, particularly that of the female, was depicted much anxiety of mind, and her footsteps were faltering at times, and she seemed as if she were unable to proceed without the support of her companion's arm.

She cast many an eager and inquiring look around her as she proceeded, and appeared to be uncertain of the way she was going. Not to keep the reader, however, any longer in suspense, it may perhaps be as well at once to state that the persons of whom we are writing were Omelia and Abdal and that they were making their way towards one of the principal of the palaces before mentioned, and in which Sir James Outram and Sir Henry Havelock had taken up their residence for the last six weeks which was the time that they had arrived to the relief of the garrison.

How they had been permitted to follow the column of the general to whom they had been first introduced, has been already shown, and that they had been also allowed to enter the residency with the relieving troops is now equally evident, but what were their motives for venturing forth at that time is yet to be seen.

As they advanced, there was much in the scene which met their gaze to call for their admiration, the bright lamp of heaven clearly revealing to them every object for some distance, and shining upon the different palaces and splendid gardens, clear ornamental waters, elegant bridges, magnificent temples with shining domes and lofty minarets soaring to the sky, whilst rich clusters of trees were grouped fantastically here and there, and forming altogether an interesting sight which none other than an eastern climate could produce.

And yet amidst all this scene of beauty, the dread effects of war were but too painfully apparent, and were calculated to excite the most melancholy thoughts and feelings in the mind of the spectator.

Omelia and her companion paused for a minute or two, and looked with anxiety and some hesitation around them, and it was quite evident that the most perplexing thoughts, and painful doubts and fears occupied and agitated the mind of Omelia especially.

"What a bold and hazardous task is this that I have ventured upon, Abdal," remarked our heroine.

"True," replied Abdal, "and there is something so strange and preposterous about it, that I cannot for a moment bring myself to encourage any idea of its success."

"And yet," said Omelia, "a singular feeling urges me on, which I cannot resist, and although nothing but the most bitter disappointment too probably awaits me, I must proceed. Something seems to whisper to me that the time is at hand when I shall at least be able to ascertain something of the fate of Stanley, and let whatever may be the consequences I will persist."

"Alas, with how little prospect I am afraid of your wild hopes being realised," remarked Abdal, "still have I consented to accompany you on your errand, and I need not say, I am sure, how great would be the gratification it would afford me should by some wonderful interposition of providence your wishes be crowned with success. The letter which the general was so kind as to give you will probably gain us admission, notwithstanding the singularity of the application, to the building where the regiment to which Lieutenant Stanley belonged, we have ascertained is at present quartered. I must admit that I far from approve of the strange resolution you have formed, Omelia"

"Why," demanded our heroine, "do you blame me for the anxiety I feel to learn the fate of him from whom I have been so long separated?"

"No," replied Abdal, "on the contrary, I most enthusiastically admire the love and constancy the self devotion that prompt you. But you cannot be ignorant of the danger we both incur by such an undertaking. Intruders as we are, we are liable to the severest punishment, nay, even to be treated as spies and traitors."

"Again, Abdal, I tell you," she returned impatiently, "that there is no risk I am not prepared to run, even death itself, with the hope of accomplishing my wishes. Besides, I have every confidence, and will not on any consideration now shrink from the task I have undertaken. Death, I repeat would be far more preferable to me than the torturing state of uncertainty and suspense I have so long had to endure. Beloved Stanley, could I but once more behold you, to assure you of the undying constancy of my love, and to hear you reciprocate my sentiments even if we were the next moment separated with the uncertainty of our ever meeting again, methinks that I could learn to be content if not happy.

"Noble-hearted Omelia." said her companion, with a look of the warmest admiration, "surely such fidelity deserves to meet with every reward, and that your fondest hopes may be realised is my most sincere and fervent prayer."

"Yes," said our heroine—and her bright eyes seemed to sparkle with redoubled lustre and her bosom heaved with the intensity of her feelings as she spoke—"my hopes again revive—although I admit they are coupled with some painful misgivings—and I cannot resist the impulse that urges me on. Last night in my dreams I again beheld my lover, I felt myself clasped to his bosom, and his heart throb to mine. I beheld his looks of affection, I listened enraptured to the melody of his manly voice, as he repeated his vows of eternal constancy, and talked of the bliss that awaited us, of the happy time when, after surmounting all the many difficulties it has been our lot to encounter, braving the numerous vicissitudes we have met with, and still remaining true to each other, our fates should be united, and the sorrows of the past if not entirely forgotten remembered only as some painful dream. Oh, Abdal, can such happiness as that which imagination thus conjured up to me be in store for me?"

"Oh, yes," replied Abdal, " most ardently do I hope and trust that it is. Most sincerely do I wish that all which was pictured to your imagination in such glowing colours may be realised. But come, let us proceed."

Omelia returned no answer, but her looks fully revealed the thoughts and feelings that were passing in her mind. Leaning on the arm of Abdal she was conducted by him towards a large building at some short distance, and which it appeared was the place of their destination.

They had not proceeded far, however, when they were startled by the sound of several footsteps mingled with the confused buzz of voices behind them, and they looked back hastily to discover the cause, but the numerous trees which grew near the spot from whence the sounds seemed to proceed, prevented them from gratifying their curiosity, although it was evident that the persons, whoever they might be, were approaching that way; and they looked hastily about them to see whether they could find some place to conceal themselves till they had passed.

Fortunately only a few paces from where they stood, and rather away from the direct road they had been pursuing, there stood a small deserted wood building, to which they hastened, and finding the door fallen from its hinges, they entered without observation, and placing themselves near a window—an eastern window it may be necessary to inform the reader, meaning a lattice work—from which they could observe all that passed without running any danger of being seen themselves, they awaited cautiously to ascertain whether there was any danger to be apprehended.

They were not kept long in suspense. The sounds approached nearer, and the voices of several men smote their ears; the moon at the same time appearing from behind a cloud which for two or three minutes had obscured it, rendered everything distinctly visible, and they then beheld a file of English soldiers emerge from behind a clump of trees that grew a short distance from the place in which they had concealed themselves, and approach quickly along the road.

Between them was apparently the tall figure of a man, apparently an officer, unarmed, and, it seemed to be, a prisoner, from his demeanour and the manner in which the men conducted him.

Why she could not understand, but Omelia felt a strange sensation of dread and dismal foreboding steal over her, and she gazed anxiously towards the approaching party, especially the individual mentioned, at the same time that her heart throbbed violently and she trembled, almost fearing to have her curiosity gratified, and that torturing feeling increased, the nearer the men advanced, and the form of him who had so particularly rivetted her attention was more distinctly revealed to her, for there was something in the commanding figure and manly carriage of the supposed stranger which was strikingly and painfully familiar to her.

The attention of Abdal was fixed on the same person, and he could not remove his eyes from him, while the most anxious doubts and fears, for which he was at a loss to account, took possession of his mind. He said not a word, however, to Omelia, but awaited impatiently the approaching party, who made their way so immediately in the direction of the building which they occupied, that it would be impossible for them to pass without himself and Omelia being able to observe them narrowly.

The nearer they came, the stronger became the anxious curiosity which the apparent prisoner had excited in their breasts, and the heart of Omelia palpitated so violently that she could scarcely contain herself, while she held her breath in painful expectation, and did not dare to give utterance to the thoughts that filled and agitated her mind.

At last the men came to within a few paces

of the building, when they halted, and Omelia and her companion had then an opportunity, by the bright light which the moon shed around, of observing them minutely, and they could no longer entertain any doubt that the surmises they had first formed were correct, and that the officer—who was in undress uniform, and carried his arm in a sling being apparently wounded—was a prisoner, who was being conducted towards the building whither our heroine and Abdal had been going.

And now as Omelia had an opportunity of more minutely scrutinising him, her agitation increased, a sickly sensation crept through her veins, and she clutched the arm of Abdal convulsively, gasping for breath, while the excitement of the latter was nearly equal to her own, and his eyes followed with the most uncontrollable anxiety and curiosity the same object that rivetted her attention.

The position in which he stood at first rendered it impossible for them to observe his features, but that manly form, so graceful in all its proportions, exciting at once the warmest admiration, could scarcely be mistaken, and the emotion of Omelia increased to such a degree that she could scarcely refrain from giving expression to it in a manner which must have betrayed herself and might possibly have been productive of the most dangerous consequences.

The soldiers, however, with their charge, by the command of the officer who accompanied them, were again about to proceed, when their prisoner raised his head, and his features were distinctly revealed to the anxious gaze of our heroine and Abdal, and a simultaneous cry of surprise and anguish escaped them, when their strange suspicions and forebodings were confirmed, and Stanley stood before their eyes.

But oh, how painful, how careworn, how melancholy was the expression of that manly and handsome countenance, what a tale of sorrow and suffering was there revealed.

The heart of Omelia was full to bursting, and her brain was distracted as she gazed at that loved being from whom she had so long been separated, and whom she now beheld again under circumstances at once so extraordinary and so torturing. She could not speak—she could scarcely breath—her faculties for the moment were completely suspended, and she was paralysed to the spot, while Abdal was scarcely less agitated, and could with difficulty believe the evidence of his senses.

Another moment and the unfortunate Stanley was conducted from the spot, and turning round an angle in the road was hidden from their sight.

———

CHAPTER CXV.

A TRYING SCENE.

For an instant, and an instant only, the distracted Omelia gazed wildly and vacantly in the direction of the spot whence her lover had disappeared, then aroused into a state of desperation, she uttered a wild and frantic cry, and before Abdal had the power to prevent her, she rushed with the speed of lightning from the building, taking her way, regardless of the consequences, towards the place whither he was apparently being escorted.

Madness was in her looks, and seemed to urge her in her wild pursuit, while she called aloud upon the name of her lover, and implored those who held him in their custody to stop and not to tear that beloved being, for whom she was willing to sacrifice her life from her sight for ever.

"Omelia!" cried Abdal, as he hastily followed her, "return, I beseech you, for little do you know the danger you rush upon. No," he added, after a moment's pause, "she hears or heeds me not; nothing will stay her in her rash pursuit, and I tremble to think of the consequences, but let them be whatever they may I must follow her."

Still the distracted Omelia hurried on, and still her frantic cries rent the air, and surely must have been heard by the beloved and unfortunate object of her anxiety, for the soldiers who were escorting him again appeared in sight, and suddenly stopped, no doubt to ascertain the cause of the alarm.

Nothimg whatever could stay the impetuosity of the poor girl's speed, and fairly outstripping Abdal, she reached the spot where the soldiers with their prisoner were standing and rushing wildly in amongst them, she threw herself in a transport of the most indescribable agony on his bosom, to their utter astonishment and confusion, so that they had not the power for the moment to prevent her, or to inquire the cause of conduct so extraordinary. Abdal immediately afterwards arrived at the spot, but was too much agitated to give any explanation even if it had been demanded of him.

But what language could possibly describe the surprise, the agony of the unfortunate Edward Stanley at that moment? Was it possible that he again held the beauteous form of that beloved being to his throbbing bosom, whom he had believed to be lost to him for ever, and in that moment of terrible misfortune? His brain turned giddy at the thought, he could scarcely believe the evidence of his senses, his heart seemed ready to burst with the overwhelming intensity of his feelings, he endeavoured to breathe her name, but could not, and as he strained her frantically to his bosom, manly tears, in spite of all his efforts to restrain them, trembled in his eyes, and a groan, which told the deep and utter anguish of his soul, escaped his lips.

With convulsive emotion Omelia clung to him, entwining her graceful arms around his neck, and gazing up in his face with such a mingled expression of love, agony, and despair, that it would have been impossible for even the most cold and insensible individual to behold it unmoved.

"What is the meaning of this?" at length demanded the officer, addressing himself to Stanley, "what female is this, Lieutenant Stanley, who thus appears so suddenly, and under such suspicious circumstances, and who is the man by whom she is accompanied?"

"Who is she?" returned Stanley, in a voice almost stifled by the power of his emotions; "oh, God! how can my lips answer that question? Ask this breaking heart which has long throbbed for her alone—ask these tears which in spite of manhood rush scalding to mine eyes—ask every feeling of my nature, every passion that glows within my breast, that guides and stimulates me. She is the idol of my soul, my hope, my beacon to happiness, the one beauteous being for whom alone I cling to life, but whom I despaired of ever beholding again. But to meet thus, when the dark clouds of sorrow and adversity gather so fast around, oh, it is torture most exquisite, agony most insupportable, and which will surely drive me to madness. Omelia—adored Omelia! most noble, most virtuous, most amiable and affectionate of human beings, oh, would to heaven that we had never met since cruel fate ever seems to frown upon us, and to triumph in our misfortunes."

Convulsive sobs again choked his utterance, and more vehemently, more fervently did he strain the lovely form of the Hindoo maiden to his bosom, while she continued to gaze upon him with an expression of countenance which no power of language could convey an adequate idea of, and for a minute or two seemed totally incapable of uttering a word.

The officer and the men who were with him appeared not only astonished but affected at the scene, and stood by without attempting to separate or to interrupt the unfortunate lovers. Abdal, too, as may be expected was deeply moved, and awaited the result of this extraordinary adventure with the utmost anxiety, doubt, and impatience.

"Stanley, my own fond Stanley," at length ejaculated Omelia, in tones of tenderness, and impressive energy which thrilled to the hearts of those who heard them, and excited the deepest sympathy in every breast, "you have formed the constant subject of my thoughts and anxieties by day, the vision of my nightly slumbers, since the sad hour of our separation, and do I again behold you, and as you hold me to your manly bosom feel your heart's response throbbing to mine own? Oh, has the sweet music of your voice, to which, in happier days, I have oft enraptured listened, once more fallen upon my ravished senses? Can this be true? or is it only some bright delusive dream which too soon must fade away, and leave me again, to all the horrors of misery and despair? Oh, tell me, tell me, I beseech you, and banish at once the torturing suspense which now distracts my brain, and leaves me lost and bewildered in amazement, uncertainty, and incredulity."

Stanley tried to answer, but could not, and the feelings of Omelia became wrought up to a pitch of the most ungovernable excitement, as she still hung affectionately around his neck, and seemed to gaze her very soul away in the brilliant light of her eyes.

"You do not speak," she exclaimed; "your looks are ghastly pale as those of death, "your limbs tremble, and there is a fearful expression in your eyes as you fix them so earnestly upon me that make me shudder to contemplate. And why do those men stand around with looks so stern and threatening? What dreadful foreboding is this which besets my mind, and bewilders my senses? Explain to me, tell me what it means, or I shall go mad?"

"Oh, agony most insupportable," groaned the wretched Stanley, striking his forehead with his clenched fist, while he looked the very picture of despair, "that this loved, gentle, and affectionate being should ever be subjected to so fearful a trial as this. Better—far better would it have been had fate continued to separate us, than that we should meet again under circumstances so terrible."

"Lieutenant Stanley," said the officer, "I can no longer suffer this extraordinary scene to continue. We must escort you to the place of your destination without any further interruption. This woman and her companion must also be detained until they have given some account of themselves."

"I know it is your duty to do so, sir," observed Abdal, too painfully aware of the dangerous position in which himself and Omelia were placed, and deeply regretting that they had ever ventured on so rash and imprudent an undertaking, "but we shall be fully able to prove, I trust, that we have been prompted in our conduct by motives which we need neither be afraid to acknowledge."

"That may be," returned the officer, "and it is not my business to attempt to dispute it.

It is only for me to perform my duty. Lieutenant Stanley, resign that young woman to the care of this man, her companion, and we must proceed without any further delay.

Stanley groaned, and his looks were quite sufficient to move any one to pity; but Omelia gazed vacantly around her, and in stupified amazement and bewilderment, her mind wandering, and evidently unable to understand what was passing.

"Omelia," at length cried her lover, with a burst of emotion it was utterly impossible for him to restrain, "Omelia, faithful, devoted girl, it is the cruel will of relentless fate that we should be again separated from each other, alas, I fear, to meet no more, and although it is a moment of trial almost too much for human endurance, there is no alternative, and we must submit. For myself I care not, but 'tis the anxiety I feel for that which may yet await you, the troubles, the sufferings it may still be your hard lot to experience, that racks my brain to madness. Oh, may heaven in its infinite mercy watch over and protect you, from the evils which I apprehend, and ultimately restore you to that happiness which your virtues so richly merit, although we may never, never more behold each other. Bless you, bless you, dearest one, and let the assurance that your Stanley's heart ever remained faithful to you to the last, that his whole soul was devoted to you, that he breathed, he lived alone for you, be to you some sweet consolation in the hour of your greatest affliction. One sweet, one fond kiss upon those loved lips, that I so oft have pressed in nameless transport and affection, and then——oh, God! how can I speak the dreadful word, farewell, farewell for ever!"

Again and again he kissed the beauteous and almost unconscious maiden, and sobbed as though his heart would break, then as Abdal approached, exhibiting by his looks the greatest emotion, he endeavoured with a painful effort gently to disengage himself from her; but suddenly aroused to terrible recollection, and awakened to a full sense of the stern reality, Omelia uttered a cry of the most intense agony, and still clinging convulsively to Stanley, in frantic accents which no one could listen to without emotion, she exclaimed——

"Ah, what fearful words were those, dear Stanley, I heard just now escape your lips? You could not mean what you said, or else my ears must have deceived me. Part—part! and for ever! No, no, it is impossible—it cannot be; all-just and merciful heaven will prevent it, or else permit us to die upon each other's bosom. Who dare attempt to separate us, now that we have so unexpectedly met again? They shall not tear you from me, I will cling to you with more than woman's strength and resolution, and

perish sooner than I will yield to a fate so terrible. Oh, mercy, mercy!" she continued, turning her despairing and half phrenzied looks upon the officer—who stood by, a deeply affected spectator of the extraordinary scene, feeling himself at the same time greatly embarrassed by the delicate and unpleasant duty he was compelled to perform—while tears of anguish coursed each other down her cheeks; "you will not, cannot surely seek to destroy the hopes, and break the hearts of two unfortunate beings so devoted to each other, by tearing them asunder. Our fates are bound together by every sacred tie; he is my husband in all but the name, the husband of my heart, in purity, and all the holiness of virtuous love, and death, aye, death alone shall part us more. Stanley, beloved Stanley! look not so upon me, or you will drive me to madness. No earthly power again shall part us, I am your's, your's for ever!"

As the unfortunate girl thus wildly gave utterance to these frantic and heart-rending expressions, her looks became more agonised than before, and her heaving bosom and the convulsive agitation of her whole frame, showed at once the dreadful state of excitement to which her feelings were wrought; and Stanley was so bewildered that he knew not what he did, and continued to hold her in his embrace, unable to attempt to resign her.

The officer, however, could no longer delay putting an end to this painful scene, and motioning to the men, they advanced, and with no more violence than was necessary drew the unfortunate Omelia, whom they resigned to the care of Abdal, away, Stanley uttering a cry of agony and despair as they did so.

For a moment or two Omelia stood in a fixed attitude like a statue, and gazing vacantly around her, her senses seeming entirely to have forsaken her. Not a word, not a sound escaped her lips, her faculties appearing to be entirely suspended; but suddenly as recollection returned to her, and some fearful thought seemed to flash upon her disordered brain, she said, with a look so firm and impressively melancholy, and in a voice of comparative calmness that it astonished those who beheld and listened to her—

"Dear Stanley, I see, I feel too fearfully that we must part; fate is against us and it must be so—I submit to its stern decree. One last embrace, then, and on this earth farewell, oh, farewell, most revered, most loved of human beings, for ever."

Stanley, who was as much taken by surprise as the others at the remarkable change which in such a few minutes had come over her, could only reply by heavy sobs, and as the beauteous girl rushed towards him, he opened his arms to receive her, and again with frantic emotion strained her to his bosom, and imprinted kisses of the most ardent affection upon her lips and cheeks, then raising his eyes towards heaven he silently invoked its choicest blessings upon her head.

A pause, a silence of a few moments ensued, which no one attempted to interrupt, for the touching pathos and solemnity of the scene completely absorbed the interest of all who witnessed it. Then Omelia gently withdrew herself from the embrace of her lover, and with a look of calm but fearful meaning, and in a tone of voice so strange, so impressive, and yet so unnatural that it was impossible it could ever be forgotten, she said—

"And now that terrible ordeal past, and hope entirely annihilated, Omelia has but one more task to perform to complete the painful drama, and to prove the strength of woman's love and self devotion. Stanley, 'tis thus I show how valueless, how hateful is life to me, without you."

In a moment, as she spoke, and without changing the calm determination of the expression of her features, she drew a dagger which she had concealed, and raising it in the air, was about to plunge it in her bosom, when Abdal, who had been watching her narrowly, and whose suspicions were excited, sprang hastily forward, and before she could accomplish her fatal purpose, grasped her wrist, and wrested the deadly weapon from her hand.

"This unexpected event took every one by surprise, and the excitement of Stanley, as he hastened towards her, may be readily imagined.

But the poor girl herself stood for a minute or two, fixed as a statue, with her eyes fixed upon vacancy, and seemed quite unconscious for the time being of what she had done or that which was passing around her; and her lover could only gaze at her with feelings of the greatest anguish and despair, but dared not give utterance to a syllable.

At length Omelia, passing her hands across her forehead, seemed to recall her scattered senses, and fixing one earnest look of mingled agony, affection, and despair upon Stanley, which told more, much more than words could have done, the insupportable anguish of her feelings, with a frantic cry she threw herself into his arms and became insensible.

——

CHAPTER CXVI.

FRESH TROUBLES AWAIT OMELIA.

For a minute or two the officer who had charge of Stanley was bewildered at this event, not knowing how to act; it was necessary that he should conduct his prisoner to the place of his destination without any more delay, and he felt himself to blame for having permitted this affecting and extraordinary scene to continue so long, but he also knew it to be his duty to detain Omelia and Abdal, but he had not the means of doing so, and therefore turning to Abdal, he said—

"I am myself inclined to think that the sentiments you have made respecting yourself and this singular and unfortunate girl, are true. Still you are doubtless aware that it is the duty of any officer or soldier to take into custody any stragglers they may find about, and who might naturally be suspected of being spies, or emissaries of the enemy: and I must therefore desire you to accompany me with her before the commanding officer, where you will be expected to render every account of yourselves, and to explain the cause of your venturing upon so perilous an errand."

"It is your duty, sir," replied Abdal, with becoming courtesy, "and, of course I will not attempt to dispute it, or to act in disobedience to it. Let me then have the assistance of one of your men to carry this unfortunate girl, and I am ready immediately to attend you."

At that moment, and when the officer was about to make some reply to Abdal, a small party of soldiers were seen to leave one of the buildings in the distance, and approach towards the spot where they were standing, and the officer stopped to await their arrival.

After a few words of explanation, Abdal and Omelia—who still remained in a state of utter insensibility—were committed to the charge of the officer accompanying the soldiers who had just arrived at the spot, and Stanley was then about to be conveyed away, when his feelings of agony, which he had so long struggled with and endeavoured to conquer, overpowered him, and rushing to the poor insensible girl, he so fondly loved, and who he had now but too much reason to fear that he looked upon for the last time, snatched her to his bosom in a violent paroxysm of grief and despair, and while the most indescribable emotion shook his whole frame, he smothered her lips and cheeks with his kisses, while every one stood by unable to interfere, and expressing by their looks the deepest sympathy.

"Omelia, sweet, gentle, and affectionate girl," cried the wretched Stanley, in tones that seemed to come from the deepest recesses of a breaking heart, "and shall we be permitted thus to part? shall two fond devoted hearts be thus for ever torn asunder? Better, oh, far better would it be if heaven would allow them now to break, and that we should perish in each other's arms, death thus at once mercifully terminating our mutual sorrows. I feel myself unarmed but cannot control the dreadful anguish that racks my brain, and drives me on to madness in this terrible moment of separation from all that I hold most precious in life. How beautiful she looks in her insensibility. Alas, that one so good, so lovely, and so innocent, should thus be doomed to perpetual misery. And shall I never more bask in the radiance of those bright eyes that ever beamed on me so affectionately? Shall I never more behold those beauteous features that ever rivetted my soul! in love and admiration; never more be gladdened by the sunlight of her smiles, or the soft melody of that voice, whose every tone was rapture? Alas, alas, it must be so, and fate can therefore have no sufferings more severe in store for me than those which I at present endure."

"Lieutenant Stanley," observed the officer, who had charge of him, "this display of weakness is unbecoming."

"I know it," replied Stanley, "but cannot help abandoning myself to it in this bitter moment of trial. But—but," he added, after a pause, and still gazing upon the insensible girl with looks of despair, "I must, I will be firm. Abdal, your hand, I know the friendly feelings you bear towards me; I thank you warmly for all the many acts of kindness, which during our short acquaintance, I have experienced from you, but oh, how much more grateful do I feel for your conduct towards that poor ill-fated girl who has now no other protector but yourself. I beseech you to continue to watch over her, to guard her with a brother's care, to endeavour to impart that consolation to her of which she will stand so much in need, and as you do so may heaven bless and reward you. And now adieu."

Abdal took his hand, and pressing it fervently to his heart while his looks sufficiently told the sincerity of his words, he promised faithfully to fulfil the duty which had devolved upon him, and to watch over the safety and happiness of Omelia with his life, at the same time expressing a fervent hope that the dark clouds which at present obscured the horizon of their destiny might shortly pass away, and that the time might at length arrive when he and Omelia would be restored to each other under every happy circumstance, and no more be doomed to part.

The distracted Stanley then fixed one last lingering look of the most intense and indescribable agony on the lovely countenance of the insensible maiden whom he never expected to behold again, struck his forehead with his clenched fist, and with a burst of agony which it was impossible for him to control, he tore himself away, and was conducted from the spot almost in a state of unconsciousness.

The officer in command of the small detachment of men who had last arrived, then gave the order and they marched off in a contrary direction, Omelia, who yet showed no signs of recovering, being carried by Abdal, assisted by one of the soldiers.

The heart of Abdal felt sad and foreboding as they proceeded, although he tried to conceal his real feelings as well as he could, and to appear firm. The unfortunate position in which Lieutenant Stanley was placed, and his ignorance of the offence with which he was charged—although he feared it was a grave one—caused him the utmost pain; but his principal anxiety was for Omelia, to whose feelings he feared this calamity—for in no other light could it be viewed—would prove a shock from which she could never recover, and under all these melancholy circumstances, he could not but look forward to the future with feelings of dread.

After proceeding some short distance, our heroine heaved a heavy sigh, and gave other signs of reviving to sensibility; they therefore stopped, and Abdal supporting her in his arms, with brotherly tenderness, watched her with the greatest fear and anxiety, the officer looking on with every feeling of kindness and sympathy.

Another sigh escaped the poor girl's lips, then opening her eyes, and gazing for a moment or two with vacant and bewildered looks around her, finding herself supported in the arms of Abdal, and beholding the soldiers standing near, some recollection of the truth seemed to flash upon her, and starting, in a voice of the most poignant anguish and despair, she exclaimed—

"Stanley, unfortunate Stanley, where are you? Why do not your arms support me? Gone—gone! Was it then but some wild dream?—some delusion of the senses and the disordered imagination? No, no, but a short time since my eyes beheld him; he pressed me to his heart, he called upon my name in tones of unutterable affection. I could not be mistaken. But why is he not present now? Oh, surely he could not willingly so soon have deserted me after our restoration to each other. Oh, no, some terrible cause has torn him from me, and I feel, I know that I have beheld him for the last time, and the cup of Omelia's sorrows is filled to the brim."

A burst of anguish followed these melancholy observations which choked her further utterance, and Abdal was too deeply affected to attempt to offer a word of consolation, which, however, it was evident would have been at that time completely useless.

Again she looked wildly and anxiously around her, and disengaging herself from Abdal's arms, she cried—

"But whither have they forced him? who are they that have dared to tear him from me? What cruel wretches are those that could separate two fond beings who have lived alone for each other, and leave them to all the horrors of misery and despair? But let me begone from hence—let me pursue their footsteps; they shall not keep me from him! Even now I hear his voice calling frantically upon my name, and imploring me not to desert him. Stanley, beloved Stanley, for you—to be with you, I have braved even death in its most terrible form, and no power on earth shall detain me from you. I come —I come!"

With frenzied looks she tore herself from No. 57.

the hold of Abdal, and staggered forward a few paces, when her strength failed her, emotions too great for human endurance swelled her bosom, her brain turned giddy, and with an hysterical laugh she sunk inanimate on the earth, and to all appearance dead.

Abdal raised her in his arms, and gazed eagerly in her countenance, in which every feeling of utter misery and despair was most painfully pourtrayed, and the officer approached, and with a look of pity, observed—

"Unfortunate girl, her's is indeed a melancholy case, and I cannot but feel for her the deepest commiseration."

"Alas, sir," returned Abdal, "this terrible shock is too much for her, and I fear the most fatal consequences. I now regret that her and Lieutenant Stanley should again meet each other, especially under such painful and peculiar circumstances."

"The sooner she receives medical assistance the better," remarked the officer, "and where we are about to remove her every attention will be paid her which the nature of the case demands and humanity can suggest."

"I doubt it not, sir," said Abdal, "and that she will find those of her own sex in the so long beleaguered garrison who will sympathise with her. But Lieutenant Stanley, I pray you inform me what is the nature of the offence with which he is charged?"

"That is a bold question," replied the officer, "and from a stranger, I must add an impertinent one; at any rate, it is one which I am not permitted to answer."

Abdal looked and felt disappointed, but he apologised for the liberty he had taken, and they again proceeded towards the series of large and magnificent buildings before mentioned, and which were now occupied by the relieving force, and the beautiful gardens attached to which, and the marble corridors communicating with the zenana's and gorgeous temples which filled the grounds, seemed strangely out of keeping with the rude soldier-tenantry; and as they approached, there was much in the different features which presented themselves to cause the most curious reflections.

"Here," says Mr. Brock, "were seen a group of rough highlanders eating their scanty, coarse food out of the finest china, and surrounded by every conceivable article of luxury; and there the dead body of a sepoy or camel polluted the atmosphere, rendering it scarcely bearable. Cashmere shawls and porcelain ornaments lay about unvalued, no one caring to preserve them, whilst of the commonest necessaries there was absolute want. Such is war."

But the mind of Abdal was too busily occupied with the melancholy subjects that engrossed it to allow him too take much notice of anything, and his anxiety for our heroine every moment increased.

These magnificent palaces, now converted into barracks, formed, as has been before stated, a continuation of the residency, in which the wounded and the women and children were located, till the opportunity should arrive for their safe removal, and in what way to accomplish which had become one of the earliest considerations of Sir Colin Campbell and his colleagues; for to stay there would have been to ensure a recurrence of the numerous hardships and disasters they had so long experienced. They must depart without delay.

This object it was the determination of the Commander-in-Chief to effect by a *ruse*; but of that more anon

At one of the palaces nearest the Residency, the soldiers by the command of their officer halted, and Abdal to his surprise and disappointment was informed that he must be separated from Omelia, whom it was necessary to convey into one of the houses in the Residency, occupied by some of the women and children, and where she might be properly attended to, while he must be detained in custody until he had undergone an examination before the commanding officer, who would decide in what manner he should be disposed of.

"Alas," said Abdal, "this is a most unfortunate and painful occurrence altogether, and I shudder to think of the result which is but too likely to take place. Poor Omelia, must I indeed leave you thus? Oh, what will be the agony of your feelings, when restored to sensibility, and the recollection of that which has occurred, and the dreadful uncertainty of the fate which still awaits your lover. That anguish, too, must be increased, to find yourself amongst strangers, who will probably feel but little sympathy in your misfortunes."

"Those she will find herself among," observed the officer, "have experienced too much of misery and suffering themselves, not to feel for that of others. Fear not, as I have before told you, every care and attention will be paid to her, and it is not unlikely that in a short time you will be permitted to meet again."

With this assurance Abdal was, of course, compelled to be satisfied, and having looked with feelings of the most heartfelt sorrow for a minute or two on the countenance of Omelia—who still remained in the same state of insensibility—and pressing her hand to his lips, he resigned himself to the custody of the soldiers who had to conduct him to the place of his destination, Omelia being conveyed with every care into one of the houses of the Residency by the remainder of the men, and under the charge of the officer.

CHAPTER CXVII.

THE MIDNIGHT DEPARTURE.

The unfortunate Omelia was received by the ladies who occupied the building to which she was removed with much kindness, and her appearance, and the melancholy circumstances that had thus accidentally introduced her to them, excited the greatest curiosity, interest, and sympathy; everybody being willing and anxious to do all in their power towards her recovery.

Great had been their own sufferings and privations during the many months that they had been pent up in the garrison, surrounded by a remorseless enemy, who thirsted like tigers for their blood, and, as the officer had remarked to Abdal, they knew too well how to commiserate with those of their fellow creatures, especially one of their own sex; and the beauty of the young Indian girl, and the peculiar circumstances connected with her fate had a more than common claim upon their humanity.

She still remained in a state of utter insensibility, and it was only by her low breathing, and the slight pulsation of her heart, that it became certain she still lived, although it was much to be feared from the alarming symptoms she exhibited that it would be some time ere she could recover, if, in fact, she ever did, from the severe shock she had received, which was the more to be regretted as the removal from Lucknow, as we have before stated, it had been resolved, must take place with as little delay as possible, and it was not likely that under any consideration the poor girl could be suffered to be left behind and abandoned to her fate.

Omelia was immediately placed on a couch in one of the apartments of Mrs. Eldred, the lady of one of the surgeons in the garrison, and who with her amiable daughter, a pretty young girl about seventeen, undertook to see to her recovery, and attended upon her with the utmost solicitude.

Mr. Eldred entered the room shortly afterwards, and immediately applied such remedies to our heroine as he considered were likely to tend towards her restoration to consciousness, but with little or no effect, and he recommended that she should be kept as quiet as possible, and trusting, as he expressed himself, that a few hours might effect a favourable change, although, on her reviving to sensibility the utmost precaution would be necessary.

"Poor girl," said Mrs. Eldred, compassionately, and looking earnestly at the handsome countenance of Omelia, as she lay calmly on the bed, as if she were wrapped in a tranquil slumber; "she is most beautiful and it is impossible for any one to gaze upon her without feeling the deepest interest in her fate. No wonder that young Lieutenant Stanley should feel a sincere passion for one so lovely, and no doubt so good and innocent, and who it is evident from all that we have heard, has ever proved her sincere and ardent devotion to him."

"True," coincided her husband, "this maiden has charms that might captivate any one, even the most cold and insensible. Who could imagine that one so gentle, and so delicate in appearance, could have performed deeds of daring and intrepidity, that justly entitle her to the name of an heroine, as all that has been related of her previous to her appearance here fully proves? Her's must be a strange, romantic history, and I cannot but feel the greatest anxiety for her recovery and in her future welfare and happiness."

Mrs. Eldred most sincerely responded to the wish, and the looks of the gentle Rose Eldred her daughter, sufficiently showed how warmly she participated in the feelings that her parents had expressed, tears trembled in her mild blue eyes as she fixed them earnestly on the beauteous features of the insensible Omelia, and pictured to herself the many troubles that too probably yet awaited her.

For who possessed a more generous, affectionate, and amiable heart than Rose Eldred? Who more fortitude and patient endurance under the most trying circumstances, as the many almost unparalleled hardships to which herself and parents had been subjected during the siege of the garrison amply testified.

No wonder then that the sympathies of one so good and affectionate should warm towards one like Omelia, who had already experienced so many misfortunes, and was at present surrounded with difficulties that might make even those who boasted of the greatest courage shrink appalled.

Rose was prepared to look upon the handsome young Indian girl with the warmest feelings of friendship, nay even the affection of a sister, and she therefore looked forward to the moment of her restoration to her senses with the greatest impatience, yet mingled hopes and fears, for the unfortunate situation of Lieutenant Stanley — whose offence will be explained hereafter — would naturally tend to increase the agony of Omelia's mind, and to retard her recovery, if it was not productive, in fact, of still more fatal results.

An hour had now elapsed since the removal of Omelia to the Residency, and she still remained in the same insensible and inanimate state, Mrs. Eldred and her daughter continuing to watch by her bedside with the same anxiety and tenderness as if she had been some dear and near relation, or intimate friend; and Mr. Eldred also paid her every attention that professional skill, and natural humanity enabled him to do.

Every now and then the loud roar of cannon rent the air, for the principal scheme of Sir Colin Campbell to deceive the enemy, and to secure the more safe removal of the wounded, and the women and children, was to make his dispositions and continue his fire, as if he intended to dislodge the foe from their position around the residency. And this was done through several days and nights.

But for some time not even this incessant din disturbed the tranquility, or rather the insensibility of Omelia, and it seemed as if all her faculties were for the time being entirely prostrated, and that her senses were steeped in comparative forgetfulness.

Happy forgetfulness; perhaps it would have been much better for the poor girl had it lasted for ever.

It was, however, satisfactory to Mrs. Eldred and her daughter that she also seemed to be totally unconscious of every feeling of pain, and the calm expression of her features was a sufficient proof of that, and was strangely out of keeping with the melancholy situation in which she was placed, and that which she probably still had to endure.

During the time that Lieutenant Stanley had been in the garrison, which was only since the relief brought by Generals Havelock and Sir James Outram, he had been on intimate terms with the Eldred's, they having been acquainted for many years in England, and esteeming them as he did for their excellent qualities, and knowing how well they could appreciate his feelings, and sympathise with him in his misfortunes, he had confided to them all the particulars of his first introduction to Omelia, and the pure and ardent sentiments that had sprung up between them; and need we say that he had mounted to a perfect pitch of enthusiasm in describing the beauties of her mind and person, and in recounting the many acts of heroism and self-devotion she had performed? They listened to him at all times with the deepest attention and pleasure, and could not but admire and esteem the Hindoo maiden, from the glowing portrait—in no way exaggerated—which he drew of her, even before they knew her.

And now that accident had so strangely placed her under their humane care, and they found that in point of personal beauty, at any rate, she more than realized all that he had described, it may not be considered surprising that they should view her with double the interest that they would probably otherwise have done, and were the more determined to do all that was in their power to serve her, and to impart to her that hope and consolation in the midst of the many sorrows and difficulties by which she was surrounded of which she so much stood in need.

The unfortunate position in which Stanley was placed, through the military offence he had committed—although it was believed that it would lead to no very serious results on a proper investigation—was rendered doubly painful and annoying at that time, when himself and Omelia had so unexpectedly discovered each other, and Mr. and Mrs. Eldred knew that it would require them to act with the greatest caution, in order to counteract the melancholy and torturing effects in Omelia's mind.

"Poor girl," said Mrs. Eldred, "it is indeed a sad trial and disappointment for her to have to experience after having so unexpectedly meeting with him she so fondly loves, to be again so cruelly and abruptly separated from him, and that, too, with the painful uncertainty as to whether they will ever be permitted to meet again."

"True," coincided her husband, "and I most sincerely sympathise with her, but trust that she may be able to endure it with becoming fortitude, and that, after all it may not turn out to be so bad as we are now inclined to anticipate. Hark! I almost thought I heard her speak or breath a sigh, and see a change has come over the expression of her countenance. Silence, and be cautious, for we must avoid as much as possible, exciting her."

The expression of Omelia's features had indeed changed, and she seemed to breathe more freely as if on the point of reviving.

Mr. and Mrs. Eldred and their daughter watched her narrowly and anxiously, and remained quiet, and in a minute or two Omelia opened her lips, and in faint but impressive accents murmured out the name of Stanley, following it with a deep and heart-drawn sigh, and again for a minute or two she remained silent without exhibiting any other signs of consciousness.

Mrs. Eldred, who was still seated by the bedside, took one of Omelia's hands, and her daughter the other, and they awaited her restoration to consciousness, which seemed likely about to take place, with no small degree of impatience.

They were not long kept in suspense, for in a few moments Omelia again breathed the name of Stanley, in accents of the utmost tenderness but melancholy emotion, and immediately afterwards she opened her eyes, and gently raising her head from the pillow on which it had been reclining, gazed with evident wonder and bewilderment around the the room, and on finding herself amongst strangers.

"Oh, what strange dream was that which my disordered imagination conjured up?" she ejaculated, fixing her eyes with astonishment and a searching look of inquiry upon Mrs. Eldred and her daughter; "or am I now awake? All things that I behold are so new to me, and so different is the scene to that in which I but a short time since imagined that I mingled, that my senses, still seem to wander. Methought that my beloved Stanley was restored to my willing arms, my throbbing bosom, that I felt his honeyed kisses on my lips, gazed in his manly face, glowing with affection—such alone as hearts as fondly attached as our's alone can feel—and again listened with nameless transport to those sincere and fervent vows of love which he has so often repeated to me. But," she added, starting up in the bed in the greatest state of agitation, "the spell is broken, it was all a mockery, a delusion of the disordered senses, Stanley is not here! No, no, and, ah! I now remember that he was present, that he held me in his warm embrace, and that again the loved tones of his voice fell upon my ravished senses, raising my very soul to bliss unutterable, when they tore him from me, all was then utter darkness and despair, and I remember no more. Oh, Stanley, only cherished being of my heart, it was cruel, it was monstrous to part us thus, and we shall never, never be permitted to meet again."

She covered her face with her hands as she gave utterance to the last melancholy words, and her bosom heaved violently, and her whole frame was convulsed with the power of her emotions.

"But," she exclaimed, after a brief pause, suddenly starting and gazing with anxious amazement and curiosity around the room and upon the persons near her, "whither have they born me? Where am I? And who are those I gaze upon?"

"Strangers to you, my poor girl," replied Mrs. Eldred kindly, and showing by her looks the deep compassion of her feelings, "but still disposed with every friendly feeling towards you. But in the present delicate state of your health I must request you not to excite yourself, and patiently to await all further explanation till a more fitting occasion."

"Ah!" said the agitated Omelia, fixing a still more eager look upon the countenance of Mrs. Eldred, and also gazing with surprise and anxious curiosity at her husband and daughter, who had hitherto remained silent, "there is a mystery in your words which I cannot fathom, and which excite my doubts and apprehensions, and yet there is a kindness in your looks which inspires me with every confidence. Oh, I beseech your pity for a poor friendless girl, whose heart is nearly broken."

"I must, as well as my wife," now observed Mr. Eldred, "request you to be calm, and to rest assured that you are with those who will treat you with every kindness and attention. Neither are you exactly unknown to us, although till to-night we never beheld you before."

Omelia stared at him with stupified amazement, but for a minute or two she could not utter a word.

"Mystery upon mystery," she at length exclaimed, "what can be the meaning of this? You torture me. But why am I here? Where is Stanley? Where the faithful Abdal, whose friendship never yet failed me in the hour of need? Ah! the whole fearful truth now suddenly rushes upon my brain, and I feel at once the full extent of my utter misery and despair."

Sobs choked her further utterance, and she threw herself back on the couch in a state of anguish which admitted of no consolation.

The torturing thoughts that crowded upon her with such rapidity and overwhelming effect, were almost too much for reason to withstand, and after giving vent to her feelings in another violent paroxysm of grief, which Mr. and Mrs. Eldred, by every compassionate means in their power tried to soothe, she again relapsed into a state of utter unconsciousness, from which it did not seem to be at all likely that she would again awaken for some time.

Mrs. Eldred and her daughter felt more keenly than ever for the deplorable situation in which the unfortunate girl was placed, and the dismal prospects that were before her, and there was nothing whatever that their limited means would allow them, which they would not willingly have done to alleviate her sufferings, and those feelings of sympathy were fully participated in by the other ladies who were residing in the same building, looking forward with anxious hopes and fears to the moment of their removal from that place, which for months had been the scene of so many horrors, and where they had had to encounter sufferings, which, fortunately had seldom before fallen to the lot of human beings.

Little change took place in our heroine during the night, but on the following day she was more composed, and was able to listen to the explanation which Mr. Eldred and his wife thought proper to give her, without any of those extraordinary feelings of excitement that might have been expected.

But most agonising were her feelings of anxiety for the uncertain fate which awaited the unfortunate Stanley, especially as she was unable to learn the character of his offence—although Mr. Eldred endeavoured to inspire her with the hope that he would triumph over all the misfortunes that at present assailed him—and at times her forebodings and apprehensions became so torturing that she was wrought up to a state of mind bordering upon distraction.

What would she have given had she been permitted an interview with the Commander-in Chief—and in the madness of her despair, she ventured to suppose that such a favour, such an honour might be granted her—that she might throw herself at his feet, and supplicate for mercy for her lover, and when she was convinced that such an idea was quite preposterous, and could not possibly be realised, she abandoned herself to all the anguish of the most inconsollable and insupportable grief, and her energies seemed entirely to forsake her.

Abdal had undergone a strict examination as to the motives which had induced himself and Omelia—who was not in a fit state to be present—to place themselves in so perilous, and at the same time, so suspicious a situation as that they had been discovered in, and his explanation being considered satisfactory, he was placed under no other restraint than was considered necessary pending the secret removal from the garrison, when he trusted he would be permitted to rejoin Omelia, for whom, of cause, he felt the greatest anxiety.

In the meantime what were the sufferings of the wretched Stanley after the affecting scene which has been described between himself and Omelia, and their separation? It is almost useless to endeavour to describe his sufferings, for they may be much more readily imagined.

At times his feelings were wrought up to such a state of excitement that he was almost driven to madness, and he would give vent to the agony of his grief in the most bitter lamentations, and wild ravings of despair. He pictured to himself in a most vivid and torturing colours the dreadful anguish of mind she must be enduring, and he almost regretted that they should have met again under such unfortunate circumstances, and which could only be productive of the greatest misery to them both.

Thus the dreary hours wore away, and as they did so the anguish of Stanley increased and all kinds of dismal thoughts and forebodings arose to his imagination, which he could not now struggle against without the greatest difficulty.

But for a brief period it is necessary that we should leave the lovers, in order that we may relate other particulars in their due course.

As has been before stated, Sir Colin continued his fire for several days until he had completed his arrangements for the deliverence of those for whom the country had so long been anxious.

Lines of picquets were at last arranged through which the women and children with the wounded were to be conducted to the Alum Bagh. The rebels were completely ignorant of this, and had not the slightest suspicion of what was being done; in consequence of which they kept on their murderous fire as they deemed it upon the garrison far into the night.

Midnight was now fast approaching, all was gloom and silence around, so cautiously and so quietly was the departure commenced. The wounded were placed in doolies, and the women and children—among the former of whom was Omelia, who had by a determined effort, summoned all her fortitude to her aid for the occasion, especially as Abdal was permitted to be near her, and Mrs. Eldred

and her amiable daughter were her companions—were disposed of in the best manner that the circumstances would allow, and thus began the all important task which Sir Colin Campbell had so bravely and so nobly undertaken to accomplish at all hazards.

"Leaving behind them many a sad memento of the losses they had suffered, and of the calamites they had endured," writes the Rev. Mr. Brock, "the rescued ones went forth hardly knowing whither they went. Probabilities were all against the hope that they might elude the vigilance of their fiendish and blood thirsty foes.

"The cavalcade moved silently and slowly onwards, unnoticed and unchallenged by any portentous token or unfriendly voice. Believing that the picquets were faithfully occupying their appointed places, and that the pathways along the many narrow lanes had been well ascertained, hope animated the fugitives, whilst the continued fire upon their abandoned prison house convinced them that the assailants had no idea of their escape.

"The generals were as anxious and as vigilant as if they had their own wives and children beneath their care, evincing the most instinctive solicitude to secure as far as possible the convenience of each wounded soldier, and the comfort of every weakly child.

"A fine subject for a congenial artist, that strange and extemporaneous grouping of young men and maidens, of old men and children, threading their dubious way from impending danger to a place of safety amidst the darkness of a long November night.

CHAPTER CXVIII.

THE JOURNEY AND ITS INCIDENTS.

The night was particularly dark and gloomy, and the thoughts and feelings of Omelia, as may be supposed were in painful unison with the dreariness and solemnity of the hour, although the novelty of the scene in which she now found herself an actress did serve in some measure to divert her mind at times from the melancholy subjects that occupied it, and her new found friends, Mr. and Mrs. Eldred and their daughter exerted themselves all that they could to alleviate the anguish and anxiety of her mind, and to inspire her with a feeling of hope

But it was impossible, when she reflected upon all the circumstances that had lately taken place, and the uncertainty of Stanley's fate, for her to be otherwise than wretched.

She recalled to her memory in the most gloomy colours, the agony of his looks, as he

...ress her with such phrenzied and convulsive emotion to his manly bosom; she again in imagination beheld the wild expression of despair that gleamed from his eyes, she again heard the mournful words that escaped his lips, as he bade her farewell for ever, and her brain became distracted, and to attempt to console her, for a time was completely useless.

It had been deemed advisable to take from the Residency the treasure which had been accumulated there, and the jewels formerly belonging to the King of Oude; this was following in the train of the cavalcade.

Hour after hour passed without the occurrence of a mishap, and as morning drew on the impression deepened and encouraged every heart that they were really safe.

At length the darkness of the night dispersed, and daylight broke upon the anxious fugitives, revealing to them their position. They saw the picquets, between whose friendly and effective shelter they had been passing all the night, closing in around them.

"To the delight of the gallant deliverers, not a soul who had left Lucknow was missing. One of the most sagacious devices with which modern warfare is acquainted was completely successful.

"The hope that had been so long deferred was realised; thus far the fugitives from the house of bondage were free. A subsequent march under the same truly patriarchal guardianship brought the rescued ones to the Alum Bagh.

"Having obtained what refreshment was available for their manifold need, the wounded and the sick, with the children and the women, were escorted on towards Cawnpore, on their way to Allahabad."

The weather was favourable, and the aspect of the country through which they were now traveling was of the most picturesque, and in some instances enchanting description, and in the contemplation of the beauties of nature, of which she was, as has been shown an enthusiastic admirer, Omelia did at length find some alleviation of the anguish of her mind, and was enabled for a time to dismiss the dismal thoughts that had previously occupied it.

A country of such vast extent as Hindoostan necessarily presents a great variety of surface. A portion of it consists of immense and fertile plains, well watered by the great rivers and their numerous tributaries, and rich in all the luxuriance of tropical vegetation. Parts of these plains are occupied by the marshes and overgrown with low underwood, which renders them unfit for cultivation. These form what are called the jungles, and there lurk the tiger, the elephant, and the hyena.

Through every variety of scene the cavalcade passed, which kept the eye constantly engaged and the mind aroused. Sometimes they came upon a wide tract of sandy desert, succeeded by table lands, or bounded by a long line of fine, undulating hill country.

Then their way lay through green valleys, well cultivated and luxuriant fields, with villages sheltered beneath groves of the cocoa-palm, and swarming with inhabitants.

We are thus particular in describing the features of Indian scenery, thinking that it may prove amusing and instructive to those who have never visited that wonderful country which now possesses a tenfold interest, from the extraordinary and exciting events that for so many months have been taking place there.

As the fugitives proceeded, so did the beauty and diversity of the scenery appear to increase, and dull and insensible must be the individual who could not as he gazed become lost in wonder and admiration. To the traveller indeed what scenes of magnificence and beauty of grandeur and sublimity meet his astonished and delighted gaze at every turn. Let him turn his eyes to the mighty range of the Himalaya mountains, rising in some parts to a height of 25,000 feet above the level of the sea, and clad in everlasting snows, or let him watch some mighty river rolling its floods through plains of boundless extent, or listen to the mountain torrent thundering down the rocky ghaut, or wander amid the pathless forest, where one leaf of the fan-palm serves for a shelter for a dozen men, and the cotton tree, with its gorgeous purple blossoms, grows to the height of fifty feet, still must he be lost in admiring wonder at the immensity of the scale of the natural objects by which he is surrounded.

Then we will suppose the traveller's way to lie through some beautiful scene such a one as is thus described by Baron Hugel in his "Travels in Kershmir and the Punjaub."

"Billaspur lies in a spacious valley, through which the Gutlez winds its long and fertilising course, while in the distance, high and waving hills, crowned with villages stretched for several miles the snowy peaks of the Himalaya mountains being distinctly visible on the horizon.

"The valley is extremely fertile, and every tropical plant flourishes in richer profusion here than in most other parts of Hindoostan, as if the Great Author of all nature had lavished his gifts on it without any reserve.

"The sun was sinking when first I gazed on this beautiful scene; the river rolled proudly on beneath the garden where I stood, surrounded on every side by a treasury of fragrant flowers, among which the rich orange and citron trees, entangled with jessamines and groups of magnolias, wafted their exquisite perfume around in the descending dews. The stars and moon arose one by one, not a breath was felt, the lofty palms rustled, and gently stirred their leaves as if some spirit breathed upon them; the trees were lighted up by fire-flies, and within their deep recesses was heard the soft twittering of the birds, and the shriller tones of a kind of mantis; which has its dwelling in the citron tree, in the distance bright lamps shining through the night, pointed out the temple where loud voices and noisy drums were sounding in the praise of their idols; the fantastic costumes, the dreamy air, all—all combining together might well have inspired the coldest spectator to exclaim as he gazed, "This is the very India of which I have dreamed.'"

It was amid a similar scene to the one thus described in such glowing colours, that the cavalcade halted to rest for a brief period, for they had now got beyond the reach of immediate danger, and hope and confidence once more began to animate each breast, while the feelings of gratitude arose to heaven for their deliverance from those dreadful sufferings which at one time they thought would only terminate in death.

As Omelia gazed upon the various beauties that met her eyes wherever she directed her gaze, she endeavoured, for a time at least, to banish the recollection of the heavy sorrows by which she had been assisted, from her brain, and to look forward with some degree of hope to the future. But vain was the effort, fruitless the task which she would fain have imposed upon herself, and the more she endeavoured to accomplish it, the greater and more insupportable became the anguish and anxiety of her mind.

Dismal indeed was the prospect before her disordered imagination, not one ray of sunshine amid the misery and darkness of despair. Stanley was lost to her, she felt all but convinced, for ever, there was a mystery, a terrible mystery about the fate which either awaited him, or had already befallen him, that was rendered still more agonising from the secrecy which every one maintained upon the subject, and which suggested the most torturing conjectures and apprehensions, and at times so powerful was the effect it had upon her, that she could scarcely contain herself, and her friends endeavoured to console and tranquilise her feelings in vain.

Could she but have been permitted to see him again, if only for a moment, to satisfy her that he still lived, had she been allowed once more to listen to the beloved tones of his voice, she could have been content, but every one seemed to mock the misery of her feelings, to exult over her sufferings, and to be kept in such a terrible state of uncertainty and suspense, was certainly almost too much for human endurance.

The journey was quickly resumed, and was continued through the same description of romantic and diversified scenery as that which has already been described. All external nature, as it then met the delighted sight, was rich in so surpassing grandeur and loveliness, that the fond fancy might well deem it some long lost relic of Eden's bowers, where sin and sorrow had found no place, and on which the primeval curse had not descended.

Was it possible that those could have been the scenes of atrocities too horrible for recital? That so bright, so fair a land could have been deluged with the blood of hundreds of unfortunate and innocent human beings? Yet so it was, and at the thought, even the most stern and insensible nature must shrink appalled, and marvel that offended heaven should so long have withheld its just, but terrible retribution from the heartless and blood-thirsty miscreants, who had so barbarously outraged all its sacred laws.

And now they approach a city, one of those oriental cities which Bishop Heber thus so graphically describes, and which we cannot do better than to quote for the information of the European stranger:—

"Behind the elegant front line of houses is ranged a town deep, black, and dingy, with various crooked streets, huts of earth baked in the sun, or of twisted bamboos, interspersed here and there with ruinous brick bazaars, pools of dirty water, cocoa-trees, and little gardens, with some fine large dirty houses, the residence of wealty natives.

"Fill up this outline with a crowd of people in the street, beyond anything even to be seen in London, some dressed in tawdry silks and brocades, more in white cotton garments, and most of all black and naked, except a scanty covering round the waist, besides figures of religious mendicants, with no covering but their long hair and beards in elf locks, their faces painted white or yellow, their heads in one ghastly lean hand, and the other stretched out like a bird's claw to receive donations, marriage processions, with the bride in a covered chair, and the bridegoom on horseback, so swayed round with garlands as hardly to be seen, tradesmen sitting on the ground in the midst of their different commodities, and old men, naked as monkeys on the flat roofs of houses, carts drawn by oxen, and driven by wild-looking men, with thick sticks so unmercifully used as to perfectly undeceive all our notions of Brahminical humanity, attendants with silver maces, pressing through the crowd before the carriage of some great man or other, no women seen except of the lower class, and even these with heavy silver ornaments on their dusky arms and ankles, while couches covered up close with red cloth, are seen conveying the inmates of the neighbouring

seraglios to take what is called the air, a constant creaking of cart-wheels, which are never greased in India; a constant clamour of voices, and an almost constant thumping and jingling of drums, cymbals, &c., in honour of their deities; and add to this a villanous smell of garlic, rancid cocoa-nut oil, sour butter, and stagnant ditches, and you will understand the sounds, sights and smells of some of the streets in the principal towns of India."

In fact, amidst all its grandeur, no other part of the habitable globe presents such strange scenes, and contains such a motley population as some of the principal towns and islands of India. Towards the evening if inclined for a stroll, you may encounter Banians (pedlars and merchants), Persian and Arab horse-dealers, Parsees, descendants

of the Guebres, Chinese, Portuguese, Armenians, Hindoo clerks, coolies, Abyssinians, Europeans, infantry, cavalry, and artillery soldiers, &c.

Nor is this diversity of objects confined to the people who perambulate the different towns. There is as much variety in the different vehicles in use. While the natives who are in good circumstances, move about in all sorts of queer carts and cars, the Europeans patronize buggies—a covered kind of gig—laudaulettes, chariots, britekas, and *shrigampoes*. The last named is a square carriage, something like a palanquin on wheels, and being surrounded by Venetian blinds, is an agreeable means of locomotion.

We have thus digressed from the regular course of our tale, in order to furnish the reader with all the information regarding the eastern empire which may prove not only amusing but instructive to him.

It was through such places that the fugitives from Lucknow frequently had to pass on their way to Cawnpore; but very different was the aspect which they now presented, all that activity, the bustle, and diversity of character, which has been described, was no longer to be seen; many of the villages had been partially destroyed, and entirely deserted by their affrighted inhabitants, and some of the towns, too, had been partly abandoned, and looked dismal and cheerless. Almost every place exhibited some fearful evidences of the horrors of war, and could not but excite the most painful and melancholy thoughts in the minds of every reflective person: and those sad feelings were even increased as the fugitives proceeded, and scenes of matchless beauty met their sight at every turn.

Alas, over this land, so abounding in the choicest beauties of nature, so rich in all its blessings, there now broods a fearful and impenetrable gloom, caused by the horrors of war, rapine, and every monstrous crime, which have, in a great measure, laid desolate the land, and shocked the feelings of the civilised world.

Man, for whose sake this beautiful earth was created, debased by superstition, and in some instances excited to feelings of savage revenge, and deeds of bloodshed, the bare recital of which makes humanity shudder, has here become its foulest, its only blot; and the sunny scene which ere while was to the fancy a new found paradise, daily grows more dark and gloomy, when we think of the frightful crimes, the fiendish deeds of bloodshed, which for so many months have polluted it, and the number of valuable lives, and innocent beings that have been wantonly, brutally sacrificed.

Such were the thoughts that occurred to Omelia—in spite of the more immediately important one's to her, which almost entirely engrossed her mind, and superseded every other feeling in her breast—as the tedious journey was continued, and they did but serve to increase her melancholy and anguish, and which, in fact, nothing at present seemed able of alleviating.

It was in vain that she endeavoured to receive that consolation which her friends sought with praiseworthy zeal to impart to her, while she was left in such a terrible state of doubt, mystery, and uncertainty as to the nature of the offence which Stanley had committed, and the probable fate which awaited him, or had already befallen him; and her brain became almost maddened the longer she reflected upon it, and, as fear conjured up the most torturing ideas and forebodings to her imagination.

It was impossible for her to banish that fond and beloved being from her thoughts even for a moment. His form was ever present to her imagination, and the agony of his looks, his words of despair, and frantic grief at their last meeting and when they were torn asunder, were never absent from her recollection.

"Why all this terrible mystery," she muttered to herself, "why do they hesitate to reveal to me the truth, if the offence with which the unfortunate Stanley is charged is of that trivial nature they would fain persuade me to believe in order to soothe my anguish? Alas, where there is all this torturing secrecy, this evasion of my anxious questions, how can I do otherwise than apprehend the worst? how can I help abandoning myself to the most horrible fears and conjectures, which gain strength every moment, and drive me to despair? My brain cannot much longer support this dreadful agony of suspense, I shall go mad."

She pressed her hands upon her aching forehead as these painful thoughts arose to her bewildered imagination; the patience and fortitude which had ever characterised her under the greatest trials and difficulties, entirely forsook her, and convulsive sobs heaved and swelled her bosom.

As night approached, the cavalcade again arrived at a deserted village, which contained a number of bungalows, and where it was resolved to stop for a few hours—although they were now at no great distance from Cawnpore, which as has been before stated, was the place of their present destination—as the fugitives required rest, and it was the great object of all connected with their escort to lighten the fatigue of their journey as much as possible.

The bungalows were principally occupied by the wounded, the women and children, the soldiers bivouacing round the village; and there Abdal, after endeavouring to impart to her some words of consolation, without, however, any effect, parted with Omelia for the night, and left her to retire with Mrs. Eldred and her daughter into the bungalow which was left for their accommodation.

CHAPTER CXIX.

THE LETTER.—THE ALARM.

Omelia lingered behind her companions for a moment, looking anxiously after Abdal —whom she now looked upon as her almost only earthly friend, and esteemed him as she would a brother—as he retired from the spot with the soldiers; and as she did so, an officer, wearing the uniform of the regiment to which her beloved Stanley belonged, hastily passed her, and whispering the words "Be secret, be cautious, and fear not," thrust a letter in her hand, and before she could recover from the surprise and confusion which such an extraordinary circumstance naturally occasioned, he had vanished from her sight.

A trembling sensation came over Omelia, and her heart palpitated violently with mingled feelings of astonishment, hope, and fear, as she held the letter which had been delivered to her in so singular and mysterious a manner, in her hand, and was so bewildered that for the moment she scarcely knew what she was about.

But looking around, and perceiving that there was no one sufficiently near to observe her, she raised the letter to her eyes, and while the greatest emotions agitated her breast, she endeavoured by the light of the moon, which fortunately at that time shone brightly in the firmament, to read the superscription. At first a mist seemed to obscure her sight, and she could not decipher the characters, but at length they were clearly revealed to her, and she could not help giving utterance to an exclamation of the most unbounded astonishment and delight, and nearly sunk to the earth with the power of her emotions, when she recognised the well known hand writing of Stanley.

But quickly remembering the words of the officer who had delivered it to her, and fearing that she might be observed, she stilled her feelings as well as she could, and thrust the letter hastily into her bosom, just as Mrs. Eldred and her daughter made their appearance at the door of the bungalow, the cry she had uttered having reached their ears, and they feeling surprised at her lingering behind.

"For heaven's sake, Omelia," said Mrs. Eldred, anxiously, "what is the meaning of this? What occasioned you to utter that exclamation? Has anything alarmed you?"

"No—no," faltered out our heroine, endeavouring to conceal her agitation, "it was nothing—I—I—it was only a slight pang caused no doubt by anxiety of mind, or from over fatigue, I'm better now."

Mrs. Eldred and her daughter looked at her narrowly, and with feelings of the deepest sympathy, yet hardly satisfied with the explanation she had given, and taking her arm the former led her into the house without saying a word.

But there was one, who unseen by Omelia, had been watching her for some moments with anxious and admiring eyes, and with feelings of a wild and bewildering nature agitating his breast, that we will not at present seek to describe; and when her and her friends had retired, he came forward, and having first looked around him to see that he was not watched, he cautiously approached the bungalow and looked eagerly in at the window.

This was the tall figure of one of the native soldiers, who had been placed at the bungalow as sentry for the night, and whose general appearance, and the expression of his dark countenance, were far from prepossessing. His features showed great craftiness and determination of character, while at the same time they could not be said to be absolutely repulsive, and his eyes beamed with intelligence, and at times even with a look of gentleness which was at strange variance with the other characteristics of his appearance.

He had formed one of the garrison which had been just relieved, and his name was Yusef. He had been looked upon with some suspicion, during the most critical period, but for what reason we will not at present stop to inquire—and his actions had been most cautiously watched, without anything of importance being detected to confirm those suspicions, and therefore no further measures were taken to guard against him.

This prejudice might probably in the first instance have been caused by the fact of its being known that the sepoy, Yusef, was a Pariah, one of those excommunicated poor creatures, who are the very outcasts of society, and consequently he was looked upon with scorn and even hatred by his own countrymen in the garrison, and they would most of them have been glad to avail themselves of any opportunity to do him an injury, or even to work his complete ruin.

The touch of the Pariah is considered contamination, and it is the duty of every true worshipper of Brahma to shun and despise them.

And here it may not be out of place to remark that to the bad effects of the caste system in India, may be traced many of the most savage features of the present war.

The Hindoo population are divided into four tribes, namely, the Brahmins, who form the priesthood, and are by the eternal will of Brahma, the first and most honoured order among men; the Kyctra, or military tribe, embracing also the princes and officers of state. On these the Veda enjoins a thirst for glory, the practice of bravery, honour, generosity, and all chivalric virtues. Buysya, corresponding pretty nearly to our middle classes, comprising merchants, farmers, &c.

The fourth is the Sooora. This last tribe contains the greater portion of the people. It embraces the artificers, mechanics, tradesmen, inferior agriculturists, and the working classes of all kinds.

These four tribes are again subdivided into many others, the members of which intermarry, eat, drink, and associate with each other. And besides there are the outcast Pariahs, of whom we have just spoken.

For a minute or two, Yusef stood looking eagerly but cautiously in at the window of the bungalow, and as he did so, the expression of his dark features, showed the violent and guilty passions that agitated his breast, and influenced his thoughts; but at length he withdrew himself, and resting his arm upon the muzzle of his musket, he muttered:—

"How beautiful is this girl, surpassing all that I have hitherto seen of my country women; even the land of the Feringhee cannot boast one more lovely in features or graceful of form. Her matchless charms bewilder my ravished senses, and kindle in my savage breast the fierce flames of desire, which nothing can ever extinguish. Yes, I, even I, the Pariah Yusef, the hated and despised of all, acknowledge myself the slave of beauty, of surpassing beauty such as this maiden possesses, and would even risk my life to gain possession of her, and to gratify the unconquerable passion she has excited in my breast. But, fool that I am, presumptuous idiot; dare I hope that one like me, hideous—as some men say—in form, repulsive in features, and in manners savage and uncouth, can ever move the heart of one so lovely and so gentle to return the sentiments she has created in my breast? No, the thought is madness, and there is nothing left for me but to endeavour to banish it from my brain."

Hearing approaching footsteps, he shouldered his musket, and resumed his measured pace, to and fro', appearing to be doing no more than performing his duty.

But there was a tempest of guilty passions at that moment raging in the breast of Yusef, which he could not quell, and which was plainly revealed in the expression of his features; and dark thoughts continued to occupy his mind, which every moment gained strength, and incited him on to deeds of desperation.

"But," he resumed, after a pause, "shall I so easily abandon my hopes, because to accomplish them appears to be at present impracticable? Shall I be daunted from my purpose because of its difficulty? No, the feeling that urges me on is irresistible; let whatever may be the consequences, I will persevere, and watch the opportunity when I may make my triumph certain. Yusef has seldom failed to accomplish anything upon which he has fixed his mind, and it shall be no fault of his if he fail to do so now."

As he thus spoke, a look of determination overspread his countenance, and he gave himself up entirely to the feelings which those guilty thoughts excited, but ventured not again to look in at the window of the bungalow, lest he should be observed.

In the meantime, Omelia's anxiety to peruse the letter which she had so mysteriously received, every moment increased, and in spite of all her efforts to do so, she found it utterly impossible to conceal the violent agitation under which she laboured from her friends, who questioned her narrowly on the subject, but were unable to elicit from her any but the most evasive answers, with which they were anything but satisfied, and were only the more convinced that something extraordinary must have happened during the brief period they left her alone outside the bungalow, to agitate her in so violent a manner.

The upper-part of the bungalow—for it was a large one—was fully occupied by women and children, who from the silence that now reigned, it appeared had all fallen off to sleep, worn out with the fatigue of the day, and the two lower rooms were left for the accommodation of our heroine, and Mrs. Eldred and her daughter, and having lighted a lamp with which they had been supplied, and spread their clothes upon the floor, Mrs. Eldred proposed that they should endeavour to snatch some repose, as the time allowed them for doing so, must necessarily be brief.

Omelia knew not what to do; she could not offer any excuse, or object to retire to the inner-room, in which it was agreed they should sleep, lest it should excite their suspicion, and yet her anxiety to peruse the contents of the important letter was so great that she could scarcely contain herself.

"Come, my poor girl," said Mrs. Eldred, kindly, "your looks convince me that you are suffering much from the fatigue of the tedious journey; time wears apace, and the weary march must soon be resumed again. Let us then no longer delay, but at once retire and seek that repose of which we so much stand in need."

"For a short time," said Omelia, in a hesitating voice, "suffer me to remain here alone, that I may endeavour to calm my feelings. It is useless my trying to seek rest till I have done so, I will follow you quickly."

"It is a strange request," replied Mrs. Eldred, fixing upon her a penetrating look; "but, of course, I have no right to oppose your wishes. Good night. We will leave the lamp with you, as we do not require it."

"No," said our heroine, "the bright light of the moon will suffice for me." It will not be many minutes that I shall remain here. Good night."

Mrs. Eldred and her daughter again fixed upon her an anxious and inquiring look— then pressing her hand in silence, retired from the room, taking the lamp with them.

Omelia felt some little relief when she was

thus left alone, but her impatience to read the letter increased, and yet she could not venture to do so till she was certain that her friends were asleep, for fear of discovery and interruption.

She took it from her bosom, where she had so carefully deposited it, and pressed it to her lips with a burst of emotion which she could not control, while her tears fell fast upon it.

Then she softly approached the door of the room to which Mrs. Eldred and her daughter had retired, and listened, but all was still—and she ventured gently to open the door, and to peep in. They had stretched their weary limbs upon the floor, and seemed to have fallen off to rest immediately, and to sleep soundly. The moment for the gratification of Omelia's anxious curiosity appeared to have arrived, and she lost no time in availing herself of it. She therefore gently closed the door, leaving the lamp behind her, thinking that the light of the moon would be sufficient to enable her to read the letter, and returned to the room she had before occupied.

Taking the all important letter once more from her bosom, with a trembling hand and a throbbing heart, and fixing herself near the window, in order the better to catch the light, Omelia attempted to commence her task—but she no sooner did so than the moon became obscured by heavy clouds, and she could not, of course, distinguish a letter

Her anxiety, however, would admit of no delay or disappointment, and she therefore once more opened gently the door of the room in which Mrs. Eldred and her daughter were, and finding that they still slept soundly, she took up the lamp, and returned, closing the door after her.

And now she again endeavoured to peruse the contents of the letter, but for a moment or two, tears dimmed her eyes, and her emotion was so great, that her brain seemed bewildered, and not a word could she decipher.

"This is a weakness," she said at last, dashing the tears from her eyes, and endeavouring to collect herself—"and I am only torturing myself unnecessarily, by remaining in this suspense. Let me be firm. Beloved Stanley, as I peruse the lines written by your hand, I may imagine I hear the dear tones of your voice breathing in mine ears, and even whatever the purport of your communication may be, it must still afford me some degree of melancholy consolation. Better, far better is it to know the worst at once than to be kept in this dreadful state of doubt and uncertainty."

Having thus succeeded in calming the violence of her feelings, she commenced the painful task, and with some difficulty, being frequently interrupted by her sobs and tears,

read the affectionate epistle in the following words:—

"My adored Omelia, sweet empress of my heart's warmest affections, of all its earthly hopes and wishes—beloved object of my constant thoughts—bright vision of my slumbers; what language can I find sufficiently powerful to describe the wild emotions of mingled joy and sorrow, of hope and despair, that torture my breast, and rack my bewildered brain, as I write these lines, with the terrible uncertainty whether or not they are ever fated to meet your eyes? But oh, may heaven in its infinite mercy grant that they may, and shed some ray of hope and consolation in the misery of your doom.

"Fain would I, although so painful the task, detail to you all that has happened to me, since that fatal night of carnage which separated us, in our retreat from the old fort. Fain would I picture to you, most loved of earthly beings, the tortures that have wrung my soul, and at times nearly driven me to madness, but my feeble pen refuses to do so, and I must be brief.

"Once more did heaven permit us to meet, but oh, under what terrible circumstances. Yet to know that that fond being, in whom is centred all my hopes of happiness, still lives, and that her faithful heart continues to beat responsive to mine own—that her bright form has been again allowed to gladden mine eyes in sorrow, is the heavenly balm of consolation to my soul, the sweet regenerator of those fond hopes that were nearly annihilated.

"And we shall again be restored to each other, my Omelia, no more I trust to part, notwithstanding the dark clouds that at present hang over our destiny, and seem to frown despair. Rest assured that we shall, and let that thought relieve the terrible anguish of mind you must now be enduring, and cheer you on to hopes of future happiness.

"You saw me a prisoner—and oh, never can the agony of your looks, your fanatic emotions at that awful moment be erased from my memory. They have haunted my imagination ever since, and added tenfold horrors to my sufferings.

"But despair not, I say again, dear girl, for happier days are yet in store for us. Perhaps ere this letter may reach you, your faithful Stanley will be again at liberty, and think not that I thus hold out to you any false or delusive hopes The offence with which I am charged was not my own seeking —I solemnly declare before high heaven that it was not; and there are those that are ready to prove that I was not the aggressor, but that I—some one comes—I can write no more. Bless you, bless you, beloved girl, and farewell till we meet again, "STANLEY."

Thus the letter abruptly concluded, and with a burst of emotion which it is useless to attempt to describe, Omelia sunk upon her knees, in humble gratitude to the Supreme Power, for the almost insupportable weight of anxiety of which it had relieved her, while her bosom swelled with the uncontrollable excitement of her feelings, and the tears coursed each other rapidly down her cheeks, and bedewed the affectionate letter as she pressed it to her lips.

"Great Spirit who ever so mercifully watches over the humblest of Thy creatures," she fervently exclaimed, "I thank thee for this. Yes, beloved Stanley, I feel sweet hope and confidence reanimate my soul in your blessed assurance. We shall meet again, we shall meet again."

"Never," exclaimed a harsh, unnatural voice, so close to her, that the word almost seemed to come from some one immediately by her side, and with a faint cry of terror she started to her feet, gazing towards the window, but she was paralysed to the spot, and trembled in every limb, when she beheld or imagined she beheld the dark and savage countenance of a man glaring in upon her.

But in a moment it was gone, vanished like a phantom, leaving the astonished girl bewildered and appalled.

For a few moments she was so terrified that she could not move from the spot, but stood gazing vacantly at the window where she imagined the fearful apparition had appeared. But at length in a state of agitation and alarm which we shall not seek to pourtray, she hastily thrust the letter in her bosom, and snatching up the lamp, she staggered into the room where Mrs. Eldred and her daughter had been sleeping, but who were aroused by the noise she made in slamming the door violently after her, and starting up, they gazed at her, noticing her agitation, in bewildered amazement, unable at the moment to ask for an explanation, which Omelia, however, had not the power to give, but grasping the arm of Mrs. Eldred, looked fearfully and significantly towards the door, as though she feared the intrusion of somebody.

"What is the meaning of this, Omelia?" at length interrogated Mrs. Eldred, anxiously, "why have you not retired to rest, and what can it be which has alarmed you in this extraordinary manner?"

For a moment or two our heroine could not reply to these questions, but continued to grasp the arm of Mrs. Eldred, and to keep her eyes fixed upon the door. But at last with much difficulty she was enabled briefly to explain what she had seen, much to her astonishment and that of her daughter.

"The excitement of your feelings, Omelia, and the confused state of your mind, must have conjured up this wild fancy. You must have been mistaken."

"No, no," returned our heroine positively, "I could not have been deceived. It was the ferocious countenance of a man, an Indian, that I distinctly saw, glaring in malignantly upon me at the window."

"'Tis strange," observed Mrs. Eldred, "and I am at a loss to understand it. But still I would not suffer it to alarm me. You seem excited in a most extraordinary manner. Surely something more must have occurred to agitate you thus than that which you have stated."

Omelia felt confused, but not wishing at present at any rate to mention the receipt of the letter from Stanley, she evaded the question as well as she could, and endeavoured to compose her feelings.

"Come, Omelia," said Mrs. Eldred, "you must try to banish this singular event from your thoughts, and as time is getting late, and in an hour or two we must resume our journey, you had better seek to obtain some little rest in order to befit you for the fatigue of the day."

Omelia assented, and Mrs. Eldred having entered the front room and secured the door, to prevent the entrance of any one, if they should really have such a design in view, which appeared to be extremely improbable, returned, and they then, accommodating each other in the best manner they could, endeavoured to compose themselves to rest.

CHAPTER CXX.

THE DREAM.

The reader will not need to be informed that Omelia had not been mistaken or led astray by her disordered state of mind at the moment. It was Yusef whom she had seen looking so anxiously in at the window, and who had given utterance to the words that had so startled her and excited her alarm; but instantly finding the imprudence of which he had been guilty, and which might lead to the most unpleasant consequences to himself, he hastily retired from the spot, and resumed his duty.

The guilty passions that had taken possession of his breast, however, were the more inflamed by what he had seen and heard, and he gave free vent to the malicious feelings that agitated him.

"So," he muttered, "the girl loves, and the object of her heart's affections is the Feringhee Lieutenant Stanley, at present under arrest. The letter I saw her perusing with such fond emotion was from him; but by what means did she receive it? That is a mystery which I cannot unravel. Oh, how do I envy him the love of one whom the mightiest monarch on the earth might be proud to possess, whose radiant smiles would repay a life of care and sorrow. But he shall never realise the fond hopes in which he has no doubt indulged, even should he be acquitted of the offence with which he is at present charged, I, yes even I, Yusef, the despised and hated Pariah, swear that he shall not, and sooner will I perish than fail to keep my word. Omelia, beauteous Omelia—for such I know to be your name—you have with your transcendent charms, and those bright eyes whose glances it is impossible to meet without delight and admiration kindled a fierce flame within this savage breast which nothing can ever extinguish; I burn with desire, and thoughts are awakened in my mind to which my uncouth nature has hitherto been a stranger, and I cannot, will not rest till the wild hopes and presumptuous wishes I have formed are realised. My determination is fixed, and no earthly power can move me from my purpose; there is no difficulty, no danger which I will fear to encounter, no obstacle which I will not surmount to secure my triumph, and I may anticipate the result with every confidence."

An expression of exultation overspread his features as he thus soliloquised, and his guilty determination increased in strength every moment.

He again passed the window of the bungalow, but the beauteous object of his thoughts was gone, and all was buried in darkness.

"She has retired to rest," he said, in low murmuring tones, "and if she sleeps, her dreams are doubtless of him who seems to hold dominion over her soul, and fond hopes follow her in her slumbers—hopes that it must now be my object to disappoint. And yet I must be a villain to entertain such base designs against one so good and innocent as I believe her to be, and to seek to throw a blight upon her prospects, and destroy her future happiness. True I am a villain, a deep, designing, crafty villain, whom all who know me look upon as such, and treat me with scorn and loathing. And since it is so, I will not fail to play the villain's part to gain my ends, let the consequences be whatever they may. But dare I, wretch, miscreant that I am, hateful in looks, in words, in deeds dare hope to supplant the noble-minded Stanley in the maid's affections, or to raise any other feelings than those of contempt, disgust, and abhorrence in her breast? No, no, too well am I convinced that I cannot, but still that shall not daunt me in the prosecution of my designs; no consideration will I suffer to change my determination. Omelia, you shall be mine,

in spite of everything that may oppose me, and I will lose no time in putting my designs into execution."

Such were the base thoughts in which the villain indulged, and he even felt confident of success, notwithstanding the insurmountable difficulties that seemed to present themselves.

The varied thoughts that crowded upon the brain of Omelia kept her waking for some time after Mrs. Eldred and her daughter had fallen off to sleep, and every moment the anxiety of her mind increased; but hope once more dawned upon her, and in some measure tranquillised her feelings, and banished those fears, doubts, and misgivings that had so long distracted her.

She took the letter of Stanley from her bosom, and again and again pressed it with the fondest feelings of emotion to her lips, but she did not venture at that time to re-peruse it, lest her companions should wake and discover her, but there was not a word which that dear epistle contained which was not stamped upon her memory in characters that nothing whatever could efface, and she pondered over every line with mingled emotions of delight and sorrow. The communication, so unexpected, had removed a weight of care and anxiety, coupled with the most terrible and dismal forebodings, from her mind, which had become almost insupportable, for the secrecy which every one had maintained on the subject, naturally led her to conclude that the offence with which Stanley was charged was of the most serious character, perhaps one involving his very life; but those fears the assurances of Stanley had removed, for she could not for a moment suppose that he would attempt to deceive her, or to raise in her breast any delusive hopes, which at the same time he knew could only end in fearful disappointment.

She had never, she could not doubt the favour and sincerity of Stanley's love, time and suffering had proved the strength of his passion, and that his faithful heart must ever remain unchanged; but still how welcome to her were the reassurances of his affection, of his undying constancy, and with what nameless feelings of rapture did she dwell upon them, and could almost imagine that she heard his beloved voice repeating them in her ear.

"And shall we indeed meet again, dear Stanley?" she murmured to herself, her heart at the same time palpitating with emotion, and tears—they were mingled tears of joy and sorrow—trembling in her eyes, "oh, I dare not cease to encourage that fond and blissful thought, notwithstanding the many difficulties that at present appear, and a ray of hope and happiness once more dawns upon my mind. But oh, when will that glad time arrive? How much longer shall I have to linger on in this state of suspense and anxiety? Every moment that shall separate me from him will appear an age, but his dear letter convinces me that the time will come, and I will be firm and patient."

These thoughts and anticipations gained strength in her mind, and the terrified fears that had before distracted it, were in a great measure removed.

She could have wished, however, that Stanley had been more explicit on the subject of the offence with which he was charged, as that would probably have had the effect of removing her doubts and apprehensions altogether; but the confidence he had expressed of his acquittal satisfied her, and she tried to rest herself upon that point content. She also regretted that he had been compelled to finish his letter so abruptly, as he doubtless would otherwise have entered into a further explanation, and thus have banished all misgivings and fears upon the subject.

But the fearful and threatening words she had heard, and the man who had given utterance to them, and who had appeared in such a mysterious and suspicious manner at the window, excited the most bewildering and painful feelings in her breast, and it was to no purpose that she endeavoured to quiet the apprehensions to which the circumstance naturally gave rise.

The strange expression of the man's features at the moment her attention was called to them, had particularly struck her and raised the most fearful conjectures in her mind, though she never remembered to have seen them before—in fact he had disappeared so suddenly, that there was little or no opportunity afforded of recognising them.

Who then could he be? and what could be the feelings that prompted him to give utterance to the threatening words she had heard? She was completely at a loss to imagine, and the longer she tried to penetrate the mystery, the more deeply involved and perplexed she became.

The waning time, however, at length aroused Omelia to a full sense of the necessity which there was for her to seek some little rest to enable her to undergo the fatigue of the remainder of the journey; and, worn out with painful thought, she did at last succeed in composing herself to sleep, but which was rendered anything but refreshing by strange and torturing dreams.

At one time she imagined herself to be wandering alone through dreary wilds, and sandy deserts—o'er rugged mountain steeps, through tangled forest, and lonely jungle, where savage beasts lurked to seize upon their helpless prey; weary, hungry, footsore, and wretched; but whither she wished to go or what errand she was upon, did not appear to her—and onward she seemed to travel, as if impelled by some invisible and inscrutable power.

And now the aspect of the scenery amongst which she was travelling underwent a most remarkable change, and all the beauties of an oriental climate were revealed to the wandering and enraptured sight, in all their surpassing and indescribable loveliness and magnificence, presenting all that the most glowing imagination could picture of fairy land.

Almost boundless seemed the prospect before her, and never had the golden sun shone upon a scene of such diversity, so picturesque, and perfectly entrancing. Swelling hills, covered with the richest verdure—vast tracts of flowery land, intersected with a winding stream or river—handsome fountains, sporting their waters in the sunlight—noble trees, bearing the most luxuriant fruit—gorgeous temples, rising here and there in the distance, amid the green foliage in which they were emblossomed; these formed some of the principal features of that charming scene, which, however, it would be difficult to find any language sufficiently powerful and eloquent adequately to pourtray.

Balmy fragrance was in the gentle zephyrs, and imparted a feeling of happiness and even transport to the senses. The fatigue which Omelia fancied she experienced before, had now entirely vanished, and her spirits were exhilerated in the highest degree. It seemed to her as if some joyful event was in store for her, and hope again reanimated her breast, and banished all those feelings of gloom which had before occupied and tortured it.

She bounded over the verdant and flower-bedecked earth with a light and buoyant step, and the further she advanced on her way, the more beautiful did the prospect become; fresh objects to excite her wonder and enthusiastic admiration at every step.

At length, as her eyes wandered enraptured over the prospect before her, the form of a man suddenly appeared advancing towards her, and at the sight of whom her heart palpitated more violently than before, and every feeling that had hitherto laid dormant in her breast, was excited with hope and expectation—for strikingly familiar was every turn of that manly form to her sight, although at present he was not near enough to enable her to distinguish his features though his face was turned towards her.

She tried to increase her speed to come up with him, and, as she did so, she fancied in her dream that strains of unearthly music filled the air, and raised the spirits to a feeling of unbounded joy.

And now the graceful form on which our heroine's whole attention was rivetted came nearer and nearer, revealing itself more distinctly to her anxious view, and increasing the emotions, which, from the first moment she had beheld it, had taken possession of her breast, to an almost ungovernable degree, and exciting hopes which she was almost afraid to encourage, but found it impossible to dismiss. Almost immediately were those bright fond hopes realised, she was enabled clearly to distinguish and recognise the features of him who had so suddenly appeared before her, and excited her curiosity, and an exclamation of the most boundless joy escaped her lips when she recognised those of her lover.

A sweet expression of love and rapture irradiated that handsome countenance, which

Omelia imagined was almost unearthly, and he extended his arms as if eager to enfold her in his embrace, while he hastened towards her, and she with a throbbing heart, and arms also extended, quickened her footsteps to meet him, calling upon his name in tones of affectionate delight, experiencing at that moment sensations of pleasure which she never remembered to have felt before.

They had nearly met, it seemed, in fact, as if only the smallest space separated them from each other; they called rapturously upon each other's name, and rushed forward to the embrace of love, when suddenly the bright and fairy scene was changed to one of gloom and horror, an almost impenetrable darkness obscured the prospect which but the instant before was so bright and lovely, a deafening peal of thunder rent the air, and the earth appeared to tremble beneath her feet with some terrible convulsion of nature, and then the dark clouds having in some measure dispersed Omelia beheld between her and Stanley a yawning gulf, down whose rugged sides the black waters gushed with a hissing, deafening sound into the dark stream beneath, while to her affrighted imagination the most ghastly and hideous phantoms seemed to flit before her, and to mock the anguish and excitement of her feelings.

With a cry of agony she gazed towards Stanley, and beheld him standing with clasped hands, on the opposite side of the gulf, and gazing towards her with looks of the most indescribable agony and despair.

Oh, how terrible was the change which that few seconds had wrought in his appearance. The smiles of hope and happiness which had then irradiated his features, were superseded by looks in which all the tortures that can rack the human breast under the most dreadful and trying circumstances were expressed, and every instant did those overwhelming, those uncontrollable feelings seem to increase in intensity.

Gradually his features became more and more indistinct, and his beloved form to fade from the sight, in the darkness that again prevailed, and Omelia imagined that worked up to a complete state of frenzy by the intensity of her emotions, she rushed to the very brink of the yawning gulf, and again uselessly extending her arms towards Stanley called wildly and frantically upon his name. But to add to her horror, at that moment fierce and threatening sounds, from savage beasts, proceeding from the direction in which her lover was being hurried, smote her ears, and she beheld the blood-thirsty tiger bounding towards him, with jaws distended, and eyeballs apparently blazing with ferocity.

What a moment of insupportable agony was that to Omelia, and she experienced the same torturing feelings in her dream, which she would have done in reality. There were no means for Stanley to escape, and being unarmed, as she supposed in her dream, he was deprived of all power to defend himself from the shock of his savage and formidable enemy.

Oh, that that fearful gulf had not intervened between them, that Omelia might have rushed to his side, notwithstanding the awful impending danger, it would have been at least a melancholy satisfaction to her to have even been permitted to perish in his arms.

She strained her eyes with the madness of despair towards the spot on which she had seen him standing, but the intense darkness had now hid him entirely from her view, but she could hear the fierce roar of the terrible beast, and which but too plainly showed the awful fate that inevitably awaited him.

In a state of the most unspeakable horror and excitement, Omelia fancied in her dream that she continued rivetted to the spot, and listened with breathless attention to catch the slightest sound, and then the voice of the unfortunate Stanley again smote her ears distinctly, calling upon her name in tones that could never be erased from her memory.

All, all was still impenetrable darkness, and now a dead and solemn silence followed the sounds that had before broke upon the air, which was even more appalling, for it seemed to proclaim the completion of the frightful tragedy, and the dreadful fate which had too surely overtaken Omelia's lover.

Her heart sickened, every faculty seemed to be suspended in horror, the spell of sleep was broken, and Omelia started up trembling convulsively in every limb, and the perspiration standing in large drops upon her quivering temples.

CHAPTER CXXI.

THE JOURNEY COMPLETED.—THE DESIGNS OF YUSEF.

With the greatest emotion, and a mind bewildered, Omelia gazed around her with vacant looks, for the moment scarcely recollecting where she was, or knowing whether the strange and torturing scene she had witnessed was reality, or only conjured up by her disordered imagination. But every incident of that dream was impressed upon her memory in the most vivid and painful colours, and each moment her anguish of mind increased to such a degree that it became almost insupportable.

It was now the break of day, and Omelia could hear the note of preparation among the troops for resuming the march, but Mrs. Eldred and her daughter still slept soundly and Omelia was not at all dissatisfied that they did so, as she did not wish them to observe the extreme agitation under which she laboured, and which might induce them to put questions to her she was in no humour to answer at present.

She endeavoured to regain some degree of composure, and to recover herself from the effects of her frightful dream; but under all the painful circumstances that was a task not easy of accomplishment, and again it destroyed those hopes she had sought to encourage after the receipt of Stanley's letter, and rekindled the most torturing doubts and misgivings in her breast.

"Alas!" she dismally reflected, "too surely is the fearful vision that has haunted my imagination prophetic—and in spite of all the flattering hopes and expectations that Stanley has held out to me, it is the cruel will of fate, I have too much reason to apprehend that there are many sufferings, many trials yet in store for us, ere we are destined to meet again, if indeed we are ever permitted to do so. Oh, heaven, how agonising is this state of suspense, this continual disappointment, and that too, when a ray of sunshine seems for a time to dawn upon the gloom of our prospects. Surely we merit not the wretched fate which so remorselessly pursues us, and is sufficient to exhaust even the greatest fortitude and patience. But let me still be firm," she continued, after a brief pause, "and not give way to doubts and fears that after all may be completely groundless. It was but a painful dream that haunted my dormant imagination, conjured up by the mingled and conflicting thoughts that naturally, in the state of suspense I have so long had to endure, crowded so constantly on my mind; and I will endeavour to look on the bright side of the question in future, and not to anticipate troubles which after all may not await myself, or he whose happiness is dearer to me than mine own existence.

She became more composed and re-assured as these thoughts occurred to her, and walked into the front room, and looked out at the door to ascertain what progress was being made for resuming the march, and beheld all bustle and activity among the soldiers and their officers, while many of the fugitives had quitted the different bungalows in which they had been lodged for the night, ready to depart on the remainder of the journey, which it was expected would be accomplished that day.

Omelia therefore returned to the room in which she had left Mrs. Eldred and her daughter, in order to arouse them, but found that they had already awakened, and were looking to see what had become of her.

She had so far succeeded in tranquillising her feelings, that she exhibited but little agitation, and her friends supposing that she had probably succeeded in obtaining a few hour's refreshing sleep, congratulated her on the same, and she did not seek to undeceive them.

In a few minutes they were joined by Mr. Eldred and Abdal, who greeted our heroine with their usual cordiality, and, having partaken with the rest of the inmates of the bungalow, of some refreshments that had been supplied to them, and the bugle having sounded the signal for departure, they hastened to take their proper places in the cavalcade, Omelia supported by Mrs. Eldred and her daughter.

They had not proceeded many paces, however, when Omelia uttered a faint cry of surprise and alarm, and evinced altogether considerable agitation, which excited their curiosity, and they eagerly inquired the cause. Omelia did not reply verbally, but motioned towards an object at some short distance, and upon which her eyes had been fixed with evident trepidation.

It was the tall figure of a native soldier, who, with his arms folded across his broad chest, was standing in a fixed attitude opposite to our heroine—so that his features might be clearly distinguished—and gazing intently at her.

It is useless to describe this man further than to state that it was Yusef, and that even for the few seconds that it was seen, the strange and sinister expression of his features forcibly struck all who beheld him.

Finding, however, apparently, the curiosity he had excited, and how narrowly he was being watched, he hastily turned away from the spot on which he had been standing, and disappeared among the soldiers.

"Why do you exhibit such terror at the sight of that man, Omelia?" interrogated Abdal.

"His behaviour was strange," replied our heroine;" besides I have seen him before, and that recently, and under suspicious circumstances. My dear madam, she added, speaking to Mrs. Eldred—I am convinced this is the same man who I beheld last night watching me so eagerly through the window of the bungalow."

"Is it possible?" ejaculated Mrs. Eldred, with a look of astonishment; "are you certain that you are not mistaken?"

"Positive," returned Omelia. "It is quite impossible that I could mistake the features of that man, and which made such a powerful impression on me when I first beheld them."

Abdal and Mr. Eldred were surprised, and they eagerly inquired the particulars of the circumstance, which Omelia briefly related.

"'Tis strange," remarked Abdal, "and I am at a loss to imagine what the object of his conduct can be; although, perhaps, after all, it is but mere curiosity, and is therefore unworthy of any further consideration."

"True," said Mrs. Eldred; "and Omelia, I am sure, will not suffer it to trouble her."

She returned no answer to this, but she again looked anxiously in the direction where Yusef had disappeared, and when she remembered the words he had uttered on the previous night, and the malignant looks he had fixed upon her, she could not but feel far from satisfied or easy.

But having now joined the cavalcade, the journey was once more resumed, and continued for some time through a part of the country presenting every variety of scenery, and which was sufficient to call forth the admiration of the travellers.

Her friends endeavoured to amuse her by conversation on different topics, but Omelia was dull and abstracted, and her thoughts were too busily occupied to suffer her to listen to them with any degree of attention or pleasure.

The letter of Stanley, couched in language so affectionate, and the exciting incidents of the remarkable dream which had occurred to her, continued to taunt her imagination, and to fill her mind with the most painful, and at the same time, bewildering ideas, and she could not but alternate between hope, fear, and uncertainty.

Alas, should the anticipations which Stanley had ventured to indulge in, in his affectionate letter, prove erroneous, and he should after all be condemned for the offence with which he was charged—and which at times she could not help thinking he had treated much more lightly than it deserved, in order to quiet her apprehensions—how terrible might be the fate which awaited him, and from which nothing whatever might be able to rescue him. She shuddered at the thought, and it was to no purpose that she sought to stifle it in her breast.

She resolved at the earliest opportunity to communicate the contents of the letter to Abdal, and to seek his advice upon the subject, although she could hope for but little assistance from him.

Could she but see the officer who had delivered the letter into her hands, and who it was certain was the friend of Stanley, she might receive that full explanation from him which she was so anxious to obtain, and which Stanley had been prevented from doing; and thus many of the torturing doubts and apprehensions she now entertained, and for which there seemed to be too much reason might be removed, and she might find again some room for hope and consolation—but at present there seemed to be no chance of such an opportunity occurring, and she could not therefore but continue restless and dissatisfied.

The sepoy Yusef, in the meantime, felt the guilty passion which the charms of Omelia had excited in his breast, increase in strength, and many were the thoughts in which he continued to indulge, and the nefarious designs which he pondered in his mind, and which he determined at all hazards to put into execution.

But it was necessary that he should watch the opportunity to accomplish his wishes with every precaution, for the least failure, the slightest mistake, might not only frustrate all his deep laid schemes, but end in his own destruction.

What these base designs were, and how far they succeeded, will be afterwards shown, but the villain was firm in his resolution, and already he anticipated the greatest success.

"Yes," he muttered to himself, "the fierce flame which this beauteous maiden has excited in my breast, is one that nothing can extinguish, and desperate and preposterous as such thoughts may seem to be, there is no danger that I will fear to encounter to obtain possession of her, and with every hope and confidence in my complete triumph. All that consummate cunning and deep laid stratagem can devise shall be put in operation to effect my object, and sooner will I perish than be defeated. Lovely Omelia, you shall be mine, for nothing whatever shall tempt me to abandon those designs upon which I have fixed my mind, and upon which I have built all my future expectations."

The looks which characterised his dark countenance at that moment, showed the infamous thoughts that occupied his breast, and the fierce determination of his designs, and a more revolting looking being than he presented as he thus expressed himself, might not very readily be imagined.

Then he thought of Stanley, and feelings of hatred and jealousy influenced his savage breast towards him, notwithstanding he had on one or two occasions received services from the generous and gallant young officer which ought to have awakened his gratitude but it was enough for him to know that he loved Omelia, and possessed her heart's warmest affections in return, to excite his most deadly feelings of malice, and he was resolved, even should he escape from the difficulties by which he was at present surrounded, that every obstacle should be thrown in the way of him and Omelia meeting again, and that it should be no fault of his if all those bright hopes and visions in which he had no doubt they had so freely indulged, should not be for ever destroyed, to accomplish which he determined to put every diabolical scheme into operation which artifice could invent, or villany suggest.

"Few, very few indeed know the power which the despised Yusef possesses to effect his object, when any desperate project has once entered his mind, and aroused all his energies," he soliloquised. "He is impelled onward by the tempest of his passions, and nothing can stay him in his wild course till his efforts have been crowned with success, and all his wishes are gratified, however bold and presumptuous they may appear to be. And shall I now fail? No, by every guilty power I swear that I will not, and that nothing whatever shall tempt me to relinquish my intentions. Arrived at the place of our destination, I will lose no time in setting about my task; then, Omelia, your fate is sealed, and I will defy you to escape it.

Such were the thoughts that continued to influence the brain of Yusef, as the cavalcade proceeded on its way, but he took good care to conceal them from observation, and not even by a look or word give cause for suspicion as to what was passing in his mind.

At length the tedious march was accomplished, and the fugitives from Lucknow arrived in safety at Cawnpore, that place which must ever occupy one of the most painfully important pages in the history of the rebellion from the frightful scenes there enacted, and which it is impossible to recal to the memory without feelings of the most unspeakable horror.

CHAPTER CXXII.

DEATH OF SIR HENRY HAVELOCK.—YUSEF AND OMELIA.

Leaving our heroine and her companions at Cawnpore for the present, and the villain Yusef to further concoct and mature his diabolical plans, we will briefly refer to the death of one of Great Britain's most immortal heroes, being in perfect keeping with the historical, matter of fact nature of our tale, and a subject in which we are certain every Englishman proud of his country must feel the deepest interest.

Need we say that we allude to the last moments of the Christian soldier, Sir Henry Havelock, whose lamented death has left a void in the list of present English heroes, which it will be difficult to fill.

We have followed him as far as our limited space would allow, through many of his most gallant achievements, in his noble and untiring efforts to relieve the garrison of Lucknow, and such unprecedented exertions on the part of a general who was advanced in years, and whose military career had been one of the most unceasing active service, were sufficient to shake and undermine even the most iron constitution.

Consequently before the final rescue of the garrison had taken place, Sir Henry Havelock evinced unmistakeable symptoms of serious illness, much to the alarm of every one, the first of which excited immediate apprehension being those of indigestion.

By the greatest care, however, these were promptly subdued, and it was considered, and likewise pronounced to be better; and that hope seemed to be sanctioned in a great measure by his not only being relieved from his recent great responsibility, but provided by that refreshing sustenance he had so much required, but of which for weeks he had been deprived.

It may be sure that every possible attention was paid to one whose life was so precious to the community at large, and whose loss must be considered as a national calamity. No one could be more assiduous than his medical attendant, and from the Commander-in-Chief down to the servants in the Residency, all were ready to render him all the assistance within their power, but as it too fatally ultimately occurred without any favourable result.

And thus till the close of the 20th of November, 1857, did the promise of continuous amendment remain, but short was the period that it did so, for before midnight unmistakeable signs of dysentery made their appearance, and the promptest attention was necessary with the best measures which sagacity and science could supply.

For a time they were apparently successful, and by the forenoon of the 21st there were again indications of improvement.

He had written home immediately on the relief of the garrison, but although this letter expressed nothing which could give occasion for alarm, others had indicated apprehensions of what might happen.

"Prospects," says the Rev. Mr. Brock, "were brigtening, and he hoped that they should ere long bear away the surviving women and children to a place of safety, and that some of their own most pressing wants would in a measure be supplied.

"For weeks they had been unable to change any of their clothing,. Just as they had come into the Residency, so had they continued night and day for forty days, harrassed incessantly by the enemy, and beset with disease and death, without even the ordinary conveniences where they could be bodily refreshed. It would be better now.

"Information had also reached him of the estimation in which his country held him for his bravery, and of the first of the series of honours which had been conferred on him by the Queen.

"This was cheering. He was grateful, but as modest and unostentatious as ever. The children were remembered in a kindly message, and their brother they were assured, though a second time wounded, was doing well.

*   *   *   *   *

"This was the last letter which Havelock ever wrote. No longer would he indite the graver or pleasanter things for perusal and pleasurable conversation at Bonn. Henceforward the wedding day and the birthdays would pass uncommemorated by the grateful references of the conjugal and parental pen. The admonitions and encouragements which had been so habitually interspersed with the periodical correspondence of the last seven years, had come to a perpetual end.

"It was now generally known that Havelock was getting worse. He was not seen about among his companions in arms, they missed him in the places of military resort. There was sorrow, lest after all his self-sacrificing exertions to save others he should himself succumb.

"To further the incipient improvement of the 20th, it had been arranged to remove him to the Dilkoosha; the change of air being deemed of importance at the crisis which he had just reached.

"Well aware was he of the danger that was impending; yet whilst he felt his jeopardy to be extreme he was thoroughly calm."

The change from the Residency had refreshed the invalid. Further improvement was observed and gladly reported.

His son, although badly wounded was with him almost constantly, and showed that care and anxiety which the melancholy situation of so excellent a parent naturally demanded.

"But that life so valued could not be preserved. Early on the 22nd the disease assumed a malignant form, and although it inflicted no severe bodily suffering it was evidently taking away his life.

"On the 24th his end was obviously near at hand. His eldest son was still his loving and faithful nurse; himself, be it remembered a wounded man, and specially needing kindly care, waiting on his father with unflagging and womanly care. He was summoned to hear some parting words.

"Come," said the hero, "come, my son, and see how a Christian can die."

"And Havelock died."

Having for purposes in our narrative, which will be hereafter explained, thus introduced the death of that illustrious man, whose glorious deeds in arms have gained for his name and memory immortality, we will return to our heroine and her companions at Cawnpore, where they had now been for several days, without anything of sufficient importance occurring to find a place in our pages.

The spirits of Omelia wavered between hope and fear, the more especially as she could gain no further intelligence regarding Stanley, Mr. and Mrs. Eldred—for what reason she could not easily imagine—continuing to maintain the most profound secrecy as to the circumstances which had placed him in his present painful and critical situation, and the nature of the offence for which he had been placed under arrest, and for which it was evident that he must undergo a court-martial.

They, however, repeatedly assured her that it was not of the serious nature her fears suggested, and endeavoured to encourage her to hope for a speedy restoration to him.

How terrible, how agonising was this suspense, and her patience was nearly exhausted her only consolation and relief being in the re-perusal of Stanley's affectionate letter, the contents of which she had communicated to Abdal only, and over which she constantly pondered with the most poignant feelings of joy and sorrow, hope, doubt, and fear. How dear was every word that fond epistle contained to her, how many were the tears she shed, as again and again she read them, and felt the more convinced of the sincerity and fidelity of the heart which had dictated them. In the excitement of her feelings she could often imagine that she heard them spoken in the beloved tones of his voice, and a feeling of melancholy transport would come over her which she did not attempt to resist.

She could not doubt the truth of what he had stated—though again she deeply regretted that he had not been more explicit—for well she knew that he would scorn to attempt to deceive her, or to flatter her by holding out hopes which he knew could only end in bitter disappointment, even more terrible to bear than the most cruel certainty; therefore she endeavoured to acquire confidence in his assurances, and to await the result with firmness and fortitude, although it was a severe trial to the patience to do so.

Abdal was almost her constant companion, and was unremitting in his exertions to calm her feelings, and to point out to her a gleam of sunshine and happiness, at those times when in the overwhelming depression of her spirits all appeared darkness and despair; and he was often more successful than he could have expected, and she would become comparatively tranquil.

Abdal also endeavoured to gain some further information regarding Stanley, but to very little purpose, any more than she had learnt from his letter, that he was at the Alum Bagh; and the hesitation to communicate anything more satisfactory was calculated to excite the most painful fears and suspicions.

The distance which now separated them, was also an additional source of torture to Omelia, and she often regretted that she had been induced to accompany the fugitives from the Residency so far, notwithstanding that she and the others were treated with every kindness, and not the least restraint put upon their conduct.

"This dreadful state of mystery and suspense, is unendurable," she observed impatiently to Abdal, in reply to some remarks he had made; "and why should I longer submit to it? What business have I here, when every feeling of affection, solicitude, and constancy, call me far away? Besides, this life of monotony and inactivity is ill suited to the mind of Omelia, and she can—she will no longer endure it. Beloved and unfortunate Stanley, again shall my wandering footsteps guide me to the place you inhabit, and no human power shall withhold me from your presence, even though it be to die in your arms, to breath my last sigh pressed to that faithful heart, whose warmest pulsations beat for me alone."

"Alas, Omelia," said Abdal, "what madness is it to talk thus. It is impossible for you to travel in the present delicate state of your health; besides, are you not completely destitute of every means of support, rendering such an idea at once as impracticable as it is extravagant."

"Oh, what danger, what difficulty is there that I would shrink from encountering, impelled by hopes and wishes which I cannot restrain?" she replied. "My woman's love will enable me to surmount everything. Why then should I longer hesitate? This suspense is worse than death."

Abdal again tried to persuade her by every argument he could make use of, but he only succeeded indifferently.

Such were the thoughts and feelings that now almost constantly agitated the mind of Omelia, and from which she could obtain but little relief or consolation.

How anxious did she feel to again behold the officer from whom she had received Stanley's letter, and she felt surprised that she did not do so. He, no doubt, could explain sufficient to remove all her doubts and fears, and, as a friend of her lover, which he evidently was, she could not believe that he would hesitate to do so.

Liking to indulge in her own meditations without interruption, Omelia sometimes left the house in which herself and her friends were at present located, alone, and would often wander to the most distant parts, or suburbs of the city, seeking such lonely and retired spots as were the most in unison with her feelings, entertaining no apprehensions of danger.

But there was one who in secret watched her movements at every opportunity with an anxious and wary eye, nurturing dark thoughts in his mind, but hitherto having refrained from revealing himself to her, or addressing her. Need we inform the reader that man was Yusef?

On the occasion of which we are about to write, the villain had been lurking for some time near the house in which Omelia resided —he having just come off duty—with the hope of seeing her, his guilty passions being now excited to a pitch which he could with difficulty control, though he had not been yet able to form any definite design as to the manner in which he could gratify them.

It was a fine clear night, the moon and stars shed their lustre in the sky—the weather was mild, even warm for the time of year, and everything presented an air of tranquillity that was in accordance with the wild thoughts which at present occupied the savage breast of the guilty Yusef, and goaded him on to acts of villany.

Having first walked cautiously round the building—which was a large one—and looked eagerly up at all the windows, as though he expected to catch a glimpse of her, he returned to the front of the house, and took up his position on a spot near the entrance, by which a cluster of mango trees grew, and where he could observe any one that came out, without any fear of being detected himself.

There was an expression of fierce determination on his forbidding features; his eyes flashed wildly, and his broad chest heaved with the base passions that agitated it, and to which, at first, he could not find vent in words.

As he stood there, his tall and muscular form raised to its full height, and his dark complexion reflected upon by the partial light of the moon, he looked like the demon of evil waiting for his prey, and any one to have accidentally encountered him at that moment might have felt a superstitious sensation of terror steal over them which they could not easily conquer, and which would have been unquestionably excusable.

A more revolting-looking object could not be very well imagined.

"She will not come to gratify my fierce desires," he said, at length, in a low and sullen tone of dissatisfaction, "yet had I come to the determination this night to address her, and to reveal the uncontrollable passions with which she has inflamed me, at every risk. It is not a trifle that can daunt the courage and resolution of Yusef, when once that resolution is formed, and shall I yield to any such coward fears on this occasion? By all my hopes I will not. I am prepared to meet the maiden's scorn and hatred, but that will have no other effect on me than to strengthen me in my designs, and to urge me on to acts of still greater daring. I have made up my mind to abandon the detested Feringhee and his course, and it will indeed be strange to me if I do not contrive to make the beauteous Omelia the companion of my flight. Either will I lose my life or I will possess her. Soft, some one comes."

He drew himself more into the shade as he spoke, and looked eagerly towards the door, which now opened, and Omelia, alone stepped forth into the open air.

She passed slowly by the spot where Yusef was concealed, and he could plainly distinguish her handsome features in the moonbeams, and their melancholy expression was sufficient to excite a feeling of the deepest commiseraton in anything but the most savage and insensible heart, but on the miscreant Yusef they had no other effect than to add fresh fire to the burning passions that goaded him on to desperation, and which nothing whatever could have the power to extinguish.

He watched her carefully till she had got to some short distance from the house, and observing the direction to which she was going, which was a lonely but romantic spot, at the further end of the city, he took his way by a more circuitous route, but quickened his pace so that he might arrive there before her.

He did so, and having concealed himself in a convenient place, watched her approach with anxious looks.

Omelia, with slow and faltering steps, and an agitated demeanour, advanced to the spot, and stepping on to a grassy mound of earth which was encircled by trees, gazed up through their spreading branches at the moonlighted and star bespangled firmament with vacant looks, and an expression of countenance which fully revealed the state of her mind at that moment, and which must have rivetted the attention and admiration of any one but such a being as Yusef, who beheld her.

He thought she had never looked half so lovely as she did at that time, and he could scarcely resist the temptation of presenting himself immediately before her, and pouring forth the disgusting avowal of his unholy passion in her ears.

For a few moments she remained fixed in the same attitude, and without saying a word, but at length in a murmuring, low, and melancholy voice, every tone of which the guilty Yusef dwelt upon with a wild feeling of transport quite new to him, and which it would be difficult to describe, she said—

"How calm and tranquil is the night, with what enchanting effect do the beautiful and wondrous works of nature appear in the soft mellow light of the moon, and the countless gems that glisten and twinkle around her. At this lovely and peaceful hour all cares and anxieties should be stifled in the human breast, and the heart beat in unison with the scene, and rebound with rapture and admiration. But, alas, how cold and insensible has sorrow now rendered this wretched breast, which once knew no other feelings but those of hope and happiness, a fairy dream which I had vainly flattered myself nothing was e'er fated to destroy. Weak credulous girl, to what a fearful reality am I now awakened, how bitter are the feelings of disappointment that now torture me and drive me to despair. There is no light, no sunshine left for me, all is darkness, impenetrable darkness, and those prospects that were once so bright and cheering now seem to frown upon me, and to mock the anguish of my lacerated heart. Oh, heaven, for what has Omelia now to live? Death would even be a relief to sufferings that have now become too terrible to endure."

For a minute or two sobs choked her utterance, and she abandoned herself to the intense grief that agitated her, and wrung her hands and wept bitterly.

But still the villain Yusef remained unmoved and unshaken in his nefarious design. In fact, the appearance of the unfortunate girl at that moment rather inflamed the feelings he had suffered to gain such powerful influence over him, than excited his sympathy, and he listened with impatience to again catch the tones of her voice.

"How long shall I have to endure this dreadful state of misery?" she at length resumed, while the tear-drops trembled on her cheek, and her lovely form trembled with emotion, "for what still more terrible fate am I reserved? Will it never again be my lot to experience one ray of peace and happiness? What have I done that misfortune should pursue me thus? Oh, beloved Stanley, on whom my whole soul's affections are so fondly rivetted, shall I never more behold you, or listen to the tones of your voice which with nameless rapture I have so often dwelt upon?"

"You will behold the proud boy no more," suddenly exclaimed the ruffian Yusef, unable any longer to control himself—placing his musket against the trunk of a tree, near which he had been concealed, and coming forward into the broad light, fully revealed his repulsive features to the astonished and terrified Omelia, who started back a few paces, and could not help feeling an emotion of dread on recognising that man who had so alarmed her on a former occasion, and at finding herself alone with him in that spot, and thus exposed to any insults that he might offer her, and which his looks fully showed that he was capable of.

Yusef seemed to enjoy her confusion and dismay, and, folding his sinewy arms across his broad chest, for a minute or two he gazed at her in silence, feasting his eyes eagerly upon those varied and transcendent beauties that had so completely ravished his senses.

"The lovely Omelia," he at length said, in the same disagreeable tones, and never for an instant removing his eyes from her countenance, "may well believe my words, for they will be realised. Lieutenant Stanley and yourself are never destined to meet again."

"What bold, presumptuous ruffian are you," demanded our heroine firmly, and with a look of indignation, as she quickly recovered herself, "that dare thus obtrude your

self upon me and address me? Your looks bespeak the guilty thoughts that occupy your mind, and excite my utmost resentment and disgust."

"One that you must learn to look upon with other thoughts and feelings than those which you have just now expressed, beauteous damsel," replied Yusef, boldly; "this is not the first time you have beheld me."

"I know it well, fearful and mysterious man," returned Omelia, who in spite of all her efforts could not exactly conquer the terror of her feelings; "for what guilty purpose do you cross my path? Let me begone; do not dare any longer to seek to obstruct me, or you may have cause to repent it."

"Nay," said the villain, resolutely, and grasping her wrist as she attempted to leave the spot, "I have long and anxiously sought

this interview, and I will not suffer you to depart till you have listened to what I have to say."

"Villain!" exclaimed Omelia, struggling to release herself, "unhand me, and begone, or my voice shall summon assistance that will not fail to resent in the severest manner this monstrous outrage."

"Nay, proud and scornful beauty," returned the ruffian, fixing upon her a look which caused her bosom to swell and her cheeks to glow with the feelings of shame, indignation and offended modesty, "you threaten in vain and much mistake the man you have now to deal with; gentle language and kindness might win me to forbearance, but mark me, Yusef possesses a spirit, humble, insignificant, and contemptible though in the estimation of some he may be, which cannot be intimidated; and scorn may only serve to arouse him into acts of violence he would otherwise avoid."

"Daring man!" exclaimed our heroine, becoming still more alarmed by the language he made use of, and the determination of his looks and manner, at the same time that she by a powerful effort succeeded in releasing herself from his hold, and retreated back a few paces, "why should you presume to act thus towards me? I know you not, and therefore can never have given you cause for offence or insult either by word or deed. this conduct is unpardonable, it is unmanly."

"The proud and disobedient daughter of the late sepoy Yunadar is no stranger to me, though she knows me not," replied Yusef; "but, if fortune frown not on me, the time is not far distant when she will know full well the man whom she now looks upon with such supreme contempt and hatred."

"Why do you thus appear before me?" again demanded Omelia, at the same time looking round to see whether there was any one approaching to whom she might appeal for protection; but as far as her eyes could penetrate through the darkness the coast was quite clear, and she could not conquer the feelings of apprehension which gained upon her every moment, for what resistance could she, a defenceless woman, worn down by long bodily suffering and mental anxiety, offer to so determined and desperate a ruffian. "Why do you thus obstruct me?" she repeated, mustering all the firmness she could, "what can be your business with me, I demand? Speak your purpose, and begone."

"Yes, lovely Omelia," he returned, and a disgusting expression flashed from his evil eyes, and too plainly showed the guilty passions that raged within his breast, and which nothing whatever could control, and as he spoke, he once more grasped her wrist, and endeavoured to encircle her slender waist with his arm, you have commanded me to divulge my thoughts, the purpose that guides me in my present conduct, and let the consequences be whatever they may, I will not shrink from the task which is thus imposed upon me. Know then, maiden, that even the savage breast of the despised Pariah, Yusef, is not insensible to the tenderest emotions, when awakened by the powerful influence of matchless beauty; and stern and inflexible as he admits his nature to be, beneath the smiles of lovely woman I could bow the veriest slave, and even bless the fetters that bound me. Nay, shrink not from me with that look of loathing, for now that the opportunity I have coveted presents itself, I must, I will give utterance to the thoughts that occupy my mind. Hear me while I declare that with such sentiments as those I have but feebly described, your tran-

scendent charms have inspired me. I love you, Omelia, and nothing whatever can extinguish that glowing passion in my breast."

As he thus spoke the expression of his eyes and looks became still more alarming, and he again endeavoured to encircle the waist of the disgusted girl, whose eyes shot forth flashes of indignation, as she exclaimed—

"Presumptuous miscreant, dare you thus insult mine ears, and outrage my feelings by an avowal of your guilty and brutal passion?"

"Aye," replied Yusef, with increased boldness and resolution, "I not only dare to do so but to repeat it, and to assure you that in spite of your opposition, and the scorn and hatred with which you view me, that I will persist till the fierce and uncontrollable desires with which you have filled my breast are gratified. But frown not so upon me, Omelia, for although rude and repulsive my appearance and manners may be, I repeat that I can be meek and submissive as a slave when beauty deigns to smile upon me. Think not that it is a mere evanescent passion with which your charms have inspired me, but one which nothing can destroy, and which time must increase in strength. Neither—strange and incredible though it may appear to your ears—is it a passion which had its origin but yesterday, but one which has existed for years, although never till now have I had the courage or the opportunity to reveal it."

"Shameless villain!" exclaimed Omelia, her breast swelling with emotions which it is useless to attempt to describe; "this is intollerable, and should meet with that punishment which it so richly merits. Think you that Omelia will tamely brook this insolence, and have her feelings thus wounded, her ears polluted? Away, I will hear no more."

"You shall, you must listen to me," said the ruffian, resolutely, "I will not have my wishes thus thwarted; and here in this lonely spot, there is no one to interrupt me. But be calm, lovely Omelia, and listen to me patiently. I marked you when but a mere child, in all the dazzling lustre of innocence and beauty, and it was then that love first inflamed my breast. Years have vanished since we met before, but never have you been absent from my thoughts, my imagination; you have haunted me like a phantom; in my dreams, and in my waking moments you have ever been present to my memory, and fed the unextinguishable fire which you so long since kindled in my breast. I see you now in all the full bloom of womanly beauty, accident has again brought you to my enraptured sight, and no earthly power shall thwart me in my purpose, no thought of danger tempt me to abandon my designs."

"Brutal scoundrel!" cried our heroine, almost overpowered by the tempest of feelings that agitated her in so alarming and revolting a situation; "release me, I again command. Oh, Stanley, unfortunate Stanley, would that you were near, how terribly but justly would you resent this monstrous outrage."

"Stanley," repeated Yusef, with a look of scorn, "bah! I loathe and despise him, and such should be my words if he were even now present. But his doom is sealed, you will behold each other no more. He has deceived you; he loves you not, but on another has he placed his affections."

"Stanley false to me!" ejaculated Omelia, indignantly, "liar!—libeller! Begone, begone!—dare not longer attempt to detain me, your touch is contamination."

"Be it so," he returned, with savage determination, and all his guilty passions aroused to the utmost pitch of excitement, and flashing forth in the expression of his eyes, "but nothing shall frustrate my designs. This hour, this very moment they shall be accomplished, even though my death should immediately follow. Proud scornful girl, resistance to my will is useless; you are mine—you are mine!"

"Help—help!—villain! miscreant, forbear!" screamed the now truly terrified Omelia, as he seized her more violently in his arms, and with fearful and disgusting looks endeavouring to force her towards a more secluded spot, amongst the thickly clustering trees: at the same time the cowardly ruffian knowing that she was powerless to resist him, again and again polluted her lips with his odious kisses.

It was a fearful and critical moment to our heroine, and terror made her desperate, as she struggled violently to disengage herself from his hold, which she at last, providentially and miraculously it might be said, succeeded in doing; and hastily retreated followed by Yusef, who gave utterance to the most dreadful oaths and imprecations.

Omelia continued to rend the air with her cries, and looked anxiously around, but perceiving no assistance at hand she gave herself up for lost, for nothing seemed likely to induce the daring miscreant to abandon his atrocious designs, and everything appeared to favour him in the accomplishment of them.

But at that critical moment, when all chance of Omelia's escape appeared to be at an end, and Yusef was again about to seize her, she caught sight of his rifle, which, as has been before stated, he had rested against the trunk of a tree previous to his approaching his intended victim, and with a cry of gratitude she immediately seized it, and levelling it at him, the villain shrunk back

surprised, enraged, and thoroughly dismayed.

CHAPTER CXXIII.

THE DEFEAT OF YUSEF, AND HIS FLIGHT.

The furious rage and disappointment of the villain, Yusef, was visible in the fierce expression of his savage and forbidding features, and the trembling emotion of his muscular limbs, whilst the looks of our heroine as she still continued to level the rifle at his head, were those of triumph and exultation.

"Now villain, shameless villain!" she exclaimed, "the chance is mine! All just heaven has interposed to save me, and to defeat your atrocious designs. Firm in virtue, Omelia, the sepoy's daughter will never yield her honour but with death. Move but a step, but a single inch to attempt to obstruct me in my retreat, and you will pay for your rash temerity with your life."

"Omelia, hear me," said the discomfitted ruffian, in faltering accents, and with cringing, cowardly looks; "I do beseech your forbearance and forgiveness for the rash conduct which the impetuosity of my unfortunate passion has precipitated me into, I—"

"Coward—hypocrite!" interrupted our heroine, with the same resolute looks and attitude, "I scorn to listen to your apologies. My answer is this, dare to offer again to molest me, and that instant I fire—if you are mad enough to rush recklessly upon death, why e'en be it so."

"The gun is not loaded," said Yusef.

"Indeed," returned our heroine, scornfully, "if it be not, then why do you thus with coward fear shrink from it? At any rate, if you are mad enough to disregard my warning, I will e'en test the truth or falsehood of your assertions."

A terrible oath escaped the lips of the defeated villain, and his features were distorted with rage, as he slowly and reluctantly retired, every now and then looking back, and observing the determined Omelia standing fixed in the same attitude, and with the rifle still levelled towards him in the most threatening manner.

He found that his guilty and infamous designs were that time, at any rate, defeated, and dreading the consequences he had no other alternative but to make good his retreat without delay, which he did, and the darkness soon hid him from Omelia's sight.

So sudden and wonderful had been her deliverance from the terrible danger which had threatened her, that she could scarcely believe the evidence of her senses, and for a few minutes after the villain Yusef had disappeared she remained transfixed to the spot and was completely lost in amazement and incredulity; but at length overwhelmed with feelings of gratitude at her extraordinary and miraculous deliverence, she laid the gun aside, and sinking on her knees, with hands clasped vehemently together, she poured forth her heartfelt thanks to the Supreme for His merciful interposion.

She was startled and aroused from this by hearing her own name pronounced in a man's voice, and looking hastily around, she beheld two persons rapidly approaching the spot where she was standing, from the direction of the city.

The darkness not permitting her to recognise them, and not knowing whether they might be friends or foes, she again seized the rifle, determined to defend herself to the last, should they happen to be the latter.

They quickly arrived at the spot, and Omelia's relief and satisfaction may be imagined when she saw that it was Abdal and Mr. Eldred, who alarmed at her long absence had come in search of her.

They were completely astonished at the attitude in which they found her, and the excitement of her looks that plainly showed that something of an extraordinary and alarming nature had happened to her.

But the mingled feelings that rushed upon her brain completely overpowered her, and with an exclamation, she again threw the gun aside, and sunk almost fainting in the arms of the astonished Abdal.

For two or three minutes she remained in the same condition, and Abdal and Mr. Eldred were left to conjecture what had taken place, till she had sufficiently recovered to afford them the explanation which they required.

At length, however, she regained her composure, and in reply to the questions which Abdal and his companion so anxiously put to her, she informed them in as few words as possible what had occurred, and their astonishment and indignation as they listened to her may be readily conceived, while their gratification at her miraculous escape from the villain's daring designs, and the extraordinary courage and presence of mind which Omelia had displayed, elicited their warmest admiration and congratulations.

"The cowardly, brutal ruffian, to commit so monstrous an outrage," said Abdal, "it is unfortunate that myself and Mr. Eldred did not arrive before he could effect his escape, he would have had to pay for his villany with his life. But due notice of this occurrence must be given to the proper military authorities who no doubt will take immediate steps for his apprehension, and bring him to the punishment he deserves."

"The fellow has ever been looked upon with suspicion," returned Mr. Eldred, "although nothing could be discovered to bring a direct charge against him. This conduct, however—for it is not likely that he will venture to return here—goes to prove that those suspicions as to his real character were not unfounded, that he has ever been a rebel at heart, and only awaited a fitting opportunity to do mischief. The effrontery of the scoundrel, however, in venturing to commit this outrage on the feelings of Omelia, and to disgust her ears by an avowal of his guilty and revolting passion, startles and astonishes me."

"Alas," sighed our heroine, "it seems to be my fate to be constantly persecuted and annoyed. I confess that after the proof I have had of the desperate character of this ruffian, and the threats that he has held out to me, I cannot think of him without feelings of horror."

"Do not unnecessarily alarm yourself, Omelia," said Abdal, "for, after this signal defeat, and now that his real character is revealed, it is more than probable that he will deem it prudent to abandon his guilty designs. But one thing is quite certain, namely, that while you remain here you must not venture forth alone, especially at such an hour as the one you have this evening chosen to do. Come let us away."

Omelia made no reply, but with strange feelings of fear and misgiving, she accompanied her two friends on their return to the city.

In the meantime, the ruffian Yusef filled with the most ungovernable rage and disappointment, at his extraordinary and unexpected defeat, at the moment when success seemed to be all but certain, and fearing that the alarm being given, an instant pursuit might be set on foot which it would be difficult for him to elude, continued his flight with all the speed he could, till he had got to some distance beyond the city, when he paused to take breath, and to give free vent to the excited feelings that raged within his breast.

Deadly malice and revenge, coupled with savage determination, were depicted on his dark countenance, he clenched his fists, and his gaunt limbs shook again with ungovernable rage and every evil passion. Then curses loud and deep escaped his lips, and for some moments he was unable to give expression to his enraged feelings in any other way.

"Curses, the most damning curses light on this misfortune," he growled forth, "it is what I never calculated upon. But with all my boasted cunning and artifice to be thus shamefully defeated, held at defiance, my life menaced, and compelled to take ignominious flight, like some craven dog, and that too by a weak girl, whom I thought would never have the courage to attempt to resist my will. Oh, the thought is most humiliating, and I hate and despise myself for my imbecile conduct. Thoughtless fool that I must be to place the very means of certain defeat in her hands. Proud, scornful girl, you triumph now, but rest assured you shall not long escape me, for let the consequences be whatever they may, nothing shall induce me to abandon my designs, and the time will ere long arrive when my wishes shall be accomplished. I have those on whom I can depend, for we are bound by solemn ties and obligations together, and who will not fail to render me every assistance in the furtherence of my wishes. The despised sepoy Yusef's day of triumph is not far distant, and when those who have hitherto looked upon him with scorn shall feel his power, and tremble at his name. Omelia's hatred does but add to the fierce feelings of desire her beauty has kindled in my breast, and which are now fanned by revenge and every malignant passion, and I swear that I will not rest until my every guilty wish is fully gratified. I will pursue her like her own shadow, and watch my opportunity to get her in my power, which I fear not will ultimately present itself. Then let her tremble, for her fate will be certain, and no earthly power shall prevent it."

Again he clenched his fists as he gave expression to these diabolical thoughts, and it was evident from his looks and demeanour that no consideration of personal danger would be able to deter him from the execution of his infamous schemes even extravagant and perfectly impracticable as they at present appeared to be.

Having thus given vent to his brutal feelings and intention, Yusef, having first looked in every direction as far as his eyes could penetrate through the darkness—for the moon was now obscured by black and ponderous clouds, to see that there was no danger to apprehend, or any one to observe him, hurried on his way by the most dreary and unfrequented route towards the jungle, which was at no considerable distance, and which he appeared anxious and from some particular and important motives to reach with as little delay as possible.

CHAPTER CXXIV.

THE MEETING IN THE JUNGLE.

The rage and disappointment of Yusef seemed rather to increase than abate as he proceeded on his way, and at the same time his determination to persevere in his guilty and atrocious designs, even at every risk.

Already sufficient has been stated to show that Yusef was a man who was not likely by a first failure to be intimidated from anything upon which he had fixed his mind, and to gratify either his feelings of revenge, desire or ambition, that there was no crime, however monstrous which he was not fully capable of perpetrating.

He was a man also, who possessed many superior intellectual qualities, much depth of thought and design, and these, of course, made him the far more dangerous for evil, and ever aided him most materially in his nefarious transactions, and rendered him tenfold a dangerous enemy.

Yet he knew so well how to conceal his real motives and intentions under a mask of hypocrisy that although he was at all times looked upon with an eye of suspicion—which was principally caused by his being one of the degraded and despised class of Pariahs—he never sufficiently openly committed himself to confirm those suspicions, and therefore secretly carried on his designs with impunity.

During the long and tedious siege of the unfortunate garrison he had often been viewed with such feelings of doubt and mistrust, that it had been more than once half resolved to place him under arrest; but he would contrive to do some act that at once had the effect of dissipating those fears and surmises, and of preventing any actual restraint upon his actions.

Yusef in reality might be said to have a deadly and inveterate hatred of all the human race—the Feringhee especially—and all his thoughts, and wishes, and passions, were guided by revenge against his fellow creatures which he determined to lose no time of gratifying at every opportunity.

In his more youthful days he had, he considered, suffered together with his kindred great wrong at the hands of the British government, and certain it was—though from what cause we are not in a position to explain—they had been deprived of their property, and reduced from affluence to a state of absolute and abject poverty.

Under these circumstances it was rather remarkable that Yusef had not been one of the first to join the revolt on its breaking out, but he nurtured his plans in secret, and bided his time to carry them into execution with greater effect.

He had those—desperate and determined villains like himself—with whom he had been for some time in secret communication, and who looking upon him as their chief, they had sworn faithfully to aid and abet in all his designs, let them be whatever they might, and it was with their assistance that he encouraged the hope to get Omelia completely in his power.

As he had stated, he had known her when

but a mere child, soon after she had been introduced to the family of the late Mr. Melville, and from that moment the guilty passion which now held such fierce dominion in his breast had had its origin; the matchless beauty of the little Omelia had made a powerful impression upon his heart at that time which nothing could eradicate; though years had elapsed that lovely child had been almost constantly in his thoughts, and in imagination he had pictured to himself those irresistible charms ripened into full maturity, and often had he wished that he might have an opportunity of beholding her again, though he was not presumptuous enough to suppose even for an instant that so contemptible and repulsive an individual as himself could ever excite any other feeling in her breast than one of disgust, if not of actual abhorrence.

He had heard too, by some means with which we are not exactly acquainted, of the passion that existed between her and Lieutenant Stanley, and it had excited his utmost feelings of rage and jealousy, though the probability of his (Yusef's) ever meeting with her again was very remote, and to have entertained the idea that he could hope to supplant him in her affections would, to say the least of it, have been preposterous.

But now that accident had again thrown Omelia in his way, and he found that she realised more, much more than his glowing imagination had pictured, his guilty passion was inflamed to an uncontrollable degree, and, as has been before frequently asserted, he was resolved to rest not till that passion was gratified.

"The defeat of to-night will but urge me on in my fierce determination," he muttered to himself, but with looks sufficient to show that he was prepared to carry his nefarious threats into execution, "and so to mature my plans as to ensure their future success. I have the means of accomplishing my designs at my command, and I will not suffer any consideration to deter me. You shall be mine, Omelia, and by every power I swear that nothing shall prevent it. For a time you have escaped through my own folly and thoughtlessness, but it shall be but for a brief period, and the delay in the consummation of my wishes will but render my final triumph the more complete. Yusef never yet suffered himself to be entirely defeated in any project upon which he had fixed his mind, and it is not likely that he will be so on the present occasion. But 'tis near the hour of appointment, and I must hasten on my way to the jungle."

He quickened his speed as he thus spoke, and continuing by the same lonely and circuitous route, and buried in the gloomy and guilty meditations that had so long occupied his mind.

The night, as has been before stated, had now become particularly dark, for there was no moon, not a single star to be seen, and a gloomy silence reigned around which was in perfect keeping with the thoughts in which Yusef at that moment indulged.

At no great distance flowed the broad waters of the Ganges, and their murmuring sound which at intervals distinctly broke upon the ear, was all that disturbed the death-like silence which prevailed.

The vast river Ganges, with its tributaries, waters a great part of the north-east of India, and finally enters the sea in the province of Bengal. This river is an object of worship, to it the natives make annual pilgrimages, on its banks children expose their dying parents, where they are either drowned by the rising tide, or perish by the burning sun and the attacks of wild beasts.

On the villain Yusef proceeded towards a deep and extensive jungle at no great distance from this river, and where he had appointed to meet several of his guilty confederates, who, like himself, were men who had lost caste, and were consequently the despised and outcasts of society.

We repeat that if through any neglect of ritual observance, a Hindoo lose caste, the wife disowns and spurns the husband, the father the son, the sister the brother. However respectable he may have been before in every social relation, henceforth he is a vagabond, a wanderer on the face of the earth, whose touch brings pollution, banished from the dwellings of men, and a victim of the just wrath of Brahma

Yusef had been supposed to be a convert to Christianity, and it was for that reason that he had been protected, and permitted to remain in the ranks of the sepoy army.

At length after wending his way through the darkness to some distance farther, he came in sight of the jungle, and which as seen at that hour particularly, when the whole face of nature was enveloped in a complete and impenetrable darkness, was indeed a wild and even fearful-looking place, and strained his eyes to the utmost through the obscurity of the night, expecting to see some signs of those whom he had appointed to meet there, but without success.

"They are not there," he muttered in accents of disappointment, "and yet the time has elapsed that we agreed to meet. Curses light upon their tardiness, what can be the cause of it? They have not repented of the undertaking, and abandoned their designs surely. Oh, no, I am too well convinced of their firmness of resolution, and of fidelity to the cause which we all have so much at heart, to doubt them. Something particular must have caused this delay, which they will no doubt be able to explain, and I will there fore endeavour to await with patience their arrival."

He entered the jungle with caution—particularly as he was now unarmed, Omelia having in so singular a manner obtained possession of his rifle—for fear of the wild beasts with which it was no doubt infested; but he met with nothing as he advanced to excite his alarm, and he felt the more emboldened to proceed, still feeling impatient at the delay of those whom he had expected to have found awaiting his arrival.

And in this manner he had advanced some short distance into the jungle when lights appeared, evidently proceeding from torches, bore in the hands of persons, and in a short time they had got so near that Yusef was enabled to distinguish the shadowy forms of several men, and feeling satisfied that they were those whom he had expected, he applied a whistle to his lips and blew a signal which was quickly answered in a similar manner, and the light became stationary, showing that the men awaited his approach.

CHAPTER CXXV.

THE CONSULTATION.—THE OATH.

The red glare of the several torches cast a broad reflection upon the singularly wild scene, partly revealing the swarthy faces of the rebels, and giving a strange effect to all around, at the same time it was well calculated to scare away the wild beasts that so numerously infested the place.

Yusef satisfied that the men were his confederates whom he had appointed to meet, advanced fearlessly and eagerly towards them, as soon as his person was recognised, he was received with a shout of welcome showing the deference with which they viewed him, and which he suitably acknowledged, and in a short time he stood in the midst of them, his tall, commanding, and athletic figure seeming to tower far above the rest.

A more ruffianly or desperate-looking set of fellows than those there assembled at that solemn hour—for it was fast approaching midnight—could not readily be imagined, and it was quite evident that they were men who were fully capable of any acts, however, daring and atrocious they might be.

They were all armed both with rifles, revolvers, and long knives, and thus fully capable of defending themselves to the utmost in case of any sudden surprise or attack. They appeared rather astonished to find that Yusef was not similarly provided.

"You are late, comrades," said Yusef, "'tis some time past the hour that we appointed to meet."

"True," replied one of the men, "business detained us longer than we expected. You, too, have tarried, Yusef, and if I may judge from your looks you are not in any of the best of tempers Has anything occurred to annoy and vex you?"

"Yes," returned Yusef, "I have met with everything to excite my feelings. My expectations have been most wofully disappointed, and what is more, I have suffered a shameful defeat, and that too by a woman."

"What, the lovely damsel who has so strangely enslaved your heart; the beauteous Omelia as she is called? interrogated the man.

"The same, Alahmed," answered Yusef, "this night she has, at any rate proved herself far too much for me."

"Ha, ha, ha!" laughed Alahmed, as Yusef had called him, "that is something for you to have to acknowledge, Yusef, with all your well known sagacity and determination."

"It is so," coincided Yusef, "but it is nevertheless true, and you will not therefore marvel at the excitement of my feelings. I ventured to avow my sentiments—if the fierce flames of desire that rage within my breast can be so termed—but the proud beauty met me with scorn and defiance for which, however, I was not unprepared."

"Of what then have you to complain?" said Alahmed.

"Listen," replied Yusef.

The rebels then gathered round him while he briefly related the particulars of what had occurred between our heroine and himself, and to which the ruffians listened with much apparent interest and could not refrain from laughter when Yusef related the critical situation in which he found himself after Omelia, had got possession of his rifle in so singular a manner. But an oath and a look from him quickly silenced them, and whatever their thoughts upon the occasion might have been, they considered it prudent to endeavour to stifle the expression of them.

"You had a narrow escape, Yusef," remarked Alahmed, "and you may thank your lucky stars for it. It was a sad oversight of your's to lay your rifle so carelessly aside where the girl could so easily possess herself of it; and I cannot sufficiently admire her courage determination and presence of mind."

"True," observed Yusef, "Omelia possesses all those quantities in an eminent degree. But the scorn and defiance with which she has met my first advances—although as I have said before, I expected her to do so—and the disgust and hatred with which she evidently views me, have mortified my pride, and still more inflamed the guilty passion which she has excited in my breast."

"This first defeat will not daunt you," said Alahmed, "or cause you to abandon your designs against the girl?"

"No," replied Yusef, "but on the contrary, it will but stimulate me to fresh exertion, and I do not for an instant doubt but that, with your assistance, I shall ere long completely succeed in the accomplishment of my wishes."

"Aye, if you persevere," said Alahmed.

"I will not fail to do so," returned Yusef, "but may I depend upon you all?"

"All, all," exclaimed the rebels, in a breath.

"You will give me your best aid in capturing the girl, and remain faithful to me in every danger?"

"We will—we will!"

"Are you prepared to swear it?"

"We swear it," answered the ruffians, and Alahmed, who seemed to be the entire confident of the villain Yusef, setting the example, sunk on his knees, his colleagues doing the same, and the oath was pledged accordingly.

"Enough," said Yusef, in a tone of satisfaction, I know I may depend upon you, and I thank you. I now feel quite certain in the ultimate and speedy triumph of my designs. You probably are aware, too, that I am not without the means of rewarding you, and in supporting the execution of our plans. I have never missed an opportunity to enrich myself whenever the opportunity has been presented. On the relief of the garrison, I contrived to gain secret access to the palace of the King of Oude, and you may be certain that I did not leave there without a goodly booty which I have got secreted.

"'Tis well," remarked Alahmed, "we shall find it most useful to us in the prosecution of our designs."

"Truly so," coincided Yusef.

"But have you hit upon any plan by which you may obtain possession of the girl?"

"I have not yet had time to decide, but we will talk of that anon."

"You must act promptly and with determination, to make success likely," said Alahmed.

"Right," agreed Yusef, "I ever do, when I have any important object in view. This night's adventure and mishap has aroused all my energies, and no time shall be lost in putting my designs into execution. Once in my power, she must become the helpless slave of my will, and will be compelled to yield to all my wishes, since resistance would be entirely useless, and would only serve to exasperate me to acts of violence which I would otherwise avoid. But this is not the only business for which we have met."

"True," said Alahmed, "you have now betrayed your real character, Yusef—which I only feel surprised that you should so long have succeeded in concealing—and should you fall into the hands of the detested Feringhee you know well the certain fate that awaits you."

"Aye," answered Yusef, "the fate which awaits us all as rebels—so, of course, they call us—should we chance to fall into their clutches. They will hang us like dogs, or blow us away from the mouth of the cannon."

"True," remarked Alahmed, "such is the only fate which we can expect from them, but it will be our own fault if we put it in their power to do so. At any rate, we will do some mischief ere that time shall probably arrive."

"Yes," said Yusef, and his large black eyes flashed with determination as he spoke, and every savage feeling that can disgrace human nature was expressed in his forbidding countenance, "I have a long list of burning wrongs to avenge, I have sworn to do so in the blood of the hated European, and I will not fail to keep my oath"

"Well said," returned Alahmed, "what course then do you propose to adopt?"

"For a day or two we can do nothing decisive," answered Yusef, "but when our plans are completed, and the girl secured, we will hasten to join Nena Sahib, who is now in the neighbourhood of Allahamed, with a large force, determined to strike a decided blow, and who, no doubt, will gladly avail himself of our services. We can make the different villages we shall have to pass through pay amply for our travelling expenses."

"True," said Alahmed, "there is every prospect of our being well rewarded for our pains, that is, if we do not happen to fall into the hands of our enemies, in which case we might chance to meet with a certain description of reward which would be far from agreeable to our wishes."

"We must have no misgivings upon that subject," remarked Yusef, "for it is only by firmness, confidence, and determination, that we can hope to achieve the object we have in view. Are ye all agreed and resolved, I once more demand?"

To this question an immediate and unanimous answer in the affirmative was given by the rebels, and they again swore fidelity to each other.

"But how do you propose to dispose of the girl should you succeed in getting her in your power, while we are on our hazardous expedition?" inquired Alahmed.

"That question is an idle one," replied Yusef, "and I wonder that you should put it. Of course, the beauteous Omelia will be my companion wherever I go. I will soon tame her proud and obdurate spirit, and make her succumb to all my wishes, depend

on it, but once let me get her in my power, and, in spite of the disgust and hatred with which she now views me, my triumph shall be rendered complete. Should she remain obstinate, force shall compel her to submit to my will. And let her beware how she attempts to oppose me, or the sentiments with which she has at present inspired me might be changed to those of the most deadly hatred and revenge, and terrible would be the fate to which she would then expose herself."

As the miscreant thus spoke he knitted his brows, shook his clenched fist in the air, and the expression of his features became more frightful and threatening than before, showing the atrocious plot he had formed against the happiness of our heroine, if not for her complete destruction.

No. 61.

"I approve of your resolution, Yusef," said Alahmed, "and I need not again assure you that you may command the aid of myself and our comrades here to carry out your designs. We have sworn fidelity to each other, and we must not, will not break our oath."

"Well spoken, Alahmed," remarded Yusef, grasping his hand, "and I thank you for it. But time wears apace, and our present meeting must be brought to a close; I have business which calls me some distance from hence before the morning.

"And where shall we meet again?" interrogated Alahmed.

"At the same hour the night after tomorrow," answered Yusef.

"In the same place?"

"No, in the ruins of the old palace on the

banks of the Ganges," replied Yusef, "there we may better confer in secret together, and I shall then be able to make you acquainted with my plans, which by that time I shall doubtless have matured."

"Be it so," said Alahmed, "we will not fail to be punctual."

"Enough, I am satisfied," returned Yusef, "give me one of your revolvers in case of accident, and then I must away."

This request was complied with, and after exchanging a few more words with Alahmed and his companions, and giving them some further instructions till the time when they had appointed to meet again, he took his departure across the jungle by a different direction to that from which he had come, and was soon lost to the sight in the darkness beyond.

Through the wild jungle the desperate villain continued his way with unabated speed, tracing his steps with the greatest ease, notwithstanding the intensity of the darkness, for every inch of the way seemed to be perfectly familiar to him, and he suffered nothing whatever to impede his progress.

But at length he paused for breath and to look around him, and then gave utterance to the following soliloquy:—

"So thus far everything promises fairly for the success of my designs. I can with safety rely, I believe, upon the fidelity of Alahmed and his colleagues, and shall find their services of every value. Omelia, think not that your triumph of this evening shall daunt me, or cause me to abandon my purpose; if you do, you can form but little idea of the real character of the man you have to deal with, and whose passions you have thus excited. Oh, there is no risk, no danger I will shrink from incurring in order to secure the accomplishment of my wishes, to get you in my power, and to break your proud spirit to my will. The thought fills me with exultation, and already I feel as if success had crowned my hopes and expectations, and that I reigned supreme master of those matchless charms that even a monarch might feel proud to possess, and anticipate the nameless, the boundless bliss that awaits me. But I must make no more delay than possible, lest something should yet occur to thwart me in my wishes, and annihilate all my hopes. Omelia, you shall be mine, and that speedily, in spite of everything which may occur to oppose me."

Thus restored, he once more resumed with hurried steps, his way to the place of his destination, without encountering any one on his way.

———

CHAPTER CXXVI.

GLAD NEWS.—ANTICIPATED HAPPINESS.

The daring outrage committed by the ruffian Yusef created the greatest surprise and indignation, as soon as it became known, while the courageous conduct and presence of mind evinced by Omelia on the occasion, became no less the theme of admiration, although it was much regretted that, on securing the rifle, and thus having him completely in her power, she did not fully avail herself of the opportunity, and ridding society of one who was likely to prove a curse to it, at the same time destroy an inveterate and deadly enemy whom she had so much reason to dread.

Means were immediately set on foot that seemed likely to lead to the apprehension of the daring miscreant, from whose treacherous designs there was every reason to fear—but without success.

Omelia, however, could not suffer the alarming subject to escape her mind, but continued to dwell long and painfully upon it, and to perplex her brain to no purpose in endeavouring to imagine what might be the future nefarious plans of Yusef, or whether—seeing the danger to which he would subject himself, and the certain punishment that awaited him in the event of his capture—he would be induced to abandon them altogether.

Our heroine was half inclined to encourage and adopt the latter opinion, and Abdal and Mrs. Eldred, by all the arguments they could make use of, endeavoured to persuade her to do so, and to dismiss from her mind the fears which at present naturally possessed it.

"The villain surely will never have the boldness to renew his atrocious attempt, especially now that he must feel certain that every means will be employed to detect and apprehend him," observed Mrs. Eldred. "However powerful may be the guilty and disgusting passion which Omelia has excited in his breast, he will not feel disposed to risk his life in the attempt to gratify it."

"True," coincided Abdal; "it would be little short of madness in him to attempt to do so, and I think Omelia may safely banish from her mind all apprehensions of future danger."

"I would fain try to do so," returned our heroine, "but cannot yet bring my mind to that conclusion. This Yusef is a desperate ruffian who is not at all likely to become daunted at the prosecution of any diabolical designs he may have in view by the fear of danger, and it behoves me then to be on my guard, and to use every precaution to render the schemes of the miscreant abortive, should he still have them in contemplation."

"Certainly," remarked Mr. Eldred, "common prudence demands the adoption of such a course, and to provide against every danger. But in a few days it is my intention to depart with many other of the persons from Lucknow, to depart from hence to Calcutta, such is the arrangement proposed to us by the authorities, as we may there receive all the accommodation and assistance that we require, till those who feel so disposed can have an opportunity of returning to England. You, Omelia, and our friend Abdal, will, I trust, accompany us, and you will then be completely beyond the reach of danger, should the villain Yusef persist in his nefarious plot against you."

"Believe me, my dear sir," replied Omelia, "that I duly appreciate the feeling of kindness and friendship which dictates this proposal, and regret that I cannot avail myself of it. But I have no business in Calcutta, where I am an entire stranger, and every affectionate anxiety for the fate of the unfortunate Edward Stanley calls me another way. Besides, why should I, a stranger to you, and without any claim upon your benevolence, continue to be a burthen to you. I feel that I already owe a debt of gratitude which it will be almost impossible for me ever to repay, and—"

"I pray you, Omelia," interrupted Mrs. Eldred, who was present when this conversation took place, "not to permit such thoughts as those which you have just now expressed, to trouble your mind. We have done no more than common humanity and justice demanded, and only regret that our means of serving you have been so limited. We need scarcely assure you I am convinced that we take the warmest interest in your fate, and that our fondest wish is to see you restored to that happiness to which your virtues so justly entitle you."

"I thank you, madam," returned Omelia, with a look which showed the fervour and sincerity of the words she was uttering, "from the bottom of my heart I thank you for your kind and charitable wishes, but, alas, I fear that happiness is never more destined to be my lot, at any rate, unless my beloved Stanley should escape the fate with which he is at present threatened, and it shall please providence to restore us once more to each other's arms,"

"Endeavour to cherish that fond hope,' said Mrs. Eldred, "and depend upon it that however gloomy your prospects may for the present appear to be, it will not be disappointed.

"True," said Mr. Eldred, "the charge against Stanley is not of that serious nature which you seem to imagine, and—"

"Ah," hastily interrupted Omelia, thinking that an excellent opportunity to elicit the truth, "if what you say be correct, and there is no danger to be apprehended as to the fate of Stanley, why do you hesitate to relate to me the circumstances of the unfortunate affair, and thus quiet the fears and banish the suspense which have so long tortured me."

"I see no reason that I should now longer hesitate to do so," replied Mr. Eldred, "since you have now sufficiently recovered from that powerful and dangerous excitement of feelings under which you recently laboured. Briefly, then, Lieutenant Stanley is accused of striking his superior officer, Lieutenant-Colonel Hartland, and—"

"Alas," interrupted Omelia, with a sigh, and a look of agony, "and call you that a charge of such trifling importance, that the position in which the unfortunate Stanley is placed, is one of no danger?"

"Under all the circumstances," replied Mr. Eldred, "I have a right to look upon it in the most favourable light, and to anticipate a favourable result."

"And what are the circumstances to which you allude?" eagerly inquired Omelia.

"In the first place," said Mr. Eldred, "Colonel Hartland was the aggressor by applying to Mr. Stanley insulting and unjustifiable language to which no gentleman could tamely submit."

"Ah," ejaculated our heroine hastily, and a feeling of satisfaction came over her, remembering as she did the assurance which Stanley had given her in his letter, "it is true then, thank heaven."

"What is true?" interrogated Mr. Eldred with a look of surprise and curiosity at her observations.

"No matter—no matter," she returned, impatiently, "proceed."

"Some difference—with the particulars of which I am not thoroughly acquainted," continued Mr. Eldred, "had for some time previously existed between the colonel and your lover, and on the occasion when the alleged offence was committed, the former made use of the most violent and abusive language towards Mr. Stanley, notwithstanding the latter was only just recovering from a severe wound which he had received in the arm, and was therefore not in a proper condition to defend himself. Nay, he even went so far as to call the gallant young lieutenant who has so frequently and so greatly distinguished himself, a despicable coward, and in his just resentment Stanley struck him a blow which felled him to the earth."

"And that was no more than he richly deserved, the base libeller," said Abdal, warmly, "it would indeed have been sheer cowardice in Lieutenant Stanley had he not at once resented as he did so gratuitous and unmerited an insult."

"True," coincided Omelia, her bosom swelling and her cheeks glowing with indignation, "even had Stanley sacrificed the life of his dastardly calumniator, he would have been fully justified. But, oh, tell me, sir, for on that now much depends, were there any witnesses to this?"

"Yes," answered Mr. Eldred, "fortunately there was; two officers of distinction, and who are bound in honour to speak the truth."

"Thank heaven," fervently ejaculated our heroine, clasping her hands together, and tears of joy trembling in her eyes; for the assertions made use of in the letter of Stanley—if she could indeed for a moment have supposed that he would have sought to flatter and deceive her with any false hopes—were fully corroborated, and a heavy weight of care anxiety, fear and suspense, were removed from her mind, which had become almost insupportable.

"There is, however," said Mr. Eldred, "one lamentable and unfortunate circumstance which I deem it right to mention. The melancholy news has just reached here of the alarming state of the great hero, General Havelock's illness, and that his death is looked forward to every hour. Lieutenant Stanley, you are aware, Omelia, formerly served under him with distinction, and no doubt would have found in him a valuable friend in his present difficulty."

"Most true," returned our heroine, "but," she quickly added, hope again sparkling in her eyes, and fluttering in her bosom, "I will dismiss the doubts, the dismal forebodings and apprehensions that have hitherto tortured me, and look forward to the result with the most sanguine hopes and the greatest confidence. Stanley, dear Stanley, will—must be acquitted, and what earthly power can then any longer separate us? Oh, blissful thought! what nameless feelings agitate my breast and throb around my heart as it occurs to me."

For a few minutes she gave free indulgence to her joyful emotions, and no one attempted to interrupt her, for they felt assured of the beneficial effects they would have, and they could not but fully enter into the spirit of them.

"But," she said at length, as a sudden idea seemed to fire her brain, and to arouse all her energies into full action, "this state of uncertainty and suspense is no longer endurable. This delay exhausts my patience, and fills my mind with fearful imaginings. Why do I longer remain here, when by retracing my steps to the place where I and my beloved Stanley were separated, and where he now awaits his doom, I may have at once my doubts removed, and be restored to comparative happiness, or be consigned to absolute misery and despair? I will run every risk, endure every trial, however severe, to meet again with him without whose bright presence life must ever remain to me a dreary blank, which it would be a release from anguish to get rid of. Abdal, my friend, my mind is made up, to-morrow I will take my departure from hence, and commence my tedious but hopeful journey."

"Omelia," interposed Abdal, with a look of remonstrance, "your brain must be bewildered by the intelligence which our kind friend, Mr. Eldred, has communicated to us, and you know not what you say. But it is sheer madness for you to talk thus. It is impossible for you to undertake such a journey, even if the accomplishment of your hopes and wishes was certain, in the present delicate state of your health, and completely destitute of resources. Be patient, and rest assured that but a short time now will serve to relieve your anxiety."

"Oh, how easy is it for you to talk," returned Omelia, pettishly and impatiently, "who cannot understand or appreciate the feelings that so violently agitate my breast, and drive me almost to distraction. What obstacle, what difficulty, however great and apparently insurmountable, should I suffer to daunt me in my undertaking. Affection, every feeling of hope and expectation that can take their place in the human breast, urge, impel me on, and let whatever may be the consequences, no matter the result, I feel as though it were absolutely impossible for me to resist the temptation."

"Be calm, Omelia," remonstrated Mr. Eldred, "and patient reflection will convince you of the folly, the imprudence, and utter impracticability of that which you propose. Wait but a day or two, and probably the violent and torturing anxiety of mind which you are at present enduring will be removed, and you may receive all the intelligence that will realize the fondest and brightest hopes you have formed."

"Oh, would that I could think so," returned Omelia, with a look of even increased anxiety and impatience, "I might then indeed learn to be content; but, indeed, even after all that you have told me, I cannot help still entertaining my doubts, fears, and misgivings, which distract my brain, and leave me not one moment free from anxiety."

Her friends still exerted themselves to the utmost to calm the agitation of her feelings, and inspire her with confidence, and they at length succeeded much better than could possibly have been expected, and, after some further observations, they separated for the night.

———

CHAPTER CXXVII.

HOPES REALISED.

On retiring to the room in which she slept, Omelia not feeling inclined for repose, seated herself in a chair and pondered over the events of the evening, and all that she had heard, and which could not fail to excite the most varied emotions in her breast; that of hope—in spite of the observations she had made use of, and the anxiety which she had expressed—still, however, being predominant.

The information which **Mr. Eldred** had at last afforded her, entirely confirmed the assertions which Stanley had made in his letter, and completed the explanation which it seemed he had been so abruptly prevented from giving, and so far Omelia could not be otherwise than satisfied, yet it was impossible for her to dismiss entirely the doubts and fears that would obtrude themselves on her mind, and which rendered her restless and unhappy.

Every moment which she might be kept in this painful state of suspense, would seem to her to be an age, and she knew not where she would be able to find the patience and resolution to endure it. But still the folly, the extravagance, and impracticability of accomplishing such a long and weary journey as that which she had contemplated, especially without pecuniary means, and in the present feeble state of her health, after the excitement and extraordinary fatigue which she had recently undergone, became quite evident to her, and she was compelled to abandon the idea as preposterous.

But oh, how fervent were her prayers for the success of all that her fondest wishes could imagine, and which she dared not to reject, and with what feelings of indescribable transport did she venture to look forward to the time when, in spite of all the numerous obstacles that had once been, and were even now placed in their way, herself and her beloved Stanley would once more be restored to each other, and the dark clouds by which their destiny had been so long overshadowed should have dispersed.

What sunny dreams of future happiness did those thoughts engender, and in which for some time Omelia continued to indulge; but should they be destined to end in bitter disappointment, what then must be the terrible consequences? She shuddered, and scarcely dared to contemplate them, but to banish such torturing and conflicting ideas from her brain altogether she found to be a task that was impossible.

The treasured and affectionate letter which she had received from Stanley in so singular a manner, at the very moment when she was driven to complete despair, and was left to anticipate the worst, she constantly carried about her, and at that time when her mind was so busily occupied with thoughts that bore so immediately upon the subject to which it referred she eagerly took it from her bosom, and with tears trembling in her eyes, and a palpitating heart, she once more perused the contents, and with feelings such as it is needless to attempt to describe, she dwelt upon every sentence, upon every word, which strengthened her hopes, and confirmed the statements she had heard from the lips of Mr. Eldred.

"Yes," she soliloquised, after she had pressed the affectionate epistle to her lips and once more consigned it to her bosom, "dear Stanley, I dare no longer doubt, I will place every reliance in the merciful interposition of providence to release you from the troubles by which you have been so long surrounded, the fate with which you have been threatened, and restore you to liberty and happiness. Severe have been the trials to which we have both been subjected, but brighter days I feel convinced are in store for us, and, faithful to each other, we shall meet with an ample reward for the many sufferings it has been our hard lot to have to endure, With what powerful emotions, and eager impatience do I look forward to the time—not far distant I trust—when all those sanguine and flattering hopes and expectations will be gratified, and we may be able to look back upon the past as only some painful dream. And that blissful time, that bright accomplishment of all that two fond hearts could wish for, will arrive, the anticipations in which I now venture to indulge will not be doomed to be disappointed, I feel confident that they will not, and that happiness to which I have so long been a stranger begins again to dawn upon my mind,"

Such were the thoughts that had now taken possession of Omelia, which every moment gained strength, and could not but have the most cheering effect upon her spirits that had long suffered under a torturing weight of care and anxiety.

She could not, however, banish entirely the recollection of the daring outrage committed by the miscreant Yusef, and the threats he had uttered, and it was impossible at present, at any rate, to stifle altogether the feeling of alarm which they had naturally excited in her breast, for she was well convinced that he was a ruffian who was fully capable of perpetrating all that he had threatened, and would lose no opportunity to accomplish his diabolical wishes, if possible, even at any risk to himself.

The difficulties that were, however, placed in the villain's way, and which it seemed to be utterly impossible for him to surmount reassured her, and with the hope of being ere long again under the protection of Stanley, she endeavoured to banish all apprehensions from her mind.

After these mature reflections, and the more cheerful prospects which by their means had opened upon her imagination, Omelia was enabled to meet her friends on the following morning with brighter looks, and in far better spirits than she had for some time experienced, a happy change which it need scarcely be said that they were most gratified to behold, and encouraged by every means in their power.

The morning passed agreeably away, and they were still engaged in conversation, when a female servant who had shared with Mr. and Mrs. Eldred and their daughter all the horrors and sufferings of the siege of Lucknow, suddenly entered the room in which they were sitting, and announced Captain Morley, who requested an interview with Mr. Eldred on important business.

"Ah," said Mr. Eldred, "what can be the cause of this unexpected visit. Captain Morley is the intimate friend of Lieutenant Stanley, and I have no doubt has taken the greatest interest and anxiety in his fate. Show him in immediately, Martha."

Our heroine trembled, and her heart fluttered with mingled hope and fear. She arose from her seat, and with Abdal, was about to retire from the room, when Mr. Eldred prevented her.

"Stay, Omelia," he observed, "one to whom Mr. Stanley is so sincerely attached, can never be considered by Captain Morley as an intruder. Besides, he may have something of importance to communicate which it may be necessary for you to hear."

Omelia felt still more agitated, but before she could recover herself, the room door was opened, and Captain Morley entered.

But no sooner had our heroine fixed her eyes upon his countenance than an exclamation of astonishment, and mingled hope and fear escaped her, when she recognised the features of the officer from whom she had received Stanley's letter, and whom she had so often wished that she might behold again.

He bowed to her politely, and fixed upon her an encouraging look, and the surprise of Mr. Eldred and his lady may be imagined, but Abdal, who had guessed the truth, awaited anxiously to hear the result.

"I am happy to see you, Captain Morley," observed Mr. Eldred. "Omelia, what is the meaning of the agitation you evince? Is it possible that yourself and my friend have ever met before?"

Our heroine was about to endeavour to make some reply, when the captain saved her the trouble by observing—

"Yes, we have met once before, on a particular occasion; it was for an instant only, but I have no doubt that Omelia has cherished the recollection of it."

"Oh, yes, yes," replied our heroine, in accents of the deepest emotion, and her heart palpitating still more violently with anxiety and expectation."

The surprise of Mr. Eldred and his wife increased, and they looked first at Captain Morley, and then at Omelia, for an explanation, when the former said—

"The cause of my seeking Omelia on the occasion alluded to, need not now be explained. It may be sufficient to observe that I come at present on business of the utmost importance, and more particularly with her. I bring intelligence of Lieutenant Stanley."

"Ah," exclaimed Omelia, with a look, and in tones of excitement which it is unnecessary to describe, "what of him. Oh, tell me sir, I beseech you, and do not keep me in suspense, what news have you to communicate of him? My heart throbs with impatience and anxiety; is it good or bad?"

"Good," returned the captain, promptly "The court-martial is over, and Lieutenant Stanley, I am rejoiced to inform you, is acquitted!"

A cry of joy and gratitude escaped the lips of Omelia, and, overpowered by her emotion she immediately sunk insensible in the arms of Mrs. Eldred, while the agitation of all present was almost equal to that of the beauteous girl, to whom the glad intelligence was of far greater and vital importance than any one.

Thus all doubts and fears were at once removed, and even the most sanguine hopes and expectations that could have been entertained, were fully realised.

"Oh, Captain Morley," said Mr. Eldred, grasping his hand in the most cordial and friendly manner, "how long, and how anxiously looked for—especially by this poor girl—is the information that you now bring us. But are you fully satisfied of the truth of it?"

"If I had not been so," answered the captain, "you may be certain, Mr. Eldred, that I should not have ventured to make the statement, which would have been, under all the circumstances, most cruel and unpardonable on my part. I do not derive my information from mere hearsay, but from Lieutenant Stanley himself, from whom I have this morning received a letter, which I now produce."

"Oh, thank heaven for that," exclaimed Mr. Eldred, sincerely and emphatically, and Captain Morley was about to read the note which he held in his hand, when our heroine revived, and fixing her eyes earnestly and searchingly upon him, in trembling but eager accents she ejaculated—

"Speak, sir, I implore you, did I hear aright; or was it some flattering delusion of my disordered senses? Oh, let me again hear the important fact upon which my happiness or misery, nay, my very life depends."

"Lieutenant Stanley has passed the ordeal bravely, triumphantly, I repeat;" said Captain Morley. "He is again at liberty. Should you doubt the truth of my assertions, this letter will convince you."

He placed it in Omelia's hands as he spoke, and no sooner had her eyes recognised the well known characters of her lover, than she again uttered an exclamation of joy and gratitude, and her limbs trembled so violently that it was with difficulty she could support herself.

Tears half blinded her, and it was a minute or two before she could decipher the contents of the note, which run briefly as follows, and which, in a faltering voice, she read aloud :—

"My dear friend,—Rejoice with me; your best wishes, which I know have ever been for my welfare, are gratified. I have passed manfully through the trial—I am free! Oh, could you see my beloved Omelia—if she is still with the fugitives from Lucknow—what a weight of care and anxiety would this remove from her mind. But I must conclude; I hope soon to rejoin you, till then, believe me to remain your faithful friend,

"E. STANLEY."

Laconic as this epistle was, every word it contained was a gem of inestimable value to Omelia, and clasping her hands together and sinking on her knees, she poured forth in language as eloquent as it was sincere, her gratitude to heaven; while the gratification of every one present, who so well knew and appreciated the manly qualities of Lieutenant Stanley, and who had felt the greatest anxiety as to the result of the court-martial, was fully equal to her own.

"Kind heaven has heard my prayers," she ejaculated; "my doubts and fears are removed, and my fondest hopes and wishes are realised, and I am happy, yes, happy. dear Stanley, in the blissful, the firm conviction that we shall meet again. "Oh, sir," she added, turning herself towards Captain Morley, and by her looks fully evincing the feelings that at that moment occupied her breast, "in what language can I convey to you my thanks for the kind interest you have taken in the fate of myself and Lieutenant Stanley, and for being to me the bearer of such welcome, such joyful intelligence ?"

"No more, my poor girl, I pray you," returned Captain Morley, who seemed to be much affected by the emotion she evinced, as he was the more struck by her surpassing beauty the longer he gazed at her; "the small service I have been enabled to render is scarcely worth mentioning, and I feel more than rewarded in seeing the relief it has afforded your mind. You must now, I think, be satisfied that the information I have communicated is correct, and that Lieutenant Stanley is again at liberty."

"Oh, it must be impossible for me to doubt it," said our heroine; "I must indeed be mad to do so. This dear letter, every word it contains; the well known characters all convince me of the joyful truth, and my bounding heart now throbs with feelings which I find it utterly impossible to describe."

"I need not, I am sure, say, Omelia," remarked Mr. Eldred, "how much myself and Mrs. Eldred participate in the feelings you have described. We most heartily congratulate you on the fortunate result of this painful trial, and fully trust that you and Lieutenant Stanley will shortly meet again."

"Oh, providence, kind providence, grant that your wishes may be realised," said Omelia, fervently; "then, indeed, will my happiness be complete, and I shall be fully rewarded for all the manifold troubles it has been my hard lot to have to encounter."

"And those wishes will be gratified, Omelia," said Captain Morley, who now addressed her with the familiarity of an old acquaintance, but with every respect; "of that you may rest assured; the letter will convince you that Stanley will seize the first opportunity of again beholding you."

"Yes, Yes," said Omelia, eagerly, "I cannot doubt it; and yet how impatiently shall I await that happy time, and tremble for fear lest some fresh calamity may interpose to prevent it. Fain would I brave all the fatigue and danger of the journey to hasten to meet him."

"Nay," observed Captain Morley, "it would be worse than folly for you to attempt to do so, and it is more than probable that you would be unable to accomplish your task. Now that you know that Mr. Stanley is out of danger and again at liberty, you must endeavour to rest yourself content, and to await that time which you so anxiously anticipate with patience."

"I will try to do so," said Omelia; "but oh, how tedious will the hours appear to be till that happy time arrives; every moment will appear to be an age."

"True," observed Mr. Eldred, "but the joy of meeting, whenever it may take place, will fully repay the anxiety you have had to endure. Captain Morley, are you fully acquainted with all the particulars of the unfortunate affair, which placed our friend Stanley in so painful and dangerous a position ?"

"I am," answered the captain, "and can

fully acquit Lieutenant Stanley of all blame. It was impossible for him to have acted otherwise than he did, in order to vindicate his honour, and Colonel Hartland must now feel thoroughly ashamed of his own conduct. But I will leave it for Stanley to explain all the facts when you see him again, which, I trust, will be in a few days. I must now beg to take my leave, with a promise to repeat my visit shortly, when I hope to have more joyful news to communicate."

Omelia again heartily thanked the gallant captain for the trouble he had taken, and he shortly afterwards departed.

Our heroine now gave the most unrestrained indulgence to the powerful emotions of joy and gratitude that animated her breast, and which her friends, who were elated at the information they had thus received, warmly reciprocated.

"Oh, Stanley," she ejaculated, while her bosom throbbed with the natural excitement of her feelings, "what words can describe the thoughts that now crowd upon my brain at this fortunate realisation of those hopes I dared scarcely once to entertain? But can it indeed be true? or am I merely dreaming? I can scarce believe the evidence of my senses. And yet it would be madness to doubt, after all the proof that I have had, and which this valued letter, written by the hand of Stanley himself, fully confirms. Heaven has indeed been merciful, and we shall meet again, I trust never more to be separated under such painful circumstances. How full is now my throbbing heart, but with what different feelings to those that lately agitated it, and nearly drove me to destruction. Oh, I could weep tears of joy."

"Yes, Omelia," remarked Mr. Eldred, "you have indeed cause to be grateful, and we can fully appreciate your feelings. The hopes which I always expressed, but which I now confess I sincerely did but faintly entertain, are now happily realised, and that too in a manner that my most sanguine expectations could hardly have anticipated, and I have no doubt that a few days only will see the completion of all your wishes; namely, the restoration of yourself and Stanley to each other's arms."

"Blissful thought," exclaimed Omelia, in a fervent voice, and tears trembling in her eyes; "my brain turns giddy as it rushes upon it, and I feel as if I were another being. Fly swift the hours that must intervene previous to our meeting. Oh, how impatiently, I am convinced, does Stanley await that happy time; with what boundless feelings of transport does he look forward to that long prayed for, yet hardly expected moment. Heaven grant that the fond expectations we have now both so justly formed may not be doomed to disappointment.

"There is no fear of that," said Mr. Eldred, "and I cannot see that you have any cause to entertain the least doubt upon the subject."

Omelia felt satisfied, and after some further conversation, she separated from her friends, and retired to her own chamber, in order that she might give vent to the thoughts and feelings that now naturally agitated her breast, without interruption.

CHAPTER CXXVIII.

THE SEIZURE.—PERILOUS SITUATION OF OMELIA.

How great, how happy was the change which only a few short minutes had wrought in the mind of our heroine. Darkness had disappeared, and all again was light, and hope, and gladness.

Again and again did she offer up her thanks to heaven for its merciful interposition, and then she pictured to herself the happiness which awaited herself and her beloved Stanley in such glowing colours that she became lost and bewildered in the mazes of her own vivid imagination.

So sudden and so joyful was the intelligence that she could scarcely have persuaded herself that it was true, had it not been for the letter from Stanley himself, that of course must remove every doubt upon the subject, and she could not therefore but feel every confidence, and encourage the most flattering expectations of the future.

But in the midst of all this, gloomy thoughts and apprehensions would occasionally obtrude themselves upon her, and which she found it difficult to banish from her mind. While the horrors of war still continued—and at present there seemed to be but little prospect of their termination—had she not everything to dread? They must quickly again be separated, and she would not be permitted to follow him, to share with him his dangers, but must ever be kept in the most torturing state of suspense as to the fate which had befallen him, her's would indeed be a life of constant anxiety, and she felt uneasy and fearful the more she thought of it.

Should her lover perish on the battle-field all her hopes would be annihilated, and life would no longer be endurable. She shuddered as the idea occurred to her, and endeavoured to dismiss it, but it was far too probable, for her to be able easily to do so, and for some time it continued to torture her.

"But no earthly power shall again separate us," she ejaculated; "I could not again endure the endless care, anxiety, doubts, and

apprehensions I have so long experienced; even death itself would be far less terrible. Disguised, unknown I will contrive to follow him wherever he goes, and all the dangers to which he may be exposed, I will myself fearlessly encounter, let the consequences be whatever they may. Providence will, I trust, aid me and protect me in my career of peril, and oh, should we both escape the horrors of the deadly strife, and our fates at length be indissolubly united, oh, how bright will be the reward for all the troubles I have so long experienced."

Her spirits revived as these thoughts occurred to her, all the natural energy of her character was aroused, and she quickly dismissed the dismal fears and forebodings that had just before occupied her mind, and looked forward to the future with all the

firmness of hope and confidence. Two days elapsed, and Omelia received no further intelligence of her lover, although Captain Morley had, according to his promise, repeated his visit, and she began again to grow restless and impatient; gloomy forebodings at times taking possession of her mind that something else had occurred which would throw an impediment in the way of the realisation of those hopes and expectations which had been so fondly excited in her mind.

Captain Morley and her other friends, however, exerted themselves to the utmost to banish those thoughts, for which they could see no just cause, and they at last partly succeeded in doing so, though she still at times felt anxious and fearful.

It was not likely that Stanley could have

the means of communicating with them, and it was a matter of surprise in what manner he had contrived to get the other letter conveyed to Captain Morley; and therefore all chance of obtaining information that way was at an end, besides it was not at all unlikely that he was at present on the march, and in a few days might arrive at the very place where Omelia was so anxiously waiting to behold him, and thus every further doubt and anxiety would be removed, and her happiness would be complete.

There was something so delightful in that thought, that Omelia scarcely dared venture to encourage it; and yet the probability of it was too great—especially after what Stanley had stated in his letter—to suffer her to dismiss it from her mind altogether.

These recent events had entirely banished from her recollection the daring outrage committed by the villain Yusef, and the threats he had held out to her, for it did not seem at all likely that he would venture to renew his guilty designs, or to venture near the city, unless he was madly determined to rush on his own destruction, which must inevitably follow should he be detected, of which there appeared to be every probability.

In spite of the danger to which she had been exposed, and the advice of her friends, Omelia again took her solitary walks, so that she might give free indulgence to her meditations, and those were generally in the cool of the evening, and in places where she was the least likely to meet with any one.

It was on the third evening after she had received the gratifying intelligence of the acquittal of Stanley, that Omelia being in one of those solitary rambles, induced by the fineness of the night, and being deeply wrapped in thought, had unconsciously wandered further away from the city than was at all prudent, or she had intended, and suddenly looking up she found herself in a dark and lonely spot, the very aspect of which was almost sufficient to excite a feeling of terror.

It was a complete wilderness, gloomy and intricate, and beyond it was a branch of the Ganges which finally discharged itself into the principal river.

Omelia felt vexed and somewhat alarmed to find that she had wandered to such a place, and at that hour, and she was about to turn in order to retrace her steps with as little delay as possible, when she was startled by hearing the rustling sound of feet in the lank grass, and the next instant the tall forms of two sepoys—in one of whom she immediately recognised the miscreant Yusef, notwithstanding the disguise he had assumed —emerged from behind the trees, and she found herself seized in the most violent manner before she had the power to offer any

resistance, which would have been entirely useless when opposed to two such desperate ruffians as those who held her.

"So, Yusef has kept his word you find, Omelia," said the villain, with a look of fiendish exultation, "we meet again under somewhat more favourable circumstances than the last, and I congratulate myself on my good fortune, though unseen I have been long in secret waiting for you. This time, at any rate, haughty beauty, you shall not escape me. Your aid, Alahmed, and now, favoured by the darkness, and the absence of any one to observe and obstruct us, we will immediately away with our prize."

"Villains," exclaimed Omelia, as Alahmed also advanced to seize her, and stilling her fears in the best manner she could, "forbear your brutal purpose, or I will pierce the air with my cries, and there may be yet those to render me timely assistance, nearer than you now imagine."

"And think you that we are to be thus intimidated?" said Yusef, scornfully; "we have carefully watched you on your way hither, and know that in this lonely spot you are far away from human aid, and that your cries would be useless. This way then, the sepoy Yusef claims his future bride."

The words of Yusef, and the fierce looks of himself and Alahmed, completely overpowered our heroine, and her courage forsook her. In vain she rent the air with her cries, the miscreant Yusef laughed at them in mockery and triumph, and then in spite of all her struggles, he and Alahmed forced her along with brutal violence, and made their way towards an opening in the wilderness, beyond which at a short distance the waters of the river before mentioned, glided.

"Ha, ha, ha!" again laughed Yusef, triumphantly, "this wild music of yours neither annoys or alarms me. You only waste your breath upon the air, no one can hear you, and in a few minutes more you will be beyond the reach of pursuit. My plans are well arranged, matured, complete, and again I tell you that you are mine, beyond the power of any one to rescue you. To the boat, Alahmed—to the boat."

Distracted with terror, for the fate of the unfortunate girl now seemed certain, Omelia again shrieked aloud, although, as Yusef had said, she knew too well that it would be useless, but she was quite unheeded by the wretches, who hurried her now almost resistlessly along, till passing through the opening they came almost immediately on the banks of the river.

The distracted Omelia now indeed gave herself up for lost, for in the power of such lawless and determined ruffians as Yusef and his companions what could she anticipate but the worst?

How rash and imprudent it was of her—especially after the narrow escape she had before from the power of the villain Yusef—to venture forth at such an hour of the evening alone.

Such were the thoughts that rapidly and naturally enough arose to the mind of our heroine as the villains forced her along, and she could not but blame herself most severely, though, alas, it was too late now to do so, and her terror every instant increased, especially as she beheld a boat moored alongside the bank at a short distance, in which two more of the savage confederates of Yusef were waiting to receive them.

Again she rent the air with her cries and struggled with all her remaining strength to free herself. But completely useless were all her efforts, and only met with the bitter mockery of the relentless Yusef and his companions.

"Away with her," said the former, his fierce eyes flashing with the exultation of his feelings; "her cries are only wasted on the idle wind; my hour of triumph, that I so long and so anxiously looked for, has at last arrived, and again I swear that I will sooner perish than any earthly power shall now foil me in my designs."

"Powers of justice," exclaimed the distracted Omelia, in accents of despair, "shall I be suffered to become the wretched and hapless victim of a miscreant like this? O, Stanley, would that you were now nigh, you—"

"Ha, ha, ha!" laughed Yusef with bitter scorn, interrupting her, "are you mad? What think you could his single arm effect against myself and my colleagues? But you will behold him no more, I repeat. He is lost to you for ever."

The unfortunate Omelia again tried to reply, but she could not, for every faculty under the desperate circumstances, was suspended by horror, and her strength almost exhausted, she was hurried towards the boat, into which she was speedily forced, still held in the arms of Yusef, who gloated with savage delight upon the charms of his hapless victim, and was perfectly regardless of her struggles.

The boat was immediately shoved off from the shore, and made with all the speed they could towards the most gloomy part of the opposite bank.

Here our heroine, worked up to a pitch of the most agony and excitement by the increasing hopelessness of her situation, again renewed her cries, her brain being too bewildered to permit her to consider the utter uselessness of her doing so.

Yusef and Ahmed tried to force her into the bottom of the boat, but she resisted.

"Daring ruffian," she exclaimed, "will nothing tempt you to abandon your guilty designs? Oh, whither are you about to convey me?"

"To where my triumph will be rendered complete," answered the ruffian, "and the scorn and hatred with which you have treated me shall be amply avenged. You may as well resign yourself to the fate which awaits you, Omelia, for henceforth you must be the slave of my will, and any attempt at resistance on your part will be little short of madness."

"Never," returned Omelia, with a look of the most ineffable horror and disgust. "there is an Almighty power above that will not permit so monstrous, so diabolical an outrage, that will prevent the accomplishment of your base and brutal designs, and wreak a just but terrible retribution on your guilty head."

"That power to which you so confidently appeal, I scorn and defy," exclaimed the hardened wretch, "my plans are too well arranged to be easily frustrated, and that you will speedily discover. But I waste words with you; abandon this fruitless resistance, and learn to submit to that which nothing can now avert. See, the shore we have just quitted is rapidly disappearing from us, and all danger of pursuit by those who would desperately attempt your rescue is at an end."

Our heroine did indeed cast an anxious look towards the shore, which was fast receding from their view, and her heart sunk within her, for all hope of deliverence seemed to be entirely at an end, and the horrors by which she was surrounded, and the fearful doom that awaited her, unless providence mercifully interposed to save her, every instant became the more apparent.

But still with a resolution most extraordinary, our heroine continued to offer every resistance in her power, and her shrieks were borne by the wind across the waters to the shore they had left but a short time before.

And while Omelia still gazed upon it with despairing eyes, she beheld the glare of several lights, as if proceeding from torches, and could also imagine that she distinguished, notwithstanding the distance, the shadows of human forms moving hurriedly about, and she uttered an exclamation of renewed hope, although there seemed to be so little cause to indulge in it.

"Ah," she cried, "my abduction has been discovered and there may yet be hope."

"Foolish girl," returned Yusef, "and think you that those whom you now behold can have the least chance of rescuing you, if even they have the desire to do so? Pursuit would now be useless, for a few minutes more will place us far beyond the reach of it. You are mine, beyond all earthly power to save you. By this kiss, I swear it, and—"

"Shameless, unmanly villain," cried the indignant Omelia, as she struggled with renewed strength to repel the disgusting advances of Yusef, "forbear."

Still he struggled determinedly to put his revolting threat into execution, Omelia resisting him all that laid in her power until they reached the head of the boat. At that moment the companions of Yusef suddenly started up in the boat induced to do so by some uncontrollable impulse, and rushing towards them the boat immediately capsized, and they were all precipitated into the river.

It has been before stated, that like most Indian females, Omelia was an excellent swimmer, and notwithstanding the suddenness of the shock, she lost not her presence of mind, but rising again to the surface of the water, she struck out resolutely towards the shore from which she had so recently been forcibly taken, and on which the lights that had before attracted her attention still glared, and she could almost imagine that she heard the shouts from the persons who bore them, as though they had witnessed the accident.

The villain Yusef and his guilty colleagues also struggled desperately in the water, notwithstanding the surprise and consternation into which they were thrown by the unforseen and unfortunate accident, and the first thought of the former was to look after our heroine, and endeavour to secure her, but at first he could not perceive her, and he had almost began to fear that she had sunk to rise no more, when again straining his eyes across the water, he beheld her by the light of the moon which shone more brightly than before, swimming rapidly towards the shore they had a short time since quitted, and which it was quite evident she would shortly reach.

To follow her would be useless, and fraught likewise with danger, for she had got a considerable way across the river, and there were those waiting on its bank who had probably come with the purpose of rescuing her if possible.

He therefore muttered a bitter oath of rage and disappointment, and made his way towards the shore whither he had meant to have conveyed our heroine if the accident had not occurred, followed by Alahmed and the other ruffians, and which they quickly gained in safety, but, of course, drenched to the skin, and in none of the best of humours at the inconvenience to which they had been put, and at the failure of their infamous designs just at the very moment when success appeared to be certain.

CHAPTER CXXIX.

THE DISAPPOINTMENT OF YUSEF.—FRESH DETERMINATION.

On reaching the shore, Yusef stood for a minute or two with his vile associates in crime, and gazed eagerly towards the opposite bank, where he could perceive the glaring lights moving to and fro, and had no doubt that Omelia had been rescued from her perilous situation.

It is almost needless to attempt to describe the violent tempest of angry passions that raged within the villain's breast at that moment, they were almost too powerful for utterance. His dark and forbidding features were frightfully distorted with rage, his eyes flashed fiercely, he bit his lips savagely, and clenched his fists, and his whole muscular frame was convulsively agitated from the effect of his feelings on the occasion.

"Now may eternal curses light upon this accident," he at length burst forth in a hoarse voice, and glowing with ungovernable passion; "this unforeseen accident which has robbed me of my intended victim, and that, too, at the very time when the envied prize, to obtain possession of which I have made such extraordinary efforts, and run so many risks, appeared to be secure. Oh, how can I patiently endure this bitter disappointment? She is now safe under the protection of friends, no doubt, and can laugh to scorn the threats I held out to her, and exult at my defeat. And now that she is put upon her guard, and will probably shortly withdraw to some distant part of the country, will not all future chance of the accomplishment of my designs be at an end? They will. What opportunity can I hope ever to present itself for getting her in my power? None that I can forsee, and once more I say may every curse light upon the accident which has thus suddenly foiled my wishes and expectations."

Again the miscreant clenched his fists and bit his lips with rage, as he still looked anxiously towards the bank to which Omelia had made her escape, and watched the lights till they moved gradually from the spot where they had shone, and gradually disappeared among the trees that grew near.

"They are gone," he muttered, "and doubtless with them Omelia in safety. Oh, well may she congratulate herself on her miraculous escape, and laugh exultingly at my defeat and disappointment. That thought excites my utmost indignation, and I can scarcely control the burning feelings that rage within my breast within the bounds of reason. But shall I abandon my designs because of this second defeat? Shall I, I say, abandon them altogether, and rest myself contented? No, I will not, my proud and determined spirit will not permit me to do that. I will continue to pursue her whithersoever she goes, and watch my opportunity when least expected to pounce upon her and to bear her off in triumph. She shall yet be mine, and there is no risk which I will shrink from incurring to secure the full accomplishment of that wish."

"Well said, Yusef," observed Alahmed, "I admire your determination, and I need not say that I wish you every success."

"It shall be no fault of mine if I ultimately fail," returned Yusef, "and I suppose I may depend upon the services of yourself and our colleagues here to aid me in my future designs?"

"Of that you have no reason to entertain a doubt," replied Alahmed.

"'Tis well," said Yusef, with a look of satisfaction, "you have hitherto kept your promises faithfully, and I therefore now place every reliance upon you. But come, let us away, our schemes this night have unfortunately failed, and it is no use tarrying longer here."

"Aye, we had better hasten to our secret haunt, where our comrades await us," replied Alahmed, "and I have no doubt that they will be greatly disappointed at the failure of our plot."

Yusef again muttered a curse between his teeth, but returned no other answer, and they instantly quitted the spot on which they had been standing, and made their way towards the most gloomy part of the country, and where they were the least likely to encounter any one; and Yusef's mind being too busily occupied with his own thoughts to suffer him to enter into conversation with any one.

They bent their footsteps as has been before stated towards a wild and dreary part of the country, where mighty trees grew thickly around, and above which the lofty summits of a chain of mountains towered at a short distance, towards which they took their immediate course.

They were not long in arriving at the mountains, and passing in between two of the loftiest of them, they stopped before a cavity just sufficiently large to admit of one person, but all was buried in profound darkness.

Yusef immediately advanced to the cavity in the side of the mountain, and applying a whistle to his lips blew a shrill signal, which was almost immediately answered by a similar one from within the cavity, and apparently at some depth below the surface of the earth. Presently the reflection of a light was seen, partially revealing a kind of narrow arched passage formed by the hands of nature, and to which the cavity before mentioned was the entrance.

Yusef and the others were not kept long waiting, for in a second or two a sepoy bearing a lighted lamp in his hand appeared, which he held above his head in order to accelerate his view, and seemed to be perfectly satisfied with his scrutiny.

"All right, Syed," said Yusef, "lead the way."

The man did so, and having conducted Yusef and his companions along the passage which widened and descended gradually as they proceeded, they stopped at the end, where a ladder was placed at an opening in the earth and which seemed to lead to some depth below.

This the rebels also descended, and alighted in a wide open space, deep in the bowels of the earth, and from which four avenues branched off, leading to different parts of this extraordinary subterraneau retreat.

Syed took the principal one, followed by Yusef and the other fellows, and after traversing this passage in a winding direction to some considerable distance, the hum of several voices might be heard, and lights observed to glimmer in the back ground.

They stopped at the end of the passage, another signal was given, which was also answered, a large stone was then removed, and revealed the entrance to a spacious cavern, well lighted by lamps suspended from the roof.

A number of armed sepoys were lounging about the cavern, regaling themselves on arack and other intoxicating beverages, and smoking vigourously.

They arose on the entrance of Yusef and his companions, and greeted them most heartily and boisterously, and the former was then conducted to a lofty seat, with some little ceremony, which showed that he held some authority over them.

This cavern was a curious looking place, which could not possibly have been formed by human hands, and contained besides a quantity of arms and ammunition, a great number of valuable articles of different descriptions, the proceeds of plunder, and which were scattered carelessly about, or heaped up together in various parts of the place, as though they were worthless.

The looks of the ruffians sufficiently testified their brutal and desperate character, and that there was no crime, however monstrous which they were not fully capable of perpetrating.

We have said that they all arose on the entrance of Yusef and those who had accompanied him on his daring expedition, and on his being seated, a tall, muscular, man, known by the name of Moolah Bhashka, advanced towards him, and said—

"So, Yusef, you have returned, but your looks convince me that the errand you went upon has not been crowned with the success you anticipated."

"True," replied Yusef, in tones of vexation and disappointment, "the girl was in my power, and success was within my grasp, when a cursed accident destroyed all my hopes, and frustrated my plans."

"The girl then has again escaped you?" said Moolah.

Yusef replied in the affirmative, and then briefly related what had taken place.

"'Twas a sad disappointment," remarked Moolah, "but I know that you are not easily to be daunted, Yusef, in anything to which you have made up your mind. You do not mean to abandon your designs, I expect."

"No," replied Yusef, "but it may be some time ere another opportunity for my putting them into effect may present itself. This second disappointment, however, has but strengthened my fierce desires, and it shall be from no want of exertion on my part, if I do not ultimately succeed. The beauty of the girl has inflamed my passions, and the scorn and hatred with which she treats me, only serves to add to the fierce fire she has kindled within my breast. I am even prepared to risk my life to obtain possession of her."

"Well said," returned Moolah, "I commend you for the spirit of determination which guides you in all your actions, they should be crowned with success, and you may rest assured that myself and our comrades here are fully prepared to assist you to the utmost in the furtherance of your designs. Say are ye not?" he added, speaking to the rebels.

"All, all," they shouted, simultaneously.

"'Tis well," said Yusef, with a look of satisfaction, "I am thoroughly convinced that I may depend on you, that you will not attempt to deceive me, and I thank you. At any rate should I fail to get Omelia in my power, I will have a terrible revenge, which I will watch every opportunity to obtain. The fates of Lieutenant Stanley and Omelia shall never be united. The hopes they have so fondly formed shall be doomed to a terrible disappointment."

A fearful expression distorted the repulsive features of the hardened miscreant as he uttered these threats, and which no one who was acquainted with his real character could doubt for an instant that he would fail to put into execution.

"But enough of this, for the present," he observed, "there is other business to which we must devote our immediate attention. To-morrow we start on our expedition which will require the exercise of our energies, and determination."

"True," coincided Moolah. "and it shall not be from any want of the qualities which you mention, Yusef, on our part, if our efforts are not crowned with success. We have sworn fidelity to each other, however desperate the cause in which we may engage, and that oath must and shall be kept inviolate."

"Aye," said Yusef, rising, "by such ties are we bound together, and what shall be the reward of he who dares to turn traitor?"

"Death, death!" was the unanimous reply, and the villains crossed their swords in token of their determination.

"Such being the compact into which we have entered with each other," said Yusef, "defeat is all but impossible. We have sworn a deadly revenge against the hated Feringhee, and that revenge we will not fail to gratify, though we have to wade through an ocean of blood to do so.

The rebels again crossed their swords and pledged themselves to act faithfully also in obedience to the words which Yusef had just spoken, and after some further conversation of no particular importance, they abandoned themselves to coarse and brutal scenes of dissipation and ribald mirth, until the intoxicating drink of which they so freely partook, had its due effect, and they one after the other fell gradually off to sleep, in which they seemed likely to remain till the morning.

CHAPTER CXXX.

OMELIA AND HER FRIENDS.—THE DANGER PAST.

The absence of Omelia was at first not known to her friends, it being supposed that she had retired to her chamber, labouring under a depression of spirits, and in order that she might give free indulgence to her melancholy thoughts without any fear of interruption.

But when the time became late, and she did not make her re-appearance among them their suspicions were excited, and which were confirmed on Mrs. Eldred and her daughter going to the chamber and not finding her there.

They became alarmed, and Abdal proposed that himself and Mr. Eldred with two or three others should immediately go in search of her, though they were quite at a loss whither to direct their footsteps, and had alone chance or accident to guide them.

In order the better to accelerate their search they took with them two or three lighted torches, and then started on their errand with considerable alarm and anxiety as to what was likely to be the result.

Accident fortunately led them in the direction of the the spot to which Omelia had gone, and where she had been surprised and seized by the villain Yusef and his myrmidons and they strained their eyes but in vain, to discover her, and their fears increased, for it seemed evident that some accident must have befallen her, or she, knowing the apprehensions which they their friends would be under, would never have remained away so long.

At length they arrived at the dismal spot where our heroine had only a few minutes before been seized, and here Abdal happening to cast his eyes to the ground, noticed from the disturbed state of the grass, and other symptoms, that a violent struggle had recently taken place, and his worst fears and suspicions were immediately excited more powerfully than ever.

While he still looked, he perceived by the light of the torches, something glittering near his feet, and picking it up, he found it was a valuable bracelet which he immediately recognized.

"This bracelet," he said, "belongs to Omelia, and my most painful apprehensions are all but confirmed, there has been foul play here, and she has, I fear, fallen into the hands of her enemies. Rash, imprudent girl, thus thoughtlessly to run herself into danger, after the escape from the ruffian Yusef, which she before so narrowly had! Hark!"

"What is it that now so anxiously engages your attention?" demanded Mr. Eldred

"I thought, at that moment," replied Abdal," that I heard female cries. Ah! I was not mistaken, they are there again more distinctly than before, do you not hear them?"

"Yes," returned Mr. Eldred; "and they proceed from the direction of the river."

Again the shrieks of a female in distress saluted their ears, and they were the more convinced that they came from the direction of the river.

"It is Omelia, I am satisfied," said Abdal, "who thus calls in vain for help, this bracelet, found on this spot, proves that. Unfortunate girl, I fear it is too late to save you and I shudder to think of the consequences to yourself, but no effort must be wanting to do so, there is not an instant to be lost. Follow, my friends, to the river, to the river!"

There was no more wanting to urge them into immediate action, and they precipitately made their way towards the river's bank, the cries still ringing in their ears, but every moment becoming fainter, till they nearly died away altogether.

They rushed through the opening in the thicket before described, and presently stood upon the very spot from whence our heroine had been forced into the boat, and where her footprints, and those of the ruffians were plainly discernible in the moist earth.

They held the torches in the air, and strained their eyes across the river and by their broad glare could plainly perceive the boat, and a female form—which they were thoroughly convinced could be no other but that of Omelia—struggling in the arms of some ruffian whom they naturally supposed to be Yusef.

"Alas! alas!" cried Abdal, in tones of the bitterest anguish; "it is too late to save her, we have no means of pursuing the villains. She is lost—she is lost, oh, what could induce her, imprudent girl, to expose herself to such danger?"

"The boat will shortly reach the opposite bank," said Mr. Eldred, "and then the escape of the villains with their unfortunate victim is certain. What is to be done?"

Abdal shook his head mournfully, and clasped his hands together in the excitement of his feelings as he said.—

"Oh, I know not, the villains have obtained all the advantage they could seek, and we are entirely without the means of offering any opposition to their atrocious designs. The fate of Omelia seems now but too certain. Herself and her lover will never meet again, and what will be his agony and despair when he hears the dreadful truth?"

Mr. Eldred keenly felt the force and truth of these observations, and was unable to make any reply, and at that moment the shrieks, of our heroine again sounded across the river, and the lights still enabled them to catch an indistinct view of her struggles in the boat with the villain who held her.

"Poor, ill-fated girl," exclaimed Abdal, "how vain are now her cries for help, she is beyond all human assistance for the present. Oh, how torturing is this. Ah! behold, they struggle more violently together towards the head of the boat, and the other cowardly ruffians rise up to the assistance of Yusef. Ah! see, the boat is suddenly capsized, and they are all precipitated into the water! All merciful Providence interpose or she will be drowned!"

"No, see!" cried Mr. Eldred, anxiously straining his eyes across the river, and in a state of the greatest excitement, "her head again appears above the surface of the water, she struggles bravely, and is swimming towards us rapidly, while the ruffians still struggle desperately, but do not offer to follow her. Nearer, and nearer she approaches, boldly surmounting every difficulty She will be saved—she will escape!"

As was described in the preceding chapter, our heroine did indeed exert herself with the greatest skill and heroism, and gained upon the shore where her friends were so anxiously waiting and watching her, but the excitement and exertion she had already undergone were too much for her, and she at last exhibited evident signs of exhaustion, which did not escape the eager eyes of Abdal and his companions, and increased their agitation.

"The poor girl's strength evidently fails her," cried Abdal. "and without assistance she will even now not be able to reach the shore. Why do I thus stand inactive here, when so precious a life is at stake? Omelia, I hasten to save you, or perish in the attempt!"

Immediately, as he thus spoke, he plunged into the river, and made with all the speed he could towards the nearly exhausted girl, while Mr. Eldred and his companions watched the result with most painful doubt and anxiety.

"The intrepid Abdal strikes out manfully," said Mr. Eldred, "and must quickly reach her. See, he gains upon her, and another moment must hold her in safety. Ah! behold. Her strength is exhausted, and she sinks! All merciful heaven interpose, or she will still be lost. And now, see! Abdal has reached the spot where she sunk, she rises again. He seized her firmly in his hold, and now speedily returns towards the shore, kind Providence I thank Thee, all anxiety is at an end, and Omelia is rescued from the awful and untimely death which but a moment since was impending o'er her!"

Another minute and Abdal reached the shore, encircling with one arm the waist of the insensible girl, while with the other he had boldly stemmed the waters, and they were both safely landed amid a scene of excitement among the spectators, which it is needless to describe. And thus the deliverance of Omelia from the perilous situation in which she had been placed was complete!

CHAPTER CXXXI.

CLOUDS DISPERSE.

Omelia was quite insensible, and from the more unusual excitement she had undergone and her immersion in the water, there was danger to be apprehended, unless some assistance towards her recovery was immediately procured.

Raised in the arms of Mr. Eldred and another of her friends, therefore, she was conveyed with all possible speed towards the house in which they at present resided, while Abdal, who was weak and almost exhausted

by the extraordinary exertion he had undergone, followed, leaning on the arm of one of the persons who had accompanied them.

They were not long in arriving at the place of their destination, where their appearance, and particularly the narrow escape of our heroine from the fate which had threatened her, excited the deepest sympathy and in interest in the minds of all.

Mrs. Eldred and her amiable daughter, were prompt in their attendance on the beauteous sufferer, and she was immediately stripped of her wet clothes and placed in a warm bed, while a medical gentleman quickly arrived to see to her recovery, and to counteract, if possible, all the dangerous effects which might otherwise ensue.

Every attention was also paid to Abdal, who soon recovered, and could never be sufficiently grateful for the preservation of Omelia in so completely miraculous a manner.

The surprise and disgust which this second and even more daring attempt of the ruffian Yusef excited, may be imagined, and it was deeply regretted that he had hitherto succeeded in escaping the punishment to which his crimes so justly entitled him, and that not the least clue could at present be obtained as to the place where he was concealed.

By the unremitting attentions of the doctor, and Mrs. Eldred and her daughter, Omelia was quickly restored to sensibility, and could scarcely believe the evidence of her eyes, when she found that she had not only escaped from the power of the miscreant Yusef, and his desperate associates, but that she was again restored to her friends.

At first she had but a faint recollection of what had taken place—which, in fact, from the daring nature of the outrage, had more the appearance of some wild vision of the imagination than reality—but at length the whole of the exciting facts recurred to her memory, and while she shuddered at the narrow and almost miraculous escape she had had, her gratitude to that Omnipotent Power, which had so mercifully and miraculously interposed to save her, was most unbounded.

"The boldness of this ruffian, Yusef," she observed, addressing herself to Mrs. Eldred, "is most remarkable, and when I think how near he was in accomplishing his infamous designs, and the horrible and revolting fate to which I must then have been consigned, my bosom swells with emotion, and I feel that I can never be sufficiently thankful for my preservation."

"True," coincided Mr. Eldred, "I can duly appreciate what the terror and agony of your feelings must have been on finding yourself in the power of a wretch from whom you had everything to apprehend, while all

assistance to rescue you seemed to be completely hopeless and I can never enough admire the courage and determination which enabled you to offer so firm a resistance. But still I must blame you for rashly and thoughtlessly venturing forth alone at such an hour, after the previous narrow escape you had from falling into Yusef's power."

"Yes," coincided Omelia, "I was indeed much to blame, and I shudder when I think of the dreadful consequences which my imprudent conduct might have been productive of, but you will make every allowance I know for the constant state of agitation and bewilderment in which my mind has so long been kept, and which at times has rendered me almost unconscious of what I have been doing. The uncertainty of the fate which awaited my unfortunate Stanley, constantly

racked my brain, and often rendered me scarcely responsible for my actions."

"And what would have been the fatal consequences," returned Mrs. Eldred, "had Yusef succeeded in bearing you away? What would have been the horror of your lover's feelings, his utter despair on arriving here, thinking once more to clasp you to his throbbing, faithful heart, to learn the terrible fate which had befallen you, and that in all probability you were torn from his arms for ever."

"How fearful is the picture you have drawn, my dear madam," said Omelia, "I tremble with fear even to contemplate it, but yet it is painfully true, and I again blame myself severely for having thoughtlessly exposed myself to so much danger. Oh, Stanley, dear Stanley, even now I dare scarcely encourage the flattering hopes that have been raised in my mind, and fear that something will yet occur to prevent our meeting again."

"Nay," said Mrs. Eldred, "why should you thus unnecessarily torture yourself by giving way to these erroneous doubts and apprehensions? The letter which you received from Lieutenant Stanley ought entirely to remove them. It is not likely that he would attempt to deceive you, or that Captain Morley would seek to impose upon you by a falsehood."

"Oh, no," returned our heroine, "it would indeed be most ungenerous, most unjust for me to do so. Away then with all such thoughts, and let me only indulge in hopes that must, that will be sooner or later realised. Henceforth I will endeavour to divest my mind of all gloomy thoughts and forebodings, and to view my future prospects and expectations on the sunniest side."

"Well spoken, Omelia," said Mrs. Eldred, "continue to indulge in hopes and thoughts like these, and heaven, I fervently and sincerely trust, will not suffer you to be disappointed. The time I feel convinced is not far distant when you and Edward Stanley will meet again, and that happiness to which your numerous virtues so justly entitle you both, will at length be your's."

"Oh, blissful thought," ejaculated our heroine, her bosom swelling with the emotion it excited, and her eyes filling with tears, "what indescribable feelings of transport does it create in my brain. I dare scarcely indulge in the halcyon vision which my imagination conjures up, and yet it is useless for me to attempt to banish it altogether. To behold each other again after so long a separation, and under such painful circumstances, when death seemed to have claimed all that my soul holds most dear on earth as his victim, and to know that his heart is as fondly and faithfully devoted to me as ever, is a thought so extatic, so redolent of every hope and happiness that it bewilders my brain, and almost overpowers my senses. Yes, Edward, I will continue to look forward to the time of our restoration to each other with the most sanguine expectation, with a firm reliance of the goodness of heaven to gratify, and that speedily, all my wishes."

A sweet expression of hope and confidence animated her beauteous features, and sparkled in her eyes as she gave utterance to these words, and all those racking thoughts and cares and anxieties which for months past had constantly distracted her mind, seemed to vanish in a moment, and feelings of a happily opposite nature to take their place in her bosom.

This change was highly gratifying to Mrs. Eldred and her daughter, and all the friends of Omelia—to none more so than Abdal—when they became acquainted with it, and they augured from it the most favourable results.

A good night's rest—which she was fortunately enabled to get after she had been able to bring her mind to that calm and even cheerful state which has been described—served to entirely recover Omelia from the effects of the shock she had received by her fearful adventure with Yusef, and she met her friends on the following morning with a change in her appearance and spirits which it was highly gratifying for them to see.

To Abdal, to whom she felt indebted for the preservation of her life, for exhausted as she was and completely senseless, she must have perished she was convinced had it not been for him, she warmly expressed her thanks, but he interrupted her impatiently, observing—

"Hold, Omelia, I beseech you, I ask not your thanks for an act of common humanity which I was bound to perform, especially for one whom I so fervently esteem as yourself. Think you that I could stand calmly and indifferently by and see a fellow creature perish when it was in my power to render that timely assistance which was so much required? No, no, I should both hate and despise myself if I thought I could."

"Kind hearted friend," said Omelia, grasping his hand, and the sincerity of her words beaming in her sparkling eyes, "who so faithfully, so disinterestedly has adhered to me throughout all the troubles and misfortunes it has been my lot to encounter since we have been acquainted with each other, friend of Stanley in the hour of his greatest adversity, oh, well do I know the warm, the noble feelings that prompt you in all your actions, and I must indeed think meanly of myself when I can cease to remember the vast debt of gratitude I owe you."

"I am more than rewarded, Omelia," returned Abdal, "in seeing the happy change which only a few short hours have wrought in your spirits. May it continue, and all care and sorrow in future cease to torture your breast. That is my sincere and ardent wish, and something seems to assure me that it will not long remain ungratified. In a few days Lieutenant Stanley will probably arrive here, and—"

"Oh, Abdal," interrupted our heroine, eagerly, "do you indeed think so? or do you only seek to flatter me with false and delusive hopes?"

"Nay, Omelia," replied Abdal, with a look of gentle reproach, "that is uncharitable. What object could I possibly have in view, in seeking to buoy you up with hopes and expectations, which my own reason must convince me could only end in bitter disappointment? If you entertain such an opinion you wrong me, indeed you do."

"Pardon me, Abdal," said Omelia, "if I have spoken a word that was calculated to wound your feelings, or to cast a doubt upon your truth and sincerity. But my brain is so bewildered by the hopes which yourself and the rest of my friends have raised in my mind, that I scarcely know what I say. But I will endeavour to be calm, and to look forward to the bright future which may soon be about to dawn upon me with confidence."

Her friends were indeed pleased to see her in that hopeful state of mind, and sought to encourage her by every means in their power, and in which praiseworthy efforts they succeeded much better than they could at all have expected, and the day passed more agreeably than any which they had experienced for some time before.

Omelia's mind was now constantly occupied with the image of her lover, and in impatiently anticipating the time when it should please Providence to suffer them to meet again. Sometimes indeed she wavered between doubt and fear, and torturing misgivings, in spite of all her efforts, would obtrude themselves, but her hopes quickly revived, and she chided herself for suffering them even for a minute to forsake her.

Since her last alarming adventure, she abandoned her former solitary rambles, and kept herself strictly confined to the building and the society of her friends, but she made strict and daily inquiries as to the arrival of any fresh troops in the city, but without being able to obtain any information in accordance with her wishes and expectations, and, as day after day elapsed with no better result, her patience became almost exhausted and at times the wild extravagant and impracticable idea again entered her mind, to take her departure from the place, and resume her wanderings till some fortunate accident should again unite her to her lover.

She was, however, quickly convinced of the utter folly of entertaining such thoughts, and she sought to banish them from her mind, and to wait patiently that happy hour which sooner or later she fondly persuaded herself would arrive.

"Kind Providence surely will not disappoint my fond hopes," she would soliloquise when alone, "for that indeed would be worse than death, and I cannot even anticipate such a thing without feelings of the greatest agony. But no it will not, cannot be, surely my troubles have already been too great to endure with any degree of fortitude, and Providence will not thus cruelly annihilate all my hopes and prospects. Beloved Stanley, 'tis to you alone my fondest wishes cling, and it is the bright anticipation of our restoration to each other which alone makes life endurable to me. Without you it must become a desert wild, a dreary blank, which must make the heart sicken even to contemplate. But away with all gloomy misgivings, all torturing forebodings, I will continue to hope on, to hope on."

She took from her bosom a miniature likeness of Stanley, which he had given her, as she spoke these words, and gazed at it with feelings it would be difficult for language sufficiently eloquent properly to describe; and her tears—mingled tears of joy and sorrow—fell fast upon it, as she pressed it to her lips with the most unbounded and unutterable affection.

The likeness was an excellent one, and no one who had seen the original, could deny the remarkable ability with which the limner had executed his task. The expression of the eyes was so true to nature, that Omelia could almost imagine it was Stanley's self that now gazed upon her with those looks of love and admiration he had ever been wont to do, and she could fancy that the lips were parted to address her, and her feelings worked up to the highest degree of excitement by this singular delusion, she listened in vain to catch the tones of that fine manly voice which had ever fell as music upon her ravished senses.

A week had now elapsed since the daring outrage committed by Yusef, and still our heroine heard no farther intelligence of Stanley, and now her patience was indeed quite exhausted, and her friends tried in vain to arose her from the melancholy thoughts and apprehensions that again took possession of her mind, and rendered her completely wretched.

Her fears suggested all kinds of dismal ideas, at one time that he was ill, and at another—which almost drove her brain to madness as it occurred to her, and yet it was too probable for her easily to dismiss it—that he had fallen in some engagement with the enemy, and so powerful and so torturing was the impression that thought had made upon her, that her friends had the greatest difficulty in persuading her that it only originated in her disordered imagination, and that the calamity had not actually taken place.

"Oh, why have my hopes been thus raised and fluttered," she exclaimed in the most mournful accents, "to be thus cruelly annihilated? Why have my feelings been thus heartlessly sported with? What have I done that I should be made the object of such bitter mockery, and finally to be plunged into all the horrors of misery and despair? Oh, I can no longer endure this exquisite, this incessant anguish of mind, I shall go mad! I shall go mad!"

She groaned aloud as she thus spoke, and covering her face with her hands, burst into a violent flood of tears, while her whole frame was convulsed with the intensity of her feelings that were quite overwhelming.

In vain her friends tried every means that they could think of to soothe her and to quiet her apprehensions, she was deaf to all their arguments and expostulations, and every moment the insupportable anguish of her mind seemed rather to increase than abate.

She was in this deplorable condition, when Captain Morley, whom they had not seen for several days, was suddenly announced, and at the mention of his name she uttered an exclamation of mingled hope and fear, starting from her chair, and her heart palpitating so violently that she could scarcely support herself.

Not knowing what the cause of the captain's visit might be, or the nature of the intelligence he probably had to communicate, whether good or bad, the friends of Omelia, in her present agitated state of mind, would fain have persuaded her to retire, but she would not listen to them, but awaited with the most painful anxiety to know the result of this visit, and upon which she could not help thinking her happiness or utter misery and despair depended.

The captain was ushered into the room, and all eyes were immediately eagerly and inquiringly fixed upon him, particularly as his looks sufficiently proved that it was some important business which had brought him here, but Omelia gazed at him with an expression which seemed as though it would penetrate his very soul, and he observing the extraordinary excitement under which she laboured, appeared to hesitate to speak.

"Captain Morley," said our heroine at length, in a tremulous voice, "this visit assures me that you bring some intelligence of our friend, Lieutenant Stanley, tell me, I beseech you, and that quickly, is it not so?"

"True," replied Captain Morley, "but before I proceed to communicate that which I have to impart, I must request you to calm the agitation of your feelings."

"Ah!" gasped forth Omelia, with a look of the most indescribable agony; "your words are ominous, you are the bearer of bad tidings, or you would not thus hesitate. In mercy let me know the worst at once, and—"

"I am happy to say," interrupted Captain Morley, "that your fears are groundless, and that the news I bring—"

"Oh, speak! speak!"

"Lieutenant Stanley then, I have to inform you, has arrived with his regiment at Cawnpore."

Omelia uttered a wild cry of mingled delight and immediately, and laying her hand upon the captain's arm. fixed upon him a penetrating and half bewildered look, and

for a moment or two was unable to speak another word, while Abdal and Mr. and Mrs. Eldred looked upon the captain for an explanation, scarcely able to credit what they heard him say

"No, no," said Omelia at length, in a still more agitated tone of voice, "I cannot, I dare not believe you, if it be true that Stanley has indeed arrived, oh, why is he not here! He could not, would not delay a moment in seeking my presence."

"Captain Morley," observed Mr. Eldred, "there is indeed a mystery about what you have stated which requires explanation."

"Which I am prepared to give immediately," replied the former; Omelia listening breathlessly, and her heart beating still more violently than before; "the regiment to which Lieutenant Stanley belongs, arrived here late last night, and I had the extreme pleasure of seeing him this morning, and finding him in good health."

"Oh, heaven be thanked for that," cried Omelia with the greatest emotion, clasping her hands together, and tears trembling in her eyes; "proceed, proceed, sir, I implore you."

"His first anxious inquiries were of you, Omelia," continued the captain, "and when I informed him that you were here, and anxiously looking forward to the time when you should meet each other again, his emotion was such that I should find it a difficult task were I to attempt to describe it."

"Dear, faithful Stanley!" ejaculated Omelia; "but is he not here? Oh, if his feelings were indeed such as those that agitate my breast, he would at once have hurried hither on the wings of love to meet me. Alas! torturing doubts and fears beset my mind, and I cannot, dare not encourage those bright fond hopes, you would fain excite in my breast."

"Compose yourself, my poor girl," said Captain Morley kindly, "I again beg of you, and I will quickly set your mind at rest. Lieutenant Stanley has particular reasons for not first meeting you here, or till you have had sufficient time to prepare yourself for the interesting and important interview. This brief note, which he hurriedly wrote during the time that I could remain with him will explain everything."

Omelia eagerly took the note which Captain Morley presented, and with trembling hands unfolding it, no sooner did her eyes behold the well-known hand-writing of her lover, than a sweet smile of satisfaction and conviction passed over her features, and eagerly she perused the contents which were in the following words:—

"My adored Omelia, the hour of bliss, so long and so anxiously prayed for, has arrived at last. I am near you, sweets, eagerly waiting to clasp you to my throbbing bosom, and press warm kisses of affection on your lips. Oh, the happiness that now agitates my breast, and bewilders my brain! I cannot describe it. But our first interview must be alone, so that we may give unrestrained indulgence to our feelings. Meet me then to morrow evening in the Temple of Fountains, whither my friend, Captain Morley will conduct you, till then beloved girl, adieu. STANLEY."

The clouds have dispersed," exclaimed Omelia, with a burst of emotion, and sinking on her knees; "the dark clouds of sorrow have passed away, oh, joy, joy!"

CHAPTER CXXXII.

THE TEMPLE OF FOUNTAINS.

It was some time before Omelia could recover herself from the excitement of her feelings which the perusal of this brief, but welcome, and affectionate note produced. She continued on her knees with clasped hands, and eyes raised towards heaven, while all who were present respected her feelings too much to attempt to interrupt her.

But at length, starting to her feet, and turning to Captain Morley, with looks, and in a tone of voice which told the sincerity of what she uttered, she said:—

"Oh, amiable and gallant sir, friend of my beloved Stanley, harbinger of joy; in what words can I properly express my feelings of gratitude towards you for the interest you take in my fate, my happiness, and that of him who is more—oh, far more precious to me than my own existence?"

"I have my reward, Omelia," replied the gallant captain, gracefully; "I have my reward for any trouble I may have taken in witnessing your happiness at the intelligence I am so fortunately enabled to bring you. I congratulate you on the joy that awaits you, and with your permission I will be here to-morrow evening at sunset, to conduct you to the Temple of Fountains, according to the wish and the arrangement of my friend Stanley."

"Oh, thanks, thanks," ejaculated our heroine, fervently; "and yet," she added, in a hesitating manner: "there is something so strange in the delay, in this appointment that my heart almost misgives me, and irrestible doubts and fears take possession of my mind.'

"Nay, Omelia," observed Mr. Eldred in a tone of gentle remonstrance; "the doubts and fears that you have expressed are groundless. Surely you can have no suspicion of deception, when you have Lieutenant Stanley's note to convince you. The arrangement he has made for your first meeting is prompted by every proper and delicate feeling. None other than yourselves should be present on that joyous occasion to interrupt the free communication of your thoughts."

"Oh, true, most true," replied Omelia, her eyes brightening at the thought; "I can, I will no longer hesitate. Captain Morley, I will attend you to-morrow evening at the appointed hour."

"I will be punctual," said the captain.

"Oh, I shall count the minutes till the happy time arrives," remarked our heroine, "each one of which will appear to me an age. Oh, Stanley, and we are indeed then destined so shortly to meet again? Transporting thought, it bewilders my senses."

She paused, and pressing her hands upon her forehead, became completely lost for a short time, in the multitude of thoughts that crowded upon her brain.

Again and again she returned her grateful thanks to Captain Morley for his disinterested friendship, and every moment the agitation of her feelings increased.

Repeating his promise to be punctual on the following evening, Captain Morley after a short time took his leave, not wishing to intrude longer upon Omelia and her friends, knowing the thoughts and feelings they naturally have to interchange with each other on so important an occasion.

When he was gone Omelia threw herself into the arms of Mrs. Eldred, and gave free vent to the powerful and indescribable emotions that filled her bosom, and overflowed her heart, and Mr. Eldred, who could fully appreciate her feelings and participated in them, embraced her affectionately, and suffered her to give unrestrained indulgence to them.

"Oh, my dear friends," said the poor girl at length, looking up, and endeavouring to smile though her tears; "share with me, I know you do, you must, in the wild joy that now circulates through all my veins, and bewilders my senses, at the happiness, the unspeakable bliss that is in store for me."

"We do indeed, dear Omelia," said Mrs. Eldred, in tones of the warmest sympathy, "rest assured that no one can more rejoice at your approaching happiness than myself and my husband. All fears, all anxieties will be rewarded for the many sorrows you have borne under all the painful and disheartening circumstances with such becoming fortitude and resignation. May such troubles be henceforth strangers to your breast, and yourself and your lover experience all that happiness to which your virtues so justly entitle you."

"Oh thanks, thanks, my dearest madam,"

returned Omelia, " for those kind, those affectionate wishes, which I know emanate from your heart. Oh, what a weight of care and anxiety is indeed removed from my mind, my heart o'erflows with gratitude to the Great Power, to which all the human race, no matter what the creed, must instinctively bow in reverence. Dearest Stanley, how tedious will the hour, the moments appear to be till we meet."

Again she gave free vent to the joyous feelings that now animated her breast, and in which Abdal and her other friends most warmly participated.

After some further conversation upon the all absorbing subject, Omelia excused herself, and retired from the room to her own chamber, where she could alone indulge the emotions that fluttered at her heart, and prepare herself for the forthcoming meeting she had so long and so earnestly prayed for, but which at times she had hardly ventured to hope would ever take place.

When there, and there was no one to observe her, she again knelt down, and poured forth her gratitude to heaven with all the eloquence that the dictates of her throbbing heart, and the joyous occasion could suggest, and it was long, long since she had experienced such happiness as she did at that moment. It seemed indeed to be some blissful dream, some bright delusion of the senses, from which she feared too soon to be aroused to misery, disappointment. and despair.

"But no," she exclaimed, as with beating heart, and tearful eyes, she once more looked upon the brief but affectionate note addressed to her by Stanley; " I can no longer doubt the happiness that is in store for me, the relief from that heavy weight of fear and anxiety which so long has pressed upon my heart, my brain, and driven at times almost to madness. This, this confirms the joyful fact, and must remove all torturing apprehensions and misgivings. But a few hours more, and I shall be pressed close to that fond and faithful heart which throbs for me alone; once more the sweet tones of that manly voice will fall upon my ravished senses, breathing those sacred vows of love that have never yet been broken, again shall I behold those beloved features which, sleeping or waking, have never for an instant been absent from my imagination. What more can I desire? My every wish will now be gratified; my fondest and most sanguine hopes and expectations will at length be realised, and the sufferings of the past be forgotten in the happiness of the present."

Such were the thoughts that continued to crowd upon Omelia's brain, and kept her in a constant state of excitement. She retired to rest, and when sleep descended upon her eyelids, how different were her slumbers to those which she had for months before experienced. Instead of the torturing dreams that had almost constantly haunted her imagination, bright visions of happiness were conjured up by her busy fancy, which on waking she could recal to her memory, and dwell upon with delight.

She awoke in the morning elate with hope and every blissful anticipation.

How tediously did the day seem to wear away, and yet as the time drew nigh at which Captain Morley had promised to be there, a strange feeling almost amounting to dread came over Omelia, and again was her mind beset by painful doubts and misgivings, for which it would have been impossible for her to assign any reason. From this, however, her friends soon succeeded in arousing her, and she awaited the arrival of Captain Morley with a fluttering heart and impatient anxiety.

As the captain had promised, he was punctual to the very minute, and after Omelia had exchanged a few affectionate observations with her friends, she took his proffered arm, and they departed on their important errand.

We will not attempt to describe the varied emotions that agitated the breast of Omelia as they proceeded towards the place of appointment, for they may be better imagined than pourtrayed. But Captain Morley exerted himself to the utmost to tranquillise her feelings, and inspire her with confidence, and he succeeded much better than he had himself anticipated.

After walking about half an hour just as the sun was sinking to rest in the western horizon, they came in sight of the place of their destination, and now as the moment of one of the most important events of her life had nearly arrived, every feeling was excited in the breast of Omelia, her heart beat so violently against her side that it seemed as though it would burst its tenement, and she was compelled to pause, leaning on the arm of Captain Morley, and endeavour to collect and compose herself.

The ancient Temple of Fountains, for by that name it is known, is one of the most beautiful specimens of Hindoo buildings of that description, and is much prized by the native population of Cawnpore and its vicinity. It was erected several centuries ago, and is partly in ruins.

It stands on an eminence, and overlooks a small river which empties itself into the Ganges.

As it was seen at the tranquil hour of which we are writing, with the last golden rays of the setting sun gleaming upon its gilded dome, it had a remarkably imposing and interesting effect. It is much larger than most of the Hindoo temples, and its architecture is most elaborate.

But it is the interior of the temple, with its numerous fountains constantly playing, strange carvings and devices on its walls, and curious statues of Hindoo deities here and there, which calls forth the wonder and admiration of the beholder and makes him linger to gaze on that which might almost be imagined some fairy scene.

This then was the place appointed for the re-union of the lover's.

CHAPTER CXXXIII.

THE SCENE IN THE TEMPLE.

It was several minutes before Omelia, on her and her companion coming in sight of the temple, could sufficiently recover herself from the state of agitation into which she was naturally thrown, by the tumult of feelings that arose within her breast at the prospect of the speedy realisation of her hopes and wishes, to enable her to proceed to the destined place, and when she did so, still supported on the arm of Captain Morley, her limbs trembled, and a sensation of giddiness and bewilderment came over her which rendered her almost unconscious of what she was about.

Captain Morley again whispered words of encouragement in her ear, and she rallied a little, and they then advanced close to the temple, all around being calm and tranquil, and not a sound, save the gentle murmuring of the wind breaking the solemn silence which reigned.

"I have fulfilled my promise," said the captain, "and shall leave you to enter the temple alone, Omelia, where my presence would only be an intrusion. I will, however, wait close by till this auspicious meeting shall be o'er in case you should require my future services."

Omelia was too much agitated to answer, but her eyes looked her thanks, and the captain abruptly departed.

Again she paused, then advanced a step or two towards the entrance to the temple, and paused again, her heart fluttering, and every feeling worked up to the highest degree of excitement.

But at length she made a powerful effort, and conquering the violence of her emotions she advanced more firmly, and almost before she was aware of it, stood within the temple.

Her brain turned giddy with the various thoughts that crowded upon it, and a thick mist seemed to arise before her eyes, so that at first she was unable to distinguish anything in particular, but when that sensation had passed away, the scene which burst upon her view, and which she then beheld for the first time, took her by complete surprise, and filled her with admiration, while at the same time her mind became so bewildered that she almost forgot the errand she had came upon.

Fountains playing in all directions, their waters descending into basins of the purest marble, strange uncouth statues ranged on either side the building, vases of porcelain filled with the choicest of flowers—which were every day renewed—the richly carved and gilded pillars that supported the matchless dome, had a most magnificent effect, especially as Omelia then beheld them, with the last red flood of light from the sinking sun, streaming in at the different windows of the building.

She was filled with amazement, while at the same time a feeling of awe stole over her which she could not resist, and which for the time banished all those thoughts that had before occupied her, from her mind.

But she was quickly aroused to recollection, and looked anxiously around the temple as she advanced towards the centre, but without beholding any human being, more especially him she had come to meet, and whom she was so anxious and impatient to see.

Fears and misgivings again beset her mind, and a trembling sensation, a feeling of the most bitter disappointment came over her.

"I have been deceived," she murmured to herself; "he is not here, he will not come; oh, 'tis cruel, most cruel thus to sport and trifle with my feelings!"

Tears gushed to her eyes as these words escaped her lips and she pressed her hands upon her forehead in the anguish and anxiety of her feelings.

But suddenly she started, and her heart beat at double its wonted pace, as the sound of hasty approaching footsteps fell upon her quick and attentive ear, and she drew herself hastily aside, behind one of the pillars which supported the dome, till she could ascertain without being observed, whether or not it was the beloved being she was so eager to behold, though hope whispered in her ear the fond assurance that it was.

She looked eagerly, but although the sounds drew nearer, for a second or two she was unable in the dim light which then prevailed, to see anything distinctly

Omelia, however, still continued to strain her eyes through the obscurity beyond, and her heart palpitated with hope, fear, and expectation.

Nearer and nearer the sounds approached, and at length Omelia could behold the indistinct shadow of a human form, which was that of a man, and her emotion became more powerful than ever. Still the dimness of the light would not permit her to distinguish clearly the personal appearance and features of the man, and in that state of uncertainty she was fearful of revealing herself.

Not long, however, was she kept in this painful state of suspense, the man having approached to nearly opposite where she stood, paused, and seemed to look anxiously, and with some degree of disappointment about him. Another moment, and the poor girl heard her name pronounced in an agitated but well known voice, that voice whose beloved tones she had never more expected to gladden her ears, and, with a frantic cry of indescribable joy, she staggered forward, and sunk fainting in the arms of her faithful Stanley!

Yes, once more, after all the cares and anxieties, the troubles and vicissitudes it had been their hard lot to have to experience, the lovers were restored to each other. The delighted Stanley again held to his throbbing, manly bosom, the form of that lovely being whom he most prized of all on earth, and the most eloquent pen must fail in trying to do justice to the feelings which at that moment of rapture agitated his breast

For a minute or two he could but press her with convulsive delight to his heart, and gazed upon her with bewildered brain; then he bore her inanimate form towards the entrance to the temple, into the pale light of the moon, which had now just risen, and raising her head gently from his bosom, once more gazed with feelings of the most unbounded transport upon those beauteous features he had scarcely ventured to hope ever again to behold, and while he did so, he could not but fancy that she looked more lovely than ever.

Oh, the bliss, the exquisite bliss of that moment! Stanley could hardly persuade himself of its reality. What kisses of adoration did he press upon her lips and cheeks, and it seemed as if he could have gazed his very soul away in looking at her.

So great were his emotions that, for a few moments the power of speech was suspended and he stood, holding the poor girl in his arms, almost as inanimate as a statue.

"Restored to me!" he at length exclaimed, "the fond being in whom are centered all my most cherished hopes and wishes, is restored to me, once more I gaze upon those beauteous features that have never for an instant been absent from my imagination, and I am happy, oh, most exquisitely, most unspeakably happy. Dearest to me of all earthly beings, one of the loveliest of heaven's works, what words can express the unbounded transport of my soul, as I clasp you in my fond embrace after all that we have suffered for each other? All merciful God, I thank Thee, this moment more than

repays me for all the sorrows I have experienced."

Still he continued to gaze with the greatest delight in her countenance, and to hold her graceful form still closer in his affectionate embrace. But a soft sigh that suddenly escaped her lips, awakened all his fondest expectations, and excited his feelings to the utmost degree.

Once more, in the most affectionate tones he called upon her name, and the sound of his voice seemed to recal her to immediate life. She opened her eyes, she fixed them upon his countenance with a look of the most indescribable affection, her bosom heaved with convulsive emotion, she endeavoured to speak, but could not, and after two or three efforts, her head again sunk upon his shoulder, and she burst into a violent paroxysm of sobs and tears.

It is almost needless to state the agitation of Edward Stanley was equal to that of the lovely being who still clung to his fond embrace, and that for a short time he was quite as incapable of speaking as herself. Such indeed was the excitement of his feelings that he could have wept tears of joy, and it was with the greatest difficulty that he was able to restrain them.

"Omelia," he at length ejaculated, in the tenderest accents, "my own, my adored Omelia, for the love of heaven, oh, look up again, I beseech you, and gladden me with the light of your eyes: speak to me, to convince me by the melodious tones of your voices that my senses do not wander, but that I am indeed so blessed, so happy as to hold you again to my throbbing heart, that heart which a much longer separation from you must have broken."

"Edward, beloved, faithful Edward, was all that she was enabled to articulate, but her looks spoke even more eloquently than her tongue could have done, the thoughts and feelings that agitated her breast were expressed in every feature, and the delighted Stanley could desire no more.

"Joy, joy," he exclaimed in accents of rapture, "our anxieties are at end, my adored Omelia, for heaven in its infinite mercy has restored us to each other."

Once more the beauteous girl raised her looks towards his countenance, and the expression of her features was transporting to gaze upon, and could not fail to banish all feelings of care and sorrow in a moment.

Tears still trembled in her eyes, in which all the affectionate and most grateful feelings of her heart were powerfully expressed. But she could not give utterance to them in words and entwining her arms fondly around the neck of her lover, she abandoned herself entirely to his embrace.

At that moment the tall, dark figure of a

E. WHIMPER Sc.

man suddenly appeared in the background, and stood for an instant, and an instant only to gaze earnestly upon the lovers. Then shaking his fist menacingly, he hurried stealthily away, but still not so silently but the sound of his retreating footsteps caught the quick ears of our heroine, who in an instant raised her head from the shoulder of her lover, and she uttered a faint scream of terror, as her eyes indistinctly caught the shadow of the man's form as it hastily vanished from the sight through one of the side entrances to the temple.

"Dear Omelia," eagerly interrogated her lover, "what is the meaning of this emotion? why do you tremble so violently? What is it that alarms you?"

"Some one has been watching us, and listening to our conversation," answered Omelia, in a tremulous voice, "I caught a glimpse of the form of a man as he retreated yonder. Alas, I fear that some fresh danger threatens us."

"Nay, my love," replied Stanley, in a voice of the deepest affection, and still encircling the slender waist of the beauteous maiden, while his whole soul was in his eyes as they were rivetted on her handsome features, "nay, my love," he repeated, "frighten not yourself unnecessarily. Not a soul is here to observe us; and whom have we to fear?"

"There is no time now for further explanation," returned Omelia, in trembling accents, "but there is one whom I have cause to fear, for he has dared to insult mine ears with the avowal of his odious passions, and attempted by force to get me in his power."

No. 64.

"His name?—his name?" impatiently interrogated Stanley, with looks of the greatest indignation.

"Yusef, a rebel sepoy," answered Omelia.

"The presumptuous miscreant," exclaimed her lover.

"It was that villain whose form I firmly believe I just now caught a glimpse of," said Omelia, gazing fearfully towards that part of the temple.

"'Tis strange," said Stanley, reflecting, "but still, my dearest Omelia, I cannot but imagine that you must have been mistaken. If any one did indeed approach it must have been Captain Morley, and he, it is not likely would intrude himself upon our privacy, unless some danger threatened; then he would not have retired so abruptly, and without saying a word."

"Oh, no, it was not Captain Morley, I am certain," faltered out our heroine, but then suddenly endeavouring to conquer the fears which had taken possession of her, she added, "and yet after I may have suffered my imagination to mislead me, I will endeavour to banish the circumstance from my thoughts, dear Stanley. You are restored to my arms, the doubts and fears, the cares and anxieties that have so long tortured me, driving my brain at times almost to madness, are removed, and I am happy."

With these words, she again entwined her arms around Stanley's neck, and gave vent to those feelings her tongue could not express

"Oh, transport, oh, bliss unspeakable," cried Stanley, in a voice of indescribable emotion, and straining her beauteous form with even greater vehemence than ever to his throbbing bosom; "away, away with all gloomy and racking thoughts, be the dreary past forgotten, buried in oblivion, the transport of this meeting, more than repays me for all the troubles and vicissitudes it has been my lot to undergo.

At that moment the dark shadowy form before alluded to again made its appearance, partly from one of the pillars which supported the roof of the temple, but this time so noiselessly, that it was impossible for any one to hear the slightest footfall, while its position was such that it could conceal itself in an instant, for it stood in the background and completely in the shade.

Could the expression of that forbidding countenance which glared upon the unconscious lovers at that moment, however, have been seen it must have startled and shocked the beholder, for it was perfectly fiendish, and showed the monstrous thoughts and passions that raged within its guilty breast.

Again the savage intruder, shook his fist at them menacingly, and then without the least sound that could reach even the most attentive ear, it glided behind the pillar, and instantly disappeared, but whether or not it had left the temple it would be impossible to say.

Omelia and her lover still continued in each other's embrace, when the sound of a distant bugle startled them, and Captain Morley hastily entered the temple.

"I am sorry to interrupt you and your beauteous companion, Lieutenant Stanley," he said, "but you heard the sound of the bugle that summonses you away?"

"Alas! alas!" sighed Omelia, with looks of the most poignant regret, and still clinging affectionately to him.

"Nay, my love," returned Stanley, in soothing accents, and imprinting a fervent kiss upon her lips, "it is but for a brief period that we must part. Captain Morley," he added, "have you before entered the temple, since myself and Omelia have been together?"

"Certainly not," replied the captain, with an offended look, "you surprise me by putting such a question."

"Pardon me, Captain Morley," remarked Stanley, "I had reasons for doing so, which Omelia will explain. Have you seen any person leave the temple since we have been here?"

Captain Morley replied in the negative, and looked more surprised than before.

"You see therefore, my dear Omelia," said her lover, "that your imagination must have deceived you, and that your fears were entirely groundless."

"I will endeavour to think so," replied our heroine, "though I must confess that I have still my doubts upon the subject. But you must leave me, Edward, and my heart misgives me, fearing that we may never meet again."

"Oh banish such melancholy thoughts from your mind, my sweetest," said Stanley, "for there is not, I assure you, the slightest cause for you to entertain them. To-morrow evening, at the same hour, I will again meet you here, and then we will talk over our plans for the future. Farewell, farewell, and may all good angels watch over your safety and happiness till then."

"Adieu, beloved Stanley, adieu," ejaculated Omelia in the most tender accents, and throwing herself again into his arms, "I will not fail, I will be punctual."

Stanley pressed an ardent kiss of affection upon her willing lips, then gently disengaging himself from her fond embrace, and resigning her to the care of Captain Morley, he hastily left the temple by one of the back entrances, and the captain and his fair charge quitted it by another.

CHAPTER CXXXIV.

A STORM AGAIN GATHERS.

The dark, shadowy form had been peering from behind the column during the latter part of this meeting, and had overheard the appointment made for the following evening.

When the three individuals had departed, the man came forward, and stood revealed in the broad moonlight, before one of the entrances. gazing eagerly after the receding forms of Omelia and Captain Morley, Stanley —as has been before stated—having quitted the place in a different direction.

As the reader will doubtless have guessed, it was the villain Yusef, and it may be imagined with what jealous feelings of rage and deadly malice he had listened to all that had passed between the faithful lovers, and beheld their fond endearments to each other. So excited indeed, were his worst passions that it was a wonder he did not betray himself.

Two or three times the miscreant's rage was aroused to such a pitch, that he presented his pistol at Stanley, and was about to fire, but remembering that he was alone, and that even by the death of her lover, he would not be able to secure Omelia, but, on the contrary, might involve himself in the most imminent danger, he restrained his murderous design, and endeavoured to wait patiently for a more fitting opportunity to put his diabolical plans into execution.

The appointment for the following evening seemed to offer the opportunity he sought, and he determined with the assistance of his villainous colleagues to avail himself of it.

"Yes," he savagely exclaimed, as he stood on the same spot, in the ancient temple, the light of the bright moon adding to the fierce fire that flashed from his eyes, "I, the pariah, Yusef, will soon crush the bright fond hopes your sanguine imaginations have kindled in your breasts, and reduce you to a state of the most abject misery and despair. I feel goaded on by a spirit of hatred and revenge as well as fierce desire, and those passions I swear either to gratify or perish in the attempt. The scorn of Omelia has mortified my pride, and aroused my indignation, and I will not fail to make her pay dearly for it. Already do I anticipate my triumph, and look forward to the future, with feelings of confidence and exultation."

As he thus spoke, he having first looked forth to see that there was no one about to observe him, the villain quitted the temple, and plunging into the most lonely and unfrequented part, he hurried on his way towards the river, where a boat with two of his colleagues, but who were not admitted entirely to his confidence, was secretly waiting to receive him.

Into this then he got, and being quickly wafted to the opposite side, the boat was left in the charge of those from whom it had been hired, and Yusef and his companions made their way towards the cavern in the mountain which has been described in a previous chapter.

It was night, and Alahamed and the other rebels, who formed the particular party of whom Yusef was looked upon as the commander, were assembled in the rocky cavern amusing and regaling themselves much after the usual style.

"Yusef tarries," observed Alahamed, at length coming forward, "something particular must have detained him beyond the time he promised to return. I trust no harm has befallen him."

"He is ever too much on his guard for that," replied another of the rebels, "yet I cannot help thinking that he was rash and foolish to venture alone."

"True, true," coincided Alahamed, "but probably he considered the errand he was going upon would not be attended with any danger, and did not therefore deem such precaution necessary."

"I am afraid that Yusef devotes too much of his thoughts to this girl, Omelia," remarked one of the men assembled, "to the injury of the cause we have all at heart, there is something more serious and important to think about now, than love making and all such nonsense. No good will come of it."

"Cease, Moolah," said Alahamed, sternly, "you're always croaking forth some dismal foreboding or the other. Omelia is very beautiful, and I do not wonder that he should feel a desire to possess her, but that will by no means destroy his zealous exertions in our cause, which is fast becoming that of the whole of our oppressed countrymen."

A shrill whistle was now heard from above.

"Ah!" exclaimed Alahamed; "the signal! 'Tis him, admit him."

One of the men taking up a lighted lamp, immediately quitted the cavern to do so, and directly afterwards Yusef stood in the midst of the lawless wretches, who looked upon him as a superior being—such was the powerful influence he had cunningly obtained over them—and who greeted him with the usual boisterous demonstrations of welcome which he likewise duly acknowledged.

"You are late, Yusef," observed Alahamed.

"True," replied Yusef, "but still the delay in my return was unavoidable."

"I had almost began to fear that some

accident had befallen you," said Alahamed, "may I inquire what it is that has detained you so long?"

"Aye," answered Yusef, "I have seen and heard that which has excited my most malicious feelings, yet inspired me with fresh hopes."

"How?" interrogated Alahamed, with some curiosity.

"Listen," returned Yusef, and the remainder of the rebels in the cavern having gathered round him, he related the particulars of the meeting of the lovers in the Temple of Fountains, of his secretly watching them and overhearing what had passed between them.

"Oh," he exclaimed, clenching his fist, and an expression of deadly malice distorting his at any time repulsive features, "with what feelings of burning rage and envy did I behold the fond endearments which Omelia lavished upon the hated Feringhee I could have buried my knife in his heart, or sent a brace of bullets through his head, but I was alone, and under the circumstances, such an act might have led to mine own destruction."

"True," coincided Alahamed; "and is a pity that you were not accompanied by myself and two or three more of our comrades, for you have lost an excellent chance of getting the girl, Omelia in your power which may never occur again."

"It will," said Yusef, with a look of satisfaction, "and that no later than to morrow evening, when Stanley and Omelia have appointed to meet each other again, at the same hour, and in the same place."

"Ah," said Alahamed, "that's fortunate, of course you do not intend to miss the opportunity?"

"No," replied Yusef, "and of course, I may depend upon the assistance of yourself and such others of our comrades as I may select for the important duty?"

"Certainly," returned Alahamed, "why need you put such a question?"

"Enough, then you will hold yourself and your companions in readiness to attend me to-morrow afternoon, and it will be strange indeed, unsuspicious as they will be of them, if my designs do meet with complete success, and Omelia to-morrow night, find herself a prisoner in these rocky caverns."

"A place of good security, certainly," observed Alahamed; "but where the girl will be rather disappointed, I reckon, if she expects to find any luxurious accommodation."

"That must be seen to afterwards," said Yusef, "one of the best caverns must be fitted up for her, for it is my determination, once having got possession of her, to endeavour to make her confinement the least painful as possible. Old Juballah, being

the only female here will have to attend upon her."

"A pleasant companion, truly," remarked Alahamed, with a grin, "for a delicate and sensitive female like Omelia."

"She is a frightful repulsive old hag, certainly," said Yusef; "but there is no alternative under the circumstances, and perhaps with a few instructions she may do moderately well. Is she anywhere about?"

"Yes," replied Alahamed, "she is in her own dark and favourite den, brooding sullenly alone, as usual."

"Let her be summoned into my presence," commanded Yusef.

"On of the fellows obeyed, and quickly returned with a miserable-looking old creature who more than realised the not very flattering description of Alahamed and Yusef, and the first sight of whom was sufficient to excite feelings of disgust, if not of absolute terror.

She was a tall boney woman, who still exhibited remarkable symptoms of muscular strength for her age. She was naked with the exception of an old petticoat, which was fastened round her waist, and her dark skin hung flabby about her.

But her features, they were of the most hideous description, and it was impossible for any one, but those who were used to her, to meet the strange and sinister expression of her eyes without a shudder.

She had a large mouth and thick lips like an African, and which sufficiently marked her origin, and her hair was wild and shaggy matted together, and upon which it would have been utterly impossible for even the strongest comb to have had the least effect.

Such was the interesting individual, the intended future attendant and agreeable companion of our heroine.

"Juballah!" said Yusef.

"Now then," answered the frightful being, —who scarcely looked like anything human —in a croaking, harsh, discordant voice.

"I've got a few words to say to you," said Yusef.

"Mind they are few," returned the old woman, surily, "and said as quick as you please."

"You are in a bad humour, Juballah!"

"I'm never in a good one."

That was true to the very letter, and Yusef therefore, did not attempt to gainsay it.

"What do you want?" demanded Juballah impatiently.

"I want your delicate assistance."

"Indeed?" she sneered, "then, if its anything delicate, you won't get it, I don't understand such nonsense."

"Come, come," said Yusef, half angrily, "this is trifling. The plain simple fact is, that I am about to bring a young female here—probably to-morrow night—upon whom

I shall require your attendance, and that you will treat her with kindness."

"She must take her chance about that," replied Juballah, "I'll make no promises. Is that all you've got to say?"

"Yes"

"Then I suppose I can go?"

"You can."

"Oh!" ejaculated the hag, and she hobbled out of the cave without saying another word.

"Ha! ha! ha!" laughed Alahamed, when she was gone, "a choice specimen that of what the Feringhee calls the fair and gentle sex."

"True," agreed Yusef, "she is a most revolting being"

"And I fancy that the beauteous Omelia will have reason to be delighted with her female companion," added Alahamed.

"Psha!" exclaimed Yusef, impatiently, "this is no subject for jesting. Savage even as the disposition of the old woman is, I will change it or know the reason why."

"Change it!" repeated Alahamed, "as well might you try to change the wild beast into a lamb."

"We shall see," observed Yusef, "at any rate we have agreed that to-morrow night the attempt to seize Omelia, and convey her hither, shall take place?"

"We have."

"I need not say that the utmost precaution as well as determination are necessary?"

"True, they will not be found wanting."

"I am satisfied, in the meantime we will make all our arrangements, so that we shall be able to be at the place at the precise moment of the appointment."

"That can be done," said Alahamed, and after some further conversation the subject dropped, and the rebels resumed their usual revels, recounting with infinite satisfaction and exultation the various acts of atrocity they had themselves been engaged in since the fearful outbreak.

———

CHAPTER CXXXV.

DISMAL FOREBODINGS.

It was with a sad heart, notwithstanding the joyous meeting with her lover, and the mutual vows of affection and constancy that had been exchanged between them—that Omelia, leaning on the arm of Captain Morley, left the Temple of Fountains, and then she looked timidly around her, fearing that she might be watched by some one, or that some danger threatened her.

But as far as her eyes could penetrate by the assistance of the moon she could see nothing that was at all calculated to alarm her, and her spirits and resolution somewhat revived.

Captain Morley eagerly called upon her to explain the strange questions which Stanley had put to him, and which he was perfectly at a loss to conjecture the meaning of.

Omelia immediately complied, and related to him the interruption that had taken place in the temple, and the retreating from which she was almost certain she had seen.

Captain Morley listened to her with the deepest interest and attention, and after reflecting for a minute or two, he said :—

"In spite of the strong impression on your mind, Omelia, it appears to me that at the time, you must have been labouring under some delusion, which the solemnity of the place and the occasion might have created."

Our heroine shook her head, and again expressed her doubts.

"I remained strictly on the look out to warn you in the case of danger," remarked the captain, "and it was impossible for any one to leave the temple without my observing them. You must have been mistaken, Omelia. Besides, who is there who could harbour a thought of evil against you?"

"You seem to forget the villain Yusef, Captain Morley," suggested our heroine.

"True," he replied, "I had indeed for the moment forgotten him. But how could your intended meeting have come to his knowledge? And is it at all likely that he would venture to be lurking about this neighbourhood, after his late monstrous outrage, and certain as he must be of the sharp look out that is kept for him and his infamous colleagues."

"I will endeavour to think so," said Omelia; "may our appointed meeting to-morrow evening not be attended with any fatal calamity, that is my devout and earnest prayer."

"Give not way to any said forebodings, Omelia," said Captain Morley, "for I sincerely trust that there is not the least occasion for them."

Omelia again assured him that she would try to conquer them, and a few more observations brought them to the place of her destination, where the captain bade her good night and departed, and Omelia entered the house to meet her friends, who had been most anxiously awaiting her return.

She dilated with feelings of the utmost enthusiasm upon the transport of their meeting, and dwelt with fond delight upon every word that Stanley had uttered, and which were imprinted upon her memory in characters which nothing whatever could obliterate, and the pleasure and satisfaction of her friends were almost equal to her own.

But in spite of all the arguments of Captain Morley, and her own exertions to do so, Omelia could not dismiss from her mind the gloomy forebodings that some danger was pending to interrupt that happiness she had that night experienced, and which she had feared, and with so much reason, it would never again be her lot to know.

Pleading fatigue as her natural excuse, she shortly after her return retired to her chamber, where she could give indulgence to her thoughts without interruption.

There was not one word that had escaped the lips of her beloved Stanley, but which she could recal to her memory with feelings of the most exquisite delight, for she was well convinced that they emanated from his heart, and that assurance was more, much more than enough to compensate her for even years of suffering, and to fill her mind with the most sanguine expectations of the future.

Still she could not remove the impression from her mind that some one had been listening to and watching them, and that evil threatened them, and the more she endeavoured to do so, the stronger and more painful that impression became.

She could imagine no secret enemy but Yusef, and him—who she was almost positive it was she had caught a glimpse of in the temple—she had every reason to dread. It was evident that a man of his desperate and determined character would not easily abandon any guilty designs he might have formed, but that he would watch every opportunity of putting them into execution, and she knew not the means he might have of doing so, so that she could not but think that there was everything to fear, and those fears she found it impossible to conquer.

She recalled to her memory the fearful dream which she had had some time previously, respecting Stanley, when he was in her imagination in the midst of all the transports of their unexpected meeting, suddenly snatched from her in so mysterious and awful a manner, and there was something so prophetic in that vision, that the more she reflected upon it, the more dismal and torturing became her fears and misgivings.

"Great Spirit that rules the destinies of the whole human race," she solemnly ejaculated, clasping her hands together, "I beseech Thee, most humbly but fervently beseech Thee to avert the evils I apprehend, and to frustrate the guilty designs of the wicked. Oh, suffer not the bright prospects of happiness which this restoration have created, to be blighted, but throw around my beloved Stanley and myself the shield of Thy protection."

She felt somewhat more composed and confident after she had uttered this prayer,

and retired to rest. She arose at her usual time the following morning much refreshed, and in better spirits than she had experienced for some time.

She abandoned herself for awhile to the varied thoughts that crowded so rapidly upon her brain, previous to her joining her friends, and now that she had, for a time at least, banished those gloomy forebodings that had before haunted her, her ready imagination drew a glowing picture of the happiness that awaited her and Stanley, and she seemed as it were to revel in a dream of delight, from which she had reason to hope that she might never be awakened.

All for the time being was light and sunshine, oh, that no dark clouds might again gather to obscure a prospect so replete with every earthly joy.

That was the sincere, the fervent prayer of Omelia, and her heart bounded with renewed hope as her lips gave utterance to it.

With a light heart she now quitted her chamber, and met her friends in the room where they were assembled, with radiant smiles upon her countenance they had not witnessed for some time previous.

The day passed away in the most agreeable manner, Mr. and Mrs. Eldred and Abdal exerting themselves in the most praiseworthy manner to keep up our heroine's spirits, and encourage her hopes for the future.

She repeated again and again in the most impassioned terms the particulars of the interview between her and Stanley, and the fond vows that they had exchanged with each other, and upon this subject she seemed never tired of dwelling, while those who listened to her could duly appreciate her feelings.

As the evening approached, her agitation increased, and her heart throbbed violently against her side with the mingled feelings of doubt and expectation.

At length, again punctual to the moment, Captain Morley arrived to conduct her to the place of assignation, and she received him with a smile of welcome, at the same time eagerly inquiring whether he had seen Stanley since the previous evening.

Captain Morley replied in the affirmative, and added—

"The happy interview with you, Omelia, after so long a separation, has had its due effect upon the spirits of my young and gallant friend, I never saw him look better or happier than he did to-day."

"Thank Heaven for that," exclaimed our heroine, fervently, "and oh, grant that such feelings of happiness may never again become strangers to his breast. May those dark clouds that have heretofore lowered upon our fate, never more interpose their baneful influence.

To this wish every one present most cordially responded, and after a few more observations, Omelia resigned herself to the friendly care of Captain Morley, and left the house with him, followed by the good wishes of her friends.

The evening, like the previous one had been, was remarkably fine, and everything in nature, seemed to smile upon the hopes, the wishes, and expectations of our heroine, who felt more elate as they proceeded on their way.

Yet when the event of the previous evening recurred to her memory—and she could not persuade herself that she had been led away by her disordered imagination—an irresistible feeling of dread came over her, and she looked timidly around her to see that no one was lurking about to observe them, though as she could perceive there was not the least cause for alarm, and almost ashamed of her weakness, she conquered her feelings quickly and became more firm and confident.

Captain Morley endeavoured to engage her in conversation on the way, and at last he succeeded, so that by the time that they had arrived to within a short distance of the temple, her spirits had reassumed nearly their natural vivacity.

And now her heart again palpitated violently, and her footsteps faltered.

As they drew nearer to the temple, Omelia suddenly uttered a faint cry of terror, and clung to the arm of Captain Morley, looking fearfully towards the building.

"What is the meaning of this, Omelia?" he eagerly and anxiously interrogated, "what agitates and terrifies you thus?"

"Again I could almost swear," replied Omelia, scarcely knowing what she said in the excitement of her feelings; "that I again beheld the dark shadow of a human form, gliding stealthily in the shade beneath the wall of the building."

"Fancy, fancy again, Omelia," said the captain with an encouraging smile, "it must have been the shadows of the trees in the moonlight which deceived you. Come, you must endeavour to dismiss these groundless fears from your mind."

Omelia made no reply, but she looked far from satisfied, and still kept her eyes fixed steadfastly upon the spot where she imagined she had seen the form, and could not help trembling as they approached the temple.

They entered it, and as they did so, both her and Captain Morley imagined, nay, were almost convinced that they heard a shuffling, rustling sound like that of retreating footsteps, and Omelia clung to him more terrified than before, but unable to speak a word, they both looked in the direction from which the sounds seemed to proceed, but saw nothing that could justify their suspicions, Captain Morley, however, drew his sword to be prepared in case of danger.

"Psha!" he said, "how silly is this, there is nothing here to alarm us, I verily believe that you have innoculated me with your weakness, Omelia. It was nothing more than the sighing of the evening breeze that we heard. The time has not yet exactly arrived, but Lieutenant Stanley will no doubt be punctual, he will not tarry when he has her that he so fondly loves to meet."

"Do not leave me, Captain Morley, I pray you," she said timidly, as he was about to retire rather abruptly, "I cannot help feeling a sensation of dread stealing over me at the thought of being left alone in this strange place."

"You are a timid little gipsy," said the captain laughingly; "there's nothing to fear I am convinced, but I suppose I must humour you."

Omelia thanked him, and they stood in that part of the temple, where the light of the moon shone clearly, and they could distinguish objects, and the former listened anxiously to catch the slightest sound.

And in this manner about five minutes passed away, when suddenly a light tread from the further end of the building smote their attentive ears, and they drew themselves back where they could observe without being observed.

They had not to wait long in suspense, the tall figure of a man appeared in the background, it approached nearer, the heart of Omelia palpitated violently with indescribable sensations, again she heard her name pronounced in that well known and beloved voice, and with a cry of delight she rushed forward, and was once more enfolded in the fond and fervent embrace of her beloved Stanley.

Captain Morley bowed, and again retired outside the building to keep watch.

CHAPTER CXXXVI.

THE SECOND MEETING.—APPREHENSIONS.

"A second time we meet, my sweetest Omelia," ejaculated Stanley, in tones of rapture, after he had imprinted the most chaste and fondest kisses on her lips and cheeks, and when he had sufficiently recovered from his emotion to express himself, "once more the feast of love and happiness is granted us, the dark clouds of our destiny have for a time, at any rate, dispersed, and all around for a time seemed bright and cheerful. Oh, what blissful dreams were mine last night, how did your beloved form, and the heavenly words you uttered, pursue me in my slumbers, renewing all those joys I had experienced but a few short hours before. All merciful heaven grant that nothing may ever again occur to interrupt those joys."

"Dearest Stanley," returned the lovely maiden, in her sweetest accents, and looking in his face with the most unbounded affection, "oh, how fondly, how fervently do I respond to that wish, and humbly beseech the Great Spirit, not to suffer anything to occur to annihilate our hopes, for that would indeed be too much for human nature patiently to endure, after having undergone so many severe trials, and I feel that my fortitude must sink under it. But, alas, situated as we are, how soon may we have to part again, and then perhaps for ever."

"I pray you, Omelia," replied her lover, soothingly and encouragingly, "do not torture yourself with that sad thought, for I trust that your fears will not be realised. True, I probably shall be compelled to leave Cawnpore, but some plan must be adopted by which you may be enabled to follow me wherever I go, and will never again be absent, only for the shortest time possible, from each other's sight."

"Blessed thought!" exclaimed our heroine with a look of the most unfeigned delight; "would to heaven that it could be accomplished, but it must, it shall be so, in spite of all who may seek to oppose it, dear Stanley, your faithful, your devoted Omelia, the simple Indian maid whose fondest love, whose only hopes are fixed on you, will ever more be by your side, for in your presence alone can she exist, and who dare attempt to tear assunder two beings so fondly united together?"

The expression of her handsome countenance was noble in the extreme as she gave utterance to these words, and a spirit of proud and fond determination flashed from her brilliant eyes, but overpowered by the torrent of thoughts and emotions that thrilled round her heart, and rushed to her brain, she threw her arms round the neck of the enraptured Stanley—who was too deeply affected to speak—and laid her lovely face upon her bosom.

At that interesting moment they were both suddenly startled by an indistinct sound, something like a half stifled laugh, and Stanley hastily but gently disengaging himself from the affectionate embrace of Omelia, drew his sword, and advanced towards the farther end of the temple, from whence the sound appeared to proceed, but not the least signs of a human being met his view.

Omelia kept close by his side, determined to share his fate, should any danger really threaten, and she endeavoured to be firm.

Stanley looked forth from the different entrances to the temple, but saw no one but Captain Morley, who was keeping watch on an elevated spot of ground, near the building.

Stanley motioned to him.

"What's the matter?" interrogated the captain, "has anything occurred to excite you and Omelia?"

"Have you seen any one near the temple?" eagerly asked Stanley.

"Not a soul."

"'Tis strange, Captain Morley, you will oblige me by continuing to make a circuit of the temple, while myself and Omelia remain in it?"

"Certainly," replied the captain, and Stanley having again glanced around without observing anything to excite his suspicion, he and Omelia returned to the temple.

"Compose yourself, dear Omelia," said Stanley, "it is evident that this time, at any rate, we have both suffered ourselves to be led away by fancy. But I will not in future expose you to the least danger, as after this evening I will invariably meet you at the bungalow at which yourself and your friends reside."

"Oh, thanks, thanks, dear Edward," said Omelia, with a look of the greatest satisfaction, "that arrangement will take a deal of care and anxiety off my mind, for I confess to feeling the strongest misgivings and apprehensions while we are here. In the garden attached to the bungalow we can converse without any fear of intrusion."

"True," coincided Stanley, "and oh, what feelings of indescribable transport will be those that we are permitted to pass together. I have much to explain, much to relate of what has occurred to me since the dreary, the fearful time that we have been separated, but that must be reserved to a future opportunity. You, too, my beloved Omelia, I feel convinced, must have an eventful narrative to detail to me, and to which I feel most anxious to listen."

"Oh, yes," returned Omelia, "I have indeed suffered much, but I am more than amply repaid, dear Stanley, by the joy of the present. But when you leave Cawnpore —since it is my determination to accompany you, or follow in your footsteps—by what means can that be the more readily accomplished?"

"I have thought upon a plan," replied her lover, "which we will fully discuss when we meet again. In the meantime, my sweet Omelia, let hope continue to animate your breast, and depend upon it that you will not be suffered by providence to end in disappointment."

"Heaven grant that your predictions may be fulfilled," ejaculated Omelia; "but I re-

peat that my determination is fixed, and I trust that providence will give me strength and the means to accomplish it. No consequence the hardships I may have to encounter, and to which I have so long been innured, in spite of the most appalling dangers that may threaten, wherever you go, I will accompany you; in the midst of every peril by which you may be surrounded, on the fierce battle-field, amid the cannon's roar, and the deadly bayonet's flash, your faithful Omelia will be by your side, dear Stanley, death alone shall again part us."

"Noble, heroic girl," exclaimed her lover, pressing her to his throbbing bosom, with even more emotion than ever, "how fond, how generous, how devoted is the spirit that prompts these words, and how proud am I to possess the heart of one who can give ut-

terance to such sentiments. Oh, when I abuse the affectionate confidence you repose in me, when I cease to honour, to revere you with all my heart and soul, may heaven curse and abandon me."

"You will not, you could not, dear Stanley," said the beauteous girl, again entwining her exquisitely moulded arms around his neck, and tears of affectionate emotion chasing each other down her cheeks; "and it is that blessed assurance that renders me happy. Oh, how glowing is the picture of the future that awaits us—when all the storm clouds of our destiny shall have passed away—that my fond and sanguine imagination would fain draw, yet which I can scarcely anticipate."

"Continue thus to hope, my own Omelia," returned Stanley, "for something assures me that all our fondest and most fervent wishes will be realised. Heaven will not suffer such transcendant virtues as your's to remain for ever without their reward."

Omelia replied not, but her looks spoke more than the most eloquent language could possibly have done, and Stanley once more enfolded her in his affectionate embrace.

Again that bugle sound!—it was the signal to part, and the heart of poor Omelia sunk within her, while a dreadful feeling of presentiment stole over her, which she found it impossible to resist. Stanley strained her delicate form still more warmly to his bosom and imprinting an affectionate kiss upon her lips, he said—

"Be calm my love, our parting is not for long, to-morrow, at sunset, I will meet you with your friends, till then heaven bless and watch over you."

The eyes of Omelia brightened, and she seemed at once to conquer the fears and misgivings she had allowed to obtrude upon her.

"Till sunset to-morrow evening then, dear Stanley, adieu," she said; he responded with a kiss, and then encircling her waist with his arm, he conducted her from the temple to the place where his kind and devoted friend, Captain Morley, was waiting, to whose care he resigned her; and then without being able to utter another word, he hurried away, Omelia following his receding form with her eyes till it was hidden from her view in the distance.

———

CHAPTER CXXXVII.

THE TRIUMPH OF YUSEF.

Not an instant had Stanley and Omelia departed from the temple. than the miscreants Yusef, Alahamed, and several more of their desperate colleagues, made their appearance from the place where they had been concealed during the interview, and approaching the entrance from which Omelia and the captain had quitted the temple, gazed after their receding forms with anxious and threatening looks.

"This time, at any rate, she cannot escape me," said Yusef, triumphantly.

"But what cause was there for any delay, Yusef?" demanded Alahamed, in a dissatisfied tone; "why not have seized the girl while her and her lover were together? He might have been got rid of at the same time, but you have allowed him to depart unmolested."

"'Tis better as it is," returned Yusef, "the discovery of her loss will be worse than death to the hated Feringhee Stanley. We will watch her and her conductor to a lonely spot, and then the prize for which I have so long panted must and shall be mine. Quick, we must not lose sight of them."

Alahamed made no reply, and the miscreants cautiously followed at a distance the footsteps of the unconscious Omelia and Captain Morley, never for an instant losing sight of them.

Everything seemed to favour their infamous designs, for no signs of a human being —save those whom they were following— was to be seen, and it so happened that Captain Morley, not apprehending danger, escorted his fair charge by a different route to what he had previously done, and which was remarkably lonely and dreary, although considerably the nearest way to which they wished to go.

"All right," said Yusef, exultingly, "they could not better have fallen into my meshes, if even they had designedly done so. Success is certain; there is nothing to prevent it that I see."

They continued to follow cautiously, but at a prudent distance.

In the meantime Captain Morley and our heroine proceeded on their way, and the latter giving expression to the various and conflicting feelings of joy and sadness, hope and fear.

"Why have you chosen this dismal way, Captain Morley?" interrogated Omelia, looking at the dreary scene before them with a shuddering sensation which she could not resist.

"Because it is the nearest by more than half a mile," replied the captain; "and I knew that you would be anxious to reach the place of your destination as soon as possible. There is nothing to fear, Omelia, while I am with you."

"Alas," returned our heroine, in tones of doubt and foreboding, "we know not that— we know not what danger may lurk amid this gloom, where the pale moonbeams are scarcely allowed to enter. I wish you had conducted me the usual way."

Captain Morley endeavoured to banish her fears, which he tried to persuade her were perfectly groundless, but he only succeeded very indifferently.

The way, in fact, which they were pursuing, or at least were just about to enter, seemed to be the only dark and cheerless spot, in the midst of all that was bright and fair; tall clustering trees interwove the long and thickly foliaged branches so closely together, that the light of the moon was almost excluded, in some places entirely so, and the ground was so rough and uneven, that to traverse it was a task of considerable labour, and Captain Morley himself now regretted that, with a mistaken idea of saving time and shortening the distance, he should have been induced to come that way, but it was too late to retrace their steps, and he therefore exerted himself to the utmost to quiet the apprehensions of his fair companion.

"Oh," she said, in a tremulous voice, "the bare aspect of this wild and fearful place chills my heart; let us return, and proceed by the usual route."

"We cannot conveniently do so," answered the captain, "but we shall soon get beyond this gloom, and I repeat that there is nothing to apprehend."

Omelia shook her head doubtfully, and looked anxiously back at the ground they had traversed, and as she did so she was almost certain that she beheld the shadows of human forms moving stealthily about in the distance, and she clung to Captain Morley with an increased sensation of fear and dismal foreboding.

"Look, sir, do you not observe human forms yonder?" she said, in a faltering voice.

The captain looked in the direction she intimated, but if our heroine had been right in her conjectures, all signs of a human being had then disappeared.

"I do not observe anything, Omelia, to excite the least alarm," replied the captain, "there are those trees that we have passed, and it must have been them which your bewildered imagination gave human shape to. Courage, Omelia, and we shall soon arrive at the place of our destination, without, I trust, encountering any danger."

Our heroine once more cast a timid look towards the place where she fancied she had but only for an instant, beheld the forms of men, and then with a sad and foreboding heart, without saying another word, she suffered Captain Morley to conduct her on the dreary way he had chosen.

As the reader will no doubt, justly have concluded, Omelia was quite right in her conjectures, it was Yusef and his guilty associates whom she had for an instant caught sight of, but the trees immediately hid them from her view.

It was with feelings of the most savage delight that Yusef watched his intended victim and her companion, as they advanced nearer to that dreary spot where he had determined that his diabolical designs should be accomplished.

"This way," he said, addressing himself to Alahamed and Moolah Bushka, "by taking this turning, and by using speed, we shall come abruptly upon them in the midst of the dreary wild, and take them by surprise the triumph which will follow will then be certain. Quick!"

The ruffians obeyed, and Yusef hastily led the way into the turning to which he had alluded, and by which means, they would be able to meet Captain Morley and his companion, so suddenly that they could not be the least prepared for it.

Captain Morley and our heroine had with much difficulty, from the thickness of the foliage, and the nature of the ground as before stated, reached about the centre of the wild, when they could plainly hear a rustling sound and the noise of footsteps, and before they had time to inquire into the cause, they found themselves surrounded by the miscreant Yusef and his ferocious associates.

Omelia with a cry of terror, clung to Captain Morley, who endeavoured to draw his sword, but ere he could do so, he was stabbed by some dastardly scoundrel in the back, and sunk bleeding to the earth, while Yusef seized the graceful but delicate form of the poor girl in his powerful arms with a shout of exultation.

Omelia shrieked aloud, and for a moment or two struggled violently, but her fears overcome her, and she fainted, thus being left entirely to the mercy of the inhuman Yusef, and her fate being apparently sealed.

"Ha! ha! ha!" laughed the hardened wretch, as he held the inanimate form of the unfortunate Omelia in his arms, "my expectations are at length realised, the beauteous Omelia is mine, I triumph, I triumph."

He dared to pollute the lips of the insensible girl with his odious kisses as he thus spoke, and a large cloak having been thrown over her, which completly concealed her person, she was raised in the arms of two of the ruffians, and was conveyed hurriedly from the dreary spot, Yusef triumphantly leading the way, and by a route which would bring them in a short time to the bank of the river, which the villains had provided every means of crossing, and that without the danger of being observed or obstructed.

CHAPTER CXXXVIII.

THE FATAL INTELLIGENCE.—AGONY OF STANLEY.

The cowardly ruffians had inflicted no farther injury on Captain Morley after the first wound, but that was a serious one, and bleeding copiously, for a time rendered him perfectly unconscious.

It was more than an hour before he was restored to any degree of sensibility, and then he felt the most acute pain, and so faint from the loss of blood, that it seemed as though he was really dying.

With the greatest difficulty, and after several ineffectual efforts, he managed to raise himself on his elbow, and then all the dreadful events that had taken place, and his own terrible and dangerous situation, in that wild and lonely place, without the least probability of any one coming to his assistance, was made fearfully apparent to him.

It was evident that Omelia had fallen into the power of the desperate and heartless villain whom, she had so much cause to dread, and if so her fate was certain.

He cast one anxious and fearful look around him, as these torturing thoughts rushed rapidly upon his distracted brain, and then with a cry of agony and despair, he sunk back upon the earth, and again became insensible.

And there in that fearful and unfrequented place, and at that time of night, it seemed not at all unlikely that unfortunate and gallant officer, who had distinguished himself in many a hard fought and sanguinary battle, would be left to die, unless All merciful providence should speedily send some persons to his assistance.

Another half hour passed away, without any prospect of assistance, and still Captain Morley remained in the same helpless and truly deplorable situation, although he was too painfully sensible of all that had taken place, and the horrors by which he was surrounded.

His wound had ceased bleeding, but he suffered the most excruciating pain, both mentally and bodily, and he was so weak that even to attempt to raise himself, or to move from the spot, where he weltered in his blood, would have been impossible.

The anguish of the unfortunate captain's feelings at that time may be imagined, and those emotions increased every moment as the prospect of his deliverance appeared to be the more remote.

The solemn silence which reigned around was alone broken at intervals by the wind which blew in frightful gusts, adding to the misery of the unfortunate captain's situation.

But even in the midst of all his sufferings, his anxiety was greater for poor Omelia than himself, and he drew a most painful picture in his own imagination of the fate which had befallen her, or which was otherwise but too probably in store for her, in the power of such a wretch as Yusef, and left entirely to his " tender mercies."

This was awful to contemplate, and Captain Morley almost forgot his own pain, and the fate which must shortly overtake him, did not providence interpose to save him, in the misfortunes and sufferings of the devoted, noble-minded Hindoo maiden, who had already to encounter misfortunes and unparalleled trials, under which the greatest fortitude might well have sunken.

Then his gallant young friend, Stanley,

how terrible, how overwhelming would be the shock his feelings would experience when the dreadful intelligence of the abduction of Omelia should reach his ears, such a calamity must surely drive him to madness, and Captain Morley deeply and sincerely sympathised with him.

But should he—the captain—perish before any one should arrive to his assistance, the cause of her disappearance would be involved in mystery, and the miscreant Yusef would be enabled to accomplish his diabolical purpose, before any one could interpose to save her.

Such were the agonising thoughts that occurred to Captain Morley, as he lay stretched and helpless, and almost in a dying state upon the earth, where indeed, it seemed but too probable that he must perish before he was discovered.

The wind lulled, and all around became as silent as the church-yard, not a murmur, not a breeze, a zephyr even the most gentle could be heard among the foliage, and nothing could be more calculated to add to the gloom and mental anguish of the unfortunate captain.

Suddenly, however, the sound of approaching footsteps—he was certain that the sounds were those of footsteps, although they were at first faint—smote his eager ears, and the anxiety and impatience with which he listened, may be imagined.

At first, as we have stated, they were very faint, but soon they became perfectly distinct, and by the measured steps he was convinced that they were those of military men, and that they were advancing immediately towards the spot where he was lying.

But now arose a torturing doubt in his mind as to what might be the character of the men who were approaching, whether they might be friends or foes. They were just as likely to be one as the other, and he felt the greatest uncertainty and suspense, and it was that doubt and uncertainty which prevented him from calling—though he had indeed, scarcely strength to do so—so that he might direct the persons who were approaching, to the exact spot where he was lying.

Captain Morley had seldom suffered more from anxiety of mind, than he did at that critical moment, and that anxiety was greatly increased, when the sound of the footsteps suddenly ceased, and it seemed as if they had taken a contrary direction, and that the chance of his being rescued was as far off as ever.

He could not help groaning in the anguish and disappointment of his feelings, but he was quickly aroused from this painful state of fear and uncertainty, by again hearing the sound of the footsteps, and they were now advancing to within a short distance of where he was lying.

Another moment and the captain could hear the voices of the men, and even catch some of the words that they said, and he could not help giving utterance to an exclamation of satisfaction when he discovered that they were Englishmen.

The exclamation of the wounded captain had reached their ears, and guided them to the spot where he was lying, so much in need of assistance

It was a small detachment of infantry under the charge of an officer, proceeding to quarters, and which, providentially for Captain Morley had accidentally been led that way.

He again with the greatest difficulty, raised himself on his elbow, and could just distinguish the bayonets of the men, and that was all, through the almost impenetrable darkness which prevailed, but he again uttered a cry for help, in order the more certainly to attract their attention.

"Who calls?" eagerly demanded the astonished officer, looking anxiously in the direction from whence the sound seemed to proceed; "where are you? Speak again."

The captain, however, could only utter a faint cry, and then completely exhausted he again sunk back on the earth, and almost fainted.

The officer had heard sufficient to direct him—for the darkness was so great that it was impossible to distinguish anything at even the shortest distance—and advancing hastily, followed by two of the men, he then beheld Captain Morley, and could discover that he was a British officer by his uniform, and that he was also desperately wounded, from the completely helpless and exhausted condition in which he was lying.

"There has been some foul work here," said the officer, stooping down, and raising the head of the unfortunate Captain Morley, "speak, gallant sir, if you can, and tell me who you are, and how this has happened?"

Captain Morley endeavoured to speak, but could not, and the officer looking more narrowly into his features, in a voice of astonishment exclaimed:—

"It is Captain Morley of the fusilliers, and he appears to be dangerously, if not mortally wounded. Unfortunate gentleman, he has fainted. Quick," he added, addressing himself to the soldiers, "he must be conveyed without a moment's delay to the hospital in the city."

This command was promptly obeyed, the soldiers forming a litter of their muskets, over which two or three cloaks were laid, the insensible Captain Morley placed upon it, and being raised on the shoulders of four of the men was conveyed with all possible expedition to the temporary hospital in the city, as the officer had directed.

The news of this unfortunate affair quickly spread, and caused the most painful sensation among both officers and men, for the gallant captain was universally esteemed, not only for his bravery in the field, but the greatest urbanity of his disposition.

As might be expected, from the nature of the injury he had received, and his long exposure without asistance, the captain was in a most deplorable situation, and totally incapable of giving any explanation of the occurrence.

But when the fatal intelligence of what had happened reached the ears of Stanley, he was in a perfect state of frenzy, for there could be no doubt that Omelia had been taken from him, and had fallen into the hands of the villanous associates, and the lonely spot in which the unfortunate Captain Morley had been found, all but confirmed that terrible suspicion.

Alas! alas! too fatally had the dismal fears and forebodings of poor Omelia been realised, and Stanley could not help reproaching himself for having exposed her to such danger by appointing to meet her in the temple, instead of himself visiting her at the place where she resided with her friends.

The agony of his mind, in such a dreadful state of uncertainty, was almost insupportable, and he rushed with frantic haste to the hospital, with the hope of being able to elicit the fearful truth.

CHAPTER CXXXIX.

OMELIA IN THE CAVERN.

The wound of Captain Morley—which was found to be not quite so dangerous as had been at first expected, although it was a most severe one—was properly dressed and upon the arrival of Stanley at the hospital, he had revived, but in beholding his young friend, he groaned, and the extreme emotion he evinced was sufficient to confirm all the worst fears of the wretched Stanley.

"Omelia! Omelia!" in convulsive accents exclaimed the latter, "for the love of heaven, tell me what has become of her?"

Captain Morley looked up at him with a most melancholy expression of countenance, but for a few seconds he could not speak a word, and that increased the agony and suspense of the wretched Stanley, who groaned aloud and beat his breast in the utter despair of his feelings.

"My dear Captain Morley," he again said, "my unfortunate friend, who have encountered this fearful calamity in serving me, once more I implore you to endeavour to muster sufficient strength to inform me of the fate of my beloved Omelia. Oh, keep me no longer in this horrible state of suspense, which is worse, far worse than the most dreadful certainty, or even death itself."

"Omelia, poor unfortunate Omelia," the captain was at length enabled to gasp forth with much difficulty, "is gone! she is taken from you, torn away from my feeble protection, by the inhuman villain Yusef, and his savage associates."

A groan of indescribable agony escaped the lips of the distracted Stanley on hearing this, and he sunk perfectly senseless and inanimate on the floor, and was conveyed immediately from the room.

Captain Morley was also quite exhausted, and sunk back on his pillow.

And now to return to Omelia.

Through the dreary wild, led on by the exulting villain, Yusef, the savage sepoys proceeded with their beauteous and insensible burthen at the top of their speed, and without meeting with anything to obstruct them, or to frustrate their diabolical plans, and very shortly they arrived near the bank of the river.

And now certainly the fate of our heroine appeared sealed, that awful and revolting fate from which nothing but the merciful interposition of providence could save her, and the heartless scoundrel Yusef, laughed aloud in triumph.

"Lovely Omelia," he said, as he commanded those who were conveying her, to pause for a minute or two, there being no danger to be apprehended, and gazed with feelings of the most disgusting nature upon her handsome features, now so fixed and sad in their expression, as if in death, "this night in obtaining possession of you, I achieve a triumph which even the most powerful and despotic monarch might justly envy. Oh, well may I exult, especially after all the trouble I have taken and the many disappointments I have experienced. Of what avail, proud beauty, will now be your scorn and defiance, when you find yourself completely at my mercy and must submit to my will? You are mine, mine only, and no earthly power can restore you from us."

Again the miscreant polluted the unconscious maiden's lips with his disgusting and lawless kisses as he thus spoke, and gloated over the matchless beauties of her face and form with feelings of the most fiendish delight and exultation.

But our heroine still remained quite insensible, and Yusef again gave the word to the ruffians to proceed, which they did without any one appearing to molest them, and at last arrived at a part of the river's bank where few persons at any time frequented,

and where a couple of boats were waiting to receive them with two of the rebels.

Omelia was placed in one of the boats, Yusef and Alahamed taking their seats on either side of her, and the rest of the ruffians having entered the other boat, they made their way with all the speed they could towards the opposite bank, which they quickly reached, our heroine not having yet given the least signs of returning sensibility.

"We are now safe," said Yusef, in a voice which showed the malignant satisfaction which glowed in his guilty breast, "our success is complete, for there is no one who would here attempt to obstruct us. Away to our cavernous retreat, through the darkness of the night, and there will I claim the full right and possession of the prize which is so justly mine."

Omelia was now removed on shore, and Yusef and his colleagues quickly following they made their way towards the cavernous retreat among the mountains, the lovely and unfortunate prisoner still remaining in a state of torpidity which had all the appearance of death, and which almost at one time alarmed the villain Yusef.

But at length they arrived at the mountains among which the extraordinary caverns were situated.

These events had necessarily occupied a considerable time, and the night was far advanced.

The usual signal was given at the entrance to the caverns, and the rebel on that particular duty having appeared with a light, Omelia by Yusef's orders was carefully and delicately conveyed down the winding descent, he himself closely following.

On reaching the principal cavern our heroine was placed on a silken ottoman which had been manufactured by two or three of the rebels for the occasion, and the whole of those assembled were about to greet Yusef vociferously, and to congratulate him on the success of his schemes, but he checked them pointing significantly to the lovely but inanimate form of Omelia, and fearful that their rude and boisterous demonstrations might, in her present state, startle and alarm her.

"I thank you, comrades," he said, "for your good intentions, "but they must be deferred to another and more fitting opportunity. True the gratification of my daring and ambitious wishes, the accomplishment of my designs is a glorious one, and I have a right to feel proud of it To our associates here I owe a large debt of gratitude for the assistance they rendered me in the furtherence and execution of my plans. Of course, I have your promises to treat my beauteous mistress with every respect?"

The mutineers bowed their assent in solemn silence, and the exulting Yusef then turned his warmest and most impassioned gaze upon the lovely countenance of Omelia, but began to feel surprised and some doubts and misgivings in consequence of the length of the time that she had been in this state of stupor or insensibility.

He placed his hand over her heart, and felt its soft pulsation, while she still breathed gently though scarcely perceptibly, and he was satisfied.

The cavern in which old Juballah slept, and performed the cooking for Yusef, leaving the other mutineers who occupied this cavern to look after themselves, had undergone a complete revolution—if we may so term it—in appearance, preparatory to the arrival of our heroine, it having been arranged by Yusef—as has been before hinted —that she should occupy it with Juballah to watch her and attend upon her.

A handsome carpet—one of the articles of plunder—covered the damp earth; the walls were tastefully hung with pink drapery, and behind a couple of silken curtains of the same delicate hue was a comfortable bed for the accommodation of the lovely young prisoner.

This cavern also, contained several other elegant articles of furniture arranged with much trouble, and altogether it was fitted up with true Oriental taste, and under different circumstances, and if it had been thus prepared with a far more worthy purpose, it might well have called forth admiration.

To this cavern then—which it should have been before stated, was secured from the intrusion of any one who might think proper so to do, by a strong door which had been constructed for the purpose—Omelia was immediately conveyed, and given in charge to the hideous looking old Juballah—who could not be persuaded to alter in the least her uncouth personal appearance — with strict injunctions from Yusef to adopt every means in her power for the restoration of the unfortunate girl to sensibility, and he then rejoined his guilty companions in the larger cavern—which was placed at some distance from the one which has just been described—and they proceeded to make merry after their own fashion, on the important occasion.

In the meantime the old woman Juballah had placed the delicate form of the insensible Omelia on the bed, with more gentleness and even tenderness than could at all have been expected, and taking up the lamp she examined her features for a minute or two with much curiosity and interest, then she bustled about with much more activity than she was accustomed to do, to procure such remedies—skillfully made by herself from herbs—as she always had handy in case of

any sudden emergency, and proceeded to apply them in the proper manner, namely, by bathing the temples and hands of the unfortunate girl, and moistening her lips with a reviving draught.

The consequence of this was that the desired effect soon manifested itself, for the death-like aspect which had before marked Omelia's features suddenly changed, she breathed more freely, and her limbs which had been cold and contracted exhibited all the signs of re-action, which, in spite of her forbidding features, seemed to afford old Juballah the highest satisfaction.

The latter again bathed the poor girl's temples, and that completed her restoration to consciousness.

With a powerful effort, which it seemed almost impossible she could have made, she started up in the bed, and pressing her hand upon her aching temples, she gazed wildly and frantically around her, her brain at first being too bewildered to allow her to have any clear recollection of what had happened to her.

"Powers of mercy!" she exclaimed, in a voice of the greatest agitation and terror, "what does all this mean? Why am I here, and where am I?"

"You are in one of the secret caverns of the rebel Yusef, and his associates, young woman, and I am your attendant," answered old Juballah—whom from the position in which she stood, Omelia had not before clearly distinguished—drawing close to her.

Omelia cast a hasty glance upon the revolting old woman, and her appearance terrified her.

"Almighty Powers!" she cried, clasping her hands vehemently together, and her whole frame violently agitated with convulsive emotion, "then I am lost! lost! The miscreant Yusef has triumphed."

"He has," returned Juballah, "and no doubt he feels highly gratified."

Omelia pressed her hands upon her forehead, and groaned aloud in the intensity of her agony.

"I remember all now," she said with a wild look, in faltering accents, and shuddering all over, "I recollect the monster seizing me in his arms, and—and then my senses left me. But the unfortunate Captain Morley, oh, what became of him?"

"Killed, no doubt," replied Juballah, coolly and carelessly, "it is not likely that Yusef would take the trouble to bring him here a prisoner."

"Oh, horror!" groaned the distracted girl, and she again covered her face with her hands and abandoned herself to feelings of the most torturing anguish and despair.

But at length she suddenly started from this excessive stupor of grief, and raising herself up again hastily in the bed, she exclaimed, with frantic gestures :—

"I must not, I will not remain here, in the power of such an inhuman wretch. He shall not hold me a prisoner in his den of infamy!"

"You had much better remain quiet," returned the old woman, forcing her back in the bed with as little violence as possible; "you would find it no easy task to leave this place, I can tell you, especially when Yusef and the other mutineers are in the way. Be calm, if you can, Yusef will not annoy you with his presence at this time of the night, I dare say."

"Stanley, dear Stanley!" cried Omelia with a burst of the greatest agony, as all the horrors of her situation, and those that awaited her rushed upon her brain; "my worst fears are realised, this time at any rate, we are torn from each other for ever!"

Completely overwhelmed, she again sunk back on the bed and her senses left her.

Old Juballah took a low seat by the bed-side, and placing her large boney elbows on her knees, and resting her chin upon her hands, she watched the insensible Omelia with an interest and anxiety that, in such a strange and repulsive-looking being seemed rather remarkable.

Even her frightful features seemed to relax in their ferocity, as she remained with her eyes fixed upon her, and there was something bordering upon humanity in the expression of her countenance, as she muttered forth in low tones :—

"Poor thing, poor thing, she must not be suffered to be lost altogether!"

Strange words these, to come from the lips of that frightful-looking being, and who was supposed to be totally insensible to every feeling of humanity. How were they to be accounted for? What was it that had prompted them? Surely she must have been moved by compassion towards Omelia, and there might yet be hope.

Juballah remained in her seat by the bedside of our heroine, anxiously watching her, and our heroine continued wrapped in a kind of stupor, from which the old woman did not offer to disturb her, as she was perfectly calm.

CHAPTER CXL.

OLD JUBALLAH PROVES HERSELF A FRIEND.

While Juballah thus sat, there was a knock at the door, and guessing who the intruder was, she arose sullenly and gave admittance to the villain Yusef, who had been anxious to visit his unfortunate victim, to ascertain how she was, but a feeling of fear which even he could not conquer had restrained him till now.

He cast an anxious glance towards the curtains that concealed the bed from view, and all being so profoundly still, he could not help feeling somewhat alarmed, and eagerly demanded of the old woman :—

"How now, Juballah? What of Omelia?"

"She sleeps," replied Juballah, "and must not be disturbed."

"Has she ever been restored to consciousness?" interrogated Yusef.

"Yes," was the laconic reply.

"And was much excited, I suppose?"

"Did you expect her to be delighted?" sneered Juballah.

"Bah, you understand me. What said she of me?"

"That you were an inhuman miscreant, and she spoke the truth."

"How?" demanded Yusef, with a look of surprise.

"I say she spoke the truth," repeated the old woman, with the same stern look, "and you know it."

"Ha, ha, ha!" laughed Yusef, "what, insensible old Juballah railing against cruelty, well that is good. But I must gaze upon my future beauteous mistress while she sleeps."

"You must put off your curiosity till day-light, when she wakes," returned the old woman, abruptly, and endeavouring to prevent his approaching the bed.

"Psha," hastily ejaculated the villain, pushing her aside, and eyeing her with a look of suspicion.

Eagerly but silently he advanced, and with a hesitating hand drew aside the curtains, and gazed with feelings of the greatest admiration upon the sleeping and unconscious girl, who breathed gently, and otherwise calmly, but there was a melancholy expression about her handsome features which even the hardened miscreant Yusef could not behold without a feeling of regret and self-reproach.

For some minutes Yusef continued to contemplate his unfortunate victim with feelings of the most guilty description, and to exult at the success so far of his cruel and infamous designs, but at length he turned away, and speaking to the old woman, who had been impatiently watching him, he said :—

"You will see carefully to your charge, Juballah."

"I want no instructions," she replied, in surly but significant tones; "I shall perform my duty."

Yusef looked narrowly and suspiciously at her for a moment, then quitted the place, and the old woman followed him to the door, which she closed and bolted, and then

resumed her anxious watching by the side of the bed, apparently determined to remain up to see after her lovely charge, for the remainder of the night.

There was evidently something particular brooding in that old woman's mind, which it was not easy to understand, and Yusef did not half like her manners and observations.

"I never heard her speak in such a way before," he muttered when alone, "I have not yet thoroughly penetrated that old woman's character, and must watch her narrowly. However, she dare not attempt to play me false, even if she should be so inclined."

This thought quieted all his apprehensions, and he retired to rest, and the subterranean retreat had now become wrapped in solemn silence.

Old Juballah continued to watch by the side of the couch on which our heroine reposed with the most unremitting attention, and evinced not the least signs of sleep.

There was a strange mingled expression of pity and anxiety in that naturally repulsive countenance, which was remarkably striking, and was sufficient to convince any one who might have seen her at that moment, that beneath that rough, uncouth exterior, throbbed a heart that was not insensible to the warmest feelings of humanity.

Her eyes were never for an instant removed from the beauteous countenance of the sleeping maiden, and if she exhibited any signs of emotion, the old woman was immediately ready to render her what assistance she might require. Then she would resume her seat, and appear to await calmly the morning.

"Poor child, poor child she again ejaculated, after a long silence, and in the strange tones of kindness and compassion that have been before remarked, "how beautiful she looks in slumber. How pure, how innocent—and even I, hideous and repulsive in looks and manners as I am, can appreciate that innocence so powerfully expressed in her handsome features, and respect and revere it. And shall one so young, so lovely, and so gentle, fall a victim to the brutal and loathsome passion of the villain Yusef? No, by every power I swear that she shall not, and Juballah never yet failed to keep her oath, even at the hazard of her life. Yusef, you may flatter yourself that your triumph is all but complete. Be it my task to disappoint your guilty hopes, and to frustrate your plans; and I will do so or perish in the attempt."

The frightful features of old Juballah became unusually animated as she uttered these words, and the change that came over their expression, so wild, and kind, and gentle, even in the midst of their ugliness and repulsiveness, was most astonishing and impressive.

It seemed indeed almost impossible that such feelings could emanate from so uncouth a being, and any one who could have seen her at that time must have become lost in wonder and bewilderment.

Tranquilly our heroine continued to sleep, as though nothing particular had occurred to pain and excite her, and Juballah could not but view her composure under the most trying and extraordinary circumstances, with the greatest astonishment.

At times a smile even was on her features, and once in her sleep she murmured the name of Stanley in accents of the utmost affection, and which struck the mind of the singular old woman most forcibly.

"Some lover of her's, poor girl, I suppose," she muttered to herself, "who is presented to her imagination in her dreams. May you, maiden, quickly be restored to his arms, and it shall be no fault of mine if you are not so. 'Tis a pity that two fond and faithful hearts should be thus cruelly divided."

Again, was it possible that such sentiments as these could be expressed by that repulsive being? one whom no person, however charitably disposed, could look upon without feelings of disgust and even abhorrence. It appeared to be almost incredible, yet so it was.

There were no means of distinguishing day from night in that subterranean retreat, but Juballah imagined from the time which had elapsed since Omelia had been brought to the cavern, that it was now about the dawn of morning; and she was gratified to think that her beauteous charge had slept so long and so calmly, as she trusted that it would greatly serve to refresh her, and to give her more strength and fortitude to meet the severe trials which she would doubtless have to encounter from the miscreant Yusef, who would lose no time in attempting to put his diabolical plans into execution, now that he had her completely in his power.

While these thoughts were passing in the mind of Juballah, Omelia awoke, and raising herself up in the bed, and gazing vacantly around, appearing at first to have no recollection of where she was, what had taken place, or the dangers of her situation, but her mind still seeming to be wandering on the subject of her dreams, in a voice of the deepest emotion and affection, she said—

"Beloved Stanley, do not leave me. I cannot live but in your presence, and why, oh, why should we again be separated? Ah, he is not here—he is gone—Stanley, dearest Stanley, where are you?"

"You are at present torn from the arms of your lover, damsel," replied Juballah, in tones of gentleness and sympathy it might have been thought impossible for her to assume; "but compose yourself, live in hopes, and all may yet be well."

"Ah," exclaimed Omelia, with a look of anguish, and pressing her hands upon her forehead, at the same time gazing with a shuddering sensation of terror upon the hideous features of her singular companion, "it was then only a delusive dream. Villany has again triumphed, and Stanley and I are once more cruelly separated."

"True," returned Juballah, in a low voice and with a significant look, lest apparently what passed between them might be overheard by some one, "but do not unnecessarily alarm yourself, and endeavour to believe that your separation will not be for long."

Our heroine turned upon Juballah a look of the most unutterable astonishment, and could scarcely credit the evidence of her senses; and there was something so remarkable and so striking in the expression of the old woman's countenance as she spoke, that it completely disarmed the poor girl's breast of those terrors which her appearance had previously created.

"Those words from you, strange being," she ejaculated in a tremulous voice, and with a searching look, "do you not attempt to deceive me, and to mock my sufferings?"

"No, maiden," replied the old woman, "Juballah has no wish to do so. You know her not yet, but the time will, perhaps, speedily arrive when you will do so."

"Dare I trust the evidence of my senses?" said Omelia, looking still more narrowly at her.

"You may," returned Juballah, "for I

speak with all sincerity. My uncouth appearance no doubt alarms you?"

"I must confess," answered our heroine, timidly but candidly, "that at first it did so, but under all the painful circumstances under which I have been brought hither, it is excusable that it should do so."

"True," coincided Juballah, "and you believe that a being so frightful in appearance and repulsive in manners as myself must be totally insensible to every feeling of humanity?"

"I would charitably believe to the contrary," answered Omelia.

"I can sympathise with you in your misfortunes, maiden," said Juballah, in a low voice, and with an impressive look.

"Is it possible?'

"'Tis true. I would prove myself to be your friend."

"Oh, thanks, thanks, if you be sincere," ejaculated our heroine, fervently, and fixing upon her a look of kindness; "may I then depend upon your assistance?"

"You may," answered Juballah; "speak low, Omelia—for that I understand to be your name—lest there should be listeners. I may ere long be able to render you an essential service, and to frustrate the guilty designs of Yusef, and it is my will to do so; but I need scarcely tell you that the utmost caution will be necessary to render the success of my scheme certain. In the presence of Yusef I must appear in my usual repulsive character, in order to prevent the excitement of his suspicions, which would retard the progress of my wishes, if not defeat them altogether."

"Oh, thanks, thanks," cried Omelia, gratefully, and warmly pressing Juballah's hand, "then I may not abandon myself to complete despair?"

"No," returned Juballah, "I have given you my word, and I will not forfeit it. Gather together all the fortitude and resolution that you can, wait patiently, and ere long you may escape the dangers by which you are at present surrounded."

"But the villain Yusef," said Omelia, with a shudder, "surely he will not delay the execution of his diabolical designs, and what can I do, completely in his power as I am, to oppose him?"

"All will depend upon your firmness," replied Juballah; "but we will talk further of this at a more fitting opportunity. You had better now partake of some refreshment, of which you must stand in need."

"Oh, I cannot eat," said Omelia, "and I do not feel to want anything. Alas, my mind is too deeply occupied with gloomy and torturing thoughts, doubts, and fears to suffer me to do so. I tremble at the thought of being again insulted by the presence of the miscreant Yusef; but I fear that I shall soon behold him again, and be subjected to his bold and disgusting advances."

"No doubt he will visit you this morning," replied Juballah, "but be firm, and he will not dare to urge his odious suit at present."

"I will endeavour to be so," replied our heroine, "and again thank you for your friendly advice, and the deep interest you seem to take in me."

Juballah returned no answer, but again pressed upon Omelia to partake of some light refreshment she had prepared for her, and with which, arising from the couch, she at length complied, more to please the old woman, in whom she had found so unexpected a friend, than any inclination she possessed herself.

CHAPTER CXLI.

YUSEF'S INTERVIEW WITH OMELIA.

The repast finished, Omelia feeling somewhat more composed and confident, entered more freely into conversation with Juballah, the alteration in whose manners was most extraordinary, and who exerted herself to the utmost to dissipate those fears which naturally beset her, and to inspire her with hope. But it was not likely that the old woman could succeed only to a certain extent, although Omelia's principal anguish and anxiety of mind was for her lover, who she had every reason to believe would be driven to a state of madness and despair on discovering what had taken place, especially as he had not the slightest means of ascertaining whither she had been conveyed, or of attempting and effecting her deliverence.

From these melancholy and torturing thoughts she was suddenly aroused by the sound of approaching footsteps, and she trembled violently, for her fears too readily suggested that it was the villain whom she had so much cause to dread.

Juballah whispered in her ear, and by a look endeavoured to encourage and re-assure her, but it was impossible for her to do so, and before Omelia had sufficient time to at all recover herself, there was a loud knock at the door, which Juballah during the night had secured on the inside, and the voice of the dreaded and terrible Yusef demanded admittance.

Our heroine clung fearfully to Juballah, and looked imploringly in her face, but the former again whispered her to be firm, and gently disengaging herself from her, went to the door and opened it, and Yusef, with a bold step and a determined look, entered.

Omelia, fearing to encounter the villain's gaze, retired to the further end of the cave, and covering her face with her hands, awaited in trembling fear and suspense the result of this interview, but at the same time endeavouring to recover herself, and to muster all the resolution that she could.

"You can retire," said Yusef, in a commanding tone, and addressing himself to Juballah.

"I suppose so," said Juballah, in surly accents, and fixing a malignant look upon Yusef.

"For mercy's sake do not leave me alone with this villain," implored Omelia, approaching the old woman, and laying her hand upon her arm.

Yusef frowned, and rudely separating Juballah from his beauteous prisoner, said in the same peremptory tone as before—

"Did you not hear what I said? Retire from here, I again command you, I will recal you when your presence is required."

The old woman grumbled something between her teeth, but Yusef thrust her unceremoniously from the door, and closed it after her.

We need not attempt to describe the terror and anguish that now agitated the breast of Omelia, for the reader may imagine it, but she exerted herself to the utmost to collect herself, and to meet the villain with that firmness and determination which were so necessary to check him in his infamous designs.

Yusef, after the removal of Juballah, stood for a few minutes near the doorway, and folding his arms across his broad chest, gazed at Omelia with looks of mingled admiration and desire, but said not a word. Omelia as has been before stated, shrunk from him and averted her looks in disgust.

But at length, unable any longer to restrain the expression of his guilty thoughts, he advanced towards her, and in a voice which he attempted to make as gentle and respectful as possible, he said—

"Beauteous Omelia, with feelings of the utmost gratification and delight, I welcome you here, and—"

"Cease, daring ruffian," suddenly interrupted Omelia, and turning round upon him with a commanding attitude, and looks of the greatest indignation, and which were sufficient to abash any but one so hardened as himself; "dare not to approach me, or to insult mine ears with your odious observations. I am a woman firm in virtue and the righteousness of my cause, and will resolutely resist to the last all your villanous designs."

"Be calm, Omelia," returned Yusef, coolly, "and do not excite yourself, for it is useless. Fortune has at length favoured my wishes, you are in my power and far beyond the reach of discovery, therefore your own reason must tell you that any attempt to resist my will, must prove to be entirely futile. But why view me with such repugnance. 'Tis true that necessity compelled me to use force to convey you hither, and the violence of the passion which your matchless charms have created in my breast urged me on. Think not, however, that it is my intention to treat you with unkindness or severity, but on the contrary, it shall be my constant study to promote your happiness, to lavish upon you every affection and indulgence Of this subterranean dwelling, and the brave fellows it contains, I am the master, and you shall reign the supreme mistress. Think me not the poor despicable being you have doubtless hitherto taken me for. I have wealth at my command, and can procure every luxury that you may require, everything which might serve to contribute to your happiness. Frown not then so scornfully upon me, but endeavour to banish all false prejudice from your mind, and to return those sentiments I so ardently, so sincerely entertain for you."

What feelings of shame and resentment swelled the bosom of Omelia as she listened to this insolent and disgusting speech; at the same time she trembled with fear at the threats which his words conveyed, and when she thought of her own utter helpless situation.

"Hateful being," she at length replied, in a firm voice, "in vain do I seek for language to express the feelings of disgust and loathing which I feel towards you. Dare such a miscreant as you insult mine ears with vows of love unknown to your insensible heart? Cease, and leave me, it is Omelia the sepoy's daughter who commands, and she will be obeyed."

"These are bold words," said Yusef, "from one who is my prisoner, and at my mercy; but I make every allowance for that under the circumstances, and heed them not. Allow me, however, to inform you that I am a man who will not suffer himself to be trifled with or set at defiance, and whatever I have fixed my mind upon I will accomplish at all hazards. You have heard the avowal of my passion, and you are aware that I have the means of enforcing its indulgence. You will do well then, to think calmly and seriously upon what I have said, and for which I will give you sufficient time. But I must again endeavour to impress upon your mind the complete folly and uselessness of attempting to offer any obstinate resistance to my will, which might probably provoke me to act in a manner which I would otherwise fain avoid."

"You dare not carry your diabolical threats into execution," said Omelia, fixing upon him a look of mingled reproach and supplication; "you will not surely persist in detaining me here a prisoner?"

"Pardon me, sweet Omelia," replied Yusef, with what he intended to be an insinuating smile, "but your observations are absurd after what I have said. Think you that I should be induced to abandon all my designs and wishes after all the trouble I have taken, and now that I have succeeded in gaining possession of you? If you have even for a moment flattered yourself with such delusive, such ridiculous hopes, I would advise you at once to dismiss them from your mind, and to endeavour to meet that destiny which you cannot avoid, with calmness and resignation."

"Villain!" exclaimed the indignant Omelia, at the same time the dignified and commanding attitude she assumed, entirely corresponded with her words; "I will hear no more; but once for all do I fearlessly hurl defiance at you, and scorn and brave your base and cowardly threats. Think not to intimidate me, for I feel firm and confident. There is a power above that will ever protect the innocent from the cruel designs of the guilty, and upon that I will place my reliance."

"Yusef laughed scornfully.

"E'en do as you say," he observed, "if you will, but I am inclined to think that the expectations you have expressed will be doomed to disappointment. In what way can you help yourself? how successfully oppose my wishes? Psha! away with such ridiculous thoughts, such erroneous ideas, which can avail you not, and try to reconcile yourself to that which most assuredly awaits you. I repeat that there is nothing I will omit to do to promote your happiness—there is no indulgence which can reasonably be afforded you that shall remain ungranted; but obstinacy will only provoke violence, and enforce that which you might otherwise gracefully and prudently yield to persuasion."

"Gracious powers!" exclaimed the disgusted Omelia, "and shall I, must I longer listen to language so insulting and revolting as this? Must the blush of shame and offended modesty be thus recklessly, thus heartlessly raised in my cheek? My very soul shrinks with loathing and horror as I gaze upon you—brutal ruffian as you are—which no language however powerful could convey an adequate idea of. Begone, I say again, and leave me to myself, to my own melancholy feelings and reflections."

"You forget, Omelia," returned Yusef, coolly, "that here at present it is my place to command, your's to obey. However, I will not suffer the proud and scornful observations you have made use of to irritate me, or to remove me from the course I have resolved to pursue. I will now leave you, and would advise you to reflect maturely and dispassionately upon what I have said, and if you are wise, you will no longer hesitate to yield compliance with my wishes. In a day or two I shall expect your answer."

With these words he attempted to take her hand, and to raise it to his lips, but she hastily and forcibly withdrew it with disgust and indignation, and he probably thinking that it would not be prudent at present to persist in his bold advances, fixed upon her one look of exultation and admiration, and then abruptly quitted the place, much to the relief of Omelia.

———

CHAPTER CXLII.

MENTAL ANGUISH, AND RENEWED HOPE.

Omelia, when the villain retired, threw herself on a seat, and covering her face with her hands, abandoned herself to all the poignant anguish of her feelings,

From this, however, she was quickly aroused by the entrance of old Juballah, whom Yusef on retiring, had immediately sent to attend upon her.

Having closed and fastened the door to prevent intrusion, Juballah approached our heroine, and laying her hand gently on her arm, mentioned her name in a tone of sympathy, which could have been little expected to proceed from her.

Omelia raised her eyes, humid with tears towards her, and beheld that the rough features of the old woman were again softened by an expression of kindness and commisseration which was most extraordinary, and could not be mistaken.

"Oh, my friend," said Omelia, looking sorrowfully at her, "for such I now sincerely believe you to be, how shamefully have my feelings been outraged by the miscreant Yusef at this interview. How bold and terrible were the threats he held out to me. I cannot think of them without a shudder, whilst my bosom swells with feelings of disgust and the greatest indignation."

"Heed them not," said Juballah, in a low tone of voice, which it would have been almost impossible for any one listening to catch, "heed them not, I say, even terrible as they may sound, for he shall never have an opportunity of putting them into execution."

"Alas," sighed our heroine, with a doubtful look, "I fear that you are seeking to delude me with fallacious hopes. Completely as I am in his power, I say again, who is to prevent his carrying his brutal designs into effect, if he has made up his mind—of which there can be no doubt—to do so?"

"I can—I will," returned the old woman,

in the same low but determined tone as before; "place every confidence in me, and fear not, I have pledged my word, and I will not fail to fulfil my promise."

Omelia looked at her narrowly for a second or two, but she could perceive nothing in the expression of her countenance to excite her suspicions, and she said—

"Oh, how flattering are the hopes that you seek to excite in my breast, but when, and by what means can you expect to realise them?"

"Leave that to me, and wait patiently," replied Juballah, "with the assurance that what I have promised shall be accomplished. Were I so resolved, or there were any necessity for it, I could at one blow have the lives of Yusef, and the whole of his savage myrmidons."

Omelia shuddered.

"No, no," she said, "miscreants as they are even, I would have so wholesale a sacrifice of human life avoided, if possible. Alas, I fear that the power which the heartless ruffian Yusef possesses, will cause him too well to succeed, if providence does not interpose to prevent him."

"Alarm not yourself with such ideas and anticipations, Omelia," remarked Juballah, "for once more, I assure you, that it is my determination to frustrate his nefarious designs, and why should you any longer doubt me?"

"Believe me, Juballah," answered our heroine, "that I do not doubt the sincerity of your wishes and intentions, and most fervently do I thank you for the feelings you evince towards me, an entire stranger to you, but I fear you will not have the means to carry your generous and humane designs into effect."

"Again I enjoin you to banish such doubts and apprehensions from your mind," returned Juballah, "for what I have said I will do—I feel for you, maiden, uncouth in manners and appearance though I be, and I will sooner forfeit my existence than my word in such a cause as this."

Omelia again returned her warmest thanks to the singular being who thus took so extraordinary an interest in her fate, and she tried to become more composed and confident.

But the critical situation in which she was placed, and the threats which Yusef had uttered, notwithstanding all the hopes and promises that Juballah held out, and which she was confident it was her earnest desire to perform, would not suffer her exactly to do that, and she still continued to waver between hope and fear.

"He has given me a day or two to consider his infamous and disgusting proposal," she said; "and it is not likely that a ruffian of his desperate character, will longer defer the execution of his monstrous purpose; if then I should not be fortunate enough to escape previous to that time, it appears too fearfully to me that my fate is all but certain."

"Not so," said Juballah, positively; "the villain shall be defeated in his guilty plans at any cost, and you shall be again restored to liberty, and I trust to the arms of your lover. Old Juballah, so hateful in form and manners, and who was ever thought incapable of performing an act of humanity, finally promises you this, trust in her, Omelia, and depend upon it she will not deceive you. She has the means to execute all she has undertaken, and she will not, she cannot fail to do so."

"Generous woman," ejaculated our heroine, and her looks fully showed the feelings with which she spoke, "again am I at a loss for words to express my thanks."

"Hold," returned Juballah, hastily, "I require not thanks; "they sound unnatural and unpleasant in my ears."

"Oh, why should you take such an interest in my fate?" inquired our heroine.

"Because," replied the singular woman, "I believe you to be good and virtuous, and therefore do I respect you. Let that suffice."

"But," said Omelia, "after running such risks to serve me, you surely must abandon this place, for the vengeance of Yusef and his myrmidons would be certain to descend upon your head."

"Fear not for me, maiden," replied Juballah, "for I am fully prepared for the consequences of my conduct, and to brave everything. I defy all that the rage and malice of Yusef and his creatures can suggest. But for a time, Omelia, I must leave you."

"Oh, are you compelled to do so?" interrogated our heroine, hastily, and with a look of alarm; "I fear to be alone."

"I shall not be absent long," answered Juballah, "but in the meantime you have no cause for apprehension. You can secure the door on the inside, and then you need not fear any intrusion."

With these words Juballah quitted the place, and Omelia immediately secured the door, as she had suggested, and returned to her seat, where she abandoned herself to the variety of conflicting thoughts that naturally crowded upon her brain.

The extraordinary and unexpected conduct of old Juballah took her completely by surprise, and she could scarcely believe the evidence of her senses. That so remarkable a being, and one so unprepossessing in every respect, should thus suddenly warm towards her, a complete stranger, was most astonishing and unaccountable; yet the manner in which she had expressed herself, and the solemn promises she had made and so often reiterated, would not allow her (Omelia) for a moment to doubt the sincerity of her words, and her heart overflowed with gratitude towards her.

But, notwithstanding the confidence which Juballah had expressed, Omelia under all the peculiar and dangerous circumstances, could not but entertain a doubt as to whether she would have the power or the opportunity to accomplish her wishes, and she still entertained the greatest apprehensions as to the fate which was in store for her—unless she was rescued by some miraculous interposition of providence—especially after the threats that Yusef had held out to her, and which she was thoroughly convinced he had the brutality and the determination to carry into effect.

How she shuddered when she recalled those threats to her memory, and thus anticipated the revolting doom which too probably awaited her; and at times she was worked up to such a pitch of excitement by her fears, that she could scarcely contain herself, and gave vent to her feelings in the most melancholy lamentations.

But the situation of Stanley, and the anguish of mind she knew he must be enduring at her loss, and the uncertainty of the fate which had befallen her—for should the unfortunate Captain Morley have been murdered by the miscreants, which it was but too probable that he had, the means of her abduction, or in whose power she was, must remain involved in mystery—tortured her more than all.

She pictured to herself the complete despair of her lover at the fatal occurrence, which must so entirely have annihilated all his hopes, and that too so soon after their restoration to each other, and her heart bled for him.

"Dear Edward," she soliloquised, in mournful accents, "what a cruel destiny is that which pursues us, and from which there seems to be no possibility of our escaping. Surely it is enough to destroy the strongest fortitude, and to exhaust the greatest patience. The fates appear to have conspired against us, and to disappoint and destroy our wishes at the very time when the completion of our happiness seems all but certain. Alas, I fear that the love which was so fervently and sincerely entertained for each other is never destined to meet with its due reward, even if we should indeed ever behold each other again, and my heart sinks within me in despair."

She could not refrain from tears as these dismal and torturing thoughts occurred to her, and afforded her some relief.

She took from her bosom the affectionate letters she had at different times received from her lover—and which she had constantly carried about her—and re perused their precious contents again and again, with mingled feelings of anguish and pleasure which it is useless to attempt to describe; while every word written therein, and which breathed the purest and most ardent affection, went immediately to her heart, and made her almost imagine that her beloved Stanley himself was again speaking to her.

She was at length interrupted in the midst of her reflections by a knock at the door, and she timidly arose from her seat, and in a tremulous voice demanded who was there.

Juballah quickly answered her, and quieted all her apprehensions, and unfastening the door, she immediately admitted her, glad that she had returned.

Yusef, on leaving Omelia, retired to an obscure part of the cavern, in order that he might the better indulge his guilty thoughts without the fear of interruption.

His interview with his beauteous prisoner had been attended with no other results than he had anticipated, although he certainly did not expect to find her so collected and firm, and altogether the villain congratulated himself upon it.

He had been prepared for her scorn and expressions of abhorrence, also for her bitter reproaches, therefore they made not the slightest impression upon him, or were in any way likely to move him to relent He exulted to think he had got her securely in his power, but still, in spite of the violence of his guilty passion, he could not but shrink with a feeling of repugnance from using violence to secure the gratification of his infamous wishes if it could be avoided; and he determined to try all his powers of persuasion to induce her to yield, although with very little prospect of success. It was certain that a woman of the character of Omelia would yield her life sooner than resign her virtue, and that she would resist to the last.

"But still so fierce is the fire which she has kindled in my breast," he soliloquised, "that in spite of all hazards, all consequences, I must and will possess her, and if not by her own compliance, by force, although the latter I would fain avoid. How beautiful she is, both in form and feature, and cold and insensible that being must be who could withstand the power of her charms. The oftener I behold her, the more must I admire her; and oh, how great would be my triumph could I but win her love. Bah! away with such presumptuous thoughts; can a wretch so steeped in crime as myself ever hope to excite any other feelings but those of horror and detestation in that gentle breast, and where the envied Stanley already reigns supreme? It would be sheer madness to suppose so, and I will therefore banish such a presumptuous idea from my mind altogether."

With these words he closed his soliloquy, and hastened to rejoin Alahamed, and the rest of his associates in crime in the principal cavern

---

CHAPTER CXLIII.

THE DESPAIR OF STANLEY.

While these events were taking place, the ravages of the sanguinary rebellion continued with scarcely any diminished fury, notwithstanding the constant victories achieved by our brave officers and troops, and the great losses invariably sustained by the enemy. In fact, his power and resources seemed inexhaustible, and no sooner had force after force been dispersed, than they concentrated again, to give fresh annoyance, and to keep our soldiers constantly employed.

In fact, the suppression of the rebellion, in spite of all that had been accomplished, seemed almost as remote as ever.

The terrible Nena Sahib had completely baffled every attempt to capture him; and he having now retired from the immediate scene of action in which he had played so conspicuous a part, and which there could be no doubt was still conducted under his main direction, not the least clue could be obtained as to his whereabouts.

It was about this period that the supposed brother of the Nena (Tantia Topee) appeared upon the stage, and although in every engagement he suffered signal defeat and immense loss, he was in no way disheartened, and ever succeeded in making good his retreat, though frequently hotly pursued, and like his brother, seemed to defy every effort to destroy or to take him.

There was a strange mystery about this man, which it would have been difficult to solve, and to which the following, recently published in the different journals, and which may not prove altogether uninteresting, bears reference—

An officer in command of a cavalry regiment, who is in full pursuit of Tantia Topee and has been within four miles of him, expresses his full conviction that Tantia Topee is no other than Nena Sahib himself. The rumours of the Nena's immediate appearance were, it seems, universal just before Tantia Topee's crossing the Nerbudda, and the prisoners and deserters, of whom the officer in question had spoken with several, he being an excellent vernacular scholar, are he says, unanimous on the point that it is Nena Sahib who is dodging our columns in Central India under the name of Tantia Topee.

However improbable this may look at first sight, a little consideration will show that there are many circumstances which coincide so well with the statement as to render it, on second thoughts, most probable that it should be true. It is now several months since we had any authentic information of Nena Sahib, and it is incredible that, after having been so prominent and restless at first, he should have suddenly become completely quiescent, or would have been suffered to do so amid the perils of his party, with a lakh of rupees offered for his head. On the other hand, Tantia Topee becomes prominent just when Nena Sahib vanishes; his army is invariably styled "the army of the Peishwa;" and finally, in the Cawnpore story of the half-caste, it is stated that Miss Wheeler is not dead, but with Tantia Topee. Why with Tantia Topee? What can he have done to require such a hostage to save his life? If Tantia Topee be the Nena, there is no mystery about it; and perhaps other Europeans may turn up besides Miss Wheeler, when his pursuers overtake him. It becomes now however, doubly important that they should do so, on the presumption that their enemy is Nena Sahib in person; for if he could once reach the Deccan, and unfurl the standard of the Peishwa, it might be the signal for a new struggle of the most serious kind.

Leaving this subject for the present, however, we will resume the main thread of our narrative.

About a week had now elapsed since the abduction of Omelia, and a terrible week of mental anguish it had been to the distracted Lieutenant Stanley.

The whole of the relieved garrison, and the women and children of Lucknow had been removed from Cawnpore to Calcutta and other places where their safety might be ensured, and the regiment to which Stanley belonged had also quitted the place.

The army were now in winter quarters, and as it is our principal object to give everything of interest regarding India and the war, we think we cannot do better than to quote the following from the eloquent and graphic pen of the *Times* correspondent—

"The army is now in the full enjoyment of the Indian winter. Like all else in this east of ours, its delights have been exaggerated, and its charms viewed through the heats of summer, disordered livers, and the oriental *siroc*, have been unduly and egregiously overcoloured. In the morning, soon after sunrise, there is a cool and pleasant air, at times keen and nipping enough. This lasts, perhaps, till nine o'clock, after which it is even now a little too warm for pleasant exercise on foot or on horseback in the sun. I tried a crusty, slow-tempered thermometer with a good deal of lead in his mercury the

other day at Allahabad, and at two o'clock it declared that the sun was 125 degrees on a bank in front of the Jumna. But it is not the heat which is so unpleasant; indeed, the temperature in tents is quite bearable and often agreeable. Soon after ten o'clock the wind arises, which flutters the walls of the tent with a heavy flapping and a noise like distant reverberation of great guns. With this breeze arises the all-permeating, inquisitive, comfort-destroying dust. In feeble Oordoo the tent klassie is ordered to close the purdah, or fly which admitted light and air to your canvas house, and that individual slowly by an internal process eliminates his person, as though a mummy were enrolling itself by slow convulsions from the folds of cotton in which head, body, and foot, he has been lying under the tent eaves, and executes the be-

No. 67.

hest. But vain the effort to conceal yourself from the dust—in India at least *non sone pulvere fama*. It comes in at every chink, and in a few moments papers, clothes, and all within the tent look as if they had been at Epsom races. A fine, light coating of powdered earth and subtle sand, and Lord knows what else, sweeps over your property, and renders contact with its gritty, harsh surface most disagreeable. Even when the breeze falls away at intervals, the dust, excited by the restless activity of men, horses, camels, bullocks, elephants, goats, and sheep rises ever, and drifts over the camp. Towards evening the breeze dies away, and then there is another short but pleasant period of the day, and the sun, like a disc of burnished copper, sets in the wall of haze and smoky vapour which bounds the horizon, and the short twilight dies away in abrupt darkness; but to enjoy those scanty hours one must ride miles away from camp. It seems as though you never can reach the limits of the wide circle in which camp followers are swarming morning and evening, shovelling up the dust with their spiky-toed, turned up slippers, as though they liked it. There they are, before and behind, and on each side of you, driving bullocks to or from water, cutting grass, drawing water, cooking, lighting fires, guarding elephants and camels on the feed, or washing themselves in the dirty ponds of stagnant water, their tents of all shapes and sizes and colours, from the regulation "pull" to a piece of cloth or cotton stretched over a stick, placed across two posts, which enclose the camp like the suburbs of some great city, and the tumult of voices is like that which rises from a huge fair when the sun is at its highest. Towards evening, when each man of those thousands lights his individual fire to cook his meal, the smoke ascending from the ground till it is beyond the influence of the fires, hangs in a well-defined mass, with a smooth horizontal line bounding its upper surface for miles over the ground like a dense low lying rain cloud. As to the ground itself no plain or desert in Arabia could look more barren than the soil which is trodden under so many feet, but all around us the dense masses of rich green foilage, the trees in every field, and the dim fretted outline of groves which hem the horizon show the fertility of the soil, which is evinced by the tall crops of coarse grain with which Oude is at present densely covered. Those crops or fields of corn (cates as they are called in Anglo-Indian speech) are excessively rich, varying in height from five to seven or eight feet, very close and thick, impassable to cavalry, difficult for infantry, and admirably adapted to afford cover to a fugitive enemy. Look out on the plain outside the camp, and you see fields of those cereals, interspersed with square patches of sandy soil of a pale yellowish dun colour. In each field of growing crops there is a rude platform, on which sits patiently some man or boy all day to frighten away the birds by loud cries, or the animals by hurling stones against them. No fence or boundary hedge is visible; a line of hard-baked earth, a few inches high, is the mark which divides one man's land from that of another. Clumps of trees dot the landscape, dark, dense, thick-stemmed, underneath which repose wearied animals and men. The crops are gloriously green, but it is strange to see all this greenness springing out of a bare barren-looking sand. Grass there is none—no rich sward refreshes the eye, and up to the very edge of the cates there is still the sand. Of the fields which are not bearing crops now, many

shine in the sun almost like a glass, and on looking at the surface you see that it is plastered smoth and slab. The process by which this is effected, may be seen going on all over the country. It is simple; a log of wood with a fine surface planed smooth is fastened to one or two oxen, a man holding on by the tail of one of the animals, or balancing himself, stands upright on this log and drives the cattle over the moistened surface of the field beneath which the young seed is lying. If long after the rains the soil is dry, water is sprinkled by hand, and the same process effected. The ploughing is more primitive—a mere scratching with a big pin fastened to two small oxen. Although there is no great reason to dread attack, all military precautions are observed, and our pickets may be seen in distant topes around. The British subaltern on his pony is pretty sure to fill up a proportion of the part of the landscape devoted to animated nature, but far and wide, through field, and lea, and swamp, in jeel or forest, are spread the inevitable camp followers—those locusts whom nothing blights save peace with its blessed canker."

But the mind of Stanley was too much distracted by the calamity which had so unexpectedly befallen him, to heed any of the annoyances and inconveniences described above, and ever since it had occurred he had been in a state bordering upon madness, and he could not admit of one ray of hope or consolation; he firmly believing that now his beloved Omelia had at last fallen into the hands of so merciless a wretch as Yusef, her fate was sealed, and that he should never behold her again, or if he did it would only be as a ruined and degraded being, which fate he knew it was impossible that she could long survive.

This thought was horrible and insupportable, and he abandoned himself entirely to all the agony of despair, and became so ill that it was necessary he should have the attendance of one of the surgeons of the regiment.

The cruel fate of Omelia excited the deepest sympathy amongst all who knew her, and it would have caused much gratification, if she could have been rescued, and the villain who held her in his clutches could have been discovered, and brought to that punishment which his crimes so justly merited, but of that there appeared to be not the slightest probability.

Captain Morley, although still very weak, was fast recovering from the injuries he had received, and he seized every opportunity of being with the unfortunate Stanley, and endeavouring to impart to him all the consolation he could, but with very little if any effect.

"I dare not hope," he would say, in the most mournful accents, "it would be madness to do so. It is now but too certain that she is lost to me for ever, and that her destruction will be accomplished by the atrocious miscreant in whose power she is. Talk not then to me of calmness and consolation with those maddening thoughts upon my brain? Oh, Omelia, poor suffering girl, that such should be your dreadful fate, and after all the severe trials you have already undergone, and with such unexampled fortitude. But it is my thoughtlessness and imprudence which has been the principal cause of this, by exposing you to such unnecessary danger—why did I suffer you to meet me in the old temple, instead of visiting you where you were residing in safety with your friends?"

"It certainly would have been better had you done the latter," observed Captain Morley, "but still you must not reproach yourself so severely, for it was impossible for any one to foresee what has so fatally happened."

Thus did Captain Morley exert himself in the most praiseworthy manner to ameliorate his young friend's anguish of mind, and to banish his despair, and in which task he was ably assisted by Abdal—whose deep sorrow at the loss of Omelia may be imagined—but their united efforts failed to have the desired effect.

CHAPTER CXLIV.

JUBALLAH MATURES HER PLANS.

Tediously wore away the hours with Omelia in the cavern, although Juballah—who in her presence had entirely divested herself of her repulsive manners, and become quite a different being—exerted herself to the utmost to divert her thoughts from the melancholy and torturing subjects that engrossed them.

Omelia fully appreciated the kind feelings and motives of the singular old woman, and felt grateful for them, but it was not to be expected that she could regain much composure under all the painful and alarming circumstances in which she was placed, and especially so soon after the hateful interview with the dreaded scoundrel who held her in his power.

Juballah's observations and solemn promises had indeed imparted to her some small portion of hope and consolation, but when she considered the immense difficulties by which any attempt to escape must be surrounded, she could not but doubt the power of Juballah to surmount them, notwithstanding the confidence she had expressed, and her heart again sunk within her, and the

most torturing fears and misgivings again beset her mind.

"You are still sad, maiden," remarked Juballah, in a tone of sympathy, and after she had been gazing earnestly at her for some time, "still desponding and anticipating the worst. I wish that I could banish those torturing fears, and arose you from this lethargy of despair."

Omelia started at the language which the old woman uttered, and could hardly believe that it had escaped the lips of one apparently so brutal and uncultivated.

"Oh, well do I appreciate your generous and kindly feelings towards me, Juballah," she said, "and most warmly do I tender you my thanks for what I firmly believe to be your earnest commiseration; but, alas, when I contemplate all the miseries of my untoward fate, and the dangers by which I am surrounded, and which threaten every hour to overwhelm me, is it possible that I can be otherwise than wretched?"

"You have a sincere friend in me," returned Juballah, "one who has made no promises that she is not able and determined to perform, and therefore let that satisfy you, and inspire you with confidence. The nefarious and infamous designs of the villain Yusef—however much he may flatter himself on the certainty of their success—shall be defeated, and here I am ready to swear it, if necessary."

"Oh," replied our heroine, pressing her hand, "I do not for a moment doubt the sincerity of your intentions, and your earnest anxiety to carry them into effect, but at the same time it is impossible for me to blind my eyes to the fearful obstacles that are thrown in your way, and the great risk you will have to run in making the attempt."

"Let not that thought trouble you," said the old woman, "for there is no necessity for it. Set your mind at rest, my plans are so well formed as to render their failure impossible."

"How mean you?" eagerly inquired our heroine.

Juballah drew her to the back of the cave, and then, almost in a whisper, said—

"Speak low, Omelia, for should our observations reach the ears of any of the rebels, I need scarcely remind you what the consequences would be. Behold!—this offers the safe key to liberty."

As she spoke, she drew forth a small phial containing a greenish-looking liquid, and which she held up to the eyes of Omelia, with a look of satisfaction.

"Poison!" gasped forth our heroine, in a whisper, and shuddering.

"No," replied Juballah, in the same under tone; "it is a powerful drug, which I intend to mix secretly with their drink, previous to their going to their usual nightly carousals, at the earliest opportunity. It will have the effect of throwing them into a deep stupor, from which they will not recover for some time, and before they do, I shall be sure to have conducted you in safety from the cavern. What think you of my scheme, maiden?"

"That it is excellent," replied Omelia; "and I thank you for the humane and disinterested motive that has prompted it."

"You will now perceive," continued Juballah, "that there is not so much difficulty about the execution of my designs as you at first seemed to imagine, and they are certain to succeed."

"Oh, may your predictions be fulfilled," ejaculated Omelia, fervently.

"They cannot fail to be," said the old woman, positively.

"And when do you propose to make the attempt?" inquired Omelia.

"Probably to-morrow night," answered Juballah; "at any rate, I will make no more delay than I can help, therefore hold yourself in readiness."

"Oh, with what anxiety, what mingled hopes and fears shall I await the important occasion," said our heroine; "but, alas, before you have the opportunity of making the attempt may not the miscreant Yusef persist in the accomplishment of his diabolical and revolting designs, and what power can I possess to resist him?"

"Do not thus torture yourself by anticipating the worst," replied Juballah, with an encouraging look, "for I assure you, and I do so with every confidence, that your fears will not be realised. When you see Yusef again, which you will probably do to-morrow, you have only to act with all the firmness you can call to your command, and he will not dare to persist in enforcing the gratification of his guilty wishes. Delay is our principal desire as regards the designs of that villain, and that obtained, there is no occasion to fear the result."

Omelia again returned her thanks for the deep, and evidently earnest interest she took in her fate, and after all she had said, she could not help feeling her spirits revive, and to be inspired with hope.

And thus the remainder of the day passed over, and night approached without anything more occurring to alarm her, and by degrees she became somewhat more tranquillised.

Omelia retired to rest at an early hour, all being quiet in the principal cavern where the rebels always assembled, and Juballah having secured the door from all intruders, also stretched her limbs upon a mat on the floor, at the foot of Omelia's couch, and soon appeared to sleep soundly.

But the thoughts of our heroine, as might be expected, were too busy to allow her for some time to seek the influence of the drowsy god, and she continued to indulge them with various feelings.

The plans of Juballah, however, were so feasible, that she could not help feeling more sanguine in her hopes and expectations, and she could not be, she thought, sufficiently grateful to providence for so unexpectedly raising her up such a friend in the hour of her greatest need. That she was sincere in offers and promises, Omelia could not for an instant doubt, for what motive or interest could she have in deceiving her, or in seeking to flatter her with false and delusive hopes? and there was that about her manner and the way in which she expressed herself that was quite sufficient to disarm suspicion.

And should those well-laid plans succeed —as they seemed so likely from what Juballah had said to do—and she should be restored to liberty, how could she retrace her steps to the place where she had left her faithful and beloved Stanley and those friends from whom she had experienced so much kindness since she had been acquainted with them, without some one to direct her, for Juballah, from what she had intimated, did not intend to accompany her? To what further dangers might she not be exposed? She almost shrunk from the idea of them.

But the hope of escaping from the fate with which she was at present threatened, completely superseded every other consideration, and to the accomplishment of that one important object, she endeavoured to devote her whole thoughts and energies.

But oh, how terrible, she reflected, must be the agony and suspense that Stanley was now enduring? What might not have happened to him since the fatal night of her seizure? She trembled to conjecture.

The shock of the dreadful intelligence might have been too great for him, when it should reach his ears, and he might even now be in a worse situation if possible than herself.

This idea tortured her, and she tried in vain for some time to dismiss it, and then she could not do so entirely.

She dreaded her second interview with Yusef which she had no doubt would take place on the following day, for she felt certain that he would urge his hateful and disgusting passion with the most unrelenting perseverance, and even proceed to the violence he had threatened, if she did not yield compliance with his guilty wishes; but still she resolved not to be easily daunted, but to act with firmness and determination, which might probably have the effect of aweing him into forbearance, and thus by delay might furnish Juballah that opportunity of putting her schemes into operation, which she at present so anxiously looked for.

This thought quieted her apprehensions and misgivings, and shortly afterwards she sunk off into a calm and comfortable sleep.

CHAPTER CXLV.

THE NIGHT OF ADVENTURE.

Omelia did not awake until a late hour on the following morning, and then felt much refreshed both in health and spirits which was fully shown by the expression of her features, which were much more animated than they had been for some time previously, while her eyes might be said occasionally, as fond hopes suggested themselves to her, to sparkle with vivacity.

The old woman Juballah had been awake some time, and had prepared the morning repast, of which she now invited Omelia to partake.

She expressed her satisfaction at the change which had taken place in our heroine's looks, and sought to keep up her spirits, and to encourage her hopes by every means in her power, and in which she succeeded much better than her most sanguine expectations had led her to anticipate.

Omelia anxiously inquired whether Yusef and his associates were in the cavern, to which Juballah replied in the affirmative, and that the former, whom she (Juballah) had seen, had made the most anxious inquiries after our heroine, which she had answered in the way that best suited her purpose, and with he appeared to be satisfied.

"Think you that he will visit me again to-day?" asked Omelia.

"It is impossible for me to say," replied Juballah, "but I think it is not at all unlikely that he will, and you had better, therefore be prepared for it."

"Alas," ejaculated Omelia, with a look of emotion, "I tremble to think of what may be the consequences of that dreaded meeting. Are there no means of avoiding it?"

"None," answered Juballah; "Yusef will not be denied, and it might be dangerous to excite his anger by doing so. But all, as I have repeatedly told you, depends upon the determination of your own conduct, by which you may awe him into forbearance. I have so managed by re-assuming my usual uncouth manners before him, as to drown any suspicions that might otherwise have been excited in his guilty breast against me. This night, if possible, I will put my designs into execution."

"This night?"

"Aye, if fortune does not frown upon me, and my hopes are most sanguine as to the result."

"Oh, may providence aid us in that on which the future happiness of myself and he who is far more precious to me than mine own existence," ejaculated Omelia, fervently, while her bosom swelled with the feelings that so powerfully agitated it at that moment. "But to you, Juballah, to whom I am a stranger, and have no more than a common claim on your humanity, I feel that I shall owe a lasting debt of gratitude for the risks you seem resolved to run to serve me. Oh, why should I expose you to such danger?"

"Talk not thus," returned the mysterious woman, "for old Juballah is a stranger to such words, and they suit her not; few have been the good actions that she has performed in her life, that she should take credit to herself for this one. Let it suffice that I seek to serve you with a free and hearty good will, and I know not what it is that so strongly urges me to do so."

"Strange woman," observed our heroine, "looking at her with amazement, "I am at a complete loss to understand you—in vain do I endeavour to penetrate your character."

"I know it not myself," replied Juballah, with a curious expression of countenance, "so it would indeed be strange if any one else could understand it. But enough of this; my object now is to prepare yourself for your departure from these caverns, which will in all probability take place this night, as I have before said."

"This night?" repeated Omelia, with a look of incredulity, "so soon?"

"Yes, I trust so," replied Juballah, "that is if no accident occur to prevent it. When the potent drug which I intend to mix with their drink shall have taken the desired effect, and steeped their senses in a deathlike sleep, which will last for hours, I can conduct you from the cavern without any fear of danger or interruption, and once again at liberty, if you exert yourself, you may soon get far beyond the reach of pursuit."

"But surely you will be the companion of my flight?" said Omelia.

"Once for all I answer in the negative," returned Juballah, possitively, "the task I have allotted to myself once accomplished, our connexion ceases, and we shall see each other no more."

Our heroine looked at her with increased astonishment, and scarcely knew what to say, and as Juballah evidently did not wish to pursue the subject further, she made no other allusion to it.

Having partaken sparingly of the repast which Juballah had spread before her, Omelia endeavoured to gain all that firmness and composure of which she stood so much in need, and succeeded in a great measure, so that she was enabled to enter more freely into conversation with Juballah, which the latter did not seek to avoid, and thus the morning passed away without anything occurring to interrupt or annoy her, and her spirits greatly revived.

All too was pretty quiet in the large cavern, and Omelia began to hope that she should not receive any visit from Yusef that day, but alas, she was doomed to disappointment, for towards the afternoon she heard footsteps, and her fears too readily suggested the painful trial to which she was again about to be subjected.

She clung fearfully to the old woman, who by a look endeavoured to encourage and reassure her.

"He comes," she said, in a tremulous voice, "the villain comes;—again must mine ears be insulted by him, and my feelings outraged. How torturing is the thought."

"Be firm," said Juballah, "meet the villain's bold advances with determination, as I have before frequently advised you, and all will be well."

Before Omelia had time to make any reply, there was a knock at the door, and the coarse voice of the dreaded Yusef demanded admittance.

Our heroine retired as she had done on the previous occasion to the further end of the room, and Juballah unfastening the door in obedience to the peremptory demand of Yusef, admitted him.

He motioned the old woman to leave the place, without saying a word, and with a surly look she suddenly obeyed, and the villain and his intended victim were again left together.

Omelia struggled with the emotions that naturally agitated her, and she quickly so far conquered them as to await the observations of Yusef with the most perfect coolness and resolution.

She had not to wait long, for Yusef after remaining silent for a few seconds, and gazing at her with the same guilty passions that always influenced his breast whenever he beheld her, he approached the spot where she was standing, in a suppliant attitude, and said—

"Has the lovely, but too cold and scornful Omelia, condescended to bestow a thought on the important subject which I left her to consider at our former meeting?"

"The only thoughts Omelia has deigned to bestow on the shameless villain Yusef's brutal proposition," she replied, firmly and haughtily, and at the same time fixing upon her persecutor a look of the most withering hatred, "are those of the most unmitigated disgust and abhorrence;—and now that you are present, presumptuous miscreant, I repeat to you my proud and firm defiance of your monstrous threats, and to demand my instant restoration to liberty."

"Ha, ha, ha!",—laughed Yusef, scornfully, at the same time he grasped the wrist of the maiden rather roughly, and fixed upon her a savage and sarcastic look; "this mock heroism and scornful bearing is most amusing, especially when I know you are so powerless to resist my will. Beware, girl, lest you provoke one to violence;—it is not by words such as those you have just now uttered, that you can win me to forbearance. More gentle language might have its due effect, e'en on the stubborn heart of Yusef."

"Gentle language to a heartless ruffian like you," returned Omelia, losing none of her firmness; it would be a bitter mockery, and I scorn to use it."

"Remember," said Yusef, "that you are my prisoner, entirely at my will and pleasure, without any one to assist you, and that this instant could, I enforce the accomplishment of my wishes. Of what use then, is this haughty defiance, and obstinate opposition? My determination, I again tell you, is fixed, and sooner or later you must yield to my desires. But away with this folly, beauteous Omelia, and listen to the voice of reason;—I would win you with the soft words of persuasion, and not those of menace and intimidation; for I love you with a passion ardent as it is sincere, and which nothing can ever extinguish in my breast. Nay, frown not, for frowns but ill become those lovely features. Conquer the feelings of hatred you have expressed towards me, and learn to view me with respect, if you cannot with affection."

It would be impossible properly to describe the emotions of shame and indignation that agitated the breast of Omelia, as the villain Yusef thus boldly expressed himself, and for a few moments she was unable to speak, but she still maintained her fortitude, and felt confident that she should ultimately be able to defeat his infamous designs.

"Daring ruffian," she at length exclaimed, "and must I be compelled to listen to words that can create no other feeling but one of horror and detestation in my mind? Must every feeling of my nature be thus wantonly and brutally outraged? Begone—leave me, for the sight of you is odious to my eyes, and your conduct cannot but excite my utmost abhorrence and resentment. You may think that at present you triumph, but beware, the time will come, and that probably much sooner than you expect, when you will have bitter cause to repent this monstrous conduct, and when a terrible retribution will most assuredly overtake you."

Yusef again laughed scornfully.

"Believe me, Omelia," he replied, "that words like those you have just now spoken, I heed not, for they are even beneath contempt. I await your answer to my proposals."

"You have it already;" returned our heroine, resolutely, "let that suffice."

"Beware, beware; decide not hastily, for for you know not what the consequences will be, if you remain obdurate."

"I will brave them all, confident that a just Providence will protect me."

"If that be your only dependence;" said Yusef, coolly, "you will find it but a weak one methinks. What should prevent me, even this instant from carrying my designs into execution?"

Omelia felt too terribly the force and truth of this, and she shuddered, although she endeavoured to conceal the real agitation and terror of her feelings from the keen observation of Yusef, who continued to feast his eyes with looks of admiration upon her.

"Yusef," at last observed our heroine, thinking it prudent under all the circumstances, to abate somewhat the severity of her manner;—"surely, hardened in guilt although I know you to be, you cannot be so entirely insensible to every feeling of humanity, as to seek to take an unmanly advantage over a weak defenseless female, whom accident has placed in your power and at your mercy. I now condescend to supplicate your forbearance, and not to urge your guilty passion to an extent which might ultimately expose you to consequences of which you can now form but little conception."

"The consequences to which you allude," he returned, "I defy and despise; but to you the sincerity of the sentiment with which your matchless charms have inspired me, I am ready to yield to your solicitations, notwithstanding that delay is so tiring to my patience, and to defer the enforcement of my wishes for two days longer, so that you may again have time calmly and reasonably to reflect upon what I have said, and come to a prudent decision. But remember, that is the utmost time that I will wait, and that on the answer you then return me, your fate most certainly depends. With these observations I now leave you."

What a relief were these words to Omelia, for in them she read deliverence, that was if the designs of Juballah failed not;—but she was unable to return any answer, and Yusef having raised her hand to his lips, which she had not the power to prevent, quitted the cave, and Omelia sunk on her knees and fervantly returned her thanks to Providence for having thus far so mercifully protected her.

Old Juballah now returned;—she had been listening attentively outside the door to all that had taken place between Yusef and Omelia, and she now congratulated the latter upon the favourable result of the interview.

"We triumph," she remarked in a low and cautious voice, after she had closed the door;

"I cannot sufficiently admire the prudence of your conduct. This delay will ensure success."

"Oh, may your expectations not be doomto disappointment," said Omelia, "if so I may again ere long hope to be restored to the arms of Stanley, who I am fully satisfied must be distracted at my loss."

"Fear not but you will," replied the old woman, with a look of encouragement

"Blissful thought," ejaculated Omelia, her eyes sparkling with renewed lustre as she spoke, "should providence permit it to be realised, I shall be happy. Oh, with what anxiety shall I await the time when we shall make the attempt to put our wishes into execution."

"You will not have to wait long," said Juballah; "to night, I repeat, should no accident occur to prevent it, the important business shall be disposed of. I will watch the opportunity, when Yusef and the others are out of the way, to mix the drug with their usual drink, arack, to which I can obtain easy access, and then no sooner shall they have commenced their night's drunken carouse, their senses will be steeped in a death like torpor, as I have said before, and I can conduct you from these caverns in perfect safety."

"Your plan possesses all the elements of succes, but," she added, with a penetrating and suspicious look, "do you state positively that it is only an opiate you intend to mix with their drink?"

"Do you doubt my word," returned Juballah, with a half angry look.

"I do not wish to do so, still I have a horror at the thought of murder, even guilty as those ruffians are."

"It would not be murder to take the lives of wretches who have been guilty of every atrocity," observed Juballah, "and for my own part, I would not hesitate to do it. But that is not now my intention, as there is no necessity for it. I have spoken the truth, so you need not be under any further apprehension on that subject."

"I am satisfied, and will place every confidence in you."

"You may do so with safety; I will not deceive you," said Juballah.

"I do believe you," observed Omelia, "and cannot but look forward to the result of this adventure with every hope. I feel most sensibly the gratitude I owe to providence, which has hitherto so mercifully watched over me, and given me strength and fortitude to resist and that successfully the daring and revolting advances of the villain Yusef, and thus obtained that delay which was necessary for the accomplishment of our plans."

"True," coincided the old woman, "and

again I commend your conduct, which was marked by firmness and decision, and was all that I desired it to be. But there is one thing I wish to ask you."

"Name it," said Omelia.

"Have you any money?"

"None."

"You will need it."

"True," returned Omelia, "but only let me escape from this fearful place, and I shall be prepared to brave every obstacle that may present itself.

"Money will be indispensable to you, as you know not what you may have to encounter," said Juballah, "and you must not be without it; here is a purse, it contains sufficient to supply your necessities for some time to come, take it, and care not by what means I have obtained it, though it may satisfy you to know that no one but the guilty will have to suffer the loss of it."

Omelia reluctantly took the purse, which was well filled, and her heart overflowed with gratitude towards that singular being from whom she had but little right to expect such extraordinary generosity and disinterested kindness.

"Excellent woman," she could not help exclaiming in the excitement of her feelings, "I am lost in wonder and admiration of your character, and again would I express to you most enthusiastically my gratitude, but cannot find words sufficient to do so."

"Cease, maiden," said Juballah, impatiently, "once for all I tell you that I am unused to and dislike flattery. If I can accomplish what I have undertaken to do, and of that I cannot entertain the least doubt, I shall feel myself fully satisfied. But we had better drop all further allusion to the subject for the present, for I hear Yusef and his companions moving about in the outer cavern, and we might be overheard."

To this Omelia agreed, and they immediately proceeded to talk on different subjects in order should any of the ruffians have the curiosity to listen, that no suspicion might be excited.

And thus the hours, to Omelia, wore rather slowly and tediously away, and she awaited with all the impatience and anxiety that might have been expected the arrival of that event upon the result of which her fate depended, and of the success of which Juballah had expressed so much confidence, that it had inspired our heroine with the most sanguine feelings of hope.

Still Omelia could not help entertaining some sad misgivings as regarded Stanley, of whose anguish and despair she could form so just and painful an idea; and she feared that something would occur to prevent their

meeting again. in which case, liberty would be valueless to her, and indeed life itself would become an insupportable burthen to her.

She tried hard to dismiss those torturing and melancholy thoughts from her mind, but she had some difficulty in doing so, and as the time elapsed her anxiety and agitation increased.

Yusef and the other ruffians still remained in the cavern, and their loud laughter frequently reached Omelia's ears, and excited feelings of the greatest uneasiness in her breast, which Juballah, however, tried to dissipate.

"They will probably shortly leave the cavern," she remarked, "and then to commence my task."

"But if the villians retire from the cavern," said Omelia, "what can there be to prevent my departing without any further trouble?"

"There would be every danger in doing so," replied the old woman.

"How so?" interrogated our heroine, "some of them might be lurking about the entrance to the cavern;" said Juballah, "in which case I need not tell you what the consequences would be. The plan I have formed is the only safe one, and must not be deviated from."

"Be it so," returned Omelia, "I will offer no further observations upon the subject, but leave everything to you Juballah."

"Do so," said the latter, "and fear not."

Omelia felt more composed, but still listened with some degree of uneasiness to the coarse voices of Yusef and his associates in crime, the more especially as once or twice she fancied she heard her name mentioned in not the most delicate or respectful manner.

However, their voices at length ceased, and Omelia, much to her relief and gratification, could hear the sound of their footsteps as they apparently retired from the cavern.

CHAPTER CXLVI.

THE ESCAPE.

Juballah and Omelia both listened attentively till the last sound died away, and then the former silently opening the door, looked cautiously out.

"All right," she remarked, "they have all quitted the cavern which is something very unusual. Now to my work. Remain you here Omelia, and fear not."

In spite of all, however, our heroine could not help trembling, and she remained at the

door, determined to watch the conduct of Juballah.

The old woman first proceeded to every corner of the cave cautiously, and listened attentively, and having apparently satisfied herself that there was no one near to observe her, she moved to one side of the cavern in which there was a kind of recess, and Omelia stepping a few paces from the door with the table lamp in her hand, watched the actions of the old woman narrowly.

Juballah took from a shelf in the recess a couple of large bottles or flasks, into which she emptied the contents of the phial, then returned them to the place from whence she had removed them, and approached our heroine with a look of satisfaction depicted in her countenance.

"'Tis well," she observed, "that part of

No. 68.

my task is accomplished, and now my success I know, is certain."

"I cannot still help thinking, Juballah," said Omelia, "that we might now with safety quit the cavern."

"No," said the old woman in reply, "it would be the height of folly and imprudence to run the risk; I tell you again that some of the ruffians are almost sure to be lurking near the entrance to the cavern. It will be better to adhere strictly to my designs, and then there will be no danger to apprehend, but I repeat that our success will be certain."

"Pardon me," said Omelia, "for my suggestions, and interference with the arrangement of your schemes; I will say no more than that I leave everything to you, and place the most implicit confidence in the honesty of your motives and intentions."

"It is not for me, perhaps, to speak thus of myself," replied the old woman, "but I again assure you that any confidence you may repose in my integrity will not be abused. Let that once for all satisfy you, and say no more upon the subject. I have some further business to transact in the cavern, so for a short time I will again leave you."

Omelia once more looked her thanks to the old woman, and the latter then quitted the place and closed the door after her.

How multifarious were the reflections which arose upon the mind of our heroine, when thus again left to herself, how sanguine were the hopes she could not help indulging in, but which at the same time, notwithstanding all that Juballah had said, and the firm reliance she placed in her sincerity were not unmingled with occasional doubts and fears. The prospect of deliverance from the revolting fate with which she was threatened, was so sudden and unexpected, that it was no wonder she could scarcely bring herself to believe it, and then the interest that so singular and savage a being as Juballah took in her fate, was even more extraordinary and perplexing.

But if all should even succeed, and she should shortly again find herself at liberty, during the time that had elapsed since her abduction, what might not have happened to her faithful and beloved Stanley, driven to distraction as he most unquestionably must have been at her loss, and especially if he should be able to ascertain into whose hands she had fallen? She shuddered to think, and, in spite of all her efforts to the contrary, she could not help again giving way to the most gloomy forebodings, and for which indeed, to her imagination there seemed to be every cause.

Then again—and that indeed appeared to her most likely—the soldiers might have quitted Cawnpore, and her and Stanley might be consequently separated for an indefinite period, if, in fact, they should ever meet again; and that idea was so improbable that it tortured her more than all.

Most fervently she prayed that her fears and misgivings might not be realised, and then she did indeed feel more composed, and looked forward to the result of this adventure with the most sanguine hopes and expectations.

Juballah was not absent long, and on her return she seemed in unusual spirits, and talked more freely to Omelia than she had hitherto done.

Our heroine could not help thinking that she had been partaking of some intoxicating drink, but she did not feel at all surprised at that, as she knew that she must require some stimulant to enable her to perform the dangerous and difficult task she had imposed upon herself.

Night approached, and still Yusef and the other rebels returned not, and Omelia, could not help again thinking, as she had suggested to Juballah, that it was folly to await the return of the ruffians when it appeared to her that they really had the opportunity of departing now unmolested. But she forebore to say anything more to the old woman upon that point, after the positive manner in which she had declared herself, and awaited anxiously the arrival of the important event on which her fate entirely depended, for that Yusef would defer the enforcement of his diabolical designs longer than the time he had threatened, she could not for a moment believe.

At length they heard the usual signal of the rebels, and that was sufficient to convince Omelia that one or more of the villains had been left behind to admit them on their return, for Juballah had informed her that, for some reason or another, that was a duty she was never permitted to perform.

Our heroine trembled, and again, in spite of all her efforts to subdue them, the most torturing misgivings assailed her, but which she endeavoured to conceal from Juballah.

"Recline on the couch, and feign sleep," said the old woman, "it may be necessary to favour our plans."

Omelia made no reply, but immediately complied with Juballah's request, who directly retired, in order to meet Yusef and his infamous associates.

The critical moment was now rapidly approaching, and the mind of Omelia, as might be expected, was in the greatest state of agitation, and which she found it impossible, under all the circumstances, to conquer.

Juballah had closed the door after her on retiring, but the quick ear of Omelia could catch every word that passed in the outer cavern, and she listened with the greatest attention.

"How now, Juballah, how fares your charge?" she heard Yusef demand.

"As badly as you might expect under the circumstances," replied the old woman, "she has been much excited during your absence."

"I must see her," said Yusef, "and endeavour to restore her to composure by gentle and persuasive means"

"Hold," returned Juballah, in a determined tone, "after becoming exhausted by the power of her emotions, she has sunk off to sleep, and must not be disturbed. Of that you can convince yourself, if you please," she added in louder accents, evidently with the wish that Omelia might hear her.

Omelia closed her eyes, and feigned to be in a sound sleep, as Juballah had enjoined her, as she heard Yusef approach the door, which Juballah opened, but she could not help trembling as the villain advanced towards the couch on which she was reclining, and drew aside the curtains.

With feelings of admiration and the most guilty passions raging within his breast, Yusef gazed at her in silence for a few moments, then stooping down, he dared to pollute her cheek with his odious kisses, need we say how much to the disgust of the apparently sleeping maiden, who, however, was compelled to stifle her feelings.

"Forbear," said Juballah, grasping his wrist, and forcing him away; "should you arouse her from her present slumber, there is no knowing what the consequences might be. Cannot you restrain your passions even for a brief period?"

"Right, right, Juballah," he replied, "I must e'en follow your advice. Pay every attention to her, and endeavour to allay her fears."

Juballah returned no answer, and Yusef, again retired, much to the relief of Omelia, who was about to leave the couch, when Juballah with a significant look prevented her, and then whispered in her ear—

"You must remain as you are for the present, for the utmost caution is now necessary. They will commence their carousals shortly, no doubt, and then the powerful drug which I have mixed with their drink will not fail quickly to have its due effect. Be firm, be patient."

The looks of our heroine were quite sufficient to convince the old woman that she would be so, and they then conversed but little, and that only in whispers.

For some time the rebels remained pretty quiet in the large cavern, and Omelia began to fear that old Juballah would be disappointed in her expectations as to their indulging in their carousals that evening, in which case all chance of their being able to put their designs into execution would be at an end.

These doubts were, however, very shortly removed, by the loud laughter of the ruffians with every now and then a ribald jest saluting her ears.

"They have commenced," whispered Juballah, "with a look of satisfaction, "and in a short time a deep stupor will steep their senses. Be calm, maiden, for the important moment approaches."

"Oh, yes, yes," eagerly replied Omelia, "I will at least endeavour to be so. Oh, would that it were over."

The noise of Yusef and his companions, however, continued for some time longer, and Omelia began to fear that the drug, notwithstanding what Juballah had said of it, would fail to have the desired effect.

All doubts upon the subject were quickly destroyed, the voices became less loud in their tone; that of Yusef could not be heard at all, and gradually they ceased altogether, and a profound silence succeeded to the riotous noise that had previously prevailed.

Juballah listened for a few moments attentively, before she ventured to ascertain the truth of her conjectures, and then approaching our heroine—who had risen from the couch, in the greatest anxiety and impatience—she said in the same low and cautious tones—

"'Tis well, they are now under the influence of the drug, from the effects of which they will not recover for some hours, when you will be far beyond the reach of pursuit I have no doubt. I can now conduct you from the cave in safety. But first let me make sure that there is no one at the entrance on the look out. Remain here till I return—which will be in a few minutes—without fear."

As the old woman thus spoke she approached the door, and Omelia cautiously followed her, and with trembling anxiety, for she was curious to see whether the drug had taken the effect which Juballah expected.

The latter silently opened the door, and stepped in the outer cave, of which our heroine was enabled to obtain an uninterrupted view, and the scene which her eyes encountered was curious in the extreme.

The rebels were all wrapped in a state of complete insensibility, some with their heads reclining on the table, and others stretched at length upon the earth, while Yusef had fallen back powerless on his seat, his features distorted and having all the appearance of a corpse.

Juballah stepped cautiously among the unconscious ruffians, and examined each of them minutely, to make sure that the drug had really taken its due effect, and Omelia anxiously watched her at the door.

One of the men moved as Juballah passed him, and slightly raised his head, and the old woman in an instant, and to the infinite horror of Omelia, seized a sharp-pointed knife, which was lying on the table, and thrust it to the handle in his breast, so effectually, that death seemed to be instantaneous and he uttered not the slightest sound.

Juballah then hastened to the rude steps which led to the entrance of the cavern, which she ascended, and was immediately hidden from the sight of Omelia, who returned to the place in which she had been confined, much terrified at the murder of the poor unfortunate wretch, which she had witnessed.

It is needless to state the anxiety and impatience with which she awaited the return of the old woman; but she was not long kept in suspense, Juballah, after an absence of only a few minutes, again made her appearance, and with looks of evident satisfaction.

"Everything favours our wishes," she said, "there is no one to observe or obstruct us, so the sooner we depart the better."

"I regret, Juballah," said our heroine, "that you should have taken that unfortunate man's life."

"It could not be avoided," answered the old woman, "but his crimes merited such a fate. Come, any delay at such a juncture is imprudent."

Omelia said no more, but suffering Juballah to take her hand, she was conducted by her into the outer cavern, and past the insensible Yusef and his companions, at whom she cast a timid but anxious glance, and having reached the steps and ascended them, they quickly arrived at the entrance, and the next moment they were both in the open air, and Omelia, whose senses were quite bewildered was again at liberty.

CHAPTER CXLVII.

THE RAGE OF YUSEF.

It was a fine clear night, and the summits of the lofty mountains and the surrounding scenery were tinged with the bright silvery beams of the moon, which was sailing high above through a cloudless sky. As far as the eye could stretch there was not a human being to be seen.

But how is it possible to describe the tumult of varied feelings that agitated the breast of Omelia, at that moment to find herself again at liberty, so soon, and so totally unexpected? It would be a difficult task to do so properly, and we shall therefore not attempt it, but leave it to the imagination of the reader. Suffice it to say that she could scarcely believe the evidence of her senses, but was almost inclined to imagine that she was labouring under a far too happy and flattering a delusion.

She could not speak, she could only look her boundless gratitude to Juballah, who still retaining her hold of her hand, led her gently a short distance from the entrance to the cavern, between the mountains, and where an open and extensive tract of country was exposed to view, with a branch of the river Ganges, which has been so often mentioned before.

"There is no one near to arrest you in your progress damsel," said Juballah, "you may proceed without fear, though I need not remind you that the utmost prudence and

precaution are necessary. My task is accomplished, and I must now leave you."

"Oh, Juballah," ejaculated our herione, with much emotion, "in what language can I sufficiently thank you for the inestimable service you have thus so generously rendered me?—But in what manner am I to proceed? Whither direct my steps?"

"The way is before you," answered the old woman; "you must cross the river at the first opportunity, and then a few hours travelling will bring you to the place of your destination. Farewell; success attend you, you may probably sometimes deign to bestow a thought of respect even on the wretched Juballah."

Omelia raised the hand of the singular and repulsive looking being to her lips, as in a voice of the most gentle sweetness she replied:

"Oh, Juballah, think you that I can ever be so ungrateful as to forget the heavy obligation I am under to you? But tell me, will you not accompany me in my flight?"

"No," answered Juballah, "it will not suit my purpose to do so. I must remain where I am."

"You surely will not venture to return to the cavern," said Omelia, with a look of surprise and incredulity, "to me it appears to be little short of madness for you to do so. I shudder at the thoughts of the terrible situation in which you have placed yourself in serving me, an entire stranger to you."

"Fear not for me," returned Juballah, "I am prepared to brave and surmount every danger which may threaten me. Again farewell, and may all your fondest hopes and wishes be shortly gratified."

In spite of the efforts of Juballah to prevent her, Omelia, overcome by her emotions of gratitude, bent one knee to the ground, and again pressed the coarse hand of old Juballah to her lips, but was unable to articulate more than the word adieu, which she did most fervently.

Juballah disengaged her hand from that of Omelia, and hastened away, but she paused just before she reached the entrance to the cave, looked back but for an instant, waved her hand, and then suddenly disappeared.

Omelia stood for two or three minutes, lost in amazement, confusion, and incredulity, and gazed vacantly towards the spot which she had just quitted, and where Juballah had disappeared; but suddenly aroused into action and recollection, and fearing the consequences of any further delay, she hurried on in the direction which the old woman had pointed out, with feelings agitating her breast such as may be better imagined than described.

It was a fine night, as has been before

stated, and Omelia had no difficulty in tracing her way, but when she reflected upon the loneliness of her situation, without a companion, or the means of protection should any danger assail her, and also thought of the weariness of the journey she would have to pursue, and with no place where she might be accommodated with rest and shelter for a few hours, she could not feel otherwise than somewhat daunted and depressed.

The thought, however, of being again restored to liberty, and the dreadful fate which had been impending over her, entirely superseded every other feeling in her breast, and she could hardly persuade herself that it was anything more than a flattering dream.

And what was now the situation of her beloved Stanley?—she almost dreaded, to think of it, for her heart foreboded the worst. He had doubtless abandoned himself to entire despair, and probably believing that her fate was already decided, and that he should never again behold her, he might in the wild frenzy of his feelings been urged to lay violent hands on himself. But that idea was so frightful and so torturing, that she almost immediately dismissed it from her mind, and endeavoured to give encouragement to the most sanguine hopes, though that was no easy task to accomplish.

She reflected again and again upon the singular conduct of the mysterious old woman Juballah, and in vain endeavoured to imagine what powerful motive could have induced her to take such an extraordinary interest in her fate, and to run such imminent risks to serve her, and the longer she reflected, the more she became involved in wonder and perplexity.

She deeply regretted, however, that Juballah, should have been so obstinately headstrong as to persist in returning to the cavern, where it seemed to her (Omelia), that she would be certain to fall a victim to the vengeance of Yusef and his brutal associates.

However, endeavouring to compose her feelings, and to muster up all the resolution and confidence she could, our heroine pursued her way, keeping as near the banks of the river as possible, with the hope of being able to meet, at some narrow part of it, with some bridge, by which she might be able to cross over to the opposite side; but after walking for about an hour, and without those wishes being gratified, she almost abandoned the thought, and continued on her journey with a sad heart, which probably would not have been the case if she had had any one to whom she might have communicated her feelings.

Yusef and his companions, as old Juballah had said, would probably not recover from the effects of the powerful drug she had secretly administered to them for several hours, by which time she hoped to be far beyond the reach of pursuit, so that in that respect she felt that she had but little to apprehend.

Being insensible all the way she was conveyed to the cavern, she could form no idea of the distance she had to travel, and she had neglected to inquire particularly of Juballah, so that it rendered her progress the more difficult and uncertain.

In the meantime Juballah re-entered the cavern, well satisfied in her own mind with the act of humanity she had so spontaneously performed, and entertaining not the slightest fears as to the consequences that were likely to ensue to herself, but rather exulting at the thought of the rage and disappointment which the villain Yusef would be sure to experience on recovering from his stupor, and learning the escape of his innocent intended victim, after all the trouble it had cost him to obtain possession of her, and at the very time when he must have considered the triumph of his diabolical designs as certain.

On re-entering the large cavern, the mysterious old woman paused for a few minutes to gaze at the unconscious ruffians, which she did with much evident gratification, and then with a malicious laugh she stalked into the place in which our heroine had so lately been confined, and taking her usual seat, she abandoned herself to the strange wild thoughts that so busily occupied her mind.

The expression of her features after the lapse of a few minutes reflection, softened, and so remarkable was the change that her looks and demeanour underwent altogether, that any one to have seen her at that moment could scarcely have believed her to be the same individual whom it had previously been impossible to view with any other feelings but those of disgust and repugnance.

"Juballah's task is accomplished," she muttered to herself; "for the first time in her life, she the hated and despised, has performed a good action, and though her death for the same appears inevitable, she is happy."

Again she laughed in the exultation of her feelings, and assuming her old position, namely, her elbows on her knees, and her chin resting on her hands, she calmly awaited the recovery of Yusef and his guilty companions, attempting not for an instant to go to sleep.

Slowly the hours passed away in that subterranean retreat, which was buried in profound silence like that of the grave; and the rebels yet gave no signs of recovering from the deep lethargy into which Juballah had thrown them, so powerful was the nature of the drug.

At length apparently tired of meditation,

the old woman arose from her seat and returned to the outer cavern, once more to feast her her eyes on the fruits of her own deep designs.

"I could have poisoned them all," she said, and her features re-assumed all their usual frightful and revolting expression, "I could at once have ended their guilty career, and perhaps it would have been better had I done so, for I should then have rid society of those savage miscreants who have already been the cause of so much misery and bloodshed among their fellow creatures. However, Juballah shrinks not from the responsibility of that which she has done; she will boldly brave the vengeance, and exult o'er Yusef's rage at the loss of that innocent being whom he had doomed to destruction.

She took her seat at the head of the table, and continued to watch in gloomy silence, but with looks of malicious satisfaction, the still insensible ruffians.

And thus another hour passed away, when Yusef suddenly aroused from the state of torpor in which he had so long been, and rubbing his eyes he looked around upon his associates with stupified amazement and bewilderment, yet hardly recovered from the effects of the drug, and without at the moment observing Juballah, who retained her seat and the same attitude unmoved.

But at length an idea seemed suddenly to flash upon the brain of Yusef that something wrong had occurred, and starting to his feet, he again gazed eagerly towards his companions just as several of them revived, and exhibited exactly the same symptoms as he himself had done.

"What is the meaning of this?" demanded Yusef, hastily; "why do you all look so strange and bewildered, and what is this sensation that steals through my veins, and still seems to work its influence on my brain? Surely this deep, lethargic sleep which it appears has wrapped us all, cannot be natural?"

A loud and malicious laugh of triumph and derision from Juballah startled him, and immediately directed his attention to her, and he beheld her large and unnatural-looking eyes glaring exultingly upon him.

"Ah," he exclaimed, "old Juballah here? What strange mystery is there in this? Speak, frightful hag, why do you thus laugh?"

"Because I'm pleased," replied the old woman.

"See," said Alahamed, "for the first time observing the corpse of the sepoy whom Juballah had slain, "one of our comrades is murdered; there has been some treachery at work."

"And of which Juballah is the authoress," added Yusef.

"Most true," replied the former, coolly and deliberately; "and I glory in the success of my designs."

"Wretch, dare you?"

"Dare I?" she repeated, with a look of scorn, "what is there that I have not already dared, and am not still prepared to brave?"

"Ha," exclaimed Yusef, again starting, and looking towards the half opened door of the place in which Omelia had been confined; "a thought suddenly strikes me now. Juballah, where is my prisoner?"

"Far beyond your power by this time, villain," returned Juballah.

"Escaped," cried Yusef, in a hoarse voice.

"Yes, and by my assistance; I had determined that she should do so from the first."

"No, no, it is impossible, I cannot believe it."

"Then e'en satisfy yourself."

Hastily, and in a state of the greatest excitement, Yusef rushed into the small cavern, and on beholding that it was indeed vacated, he gave utterance to a most dreadful oath, and darted back into the outer cavern.

"It is true," he exclaimed, in a voice of the most ungovernable rage, "the girl is gone. I see it all now. Our drink last night was drugged by Juballah, and while we were wrapped in a state of torpor, she seized the opportunity to restore Omelia to liberty."

"Totally regardless of the consequences," added the old woman, again laughing exultingly, and without offering to remove from her seat, or to change her attitude.

"Wretch! traitress!" exclaimed Yusef, fiercely, drawing his sword, rushing towards her, grasping her wrist, and dragging her from her seat into the centre of the cavern, "for which daring act your worthless life shall pay. Die!"

"Hold," exclaimed several of the rebels in a breath, rushing upon him, and wresting the deadly weapon from his hand, just as he was about to plunge it into the old woman's bosom; "Juballah must not perish thus?"

The villain's eyes become bloodshot, and he perfectly foamed at the mouth with rage, as he exclaimed—

"Confusion! have ye all then conspired against me? Do ye no longer acknowledge my authority?"

The rebels who now all, with the exception of Alahamed, seemed to be unanimous, returned no immediate answer to this, but merely released Juballah from Yusef's hold, and took her under their protection.

He stared at them with stupified amazement, and his whole muscular frame seemed agitated and convulsed by the violence of his passions.

"Is this a dream?" he said, "or can I believe the evidence of my senses? Is it thus you reward my fidelity to ye?—the many services I have rendered ye? Do ye all mean to desert me at this particular juncture?"

"Aye," replied one, who seemed by his manner to be appointed by his comrades as their chief in this mutiny, "we have submitted to your authority too long, Yusef. From Juballah, uncouth and repulsive as she has appeared to be, we have received many valuable services, and we are determined to protect her."

"It is impossible that you can mean what you say," said the astonished and terrified Yusef, "you do but jest with me."

"Indeed," sneered the man who had before spoken, "but you will quickly find that it is no jest, to your cost."

"Ha, ha, ha!" again laughed Juballah, "you hear that Yusef? Can you now deny that my triumph is complete?"

"I still cannot believe that you are in earnest," said Yusef, addressing himself to his late associates in a faltering voice, "or that you will throw the shield of your protection around this old woman, who has murdered one of your comrades in cold blood."

"He was a fellow after your own heart," returned another of the men, "and richly merited the fate he has met with."

"What are your motives for this conduct?" demanded Yusef, with looks of alarm.

"Simply that we are tired of the authority of the contemptible Pariah Yusef, who has hitherto made us the mere instruments to serve his own ambitious and mercenary purposes, and would be ready to betray us at any time into the hands of our enemies. We go to join one from whom we may expect to receive every encouragement and reward for our services, and Juballah will accompany us."

"You cannot mean what you say," again ejaculated the villain, with increased terror and looks of remonstrance and supplication, "you can never abandon me in this cruel and treacherous manner."

"That you shall quickly see," returned the first speaker; "comrades, seize and secure him and Alahamed, and then to complete our designs."

Yusef and Alahamed were completely thunderstruck at an occurrence so totally unexpected; but the order was no sooner given than obeyed, and before the ruffians had time to offer any resistance, which would, however, of course, have been entirely useless.

They were immediately seized and bound hand and foot with strong cords, and thus rendered completely helpless, and loud shouts of derision and exultation escaped the rebels when this task was accomplished, in which it is hardly necessary to add that old Jubal-

lah heartily joined, at the same time fixing upon Yusef looks of the most deadly malice and triumph.

The two villains were now secured to a strong post at one end of the cavern, in which position it seemed to be the intention of the rebels to leave them.

To describe properly the furious rage of the defeated sepoys, particularly that of Yusef, would be indeed a difficult task. So completely discomfitted and taken by surprise were they by this sudden revolt among their own associates, and in whom they had thought they could place every confidence, that for a few minutes they could not give utterance to a word, while old Juballah folded her arms across her chest, and eyed them with the same almost fiendish expression as before.

Some of the rebels proceeded to collect in a heap all the money, and everything that was valuable and portable in the cave, previous to removing it with them, while the wretched Yusef, and his equally miserable companion watched them with looks of the utmost dismay.

"You cannot, surely do not mean to leave us here to perish of want?" at length gasped forth Yusef in a voice of horror and expostulation.

"Aye," returned Juballah, "to linger on in all the horrors of hunger, without any one to pity and relieve you; till death shall put an end to your sufferings. See, the table is still loaded with provisions, on which you may feast your longing eyes without having the power to reach them. Ha, ha ha!"

"Fiends! wretches! traitors!" exclaimed the distracted Yusef, his eyes almost bursting from their sockets, and every feature frightfully distorted with the terrible and almost insupportable agony of his feelings, "you dare not be guilty of a crime so monstrous as that with which you threaten us. What hideous and sanguinary feeling urges you on? What have we done to merit such a fate?"

Loud laughter and bitter mockery was the only reply the wretched guilty men received to this, and Yusef's feelings of anguish and despair were excited to such a degree, that madness almost seized upon his brain, and the once bold and reckless Alahamed, whose courage and fortitude had entirely forsaken him, was in very little, if in any better condition than himself.

The rebels having completed their task of collecting together the valuables which they meant to take away with them, sat down to the table and regaled themselves heartily, and in which Juballah joined them, and thus they continued throughout the day, they having arranged not to take their departure from the cavern till the dark of the evening, when they could do so with greater safety.

Yusef and his companion in misfortune, made frequently very humble and piteous appeals to them for mercy, of which they took no heed, at least, only to deride and exult over them, and at length the wretched prisoners finding that all they could say was of no avail, and being worked up to almost a state of frenzy, abandoned themselves to complete despair.

Evening came at last, and all being in readiness, the mutineers, accompanied by Juballah, prepared to depart.

To attempt to describe the anguish of Yusef and Alahamed, at this moment when their frightful fate seemed to be all certain, would be a fruitless task, all the desperate courage they had previously possessed had now entirely left them, and two more abject and pitiable objects than they then presented could not very well be imagined.

They absolutely shrieked aloud for mercy, in the horror and excitement of their feelings, but without the least effect, and in a few minutes they found themselves alone—in what seemed destined to be their tomb—and in total darkness.

CHAPTER CXLVIII.

THE FEARFUL SUFFERINGS OF YUSEF AND ALAHAMED.

What the principal motives of the sepoys —who had hitherto implicitly obeyed the authority of Yusef, and exhibited no signs of dissatisfaction—were for this sudden, unexpected and extraordinary mutiny, and the brutal spirit of revenge in which they had acted, we will not here stop to inquire, but at once proceed to relate the particulars of what happened to the guilty Yusef and his fellow prisoner in the terrible situation in which they were placed, after the ruffians had quitted the cavern.

For some time after their departure, the feelings of the unfortunate wretches were so bound up in horror, that every faculty was suspended, and they remained in a complete state of stupefaction, and as though they were labouring under the influence of some frightful dream; but when the dreadful truth flashed with overwhelming force upon their brain, they groaned aloud, and made the dismal place resound again with their bitter lamentations, and fearful oaths and execrations.

Then they made a desperate attempt to release themselves from the cords that bound them, but which were completely futile, and

convinced them that their fate was inevitable, unless something perfectly miraculous, and which they had not the slightest reason to anticipate, should interpose to save them.

The impenetrable darkness which reigned around—for the rebels had extinguished every light on their departure from the cavern—added to the horror of their situation, and filled their disordered minds with all kinds of fearful ideas and images.

To be left there to die a lingering death of starvation, was so dreadful to think of, that it seemed to freeze the blood in their veins, and they shrunk from the bare contemplation of it even with more than childish terror.

"May eternal curses light upon the head of Juballah," exclaimed Yusef, in a hoarse voice, and gnashing his teeth together as he spoke, "'tis her that has been the cause of all this. 'Tis her that has inflamed the minds of our comrades against us, and 'twas her that aided Omelia to escape, after all the trouble it had cost me to obtain possession of her."

"You have yourself alone to blame for all the troubles that are now brought upon us," said Allahamed, in savage tones. "I wish I had never had anything to do with you."

"What mean you?" demanded Yusef.

"I should not think," answered Alahamed, "that what I have said requires any explanation. I repeat that you have brought all this upon yourself and me."

"How so?"

"By your own rash and overbearing conduct towards our associates, and by appropriating nearly the whole of the proceeds of our plunder to yourself, thus giving them no encouragement to remain faithful to you."

"'Tis false," said Yusef, sternly.

"'Tis true," retorted Alahamed positively, "and you cannot conscientiously deny it. The money that should have been shared equally among us, you have recklessly squandered in such expensive freaks as your late adventure with the the girl Omelia. Men engaged in the desperate cause that we are should find something else to employ us than amorous toying. And then the great risks we have so often run, merely to obtain the gratification of your wishes."

"Have you then turned against me, Alahamed?" said Yusef, "and load me with your reproaches?"

"It's time I did, I think," replied Alahamed, "since I have so unjustly got to suffer with you. Our fate is inevitably sealed, and thus buried in the bowels of the earth, without the least chance of making our situation known to any one, to escape from it is impossible. We now occupy the grave that shall enclose our future remains when starvation has done its frightful work."

Yusef groaned, and the perspiration stood in large drops upon his forehead, with the terror and anguish of his feelings.

Again the wretched guilty man uttered a volley of the most fearful oaths and execrations, and made another determined but futile attempt to release himself from the cords that bound him, for the man had taken too much care to secure, to render the accomplishment of that task at all possible.

"And shall the villains thus be allowed to triumph in their brutal schemes of vengeance?" said Yusef.

"They do triumph," returned Alahamed, "and we cannot help ourselves; there is nothing now left for us to do than to learn to submit to that fate which we cannot avoid, and which must overtake us in two

No. 69.

or three days. Already, methinks, I feel the dreadful vultures of hunger preying upon my vitals."

"Forbear! forbear, Alahamed;" said Yusef, in a voice of terror, "or you will drive me mad!"

"Drive *you* mad," repeated Alahamed, in accents of scorn; "where is now your boasted courage and recklessness of disposition, that you tremble even at the prospect of approaching death? Bah!"

"*Such a death*," returned Yusef, emphatically, "but taunt me not, Alahamed, my feelings are sufficiently excited without that."

"And do you suppose that I have no sense of feeling?" demanded Alahamed, sternly. "Oh, it was a cursed evil hour when I first became acquainted with you."

Yusef was too much agitated to return any immediate answer, and, as he reflected upon all the horrors of the awful and lingering death which seemed too surely to await him, his agony increased to an insupportable degree.

That his associates in crime should thus so suddenly rebel against him, and espouse the cause of old Jubullah, was to him the more extraordinary and explicable, as they had never given him the least hint of their disapprobation of his conduct; and even now he could hardly persuade himself that he was not dreaming, for the stern reality was by far too dreadful to contemplate.

The guilty ruffians continued to taunt and upbraid each other at intervals; at other times to utter the most dismal lamentations on the cruelty of their destiny, (forgetting the many atrocities they had committed on others), and to heap their bitterest curses on the heads of those who had consigned them to it.

They had not the least chance of releasing themselves, for they were bound in such a manner that they could scarcely move, and the cords penetrated their flesh and caused them the most excruciating pain; and thus they were deprived entirely of the means of sleep, which might have afforded them at least some temporary respite from their sufferings.

The rebels on their quitting the cavern, having, as has been before stated, extinguished every lamp, they were involved in complete darkness, which, to their distracted imagination, appeared to be the more intense, under the dreadful circumstances in which they were placed, and it was no wonder that their patience and fortitude entirely forsook them, and they abandoned themselves to all the anguish of despair, in the midst of which they could almost fancy that they still heard the voices of the ruffians shouting, and laughing in bitter mockery of the tortures they were enduring, and of the still far greater sufferings that most assuredly awaited them.

Slowly and tediously the hours passed away, and every moment their misery increased, and which there were not the least means of alleviating. The terrible excitement of their feelings almost drove them to madness, and at times their wild ravings would have been quite appalling to hear, and in spite of their guilty character, could not but have excited a deep feeling of pity.

"Every evil earthly power seems to have conspired against me," cried Yusef in in the agony of his feelings, "to disappoint my wishes and expectations, to frustrate my designs, at the very moment when their complete success appeared certain, and to hasten my destruction."

"And because I have been fool enough to aid you in your mad-brained schemes," said Alahamed, in surly tones, and writhing with pain, "I am doomed to share the same fate. Curses light on the girl Omelia, and on you for involving yourself and me in so much danger, to gain possession of her, it is her that we have principally to blame, as being the cause of all our present misfortunes."

"The fierce passion I once entertained towards her," returned the wretched Yusef, "is now turned to deadly hatred; and should I be released from my present terrible situation, I will pursue her to the remotest corner of the earth, rather than suffer her to escape my vengeance."

"Fool," exclaimed Alahamed, in fierce but at the same time scornful tones, "flatter not yourself with such preposterous and fallacious ideas; the opportunity you so long for, as you say, to gratify your feelings of revenge, will never be afforded you, from this place, neither you nor I can escape, we shall never more be permitted to see the light of day; lingering tortures await us, compared with which immediate death, even in its most frightful forms, would be mercy."

"Cease, Alahamed," supplicated the distracted Yusef, with a groan of agony, "I cannot, I dare not listen to the hideous description your disordered imagination portrays. You seek to torture me."

"Torture you?" repeated Alahamed, scornfully, "what have I to gain by that, since I have to share your fate? But 'tis no use seeking to deceive ourselves with false hopes and expectations. The picture I have drawn of that which awaits us, is a true one, and in a day or two, if not in a few hours, depend upon it, it will be realized. Already I begin to feel the pangs of hunger and thirst upon me."

Yusef agained groaned, for by the observations that Alahamed had made, he felt were too fearfully true, and he could not think upon his approaching fate, without feelings of the most cowardly dread. In fact, the daring brutal man whom nothing whatever seemed capable of daunting or subduing, was, in the course of a few hours reduced to all the weakness of a child.

The limbs of the wretched prisoners were cramped and stiffened, by being compelled to remain in one position, and the blood flowed from several parts, in their violent but fruitless efforts to release themselves from the cords which bound them. As well might they have sought to burst asunder fetters and chains of iron of the strongest description.

A burning thirst was also upon them, caused by the anguish and excitement of their feelings, and that was, if possible, more torturing and insupportable than all.

And thus the first night of their fearful incarceration passed away, at least as well as they could imagine, for they had no means of judging of the exact lapse of time, or distinguishing the night from day.

The next day, as might be expected, found them in a still more fearful and deplorable state than before, and the intensity of their sufferings was almost beyond description.

Alahamed supported himself, after all, with much more patience and fortitude than might have been expected, but the wretched Yusef was brought to the most pitiable condition imaginable, and at times his senses wandered.

Many hours had now elapsed since they had taken food or drink, and the consequences now began to show themselves in the most violent and alarming manner; and what added to their torture was the fact that the men on leaving the cavern had left abundance of food and drink upon the table, which they had not the power to reach, and that had the effect of aggravating their thirst and hunger tenfold.

The guilty wretches talked but little together, and when they did, it was in wild and incoherent sentences, but the groans and lamentations that almost incessantly escaped them, spoke more of the agony of feelings they were enduring than words could have done.

All the crimes they had committed throughout their guilty career, rushed with tumultuous and overwhelming fury upon their memory, and while it convinced them that the retribution which at last had overtaken them, though terrible, was just, added to their dreadful agony; and, in fact, at times drove them to complete madness.

When the distracted Yusef could calmly reflect upon the causes which had led to his present horrible fate, which was seldom, how deeply he regretted that he had ever beheld Omelia, whose matchless charms had excited so powerful, guilty, and irresistable a passion in his breast, and urged him on to acts of desperation to gain possession of her, which had placed him in his present situation, and without his being able to obtain the gratification of his guilty wishes after all.

That day wore away, and still no hope, no prospect, no chance of relief to the miserable prisoners; in fact, it would have been madness to have entertained even for an instant, any such delusive idea, and the horrors of their cruel destiny now presented themselves in the most awful array before their imagination.

All the pangs of the most gnawing and insatiable hunger were upon them, their throats were parched with a burning and maddening thirst, an intense fire seemed to consume their brains, and their eyes rolled wildly, and appeared ready to burst from their sockets; in fact all that human nature might have to endure and still to live, they suffered, and even fearful miscreants as they were, it must have been a cruel and insensible being who could have witnessed their dreadful agonies unmoved.

It seemed utterly impossible that they could continue to live in such a frightful condition much longer; and, in fact, when their senses did not wander, they earnestly wished that death would speedily put a period to their sufferings.

As night again approached, completely worn out, they became unconscious, and in that fearful and melancholy condition, we will, for the present, leave them, and follow the footsteps of our heroine.

CHAPTER CXLIX.

THE PROGRESS OF OMELIA IN HER FLIGHT.

NOTWITHSTANDING the loneliness of her situation, being as she was without a companion, Omelia proceeded on her way with much better spirits than might have been expected, and to which the fineness of the night, to which we have before alluded, served not a little to contribute.

The prospect before her, although it presented no signs of a human habitation where she might obtain temporary shelter, was bright and cheerful beneath the silvery moonbeams, and the myriads of twinkling stars; and even amid all the bewildering and conflicting thoughts that naturally occupied her mind, she could not help being lost in wonder and admiration of the beauties of nature, as they were then so strikingly and so advantageously displayed.

Nothing could be more diversified, picturesque, and so romantic, even in the Eastern world, than the scenery upon which the eyes of Omelia rested in every direction, and for a time the contemplation of it diverted her mind from the reflections that must otherwise have engrossed it.

She proceeded with renewed hope and confidence, still keeping as close as possible to the bank of the river, with the expectation of meeting with some means of crossing it, but in which she was unfortunately doomed to disappointment, which she deeply regretted.

She could never be sufficiently grateful to Providence, she considered, for her miraculous deliverance from the cavern, and the revolting fate which was impending over her; and when she reflected upon the extraordinary means by which that escape was effected, it seemed to her to be incredible.

She felt most anxious about the probable fate of that singular and mysterious woman, Jubullah, to whom she was so highly indebted; and she could not at all understand the motives that could induce her so obstinately to persist in returning to the cavern, after having effected her (Omelia's) escape, which appeared to be nothing more nor less than to rush upon certain destruction; for it seemed scarcely possible that she could escape falling a victim to the deadly vengeance of the bloodthirsty miscreant, Yusef, and his infamous associates in crime. Uncouth and frightful as that strange old woman was in appearance, Omelia would have felt much more gratified had she accompanied her, not only for the assistance she might have afforded her on the road, but that she might at some future period have evinced her gratitude in a manner which could not be misunderstood.

Then the thoughts of the affectionate maiden wandered to her beloved Stanley, in fact, he had never been absent from them, and various and conflicting were the conjectures she formed as to his present situation, and the effect which her disappearance, under such alarming circumstances, had had upon him, though after mature and painful reflection, she could not but anticipate the worst, and entertain the most dismal forebodings.

Indeed, was there not sufficient to drive him to despair, after those repeated separations, and so soon after being restored to each other? There was, and the longer that Omelia reflected upon it, the more miserable and apprehensive she became.

It seemed as though the fates had conspired against them, and had resolved to throw every obstacle in the way to the completion of their happiness, and strange and powerful doubts, which she could not resist or conquer, beset her mind, as to whether they should ever meet again.

"And if so it is decreed," she soliloquized in the most melancholy accents, as she continued on her way, "of what value is liberty, nay, even life to me? What all my hopes and prospects if happiness must be annihilated, and death would be a mercy to me.

Dear Stanley, how severe have been our trials since we have known each other, and it seems as if they were never to have an end. Surely it is enough to exhaust the patience and fortitude of even the most firm and resolute. When will our fond and untiring devotion to each other meet with its due reward?"

She paused for a minute or two to rest herself, standing on an elevated spot in an open space, and upon which the bright moonbeams fell with uninterrupted splendour, she drew the miniature likeness of her lover from her bosom, where she had constantly worn it since he had given it to her, and gazed at it earnestly, and with feelings of fond emotion and admiration which it is needless to attempt to describe.

It was a most faithful likeness, and as she continued to gaze upon it, she almost fancied that the eyes beamed upon her with that feeling of affection which the original was ever want to express, and that the lips were about to part to pronounce her name, coupled with a blessing.

Such was the impression that this idea made upon her, that Omelia could not remove her eyes from the miniature, and her tears fell fast upon it, while various were the thoughts that crowded tumultuously upon her brain.

She pressed it fervently to her lips again and again, and then reconsigned it to her bosom, and endeavouring to tranquillize her feelings, she once more resumed her journey.

The scenery even appeared to be more beautiful the further she advanced on her way, and Omelia's thoughts were again for a time diverted from other subjects and she gazed on everything that met her eye with feelings of the most enthusiastic admiration.

The place, too, seemed the more familiar to her as she advanced, though she did not remember when, or if ever she had travelled that part of the country before; but she proceeded with renewed courage and expectation, but still with no better prospect of meeting with a human habitation where she might meet with the accommodation she required for a few hours, than before.

It was now that she felt more than ever the want of a guide, and had the more reason to regret that old Jubullah had not accompanied her, as she was doubtless well acquainted with the country.

She already began to feel fatigued (for she had travelled some distance from the cavern, and the thought of having to wander during the whole of the night (which was now considerably advanced), and in a strange place, where she knew not what danger might threaten, filled her with much alarm.

From these thoughts she was suddenly aroused by hearing the sound of hasty footsteps behind her, and timidly looking back, she was somewhat startled and alarmed by beholding two men approaching her, who, as well as the dim light of the moon, (for it was now partially obscured by a cloud) would permit her to distinguish, appeared to be native villagers, and seeing that they were close upon her, she stopped to await them, though it was not without some doubt and hesitation that she did so, uncertain, of course, as she was, whether they might prove to be friends or foes. Still she did not lose her presence of mind, and resolved to answer the questions they might put to her with every precaution.

The men soon came up with her, and although they naturally looked surprised to see a young female travelling alone at that hour of the night, there was nothing at all in their appearance to excite any apprehensions within her breast,

They asked her civilly if she was going far, whether or not she was a stranger in that part of the country, and if they could be of any assistance to her in guiding her on her way.

This inspired Omelia with confidence, and she answered accordingly, namely, that she was unacquainted with that part of the country, that she had wished to cross to the other side of the river in the early part of the evening, could she have met with the opportunity, but as she had travelled some considerable distance, and felt fatigued, she was anxious to meet with some dwelling where she might obtain rest till the morning.

"'Tis fortunate," remarked one of the men, "that the village we inhabit is only a short distance ahead, and there you can obtain all the accommodation you require, at either my bungalow or that of my companion here, and our wives will pay you every attention.

There was something so candid in the manner of the stranger, that it immediately won the confidence of our heroine, and thanking him, she gladly accepted his offer, and they proceeded on their way in the direction which had been intimated.

CHAPTER CL.

OMELIA'S VAIN SEARCH FOR HER LOVER.

THE strangers put no idle questions to our heroine on the way, but merely talked upon common topics, and that inspired her with still more confidence, and she felt gratified that she had met with them, as she seemed now certain to obtain that accommodation for the night of which she stood so much in need.

They had not to walk long, when, the village (which was a small one, containing only a few dwellings), appeared in sight, and the men then separated, the one who had first addressed Omelia, remaining with her.

"Yonder is my bungalow," he observed, pointing to one close by where they stood," if you will wait here a few minutes, I will inform my wife of your requirements, and no doubt, make all the arrangements that are necessary."

Omelia again thanked him, and the man retired into the bungalow, leaving her at the door.

He was not absent long, but reappearing at the door, he beckoned our heroine to approach, which she did without any hesitation, and he then conducted her into the bungalow, the interior of which was exceedingly clean and neat.

A middle aged woman, and a young girl, no doubt her daughter, were in the room. They seemed much struck with the appearance of Omelia, but greeted her with kindness and civility, the elder female handing her to a seat.

"Your husband, I presume, has acquainted you with the accommodation I require?" said Omelia.

The woman replied in the affirmative, and added :—

"All the accommodation our humble dwelling can afford, I am sure you are heartily welcome to. You can sleep with my daughter, and, as you say that you wish to cross to the opposite side of the river, if you please, Doolab, my husband, will conduct you at any time you think proper in the morning to the bridge."

Our heroine again returned her warmest thanks, and then the woman and her daughter, without asking any questions, which at that time would certainly have been particularly annoying, quitted the room.

They were only gone a few minutes, when they returned, bringing in a humble and light repast, which they placed before Omelia, and warmly invited her to partake.

Of this invitation our heroine, not having tasted food for so many hours, gladly availed herself, and having eaten heartily, and feeling much fatigued after the distance she had travelled and the extraordinary excitement she had experienced, she requested to be shown to the room in which she was to sleep.

The young girl bade her parents good night, and taking up a lamp, conducted Omelia up the stairs to the chamber, in which was a clean but humble bed, which to our heroine, under the circumstances, was a very welcome sight.

The young girl was very interesting in her appearance, and remarkably civil and prepossessing in her manners, and Omelia having exchanged a few observations with her in conversation, in which she found her to be very intelligent, they both retired to bed.

Her bedfellow was soon sound asleep, but Omelia, notwithstanding she felt so tired, was too busily occupied with the various thoughts that crowded upon her mind, to suffer her for some time to yield to the influence of the drowsy God; and the novelty of her situation likewise kept her waking.

She placed every confidence in the good people with whom she had found accommodation, for their manners were beyond suspicion; and she could not but congratulate herself in having so fortunately encountered the two men, when she was at a loss what to do—what course to pursue.

According to what Jubullah had said of the strength of it, it was more than probable that Yusef and his associates had not yet recovered from the effects of the drug, and when they did, they would certainly abandon the idea of pursuit as completely useless; therefore she considered that, so far as she had proceeded, she was perfectly safe, and she fervently returned her thanks to Providence for it.

She was anxious for the arrival of the morning, when she would resume her journey, and under the guidance of Doolab, be able at last to cross the river, and pursue her way, she trusted, in safety and without difficulty, to Cawnpore, where she continued to indulge the hope that she would again be restored to the arms of her lover.

Oh, what happiness was in that thought! Yet, in spite of her endeavours to banish them, torturing doubts and misgivings would obtrude themselves; and at times so strong was the impression on her mind, that she could scarcely contain herself, and she almost dreaded the time to arrive when she should ascertain the truth or erroneousness of her conjectures.

At length, however, completely wearied with thinking, Omelia did sink off to sleep, and for some time, notwithstanding she was in a strange place, she slept soundly and tranquilly, and dreams of varied description presenting themselves to her busy imagination.

The early morning's sun was streaming into the little chamber she occupied, when she awoke, and she felt considerably refreshed after the few hours' repose she had so comfortably enjoyed.

The young girl who had been her bedfellow was already arisen, and seemed to have been so for some time. She complimented our heroine on the improvement in her looks after her night's rest, and then assisted her to dress, after which Omelia accompanied her below, where she found Doolab and his wife ready to receive her, and to give her a cordial greeting.

In fact, Omelia was quite overwhelmed with the kindness and hospitality of these humble people, and she expressed herself accordingly. But they heard her with evident impatience, and when she had concluded her observations, assured her that they needed no other return for what they had done, than the conviction that they had done their duty. It was, indeed, not without the greatest difficulty that our heroine could prevail upon them to take the least remuneration, and they did that with evident reluctance.

During the morning meal Omelia put some questions to her kind host and hostess regarding the present state of that part of the country, and their answers were of a most satisfactory description, and revived our heroine's hopes of the successful and happy issue of her journey, and of the startling adventures which had naturally caused her so much excitement and alarm.

Upon mature consideration, Omelia thought it would be more prudent and advisable, as she had slept far beyond the time she had intended to resume her journey, not to take her departure from the bungalow till towards the evening, and telling Doolab and his wife that she felt to require still further rest after the unusual fatigue she had undergone, before she continued on the way to the place of her destination, she asked them whether it put them to any inconvenience to afford her the extra accommodation she required, which they readily answered in the negative, and added that it would give them every satisfaction to be able to render her any further service in their power.

Omelia felt grateful for this, and after some time passed in conversation, in order that she might not present any obstacle to the performance of their domestic affairs, and also to indulge uninterrupted in her own thoughts, she retired to the little room above, which she had occupied for the night.

There she seated herself by the window which commanded an extensive view of the surrounding country, and in the contemplation of which she for some time amused herself, and felt her spirits greatly revive as she gazed upon the boundless beauties of nature which were there displayed to such advantage,

Nothing could be more lovely than the weather; the sky was clear, cloudless, and transparent, the sun shone brightly, but a brisk and refreshing breeze cooled the atmosphere, and counteracted in a great measure the effects of the oppressive heat which would otherwise have prevailed.

Omelia could not but feel grateful for the success which had hitherto attended her in her escape from the cavernous retreat of the rebels, and she augured well from it for the future.

Many were the reflections that crowded upon her mind during the day, but though sometimes a gloomy thought or a sad misgiving would obtrude itself; yet altogether her hopes were sanguine, and she awaited with impatience the arrival of the time, which was fast approaching, when all her doubts would be removed.

She pictured to herself the fierce rage and disappointment of the villain Yusef on discovering her escape, and that his diabolical designs were thus completely frustrated; but she felt the utmost anxiety for the fate of poor old Jubullah, to whom she was so much indebted, and who, she feared, would be sure to be sacrificed to the inhuman miscreant's vengeance, and again Omelia deeply regretted that she could not be persuaded to accompany her in her flight.

All these thoughts, however, gave way before the idea of again beholding her beloved Stanley, and she buoyed herself up with the fond hope that that joyful event was on the eve of taking place. If those hopes should not be realised, how terrible would be the disappointment. She shuddered at the thought, and felt as if madness must certainly seize upon her brain, if fate had destined that her and Stanley should meet no more. Life would then possess no charms for her, in fact it would become a complete and insupportable burthen to her, and she felt the sooner (under such circumstances) she was rid of it the better.

She endeavoured, however, to banish all such apprehensions from her breast, and she succeeded even much better than might have been anticipated.

At length, tired of thinking, Omelia rejoined Doolab and his wife in the room below (as the time was fast approaching when she must take her departure), and they engaged in conversation for a short time, of the most friendly and interesting description, which served to divert the mind of Omelia from painful and gloomy subjects, that otherwise might have obtruded themselves.

At length the golden monarch of the day began to decline in the western horizon, and our heroine now intimated her wish to depart, she having succeeded in banishing all fear of the dangers of pursuit.

Doolab expressed his readiness to accompany her without any further delay, and Omelia having again warmly thanked his wife and her daughter for their kindness during the short time she had been with them, bade them adieu, and then accompanied Doolab from the Bungalow.

They passed quickly through the village, without meeting with, or being observed by, anyone, and pursued their course by a pathway that skirted the river's bank.

Omelia inquired if it was far to the bridge which Doolab had spoken of, and the latter replied in the negative, and that about half an hour's walking would bring them to it, with which she felt satisfied.

The river gradually narrowed as they proceeded, until the bridge (a roughly-constructed wooden one), and a most welcome sight it was to Omelia, who now anticipated that her journey would shortly be at an end.

Doolab conducted her across it, and on arriving at the opposite side of the river, inquired whether she had any further occasion for his services, as he was perfectly willing, if she required it, to conduct her any distance on her way.

Omelia replied in the negative, and again thanked him most fervently for the services he had already so kindly rendered her. She then, after having in vain tried to persuade him to receive some further remuneration for the trouble he had taken, bade him adieu, and they separated, Omelia making her way in the direction of a road which Doolab had pointed out to her, as leading almost direct to the city of Cawnpore, whither he had understood her to say that she wished to go.

He watched her receding form from the bridge apparently with much interest, till it was hidden from his sight in the distance, and then proceeded on his return home.

The heart of Omelia now palpitated

violently with mingled hopes and fears, and she was frequently compelled to pause to give free vent to her emotions.

Not a human being met her observation, and there was nothing therefore to create the slightest apprehension of danger within her breast.

Every spot that she was now traversing seemed familiar, and that increased her hopes, yet a melancholy thought and fear would occasionally steal in which she could not resist.

She, however, collected herself sufficiently to proceed with all the speed she could, and after nearly two hours sharp walking, the City of Cawnpore, in which all her hopes and fears rested, burst upon her sight.

The feelings that now agitated her may be much better imagined than described, and she was compelled to pause to tranquillize them.

The moon had risen in all its splendour, and revealed distant objects as distinctly to the sight as in the light of day, and our heroine, standing as she was upon an elevated spot of ground, could clearly trace the outlines of some of the principal buildings in the city to which she was going, and among others the ancient Temple of Fountains.

Oh, what a tempest of tumultuous and mingled feelings rushed upon the heart of Omelia, almost overwhelming her, as she did this! What tender yet painful reminiscences did it recall! She remembered with emotions of the most powerful description every affectionate word that her lover had uttered on the two occasions of their meeting there; they still seemed to breathe in her ears, and the looks of boundless love which he fixed upon her as he spoke them, were still vividly present to her imagination.

Alas! that bliss like that should have been so cruelly interrupted, if not completely destroyed; and that they should again be doomed to experience all those torturing disappointments and trials of the heart it had before been their lot to undergo.

She shuddered when she thought of what might but too probably have happened to the wretched Stanley even during the brief period of their unfortunate separation, and again her heart misgave her.

But from that melancholy feeling she endeavoured to arouse herself, and to become more composed.

"Away with these dismal thoughts and fears," she ejaculated; "why should I distract and rack my brain by giving encouragement to them? Surely an All-merciful Power, who knows the patience and resignation with which I have endured all the many severe trials and vicissitudes which it has been my hard lot to encounter, will not suffer my fond and anxious hopes to be again disappointed, and I will endeavour to be firm and confident. Beloved Stanley, your faithful Omelia, with wildly throbbing heart, again hastens to seek you, and to be once more enfolded in your fond and fervent embrace!"

How bright, how beautiful was the light that beamed from the eyes of the lovely girl as she thus spoke, and how animated and striking the expression of her features. She felt renewed strength and confidence, and having cast one hasty glance around her, to see that she was not watched, but without observing anyone, she again hurried on her way, her heart still palpitating violently with the powerful and almost uncontrollable agitation of her feelings.

She felt rather surprised that she met with no one on her way, and as she approached nearer the City, a faint and sickly sensation came over her, which she found it impossible to conquer, and she was again compelled to pause in order to endeavour to compose and collect herself.

Notwithstanding the extreme fineness of the night, and the radiance of the moon, which tinged all around with its silvery hues, to the imagination of Omelia, everything seemed to wear an aspect of gloom; the solemn silence of the grave to reign around, and her spirits again droopped beneath the influence of that sad impression.

She almost dreaded to proceed, for it seemed to her distracted imagination, as though some terrible disappointment—some fearful shock awaited her, and her heart sank within her.

"Oh, may the Great Spirit," she fervently exclaimed, "avert the evils that I apprehend. Let not the sanguine—the fond hopes I have ventured to cherish, be doomed to be disappointed, for that, I am convinced, would indeed be a shock that my reason could never be able to withstand. Oh, suffer me once more to be restored to the arms of my beloved Stanley, no more to be separated from him, and my happiness will be complete."

Her bosom swelled with the power of the emotions which those thoughts excited, and she looked around her with a sad expression of countenance, and her eyes were humid with tears.

"But why should I suffer such gloomy ideas and fears to haunt and torture my imagination?" she said, after a pause; and suddenly arousing herself;—"why should I thus delay, when in a few minutes I can have my doubts and fears removed, or ascertain the truth, which even at the worst

is better than suspense and terrible uncertainty. Let me at once proceed."

Thus armed with fresh resolution, she quitted the spot on which she had been standing, and with a firmer step she hastened towards the city.

CHAPTER CLI.

HOPES DESTROYED.

A few minutes brought Omelia to one of the entrances of the city, upon which the moon was shining brightly; but a deadly chill again fell upon her heart at the solemn silence which reigned around, and at the apparent desertion of the place; for no signs of a human being could she see.

No. 70.

"But why do I again suffer my fears to overcome and unnerve me?" she again exclaimed; "I am ashamed of my weakness; it is unworthy of me, let me again proceed."

This time she seemed to have mustered up every resolution, and she walked on towards the city with a firm step.

But there was nothing whatever to encourage her hopes, for the silence which reigned around remained unbroken, and still proceeded without encountering a human being. It seemed indeed as if the place was entirely deserted, and again the poor girl felt a depression of spirits and torturing misgivings that were almost overwhelming.

And now she reached the Temple of Fountains, which was immediately in her way to the place of her destination, and by this time the excitement of her feelings had arisen to such a pitch, that it was not without the greatest difficulty she could control them within the bounds of reason.

She paused within a few paces of the temple, fixed her eyes earnestly upon it, as it stood out from amidst the surrounding and romantic scenery in bold relief in the bright moonlight, trembled, and how bewildering were the thoughts that rushed upon her brain.

Short as was the time which had elapsed since her and Stanley had last met here, on that never to be forgotten evening which had so fatally separated them, what might not have happened to him to prevent their ever being again restored to each other, and what fresh troubles and struggles of the heart might await her? She could not help shuddering at the thought, and again the most sad misgivings tortured her mind, and she almost dreaded to proceed any farther on her way, and to ascertain the truth.

At any rate, before she did so, she could not resist the temptation to enter the temple, and with faltering but anxious steps she did so, while a trembling sensation came over her, and melancholy feelings agitated her which she could not conquer.

A solemn silence yet more impressive than that which prevailed outside, reigned within the sacred place; but it was illumined by the bright moonbeams, which streamed in at the different windows, and played and glittered among the silvery waters of the numerous fountains, adding greatly to their beautiful effect.

Omelia supported herself against one of the marble pillars, and though she could not but contemplate the beauties of the place with the most enthusiastic admiration, it was mingled with feelings of the greatest sorrow and anguish.

Where was he to whose manly and affectionate bosom she had been so warmly and fondly pressed on the last occasion of her visiting there? Alas, echo answered— "Where?"

No more she listened to the tender and fervent vows that his lips then gave utterance to; although she could almost imagine at times that she heard the beloved tones of his voice, and that she again beheld those looks of indescribable affection he had then fixed upon her.

How sad, how dreary was everything around her to her imagination, without his presence, and, alas, under all the melancholy circumstances, it did not appear likely that it would gladden her eyes again.

She pressed her hands upon her forehead as these painful thoughts occurred to her, and she endeavoured, but with little success to banish them from her mind.

At length, urged by emotions which she could not resist, Omelia sunk on her knees, and fervently besought that Great Spirit, in whom she had been taught to believe, to watch over and protect her lover and herself, and not to suffer those doubts and fears, which notwithstanding all her efforts to the contrary assailed her, to be realised.

She felt somewhat composed and confident after this, but still she lingered in the temple and seemed loath to leave it, notwithstanding the night was so far advanced, and that it was necessary she should endeavour to as certain that she was so anxious to learn without any more delay than possible.

Slowly and reluctantly she at last, however quitted the place, and, trying to reanimate her spirits, and to revive her most sanguine hopes, she once more with a palpitating heart, and eager eyes, pursued her way in the immediate direction of that part of the city in which Mr. and Mrs. Eldred had resided, and whom she hoped, with her other friends, to find there still.

But as she walked on, there was nothing whatever to encourage her hopes and expectations; not a human being met her eye, and every portion of the city was dull and silent, and appeared to be entirely deserted.

At length our heroine reached the bungalow in which the fugitives had resided, but all about them was dark and silent, and gave no signs of being any longer inhabited, and again the most torturing forebodings rushed upon her mind, and her heart sunk within her.

She once more pressed her hands upon her forehead, and paused a moment to reflect, and then imagining, from the lateness of the hour—for it must now have been near eleven o'clock—that the inmates had retired to rest, and that her fears of the buildings being abandoned might turn out to be erroneous, with a trembling but eager hand she knocked loudly at the door of that bungalow which had been occupied by herself and her friends, and awaited with the most trembling impatience the result, looking up at the different windows to see whether it had any effect.

A few moments, however, elapsed, and no answer was returned, which, of course, increased the doubts and apprehensions of the greatly and naturally agitated Omelia.

Worked up to a pitch of the greatest excitement, she repeated the knock still louder than before, and again impatiently awaited the result.

The distracted girl repeated the knocking at the adjoining buildings, but still with no better success than before, all her expectations were doomed to disappointment; it was evident that the houses were no longer inhabited, and she wrung her hands in the agony and despair of her feelings, and tears which she could not restrain started to her eyes.

"Alas, alas," she ejaculated in the most mournful accents, and with looks of intense and unutterable anguish, " all my worst, my most dreadful apprehensions are realised. Those friends so dear to me, no longer are here to greet me, and I shudder with horror to anticipate that which yet too probably awaits me. Oh, what have I done that I should still be doomed to so terrible a fate? Human patience and fortitude can surely never long endure such fearful trials as those to which it has been and is now my hard lot to be subjected."

Sobs choked her further utterance, and leaning against the door-post of one of the buildings, in order to support her trembling frame—for she must otherwise have sunk upon the earth—she abandoned herself for a few minutes to all the poignant anguish of her emotions, and felt herself totally incapable of moving from the spot.

At last aroused once more into action, and made desperate by the nature of the painful and now but too apparently hopelessness of the circumstances in which she was placed, the poor girl, pronouncing the name of her lover, rushed as precipitately as her trembling limbs would carry her, and with distracted looks towards that part of the city in which the temporary barracks was situated.

Still more brightly shone the silvery moon upon all around, but to the eye of the agonised Omelia the aspect of everything upon which her eye rested as she breathlessly proceeded, was one of disheartening gloom, and she continued to strain her eyes in every direction, but without encountering the least signs of a human being, and at length quite exhausted, and worked up to a pitch of the most feverish excitement, she was compelled to pause in her rapid progress to endeavour to recover herself.

With what distracted eyes she gazed around, her brain bewildered, clasping her hands in agony together, and her whole delicate but graceful frame agitated and convulsed with the power of her emotions.

"Unfortunate and beloved Stanley," she gasped forth as well as her sobs, which swelled her bosom would permit her, "our doom is sealed—we are lost to each other for ever. Vain are all my efforts, useless my endeavours to realise the hopes I had too hastily and too fondly suffered myself to indulge in, and there is nothing now left to me but despair. Would that I were dead, for every prospect of happiness for me in this world is completely destroyed; and everything must become hateful and unendurable to me."

One more look of bitter anguish the wretched and distracted maiden cast around

her, her hands still clasped convulsively together, and her heart seeming to swell in her bosom as though it would burst, her brain turned giddy, her limbs failed her, and then with one intense groan, she sunk upon the earth and became insensible.

CHAPTER CLII.

THE PRISONERS IN THE CAVERN.

We will leave our heroine for awhile in the melancholy and critical situation which has just been described, and return to the wretched and guilty Yusef and Alahamed in the cavern.

Their doom appeared to be inevitably sealed, for there was not the slightest prospect of their being rescued from their frightful situation, and it was utterly impossible that they could much longer exist under such fearful circumstances

It must have excited feelings of horror and compassion—notwithstanding the brutal nature of their character, and the atrocious crimes they had in the course of their guilty career committed—in the breasts of those who could have witnessed their dreadful sufferings, and the appalling expression of their at any time repulsive features, and it might be said that such a hideous and lingering punishment as that to which they were consigned, could only have been suggested by the minds of fiends in human shape, and that nothing of which they might have been guilty could ever have merited so terrible a retribution.

Their eyes were bloodshot, with the intensity of their sufferings, and at times madness was upon their brains, and they uttered in hollow and sepulchral voices the most awful lamentations and execrations.

We left them, in a former chapter, in a kind of torpor, apparently but the prelude to death—which, under the dreadful situation in which they were placed, must be admitted would have been a mercy—and from which they did not recover for some hours; but to what horrible sufferings were they awakened, too much for even the most firm and insensible to endure patiently, and language must fail to give an adequate description of it.

All the horrors of the most intense hunger were upon them, but even these were comparatively trifling to those of the burning thirst that was upon them, which seemed to fire the blood in their veins, and to prey upon and consume their vitals.

Their limbs were stiff and benumbed by being so long fixed in one confined attitude, and they had lost all power to attempt to relieve themselves, though that, as has been before shown, would have been completely useless.

And then the impenetrable darkness and solemn silence that reigned throughout their subterranean prison, was sufficient of itself to have excited the utmost terror, and to render approaching and unavoidable death the more appalling.

And yet it was truly wonderful how the poor wretches rallied at intervals, and thus struggled miraculously against their impending fate.

The tortures of their guilty consciences might be said to be even equal to their bodily sufferings, and drove them at times to madness. All the frightful crimes that they had so savagely committed, were arrayed before their memory in the most ghastly form, in vain they sought to conquer them, and they endured all the torments of an earthly perdition.

They raved against each other in the most fearful manner, when they could manage to find strength sufficient to give vent to their feelings in words, and each accused the other of being the cause of the dreadful fate which had befallen them, and from which there was evidently no means of their escaping.

"My mad infatuation is justly rewarded," said Alahamed, in a hoarse and almost unearthly voice, "my folly in making myself the mere tool to effect the accomplishment and gratification of your ambitious and avaricious wishes, is properly punished. Cursed fool that I have been; but for that I might now have been at liberty, and not have been exposed to this horrible and lingering death."

"Miscreant! taunting dog!" retorted Yusef, in a savage voice, "you accuse me wrongfully. You sought to serve your own guilty purposes, and not mine, and I owe you nothing but the most deadly hatred."

"Liar!" cried Alahamed, with increased fury, and the blood seeming ready to burst his swelling veins with the excitement of his feelings as he spoke, "had I not been mad enough to aid you in your amorous and guilty designs against the girl Omelia, which, together with the unfair and greedy manner in which you appropriated the principal portion of the proceeds of our plunder to yourself, excited the hatred and revenge of our comrades, I might have been permitted to join them in their schemes, and you alone would have been consigned to this dreadful doom which you so justly merit. Oh, would that I were myself at liberty, what delight and satisfaction it would afford me to gloat and exult over your sufferings."

He bit his lips till the blood came, as he thus gave utterance to his savage and revolting feelings, and could the wretched Yusef have beheld the dreadful expression of his features at that moment, he must have been even more appalled and dismayed than before.

However, he could return no immediate answer, and the two unfortunate wretches relapsed once more into the most gloomy silence, which they only broke at intervals by giving utterance to a groan of agony.

The time which had elapsed since their former associates had departed from the cavern, and left them in their present hopeless and torturing situation, was considerable, and it was wonderful how they had been able to bear up against their fate, so long and so well, but it appeared impossible that they could do so much longer, for their strength which had been put to such a severe and almost unexampled trial was nearly exhausted, and they became again in a state bordering upon insensibility.

What the exact time was that had elapsed it was not possible to ascertain, but probably an hour, in the manner we have described, had passed away, when suddenly Yusef and his miserable companion were aroused from the kind of lethargy, which, as has been before stated, they had fallen, by imagining they heard footsteps near the entrance to the cavern above, and instantly they were thoroughly convinced that they were not mistaken, and were not labouring under any delusion of their disordered imagination, for looking anxiously in that direction they perceived the glimmering of a light, as if emitted by a lamp carried in the hand of a person who was evidently approaching.

The wretched men uttered a wild and frantic cry as the prospect of deliverance seemed to burst upon them, and they kept their eyes fixed upon the rude steps that conducted to the cavern, and watched for the descending form with the most breathless impatience.

They were not long kept in suspense, for the light almost immediately revealed to them the person of one whom they had never expected to behold again, namely, old Juballah.

They uttered a simultaneous groan of anguish and disappointment, and their hearts sunk with despair, for they knew too well that they could expect neither pity nor mercy from her.

The mysterious old woman—who had undergone no change in her personal appearance—placed the lantern—for such it was—on the table immediately before them, and folding her arms across her naked chest, she fixed upon them a look of the most deadly malice and exultation, and laughed aloud, which sounded awful in that fearful place, and under such peculiar and frightful circumstances.

It would be a difficult task to attempt

properly to describe the dreadful anguish of the helpless and disappointed prisoners, at the sight of Juballah, for they felt satisfied that whatever might have induced her to return so unexpectedly to the cavern, it was not from any motives of pity or compunction on her part towards them, but, on the contrary, to triumph over their sufferings, and to mock at their despair.

They could not speak, however, but continued to gaze at her with looks of the utmost terror and supplication, and which she only returned with those of the most unfeeling indifference and scorn.

Yusef and his exhausted companion looked greedily at the viands and drink upon the table, and Juballah, who observed them, again laughed aloud, and appeared to enjoy their maddening agony vastly.

In this manner several minutes passed away without Juballah changing her attitude or the expression of her ugly features, but at length, in a voice which perfectly corresponded with her looks, she said—

"So death has been tardy in his work, and has not yet put a period to your lingering sufferings. 'Tis well, 'tis well; 'tis fit that those who have committed such unparalleled atrocities should experience all the horrors they have so recklessly inflicted on others."

"Fearful woman," with difficulty ejaculated Yusef, "come you here with fiendish malice to taunt and torture us?"

"Yes," she replied, with a savage grin: "it is the most welcome sight that old Juballah has experienced for many a long day, to behold your excruciating agonies. The fierce tortures of hunger and thirst are preying on your nearly exhausted vitals; I see it in your bloodshot eyes, your ghastly looks. What would you not give even for a taste of the most disgusting and unwholesome food? —a drink of even the most filthy and poisonous water. Oh, surely it is hard that such envied indulgence should be denied you."

"Monster!" exclaimed the horrorstruck and distracted Alahamed, his eyes appearing to be ready to start from their sockets, and aroused into a state of desperation by the brutality of her observations, "devil—for woman you cannot be, though in some respects you bear the faint resemblance of one —are not your deadly and unprovoked feelings of revenge yet satisfied?"

"No," answered Juballah, again laughing triumphantly, "but the time is coming when they will be completely so. Despair, for all hope of relief for you is at an end. This frightful place will form your tomb, where your bones will rot and moulder, and you cannot escape the fate which now quickly awaits you."

"Mercy — mercy, Juballah," exclaimed Yusef, wildly, and now worked up to a perfect pitch of frenzy, and with looks of the most abject supplication.

"Mercy to a wretch like you," she repeated disdainfully, "you appeal in vain, and your frantic anguish does but serve to add to my triumph."

"What have I done to excite such horrible feelings of vengeance in your breast against me?" he anxiously interrogated.

"Quite sufficient," was the fearful old woman's answer, "and I do not think proper to explain further."

"Oh, release us from these cords that bind our limbs," implored the wretched man, "and do not suffer us to end the few short moments that but too probably remain to us in this dreadful manner. Starvation has already nearly accomplished its awful work, and we are too much exhausted to attempt to leave the cavern without assistance, which, after what you have said, we cannot expect to find."

Juballah grinned contemptuously and inexorably, and returned no answer.

"Forbear to appeal to this heartless wretch," said Alahamed, suddenly mustering up the most wonderful resolution, and even fixing upon Juballah a look of defiance, which, however, she heeded not, "it is only a waste of time to do so, and since it seems we must perish, I will endeavour to meet my fate as a man."

"Be it so," returned the old woman; "your boasted courage will soon be put to the test. My task is now completed," she added, taking up the lantern, "and I leave you to the full and uninterrupted enjoyment of your last moments."

With a frightful and withering look she moved towards the steps as she spoke, and Yusef worked up to an uncontrollable state of madness at the idea of being again left, and in darkness, with his wretched companion in that frightful place to perish, shrieked aloud in horror and agony, and called upon Juballah in mercy not to leave them, but to which she only replied as usual with a scornful and triumphant laugh, though she paused for a moment at the foot of the steps to bestow a parting look upon the unhappy and ill-fated prisoners.

"Fearful woman," exclaimed Yusef, in a voice half choked by the overwhelming power of his terrible emotions, "again I implore your mercy, though I ask you not to endeavour to save my life, for that I know would be useless, and I abandon all thoughts of it I beseech you to release me from those lingering and insupportable tortures, and let your dagger's point at once terminate my wretched existence."

"No," returned Juballah, inexorably, "that

would indeed be too great a mercy for a mis-creant like you. Your fate is sealed, and nothing whatever can release you from it."

Yusef closed his eyes with a sickening sensation of terror, and Juballah having said no more, ascended the steps, and quitting the cavern, left the doomed men again in total darkness.

CHAPTER CLIII.

THE FATE OF THE PRISONERS.

It seemed impossible for human nature to endure more, and for some time after the de-parture of the revengeful old Juballah, the miserable men sunk into a complete state of exhaustion and insensibility, and it seemed as if the final and fatal moment was rapidly approaching. But death was most wonder-fully retarded, though they had now been nearly three days and nights in their present frightful situation, and without the slightest portion of food or drink.

Indeed, after a little time, they again rallied in the most remarkable way, and ap-peared to be determined to battle with their fate to the last.

A strong current of air which suddenly entered the cavern from the direction of the steps which led to the entrance, served in a great measure to revive them, and excited their astonishment.

It seemed as if old Juballah must singu-larly enough have neglected to secure the entrance in her usual manner on her depar-ture, and if so, should any one pass that way they might be induced to examine farther, and all chance of deliverence might not yet be at an end.

This was a wild and extravagant hope, but "drowning men will catch at a straw," and the wretched men could not banish it.

Oh, that they could but release themselves from the cords that bound them helplessly, even in their terrible and completely ex-hausted condition, they ventured to encou-rage the desperate idea that they might yet, after appeasing their hunger, and quenching their thirst, be able to crawl from the cavern into the open air, and probably be discovered by some one ere it was too late to save them.

How fallacious and unreasonable was such a thought, in fact it was madness to enter-tain it even for a minute; and they were at length fully convinced of that, and again abandoned themselves to all the horrors of despair, for what person was likely to ap-proach that unfrequented place, and espe-cially at such a hour as they imagined it to be?"

"All hope is at an end," groaned Yusef, in the most melancholy and pitiable accents,

"there is nothing left for us but to resign ourselves to our fate, horrible though it is."

"And the quicker it arrives the better," observed Alahamed, in a faint voice, but still endeavouring to maintain his firmness in the best manner he could; "I am tired of this lingering torture so fearful to endure, and wish that I had but the means and the opportunity of putting an end to it; curses light on it, and the infernal wretch who has been the means of bringing us to it."

Yusef again groaned, but his feelings were too much excited—when he became con-vinced of the utter folly and extravagance of the idea of any one accidentally coming to their deliverence—to suffer him to make any reply to the observations of the frantic wretch Alahamed, and they both remained buried in a solemn silence for some time, gradually becoming fainter and fainter, and evidently rapidly sinking.

Suddenly, however, Alahamed exclaimed, as if awaking from some frightful dream, while all his energies for the moment seemed to have returned—

"Ah, what sounds were those that just now smote my listening ears?"

"Has madness seized upon your brain, Alahamed?" demanded Yusef, in a tremu-lous voice, that almost seemed to come from the grave; "what mean you?"

"Did you not hear the muttering of voices above?" returned Alahamed; "there, again."

"'Twas but the murmuring of the wind," said Yusef, in tones of despair, "'tis folly to encourage such wild and delusive hopes and fancies; there is no escaping from our fear-ful and quickly approaching doom. Oh, that death was not so tardy in his awful but merciful work."

"Silence, coward," said Alahamed, scorn-fully; "listen."

They did both listen attentively, but for a few minutes without hearing anything but the dismal moaning of the wind, and which the more strongly convinced them that the entrance to the cavern, by some strange oversight, had been left unsecured by Jubal-lah on her departure.

Still the two wretched prisoners continued to listen with breathless attention, and in a state of mental anguish which it is quite un-necessary to describe, and presently between the pauses of the wind they both now ima-gined that they heard the low and distinct mutterings of human voices, which sounded immediately above and near the entrance; and so strong was this impression, that with a powerful effort which seemed scarcely pos-sible for men in their awful and exhausted condition, they shouted aloud, and in the most piteous accents supplicated for help.

The hollow voice of the wind was the only answer returned to their cries, and then all became hushed in silence, and the distracted Yusef and his companion were again left in terrible disappointment and despair.

About half an hour passed away in this manner, and then the frightful agonies of the apparently doomed men became most intense, driving them to a perfect pitch of frenzy, so terrible were the pangs of hunger upon them that they could have gnawed their own flesh, and their dreadful thirst was even more intolerable.

"Water—water," they cried in their frenzy as though there had been any one near to hear them, and to take compassion on their sufferings, "oh, but one drop of water to wet our burning lips."

In the wild paroxysm of their madness they mingled the most awful oaths and curses with their supplications, and foamed at the mouth and bit their lips with insupportable agony till the blood flowed.

And now the final struggle, the termination by death of their unexampled sufferings, appeared to be evidently at hand; a weight of molten lead seemed to press upon their brain; their eyes were like balls of fire, and ready to start from their sockets; a cold tremor convulsed their swolen and bleeding limbs; gradually their groans and moanings became fainter and fainter till they died away altogether; their heads drooped, their eyes closed, the "grim tyrant" seemed at length to have completed his task, and silence reigned in the dreary cavern.

Some minutes had elapsed, and the ill-fated men seemed indeed at last to have been relieved from their excruciating sufferings by death; when suddenly the sound of voices might have been heard, mingled with that of the storm—for it appeared that one had arisen, and threatened soon to rage with the greatest violence—and a broad glare of light immediately afterwards illumined the cavern.

———

CHAPTER CLIV.

UNEXPECTED RELIEF.

Four men, dressed as natives of the middle class, armed, and one of them carrying with him a lighted torch, quickly made their appearance on the steps, descending cautiously into the cavern.

They had evidently been benighted in that dreary and but little frequented part of the country, and having accidentally lighted upon the entrance to the cavern, had been induced to seek shelter there from the storm.

The man with the torch held it above his head, in order to accelerate his view, and that of his companions, and they gazed with amazement at the strange place, and hesi-tated to proceed, perceiving the table with the remains of the food and drink, as the rebels had left them on their departure from the cavern, therefore concluding that the place was inhabited, and with what description of individuals it was not very difficult to conjecture.

They were about to make a hasty retreat, not knowing what danger they might probably be involving themselves in, when an exclamation from the man who carried the torch arrested their footsteps, and drew their attention in the direction he was eagerly gazing, with looks of astonishment and terror, and they then, for the first time, discovered the apparently lifeless forms of Yusef and Alahamed, secured to the post, in the manner which has been before described.

Thunderstruck at this unexpected sight, and imagining for the moment that they were two of the sepoys who had remained faithful to the British cause, and being captured by some of the rebels, had fallen victims to their vengeance, the travellers listened first attentively, but hearing no sound they concluded that the cavern was deserted, and they therefore descended the steps hastily, and advanced towards the spot where the ill-fated men were secured, and gazed with horror and the deepest commiseration at the truly awful spectacle which they presented.

They raised their heads, and gazed at them more minutely, and ghastly indeed was the expression of their features, showing in characters that could not be misunderstood the dreadful agonies they must for some time have endured.

"Unfortunate men," said one of the strangers, in a voice of compassion, "their death has evidently been a horrible one of starvation, which none but the most atrocious miscreants could inflict. I regret that we did not arrive before, when we might probably have released them from their dreadful fate."

"True, Zelib," coincided the man with the torch, "the sufferings of these unfortunate men have doubtless been of the most frightful and lingering description, to judge from their appearance, and it is a mercy that death has at length put an end to them. But let us unbind them from the cords, and we may then place their remains in the earth here, as well as we can."

This suggestion received the approbation of his companions, and they accordingly proceeded to release the bodies of Yusef and Alahamed from the post to which they had been so mercilessly bound; but no sooner had they done so, than one of them uttered an exclamation of surprise, as a faint sigh escaped the lips of Alahamed, and Yusef also gave symptoms that life was not extinct.

"They are not yet dead," observed one of the men, "the removal of the cords has doubtless caused the sudden re circulation of the blood, and even in their deplorable and exhausted state, with prompt care and attention, it may not yet be too late to save them."

They immediately placed the inanimate forms of Yusef and Alahamed upon one of the benches which the cavern contained, and taking a flask from his pocket, the man who had just spoken proceeded to moisten their lips with a certain reviving beverage it contained, not knowing what might be the contents of the different bottles on the table, at which the rebels had been regaling themselves, after they secured their victims, previous to their departure.

Placing his hand over their hearts, the man who had been called Zelib, felt them slightly palpitate, and that encouraged them to pursue their humane exertions to endeavour to restore the miserable men to consciousness—although they appeared to be too far gone to recover altogether—with increased perseverence, and with some little prospect of success.

The features of the unfortunate men became less distorted, and their hearts seemed to beat more freely and distinctly, but still they remained perfectly insensible.

In the meantime, while these humane proceedings were going on, such as chafing the limbs of Yusef, and Alahamed, in order to impart freer circulation to the blood, and applying such other remedies as were at all practicable at present, one of the travellers, whose curiosity was more excited than the others, took a more minute survey of the cavern, and discovering the place where Omelia had been confined, and which remained the same as when she had left it, he uttered an exclamation of surprise, and drew the attention of his companions towards it.

The taste and even elegance with which this cavern was fitted up, could not fail to excite their utmost amazement, and left them in a still greater state of mystery as to the real characters of the men who had inhabited this singular subterranean retreat.

The sight of the bed, however, was most welcome to them, and they immediately removed the insensible Yusef and Alahamed to it, and laid them upon it, redoubling their praiseworthy efforts to restore them to animation, which, however did not seem likely to take place for some time.

The storm was now at its height, and the rain poured down in torrents, and the thunder roared, and the wind howled in tones sufficient to awaken the dead. It was a terrible night to be exposed in, and the travellers could not but congratulate themselves upon having so fortunately and so unexpectedly found a place of shelter, but more especially in having the opportunity of performing the act of humanity they were now doing.

They could not but entertain some apprehensions of the return of the persons who had lately occupied the cavern, but these they endeavoured to conquer, and to content themselves by proceeding with their humane task, with the hope of their efforts being ultimately crowned with success.

In this they were not disappointed; at length warmth was imparted to the sufferers' limbs, the expression of their countenances became less ghastly, they breathed more freely, and opened their eyes, although by their vacant stare it was quite evident that they were not yet restored to consciousness.

This again encouraged the benevolent travellers, and having now the opportunity of administering to them a gentle stimulant, the two unfortunate men seemed to progress much more favourably than could have been at all expected under the desperate and apparently hopeless circumstances.

There was something, however, in the appearance of the guilty wretches which could scarcely fail to excite the suspicions of the travellers as to their real character, and what had brought them into the dreadful situation in which they had discovered them, and they were not a little anxious that they might recover, so that they might possibly afford them some explanation.

"Their looks are ferocious," observed Zelib, "and there is something in the expression of their features, which would almost induce one to believe that they were capable of committing any crime however atrocious. They may be two of the bloodthirsty rebels, who have proved themselves to be so totally unworthy of the land which gave them birth."

"True, Zelib," coincided one of his companions, "but the mystery is how they came into the frightful situation in which we found them. Such tortures could only be inflicted by the heartless wretches engaged in this revolt, and if these are two of them, they must have done something extraordinary thus to excite the vengeance of their associates in crime. The elegance of this place shows that those who occupied the subterranean retreat, know how to enjoy themselves, and could fully appreciate all that is luxurious."

To this Zeleb and the others also agreed, and the conversation upon that subject dropped, while they renewed their exertions for the recovery of Yusef and Alahamed.

———

CHAPTER CLV.

WHAT BEFEL OMELIA.

The situation in which we left Omelia in a former chapter, was a melancholy and a critical one, and it is now necessary to relate what befel her.

On recovering her consciousness, but with only a vague and dreamy recollection of what had happened, she found herself being supported in the arms of a strange man, a non-commissioned officer, and who was treating her with every respect, and gazing at her with looks of the deepest compassion and interest.

The sight of a human being, when she had supposed that the city was entirely deserted, and that a man, a British soldier, too, instantly aroused her, and revived her hopes, and with eager haste she inquired of the stranger whether the regiment to which her lover belonged was still in the city.

He replied in the negative, and added that only two days before it had departed for Calcutta he had been informed, though he had every reason to believe that it was to some distant station, where its services were required.

This information, this confirmation of her worst suspicions, came like a death blow to our unhappy heroine, and uttering an exclamation of the most poignant grief and despair she again became insensible.

On again recovering her senses, she found herself reclining on a sofa, in a comfortable, if not extravagantly furnished apartment, with two females of respectable and prepossessing appearance, who seemed to have been paying her every attention that kindness and humanity could suggest, and who by their looks evinced the utmost satisfaction at her recovery.

Eagerly the poor girl raised her head from the pillow on which it had been resting, and fixing her eyes anxiously on the fair strangers who were in attendance upon her, attempted to address them, but a sickly sensation came over her, and choked her utterance, while the wildest and most painful thoughts and apprehensions crowded upon her brain.

They, however, seemed to anticipate her thoughts and wishes, and the eldest of the females, in a kind and gentle voice, said—

"Do not disturb or excite yourself, my poor girl, but endeavour to compose yourself with the assurance that you are with friends, and in the morning you shall receive every information that you may require."

"Oh, no," replied our heroine, impatiently and with an agitated look and manner, "I cannot wait till then, with my mind in this terrible state of suspense. Tell me, I beseech you, where am I, and who are you that seem to look upon me with such kindness and sympathy?"

"Perhaps," answered the female, "unless you are a stranger here, "it may be unnecessary to inform you that you are in the city of Cawnpore, made painfully notorious by one of the most horrible slaughters that was ever perpetrated upon the human race. Myself and my sister here are the daughters of a distinguished British officer, by whose orders you were brought here about an hour since, by Sergeant Simpson, who had discovered you lying in an insensible state in a, at present, unoccupied part of the city.

"Alas," sighed Omelia, with the greatest emotion, and pressing her hands on her forehead, while tears gushed to her eyes, "the painful, the agonising truth now flashes upon my memory with all its overwhelming effects. Stanley, dear Stanley, lost, lost to me for ever."

Convulsive sobs prevented her saying more, and burying her face in her hands, she wept bitterly.

The ladies who were in attendance upon her, and to whose residence she had been so fortunate as to be conveyed, again sought to tranquillize her feelings, but, although she could not but feel grateful to them for their kindness and commiseration to one who was a complete stranger to them, their endeavours to soothe her in her present distracted state of mind, when all the fond hopes she had dared at times to cherish, were attended with very little if any success.

From these ladies, in answer to questions she put to them, she received a corroboration of the statement made by Sergeant Simpson, namely, that the regiment to which her lover belonged had left the city, but whither it was gone was not exactly known.

She was also informed of the departure of Mr. and Mrs. Eldred, their daughter, and most of the other fugitives from Lucknow, and thus she was deprived of every friend and acquaintance from whom she might expect consolation, advice, and protection.

This thought of itself was quite sufficient to cause her the utmost pain, and she again burst into a violent flood of tears, which the two ladies, probably thinking it might afford some relief to her overcharged heart, did not offer to interrupt.

They were right, in their conjectures, as Omelia did, by dint of great exertion—especially as she did not wish at present to obtrude her sorrows upon those who were strangers to her—become considerably more calm, and thanked the two fair sisters—who were very beautiful—most warmly and sincerely for their kindness and hospitality.

She also begged that her acknowledgements might be presented at the earliest opportunity to Sergeant Simpson for the service he had rendered her, when he discovered her in so critical and dangerous a situation, and which request the eldest sister promised to comply with.

They then prevailed upon her to partake of some slight refreshment, and bidding her good night, she expressing a wish to be alone, they retired, having arranged for a young ayah to sleep in an adjoining chamber, in case Omelia might require any assistance in the night.

What a strange, chequered, adventurous life was our heroine's, and so it seemed likely to remain till the day of her death. She had been gladdened by the brightest sunshine of earthly happiness; but for some time past the black storm-clouds of adversity had more generally pervaded her destiny, disappointment had followed disappointment in rapid succession, hope after hope had been destroyed, until her patience was nearly exhausted, and no wonder that, even with all the heroic fortitude she had displayed on so many trying occasions, she could at times abandon herself to despair.

And for what fresh troubles might she not still be reserved? What future sorrows might be weaving her in the web of destiny?

Such were the torturing thoughts that naturally occurred to Omelia when she was left alone, and which, coupled with the novelty of her situation, for some time banished sleep from her eyelids.

How sad and dreary was the prospect that now opened before her; it was almost too dark and cheerless for her to contemplate, and she shuddered with an instinctive feeling of terror, which she could not resist, as she did so.

Stanley it now appeared too certain to her, and she could not remove the impression, was indeed lost to her for ever, every hope of her future happiness was at an end, and that thought was of itself sufficient to drive her to destruction.

And what course could she now adopt in her present difficulties? was a question she asked herself, and which she found it difficult to answer; whither could she go?— where seek a home and asylum? Her present means, the money which she had received from old Juballah, were very limited, and they would soon be exhausted, and it was not likely that she could long remain a burthen to strangers; so that she knew not where to direct her steps, where to seek a refuge.

Had her friends the Eldreds—to whom she had become greatly attached—still been residing in Cawnpore, she would indeed have had those to whom she could confide her thoughts, and who would sincerely have sympathised with her sorrows and misfortunes, but now she was left completely alone —she had not a friend near her to whom she could look for advice and protection.

The faithful and generous-hearted Abdal, too, whom she had so much cause to esteem, and to whom she was already so largely indebted; what had become of him? How inestimable would have been his friendly advice and friendship at this particular juncture; but fate seemed to sport with her and to mock at her misfortunes and disappointments, and the longer she reflected, the greater her anguish became.

"Oh, would that I were dead," she sighed, "since the greatest and most insupportable misery alone seems destined to be my portion, and there is not the least prospect of a favourable change to cheer me on to renewed hope. My life is a dreary waste, without one solitary plant to relieve my weary sight, and over which the rude winds of sorrow constantly sweep and howl around my defenceless form. Not one ray of sunshine is there now left for me, and surely I had better be no more—be reposing in the peaceful grave, than continue to drag on this lingering life of misery."

She clasped her hands with anguish together as she thus spoke, and the tears coursed each other down her cheeks.

But at length fatigue and anxiety of mind overpowered her, and throwing her head back on the pillow, she sunk off into anything but a refreshing sleep.

No the thoughts that had so tortured her in her waking moments, pursued her in her dreams, and conjured up things and scenes to her disordered imagination of the most fearful description, and she frequently started from her slumbers with terror convulsing every limb, and the perspiration standing in large drops upon her forehead.

Her beloved Stanley was presented to her imagination in various of the most appalling situations; at one time she fancied that she saw him stretched in the agonies of death, bleeding copiously from many frightful wounds, upon the dreadful battle-field, she beheld the ghastly expression of his fine manly features at the awful moment, she heard him call frantically upon her name, but although she was only a few paces from him, she was transfixed to the earth like a statue, and could neither move from the spot or utter a word.

Oh, what was the terrible agony of her feelings at that moment; her heart seemed ready to burst its tenement—the blood ran icy chill through her veins, though the perspiration started from every pore.

The next moment, she imagined, that the enemy rushed over the bloody field in a host, crushing the dead and the dying; a mist arose before her eyes and she beheld no more.

Again she dreamt that she beheld her lover in the power of the bloodthirsty and remorseless foe, bound to a tree, and the wretches inflicting every torture upon him that the inhuman minds of demons could invent, and mocking at and exulting over his frightful sufferings. Distinctly did she witness all, but yet, as in her previous dream, she was unable to approach him; and with the agony caused by this vision she again awoke.

The young ayah—who was an interesting-looking girl—was seated by the side of the sofa, anxiously watching her, when our heroine started from her slumbers, greatly agitated by the fearful dreams that had been presented to her imagination, but she requested her to retire for a few minutes, that she might give free indulgence to her thoughts, and, of course, the girl immediately obeyed.

CHAPTER CLVI.

OMELIA'S NEW FRIENDS.

For a minute or two the brain of Omelia was so bewildered by the painful and alarming nature of the dreams that had occurred to her, that she could not collect her thoughts sufficiently to reflect with anything like calmness or reason upon them, but when she did, to what bitter feelings of anguish did those dreams give rise to in her breast. They appeared to her to be prophetic, and she was too ready to believe that they would be, if they had not already been realised, even in their most horrible form, and that idea for a time drove her to complete distraction.

What could be more probable than the occurrence of such dreadful facts, when she considered the great dangers to which her lover was doubtless exposed? Nothing; and Omelia could not divest her mind of the impression, that their fate was sealed and they should behold each other no more.

That idea gained strength every moment in her mind, until she was worked up to such a pitch of torturing excitement that she could scarcely contain herself within the bounds of reason.

A flood of tears, however, at length came to her relief, and she was then able to reflect upon all the peculiar and unfortunate circumstances by which she was surrounded more calmly.

But in vain she endeavoured to discover anything in the dismal prospect before her, which was calculated to dissipate the apprehensions that assailed her, or inspire her with the least degree of hope. In which ever way she directed her thoughts, all was gloomy, cheerless, and disheartening, and the longer she reflected the more terrible her situation and prospects appeared to be.

Had she but been enabled to learn whither the regiment to which Stanley belonged had gone, it would have afforded some little relief to her anxiety, for in spite of all the hardships and perils she might, and probably would have to encounter, she would then have followed him, and, if she should be destined to be disappointed in her hopes of again beholding him, she might at least be able to ascertain the fate which had befallen him, and certainty, however dreadful, would, she could not help considering, be better than to be kept in this torturing state of suspense.

"Oh, best beloved of all earthly beings," she ejaculated, in tones of the deepest emotion, "surely it was cruel, it was unfortunate that we should ever have been permitted to know each other, if thus all our fond hopes and wishes should be continually doomed to disappointment, and that we were ever to be exposed to such terrible misfortunes, constantly tossed about on the rough sea of adversity, without any pospect of ever being able to reach the bright haven of peace and happiness. But if it is your fate to fall by the hands of the ruthless enemy, dear Stanley, oh, that I might also be suffered to perish with you, to die upon your manly bosom, and that we might mingle our last sighs together. That, even that would indeed have been some melancholy consolation, but alas, it is denied us."

Once more she wept bitterly in all the poignancy and uncontrollable anguish of her feelings, and not one thought occurred to her that could afford her the least relief.

But suddenly she dashed the tears from her eyes, as a fresh idea seemed to flash upon her brain, arousing her dormant faculties, and exclaimed—

"But why should I thus remain inactive, and abandon myself to despair, when there may yet be the means of confirming or removing my worst apprehensions? I will again resume my weary wanderings in search of that beloved being, deprived of whom life must become to me worthless and insupportable. If he lives, providence will, I trust, aid me in my efforts, and guide me to his presence. Oh, yes, I feel fresh hopes arise within my breast, and urge me on, and I must not, will not delay the commencement of my arduous and perilous task any longer than possible. There is no danger, no trial, however severe, which I will not fearlessly encounter for your sake, dear Stanley."

Fresh hope and courage reanimated the breast of the beauteous maiden, as she thus gave expression to the thoughts and feelings that agitated her, and she endeavoured to arise from the couch on which she had been reposing during the night, but to her utter disappointment and dismay, she found she was so weak that she could not, and, with a sigh, she sunk back on her pillow, and for a few minutes she was so distracted by the various emotions and confused ideas that stole over her that she became stupified and almost unconscious.

"Alas," she sighed at last, "how fruitless is it for me to form resolutions, when everything seems to conspire to mock and thwart my wishes? The troubles and almost unexampled exertions I have so long had to endure have at last proved too much for me, and just at the very time which requires the exercise of all my energies, I am rendered completely powerless and exhausted. Oh, misery most unendurable—disappointment too great for even the utmost patience to endure. I shall go distracted."

She covered her face with her hands, and a sickly sensation stole over her, while the most terrible presentiments arose to her mind. It seemed to her that she was about to experience a severe illness, and no wonder that her apprehensions should excite her feelings to the utmost degree, the more especially as she was so awkwardly and delicately situated among strangers.

The ayah now entered the room, although she had not been summoned, and alarmed at the appearance of Omelia, she immediately retired, in order to make her two young ladies acquainted with the fact, and they quickly repaired to the chamber.

On entering it they found the unfortunate

and deeply afflicted girl in a complete state of exhaustion, and quite insensible, and seriously alarmed, they made their gallant father —who happened to be in the house at the time — acquainted with the circumstance without delay, and he summonsed the attendance of a surgeon with whom he was acquainted, and who attended with the greatest promptitude.

He immediately applied such remedies as the nature of her case required, pronounced her to be seriously ill from over exertion and anxiety of mind, advising that she should be kept perfectly quiet, and on no account to suffer anything to excite her, if possible.

He then took his leave for the present, as his services were required elsewhere, but promising to visit Omelia again in an hour or two, and the two sisters continued to watch by her with the most anxious solicitude.

The extreme beauty of our heroine had not failed to excite the warmest admiration in the breasts of those two amiable girls, while the peculiar and melancholy circumstances under which she had been introduced to them, had naturally caused them to feel the deepest interest and sympathy towards her, and which they were thoroughly convinced, from her appearance and manner, she so well deserved.

It may, perhaps, here be thought necessary to say a few words respecting the new friends among whom Omelia was so accidentally thrown.

Colonel Bridport—which was the name of the two interesting and amiable young ladies who have already been introduced to the reader—was one of the most gallant officers in the British army, and on several occasions had greatly distinguished himself in the present war. He was much esteemed by the officers and private soldiers of the regiment to which he belonged.

The colonel was a man about sixty years of age, and had seen much service, though he probably, like too many others, not being connected with some aristocratic family, had been far from adequately rewarded for them.

He was a man of the most sterling private character, and there was no one who might become acquainted with him but must be anxious to secure and continue his friendship.

Colonel Bridport, as soon as he was made acquainted with the extraordinary and painful circumstances under which our heroine had been discovered, had felt the deepest interest and commiseration for her, and had ordered that she should immediately be conveyed to the temporary residence of his daughters and himself, where every attention should be paid to her, and it has been shown how promptly and faithfully those instruc-

tions had been complied with. The gallant colonel though, with all his amiable qualities, had experienced severe troubles and afflictions in the course of his life, which must have borne down many a less courageous spirit.

Early in life he had contracted a marriage of pure affection with one of the most lovely and virtuous of women, but against the stern will of his father, who in consequence discarded him, leaving him nothing but his limited income to support himself and his wife.

This, however, himself and his amiable partner bore with the most exemplary fortitude and resignation, and with a firm reliance on the goodness of providence, with their own perseverance to enable them to struggle against and to surmount all vicissitudes and difficulties.

Nothing could be greater than the domestic happiness which this union produced. The fruits of it were two sons and three daughters, the former of whom, following the example of their gallant father, entered the army at an early age.

Alas, both these young men perished in the same engagement, in the early part of their career, and thus were all the fondly cherished hopes and expectations of their affectionate parents blighted, and their happiness received a blow from which it was difficult for them to recover.

But their peace of mind and domestic happiness was soon fated to receive another melancholy shock, which occurred in the premature death of their youngest daughter, a fair and gentle being, who fell a victim to consumption at the early age of twelve.

Some years elapsed, and the whole care and attention of the affectionate mother, during the absence of her husband on foreign service, was devoted to the cultivation of the minds of her two surviving daughters—Julia and Charlotte, the two lovely girls who have been already introduced to the reader—and well did they repay her for her maternal exertions, by evincing the most superior intrinsic qualities, emulating her's and their father's virtues, at the same time that their matchless personal charms excited the admiration of all who knew them.

Some time before the rebellion broke out, Mrs. Bridport, with her daughters, joined her husband in India, where he was likely to have to remain for some years, and they took up their residence at Delhi, in which capital the regiment to which he belonged was stationed, and there their time passed happily, till the sanguinary war, which had long been looming in the distance, commenced, spreading terror and dismay among all classes of society around.

It was then that Colonel Bridport and his

daughters received a blow which was far more terrible than any they had yet experienced; Mrs. Bridport was brutally murdered before their eyes—as they gazed from the window of their dwelling—when returning home, and they themselves only escaping by a miracle.

What subsequently happened to them, and the various horrors, dangers, and hairbreadth escapes they had to encounter, space will not allow us here to relate, and having mentioned those few most prominent features of their history, in order the more clearly to show the characters of the individuals to whom our heroine had been accidentally introduced, we will return to that part of our story from which we have thus shortly digressed, and which the reader will doubtless feel anxious for us to do.

CHAPTER CLVII.

HOPES REVIVED.

Contrary to the expectations of the surgeon, and Julia Bridport and her sister, our heroine in the course of an hour or two so far revived as to be able to speak, and to thank her amiable friends for the care and attention they had paid her, and for the anxious solicitude which they evidently felt in her welfare.

But she still felt too weak and ill to leave her couch, and following the advice of the surgeon, the sisters desired her to become composed if possible, and not to suffer anything to excite her unnecessarily.

This was excellent advice, but much sooner given than followed, but Omelia exerted herself to the utmost to do so, and succeeded much better than might have been expected.

She listened to the conversation which Julia and her sister occasionally addressed to her with pleasure, and it served in a great measure to divert her thoughts from the melancholy subjects that would otherwise have engrossed them; and the fair sisters were no less captivated by the sound sense of Omelia's observations, and the bewitching simplicity of her manners, and although they were aware that it would not be prudent or advisable to fatigue her with conversation for the present, they could never have become tired of listening to her.

They felt the greatest anxiety and curiosity to become acquainted with the particulars of her history, which they were satisfied must be a most extraordinary and interesting one, but that of course they could not expect to elicit under the present circumstances, if indeed they should ever receive that gratification.

But in spite of all her efforts, Omelia found it impossible to banish entirely the gloomy and torturing thoughts that would at intervals crowd upon her brain, although she felt grateful that providence had placed her under the protection of those who evidently so warmly sympathised with her.

Julia and her sister continued unremitting in their attentions to Omelia throughout the day, and in the evening finding that she had sunk off into a tranquil slumber, they left her, as on the night before, under the care of the young ayah.

Our heroine passed an excellent night undisturbed by the strange and fearful dreams which had before distracted and bewildered her imagination, and she felt so much recruited both in health and spirits in the morning, that Julia and her sister were surprised, and, it is almost unnecessary to add, sincerely gratified on witnessing the favourable and unexpected change, and they congratulated her accordingly.

Indeed Omelia felt so far recovered as to be able to leave her bed, and, after partaking of a slight repast, at the express wish of the two sisters, she suffered them to conduct her to a room below, in order that she might be introduced to their father who was anxious to see her.

On her entrance the colonel greeted her with much friendship and kindness, and she was no less favourably impressed with the urbanity of his looks and manners, than he was forcibly struck with her great beauty and modesty of demeanour.

The cordiality of her reception, and the kind observations of Colonel Bridport, soon banished the natural confusion and timidity of Omelia, and she thanked him most fervently for the humane part he had acted in taking her, an entire stranger, under his roof, at a time when she might have been exposed to so much danger, and for the great care that had been taken of her by him and his amiable daughters since.

Her looks confirmed the sincerity of her words, and the gallant colonel was more prepossessed in favour of her than ever.

"My poor girl," he observed, "much as I admire the feeling of gratitude which prompts you, I cannot but deem thanks, under such peculiar and painful circumstances as those in which you were discovered, as almost unnecessary and uncalled for. Brutal and insensible indeed must that individual be who could have beheld one of their fellow creatures, and that, too, a woman, in so deplorable a situation, without being moved to compassion, and rendering all the assistance in their power. It is a source of the highest gratification to me that I have been enabled to do so, and I require no acknowledgements."

Omelia's eyes filled with tears, and she could not withhold her eloquent looks of gratitude and admiration from her generous friend in the time of need.

"Oh, dear sir," she said, unable to restrain the expression of her feelings, "how kind, how humane, how truly benevolent is this. Would that there were more, many, many more in the world like you than there are, there would not be half the misery that there is. I must, I cannot resist the temptation to repeat my humble, but most earnest and fervent thanks. To your amiable daughters too, sir, who have treated me with even sisterly kindness, how much am I indebted, a debt that it can never possibly be in my power to repay?"

"Name it not, we beseech you, my poor girl," said the gentle Julia, taking her hand, and pressing it fervently, "we feel satisfied in the sweet consciousness of having performed our duty."

The looks of Charlotte showed how sincerely she coincided with her sister's observations.

"Truly spoken, my love," observed the colonel, with an approving smile, and politely handing our heroine to a seat, "and there e'en let the subject drop. May I take the liberty of inquiring your name, my good girl?"

"Omelia," replied our heroine, in a timid voice.

"Omelia?" repeated the colonel, after a moment or two's reflection; "methinks I have heard that name before; but probably I am mistaken. Oh, what strange misfortunes could have brought you into such a distressing situation?"

Omelia hesitated, and pressed her hands upon her forehead, then sighed, and replied,

"Alas, mine is a sad, sad history, sir, but it is too long to relate now, neither have I the strength or fortitude to do so."

Colonel Bridport gazed at her for a few moments with looks of compassion, without speaking, but at length in a voice of the tenderest feeling he said—

"Believe me, Omelia, that the questions I may take the liberty of putting to you are not prompted by mere idle curiosity. Heaven forbid that they should be. But allow me to ask you, have you any friends?"

"Alas," sighed our heroine, I know not."

"How?" interrogated the colonel, with a look of surprise.

"Oh, sir," replied Omelia, with increased agitation, and tears gushing to her eyes, "I once had friends, dearly beloved friends, whom I prized more than my life. They were here, in this very city, but cruel fate separated me from them in an evil hour, and now I know not whither they have gone, or whether they be living or dead."

"And their names, my poor girl?" anxiously inquired Colonel Bridport.

Omelia again hesitated, and it was some moments ere she could sufficiently conquer her emotion to answer, but at length she said, in a faint and tremulous voice, at the same time averting her looks from the gaze of the colonel and his daughters—

"There was one who—his name was Lieutenant Stanley, of the Fusileers, and—"

Her voice failed her, and she could say no more.

The colonel looked steadfastly at her for an instant, and he seemed perfectly to understand and to sympathise with the feelings that so violently agitated her, but he delicately forbore to press her on the subject.

"The Fusileers and other regiments left here some four days since," he remarked; "as soon as we arrived; and it being considered of importance the place of their destination was not made known."

"Alas, alas," said our heroine, wringing her hands with the anguish of feeling which she could not conceal.

"Unfortunate girl," said Colonel Bridport, "I sincerely pity you, and regret that it is not in my power to relieve your anxiety by giving you the information you require. But wait patiently for a day or two, and something may luckily transpire to promote your wishes."

"Oh, do you really think so, my dear sir?" interrogated our heroine, anxiously.

"It is more than probable that it will," returned the colonel, "so live in hope, and I trust that you will not be disappointed. But try to compose yourself, and with the assurance that you are here among friends. With your permission, we will drop this subject, which is so painful to your feelings, for the present."

Omelia duly appreciated the kind feeling of consideration with which this was spoken, and she did endeavour to tranquillise her feelings, and to banish her gloomy and painful thoughts, in which she was far more successful than might have been expected.

The observations of Colonel Bridport had revived her hopes to a certain degree, and the evident sincerity and kindness of his expressions of sympathy inspired her with confidence.

They passed two or three agreeable hours in conversation upon different topics, in which Omelia displayed an intelligence that rather took the gallant colonel and his daughters by surprise, and filled them with admiration.

But at length our heroine feeling tired, requested permission to withdraw to her chamber, and there, when left alone to her own melancholy thoughts, her spirits again became depressed, and she ruminated sadly on her hard and cruel fate, on the severe trials and misfortunes that constantly attended her, and though she tried hard, she could find but little, if any consolation

"Alas," she sighed, "it seems to be my fate to be in a state of dependence upon strangers, and to place myself under obligations which I can never repay."

She checked herself, however, before she proceeded farther, for such observations she considered, when she reflected upon the kind and disinterested conduct of Colonel Bridport and his daughters, and the delicate way in which they had tendered their services, savoured very much of ingratitude, which base passion she abhorred and despised.

The hopes that the colonel had, with such apparent confidence, held out to her, that a day or two, if she waited patiently, might furnish them with the desired information as to the place where the regiment to which her lover belonged had gone, she could not help encouraging, in fact, had she not done so, she must have become one of the most miserable of human beings, and sunk into complete despair.

"Oh, all merciful powers," she most fervently ejaculated, clasping her hands vehemently together, her bosom swelling and her heart palpitating violently at the thought, "grant that those hopes may at least be realised, with what eager haste would I resume my weary wanderings in search of you, dear Stanley, fearless alike of dangers which might beset me on every side, and of the fatigue, the privations, and the sufferings I should doubtless have to undergo. And should my exertions be crowned with success, and providence once more guide me to your fond embrace, even, though worn out with terrible anxiety of mind, I should expire upon your bosom, and thus prove my heart's fond devotion, methinks I could die happy, since I had beheld you again and received your blessing. Blissful thought, my brain turns giddy as I dwell upon it."

She was worked up to a pitch of the most feverish excitement as she thus reflected, and her emotions were too great to suffer her to say more.

And thus Omelia continued to waver between hope and fear for some time, and until she was rejoined by Julia and her sister, who were anxious to know how she felt after her interview with their father, and the conversation that had taken place.

She stifled her emotions as well as she could, and even endeavoured to appear comparatively cheerful, as she expressed her high sense of the kindness and sympathy Colonel Bridport had evinced towards her, and which she said under any circumstances in which she might in future be placed, must be stamped upon her memory, and awaken feelings of the most lively gratitude in her breast.

"To me, a poor, humble, lonely girl," she added, "to receive such unexampled kindness and assistance from those to whom I am an entire stranger, and with whose character and real claims upon their humanity they are totally unacquainted, the sense of the deep obligations I am under must be doubly keen, and in vain do I endeavour to find words sufficiently powerful to express my feelings. May the Great Spirit Who watches over the destinies of the whole human race, shower its blessings upon your heads, that indeed is my sincere prayer."

The sisters were strongly impressed and deeply affected by the fervour and sincerity of Omelia's words and manner, and for a moment or two they pressed her hand in silence.

"Unfortunate Omelia," at length said Julia, in the kindest accents, "I pray you to banish from your mind all unpleasant thoughts of obligation, and to rest assured that our conduct towards you is prompted by the most unselfish and disinterested motives, and that we are only too happy in being able to render you the assistance you so urgently require, under the extraordinary and truly painful circumstances in which you are placed. The child of misfortune must ever have the most undeniable claims upon the sympathies and assistance of the benevolent and humane, and surely there cannot be a greater gratification than in being afforded the opportunity of doing good. Besides, both our father and ourselves are convinced that your virtues as well as your misfortunes entitle you to our kindest consideration and esteem."

"Oh, how noble, how generous is this," ejaculated our heroine, overwhelmed with feelings of the warmest gratitude, "how truly kind and charitable is the confidence yourselves and your gallant father repose in me, and which, if I could ever abuse, I must hate and despise myself. I hope at some future time to be able to explain to you some of the most important particulars of my wayward life, and then you will indeed perceive that I have at least those claims upon your sympathy which Colonel Bridport and yourselves acknowledge me to possess.

The fair sisters expressed their anxiety to hear the particulars of Omelia's doubtless remarkable history, and the conversation was continued throughout the afternoon upon different subjects, and at an early hour in the evening Omelia retired to rest, feeling much more tranquil and hopeful in mind than she had done for the last few days.

———

CHAPTER CLVIII.

OMELIA'S RESOLVE.

The following day Omelia had a second interview with Colonel Bridport in which he renewed his expressions of friendship, and again assured her that he would exert himself to the utmost to obtain the information she so anxiously required, regarding the part of the country to which the regiment to which Lieutenant Stanley belonged had been sent; for which our heroine returned her warmest thanks, and trusted that the gallant colonel's praiseworthy efforts would be rewarded with success.

Colonel Bridport became more pleased with Omelia, the longer he remained in con-

versation with her, and he felt thoroughly convinced, from the observations which occasionally inadvertently fell from her lips, that her troubles and misfortunes, had not been brought upon her by any improper conduct of her own, and that she was worthy of a far better fate than that which had befallen her, and he deeply commiserated her accordingly.

He had the greatest anxiety to hear the narrative of her sorrows, but, of course, in her present delicate and agitated state he forbore to press her to gratify his curiosity.

This interview was a short one, the colonel's duties calling him away, and Omelia and the two sisters being left together, the former feeling so much better, and thinking that her strength was adequate to the task, expressed a wish to take a walk through the streets of Cawnpore, that she might once more dwell upon those scenes that were endeared to her by their association with her lover.

Julia and her sister complied with her request, at the same time expressing a wish to accompany her, which, it is almost needless to say, Omelia willingly acceded to, and in a few minutes they issued from the house, and proceeded on their ramble.

They went through the principal streets of the city, in which Omelia felt any interest, and how mingled were the feelings which agitated her breast as she did so.

Every spot seemed to recal some recollection of her lover—if indeed her memory required any refreshing upon the all important and affecting subject—to her mind. She could imagine that every spot upon which she gazed had been trodden some time or the other by him, and thus was it endeared to her—viewed as hallowed ground.

But where, oh, where was that beloved being now? she dared scarcely attempt to answer the question she put to herself. Alas, it was too probable that his cold and mangled remains were left, with many other of his brave companions in arms, to moulder on the gory battle-field, or, even still more horrible, that, having fallen into the hands of the remorseless foe, he was enduring all the fiendish and lingering tortures that such wretches could inflict upon him.

This thought was so dreadful that she could hardly endure it with any degree of fortitude; she groaned, beat her breast, turned so ghastly pale, and trembled so violently that Julia Bridport and her sister became seriously alarmed, and the former taking her hand, and looking anxiously in her face, said, in a voice of the utmost kindness and solicitude—

"I am fearful that you are again taken seriously ill, Omelia; this exercise is too much for you. Had we not better return?"

"No, no, my kind friend," returned our heroine, as calmly as she could, "it was only the agony of thought that overpowered me for a moment; but—but it is past now. Oh, Edward."

The sisters saw the anguish of mind she was enduring, with much painful regret, and perfectly understood the thoughts and feelings that agitated her, after what she had said of Edward Stanley, but delicacy prevented them from obtruding any observation upon her.

"I am better, much better now," said Omelia, after a few minutes pause, and even attempting to smile through her tears; "I am very weak and silly thus to give way to my feelings. Let us proceed."

They did so, though at a slow rate, for the strength of our heroine would not permit her to do otherwise, and, after visiting several places of minor importance, they at last entered upon the deserted part of the city, and there fresh and melancholy objects arose for the contemplation of Omelia.

She viewed with a sad heart the building which had formed the residence of herself, and those friends—who had ever evinced such disinterested kindness and sympathy towards her in her misfortunes—after their escape from Lucknow, and sincere and fervent was her regret at their separation, and many were the prayers she mentally offered up for their future welfare wherever they might be.

Had they remained in the city, she might possibly have received such information from them respecting Stanley as would have set her doubts at rest, if not revived her hopes.

Her faithful, her devoted friend, Abdal, too, was gone, and thus was she at once deprived of all those upon whom she could strictly depend, and left to the pity and benevolence of those who were entire strangers to her, an obligation to which her proud and independent spirit could not very well submit.

There being nothing more to excite her particular attention and curiosity, and Omelia beginning to feel faint and tired, she expressed a wish to Julia and her sister that they should return, and they did so by the Temple of Fountains, and notwithstanding she had so recently visited it, Omelia could not resist the temptation to again enter a place which was so painfully connected with the latest and most melancholy events of her life.

Yet as she did so, she could not help shuddering with a feeling of unconquerable awe, for, to her disordered imagination, the spirits of the dead seemed hovering around, and she could almost fancy that she heard the voice of despair in every breeze that was wafted through the ancient and remarkable place; and so strong was that superstitious fear, that she paused at the entrance for a minute or two, and hesitated to advance, but at length the anguish of her thoughts and recollections became too powerful for control and she burst into a violent paroxysm of sobs and tears.

Julia and her sister were much alarmed, and deeply affected, but, of course, being unacquainted with the particulars of our heroine's melancholy history, they were totally at a loss to conjecture the cause of her extraordinary and violent grief.

"For heaven's sake, Omelia," interrogated the anxious and tender-hearted Julia, "what is it that affects you in this distressing manner? Tell me, and think me not impertinent for putting the question, and I may be able to impart to you some degree of consolation."

"Consolation, my good girl," replied our heroine, in a voice half stifled by sobs, "alas, that is not for me; black despair, and heart-rending misery must ever more be my doom."

"Oh, say not so, my poor friend," said Julia, in a soothing voice, "there is hope for all, however sad and dreary their lot through life may have been."

"None for me, none for me," returned Omelia, wringing her hands, and sighing deeply, "the dense clouds of adversity have long since obscured every ray of sunshine and hope that was left to shine upon my pathway. How solemn and death-like is the silence that now pervades this sacred building."

"Why does it inspire you with such evident feelings of awe, if not absolute terror?" interrogated Julia.

Our heroine was too much agitated by the question to reply immediately; but at length she said, while the tears chased each other down her cheeks.

"Why does it agitate me as you see me now? Oh, the bare contemplation of it, and the thoughts it recals should break my heart. 'Twas here our last meeting took place, 'twas here we exchanged our last vows with one another, and parted, unknowingly to meet no more. Oh, Stanley, Stanley."

Julia Bridport read all the painful and fatal truth in these words, and she did not offer to make use of any further observations upon the dismal subject, fearful that they might only serve to agravate the poor girl's feelings.

For some minutes Omelia remained gazing with bewildered and agitated looks around the temple, then with a heart-drawn sigh, but without uttering a word she took the arms of Julia and her sister, for support, and they immediately quitted the place.

But few words escaped the lips of Omelia on their return, and they were of that singular and rambling description that shewed her brain was bewildered and that she knew not what she said.

They met with no one on the way, and on their arrival at the residence of Colonel Bridport and his daughters, our heroine immediately requested permission to retire, desiring at the same time that no one might interrupt her for the present, and trusting that they would not feel surprised or uneasy if she did not make her appearance again for the night.

Her wishes were, of course, complied with, and she left the room, after bidding the sisters good night, and sought her chamber without any further delay, where she sunk exhausted on a seat, and for some time was unable to give utterance to her thoughts in words.

Her anguish of mind was almost unen-durable, and at times she regretted that she had been tempted to make the melancholy ramble, since it could do no possible good, but, on the contrary, was only calculated to raise the most torturing ideas—which it had done—in her breast.

She felt her prospects to be more wretched and cheerless than they had been before, and what few hopes she had ventured to encourage were again for the present entirely banished.

All that the gallant Colonel Bridport and his amiable daughters had said to try and console her, and to ameliorate the violence of her grief, was forgotten, or had, at least, lost its effect, and she felt herself to be one of the most forlorn and miserable beings in existence.

She was tired of life, for it had become a dreary blank to her, and she earnestly prayed for death.

"But why should I remain here?" she suddenly exclaimed, "why continue to linger on day after day in this terrible state of suspense and uncertainty? The colonel thinks not what he said, and only did so to try to comfort me. My torturing anxiety and impatience will not allow me to wait. I must away from here; again renew my lonely wanderings, and leave the result of my weary search after my beloved one to the mercy of providence, and if I fail in the accomplishment of my soul's desire, I can but lay me down and die."

The poor girl's handsome features were animated with an expression of determination as she thus spoke; and the fire of her eyes became still more brilliant.

"Why should I hesitate?" she again soliloquised; "what dangers that I may have to encounter can possess any terrors for me? None, none; I am prepared to brave them all, even at the hazard of my life, a life now rendered valueless to me, if deprived of that beloved being for whom alone I wish to live. Let me then no longer delay; it is but a waste of time that can be productive alone of disappointment. At all hazards I will depart from this place, which does but serve to recal the most melancholy and painful events to my memory, and to fill my breast with feelings of anguish and despair, and at once resume my anxious search, let the consequences be whatever they may."

Such was the rash resolve which Omelia formed, and from which nothing whatever, after having come to the decision, could move her.

She had not the least idea whither to direct her course, having not the slightest clue to the place whither the regiment to which her lover belonged had gone, and there was nothing therefore left for her to do but to leave it to chance and providence.

CHAPTER CLIX.

The agitated state of Omelia's mind would not allow her to seek the society of the fair sisters again that evening—though they sent two or three times to inquire after her health —and she retired to bed at an early hour, but so busy were her thoughts, that it was some time ere she sunk off to repose.

The longer she reflected upon the decision to which she had come, the more determined and confident did she feel, and the more impatient for her departure, which she had made up her mind should not be delayed longer than the following evening, if nothing occurred to prevent it.

She deeply regretted that she should thus clandestinely be compelled to leave those who had acted with such kindness and friendship towards her; it appeared indeed like the worst of ingratitude to do so; but she determined to leave a note behind her, explaining everything as far as she was able, and with which she trusted they would be satisfied, and forgive her.

She now felt more than ever the loss of the faithful Abdal, who would have, on this important occasion, been to her most assuredly friend, counsellor, guide, and protector.

She also regretted that old Juballah had not accompanied her in her escape from the cavern, for she had no doubt that she would now have found her services of the greatest value.

She could not but think it complete madness for the mysterious old woman to return to the cavern, and thus to incur the certain vengeance of Yusef and his base associates; and she felt the greatest and most painful anxiety about the fate which had befallen one to whom she was so largely indebted.

Yet, in spite of the many difficulties and dangers which presented themselves in the way of the accomplishment of the arduous task she was about to undertake, Omelia could not help at times encouraging the most sanguine hopes of success, and that still further urged her on, and stimulated her to exertion.

"The Great and All merciful Power," she soliloquised, "after all my sufferings, cares, and anxieties, will not surely permit my self-devotion to go ultimately unrewarded. Dear Stanley, I feel confident that I shall yet behold you again, if it be only to receive your blessing, and to expire upon your bosom. Away then with all childish doubts and fears —all dismal forebodings, and let me remain firm in my resolution."

These thoughts revived her spirits, and inspired her with fresh courage, and, becoming more composed and tranquil in her mind, she at length sunk off to sleep in which state she continued till the morning.

She arose refreshed, and firm in the resolution she had formed, but she could not help meeting her new found and generous friends at the morning repast with reluctance, for it pained her to be compelled to act the part of the hypocrite towards them, though, if she candidly acknowledged to them her intentions, she was fully aware that they would meet with their strongest opposition and cause the utmost pain and regret to all parties.

Colonel Bridport remained at home for two or three hours—having no particular business to call him away—for he seemed more and more charmed with the society of the beautiful young Indian maiden, and in whose fate he could not but take the deepest interest, under the peculiar and distressing circumstances in which she had been introduced to him.

In order to divert her mind from the melancholy subject that he knew must otherwise engross it, he engaged her in conversation, into which she entered with a spirit and vivacity that could hardly have been expected, and which indeed surprised herself, when she considered the important designs she had in contemplation.

To Omelia's eager questions, however, as to whether he had yet been able to ascertain anything as to the destination of the regiment to which Stanley belonged, the colonel was compelled to answer in the negative, and that, although she carefully concealed her real thoughts, or anything that might excite the least suspicion, the more fixed and decided her in her determination.

Anxious that the colonel and his daughters should not labour under a wrong impression after she was gone, or imagine that she had imposed upon their sympathies by false representations, our heroine mustered sufficient courage and composure in the course of the day to relate the more important features of her extraordinary and affecting history, and to which they listened with that breathless attention, and degree of interest which may well be imagined, while they could not help the more admiring the noble character and glowing virtues of the heroic girl.

"Unfortunate Omelia," observed the colonel, when she had concluded, "your's has indeed been a life of sorrow, care, and anxiety, with but few days of real happiness to intervene. Let us hope that the fortitude, the patience, and resignation that you have throughout displayed, will ere long meet with their due reward."

"Need I say, sir," replied our heroine, with the utmost sincerity, "how much I thank you for your kind wishes? But, alas, under all the painful circumstances by which

I am surrounded, there is, I fear, but little room for hope.

"Say not so," returned the colonel, in his most soothing accents, "sad though our lot may hitherto have been we know not what yet may be weaving for us in the web of fate. Look on the brightest and sunniest side of circumstances, and live in hopes for the future."

Omelia again thanked the colonel for his friendly wishes and advice, and he then left home on business, promising to return in about an hour, and in the meantime leaving her to the agreeable society of his two amiable daughters.

Omelia endeavoured to join in the conversation with spirit; but at times a cloud of sorrow overshadowed her brow, when she thought of what she was so soon about to do, that it could not possibly escape the notice of Julia and her sister, although fearing that it might only pain her feelings the more, they forbore to mention anything about it, but engaged her in conversation, which was the more calculated to raise her spirits and to banish gloomy thoughts from her mind.

In this praiseworthy effort they succeeded beyond their expectations, and when their father returned, which he did shortly afterwards, he was agreeably surprised to see the favourable change which was wrought in so short a time, in the looks and manners of our heroine.

The afternoon was passed away in the most pleasant manner possible, Colonel Bridport possessing a fund of anecdote, which given in his peculiar style, could not fail to be both amusing and instructive to those who listened to him

In fact, the gallant officer was a most accomplished man, and agreeable companion, and his society in the hours that his duty did not call him to the field of strife, had always been much courted and admired.

But as the time approached when they must separate for the night, and Omelia knew that they would meet no more, that she was about to repay the most disinterested kindness with apparent ingratitude, her emotions became so great that she could not without the greatest difficulty restrain or conceal them, and she was several times worked up to such a pitch of excitement, that she was on the point of acknowledging her intentions to the colonel and his daughters, and imploring their forgiveness for the rash resolve she had formed, and which, as they must be aware, she was urged to by the insupportable anxiety and suspense of her feelings.

But she resisted that temptation, and conquering her emotions as well as she could, she bade them a fervent good night, and

hastily retired to her chamber. Here she sunk upon a seat, and unable any longer to restrain the tempest of agonising thoughts and feelings which burst upon her brain, she gave free vent to them in convulsive sobs, and a violent flood of tears.

It seemed to her disordered imagination as though she was about to commit some fearful crime, and several times she was half inclined to abandon the idea, and to remain where she was, at any rate, for a few days, but her impatience and anxiety triumphed over every other feeling, and she remained firm to her first resolution.

In one respect, however, she changed her mind, namely, instead of taking her departure at night, as she had at first determined upon, she had come to the resolution to defer it till an early hour in the morning, which would give her more time to prepare herself for the arduous and perilous task she had undertaken, and might be done, she thought, with greater safety.

Having, after considerable reflection and exertion, somewhat regained her composure, Omelia secured the room-door, to prevent the intrusion of Julia Bridport and her sister, whom she could not muster fortitude to see again, and then resumed her seat and her reflections.

The nature of the latter, the reader may pretty well imagine, so that there is not much occasion to describe them. It may be sufficient to state that for some time she alternated betwixt hope and fear, and occasionally she wavered in her resolution, and was half disposed to abandon it. Not that she shrunk intimidated from the dangers and sufferings with which the enterprise was sure to be fraught, but the idea seemed so wild and extravagant, and the improbability of its success so great, that she almost wondered she could ever have been mad enough to entertain it.

Then the course it would be most desirable for her to take, the road she should pursue, with the greatest probability of success, was a perfect problem to her, and one which she found it utterly impossible to solve.

This showed her at once the absolute necessity of delaying her departure, in order that she might probably obtain the desired information, which she might do in a day or two. But her impatience prevailed over everything, and she again became fixed in her determination.

She counted the tedious hours as they passed, and awaited anxiously to hear the colonel and his daughters separate for the night, and retire to rest, for she discovered that they were still engaged in conversation, and at length her wishes were gratified, and she heard the sisters ascending the stairs to their chamber, which was above the one in which she slept, and she concealed her lamp, in order that in passing the room-door they might conclude that she had retired to bed.

This had the desired effect; she heard Julia and her sister stop at the door of her chamber for a moment or two, and then having exchanged some observations with each other in a low tone, they ascended the stairs to their own room, and the house was soon after wrapped in solemn silence, which to Omelia, in her present state of mind, appeared doubly so.

She had hitherto quite forgotten the letter she had intended to write to the colonel and his daughters, explaining the cause of her sudden flight, thanking them warmly for the many acts of kindness she had received from them, during the short time she had been with them, and praying their forgiveness for the desperate step she had been induced to take, and which seemed to convey a feeling of ingratitude towards them.

But this now recurred to her recollection, and having taken care during the day to provide herself with writing materials, she immediately set about her task, which she quickly accomplished, and much better than she expected she could have done.

This she placed open upon the dressing-table, where she knew they must immediately see it on entering her chamber, and that business over she felt some little weight removed from her mind.

She then resumed her seat, and endeavoured to collect her thoughts, and to reconsider her projects, before she finally retired to rest for the two or three short hours that she must venture to indulge in.

Money she knew was one of the most essential things she would require on her uncertain but doubtless tedious journey, but of that she stood in no immediate need, having that which old Juballah had given her—and which was a considerable sum—still by her untouched, besides she had been long used to the greatest privations, and looked upon them with comparative indifference.

That matter did not seriously disturb her, therefore, and she gained courage as she continued to reflect.

"All merciful powers," she solemnly exclaimed, sinking on her knees, and clasping her hands together, "guide me how to act in this desperate and perilous undertaking, and grant, I beseech Thee, a poor humble girl Thy protection through the many and, perhaps, terrible dangers that may beset her. Thou knowest the pure motives that guide me in my conduct, and will, I trust, watch over and aid me in my efforts accordingly."

She felt much more composed and confident, after this solemn invocation, and arising from her knees, she immediately sought her couch, without undressing, so that she might be prepared to depart at the earliest moment in the morning.

She, however, slept but little, for her mind was too busily engaged with the important subject that engrossed it; and at the earliest dawn of the day she arose from her couch, and commenced making preparations for her departure with a palpitating heart, and trembling anxiety.

These were soon completed, for there were but few to make, and now the important moment had arrived, and the courage and resolution of Omelia for the moment failed her, as she reflected upon the desperate character of the undertaking upon which she was about to enter.

She walked cautiously to the room-door, which she opened, and stepping lightly on to the landing, she listened attentively to endeavour to ascertain whether or not there was any one stirring, although at that early hour of the morning it was not likely that there would be, but all was perfectly silent, so she returned to the room, quite satisfied in that respect.

She looked from the window on to that part of the city, a view of which could be obtained of it The grey mists of early morn were upon it, but she could not perceive a human being as far as her eyes could reach, and a profound silence pervaded everything.

"All is secure," she whispered to herself, "there is nothing to excite the least apprehension; everything seems to favour my designs. Now then for the commencement of my arduous task, and kind providence assist me in it. Courage, Omelia, and all will yet be well."

For the moment she became firm, but again she hesitated, as strange thoughts came over her, and her heart throbbed violently.

"This is childish weakness," she said, at last; "I am ashamed of it; let me arouse myself; what have I to fear? May the Great Spirit bless you, my friends, for the kindness I have received from you, is the sincere prayer of the wandering and unfortunate Omelia."

Tears—but they were those of gratitude—started to her eyes as she spoke, and she felt the keenest emotions; but she quickly recovered herself, and issuing from the room, with noiseless footsteps she descended the stairs, and opening the outer door cautiously, the next moment found herself in the street.

———

CHAPTER CLX.

THE JOURNEY.

It was a fine morning, and there was a refreshing breeze stirring, which made it particularly pleasant and grateful to the senses, in that scorching climate.

And then all was so calm and tranquil at that early hour, that it was sufficient to "soothe the heart bowed down with care," and to raise the spirits into hope and cheerfulness.

Omelia walked a few paces from the house with faltering and timid footsteps, and a brain so bewildered that she scarcely knew what she was about; then pausing for a minute or two, and pressing her hands upon her forehead, she endeavoured to recall her scattered thoughts, and to collect herself.

This was soon done, though she was greatly agitated, as might be naturally expected, under the circumstances, and then she gazed cautiously and anxiously around her, to see that there was no one at hand to observe her, but saw nothing of the kind to alarm her, and her firmness and confidence returned.

She cast a melancholy look up at the different windows of the house she had quitted for ever, and could not help feeling a pang of regret at leaving so abruptly those who in the short time she had known them had gained so large a place in her heart's esteem.

Again she looked anxiously around her, and for a minute or two hesitated which way she should direct her course, so that she might the more quickly get out of the city, into the suburbs, without encountering any one.

But at last she resolved on leaving it by the same way she had entered it, after her escape from the power of the villain Yusef, and having once more breathed a prayer of gratitude for the good colonel and his daughters, she proceeded from the spot in the direction she wished to go, at first with trembling footsteps, but which grew firmer the farther she went.

Sad and conflicting were her thoughts, bewildered and wandering her ideas, and gloomy the prospect before her, as regarded the result of her wild and hazardous journey, but still she endeavoured to arouse herself and to become cool, firm, and collected, and after a while she succeeded much better than might have been expected, and proceeded on her way with a quicker and lighter step.

Ever and anon, however, she would pause and look back, to see that she was not observed or followed by any one whom she might have cause to fear, but she saw no one, and, in fact, could hardly expect to do so at that early hour in the morning, and especially by the little frequented way she was proceeding.

The first red glow of the rising sun might now be seen in the eastern horizon. Gradually that bright, golden stream expanded itself until its glory pervaded the whole of the eastern sky, making the distant scenery which had before been left obscured in the grey mists of early dawn, clear and distinct, and imparting to it an aspect of grandeur and sublimity.

Everything betokened a beautiful day, though one of scorching heat; but, of course, Omelia, as a native, was prepared for that, and, in fact, her thoughts were so busily occupied on other subjects that the weather never for an instant troubled her mind.

On she went with the same light, quick step, and arrived at the Temple of Fountains so suddenly and unexpectedly, that she could scarcely believe it.

She paused before it, and gazed at it with melancholy looks, and a heavy heart, for a few minutes, but she did not venture to enter it, for her feelings would not suffer her to do so; then with a heavy sigh, and unable to bear the contemplation of the temple any longer, she covered her face with her hands and hurried on her way.

On she went, almost regardless whither, and such was the confusion of her mind, that she could hardly distinguish anything until she found herself beyond the city; and she felt thankful that she had been enabled to proceed so far without obstruction or interruption.

Here she again stopped to compose and collect herself, and she gazed back upon the city she had quitted with mingled feelings agitating her breast.

"Thus far," she soliloquised, in melancholy tones, "my task is accomplished, and the wide world is again before the lonely wanderer. For what fresh trials and vicissitudes am I now reserved? Am I still to be the sport of fate, and after all my painful struggles, shall the hopes I sometimes venture to indulge in, end in disappointment? Great Power above, have mercy upon me, and at least deign to reward me for the many troubles and sufferings which love's devotion has led me to encounter. Oh, guide my footsteps in the right way, and if he be still living, restore me to the arms of my beloved Stanley."

Her tears flowed fast as she thus spoke, and a variety of the most painful emotions agitated her bosom. But again she exerted all her energies with success, and pursued her way with renewed perseverence.

In a short time she once more found herself in the road, which she had taken on leaving the friendly Doolab, after they had crossed the bridge, and in which direction something induced her to retrace her steps.

She also consulted with herself whether or not she should re-cross the bridge, and prosecute her search in that part of the country on the opposite side of the river, and, in spite of the danger which presented itself of her again falling into the power of the dreaded Yusef and his miscreant associates, she quickly decided on doing so, and leaving everything to the mercy and will of providence.

Something seemed to convince her that the resolution she had thus promptly formed was right, and that it would lead to some satisfactory result, and she therefore continued on her way way with increased spirits.

She considered also that she might stop at the bungalow of Doolab to rest and refresh herself with safety, and probably obtain from him some useful information, and that thought still further urged her on, and tended to revive and strengthen her hopes and expectations.

Omelia had now long lost sight of the city, and was proceeding at a quick pace along the road, anxious as she was that she might reach the bridge and re-cross the river with as little delay as possible.

The sun was shining brightly on the truly magnificent scenery which presented itself to the eye at every turn; but a sweet and refreshing breeze was wafted around, which greatly counteracted the effects of the excessive heat, and enabled the traveller unused to the climate at least to breathe.

It was strange, but still Omelia met no one as she pursued her way, which was a great gratification to her, as she wished not to encounter observation any more than could be helped.

The various thoughts that crowded upon it, kept her mind continually engaged, so much indeed, that she scarcely heeded whither she was going, or the distance she had accomplished.

But at length feeling tired—for, as has been before stated she had travelled at a pretty rapid rate—she stopped to rest herself, and she then perceived to her surprise but satisfaction that she had nearly arrived at the extremity of the road, which was a long one, and required some time to traverse.

It must have been at least two hours since she had quitted the house, yet her thoughts had been so occupied another way, that she had passed unnoticed the lapse of time.

She felt truly grateful that she had been enabled to proceed thus far unmolested, and therefore was the more encouraged to advance on her journey, making up her mind to travel no further than the residence of Doolab that day, where she could rest, and give herself time the better to mature her plans.

After resting a few minutes, Omelia, reinvigorated both in mind and body, once more proceeded on her way, and stopped not again till she arrived at the foot of the bridge, by which time morning had far advanced, although it appeared most extraordinary how she could have accomplished so great a distance in so short a period.

After a few minutes reflection she stepped on to the bridge, and quickly arrived on the opposite side of the river.

CHAPTER CLXI.

OLD JUBALLAH IN THE TIME OF NEED.

For some short distance, after she had crossed the river, Omelia proceeded with hope and energy until she reached a romantic spot, not more than an hour's walk from the place of her destination, namely, the small village in which the bungalow of Doolab was situated.

Here, probably caused by over excitement and exertion, her strength suddenly completely failed her, a deathly faintness came over her, a cold shuddering ran through her veins, her brain turned giddy, and with a deep sigh she sunk upon the earth insensible.

At that moment a strange looking form might have been seen to emerge from a grove of trees at a short distance, and after looking round for a second, approach in the direction of the spot where Omelia was lying.

It appeared to be the form of a woman, but so strange and uncouth was its appearance, that at the shortest distance it would have been difficult to form a correct judgment.

It advanced nearer, with a stealthy kind of step, and all further doubt might then have been removed, for it was the mysterious being old Juballah.

It was a most extraordinary circumstance that Juballah should have arrived at that spot at the very time when her services were so much required, but so it was, and most fortunate it was for Omelia that it had so happened.

As Juballah approached nearer, her quick eye caught sight of an inanimate form upon the ground, and with a wild exclamation of surprise, she rushed forward, and stooping down she raised the form of Omelia from the earth, and supported her head and shoulders on one knee, with as much tenderness as if she had been one of the gentlest of human beings.

But when she discovered who it was, the strange wild cry that escaped her lips, the

remarkable expression of her features, and the powerful emotions that agitated her could scarcely be properly described.

"Poor thing," she said, in the most gentle accents, and parting the dark silken hair from her forehead with as much affection as if she had been her own child, "that we should thus meet again. Poor thing—poor thing."

Again the poor old woman fixed upon the insensible girl a look of the utmost tenderness and sympathy, and passed her hand across her forehead; but suddenly seeming to recollect herself, she hastily took a flask which was suspended by a small chain by her side, and contained a powerful restorative which she always carried about with her.

A small portion of this she poured into the palm of her hand, and with which she bathed the forehead and temples of Omelia, and then applying the flask to her lips, she moistened them with a few drops of the liquid.

This had an almost instantaneous effect, a deep sigh escaped Omelia's bosom, then she opened her eyes, and finding herself supported in the arms of some one, she fixed an eager but vacant look upon Juballah, but so confused and agitated was her mind that she could not for the moment recognise her.

But when she did so, she uttered an exclamation of astonishment, and throwing herself upon the dark and naked bosom of the old woman, the mingled emotions that agitated her were so great that they almost overpowered her.

And, strange though as was the way which Juballah had of showing them, her feelings were evidently almost as violently agitated as those of the poor girl for whom her sympathy was excited. Even her repulsive features could not conceal the real and tender emotions which she felt, and there was a peculiar expression in her large dark eyes, as they were rivetted upon the handsome countenance of our heroine, which seemed to speak volumes.

Neither of them for a few minutes could conquer their emotions sufficiently to speak, but at length Omelia, looking with an expression of the utmost pleasure and affection in the countenance of old Juballah, said—

"Juballah, dear, good Juballah, alive, escaped the vengeance of Yusef and the other bloodthirsty miscreants, and here again restored to me in this, the hour of my need? Great Spirit, I thank Thee. But tell me, I pray you, most kind but mysterious woman, by what strange accident do we so fortunately meet again?"

"Juballah is glad, very glad," she replied, attempting to smile, and the expression of her features proving the sincerity of her words; "and will remain with you, and aid you in your endeavours to discover him to whom your fond heart is devoted; but at present there is not time to explain. You are faint, and require rest; lean on me for support, and I will conduct you to a place of safety, and where you can obtain all that you require."

Omelia pressed her hand in silence, for she was unable to find words to give utterance to her feelings of gratitude, and supporting herself on the arm of Juballah, they moved slowly from the spot.

"Not far from this place," observed the old woman, "is a small village of friendly natives, and there we shall be received in any of the bungalows with the greatest kindness and cordiality."

"I know it," replied Omelia.

"Know it?" repeated Juballah, with a look of surprise.

"Yes," said our heroine, "I know it, from experience; "it was in one the bungalows of that village that I was received with every kindness and hospitality after my escape from the cavern, and found many hours of rest, shelter, and refreshment. It was thither I was directing my footsteps, when my strength failed me, and I sunk into that state of insensibility in which you found me."

"And did you hear the name of those who thus befriended you?" interrogated Juballah.

"The name of the man is Doolab," replied Omelia, "he has a wife and one daughter, from whom I also received every kindness and attention.

"Doolab," repeated the old woman; "ah,

I know him well, he is good and faithful, and may be depended upon. We will make our way to his residence, for there is no danger to be apprehended in this part of the country."

"But the villain Yusef and his associates?" said Omelia, with an anxious look.

"You have nothing to fear from them," replied Juballah; "Yusef and Alahamed must long before this be dead, and the others —who have abandoned the cavern—are not disposed to molest you."

Omelia looked surprised, as she certainly was, at what the old woman said, and she anxiously inquired—

"Dead, Juballah? Can you really mean what you say?"

"It is true," answered Juballah; "you may always place implicit confidence in what I assert; I never attempt to deceive those whom it is my desire to serve. But we delay —come my poor girl, let us proceed on our way to the dwelling of this Doolab, whose hospitality you say you have already experienced."

Our heroine felt more surprised than ever at what Juballah had said respecting Yusef and the other rebels, and was anxious for a full explanation of all the circumstances; but she knew it would be useless to urge the old woman farther, and she likewise agreed with her that that there was not now time to enter upon the subject; and she therefore said no more about it at present, but proceeded with Juballah, at a moderate speed towards the bungalow of Doolab.

Omelia's hopes and spirits revived, as it may be expected, at this fortunate meeting with the singular, but evidently kind-hearted woman, Juballah; and she placed the utmost reliance in her honesty and faithfulness of purpose. Her strength seemed suddenly recruited now that she had a companion and guide on whom she could so thoroughly depend, and even already her prospects appeared to brighten.

Juballah seemed to be no less pleased than Omelia at their meeting again, and her looks, whenever she directed them to the handsome countenance of her young companion, fully revealed it.

But they did not converse much as they proceeded, and after walking for about half an hour without encountering any one on the way, they came in sight of the village, which was most welcome to Omelia, as she knew they could rest there in safety, and she really felt tired with the distance she had travelled since leaving Cawnpore, and the heat of the day being now most oppressive.

Several of the villagers were about, who seemed to know Juballah, and to respect her, from the manner in which they greeted her, as she and Omelia passed on their way to the bungalow of Doolah, and that inspired the former with fresh confidence.

On arriving at the bungalow, and the door being opened, Doolab made his appearance, and welcomed old Juballah, but on perceiving Omelia, which he did not at first, he started back a little in surprise, but not without evident pleasure on beholding her again.

He, however, without any further ceremony or hesitation ushered them into the room, in which were his wife and daughter, who betrayed no less astonishment than himself at again beholding Omelia, especially in the company of Juballah.

But they welcomed them both with every respect and kindness, and our heroine, gratified with her reception, although it was no more than she had expected, taking a seat, felt herself quite at home.

Juballah had scarcely any occasion to say what it was that Omelia and herself would require, namely, refreshment and accommodation till the following morning—she having suggested to her companion on their way to the village that it would be advisable to defer the resumption of their journey till then, as it would give them time to arrange their plans—for Doolab voluntarily offered them all the accommodation in his power; and at the same time having given his wife and daughter some instructions, they departed from the room, and quickly returned, bringing in an ample supply of refreshments, which they placed before their guests and cordially invited them to partake of.

"My good friend," said Omelia, addressing herself to Doolab, "I did not anticipate the pleasure of again seeing you and your wife and daughter so soon, and of having the opportunity of once more expressing my acknowledgments for the services you have already rendered me, and I assure you it affords me much gratification to be able to do so, especially in the company of one to whom I am so highly indebted."

"The gratification is as great on my part as it can be on your's, young lady," replied Doolab, with every mark of respect and sincerity, "and I must again be permitted to assure you that I require no thanks for that which I have done. As to my old friend, Juballah, it always gives me the greatest pleasure to see her—which, however, I have seldom had the opportunity of doing for some years past—for I am under a weight of obligation to her which—"

"Say no more, Doolab," interrupted the old woman, impatiently, "you know the character of Juballah, I believe, pretty correctly, and are aware that there is nothing more distasteful to her than idle flattery. She is, however, not the heartless monster that most of those who have seen her have supposed her to be."

"Oh, no, no," said our heroine, fervently, and looking in the strange old woman's face with an expression of gratitude and tenderness, "how cruel, how unjust, and uncharitable must those be who could think so. Dear Juballah, I, at least, must ever look upon you with esteem and reverence; and I should both loathe and despise myself, could I believe myself capable of doing otherwise, after the services you have so spontaneously, and at every personal risk, rendered me, an entire stranger to you."

The poor old woman took her hand eagerly and fervently, and raised it respectfully to her lips, then gazed at Omelia for a minute or two with such a look of tender feeling that it would be difficult to describe, but without saying a word.

A silence of several minutes, which no one seemed inclined to break, ensued, but at length Juballah gave a motion with her hand to Doolab, which he seemed to understand, and saying a few words apart to his wife and daughter, they quitted the room together, leaving our heroine, and her aged companion to themselves.

CHAPTER CLXII.

YUSEF AND ALAHAMED AGAIN.

Juballah remained silent for a few minutes after Doolab, his wife and daughter, had quitted the room, and appeared to be lost in thought; but at length arousing herself, and turning to Omelia, she said—

"You have expressed a natural curiosity, Omelia, to hear what happened at the cavern after your escape from it; and therefore, as we are now alone, and there is no one to listen to us—for I can, as I have before stated, depend upon Doolab and his wife—I will, if you please, relate to you the particulars."

Omelia expressed her willingness and anxiety to hear her, and Juballah immediately proceeded to relate all those startling facts with which the reader has been already made acquainted, and to which it need scarcely be added, that our heroine listened with the most profound attention, and mingled feelings of surprise and terror.

"I cannot for a moment, my good Juballah," she observed, when the latter had concluded, "attempt to extenuate the heinous crimes of which the villains Yusef and Alahamed had been guilty, and which deserved severe punishment; but I cannot help shuddering with horror at the thought of the frightful and lingering death they were put to."

"The blood-thirsty miscreants deserved

no mercy or commiseration," replied Juballah; "they had been guilty of the most fiendish atrocities upon innocent women and children, and the retribution which overtook them, though terrible, was just and merited. You are now released from brutal enemies from whom you had everything to dread."

"True, most true," coincided our heroine, "and most grateful am I for it. But for you, my good Juballah, I shudder to think of what my fate might, nay, would inevitably have been."

"Enough of that, Omelia," returned Juballah, impatiently, "it is sufficient for me that I was enabled to rescue you, and that is the greatest self gratification I can experience."

"But," interrogated Omelia, after a pause, "what could be your motive for abandoning those with whom you had quitted the cavern, Juballah?"

"I had other business than to follow them in their wild and lawless career," replied the old woman; "but it matters not; I have no wish to pursue that subject any further. I rejoice to think that accident has again guided me to you, and that I shall thus be enabled to afford you my humble advice and assistance. But tell me what befel you after I parted with you on the night of your escape?"

"I have but little to relate," replied Omelia, "and know not whether my conduct and the resolution I have formed will excite your censure or approval, but I will lose no time in complying with your request."

She then proceeded to relate all those circumstances as they have been detailed in some of the previous chapters, and concealing nothing whatever from old Juballah, for she did not consider it necessary.

She awaited anxiously to hear the opinion of Juballah, and she was not long kept in suspense.

"I have listened to your short and simple narrative, Omelia," remarked the old woman, after a few minutes' reflection, "with the greatest interest. You were most fortunate in falling into such kind and humane hands as those of Colonel Bridport and his daughters, and I cannot but feel some regret that you should have quitted those to whom you were so highly indebted, so abruptly and clandestinely."

"Oh, it pained me much to do so, I assure you, my good Juballah," replied Omelia, "but unable to obtain any satisfactory information respecting Lieutenant Stanley, and it not appearing at all likely that I should do so, my patience was exhausted. Can you blame the motive which urged me to take the step I have?"

"Poor thing, poor thing, no," replied old Juballah, reassuming her usual simple and impressive style; "you love; and who that has a heart to feel can help admiring your unceasing devotion to the object of your passion? Juballah will remain your firm friend, and accompany you in your wanderings, and happily she may be the means of once more bringing you to the arms of your lover."

"Oh, thanks, thanks, most excellent of women," ejaculated Omelia, fervently, but Juballah, hastily interrupted her, and their host and hostess returning to the room at that moment, put an end to the conversation

Having pursued the adventures of Omelia so far, since she had left the city of Cawnpore, we will resume the particulars relating to the unfortunate wretches, Yusef and Alahamed.

It was the dusk of evening, and dark shadows were fast gathering o'er the face of nature, showing the rapid approach of night, and a solemn silence reigned around.

The scene to which the attention of the reader is directed, was a wildly romantic one, with wood and jungle on one side, an open landscape of vast extent on the other, and finally closed in by a range of lofty mountains in the distant back ground.

In the midst of this, and occupied by the wide-spreading branches of tall trees, stood a solitary bungalow, but for what purpose it had been erected there, or whether it was at present occupied, did not appear, though that will be explained shortly.

Towards that spot, and at that silent hour, approached, with slow and feeble footsteps, the bent forms of two men (Indians), leaning on each other for support, apparently in the last stage of exhaustion, and ready to sink powerless to the earth.

The horrible ravages of want and other sufferings were plainly visible in their countenances and emaciated forms; but the reader will require no further description, when he is informed, as he has doubtless already anticipated, that the two wretched beings—who seemed indeed to have just escaped from the grave—were Yusef and Alahamed.

How they had left the cavern, where we left them, under the humane care of Zelib and his fellow travellers, who had been so fortunately led thither, at the very moment that the immediate death of the two guilty men seemed certain, will be explained presently.

What a terrible change had the dreadful sufferings to which they had been subjected wrought in their appearance; misery and despair had usurped the place of that savage ferocity which had before marked their features; their once robust and athletic forms were reduced to comparative skeletons, and their limbs were weak and tottering as those of infants. Their hardened and reckless spirits were also completely crushed, and they felt quite humbled and subdued.

The place to which they had now wandered was at least a day's journey from the cavern, and how they had contrived to reach that distance in their present wretched and deplorable condition is a problem which it is almost useless to attempt to solve.

It appeared that they had proceeded some little distance in the direction of the solitary bungalow before mentioned, before they perceived it, and completely worn out, and scarcely able to drag one limb after the other, they were about to abandon all efforts to proceed further, and to resign themselves to their fate.

"It is useless our longer struggling against the certain and terrible doom which awaits us," said Yusef, in a faint voice; "my enfeebled and trembling limbs will not allow me to proceed. Here then we must remain and die."

"No, no," returned Alahamed, who was a little more firm than his companion, "we must not give up while there is the least shadow of a chance; if so, we might as well have saved ourselves this trouble and exertion, and remained at the cavern to die. Arouse yourself, Yusef, and something will yet, I trust, turn up for our relief."

Yusef returned no answer, and again leaning on each other for support, they slowly proceeded on their uncertain way.

But suddenly an exclamation of surprise and satisfaction from Alahamed caused Yusef to look up, and in the direction in which he was gazing so eagerly, and it was not till then that the bungalow was first observed.

CHAPTER CLXIII.

HOW THE FUGITIVES FARED.

"See," said Alahamed, in a voice of the utmost gratification, "the expectations I ventured to express so confidently, are quickly realised; yonder is the place of shelter we seek, and where we shall no doubt find that rest and refreshment of which we stand so much in need. And that may enable us in a day or two to resume our journey, and to reach the quarters of Tantia Topee, or one of the other great chiefs."

"We must not be too sanguine in our expectations, Alahamed," observed Yusef, lest they should be doomed to be disappointed. The inhabitant of the lonely bungalow before us may prove to be an enemy, if so, we can hope for no relief from him."

"Meet not troubles half way, Yusef," returned Alahamed; "in our present wretched condition, there are few indeed I should think who could resist the demands of common humanity. Besides, you recollect what we are both agreed upon, namely, to conceal, to the best of our abilities, from the prying eye of curiosity, our real character?"

"True," answered Yusef, "but I doubt much whether we shall long be able to carry on the deception with success."

"Psha," ejaculated Alahamed, impatiently, "you alarm yourself without a cause; we have but to act with due precaution, and all will yet be well."

Yusef returned no answer to this, and they advanced with quicker footsteps and renewed hopes towards the bungalow, in one of the lower rooms of which, as it had become dark, they perceived a light glimmering, which was sufficient to convince them that the place was inhabited.

Alahamed knocked at the door, which was almost immediately opened by a middle-aged native of rather uncouth appearance—at least as far as Yusef and his companion could see—holding a lamp in his hand, and who demanded, in rather surly tones, what they wanted?

"We are two poor weary travellers," replied Alahamed, "faint, hungry, and weary, and would fain solicit food and shelter, be it ever so humble."

"I am poor," returned the man, in a hesitating voice, "and can ill afford to be hospitable. Who and what are you?"

"My companion in misfortune has already informed you, and he has spoken the truth," observed Yusef.

"Ah!" exclaimed the man, starting; "that voice; surely I have heard it before."

He held up the lamp to accelerate his view as he spoke, and gazed eagerly in the face of Yusef, who also followed his example with no less curiosity.

"Yusef, my old friend," exclaimed the man, recognising him; "well, after the lapse of so many years since we before saw each other, this is indeed an agreeable surprise."

"Mahmoud," returned Yusef, looking at him with the most unbounded astonishment and almost incredulity, "can it be possible it is you? This is indeed a surprise. This is my friend and brother unfortunate, Alahamed."

The feelings of Yusef and Alahamed at this fortunate occurrence in the midst of their most urgent distress may be easily imagined, and they suffered Mahmoud therefore to conduct them into his bungalow, without making use of any further observation, where they each sunk on a seat quite exhausted.

Mahmoud was a fellow who was inured to crime, although he had hitherto contrived to escape detection. Himself and Yusef had been connected together, many years before their present unexpected meeting, in several acts of villany, but accident separated them, and they believed each other dead.

Mahmoud called loudly on the name of his wife—who was in a room above—on ushering his guests into the bungalow, and she slowly made her appearance.

She was a decrepid, haggard, disagreeable looking old woman, and she looked still more unpleasant on beholding strangers intruding in their dwelling.

"This is our old friend and acquaintance, Yusef, Aelah," remarked Mahmoud; "do you not remember him?"

"No," was the laconic reply, and in no very agreeable voice.

"There," said Mahmoud, peremptorily, and frowning upon her, "you see that they require refreshment, so be quick in bringing it them; the best our dwelling affords; they will be our guests for the night."

Aelah, as her husband had called her, muttered some surly reply, then hobbled from the room, and Mahmoud, turning to Yusef, said—

"My curiosity is naturally excited, Yusef, to know by what strange accident this meeting, after the lapse of so many years, has been brought about, and how it is that I behold yourself and your companion in so sad a plight. But I will restrain the gratification of my curiosity to some more fitting occasion. You appear quite worn out, and therefore as soon as you have partaken of what you require, I would advise you to retire to rest.

Yusef and Alahamed thanked him for his consideration, and Aelah shortly afterwards appeared with the provisions, which she placed on a table before them without saying a word, and retired sullenly into a remote corner of the room, but Mahmoud urged them to eat heartily, and then addressing himself to his wife, said—

"And in the meantime, Aelah, you prepare our guests a bed up stairs, and be quick about it, d'you hear?"

Aelah did not condescend to make any reply to this, but again hobbled out of the room, and Yusef and Alahamed partook most greedily of the food, Mahmoud watching them with looks of much satisfaction, but not offering to interrupt or annoy them by conversation.

By the time they had done the old woman returned, and Mahmoud without having the patience to hear their acknowledgements advised them to let him conduct them to a chamber for the night.

To this, of course, so much requiring rest as they did, they willingly assented, and Mahmoud, taking up the lamp, and motioning them to follow, preceded them up a short flight of stairs, to a small chamber above, where a mattress had been spread for them on the floor, and bidding them briefly good night, retired from the room, and left them to themselves.

Yusef and Alahamed merely congratulated themselves on their good fortune in meeting with this seasonable and much needed relief, and then feeling too much fatigued to enter into further conversation that night, they stretched their weary limbs upon their rough pallet, and were soon sound asleep.

The reason of Yusef and Alahamed being left to do the best they possibly could for themselves, after the humane attentions of Zelib and his friends in the cave, may be briefly explained.

By the exertions of those kind-hearted people they had been so far restored as to be able to sit up and to converse pretty freely. They told a plausible tale of the cause of their being placed in the frightful situation in which Zelib and the others had found them, which they believed, and sympathised with them more than ever; but important business would not allow them to remain with them longer.

So having seen that there was plenty of eatable food in the cavern for their consumption for some time, and promising them the means of leaving, and a place of refuge in a day or two, they departed from the cavern, and again left the unfortunate and guilty wretches to all the horrors of their loneliness.

They were fearful, however, to remain longer in the cavern than that night, and the following day, lest old Juballah and their other enemies should return, in which case their fate would be certain, and accordingly, notwithstanding their weak and almost hopeless state, they determined to endeavour to make their escape at once, while the opportunity was afforded them, though they had not the least idea at that time whither to direct their course, or what plans for the future it would be advisable for them to adopt.

Securing as much of the provisions—as were fit to eat—as they could conveniently carry with them, they cautiously left the cavern without much difficulty, and commenced their weary journey.

What happened to them on the road, and the sufferings they endured, till they arrived at the bungalow of Mahmoud, our limited space will not allow us to relate.

———

CHAPTER CLXIV.

THE ROMANTIC ADVENTURES OF OMELIA AND JUBALLAH.

Omelia and old Juballah retired to rest at an early hour, in the same chamber, in the bungalow of the worthy Doolab and his wife, and there they sat for some time discussing the strange and fortunate circumstances that had brought them together again, and in trying to arrange their plans for the future; and in which Juballah showed much clearness and ingenuity of intellect, while the strict integrity of her motives could not for an instant be doubted.

Omelia was indeed astonished at the wisdom and superiority of mind which the mysterious old woman displayed, and which, no doubt, to suit her purpose, had been concealed under so uncouth an exterior.

" The thought strikes me, the course to be pursued, with the greatest certainty of a successful result, is now clearly revealed to me," Juballah suddenly exclaimed, after a few minutes of deep thought, " be patient, be hopeful, Omelia, and your fondest and most anxious wishes shall yet be gratified."

"Oh, what mean you?" interrogated our heroine, eagerly; " what makes you thus express such sanguine and flattering hopes?"

" Question me not, Omelia," returned Juballah, " for I cannot answer you at present. An idea has struck me, which I am all but certain must succeed, but it will probably take some little time before it can be carried into full effect. Depend upon, be guided entirely by me, and you may be certain that old Juballah would sooner sacrifice her own life, than deceive or lead astray any one whom she has promised to serve."

"Excellent woman," replied Omelia, " I do believe you, and with every confidence I place my fate in your hands."

" Enough, my poor girl," said Juballah, "you will have no cause to repent the confidence you repose in me. If your lover be still alive, he shall be discovered, and you shall be conducted in safety to him."

"Oh, blissful assurance," ejaculated Omelia, with much emotion, " dare I hope that it will ever be fulfilled?"

" I have said it," replied the old woman, " and I am seldom wrong in the ideas I form. We depart from hence at an early hour in the morning."

"And what direction do you intend us to take?" inquired our heroine.

" I have before requested you to leave everything to me, and you have agreed to do so. Be satisfied, and your hopes may be realised much sooner than you anticipate. But come, let us retire to rest."

Omelia knew the necessity of this in order to recruit her strength for the probable fatigues of the following day, and she therefore, of course, did not offer any objection, and a few moments afterwards she sought her couch, the singular being, Juballah, in spite of all our heroine's remonstrances and persuasions, obstinately persisting in sleeping on the rug at the foot of the bed.

The busy thoughts of Omelia upon the fresh and extraordinary adventures she was probably about to experience, however, kept her some time waking, and various were the feelings which they naturally excited in her bosom.

In the promises and hopes which Juballah had expressed, extravagant and even improbable though they might appear to be, she placed the most implicit confidence, and she could never feel sufficiently thankful for the accident which had so providentially brought them together again.

While the strange mystery and eccentricity that marked the character of that singular being completely bewildered her, her evident excellent qualities of heart, and the services so inestimable which she had herself already received at her hands, could not but win her utmost esteem and reverence, and that feeling she was convinced her future conduct must entitle her to.

With such a guide and adviser, the uncertainty of success, and the perils of the journey seemed half diminished, though she would have been better satisfied if the old woman had been more explicit as to the course she intended to take.

Again the hope that her beloved Stanley still lived, and that she should once more behold him, revived in her heart, and a feeling of ecstacy animated her as it did so, which she neither could or attempted to subdue.

Tired of thinking, however, she at length fell asleep, and her mind being comparatively at rest, she slept calmly for the remainder of the night, and until she was aroused by Juballah at an early hour in the morning.

Juballah greeted her with even more than usual tenderness, and having assisted her to dress, they proceeded to the room below, where they found Doolab and his wife and daughter, notwithstanding it was only just daylight, waiting to receive them, and a light repast prepared, in case they should require it. But they did not, and after Juballah had with much difficulty persuaded Doolab to accept of some remuneration, and our heroine had returned her warmest acknowledgements to him and his wife for their great kindness and hospitality, they quitted the bungalow without any more delay, and recommenced their journey, proceeding at a pretty brisk pace in the cool of the early morn.

And what a strange contrast did that mysterious, ugly, and half naked old woman, and the lovely and gentle Omelia present. It must have created the greatest wonder in the breasts of all who could behold them; but at that early hour, and the way which Juballah had chosen to take, it did not seem likely that they would meet with any one to observe them.

Omelia, as we have said before, felt revived in spirits, and her strength greatly recruited after the few hours refreshing sleep she had obtained, and now that she was accompanied by the faithful Juballah, and they continued to travel cheerfully on for some time, and until they had got to a considerable distance from the village in which the bungalow of Doolab was situated; but at length they stopped for a short time and seated themselves on the grass to rest themselves.

The country they were travelling through was pleasant, and every way calculated to invigorate the spirits, and it had happily taken its due effect on those of our heroine, who felt herself contented, hopeful, and confident.

"Shall we find any friendly place of shelter to night?" she interrogated.

"Oh, yes, though we shall have to travel some coss before we reach it," answered the old woman, "the route I have chosen, and which leads to some of the latest destinations of the British troops, will afford us every accommodation when we require it, so that you may make your mind quite easy on that point."

Omelia was gratified to hear this, and expressed herself accordingly, and after having taken sufficient time to rest themselves, they once more resumed the journey; the beauty of the country, and the occasional conversation of old Juballah, serving to divert the thoughts of our heroine from the less cheerful subjects that might otherwise have engrossed her mind.

And thus they continued to travel, stopping at intervals to rest themselves, till late in the afternoon, when the character of the scenery became changed, assuming a wild and cheerless aspect, notwithstanding the golden sun was streaming its brightest beams upon it.

The road, too, was difficult and rugged, and Omelia needed all the support and assistance of her more experienced and hardy companion, to enable her to proceed.

They were travelling amidst wild mountain scenery, with a stream of water and a foaming, roaring cataract on one side, and a woody country on the other. The noise of the cataract was the only sound that broke upon the solemn silence, and which imparted a sensation bordering upon awe to the breast.

Juballah, however, held the hand of our heroine in her's, and encouraged her on.

"We shall shortly emerge from this cheerless place," she remarked, "and enter upon a more agreeable part of the country. I see, Omelia, that you are getting faint and exhausted."

"True," answered the latter, "for we have travelled far, and without refreshment."

"Another hour's walking will bring us to a friendly village, where I am known," said Juballah, "and where we can obtain all that we require. Courage, Omelia, and depend on me."

"Believe me I do so, and have every confidence," returned our heroine.

Juballah smiled her approval, and they again advanced on their way, though not without considerable difficulty.

They avoided the stream and the cataract, and Juballah leading the way along a mountain pass, they presently came upon a more cheerful part of the country as she had promised they would, and the spirits of Omelia, which had become somewhat depressed, again revived, and she proceeded with renewed strength.

They had met but a few native men and women throughout the day, and they took little or no notice of them, so that Omelia had had no cause for alarm, or anything to shake her confidence.

"Have we much further to travel ere we shall arrive at the village you lately spoke of?" inquired Omelia, anxiously.

"Another half hour will bring us to it," answered Juballah, "and I am anxious, for your sake, to reach it, for I know well how much you must stand in need of refreshment."

"I do indeed feel faint," returned Omelia, "and so must you, my good Juballah, for it is many hours since we tasted anything. I am afraid you will expose yourself to many troubles and privations in trying to serve me."

"Mention it not," said the old woman, "there is no difficulty or danger that can daunt the spirit and determination of Juballah, when she is engaged in a good cause. Set your mind at rest, Omelia, for I am perfectly content."

Omelia returned no answer to this, and on they went in silence for some distance further, till arriving on elevated ground, the welcome sight of the village which Juballah had spoken of, at a short distance before them, met the eager observation of Omelia, just as the sun was about to sink to rest in the western horizon.

"There," observed Juballah, pausing, and pointing to the village with a look of satisfaction, "you see I have been as good as my word, Omelia. Your cares for this day will

soon be over, for yonder we shall find a friendly welcome, and all the accommodation we require."

"Oh, thanks, thanks, my good Juballah," replied Omelia, "how much am I already indebted to you."

"Cease, Omelia," returned Juballah, somewhat impatiently, "I have already repeatedly assured you that I require no thanks. There is nothing I can possibly do to serve one whom I so highly esteem, which I will not willingly, nay, anxiously perform. But come, let us no longer delay."

Omelia pressed the poor old woman's hand in silence, and quickening their speed, in a few minutes they arrived at the village.

———

CHAPTER CLXV.

A WELCOME MEETING.

The village was pleasantly situated amidst a grove of trees, and the bungalow at the entrance formed a kind of caravansary, not much frequented, except by casual travellers whose way happened to lay in that remote part of the country.

"We cannot do better than to put up here for the night," observed Juballah, "for the host and I are well acquainted, and we are sure to receive every kindness and attention."

"I leave everything to you, Juballah," replied Omelia, "knowing it will be for the best."

Juballah nodded her approval of the confidence which our heroine reposed in her, and they immediately entered the bungalow.

The host, who was a good-humoured, well behaved man, met them at the door, and welcomed Juballah most cordially, but observing Omelia, he evinced by his looks some surprise and curiosity.

Juballah, however, said a few words to him aside, and he then greeted our heroine most politely, and invited her into a private room at the back—though there were at that time no other guests in the caravansary—while Juballah remained for a time behind, doubtless to explain, and to make the necessary arrangements for their accommodation.

She was not long kept in suspense, for Juballah entered the room, followed by the host bringing in the viands she had ordered, and which were most welcome to Omelia, who, as might naturally be expected, after long fasting and travelling much needed them.

The host eyed our heroine for a moment with much interest and sympathy, and then retired from the room.

"I have made every arrangement for our accommodation for the night, Omelia," remarked the old woman, "which, no doubt, will meet with your approbation. What is more, I have obtained such information from my friend as I believe will prove most valuable to us in our search."

"Ah!" exclaimed Omelia, eagerly, "tell me, I beseech you, and that quickly, my good Juballah, what is it?"

"To questions which I put to him," re-replied the old woman, "Tasmia Hoolkar —which is the name of our host—informed me that more than a week ago, British troops passed through the village in the direction we are about to go, and a portion of which though he is not certain, he believes to have been a regiment of Fusiliers."

"Oh," exclaimed Omelia, clasping her hands vehemently together, and her heart palpitating violently, "grant that this may prove to be correct, there will then indeed be some cause for hope."

"Yes you have every cause for hope, since I have fortunately met with you again," said the old woman and her features, as she did so, expressed as much kindness as it was possible for features so naturally repulsive to do; "I can depend upon the statement of my friend, the master of this caravansary, for he is intelligent and honest, and that's more than we can say of many of our countrymen in his station of life."

"True," coincided Omelia, "but there is one question I particularly wish to ask you, my good Juballah."

"Name it," requested the latter.

"Did your friend give you any information," interrogated Omelia, "which might afford you some idea as to the destination of the troops he spoke of?"

"Yes," replied Juballah, "although he was unable to obtain any direct information from the officers or men themselves he watched the route they took, and from the present state of Oude, where the utmost energy and constant action are required to suppress the rebellion, he is strongly inclined to think that to be the place of their destination; and of that opinion I am now also, thither, therefore, we will direct our course."

"Oh, yes," returned Omelia, eagerly, "anywhere, no consequence how long, tedious, and weary the journey, if it be only at all probable to conduct me again to the presence of my beloved Stanley. I am prepared to endure any fatigue, to brave any danger, however imminent for his sake."

"Poor girl—poor girl," ejaculated Juballah, feelingly, "and may your affectionate self devotion be fully rewarded by the realisation of all your fondest hopes and wishes."

"Thanks, thanks, kind-hearted Juballah," replied our heroine, "your generous sympathy doubly encourages me to hope, and the doubts and misgivings I have lately entertained all but vanish."

"Continue in the same state of mind, Omelia," said the old woman, "and I feel confident that you will not be doomed to disappointment, of which you have, I know, experienced too much already. A good night's rest will, I trust, enable you to resume our journey, which must extend over many days, early to-morrow morning."

"Oh, yes," returned Omelia, "recruited in strength, and re-animated with hope, I shall be prepared to do so."

Omelia and her friendly companion continued in conversation upon the subjects most interesting to themselves, regardless of the lapse of time, and the necessity of their seeking repose to recruit themselves for the following day's exertions, till the darkness of night enveloped everything around, and, very unusual at that time of year in India, a storm had commenced with considerable violence, and which threatened to last some time.

"It threatens to be a stormy night," remarked Juballah, "but I trust it will clear off before the morning. Come, Omelia, you had better retire to rest, for you must be fatigued; it is getting late, and I hear that they have closed the caravansary for the night."

"But a little longer yet, good Juballah," replied Omelia, half thoughtfully, "and I will gladly do as you suggest, for I am indeed tired. Hark, what noise is that?"

"It is some one knocking at the door of the caravansary, some weary traveller, no doubt, like ourselves, seeking admission."

The knocking was repeated, and then they heard the door opened, followed by the faint and mournful voice of a man, who seemed to be in great distress, exciting the sympathy and curiosity of Omelia and Juballah.

"Excuse me, Omelia, for a few minutes," said the old woman, "my services may be needful below, and they shall never be withheld from those who require them."

Our heroine smiled her approval, and Juballah immediately quitted the room on her humane errand.

Omelia's curiosity to know who the stranger was, was greatly excited, though she knew not for why, and hearing the murmuring of voices proceeding from those below, she silently opened the room-door, and stepping on to the landing, she listened with the hope to catch some of the observations that might pass, although it was quite certain that Juballah would make her acquainted with all the particulars on her return to the room.

At first the voices of Juballah and the host alone distinctly reached her ears, but at length she clearly heard that of the traveller —who appeared to be revived by something which had been administered to him—and she started, for she was quite certain that she had heard it somewhere before.

Then followed a confused mumbling of voices, in which Omelia was unable to distinguish a word, and after the lapse of a few moments an exclamation of surprise and emotion, and hearing footsteps hastily ascending the stairs, she returned to the room.

Juballah immediately afterwards made her re-appearance, her strange countenance expressive of mingled feelings of surprise and pleasure, and laying hold of the hand of our heroine, was about to hurry her from the room without speaking a word, when Omelia eagerly inquired—

"What means this excitement, Juballah? what has happened?"

"There is an agreeable surprise for you," replied the old woman, "but ask no questions. Come, come."

Astonished at the manner of Juballah, and not knowing what to conjecture, Omelia obeyed, and the old woman hurried her down the stairs.

At the door they paused for a moment, Omelia being in a state of great suspense; but Juballah quickly opened it, and drew her inside the room.

The stranger's back was towards them, and the host was engaged in talking to him in a low tone; but on hearing the door opened, the man turned hastily round, with an exclamation of delight, and the light from the lamp fully revealed his features.

Omelia no sooner recognised them, than with a cry of astonishment and unspeakable gratification she rushed towards him, for it was no other but her esteemed and well tried faithful friend, him whom she had been so anxious to behold again, but had despaired of doing so, Abdal!

CHAPTER CLXVI.

THE GREETING OF ABDAL AND OMELIA.

The host immediately retired from the room, and Juballah would have done the same, but Omelia, as well as her agitation would permit, motioned her not to do so, and the old woman remained, and retiring to the opposite side of the room, looked on all that took place between the two friends, and listened with the greatest interest and gratification.

It was some minutes before either Abdal or Omelia could find sufficient composure to speak. Abdal looked wan and careworn, but in other respects there was no material alteration in his appearance, and his intelligent and fine manly features were now lighted up with pleasure again at beholding Omelia, whose handsome countenance fully showed that she warmly participated in his feelings.

"Dear Omelia," at length said Abdal, in tones of the utmost respect, "for such the feelings of esteem and friendship which I sincerely entertain towards you, will, I trust, entitle me to call you, oh, what can equal my astonishment and delight at this strange and unexpected meeting, when I had abandoned all hope of ever beholding you again?"

"Oh, my kind, my faithful friend Abdal," returned our heroine, with equal sincerity and emotion, "need I say how warmly I reciprocate the feelings that you have expressed? But there is one thought, one anxiety that supersedes all others in my breast. Stanley, here."—

She could not finish the sentence, for the power of her emotions choked her further utterance.

Abdal shook his head mournfully, but could not return any immediate answer, and that increased the poor girl's agitation.

"Oh, tell me, I implore you," she with difficulty ejaculated, and the most terrible apprehensions beset her mind; why do you look so melancholy at the question I have put to you, and remain silent? Oh, keep me not in this horrible, this insupportable state of suspense, if you are capable of giving me the information I seek.—Stanley,—my Stanley,—Oh, tell me, does he still live?"

"I trust he does," replied Abdal, earnestly, "but, alas! I know not."

"Dreadful state of uncertainty," cried Omelia, in a voice half choked by sobs, "Oh,

when will my torturing doubts be removed?
you know not then, Abdal, where the unfortunate Stanley is, if indeed he be still in existence."

"Be calm and patient, Omelia, I beg of you," replied Abdal, "and I will tell you all I am acquainted with, in a few words."

Omelia endeavoured to be so, and Abdal, after a brief pause, to recollect himself, thus proceeded—

"I will not attempt to describe the agony of Lieutenant Stanley and myself, when Captain Morley was brought into quarters, apparently mortally wounded, and quite insensible, and it became quite certain, after every inquiry had been made, that you, Omelia, had been torn away."

"Oh, tell me, before you proceed further," interrupted our heroine, anxiously, "did the gallant captain survive the serious injuries I have too much reason to fear he received?'

"Fortunately he did," answered Abdal, "and it was from his lips that we received the terrible information of your brutal seizure by the daring miscreant Yusef and his infamous associates, and to seek to pourtray the maddening effect which that dreadful intelligence had upon your lover, Omelia, would be a completely fruitless task. For some days he was unable to leave his bed, and no sooner was he capable of doing so, than orders came down from head quarters for the troops to vacate Cawnpore, and to prepare themselves for a series of long and rapid marches."

"Ah, whither? in what direction?" anxiously and breathlessly interrogated Omelia.

"That was kept a profound secret from all but the principal officers," replied Abdal.

Our heroine sighed.

"Two days after the order had arrived," continued Abdal, "the whole of the troops left the city, others having arrived to take their place. I was not permitted to accompany them, and outside the city I bade adieu to Lieutenant Stanley, he solemnly enjoining me to make every effort to discover you, and to endeavour at every hazard to rescue you from the inhuman villain who held you in his power, a task, which I need scarcely say, I willingly promised to perform, and have faithfully kept my word, travelling many many miles, and encountering perils and privations out of number in search of you, but all to no purpose, till accident fortunately, this night, brought me hither, for which circumstance I know not how sufficiently to return my thanks to Providence. Of Lieutenant Stanley, or the regiment to which he belonged, I have not been able to learn anything since they left the city of Cawnpore."

Thus Abdal concluded his brief narrative, which had thrown not the least light on the mystery in which the part of the country

whither the troops from Cawnpore were gone, was enveloped, and Omelia was left in the same torturing state of doubt and uncertainty.

She consoled herself, however, with the hopes that Juballah had inspired her with, and which were greatly increased by the fortunate and unexpected restoration of Abdal to her, whose services she was certain would be found so useful in their search.

She related to him, at his earnest request, but in as few words as possible, the particulars of her seizure by Yusef; the great danger in which she was placed, and the manner in which she had been rescued by the humanity of the kind-hearted though uncouth looking Juballah, to whom Abdal was about to pay the most flattering compliments, but the old woman hastily and impatiently interrupted him.

They then discussed their future plans, of which Abdal entirely approved, and shortly afterwards separated for the night, resolving the following morning to change their course, and make their way as well as they could towards Oude,

The storm had passed over in the night, and when Omelia and her two friends met at the appointed time the next morning, the weather was remarkably fine, and they started on their journey in the best of spirits.

And here for a time we must necessarily leave our heroine and her companions to their adventures, having many other exciting and interesting particulars to relate.

———

CHAPTER CLXVII.

OUDE.

Hindoostan Proper, containing the more central provinces of India, holds the most important place in its ancient Mahommedan dynasties. It extends southward to the Norbudda river, and includes thirteen provinces, of which Oude is one of the largest.

We will take the liberty of quoting Mr. Russel's masterly description of it:—

"The country through which our column is advancing is fertile—in Indian crops perhaps unrivalled, and is cultivated to a degree of perfection which capital and science could not surpass. No scrutiny can detect a single weed in the fields of wheat and rice which are spread far and wide. Cleaner and more beautiful agriculture the Lothians could not show.

"Without steam ploughs or scarifiers, or chemical laboratories, malodorous manures, or armouries of weapons, the Hindoo manages by patient, untiring hand labour, aided by the rudest traditional implements and traditional knowledge, to extract from *alma mater* the richest rewards of cereal industry.

"The fields are generally square, and each well defined by a small bank of earth eighteen inches or two feet high, and broad enough at top to serve as a pathway for man or horse.

"There is considerable uniformity in the size of the rice fields, which average here about 200 feet square.

"The banks serve to keep in the irrigation waters; they are hard and solid, and offer considerable difficulties to the rapid advance of cavalry in order, or of artillery.

"The dall and Indian corn-fields are not defined by banks, but are all sown and planted in regular parallelograms. In places where the water lies, making jeels or marshes, the ground is left uncultivated, but the long tufted grass with which it is covered naturally yields fine pasturage to domestic animals, and gives shelter to quantities of game —antelopes, dear, hares, as well as to jackals, silver foxes, and wolves.

"The most striking feature of the whole district, however, is the absence of towns or even villages. The towns marked on the map, such as Churdah and Bankee, are not to be found on the spots indicated, but in lieu of them are collections of cottages, with a small Hindoo temple or Mussulman mosque, and a mud fort, and a strip of wild forest and brushwood, a jeel, and a tank.

"The misery and vices, idleness and discontent engendered by large oriental towns and cities are thus obviated. Instead of being concentrated in one spot the population is scattered all over the face of the country.

"Look where you will in this part of Onde, you will be sure to see one or two petty hamlets in view at the least, each consisting of only three or four cottages, with outhouses and inclosures, fenced round by neat hurdles filled in with plaited grass and reeds.

"The cottages are one-storied, covered with good roofs of thatch or tiles, and very clean outside; of the inside, alas, one cannot judge. Religion, prejudice, and priestcraft have raised up a great barrier between the Hindoo and mankind. His threshold you cannot cross; hospitality in its finer sense he cannot display.

"I was almost amused at the indignation of a 'farmer,' from whose house I drove away a set of rascally camp-followers, who were plundering his little store of grain and corn. Of the robbery he seemed to think nothing; his complaint was that these Mussulmans should have violated the sacredness of a Hindoo's cottage.

"There are no windows of glass in the houses, and the interiors must be dark enough. The apertures which serve to admit air and light, are closed by wooden shutters.

"Each cottage is surrounded by its own hurdled enclosure, within which are its domestic offices, the women's cottage—if the proprietor has a large family—the granary, the storehouse, the cattle-sheds, and the mill for expressing mustard oil, which is in common use among the people—perhaps a private well. The threshing floor is frequently outside the village. The whole of the enclosed space is swept as clean as a Dutch parlour, the surface of the ground within being smoothed down till it is like a tile. The cottage roofs are covered with green creepers, pumpkins, and a coarse sort of melon.

"Hideous images of clay, and rude drawings in coloured ochres on the walls of the buildings of Vishnu, Siva, or Rana remind us that we are not in Arcadia; though, indeed, I am not sure that the paintings or worship of that happy apocryphy were any better or purer.

"The ryot, under good government, ought to be happy enough, and, notwithstanding the cruelties and oppression to which he has been subjected in Oude, his maternal condition, as indicated by the state of his dwelling and farming, contrasts by no means unfavourably with that of peasants in some of the most civilised parts of Europe.

"In this district cotton is grown in considerable quantities, and, though I do not pretend to be a judge of the staple, I should say it was fine and good. No doubt, it could be produced here to any extent, but at present the natives merely grow it to supply their own wants. They use it to stuff their 'resais,' or bed covers, which serve them in lieu of blankets, and to quilt their winter clothing.

The absence of roads, of no great consequence now, must prove a serious obstacle to any extensive export during the rainy season, and long afterwards.

"The roads which do exist are called by the natives by a name ('leek') which signifies a wheel-mark; arbitrary tracts across the country connecting village with village."

In fact, one of the principal things to complain of in the province of Oude, is the badness of the roads, in all other respects the country is beautiful; abounding in sublime and magnificent scenery, rich in vegetation; teeming with all the blessings that all bounteous nature can produce, but, alas, cursed with the ravages of sanguinary and all devastating war.

Hear Mr. Russel in conclusion—

"I am begining to disbelieve in the 'terai,' and to be an infidel as to the impenetrable jungle.

"As we advance the 'terai' recedes. We can see the ranges of the southern Himalayas which bound Nepaul close at hand, and above them the tremendous crest of the Snowy range, which forms the dread northern barrier of the Ghoorkas from central Asia; and if we ask for the 'terai,' we are told it lies generally in the direction of the O'Mulligan's residence, 'down there;' but our column is now at the place where this deadly region, sacred to witches, serpents, malaria, and tigers, and saul-trees, was said positively to commence its awful sway.

"Popular superstition has assigned to the Himalayan border a sort of mystical character, such as in olden times attached to Colchis or the Cimmerian solitudes. The Punjaub soldier, the Madrassee, the Bengalee approach the junction of mountain and plain with reluctance and horror.

"The women are all versed in witchcraft, and can by a glance deprive a man of his entrails—a pretty fancy enough if the power were restricted to his heart. The men are satyrs; the voices of Pan and his friends are heard sounding through the dreary wood. Such are the delusions we are about practically to dispel if our military necessities compel us to another march northwards.

"Nepaul is not more than twenty miles on the north, and ten miles on the east. Rarely, indeed, do we see the magnificent framework of mountain in which the kingdom is enclosed, for in India, so far as I know, a clear day, such as lends enchantment to an Alpine landscape, where every snowy pinnacle, every mountain side and farthest peak stands out sharp and bright in the light pure air, is scarcely known. In summer, the haze, the heat incorporate, broiling and waving and dancing across the weary eyes, perplexes vision and destroys perspective; in winter there are clouds, fogs, and vapours. In the hills after the rains I have indeed seen some fine clear days, but never the distinctness which characterises such days in Switzerland or the French Pyrenean frontier. But occasionally and for a moment the veil is raised here, and we see the grandest mountains in the world towering towards heaven, and clad in dazzling white.

"What future Albert Smith will describe the glories of Dwalagiri, which we saw revealing itself the other day, to which the summit of Mont Blanc would be but a poor half-way house in its sheer flight of nigh 27,000 feet?

"One would think that in the vicinity of these stupendous ranges the heats of summer would be pleasantly tempered by the comparative proximity of the snow, but in no part of Indian is the sun more powerful, or its influence more painful, than in the plains bordering on the 'terai.'

"Much has been done under native government to clear the jungles of this district. Maun Singh told us that when he was here, seven years ago, collecting the taxes—an operation which he conducted in a way that would very much astonish the formidable gentleman who, in the guise of ecclesiastics with white neckcloths and black coats, make war against so many households with no more formidable weapons than a notice-book, schedules, and pencils—the whole of the country round Churdah, Mejiddiah, and Burjiddiah was covered with forest and jungle. It is now cleared and cultivated. Evidence of the truth of the whole of Maun Singh's story remains in stripes of jungle still left, and in the numerous stumps of trees in every field, which have been charred to prevent shoots sprouting out.

"But jungle, in the sense of dense impenetrable forest and undergrowth, I have not seen in Oude. Through the thickest there are paths and traks, the jungle at each side being, indeed, lacerating and savage to the utmost. It abounds, however, with passages made by wild beasts, through which a man can go on bended knees, but since our mail was interfered with by tigers the day before yesterday at Nanparah, and the postmen waylaid by a more formidable antagonist even than Lord Colchester, no very vehement desire for exploration has been expressed by any of us, lest in such an excursion we might meet the original proprietor of the soil where there would not be room for both to pass, and his action in trespass on the case is summary.

"As the jungle disappears, the mud fort becomes a poor defence; few of these forts were really formidable, except to the rabble armies of native chiefs and chuckledars with bad artilery. To any infantry they would be serious obstacles, never to be taken by assault without heavy loss, but they are mere 'shell traps.' There are no defences against vertical fire, a few mortars could at any time empty them completely. To keep them in repair was expensive, for the rain and the sun united each year to make war upon the mud bastions and curtains, and the walls were apt to be washed into the ditch. Under any circumstances it was costly enough to the owner to maintain the petty corpse of matchlockmen and their followers, who lived in huts within the *enceinte* of the fort, and the whole class of Oude nobles will be richer, if not more happy, secure, and contented, when their strongholds are levelled to the earth, and their defence confided to the police and government of the country."

Such is the province of Oude, in which so many startling events have for some time taken place, and the annexation of which there can be little doubt was the principal cause, if not the origin of the rebellion.

———

CHAPTER CLXVIII.

OMELIA'S LOVER.—THE BATTLE.

The desperate state of Oude was most alarming, and sadly harrassed the British army. Engagements followed engagements in rapid succession, and although the enemy were invariably defeated with great loss, it was only to re-appear in double force in different parts of the country.

It required all the troops that could possibly be spared to meet this emergency, and thither it was that those from Cawnpore were despatched.

Stanley knew not the place of their destination, but he was certain that it was where he should have to face death in its most appalling form, and he hailed it with a feeling of melancholy pleasure, for life had become to him an insupportable burthen, since his beloved Omelia, he now firmly believed, was lost to him for ever, in fact, that she was no more, for it was impossible that she could long survive the atrocities of the savage miscreant who had got her in his power.

What he had suffered since that fatal evening when she had been torn away, it would defy the power of language to describe, and every hour, every moment his anguish and despair increased, in spite of all the efforts of his friends to soothe him.

"Why talk to me thus!"—he would say, impatiently, "you do but seem to try to mock and trifle with my feelings by doing so. Can I be calm, resigned, and know that she in whom all my hopes, all my joys, all my wishes are centered, is in the power of a monster capable of any crime, however atrocious, is at present suffering all the horrors that can be imagined, and to which immediate death would be preferable, while I, not knowing where she is concealed have not the power of flying to her rescue?—Oh, Omelia, beauteous, gentle, affectionate, but most unfortunate of human beings, we shall see each other no more, and that fatal conviction seals my doom."

He beat his breast in the agony of his sufferings, and his friend, who could return no answer to his observations, saw that to endeavour to impart consolation to him, under all the melancholy circumstances, would be a completely useless task.

In fact, he was reduced to such a deplorable state from mental anguish, that he was rendered almost incapable of performing the necessary duties that devolved upon him, and there was not an individual in the regiment to which he belonged, from the highest officer to the humblest soldier of the ranks, (so universally was he esteemed by all who knew him), who did not deeply and sincerely sympathise with him, and who would not willingly have done anything in their power to serve him and alleviate his sufferings.

And thus matters stood when the order came down from the commander in chief for the departure of the troops from Cawnpore.

This instead of disturbing the mind of Stanley, in its present delicate state, was received by him, as has been before stated, with a melancholy kind of pleasure, for since the fate of his Omelia seemed too fatally sealed, and there appeared to be not the least probability of their ever meeting again, he could more boldly rush on danger, nay, wished to die the death of a soldier on the battle field.

On the morning therefore of the departure of the troops from Cawnpore, he might be said to be in comparatively good spirits, and his friends were surprised to see him.

He felt the deepest regret at being compelled to separate from the trustworthy and kind-hearted Abdal, and implored him, as the latter had stated to our heroine and Juballah, in their meeting in the caravansary, to use every exertion to endeavour to discover Omelia, and if possible to rescue her from her awful situation in the power of the villain Yusef, which Abdal having promised faithfully to perform, they parted with the greatest reluctance, and the troops proceeded on their weary march, beneath a burning sun, and over land so broken and so rugged, frequently intercepted by deep swamps, or rendered almost impassable by dense jungle, that the difficulty and fatigue were rendered doubly trying, even to the oldest and most experienced soldiers, who were used to the country.

But Stanley seemed to heed not in the slightest degree, these obstacles and difficulties, his mind being entirely occupied with other thoughts and subjects, and he bore up against them in such a manner as completely astonished all who saw him, knowing what he had suffered both mentally and physically for some few days past.

Captain Morley had quite recovered from the injuries he had received on the occasion of the abduction of Omelia, and on the march, they being together, he exerted himself to the utmost to banish the gloomy thoughts that beset Stanley's mind, and to raise his spirits, but although he listened to him with every attention and respect, his arguments and persuasions could have but little effect upon him, or serve to ameliorate the violence of his mental anguish.

When they had been on the march above a day, they heard for the first time the place of their destination, and the desperate nature of the dangers they would have, without doubt to encounter; but Stanley received the information with every mark of satisfaction, and seemed to look forward to the scene of sanguinary strife in which he would so shortly be engaged with feelings of impatience

As has been before stated the march was a most weary and tedious one, and as the occasion was one of the greatest emergency, the rebels pouring down upon Oude, under the command of some of their most distinguished chiefs, in overwhelming numbers, there was but little time given to the troops for rest.

A great portion of the country through which they had to pass, also presented the greatest obstacles, and necessarily retarded their progress. The heat was so excessive, that it was almost insupportable, and many of the men sunk beneath the effects of sunstroke.

But it was most surprising to see the firmness, nay, even indifference with which Stanley bore up against all these difficulties, in fact, his mind appeared to be too much occupied upon other subjects for him to bestow a single thought upon them.

After a most fatiguing march of five days, they came quite unexpectedly on a large body of the enemy, well provided with guns, in a good position, and presenting all the means for a most determined and obstinate resistance, if not a most certain and decided victory.

In a moment all was activity and excitement among the British troops and the officers commanding them, and Lieutenant Stanley turning suddenly round to his friend Captain Morley, and pressing his hand warmly, said solemnly and impressively—

"Morley, I have every reason to believe that you regard me with the same feeling as that of a brother, and that feeling, I am certain I need not assure you that I most cordially and sincerely reciprocate. Before we enter upon the deadly strife, I have a request to make."

"Name it, my dear Stanley, and I swear that, if I have the power, I will comply with it," replied Captain Morley.

"Should it be my fate to fall in this engagement," remarked Stanley, impressively, " and yours to survive, will you pledge yourself to use your utmost, your untiring exertions to discover Omelia, to impart to her the intelligence of my death, to assure her that my heart's last pulsation was for her, and to offer her all the consolation in your power, and to see to her future safety, if possible, happiness?"

" I promise, most solemnly, most sincerely promise," answered Captain Morley, pressing his hand with every warmth of feeling.

"Enough, I am satisfied," said Stanley, " dear Morley, your assurance has made me comparatively happy."

There was no time for more, the bugles sounded the attack, and the deadly combat commenced.

It would require far abler pens than our's to do adequate justice to the scene which ensued.

The British were composed of a select force of cavalry, artillery, and infantry, and they had come as has been before stated, quite unexpectedly upon the enemy at Bankee.

So completely, in fact, were the rebels taken by surprise, that a portion of the cavalry brigade, consisting of the 6th dragoon guards and two horse artillery guns, under the command of a most able and gallant officer, were at one time within 150 yards of their guns. In consequence of the infantry not being up in time, or the cavalry and guns being too far in advance, the latter were forced to retire under a heavy fire.

There were only, however, three men wounded, and one so slightly as not to be reported. The behaviour of the 6th dragoon guards was particularly deserving of mention.

These advanced rapidly to the front, over bad ground and deep ditches, where two horses were obliged to be left; and, after standing under fire for a quarter of an hour, retired by alternate squadrons, supporting the guns, as if it had been a field day.

When the infantry came up, the 7th huzzars advanced through the jungle, and, in the eagerness of pursuit, followed the rebels into the Raptee—a rapid stream, where an officer, two men, and several horses were drowned.

About 300 of the rebels were killed or drowned, and six guns, five elephants, and many horses were captured.

This was an important victory; the country into which the enemy were driven, contains no villages and is quite uncultivated, and unless they surrendered they must starve.

And during this fierce and terrific battle, where was Stanley? Where danger was the greatest, where death stalked most awfully, there was he to be found, regardless of consequences, and performing perfect prodigies of valour.

At one time he was engaged in deadly combat with two of the enemy; one he slew, but by that time he was nearly exhausted with the extraordinary exertions he had undergone, and the adversary he had now to contend with being a most powerful man, his fate seemed all but certain, when a well directed shot from an unseen hand stretched the fellow a corpse on the earth.

The next minute the enemy was in full retreat.

CHAPTER CLXIX.

THE STRANGER.—THE WANDERER.

Leaving Omelia and her lover for awhile, we will now proceed to introduce into our eventful narrative some incidents of a startling and interesting description, and which will be found ultimately to be immediately connected with it.

The surprise and regret of Colonel Bridport and his amiable daughters on discovering the abrupt departure of Omelia, and perusing the letter she had left behind her, may be readily imagined; and they could not but blame her for the rash and dangerous course she had thought proper to take, while they deeply lamented the loss of the society of one whom they were so well prepared to esteem.

"Foolish, headstrong girl," said the gallant colonel, in tones of the most unfeigned regret, "she has been hurried into a course which, I fear, is fraught with every peril, while the gratification of her purpose, or that she will ever be able to accomplish her wishes, seems all but hopeless. Whither can she go, destitute and unprotected as she is? How will she be able to brave and withstand the numerous dangers by which she will be sure to be surrounded?"

"Yes, I shudder at the thought, my dear father," said his daughter Julia, "especially in the present disturbed state of the country. Oh, why did she not follow your advice, and await patiently for a few days, at least, under your protection? She might be certain that

No. 75.

from us, after the manner in which we had received her that she would meet with every sympathy."

"Most true, my dear Julia," returned her father, "of that she was evidently herself convinced, and she has warmly expressed herself to that effect in her farewell letter. Poor girl, how wild, how extravagant, and perilous is the task she has imposed upon herself. May heaven protect and guide her through it, safely and successfully."

To this wish the amiable sisters most fervently responded, and their father soon afterwards left them to themselves.

The next day was an equally melancholy one to them, so greatly did they miss the company of Omelia, so much had that beauteous maiden charmed them by the sweetness and gentleness of her manners.

The colonel had been absent all day, and therefore they had felt more than usually dull, but towards the evening he returned, and his conversation somewhat reanimated their spirits.

The night—which was rather unusual at that period of the year—turned out dark and tempestuous, and the rain, at intervals, descended in heavy showers.

The streets of the city were, of course, entirely deserted, and the misery that reigned around was most intense.

"It is a fearful night," remarked the colonel, as him and his daughters sat together in one of the lower rooms of the place where they were residing, listening to the storm which raged with such violence without; heaven help the poor friendless creatures who have no place of shelter from the tempest."

"Amen!" devoutly responded Julia, with a mournful look; "alas, where is poor Omelia now? What will become of her, if she should be exposed to such a storm as this?"

"Most true," coincided her father in a voice of sympathy, "but I sincerely trust that such is not the case, but that she has found friends who will pity and relieve her. Hark; surely I heard the faint cry of a human voice outside."

They listened with some curiosity, but could hear nothing but the voice of the howling tempest which had increased in fury.

"I might have been mistaken," said the colonel, "yet I could almost have sworn that I heard the mournful voice of a female in the pauses of the storm. There again, that, at any rate, was distinct enough."

It was, and Julia and her sister were violently agitated; for the thought struck them that Omelia had repented of the rash step she had taken, and returned.

They took up the lamp and looked from the window, but as far as their eyes could penetrate through the darkness they could

not perceive anything, and they were about to return disappointed to their seats, when the cry was repeated, and it then sounded nearer than before.

"It is some unfortunate being who claims our immediate assistance," said the colonel, entering the passage, and moving towards the outer door, followed by his daughters, in a state of great excitement and suspense, "come, we must not delay a moment."

As they advanced towards the door, there was a low moaning sound, as if proceeding from some unfortunate being in their last extremity, and which confirmed their surmises, but it ceased immediately, and the colonel hastily opened the door, and holding the lamp up, he and his fair daughters beheld stretched inanimate on the wet earth, and the rain still streaming upon her, a female form, but they immediately perceived that it was not that of Omelia.

Shocked and deeply affected at so deplorable a sight, and almost fearing that the unfortunate stranger was dead, the poor girls were completely transfixed to the spot on which they stood, and were unable to render the least assistance, but their father quickly putting down the lamp, raised the cold wet form of the wanderer from the ground, and then found that although she was quite insensible, and apparently in an almost hopeless condition, she still breathed, and he lost no time in carrying her into the room, so that means might be immediately resorted to for her recovery.

CHAPTER CLXX.

THE MYSTERY.

It would be almost impossible properly to describe the deep feelings of emotion that pervaded the breasts of the colonel and his daughters, as they gazed for a moment or two at the hapless stranger, after the former had placed her in an easy chair.

She appeared to be a young English woman of not more than two or three and twenty years of age. Her features were extremely handsome, with an innocence and gentleness of expression—as far as they could see, in her present deplorable state—which rendered them doubly interesting; but they were pinched and careworn evidently from long mental and bodily suffering.

Her hair, which was a beautiful glossy auburn, had become unfastened, and hung loose and dishevelled over her neck and shoulders. She appeared to be respectably and neatly attired, but her clothes were now disordered and saturated with rain.

"Ill-fated girl," said Colonel Bridport,

in a voice of great feeling, "who can she be? and what can have brought her into this wretched situation? But this delay is dangerous, let me convey her up stairs to a chamber, where you, my dear girls can immediately strip her of her wet clothes, and place her in bed, while I hasten to obtain the assistance of my friend, Mr. Hamilton, the surgeon."

He again raised the poor insensible girl in his arms as he spoke, and hurried up stairs, accompanied by Julia and Charlotte, in a state of great anxiety.

Here the colonel left the young stranger in charge of his daughters for a few minutes, while he went to request the attendance of his friend the surgeon; and they lost no time in following his instructions, in stripping her of her wet clothes, and placing her in a warm bed, and bathing her temples with vinegar, but without showing the least signs of returning life.

"Unfortunate girl," ejaculated Julia, in accents of the greatest sympathy, "she is very beautiful, but appears to be worn out with sorrow and suffering. I wonder what will be the result of this romantic adventure."

Before her sister could make any reply, their father returned, accompanied by Mr. Hamilton, and entered the chamber.

Mr. Hamilton appeared much struck with the appearance of the fair unknown, and to commiserate her melancholy condition. He immediately set about adopting all the necessary remedies for her recovery, stating it as his opinion that she was in a very precarious situation from complete exhaustion, and that she would require the utmost attention to prevent her from sinking under it.

Colonel Bridport was fully prepared to hear this, and having desired his friend to exert himself to the utmost for the restoration of the unfortunate girl, for whom his feelings of pity were fully aroused, he quitted the room, and left her in charge of Mr. Hamilton and his daughters.

The worthy surgeon humanely exerted himself beyond all praise, while Julia and her sister rendered all the assistance in their power. But for some time all their efforts were of no avail, and the gentle sisters watched the poor sufferer with the most painful fear and anxiety.

Their hopes, however, were at length slightly revived, for the stranger evinced signs of returning life, a faint sigh escaping her lips, and opening her eyes, but glaring upon vacancy, which showed that consciousness was not yet thoroughly restored to her. This afforded Mr. Hamilton, however, an opportunity of administering to her a reviving cordial, which he trusted would have the most beneficial effect, and she then once more relapsed into a state of insensibility, though she breathed much more freely than she had done before.

Mr. Hamilton being of opinion that she might remain in that state for hours, and that it would be all the better for her to remain quiet, having given the sisters some necessary instructions how to act, promising to attend immediately if any unfavourable change should take place, took his leave for the night, and previous to his departure from the house, visited the colonel, who was anxious to see him in the parlour.

Colonel Bridport felt more satisfied with the report of the surgeon, and expressed a strong hope that the unfortunate girl would soon recover sufficiently to satisfy the great interest and curiosity that was excited in his breast by the mystery which was attached to her, and he could not but naturally feel anxious to know who she was, and what strange and unfortunate circumstances had brought her into the truly lamentable situation in which he and his daughters had discovered her, not only exposed to all the fury of the tempest, but apparently famishing from want.

This adventure, so soon after that of Omelia, and so similar in its circumstances, surprised and bewildered the good old colonel, and he scarcely knew what to think; however, all the best feelings of his excellent heart were awakened, and he determined to act with the same kindness and attention towards the young stranger as if she had been one of his own daughters.

Having heard the opinion of Mr. Hamilton, and that gentleman, after promising to call again early in the morning, having departed, the colonel could not resist the temptation to visit the chamber of the fair sufferer, in order to ascertain personally how she was, and to see whether he could be of any assistance to his daughters before he retired to rest.

On entering the room, which he did as quietly as possible, he was gratified to find the object of his anxious solicitude apparently in a calm and refreshing sleep; while the extreme pale, and even ghastly aspect of her countenance had disappeared, a slight flush suffused her cheeks, and made her uncommon beauty appear to still greater advantage.

Colonel Bridport, as in the case of the other object of his humanity, namely, our heroine, could not but wonder and admire while he felt the more anxious for her recovery, so that he might probably learn who she was, and whether he could do anything to serve her, and to extricate her from the frightful difficulties in which she was evidently at present involved.

He inquired of Julia and her sister whether she had shown any symptoms of returning consciousness since the doctor had departed; and they replied in the negative, adding that it was not till within a few minutes previous to his (their father's) entrance that the present change had come over her, which they could not but feel glad to see.

"Poor girl," remarked the colonel, "she has evidently suffered much, and is greatly exhausted; but I trust that with proper care and attention, which she is sure to receive from us, she will shortly be restored. She appears very young."

"Yes," replied Julia, "and she is most beautiful. How melancholy it is to think that so useful and interesting a being should be thus exposed to such fearful trials and vicissitudes as those which she has evidently had to encounter."

"Most true, my dear child," coincided her father, "and I admire you for the sympathy which I see clearly she has excited in your breast. You propose sitting up with her, I believe, but the fatigue might be too much for yourself and your sister, unaccustomed as you are to it; so you had better have the assistance of the ayah, Mira, so that you may be able to snatch an hour or two's repose at intervals.

To this the sisters gladly assented, and the colonel having summoned Mira into their presence, and given her his instructions, quitted the chamber, strictly enjoining her and his daughters to give him immediate notice, should any unfavourable change take place.

The sisters resumed their watching with Mira for some time longer, by the bedside of the stranger, but she continued to sleep tranquilly, the composing draught which Mr. Hamilton had administered to her during the brief period he had the opportunity of doing so, having had the desired effect, and in that state of repose she seemed likely to remain till the morning.

Once or twice indeed she started, as if disturbed by some unpleasant dream, and muttered some incoherent words, but she quickly dropped off again, and became as calm as ever.

At the request of Mira, as their services were not at all required at present, Julia and her sister now retired to an adjoining chamber to snatch an hour or two's repose, and the young stranger was left entirely to the care and attention of the former, who watched by her bedside during the dreary hours of the night almost with as much sympathy and anxiety as they could have done.

———

CHAPTER CLXXI.

WHO IS THE STRANGER?

Not once did the fair unknown awake till the colonel and Doctor Hamilton entered the chamber in the morning, when the latter having felt her pulse and pronounced favourably of her, she suddenly gave signs of returning sensibility, murmured a few words in a low and plaintive voice, which those present could not hear distinctly; then pressing her hands upon her forehead for a moment or two, she gently and with difficulty raised her head from the pillow, and stared vacantly, evidently not being able to distinguish anything around her clearly, while there was a wild and unnatural expression about her bright blue eyes which Mr. Hamilton did not like to see. He, however, motioned the colonel and his daughters to remain silent, and not to thrust themselves too suddenly on her notice.

A pause of two or three minutes ensued, during which those present awaited with breathless attention and curiosity to hear what she might have to say, while the poor girl still remained with her eyes fixed upon vacancy.

"How still—how solemn," she said at length, in a low and melancholy voice, "how icy cold—too cold, cold! This then is death. And yet this looks not like the tomb in which the ashes of the dead should repose. Hark, what dismal sounds were those? Clara—dear Clara! methought I heard, and it was uttered in *his* voice. Ah, no, it was all a delusion; the wretched outcast never was, and never can be dear to him. Strange shadowy forms seem to move before mine eyes; ah, me! my poor brain's bewildered, I—"

She was unable to finish the sentence, but with a deep and heart-drawn sigh she sunk back on her pillow, and again became insensible.

The curiosity and anxiety of Colonel Bridport and his daughters were more excited than ever, and they felt disappointed that they had not been able—with the exception of her name being Clara—to elicit more from her wild and rambling observations.

"Poor girl," said the kind-hearted Doctor Hamilton, "some terrible misfortunes have clearly impaired her intellect, and her mind at present wanders. She seems to labour under the singular delusion that she is dead, but that may be accounted for by the many severe trials it may have been her lot to encounter, the fearful sufferings she has had to endure."

"Very true," remarked Colonel Bridport, "and therefore is my sympathy, if possible, still more warmly excited for her, and I feel the more anxious to become acquainted with the melancholy circumstances that can have brought one so young and so lovely into so wretched a situation."

"I do not wonder at your curiosity, colonel, which is no idle one," replied Mr. Hamilton, "and that you should feel anxious that the mystery should be unravelled, but my patient must not be disturbed, for the least excitement might be productive of the most fatal consequences."

"Heaven forbid that I should be the cause of anything of that kind," said the colonel, fervently, "myself and my daughters will be guided entirely by your instructions, Mr. Hamilton."

"Enough," returned the latter; "then I have not the least doubt, but that with proper care and attention, she will soon recover her senses, and will be able to converse and probably feel disposed to gratify your wishes."

"I trust, my good doctor," remarked the colonel, "that your surmises will prove to be correct. But is it not strange that in so short a space of time, providence should have guided two unfortunate beings hither, and whose fate appears to be so similar."

"It is," replied Mr. Hamilton, "and it is no less fortunate for the two sufferers themselves, that they should have fallen into such good and humane hands. But come, colonel, perhaps it would be better for us to retire, and leave the patients to the tender care of your amiable daughters and their attendant. It may be a day or two before she is restored to complete consciousness, but I am happy to state that I consider all immediate danger is past. Should she sufficiently revive during the day, it will be necessary to contrive to administer to her the light nourishment provided; but on no account whatever suffer her to become the least excited, if it can be helped."

Julia and her sister promised strictly to follow the worthy doctor's instructions, and the latter and their father then again retired from the chamber.

After some further conversation, Mr. Hamilton took his leave, and the colonel, who had nothing to call him away for an hour or two, was left to the undisturbed indulgence of his own reflections.

The reader will, of course, conclude, that his whole thoughts would naturally be devoted to the fair young stranger, who was so singularly placed under his care and protection. Various were the conjectures, in fact, that he formed upon the important subject, but without being able to come to any satisfactory conclusion, and he was even more deeply interested in the fate of this young girl, then Omelia's, because it seemed to be still greater involved in mystery.

From the few rambling and disjointed observations that had escaped the poor girl's lips, he was led to imagine that one portion of her sorrows at least, originated in some disappointment in love, but there must, he believed, be something far more terrible and important than that which had driven her forth, a wretched wandering outcast on the wide world, without the means of existence, or a place to shelter her weary head, and he was lost in wonder and in vain conjecture.

Although he knew not whether it had been her own misconduct that had brought her to so awful a situation, the benevolent heart of Colonel Bridport bled for her, and he was inclined to take the most charitable view of the subject.

"Unfortunate young creature." he soliloquised, "what a melancholy history, like Omelia, methinks I can read in her looks. And even though her own errors may have been the principal cause of producing her present sufferings, it must be a hard and insensible heart indeed that could withold pity and commiseration from so young and fair a creature, exposed to such unexampled misfortunes, and so far away from her native land. And may she not have been the victim of some heartless villian, who having gratified his base passions, has driven her forth to want, and shame, and misery?—The few words she uttered would almost seem to imply as much, and in that conjecture, my sympathies are even more strongly enlisted for her."

The colonel did but sincerely express the nature of his feelings and sentiments, as the reader will willingly believe, after what they have already been informed of his character, and such feelings were never strangers to his breast.

Previous to his leaving home, the colonel sent to inquire after the state of the unfortunate Clara,—for by that name she had called herself,—and Julia sent word that there had been no unfavourable change, but that she remained much about the same as when he—the colonel—and Doctor Hamilton had quitted the chamber.

Julia and her sister Charlotte continued unremitting in their attentions by the bedside of the unconscious Clara, and every moment they became more anxious and impatient to become better acquainted with her and her misfortunes, so that they might at least have the opportunity of endeavouring to impart to her some degree of consolation, and of which she evidently stood so much in need.

The fatigue consequent on the task which had thus unexpectedly devolved upon them, they regarded not; in fact, they felt a melancholy kind of pleasure in being able to perform it, and only sincerely hoped and trusted that it would be attended with the favourable results which they so devoutly wished; but when they remembered the wild observations she had made use of, and her vacant stare, they could not but entertain the strongest apprehensions that her reason had fled for ever.

And yet there was that gentle, intellectual, but sorrowful expression in her handsome countenance as she now slumbered, which was calculated to banish such dismal fears, and the sisters earnestly endeavoured to do so.

Only twice during the day, did she arouse from the kind of torpor in which she had been wrapped, and Julia then succeeded in administering a portion of that nourishment which she had been instructed by Mr. Hamilton to do; and the poor girl only stared at her wildly, apparently not knowing what she had done, laughed hollowly without seeming to notice her, and sinking back on the bed, sleep or stupor again closed her eyelids.

In the evening the colonel with Mr. Hamilton, again entered the chamber, and were rather surprised to find that the patient still slept, and that too, soundly, but the doctor repeated his opinion that it was anything but a bad sign, and trusted that when she did awake, it would not only be to recruited strength but to reason.

They had not been in the room many minutes, however, when a convulsive tremor shook the frame of the fair stranger, a deep sigh escaped her breast, and starting up in the bed with a strength and energy which astonished all those who beheld it, so much so that they could scarcely believe the evidence of their senses, she pressed her hands upon her temples with a wild and agitated expression of countenance, and ejaculated in accents louder and more distinct than she had before done—

"It is not death which has laid me thus prostrate, no, no, I did but dream, and now I awake to all the horrors of my dreadful doom. Ah, what place is this in which I find myself, with every comfort, nay, luxury surrounding me, as if in bitter mockery of my poverty and my misery? How came the wretched outcast wanderer here? Surely she must still be labouring under the delusion of a dream. It cannot be real, it must be my senses that wander. And now, what human forms are those I see, which seem to gaze on me so kindly, and yet so sorrowfully? Speak —speak, I beseech ye, and end the torturing suspense which racks and bewilders the hapless Clara's brain; are ye mortal? How came I hither? Why was I not left to perish in the frightful storm, which I now remember?"

She spoke all this in breathless haste, and her bright, and almost unearthly eyes glared eagerly and searchingly upon them all, as though she would penetrate to the inmost recesses of their souls.

Julia and her sister were on the tip-toe of expectation, but at a motion from their father and Mr. Hamilton they held themselves reluctantly back, while the former advancing nearer to the couch, said, in tones full of tenderness and compassion—

"Unfortunate girl—"

He could proceed no farther for the suffering Clara started, and uttered an exclamation of surprise not unmingled with fear on hearing the voice of a man.

"That voice," she cried, rubbing her eyes, and gazing at Colonel Bridport, earnestly and incredulously, "so strange to me, surely my ears did not deceive me? Who are you who speak so kindly to the friendless and wretched Clara?"

"One who sincerely pities you," replied the colonel, in the same gentle and compassionate accents, "and who would do anything that might tend to alleviate your sufferings."

"Ah," she exclaimed, in a voice of extreme agitation, and looking at him still more wildly and earnestly, "a soldier and an officer? Away—away! they are heartless, cruel, all; they know not what it is to feel the tender emotions of love for devoted woman, even when she could willingly lay down her life to hear one word of affection from the lips of him who holds possession of her heart, her very soul. Away—away, the sight of you appals me!"

Colonel Bridport felt hurt and confused at these unexpected observations, and he knew not what to say.

"My good girl," said Mr. Hamilton, now for the first time venturing to speak, which he did with every feeling, "misfortune has, I am afraid for a time shattered your reason, and you know not what you say. Believe me that you are with those who are disposed to treat you with every kindness and humanity. Behold," he added, taking the hands of Julia and her sister, and leading them forward, "here are those of your own sex, who are ready to sympathise with your misfortunes, great as they doubtless have been, and to tender you all the consolation in their power. The amiable daughters of Colonel Bridport, to whom you have just now spoken."

The young stranger fixed her fine expressive eyes upon Julia and Charlotte for a moment, and seemed excited to admiration. A faint smile passed over her handsome features, and she beckoned them to come nearer, which they did, and in strange and mournful accents, addressing them, she said—

"Maidens, you are gentle, you are fair,

and innocence shines forth in every feature. Tell me," she added, in a voice still more wild and agitated, "did you ever know what it was to love and to meet with no return from the cold and insensible object of your passion? To be treated with scorn, with disgust, nay, even hatred? If you have not you have never known what sorrow and suffering were, and you should feel grateful and happy. But oh, I have been spurned, despised, as something loathsome, by him to whom my whole heart's fondest affections were devoted, and for whom I was willing to make any sacrifice, however great. I have had my brain racked to madness, as I feel it to be now, at the terrible remembrance, and my blood turns to ice. Why was I ever permitted to return to life, to endure this terrible agony of the soul? Behold the beloved, the cold, and insensible one stands there! He points at me the finger of scorn, he mocks and derides my sufferings I cannot endure it; the tortures of perdition cannot be worse than this. Bury me in the deep bowels of the earth; hide me from his sight. Oh, mercy, heaven."

She sunk back on her pillow, and again her senses left her.

CHAPTER CLXXII.

THE MYSTERY PARTLY SOLVED.

We need not, we are sure, describe the feelings of all present at this melancholy scene; it may suffice to say that they were greatly affected, and they deeply regretted the excitement it had caused the poor suffering girl.

"Poor girl," said Mr. Hamilton, "it is as I feared, long and terrible anguish of mind has impaired her intellect, and I am apprehensive that the excitement which she has just experienced may retard her recovery for some days, and then the utmost precaution must be used to secure a favourable result. Her sufferings must have been great indeed to reduce her to so lamentable a condition."

"True," coincided Colonel Bridport, "and I know I need not urge you, Mr. Hamilton, to do all that skill and humanity can dictate for the unfortunate girl. It is evident that from her observations she has been made the sport of some unprincipled villain, on whom she has unhappily placed her affections; and from the words that escaped her on beholding me, that he is a military officer. I hope that such a man does not disgrace the British army."

"I fear there are too many of them, colonel," replied Mr. Hamilton, "although they may have hitherto escaped detection. But

you had better retire and leave the patient to myself and your daughters, though I do not expect from her appearance that she will revive again to-night,"

The colonel fixed one more look of compassion and regret upon the insensible girl, and then replied with the doctor's request.

The poor girl seemed gradually to sink into sleep, remarkable for its calmness, after the passionate burst of agonised feeling she had displayed; and that sleep appearing likely to continue for some time, and no immediate danger to be apprehended. Mr. Hamilton—after giving Mira and the sisters some necessary instructions, but above all cautioning them if the unfortunate Clara should awake, to avoid saying anything which might excite her again retired from the room.

Julia and her sister had been greatly affected, as has been before stated, by the scene which had recently taken place, and they now watched by the side of the sufferer's couch with double, and the most sorrowful interest.

They remembered every word she had uttered in the wild delirium of her anguish, and it had made the deepest and most painful impression on their minds, while their curiosity was even the more excited to hear the history of her sorrows and misfortunes, which they were convinced must have been terrible to have so deranged her intellect, and brought her into the awful and deplorable situation in which she then was.

They were glad, however to find that she slept so tranquilly, and seeing that their services were not likely to be required for the night, and being ready in a moment at a call, they at length retired to the adjoining chamber, and left Clara—for by that name we will in future call her—to the care of the faithful Mira.

Mira, who was a kind hearted, and intelligent young Indian girl, felt as much sympathy for the suffering Clara, as her master or his daughters could possibly do, and therefore now that she was left alone with her, she watched her with the most anxious solicitude, and started, and hastily hung over her if she was the least disturbed in her slumbers, ready to render all the prompt assistance that might be required.

But with one or two trifling exceptions, Clara continued to sleep soundly and calmly till an early hour the following morning, by which time Julia and her sister had arisen, and were by her bedside.

Clara raised herself on her elbow in the bed, and from the expression of her eyes and features, returning consciousness was quite evident.

With a sweet but faint smile she motioned Julia and her sister to come nearer, which they did immediately, and each taking a hand of the fair stranger's in her own, anxiously and affectionately inquired after her health.

"Better, better," replied Clara, in a gentle but melancholy voice; "oh, I have had such a sweet dream. Methought that I was rambling through delightful groves of odoriferous flowers with him who—but no, why should I tire the patience of those who are strangers to me, by relating that in which they can feel not the slightest interest?—Fair, gentle maidens, who fix upon me such tender looks of sympathy, tell me for my brain does not wander now,—who are you, to whom we are thus indebted?"

"We are the daughters of Colonel Bridport," answered Julia, "whom"—

"Ah," hastily interrupted Clara, and passing her hand lightly over her forehead, as if endeavouring to recal her memory, "I remember now seeing a venerable gentleman, who spoke to me in words of kindness which I have long been unused to. Was he your father, maidens?"

Julia replied in the affirmative

"And how came I here?" eagerly interrogated Clara.

Julia briefly informed her, and a slight change for the moment came over the countenance of Clara, and she shuddered.

"Oh, that fearful night," she ejaculated in a voice of great emotion, "which I thought and sincerely wished might be my last;—what I then suffered no imagination can conceive."

At that moment Colonel Bridport and Mr. Hamilton entered the room, and, as might be expected they were greatly astonished, and extremely gratified to behold the sudden and wonderful change for the better which had come over the fair object of their anxiety.

The eyes of Clara brightened, a slight blush suffused her cheeks, and she uttered a faint exclamation of melancholy pleasure, on beholding and recognizing the colonel and Mr. Hamilton, and the former hastened to her bedside.

Clara extended her fair and delicate hand to the gallant officer, which he pressed warmly in his own, and after a slight struggle with her feelings, in gentle but mournful tones, tears of mingled sorrow and gratitude at the same time trembling in her eyes, she said—

"Oh, my dear, benevolent sir, your fair daughters have told me all, and thank heaven for restoring me sufficiently to reason to understand them. Oh, how greatly is the wretched wandering outcast indebted to you for your humanity? and yet you have preserved a life which was not worth prolonging.

"Say not so, my poor girl," replied the colonel tenderly, "I feel most thankful that I have once more been enabled to perform my duty towards my fellow creatures. I would not appear inquisitive, but it is no mere idle curiosity which prompts the question, but tell me, who are you, in whom I feel so deeply interested?"

"A poor friendless being," she answered, with a heavy sigh, and a look of agony that was sufficient to go to the heart of all who saw it;—the child of sorrow and untoward fate, to whom existence has long been an insupportable burthen."

"But your name?"

"Clara."

"Aye; but your surname?"

"I know not."

"Know not?" repeated the colonel, with a look of the greatest astonishment and incredulity.

"Alas, no," sighed Clara, "from the earliest days of childhood I was brought up amongst strangers, unfeeling and uncouth, and never knew my parents or their name."

"Astonishing."

"Oh, sir, mine has been a strange mysterious life, one of constant care and suffering."

"Poor girl, how deeply do I sympathise with you. You are a native of England, are you not?"

"Yes; at least, I have every reason to believe so, as I was brought up there, as I have before stated, from the earliest days of my childhood."

"And what strange accident, friendless as you say you are, brought you so far from your native land, and reduced you to the deplorable situation in which I found you?" asked the colonel, eagerly.

Clara hesitated to make any reply, and covering her face with her hands, exhibited much emotion.

"Oh, sir," she returned at last, with pale looks, and quivering lips, "how can I answer that torturing question? What scenes of anguish, nay, even horror, does it awaken to my memory. Flying from those who had treated me with such cruelty, I found an asylum accidentally with—but some other time, not now, I may relate the particulars of my eventful history.

"And has love, unrequited love had nothing to do with your sorrows, Clara?" interrogated the colonel, with all the delicacy and feeling he possibly could.

The emotion of Clara increased to a most violent extent, and the colonel almost regretted that his anxiety and curiosity had urged him to put the question.

Convulsive sobs escaped the poor girl's bosom, and she wrung her hands, and wept bitterly for several minutes, without being able to give utterance to a syllable, but at length, by a determined effort, she conquered her feelings sufficiently to remark—

"Oh, what a question is that you put to me, Colonel Bridport; but your kindness and sympathy have inspired me with every confidence, and I will endeavour to answer it faithfully and candidly. Alas, I have indeed madly suffered a fatal passion to take possession of my bosom, and to kindle into a flame which nothing whatever can extinguish; but he whom I own I love to adoration, returns not my sentiments, but views me with cold indifference, if not with absolute scorn and loathing, not that I believe his affections to be placed on another. It was indeed presumption in me, humble and unknown being as I am, to aspire to the love of one placed so far above me in station, but it was my fate to do so, and severely have I suffered for it."

"And how did you first become acquainted with him, Clara?" interrogated Colonel Bridport.

"By his visiting the family with whom I lived, to whom he was closely related. He is an officer in the army, and about two years before the present war broke out, he was ordered with his regiment to this country. What was my agony of mind when he departed, and I believed that I should never behold him more? It is impossible for me to describe it. A few months afterwards called the family with which I resided, also to India, and my hopes revived, but why they should do so, I knew not. In due course we arrived here, but I never could ascertain anything of him whom I so fatally but devotedly love. My poor master and mistress were among the unfortunate victims who perished in the frightful slaughter by the

No. 76.

monster Nena Sahib at Cawnpore, and I and several others escaped by a complete miracle. What I have had to suffer since that period, I must relate at some future opportunity. A wild, a mad idea seized me to endeavour to discover the possessor of my heart's fondest affections; and it was on that hopeless errand I was when I sunk exhausted with hunger and fatigue at your door."

"And the name of this cold and insensible young officer?" inquired Colonel Bridport.

Clara started and turned ghastly pale, as the Colonel put this question to her, and she evinced so much emotion, in fact, covering her face with her hands, and sobbing as though her heart would break, that those around her became much alarmed, and were fearful that from the excitement of her feelings might cause her to relapse into her late deplorable state.

Mr. Hamilton, however, after allowing her two or three minutes to give vent to her feelings, administered something to her which served to revive her, and she became more composed, though the tears still trembled in her eyes, and frequent sighs escaped her bosom.

"You ask me *his* name," she said at last, in a faint and agitated voice, "but oh, of what interest can it be to you to know? He is good, he is honourable, no act of his need he blush to acknowledge. All who know him esteem him for his virtues and manly qualities, and yet, alas, he has no heart for me; he loves me not."

"Then, my good girl," said Mr. Hamilton, compassionately, "since it is so, you should try and conquer your hopeless passion, and seek to forget one whose affections you can never expect to gain."

"Forget him," repeated Clara, with a look which expressed even more than words could do; "oh, what is it that you advise the wretched, heart-broken Clara to do? Forget him! oh, his image is so deeply enshrined within my heart, that it is utterly impossible for me to do so. You might as well ask me, by my individual efforts alone to suppress the sanguinary war which has so long been raging in this unhappy country. He is ever before mine eyes, sleeping or waking; he is the constant subject of my thoughts, by day, by night. Methinks I see his manly face in the bright moonlight, behold his flashing, eyes looking down from the stars, and hear his beloved voice in the fragrant breeze. Forget you, dear Stanley, oh, never never."

"Stanley," repeated Colonel Bridport, with a look of the most unbounded astonishment, while his daughters and Mr. Hamilton were equally surprised and anxious.

"Ah, my rash tongue has divulged the secret," ejaculated Clara; "but why should

I seek to conceal it from those who evidently sympathise with me in my misfortunes, and to whom I am already so greatly indebted? Yes, Stanley, that is his loved name, that name which is ever uppermost on my lips, and forms the constant subject of my prayers and blessings. Lieutenant Edward Stanley of her Majesty's gallant fusiliers. But you started, and seemed agitated, my good sir, when I mentioned his name; oh, tell me, do you know him?"

The colonel hesitated to reply, and almost repented having exhibited the emotion he had done; but at length thinking that it might only serve to excite her the more, if he sought to evade the question, and kept her in a state of painful suspense, he said—

"You ask me, Clara, if I know Lieutenant Stanley of the fusiliers. I reply that I do, and honour and esteem him."

"Bless you, bless you, my dear sir, for those words," ejaculated Clara, fervently, and warmly pressing the colonel's hand.

He looked at her with a feeling of sorrow and regret, in which those who were present participated, as he observed—

"And yet, my poor girl, I pity you with all my heart."

"Oh, this is indeed most kind," she returned, tears starting to her eyes, "alas, did you but know my melancholy story—which I hope ere long to be able to relate to you—you would indeed be able to convince yourself how much my misfortunes, the strange and almost improbable events of my life, claim your pity. But Stanley, oh, tell me, I beseech you, does he still live?"

"I trust so," replied the colonel, "and have every reason to believe he does. He, and the regiment to which he belongs, was quartered in this very city."

"And I not here to behold him," sighed the poor girl:—"but, oh, tell me, if you know it—where is he now?"

"I know not," replied Colonel Bridport, "the destination of the troops when they left this city, was kept a profound secret, and so it remains up to the present time; but in the course of a few days it probably may be made known."

"But alas!" remarked Clara, in the most melancholy and despairing accents, and with the greatest emotion; "ere this he may have fallen on the deadly battle field."

"Try to banish such dismal thoughts and apprehensions from your mind, my poor Clara," returned the colonel, soothingly; "kind and merciful providence, I trust, will watch over and protect my brave young friend."

"Oh, may the wishes you have thus so generously and feelingly expressed, my dear sir," ejaculated Clara, "be realised, that is my most sincere, my most fervent prayer."

"And that you will not in that respect be disappointed," remarked Colonel Bridport, "I feel all but certain. But you require repose, Clara, after this excitement, and for the present then, we will drop the subject we have been conversing upon, and myself and Mr. Hamilton will retire from the chamber, and leave you in the care of my daughters and Mira."

Clara again thanked the colonel and Mr. Hamilton, warmly, and they quitted the chamber accordingly.

CHAPTER CLXXIII.

A TRAGIC SCENE.

The revelation which the unfortunate Clara had made, greatly astonished and hurt Colonel Bridport, as it had likewise a similar effect upon the kind-hearted Mr. Hamilton; and they both saw in it a long train of misfortunes, trials, and disappointments to her and Omelia, if the latter still lived, and they should accidently meet, and become acquainted with each other's love.

The young Indian girl, they were fully aware, was possessed of all those romantic, yet wild and strong passions, which characterised the generality of her countrywomen, which were ready to be rekindled at any moment, and burst forth into a flame that might be productive of the most fatal consequences, and should she acquire the knowledge before mentioned, there was no knowing to what lengths her feelings of jealously and revenge might induce her to go.

"They are both most unfortunate," remarked Colonel Bridport, "and in one or two respects, their fates appear to be similar to each other, while they must both enlist our warmest sympathy."

"True,' coincided Mr. Hamilton, "and they sincerely have mine, as I know they have yours, colonel. But the misfortunes of Clara appear to be greater than those of Omelia, and there is a mystery about her fate, which cannot fail to excite our deeper interest and curiosity. Besides, Omelia's love is returned by the being on whom it is irrevocably fixed, that of poor Clara's is hopeless.'

"Yes," returned the colonel, "that is indeed the case, and therefore, our pity is naturally more excited for the latter than the former. Should they both by accident encounter Stanley at the same time, I almost shudder at the idea of the consequences that might follow, and feel for the delicate and painful situation in which Lieutenant Stanley would be placed. I almost regret my having acknowledged my acquaintance with him to Clara, for the present."

"Well," observed Dr Hamilton, "perhaps it would have been better if you had not; but still I do not see how any particular harm can arise from it, if only necessary caution and prudence are used. Should we obtain any information as to the place where the troops are gone, it will be as well to withhold it from her for the present, or to break it to her carefully, when she has made us acquainted with the particulars of her history, which she has promised to relate to us."

With that opinion Colonel Bridport agreed, and added—

"That history, extraordinary as no doubt it is, I am most anxious and curious to learn, for I think there is something about the circumstances of the poor girl's life, even more remarkable than we can now form the slightest conjecture of."

Mr. Hamilton expressed the same belief, and the conversation dropped, and the worthy doctor then took his leave, and the colonel remained for some time longer absorbed in thought.

And here it is absolutely necessary that we should return to Omelia and her friends for a brief space, in order that we may relate an incident of the greatest importance to the thread of our narrative.

With renewed hope and recruited strength —after the information she had received— our heroine proceeded on her journey, conducted by the faithful Abdal and Juballah.

It seemed as if an almost intupportable weight of care which had previously oppressed it, was removed from her mind, which feeling her friends sought to encourage, and she entered cheerfully into conversation with them on different subjects as they journeyed on their way.

The scenes they travelled among were of the most diversified description, ever varying, sometimes enchantingly romantic and picturesque, at other times wild and uncouth, but at all times beautiful, grand and sublime, and such as could not fail to draw forth the most enthusiastic admiration of Omelia.

At night they usually stopped at some friendly village, and at one or two of which they received such satisfactory information, that confirmed them in the belief that they were in the right track, and redoubled the hopes and expectations of them all, Omelia especially.

But on the third day of their journey, they entered upon a wild and dreary tract of the coutry, where not the least signs of a human dwelling was to be seen, and Juballah, who knew the country well, and was certain that they had not wandered out of the right track, stated that they need not now expect to meet with any human place of shelter for many weary miles, and they must endeavour to meet the fatigue with all the fortitude they could.

It was then that the hopes and courage of Omelia drooped for the first time, and her companions found all their efforts of no avail to arouse them.

Night set in just as they had entered upon a dreary and deeply entangled forest, and the spirits of our heroine became more depressed, and her fears increased.

Many were the weary miles they had travelled that day from "the earliest blush of the morn," with little or no rest, and our heroine was completely exhausted, and had it not been for the support of Abdal and Juballah—who, in fact, totally regardless of their own fatigue, almost carried her—it would have been impossible for her to proceed much farther.

"Alas," she sighed, "what is to become of us in this dreary part of the country; and without any prospect of a place of shelter? It will be quite impossible for us, fatigued as we already are, to travel all night without rest."

"Do not give way entirely to despair, Omelia," replied Juballah, in soothing and encouraging accents, "for gloomy as our prospects certainly appear to be, accident may befriend us. It is not likely, as I have before said, that we shall meet with any human habitation, but before we have proceeded much farther we may light upon some place of temporary shelter, and where we may at least rest our weary limbs till the morning. Endeavour to bear up a little longer, my poor girl."

"I will try to do so," replied Omelia, faintly, "but shall, I fear, find it a most difficult task. Could not this cheerless part of the country have been avoided? Might we not have proceeded by a different and more friendly route?"

"No," answered Juballah, "or you may be certain that I would have chosen it in preference to this. But cheer up, Omelia, and let the remembrance that every hour brings us nearer to the place of our destination, and you probably to the arms of your lover, inspire you with fresh courage."

"Oh, would that I could do so," returned our heroine, with a deep sigh, and a melancholy look, "would that I could think as you suggest, good Juballah; but, alas, melancholy fears and misgivings again beset my mind, and make me feel wretched."

"Try and banish such gloomy ideas, Omelia," said Juballah, "come, lean on me, and Abdal, and we will support you on the tedious way."

They were now approaching a more open part of the forest, where the light of the moon might be seen, when the report of a pistol was suddenly heard, this was instantly followed by an exclamation of agony from poor old Juballah, and she sunk wounded and bleeding in the arms of the astonished and horrorstruck Abdal.

So sudden and so terrible was this unexpected event, that Omelia stared aghast with stupified amazement, incredulity, and horror, and for the moment she was completely paralysed to the spot; but when she was awakened to a full sense of the dreadful tragedy that had occurred, she threw herself on her knees in an agony of grief by the side of the unfortunate old woman, whom Abdal still supported in his arms, and grasping her hand, and pressing it to her lips, in a voice of the most indescribable emotion, she exclaimed—

"Juballah, dear Juballah, one of my best earthly friends, oh, speak to me, if it be only one word. Oh, what fiend in human shape hath done this frightful deed?"

The poor old woman returned the pressure of Omelia's hand, looked in her face with a melancholy expression which she could never forget, and tried, but could not speak.

Hastily Omelia tore away her scarf, and binding it across the wound, endeavoured to staunch the blood which was flowing fast from it; but she saw plainly that the unfortunate Juballah had received her death-blow, and the agony of her grief was insupportable, while that of Abdal was almost equal to her own.

"Ill-fated old woman," ejaculated the latter, "it was no accident which caused this terrible calamity, but the hand of some cowardly assassin I am certain. I plainly heard a laugh of exultation, and a shuffling sound among the grass yonder, after the discharge of the pistol."

"Yes, yes," now with difficulty gasped forth poor Juballah, "it was the hand of the villain Yusef which committed this fiendish crime. I caught a glimpse of his features in the opening yonder, but before I had time to raise any alarm he deliberately aimed and discharged the pistol at me."

"Oh, villain—monstrous villain!" cried our heroine, fixing upon the wounded old woman a look of anguish and despair; "but oh, what, dear Juballah, is to be done in this dreadful emergency, and far away from every place where assistance might be obtained? Oh, agony."

"Weep not for me, Omelia," said Juballah with difficulty, and with a faint smile of resignation, "I'm dying, the race of the aged Juballah is nearly run, and she can meet her death calmly and without one emotion of fear or regret. Bless you, bless you, child, may every earthly happiness be your's. You will not sometimes I know begrudge a tear to the memory of the poor old woman who loved you so fondly."

Omelia sobbed as if her heart would break, and looked with an expression of the most intense sympathy and anguish in the face of the dying woman, but in vain she tried to speak in answer to her last feeling observations; and Juballah then for an instant turning her gaze upon Abdal, in a faint and tremulous voice, said—

"Abdal, you will not forget the instructions I have given to you, and strictly to follow them. You will be now the only protector of poor Omelia, be so, even at the hazard of your life, and as you faithfully perform your duty, so may the Great Spirit bless and prosper you. And now," she added, with a slight pang, but in tones perfectly calm and collected, "my last moment approaches, I feel that the grim tyrant is near, and I hail him with pleasure; a mist gathers before mine eyes—I cannot see you, dearest Omelia, but I her your sighs and sobs of sorrow; do not weep, poor child—Juballah goes where the good spirits dwell. Bright, bright, all his bright. Omelia, bless bless—"

Before she had power to finish the sentence, her eyes closed, she sunk back in the arms of Abdal, and without so much as a sigh expired.

Such was the untimely death of the mysterious but noble-hearted Juballab.

CHAPTER CLXXIV.

CLARA COMMENCES HER EXTRAORDINARY NARRATIVE.

The following day when Mr. Hamilton called, to his surprise he found the fair stranger so far recovered as to have left her chamber, and that she was engaged in deep conversation with the good old colonel and his daughters; and he congratulated her warmly and sincerely upon the circumstance, which she acknowledged in the most gentle and appropriate terms.

"The fair Clara," remarked the colonel, "feeling herself now competent to the task, was just about to commence the history of her misfortunes, on your entrance, Mr. Hamilton."

"Then I am afraid," replied the latter, "that I should be an intruder, were I to remain."

"By no means, my dear sir," said Clara, eagerly; "the kindness and sympathy expressed by you towards me, claims my confidence. Pray be seated, sir, and if it will not occupy too much of your valuable time, listen to the strange, but no less true events that I have to relate."

Mr. Hamilton bowed, and took his seat accordingly, and Clara having waited a minute or two to refresh her memory, while her friends were all attention, anxiety, and expectation, commenced her tale in the words that follow.

CLARA'S NARRATIVE.
"A STRANGE EVENTFUL HISTORY."

"My tale is one of simple facts, without embellishment or exaggeration, but recording circumstances just as they occurred; however wild, romantic, and extravagant they may appear to be at times. I do not seek to conceal anything, neither do I wish to paint in false colours, any conduct of mine which might appear deserving of censure. With this brief explanation then, I commence.

"From the earliest period that I can recollect, I found myself a little half-naked thing, rolling about and gambolling with other little sun-browned children, about my own age, on the green sward before a gipsy encampment, in which aged men and women, stalwart young men, and bright-eyed nut-brown damsels were to be seen, and whose very looks would fascinate you to believe them when they professed to tell you your fortune.

"At first I knew myself by no other name than the Wildflower, and those who called themselves my parents were Gipsy Jem, and dark Morna, two uncouth, repulsive beings, who were constantly quarrelling and fighting, and whom I could not look upon, even child as I was, without instinctive feelings of dread and repugnance.

"And I had a vague idea, but it was doubtless only a childish notion, that I had not always been among the strange beings that I was then. Something like elegant rooms, and smiling faces, and gentle words, flitted before my childish imagination, but it could only have been a dream, and it was quickly unheeded and forgotten.

"I never remember receiving a smile or a word of kindness during my childhood, from those who called themselves my parents, and I must candidly acknowledge that I looked upon them with an instinctive feeling of repugnance, nay horror, and shuddered at their approach. Their behaviour to me was cruel, beating me severely without any cause; but I bore it all with remarkable fortitude for a child, and it was only when out of their sight, and away from my little gipsy playfellows, that I suffered my tears to flow.

"As you may expect, among such people, education was unknown, and therefore it was not till within the last two or three years that

I acquired the little I now possess, thanks to those who became my benefactors.

"What a wild, wandering life is that of the gipsy tribe, and yet withall possessing many pleasures that even the most fastidious might enjoy.

"What life can be possessed of greater change?—scenes ever varying; wandering through every description of the romantic, beautiful, and picturesque, beneath a clear bright summer sky; through shady lanes, o'er flowery meads, now through golden corn-fields, anon by lake or silvery streamlet; climbing rich verdant hill; traversing fer-the vales, passing through pretty rural vil-lages, then some quaint old mansion, whose very aspect seemed to speak of hospitality; or the moss and ivy-covered ruins of some venerable castle or abbey; through forest wild, and woodland glade, finally, perhaps to pitch their tents in a romantic dell, beneath the umbrageous foilage of stately trees, with the emerald turf for a carpet, and wild flowers peeping forth to charm the eye.

"Pardon this tedious, and apparently un-necessary digression, but I could not help describing faintly the impression which the wild rambling life which I led in my younger days has left upon my mind, and notwith-standing the many vicissitudes I had to en-counter, I must confess that there are times when I almost regret I ever quitted it, that I am not still the wild gipsy-girl that I then was.

"I have said before, I think, that even from my earliest recollection of them, I could not look upon the brutal and repulsive beings who claimed me as their offspring with those feelings which nature would dictate a child to do towards its parents; and as I became older, they became stronger and stronger, until they amounted to disbelief, and abso-lute abhorrence.

"And they seemed to read my thoughts, for their behaviour towards me became more severe, nay savage, and their companions were frequently compelled to interfere, or heaven only knows what my fate might have been.

"There was one simple thing which cost me many hours of anxious thought and fruit-less conjecture, and continues to do so up to the present time. That was a small locket which was suspended from my neck, and my pretended parents never sought to deprive me of it. It contained a lock of silken hair, and on the back was inscribed the name of Clara.

"But it is a waste of time to describe it more minutely, as I have it now—'tis here."

As Clara thus spoke she took it from her bosom, and presented it to the colonel for the inspection of himself and Mr. Hamilton, which they did with some curiosity.

"No doubt this was the christian name of her who was really your mother," observed the colonel.

"Yes," returned Clara, "such has ever been the impression on my mind, and con-sequently have I treasured it as the only precious thing I ever possessed. For hours and hours have I pondered over it, when I could do so without the fear of being ob-served, and often were my feelings worked up to such a pitch of excitement by the strange and bewildering thoughts and fancies that rushed upon my brain, that I could scarcely contain myself, and hardly knew what I was about. Yet do I still remain involved in the same state of mystery, a mystery which it does not appear at all likely will ever be unravelled.

"I will not tire your patience, however, by dwelling too long upon one subject, but come to the more important events of my ro-mantic history as quickly as possible.

"Thus time flew on with very little change, until, as near as I could imagine, I might have been about fifteen or sixteen years of age, and I might be considered to have be-come a perfect gipsy-girl, having to play my part with the other young girls, in fortune telling, and other like impostures.

"Morna and her husband somewhat re-laxed in the severity of their conduct towards me, but notwithstanding, I felt more truly wretched than ever, and the course of life I was thus compelled to lead was more dis-gusting to me. Nothing could be so repug-nant to my feelings as the false character I was forced to assume; the impositions I had to practice in common with my companions, in order to extort money from the simple and unwary, and many were the hours of painful thought it cost me, many the feelings of shame and anguish to torture my breast.

"I had often felt an anxiety, nay an almost irresistable temptation to question my sup-posed parents respecting the locket and the name engraved upon it, but fear of the con-sequences, and that they might take it from me, prevented me. But at last I could re-strain my curiosity no longer, and one day, when they were alone, and apparently in a better humour than they had been for some time, I did venture to break the ice, and to put the question in the best terms that I could.

"There was a fearful change came over the countenance of them both, and I could not help trembling, and repenting that I had ventured to interrogate them at all upon the subject.

"They exchanged looks of mysterious meaning with each other for a moment, and then Gipsy Jem, as my pretended father was commonly called, turning sternly to me, and his dark repulsive features looking still more fierce and forbidding, he said, in his usual coarse and hateful voice—

"'What devil's notion have you now suffered to take possession of that foolish head of your's, girl? I was a fool not to take that worthless trinket away from you long ago.'

"'Oh, you will not deprive me of it surely now?' I cried, with looks of the greatest fear, supplication, and anguish.

"'That depends entirely upon your own future conduct,' he replied in the same morose and threatening tones; 'why do you seem to prize the bauble so highly?'

"'Because,' I returned, though not without some hesitation, 'I believe it to have belonged to one who should be dear to me.'

"'Bah!' he exclaimed, impatiently, 'that is not your only motive for putting the question, I am certain.'

"'Oh, tell me, I beseech you,' I once more dared eagerly to inquire, 'who's is the name engraved upon the back of that locket?'

"'Your own,' he answered, 'let that suffice you. Ask no more questions upon the subject, or you may have bitter cause to rue your boldness. Away, and remember what I have said.'

"He motioned peremptorily, and I immediately withdrew from the tent, not at all sorry to escape from his presence.

"The mystery was no further penetrated than before, and my fears and suspicions were rather increased than otherwise.

"It was quite evident to me, however, that Morna and Gipsy Jem were not my parents, but how I had fallen into their hands, and what could be their motives for seeking to detain me, it was in vain for me to seek to form the least conjecture.

"And now another circumstance occurred to me, which I must ever consider to be one of the most important of my life, and cannot dwell upon without mingled feelings of pleasure, regret, and sorrow."

At this point of her narative, the unfortunate Clara was compelled to pause to regain her composure, and it was some minutes ere she could proceed, which she die, however, at length as follows in the succeeding chapter.

CHAPTER CLXXV.

CLARA CONTINUES HER TALE. STARTLING EVENTS.

"We had pitched our encampment in a pleasant spot in the beautiful county of Kent, the Garden of England, as it is justly called, and where we were well known, always received with kindness, and never molested.

"It was just the commencement of summer, and nothing could be more beautiful and healthy than the weather. Everything wore an aspect of cheerfulness, while it must have had a most invigorating effect upon those even who were the most melancholy and depressed in spirits.

"The females belonging to our tribe were all busily engaged, in the neighbouring green lanes, and elsewhere, in telling the fortunes of simple country maidens, credulous servant girls, and others, and I, of course, made one of the number, and had been more than usually successful, and was thinking of returning to the encampment, when looking before me, I saw approaching a young gentleman, of graceful and commanding figure, which somehow rivetted my attention, and I already began to feel my heart flutter, although I was at a loss to understand the meaning, I being too young to know what it is to love.

"I could not move from the spot, but, scarcely knowing what I did, I continued to gaze as he approached, and until I had even a distinct view of his features.

"That view was enough, never, I imagined, had I beheld so handsome and manly a countenance before. I felt the crimson blushes burning in my cheeks, and my heart palpitated violently. Never had I felt so strange a sensation before.

"The young man had nearly got up to me, and I was still unable to move from the spot, when suddenly a brutal oath, proceeding from some one behind me, saluted my ears, and turning round, I beheld Gipsy Jem, who, it appeared had been watching me, and the expression of whose countenance was savage in the extreme.

"I trembled, for I knew too well what it was to incur his anger, though I was at a loss to conjecture how I could have done so in this instance. But he did not give me time to question him, for, grasping me roughly by the wrist, hurried me on.

"On passing by the gentleman, to whom I dared scarcely raise my eyes, he did not show him the usual mark of respect, but on the contrary, frowned darkly, upon him, and muttered some words between his teeth which I could not understand.

"'So,' he said, sternly, 'the young Wildflower has eyes for those of the opposite sex, beyond those of her people in the gipsy tent.'

"'I do not understand you, father,' I faltered out, trembling.

"'You lie, girl,' he replied fiercely, and frowning more darkly 'did I not notice the looks of transport and admiration which you fixed upon the form and features of that stripling yonder? Beware, I know him, and have cause to hate him, and all who are connected with him.'

"I trembled more than ever as you may

be certain, blushed, and was so confounded and confused that I could not give utterance to a single word. The gipsy, however—for I will not call him father—did not wait for any observation from me, but hurried me, nay, almost dragged me away to our encampment, and taking me into one of the tents where his wife was awaiting him, he strictly enjoined me not to attempt to leave it again that day, under any pretext whatever, and then drawing Morna aside, they continued to converse together for some time in a low tone, but from their gestures it was quite evident that they were much excited.

"At length they removed to their own tent, commanding me to follow them, which I did hesitatingly, and fearfully, expecting as I did a torrent of abuse from them; but to my agreeable disappointment, nothing of the sort occurred that night, and I was ordered to retire to rest, and which I was glad to obey.

"But not to rest did I retire, oh, no, that was impossible. I could not banish the form and features of the handsome young stranger from my memory, yet why he should have taken such a strong hold of it, my young heart could not then understand. Alas, I too soon knew and felt the hopeless sentiments with which that, the first sight of him, had inspired me.

"Fatal, unfortunate meeting it was for me, for it has made me one of the most wretched of human beings ever since.

"When I sought my humble pallet of leaves and rushes—for such was all that was allowed me, with a coarse rug to cover me, although the gipsies always brought with them a supply of mattresses in their covered carts—and sleep closed my eyelids, the same form haunted my imaginatin in my dreams, exciting mingled feelings of pleasure and pain, of hope and despair.

"In fact, from the moment that I first saw Edward Stanley, his image has never for an instant been absent from my memory."

"He it was then who had so strangely captivated you at first sight, Clara?" interrogated Colonel Bridport.

Clara blushed deeply, her fair bosom heaved with emotion, tears trembled in her eyes, and it was some moments ere she could return a reply, but at length she said, in a tremulous voice—

"Alas, it was, but of course I knew not so then, nor for a long time afterwards, and in fact it was impossible for me to suppose that I should ever again behold him; and oh, how much misery it might have saved me if I never had.

"My emotions, so new and so strange to me, increased every day and every hour; although I exerted myself to the utmost to conceal them from the gipsy and his wife,

for I dreaded the consequences that would be almost sure to follow should they discover them.

"The dark hints that Gipsy Jem had thrown out respecting the stranger, were constantly present to my recollection, and while they filled me with astonishment and fruitless conjecture to endeavour to fathom the mystery of them, excited in my breast feelings of the utmost dread and suspicion.

"He had said that he knew him, and that he had cause to hate him, and all who were connected with him, and that still farther increased my alarm, for I knew too well how terrible, slow, probably, but nevertheless certain as the rising of the sun in the east is the gipsy's vengeance.

"But why should the recollection of this handsome young stranger exercise such a powerful influence over me? Why should I feel so deep and absorbing an interest in his fate? These were the questions which I again and again put to myself, but was unable to find any answer to them, and I therefore racked and bewildered my brain to no purpose.

"Day after day, when I thought that none of the gipsies were near to observe me, I would wander to the neighbourhood of the place where I had beheld him who made such a strong impression on my mind, but it was only to meet with disappointment, for I saw no more of him till after the lapse of three years, during which interval the various trials and vicissitudes it was my fate to have to undergo, were more than sufficient to crush the spirits and destroy the energies of even the strongest.

"In another month after the circumstance I have just been relating to you, the tents were struck and we commenced our journey to another and more distant part of that romantic country.

"I felt as if I were then about leaving some dear relation whom I might never behold again; I scarcely ever remembered to have been so painfully agitated, and it was not without the greatest difficulty that I could conceal my emotions from the keen and penetrating observations of Gipsy Jem and his wife.

"If I could only have caught one more sight of the young stranger who had so captivated me, and bewildered my senses ever since, I felt as though I could be content, at any rate, if not happy. But vain were all my wishes, we quitted the locality, and when we did so, my anguish of mind became still more intense and insupportable, and I thought I should have broken my heart.

———

CHAPTER CLXXVI.

CLARA WITNESSES AN AWFUL SCENE.

"I will here take the liberty," continued Clara, "of hastily passing over two years of my wandering life, as otherwise I fear I might become tedious; it may be sufficient to state, that Stanley had never been absent from my thoughts, and something seemed to assure me at times, improbable though it was, that we should yet meet again, and with that fond and flattering idea I endeavoured to console myself, and indeed partly succeeded in doing so.

"Two years, as you may suppose had wrought a considerable change in my personal appearance; I had ripened from youth

into womanhood, and my mind kept pace, I believe, with the other alterations to which I have alluded.

"But the conduct of the ruffian, Gipsy Jem and his wife towards me, daily became even more severe, and they endeavoured to keep me under the same state of coercion and subjection as if I had been a child.

"I was compelled in a manner to submit, yet my heart revolted at it, and feelings of shame and indignation swelled my bosom.

"The wandering gipsy's life hourly became more disgusting and hateful to me, and I would have given anything, had it been in my power, had something occurred to have released me from it; but the members of the gipsy tribe constantly watch with jealous and suspicious eyes those who have become associated with them, and should they happen to be detected in any attempt to escape from them, they were almost sure to be followed by their deadly vengeance.

"And now a fresh source of misery was in store for me, which I will proceed at once to relate.

"Among those who formed the members of our tribe, was a brutal ruffian, revolting in manners as in deeds, who was known by the name of Wild Rob, and was the complete terror of every one.

"He was a man about thirty, tall and powerfully built, with a most forbidding expression of countenance; high check bones. large black, bushy whiskers, piercing eyes sunk deep in their sockets, with shaggy eyebrows and low forehead. In fact, he was such a man as the defenceless traveller might well dread to meet alone, and indeed, I not only believe, but am certain that he was capable of committing any crime, however monstrous.

"This man, then, had dared to raise his thoughts to me, and every day he became more bold and determined in his advances, notwithstanding I disdainfully and resolutely repulsed them, and avoided him as much as possible.

"Gipsy Jem encouraged him in his hateful suit, and endeavoured by threats to intimidate me into compliance, but Morna—for what reason I am totally at a loss to account—was obstinately opposed to them, and her and her brutal husband often quarrelled upon the subject, and frequently came to blows.

"My life was now truly wretched, and I was kept in a continual state of dread of some desperate and fearful outrage being attempted, which caused me never to have a moment's rest.

"I often contemplated escape, though whither to go, poor and friendless as I was, I knew not—but I was so strictly watched that there was not the least opportunity of my doing so, and it appeared as if my fate was inevitably sealed.

"And now I come to one of the most dreadful events of my life, and the blood freezes in my veins, and I shudder with horror as I recal it to memory.

"Wild Rob, Gipsy Jem, Morna, and several of the other of the gipsies had been absent from the encampment from an early hour in the morning, and although the afternoon was far advanced, and the weather was anything but cheerful, the gathering clouds at times, indeed, threatening a storm, I seized the opportunity of rambling to a neighbouring wood, in order that I might indulge in the painful thoughts that continually racked my mind, unseen; but the idea of attempting to effect my escape never occurred to me, for at that time it appeared fraught with every danger, and totally impracticable.

"I plunged into the depths of the wood, frequently looking back to see whether or not I was watched, and at length seating myself on a mound of earth in a retired spot, I abandoned myself to the melancholy thoughts that arose upon my brain with, at times, such overwhelming force, and totally unconscious of everything around me.

"All the many instances of my chequered life, were, placed before my imagination in dismal array, and the retrospection was almost too much for me.

"The mystery of my birth—who were my real parents, by what extraordinary and unaccountable means I had fallen into the hands of the gipsies, all passed through my thoughts, but I only bewildered my brain the more by endeavouring to find a solution to the apparently impenetrable mystery.

"And then the disgusting advances of the miscreant Wild Rob, was one of the principal causes of my terror, and, powerless as I was, and surrounded by cruel enemies, what means had I of resisting them?—so that, without the merciful interposition of providence, his triumph and my destruction seemed all but certain.

"In the midst of these torturing reflections, the beloved form of Edward Stanley, —for so I must now express it—arose to my imagination, and excited in my bosom emotions of the most mingled and powerful nature, and which gained strength the longer I encouraged them.

"Every feature of his manly countenance was stamped in vivid characters upon my memory, as though I had seen him but yesterday, and from which I felt assured nothing whatever could tear him; and I could not entirely divest my mind of the idea, that we should yet be permitted to behold each other again.

"But how dare I, a wretched, friendless girl, aspire to the love of one who was placed so far above me, and besides, stranger as I was to him, who could believe him likely to entertain one thought towards me, or even to trouble himself to think whether there was such a being in existence? the idea was completely preposterous, and I abandoned it nearly as soon as it had been formed.

"The darkness of night, which had set in, and a heavy peal of thunder, for the storm had at last commenced, now aroused me from this gloomy train of meditation, and alarmed, at the consequences that might follow, should Wild Rob, Gipsy Jem, and their companions return before me, I started from the place where I had been seated, and hurried on through the darkness and the storm—for the latter had now commenced in earnest—as well as I could, although I trembled so violently with apprehension that I had great difficulty in doing so.

"I had reached a most secluded part of the wood, which was all in my way, when I was alarmed and arrested in my further progress, by hearing the loud voices of men and a woman, in which I immediately recognised those of Wild Rob, Gipsy Jem, and Morna, engaged in a noisy altercation, and my terror you may easily imagine. I was transfixed to the spot at which I had arrived, and knew not how to act.

"To retreat by the way I had come, was the first thing that suggested itself to me, but fear, and a feeling of curiosity which was irresistible, withheld me, and I resolved, in spite of whatever might be the consequences, to see the result of this adventure.

"Besides, they were in an enclosure of trees, between which I might observe them, or, at any rate, listen to them, without any danger of being seen myself, and I therefore took courage, and approached a convenient spot where I could both see and hear.

"I had scarcely done so, when I heard fierce and terrible oaths from the ruffians Rob and Jem, then a loud exclamation of agony from the guilty but unfortunate Morna, followed by the fall of some heavy weight upon the earth, and the blood seemed to freeze to ice in my veins; for it was very evident that murder either had or was about to be committed.

"'As we have gone so far,' I heard the blood-thirsty miscreant Wild Rob, distinctly say, 'that we may as well finish her;—she knows too much, and our associates will be glad to get rid of her.'

"'Aye,' answered his companion, 'we could not have a fitter spot or a better opportunity, and now that she is in a state of insensibility, she will know nothing about it.'

"All merciful powers! what feelings of unutterable horror came over me, when I heard these dreadful words?—But some strange and powerful feeling which I cannot describe, rivetted me to the spot, and urged me to become a spectator of the horrible scene.

"What feeling it was that impelled me to witness so frightful a sight, I cannot imagine. Surely I must have been mad, or labouring under some strange infatuation; but as I recall it now to my remembrance, all my faculties seem as though for the moment they were suspended with horror, and I scarcely know how to proceed with the task I have imposed upon myself.

"Let me, however, endeavour to accomplish it as well and as quickly as I can.

"I heard a gurgling sound, then a few convulsive struggles on the grass, and then all was silent.

"Scarcely venturing to breathe, and I

should be overheard, I peeped through the opening at which I had placed myself, and beheld the unfortunate Morna stretched upon the earth, apparently lifeless, and Rob and Jem were rising from the body, each with a long-bladed knife in his hand. There was just sufficient light for me to perceive that the wretched and ill-fated woman was bleeding copiously from a deep and frightful wound in her throat, and I could restrain my feelings no longer; I uttered a shriek, which was fortunately drowned by the voice of the thunder, or I must have been betrayed, and my life would also have been sacrificed; and covering my face with my hands, I precipitately fled from the fatal spot, but in what direction I at first knew not.

"But my feelings are too much excited by the recollection of this terrible adventure to suffer me to proceed with my eventful narrative for the present, and I must therefore claim your indulgence for the continuation of it till to-morrow."

To this the colonel and his companions—who had listened with the most breathless attention to the startling narrative of Clara, without offering to interrupt her for an instant—of course, readily assented, and she became silent and thoughtful for a time; and after some conversation for about half an hour, of no importance, they separated for the night, and Clara retired to her chamber.

CHAPTER CLXXVII.

CLARA FURTHER PURSUES HER EXTRA-ORDINARY ADVENTURES.

The next morning, Clara, Colonel Bridport, his daughters, and Mr. Hamilton again assembled at an early hour, and the former thus continued her interesting tale—

"Appalled, distracted, bewildered, by that which I had witnessed, and which still seemed to be presented to my horror-struck sight, I continued in my wild and rapid flight, regardless of the storm—which was at its most violent height—and the many impediments that were thrown in my way, until I could proceed no further without resting, and, making a sudden stop, and looking anxiously but almost unconsciously around me, I was somewhat surprised to find myself just upon the borders of the wood, and at some considerable distance from the gipsy encampment.

"What was now to be done?—my situation was a desperate and deplorable one. I durst not return to the gipsies, for then the fate which awaited me was certain; yet whither could I go, penniless, destitute, and inexperienced as I was? Where find a shelter for my weary limbs from the raging storm? How in future exist?

"My brain was distracted, and I beat my breast and tore my hair in the utter despair of my feelings.

"There was one fear which urged me on, however, more than all, and that was the idea of pursuit; and hastily committing myself to the care of the Supreme, I made my way to emerge from the wood, as well as my feeble and trembling limbs would allow me.

"The war of elements still continued with unabated violence, and, of course, I was soon drenched to the skin, and felt that if had to proceed much further, without some place of shelter, let it be ever so humble, I must sink and perish, from the effects of what I had already endured.

"Still the fear of pursuit, I repeat, urged me on; the rustling of the wind among the branches of the trees, startled and alarmed me, and I frequently imagined that I heard the voices of my pursuers in the pauses of the storm; and I looked timidly around through the darkness to see if I could behold them.

"But this was all imigination, and mustering all the fortitude I could under the wretched circumstances, I once more resumed my way, and proceeded much better than could have been expected, until I emerged from the wood and entered upon a more open part of the counrty, but still presenting not the least prospect of relief.

"My first idea had been to endeavour to hurry on my way to the nearest town, and reveal to the proper authorities the dreadful crime which I had seen committed, but on more mature consideration, fear caused me to abandon it; for although the murderers would undoubtedly be brought to justice, and receive the punishment due to their monstrous crime, their comrades in guilt I well knew would never cease to pursue me with the most deadly vengeance until they had accomplished my destruction, and I had no means of escaping them.

"Nothing surely could be more horrible than my forlorn and hopeless situation, and hard indeed must have been the heart which could not be moved to pity for me. A poor friendless girl, inexperienced in the world, without one individual to whom I could apply for advice or assistance, destitute alike of food or the means of procuring it; exposed to all the horrors of the raging tempest, and without the smallest prospect of procuring a place of shelter, faint, wet, weary, and completely exhausted; good God! could there be another such a miserable wretch in the world, and what was to become of me?"

"It was indeed a most terrible situation for a poor helpless girl to be placed in," remarked Colonel Bridport, "and I shudder to think of it. From what you have already related, Clara, your misfortunes must have been great—greater indeed than I could have imagined."

"Alas, my dear sir," replied Clara, "they were indeed; no one can possibly form the least idea of the dreadful sufferings I have had to undergo, and heaven only knows how I found strength to support them. I often wonder that I am still alive."

"True," said Mr. Hamilton, "but providence must have sustained you, or you must inevitably have sunk under it. But we are interrupting you; pray proceed."

Clara paused for a minute or two, in order to regain her composure, which the recollection of the awful past had somewhat disturbed, and then complied.

"While I thus stood, ' amid the pitiless pelting of the storm,' considering what to do, and my brain, as may be imagined, completely distracted, I was alarmed by the sudden appearance of lights, as if from torches, moving about in the wood I had only just quitted, and then the distant voices of men I felt certain saluted my ears, and added to my terror.

"I could have but one idea upon the subject, namely, that it had been discovered I had quitted the gipsy encampment, and that these were my pursuers.

"A frightful death, or treatment most cruel, I knew awaited me, if I were caught, and that thought, even exhausted as I was, aroused me into action, and I fled with all the precipitation I could, sometimes venturing to look back, when to increase my alarm I beheld the lights approaching in the direction I was pursuing, and I could just catch a glimpse of the men who carried them.

"My suspicions were confirmed, and I almost gave myself up for lost, for as yet I could perceive no signs of a place of concealment.

"However, I kept on my way with unabated speed in the shadow of the trees that grew by the road-side, and committed myself to the mercy and protection of providence.

"If I were once seen, my capture must be certain, and that it would be entirely useless for me to continue my flight, but the silence of the men in pursuit, all but convinced me that I had not been observed, and again looking back, was gratified to find that the lights were moving in a contrary direction and were gradually disappearing.

"Another minute or two, and they were no longer to be seen, and I clasped my hands vehemently together, and raised my eyes towards heaven in heartfelt thankfulness.

"What an overwhelming weight of fear was removed from my breast, although indeed my condition was as hopeless and wretched a one, you must admit, as any poor, unfortunate young creature could possibly be reduced to.

"The thunder and lightning had ceased, but the rain still descended in torrents, and rendered the night as miserable as possible. My wet clothes clung to my weary limbs, and impeded my progress more than anything.

"But it was no use to hesitate or delay, I had better continue on my way as well as I could, and leave the rest to chance. And dreary enough was the prospect before me, and I felt as though I must sink to the earth every moment.

"At length the rain somewhat abated, and the moon arose, making the scene appear somewhat less dreary.

"Straining my eyes, with the hope of discovering some place of shelter, the dark outlines of some building in the distance caught my attention, and revived my hopes, though why it should do so, not knowing the kind of reception I might meet with, if even it should prove to be inhabited, I know not.

"There was at least a chance, and therefore I proceeded towards it with renewed strength, and in about ten minutes stood before it, and surveyed it eagerly.

"It was an old barn, which appeared not to have been used for many years; and there were the mouldering remains of some other buildings near it, that had been suffered to go to decay.

"The door of the old barn had dropped off its hinges, so that there was nothing to prevent ingress; but such was the chilling gloom which reigned about it, that for a few minutes I hesitated to enter.

"This timidity, however, I exerted myself to the utmost to conquer, and having listened at the entrance for some moments, without hearing the least sound which was calculated to alarm me, I took courage and stepped into the building.

"It felt damp and chilly, and there was a heavy, noisome atmosphere about the place, which rendered it anything but agreeable.

"It was involved almost in complete darkness, the only light that was admitted being through a narrow crevice in the wall; and that merely served to make darkness visible; but wretched as the place was, I hailed it with feelings of melancholy gratitude, for, at any rate, it would give me the opportunity of resting my weary limbs for awhile, and of collecting my thoughts, and had I not met with it, I certainly must have perished in the open air, and amid the howling tempest,

"There were heaps of half decayed and damp straw in different parts of the barn, and which I eagerly examined, thinking it might afford me a rough pallet, and which was what, in fact, I had been used to nearly all my life, and I might be said to be innured to it.

"I selected some of the dryest of the straw, and spreading it in a convenient corner, which seemed to be the least exposed to the weather, I stretched my tired limbs upon it, and endeavoured to compose myself to sleep.

"But even worn out with fatigue as I was, that was for some time a fruitless task, and my excited imagination wandered upon different subjects of the most torturing description, which sometimes worked me up to a pitch of terror that was almost insupportable.

"The whole of the frightful scene I had witnessed in the wood was vividly and appallingly recalled to my imagination; I again thought I beheld the ghastly, distorted features add the gaping wound of the murdered woman, and every limb was convulsed with horror, and I almost feared to remain where I was

"At length, however, nature could hold out no longer, and I fell into a sound if not a refreshing sleep.

———

CHAPTER CLXXVIII.

THE TALE CONTINUED.

"I must have slept some hours, for when I suddenly awoke, which I did from some frightful dream, which had occurred to my disordered imagination, it was broad daylight which I could perceive by the crevice in the wall and the open door.

"I arose from the humble pallet on which I had been reposing with difficulty, for my limbs were stiffened and benumbed with the damp and cold.

"The first thing I did was to sink on my knees, and fervently to return my thanks to the Almighty for my preservation so far, and implored his protection and assistance for the future, especially in this, the greatest and most terrible hour of my need.

"But what was I really now to do, lonely and destitute? The question was unanswerable, and the thought distracted me.

"There were no visible means of sustaining a miserable existence, but from what I might obtain from the hand of charity, and from the idea of that I shrunk with a feeling of pride and repugnance which I could not conquer. But, alas, I had no alternative.

"Then there was the constant fear I should be in of encountering some of the gipsy tribe, and being detected, in which case I was fully aware that the consequences to me would be dreadful, and I shuddered with horror at the bare contemplation of them.

"It was useless to remain where I was,

and having resolved to resume my journey, and leave the rest to providence, I walked to the entrance to the barn, and looked out to ascertain what sort of weather it was.

"All traces of the previous night's storm had disappeared, and the morning was clear and fine, the sun just beginning to rise above the eastern hills, and imparting warmth and radiance to the scene.

"I was considering which was my best way to pursue—though all roads for that matter to me, might then be said to be alike—when I suddenly beheld several men emerge from behind a cluster of trees at some distance, and approach towards the barn.

"I gazed more eagerly, and you may imagine my absolute terror, when I recognised in their persons some of the most brutal of the gipsies.

"They were probably those who had pursued me the night before, and were now returning to the encampment.

"There was not a moment to be lost; the gipsies were approaching nearer, their intention, no doubt, was to examine the barn, and there were therefore only a few seconds given me for my attempted escape, I quitted the barn, and stooping down I crawled on my hands and knees, so that they should not by any possibility observe me, round to a contrary direction to that in which they were coming, and then rising to my feet, I fled with the greatest rapidity along the road, or rather lane, which was shaded on either side by trees, and did not stop till I was fairly exhausted, and I must have run a distance of above a mile, at any rate, nothing was to be seen of the old barn in which I had slept, and, what was still more gratifying, of the gipsies, whom I had such cause to dread.

"It was truly wonderful how I had found strength sufficient to accomplish this task, especially in the continual state of excitement I was. But how thankful to heaven I was that the gipsies did not come to the old barn at night, for then escape would have been impossible, and my doom would have been sealed.

"Having regained my breath, I walked leisurely along, for the great exertions I had undergone would not allow me to do more, trusting that I might reach some town or village where my destitute and deplorable condition might ensure me some relief.

"But many was the weary mile I travelled—faint and hungry as I was—without meeting with anything of the kind, and the horrors of my situation every moment became more alarming.

"'God of heaven help me in this my dreadful emergency,' I said in a faint but earnest voice, 'for without Your merciful aid I am lost; nothing but a frightful death awaits me.'

"I had never, you may be sure, been taught to pray in the gipsy tent, by the guilty wretches who had brought me up, but instinct prompted me, or some more powerful feeling which I cannot describe, and I never prayed more fervently in my life than I did on that dismal occasion.

"And it seemed to revive my hopes, and recruit my strength, and I again pursued my way, although I was compelled to do so slowly, for my clothes were almost as wet as when I had entered the barn, and they clung to my trembling limbs, with a most miserable effect.

"At length, when my footsteps could not possibly have carried me much further, I came to a humble and lonely cottage, at the door of which, a kind, homely, motherly looking old woman was sitting.

"This encouraged me, and I walked, or rather tottered up to the cottage. But before I could speak, the old woman raised her eyes, and observing me, seemed much struck with my wretched and deplorable appearance.

"'For heaven's sake,' I said, in a voice scarcely audible, 'take pity on a poor friendless, starving girl, and give her but a mouthful of bread, a draught of water, and allow her to rest her weary limbs for a time in your humble dwelling.'

"'Poor child, poor child!' replied the old woman, compassionately—and being the first words of pure kindness that I had ever heard in my life, I could not refrain from tears—'oh, what terrible misfortunes can have reduced one so young to a state like this? Poor child, poor unfortunate child. Here, Bridget, Bridget lass,' she called, and a neatly clad, and buxom-looking young woman, apparently about twenty years of age, quickly made her appearance from the cottage, and was evidently as much moved on beholding me as her mother, for such the old woman was.

"'Help this poor creature into the cottage Bridget,' said the kind old dame, in the most feeling accents, 'and we must see to her immediate necessities; we are poor, but the Almighty will not suffer us to be any poorer for the performance of an act of charity towards one of our unfortunate fellow-creatures.'

"Completely overwhelmed by such unexpected and spontaneous benevolence, I was going to pour forth my thanks, but the good dame by a motion of her hand, prevented me, and she laying hold of one of my arms, and her daughter the other, they gently led me into the cottage parlour, the clean and neat appearance of which was sufficient to strike the beholder with admiration at first sight.

"Here, my damp and ragged cloak being

removed by the attentive hands of Bridget, I was immediately placed in an arm chair before the fire—on which was a quantity of boiled milk, which, with some home-made bread, was prepared for the morning meal—and every attention paid to me, that the necessity of my case required.

"But so sudden and extraordinary a change, in the weak condition to which I was reduced, was almost too much for me, and I nearly fainted; but the dame immediately administered to me a simple cordial, which she took from her little closet, and that quickly revived me.

"By this time, the humble repast was spread upon the table by Bridget, with the addition of some ham and new laid eggs; such a meal, in fact, as I had not seen for many a day, and taking me, as it did, by surprise, and when nothing but starvation only a short time before, met my eyes, I could scarcely now believe the evidence of my senses.

"Of this I was kindly and warmly invited to partake heartily, and certainly it looked most tempting.

"'Oh, my good friends,' I ejaculated, 'I did not ask you for this; the humble object of charity can have no such pretensions. I am intruding upon your kindness.'

"'Mention it not, my poor girl,' replied the old woman, in tones that showed her sincerity, 'or I shall feel hurt and offended, you are truly welcome.'

"I pressed her hand in silence, and a tear, I trust, fully explained to her my feelings.

"I complied with her request and that of Bridget, but I was so weak from long fasting, and the extraordinary fatigue I had undergone, that I could only eat sparingly, but what I did take, I felt recruit my strength and refresh me.

"Overwhelmed with gratitude, I was again about to return my thanks, but the old woman again stopped me, and seemed annoyed by my acknowledgement for what she had done.

"'You seem to have travelled far and exposed to the terrible storm of last night—it did come down, sure enough—and I should think that an hour or two's nice refreshing sleep now, would do you a world of good. What do you say, my dear?'

"What could I say, I could only acknowledge that it would, but again express my fears of the great inconvenience that I, a perfect stranger to her, and for aught she knew to the contrary—some impudent impostor, must put her.

"'I won't hear it, my poor girl,' she said, impatiently, 'you are unfortunate, and that is quite enough for me. Up stairs is my daughter's little bed-room, and there you may sleep comfortably, without any fear of being disturbed. My old man—bless his kind heart—does not come home from his daily labour till night, and so far from feeling offended at what I have done, he will commend me for it, for he is one of the best old creatures in the world, is Andrew Bramble; so everybody says that know him, and what everybody says must be right. There now, my poor girl, I will not hear anything you have to say, for you are not in a fit state to talk just now, I'm certain. Now Bridget, my lass, conduct our young guest to your chamber, and see to her comfort'

"I raised the excellent old woman's hand to my lips, and tears, which I could not restrain, fell upon it. Bridget then kindly taking my arm, with an encouraging smile, conducted me up a small flight of stairs to a bed room, which, for cleanliness and comfort, vied with the parlour below.

"Here she immediately commenced stripping me of my wet clothes, replacing them by others of her own, and she then assisted me to the first clean and comfortable bed I ever remember to have slept upon in my life.

"'My father and mother sleep down stairs,' said Bridget, 'and this is my snug little chamber, where there will be plenty of room for you and I, if you should remain here any time. What's your christian name? It's a foolish whim of mine, but I have always a strange curiosity to know people's names.'

"'Clara,' I faltered out.

"'Clara,' she repeated, 'that's a sweet pretty name, and I'm sure not to forget it. But dear me, if I ain't talking to you all the time you ought to be asleep. Good bye; if you want anything, you have only to ring this small hand bell, and I will be with you in an instant.'

"With these words she retired from the room.

CHAPTER CLXXIX.

THE COTTAGE.—GENEROUS HEARTS.

"What a remarkable change, had only an hour or two effected in my circumstances—it seemed incredible.

"Could it be real or only imaginary? I could with difficulty bring my mind to believe it; but when reflection convinced me that it was absolutely the fact, my bosom swelled with the most unbounded feelings of gratitude to that Supreme power which had hitherto so mercifully interposed to save me when the most fearful dangers threatened me, and in the midst of my greatest adversity, when death in its most appalling form seemed to stare me in the face, had guided my footsteps to these humble but benevolent people, and procured me that relief, without which I probably must have perished.

"It was impossible that I could restrain my feelings; convulsive sobs agitated my breast, and my tears flowed fast.

"And yet the dreary and hopeless prospect which was before me, was fearful to contemplate, I shrunk from it with a feeling of dread, if not absolute horror, which I could not control.

"But these thoughts so conflicting and so torturing, were at length compelled to yield to the fatigue which had quite worn me out, and throwing my weary head back on the pillow, I almost immediately sunk off to sleep.

"No troublesome dreams, such as might have been expected from the state of my mind, disturbed me, and so calm and sound was my repose, that I awoke not again till the bright moonlight was streaming in at the window, and I found Bridget seated by my bedside.

"My brain was bewildered, and for a moment or two I hardly knew where I was, or what had happened to me, but the voice of Bridget aroused me to recollection.

"'You have had a nice, and I hope refreshing sleep, Clara,' she observed, 'and I am sure you look all the better for it.'

"'I am indeed better, much better, my good young friend,' I replied, 'for which I have to thank your mother and yourself. Such christian charity towards a destitute stranger is beyond all praise, and I am at a loss for words to express my gratitude.'

"'And I am sure neither mother or myself require anything of the sort,' returned Bridget, 'we should be ashamed of ourselves if we neglected to do our duty, at least, as far as our humble means will allow us, towards our unfortunate fellow creatures; so make your mind happy on that subject, Clara. Dear me, how pat I have got your name already; but then it is such a pretty name.'

"I smiled, and pressed her hand.

"'What time is it, Bridget?' I interrogated.

"'It's past eight o'clock,' she replied, 'so, of course you will remain here for the night. Father has returned from his daily toil, and is now enjoying his pipe and his jug of ale in the chimney corner.'

"'And does he know of my being here?' I eagerly asked.

"'To be sure he does,' answered Bridget, 'we had no occasion to conceal it from him, for he is never so happy as when he is enabled to perform a good action. He commended mother and myself for what we had done, and expressed his pity for the melancholy state in which you came to our cottage. So you lie still, Clara, and I will bring you something nice to eat and drink presently. I must let father and mother know how you are now, for they will be anxious to hear.'

"Thus speaking, and without giving me time to say a word, the kind-hearted girl hastily quitted the room, and left me to my own reflections.

"I may appear tedious and prolix in relating all these particulars, but I cannot help attempting to delineate, to the best of my ability, the character of those simple but excellent people whom I must ever remember with feelings of the warmest gratitude.

"Here then, where I had already met with such a charitable and hospitable reception, I could probably remain for a day or two—although I felt reluctant to encroach upon their kindness—until I had recruited my strength, and had time to arrange in some measure my plans for the future.

"The latter, however, was a most difficult task, and I scarcely knew how to set about it; but probably I might receive some useful advice, when I had made them to a certain extent acquainted with my circumstances.

"In a few minutes Bridget re-entered the room, bringing with her a light and homely meal, which she placed on a tray before me as I sat up in the bed, and requested me to partake of freely.

"I again thanked her for her kindness but she grew impatient and would not listen to me, and I therefore had nothing to do but to comply with her request.

"But I really did not now feel disposed for eating, though I did so, sparingly, to satisfy Bridget, and she then again seemed inclined to enter into conversation with me, being rather of a loquacious disposition.

"'Mother will be here presently to bid you good night, Clara,' she observed, 'for it is near the usual hour of her and my father retiring to bed. I shall not again leave you, but be your companion for the night.'

"I expressed my satisfaction at that circumstance, and soon after the good old dame made her appearance, and congratulated me warmly on the improvement which rest had made in my looks.

"After some conversation the dame bid me good night, and retired from the room, and myself and Bridget were left to ourselves.

CHAPTER CLXXX.

THE TALE PROGRESSES.

"'I will not tire your patience,' resumed Clara, after a brief pause, by detailing matters of minor importance, but come as quickly

as possible to the principal incidents of my remarkable and melancholy history, which you are anxious to hear."

"Yes, Clara," replied the colonel, "that which you have already related, is of the most deep, pathetic, and startling interest, and I'm sure has rivetted my most profound attention, and that likewise of Dr. Hamilton and my daughters. Seldom, I hope, has it fallen to the sad lot of one so young and perfectly friendless to experience such terrible misfortunes, and I cannot but again and again admire and wonder at the fortitude and patience which enabled you to endure them."

"Yes," remarked Clara, "and I often reflect with astonishment and heartfelt gratitude to heaven that enabled me to do it. Alas, I have been the child of sorrow and adversity

from the earliest days of my recollection, and perhaps it would have been far better had I never been born, or perished in my infancy."

She pressed her fair hands upon her forehead as she thus spoke.

"Say not so, my poor girl," said the colonel, soothingly, "but endeavour to live in hopes of future days of peace and happiness."

"Happiness," she repeated, in the most melancholy and despairing accents, "oh, that would be fruitless, happiness, I fear, is never destined to be my lot. But away with these sad thoughts, and let me proceed with my narrative."

Colonel Bridport and the others made no reply to this, and Clara thus resumed—

"The following morning I awoke at an

early hour, being much recruited in strength and greatly revived in spirits.

"Bridget was already risen, and seemed to have been so for some time. I could hear the old people bustling about below, for Bridget informed me that her father had not yet departed to his labour.

"As that was the only opportunity I might have, I expressed a wish to Bridget to be introduced to her father before he left home, that I might return him my thanks for the kindness I had received from him and his worthy dame since I had been in their humble dwelling.

"Bridget, therefore, assisted me to dress, and we descended the stairs into the little parlour in which the old people were.

"Andrew Bramble, like his wife received me with the greatest kindness and cordiality, and appeared to view me with the greatest sympathy.

"He was a fine, robust, hale old man, with a countenance that spoke of nothing but good humour and kindliness of heart, from which every word that he uttered evidently came. Plain and simple in his manners, he was moderately educated, possessed of natural good sense, and was far above the common class of rustics.

"May heaven bless and prosper him and his dame, and his amiable daughter, if they be still living, though I fear it will never be my fate to see them more, or to make them any returns for the obligations I am under to them.

"There was not time for much conversation, but before departing from the cottage, the good old man kindly took my hand, and in a voice of great feeling, said—

"'My poor lass, I am satisfied that you are no impostor, but have suffered much, and therefore do I pity you from my heart. A day or two's rest will refresh you, and here you're welcome to remain, and partake of all the comforts that my humble dwelling can afford.'

"'Oh, my dear sir,' I exclaimed, 'I could not think of such a thing; already I have intruded too much upon your kindness and generosity, and I should despise myself if I—"

"'Tut, tut,' he interrupted, impatiently, 'I will listen to no excuses, I have not time to do so; old Andrew Bramble is not without a bright pound or two, the honest savings of industry, and he is not afraid to spend them either in a worthy cause. See to the poor girl's comfort, dame, and Bridget, my lass, while I am away. Mind, I shall expect to see her in the evening when I return.'

"With these words, the good old man fixing upon me a friendly smile, hurried from the cottage.

"'Bless his kind old heart,' said the dame, looking affectionately after him, as he disappeared among the clustering trees, 'I knew how it would be, and I feel so happy. Now, my dear child, you must make yourself quite at home, for you see what we are, and what we say we mean. It shall be no fault of mine or Bridget's if you are not comfortable.'

"I knew not what reply to make to the good old dame—my heart was too full. She read my thoughts, however, at least, so it seemed, for she good-humouredly kept on talking, in order, as I suppose, to prevent me answering, and Bridget expressed herself in terms of the highest satisfaction and pleasure at the thought that she should have, for a short time at least, a companion of her of her own age, and one in whom she felt so great an interest.

"Most pleasantly did that day pass away, and the dame and her daughter did all that they could to amuse me, raise my spirits, and render me as comfortable as under all the peculiar circumstances of my fate, I could hope to be.

"About six o'clock in the evening old Andrew returned home, and the affectionate meeting which took place between him, and his wife and daughter, as if he had been absent a twelvemonth, gladdened my heart to witness.

"And the greeting which the good old man gave me, was so kind, so friendly, nay, almost fatherly, that it quite overpowered me, and I could not refrain from tears.

"'In a short time, however, we were all comfortably seated at the evening repast, and I quickly regained my composure, indeed I might almost say that I felt comparatively happy.

"In the course of the evening I related such of the particulars of my sad history as I thought it prudent to do, in order the better to satisfy them; accounting for my flight from the ill-treatment I had received.

"They listened to me with the greatest attention, though they frequently interrupted me, to express their astonishment and sympathy.

"'My poor girl,' said Andrew, when I had concluded, 'your simple and affecting narrative has excited in my old breast feelings of the deepest pity for you, and those of hatred and disgust against the wretches who could so cruelly treat you; and I cannot but warmly congratulate you on your escape from their power, and that providence fortunately guided your footsteps hither.'

"I thanked him, with tears in my eyes, for such disinterested kindness from one who was a complete stranger to me, appeared to me to be almost unexampled.

"'You must remain here, Clara,' said the old man, 'until you have quite recovered yourself, and some arrangements have been made for the future; indeed I care not if you take up your residence here for good, for thank God, I'm not exactly a poor man, though I work hard, for it is not my disposition to be idle, while I have health and strength. Now, now, I will not listen to any excuses and objections, I insist upon what I have said.'

"'To be sure, Andrew, my good old man,' observed the dame, 'and so do I, too.'

"I threw myself at the excellent old people's feet, and taking their hands and raising them to my lips I bathed them with my tears of gratitude, but could not utter a syllable.

"They raised me tenderly, and endeavoured to calm my feelings, and to re-assure me, which at length they succeeded in doing, and the remainder of the evening was one of the happiest I ever remember enjoying.

"That night I slept more calmly than I had even done the night before, and pleasant and hopeful dreams were presented to my busy imagination, which, alas, have never yet been realised.

"I will not dwell unnecessarily upon all that took place while I remained at the humble, but hospitable dwelling of these good people. I was there for more than a week, during which time I heard of the apprehension of Jem, Rob, and two or three others of the gipsies, on suspicion of being the murderers of old Morna, and that circumstance still more excited the sympathy of my new found friends towards me, to think what I must have suffered while in the power of such monstrous wretches, though I carefully —for I thought it prudent for many reasons —concealed from them the dreadful fact that I had been an eye-witness of the frightful deed."

"And I consider, Clara," remarked the colonel, "that it was wise on your part to do so. I need scarcely inquire of you what was the fate of the bloodthirsty miscreants?'

"Gipsy Jem, and Wild Rob," answered Clara, "were convicted, and suffered the penalty of their atrocious crime upon the gallows; but there being no evidence to prove the guilt of their companions, they were, of course, acquitted. The gipsies, were, however, compelled to quit that part of the country, or they would soon have found themselves in prison as rogues and vagabonds."

"That was a fortunate circumstance for you, Clara," said Mr. Hamilton, "and must greatly have quieted your fears."

"It did," she replied, "for the time being. But still, well knowing the character of the gipsies, and that they will run any risk to accomplish their object, I could not consider myself completely out of danger. But to continue my tale.—Although I well knew that everything my kind friends did for me came freely from their hearts, I could not endure the sense of the weight of obligation I was under to them, the degrading state of dependence in which I was living; and though I deeply regretted having to part from those whom I so highly esteemed, and had such good cause to do so, I determined to leave them, and commit my future destiny into the hands of providence.

"It cost me a severe pang to reveal this resolution to them, but after a hard struggle with my feelings I did so, and they heard me with looks of the greatest sorrow and regret.

"'I admire your spirit of independence, Clara,' remarked Andrew, feelingly, and after a pause, during which time he had been watching me earnestly and with evident emotion, 'but, alas, my poor child, what are you, young, and totally inexperienced, destitute, alone, unprotected, to do in this wide and dreary world—at least, to those who are unfortunately situated like yourself—surrounded by dangers as it is, and so full of villany?'

"'It is a fearful picture, my dear sir,' I replied, 'and, alas, I feel convinced that it is a faithful one; nevertheless—oh, pray think me not ungrateful—I cannot, dare not consent longer to remain a burthen upon you, on whom I have not the slightest claim.'

"'Oh, Clara, my poor girl,' said the dame, in a voice of sorrow, 'did you but know the anguish it causes us, you would cease to talk thus. Short as is the time that I have known you, I could almost love you as my own child, and so could Andrew, I know, and Bridget, she has already learned to look upon you with the affection of a sister. See, she is even now in tears, poor lass.'

"It was true, and you may guess how deeply I was affected.'

"'Best, kindest, and most benevolent of women,' I at length found strength to articulate, in a voice half-choked with emotion, looking in her mild and venerable countenance with the utmost reverence, and tears streaming from my eyes, 'oh, where can the poor outcast unknown girl find words to express the feelings that make her heart throb and yearn towards you. She could reverence yourself and your aged partner as superior beings, and such must ever be the sentiments she will entertain towards you, though distance may separate us, and perchance it may never be ordained that we should meet again. But all language, however powerful, must fail to portray my thoughts, my emotions. I can no more; dear, dear friends, I—'

"I could not finish the sentence, the words died upon my lips, I sunk into the arms of the good old dame, who embraced me fondly, while poor Bridget sobbed as though her heart would break.

"'This scene has lasted long enough,' said the old man, in an agitated voice, 'and has excited poor Clara more than she has sufficient strength to bear. For the present let us drop the melancholy subject, and resume it to-morrow evening, by which time we shall probably all of us have had sufficient time to mature our ideas, and calmly to come to some decision. Come, my poor Clara, and Bridget, child, retire to rest, and may heaven and all good angels watch over you.'

"I again knelt at the feet of himself and his wife, and raised their hands to my lips, without being able to utter a word; then, leaning on the arm of the still weeping Bridget, retired from the room."

CHAPTER CLXXXI.

THE JOURNEY DETERMINED ON.

"Excellent, amiable beings," said Colonel Bridport, in tones of honest admiration, "they are, or were, an honour to the human race, I never before heard of their equal."

"Most true," coincided Mr. Hamilton, "they form a bright pattern of human nature. How fortunate it was for you, Clara, that you happened to fall into such hands, so soon after your escape from the gipsies."

"It was indeed, sir," coincided Clara, "and I must even now look back upon it with feelings of the deepest and most overwhelming emotion. But let me not delay, for at present my melancholy narrative has far exceeded the limits that I thought it would.

"That night, such was my agitated state of mind that sleep was driven from my pillow, and I felt, if possible, still more truly wretched than I did during the last few days I was with the gipsies; but it was a misery of a different description. I cannot portray it in words, though I have still a vivid recollection of it.

"I was about to leave the only friends I had ever known in the world, without the least prospect of beholding them again, and to rush upon all the vicissitudes and cares and anxieties of the world, without the means of obtaining even a bare existence unless accident should throw it in my way, and with no one to sympathise with me or to guide me.

"The picture which my imagination thus drew was a fearful, but, as I afterwards experienced, too faithful a one; I shuddered at the contemplation, and hesitated.

"But still the painful thought of remaining a burthen to strangers urged me on, and I became determined, although my heart was almost breaking at the same time at the thoughts of being compelled to abandon those amiable beings, who had become, in so short a period, as much endeared to me as if I had known them from the earliest days of childhood.

"The violent grief of poor Bridget also affected me greatly; she slept but little during the night, and did nothing but sob and sigh and implore me not to persist in the resolution I had expressed, but to continue to remain at the cottage for at least some time longer. I found it impossible, although I exerted myself to the utmost to do so, to console her.

"We both arose at an early hour in the morning, for I was anxious to see old Andrew Bramble before he left home.

"I entered the presence of himself and dame with with a throbbing heart, and faltering footsteps, and found them both deeply and earnestly engaged in conversation.

"They arose eagerly on my entrance, and my melancholy looks and agitated appearance seemed to affect them greatly. They both advanced towards me, and with looks of sorrow and sympathy.

"It was some minutes before either of us could speak, but at length poor old Andrew with feelings of emotion, which he could not restrain, said—

"'I see by your sad and careworn looks, Clara, the anguish of mind that you have suffered during the night. I fear, also, that your resolution remains unchanged.'

"'Oh, my dear sir,' I replied, 'I am sure I need not repeat to you and the good dame here, the sorrow and regret I feel at being compelled to leave you, but indeed, indeed I cannot any longer continue to encroach upon your kindness and benevolence.'

"'Silly girl,' said the dame, 'to talk thus, when you know that you are as welcome to what we can do for you as if you were our own child. We have the means, thank God, and we are only too happy to know that we have, therefore, why make your mind miserable and uneasy upon the subject?'

"'True, true, dame,' remarked her husband, 'and poor Clara is very foolish for doing so. But, my dear child, let me ask you one question. What course do you propose to pursue, if you leave us?'

"'I scarcely know, my good friend,' I replied, 'but I have been thinking that if I could only make my way to London, I might by perseverence surely obtain some situation.'

"'The idea is little short of madness,' said Andrew; 'what chance have you, think you, a poor, friendless, unknown girl, without any one to recommend you, of obtaining a situation? Besides, how are you to reach London, without money, a complete stranger to the road, and with no one to guide you? Besides, even if you should succeed in doing so, know you not, that you would find yourself in a city intersected by evils of a most dangerous nature, where vice stalks unblushingly abroad, almost at every turn, and villany lurks about to entrap the innocent and unwary.'

"The picture thus briefly, but graphically drawn, startled me, and I could return no answer.

"'But I must begone,' said Andrew, 'I cannot stop to argue this painful subject now. We will resume it in the evening. Clara, remember what I have said, and weigh it well in your mind. Good-bye, Bridget, good-bye.'

"He warmly pressed my hand, with a feeling and significant look, then hurried from the cottage to his labour.

"The day was a melancholy one to us all, the dame used all her powers of persuasion to induce me to change my mind, and her daughter scarcely ever ceased weeping. I felt my resolution at times giving way, and my mind waver; my brain was bewildered by the variety of thoughts that crowded upon it, and I could come to no final decision.

"Evening came, and with it the return of Andrew, who was welcomed with unfeigned pleasure. He did not make any allusion to the subject which was nearest to all our hearts, till after he had taken his usual meal, but which he seemed to do with little appetite, and he then said, addressing me, in as calm a voice as his feelings would permit—

"'My dear Clara, you may be sure I have been thinking most seriously upon your observations this morning, and I have come to this decision, to which, I am certain, you can raise no reasonable objection.'

"'Oh, my kind friend,' I returned eagerly, 'name it, and you know that I will, if possible abide by it.'

"'If you still adhere to your resolution, which I hope you do not, I have formed some arrangements in my own mind, which I trust will promote your views and wishes.'

"The dame looked sad at this, and anxiously inquired—

"'What mean you, Andrew? You surprise me.'

"'Listen,' said the old man, 'in the first place, I must insist, I will not be denied, that Clara shall remain here for another week.'

"The countenances of the dame and her daughter brightened, and Andrew thus proceeded—

"'In the course of that time I will write to a sister of mine, who has resided for many years in a nobleman's family in London, and who will be prepared to receive you with every kindness, I know, for my sake, and afford you all the assistance in her power.'

"'Aye, that she will, I am certain,' said the dame, 'for she is a good, kind creature, and ever ready to perform a generous act towards her fellow creatures.'

"'Oh, how kind and considerate is this,' I ejaculated, overwhelmed with gratitude.

"'Hear me out,' said Andrew, 'for I have not done yet. The coach for London passes by here once a week, in which I will secure you a place, and supply you with money sufficient for your necessaries for some time to come.'

"'This is too much,' I ejaculated, tears gushing to mine eyes, and in a voice half choked with emotion, 'such generosity, and to one with whom you have so short a time been acquainted, is unexampled, and quite overwhelms me.'

"'Say no more about it,' returned the good old man, 'for my mind is made up, and whatever I do, my heart prompts me to, and nothing can remove me from it, when I know that I am acting for the best. Come, lasses, now dame, since that point's settled, therefore let us drop the melancholy subject, and endeavour to banish all sad thoughts for the present, at any rate.'

"It was impossible to refuse compliance with this request, and the conversation that took place for the remainder of the evening was of a much more cheerful description than could have been expected under the circumstances.

———

CHAPTER CLXXXII.

THE DEPARTURE.

"How rapid seems to be the flight of time when you are looking forward to some important event, and which you yet wish to be delayed.

"Such was the case with myself and my friend during the week previous to my departure from the cottage, and when I thought of the many risks I was about to run, and which poor old Andrew Bramble had so truly described, my mind wavered, and I almost repented that I had ever suggested the idea, but it was too late I imagined to recal it, and I endeavoured to stifle and conceal my feelings as well as I could.

"As the time, however, approached, our melancholy increased, at times the good old dame and the affectionate Bridget were so overpowered by the violence of their emotions, and the dismal anticipations and apprehensions that distracted their brains, that they were quite inconsolable, in fact, no one felt in a state of mind to attempt to offer it, if even it could have been of any avail.

"Poor old Andrew, notwithstanding he struggled hard to conquer his feelings and to conceal them from observation, was evidently greatly affected, and looked forward to the moment of separation with emotions of dread and regret.

"Every word that he uttered to me, the sage advice he gave me, I dwelt upon with melancholy pleasure, and have fondly and carefully cherished in my memory ever since. There are they imprinted in characters which nothing can ever efface.

"Andrew had written another letter to his sister—of whom he spoke in the highest terms of praise—in the superscription of which he had taken care to give the clear and direct address of the nobleman's family where she resided in London; and this he committed to my care, with strict injunctions not to lose it, but deliver it safe into the hands of her for whom it was intended.

"This, of course, I promised faithfully, but it was with sad feelings, which I could not dismiss that I did so, and on the following day a letter arrived in answer to the first one sent by Andrew, and was written with the most sisterly affection and good sense; expressing in the most simple but at the same time most forcible terms, her warmest sympathies with me in my misfortunes, and her readiness to receive me under her protection until something permanent and suitable could be obtained for me.

"Oh, how heartily grateful was I for this, of what a weight of care and anxiety did it seem to relieve my mind, although I could not for a moment doubt that so it would happen, after the feeling and noble portrait which Andrew Bramble had drawn of the character of his sister.

"The days rolled rapidly on, and at length it wanted but two days of the fatal and melancholy Monday of my departure from the humble but hospitable dwelling of my inestimable friends, and, of course, the excitement of us all was painful, although I endeavoured to muster all the calmness and resolution I could.

"During that sad week, the dame and her daughter had been busily employed—though I knew it not at the time—at every opportunity, in preparing me a complete double change of useful and comfortable wearing apparel, of which, as you must be aware, I stood so much in need, which they carefully secured in a bundle, and said nothing to me or the old man till the morning of my departure.

"It came at last, bright and cheerful, how sadly in discordance with the torturing feelings that agitated our breasts.

"We had all arisen at the earliest dawn of for it was impossible that any of us could sleep under the circumstances, and the morning meal passed over without any one scarcely partaking of it.

"The good old man tried his hardest to restrain the expression of his feelings on this trying occasion, and to appear calm and collected, but indeed it was a difficult task to accomplish, and I could clearly read the thoughts that were passing in his mind, though I pretended not to do so.

"As for the poor old dame and her amiable daughter, they abandoned themselves entirely to the violence of their grief, and would not listen to a word of remonstrance or consolation.

"Let me hasten as quickly as possible over this painful scene, one of the most poignant anguish in my whole existence, and which I cannot now look back upon without feelings of the greatest sorrow and regret.

"Andrew had paid my coach fare to London two or three days before, and he now insisted upon me taking a supply of money, namely, two five pound country notes, in an old pocket-book, and some silver in a purse, both of which I consigned for greater security, as I thought to my bosom.

"Again and again the poor old woman and her daughter and myself embraced affectionately, and mingled our tears together, and indeed altogether a scene ensued which I will not attempt to describe, but must leave it entirely to your imagination.

"Old Andrew Bramble, as I have before repeatedly stated, assumed and maintained all the firmness he could, but his melancholy feelings would, in spite of all his efforts, burst forth at times, and he could not restrain them.

"The fatal, the dreaded moment came at last—the wheels of 'The Dart' coach were heard rolling in the distance, and soon afterwards the vehicle was seen dashing along the road, and approaching the cottage.

"My feeling of emotion, as you may guess, were of the most powerful and agonising description; but still I controlled them much better than could have been expected on such a dismal occasion.

"I embraced the good old people, and the weeping, sobbing Bridget, fervently, as if they had been my own dearest relations, and they invoked the blessings of heaven upon mine head; the coach arrived and stopped near the door of the cottage. With trembling emotion they conducted me to it, and assisted me inside; they could not speak a word, neither could I; a mist seemed to float for an instant before mine eyes; the guard sounded his bugle—the coachman smacked his whip, and the next instant the vehicle was on its way to London.

CHAPTER CLXXXIII.

THE JOURNEY AND ITS DISASTERS.

"The coach proceeded pretty quickly on its way, I believe, for I took little or no heed of its progress, my mind being too fully occupied with the dismal thoughts that crowded upon it.

"There were only three individuals inside beside myself, namely, a surly looking old gentleman, and two crabbed visaged females, who, from the likeness they bore him, I took to be his daughters.

"They said not a word, but from the contemptuous glances which they frequently fixed upon me, I imagined that they did not think themselves highly honoured by my presence, but that did not trouble me the least in the world.

"The coach proceeded for about an hour, when it arrived at the market town, and having watered the horses, and taken up two or three more outside passengers, resumed the journey without any more delay, for the present, my silent fellow travellers remaining in much the same agreeable mood, the old gentleman, however, having fallen off to sleep, and snoring loudly, with his hands thrust into his breeches pockets, while his amiable daughters talked together occasionally in whispers, and casting sinister glances towards me, which I treated with the utmost disdain.

"The day passed away without anything particular or worthy of being recorded taking place, and although I had no one to speak to, or to communicate my thoughts and wishes, I gradually became more composed, and looked forward to the result of my journey with far more confidence, and sanguine expectations than I had hitherto done.

"Towards the evening the coach stopped at a roadside inn, in order to change horses, and to give the passengers an opportunity of obtaining some refreshment; and I alighted with the rest and entered the house, though I did so timidly.

"But I felt somewhat re-assured on meeting an elderly woman, whom I took to be the hostess, in the passage, whom I asked whether I could be accommodated with a private room and some necessary refreshment.

"She showed me into a small apartment which was unoccupied, and in a short time supplied me with what I required, and retired without saying a word.

"I drank pretty freely of some wine which she had brought me, for I felt faint, and I thought it might revive me; but it had a most pernicious and unfortunate effect upon me. A strange sensation came over me, my brain turned giddy, my faculties seemed for a time to leave me, I was powerless as an infant, my eyes grew dim, and my head dropped upon the table, and I became insensible to everything around me.

"How long I had remained in that torpid state I had no means of forming the least conjecture, but I was suddenly aroused by some one shaking me roughly, and starting up in a fright, and with stupified amazement, I beheld the woman who I had supposed to be the hostess standing over me, and with no very agreeable expression of countenance.

"'Are you going to sleep here all night?' she demanded, in surly accents, 'I'm surprised and ashamed at a young girl like you drinking more than will do you good.'

"'What has been the matter with me?' I eagerly interrogated, scarcely taking any notice of her latter observations.

"'That's best known to yourself,' she replied, in the same disagreeable tones, 'though I daresay I could form a pretty good guess, if I were to take the trouble.'

"'Pray conduct me to the coach,' I said.

"'I should be puzzled to do that,' she returned, with a half vulgar laugh.

"'What mean you?' I hastily demanded, in a tremulous voice, and with a terrible misgiving.

"'Why bless the girl,' answered the old woman, 'the coach has been gone these three-quarters of an hour.'

"I stared at her aghast, and could scarcely believe the evidence of my senses.

"'Gone!' I repeated, in a voice of consternation and incredulity, 'gone, and without me, after my fare all the way to London has been paid? Oh, it is impossible, you are only joking with me.'

"'Indeed I am not,' she replied, 'do you think that the coach can stop for every drowsy passenger? I tell you again that it has left here more than three-quarters of an hour, and is far enough off by this time.'

"'Are there no means of overtaking it?'

"'Not unless you've learnt how to fly, and that's not very likely.'

"'Are there no other means of conveyance?'

"'None.'

"'Good God! what then is to become of me?' I exclaimed, wringing my hands in terror and despair, 'and they have got my bundle, containing my articles of property.'

"'It's a pity, but it can't be helped. You should have taken more care though.'

"'What is to be done?'

"'I can't tell you.'

"'How far is it to London?'

" ' About a hundred and thirty miles.'

" ' Can I sleep here to-night?'

" ' No; no room, every bed engaged.'

" ' Gracious powers,' I exclaimed, with still greater agitation, 'this is worse and worse. I must, at any rate, remain here to-night, let the accommodation be whatever it may. I can proceed no further, and on foot.'

" ' But you must, and that quickly too,' replied the disagreeable old woman; for we shall want to clear the house of all strangers and retire to rest.'

" ' What time is it then?' I eagerly interrogated.

" Past nine o'clock, and quite late enough for all honest, sober people. Early to bed, and early to rise, makes one wealthy, healthy and wise. That's our maxim, and I hope we shall keep to it, for we have already found the benefit of it.'

" ' Surely you will not, cannot be so cruel, as to drive me hence,' I ejaculated, in tones of agony, 'under the unfortunate circumstances, stranger as I am to this part of the country, with no one to guide me, alone, and unprotected.'

" It's rather awkward, certainly,' returned the unfeeling woman, ' but I can't help it; it's no fault of mine, and I can't assist you.'

" ' Alas, alas,' I sighed, as I saw that any appeal to the sympathy of such a woman as this—who seemed to be totally insensible to the common feelings of humanity—would be quite useless, ' thus early, then do my misfortunes re-commence, and most dismally augurs for the future. What will become of me? Tell me, I pray you,' I continued, addressing myself to the landlady, 'since you will not permit me to remain here for a few hours longer, is there no other town or village near here where I might obtain the accommodation I seek?'

" ' About three miles from here, along the road,' replied the woman, ' is a village where you might meet with what you want, that is if you make haste.'

" I fixed upon her another look of supplication, which was passed almost totally unheeded by her, and, resigning myself to my cruel fate as well as I could, with a heart almost full to bursting, I slowly and reluctantly quitted the house, the doors and shutters of which were immediately closed, and the building wrapped in the same gloom and darkness as if it had been midnight, instead of scarcely half-past nine o'clock.

" I stood in the road for a few minutes, with my hands pressed upon my forehead, and what the feelings were that then agitated my breast, I must entirely fail were I to attempt to describe.

" In what a terrible and ominous way had my entrance upon the new and important scenes of my life commenced; and had I not a right to entertain the most torturing fears and misgivings, and bitter cause to regret that I had quitted the happy dwelling of my best friends, probably never to behold them again

" Would it be better for me, under all the melancholy circumstances, to endeavour to retrace my footsteps, and to return to them? But this idea I rejected, almost as soon as I had formed it; the distance was too great, and I knew not that I should be able to find my way again to the locality in which they resided. Besides, I had resolved to communicate all the particulars of my journey to them, as soon as I should have arrived at the end of it, for I well knew how great their feelings of anxiety and suspense would be to hear what had happened to me.

" But was not my present situation most fearful and disheartening? It seemed as though the fates had conspired against me, and that there was nothing but misfortune and disappointment for me in whatever I might undertake. But to remain here hesitating was only a waste of time, and might render all chance of my obtaining a shelter for the night hopeless; and, therefore, solemnly and fervently committing myself to the care and protection of the Supreme, I hurried along the road as fast as my feeble limbs would carry me, and in the direction which the disagreeable landlady of the inn had pointed out to me, my heart palpitating violently with mingled hopes and fears.

" The night was fine, and the moon shone so brightly that objects could be distinguished clearly for some distance along the road; but for some way I proceeded without meeting with anything to arouse my curiosity or excite my alarm.

" But suddenly I was startled by loud laughter in the voices of men, though I could see nothing of them, but immediately afterwards they broke through a hedge, and appeared in the road a short distance before me, and from what I could then see of them, I was not inclined to form any very favourable opinion of them.

" I hesitated to advance, I was at a loss what to do, for I could not avoid them. The men from their general demeanour appeared to be intoxicated, and it was then that I felt the loneliness of my situation most keenly; the want of a protector.

" They approached nearer the spot, on which I was standing unable to move, and I could then perceive that they were dressed in the extreme of vulgar taste, and that their features were coarse and flushed, evidently from the effects of drink.

" I dreaded to encounter them, but would be compelled to do so, for, as I have said before, there were no means of avoiding them, and I looked around in vain for any one to

afford me assistance in case I should require it—not a soul was to be seen.

"The men quickened their speed—having it seemed immediately caught sight of me—and quickly came up with me, and eyed me with looks of vulgar and insolent curiosity, and, as it appeared, admiration, which called the crimson blushes to my cheeks, and swelled my bosom with shame and indignation.

"'So, my pretty damsel,' said one of them approaching me nearer, and continuing to eye me with the greatest boldness, though I carefully endeavoured to avert my looks, and my fears increased every instant, 'you are out alone, taking the benefit of the night air, although it is rather late for a solitary ramble. I say, Ned,' he added, speaking to his companion, who was, if possible, a still

more repulsive looking being than himself, egad! this is fortunate, is it not?'

"'True,' replied the fellow, who the other had called Ned; 'she is a charming creature, and will serve us to pass the time away for a few minutes in conversation.'

"How I trembled, and what horrible fears rushed upon my mind, which it was quite impossible I could conceal. It was evident that these were two desperate ruffians, and their object might be robbery or even worse. And what would become of me, should the little stock of cash with which the kind-hearted Andrew Bramble had so generously supplied me with, be taken from me, and I should be left entirely destitute? I shuddered at the thought.

"Oh, how I prayed for some persons to appear in sight, who might render me some assistance, if I should require it, and which it seemed not at all unlikely I should do.

"But it was all to no purpose, and there was no time for reflection, I was entirely at the mercy of these suspicious-looking men; they seemed to be fully aware of that, and, if I could judge by the bold and disgusting looks which they continued to fix upon me, appeared resolved to take every cowardly advantage of.

"'Now, my dear,' remarked Ned, endeavouring to take my hand, which, however, I hastily withdrew, with looks and feelings of the greatest resentment: 'you must not be bashful. What do you say to your taking a little bit of a ramble with myself and my friend? Oh, you will find us the most agreeable persons in the world, I can assure you. Ain't we, Jack?'

"'To be sure we are,' answered the other, 'very pleasant companions indeed; so every one says, and so the young woman will find, after she has been in our society for a short time. So, come, my dear, as it is a fine night, and I and Ned Clinton always like to do the amiable, we will take a bit of a walk in the green lanes. We'd like to form your acquaintance very much.

"I almost gave myself up for lost, for I noticed the expression of their eyes, and imagined I could read the guilty thoughts that were passing in their minds. But I mustered all the courage I could, and behaved altogether with much more firmness than could have been anticipated.

"'If you are men,' I said, 'and have any regard for a poor friendless female, who having by accident missed the coach by which she was on her way to London, now seeks a shelter for the night, you will no longer detain me, but suffer me to proceed on the road.'

"'Oh, you are a traveller, after all, my pretty one, it seems,' remarked Ned Clinton, with a searching look, that served to add to the fears which already agitated my breast. Well, then, myself and my friend will conduct you in safety to some place of shelter for the night.'

"'No, no,' I faltered out, scarcely knowing what answer or excuse to make; 'what necessity is there for that? Why should I put you to so much trouble and inconvenience, strangers as you are to me?'

"'That's where it is,' replied Clinton, 'we don't want to remain strangers any longer, and this job will just do it. So come, Jack, you lay hold of this young woman's arm, I'll lay hold of the other, and we'll be as happy and cosy as possible in no time at all.'

"They seized my arms rudely, as Ned Clinton thus spoke, and my terror was so great that I could scarcely contain myself,

for it seemed that my worst fears were too likely to be realised.

"'Unhand me, ruffians,' I exclaimed, 'for you have now unmasked yourselves, and appear in your true colours. Unhand me, I say, and suffer me to proceed without any further insult.'

"They were totally unmindful of my supplications and remonstrances, and in spite of my struggles, they were hurrying me along towards the most gloomy part of the road, for what purpose I shudder even to think.

"I rent the air with my frantic cries, but they seemed alike lost upon them, and equally futile as regarded myself, for there were no persons at hand to hasten to my rescue, and there did not seem likely to be.

"That they were characters of the very worst description I could now no longer doubt, and what would become of me in such villanous hands I trembled to think. The money, the only means of my present support, and upon which the accomplishment of my journey to London entirely depended, would be lost to me, stolen from me, and then my situation would be even more truly wretched than it had ever been in my existence before.

"I still rent the air with my cries, and struggled hard to release myself, but all to no purpose, in the hands, as I was, of two such powerful and determined ruffians, who appeared to laugh my efforts to scorn, and to become even more resolute.

"And now, in the struggle, I plainly distinguished the hand of Clinton in my bosom, as though I had revealed to him the place where my money was deposited, which you may very well be certain I had not, and my heart sunk within me, for my fate seemed to be inevitably sealed.'

"Mercy, mercy,' I implored, tears coursing each other down my cheeks, and worked up to a pitch of the most violent excitement, 'do not rob me of my last farthing, and leave me destitute and starving, and a stranger in the wide world. Oh, for the love of heaven, if you have still one spark of humanity left, do not; but take pity on my forlorn and wretched condition.

"Derisive laughter was all that I received in reply to this, and they continued to force me away, while I made the place resound again with my cries and lamentations.

"At length, when I had become almost exhausted, I heard the shouts of men from that part of the road which I had traversed, or been forced along, and looking eagerly back, I saw several persons hurriedly approaching the spot, doubtless alarmed by my cries, and hastening to my rescue.

"The ruffians uttered a mutual oath, and relinquishing their hold of me, sprang over the hedge, flying as if for their lives, and I, quite worn out with terror and exertion, sunk inanimate on the earth.

CHAPTER CLXXXIV.

HOW CLARA ACCOMPLISHED THE JOURNEY.

"I did not remain in this insensible condition many minutes, and when I recovered, I found myself supported in the arms of two of the men, while there were several females standing by, who, it appeared afterwards, had been rendering me all the assistance in their power, and were at present eyeing me with looks of kindness and pity.

"All the terrible misfortunes that had occurred to me in so brief a period of time, rushed upon my memory in an instant, and I wrung my hands in despair.

"But the people who had so fortunately rescued me, did not give me much time to indulge in these painful feelings, but anxiously inquired who I was, and what had brought me into the dangerous situation in which they found me.

"I informed them in as few words as I could, and they—the females especially—seemed to feel much sympathy for me, and told me—quite contrary to that which the disagreeable hostess at the inn informed me —that a little further on was a village, in which they resided, and where I could receive all the accommodation I required

"This was a great relief to my mind, and composing myself as well as I could, supported by two of the females, I was conducted from the spot.

"It was not long before we arrived at the village, and I was received with every possible kindness at the little inn, thanks to my preservers.

"I requested to be shown without delay to a chamber, for I was completely worn out with fatigue, terror, and anxiety of mind.

"This was complied with, and I was left to my own reflections, the nature of which after such a night of terrible adventure you may readily imagine.

"In the confusion and excitement of my thoughts and feelings, I had hitherto forgotten to examine whether or not I had really been robbed. But I now with trembling apprehension did so, and to my utter despair I found my worst fears realised; at least, the pocket-book, in which were the two notes, was gone, but the purse, containing about a pound in silver, had somehow escaped the thief.

"The letter, too, addressed to his sister, by Andrew Bramble, was also in the pocket-book, and therefore, like the money, was lost to me, and what rendered this part of the fatal business still more serious, was that I had had not the slightest recollection of the address in London—no more than that it was some fashionable mansion, near a large park—or that of old Andrew Bramble; and therefore all my hopes and prospects seemed at one blow to be annihilated.

"What could now be more deplorable than my situation? Was not such a rapid succession of misfortunes in one night sufficient to distract any person's brain, and drive them to despair?

"I know not how I was enabled to withstand so fearful a shock, but I did, and it must have been providence that assisted me to do so. I even so far recovered myself as to be able to go to sleep, and, for a time, at any rate, to forget all my cares, my sorrows, and anxieties.

"I have already detained you too long, and I shall therefore hasten as quickly as possible to the conclusion of my eventful history.

"For that reason I will not dwell upon all the particulars of the remainder of my journey to London, for, notwithstanding I knew not what to do when I arrived there, thither I was resolved to direct my footsteps.

"I sometimes was enabled to obtain a ride in a waggon, where I could rest myself, and obtain some repose, and at length, after numerous trials and vicissitudes, I accomplished my tedious journey, and arrived in London, with above ten shillings in my purse, such was the careful and economical manner in which I had used my remaining cash.

"The winter had now set in, and that severely, the snow was falling fast when I allighted from the waggon at some old fashioned inn, the sign of which I forget, near Holborn.

"I wanted some trifling refreshment, but hesitated to enter this wild lumbering place, where all was bustle and activity; however, I did so, and found my way to a side room, where the waggoner, who had kindly brought me some distance, refusing to take any remuneration, shortly entered, and procured me all that I required.

"He asked me, but with anything but vulgar curiosity, whither I was going, in order that he, I being a stranger to London, might direct me.

"Alas, that was a question which confused, distracted, and agitated me, and I knew not how to reply. I racked my brain to no purpose to endeavour to think of the address of Andrew's sister, but the greater became my bewilderment the more I tried to do so.

"The waggoner evidently pittied me, and gave me the address of his sister, a poor widow, he said, but who he was sure would afford me all the accommodation that her humble means would permit her to do.

"For this I thanked the honest man most gratefully, but he not having time to accompany me, I was compelled to go by myself, a task which I own I shrunk from with feelings of dread.

"However, I quickly conquered this unpleasant feeling, and proceeded on my way with much more firmness and composure than could have been anticipated.

"It was yet early in the afternoon, and I therefore went on my way with much more fortitude than if it had been night, and I made frequent inquiries after the street to which I was directed, as I proceeded.

The noise and confusion, the lumbering of carriages and other vehicles, the number of pedestrians, all seeming intent on business; the great variety of handsome shops, the stately mansions, the constant change, astonished and bewildered me, but at length after walking considerably out of my way, either through misdirections, or my not being able to understand them, I arrived in the street where the sister of the waggoner resided.

CHAPTER CLXXXV.

ADVENTURES IN LONDON.

"The street where the poor widow dwelt, with her family of three little ones, was one of the most humble and neglected at the east end of the metropolis, but nevertheless, it was a most welcome sight to me.

"The widow's appearance—who had evidently been a good looking woman—exhibited the very lowest depths of poverty and mental anxiety, and she started back with amazement on beholding me, for which, of course, I was fully prepared.

"However, I quickly explained everything by giving her her brother's note, and telling her what it was I wanted.

"'Alas,' she sighed, 'what could my brother be thinking of by sending you to me, wretched and destitute as I am? I have no means of accommodating you, my good girl, would that I had.'

"'I do not ask you to do so, my poor woman,' I replied, 'without intending to remunerate you for it, and that might be some assistance to you. A mere shelter is all that I at present require.'

"'And that is barely mine,' she returned, in the most melancholy tones, 'but see, if it be not too much trouble, and judge for yourself. This way, if you please, and mind how you go, for the stairs are broken, and dangerous in some places.'

"She held her squalid infant closer to her breast as she thus spoke, and began to ascend the crazy staircase, I following carefully, as she had advised.

"The house was very old and very large, containing many wretched rooms, and all in a most dilapidated and dangerous state, in fact, it had not been fit or safe for human habitation for several years.

"Two or three of the houses in the same street had fallen with a great destruction of human life. The rest certainly were shored up, after a fashion, but with that exception the parochial authorities troubled themselves not the least about the business.

"Of course not, the sacrifice of the lives of a few dozen, or even hundreds of wretched paupers was rather a God-send than otherwise to them. They deposited their humanity with their cash, which never under any circumstances was used for charitable purposes.

"Pardon this slight digression, my friends, but experience, sad experience sometimes makes me bitter and sarcastic.

"In this filthy and ruinous place, then, about a dozen miserable families, for a small sum weekly, were allowed to herd. How they contrived to exist from day to day was a mystery which they probably themselves would be puzzled to unravel.

"At length, after much difficulty, we arrived at the door—which was standing open —of a miserable garret, with not a morsel of fire in the skeleton grate on that bitter cold winter's day, and containing no other articles of furniture than a ricketty deal table, a mattress laid upon the floor, and two or three broken chairs. The window contained scarcely a square of glass, and old rags and paper were used to try and shut out the keen wind.

There were two or three cups and saucers, and a couple of plates on the table, an old gridiron and wooden coal-skuttle in one corner of the room, and a tea-kettle and saucepan in the fire-place, and these domestic articles completed the poor widow's property. Two half naked children were on the floor, apparently, poor things, too cold and too hungry to play together, or even to get up a smile.

"It was a sad sight, and my heart bled.

"'This is my wretched home,' said the widow, in tones of the deepest pathos, and tears starting to her eyes, 'to which my brother has recommended you on your arrival in London.'

"I own I was startled; but I was moved by compassion, and I quickly recovered myself.

"'I will stay here to-night, at any rate,' I said.

"'Oh, it is impossible,' replied the widow, with a look of astonishment and incredulity.

"'I am resolved,' I returned, firmly; 'that is, if you will permit me. Have you no firing?'

"'No firing, no food since yesterday morning,' answered the unfortunate woman, in a sorrowful voice, 'and the poor children—'

"I was shocked.

"'For God's sake get food, firing, all that you may require,' I hastily said, thrusting two or three shillings out of my scanty stock into her hand; 'do not delay a minute, I will see to the poor children while you are gone. No thanks, they are not required.'

"She fixed upon me such a look as I can never forget, then hastily snatching up the coal-skuttle, she left the room, and with the poor little infant in my arms, which I pressed to my breast for warmth, I seated myself in one of the old chairs, and anxiously and impatiently awaited her return.

"What my feelings were at that time, I cannot properly describe. Such a scene of perfect misery I had never witnessed before, and I was appalled.

"My own misfortunes appeared to sink into perfect insignificance before those of the poor widow, and from my very soul I pitied her; and had I not been so cruelly robbed, what gratification would it have afforded me, much even as I needed it myself, to have relieved her.

"The poor woman was gone but a short time, and when she returned it was with the necessary firing, and the articles of food, the latter in her apron, and which she deposited on the table.

"'Oh, my good, kind miss,' she ejaculated, unable to restrain the expression of her feelings; 'I have nearly laid out all the money you gave me, and heaven bless you; here is the change. Dear, dear, that I should meet with such kindness and generosity from a stranger.'

"'Pray cease, my good woman,' I observed, 'and hasten to prepare that food for yourself and children, which you so much require. Can I render you any assistance?'

"'Oh, why should I trouble you, miss?' she replied.

"I, however, heeded not what she said, but placing the infant, who was asleep, gently on the mattress, I set to work in earnest.

"The cheerful fire was soon glowing in the grate, the water singing in the kettle, the bread and butter cut, and a slice placed in each of the two little one's hands, who seemed taken by surprise, but commenced munching greedily immediately, the tea was prepared and made, and a nice steak cooking, and the next minute myself and the poor destitute family were all seated at the table partaking of the humble but wholesome and timely meal.

"My heart, however, was too full with the misery of this unfortunate woman, to suffer me to eat any more than slightly, and I was too busily occupied with my melancholy thoughts to suffer me to say a word till the meal was over.

"When it was so, the widow seized my hand, and raising it to her lips, before I could prevent her, in tones of heartfelt gratitude, she said—

"'Oh, where can I find words to express my feelings for this unexampled act of philanthropy and true Christian charity? The widow's prayers to heaven, for blessings on your head will never cease to be offered up. But for you, myself and children would probably this night have perished.'

"'It was providence that surely guided my footsteps hither, my good woman,' I replied, 'and I feel happy to think that I have been enabled to do the little I have done to serve you; would to heaven that my means were not so limited. But I am only a poor, friendless girl myself—the child of sorrow and adversity—a stranger to London, and unknowing whither to go. It is for that reason I feel grateful even for this humble shelter.'

"'Oh, surely you cannot think of remaining in this wretched place?' she said.

"'Till to-morrow I undoubtedly shall,' I answered; 'besides, you make it your residence, and why should I object to one night? But your brother, cannot he do anything to assist you in your misery?'

"'My brother, poor fellow,' she replied, 'his will is good, though he has not the means. He often gives me a sixpence, however, and something for myself and children to eat, though he can ill spare it. Poor man, what is he to do, with a wife and seven children, and all to keep upon ten shillings a week?'

"'True,' I replied, 'excuse the liberty I may appear to take, but what are your means of existence?'

"'Alas,' she sighed, 'that is a question which I scarcely know how to answer. For some time I used to earn about eightpence a day at needle-work; but I'm now so poor that they will not trust me with the work without a security, and how am I to procure that?'

"'Most true,' I coincided; 'but pray proceed, my poor woman, for you excite my deepest interest.'

"'I was compelled to apply to the parish,' she continued, 'where they at first refused to relieve me, abused and insulted me. At last, through the recommendation of two or three respectable housekeepers, they agreed to allow me three shillings per week, two quartern loaves, and sometimes a bit of uncooked meat. This I now receive every Friday. Then there are two or three Christian ladies, who call upon me now and then, and talk to me, and give me religious tracts to read. Sometimes, too, but it is very seldom, they give me a shilling, or a ticket for a hundred of coals. Out of this I have to pay a shilling per week for this wretched place, and that must be ready every Monday morning, or the hard hearted landlord would turn me and my poor children into the streets. These are my only means of existence, my kind friend.'

"I was deeply touched by the simple, artless, but truly impressive manner in which the unfortunate woman had related her miseries, at the same time, I was very much shocked and surprised, and for a few minutes my emotions would not allow me to make any observation, though I reflected the more.

"This then was a fair sample of the way in which the struggling poor of London were treated; these were the miseries and privations they had daily and hourly to endure, in their fearful battle with life, and that in the land of plenty. The picture was a fearful one to contemplate, and I shuddered, for I reflected that in my destitute and helpless condition, it was the only one before me.

"We interchanged a few observations with each other, and then thought of retiring to rest for the night.

"Rest!—How was that to be accomplished? That was rather a difficult and perplexing question to answer. But it was done in a way that I cannot describe, all huddling on the floor together.

"And thus passed my first day and night in London.

CHAPTER CLXXXVI.

CLARA CONCLUDES HER TALE.

"The next morning I felt anxious to procure a decent but reasonable lodging, for it was impossible for me to remain in the wretched place where I was, and yet I shuddered when I thought of the scanty means of support I had for any more than a few days, and when that was exhausted, what was to become of me?

"I tried hard, however, not to meet troubles half way, and endeavoured to put my trust in the mercy and goodness of providence.

"The widow Sadgrove—for that I understood to be her name—now recollected a single woman, with whom she was well acquainted, who resided some short distance off in a more respectable house, because she was much better off than herself, having no children, and plenty of needle work, and who, she said, no doubt, would be glad to receive me.

"I liked the description she gave, and therefore agreed to accompany her to the residence of the person alluded to, she leaving the two eldest children under the care of a female lodger, on whom she could depend, while she was gone.

"In a few words, we reached the place of our destination, and were received kindly by the young woman—for she did not seem to be much older than myself—and with whose clean and neat appearance, and that of the little room she occupied, I was most favourably struck.

"It did not take long to come to terms, and notwithstanding my money was short, I could not help giving poor Mrs. Sadgrove another shilling at parting, leaving me, as I imagined, the small sum of seven shillings; but you may guess my agreeable surprise on discovering a sovereign among the silver in the purse.

"I paid Mary Melrose—for such was my new companion's name—a month's lodging in advance, so as to have that off my mind, and that seemed to her, poor girl, like a little fortune.

"Our arrangements for the future were then quickly made, I agreed to assist her at needle-work—though at that time I knew little about it—and were to board together, living in the most frugal and economical manner we could.

"I found Mary a most agreeable and amiable companion, and no two persons could be better matched.

"But I frequently thought of poor old Andrew Bramble, and his wife and daughter, and pictured to myself what their anguish of mind must be, on learning that I had been left behind by the coach, and that his (Andrew's) sister, had neither heard or seen anything of me.

"It was strange that the idea never occurred to me to inquire at the inn in London what time the Dart coach was there, for then everything could have been explained, Andrew communicated with, and all the misfortunes I encountered, probably avoided. But so it was, and my evil destiny still continued to pursue me.

"We worked hard at the needle, early and late, and scanty enough was the pittance we received, but by ekeing out my little capital, we managed to get all our humble wants supplied, and were content and comparatively happy.

"But, alas, this was not fated to last long. Poor Mary was seized with a violent fit of illness, which confined her to her bed.

"I had the parish doctor to her, but he did her no good, and did not appear to trouble himself to do so. She became worse.

"I attended her with all the affectionate anxiety of a sister, working hard all the time.

"Alas, it was all of no avail, she died.

"Poor Mary Melrose, she was buried in a pauper's grave, over which there was no one to shed a tear but myself.

"My situation was now desperate; every farthing of my money was exhausted, and without the means of procuring more, for the work was withdrawn, and I was likewise in arrears for rent, which, of course, I had no means of paying, and there was nothing before me but to be driven from this humble home, without the least means of procuring another, or even food, unless I received it from the hand of charity.

"The fatal moment came; I was driven from this place, which for a few weeks had formed for me a comparatively happy home; like something loathsome and contagious I was driven forth starving, destitute, and brain distracted.

"I will pass as hastily as possible over that day and night of horror, during which I wandered in a violent snow-storm, I know not whither.

"At length, unable to proceed further, being completely exhausted, I sunk insensible on the door-step of a gentleman's mansion, situated as I afterwards discovered at the west end of the town.

"On recovering my senses, what was my astonishment to find myself in a warm and comfortable bed, in a spacious and handsomely furnished chamber, undressed, and a lady of the most amiable aspect, a medical gentleman, and two female servants watching over me with the most anxious solicitude.

"I stared upon them with amazement, and thought that I must be under the influence of some extraordinary dream; but the lady quickly convinced me to the contrary, and in the most kind and gentle accents inquired how I felt, and if there was anything that could be done for me to add to my comfort.

"My brain was quite bewildered, I was overwhelmed with emotion, and could not utter a word. But my tears burst forth, and told all and even more than language could have done.

"The lady seemed much affected.

"'Poor girl, you have evidently suffered much,' she said in a voice, and with a look of the deepest compassion; 'and I thank heaven that guided your footsteps hither, at the time of your dreadful emergency; for you are with those who will not fail to see to your necessities. I will now leave you to the care of those present, and hope to find you here in the morning.'

"With these words, after giving some instructions to the female domestics, the lady quitted the room, accompanied by the physician.

"The circumstances which had occurred to rescue me on the fearful occasion described, were of that extraordinary nature that they were more than sufficient to rack and distract my brain, and I found it impossible to put any questions to the domestics.

"But they enjoined me to silence, assuring me that I was with those who would not fail to treat me with every kindness, and having administered to me some refreshing beverage, they requested me to endeavour to compose myself to sleep.

"This advice I speedily followed, and slept so calmly and soundly that I did not awake till the morning, and I then felt as if I had entirely recovered.

"The females who were in attendance upon me, seemed gratified to behold this, and spoke to me words of kindness and condolence, which I gratefully acknowledged, and eagerly inquired where I was, and who was the lady whom I had seen the night before, and who had expressed such sympathy towards me.

"It was then I learnt that the mansion in which I then was belonged to Mr. and Mrs. Hastings, a lady and gentleman who were celebrated and admired for their Christian virtues, and their whole time being passed in acts of benevolence, of the most exemplary description, and that although they were persons of great wealth, pride or ostentation were entirely unknown to them.

"They looked upon the most humble individual, so long as his or her character deserved it, with the same respect as they did upon those in the most exalted station, and they themselves were revered by all who knew them.

"Oh, what a mercy of providence it was to place me in such hands.

"I will say no more than that those were the friends you have heard me speak of, and eulogise. They took me under their protection, and treated me as their own daughter. They educated me, cultivated my mind, in fact, to them I am entirely indebted for all I know.

"Heaven bless their memory, and rest their souls in peace.

"It was there, after the lapse of years, that I again beheld the object of my strange and unconquerable passion, Edward Stanley, and what my feelings were on that occasion, I must leave you to imagine.

"My heart throbbed at double its wonted pace, and I was compelled to form some excuse to retire from the room, for fear of betraying myself.

"When alone, I gave free vent to my passionate emotion, caused by this unexpected event. The love which I had always entertained for this hitherto unknown being, seemed to increase in strength; and I imagined that he looked upon me with pride and haughtiness, nay, even contempt; and what bitter anguish of mind did I experience, as I thus reflected.

"I will pass over many other incidents of my extraordinary and eventful history which I have already sketched to you, namely, Stanley's departure for India, followed shortly afterwards by Mr. and Mrs. Hastings and myself; the slaughter of my benefactors, and my own miraculous escape, and come at once to the dreadful night when you, Colonel Bridport, and your amiable daughters, discovered me lying exhausted and senseless at your door. What I that night suffered is almost impossible for language to describe; still I will endeavour to do so.

"I had been wandering about for several days, I knew not whither, but with the wild hope of discovering Stanley. I must certainly have been mad.

"At length I found myself in one of the wildest parts of the district in which I had been travelling, and which it would seem could scarcely ever venture to be traversed by human being.

"Savage beasts might be supposed ready to spring upon you at every turn, and every step you took you knew not whether you might not be hastening upon death.

"Night was approaching when I entered this frightful scene; and one of the most fearful storms was raging that I ever remember.

"With hair loose, and flying in the wind, and clothes wet and torn, with the air of a maniac I hurried on, and suffered nothing whatever to impede my progress; but I was suddenly startled by the loud voices of men behind me calling upon me to stop, and looking back, I was alarmed by beholding in the glare of the lightning, two or three armed sepoys in rapid pursuit of me, and appearing determined to overtake me.

"Terror added to my speed, for I felt certain what my fate would be, should I fall into the hands of such bloodthirsty miscreants, being an English woman.

"I firmly believe that I never ran so fast before in my life, although exhausted by my previous extraordinary exertions, but I could hear the dreadful threats and curses of the men behind me, and, without venturing to look back again, I felt too painfully certain that they were gaining fast upon me, and that it could only be by the merciful interposition of providence I could escape them.

"Still, however, wrought up to a pitch of desperation, I even increased my speed, making my way towards the city of Cawnpore, which I knew could not be far from the place I was traversing, and was at present occupied by British troops; when one of the villains fired after me, but fortunately I escaped the intended shot, and continued to hurry on my way, as fast as I was able.

"At length, quite exhausted, and panting for breath, I was compelled to stop, and support myself against a tree, let the consequences be whatever they might, and looking fearfully round, I was greatly relieved to find that there was nothing of the men to be seen, and I therefore naturally concluded that they had abandoned the pursuit, especially as it would not be safe for them to approach too near the city of Cawnpore.

"My brain was in the most distracted and bewildered state, and I scarcely could recollect where I was, or what had happened to me.

"Still the wild thought of Stanley continued to haunt me, and to urge me on, and at length, through the fierce tempest and this fearful scene I continued my flight, till I emerged into the open road, and I beheld lights, which I knew proceeded from Cawnpore, and were only a short distance off.

"I reached it—I darted madly along, till nature could do no more, and I sunk, worn out and insensible, at the door of this building.

"The rest you know.

———

CHAPTER CLXXXVII.

TORTURING INCIDENTS.

Thus Clara concluded her remarkable and romantic narrative, and to which her friends had listened with the most breathless attention, and absorbing interest, dwelling with mingled feelings upon every paragraph, but seldom venturing to interrupt her.

Such a strange variety of incidents and misfortunes for one so young to have experienced, they had never before heard of, and it seemed almost impossible that human fortitude could stand against trials so severe.

They allowed the poor girl to rest awhile, in order that she might try to compose her feelings, and collect herself, after the pain naturally caused by the recital of so many sorrows and misfortunes; and scarcely heeding their presence, she gave unrestrained indulgence to the emotions that agitated her bosom, and her tears flowed copiously, but of which those present pretended to take no notice.

"Dear Clara," at length Colonel Bridport ventured to say, "I am afraid the long narrative of your woes, and the torturing thoughts and recollections it has naturally awakened, has proved too much for you, and we should have been less anxious to urge you to a task so difficult."

"Ah, my good sir, they are indeed no

trifling sorrows to recal to one's memory, and I hope you will pardon my emotions," returned the poor girl, "when I look back upon them, through the long dreary waste of years in which they took place, I can scarcely persuade myself that they could have happened, but that they are merely the offsprings of my diseased imagination. Not long, however, am I suffered to indulge in that idea, the whole—the painful truth rushes upon my recollection in characters too vivid and impressive to be mistaken or rejected. And then the strange mystery connected with my birth, and which seems as though it would never be unravelled, tortures and bewilders my brain, and gives rise to a variety of conjectures in my mind, which only leave me in a still greater state of doubt and uncertainty than before."

No. 80.

"You never heard of anything then that was calculated to throw any light upon that mysterious and important subject?" interrogated the colonel.

"Alas, no," replied Clara, "and I'm fearful that I never shall; though I should dearly like to know the real authors of my being, so, that, if they be no more, I might shed a tear, and offer up a prayer to their memory."

"But should they have abandoned you to the mercy of those guilty wretches in your childhood," observed Mr. Hamilton, "they have forfeited all claims to the feelings of nature, or even those of common humanity."

"Most true," coincided Colonel Bridport, "and they could only be remembered, or at least, deserve to be remembered with feelings of disgust and detestation."

"Oh, I cannot, I dare not believe that such could be the case," replied Clara, shuddering, "I cannot think so uncharitably of my fellow creatures, as to suppose that there are parents in the world that could be guilty of or even contemplate so monstrous, so revolting a crime. I have often thought I was stolen by the gipsies, either for the purposes of begging, or from motives of revenge."

"That is by no means an improbable idea," returned the colonel, "and if so, the sufferings of your parents must have been fearful, Clara. Still, I hope that something will yet occur to unravel this perplexing mystery, and that you will discover who you really are. There is one question, however, which I feel particularly anxious to ask you."

"Name it, my good sir, and, if possible, I will answer it."

"Those excellent people, Andrew Bramble and his dame, did you ever behold them again?"

"Oh, yes," eagerly replied Clara, tears starting to her eyes at the recollection, "but not till long after I had been in London, and was living under the protection of Mr. and Mrs. Hastings, and that happy occasion must ever be treasured in my memory, although I inadvertently omitted it in my narrative. I had been out for a morning walk with Mrs. Hastings, when in turning the corner of a street, I abruptly and accidentally encountered poor old Andrew, looking much the same as formerly.

"We were paralysed, and absolutely stared aghast at each other, as though we could not believe the evidence of our senses.

"Mrs. Hastings, too, she was not much less surprised, for from what I had related of the poor old man and his family, she concluded it was him.

"The scene which followed, even in the public street, and with several people, tempted by curiosity, looking on, defies all my powers of description, so I will pass as hastily over it as I can.

"Andrew embraced me with the same warm affection as if I had been his own daughter; looked close into my features to see that he was not mistaken: laughed with joy, then sobbed and wept like an infant, and was totally incapable of giving full vent to his powerfully excited feelings, so pure, so truly genuine.

"'Dear, dear Andrew,' I at length ejaculated, 'and one of my best earthly friends.'

"'Ah!" he joyfully interrupted, 'it is her—it is my own dear child, whom I never expected that these poor old eyes would ever behold again.'

"'Poor, kind-hearted old man,' I replied, deeply affected, "oh, how can I speak my feelings at this joyful—this unexpected meeting. Oh, how constantly have my prayers been offered up to heaven upon that subject, but I had begun to despair of their ever being realised. But the dame, the dear old dame, and your amiable daughter, do they still live?'

"'Live,' repeated the old man, 'oh, yes, bless their hearts. We've been in London now more than a week, and are staying at my sister's near St. James's Park. Oh, Clara, you may guess what we all suffered when we could hear nothing what had become of you, no more than from that stupid coachman, who told us about his leaving you at the inn, you having fallen asleep. But dear me, my heart is so full, and my brain so bewildered, that I scarcely know what I am saying or doing. But this is not the place for explanation. Come along, Clara, you'll come and see the dame and Bridget without delay. It is not far from here; they'll go mad with joy. Your pardon, madam.'

"'Compose yourself, my good Andrew,' I said; 'this is my kind benefactress, Mrs. Hastings; I must attend her home, but if you will give me the correct address, I will make no delay in visiting you.'

"'If my presence be not an intrusion,' said Mrs. Hastings, "I will accompany you, my dear Clara, and we will attend this good old man to his sister's at once.'

"I could see a tear glisten in poor old Andrew's eye, as my benefactress thus spoke, and his features became more animated, and his countenance glowed with the warmth of his feelings.

"Most respectfully taking the hand of Mrs. Hastings, which she had extended towards him, he said, in a voice of great emotion—

"'Heaven bless you, my dear lady, for this. You have made me one of the happiest of human beings, by your kind condescension. Pray follow me, madam, and you, Clara, and we will be there in no time at all. Dear, dear, how surprised and delighted they will be.'

"Thus talking and congratulating himself, the poor old man hurried on his way, and Mrs. Hastings and myself followed deeply interested.

"I need scarcely say what pleasure this unexpected adventure caused me, and the anticipation of the delight of the worthy dame and her daughter on beholding one whom they must long since have concluded to be no more, again; and I was almost afraid that the sudden surprise would be almost too much for the dame's strength to bear.

"It was not more than a quarter of an hour before we arrived at the door of a stately mansion, which Andrew informed us belonged to the nobleman in whose service his sister was, as housekeeper, and had been for a period extending over more than twenty years, and where himself, the dame, and Bridget were at present staying, and now the moment of trial was approaching, though I felt myself pretty well prepared for it.

"Andrew knocked at the door with a tremulous hand, and it being answered by a female domestic, Mrs. Hastings and myself were ushered into one of the parlours—the family being out of town—while Andrew hastened to his sister, the dame, and Bridget, in order to break to them the extraordinary and agreeable intelligence, which I was certain must be received by them with the most unbounded and extravagant astonishment and delight.

"But a few minutes alapsed from the departure of Andrew on his important errand, when I heard exclamations of surprise and emotion, and immediately afterwards footsteps hastily descending the stairs from the housekeeper's room, and my heart palpitated at double its wonted pace, while my kindhearted benefactress, Mrs. Hastings awaited the result of this adventure with the greatest anxiety.

"We were not long kept in suspense, the room-door was thrown hastily open, there was a loud and simultaneous cry of joy and astonishment from Bridget and her mother, and the next moment I was fondly locked in the embrace of them both.

"What an extraordinary and affecting scene was that which followed; no language of mine, I am sure, my dear friends, can give a faithful picture of it, and therefore I must leave it to your own imagination.

"The poor old dame seemed half stupefied and bewildered with joy, and Bridget's emotion was equally as great. They embraced me again and again, and we mingled our tears together.

"It was some time before we could at all compose our feelings sufficiently to enable us to talk calmly and to enter into explanations, and then for the first time, I was introduced by the delighted Andrew to his sister, an amiable, gentle-looking woman, the very counterpart of himself, but evidently several years his senior.

"Nothing could possibly be more affectionate than the reception I met with from that good old woman, and I was prepared to view her with the utmost esteem.

"This interview lasted for more than a couple of hours, and the poor old people would fain have prolonged it, for the idea of parting was torture to them; but it was getting late, and Mrs. Hastings was impatient to depart, as she knew her husband would be anxiously awaiting our return; we therefore at last arose to separate, I promising faithfully to re-visit them in the morning,

and remain with them during the whole of the day.

"With this they were satisfied, and with feelings such as may readily be imagined, we bade each other adieu, and myself and Mrs. Hastings made our way as quickly as possible towards home, deeply affected by all that had taken place, and my benefactress expressing herself in the highest terms of Andrew, his wife and sister, congratulating me warmly at the same time on the accident which had brought us together again, after so long a separation.

"I think that I have now fully and satisfactorily answered your question, Colonel Bridport, though perhaps it may be as well to add, that Andrew and his wife prolonged their stay in London a week over the time they had originally intended, and I was with them every day, and when they finally departed, they begged me to correspond with them, and to visit the sister as frequently as possible, which I promised to do, and you may be sure that I kept my word.

"I never saw them afterwards."

"Amiable beings," said the colonel, "they were indeed worthy of your esteem. But there is another question I wish to ask you, Clara: what became of the poor widow with whom you lodged on the first night of your arrival in London?"

"I thought I had told you, my dear sir, in my narrative," replied Clara, "but if not, a very few words will suffice to explain every thing upon that subject.

"As soon as I had become permanently settled with Mr. and Mrs. Hastings, I availed myself of the earliest opportunity to make them acquainted with all the melancholy particulars connected with that unfortunate creature, by which they were much moved, and determined to visit her in order to see what could be done for her to better her condition.

"She, with her family, were removed without delay to a comfortable little two-roomed dwelling, and which was decently furnished with everything necessary at the expense of my benefactors: she was supplied with a good stock of clothes for her and the children; plenty of needle-work, for which she was well, nay, liberally paid, was procured for the widow, at which she most industriously employed herself; the consequences of which were that, in a short time, she was rescued from a state of the most squalid poverty to one of absolute comfort and happiness."

"What excellent people your benefactors must have been, Clara," remarked the doctor.

"Oh, they were indeed," she replied; "but I can never find language sufficiently powerful adequately to describe their brilliant virtues."

" There is still another, and a delicate and important question which I wish to put to you, Clara," said Colonel Bridport, " and I hope you will pardon me for it."

" Name it, sir," she returned, " for there is now no question which I am not fully prepared to answer."

" Do you, my poor girl," said the colonel, in a hesitating voice, " still entertain the same unfortunate sentiments towards Lieutenant Stanley?"

" Oh, yes—yes," Clara fervently exclaimed, " I must ever continue to do so."

" My dear girl," returned Colonel Bridport, tenderly, " you must cease to remember him in any other character than that of a friend ; he can never be your's?"

" Why?—oh, why?—tell me, I implore you."

" Because he loves another."

" Ah," exclaimed, Clara, eagerly, an expression of jealousy flashing from her fine eyes, and every limb convulsed with powerful emotion ; " who—who is she who has presumed to aspire to, and won dear Stanley's love?"

" A beauteous Indian maiden, whose virtues entitle her to esteem and admiration."

" Her name?—her name?—torture me not."

" Omelia."

Poor Clara could hear no more, but with a wild cry of agony and despair, she sunk insensible in the arms of the colonel.

—

CHAPTER CLXXXVIII.

CLARA'S MENTAL ANGUISH.

Every one present, of course, were deeply affected at this scene, and could not but keenly feel for the painful situation in which the poor girl was placed, and the melancholy consequences that were too likely to follow.

She was immediately placed on a couch, and every proper means resorted to for her recovery, though it was not without something like dread that that was looked to.

But it was some time ere she gave any signs of returning life, and that was but slowly.

Frequently she murmured the name of Stanley, during the time that she was in this half insensible state, and heavy sighs and sobs escaped her bosom, which pained those present to listen to, and Colonel Bridport now regretted that he had not waited for a day or two, until the feelings of Clara had become a little more composed, ere he had mentioned the delicate and important subject to her, and which he might have been

certain would cause her such intense mental anguish.

And what a strange passion her's was : for years she had suffered it to exist in her breast, without giving the object who had inspired it the least cause to suspect the sentiments she entertained towards him. And she accused that man of being cold and insensible to a passion which she had never acknowledged, and now she found that he loved another, all the pangs of jealousy racked and distracted her brain.

Some few minutes more elapsed, without a change, and Colonel Bridport and Mr. Hamilton were about to retire from the room, leaving Clara to the tender care and attention of the females, when she suddenly awoke to consciousness, and started hastily up from the couch on which she had been reclining.

There was a wild, wandering expression in her eyes, which it was painful to look upon, and her cheeks glowed with the excitement of her feelings.

She pressed her hands upon her temples as if endeavouring to recal what had happened to her memory, and then, in a strange wild voice of agony, she exclaimed—

" Who said that he loved another? 'Tis false, no other but myself can feel a sincere passion for him, and they must be mad who would try to persuade me otherwise. But they only do so to mock and torture me. And yet what claim have I, a poor wretched, unknown, friendless girl, upon his affections? Happy Omelia—miserable, heartbroken Flora!"

It was evident that her mind was somewhat affected by the sudden shock of the melancholy intelligence, and Colonel Bridport and his companions did not venture upon an observation, for the present therefore, but awaited until she should in some measure have regained her composure.

She pressed her hands upon her forehead, and abandoned herself to the utmost intensity of mental anguish, to thoughts and feelings that seemed to rack her very soul to madness.

The fair Julia and her sister were so powerfully affected, and could so fully appreciate the unfortunate Clara's feelings, that they could not refrain from tears, and they watched her with the utmost anxiety,

At length Clara again aroused herself from the state of lethargy in which she had been, and, in the most melancholy accents, she ejaculated—

" But who is she, I repeat? Who has dared to usurp the heart of that beloved being to whom, although he knows it not, I am ready to make any sacrifice, nay, even that of life itself? Where is she? Where can I find her, that I might wreak my feelings of jealousy and revenge upon her head?"

" Hold, Clara," said Colonel Bridport, hastily, and shocked at the dangerous extent to which the poor girl had suffered her excited feelings to carry her. "You surely cannot know what you say, or you would never talk thus. Jealousy, revenge—oh, for heaven's sake, my unfortunate young friend, endeavour to stifle such fearful passions in your breast. Try to tranquillise your feelings and to reflect more calmly and dispassionately upon the melancholy, and, I admit, painful circumstances by which you are surrounded. Such sentiments as those you have just now, in the excitement of your feelings, expressed, are quite opposed to your nature, I know."

Clara looked at him earnestly and despairingly for a moment or two, sighed deeply, then burst into a copious flood of tears, which her friends were glad to see, as they hoped that by thus giving free vent to her emotions it would afford her some relief.

"Oh, my dear friends," she at length said, in calmer accents than before, but still her countenance expressive of sorrow and regret, "pardon the rashness of my tongue, I beseech you, which caused me to give utterto observations which I meant not, and which I would fain have avoided and restrained. What cause have I to encourage feelings of malice and revenge against this fortunate being who, it appears, has won the heart of Edward Stanley? As I have stated again and again, he knows not of the fatal passion I entertain for him; he can never have the least idea or suspicion of it, for never did I venture to hint at it, though my looks frequently when I was in his company were almost sufficient to betray my secret. And even if he had discovered the sentiments I had presumed to encourage for him, could I expect that he could ever return my love? Ah, no—the idea was preposterous, and could only have originated in the madness of despair. Still, in spite of all I have said, I cannot but envy this fortunate girl her happiness."

"Alas," replied Colonel Bridport, " Omelia is far from happy. In fact, in many respects, like yourself, she has long been a wretched wanderer over distant lands, to endeavour to discover her lover, or to ascertain the fate which has befallen him. A short time since, accident guided her hither, in the most miserable condition that can well be imagined, and she remaiued for a few days under my protection; but her impatience would not permit her to stay longer. She secretly absconded, and, if she be still living, heaven only knows what has now become of her.

"Poor girl—poor girl," sighed Clara, with true womanly feeling, "her passion then is sincere, and therefore, even rival though she is, am I almost prepared to love her as a sister for it."

"Nobly—generously spoken, Clara," said the colonel, admiringly, and pressing her hand, "those are sentiments that alike do honour to your head and heart. Endeavour to encourage them, and gloomy and hopeless though your present prospects may appear to be, there are yet bright, happy days in store for you, depend upon it."

"Ah, would that I dare hope so?" Clara replied with a sigh, "but in spite of all my efforts to do so, I cannot. But this Indian maid, Omelia, she must be very beautiful both in person and manners, to have made such a powerful impression upon the heart of Stanley."

"She is most lovely," said the colonel, warmly, "and her intrinsic virtues even outvie her personal charms. Did you but know her, with sentiments and feelings so much in unison with your own, you must indeed love her as a sister."

"Dear Stanley," ejaculated Clara, with emotion, "I marvel not that so gentle and amiable a being as Omelia is described to be should win your heart's warmest affections, but," she added, after a pause, "'tis hard to think that all my fond but delusive hopes should be thus cruelly, totally annihilated, and that by one who claims the blood-stained land of India, land moistened by the blood of our innocent women and children, as her country. I should hate her as something loathesome."

"Forbear, Clara," remonstrated the colonel, "utter not such sentiments against the noble-minded Omelia, for then would you be doing her a monstrous injustice. No one can more execrate the inhuman conduct of her countrymen than herself, and she run the most awful risks to oppose them. Think you that she could ever obtain the love of Stanley had not her conduct been all and more than I have feebly attempted to describe?"

"Ah, no," sighed Clara, and the tears chased each other down her pale cheeks; "and I despise myself for having for a moment, entertained such thoughts towards her; but my poor brain is bewildered by the various thoughts which rush tumultuously upon it; my tongue runs riot, and I know not what I say. Allow me a few hours reflection, and I probably, by exertion, may be able to collect and compose myself."

To this the colonel could raise no reasonable objection, and after an affectionate and friendly observation or two, himself and Mr. Hamilton retired from the room.

CHAPTER CLXXXIX.

UNEXPECTED INTELLIGENCE.—DEPARTURE
FROM CAWNPORE.

For some minutes after the departure of Colonel Bridport and his respected friend, Mr. Hamilton, from the room, Clara remained wrapped in silent and melancholy meditation, upon which Julia and her sister did not think it prudent to obtrude by any observations of theirs, but they watched her as usual with feelings of the deepest interest and sympathy.

Indeed, after the conversation which had just taken place between herself and the colonel, poor Clara had much room for varied and painful reflection, and no wonder that she felt her brain bewildered, and it was some time before she could arrange her thoughts into anything like order, or at all regain her composure.

The principal cause of her anguish, it is almost needless to state, was the too certain love of Omelia and Stanley; and there were moments that she felt as if her heart was ready to break, or that madness was about to take possession of her brain. Her bosom swelled with mingled emotions, and it was not without the greatest difficulty that she was able to contain herself within the bounds of reason.

"My fate is sealed," she at length murmured forth in mournful accents, and arousing from her train of dismal meditations, as if awaking from some fearful dream, "it is madness for me to encourage hope when all hope is at an end. He loves her, fondly, devotedly loves her, and she is worthy of his love; what ray of hope is there then for me, when the passion I entertain for him is unknown to him, and he probably has never even bestowed a thought upon so insignificant a being as myself? Oh, why did I not make an avowal of my unfortunate passion to him, when I had the opportunity of doing so? I could then at once have known my fate from his own lips; for, dear Stanley, I know you to be the very soul of candour and honour. And since it is so, for what have I to wish to live? Wretched, friendless, unknown being as I am, what business have I in the world? Why should I still continue to cling to that which must now become hateful to me, and in which I can find no ray of sunshine or happiness? Oh, that I could die—that I could die!"

Convulsive sobs choked her further utterance, and covering her face with her hands, while her whole frame was violently agitated, she gave way to a wild paroxysm of grief, which caused the fair sisters the greatest anguish to witness.

They would willingly, in their own gentle and persuasive manner, which no one could have listened to with indifference, have endeavoured to impart some degree of consolation to her deeply lacerated heart, but they were fearful of interrupting her, and considered that the uninterrupted indulgence of her grief might afford her some relief.

They, however, drew nearer the chair in which she was seated, and awaited her recovery from the violence of her emotions with anxiety and impatience.

But although they spoke not, even in a whisper, she became almost immediately conscious of their proximity, and looking up through her tears, in a mournful, but affectionate voice, she said—

"Heaven grant that you may never know what it is to cherish a hopeless passion in your bosom—to love one who can make you no return, but with scorn and indifference. Better had you never been born than have to endure such misery—such ceaseless torture of mind—such fierce racking of the brain. Ah, no, may you, on the contrary, live to have all your fondest hopes and wishes gratified; may your pathway through life be one of sunshine and flowers, no gloomy cares beset your minds, but every day, every hour, be one of prosperity, peace, and happiness. This is my sincere, my fervent prayer, and heaven grant that it may be realised."

Julia was about to return some appropriate reply to this affectionate speech, when the attention of them all was arrested by a confused noise in the street, followed by the cheerful and inspiring music of a military band, and hastening to the window, which looked on to the main street, they beheld a sight which made the blood glow within their veins, and caused them the most pleasurable feelings of excitement.

It was a regiment of British troops which had just arrived, and were marching into the city, with colours gaily waving in the air, and to the merry sound of the fifes and drums, while those troops that were and had been for some time quartered in the city, were arranged on each side of the road, and as the new comers passed along, they gave each other a deafening English cheer, which re-echoed far and wide. In fact, it was a most animated scene

The heart of Clara palpitated violently, and nameless feelings came over her, which she could scarcely herself understand.

With anxious looks she watched the soldiers as they passed—and that so near the window that she could see them all distinctly—with the wild hope of beholding her beloved Stanley, although at the same time she well knew that it was not the regiment to which he belonged; and when they had all gone by, she could not resist a feeling of sorrow and disappointment, and throwing herself back in her chair, she burst into a flood of tears.

Julia and her sister's curiosity was also excited to the highest pitch, by this unexpected arrival; but they were not long kept in a state of doubt and suspense, for Colonel Bridport hastily entered the room, and the expression of his countenance plainly showed that he had some intelligence of an important nature to communicate to them.

Clara and the sisters looked eagerly and inquiringly at him, but the gallant old colonel understood their feelings perfectly, and did not delay an instant in gratifying their very natural curiosity.

"I have unexpected news for you," he said; "the troops you just now saw march into the city have come to relieve us, and instructions have arrived for us to depart without any more delay than possible to the kingdom, or rather province of Oude, where the disturbances seem rather on the increase than otherwise."

"Ah," exclaimed Clara, her eyes flashing and her countenance glowing with the sudden excitement of her feelings, "Oude?— that is whither you told me the noble Stanley went, is it not?"

"True," answered the colonel; "but why, my dear girl, still suffer him to occupy your thoughts, after what I have told you?"

"Oh, it is impossible for me ever to banish his beloved image from them," she returned, clasping her hands vehemently together, and looking piteously in the colonel's face; "my fond heart yearns to behold him again under any circumstances, and methinks I could then learn to be content, though not happy. But, oh, tell me, my dear sir, I beseech you, if I may be permitted to follow you, with your amiable daughters, to the place of destination?"

"I have little doubt," answered the colonel, "that I shall be able to gain that permission as you are under my protection, and the same as one of the members of my family."

"Oh, thanks, thanks," ejaculated Clara, gratefully, "but when will the time of departure be?"

"To-morrow afternoon at the latest," replied Colonel Bridport, "but hark ye, Clara, I wish not to wound or distress your feelings, but I would warn you in a friendly spirit not to cherish any sanguine hopes and expectations, that after all may turn out to be illusive, and thus end in the most bitter disappointment. Lieutenant Stanley left here for Oude some time since; there have been some fierce engagements with the enemy in that district since then, and Stanley may unfortunately, though I sincerely hope not, be one

among those gallant officers who have fallen in the deadly strife."

Clara turned ghastly pale, her lips quivered, and a convulsive shuddering ran through her frame, as with the greatest difficulty she faltered out in a tremulous and agitated voice—

"Ah, that fearful idea—oh, why have you hinted it to me? for every faculty is enchained in horror as I reflect upon it. The noble-minded Stanley among those who have fallen upon the sanguinary field of battle; it cannot be, I dare not encourage the dreadful thought."

"Remember, Clara," replied the colonel, "that we soldiers all have to take our chance in the perils of war, and, on entering the field of carnage, we none of us can tell whose lot it may be to return from it. But we never suffer that thought to trouble us— our war-cry is 'Death or Victory,' and he is a dastard, who deserves to be hung up at the nearest tree, to whose heart fear is not a stranger. But you must endeavour to compose your feelings as well as possible, and prepare for your departure from hence to-morrow. You had better now retire to your chamber, after the excitement you have experienced this last few hours."

"Thank you for your kind and considerate advice, my dear sir," returned Clara, "I will gladly accept it, but permit me to retire alone, that I may for a time give free indulgence to my thoughts, and endeavour to tranquillise my feelings."

To this, of course, the colonel could raise no objection, and Clara having wished him good evening, and quitting the room, ascended th stairs to the chamber which had been appropriated to her use, since she had been an inmate of the building.

It is useless to describe the state of her mind, as the reader must be aware that she must be suffering much from mental anxiety, which the events of the day, particularly the intelligence which had just been communicated to her could scarcely fail to produce.

Mingled hopes, and doubts, and fears agitated her, and distracted her brain; but the last observations of Colonel Bridport, and the too fearful probability of their being verified, tortured her more than all. She shrunk and shuddered with horror at the idea.

"Great God of heaven," she exclaimed, worked up to a pitch of the greatest emotion, clasping her hands, and raising her eyes devoutly, "oh, I implore Thee in Thine infinite mercy to avert so dreadful a calamity; spare the life of the gallant Stanley through every danger and difficulty, so that providentially, when this sanguinary war is at an end, he may return to his friends full of honours, and pass the remainder of his days in the uninterrupted enjoyment of all the happiness that human being can experience. Happiness," she repeated, after a moment's reflection, a change at the same time coming over the expression of her handsome features, "happiness! and she, my rival may share it with him, and bask in all the enjoyment of his love, while I am left to all the horrors of despair. Oh, agonising thought, sufficient to drive this poor brain to madness. Ah, and perhaps even now she is with him—she is locked in his embrace of affection—they breathe soft vows of love and constancy—and now their lips meet, and fond kisses are exchanged between them; they— oh, the picture which my too vivid and ready imagination draws, is too torturing; I cannot, dare not contemplate it."

Her emotions overpowered her, and throwing herself back in her chair, she could say no more, but abandoned herself to all the agony of thought.

"But let me be calm," she suddenly ejaculated, arousing herself somewhat from the excited state of mind she was in before, "let me not do the poor girl, Omelia—whose virtues have been described to me by the good old Colonel Bridport—an act of injustice. Her's, I believe, is a pure and virtuous love, emanating from the heart, sincere, fervent, and unconquerable: and therefore worthy of every respect and admiration. And to that love Stanley warmly responds; why then should I envy them their happiness, or entertain any jealous feelings towards the Indian girl, Omelia? Mine is a wild, hopeless passion, receiving no encouragement from the object of it, in fact, entirely unknown to him, and I should have exerted all my energies to have stifled it in its infancy."

She again paused and reflected deeply.

"But could I behold him once more," she sighed, "could I have the opportunity of speaking to him, of confessing to him how fondly I love him; even though I should receive a firm but cold rejection from his lips, oh, what a weight of care it would remove from my breast, and methinks I could then calmly resign myself to my fate. Grant me this, oh, heaven, and, powerful as the effort may be, I would endeavour to be content; although nothing whatever, I feel convinced, can eradicate my fatal passion from my breast. There it must remain until I breathe my last sigh."

These thoughts, melancholy even though they were, seemed to tranquillise her feelings, and she remained for some time comparatively undisturbed, but still wrapped in deep meditation.

The evening was now somewhat advanced—and a beautiful one it was. The moon shone brightly in the clear cloudless sky, and myriads of brilliant stars lent their twinkling lustre to her chaste and mellow radiance. Clara seated herself near the window, in order to try to enjoy the delightful serenity of the hour, and as she did so, the gloomy thoughts which had before tortured her, seemed for the time being to forsake her, and she felt comparatively happy.

A gentle knock at the room-door somewhat startled her from a reverie into which she had fallen, but she quickly guessed the cause, and instantly afterwards Julia and her sister stepped lightly into the chamber.

Clara received them with a faint smile, sufficient to mark the esteem in which she held them. and hastening closer to her, they inquired tenderly and earnestly after her health.

"Better, better," she replied, again endeavouring to assume a most cheerful aspect, but sighs, in spite of herself, escaping her bosom, "you must indeed deem me week, my dear young friends, thus to give way to such violent grief; but oh, in calmer reflection, can you marvel at my excessive anguish and despair, after the fatal and melancholy intelligence which your gallant father but recently communicated to me? Can you wonder that it should make so powerful and agonising an impression upon my mind?"

"Most true, dear Clara," coincided Julia, "and rest assured that mine and Charlotte's sympathies are warmly and sincerely with you. Still we would earnestly implore you to endeavour to conquer the emotions that are torturing you, and try to encourage at least some degree of hope."

"Psha, you talk like an inexperienced girl which you are," replied Clara, impatiently, and her cheeks glowing with excitement, "that which in your ignorance—pardon the harshness of the word, it is spoken without the least angry feeling—you have advised is utterly impossible, and it would be little short of madness to encourage the idea. Oh, how futile is it to attempt to efface from the memory the image of that beloved, that adored being which is enshrined in the deepest recesses of the heart; how agonising to know that the love you have aspired to is possessed by another, and that, too, one whom from her country, would appear the least likely to obtain it. Oh, thrice happy Omelia, miserable, hopeless, wretched Clara."

Again the power of speech was denied her, and unable to control the power of her feelings any longer she burst into a violent paroxysm of sobs and tears, which it was quite painful to listen to, and moved the amiable and gentle Julia and her sister to tears; but they would not have ventured to interrupt the wretched and unfortunate girl in the expression of her anguish for the world.

However, they sat and watched her with looks of the greatest commiseration and sorrow.

After some time had elapsed, Clara revived, and in a voice of diminished anguish, without the least allusion to the torturing thoughts that occupied her mind, she expressed a wish to retire to rest.

Mira was, therefore, immediately summoned to attend upon her, and the two sisters having affectionately bade her good night, also retired to their chamber, which, as we believe has been before stated, adjoined that of Clara's, so that they could hasten to her assistance in an instant should it be required.

Clara, however, passed a wretched night, and had but little calm sleep, fearful dreams continuing to torture her imagination.

No. 81.

She arose at an early hour in the morning, and her pale and languid appearance, and bloodshot eyes, plainly showed the intense anguish of mind she was enduring.

But she made every effort to conquer or subdue it, and succeeded so remarkably well, that she met Colonel Bridport and his fair daughters at the breakfast-table with comparative composure.

The keen eye of the colonel, however, could not fail to read the agonising thoughts that were passing in her mind, but he carefully avoided making any allusion to the painful subject that caused them, and tried all that he could to divert her attention to somthing else; and this he did, by urging the necessity of her and his daughters making hasty preparations for the commencement of the march, which would be towards evening.

He added that it had cost him the greatest difficulty to obtain permission from his commanding officer for even his daughters to accompany him, and he was compelled to represent Clara as a dear and near relation, in order to obtain the like usual favour, and then it was only under the most severe penalties and restrictions.

Clara could scarcely find words to express her thanks, but Colonel Bridport would not listen to them, and hastily dismissed her and his daughters to their preparations.

We shall not dwell further upon this subject, suffice it to say that, about four in the afternoon the troops left the city, and commenced their long and tedious march to the scene of strife.

CHAPTER CXC.

THE SUFFERINGS OF ABDAL AND OMELIA.

Again for a brief period we are compelled to leave the unfortunate Clara and her excellent friends, and return to Omelia and Abdal, after the awful and unexpected death of the faithful old Juballah.

For a few minutes after the last breath had departed from the body of the ill-fated old woman, Omelia was transfixed to the spot, and stared aghast at the corpse, as though scarcely believing what had taken place.

But when she was at length awakened to a full sense of the dreadful truth, she uttered a cry of horror, and throwing herself distractedly by the side of the murdered woman, she became, for a time, totally insensible.

The situation of Abdal was now most awkward and trying; he was in a strange part of the country, worn out with fatigue, on one side the corpse of poor faithful old Juballah, on the other the insensible form of Omelia, who, independent of the late frightful catastrophe, was quite exhausted by the extraordinary and almost unparalleled fatigue she had undergone.

Nothing could possibly be more awful and disheartening than the prospect before him, and in spite of his natural courage, in facing dangers and difficulties, Abdal shrunk from the contemplation of it with a feeling of horror and dismal foreboding which he could not resist.

At length, for the first time, he remembered the reviving draught which the murdered woman always carried in a flask by her side, and immediately seizing it, he applied it to the lips of the inanimate Omelia.

It had an almost instantaneous effect, the actions of the limbs showed returning life; then a sigh escaped the poor girl's swelling bosom, and she gradually opened her eyes, and gazed with astonishment and bewilderment around her.

Abdal did not at first attempt to speak, for his agitation and confusion would not allow him to do so, and Omelia, hearing all so silent at first imagined that she was abandoned to her fate, left all alone, and she looked around upon the dreary scene before her with the most indescribable feelings of horror and despair, and groaned.

Abdal remained in the same stupified state, and his senses seemed, for the time being to have left him.

At length a faint ray of moonlight forced its way through the branches of the trees, and fell upon the corpse of old Juballah, which again met the gaze of Omelia, with a frantic cry that re-echoed far through the dreary wild, she sunk on her knees by the side of the corpse of that extraordinary being to whom she was so largely indebted, and tenderly raising the head of the murdered woman in her lap, as if she had been still alive, she gazed at the ghastly features with a degree of earnestness and intense horror that almost drove her into the same state of insensibility from which she had only just recovered.

"Juballah," she groaned, "friend, protector, guide, and do I indeed gaze upon your ghastly corpse! Hold your cold and inanimate form in my arms? Oh, it was a monstrous deed to deprive the poor old woman of her life, and the curses of the Great Spirit will pursue the cowardly and bloodthirsty assassin for it. It was the hand of the miscreant Yusef that perpetrated the atrocious crime, and it therefore appears that he must by some miracle have escaped from the frightful death to which he and Alahamed were doomed, and which seemed to be inevitable, and that by some unfortunate accident he is lurking about in this locality, and therefore that I have now the greatest danger to apprehend. Oh, Juballah, my best earthly friend, how sincerely, how irreparably do I already feel your loss. Would that I could die, while I thus gaze at your lifeless features. There, at any rate, would be an end to all my earthly cares and sorrows."

"Omelia," said Abdal, in low solemn tones of remonstrance, having but a minute or two recovered from his state of stupefaction.

She started at the tones of his voice, and could scarcely believe that it was him, such was the bewildered and distracted state of her senses.

"Ah, Abdal," she faintly ejaculated, and in the most melancholy accents, "you here? then the wretched Omelia is not entirely deserted, in this, the most terrible hour of her adversity.

"Deserted, Omelia," repeated Abdal, in tones of gentle reproach, "oh, think you that Abdal could ever be that miscreant to remorselessly abandon you to your fate while the purple current of life continues to circulate throughout his veins? You wrong me, Omelia, and I feel hurt at it."

"Oh, pardon my rash tongue, my good friend, Abdal," sighed Omelia, "pardon me, I implore you; my poor brain is so bewildered, that I know not what I say. Look on this appalling sight, the lifeless features of this poor murdered old woman, and say is it not enough to drive the brain to madness."

"True, most true, Omelia," coincided her friend, "and no one can feel more bitter resentment against the cowardly assassin than myself. But we must endeavour to collect ourselves, and to be firm, in this, the terrible hour of our affliction. It is getting late, and we must endeavour to find some place of rest and shelter."

"Oh, let me remain here and die," sighed Omelia, "all hope has forsaken me."

"Nay, 'tis madness to talk thus, while there is the least chance of relief," returned Abdal; "but first to consider how to dispose of the cold remains of the unfortunate Juballah; they must not—they shall not be left here to be devoured by the wild beasts or birds of prey."

"Gracious powers forbid!" exclaimed our heroine, emphatically and solemnly, "they are far, far too precious for that. But where—where, Abdal, can we find the spot or the means of placing them into their final resting-place? I feel myself aroused into fresh strength and energy, and am prepared to act in any way you may think proper to advise."

"Be calm, Omelia," said Abdal, "and listen patiently to me. You will remember that a short distance from here, we passed the borders of a clear silvery river, and—"

"Oh, yes, yes—pray proceed."

"To the waters of that river I would fain consign the remains of poor old Juballah, as the only fitting resting place, under the peculiar and difficult circumstances in which we are placed."

"Ah, fortunate thought, good Abdal; it is a solemn and sacred duty which we owe to the deceased, and it must be performed without delay; let us at once proceed, and—"

"The task will be too much for your strength to accomplish, Omelia," interrupted Abdal, "and you had better not attempt to accompany me. Remain here, where no harm, I trust, will beset you, and endeavour to rest yourself. I will quickly return—"

"Remain here," repeated Omelia, impatiently, and seeming inspired with sudden energy and determination, "remain here,

and not pay the last respects to her to whom I am under such an incalculable debt of gratitude? Never, never, I should hate and despise myself if I thought I could entertain such a disgraceful idea for an instant."

"Be it so," said Abdal, seeing that she was determined, and that it would only be a waste of time to attempt to dissuade her, "and may providence give you strength to support such extraordinary exertion. Come, we must no longer delay. I think I can retrace my footsteps without much difficulty to the river, but you must keep close to me, for in the darkness which prevails we might lose sight of each other."

With these words, he raised the cold remains of the unfortunate Juballah in his arms, and followed closely by the agonised Omelia, he retraced his steps as quick as he could towards the river of which he had spoken, and which was only a short distance from the fatal spot where the poor old woman had met her awful and untimely death.

As if to favour him in his solemn and sacred purpose, the moon suddenly shone between the branches of the trees, and lighted him and Omelia on the way, and in the course of a few minutes more they arrived on the banks of the river, upon whose waters at that time the moon beams were shining clearly.

Abdal deposited the cold remains of his sacred burthen on the green grass near the water's edge, amid the convulsive sobs of poor Omelia, and then commenced immediately the last solemn and impressive ceremony.

It lasted but a few minutes, but on the minds of those who might have beheld it, and who were strangers to the customs of the country, it could scarcely fail to have the most powerful effect, so truly solemn was it in all its particular bearings.

Omelia knelt by the side of the corpse, holding both hands of the same in hers, and muttering strange unintelligible sounds, swaying her body to and fro, as if in the most violent convulsive agony; but Abdal stood erect, his eyes raised towards the moon, and his hands crossed upon his breast, and not a single word escaped his lips.

Suddenly, however, at a signal from Abdal, there arose between him and Omelia a strange wailing dismal sound, which it would be almost impossible to describe, they putting their bodies during the time into curious contortions.

This lasted, however, only for two or three minutes, when the countenances of the mourners suddenly became animated, as if inspired by some holy spirit, and they both burst forth in a solemn prayer for the dead. in the Hindoo language; they then kissed the forehead and lips of the deceased, Omelia continuing on her knees; Abdal raised the corpse in his arms as tenderly and affectionately as if it had been that of his own parent, there was one more wailing cry, and Abdal gently suffered the corpse of poor old Juballah to glide into the river, the waters seeming to part to receive it, and the moonlight to hallow it with its beams.

Slowly, silently, and solemnly they retraced their steps from the spot, Omelia leaning for support on the arm of Abdal, and soon regained the spot they had so recently quitted, but there the extraordinary exertions that the poor girl had undergone, completely overpowered her, and she trembled convulsively in every limb.

"I can no more," she sighed, in a faint voice; "thank the Great Spirit Who has given me power to perform my duty; bless you, Abdal, Omelia's earthly career is at an end—darkness closes around me—let me here remain to die, to die hap—"

The finish of the sentence died away upon her lips, and she sunk totally powerless and insensible in the arms of the distracted Abdal!

CHAPTER CXCI.

UNPARALLELED TRIALS.—THE NOBLE HEART.

Who is there, so destitute of all the feelings of common humanity, who could sympathise with the noble-minded Abdal in his present desperate and apparently entirely hopeless situation?

For a few minutes, with the inanimate form of Omelia in his arms, so ill able to support it, he stood transfixed as a statue, and apparently unconscious of anything. A more ghastly or deplorable an object could not readily be imagined. His bloodshot eyes glared upon vacancy, and he had more the ghastly look of a corpse, than anything else the imagination could possibly conceive.

The darkness gathered more thickly around—there was scarcely a ray of light to be seen in that wild and fearful spot, horror of the most marked and awful description seemed to be its principal characteristic, and to breathe of despair to the poor hapless wretch who should be entangled in it.

And there the tortured imagination might picture to itself the wild and threatening howlings of savage beasts, and anticipate every moment an awful fate, which it would be impossible to avoid, and stand paralysed with agony and uncontrollable despair.

And in the midst of a frightful scene like this, with horrors accumulating every instant around him, the wretched Abdal, worn with fatigue, and sinking for the want of food and water, still stood transfixed as a statue, with the inanimate form of the apparently dying Omelia supported in his arms, as though providence had by some extraordinary miracle allowed him to retain his hold of his senseless burthen, even when human nature was completely exhausted.

But suddenly he started from this deplorable state as if awaking from some frightful dream, the effects of which he now severely felt.

The perspiration stood upon his quivering temples, his eyes glared wildly around, and he trembled convulsively in every limb. He was compelled to place the form of Omelia on the ground for a minute or two, until he could recover himself, and he then panted for breath, so great and unusual had been the exertions he had undergone.

He gazed around with despairing looks and nothing could possibly be more dreary, and even frightful than the scene before him now enveloped in complete darkness.

Even the courageous heart of Abdal seemed to sink within him as he gazed upon it, and, under all the melancholy circumstances, he could not but abandon himself to despair.

"Oh, how can I act in this terrible emergency?" he exclaimed in a melancholy voice, and beating his breast; whither can I direct my footsteps through this impenetrable darkness, with my senseless burthen, where find a place of rest and shelter for myself and the unfortunate Omelia? The thought distracts my brain, and I am so bewildered that I know not what to do."

He seated himself on the ground for a few minutes, and reflected what to do, but the more he did so, the farther he became lost in confusion and perplexity.

One thing, however, he now remembered which he had before forgotten, namely, the reviving cordial of the late Juballah, which he had taken care to secure. He took some himself, and felt the immediate benefit of it, he then administered some to Omelia, but was surprised to find that it now had not the least effect upon her.

He became alarmed, for it now appeared too certain that Omelia was much more seriously ill than he had at first imagined.

"Alas," he ejaculated, in a voice of intense anguish, "should she die—meet with her fate in this awful manner. Dreadful idea, I shudder as it occurs to me."

The thought seemed to inspire him with fresh energy and determination—he started to his feet, and once more raising the inanimate form of Omelia in his arms, he resolutely penetrated his way through the dreary mazes of the forest.

At any time, and even under the most favourable circumstances, this would have been one of the most difficulty tasks imaginable, for the forest was so entangled, the spreading branches of the trees so closely entwined, with here and there the jungle growing, that it was completely impassable.

But for any one to attempt it on such a fearful night as the one on which Abdal and Omelia were exposed to its horrors, when there was not the least ray of light to be seen, seemed little short of madness.

Abdal, however, with a courage and determination that was truly astonishing, continued on his way, suffering no impediment to obstruct him, and carefully guarding the form and features of Omelia from any injuries they might otherwise have received from the branches of the trees.

There was but one idea which seemed to urge him resolutely on, and to set every difficulty and danger at defiance, and that was the life of Omelia, which was placed in so critical a situation.

Difficulties seemed to accumulate the farther the unfortunate Abdal proceeded, but he struggled with them manfully, and never once suffered a murmur of complaint to escape his lips; and his resolution even appeared to increase with every fresh danger that beset him.

In this manner some time necessarily elapsed, and Omelia still gave no signs of returning life, though Abdal felt her heart throb, and knew, therefore, that there was still hope, and this further encouraged him.

He paused for a minute or two to take breath, and to rest himself, and he again administered some of the cordial to Omelia without the least effect.

He renewed his perilous and dreary journey with renewed courage, and at length to his utter astonishment and delight, he suddenly burst from the darkness of the dreariest midnight into comparative daylight, and the obstacles that had before presented themselves had entirely disappeared.

The change was so sudden and so totally unexpected, that Abdal could scarcely believe the evidence of his eyes, and stared about him with amazement.

It was a fine open country, in some places completely romantic, with rich tracts of land, lofty hills, clothed with continual verdure, and the whole lighted by a bright moon, which added to the beauties of the cheerful scene.

Abdal gently laid the form of Omelia on a grassy mound of earth, and sinking on his knees, he fervently returned his thanks to the Deity he worshipped for this miraculous deliverence from the horrors and dangers by which he had so recently been surrounded, and from which there seemed to be no probability of escaping.

Again he arose, and raising Omelia in his arms, proceeded in a direct line before him,

for he could almost imagine that he beheld the outlines of a building in the distance.

The farther he advanced, the more he was convinced that he was not mistaken, for the building became more distinctly revealed to view, standing as it did, on elevated ground.

His most sanguine hopes were revived, and he proceeded as quickly and as freely as if he had actually suffered no fatigue at all.

A few minutes more brought him to it, when he discovered it was the remains of a temple, and evidently in some parts as perfect as the first day it had been erected, so nobly had it withstood the ravages of time and decay.

Nothing, as the reader may expect, could be more welcome to the sight of Abdal under the peculiar circumstances especially, than the sacred building, and, without delaying a moment, he bore the form of Omelia up the elevation on which it stood, and entered the temple with a degree of confidence which he had not experienced for some time before.

The hopes he had formed on beholding the temple, were not destined to be disappointed, and he felt more than satisfied. The part of the building in which he now stood, was all but perfect, and the roof totally unimpaired, so that there were every means of shelter, and that terrible anxiety was thus removed from his mind, and most grateful he was for it.

He placed Omelia in a convenient spot, where she could probably snatch a few hours' repose, and he then again tried the late Juballah's reviving remedy, and this time with the desired effect. Omelia immediately gave signs of returning life after her long insensibility, and opening her eyes, she gazed with the most bewildered astonishment around her, so extraordinary was the change of scene which had taken place during the time that she had been in a state of insensibility.

She could scarcely persuade herself that she was not under the influence of some flattering and delusive dream; but perceiving the faithful Abdal standing near her, and anxiously watching her, in a voice of the greatest curiosity, she said—

"Oh, my kind friend, Abdal, tell me, I pray you, how is this? By what strange and miraculous means have you managed to escape from the horrors to which we were so fearfully exposed, and what place is this?"

"Some Almighty power surely must have done it, Omelia," replied Abdal, "and enabled me to surmount the difficulties by which I was surrounded. This place is the ruins of an old temple, and here we may find rest and shelter for the night, secure from all danger. There is a fine open country before us, and we shall probably soon light upon some village in the morning where we can obtain all that we require. It is a fortunate thing that we happen to possess the means of procuring all we want."

"I am completely overwhelmed with astonishment and gratitude," said our heroine, still looking round incredulously, while tears which she could not, and did not attempt to restrain, started to her eyes, "how wonderful and unlooked for is the change—I can hardly believe the evidence of my senses. It is evident that there is some Almighty power watching over us, and I will not, cannot despair of the future. But oh, Abdal, how terrible must have been the dangers you have had to encounter in arriving here. How can I sufficiently praise your manly fortitude, courage, and perseverence? Such noble deeds are beyond all praise."

"I own," replied Abdal, modestly "that the task I had to perform was a most frightfully difficult one, but I have been able to accomplish it, and I am more than satisfied. But pray let us not delay time in conversation, here you may obtain a few hour's repose; I will sleep near the entrance, so that I may be able to give the earliest alarm should the least danger threaten, which I trust it will not."

Omelia again thanked him for his unceasing kindness and attention, and having bade each other good night, they sought that repose of which they both stood so much in need.

CHAPTER CXCII.

LIEUTENANT STANLEY AND CLARA.

We are about to record a series of the most startling, pathetic, and romantic events that have probably yet appeared in our tale —events in which the fates, the happiness, nay, the very lives of several individuals are involved, and which must rivet the attention of the reader.

In order to proceed to do this in a regular way, we must once more return to Lieutenant Stanley, whom we left after his perilous adventure on the field of battle, from which he was so fortunately rescued by his friend Captain Morley.

The battle over, and attended, as has been shown by the most favourable results, the gallant troops were allowed a short rest, which was a great relief, after the harrassing life they had for some time led.

Captain Morley and his melancholy young friend had now the opportunity of enjoying each other's society, and the latter was lavish in his thanks for the great service which Captain Morley had rendered him, but the captain checked him, and expressed his great satisfaction at having arrived at the critical time, when his life must otherwise have been sacrificed by his powerful adversary.

Stanley sighed, and otherwise exhibited much uneasiness and agitation of manner.

"Alas," he ejaculated, after a brief pause, "and why should I congratulate myself on my escape from death when life is no longer valuable or endurable to me?"

"Nay, say not so, Stanley, you have no cause for such dismal thoughts," said Captain Morley.

"No cause," repeated Stanley, with a look of astonishment and impatience, "no cause. Good God, Captain Morley, surely you cannot be serious. Oh, surely I have more than ample cause in the loss of my adored Omelia, and the terrible uncertainty of the fate which has befallen her."

"Still cherish hope—still cherish hope."

"Oh, how idle is it to talk thus—my heart sickens at the fallacious thought, and to me the words sound only as a bitter mockery. She could never find fortitude to support the dreadful trial, many, however, as it has been her lot to undergo, and doubtless long ere this, driven by despair, she has rushed recklessly, wantonly rushed upon death. Indeed, indeed I cannot think otherwise.'

"And I am firm in hope," said the captain.

"And what reason have you to be so?" hastily demanded the wretched Stanley.

"Oh, I have many," replied Captain Morley, trying all he could in some measure to raise the spirits of his distressed friend; "we all know the undaunted, firm, and heroic character of Omelia, so often displayed under the most terrible and desperate circumstances, and it is not likely that they will fail her now."

"But she never was placed in a situation of such imminent danger and utter helplessness before," said Stanley, "in the power of such an inhuman miscreant as this terrible Yusef, her fate is too horribly certain, and she cannot resist it."

"Fear not, providence will interpose to save her," returned the captain, "and she will escape."

"Oh, it would be sheer madness to entertain such a preposterous thought," said Stanley, "and pardon me, but I have not patience to listen to you."

"You suffer yourself to get too much excited," observed Captain Morley, "but, at any rate, let us drop the melancholy subject for the present."

Stanley reluctantly complied, but although they talked upon different topics, he scarcely knew what was said on either side, for his whole thoughts and anxieties were still fixed upon his beloved Omelia, about whose fate he still continued to entertain the most dismal forebodings. Captain Morley, and two or three brother officers who dropped in, tried all they could to cheer him, but with little or no success, and he took the earliest opportunity of retiring, where he could indulge his melancholy thoughts alone and without interruption.

There were yet no orders for the troops to march, since the last sanguinary engagement as described in a previous chapter, but in a few days they were taken by surprise by the sudden arrival of troops from Cawnpore, and it then appeared evident that the Commander-in-Chief was concentrating his forces for some great enterprise.

On the same day Stanley and Captain Morley were standing on an eminence commanding a most magnificent and romantic prospect, engaged in conversation, and admiring the grandeur of nature's works, as they appeared at that moment.

The bright sun was at its height, and the heat was excessive, but Stanley and the captain had become almost inured to the climate, besides, there was a refreshing breeze wafted occasionally from a fine grove of trees that grew close by where they were standing.

It was indeed a delightful scene, and one well calculated to calm the troubled feelings of those who were assailed by grief, and even Stanley could not help feeling its influence.

"It is a noble prospect," he observed enthusiastically, "certainly not to be surpassed, if equalled, by any other in the world. How sad is the thought that a land so rich in all the bounteous gifts of nature, should be the scene of all the deadly horrors of war."

"True," replied Captain Morley, "but the blood-thirsty miscreants, the wholesale butchers of innocent and helpless women and children, have nearly all met with their deserts; they have learnt the terrible force of British soldiers, especially when avenging the monstrous atrocities so wantonly committed by them. I trust that this rebellion will shortly be entirely suppressed."

"I wish I could share in your opinion, captain," remarked Stanley, "but while those two monsters Nena Sahib and Tantia Topee still remain at large, I cannot help thinking that there will be constant work for our troops to do."

"It certainly may be so," returned Captain Morley, "but I hope and trust that those unequalled monsters will shortly be captured, Ah! whence came that piteous cry?"

"A cry?" repeated Stanley, with a look of surprise and agitation.

"Yes," said the captain, "I imagined, nay, I am all but certain that I heard the cry of a female as if in distress."

"Oh, you must have been mistaken," replied Stanley, still trembling with unaccountable emotion."

"No, I am positive," said the captain; "hark, there it is again; surely you must have heard that, Stanley."

"Oh, yes," replied Stanley, in a voice, and with a look of extreme agitation; "I did indeed hear it: it came from yonder grove of trees—what can it mean?"

"Some unfortunate female may require our assistance," said the captain, whose interest and curiosity were greatly excited; "let us hasten to the spot from whence the sound proceeded."

"Oh, should it, by some miraculous interposition of providence, be—"

"Who?" demanded the captain, hastily.

"Omelia," faltered out Stanley, and his lips quivered, and his limbs trembled as he did so.

"Beware," hastily cautioned Captain Morley; "flatter not youself with delusive hopes which can only end in disappointment. Let us proceed without delay. Ah, behold.'"

At that moment there emerged wildly from the grove of trees, the figure of a young English woman, at least as well as could be distinguished at the distance, and when she beheld them, she seemed to hasten more quickly towards them.

They were both surprised and agitated, Stanley particularly so; for the form of the young girl seemed remarkably familiar to him.

Before he could collect his thoughts, she rushed to the spot, passing the captain unheeded, and with an exclamation such as it would be impossible almost to describe, she sunk convulsively at the feet of Stanley and gazed up piteously in his face.

It was Clara.

CHAPTER CXCIII.

AN AFFECTING SCENE.

By what means the unfortunate Clara had contrived to elude the vigilance of her friends and to reach the presence of Stanley, we cannot undertake to say, but the scene which followed almost baffles description.

Captain Morley stared with astonishment, of course not being able to understand the meaning of it, though his curiosity was excited to the utmost degree.

But how great was the astonishment of Stanley, at this unexpected appearance, and the strange looks which the poor girl fixed upon him, as she knelt before him, with clasped hands, and convulsive sobs heaving her fair bosom.

"Clara!" he ejaculated, in an agitated voice.

"Ah, you do recognise the wretched wanderer, and I again hear the loved tones of your voice," she replied with the most indescribable emotion, "dear Stanley!"

Stanley started, and gazed at the fair sufferer in perfect bewilderment, and Captain Morley, although his curiosity was excited to the utmost pitch, could not think of obtruding himself upon so delicate a scene. retired to a short distance off but awaited with impatience the result of this extraordinary adventure.

For some moments after the last observations of Clara, Stanley was so completely taken by surprise that he was unable to utter a word, but at length he said feelingly, and raising her from her knees—

"Clara, my poor girl, how is it I see you thus alone, a wanderer."

"To endeavour to discover you," she replied in a voice half stifled by convulsive emotions,—"to have the happiness of once more beholding you, and listening to the tones of your voice, dear Stanley."

"Dear Stanley!" repeated the latter, with a look of the utmost surprise and confusion, "what mean those words, Clara? Has long suffering impaired your reason?"

"Yes," she replied, while deep blushes suffused her cheeks; "but not on that subject. The long hidden secret must at length out; Stanley, dear Stanley, the unknown girl, loves you!"

She sank in his arms as she spoke in a violent paroxysm of emotion, and the agitation and excitement of Stanley may be better imagined than described.

How deeply did he sympathise with the unfortunate girl; but at the same time he was completely thunderstruck at the extraordinary and startling confession; he never having encouraged such a passion by a look or a word, or ever imagined for a moment that it existed.

And what answer could he now return to her, how act in the delicate situation in which he was placed?—He was quite bewildered, and at a loss what to do.

At length Clara having partially recovered from her first burst of emotion, and feeling somewhat relieved now that her torturing secret was at last revealed, though she knew too well that there was no hope for her, raised her head from the shoulder of Stanley, where it had rested; her eyes streaming with tears, her cheeks colourless, her bosom heaving with emotion, and yet unable to say a word.

It was no use, however, Stanley thought, to remain thus, and he was fearful that some of his brother officers might wander near the spot, and behold him in so questionable a situation. He therefore made a powerful effort to arouse himself, and in a voice in which pity and surprise were blended, he said—

"Unfortunate Clara, how I am startled by the confession you have made; and how sincerely do I feel for your painful situation. Oh, how have you suffered this fatal passion to take root in your bosom?"

"It has been growing there for years," replied Clara, "from the first moment I beheld you, when a poor friendless gipsy girl, the hapless victim of the most brutal wretches. From that moment you were never absent from my thoughts, your form and features were ever present in my imagination. It was presumption, but I could not stifle the passion, and it must continue to exist while life remains."

"Poor girl, poor girl," said Stanley, tenderly, and with the deepest sympathy, "your words pain me."

"Pain you, Stanley," she hastily replied, her looks told the sincerity of what she uttered;—"pain you, oh, not for the world would I cause your breast one single pang; sooner, far sooner would I perish at your feet, although I know full well you love another."

"Love another," said Stanley, with a look of astonishment and incredulity.

"Yes," replied Clara in a melancholy voice, and an expression of sorrow and regret passing over her pale but handsome features—"the Indian girl, Omelia."

Stanley started

"Ah," he exclaimed, "how know you this?"

"It is the truth, you cannot deny it."

"I will not seek to do so—I love her to distraction."

Clara groaned.

"Oh, how do I envy the happiness of that fortunate girl," she at length ejaculated, a slight expression of jealousy and malice which she could not control, passing over her features, and which Stanley noticed with a sensation of dread and dismal foreboding.

"Happy, Clara," he sighed, "ah, no, that is impossible, even if she still lives, snatched from me as she was, under such dreadful circumstances, that it makes me shudder to think of it."

"But, if she died," said Clara; she would still be happy in knowing she possessed your love, dear Stanley, for such I must persist in calling you; while I, friendless, and unknown, are looked upon with scorn. Oh, could I hear but one word of affection from your lips, I could be content to die in your arms, to breathe my last sigh on your loved bosom."

Stanley was much moved, and every moment became more bewildered.

"Poor Clara," he said, "again I tell you, how deeply I sympathise with you; but this

scene is torturing to us both, and can end in no favourable result, and the sooner it is brought to an end the better. Come, my poor girl, allow me to conduct you to your friends.'

"Friends—friends!" exclaimed the poor girl, wildly, and fixing upon him a look which seemed as if it would penetrate his very soul; "I have no friends: I am a wretched, unknown wanderer."

"No friends?" repeated Stanley, with a look of surprise and incredulity: "where then are those excellent benefactors, Mr. and Mrs. Hastings, to whom you are so largely indebted, and who would do anything to contribute to your happiness?"

Clara burst into a violent flood of tears, and wrung her hands, but could return no immediate answer, and Stanley awaited im-

patiently, and in a state of the most melancholy foreboding.

"Alas, alas!" Clara sighed, when she again found the power of speech, "they were the first that fell in the frightful slaughter at Cawnpore."

Stanley seemed horrorstruck, and could scarcely believe the evidence of his senses.

"Unfortunate relations," he ejaculated, in a voice of the deepest emotion, and his manly bosom swelling with disgust and indignation, "to meet with such a fearful and untimely fate; may heaven's most terrible curses pursue the perpetrators of it. But you were with your murdered benefactors, Clara?"

"Oh, yes, yes," replied the latter, with another burst of grief.

"And how did you then manage to

escape, my poor Clara, eagerly interrogated Stanley.

"I know not," answered Clara; "it must have been by a complete miracle; but why did providence preserve my wretched existence? oh, why was I not allowed to perish with them?"

"Oh, talk not thus, Clara," remonstrated Stanley; "but surely you have not been a wretched wanderer ever since that frightful occurrence"

"Till within a fortnight I have, in the wild hope of discovering you, dear Stanley," she replied; "when arriving at Cawnpore I sunk exhausted at the door of those who have since protected me, and behaved to me with every kindness, and brought me hither this day."

"Their names—their names?" eagerly asked Stanley.

"Colonel Bridport, and his two amiable daughters," replied Clara.

"Ah!" ejaculated Stanley, in a voice of surprise and satisfaction, "my old and esteemed friend, whom I have not encountered for some time. You could not possibly have fallen into better hands, Clara, and I warmly and sincerely congratulate you upon it. But you have deceived them, I fear, and seized some favourable opportunity of coming clandestinely hither, leaving them in a state of fear and suspense as to what has become of you. Oh, it was wrong—very wrong."

"Reproach me not, Stanley," said Clara, with a piteous look of supplication; "I heard that you were still in existence, and could not resist the temptation to endeavour to discover you."

"Strange infatuated girl," said Stanley, "it must be madness that thus urges you on in your wild and hopeless career. Oh, why not persevere, and endeavour to banish the fatal feeling from your breast?"

"How easy it is thus coolly to advise," returned Clara, impatiently, but to a poor unfortunate wretched being like me, how difficult the task to follow it. The same feelings must remain within my breast, till my poor broken heart shall cease to beat."

Stanley remained silent for some minutes, much moved by the melancholy observations of the unfortunate Clara, but quite bewildered under the peculiar, painful, and delicate circumstances, what to do.

"It is folly," he said, at last, "and cannot possibly do otherwise than have the most injurious effects. Oh, banish this strange and hopeless passion ere it be too late. You shall ever have my warmest esteem, assistance, and protection. More it is not in my power to promise you; and I would not trifle with your feelings, by holding out any false hopes to you. Suffer me then to conduct you to your excellent friends.

"Oh, I cannot, dare not leave you, dear Stanley," she said, with a burst of emotion, and clinging convulsively to him.

Stanley felt more confused and agitated than ever, though he could not attempt to disengage her from his arms, so strange and unaccountable was the feeling that came over him.

"You tire my patience, Clara," he said, "heaven forbid that I should say anything that might appear harsh to you, or that was calculated to wound your feelings, but I feel the delicacy of my situation, that this torturing scene has been carried too far, and I must put an end to it."

Poor Clara slowly withdrew herself from Stanley's arms, and, as she did so, she fixed upon him a look that it would be almost impossible for him ever to forget.

She stood in this way for a minute or two, transfixed as a statue, while every limb at the same time was convulsed with powerful emotion, and a more perfect picture of anguish and despair could not easily be imagined.

Stanley was shocked to behold her, and almost repenting what he had last said, he advanced towards her with the idea of endeavouring to impart words of consolation to her, but the poor girl shrunk from him with an apparent feeling of dread, gazed at him for a minute or two in silence, and with a mingled look of regret, reproach, and sorrow, then pressed her delicate hands upon her pale forehead, and burst into a violent paroxysm of grief, which seemed to be quite overwhelming, and which was truly piteous and heart-rending to witness.

The noble-hearted Stanley was affected in the highest degree, and gently encircling her slender waist with his arm, he whispered to her, in the most tender accents, words of consolation.

But she heard him not, and the ebulition of her grief continued unabated, and had it not been for the support of Stanley's arm, she must have sunk powerless to the earth.

And this affecting scene continued for several minutes.

———

CHAPTER CXCIV.

THE SECRET REVEALED.—THE ORIGIN OF CLARA DISCOVERED.—STARTLING APPEARANCE.

"No, no," at length said the unfortunate Clara, with a look of such deep sorrow and regret, such intense agony of feeling, that those who had once beheld it, it would be almost impossible for them to forget; "this poor unknown being must be presumptuous to encourage her fatal passion, when she of the land of crime and bloodshed, Omelia, the Indian girl, holds possession of your heart, Stanley. She who loved you in the gipsy tent—she who has never ceased to love you, to adore you, and has braved every danger to behold you, is worthy only of your scorn, nay, perhaps your hatred."•

"Clara," replied Stanley, deeply affected by her observations, but with a look of gentle remonstrance, "how much you wrong me by these surmises. Heaven knows how sincerely I esteem you and sympathise with your misfortunes, and that I would gladly do anything to serve you, or that might contribute to your peace of mind. But I pray you be calm a few minutes and listen patiently to me, for I have some questions to put, and some observations to make to you, on which your future welfare in life, your happiness may depend."

"My happiness?" she repeated mournfully.

"Yes," replied Stanley, " but listen. Have you never by any means discovered your surname ?"

"No," answered Clara, carelessly, "and I have long since cared to trouble myself upon the subject, for of what consequence is it to me?"

"Oh, yes, it is of every consequence, Clara," returned Stanley.

"And why do you seem to take so great an interest on the subject Stanley?" interrogated Clara.

"Because I have particular reasons for doing so," answered Stanley; "but listen attentively, for that I am about to relate and explain, is of the greatest importance, and may lead to the most wonderful and fortunate discoveries."

Clara was indeed much struck by the seriousness of Stanley's observations, and she listened to him attentively and with anxious curiosity as he proceeded.

"Your gipsy story, Clara," he remarked, "has often occupied my thoughts, and I have blamed myself for not having questioned you more minutely upon the subject. You will naturally ask, why this anxiety on my part? Listen, and I will tell you.

"My father had a younger brother, good and virtuous, but who was doomed to be the victim of many misfortunes sufficient to bear him down, but he bore with them manfully, his whole hope and joy being centred in his lovely and amiable wife, and only child, a beauteous and innocent girl."

"Proceed, proceed," said Clara, breathlessly, and her excitement now worked up to the highest pitch.

"In the family of my uncle," continued Stanley, "was a man who for years had been in the service of my late father, and had obtained his confidence. He was a man of uncouth aspect, and abrupt and forbidding manners, and my uncle and his wife had always looked upon him with an eye of suspicion, though they still retained him in their service out of respect to my late father, though he was then living, and for many years after, though he had transferred the services of Roland to my uncle, at his own request."

"My interest and anxiety increases," said Clara, in a tremulous voice, and with a look of the greatest curiosity and mental emotion, "oh, what mean these strange thoughts that rush upon my bewildered brain? Keep me not in suspense, I implore you, dear Stanley, for such I must still call you."

"Roland," resumed Stanley, "was at length detected in a daring act of robbery in my uncle's house, which he had no doubt carried on to a great extent for some time. My uncle naturally reproached him bitterly for his base ingratitude, but declining to prosecute him, as he so richly deserved to be, he immediately dismissed him from his service.

"The villain left, swearing the most deadly and diabolical vengeance, which he was not long before he most terribly carried into execution.

"The beauteous innocent child, the chief joy and comfort of its doting parents, was sent out one lovely summer's day in the charge of its nurse, no fear or suspicion haunting my uncle and his lady's mind. An hour afterwards she returned distracted, raving wildly, and wringing her hands, but without the child.

"You may judge of the agonised feelings of my uncle and his wife; they were completely distracted, but such was the state of the wretched Alice, that it was some time ere they could obtain any reasonable reply to the anxious questions they put to her, or elicit the least word in explanation of the terrible, torturing, and mysterious subject.

"But oh, how frightful was the shock that awaited them, when Alice had sufficiently recovered from her paroxysm to explain. It was a marvel that its effect did not immediately deprive them of life.

"Walking near the woodlands, she was suddenly blindfolded by some persons from behind, and her arms held tight.

"She was so terrified that she could not utter a sound, but she heard the poor child cry loudly."

"The next minute she was released from the hold of the person behind; and when she removed the bandage from her eyes, there was no one near, the little one was gone, alas, from its wretched parents for ever."

"Good God !" exclaimed Clara, tears of sympathy gushing to her eyes, and her bosom swelling with the most powerful emotion, which it was impossible for her to control; "how terrible. I could scarcely have believed there could be such monsters in existence. Unhappy Mr. and Mrs. Stanley, ill fated beings, poor bereaved parents. But there is no proof that the cruel stealing of the poor child was the crime of the gipsies, Alice being blinded."

"True," coincided Stanley, "but there can be no doubt that monstrous act was that of the miscreant Roland, whom we knew to have joined the gipsies shortly after his dismissal from the service of my uncle."

"Alas," sighed Clara, "there is too much reason for so fatal and agonising a suspicion."

She pressed her hands upon her forehead, and seemed to be in the greatest agitation of mind, Stanley watching her anxiously and narrowly.

"And long is it since this dreadful event occurred?" she at length interrogated eagerly, and looking up.

Stanley hesitated for a minute or two and reflected.

"As near as I can recollect," he at last replied "it must be some fifteen or sixteen years ago, but certainly not longer."

"Strange coincidence," observed Clara, in an agitated voice, and her heart fluttering; "it was about that time, as near as possible, that I found myself a poor half naked little thing among the gipsies."

"Ah!" exclaimed Stanley, with a look of surprise and emotion; "I am lost in amazement and bewilderment."

"And could no clue ever be obtained as to what had become of the unfortunate child?" inquired Clara.

"None whatever," answered Stanley, "though you may rest assured no means were left untried to discover her, and to restore her to the arms of her distracted parents; large rewards were offered to those who might be able to furnish information. Many of the gipsy tribe were apprehended on suspicion, but all was unavailing, not the least clue could be obtained, and from that fatal day to this all has been involved in the most fearful and impenetrable mystery.

Clara again paused and reflected, with evident emotion, and Stanley seemed as agitated as herself.

"And the unfortunate parents?" at length anxiously demanded Clara.

"Oh, need I tell you," replied Stanley, "that the terrible blow was too much for them, and that they never recovered their irreparable loss? My poor aunt gradually sunk into a decline, and breathed her last in her fond husband's arms.

"But a few short months, and my uncle followed his faithful and affectionate partner to the silent grave."

Clara was deeply affected, sobs escaped her bosom, and strange sensations came over her which she never remembered to have experienced before, and she could not understand them or conquer them. She stood as one stupified, with her hands pressed upon her temples.

A thought seemed suddenly to flash upon her distracted brain, and turning hastily to the agitated Stanley—for he foreboded that some extraordinary discovery was on the eve of taking place—in a faltering voice, she demanded—

"And did the poor child, when it was stolen, bear nothing about it which might trace its origin?"

"Yes, if the wretches did not remove it when the poor little innocent fell into their hands."

"The nature of it?"

"A small silver locket, bearing its own and its mother's names."

"Gracious powers!" ejaculated Clara, in a faint voice, and sinking overpowered in his arms.

"What means this extraordinary emotion, Clara?" eagerly interrogated Stanley; "speak —speak!"

"Behold," she replied, breathlessly, thrusting her hand into her bosom, and producing the locket.

Stanley started when he beheld it, and trembled convulsively in every limb.

"Almighty powers!" he exclaimed, as he gazed at the locket, scarcely able to believe the evidence of his senses, "what do I behold? The very locket which was suspended from the unfortunate child's neck when it was stolen. See it bears the name of Clara."

"Yes," said Clara, "but that is unsatisfactory, there is no surname. The initials might have proved everything."

"There is another secret spring," said the agitated Stanley, "which doubtless you have overlooked; 'tis here."

He touched a spring close to the other as he thus spoke, while Clara looked on half stupefied, and in a state of the most indescribable anxiety.

She was not long kept in suspense: the spring immediately yielded, revealing an inner portion of the locket which contained the extreme miniature likeness of a lady, round which, in very small letters, was the name in full of "Clara Stanley!"

"Stanley became transfixed as a statue with astonishment, and for a moment or two could not speak a word, while poor Clara, whose brain was bewildered, stood vacantly gazing at him, and apparently totally unconscious of what was going on.

"Gracious powers!" at length exclaimed Stanley, as he continued to gaze on the miniature, and in a voice of the most indescribable emotion; my surmises and forebodings are verified. There can be no doubt upon the important—the all important subject. Dear Clara, it was nature's voice that guided your love towards me; *you are my long lost cousin !*"

A cry, such as no language could possibly describe, escaped the lips of poor Clara when she heard this, and rushing to the arms of the equally agitated Stanley, she immediately became insensible.

Hitherto Captain Morley had patiently stood in the background, and watched with curiosity the remarkable scene, but now his anxiety and amazement were worked up to such a pitch of excitement that he could not resist them, and hastening to where Stanley and Clara stood, apparently unconscious of all around them, and addressing the former, said—

"For heaven's sake, Stanley, what means this? Why do you hold with so much emotion and apparent affection this young woman in your embrace?"

"Aroused by his voice, Stanley looked up, and the expression of his features fully showed the extraordinary agitation and excitement of his feelings.

"Oh, Morley," he at last replied, "I have just made such a remarkable and astonishing discovery. This poor senseless girl whom I now hold in my arms, is no other than my long lost cousin, Clara Stanley."

"Your cousin!" repeated Captain Morley, with a look of the most unqualified astonishment, nay, almost incredulity; "is is possible? How was this extraordinary discovery made?"

"There is not time to explain here," replied Stanley, impatiently; "suffice it to say that the proof is unquestionable."

"You surprise me, Stanley," remarked the captain; "you have spoken to me before about your uncle having had a child stolen, probably by gipsies, but is it possible that after the lapse of so many years you should discover her in this distant land?"

"It is true," answered Stanley; "and I am completely lost in amazement and bewilderment."

"It is indeed most astounding," said Captain Morley; "but arouse yourself, Stanley, and let us conduct this poor girl to her friends Should any of our brother officers accidentally stroll hither, and behold us in our present delicate and questionable situation, we should not only draw upon ourselves their redicule, but their extreme censure and unqualified reprehension."

"True," replied Stanley, with an agitated and bewildered look, "but what can I do?"

At that moment, and before Captain Morley could make any reply, there arose near them a cry so frightful, so unearthly, so full of anguish, yet of deadly malice, so indescribable in its unnatural intensity, that it was quite sufficient to appal and paralise all who heard it.

Stanley raised his head, and looked fearfully towards the spot whence the alarming sound had proceeded, but what was his surprise and horror on beholding the distorted features and unnatural and revengeful eyes of Omelia glaring full upon him and the senseless being he held in his arms.

Had a thunderbolt at that moment struck the wretched Stanley he could not have felt more astounded and appalled, but Omelia never for a moment changed her looks or her attitude, in fact, they seemed to become more fearful and revengeful every instant, and the perspiration streamed down the cheeks of Stanley, his lips quivered, and he trembled convulsively in every limb.

Captain Morley also was greatly shocked and alarmed, for he dreaded from the truly frightful looks of Omelia, the scene which was too likely to follow, and which his unfortunate friend Stanley, he feared could never muster fortitude to combat.

Fate had indeed at length brought them to the very highest degree of misery, suffering and adversity.

CHAPTER CXCV.

THE FRENZY OF OMELIA.

Our heroine moved not, the expression of her features every instant became more unearthly, so that it was almost impossible to recognise them, so frightfully distorted were they, and she scarcely seemed at intervals to breath, though her bosom heaved and swelled convulsively with the intense power of her emotions.

There was a fearful and solemn pause of a few minutes ensued, which no one seemed disposed or to have the power to break.

It was indeed an awful interval.

Suddenly a deep sigh escaped the lips of the unfortunate Clara, and she opened her eyes, but they immediately encountering the appalling looks of Omelia, she uttered a cry of horror, and again became insensible.

A laugh from Omelia immediately followed, so wild, so supernatural, so fearful in every degree, that it re-echoed far and near, and made Stanley and Captain Morley absolutely tremble with terror.

It was some minutes ere they could recover themselves in the slightest degree, when the wretched Stanley, resigning his insensible burthen to the care of the almost equally agitated Captain Morley, with faltering steps, and feelings of agony and despair which it would be quite impossible to describe, he ventured to approach our heroine.

"Omelia," he tremulously ejaculated, in a voice scarcely audible.

But oh, the look the distracted girl fixed upon him the moment she caught the sound of his voice, was even more appalling and unearthly than ever, and she stretched forth her hand, in which she clasped a dagger, menacingly towards him.

"Monster!—deceiver!—traitor!—villain!" she exclaimed, with blood shot eyes, and in tones that were calculated to make a lasting impression upon him, "dare not to approach the wretched being you have so cruelly deceived, the poor, simple, confiding Indian girl, who could have worshipped you, believing you all truth and honour, lest this determined hand, guided by a deadly feeling of revenge which now circulates throughout my veins, stretch you a corpse at my feet. Go bask in the lewd caresses of yon shameless wanton, and bear with you the bitter curses of her whose hopes you have destroyed for ever!"

The emphasis and fearful meaning with which the wretched and distracted girl uttered these words, was truly awful to listen to, and Stanley stood transfixed with terror, and totally at a loss how to act.

"Oh, Omelia," he at length found strength to utter, in a voice, and with a look that showed the dreadful mental suffering he was enduring, "I implore you to forbear, and to listen to the voice of reason. Oh, how fearfully have you wronged me, and your poor suffering, innocent girl by the terrible aspersions you have so undeservedly cast upon us. This is my long lost cousin, stolen in her childhood, and only this hour miraculously restored to me."

Omelia burst into a loud and scornful laugh, which completely startled and terrified her listeners, and her features became still more frightfully distorted than before.

"Your cousin," she repeated, with a sneer, "liar! shameless, heartless villain, I am no longer to be deceived. My eyes are now opened, and oh, how dreadful is the truth that is revealed to them. How dark and dreary is the prospect that once was all sunshine and hope. Cruel, cruel, thus to trifle with a poor girl's feelings, and destroy her happiness for ever. And was it for this that I devoted all my thoughts—my woman's fondest affections to you? Is it for this that I have braved every danger, scorned every suffering, privation, and vicissitude to again behold you, to revel in the sunshine of your smiles, and listen to those oft repeated vows of affection which I thought were so sincere? Cruel—cruel!"

The wretched suffering girl covered her face with her hands as she uttered these mournful lamentations, and sobbed as though her heart would break.

Stanley stood by in a dreadful state of excitement, and shuddered at the thoughts of the result this fearful and unexpected recontre was likely to produce, maddened as the wretched Omelia evidently was, and deaf to all the expostulations of reason.

Captain Morley stood transfixed as a statue, and appalled at what he saw and heard, supporting the still insensible form of Clara in his arms.

At length, however, the distracted Stanley partly aroused himself, and approaching tremblingly the spot, he ventured to mention her name.

Had some savage monster at that moment crossed her path, Omelia could not have started with greater horror and disgust; and the look she fixed upon him, as she exclaimed in a voice truly fearful, was perfectly hideous, and could never be forgotten—

"Back, back!—traitor, deceiver, miscreant!—back, I say, there is contagion—contamination in your very presence; from this moment I tear you from my heart, blot you from my memory, hate, loathe, scorn, and curse you, with my heaviest curses. May all the horrors of madness and despair pursue you; may your future course through life be one of terrible sorrow and vicissitude; may you never know peace, but wander madly over the face of the earth, hated and accursed of all mankind. But keep your abandoned mistress from my path, or her heart's blood will have to pay for it!"

Such were the terrible maledictions of Omelia, and the voice in which she uttered them, and the looks with which she accompanied them, must completely defy description.

The brain of the wretched Stanley was bewildered, and again his limbs trembled with convulsive emotion, and could scarcely support him.

At last, with a desperate effort, and in a hoarse voice, he cried—

"Omelia!—ever dear Omelia!"

A wild, scornful, and unnatural laugh was the only reply, and Omelia rushed from the spot with the speed of lightning, and the air of a maniac.

She paused on reaching the eminence where Stanley and Captain Morley had lately stood, and which was but a short distance off, and turning suddenly round she fixed upon Stanley a look, if possible, more full of loathing and deadly malice than before; a wild, indescribable laugh, which seemed to re echo far and near, followed, and turning away the wretched Omelia bounded with wonderful rapidity from the spot, and was soon lost in the distance.

Stanley and Captain Morley stood and

gazed at each other for a few minutes in stupefied amazement and consternation, and could scarcely persuade themselves that they had not both been under the influence of some frightful dream; for the event appeared too dreadful and too startling to be real.

"Gracious powers!" the agitated Stanley at length found strength to utter, "what a terrible, torturing, and unexpected event is this, Morley, and what will be the result of it? I shudder to think, my brain is distracted; I shall go mad."

"It is indeed a fearful adventure," replied Captain Morley, "and I know not what to advise, what to say upon the agonising and bewildering subject. How strange, how unfortunate that Omelia should appear at such a critical, such a painful moment; it seemed as if the fates had conspired to bring about such a dreadful result. How perfectly hideous were her looks. I shall never forget them, and although I am a soldier, and could never, I trust, be accused of want of courage, I must confess the terrible and irresistible effect which this startling adventure has had upon me. Poor Omelia, I fear that she will never more be able to get rid of the fatal impression which has got possession of her maddened brain, and that her doom, her mournful doom is inevitably sealed."

"Alas," groaned Stanley, beating his breast, in the agony of his feelings, "oh, that this should have happened."

"It is most unfortunate, most lamentable. And this poor girl. Oh, what will become of her under such an accumulation of dreadful misfortunes, sufficient to try the stoutest constitution? Ah, see, she revives."

The unfortunate Clara did so, and looking up and beholding herself supported in the arms of Captain Morley, she turned ghastly pale, thinking that Stanley had abandoned her, and she almost relapsed into her former state of insensibility.

"Stanley—dear Stanley," she at length sighed, "oh, where are you?"

"Here, dear Clara—cousin," he replied, in a voice of the deepest emotion, and drawing near her, with looks of sympathy and affection.

At the sound of his voice, she fixed upon him a mingled look of joy and sorrow, uttered a faint cry of emotion, and withdrawing herself from Captain Morley's arms, she threw herself on the distracted Stanley's heaving bosom, and looked up so piteously in his face, that it was enough to move even the most insensible heart to compassion.

The sun was now slowly declining behind the western mountains, and everything began to give token of the time that had elapsed.

Stanley and Captain Morley could not but feel uneasy, for their long absence must appear strange and unaccountable, and might get them into some difficulty which they were not very well prepared to encounter in the present agitated state of their minds.

"Stanley," said Clara, in a terribly earnest voice, and looking up solemnly and searchingly in his face, "whose were those eyes of deadly malice which glared upon me and still seem present to my sight? They were her's were they not?—Omelia's."

The question rather startled Stanley, but there was no evading it, in fact, it would have been entirely useless to attempt to do so, he therefore said—

"Yes, Clara, it was indeed Omelia that you saw, my own loved, but I fear now to me lost for ever. Some cruel accident brought her to the spot at the moment I held you to my bosom, and she was excited to frightful feelings of rage and jealousy, believing me faithless to her. She has left with the same impression on her disordered mind; she has denounced me as a villain, a monster of the deepest dye, and has breathed her curses on my head. Heaven alone knows what will be the result of all this, but I am distracted."

"Oh, never, never," said Clara with a shudder of horror, "can I forget those awful looks she fixed upon me; there was nothing earthly or natural about them."

Stanley was about to make some reply, when Captain Morley stepped up to him, and drew his attention to Colonel Bridport, who, with his servant, was riding towards the spot.

"This is most fortunate," said Stanley, "for our long absence will create the greatest surprise and censure."

The unfortunate Clara cast a hasty glance towards her approaching friend and benefactor, Colonel Bridport; then throwing her fair arms affectionately round his neck, and looking up piteously in his face, in the most melancholy accents, she said—

"Dear Stanley, for such I am now lawfully entitled to call you, and must I leave you?"

"Clara," remonstrated Stanley, "it is ridiculous and unreasonable to talk thus, there is, you know, no alternative, so why torture yourself uselessly? I will see you again shortly. Be calm, be comforted. But here is one of your best earthly friends, Colonel Bridport."

"Clara, headstrong, foolish girl, thus to alarm me and my daughters," said the colonel, dismounting from his horse, and giving it in charge of his servant. "Ah," he added angrily, and with a look of suspicion, "Lieutenant Stanley. How is this, sir?—speak, I command you."

"I pray you, my dear colonel, to be patient, and judge me not hastily," replied the agitated Stanley, imploringly; "it was not I that sought this painful and fatal interview, and which has been productive of such torturing circumstances to me; there is nothing criminal in the conduct of poor Clara and myself; a wonderful discovery has been made, she is my own nearest and dearest relation—she will explain, I cannot."

Colonel Bridport looked alternately at Stanley and Captain Morley with the most unbounded and indescribable amazement, and thirsted for an explanation of that which appeared to be so perfectly extraordinary and incredible; but there was evidently not the slightest chance of his obtaining it, and Clara suddenly breaking from his hold on the impulse of the moment, threw herself again convulsively on the bosom of Stanley, who did not attempt to prevent her, and sobbed and sighed as though her heart would break, then in the most piteous accents that were sufficient to thrill to the heart of the listener, she said—

"Oh, farewell, dear Stanley, cousin; that we must part. But let it not be for long, for Clara must certainly die, if for any lengthened time out of your loved presence."

She looked up mournfully and imploringly in his face as she thus touchingly spoke, tears gushed to her now lustreless eyes, and sighs swelled her gentle but agitated bosom.

The distracted Stanley still held the poor girl to his bosom, almost unconscious of what he did; he even pressed an affectionate kiss upon her pale lips, which seemed to glow through all her veins, as he said in a voice of most painful agitation and excitement—

"Dear Clara, I beseech you to be calm; I will endeavour to see you again before long, and try to impart comfort and consolation to your deeply lacerated breast. But you must persevere and be patient, for this violent and useless excitement can only be productive of the most unfavourable results. This agonising scene has already lasted too long, and must be put an end to; I must resign you to the care of the excellent Colonel Bridport, who, fear not, will bestow upon you every affectionate and fatherly attention, especially when he hears the wonderful and astounding secret you have to disclose."

He withdrew himself gently from her arms, with a look of the greatest sympathy and distress as he thus spoke.

Clara seemed unconscious of everything, she stared on vacancy, and Colonel Bridport whose astonishment was at its greatest height, and whose impatience was now indeed completely exhausted, advanced hastily, and taking Clara gently in his arms, looked sternly at the wretched Stanley for a further explanation than that he had already given.

But the latter could not speak—he looked with agony and supplication at the colonel, waved his hand significantly towards him, beckoned to Captain Morley, and they both hurriedly quitted the spot in a state of mind it would be quite impossible for any language however powerful to describe.

The agitated Colonel Bridport led his fair, unfortunate, and unconscious charge tenderly from the spot, his servant following with the horses, and ready to render any assistance if required.

CHAPTER CXCVI.

THE BUNGALOW AND THE INVALID.—THE MANIAC.

It was night, and the interior of a comfortable bungalow. On a mattress was stretched the form of a sufferer; a kind-looking Hindoo watching anxiously over him, and eagerly attending to his wants.

It was Abdal.

Yes, it was the poor friend of the ill-fated Omelia, who thus for several days past had been stretched upon a bed, or rather a pallet of sickness, quite exhausted and worn out by the unusual excitement, fatigue of body, and mental anxiety he had experienced, and there were times when his illness seemed likely to prove fatal.

His appearance was sadly and painfully changed, and those who knew him, and the true manly truthfulness and nobleness of his heart must have sincerely sympathised with him to see the truly wretched and deplorable state to which he was reduced.

His features were languid and careworn as if with the sufferings of years, and his eyes were deep sunk in their sockets and entirely without lustre.

But there was now a feverish expression in his countenance, and he had raised himself by an effort on his elbow on his pallet, and was gazing anxiously around him

All was completely silent, and the bright moonbeams streamed full into the room.

"Jungh," said the suffering Abdal, at length, addressing the watchful Hindoo, in a faint but anxious voice, "what time is it?"

"It is night," replied Jungh, "but I know not the hour. See the moon shines brightly."

"And she still absent," groaned Abdal; "oh, this terrible, this insupportable agony and suspense. Omelia, oh, whither have you wandered?—what fresh danger have you rashly plunged yourself into? What can have befallen you to detain you thus long? And I unable to go in search of you?"

The unfortunate man swayed his body to

and fro, groaned, beat his breast, and was in the most dreadful state of excitement, while the kind-hearted Jungh was deeply affected, but knew not what to say, under the peculiar circumstances, which might comfort him, or impart consolation to him.

A pause, a solemn pause of a minute or two ensued, when Abdal suddenly called the Hindoo to him, and in a faint but eager voice, said:—

"Jungh, the moon still shines brightly, and will enable you to see far-off objects distinctly. Hasten, I implore you, to the door, and watch the approach of the wretched Omelia, if indeed she ever again return. I cannot endure this dreadful state of suspense."

Jungh immediately complied with this

No. 83.

request, and hastening to the door, looked eagerly forth.

"It is as clear as daylight," said Jungh, "but at present I observe nothing but the tall trees, and the shadows of the distant mountains."

"Alas! Alas!" groaned poor Abdal, his excitement and impatience increasing; "but I pray you continue your watch, good Jungh."

Jungh did so; but for some time, strained his eyes in vain.

"Jungh," said Adbal, after a pause, during which time, he was suffering the most terrible mental and bodily agony, "see you anything approaching now? Speak, quick!"

Jungh replied in the negative, and Abdal groaned and beat his breast in the utmost despair.

"Ah!" the Hindoo suddenly exclaimed, and in tones that rather startled Abdal, "in the distance I now behold a female form, and apparently with wild and disordered steps approaching this way!"

"Great Spirit!" said Abdal, with the most powerful emotion; "it must be her. Oh, my good, my faithful Jungh, do not remove your eyes from the coming object, till you have ascertained the truth!"

"And now," continued Jungh, "she approaches nearer, swinging her arms madly in the air,—bounding wildly over every difficulty, as if some savage beast pursued her, suffering nothing to impede her progress, and making the air resound again with her frenzied laughter, do you not hear her?"

"Yes, yes," replied Abdal, hastily, "but on your life, do not remove your eyes from her for an instant. Now,—now?"

"And now," said Jungh, "the bright moonbeams fall full upon her features, and reveal them distinctly; they are those of Omelia!"

Abdal uttered a cry, or rather a yell, which it would be totally impossible for the most powerful language to portray, and his strength became almost exhausted, not withstanding which he managed after an effort, to observe, in an agitated tone of voice which requires no description.

"Miserable, unfortunate girl, oh, whither have you now been? and what has happened to bring you to this frenzied condition?"

Again the wild, frantic laugh of the maddened Omelia sounded in the air, and Jungh continued to watch her as she advanced towards the bungalow with the greatest anxiety, but without attempting to meet her.

Omelia now came more slowly on, but her looks and general deportment were none the less wild and disordered, and it was but too painfully evident that madness had seized upon her brain.

Within a short distance of the bungalow, the wretched Omelia paused, pressed her hands upon her forehead, and seemed to hesitate; and in that attitude she stood for several minutes; but suddenly she started, a faint, mournful cry escaped her lips, and she rushed wildly into the bungalow, (pushing Jungh violently aside as she did so), and stood erect before Abdal, her eyes glaring vacantly upon him.

Abdal could not but gaze aghast at the unfortunate girl, in whose fate he had taken so untiring an interest, so awful, nay, so frightful was the change.

His heart bled for her, and his brain, for the moment, was almost as distracted as her own.

But from these melancholy thoughts Abdal was quickly aroused by a fearful cry from Omelia, sufficient to strike terror into the breasts of all who heard it, and she placed her hand upon his shoulder, and at the same time fixed upon him a look so piteous, so full of regret and despair, that his heart was full to bursting, and it was with difficulty he could restrain the expression of his feelings.

Jungh, who was deeply and sincerely affected, stood by with looks of the greatest compassion, and awaited the result of this fearful adventure with the utmost anxiety.

"See," at length said Omelia, in the most mournful and wandering accents, "see! he is there, locked in the abandoned wanton's arms—the deceiver!—the betrayer of fond confiding innocence!—the heartless villain;—but I have breathed my curses on his head, and torn him from my heart for ever. Yes, and I will pursue him with my deadliest hatred and revenge. Yes, to the world's end I will pursue him and his shameless wanton, and rest not till I have worked their destruction."

The distracted Abdal still gazed completely appalled, but could not utter a word. The whole dreadful truth was now revealed, clear as if it had been reflected in a mirror; and in his heart, Abdal also cursed the wretched Stanley, who could basely play so base, so villanous a part.

Yet it was so truly monstrous, that he could scarcely bring his mind to believe it. But it was evident that the wretched Omelia had seen Stanley—seen him under the most fearful and guilty circumstances, and Abdal could no longer doubt.

But what a heartless miscreant must Stanley be, so long to trifle with a poor girl's feelings, her heart's purest and most ardent affections, and then to leave her to madness and despair; it seemed scarcely possible that there could be such a monster in existence, and no punishment, however terrible, could be severe enough for him.

A solemn pause of a few minutes ensued, Omelia remaining in the same fixed attitude, and the wretched Abdal continuing to gaze at her appalled, and entirely incapable of uttering a word.

At length Omelia suddenly started, though her looks remained the same, if possible more wild, and addressing herself to Abdal, said:

"Why stand you there dumb-founded, or as if you were some wretched idiot who could not comprehend what I said? Do you doubt what I say? Ah! you may well do so, for who could believe that such base treachery existed in the world? But hear me again utter my most deadly curses on the villain's head, and see, see, see!"

As she thus spoke, she hastily took forth the likeness of Stanley which she always wore in her bosom, nearest her heart, and trampled it to pieces under her foot, all the time laughing frantically.

"So would I willingly serve the wretch who has so basely deceived me, and his unprincipled strumpet," she exclaimed, and she gnashed her teeth, and clenched her hands vehemently and passionately together as she spoke.

Again a dismal silence prevailed, for Abdal still remained too dreadfully agitated and distracted to speak.

Powerful and convulsive sobs at length escaped the bosom of Omelia, and she was compelled to lean against Abdal for support, who was in hopes that this ebullition of grief would tend greatly to relieve her.

It continued for several minutes with unabated violence, when in a truly pathetic and mournful voice, enough to move the most insensible being to tears, she ejaculated:

"But oh, it was most cruel, thus to trifle with a poor inexperienced girl's pure affections, to lead her on by the most solemn and oft repeated vows of ceaseless love and constancy to the brightest hopes of earthly happiness, then to cast her from him, for the embraces of an abandoned wanton, leaving her to all the horrors of misery and dispair; oh, cruel, cruel, cruel!"

Again she sobbed as though her heart would break, and pressed her hands upon her forehead.

Oh, what a lamentable scene was it for anyone to witness.

And what was the agony and the power of the emotions of Abdal all this time?—They might baffle description.

Again Omelia spoke, in the same pathetic and heart-thrilling tones.

"Yes, yes," she said, as if ruminating; "he came to me in all my happy innocence, and breathed soft vows of love and constancy. And could I for a moment doubt those delightful words of apparent sincerity? Could I resist those bright smiles of affection? No, from that moment I resigned to him my heart, solely, entirely; and how basely has he served me for my confidence,—base, brutal, unnatural villain!"

She again burst into sobs and tears, and could say no more.

Again this lasted for several minutes, and Abdal did not attempt to interrupt her or to utter a word, in fact he knew not what to say.

The distracted Omelia's features became more calm and placid, but it was quite evident it was not for long, and that the fierce tempest would again burst forth in all its terrible and awful violence.

Abdal felt convinced of the approaching shock, and he shuddered at the thought of it.

Once more the unfortunate Omelia resumed her mournful lamentations, and such was the breathless attention with which Abdal and the kind hearted Jungh listened to her plaintive and impressive words, that not the least sound broke upon the profound and solemn silence of the scene.

Omelia dashed hastily away her tears, as though she were ashamed of them, a proud and even scornful expression for a moment passed over her fine handsome countenance, but it was gone instantaneously, all was grief, and mental anguish, and after a deep sigh which came from her heart, she seemed to regain her composure, and thus commenced:—

"Oh, how blissful were the scenes we passed together. What dreams of nameless happiness did this poor, confiding, silly girl indulge in, and which every hour, every moment served to strengthen. I breathed an atmosphere of odoriferous flowers,—I basked perpetually in the sun's brightest beams. I knew not what sorrow meant. Mine was a life of sunny hopes and ceaseless happiness What more could mortal wish? what more could the heart crave for? And he seemed never happy but in my presence; and my thoughts were constantly fixed on him day and night, sleeping or waking. I could have died to serve him, and to prove the truth, the sincerity of my love. Time wore on, months passed away, and I could see nothing to excite my suspicions, or to awaken me from this fond dream of love. Would that nothing had ever occurred to do so.

"But sorrow came at last, and I met it with fortitude and resignation, confident of my Stanley's love.

"Terrible war broke out, and it became necessary that we should part. What dreadful anguish was this to me; I cannot describe my feelings. Stanley in vain tried to comfort me, and to impart consolation to me, even his words were powerless.

"When the final hour of separation came I thought my heart would have broken; I became insensible, when I recovered he was gone!

"I now felt almost as though I had parted with my soul, and had nothing to live for; but still there was a powerful innate feeling which seemed to sustain me, and to impart to me a feeling of hope, nay, even joy.

"With what eagerness and anxiety did I watch the daily intelligence from the seat of war, and how did my heart bleed for the scenes of horror that were hourly being enacted, and what terrible doubts and fears haunted my mind at the fate which had too probably befallen my beloved Stanley.

"Still a certain degree of hope never forsook me."

A brief pause again ensued, during which interval Omelia seemed quite lost in reflection, and to take not the slightest notice of the persons present.

Abdal was deeply affected, how indeed could he be otherwise, especially when he might plainly see that the poor girl's reason was fled for ever?

Abdal awaited with utmost anxiety and impatience, the unfortunate sufferer to speak again, but for several minutes more she kept him in suspense, fixed in the same statue-like attitude, and lost to everything in silent mediation.

This appeared to be even more awful and threatening than her wildest ravings.

But suddenly she started as if a thunderbolt had struck her, and her looks resumed all their former frightful and frenzied expression, as she raved out in tones that were sufficient to appal the listener.

"But the betrayer and his wanton partner in crime shall not be suffered to escape my just but terrible vengeance. See, they mock at me—they deride me in the frenzy of my despair! And shall I tamely submit to this? No, no, no; let me at once begone, and wreak my most deadly revenge upon their accursed and guilty heads. Off, off—who dares detain me? I will pursue the wretches to the world's end, but I will accomplish my will. Ha! ha! ha! I come—I come upon my deadly mission. Oh, how they will writhe in agony and despair, and how I shall gloat over their sufferings. Ha! ha! ha! I come—I come."

And laughing wildly, flinging her arms madly in the air, she rushed from the bungalow before any one had time to prevent her, if even it had been at all possible to do so; and already had she proceeded some distance, bounding madly on, and Jungh watching her with the greatest emotion and anxiety, until her fine form was hidden from the view in the darkness beyond.

"'Tis all over; 'tis all over," said Abdal, in a voice of the most indescribable anguish—lost, for ever lost, oh, agony and despair."

He groaned, then threw himself back on the pallet, totally insensible and apparently dying.

CHAPTER CXCVII.

THE AGONY AND DESPAIR OF STANLEY.

EVENTS of such terrible and startling an interest as those that have been so faithfully described in the previous chapters, it is needless to say, must have the most appalling and distracting effect upon the unfortunate individuals immediately connected with them, and the reader may therefore easily judge of the torturing and almost insupportable state of mind in which the wretched Stanley quitted the fatal spot.

He looked the very picture of intense agony and despair; the perspiration stood upon his forehead in large drops, his limbs trembled convulsively, and at one time he must have sunk helplessly upon the earth, had not his faithful friend Captain Morley, who was nearly as agitated as himself, caught him and supported him.

The eyes of Stanley rolled wildly in their sockets, and his whole appearance was ghastly and appalling in the extreme.

"Oh, what a fine intellect have I destroyed for ever, he groaned, I shall go mad, I shall go mad!"

"Be calm, for Heaven's sake, be calm, Stanley," said Captain Morley, in a soothing voice.

"Be calm!" repeated Stanley, wildly, and impatiently, and at the same time looking not at all like himself; "who is it that talks of calmness to a guilty wretch like me? I have destroyed one of the most beauteous and innocent beings that ever existed, and I deserve, oh, richly deserve, all the just but terrible curses she has invoked upon my devoted head; and they will pursue me, aye, pursue me, even to the end of my existence, making that wretched existence an earthly perdition."

"You shock me, Stanley, by your terrible observations," said Captain Morley, with a look of the most sincere sorrow and sympathy, at the same time almost fearful to address him; "for the love of Heaven, forbear these torturing and dismal lamentations, and try to·collect yourself and be firm."

"You talk to me like an idiot," said the wretched man, impatiently, and almost savagely;—"I am a villain of the deepest dye,—a base, perfidious villain, and the curse of Heaven is upon me for it."

He groaned aloud as he spoke, and beat his breast with insupportable agony.

Captain Morley still supported him, and tried, but in vain, to induce him to leave the fatal spot; but his words fell unheeded on his ear, and their situation now became truly alarming.

"Off, off!" he exclaimed, wildly, and his brain evidently distracted and wandering; "who dares to seek to hold me, to restraint me thus? I tell you again that I am a wretch, unworthy of anything but disgust and hatred; all the hideousness of my character is now made evident to me when it is to late; and I shudder with horror at the contemplation. I see how step by step

I have led that poor innocent, confiding girl to destruction, till at last, I have sent her forth, a wretched wandering maniac. And can there then be any pity or solicitude for an odious monster like me? no, all mankind should shun me, despise me, loathe me, even as they would a murderer."

He swayed his body to and fro in the most dreadful agony, covered his face with his hands, and groaned aloud.

It was a terrible and most critical moment, and the bewildered Captain Morley knew not what to do, for the awful circumstances that had taken place seemed to have made a powerful impression on the unfortunate Stanley's mind, which nothing whatever could remove.

And thus for several minutes everything remained, and Captain Morley was worked up to a state of the most horrible excitement, which was truly deplorable to behold.

At length Captain Morley saw that it was completely useless trifling any longer, and mustering up all his fortitude and determination for the painful and arduous task he had to perform, he laid gently hold of the arm of Stanley, and led him in a perfect state of unconsciousness from the spot.

Stanley never once looked up, he said not a word, he seemed to be in a complete state of mental torpor, and did not attempt to offer any resistance.

It was a most fortunate circumstance, and Captain Morley's hopes began to revive, for they had now got a considerable distance towards the place of their destination, and he flattered himself with the idea that he should be enabled to accomplish the rest of his task with success.

But he was doomed to bitter and painful disappointment.

Suddenly the wretched Stanley burst violently from his hold, with a wild look and a frantic cry, and clenching his fists in a menacing manner, he exclaimed in a thrilling voice:—

"Away!—away! Seek not to control me, lest you drive me to desperation, and you will then have bitter cause to rue the consequences. Away, I say; whither would you lead me?—to some horrible earthly punishment? Yes, I see deadly malice, hatred, and revenge lurking in your bloodshot eyes. But 'tis fit that you should hate me; 'tis fit that all mankind should view a guilty wretch like me with horror and disgust!"

He again covered his face with his hands, and groaned with agony.

"Good God!" exclaimed Captain Morley, worked up to a state of utter despair, and striking his forehead with his clenched fist, "what is to be done? I never was placed in such a terrible situation before, even upon the deadly battle field."

He looked around him in despair, and his agony increased every moment. Yet, as he still gazed eagerly, he could almost imagine that he beheld the shadow of a human form approaching, but it was too indistinct to be certain.

"Stanley," he at length ventured to remonstrate, gently laying his hand on his arm.

The wretched man started as though some venomous reptile had bit him, and his looks were perfectly frightful.

"Stanley!" he repeated in a hoarse voice, who dares to call me by that hated name? I have no name now but that of monster—betrayer of female innocence—villain—basest of villains; and I will hasten to some remote corner of the earth and hide myself from mortal sight. Let me begone—let me begone!

He was about to rush madly from the spot, and the distracted Captain Morley, exhausted as he already was, found that it would be impossible for him to detain him, when the voice of a man, calling upon his name, saluted his ear, and looking in the direction from whence it came, he was relieved on beholding that it was Captain Robinson, an officer belonging to the same regiment, and one with whom he was on the most intimate terms of friendship.

Captain Robinson gazed with perfect amazement and bewilderment on the singular scene before him, and turning to Captain Morley, said:—

"Captain Morley, what am I to understand from this?"

"Question me not, I pray you, Captain Robinson," replied Captain Morley, "for I cannot now explain; only assist me to conduct the unfortunate Stanley from the spot; he's mad."

All this time, the bewildered Stanley stood transfixed as a statue, and gazing at them vacantly.

But he seemed terrified at the sight of Captain Robinson, consequently, when he approached and gently laid hold of him, he offered not the least resistance, but became passive as a child, and the two officers were enabled to conduct him from the fatal spot without the least difficulty.

CHAPTER CXCVIII.

AN APPALLING SCENE.

A fortnight must be supposed to have elapsed; and terrible had been the suffering that the unfortunate Stanley had endured during that period.

But youth, and a naturally strong constitution, surmounted every difficulty, and Stanley so far recovered as to be permitted to leave his bed.

During the most afflicting parts of his malady, Colonel Bridport visited him, and great was his sympathy and regret, at the deplorable situation in which he found him, and from which he feared he would never recover.

To the anxious questions of Stanley regarding the hapless Clara, the Colonel was compelled to be very cautious in the answers he returned.

He said that she was comparitively calm; that she had every care and attention by himself and his daughters.

He (the Colonel), also informed the invalid, that he was perfectly satisfied with the explanation she had given, and could never help wondering at the extraordinary discovery.

He, however, strongly advised him not to attempt to visit her for a few days, as the excitement might prove too much for him, and Stanley promised to adhere faithfully to his wishes; Colonel Bridport then took his leave, much hurt by what he had seen.

Stanley was permitted to go at large for it was thought there was no further danger in his malady, and that consequently there was nothing to fear.

But one evening he was missed, which caused great alarm, and persons were immediatley sent out in search of him.

It was a lovely moonlight night, and myriads of stars twinkled in the clear, cloudless sky.

But it is to a far different scene we must call the attention of the reader.

Huge masses of rock piled upon each other, and that looked as though they would every moment fall and bury themselves in the earth with ponderous weight; a wild, frightful scene, with withered trunks of trees scattered here and there, and above all, the bright moon shining, and the stars glittering; such is the description of the dreary spot we are now endeavouring to picture.

Not a sound disturbed the solemn silence of that awful place, and you might imagine yourself out of the world.

But hark! what awful, wild cry is that which suddenly resounds upon the air? Can it be that of a human being?

It is there again! It approaches this way, and now behold, a female form rushes madly on towards the rocks; she is pursued; it is the form of a man that does so.

It is Omelia and Stanley!

Frantically he calls upon her nam ; and implores her in piteous accents to stop. She replies to him only by loud laughter, and her wild speed increases, as she proceeds towards the rocks, and there is no one to impede her in her mad progress.

And Stanley does not abandon the pursuit; he seems determined to brave the result, even though it be death.

Breathlessly he hurries on. He gains upon her.

And now again he calls frenziedly upon her, and implores her to stop, the same wild laughter is his reply.

She reaches the rocks, she rushes up them with astonishing agility.

She reaches one of the highest of them, Gracious Powers! what are her terrible intentions?

But he was worked up to state of a madness almost as great as that of the poor wretched being he was pursuing, and hurried on, totally regardless of the consequences.

He reaches the rocks, he hurries up them with the footsteps of despair;—once more he imploringly and piteously called upon her name; she laughs wildly, fixes upon him one fearful look, and with a wild cry, such as no language can describe, precipitates herself headlong into the frightful depth beneath.

With a frantic cry the wretched Stanley is about to follow Omelia's terrible example, making sure that she was dead, when he was fortunately and unexpectedly arrested in his terrible purpose by the officers who had been sent in pursuit of him, and who had just arrived in time to save him.

He uttered a wild cry of despair on beholding them, and at first offered a desperate resistance, but it was all useless, and the officers forced him down the rocks, and hurried him along, in spite of his wild cries of madness and despair.

CHAPTER CXCIX.

THE DREADFUL SITUATION OF OMELIA.

FOR some time Omelia lay in her terrible position, in a perfect state of insensibility, but it seemed as nothing could destroy the life of that wretched unfortunate being.

Suddenly she opened her eyes, and gazed vacantly around her.

Above was piled the frightful rocks, from which she had precipitated herself, apparently to certain death, frowning in all their natural horror, beneath, where Omelia lay, was a grass flat, opening on a scene of vast extent, beautifully romantic, picturesque, and inviting to the eye, and upon this at that time, the bright sun was shedding its golden beams, rendering it still more lovely.

"Why am I still living?" said Omelia at length, "why am I still doomed to carry out this wretched, accursed existence?—Why cannot I perish, and sleep in peace?—Ah!—what lovely scene is this that bursts before mine eyes, as if by magic?—Is it to cheer me on to hope?—Hope!—Ah no, there is none, none,—for the mad, the heart-broken Omelia!"

She pressed her hands upon her forehead, and sobbed bitterly.

Suddenly she started with all her former violence, and exclaimed,

"It is mockery all; they think to deceive the wretched maniac by these bright delusive visions, so wildly opposed to my feelings, and the tempest of furious passions that rage within my distracted breast. No, let mr hasten where all is dark and dreary, and fearful as my own thoughts. Where the foot of human being never yet trod, and the howling wind in its mad fury has alone broken the frightful silence. I cannot remain here amid this bright scene of sunshine and peace."

She paused for a minute or two in reflection, during which time she said not a word, then suddenly starting, as if from some frightful dream, and with a frenzied cry that resounded far and near, she hurried madly from the spot on which she had been standing.

More beautifully romantic and picturesque became that favoured spot at every turn; it seemed as though all charms of nature were concentrated there, and with the bright sunbeams shining over it, it looked like some scene of fairy land.

Omelia hurried on, heedless of all around her; she passed several bungalows, at the doors of which the inmates were standing, and were prepared to render her any assistance.

But she looked at them with alarm, as though they sought to detain her, and dashed madly on towards the gloomiest part of the country, and her wild cry and laughter resounded on the air as she did so.

Nothing could stop her in her mad and frightful career, and the further she proceeded the wilder she seemed to become.

Every minute that noble form, so lovely and so graceful, became more and more indistinct, but still her voice could be heard, as she hurriedly wended her way to the gloomiest part of the country, where all was darkness and horror, and no eye to observe her.

She seemed to exult with wild pleasure

as she did so, and rushed on her way till lost in the gloom beyond.

CHAPTER CC.

A CHAPTER OF GREAT INTEREST.

CLARA, with her friends the excellent Colonel Bridport and his amiable daughters, continued for several days calm and resigned: gloomy thoughts again came over her, and she became deaf to consolation.

One beautiful afternoon, when all above or below was lovely, and nature shining forth in all its beauty, Clara, by the urgency of her friends, retired to her couch; and falling off to sleep, suddenly a tall, majestic form entered the room, and approached the couch on which Clara was sleeping, stood over her with deadly malice, and was about to stab her to the heart, when celestial strains of music were heard, at which she paused. They swelled higher and higher; a heavenly light filled the room, and there stood the spirit of the mother of the sleeping girl.

Omelia gazed appalled—gave one frantic cry, and rushed madly from the place. The strains of celestial music reached the ears of the sleeper, she awoke; she gazed with wonder, dropped on her knees before the spirit of her mother, but was too awe-struck to speak a word. The heavenly shade, passing its arms above her head, said :—

"Child of sorrow, the spirit of thy mother will watch over thee and guard thee from all danger; be comforted; be happy."

And thus the celestial music still continued; gradually the vision faded away, and all in the room was the same as before.

Colonel Bridport and his daughters immediately entered the room, and being informed of what had occurred, rendered all their most excellent advice and assistance. But the heavenly spirit had performed its mission, and Clara was happy.

Through jungle, over hillock, suffering nothing to impede her progress, madly rushed the wretched creature after leaving the bungalow; over rock, through stream, she reached that region of gloom, which had never yet been trodden by human foot. 'Twas there the savage monsters found a lair, and with their fearful howlings broke the silence that constantly reigned in that place of horror and gloom. As Omelia entered it, she laughed loudly and madly with frantic feelings of joy, and in wild accents, exclaimed:—

"Here, here, I reign in the region of perpetual gloom, and laugh—laugh—laugh to scorn the noted world. Here—here would I sit on my throne, my mystic throne of all that is frightful in nature, and those who dare approach me, or venture to breathe the sounds in my ears, let them pray for their sins, for they will have rushed on death."

Thus days and nights passed on, and Omelia sat in her region of gloom and horror; if the wind howled, she laughed exultingly; if it breathed not, she sat on the point of a rock, her elbows on her knees, her chin resting on her hands, and her wild eyes seemed to penetrate through the frightful region.

Hark! even through the dreary wild, a footstep might be heard, nearer and nearer it approached the awful spot where Omelia was sitting. Woe, woe, to the poor unfortunate wretch whom fate led that way, nearer and nearer it approached the fatal spot: a shriek—a fearful shriek, and that rang through all the horrors of the dreadful night; a frantic laugh, and death had done its work, and there Omelia sat with exultation and triumph in her looks.

On came the dusky torrent, the rain, the howling of wind, fiercer and fiercer still, and still sat there Omelia laughing wildly in her madness, on holding the tempest to scorn.

Fiercer and fiercer still it became, and louder and louder laughed Omelia.

"I'm here," she wildly exclaimed, "I'm here, queen of the region of horrors, here let no one intrude, or death is there; even as the poor wretch just now received it from the hands of Omelia queen—great queen of the region of death. I cannot die —I will not die. Heaven has no power over me. I live to torture and destroy. Where art thou, Stanley? Oh, that I had thee now in my grasp, to send thy worthless carcass dashing, crashing, from this rock; without time to give thy wretched soul to breathe a prayer to eternity. I'd do it, with glad triumph I'd do it; granting thee not one moment to breathe a prayer to Heaven. And it will come—it will come, and I shall hear thy frightful shrieks, as thine hated soul rushes on its way to eternity."

And it did come—that hoped for moment of horror did come—and Stanley, led on by madness, approached this moment of destruction. Sitting on that wild rock remained Omelia, in all her native horror, as queen of the frightful region she had chosen for her region of death; and there she continued to sit and laugh exultingly

at the howling blast. It came—it came—a footstep is heard, it reached the ears of the wretched maniac, who there sat still howling with the blast. What fate could have led that poor maniac to his doom of death —of certain death, and destruction? But it was fate, and so the poor wretch passed on his way to eternity.

Nearer and nearer—nearer still the doomed one rushed upon his fate—his frightful fate; and it was Stanley. Madly, frantically, the wretched man passed to his doom. One frightful howling shriek, and the queen—the great queen of horrors had performed her dreadful mission—she was there to destroy, and she had done her terrible work. The wretched, guilty Stanley was no more; might hear his body dashing from rock to rock; 'twas a terrible and frightful doom he had appeared to seek.

And thus still sat the wretched maniac, in her region of gloom and horror, laughing exultingly; triumphing in her region of darkness and perpetual horror; the blast howled fearfully around, and the louder it howled, the more frightful became the shrieks and laughter of the queen of horrors, in her dark region of perpetual gloom. She triumphed—she exulted in her hideous work of destruction.

Again through the whole of that frightful night, another wretched being, led on by fate, rushes madly to eternity. Nearer nearer it approaches the frightful scene of death, a dreadful yell, a loud laugh even above the blast, and another wretched being had met its death doom; it was Yuseff, and the hideous laugh was the maniac's, and she continued to laugh and howl with the blast.

And she continued to sit laughing and yelling with the blast, and no earthly power could stay that wild and frightful cry.

"They have come," she said, "the death-doomed have rushed upon their fate, and now is Omelia's hour of triumph! Laugh, queen of horrors, in all thy frightful work of destruction! Let them come—I look for them, the poor mad wretches!—'tis music, heavenly music to my soul, to hear their shrieks as their worthless souls sink into eternity! I've come again! I've come to hear the poor guilty victims dash on their way to the unknown regions of death and endless eternity! And I will laugh, I will howl and yell in the frightful work of destruction! 'Tis my triumph! 'tis my triumph! 'tis my hour of triumph! and oh, how I glory in it! and they shall hear me in the deepest recesses of the earth, for the queen is here in all her majesty of destruction!

Thus raved the miserable Omelia, whose better instincts were, for the time, entirely obliterated, by the overpowering feelings of jealousy which had been aroused in her bosom, against the apparently doomed Stanley.

"Thus have I lured him to his doom!" she exclaimed, as she glared round upon the savage scenery she had chosen for her purpose. Thus perish all who betray a too confiding heart. I trusted him—and ah!—I loved him, and now what remains but an empty casket that enshrined the heart I once worshipped?"

She passed her hand across her brow, and looked stupidly through her fingers with a demented gaze, at the silver cresent now high up in the heavens.

"What remains?"

No. 84.

Again a terrible shudder passed through the frame of the unfortunate girl. Wild and ferocious as had been her words, she still seemed to avoid turning her gaze towards the spot where Stanley had fallen from the rock above, and where indeed he now lay insensible and to all appearance dead.

He had fallen from such an appalling height, that it seemed utterly impossible to imagine any human being surviving so awful a concussion. And to the excited and frenzied imagination of Omelia who imagined herself an avenging spirit of betrayed innocence, or queen of horrors for the time, to her mind he was crushed to a shapeless mass. For had she not heard his wild shrieks borne upon the blast?—his body dashed from rock to rock—yet for all this, although for a time Stanley, to the things of this world, was no more; still "life's fitful flame," although well nigh extinguished, yet feebly flickered within his bruised and shattered frame.

The height from which he had fallen, as we have observed, was terrible to contemplate, but the ground upon which he fell was soft, and covered with tall grass. It was, in fact, a morass, being frequently flooded by the overflowing of the Jumna, and although vegetation was prolific in this spot, it was all of a savage character, and uncultivated by man. It was, in fact, one of those wild wastes of ground so common in India, where the traveller may journey for miles through jungles and forests tenanted only by wild and ferocious beasts of prey and noxious reptiles. When perhaps he may, after some hours travelling light upon a few huts, so issolated in their situation, so surrounded by wastes and jungles, and so entirely cut off from other human habitations by miles of deserted country, that one would hardly believe it possible for persons to exist in such barbarously wild spots.

There is a natural grandeur in contemplating a wild country in the deep recesses of which the foot of man has never fallen. In the very stillness of the scene there is delight, and a mournful silence in the calmness of the evening, as the silver moon looks so calmly upon the savage regions. No hum of distant voices—no rumbling of busy wheels—no cries of domestic animals meet the ear. Before lies a wilderness pathless and untrodden by the foot of civilisation —where no sound is heard but that of the elements—where the thunder rolls among the towering forests, or the wind howls along the plains, and far, far in the distance the blue mountains melt into an indefinite haze.

Above are the rocky pinacles which spring from the level plain, their swarthy cliffs glistening from the recent shower, and patches of rich verdure clinging to precipices a thousand feet above.

The eye stretches along the grassy plains, taking at one full glance a survey of woods of rocks, and streams; and imperceptibly the mind wanders to the thoughts of home, and in one moment scenes long left behind are conjured up by memory, and incidents are recalled which banish from the mind the immediate scenes it is contemplating.

Lost for a moment in the enchanting power of solitude, where fancy and reality combine in their most bewitching forms, the hunter or traveller is suddenly roused, perhaps, by the shrill trumpet of an elephant, or the roar of a lurking tiger.

He wakes from his reverie—the reality of the present scene is at once manifest. He stands within a wilderness, where the monster of the forest alone holds dominion, knows not what a day or an hour may bring forth; he looks to his rifle of heavy calibre, and is, perhaps, shortly upon the track of beasts.

Spots like these are frequent enough in Hindostan, where, of course, it is dangerous at any time to travel alone; yet for all this there may be found some native Hindoos who build a few huts, and a small village springs up, and an acre or two of cultivated land may be seen. The sight of these habitations having been thus purposely chosen to avoid the payment of the collector's rates. Their approach is so dangerous, and they are frequently so concealed from sight that in many instances they are not known to be in existence at all.

———

CHAPTER CCI.

THE PERILOUS ENCOUNTER.

But the spot chosen by Omelia for her wild ravings was a complete wilderness, without hut or hovel near, and certainly from the rugged character of its appearance it was in consonence with her savage mood of mind. The noise of the jackalls, the roaring of the tigers and other beasts of prey, enhanced the horrors of the scene. Still Omelia, heedless of her situation, sat immovable, regardless of danger. Far more stormy thoughts agitated her heart, thoughts that matched the tiger in ferocity, and held her in bondage.

But hush! there is a rustling of leaves— a slight movement in the jungle—something is stealing along with cautious steps—hark! the tall Indian grass casts fantastic shadows on yonder rock—it quivers like an aspen bow. Omelia's eyes are directed to the spot and are eagerly watching with intense anxiety. Despite her frenzy, her heart beats audily, and a new and undefined fear takes possession of her. Is it a spirit? her suspicious fears are aroused, and she asks herself—"Is it a spirit of my murdered lover, come to upbraid me for my treachery?"

"She is answered by a horrible roar, which is reverberated from rock to rock, and is re-echoed in the distance like terrible thunder.

Omelia's eyes are directed to the spot from whence the noise proceeds, and there, over the prostrate body of Stanley, what a sight met her gaze, for a moment it froze her with horror.

Yes, standing over Stanley, with one gigantic paw on his chest, stood a large Bengal tiger in all it's native ferocity—his lurid eyes glancing round indicative of his being monarch of the place. Omelia held her breath, and dared not move; there was a fascination to her mind—mad as she undoubtedly was—in beholding something even more savage than herself.

Presently the animal began turning her lover over with his paw, as a cat would play with a mouse before she devours it, then the tiger put his nose to the face of the prostrate man, and sniffed as if doubtful whether any spark of life yet remained.

"Ah, ah!" shrieked Omelia, now in her wildest accents, as she now believed the animal was about to devour her lover.

"Ah, ah! I am avenger here! who dares usurp my rightful throne? I am the queen of horrors, and more savage and terrible in my nature than thou, cruel and bloodthirsty as is your nature. For have I not cause—too terrible for human heart and brain to bear? Have I not cause—mightier and more potent than thy instincts, savage as they naturally are? Stay thy work of destruction; living or dead he belongs to me! to me! Do'st hear?"

The tiger raised his head and looked towards the speaker with a proud disdain. It was a fine sight to see the beast in all his native glory; those only who have seen savage animals in cages, can form a very faint idea of their majesty in their native lairs. Their roar is paralizing beyond description, and the lower animals are rendered incapable of moving under its influence.

The tiger did not seem, however, to be inclined to alter his position, and the poor maniac cried out again in her rage—

"Do'st hear me fool? Begone, and leave me undisturbed in my proper sphere. 'Tis I alone have power to reign here; I, whom the gross inhumanity of man has made more savage than tigers, wolves, panthers, hyenas, or any beast beneath heaven. They have not the great cause that I have. They never knew ingratitude—never having given kindness—while I, I— Begone I say!"

Rising from her position, she now advanced boldly towards the tiger, and looking him full in the face, raised one hand menacingly.

The beast seemed astounded at her temerity. Much has been said about the power of the human voice and the human eye, upon savage animals, and there is no doubt that to a certain extent it has its power; but this is only for a time, and in another moment Omelia's fate seemed likely to be sealed, for with a roar that shook the rocks with its fearful tone, the tiger made a bound from the prostrate Stanley towards Omelia, with one blow of his paw he struck her to the earth senseless and inanimate, whilst he indulged with another roar over his victim. But hark! his quick ears detect some movement in an adjoining mango tree. His enemy is on his scent. And now may be seen another actor in this drama of savage life. "A shikaree," or native hunter, is on watch for his natural enemy, the tiger. His practised eye measures the distance, and he seems to hesitate in firing his rifle. Again his eye wanders lovingly along the barrel which is levelled at the beast, but he seems to hesitate as if doubtful of his distance.

There appears to be no probability of the tiger leaving his prey, although he is evidently aware of the close proximity of the shikaree, and seems disturbed in his expected meal.

Another minute, and with steady aim the hunter discharges his piece. The ball has taken effect, as is surely told by a dark streak of blood staining the white garments of Omelia.

The animal roars with pain and rage as he rolls over in agony. In an instant, with surprising agility, the hunter drops from the mango tree, and his lithe form is seen standing erect in the jungle. He is armed with a tulwar, or short scimitar. This weapon is a knife about two feet long and three inches broad, and is used with surprising dexterity by the native hunters of India as a weapon of defence, it being swung round in the hand before a blow is inflicted, and then brought into contact with the object intended to be struck with a force truly astounding.

On his left arm the hunter bore a small shield formed of leather. The upper portion of his person was perfectly naked, and his appearance and expression of countenance, as he fixed his eye, in his advance, dauntlessly and threateningly upon the beast, was grand in its determined courage. It was the very concentration of moral energy, the index of high and unconquerable resolution. His erect and commanding figure, as seen in the moonlight, in that lonely and deserted spot, seemed the very personification of an avenging spirit

It was a magnificent picture, the two, brute and man, now destined for single combat, for life or death.

The animal was evidently not very severely wounded, but crouched down before the stern gaze of his fearless opponent. A low growl of suppressed rage and pain still continued from the beast, and his tail was vibrating to and fro with excitement: but he did not appear to be at all desirous of making an attack. The practised eye of the shikaree well knew the character of his antagonist. One movement on either side, and the foe would be upon him. He still fastened upon him the same settled look of determination, as he continued to waive aloft his heavy scimitar.

Presently the tiger retreated a few steps, crawling cautiously backwards, his belly touching the ground, as he trailed himself along with a subtle movement from his antagonist's gaze. The hunter nears him now—can almost feel his breath upon his face. Another moment, and the animal with a growl makes a sort of spring forward, dropping from his mouth the inanimate form of the Indian maid, whom he had dragged some few yards with him upon his retreating from the hunter. The man moved a step on one side, at the same time partially covering himself with his shield. Then, again advancing towards the animal, with a slow and measured step as the tiger retreated before him, still however keeping his head towards the hunter, who now paused with the same look of settled determination fixed upon his enemy, when, after viewing him steadily, he in his turn retreated back several paces. He saw now that the tiger was preparing himself for a final spring. His tail became twice its usual size, with which he lashed his sides furiously.

There was a pause of breathless suspense, when, with a ferocious cry, the furious brute made a savage bound at his antagonist. He was prepared for this, and with an agility almost miraculous, leaped adroitly on one side, and upon the tiger alighting on the ground, he swung round his knife, and with a single blow severed the animal's hind leg above the joint, leaving it hanging uselessly by the skin.

A loud shout and taunt, in the Indian language, now burst forth from the *shikaree* The wounded beast sent forth in answer a frightful cry of rage and anguish, and advanced in a state of maddened anger upon his opponent, who had, however, retreated back a few yards after the infliction of the wound. He now waited with perfect presence of mind, well knowing he could no longer make a spring with any effect; but rendered blind with impotent rage, the tiger now advanced upon his three legs, when having arrived within reach of the avenging knife, it was again brought down with such terrible force upon his head as to sever the skull, and to lay the animal dead at his feet.

The hunter wiped the drops of perspiration from his face, and presently gazed round with inquiring glances for the maiden whom he had seen in the tiger's grasp. He found her senseless, with a dreadful wound in the head from the first stroke of the tiger. She was covered in blood, partly from the wounds inflicted by the tigers claws, and partly from the animals own wound, which had flowed over her when the rifle ball took effect. The *shikaree* believed her to be quite dead; indeed it was hardly possible to suppose otherwise. He debated with himself what had best be done under the circumstances, but was more astonished when he discovered Stanley bereft of life, and a few paces from him he discovered Yusef, with his skull fractured, his back broken, and unmistakeably gone to his account. Yussef had fallen from the rock upon a jagged point of another rock; not having leaped so determinedly as Stanley, he had not alighted upon the soft jungle, consequently he had met a fate worthy of his dark character.

It must be understood, that the scene we have just described, was quite accidental as far as regards the presence of the *shikaree*. It may appear strange, that in this deserted region there should be any one to have been cognizant of the situation of our characters, or come so suddenly upon the scene. But the *shikaree* was but following his natural avocation. In India the tiger still disputes every inch of ground, and many years must necessarily elapse before these animals are sufficiently exterminated, to render the establishment of villages for new settlers secure from their depredations. But the work of redemption gradually goes on, and a course has been pursued by the Hon. East India Company which has done much towards meeting this evil. Rewards are given by them for the destruction of the tiger. In consequence of this, a large class of men have sprung up called *shikarees*, and it is one of these who had chosen this wild and deserted region for his operations, that we have seen come so opportunely to rescue our heroine. These men follow no other occupation than hunting and destroying beasts of prey, and a perilous warfare they oftentimes wage. They are the pioneers of civilisation, clearing away the impediments to the cultivation and occupation of the uninhabited portion of the globe. A donation of ten rupees, equal to twenty-five pounds of our money, is bestowed upon the *shikaree* for every tiger he destroys, and he makes something considerable by the sale of his skin, claws, &c., so that a great temptation is thus offered for many to follow this dangerous calling.

The man whom we have described as having fought so courageously with the tiger, was a celebrated tiger-slayer. His name is Moorsha, and he had a great celebrity for his fights in the arena, amongst the neighbouring Rajahs, who sometimes hold entertainments with battles fought between men and entrapped animals, but we shall in the course of our story have to recur to this subject—at present we have other matters to describe.

CHAPTER CCII.

THE HAVEN OF REFUGE.

When Moorsha, the *shikaree*, discovered the bodies of Stanley and Yusef, he was more than ever puzzled in his conjectures.

"For what possible purpose," exclaimed he, "can these persons have come unarmed in such a locality? and what can I now do with them? If alive, which is doubtful to me, it will be hazardous to leave them here, while I go for assistance. Let me see! Jahnsah—the good Jahnsah—the Brahmin priest should not be far hence, but then how to leave them. Ah, yonder's a cave. I have it! I will secure them there as best I can."

So saying, Moorsha disposed of Omelia and Stanley in the cave, as well as circumstances would admit, cutting down much of the grass and superabundant vegitation with his tulmar, he made a rude couch, upon which he laid the bodies of the two unfortunate victims—Stanley and Omelia.

As to Yusef, it was but too evident that he was past all human aid, so he left him to his fate.

Having accomplished this task, he next proceeded to roll a large stone against the mouth of the cave, to prevent the entrance of any marauding animal, and then proceeded on his journey, amidst the deep recesses of a country even still more rugged and gloomy than the spot he had but just left. It was indeed a wilderness of the most savage character, through which Moorsha had now to journey.

But presently he came to the outskirts of a wood, where there would have been to the casual observer, no visible signs of any human habitation; but Moorsha knew the spot he was making for, as close by the river Jumna, which was now distinctly visible, there might be observed a natural and small mountain or rather bank of rising ground, overgrown with trees and thick vegetation. Pursuing his way through thick underwood, the form of Moorsha paused before a small entrance, and shouting loudly in his native tongue, a voice was heard in reply, and presently a venerable form appeared to his summons. It was the good Jahnsah—or "old man of the mountain" as he was sometimes called. He had been one of the few who had rendered signal service to the English on the occasion of the late Indian outbreak; and many lives had been saved through his instrumentality.

Crossing his arms over his breast, he bowed reverently to Moorsha, and said—

"What would'st thou, my son? What is it that brings thee to my silent retreat from the world's strife and cares?"

"Father!" hastily answered Moorsha: "not far hence, lie three Europeans—no not three—one, only one European—one is dead to a certainty, and it may be the other two are also; but your better judgment will know as to that. Hasten with me and see what had best be done."

"If it be an errand of mercy, my son, it is enough, I will at once accompany you thither." So saying the two retraced their way to the cave, where the *shikaree* had left Omelia and Stanley. They were insensible, and the old man made a careful examination of them.

"All but gone, my son! I fear me much that their troubles are over in this world," he gently observed; "still if we can get them safely lodged in my humble abode, I will do my best for their recovery, although I much fear all my attempts may be futile to propitiate the Great Spirit. It is but for man to humbly hope."

They succeeded by means of a rude palanquin, in conveying them to the interior of the Brahmin priest's abode. It was a commodious habitation, fitted up with every convenience and luxury of the country, and no one would have dreamt of the internal comfort within; in fact it was part of an ancient Hindoo temple, which had stood perhaps for centuries; but latterly had been quite overlooked. There are many temples of this nature throughout British India.

Stanley was conveyed to an inner apartment, while Omelia was out of hearing, and far removed from her companion in misfortune. The good Jahnsah brought all the knowledge he was possessed of to endeavour to restore the sufferers to animation; and, after dressing the wounds of Omelia, he applied what medicaments he had to both his patients. For a time, the spirits of each seemed to hover between two worlds; but the morning sun saw Stanley restored to consciousness, but so weak that he appeared entirely prostrated.

Omelia reclined on a couch of carved ivory, around which hung curtains of lace. On her right side there was an opening or small fissure in the rock, which was interlaced with bamboos crossed in lattice-work, upon which crept several climbing plants. Through this opening might be seen the river Jumna.

It was altogether in its appointments, as well as situation, a lovely apartment, and seemed like an abode in fairy land. Still no other indication of life was evinced by Omelia, but occasionally uneasy breathing, and now and then a deep drawn and prolonged sigh.

Thus she continued for hour after hour.

When at length, after awakening as from a deep sleep, she gently opened her eyes and gazed wonderingly round the apartment. Passing her hand across her eyes she was made sensible of her situation by a sharp pain from her bruised body and bound-up wounds. She would have fainted perhaps, but Jahnsah was at her side immediately, and administered a slight restorative. Her large lustrous eyes opened in wonderment, when she beheld the venerable and benign countenance of the Hindoo. Seen in that apartment, under all the circumstances of her bewildered imagination, he looked like a denizen of another world. His aged beard swept his breast, and the slanting rays of the sun coming through the interstices of the bamboo lattice-work, lit up his fine countenance in all its melancholy beauty. Omelia gazed round the apartment with wonder, and then again at her attendant.

"Where am I?" she said in a soft whisper; "and you?" she paused, and looked at her blood-stained dress and shuddered.

"Hush, my child," said the old man, softly; "seek not to know all now. It is enough you are restored to life and consciousness. Thank the Great Spirit for that. You have passed, my daughter, through great dangers, and I had almost despaired of ever seeing you recover, and indeed now you are still in imminent danger. Therefore be careful, and let not your mind be too soon agitated with worldly cares."

"Oh, father, where am I?" she exclaimed, in imploring accents. "I have been mad—fearfully mad, and I have been wicked, I know that—indeed I have; but I am calm now—quite calm. You see I am, but oh, I have had cause for sorrow, more than even you can guess. What of him—what of Stanley?" she continued, as she endeavoured to raise herself up to approach nearer to Jahnsah. "What of him? tell me, father. Was it a dream only?—oh, would that it were!"

"My daughter, you must not agitate yourself thus, or I will not answer for your life. In good time, if aught weighs upon your mind—as I much fear there does—it shall be my business to do my best to relieve you. See, yonder flows the noble Jumna; you are not, I dare say, far from your own home and from those you love."

"Love," passionately ejaculated Omelia, "Talk not to me of love, father, "it has been my direst curse. It has turned all my fondest hopes to bitterness and gall. It was I who lured on two unhappy beings to destruction. Oh, I have been driven to desperation past all human endurance."

"How so, my daughter?—love should bring peace and comfort to the bruised spirit, and anguished mind, not evoke such maddening thoughts as you describe; beneath its soothing influence we should learn the mysteries of our better nature: all our relations in life are, or should be, under the influence of a humanising love. Calm yourself now, and when in a more fitting state we will talk more upon the subject. At present you are not able to bear further converse. See, I have prepared something to give you a little strength—eat."

So saying, the worthy priest placed before our heroine some light repast, which she gratefully accepted.

Although suffering from her wounds, and the shock attendant upon the events described, her reason was comparatively restored to her.

Still the remembrance of all she had gone through—the agonising thought of her last interview with Stanley and Clara, when she cursed him so bitterly and let her worst feelings rush on like a wild torrent, giving vent to the most bitter invectives against the perfidious deceiver, and eventually how he had followed her to that wild region and heard her maniac laughter.

An indistinct hazy recollection of these things, like the disjointed fragments of a hideous nightmare, still weighed heavily upon her mind. Byron says the "cold of clime are cold in love;" but with Omelia it was like the lava flame;" too ready to respond to the promptings of a false jealously, which distorted the whole current of her thoughts, and hurried her as by a fascination into a vortex of destruction,

Who can probe the heart of woman?—Who understand its main spring of action, or define its character! a mystery unsolved by the most profound philosopher, or most observant student of human nature.

Under the watchful care and good precepts of Jahnsah, Omelia began daily to increase in strength, and recover to a considerable extent the balance of her mind.

This excellent man by studiously avoiding any discussion that might remind her of her sufferings, and, by excellent advice, and unremitting attention, he managed to bring her to a much better feeling; and the deep sense of gratitude she entertained for him, naturally added weight to all he said. He had given her a brief and succinct account of the miraculous combat by Moorsha with the tiger, and had also told her how he had conveyed her, assisted by his friend, to her present habitation, but at the same time he had suppressed all mention of Stanley.

It was a subject he dreaded to broach, and thought very wisely that if he was too precipitate in undeceiving her as to the supposed fate of her lover, as he supposed him to be, the consequences might be disastrous in the extreme.

One day, however, when our heroine was comparatively recovered, the question was again for the hundredth time asked.

"Father," said Omelia, "I feel so calm, and happy under your kind care, that I shall almost dread going again out into the living world. Here at least I have had peace, the best and kindest of care and advice; but," and she paused.

"But what, my daughter," said the old man, smiling.

"Why, as I can learn nothing of him—of Stanley—why, no wthat I am capable of doing so, I must endeavour to learn if he perished on that horrible and fearful night."

"Will you make me a promise?" said Jahnsah, gently, laying his hand upon her arm.

"Unquestionably," was the prompt reply.

"Good. And keep it?"

"Assuredly, without doubt."

"Then promise now, if I tell you aught of Stanley, to seek to know no further of him for three days?"

"I promise, by all that's sacred."

"Then make your mind happy upon one account. Stanley was stunned and senseless; but he has been restored again to life. He still lives."

"Oh, incomparable happiness," wildly exclaimed Omelia, in a paroxysm of delight; "bless you, father, a thousand, thousand times, for this welcome intelligence. A fearful weight is taken off my mind. I live again, if not for his love. If the poor Indian girl is not worthy of all his fond professions, and another has stolen the heart she prized beyond all else so fondly, at least she will learn now how to master the fatal passion, hopeless as it may be; and bear herself more worthy of her humble race. Ah! it indeed is too true, how I have sought him after many a weary search in the vain hope, the delusive hope, that his heart was mine, and mine only; but the vision, too flattering to be true, is now for ever dispelled, like the deceitful mirage of the desert. His love will never now be mine—"

And the unhappy girl broke down in an agony of tears. She ceased speaking, but continued sobbing convulsively, whilst the Brahmin priest did all in his power to comfort and assauge her troubled spirit.

CHAPTER CCIII.

THE RECOVERY AND RETURN OF STANLEY.— MYSTERIOUS APPEARANCE.

It will be seen that there was good cause for Jahnsah to extract from Omelia her promise not to endeavour to seek Stanley for three days. It was an onerous task the old Brahmin had in dealing with the two inhabitants of his distant and obscure retreat. Stanley had been in a much more forward state of convalescence than Omelia, and Jahnsah had detailed to him all the particulars of his interviews with the latter, as also her tone of mind, which he had done so much to restore. To say the truth, Stanley himself was not in the most placid state, and the poor old Brahmin began to think that he had never had so hard a task as he experienced with these two unfortunate lovers. After Omelia had somewhat recovered her grief, he left her to her reflections, and proceeded through a different entrance to that part of the habitation where Stanley was located. He found the latter waiting his appearance with considerable anxiety.

It had been arranged between the two that the intelligence should be broken to the unhappy Indian girl respecting his recovery; but at the same time not a word was to be said as to his whereabouts. He was anxious to return to his friends, now that he was sufficiently recovered. He had communicated with them through the medium of Moorsha—and indeed Captain Morley and Clara had been to see him more than once during his illness, but of course with the utmost caution.

"How goes on your patient now?" said Stanley, as the Brahmin entered; "have you told her of my existence?"

"It has been done as you desired," was the reply; "the poor girl is broken down with joy at the intelligence."

"It is well, kind, father. How can I ever recompense you for all your trouble on my behalf."

"Enough, my son, I require no recompense from man. It is sufficient that we endeavour to do our duty in this world, without seeking rewards from mortal hands."

"Notwithstanding, I can never forget your kindness. Indeed, how much we all owe you for rescuing so many of our countrymen, frequently during this terrible revolt; but more of this hereafter. I have arranged to return to my friends; Moorsha has kindly undertaken to be my guide back to my quarters, and so kindest and best of protectors, I must say farewell for the present, to my excellent benefactor."

Moorsha soon appeared, and Stanley after another farewell and expression of his sense of gratitude, took leave of the old Brahmin and proceeded on his journey.

As Stanley and the *shikaree* passed by the spot where the terrible scene had taken place, the former seemed to pause as if spell-bound, and turning to his guide, inquired of him how it was he had chosen so wild a locality for the exercise of his calling.

"Why I should have imagined," now he observed; "that a man might be weeks or months here without ever being discovered."

"'Tis more than probable," said Moorsha, "but it so happened that I had been on the track of a tiger for some time past, and hearing the roar—when he stood over you—hastened to the spot. Yonder tree is a favourite, and an old station of mine. You may observe a stage has been erected between its branches."

"I see," was the reply.

"But why be surprised?" continued Moorsha, "it is the old, old story from our earliest childhood to the last moment of our existence. Fate, through long and perhaps many painful years of trouble we endeavour to altar its decrees. But it is seen throughout every transaction of our lives. 'Tis fate that decrees what is to be, and no man can alter his destiny."

Stanley looked furtively at his companion to know if there was any hidden meaning in his observations, but he could discover nothing from his grave and immovable features.

He knew well enough from his intercourse with the natives of India, that very many, and, indeed, most of them, were believers in predestination.

The nature of their religion encouraged this feeling, and it has been found almost impossible to divest their mind of the strong prejudice let, their intercourse with Europeans be ever so great. *Shikarees* especially are perhaps more than any other class imbued with this belief.

"Ah," exclaimed Stanley, "fate or no fate without your timely aid, my excellent friend, I should have been by this time food for a pack of savage beasts."

"Destiny again," curtly answered the other. "Now, I can never be injured by them," seriously continued Moorsha, with a countenance of the utmost gravity.

"And wherefore not?"

"Because it is ordained otherwise, and can never come to pass, that I should fall a victim to any of those rapacious monsters. I have met them in all sorts of places and ways. In the jungle—in the wood—in lonely huts—in the arena—I have watched for them all the lonely hours of night, but have, as you see, come off scathless. It was not to be, whilst—" he paused, and heaved a deep sigh—"whilst, ah! it was many, many years ago now," he muttered to himself, and seemed lost in his own reflections, entirely unconscious of the presence of his companion.

There was something peculiar and strange about the bearing of this man, very different and altogether superior to most others of his class. Stanley had been impressed with this from his first interview with him, and from the short chance observations that he occasionally let drop, Stanley augured that he had been intimately connected with Europeans in some earlier part of his life, for he was now past his meridian.

"Ah, my friend! at another time," said Moorsha; "perhaps I will tell you how and why it is I appear to bear this charmed life more than this. I will give you an unmistakeable instance of the degrees of destiny. For the present, we must let the matter rest, for see we are within sight of your friends!"

It was indeed true, Colonel Bridport and Mr. Hamilton were in sight, and advanced to meet him, and immediately behind them was Captain Morley.

"My dear friend," exclaimed the colonel, with more than his usual warmth and cordiality; "my dear friend, restored again to life! Welcome back to your quarters once again. We have had a pretty time of anxiety on your account, and had it not been for our worthy friend here," turning to Moorsha, "we should, I fear, have gone almost as distracted as yourself."

Stanley was warmly received by the others of the party, and of course, by no one more so than Clara, upon whose features there now sat a grave and settled melancholy. Stanley had not entered into any particulars to her of his wild and sudden flight. It is true she had been to see him with Captain Morley, when confined at Jahnsah's, but the painful subject had not been mentioned. All she had heard therefore was through Moorsha.

Towards the evening, however, she was alone in an apartment of the bungalow, when Stanley somewhat suddenly entered. He was not aware of being there, and she looked up with a heightened colour in some surprise. Stanley approached her, and placing his hand kindly on her shoulder, began thus—

"My dearest Clara, I hardly know what to say to account for my seemingly strange and wild conduct. Alas, it appears to me that I am the sport and victim of a series of disastrous circumstances. This girl, this Omelia, the saviour of my life—again and again—so faithful to me in many hours of trial—I cannot deny that I have learnt to love her with a mad, stupid, infatuated love, if you will. It has driven me to desperation, and made me forget for a time all else. Well, is it my fault? Is the growth of love in the human breast spontaneous, or does it come there by our own planting? You know—you surely know this. Ask yourself the question, and if you can, pity me; for I know what you will call it, a mad infatuation."

"I have not said so," rejoined Clara, "I have not said so. Rather call mine a mad

infatuation," she continued, the tears rising in her eyes, "rather call mine the wildest, most fatal passion, that ever wrung the breast of a poor suffering woman. "Go," she continued—"go to your Indian girl, who holds your soul in such perfect bondage. Go, it is not for me to control your actions. It is enough for poor women to suffer in silence—to bear patiently the scorn and taunts of the world. Enough! it is their vocation. Of what moment is it to the world if a woman nurses a hopeless passion, and, day by day, hour by hour, sinking under the load weighing at her heart, a load too heavy for mortal to bear long. No man heeds. It is her duty to suffer in silence, as hundreds, as thousands have done before, and will do again, I suppose."

No. 85.

"My dearest girl," said Stanley, "be not so unjust. No one has a greater esteem or consideration for you than myself, anything that pains you or causes you anxiety, finds, I am sure, a ready sympathetic response in my breast. And anything that is possible for me, as an honourable man, to do to serve you, you have only to command, and——"

"Cast off Omelia—your Indian idol— at once and for ever!" exclaimed Clara, with such sudden energy, that Stanley started back with surprise.

"Ah!" she scornfully continued, ' now, about your great professions. Does the very proposition arouse your alarms, so that you start like some guilty thing from its own thoughts? Oh, Stanley! I do indeed fear this girl is our evil genius—I cannot help thinking so—at least, I know she is mine. She has turned the whole current of your thoughts. Can you? Do you love her to that extent that places your feelings so completely beyond your own mastery? tell me, for once and for all—that I may at least know my worst fate. You surely need not me to tell you again how my love has been now the growth of years; the fondest dream of my life; and how entirely unconscious I was, until recently, of the Indian enchantress—this magician, who holds the master key of love's mysteries, and has such potent sway over the human heart. Who by sorcery, or some unholy rights, has bewitched and stolen from me all that I cared for in this world. Tell me, Stanley."

"My ever dearest Clara," said Stanley, as his arm gently encircled her waist, and he imprinted a kiss upon her forehead—"be not thus inveterate against one who perhaps deserves as much sympathy as any other of her sex, believe me no arts of sorcery or unholy rights have ever been practiced upon me, but I am in a measure bound to her, you must admit, by feelings of gratitude for her devotion and self sacrifice on my behalf. You do not know all her acts of kindness. You have only seen her when under the influence of a savage jealously, and she uttered words and execrations which where quite foreign to her nature, and which her better reason would at once repudiate; she is, I am told, now quite calm and reasonable, although I have not seen her myself."

"Not seen her?" exclaimed Clara,—"not seen her?—have you not been living under the same roof as that—that Brahmin priest's?"

"Certainly I have, but she has been utterly unconscious of this fact, and, as I tell you, I have not seen her since the last terrible interview we had here."

"Oh, Stanley!" shudderingly exclaimed Clara, "I tremble when I reflect upon the fearful expression of that girl's countenance. Would that we were far away from here— once again in dear old England, you might— you might learn to forget her, and perhaps learn to love me."

At this moment Stanley bent fondly over Clara, as if to reassure her of his good feelings towards her, when he was surprised and horrified at her frantically and suddenly grasping him convulsively, and uttering a scream of alarm and horror.

"Ah!" she said, wildly, "ah! again that face!" and she pointed to the closed windows of the apartment. Stanley looked in the direction she pointed, but could discern nothing that gave occasion for any alarm. "The window! the window! that face!" she exclaimed," again I have seen it, as it

harrows up my soul to contemplate—who or what can it be?"

"My dear girl, there is nothing there, it must be conjured up only by the aid of your too vivid imagination, see! all is quiet," he continued, as he approached the window, "and we are quite alone; what strange fancy is this, dear Clara?"

"No fancy, Stanley, I saw it as plainly as I now see you, two fearful stealthy looking eyes peering through the window pane. I saw it before—the same lineaments some day or two since. Oh! would that this dreadful war were over, that we might return again to our own peaceful, happy clime."

Stanley hardly believed even now that Clara had anything to occasion alarm, and tried his utmost to re-assure her, and restore her confidence.

"You have gone through much suffering and many trials, my dear girl, and start and tremble at imaginary ills," he said.

"And I have still a greater trial to bear —a trial that will endure as long as life lasts, and end only with it, I fear," said Clara, sadly; "but yet, Stanley, while you are by my side, I ought at least to try and be happy—this Indian girl——"

"Was it her you saw, or fancied you saw at the window just now?" said Stanley, somewhat hastily. He had imagined that possibly Omelia had, by some secret agency, discovered his whereabouts, and had heard their voices, and looked in at the window. He was in this, however, mistaken.

"Oh, no," said Clara, "it was the face of a man, quite different to any I have seen about here, and who it can possibly be, and what can be his intentions, I cannot possibly imagine." While she was yet speaking, Stanley observed against the window, too plainly to admit of any mistake, the face of a man endeavouring to see into the interior of the apartment. There could now be no mistake about it. He did not appear to observe them, but was at the same time very quiet and cautious in his movements, as if he would avoid observation or detection. Stanley's looks were fascinated to the spot, and Clara, following the direction of his eyes, uttered one wild shriek as she exclaimed, "that face again!" and immediately sunk senseless to the ground.

In an instant, fearing some treachery, Stanley flung open the window, dashed through the opening, pistol in hand, and was just in time to catch sight of the figure of a man retreating into a neighbouring clump of trees which formed the outskirts of a wood. He shouted loudly and fired one barrel of his revolver, but with no other effect than arousing Colonel Bridport and Captains Morley and Robinson to the spot.

"How now!" they shouted; "Stanley! Stanley!"

"Here! here!" exclaimed the other, in answer, as they rushed towards him.

"What's amiss?" was the instant enquiry.

"Some figure—some strange looking mysterious fellow has, it appears, been lurking about here for the last two or three days."

"Clara has spoken of such," said Colonel Bridport.

"Well?"

"Well—I fear it is not well, Colonel, I saw him looking through yonder window, saw him, as I am a living man, as plainly as I see you now. I opened the window and went after him, and only caught sight of his retreating figure, which I lost sight of in yonder bushes. He can be after no good, so I fired at him, although I believe the rascal was out of range of pistol shot."

"Ah!" said the Colonel, "I have my suspicions, but it will not do to rely on these alone, we must endeavour to make sure. What, ho!—ho, there! Horses!—at once! do you hear!" he said to the servants that answered his summons. "We will see to this at once, if it be possible."

Having attended to Clara, and placed her under the gentle care of the Colonel's daughters, the party sallied forth on horseback, to see if they could discern any traces of the missing fugitive.

"Hold!" said the Colonel. "The dogs! Let loose Hector and Juno!" This was addressed to a servant; and in a few moments two magnificent hounds—prize beasts of the Colonel—came bounding towards their master.

"So ho! we are pretty well equipped. Should you know this beauty, Stanley, if you should chance to see him again?" said the Colonel.

"Yes, out of a thousand," was the reply. I saw him so plainly through the window that I had ample time to observe his features."

"It is well! let us hope we may unearth him from his hiding-place, wherever it may be. It can be for no good intent that he was lurking thus mysteriously at our bungalow, and I think these are not times to pass by unheeded any suspicious circumstance. Was he in any way familiar to your recollection?—I mean in features or person. Did you ever see him before?"

"Never, to my knowledge. He did not appear to be any native who was out upon a marauding expedition, to see what he could pick up. On the contrary, he seemed more as if he were looking for some one, or it may be that he was reconnoitring preparatory to making an attack upon our habitation; any way his movements were of a most stealthy character, such as to give rise to my worst suspicions."

CHAPTER CCCIV.

THE CHASE AND ITS CONSEQUENCES.— TERRIBLE ENCOUNTER.

THUS prepared for any emergency, with some few private soldiers and the dogs, the party hastened to the spot where Stanley had missed sight of the fugitive. A careful inspection was made of the place, which was, as before mentioned, on the outskirts of an Indian forest. The clump of trees into which the figure had disappeared were thickly covered with underwood and densely tangled vegetation. In these a search was made, the dogs sent in, but with no satisfactory result.

Beyond lay a forest, through which a rude and circuitous path had been made by occasional travellers.

"We will proceed onwards, at any rate," said Colonel Bridport, "it is now no use giving up the search on the outset. There are animals of no very mild dispositions lurking about, but there are plenty of us— a quick eye and a steady nerve, and we have nought to fear."

"Hurrah! I like the spirit," said Captain Morley, "anything is better than doubt and suspense. Ah! what is that?" and he pointed to a spot where the trees had been cleared from the surrounding vegetation.

"I know not—dismount and see," was the reply.

No sooner said than done.

"Ah! ah!" said Morley, as he inspected the place, "here has been a fire, at all events, and I fancy some party has bivouaced for the night. See! there are the remains of half-burnt faggots and bones, the latter evidently the remnants of their repast. And what have we here?—a portion of a dress—a woman's dress—it seems to have belonged to an European lady—and here is a portion of a belt, if I am not mistaken—yes, it certainly is———"

"Let me look at it," said the Colonel, "we may possibly learn something therefrom. Ah! what is this? my worst suspicions are confirmed," and he at the same time carefully examined the object which Morley had handed to him.

"This belt has belonged to a Thug!" he exclaimed, turning to Stanley, with looks of surprise; "I know the marks engraved on the buckle to be the signs of their accursed order. See !" he said, handing it round for inspection; "do you notice those characters? they are the mystic signs of Thugism; I have had them come under my notice before this."

No one doubted the words of the Colonel, most present knew his experience to have been too great to admit of his being mistaken upon the subject. Stanley had heard and knew of the existence in India of a race of men called Thugs, or stranglers, who make it their horrible and unholy business to commit daily murders in the most secret and silent manner by strangulation. He knew moreover that their subtlety and treachery was beyond all precedent. It is not till lately that Europeans have been able to comprehend the enormous extent these men carried on their hateful practices. Thousands even now perish every year victims to this detestable race of men, who perform their unholy calling under the cloak or name of religion.

There is no reason to believe that Europeans were not aware of the existence of such criminals as the Thugs, until shortly after the conquest of Seringapatam, in 1799, when about a hundred were apprehended in the vicinity of Bangalore. They did not then engage general attention, nor would it appear that they were suspected to belong to a distinct class of hereditary marauders, settled in various parts of India, alike remarkable for the singular and secret mode they followed their terrible calling, and the extent of their practices. In the year 1807, between Chittoor and Arcat several of these wretched beings were apprehended, belonging to a gang which had just returned laden with booty from an expedition to Travancore, and information was then obtained which ultimately led to the development of a system of secret and insidious wholesale murder, so appalling that the mind turned from the details with disgust, and was disposed to seek refuge by endeavouring to disbelieve the facts which were, however, but too truly proved to admit of there being any doubt upon the subject.

"Yes," said Colonel Bridport, "I fear me much that this is a key to the mystery. Here has been an encampment of Thugs, and I should not be surprised if the man you saw at the window was not one of their abominable gang, but for what purpose he was there, or who he was seeking for, remains at present undisclosed. However, we will on, and see if there be any further traces of them. Forward, then, at once ! and keep a sharp look out. It is not their practice generally to attack any party openly, they watch and wait to entrap them unawares."

The party moved forward, and soon became enveloped in the deep recesses of the forest, and the way became so choked up with underwood, that it was with difficulty they could thread a passage through. It was indeed a gloomy path they were traversing, and one not unattended with immediate damage, as there was no telling what denizen of the wood might confront them in their path and dispute their passage. The foliage concealed numberless beasts of prey and noxious reptiles, who might be upon them without a moment's notice.

"Don't you think, Colonel," said Morley, "that it would be as well, by way of caution, to scratch and mark the trees every now and then, so that we may know, if it be necessary, how we may best retrace our steps. I observe there are other smaller pathways which diverge from the one we are now tracing; should we by chance take one of them as we return, there will be, I fear, some trouble to find the way."

"A good thought, Morley," was the reply; "we may be, after all, pursuing a phantom, but it is not the characteristic of Englishmen to give up for trifles. It shall be done. Hawkins, take your knife, and, with one or two others, you can just cut the barks of the trees at convenient distances, for, to say the truth, it is getting more of a wilderness of a place every step we take.

This precaution was carried into effect by the attendants, whom, I think, began to have some serious misgivings as to the utility of their search.

"Hush !" said Robinson: and they all came to a dead stop. "There is a sound or movement of something." They listened attentively; in the unbroken stillness of the forest the rustling of the smallest leaf might be heard.

"Hush !" again said Robinson: and there was now heard distinctly the movement of some figure a few paces off; it did not appear to be in the path, but was creeping amongst the underwood; they could hear the branches being disturbed by its progress.

"Ah ! there !" called out Stanley, "speak, or I fire !" These words were scarcely uttered, when a sharp report followed from Stanley's rifle.

"Gracious Heavens ! It is he—it is the man we are in search of," he exclaimed, in a half suppressed whisper.

"Where? where?" was the enquiry of all.

Stanley had dropped from his horse and was about to proceed in the direction he indicated, when Colonel Bridport secured him somewhat suddenly, and pulled him back.

"Are you mad?" he exclaimed.

"No! I hope not. Let me go, Colonel; I will run all risks myself. I saw him distinctly; the same man. Let me go, I entreat."

"Tush, man, never! you seek certain death. Do you suppose you will ever be able to find us again when once entangled in that barbarously wild spot? you cannot expect to return alive. It is rushing to certain destruction—and what is more—it is worse than useless. That fellow is now, without doubt, belonging to a party of Thugs, and it is utterly hopeless for you to endeavour to compete with him in fastnesses with which he is well acquainted. No doubt he is going to join his party. Let me see; I wish I knew where his gang was located, I might know some of the rascals, at any rate I would bring them back prisoners upon suspicion. What had best be done now? How far is it through this forest—do you know, Hawkins?"

"We are hardly half through it yet, sir," was the reply; "but if you continue on you will shortly come to an open plain in the midst of the forest, where the trees have been levelled to the ground."

"And in the event of our going completely through the forest, is there not a way by the river, somewhere, by which we can return?"

"There is a way, sir, but it is a long distance round, and, moreover, anything but an agreeable one."

"How so? It must be surely better than this, seeing that it can hardly be worse."

"Well, sir, it is a long way round, and the river abounds in crocodiles, who prowl about at night, to snap up a stray animal or two as they come down to drink, leopards, tigers, and peumas, are constantly at the water side."

"Umph. Well, we will push on as fast as possible to this plain you speak of."

By the time they had proceeded a little farther on their journey, Robinson and Lieutenant Seagraves, who was another of the party, journeying through the wood, were, with one or two attendants, some little distance a-head of the others, when, to the surprise and horror of these behind, they saw Robinson and Seagrave's horses both fall, and the riders both disappear as by some invisible agency; both the dogs began baying vociferously, and seemed engaged in some struggle close by.

"Push forward! in mercy's sake," exclaimed Colonel Bridport, "not a moment is to be lost," and clapping spurs to his horse he rushed on hastily, the rest following with the utmost speed. They had not gone far when the Colonel's horse stumbled;

Morley and Stanley, who were immediately following, would have shared the same fate, but the former drew up his horse suddenly and at the same time applied his other hand in pulling the check rein of Stanley's steed, who was at a loss to comprehend its meaning.

"Dismount!" said Morley, as he dropped from his own horse. The order was obeyed instantly and then was seen the cause of the order being given. Across the narrow pathway there were two or three ropes drawn about a foot and a half from the ground, which being risen under the horses' feet as they passed had effectually thrown them as described. Morley saw that some insiduous foe was at work, and the emergency of the case did not admit a moment's delay; already his countrymen might, and no doubt were, in their enemies' clutches.

"Cut the ropes and forward on foot!" were the orders he gave, and at the same time he proceeded to demolish the first rope himself with his drawn sword.

While this was going on, the baying and growling of the dogs as if engaged in an angry contest, and the noise as of a desperate struggle could be heard. Morley and Stanley with the others pushed forward and emerged into the open plain described by Hawkins; it was well they did so; Seagrave and Robinson were in the hands of Thugs.

They were prostrate on the ground, rendered powerless and apparently dead or senseless. A Thug knelt on the chest of each, and was compressing the cord round their necks to deprive them of life noiselessly. Colonel Bridport was on his feet, however, and contesting manfully with several assailants. He also had a cord round his neck which one had hold of, and compressed so tight that it nearly suffocated him. Nevertheless, the gallant Colonel was fighting desperately against such odds, in which he was materially assisted by his dogs, who had inflicted severe punishment upon several of the assailants. These noble brutes had divided their attention to the protection of their master, and at the same time had assisted in some measure both Seagrave and Robinson. Indeed it is more than probable that without their assistance they would all three have perished before their friends had arrived. Not an instant was to be lost. Stanley let fly his rifle; luckily now with better success. The wretch who had Seagrave in his clutches received the contents of the barrel, and made a hasty retreat, although in all probability mortally wounded. The other miscreant was seized hold of by some of the soldiers, and bound hand and foot with his own cord. While this was going on,

Morley and several others rushed to the relief of their Colonel. The villain who had hold of the rope had the honour of receiving Morley's first sword cut. It was a back stroke, and cut completely through the thick white head dress worn by these rascals, and laid open his scull, sending him instantly to his account. Relieved from this villain, the Colonel felt like a ship that had righted herself in a overpowering storm. It was long odds to fight some half-dozen ruffians with one lugging at a cord round your neck, besides this the Colonel had been unable to draw his sword, in consequence of those who clung with such tenacity to him. He did so now, and was able "to have at them," in good earnest. They now observed a large body of dusky figures in the further part of the open plain. These had hitherto been concealed, or had else escaped the notice of the European party; but now seeing their countrymen being cut to pieces, many rushed to the rescue.

Hitherto the battle had been waged in a sort of pell-mell fight, without order or arrangement, but the Colonel when he perceived the other body of Thugs, thought it advisable to form his few troops in order.

"Forward men! keep compact together. March!" And the gallent Colonel advanced upon his foes. There were not perhaps a dozen men in all of the British troops, while it was impossible to imagine how many the others numbered. Certainly if they had attacked all at the same time with any thing like spirit and determination, they must have overwhelmed the Europeans; but they are naturally cowards, and nothing but the fear of being taken prisoners, and meeting condign punishment, commensurate with their deserts, would induce them to fight at all.

The Colonel called out to them to surrender, but the only reply was a confused babel of sounds, amongst which could be heard. "Accursed Feringee! death to the Feringee!"

"Make ready, present, fire!" shouted the Colonel. A rattling report was the answer, waking up the quiet solitude of the forest with an hundred echos. The shot appeared to do deadly havoc, as numbers seemed killed or wounded from its effect, but not many seconds had elapsed before it was answered by the Thugs, amongst whom however there happened to be many of the revolted Sepoys. Either four or five of the little band of British soldiers were wounded by this volley, three of them mortally. This was more than could be spared out of less than a dozen men. The Colonel saw that if they intended really to show any thing like fight his situation was critical.

Inwardly cursing his imprudence in following the fugitive to such fastnesses, and thus being caught, as it were, in ambush; he nevertheless determined to be prompt in his resolves, and make the best of the case.

"Fix bayonets—charge!" shouted the Colonel. On rushed the troops, completely through the band opposed to them. Again they charged with desperate determination, bayoneting many in their progress. Nevertheless, although their foes were errant curs, they were, nevertheless, very numerous, and shots from all quarters came against the gallant band. It would have been hard to say what might have been the issue of this unequal contest, had not Morley, Stanley, and Robinson come to the rescue. The former, seeing how matters stood, and having mastered and put to flight those who originally commenced the attack, now sought to recover the horses, and mounting them, at once proceeded at full gallop to the scene of action. They rushed on infuriated into the very midst of their enemies, and a terrible slaughter ensued.

The mounted officers sabred all that were within reach, and committed frightful slaughter amongst their foes, who fled in all directions. Those who remained of the English infantry loaded and fired repeated volleys at the flying miscreants, who sought shelter in the surrounding wood. Stanley, in the *meleè*, had caught sight of the man whose mysterious appearance had been the cause of their present expedition; he rushed furiously upon him and commanded him to surrender. An insolent laugh was the reply. Clapping spurs to his horse, Stanley succeeded in giving the ruffian a stroke with his sabre, inflicting a severe wound in the left shoulder; he, however, still continued the retreat, crying as he did so:—

"I will remember this with other favours, Lieutenant Stanley: a day of requital will assuredly come."

He spoke this in tolerably good English; Stanley was rendered doubly savage at the prospect of his enemy again escaping him, and seeing he was getting entangled in the wood, where it was impossible to follow with a horse, Stanley again dismounted, and, on the impulse of the moment, followed his adversary on foot. Morley caught sight of the action, and dismounted with the intention of staying him, if possible, in his imprudent resolve, shouting as loudly as he could for Stanley to halt—he hurried on. A dark streak of blood guided their footsteps, which no doubt was still flowing from the wound inflicted by Stanley's sabre. After some short distance had been gained, Morley succeeded in overtaking Stanley as they came into a small passage or foot-path in the wood.

"Headstrong as usual," exclaimed Morley, as he arrived up with the other. "How could you be so imprudent? It was a thousand to one but you were rushing into the very midst of your foes to certain death, and what is the result?"

"My dear fellow, it is that accursed fellow who has again eluded me. I would rather have lost my commission than he should have escaped. He cannot be far, however, as I fancy he must soon give up from loss of blood." And he paused, breathless with his exertions, and looked round to see where next to bend his footsteps. Morley, however, persuaded him, after some little reasoning, to seek their companions in arms; and the two endeavoured to retrace their steps; what was their horror, however, after many fruitless attempts, they could neither find their way out of the intricacies of the forest, nor discern any traces of their friends.

CHAPTER CCCV.

MORE ADVENTURES.—A NIGHT OF PERIL IN THE FOREST.

VAIN and futile were the many attempts made by Stanley and Morley to discover any path that might lead them to the open plain where the scene of the conflict had taken place. They shouted loudly to their companions, calling them each by name repeatedly, but with no success, and it was with dejected looks and heavy hearts that they considered what course had best be adopted under their present circumstances. It was impossible to know, whether any of their foes where lying in ambush in the immediate vicinity, and every nerve was strained to the utmost degree of tension as the fearful contemplation presented itself to their mind, that after all they might fall victims to the invidious manœuvres of the hateful Thugs. The thought was agonizing to the last degree.

"There is, however, no help for it," said Stanley; "I deeply regret, my dear friend, that any imprudence on my part should have led you into this trouble as well as myself. To say the truth, it was not the best of judgment that directed us to follow the footsteps of this scoundrel at all, whoever he may be, and that he knows me is very clear, by his calling me by my name as he retreated."

"Ah!" replied Morley, "it is of no use now talking about what is passed. I am much pleased with the reflection that I had the prudence to follow you as I did, otherwise you would have been entirely alone, and if we are either or both of us to meet an untimely end—to be strangled by Thugs—devoured by wild beasts, or starved to death in the forest, why, it is better to die in company than to meet our fate alone, cut off from all human sympathy. Let us see, Hawkins said that the open glade was about half way through the forest. This appears a regular path, and must surely lead to somewhere; we have no other alternative I suppose, than to follow this, and trust to Providence."

"I suppose not; but it is a thousand to one if it leads us out, for it is evidently not the one Hawkins spoke of, and then again we must be especially favoured by Providence to escape the numerous animals in our passage. Have you any powder left in your flask? I have hardly enough for another charge."

"Oh, yes, enough for both of us."

"Then let us load at once."

"I think," said Morley, "it would be advisable for us to stay on this spot for a short time; it is just possible that when the Colonel calls over the muster roll he may miss us and send in search. Should that be the case, they may be able to find us when we cannot find them. It is certain we cannot be so very great a distance off, and I should almost have thought within hearing of some of them."

"Oh, there is no telling as to that," was the reply; the echoes of the forest are so deceptive, that the voice appears to come sometimes from quite a different quarter than it in reality does."

They waited for a considerable period, agreeable to the suggestion of Morley, but neither saw nor heard anything of their companions, and it was with many an anxious look that they took their way from the spot. After proceeding some distance the path diverged into two sinuous courses. Which of them were they to take? It was necessary to hold a council war. They paused irresolute, when in the distance they could discern a figure. They paused again, not to be too precipitate, before they knew if it were friend or foe. When, oh! joyful sight, the figure was dressed in English uniform, and was without doubt one of their countrymen. They shouted and received a reply; when, upon hastening on, they discovered it to be Hawkins, who was wounded rather severely in the leg and side. Never, surely, was there any man greeted with more heartfelt gladness than this individual. They both thought he had been sent in search of them.

"Well, Hawkins, all alone?" said Morley. "Has the Colonel sent you to seek for us by yourself?"

Hawkins seemed, if possible, more delighted even than they were at the meeting, but shaking his head he replied:—

"Indeed, no, Captain, I am sorry to say I am in this wood without the Colonel's orders. Indeed, to say the truth, without any orders at all. I have missed my way, and am out of my reckoning."

"Indeed! and so are we! How comes it you left the open plain?"

"Well, sir, you see I really ought not to have done so, but one of our men, Mat Parker, was set upon very hardly by several of these *varmints;* I knocked over one or two of them, and the rest made off like a pack of sneaking hounds, as they are. Well, one comes behind Mat, and runs him through, before I had time to put him on his guard. Well, this so enraged me that I pursued the scoundrel, who made off for the forest, and, thank Heaven, I succeeded in overtaking him and settling his business off-hand; not without, however, receiving a nasty wound or two; but no matter for that, I have had my revenge upon the coward. After this I could not find my way back, and have been wandering about till by good luck I chanced to meet with you."

The two officers were glad enough to have the companionship of the faithful Hawkins in their present predicament, more especially as he knew the country about their quarters better than any other party, he having had opportunities of observing the locality arround, from his frequent foraging expeditions for the mess table. He was, however, quite at fault now respecting the course to take; so the three continued their course, urged on by the hopelessness of despair. The roaring of wild beasts added to the horrors of their situation. They had not gone very far, when they observed, over their head, crouched on the the branch of a tree, apparently preparing to make a spring, a small species of leopard or tree tiger as it is called in India. They fell back immediately, and Morley's piece was at his shoulder in an instant; another second or two and it was discharged, and down dropped the animal severely wounded, but not dead. They, however, finished him with their swords.

"This bids fair to be a tranquil and charming night for all of us," said Morley, "however, come what may, we will fight while we have a shot in the locker."

"I have been debating with myself if we had not better endeavour to fix our quarters somewhere for the night," observed Hawkins.

"Yes, a charming—spot to do so," observed Stanley, "why, what chance have we of safety in such a place as this?"

"There are but two courses that I know of," said Hawkins. "One is, to clear a spot as well as we can, and gather all the combustible materials that may be needed, and make a circle of fire round us; as long as that burns we are safe."

"And the other alternative?"

"The other would be, to find if possible, two or three hollow trees, into which we might creep, and, by covering up the aperture with the bark of another tree, we might get a little rest in a perpindicular position."

"Well, we may be compelled to have recourse to some such alternative, but at present we will not give in without endeavouring to see if it be possible to catch a glimpse of the heavens again." And so " with weary steps and slow," did the three disheartened travellers take their lonely way. They had numberless alarms, and two or three narrow escapes from snakes, but the longest period of trial must have an end, and after hours of painful and anxious wanderings, to their infinite joy they emerged from the forest into open country again; and oh! with what heartfelt thanks did they greet the sight of an open field. They were by the margin of a river upon emerging from the forest, and a lovely landscape lay before them. The moon interlaced the water with silver streaks, and there was a calmness and serenity in the scene which lay before them, which struck them with awe.

"Where are we now?" was enquired immediately. Hawkins looked carefully round.

"Ah, very many miles from our quarters, sir; we are at the farther edge of the forest, and the only way back is by the side of the river, and that is miles round. Unfortunately this part is a perfect waste or wilderness, without hut or hovel near. We must see if we can find some place to pass the night in safety, when, perhaps, in the morning, we may get some conveyance down the river." They had not walked many yards when Morley, who went first, suddenly discharged his piece at something in the water; the other two drew back with guns shouldered, when they were horrified to behold a monstrous crocodile emerge from the water and pursue Morley with a determination to snap him up.

"Fly! Fly! Captain," shrieked out Hawkins. "It's your only chance, climb yonder tree and you are safe!"

Morley hastened on at his utmost speed, and flung his discharged rifle at the brute's head, at which the monster savagely snapped, bringing his jaws together with a dreadful crash.

"Fly! Fly!" still shouted Hawkins—"the tree! the tree!"

The scaly monster was evidently gaining upon Morley, and the two spectators absolutely trembled with excitement. Stanley would have fired, but Hawkins restrained him as saying it would be only adding wings to the speed of the brute. So the two followed the footsteps of both at some distance off. The scaly reptile was within a few feet of the pursued officer, and there was yet many yards to gain before he could reach a tree. What time would he have to make an ascent? The two comrades were frozen with horror and closed their eyes as though unable to bear the sight of their companion coming to such an untimely and shocking end, without their being able to render any the

No. 86.

smallest assistance. Another moment and all would have been over with poor Morley, but with a superhuman effort that matched the antelope, in speed he reached the tree, the beast following at his heels with open jaws.

As he came at full trot, Morley slipped round the tree with miraculous agility and eluded the animal's onslaught. By the impetus of his own speed, the crocodile was carried some yards past the spot before he could discover that his prey had so dexterously eluded him. His length of body prevented him turning upon his intended victim with very great agility; this gave time for Morley to ascend the tree, of which he did not fail to avail himself. The animal returned to the charge, but Morley looked down upon him from an overhanging branch, safe from his further molestation while seated there.

"Heaven be praised," exclaimed Stanley. "Safe for the present, at any rate."

There did not appear any probability of the crocodile's departure, for he took his station at the base of the tree, and looked up at Morley with wistful and eager eyes. Morley hooted at him, and threw down what missiles he had, at the enemy, who would not however quit his post. Stanley and Hawkins had crept round to a bank covered with bushes, to get out of the animals sight.

"Now, what is to be done?" said the former. "We are all three prisoners, and I think I can have a quiet shot from here, with a tolerable certainty of rolling the fellow over."

"By your leave, sir! No!" replied Hawkins. "Let us wait a short time. I have had a brush or two with these animals before now, myself, and know how hard they are to hit with a rifle ball, which generally glances off their cursed hides perfectly harmless. There are but two places where they are vulnerable: that is, in the eye, or the soft part of the body, immediately under the shoulder, and, at this distance, it is very improbable that you would hit either."

Hawkins, moreover, informed his companion, that he had, in company with others, hunted the crocodile on one or two occasions; and they found the most efficacious weapon to be a long spear, and when that could not be obtained, they used to fix their bayonets on long poles. Hawkins had his bayonet with him, but where to find a pole? He crept cautiously about, and luckily succeeded in getting a tolerably straight branch of a tree about seven feet in length. To this he firmly tied his bayonet. "Now," he observed, "we are somewhat better prepared; my leg is so stiff from the wound that it will be impossible for me to run away. We will get a little nearer to him, if possible. So, now, sir, if you please, you may try your hand at a shot. He will, in all probability, make for this spot if not mortally wounded, so I will take up my station here to receive him on my bayonet," continued Hawkins, as he advanced some little distance from his officer.

"I am all ready, sir; I think you had better try the shoulder, just underneath the fore leg," he called out to his lieutenant.

A sharp report was the reply, and the shot had hit its mark, although the animal was but slightly wounded, and appeared still to have lots of fight in him, for he turned round and rushed furiously at his assailants. Hawkins was the first who attracted his attention, and, as he came towards him, Stanley let fly his other barrel in the hopes of hitting his eye. The ball struck the skull, and seemed for a moment to stagger him, but he soon recovered, and was up with one of his assailants. Hawkins dropped upon one knee, and firmly grasping his temporary spear, awaited with admirable coolness the animal's onslaught, when, as he approached, he raised the head of the spear, or rather bayonet, and thrust it into the animal's open jaws. If it had passed down his throat, or into his skull, Hawkins might have been declared victor, but, from the weight of the monster, the bayonet was twisted, and passed through the upper jaw, inflicting a severe, but not a mortal wound; however, the bayonet protruded through the creature's head for more than a foot, and therefore was a prisoner. Stanley now boldly advanced upon the enemy, and succeeded in inflicting a mortal wound with his sword, upon which Morley droped from his tree, and joyfully rejoined his companions. It was a fearful looking monster, the three contemplated being a crocodile of the largest species known in India.

"That's as near a touch as ever I had," said Morley, "what a voracious brute!"

"Yes, sir," said Hawkins, and we are not safe a moment here. "Look yonder!" They did so, and saw a long distance off, two tigers, or else a tiger and leopard, lapping up the water on the opposite bank. The animals did not however apparently observe them. The three wayfarers now searched anxiously about for some place of shelter for the night.

CHAPTER CCCVI.

THE BIVOUAC FOR THE NIGHT. MORE PERILS. THE RETURN TO QUARTERS.

It was with anxious thoughts and eager eyes that the three unfortunate travellers sought some protection from the dangers which now surrounded them. It seemed a miracle that they should have escaped as they had, for the river was perfectly swarming with reptile life, and rhinoceroses and alligators were known to frequent its banks. After a search for a short time they succeeded in finding a cave not far from the bank of the river. This they joyfully hailed with delight, and by the united exertions of all three they contrived to roll a large stone against the mouth of it; but before this was finally fixed in its place, they provided themselves with a sufficiency of fuel to last them the night. Not that it was necessary for warmth, but they thought it best to light a rousing fire before they settled themselves —first that they might light up the innermost recesses of their retreat, and make a careful inspection of it, and at the same time it would ward off any intruders. Before entering the temporary domicile, Hawkins cut a number of canes from the laul trees and bamboos, which were near, with which he formed a sort of fence behind the stone by sticking them in the ground at equal distances, and forming them into lattice work. Thus protected, the little party were comparatively comfortable, and awaited the issue of the morning with tolerable composure. Sorely fatigued, as they undoubtedly were, rest appeared out of the question.

The terrible scenes they had witnessed, and the trials they had gone through, within the space of a few hours, all acted upon their minds too powerfully to admit of calm repose.

So lighting their pipes they began to fumigate their retreat with the fragrant weed. Hawkins whose experience in savage life was much greater than either of his officers had ever imagined, entertained them with discriptions of the dangers he had passed through, when following, and hunting many savage animals, and with such converse they contrived to wear away the hours through that lovely night. When at length tired nature asserted her supremacy, and the three dropped off to sleep.

How long they had continued so it was uncertain, when Stanley was awoke by some unnatural noise, which seemed to strike against the cave, and reverberate in its deep recesses. He looked towards the opening, when he was horror struck to see the stone pulled forcibly back two or three times, and strike against the sides of the rock, as it returned to its position again. It was this noise that had awoke him.

He hastily aroused his companions, when what was their surprise to see a monstrous tiger coolly pulling the stone on one side, and snifting in, as if he smelt some tempting dainty inside. It was now seen how useful Hawkins' precautionary measures were, in fixing up a pallisade behind the stone, for the animal at last succeeded in removing the stone several inches, and got between it and the pallisade. It was evidently a full grown tiger, and a huge mass of yellow-striped fur, and a pair of mischievous looking eyes, were visible to the inhabitants of the cave. The animal was on his hind legs only, and began with his fore paws, to pull down Hawkin's temporary defence. He had not much time

for his purpose allowed him, for Stanley and Morley passed their swords through his body, almost simultaneously, and she sent forth a series of sharp roars or cries of rage and pain, appalling to hear. The cry of the tiger is even much more horrid then that of the lion; there is a grandeur in the deep full tones of the latter animal, but there is neither majesty or music in the voice of the tiger. It begins with a deep, slow, and melancholy howling, these become more acute and hurried, till they terminate in a piercing cry, of which no description can be given, and this cry finishes with a convulsive jarring, as if the rocks around were shaking to pieces. This voice is very loud, and when it is uttered in the forest, it is so repeated in echoes that the roaring of one tiger is heard as though the place was surrounded by numbers of them. It would have led any hearer to such a supposition, in the present instance, for the noise resounded in the entrance of the cave as if there were at least a dozen animals within and around.

"I think that will be enough to satisfy his enquiring mind for to night," said Morley, as the tiger managed to crawl from between the stone and palisade, evidently in the greatest pain and agony.

"Now, what's the next proceeding?" said Stanley; "it will never do to let the opening be so visible as it is now, in consequence of the removal of the stone. How are we to return it to its position?"

"Let us wait a short time and see if we hear anything more of our feline friend," said Morley, "and if not, we will venture out and put it back — or stay — we can manage it, even here."

They now passed a rope round part of the stone, and succeeded in fixing it firmly again, and had no more disturbance or alarms for the remainder of the night.

The rays of the morning sun found their way into the cave, and indicated to its three occupants the dawn of morning; upon the appearance of which they emerged from their place of safety, and found the tiger by the water side quite dead; he had crept thither no doubt to slake his thirst.

After waiting some time, they were lucky enough to descry a boat laden with grain, which conveyed them partly towards their destination, and after a short march, they were again at their quarters.

Colonel Bridport and their comrades, after many perils had reached home the previous night, and were in the utmost state of anxiety about their missing companions, hardly ever expecting to see them again alive.

It appeared that three soldiers had lost their lives in the contest with the Thugs, and four more were severely wounded. Colonel Bridport had also received several contusions and surface wounds, but Lieutenant Seagrave's injuries were of so severe a character that it was questionable if he could possibly survive them. They had succeeded however in making two of the Thugs prisoners. The rest of the scoundrels had flown in all directions.

No key was as yet obtained as to the cause of the appearance of the man who had so suddenly startled them. Stanley found Clara still very dejected, but the charming daughters of the worthy Colonel Bridport did all in their power to cheer her drooping spirits.

In a day or two after Stanley's return, he was informed that a venerable Hindoo desired to have audience with him, and he was both surprised and pleased to see that it was his late host and friend the good Jahusha.

"My worthy kind-hearted and most esteemed friend and saviour in the hour of need," said Stanley, upon the old man's entrance, "how can I ever sufficiently express the deep sense of gratitude I owe you? without your timely aid, I shudder to think of my own fate and the fate also of her whom I hold still dearer even than mine own life. But father, since I saw you I have had more adventures and trials—my comrades had almost again given me up as lost."

"We have all our trials, my son," answered Jahusha, mildly; "this life to many, and alas, indeed, to most of us, is but as a crucible wherewith we separate the worthless drop from the purer essence? this done, we are fit, let us hope, for a better sphere. For ah, the noblest sight beneath the sun, is an erring mortal—as we all are, at best: but to see one who under overwhelming trials, dangers, and misfortunes, keeps his heart in tact, and never loses sight of the high path of honor and rectitude, or is unmindful of the light that is shed upon him, from far—far beyond those stars; and who in the most grinding penury, and the utter abasement of man's wretchedness, never stoops to fawn and flatter, or barter his free spirit for the world's idle wealth. For does he not then hold within himself a brighter jewel than gold can ever produce—a jewel that will shed its light upon him in the loneliest and darkest hour of his existence?"

"It is indeed truth you are uttering, Father," said Stanley, as the mellow and mild voice of the Hindoo fell softly upon his ear, and gave additional weight to the words he uttered, while at the same time it impressed the hearer with the speakers sincerity. There was a pause of a few moments. Then Jahusha proceeded to take a packet from his robe, and placed it on the table before Stanley.

"I am charged," he said, "to deliver this into your hands alone. You will doubtless guess from whom it comes."

Stanley changed colour as he answered quickly :—"Yes—I suppose—that is—from my Omelia! How is she, Father? Is she quite restored to her original self?"

"Well, my son," said the Hindoo, with a half-smile upon his naturally grave features, "I have not known her long enough to be aware what her original self was—but this I know, she is now mild and gentle, and resigned to the course she has thought best to adopt under the circumstances—she loves you, young man! with all the sincerity of her trusting and impetuous nature. I believe, and indeed know, from my short acquaintance with her, this much, that she loves you most sincerely, but there are circumstances, it appears, which it would be out of my place to dwell upon. Read what she says herself."

Stanley tore open the packet, and read as follows :—

"My ever dear Stanley,—You need not be told how, under the fatal influence of a distracting jealousy, I was driven to a desperation which well nigh ended in the distruction of us both. Neither will it be necessary to remind you, that in our last interview, I forgot the natural promptings of my nature, and uttered words which I dare not think of now without shuddering. It is past—let it be forgotten. I thank Heaven that you are restored to life, and, let me hope, happiness. Although I shall never cease to love you—although my thoughts will be for you, and with you to the last and latest period of my existence, I think it best no longer to trouble you with my presence. Do not think this harsh or unkind. It is for your sake, dear Stanley, I make the sacrifice. If you love another, be happy with her! and think no more of the poor Indian girl. Forget her—as she is not so selfish in her nature as to force you from one whom you deem (and perhaps is) more worthy of you. Enough! let that pass. Although no one I am sure can ever love you with a greater sincerity of purpose than I do; still, she may in your opinion be more adapted by birth and position to be your companion through life. For me, there is but one course remains—to suffer in silence; I have but your happiness to consider, and therefore now take that step which I think is most likely to secure it. You will see I can reason calmly now, Edward. The wild and strong passions which oftentimes shook my too headstrong nature are, let me hope, under better control. For this I have to thank the good and inestimable Jahusha. It is his kind advice that has made me see the wickedness of allowing our passions to bear us on as a roaring torrent with ungovernable fury. He will give this to you, when I shall have left his kind home. And so, my ever dearest Stanley, I bid you for once and for all, adieu! I can hardly see for my tears, how to write these words—but, 'tis done, farewell! May you meet with a heart that loves you with the sincerity and devotion of the poor and despised Indian girl.

"Yours ever
"OMELIA."

Stanley read and re-read this letter over and over again, and became deeply impressed as he did so with the altered tone of his still ever beloved Omelia. Then, turning to Jahusha, he said, in tremulous accents—

"You know the purport of this letter, I suppose, father?"

"I do, my son."

"And my Omelia—do you know whither she has gone?"

"Indeed, no! To my most urgent request upon this head, she would not yield, or let me know her future intentions, further than this, that she was going somewhere to suffer in silence, and would no longer trouble you with a love she feared you could now never return."

"What is the cause of this sudden resolution?"

"She is under the impression that you love another—at least, so she said."

"It is a false supposition!"

The old Hindoo bowed his head.

"Perfectly false! What did you tell her?"

"I said she had better see you, and not come to so hasty a resolve, without first ascertaining your sentiments, when you were both in a sufficiently calm state to talk dispassionately upon the subject."

"And could you not succeed in making her see the policy of adopting your good advice?"

"No—all my persuasions were futile."

"Unhappy girl!" exclaimed Stanley. "Why be thus precipitate? Still acting under the influence of a false creation, or phantom of your own brain. Father! I am more than ever concerned regarding her. I do not, I cannot conceal from you that I love her, and there is really no reason for her to doubt this; it is true."

And here he explained to Jahusha the whole particulars respecting Clara; and how this feeling of jealousy had been at first engendered.

The old priest listened attentively, and gave the best advice and consolation he could under the circumstances, and at the same time informed Stanley that Omelia had promised to meet him occasionally, and always seek his advice in any emergency. When after some further discussion Jahusha withdrew, with the impression that it was a harder task than he had at first imagined, to square accounts with lovers. He had tried his utmost, and certainly done much, still all was not quite straight, as matters stood at present.

CHAPTER CCCVII.

OMELIA VISITS ABDAL.—TERRIBLE DISCLOSURE AND PAINFUL PARTING.

WE must now return to the humble dwelling of the faithful friend of Omelia, whom, it will be remembered, she left, apparently dying, upon the occasion of her last visit to him. Abdal had gone through much suffering, both bodily and mentally, so much indeed that he was very nearly being past all trouble again in this world: and had it not been for the unremitting attention of the watchful Jungh, he would never in all probability have seen our heroine again. When he did recover his strength in some measure he was thrown back by the reflection of his last painful parting with Omelia, and the sad reflection as to what had become of her. Day after day passed and his unceasing inquiry was, "Have you heard any tidings of Omelia?" Since then a more painful circumstance had transpired to rack his thoughts, which will presently be seen.

Abdal was sitting partially up on his couch very depressed and melancholy. It was evening—and he was reading, or endeavouring to read a small book by the light of an Indian lantern, which was suspended from the ceiling of his apartment. Jungh had left him for awhile upon some trifling mission, but he was expected to return every minute. In a very short time his faithful attendant entered, and looked furtively at his master, who saw in a moment from the expression on Jungh's features that he had some news to communicate.

"Well, my good Jungh, what news? have you heard anything of my dear friend? tell me at once, I pray. If it be bad news, tell it me at once, I can bear anything but this dreadful suspense."

"I have," replied Jungh. "Now do not agitate yourself. I have seen her, and she desires me to say she will be here shortly."

The eyes of the sick man grew bright again at these words, and he clasped his hands with joy.

"Oh joyful news!" he exclaimed, "shall I again behold you once more, my unfortunate Omelia, after our painful parting, and after many weary and expectant hours passed, day after day, and night after night, I know not how many, but to me it appears half a lifetime.

"Oh! this news puts fresh vigour into my poor enfeebled frame. I think—yes, I think I could get up and walk anywhere to be assured of the safety of my attached friend." While he was still speaking, he was surprised and delighted to find Omelia by the side of his couch kneeling, and at the same time she clasped one of his hands in hers, and wept abundantly. Her feelings were quite overpowered for some time; they were of a mingled character, joy, sorrow, doubt, and pity for Abdal's emaciated appearance, all agitated her breast with conflicting emotions.

"My ever kind and faithful Abdal," said Omelia, "how shall I express my delight at again beholding you alive, and if not well, let me hope soon to be again restored to your usual health and strength. You behold me now, carrying about with me a silent sorrow, it is true, but no longer a prey to the violent and stormy passion which distorted my whole being. My mind has recovered its equilibrium, and can look calmly now upon all my trials and misfortunes, however great they may be."

"It gives me joy to hear you say so," replied Abdal. Oh, I have been a prey to the most terrible doubts and fears regarding your fate, for indeed when you were last here, your injuries appeared to have driven reason entirely away. How joyful, therefore, am I to see you now in such serenity of mind. How has all this been accomplished?"

Omelia now informed Abdal of all she had passed through; how she had been miraculously saved, and how the kind Jahusha's counsel had worked a perfect regeneration to her bewildered intellect; she told him, moreover, of her determination with regard to her lover, and also the substance of her letter to him. To this Abdal only said, he supposed it was a wise course to adopt. He did not venture to dilate upon a subject which he never as yet had deemed it advisable to thrust forward any officious advice. Some time had passed between the two friends in familiar and pleasant converse, when Abdal, who had betrayed considerable anxiety in the expression of his countenance, addressed our heroine thus:—

"My dearest Omelia,—I cannot tell you how it pains me now that we are so happy, to be obliged to tell you that which I am afraid must cause you the most serious alarm; but your own safety may perhaps depend upon it, and therefore it is my duty to let you know what I have heard."

Omelia looked at her friend in some astonishment, scarcely knowing what this speech prefaced, but said—

"Oh yes, if you have any news, however bad it may be, do not keep it from me. It is the last thing I should wish you to do."

Abdal proceeded:—

"You must understand," said he, as he settled himself in the pillows that supported him, "that what I am about to tell you has come to my knowledge in an extraordinary manner. I have not of course, since your last visit, ever been able to leave my couch, or I might have been able to ferret out something more than I know at present. There has been occasionally to visit me since your absence, a woman who knew me many years ago. Her name is Tallee Sheeboo. You may perhaps have heard me speak of her?"

"Yes, I have."

"Well, this woman has been very kind in doing what she can to make me comfortable during my illness. She has read to me, and told me all the news, and cheered me up as best she could under the circumstances; but she has more recently horrified me by making me acquainted with the details of some plot against your life, at least there is every reason to believe so. It appears that there have been a party of Europeans and Natives murdered by the Thugs, near the place where she resides. One of the females she thought was you, and you may judge of my despair when she told me this; however, she ascertained upon enquiry, that she was wrong in her supposition. She has never seen you, but heard my description of you, and knew also my great anxiety. One night, upon her returning home after a visit to me, she saw in the distance, coming along the pathway, two figures in close converse. She did not like their appearance, thinking they boded no good, so, to avoid them, she crept into the jungle until they had passed; while concealed she distinctly heard their conversation.

"'Have you heard anything of this girl Omelia?' said one to the other.

"'No,' was the reply, 'but I do not doubt about being able to find her—either alive or dead.'

"'Ah! you must find her dead!' was the reply, '100 rupees for the proof of her death.'

"'You may rely upon me; I have been on her track; she will not keep long from the quarters of her lover, Lieutenant Stanley; she has not returned there as yet, but I am on the watch, and shall be able to bring down the bird when once in sight.'

" 'Good! she must be found dead you know?'

" 'Of course, it will not be worth finding her till she is dead. I understand; she will be very dead no doubt when she is found. Of course she will—dead from a broken heart, brought on by unrequited and misplaced confidence,'" and Tallee Sheeboo heard both the villains laugh sardonically. She ventured after they had passed, to emerge a little from the jungle which had concealed her, and had a good look at them. She was convinced that they were Thugs, and her alarm was increased on your account. She hastened the next day and acquainted me with what she had heard and witnessed, and I have since ascertained through Jungh, that a Thug was observed a day or two after this circumstance loitering about the quarters of Colonel Bridport; several officers went in pursuit of him, but whether they succeeded in capturing him I know not; so you see what new danger now surrounds you; no one can tell what is the reason that actuates this persecution of you; but do, O! pray do, my dear friend, leave here, and disguise yourself until you are far hence. You have a terrible and insiduous foe on your track, who, animated by the thought of gaining the 100 rupees, will pursue you till death Oh! the thought is dreadful, and made doubly dreadful by the reflection that I am unable to accompany you, or be of any assistance."

" Fear not," replied our heroine, " I have already arranged to go far away from here; I will no longer be near him, who now is as nothing to me, and it only makes the bitter hours doubly bitter to hover about the cold ashes of a consumed love; although I can hardly tell who it is that has thought it worth while to offer so large a sum for my death, or what can be the motive; this to me is a mystery; we have all our enemies, but this malignity is far beyond my comprehension. If it is my life that is wanted, they have only to wait a short time and perhaps they will be satisfied, without adding the sin of murder to the catalogue of their other crimes."

" Do not talk thus despondingly," said Abdal, " you have youth, strength, and beauty, and let us hope a long and happy life before you; therefore pray act with caution. Let me know where you are, and I shall, I hope, soon be well enough to join you, only it would be as well perhaps not to send direct to me, as it may put your enemies on your track; send to Tallee Sheeboo, and she can bring me word every now and then, till I get round again. Oh, it is sad now that I am cheered again by the sight of you, to find that you must leave again so suddenly; but caution; it never would do to run any risk. It would be madness to remain near so appalling an enemy."

Fully awake to the danger of her staying, Omelia took a sad farewell of her faithful Abdal, and it was with a heavy heart and drooping spirits that she left her attached follower.

There was every reason for the greatest apprehension, for a dark cloud hovered over her path, and an active, though concealed enemy was seeking her destruction. We would fain drop a veil over the dark machinations of her secret foe, but the faithful chronicler of human actions cannot ignore the more wicked and sombre portions of man's character, however much he may be disposed to do so.

It will be seen as this narrative proceeds the cause which led to this plot against our heroine, the bare contemplation of which fill the mind with horror at its wicked atrocity. It was not from feelings of hate, revenge, or jealousy that our heroine was thus pursued—no! it was at the shrine of mammon she was to be offered up a sacrifice; at whose shrine so many thousands are annually prostrated. A wicked and guilty man, with as guilty accomplices, sought to imbrue his hands in innocent blood, and all to obtain a few ounces or pounds, as the case may be, of this precious, but demoralizing metal.

CHAPTER CCCVIII.

THE THUGS.—MOORSHA THE SHIKAREE.—HIS TALE.—EVENTS THICKEN.

THERE had been no more alarms in the officers' quarters since the chase and conflict with the Thugs. The two scoundrels who were brought home prisoners maintained an obstinate and impurturbable silence. They would ere this have been tried at a drum head court martial, but they were so severely wounded that Colonel Bridport thought advisable to detain them prisoners for the present. He wanted to get a full confession, and if possible obtain some clue to their companions in crime. The Colonel lost no opportunity when any occurred, in hunting down there secret assassins, and endeavouring to bring them to justice.

To many persons in England who may perhaps never heard or read of these bands of professed robbers and murderers, this account from the Asiatic Journal, vol. 13, will prove that the scene described is not one entirely of romance, or conjured up by the agency of imagination.

In some parts of India these men are called Phansigars or stranglers, in the more northern parts of India they are called Thugs. These set of men were a few years ago particularly numerous at Chittoor. This sequestred part of the country, abounding in hills and fastnesses, afforded them a convenient and secure retreat. The men never commit a robbery unaccompanied by murder. Their practice being first to strangle, and then rifle their victims. It is also a principle with them never to allow any one of a party to escape if they can help it. The only exception to this rule, are boys of a tender age, who are spared for the horrible purpose of being, (when old enough) initiated into the practices of their detestable calling. A gang generally consists of from ten to fifty or even a greater number of persons. Their victims are generally travellers whom they fall in with on the road. Each gang has its leader, who directs their movements. In appearance they resemble ordinary inoffensive travellers, and seldom assume any particular disguise, frequently pretending to be traders.

They are accustomed to wait near towns, on high roads where travellers are wont to rest; on such occasions, some of the gang are employed as emissaries to collect information and ascertain if persons of property are about to undertake a journey. Sometimes children of tender years of age will be employed to ingratiate themselves by obsequies into the good graces of travellers, and having gained their confidence, learn whither they are journeying, and all the necessary particulars, and also what property they possess; this

——" Under fair pretence of friendly ends,
And well placed words of easy courtesy;
Baited with reasons, not unplausable,
Wind them into easy-hearted man,
And hug him into snares."

When these men determine upon attacking a traveller, they will sometimes propose accompanying him for the sake of mutual society and protection; when they easily find an opportunity of effecting their purpose. One of the gang puts a rope or sash round the neck of the unfortunate person, and thereby strangles him. If circumstances favour them they will commit murder in a jungle or unfrequented part of the country, near to a sandy place or dry water course. A hole of three or four feet is then dug, into which the body is placed

with the face downwards, and shockingly mangled. Deep and continued gashes are made from the shoulders to the hands and feet, which lay open the abdomen, and divide the tendon of the heel. Wounds are also made between the ribs into the chest. The body is thus cut and mangled to expedite its decomposition. It will therefore be evident that the system of the Thugs is but too well adapted for concealment. The precautions they take; the artifices they practice to destroy their victims, are calculated at once to almost preclude the possibility of rescue or escape.

There are no witnesses to the deed; no cries for help; no effusion of blood; nor, in general, any traces of the murder. These circumstances conspire to throw a veil of darkness over their atrocities. The instrument of death they use is a long silken cord with a running noose with a loop at one end. They sometimes use a long narrow cloth, such as worn round the waist; when such a cloth is used, it is previously doubled to the length of two and a half feet, and a knot is formed at the doubled extremity, and about eighteen inches from it a slip not is tied. In regulating the distance of the two knots, so that the intervening space, when tightly twisted, may be adapted to embrace the neck, the Thug who prepares the instrument tries it upon his own knee. The two knots give the Thug a firm hold of the cloth, and prevents it slipping through his hands in the act of applying it.

In attacking a traveller on horseback. the Thugs arrange themselves in the following manner: one of the gang goes in front of the horse, and another has his station in the rear, whilst a third walking by the side of the traveller keeps him engaged in conversation till finding him off his guard, he suddenly seizes the traveller by the arm and flings him to the ground, the horse being at the same time seized by the foremost villain, the miserable sufferer is then strangled in the usual manner. It must be obvious that arms and ordinary precautions against these robbers are unavailing. When a person is armed with a dagger, it is usual for one of the villains to secure his hands.

It sometimes happens that a party of travellers consisting of several persons possessed of valuable effects are, while journeying in imaginary security, suddenly cut off, and the lifeless and mutilated removed, that not a vestige of them appears. Instances have occurred of twelve and fourteen persons thus being simultaneously destroyed. It must be obvious that no estimate, except what is extremely vague, can be formed of the number of persons

that have annually fallen victims to these class of men. There is every reason to believe that many hundreds still perish every year.

It must be understood that the pursuit of the Thug, by the party of English officers already described, took the former by surprise. The man who had reconnoitred at the bungalow was anxious to rejoin his companions without letting any one know of their whereabouts, but finding he was obstinately pursued, he hastened to his companions, and they, seeing how matters stood —that it was certain they would be discovered — determined upon their plan of operation, to offer what resistance it was possible under the circumstances.

They had not sought the engagement; on the contrary, would rather have avoided it,

but it was forced upon them from the exigency of their situation.

Let us, however, now return to the characters more immediately connected with our story.

In the garden adjoining Colonel Bridport's bungalow, there were collected together, lounging in various easy attitudes, the several officers under his command, amongst whom there were, of course, those whose acquaintance we have already made.

Clara, the colonel's daughters, and many other ladies were seated underneath a temporary tent.

The whole party had been partaking of a a *tiffin*, or Indian luncheon, and the ladies were now some sipping their perfumed sherbet, whilst others partook iced claret. The gentlemen mostly reclined on the grass, smoking the fragrant weed in its various shapes, either in pipes, cigars, or cigarettes. Poor Seagrave was still very weak, but was, however, now supposed to be out of danger. He had been brought down upon a palanquin, upon which he reclined beneath the shade of the tent.

"Not far from him was Mr. Hamilton, the worthy doctor, in his hand the last number of the "Bombay Times;" he had been reading several scraps of news aloud for the general benefit, and was still glancing his eye over its columns to see if there was anything more that might interest the company.

"Ah!" he presently exclaimed, "what have we here? Good news for some one I suppose."

"Hope it's for me," said Captain Robinson, "or else one of us here present What is it, doctor? a few thousands or so going begging?"

"I can hardly tell you. Listen, and judge for yourself:—'Advertisement.—Next of kin. —Wanted the next of kin to an English lady, named Rose Harcourt. The said Rose Harcourt married an Indian gentleman named Kerah Bardah Singh, who has been many years deceased. By this marriage she had one daughter, who is supposed to be still alive. After the death of her first husband it is believed she married again, and gave birth to another daughter by her second husband, whose name is unknown. The said Rose Harcourt has been dead many years, but whoever will give information respecting either or both of her daughters, as to where they are to be found, if alive, or certificate of death, if deceased, will be handsomely rewarded, by applying to Messrs. Cottle, Leaf and Cottle, Conveyancers and Commission Agents, Dipdownayah Wharf, Calcutta.'"

"Ah," said Robinson, "that don't concern me, doctor, I am sorry to say. I am not an interesting young lady, sole heiress to the Harcourt estates."

"Nor me," said Morley.

"Nor me," said another and another of the gentlemen.

"Ah, but you forget," observed the doctor, smiling. "Perhaps some one of the ladies may be a fair candidate for the munificent bequest, for such I am sure it is, who knows?"

With many jests, and some considerable amount of merry laughter, the paper was handed round for their inspection, but none appeared to have any claim to be considered the daughter of either Rose Harcourt or Kerah Bardah Singh.

The former name struck Stanley as being in some way familiar to him, and he endeavoured to unravel the thin thread of re-collection with which he was impressed concerning it.

"Harcourt," he repeated several times; "I surely have a distinct impression that I have heard it before. Yes, most assuredly. I remember now. She was the mother of—" he paused suddenly, as he caught Clara's eye directed towards him.

"Well," said the colonel, "the mother of whom? The mother of pearl, perhaps A pearl beyond price. Out with it, man, if you know anything that may be good news to your friends, let us know it at once."

Stanley still hesitated, but at length continued—

"I fancy I know one, and, indeed, did know both of these daughters mentioned in this advertisement. One poor girl is long since dead, and the other is Omelia."

"Omelia!" several voices exclaimed. "How extraordinary! What a remarkable coincidence!"

Stanley then explained the circumstances connected with the death of Miriami, and the particulars of the narrative which she left behind for her sister's perusal. That sister being no other than our heroine.

The reader will no doubt remember the circumstances, which were detailed in an earlier portion of this work.

It was indeed Omelia, who appeared now to be the only surviving daughter of the late unfortunate Rose Harcourt. He read again the advertisement, and became fully assured of the fact, and was doubly pained to think that he had no clue to find out the missing girl.

"I cannot possibly tell how to have this information conveyed to her, as I am utterly ignorant where she has bent her course."

"In that case," said the colonel, "you had better draw up a memorial of all the particulars you know, and forward it to Messrs. Cottle, Leaf and Cottle, at Calcutta. At any rate, there can be no harm in putting them in possession of the fact that one of the daughters is still in existence."

Stanley at once made up his mind to adopt the advice of his excellent and judicious friend. Omelia had possession of Miriami's narrative, as also the portrait of her mother, which, it will be remembered, the latter bequeathed to our heroine.

Pondering over the circumstance, Stanley became grave and abstracted, and his altered demeanour could not fail to be observed by most present, although they did not appear to notice it.

He was awoke from his reverie shortly by the entrance of Moorsha the *shikaree*, whom he had not seen since he left Jahnsah's to return to his quarters.

He greeted Moorsha with great cordiality, as indeed did most present.

The *shikaree* was a great favourite with the officers, as, also, with the ladies. The colonel insisted upon his staying some little time to partake of refreshment, and Stanley anxiously inquired if he knew anything of Omelia, and, at the same time, informed him of the advertisement in the "Bombay Times."

"Fate again," said Moorsha, "whose ways to us blind mortals are still inscrutable."

"What do you mean?" said the colonel. "Do you think then that my friend here will never be able to find out the fugitive? Or do you imagine that she herself knows of this, and has gone to Calcutta to present her own proper person as the claimant?'

"Who knows?" was the reply.

"Ah, who indeed! Perhaps you do. If so, oblige us, my friend, by telling."

"I think not," said Moorsha, "indeed I may say I am sure not: at least, up to the time of my parting with her, I am confident she was quite ignorant of any inquiries having been instituted for the daughters of the late unfortunate Rose Harcourt."

"Why unfortunate?"

"For many reasons that it would be useless to dwell upon now. To be the wife of such a man as Yunadar was unfortunate enough for any woman, and which could not fail to embitter her life, and bring her where it did, to an early grave."

"You knew him then?" said Stanley, in some surprise.

"Oh, yes, I knew him well enough—for the matter of that, too well, indeed."

"And the lady—his wife—did you know her?"

"Yes, perfectly well."

"Dear me, you do indeed surprise me."

"And I knew, when but a boy, Kerah Bardah Singh, her first husband. I did not, however, know, till within the last few days, that Omelia was the daughter of Rose Harcourt. Indeed, I had never seen her till I found you both senseless at the foot of the rock on that eventful night."

"You surprise me more and more. How came you acquainted with Bardah Singh? You must pardon my asking the question so abruptly, but it is a matter upon which, of course, you know I am considerably interested."

"Certainly, it is but natural you should be. My father knew Kerah Singh, and I was myself, at one time, in his employ. A better nature never existed, I believe: kind, generous to a fault, and considerate to all around him. Oh, what a contrast to the cruel, vindictive, and hateful Yunadar."

Stanley did not much like to hear Yunadar thus abused before all present. He knew the man's detestable nature well enough, it is true, but still he was Omelia's father, and he did not want all his darker qualities paraded before his companions and friends, so he said, somewhat hastily—

"You were saying, when we were last together, that you would give me unmistakeable proof of the decrees of fate, and why it was that you considered yourself invulnerable from the attack of tigers. To say the truth, you have certainly given a pretty good sample of your prowess and daring already"

"Well," said Moorsha, "the very name of Kerah Singh, calls to my mind the particulars of my first proof, and if you like, and as you appear to be interested in it, I will tell you."

Colonel Bridport and all said they should be too delighted to hear, and Moorsha began:—

"You must understand, that my father was well acquainted with Kerah Singh, who entertained a great respect and esteem for my parent. Kerah was acquainted with many Europeans; indeed, I believe he mixed more in their society than with his own countrymen.

"My father, at the time I am now speaking, kept a small farm, and was what is called tolerably well to do, as the phrase goes; and my mother was also alive.

"Well, it appears that Kerah had been very intimate with an English gentleman whose name I never knew; but he had stopped with Kerah for months together, in fact they appeared to be on the most intimate and friendly terms.

"I do not think at this time he was married to Rose Harcourt, but will not be sure of that, being myself young at the time, and by my father generally going to the house himself, I had not so much opportunity of knowing this. But it appeared that the English gentleman was either taken ill, or had to return home from some cause or other, whatever it might be; but he left behind him a little boy of about seven years of age, with instructions for Kerah to place him out in some family where he knew he would be well taken care of, until the gentleman should return. Kerah thought of my father, and mentioned the circumstance to him, asking if there would be any objection to his taking charge of the boy till the return of his parent, adding at the same time, that every care was to be taken of him, as he was a favourite, and as I understood, an only son.

"My father undertook the charge, and the young gentleman soon afterwards came to reside with us, and became much beloved by us all. We lived in a cottage with a thatch roof, at a small village near Shaunpore, and I was myself about sixteen years of age at the time, as nearly as I can recollect. The youth was my constant companion and playmate, and I had formed, after he had been a few months with us, a very strong feeling of friendship for him. Near to where we resided there dwelt a *faker*, named Jagula Kayoo. He paid us occasional visits, and upon one occasion I recollect his noticing the young child under our care, when after some conversation with my father, I remember he shook his head somewhat ominously, and said, after the boy had left the room, that he feared he was doomed to come to an untimely end before he arrived at manhood.

"I know at the time that this made an impression of a very painful character upon us all, and my father questioned him more closely as to the cause of his making such a remark, observing that 'it was impossible for men to tell. The same thing might be said of me or any one else, with perhaps just as much truth.' The *faker* said 'No, I was not to meet any such fate; on the contrary, I should be exposed to many dangers, out of which I should come off uninjured.' This he repeated several times. My father, who felt quite oppressed in spirits at the remark, although he did not like to appear so, asked him if he could tell what disaster would happen to our young charge. The *faker*, after a little consideration observed, that in all probability, as far as he could at present tell, he was doomed to fall a victim to the rapacity of a tiger.

"'Well,' observed my father, 'if that were to be the case, I do not know how Tallee (that was me) is to escape, seeing that he and the boy are almost always together.'

"'No matter,' said the *faker*, 'Tallee *can never be destroyed by the tiger*. There are some who *never can* be, but the boy does not possess any such immunity as your son.'

"Well, you may suppose these prophetic words threw a great damper upon our spirits, which it was in vain for us to endeavour to shake off. I believe my father was so impressed with them at the time, that he debated with himself the propriety of conveying the child back to Kerah Singh. He, however, did not do so, but the boy's movements were watched with more than usual care. Months rolled on, and the effects of the prophecy began to wear away. And then my mother died, and I think my father would, after her death, have taken the boy back, and declined having further charge of him, but there were two circumstances which prevented, in a great measure, his doing so. The first was that, I believe, he almost daily expected his parent to return, and was anxious to keep him now till he did so; and at the same time, having become really and sincerely attached to the child (almost as much, and, indeed, I believe, nearly more than if it were his own), he was loth to part with him. My father had felt my mother's loss severely, and could not, I imagine, bear to have any other member of his little household taken from him. Be this as it may, the child still continued an inmate of our humble abode.

"One day my father had to journey several miles upon business, and told me that he was afraid he should not be able to be back till night; he would be as early as he could, but the distance precluded the possibility of his returning before the evening. He then charged me not to allow the boy out the whole of the day, but I was to amuse him as well as I could in the cottage. He really seemed to have a prescience of his coming fate.

"I promised to follow his instructions, and did as he desired.

"Towards evening I closed the door of our cottage and was sitting in our apartment with my sister and our young charge, anxiously awaiting the return of my parent, I heard a noise as of something scratching at the roof of our abode. I looked up, and could see to my intense horror, that the thatch was being removed from the outside. I shouted out, but to no purpose, for the scratching continued; and I could now distinctly see the claws of some animal inserted into a small aperture it had made in the thatch, and at the same time large pieces were every moment being dragged away to make the hole larger. I was completely petrified with horror as the light of heaven streamed in from the roof. I knew not how to act, but did what was perhaps the most imprudent thing I could do, and that was to rush to the door and scream for assistance. You may judge of my feelings when I saw, on emerging from the cottage, a large tiger on the roof, actually tearing away vigorously with his claws at the thatch with an evident determination to effect an entrance.

"He stopped an instant and glared at me. I instinctively rushed in and closed the door. He had now made a hole nearly large enough to admit himself into our apartment. I was so completely overpowered with my feelings, that my knees actually knocked together with fear. I was utterly at a loss to know what to do, but my little sister, when she saw the danger to which we were exposed, set up a series of piercing screams, loud enough for many of our neighbours to hear, as indeed many of them did; but it was not likely they were coming to meet a tiger. The only effect it had was to make them all close their doors and windows, and fall upon their knees in helpless fright. Seeing the animal would now soon effect an entrance, I seized hold of the nearest weapon, which was a stout spear, and with this I made up my mind to receive him. I had not much time for reflection, for in a few more seconds down he droped. He fell almost upon me, and my spear, as nearly as I could make out, must have entered his shoulder and broke off, about a foot and a half from the head. I was prostrated to the earth almost stunned with the concussion; but I distinctly remember my sister running to the door, opening it, and screaming for assistance, which of course never came. And while I was prostrate on the ground, and the tiger over me, the youth who was under our charge came forward, as though he thought, poor child, he could render me assistance, when with an angry snarl the tiger flew at him, snapped him up in his mouth, and rushing through the open doorway, tore off at headlong speed.

"The prophecy of Jagula Kayoo was fulfilled to the letter," said Moorsha, as he looked at each of his hearers for their approval.

"Other persons are carried off by tigers," said the colonel, "without any prophecy. It is merely a coincidence; but it is of no use our endeavouring to prove to you that it was not fate, so we will not attempt it."

"It is of no use indeed. Had it not been so ordained, and had I have been allowed to act according to the dictates of common sense, I should, when I saw the beast endeavouring to effect an entrance, have gone to the door with my two companions, waited till the animal was about to jump down, and then closed him in, leaving our three selves outside. He would have been then caught in his own trap, and this is a course frequently adopted by villagers in such an emergency; but it was ordained otherwise."

"Ah, it is a melancholy narrative," said Clara. "But what said your father upon his return?"

"Oh, he was, as you may imagine, perfectly frantic, and Kerah Singh was inconsolable at the loss. I do not remember, though, to have heard anything about the father ever returning to inquire after him, but I suppose he must have done so."

"This is certainly a charming country." said Morley. "What with savage animals, sepoys, and Thugs, you require to have your eye-teeth about you."

It was now explained to Moorsha the particulars respecting the Thugs, as also the suspicious circumstance of the scoundrel who was seen through the window.

The hunter said he would make all the inquiries he could to elucidate the mystery, and informed the colonel that a man answer-ing to his description had been observed near where Jahnsah resided.

"It might be a coincidence," he observed, smiling, "but it was one that was worth taking note of."

Stanley had still further misgivings when he heard this. If it were the same man, or one of his gang, there could be no doubt it was either himself or Omelia he was after; and a terrible foreboding seized him as this reflection presented itself to his mind. The colonel begged of him to banish such thoughts; but nevertheless the circumstances were very suspicious, and the reflection anything but an agreeable one.

Moorsha agreed to lay in wait near the residence of Jahnsah, to observe any further movement on the part of the Thug.

CHAPTER CCXI.

SCENE IN CALCUTTA.—THE INSIDIOUS FOE.

The office of Messrs. Cottle, Leaf and Cottle was situated near to the water's side. Their business was rather of a mixed character; although ostensibly attorneys, they nevertheless were owners of a large wharf, and had much to do with the embargo of vessels sailing to and from Great Britain, and had also various mercantile agencies, which have little or nothing to do with the present story.

It will be enough to observe, therefore, that they were a highly respectable firm, and were generally held in excellent repute by most of those with whom they had business transactions.

Some few days after the incidents occurred which have been recorded in the last chapter, the two partners of the firm, namely, the elder Mr. Cottle and Mr. Leaf, were engaged in conversation with a gentleman apparently a little past the meridian of existence.

It will be neccessary, for more perfect developement of our tale, for us to listen to a portion of the confidential conversation taking place in the counting-house of the respectable firm.

"Have you had any application or reply to your advertisements?" said the gentleman, who was with the partners.

"No, indeed. As yet not the slightest notice has been taken by any single individual, but we are in hopes, nevertheless. You see, the affairs of the country are in so unsettled and confused a state that it is peculiarly difficult to get news conveyed to the remote districts of India; and, indeed, if there should not be any answer for some time to come we have no right to despair."

These observations were made by the senior partner, Mr. Cottle.

The stranger ruminated for some little time, and then said, in as careless and indifferent a tone as he could assume—

"And in the event of your not receiving an answer after the lapse of—of some months?"

"Well, I hardly know what is to be done, the matter must of necessity rest in obeyance. You see, although we may have made every effort it was possible to do under the circumstances, and our endeavours may have not been crowned with the success we had anticipated or desired, we have even then no right to assume that they will not ultimately be so. We know positively that the late Rose Harcourt left two daughters. Of the decease of one there is, I think, sufficient proof without a doubt, but the other, if she be in existence, is certainly the sole heir to the Harcourt estate."

"Unquestionably," said the gentleman, whom we may as well introduce by his right name, Mr. Natterly. "There can be no doubt about that, of course not; my only object in being thus troublesome and importunate upon the subject is, as I have already explained, because I want the matter settled one way or the other as speedily as possible; you must pardon, therefore, my seeming impatience. As I have before observed, I am anxious to return to England, now that all my other business is completed, and, of course, I need not endeavour to conceal from you that this is too important an affair for me not to feel some considerable anxiety about; of course, I know that I may have nothing at all to do with the matter, but still, in the event of no claimant turning up, I am, although remote, nevertheless the heir."

"No doubt," said Mr. Cottle, "no doubt, I should say, of that; but you must understand, that even in the event of our not finding any claimant, you could not have the matter settled in any satisfactory way before you left for England, and therefore I should be sorry for you to deceive yourself. The property would be placed in trust for the rightful heir whenever she presented herself."

"Oh, in that case," said Mr. Natterly, "it would remain unsettled for ever."

"Well, it must necessarily do so for a very long period of time, and then there could be no possibility of bringing it to an issue without an expensive and intricate course of proceedure, unless—"

"Unless what?" eagerly exclaimed Mr. Natterly.

"Unless, of course, there could be direct proof obtained of the death of Rose Harcourt's second child."

"Oh," said Mr. Natterly, "I have every reason to believe, from the inquiries I have made, that she perished some short time since in one of the late conflicts. Indeed, I am almost confident upon this point, and her not answering your advertisement still more strengthens this supposition. Would it not be best to advertise again, saying that such is supposed to be the case, and offering a reward for proof of the same?"

"I think not," observed Mr. Leaf. "It would really be offering a premium for deception; the identity must be always difficult to establish. No—let the notice stand as it is."

While these observations were being made, one of the clerks put in his head, and said there was a packet addressed to the firm labelled "immediate," and he placed it on the table and left the apartment. Mr. Cottle, apologising to his visitor, opened it and perused its contents. As his eye glanced over the lines he saw the nature of its contents. It was Stanley's memorial, which he had drawn up at the suggestion of Colonel Bridport.

"There," said Mr. Cottle, "there is a communication upon the very subject we were discussing. It is indeed singular that it should come while you were here," and he laid the packet upon the table before Mr. Natterly for his inspection.

The latter eagerly devoured its contents, and, in spite of the habitual command he had over himself, he betrayed evident signs of vexation and chagrin at the contents of Stanley's communication, as it left no doubt of the existence of Omelia a few days prior to its being penned.

"There, you see, this will now only act as an incentive for us to renew every exertion to trace out the missing fugitive. It is quite clear she is the rightful and, indeed, only claimant, now that her sister Miriami is dead. Lucky girl, she little knows the joyful news that awaits her appearance," said Mr. Cottle, smiling, and rubbing the palms of his hands together.

"Y—yes," returned Mr. Natterly, with a forced and sickly smile in return; "very lucky, indeed. I suppose this is a legitimate communication?"

"Oh, I should say so—most certainly. It is, you see, from an English officer, whom I believe has distinguished himself on many occasions during the late fearful outbreaks. I do not think there can be any reasonable doubt about its veracity."

"No, perhaps not; only, to speak frankly, the proof I have had, apprising me of her death, appeared to me to be so positive at the time, that it makes me look upon everything with a suspicious eye. Mr. Leaf was but just now observing that the identity would be difficult to prove. It is not for me to suggest to you what course you may think proper to adopt, but I may be pardoned in saying, that I should be extremely cautious in arriving at any hasty conclusion; and nothing but the most positive evidence of her actually being the individual in question, would induce me to entertain her as a claimant."

"Oh, we will look well after that," said Mr. Cottle, with a quiet smile. "We shall not evince any undue haste in so important a matter. Indeed, I believe, in affairs of this sort, it is not the usual characteristic of any of our profession to do so."

Mr. Natterly inclined his head in reply, and continued to bite the end of his stick, and gaze abstractedly at the pendulum of the clock, as it told off the seconds. In a minute or so he rose from his seat suddenly, with a smile, as if he had only just recollected that he had had an appointment of a pleasing character. For with a countenance beaming with radiance, he grasped the hand of Mr. Cottle, shook it warmly, and did the same by Mr. Leaf, and was taking his departure with really quite an easy and jaunty air. When he got to the door, Mr. Cottle said—

"You will not be leaving as yet, I suppose, for England?"

"Oh, no," smilingly replied their visitor; "oh, no; I shall want to have a peep, if possible, at this Indian heiress of yours."

And he went away laughing as if really he had uttered something extremely witty.

The two partners looked at one another meaningly, and smiled also. They were used to contemplate the various emotions of men under both adverse and prosperous circumstances, and knew what value to attach to Mr. Natterly's self-satisfied jocose bearing.

We must, however, follow that individual himself for a short time. He had not got many yards clear of the premises of the firm of Cottle and Co., when his whole demeanour changed, and the countenance of the easy pleasant gentleman became disturbed by the expression of malignant hate, rage, and disappointment.

"Curses!" he muttered, to himself; "curses on the officious fool for his confounded packet—a meddling idiot! What business was it of his? He intends to marry the girl, I suppose. Of course, now he will be glad to do—if he can. Ah, ah! if he can—we will see about that. I have said she is dead—I have said so—and she is—or will be! Ah, ah! or will be. She shall and must be!" he screamed out, as though he were addressing some imaginary figure who had expressed doubt upon the matter, "shall and must be, and that as speedily as possible; and then this immaculate firm will not have the delight of hand-ing over all the large fortune and magnificent estates of the late bankrupt Harcourt. For years have I been anxiously watching for the day to come when I could laugh to scorn my quandom friends: and shall I be cheated now out of what I have so laboriously sought, by a half-bred girl, who has neither taste to appreciate, nor sense to make use of, the favours fortune throws into her lap? No, it must not, cannot be. She shall be removed at once. Confound that sentimental lover of hers, for sending his cursed memorial at such an inopportune time. It will look awkward, her sudden death, now; and yet, I don't know, such matters are of daily occurrence. But I think my esteemed friends, Messrs. Cottle and Leaf, look upon me with rather a suspicious eye. With what glee the old gentlemen received the news contained in this—this Stanley's paper. No matter, I will match them all yet, or I am much mistaken."

Thus did this bad man ruminate, muttering his wicked thoughts to himself, as he went through the bye streets of Calcutta.

In a short time he emerged from the town, and then proceeded at a more rapid pace, as though he were anxious to arrive at some particular spot or place of rendezvous. Indeed such was actually the case, for after a journey of about two miles, Mr. Natterly stopped at a bungalow situated in the midst of a mass of tropical foliage of such a dense nature as to entirely screen it from sight. He, however, seemed to know the locality well, for shouting out some Indian name, an old woman made her appearance in answer to his summons.

"Well," said Mr. Natterly, "what of Goryeboo? Is he on duty, or off?"

"He is within," was the reply. "Will it please you to enter?"

And the old woman led the way into the interior of one of the lower apartments.

Upon Mr. Natterly's entrance he observed the man whom he sought reclining on a rude couch, with one of his arms in a sling swathed in bandages. He rose at the entrance of the visitor, and made a sort of moody recognition of him by a short bow; then turning to the old woman, he gave her a look which she appeared to understand, and immediately left the room.

"Any good news for me?" said the Englishman, as soon as they were alone.

"No, indeed," was the reply, given rather sulkily; "there has been nothing but bad news for us all. This cursed girl has been the cause of numbers of my companions being cut to pieces. And it was by a perfect miracle that I escaped with my life."

"Dear me! ah, you are wounded, I see," said the other, with an affectation of sympathy. "Why, what has been the matter?"

"Matter, indeed! I would not undertake such another job for ten—twenty times your reward. It has been well nigh the ruin of us all."

"How so?"

"Why this is how it occurred. I was watching by the quarters of Colonel Bridport for the return of this girl Omelia, who you take such deep interest in; of course, I knew she would in all probability return to see her lover, and I could then have dogged her footsteps until a convenient opportunity occurred—"

"Yes—of course—quite right, so you could."

"Yes, so I could indeed. If she had come, which she didn't; but instead of my dogging her footsteps I had a lot of men and bloodhounds racing after mine."

"How so?"

"Why, I was discovered by her lover, curse him, and I was obliged to beat a hasty retreat. He followed, aroused his companions, and a pretty chase they gave me of it. Unfortunately this drew them into the forest, and put them upon the track of my companions, and a regular slaughter they have made amongst them. That cursed Stanley nearly cut me in two with his sabre, and I had a hard job to escape from him, but I'll be even with him some, day or other a time will come."

"Dear me, this is sad news; and after all the girl has not been found?"

"No. I wish she had never been sought after; it has been at the cost of I know not how many lives"

"And your companions?"

"Oh, there are two of them taken prisoners by the accursed Feringhees."

"Prisoners! dear me, that is very disastrous; why, they may betray all."

"No fear of that, as they know nothing respecting this transaction — none of my companions are in the secret of our engagement together. Indeed, if they had known that I could not have been so rash and imprudent as to have run the risk I have for the sake of obtaining one girl; my own life would not be safe. They imagine that the affray was accidental."

"My excellent Goryeboo, you have managed well in this respect, however. Now about your future proceedings. It is essential the girl is put to rest at once."

He took from his purse several pieces of money, and gave them to the Hindoo.

"There is a plaster for your wound," he continued, "and now mind I double the reward, if the certificate of her death can be obtained within a fortnight, as it is now of some importance."

"Ah," replied the other, "that may be all very well, but I would not undertake the offer, even with all that, unless I had my own revenge to gratify. I run great risks—"

"Run great risks? What do you mean? are you sick of your task, and intend to desert me, now that I most need your services? Now look here, Goryeboo, let us understand one another. I will have no faltering, hesitating, or shuffling in this matter; you must do this, and do it speedily, or else— but you need not be told that I hold your life in my hands. One word from me, and you and your family would be consigned to an ignominious death."

"I know that."

"Well, then, it is better to have me for your friend than your enemy—indeed, I don't conceal that it is better for both our interests that we should understand each other. You must use every exertion; I tell you the reward shall be doubled, if the matter is settled, say within three weeks or a month, only lose no time."

"And how about my son?"

"Oh, I give you my word he shall be restored to you the moment this is accomplished—I pledge myself to this."

The other still hesitated.

"Eh, what do you say to that? Double the reward—your son returned, and all those papers which criminate you, given into your hands."

"Oh, I cannot, of course, object; only will you return my son? What security have I—"

"Do you doubt my word?"

"No—oh, no."

"Then why hesitate? Take a common sense view of the question: you are going to render me an essential service, and I, in return reward you partly in money, partly by saving you from the punishment of offences you have already committed, and to complete all, I restore your son to you who is completely at my mercy. Why do I do this?—Because it is my interest to do so. When our bargain is completed I shall return to England, and you will not be troubled with any further fears about me."

"I understand. It shall be done, sahib, as you desire. The murderous, bloodthirsty Stanley shall find to his cost what it is to hunt down human beings like wild beasts. Oh, sweet is revenge. Never fear, sahib, you shall soon hear of her death; only we must find her first. I have been watching at that old priest's, but have not been able to learn anything of her."

"Indeed. Have you been to her cousin Abdal's?"

"Yes, but with no better success. She has been there once since the night of attack, and only once. I must keep a sharp look out there. Oh, I have no doubt about managing it all comfortably enough for you.

and then you will keep your word as to your part of the engagement."

Thus did these two scoundrels bargain and haggle about terms for the destruction of a human creature.

It will now be seen the cause of the mysterious appearance of the Thug at Colonel Bridport's. It was no other than Goryeboo, who at the instrumentality of the wicked Natterly, was seeking to do his behests by the destruction of our heroine, who was now sole heiress to immense wealth, inherited from her maternal grandfather. By removing Omelia out of the way, Natterly would, with a little chicanery, manage to lay hold of the property himself. He had laid his plans deeply: Goryeboo was in his power, for he had been taken prisoner and condemned to death, by the military authorities,

No. 88.

some months before, for several murders. There was not a shadow of doubt of his guilt, and he would have met a fate commensurate with his deserts, but Mr. Natterly, foreseeing the probability of rendering him serviceable in his wicked plots and machinations, contrived to facilitate his escape, and consequently now completely held him in his power—the more so as, in one of the recent revolts, Goryeboo's son had been taken prisoner, and was now in charge of Mr. Natterly, who held him as a hostage until the fulfilment of the contract respecting the death of Omelia.

Thus we see the main spring of action which has set in motion the machinery—or rather human agency—which sought to compass the death of our heroine, who was completely unconscious of the importance which was now attached to her, or the large guerdon which was to be won by her removal.

For the credit of our country we could have wished there had been no such a person to describe as the iniquitous Mr. Natterly, who, lured by the prospect of immense wealth, seemed regardless upon what terms he obtained it; and from petty shuffling and chicanery, which he had practised for years, now halted not at the heavier and more heinous crime of murder.

But what will man not not do, when actuated only by a yearning for the lust of wealth and power? His mind becomes distorted—his better qualities entirely prostrated before the unholy shrine he has himself set up for his idolatrous worship. A few years pass, and where are all his hopes and aspirations? The wealth he may have obtained is, in all probability a source of misery to him; he sees other eyes watching eagerly for his death, and becomes aware, perhaps, that the same spirit of cupidity which prompted him—some years ago—now actuate the feelings of his nearest relative, and he finds, when too late, that the sordid gold he has worshipped has failed to give him contentment or a tranquil mind; and now that the fruition of his hopes are realised, he sees himself still farther removed from happiness, and longs for the happy days when, in the spring time of his youth, ho had a conscience unstained by sin, and a heart unpetrified by crime.

Mr. Natterly was the type of a large class of men who, in their greedy appetite for wealth, think gold all-sufficient for the purchase of every comfort this world affords. But let us not stigmatise the whole class of gold worshippers as being stained with the crimes which defaced the character of Mr. Natterly. His was an extreme case, and his mind was carried on from one petty sin to another till he lost sight completely of the path of honour and rectitude.

CHAPTER CCX.

OMELIA'S FLIGHT.—THE CONFLICT.—THE MEETING WITH TAMNEEGAL.

We must now return and follow the footsteps of our heroine. Depressed in spirits, and with the feeling as of heavy weight at her heart, she nevertheless endeavoured to bear up against her misfortunes with a calm and dignified heroism, yet with a mind sorely distrought, she bent her footsteps far away from scenes, the contemplation of which only served to open fresh wounds to her troubled spirit.

It was with no very definite idea as to her ultimate destination that she now proceeded on her journey; anywhere, it was all the same to her—" anywhere—anywhere out of the world." She endeavoured, " poor fluttering moth," to school her mind to act what she deemed a noble part. Firm and inflexible in her resolve, she really meant never again to see her lover in this world, being under the full impression that Stanley in reality did not now care for her, and would perhaps be rejoiced to find himself no longer troubled with her presence.

" And yet," she exclaimed, bitterly, as she went along, " he loved me once! Oh, yes, I know he never deceived me. He loved me once!—but now he sees other and more attractive subjects to interest him, and it is not for me to come between him and them. Oh, no—poor, despised, and discarded as I am, I shall certainly never stoop to beg the return of a love which, though once mine, he can now never more give. No, he shall not have cause to say I torment him with any importunities. Never!"

Thus determined in her resolve, she journeyed many weary miles, apparently sustaining little or no fatigue. The course she was taking would lead towards Merud—a town in Hindoostan. In the early period of the revolt, this town had been assailed like many others by the sepoys, and numbers of the European inhabitants ruthlessly slaughtered. In one of these outbreaks, Omelia had been instrumental in saving the lives of an English family of the name of Forrester. The lady—the mother of several young children—was about to meet a fate perhaps worse than death, when Omelia rushed up in time to rescue her, and eventually effected her escape.

In parting with our heroine, Mrs. Forrester was profuse in protestations of gratitude and friendship, and presented her preserver with a signet ring, telling her that if she should ever be in trouble and need assistance at any future period, she might command her, saying at the same time that, should she not be able to come herself, if she sent her this ring at any time it would be enough to let her know to whom she was indebted for her own life, as well as those of her children, and any request she made that it was possible to be granted, should meet immediate attention. Omelia thought little enough of the incident at the time, such scenes were of too frequent occurrence to make much impression on her, but now wishing to fly from old connections and associations the circumstance occurred to her, and it was with a vague notion that she might possibly hear of her friend, Mrs. Forrester, that she now wandered towards the town of Merud.

Night was far advanced when our heroine

began to think of seeking some place of shelter, and observing a woman of prepossessing features outside a cottage on her road, she asked how far it was to the nearest town, or if she could tell her where she might obtain accommodation for the remainder of the night. The woman looked at her in some surprise, and then said—

"Indeed, I am thinking you had better not go much farther, late as it is now. Accept, therefore, such accommodation as I can offer."

This was thankfully accepted, and Omelia discovered that the woman was a widow, and had an only son in the army in the East India Company's service. He was stationed at Calcutta, and was in one of the few regiments which did not revolt. In all probability owing to the fact of their being overawed by the British. After some hours sound repose, Omelia was enabled to resume her journey early on the following morning.

After proceeding many more miles her ears were assailed with screams and shouts, together with the firing of muskets, which too surely told of some terrible encounter. As she neared a village, the cause of the sounds of strife became painfully manifest. A fierce contest was taking place between a few Europeans and revolted sepoys; the latter of whom were attacking on all sides the little party of fugitives.

Our heroine shuddered as she paused and beheld a repetition of horrors she had too frequently had occasion to witness. She observed a covered caravan which appeared to contain several European ladies; a wild and mad rush was made towards this vehicle by numbers of the sepoys; as they approached it, thinking to make an easy prey of its inmates, they were thrown into the utmost confusion by receiving a well-directed fire of musketry. Numbers fell dead or mortally wounded, and the remainder fell back in disorder: when at length somewhat recovering themselves, they again made another onslaught. Once more they were received with a terrific and murderous fire, and the caravan was then driven on for some distance, followed by the infuriated mob of depredators. A desperate battle ensued between the occupants of the vehicle and its assailants, the latter of whom rushed into it, and many received their death wound. It appeared that it was a *ruse* adopted by the occupants of the caravan. They were English officers and civilians, who had disguised themselves in female attire to lead to the supposition that their enemies would find them an easy prey, instead of which they met with such a stout resistance that the slaughter was terrific. Omelia watched the retreating van with its burden of life and death, and in the interior of which

still raged a most deadly and unequal struggle.

"Ah," she sighed, "no wonder I am turned from as something despicable, to be the daughter of such a race of murderers as those. No wonder that one who bears the semblance of any Hindoo caste should be a thing to shudder at by the noble-minded and the just. Oh, cruel fate, that should have given me hopes and aspirations which were doomed never to be realised—hopes that vanish into air, even as a bubble at an infant's touch. Why was I ever born, or being born, why was I made the sport and toy of feelings which, alas, have carried me far out of my natural sphere, and above my own class?"

Whilst thus soliloquising, Omelia could observe that a terrible *melee* was raging in various quarters. The report of fire-arms, the shrieks of women and children, and the confused shouts of infuriated sepoys, all proclaimed the contest to be still continued, and a work of dreadful destruction being enacted. She would fain endeavoured to afford what assistance she might under the circumstances, but hardly knew how to render any. She had not, however, remained long in doubt as to what course to adopt, when an end was suddenly put to her ruminations Several ferocious sepoys rushed past apparently in hot pursuit of some fugitive, when one of them suddenly glanced at Omelia, and darting forward, caught her savagely by the wrist. His face and form were half covered with blood, and his aspect terribly ferocious.

"Ah, ah," he exclaimed, in fierce accents, "you belong to me! Henceforth I am your natural protector."

"Unhand me, sir! What would you?"

"Know, girl, that I am your future parent. Your father, Yunadar, bequeathed you before his death to my protection—I am to fill the duties of a parent, and teach you to avoid the Feringhee. You have had a long chase after the false god of your idolatry, and I hope you found that he had met with his deserts."

"Unhand me," said Omelia, "and dare not to speak of one whose noble nature you can never understand or appreciate. Is it not enough for you to indulge in wholesale and merciless slaughter, such as has now been enacted, without carrying your malevolence so far as to defame or injure by your wicked thoughts one whose conduct is governed by the highest sense of honour and mercy. Forbear, misguided man, and learn from me, ere it is too late, that a terrible fate awaits both you and your guilty companions. Repent, whilst there is yet time."

"Oh, indeed, so you have learnt to preach

their cant, and lecture with the oily tongue of the accursed race, have you? We shall see. The fate that awaits you, is to become a dutiful daughter to me, and not longer disgrace or dishonour your name and family by siding with their bitterest enemies. I have a most trusty friend, who has solicited the honour of your hand, and, in consideration of faithful services to me, I have promised you will accept him. Do you hear? See that you make yourself agreeable; I shall introduce you to him shortly. Do you understand? Mind I will be obeyed!" and he shook her savagely.

"Understand, once and for all, that both my heart and hand are my own to bestow upon whom I think best; and therefore you may tell your friend, whoever he may be, that he must seek elsewhere for his bride, for it would be easier for him to lift up with his own hand one of the Himalaya mountains, than it would be for him to ever gain either mine or my love."

"Disobedient girl! we will see, and teach you your duty. Never more shall you be allowed to follow the footsteps of your destroyer, for such he will be if you are not checked in your mad infatuation. I have you now, and intend to keep a sharp look out after you. You leave not again without my permission."

"I go whither I please, in spite of you and your desolute companions," answered Omelia, endeavouring to assume a bold demeanour she was far from feeling.

"You'll home with me now, at all events," was the answer, as he fixed upon her a savage and determined look.

"What, oh! Alahamed!" he shouted, and in answer to the summons Alahamed appeared. He was surprised to see Omelia, and turned to the other for some explanation.

"The long lost daughter bequeathed to me," said the latter. She has been spirited away by one of our enemies, as you know, but luckily I have again met with her after many months of anxiety."

And so saying, he proceeded to drag his unfortunate victim along with him. Omelia was horrified when he told her she was for the future under his charge. He informed her that he was the only surviving relative of her father, Yunadar, in fact, his half brother, and some time prior to his death he had, by a written document, appointed his half brother, Tamneegal, her future protector and parent.

It is a common thing for the native princes of India to will away their sons and daughters, and appoint those whom they wish to officiate as their parents, and this is a course frequently adopted by many of the other classes of that country, and one which had been followed in this, our time,

by the wicked Yunadar. Omelia now remembered to have seen Tamneegal in her earlier youth, and knew that he was her father's half brother.

"We will home to our quarters," said Tamneegal, as he proceeded hastily along.

Omelia had no idea where he was about to conduct her, but she passively resigned herself to her fate, be it whatever it might. To say the truth, she was so borne down with one trouble and another that she did not appear to have the capability of offering any resistance, and, therefore, thought it advisable to remain passive, and not excite the rage of her wicked and guilty conductor. She was soon conducted to a large cave which appeared to be the haunt, as indeed it was of Tamneegal and his lawless companions. It was their secret retreat, being unknown to Europeans. From this cave they would sally forth to attack any party whom they thought were not sufficiently strong to offer much resistance.

The place was hung round with numberless weapons of defence, and several barrels of gunpowder and shot were strewed around on the floor. A party of half inebriated sepoys were at their carousals. They greeted Tamneegal with loud and voiceferous cheers; he returned their salutations, but stalked on into an inner apartment, before which was hung several thick curtains.

On entering Omelia observed a female of mild features, about the middle age; she arose and greeted Tamneegal who turned to Omelia and said, what he intended to be impressive—

"I introduce you now to your future mother. This is my wife, Meugriah; and this is the long lost daughter bequeathed to me, and of whom you have often heard me speak. I now place her in your charge, and understand I do not wish her ever to leave here without she is accompanied either by myself or one of my most trusty friends. Do you understand?"

The woman bowed in acquiescence, and handed her new charge to a seat.

The appartment appeared to be tolerably comfortable, and our heroine was apparently reassured for the the present. The more so as Tamneegal said he had some business to transact, and left the two females to themselves.

The elder one was very corteous to her young charge, and placed refreshments before her, and appeared to be solicitous of making her as happy as the circumstances would admit.

"So you have been for many months away, I understand," she said; "an affair of the heart, I believe?"

"I have been chasing a phantom of that kind," replied Omelia, "but that has all past now, still I cannot consent to live with my parent; his habits are of too lawless a nature for me to even be a spectator of them."

"Ah," said the other, "poor girl, no doubt they are, but you know his determined nature; he will, I am afraid, keep you prisoner. There are always numbers of his companions in the other apartment who will be on the continual watch. Your chance is but a feeble one to get out of his power."

"Ah, I fear so. He spoke to me of some friend of his who sought my hand, do you know to whom he alludes?"

"Yes, I fancy it must be young Goolooh. He is particularly friendly with my husband, and I believe some time since saved his life."

"Indeed! and so out of gratitude he would sacrifice me."

"He would I suppose wish you to marry him."

"And you, how long have you known my uncle?"

"Oh, a very long time; it is only recently however that he has been able to persuade me to become his wife."

"And—and does he use you well?" was the prompt question which followed. No answer when it was repeated.

"You must pardon my freedom," said Omelia. "Alas, I know know but little of him, but always heard he had a cruel nature, and can hardly believe he would behave better to you than he has done to others."

"Oh, as to that, we have all our faults, I suppose."

There was a pause after this. Omelia found her not deficient in candour or frankness, still, at present, they were strangers, and she was at a loss to discover in what way this woman had been identified with her uncle; for it certainly appeared that she leant towards him to a considerable extent. Omelia thought it best therefore not to be too inquisitive. She made her companion a confidant and related to her all the circumstances connected with her lover, with which the reader is already acquainted.

In the course of a short time Tamneegal returned, accompanied by a young man, whom he at once introduced to our heroine by the name of Goolooh.

"And you will understand," he observed, "that this is one of my most esteemed friends, and is, moreover, the same one of whom I have already spoken, but I wish him to be to me more than a friend. Do you understand?"

Omelia made no reply to this, and her uncle concluded that she gave a half consent, at least that was, at any rate, the con-

struction he chose to put upon her conduct, so he assumed quite a pleasant bearing—to say the truth, bad man as he unquestionably was, he had some natural latent affection for his niece, and seemed to be proud of her beauty, and the superior tone of her mind. Goolooh paid her marked, but respectful attention. He appeared to be very superior to the majority of her uncle's companions, and she received his attentions with cold civility. So thus the first night of initiation into her uncle's mode of living wore away.

On the following day, Goolooh again made his appearance, and when left alone with Omelia, began thus to urge his suit:—

"It is true, we are as yet comparative strangers to each other, although I have seen you many times when you were not aware of it; but you know as yet but little of me. You will perhaps think it premature in me to tell you that, for a long time past, I have learnt to love you. I have asked your uncle's consent to become a suitor for your hand; but this is not all—I have to know at the same time whether I dare hope I shall meet with a consent from you."

He was about to go on, but Omelia stopped him by saying:—

"I do not understand how it is possible, sir, I can have inspired you with so sudden a passion as you pretend to have; but of this be assured that it is utterly out of my power to offer you the slightest encouragement. I will not endeavour to conceal from you, sir, that my heart is not my own to give. It is already another's."

"Indeed; I—ah—that is, I understood —certainly I understood you had an attachment some time since; but I thought that was all over."

"Then know, sir, that when a woman has once an attachment, it is never all over, as you term it—never, except with her life. I am not going to enter into details and particulars which would be extremely painful and distasteful for me now to do. Indeed you would hardly wish it. It is sufficient for me to tell you, that it is not at all probable I shall ever listen to another man's suit."

"Well, if not now, let me hope at a future period."

"No, sir, at no period however remote. Do not deceive yourself, there are numbers of fair young women for you to choose a companion from, whose hearts are as yet untouched by the aching pangs with which mine are wrung."

"Well, if you have been badly treated, you surely might endeavour to forget one who is unworthy of you, by listening to the attentions of him, whose life should be devoted to make you happy, and anticipate your every wish."

"Who dares thus to have the audacity to tell me that my lover is unworthy of me, or that I have been badly treated; learn, ignorant simpleton, that he upon whom I have set my affections, is worthy of an empress's love, of the highest and noblest in the land; it is me who feel myself quite unworthy of him—unworthy from my connection, unworthy——but why am I talking thus," suddenly said Omelia, as she found her passions beginning to hurry her on beyond her own control. She ceased abruptly, and paced the apartment several times.

"Perhaps," she said sharply to her companion, you will tell me why I am kept a prisoner here; you say you have conceived a friendship for me, tell me why I am detained prisoner here."

"I was not aware of your being so."

"Indeed! then you are now; I am not allowed free passage, it seems."

"I will speak to your uncle about it, if it so please you.

"Do so, and you will oblige me."

"I am sorry I should have offended you."

"You have not offended me. If you are sincere in what you have said, I see no cause for offence. None whatever, you have my answer, and furthermore, I would have you bear in mind that I am not one of those natures who are vacilating or fickle in their character, and what I have once said I mean."

The young man bowed, and took a respectful departure of our heroine. He had really been an ardent admirer of her for a long period, and had hoped the affair with Stanley was off—to use a sporting phrase. He was convinced now, however, of his mistake.

CHAPTER CCXI.

OMELIA AND TAMNEEGAL.—THE BESEIGED BAND OF ENGLISH.—THE FORT AND ITS INMATES.

FOR the next few days Omelia saw but little of either Tamneegal, or his friend Goolooh. There was evidently some active business on hand, as she could hear him holding long discussions with his comrades in the next apartment, but he did not deign to enter into any particulars either to his wife or our heroine. One evening, however, there was a scene of more than usual confusion, and numbers of sepoys were conveyed into the cave very severely wounded, and the groans of the sufferers became painfully audible.

"What terrible scene has been enacted?" enquired Omelia of Goolooh, as he hastily entered the apartment.

"The fort! There has been an attack made on it, and we have been repulsed with great loss. They cannot possibly hold out long though."

"What do you mean? What fort?"

"Oh, don't you know? I will explain the whole affair whenever opportunity serves; at present I am officiating as surgeon to the sufferers."

And with these words he left the apartment; Omelia turned to Mengriahas though she would ask some information upon the subject, or an explanation of the meaning of the words that had been just spoken.

"Where you not aware," said Mengriah, "that a short distance from hence a few of our oppressors are shut up in a small fort, and are undergoing a siege, being surrounded on all sides. It is, I believe, quite impossible for them to eventually escape."

Omelia was much pained to learn this sad intelligence, and still more so, when she was informed that another attack was meditated, to compel the Europeans to surrender. Sympathising as she did with the besieged party she was grieved, when she reflected upon her incapability of assisting them in their present hour of imminent peril.

Later in the day she over-heard Tamneegal planning with Alahamed some new species of attack; the nature of which she could not quite comprehend, from the few disjointed sentences she could manage to hear. It was quite certain, that some fresh scheme was on the tapis, which her uncle and his worthless associate were discussing in an undertone.

Some time afterwards, Tamneegal entered accompanied by Goolooh.

"Let my advice be followed, and I think you will find it effectual," said the latter to his companion, shortly after their entrance.

"There could be no harm done, and it might result in a great benefit to us all."

"Oh," answered Tamneegal, "it might be so, if we had a different sort of ambassador; however, let it be as you say. Come hither, girl!" This was addressed to Omelia.

"You are, I believe, fond of errands of mercy. I have one to propose to you."

"Name it," was the answer, "and if it be nought that affects my honor, I shall be too glad to undertake whatever you may desire."

"There is a small band of our most bitter enemies shut up in fort, they are surrounded on all sides, that it is impossible for them to escape their just fate. Now we are disposed to be merciful, and if they will surrender themselves into our hands we will deal with them leniently; but if they refuse to do so, they will most assuredly be all destroyed."

"Cruel, remorseless, men; a terrible vengeance will overtake you for such monstrous crimes."

"Indeed," replied Tamneegal with a sardonic smile, "I'm not going to be preached to by a silly disobedient girl, so enough upon that head. "I am simply stating the present circumstances of the case, and what I would have done. You are so monstrously friendly with the enemies of your house and home, that I thought you might be glad to avail yourself of the offer I am about to make. If you like to take a flag of truce, and accompanied by Goolooh and a few of my trusty companions in arms, declare an armistice, and then offer them the terms I propose, provided they surrender themselves prisoners into our hands.

"What are those terms?"

"We shall deal with them leniently, and of course spare their lives."

"I accept the mission," said Omelia.

"And may it be crowned with success; but in the event of their acceding to the offer you make through me, you promise to let them pass unmolested whithersoever they please?"

"I have not said that; they must certainly remain prisoners till I and my companions have consulted upon the subject, and also ascertained who they are."

"Ah! would you play me false then!"

"No!—go to—do my bidding, without useless parley."

Goolooh now interceded in the matter, and pointed out the impossibility there was of their escape, and therefore it would be advisable to make an offer of terms.

On the following morning Omelia sallied forth with Goolooh and several fierce vindictive looking Sepoys. The country they went through was laid waste by the scenes of repeated contests. In an isolated part she soon observed a small fort; this was surrounded by a number of mutinous Sepoys, who hailed her party with loud shouts, and Goolooh briefly explained the object of their mission. Waving her flag of truce, she called out loudly in the English language, which she spoke with the purity of a native. Through one of the loop-holes of the fort she beheld several muskets directed towards her and her companions.

"A truce! A truce!" she called out loudly. "I come a messenger of peace,

and like the dove of old, bear an olive branch. Listen to the terms offered!"

"Stand off," was the reply. "Endeavour to approach one step farther, and your life shall pay the forfeit of your temerity."

"Fall back at once," she said, in an imperious voice, to her companions, "I will perform this task by myself."

They did as she desired.

"Now I am alone, and unarmed. It is not usual for Englishmen to fire upon a defenceless woman."

"What would you?" was asked, in a masculine voice.

"I come to offer terms. It appears impossible for you to withstand the attacks which are made upon you, and if you will surrender yourselves prisoners without further resistance, you shall have full assurance given of your safety."

"Never!" was the reply immediately given. "Never! we know how much faith is to be placed in the promises of your countrymen. If we are to fall, we shall sell our lives as dearly as possible under the circumstances. This fort may be our tomb; better that than trust to faithless promises—that would only lead to a worse fate than death. The British soldier knows his duty, and prefers to die at his post."

"Believe me," said Omelia, "I am your best friend, and would not urge you to a course which might be dishonourable. I am a friend to all your countrymen. The greater and happiest portion of my life has been passed with them. Although I bear the form and features of an Indian, my best sympathies have been and ever will be, with the noble English. Do not, I pray, therefore, turn a deaf ear to my appeal. Alas, I shudder to think of your unhappy fate, and wish it were in my power to convey you far from hence to a place of security.

There was a tone of sincerity in the manner these words were uttered, which seemed to have an impression on the inmates of the Fort. They hesitated and consulted together.

"Who are you? and what is your name?" was asked by another voice.

"My name is Omelia, I have been befriended by many of your countrymen, and have been in sad trouble myself—I am here now against my own will, being, indeed but a prisoner myself.

She was not allowed to conclude the brief history of herself, but was startled to hear a female voice scream out in wild accents :—

"Oh! that voice and name, it is as I thought—my preserver—oh! joyful meeting —noble-minded, kind, generous girl—this is indeed a prestige of better days."

What was our heroine's astonishment

when she recognised the speaker's voice to be that of Mrs. Forrester.

"We do not doubt your word," said the voice of the first speaker—"but we naturally are very dubious regarding the sincerity of your companions, and do not at all feel disposed to place ourselves in their power."

"Oh, yes, yes," exclaimed Mrs. Forrester, "she will be a surety on the good faith of her companions. What had best be done, you surely might admit her into the fort, when we could consult upon our ulterior proceedings."

Omelia drew back, and rejoined Goolooh and the others. She explained to him that the party desired her presence in the fort, and by acceding to their request, there was every probability of their consenting to surrender themselves prisoners. Goolooh was very reluctant to permit Omelia to trust herself to the mercy of the occupants of the fort, when our heroine indignantly exclaimed, "what think you that I fear to trust my life with those whose actions are ever dictated by the highest sense of honor, I would not do those illfated individuals the injustice to imagine for one moment that they could injure an unprotected girl who seeks to do them what she hopes and believes to be a signal service. No! I will accept their offer, and enter alone: you, therefore, keep back out of gun range, otherwise you will peril your own lives as well as mine, for of course they will be justified in firing, if they see me followed by armed men."

It must be understood, that the fort itself was surrounded by a low wall on all sides. On the inner side of this wall was a deep ditch or moat, it had been originally well supplied with water, and formed an almost insurmountable barrier from an attacking party; but it was now perfectly dry, nevertheless it afforded considerable protection to the inhabitants of the fort from their aggressive foes repeated attacks, indeed the sepoys had been so fearfully punished in the last two or three onslaughts that they dared not again venture upon another, and contented themselves by indulging in threats and execrations out of the range of gun shot. It was in the last attack that so many had been killed and wounded, and were carried back to Tamneegal cave, as already described.

Tamneegal himself began to despair of ever taking the fort by assault. All the attacks had been repulsed with such obstinacy and determination, that the case appeared hopeless. It is impossible to guess how many lives had fallen before the walls of this brittle building—or rather the remains of a building; for there was only a portion of that originally built by the British. Smarting under the determined resistance offered to them, Tamneegal and his lawless companions thought it best to try another course, with what success we shall presently see. They did this, thinking that by getting the few Europeans in their power, they might dictate their own terms, and obtain a free pardon from the British military authorities at some future period, by restoring the prisoners to their friends.

They knew by this time, that in most districts of India, the Europeans were fast gaining the ascendancy, and the more wary portion of the revolted population thought it advisable to lay up in store one or two humane acts, whereby they might propitiate their rulers to grant them mercy at some time when it might be needed, Tamneegal, Alahamed and their associates had planned this scheme together as quite a piece of diplomacy. First it placed their enemies in their power, and next, they thought they should have a large booty, as they were under the full impression, that an immense treasure was contained in the fort, but a treasure that was perfectly useless to its inhabitants, situated as they were at present; scarcity of food, and almost worse than that, very short of ammunition.

When our heroine approached the low walls which surrounded the building, the beleaguered party called upon her to declare upon her soul that she was alone and unattended by even one companion. She gave her solemn adjuration in reply; and then a small iron bridge was lowered for her to enter by, and immediately drawn up upon her passing it. Immediately upon her entrance, Mrs. Forrester clasped her in her arms and shed tears of mingled joy and sorrow over her; and her three children, with the imitative characteristic of youth, immediately followed their mother's example. Our heroine was shocked beyond expression to observe the alteration in her friends' appearance, and the gaunt features of those of her companions.

It would be a vain effort to describe the sufferings of the few occupants of the little stronghold. For weeks they had been shut up, surrounded on all sides, a prey to continuous alarms, and requiring their utmost vigilance both day and night. Latterly they had been compelled to live upon the remains of a horse they had shot, and for which they had been unable to find in a sufficiency of food. They had lost many of their companions during the siege they had undergone; some had perished from exhaustion or disease, and some had fallen whilst defending their position from the attacks of their enemies. The present

occupants of the fort consisted of eight individuals besides the three children of Mrs. Forrester. There were two other laidies besides Mrs. Forrester, namely Mrs. McDarvish, and Miss Hilayard, and five gentleman, amongst whom were Major Forrester, and Quartermaster McDarvish.

"Kind, generous, noble-hearted girl," passionately exclaimed Mrs. Forrester; "the sight of you gives me renewed hope for myself and unfortunate companions; what strong proofs have I not already had of your honor and integrity of purpose; alas! I thought to meet again under very different circumstances to these, when I might have been able to requite your noble conduct in some befitting manner."

"I seek no requital but my own thoughts of having saved the just whenever an op-

portunity occurred, and now I hope I come on an errand of mercy."

Omelia was introduced to Major Forrester, who was the senior in command. She explained to him the full particulars of the offer she was desired to make from Tamneegal and his companions, and was pained to be obliged to acknowledge the former to be her half-uncle. She however fully explained how she had been met, and indeed captured by her pretended parent.

A consultation now took place as to the propriety of accepting the offer of Tamneegal, and Mrs. Forrester, having full confidence as to their assured safety, was particularly solicitous for them to at once acceed to the terms proposed. Some of the others seemed, however, to be of a different opinion.

"In any case," urged Miss Hilayard, "we shall be obliged to let them take us prisoners when all our ammunition's gone."

"Hout! my friend, wha so? have we not our ain swords and bayonets? aye and een without them we've such weapons as nature has gaen us. Na, we'el hae na surrender—na surrender—ye ken weel enoo," she continued, addressing her husband,—"ye ken weel enoo that the McDarvishes never yielded to man or fiend—na, not for centuries past."

"That's e'en true, I believe," said her husband; "and neither will I ever quit my post. If we are to fall, ye'l jist see that I'l e'en die in harness, and never yield while I've life."

"Nor I," said another of the party.

"I cannot," said Major Forrester, "under these circumstances, accede to your proposition. In refusing it, you must not imagine that I or any of us doubt your sincerity, or, indeed, that of your companions; but the duty of an English soldier is never to desert his post; better a certain death upon the bed of honour, than an ignoble surrender. We shall hold this place as long as we can, and if no chance succour arrive, we must submit to whatever fate is in store for us."

All further arguments appeared futile, as the beseiged were inflexible in their resolve; and Omelia was compelled to take a reluctant leave of those who had excited her sympathy so powerfully on their behalf. She, however, said that she intended to inform Tamneegal and his associates, that she had given her promise that there should be a cessation of hostilities for two days, as an earnest of their good intentions, and hoped that before that time they would deem it advisable to think better of the proposition.

The major said it would be useless. His path of duty lay before him, from which nothing should turn him.

"At any rate it will afford me an opportunity of paying you another visit," said our heroine; "and I will avail myself of it to receive your final answer."

Upon her returning to Goolooh, he evinced little or no surprise at her non-success. It was, indeed, no more than he had expected. Observing, however, at the same time, that they must eventually yield, or be starved to death.

"Well," said Tamneegal, tauntingly, upon their return, "much confidence your friends appear to have in you, after all your boasting. They know the fate they deserve at our hands. They would have been safer with our party than they will even likely to be with any other. How-

ever, let them take their chance, now, as they choose to refuse a fair offer."

"I do not say they positively refuse," replied Omelia, although her heart could not respond to the words she uttered. "Give them time to consider, and I will make another attempt, let us hope with better success."

"I do not see that we have any right to guarantee them two whole days' rest to recruit their strength, that they may be enabled to massacre more of our countrymen; we will compel them to surrender before then."

"No, no, you would never be so unjust after I have passed my most solemn promise in the name of yourself and companions, you dare not violate it!"

"Oh, as to my daring to violate, we will very soon see about that if it is necessary. Who is there to prevent it?"

"You, yourself! your own conscience!" Goolooh now interposed, and it was eventually agreed, after some further discussion, that Omelia's agreement should be respected and hostilities cease. It was not, perhaps, so much from motives of mercy that occasioned this, but owing more to the fact of their having received so sound a dressing, which made them unwilling at present to make another attack.

CHAPTER CCXII.

THE FORT.—THE MIDNIGHT SURPRISE.— FEARFUL MOMENTS OF PERIL.

It has been a fact incontestibly established throughout the whole of the late wars in India, that the native army or inhabitants have no confidence in one another. The revolted portion were but predatory hordes of marauders, some seeking to gratify their revenge, whilst the major part were actuated more from motives of plunder and rapine. But it appears remarkable that, out of the many thousands of well disciplined troops, as unquestionably many were, that no well organised stand was made against the few faithful British heroes who sustained the first shock of the fearful mutiny. No leader of any note has been called forth out of the native regiments of India, and no successful battle has ever been won by the Sepoys in a fair-fought field. This is, no doubt, attributable to their being split up in sections or classes, and having no confidence in one another. This was exemplified in the present instance. Tamneegal and his associates belonged to one class, each individual of which had but his own selfish purpose to serve. Still, for their joint interest, they, to a certain extent consented to pull together as long as they thought it answered their purpose.

But the unfortunate inhabitants of the fort were surrounded by other sets of men who had no sympathy with Tamneegal and his associates, on the contrary, they were jealous of his gaining any advantage. It became pretty generally bruited about that terms had been offered to the few Europeans, and consequently, so treacherous were these men to each other, that this only acted as an incentive for the other party of Sepoys to concoct surprise and attack. They had heard that two days had been granted for a cessation of hostilities, and thought this was an admirable opportunity for them to commence an attack on their own account, and sack all the plunder they could lay hold of. Their plan of operation was artfully devised, and whilst Alahamed and Tamneegal were pluming themselves upon what they deemed a master-stroke of policy, the opposition members of the community were hatching a pretty little plot on their own account. Their scheme was to dress up one of their Hindoo maidens as much like Omelia as possible, and in the dusk of the evening let her proceed to the fort as though she had come for their final answer. The men would be as near as they dare venture to the fort, and, should the supposed Omelia succeed in deceiving its occcupants, they intended, when the drawbridge was lowered, to make a rush for it, and, if possible, carry it by a *coup de main*.

So far, all was very cleverly contrived, but they had a difficulty presented itself in the perfection of their scheme—they could not get any one who was able to assume the voice of our heroine, or speak English with sufficient purity to deceive the unfortunate Europeans—however, they put up with the best they could find, and determined to endeavour to put their arrangements in practice on the following evening. It was suggested by some of the most hardened of these scoundrels to watch Omelia herself when she came to the fort, and then make a rush for it, but this proposition was negatived by the majority, and it was therefore determined upon the course.

We must now take a glance at the inmates of the fort. Alas, what hollow cheeks and a worn expression was observable on the countenance of each; weeks of anxiety, long and painful vigils and want of food told a sad tale upon the gallant band. Since the interview, they had been lulled into comparative security, but they were nevertheless not thrown completely off their guard. In the early part of the day, Ensign Lightfoot had been fortunate enough

to shoot two good sized birds that were flying over the immediate proximity of the fort; one of the party was busily engaged by a fire cooking them for their repast whilst McDawlish was melting in an iron ladle sundry buttons cut from his comrades' jackets for the purpose of casting them into bullets; thus was the fire made an agent for preparing, both at the same time, sustenance for the living and the instruments of death.

"A wise mon never should leave himself unprovided for any emergency," observed the stoical Scotchman.

"Ah, this is the most disastrous affair of all," was the reply, "to be so cursedly short of ammunition; luckily I have found out a good stock of small pebble stones, see here!"

"Excellent, i'faith; they will not go very sure of the mark, but a random shot is better than none at all—hurrah!—we are not used up as yet, but shall be ready when needful."

"Oh, let us hope some succour will arrive," said Mrs. Forrester, "before the time is expired for us to give the required answer. Surely some of our brave troops will be on the march this way shortly, and they cannot fail to see the English flag still flying, which will be a sufficient indication of our situation."

"Let us hope so," was the general response.

The party then set down and partook of a slender repast from the two birds which had so luckily chanced to fall into their hands. It was a rude meal enough, but was quite a luxury to anything they had tasted for a long period, and this was a fact of which they were quite confident; they did not need an appetite to enjoy it. Towards the dusk of the evening they descried a female figure approaching the fort, waving aloft a flag of truce precisely like the one carried by Omelia on the day previous.

"Ah," exclaimed Mrs. Forrester, "here comes again our good friend; see, she is waving the flag to attract our notice. Pray heaven she may have devised some scheme for our deliverance."

"It is not from the hands of her or hers that we are like to get much assistance," said Ensign Lightfoot, who was too prejudiced against the whole of the natives of India to admit that any faith could be placed in any one of them.

"Let us admit her, and hear what she has to say, at any rate," said Miss Hilayard.

"What, ho, there!" shouted the major. "Your business? Speak at once!"

"I come, as you know, on an errand of

mercy, and crave admittance again," was the answer.

"Let down the bridge," said one of the inmates of the fort.

"Stay! be not too hasty!" answered the major. What is the meaning of this? she speaks apparently in a feigned voice—not like the one when here last. Perhaps there may be a motive for this. She is sincere?"

"Sincere!" replied his wife. "I will answer for her with my life; she is incapable of deception or subterfuge."

"I hope not; but her voice sounds to me quite different to what it was; and indeed now I observe her more attentively, she certainly seems to be altered in appearance. And yet there can be not much harm in admitting a single woman; we are not so poorly garrisoned as to fear her taking us by surprise."

These words seemed to be prophetic. The drawbridge was lowered, and the representative of our heroine walked forward; and when she had placed her foot on the bridge, she pretended to have caught her dress in one of the joins, and stooped down to remove it. This was done purposely to give her companions time to come up. It was the signal for them to follow, and afforded them greater facility to do so. Standing, as she did, immediately in front of the port hole of the fort, with every eye of its occupants upon her, she intercepted their view of the advancing party, who rushed on, elated and uproarious, at the success of their *ruse*, and feeling confident in the plan of their enterprise. A rush of armed and ferocious men was the first indication the poor inmates of the fortress had of the preconcerted and desperate attack. It was now quite impossible to draw up the bridge, as it was filled with armed men.

"Treachery!" shouted the major. "Club your bayonets."

A bristling array of bayonets received the first shock, and numbers were impaled upon them, amidst cries of agony. They would have retreated, but were now urged on by their eager companions who were behind, out of the reach of weapons.

A dreadful and murderous contest was now waged at the entrance of the fortress. Its gallant defenders held their ground with a determination that appeared almost superhuman. The entrance was so narrow that it was not possible for many to come up at the time; still a large body, or rather a column of men, passed on to effect a passage; shouts, screams, and execrations, resounded on all sides. The unfortunate girl who had the temerity to represent Omelia paid dearly for her duplicity; she fell into the ditch pierced with two deep wounds from which the life-blood was fast flowing. Several Sepoys, rendered desperate by their situation, made a breastwork of the dead bodies of their companions, and effected an entrance. One was seized by the intrepid McDarvish, and flung back over the heads of his companions. He fell never to rise again, but was trampled under foot by the assailants, the other two were cut down by the swords of an English officer of the party.

"Load, and fire from behind," shouted the major, "we cannot all be at the entrance at once; those behind us, therefore, pick down as many as you can; ladies to your duty."

There was no time for reflection, all was action, and the three ladies of the party were actually occupied in loading the weapons one after the other, and supplying them to their companions to fire as rapidly as possible upon the assailants. Volley after volley was poured in upon the attacking line, and did dreadful havoc, as every shot told. The carnage was fearful: a heap of dead lay strewn around, and bid fair to block up the passage.

"Have at the rascals," shouted out the major; "they must walk over our dead before they effect an entrance yet, hurrah!" this was caught up, and three hearty British cheers were sent forth upon the night air.

Immovable as a rock, the stalwart form of McDarvish confronted his foes with steady determination, and stopped their entrance. They had fallen back with some confusion, appalled at their reception, and now began to fire their pieces. Amidst the smoke and confusion, several having crept round on their hands and knees in the ditch, now managed to effect an entrance. Then a fearful struggle took place inside the fort, and eventually they were slain: not, however, without the loss of one of the English party. How long this dreadful contest would have lasted, it is hardly possible to say, but a new cause of disturbance took place; Tamncegal and his band hearing the shouts, the shots and noise occasioned by the affray, now rushed to the spot, to see what was the occasion of all the disturbance. Upon arriving there, they immediately devined the cause of the whole affair, and instantly commanded a cessation of hostilities. They might as well have spoken to the winds, for they were only greeted with taunting jeers, irritated beyond measure; they charged the attacking party, and then a fierce contest was waged outside the walls of the fort, which gave its inmates a little breathing time to recover themselves.

Never was there seen such a confused mass of combatants. The attacking party, bent upon effecting an entrance, were now themselves assailed on all sides. The Eu·

ropeans did not know the cause of this new incursion, but had only to think of defending themselves as they best could under the circumstances; so as fast as the guns were loaded they were discharged indiscriminately upon the nearest foe. Presently a new cause of alarm occurred which threatened to end in their complete destruction. Several of the originators of the onslaught had succeeded in bringing up a field-piece, and were directing it to the exposed opening of the fortress. The muzzle was brought to bear upon the exposed place, and death and utter annihilation seemed to be the fate of the small band of English warriors, when Omelia, who was with the new comers, seeing the imminent danger of her friends, snatched a revolver from one of her companions, and levelling it, discharged it at the gunner, who was about to fire the piece. He fell, mortally wounded. Another came into his place and was served the same. She then called the attention of Alahamed to the proceedings of their enemies, and he charged with several of his companions, and took possession and captured the piece in question. Before there was time for much discussion upon the point, our heroine spiked the gun, thus rendering it harmless for the present in the hands of either parties. Still the fight was raging with determination on both sides. Seeing the whole of the Sepoys belonging to both parties pretty well engaged, Major Forrester endeavoured to clear the bridge of its burthen of life and death, but many living foes still offered an obstinate resistance, and kept pressing on in the hopes of effecting a passage. The Europeans had received numerous wounds, and it was a matter of surprise how nature could endure what they had gone through, but "a stag at bay is a dangerous foe," and few resolute Englishmen in the way of defence when driven into a corner are not likely to dispair while they have life.

In the midst of the confusion and darkness which was now beginning to enshroud the combatants, Omelia managed to press on towards the bridge unobserved, and, calling Mrs. Forrester by name, received a feeble answer in return.

"It is your friend Omelia!" said our heroine, "by this ring which you gave to me in a former hour of trouble you should know me," and heedless of danger she pressed forward for the bridge.

"Stay," shouted out the major, "fire not upon her." This was said only just in time, as the levelled pieces were about to be discharged through the opening. Our heroine rushed on and was received in the athletic arms of the inflexible McDarvish.

"Heaven be praised," she exclaimed, as she once more found herself an inmate of the fort. "Here will I now take my stand, and share your fate, whatsoever it may, for weal or for woe. Alas, I have been compelled to be with those against whom my heart and feelings revolted, but now come what may, if certain death stares us in the face, I will lay down my weary life cheerfully at the shrine of honour and justice."

"Heroic girl," said Mrs. Forrester. "I much fear our fate is doomed to be a dark and sorrowful one, but let us not drag you down to destruction along with us; you are safe, and would be only seeking certain death perhaps by espousing our cause, and taking part against those whom you own as your kindred."

"Better that than to be doomed to follow the footsteps of those from whom the sad heart turns from with loathing and disgust."

"Have you no parents whom your are leaving, and who perhaps, with all their faults, have a natural affection for their offspring, and may possibly mourn your loss, as something irreparable, and feel bitterly aggrieved that you should desert over to those whom they may consider their enemies."

"Indeed, no! I have not any parents living. My mother—I do not remember, and my father perished in a mortal conflict some time since; I have no ties or relations save my father's half-brother, who is a man at which my soul shudders; he lays claim to be my natural protector, as it appears my father bequeathed me to him. I will not, however, consent to be guided in my actions by one whose character and sentiments I hold in no kind of respect."

The fight still continued here and there feebly, but the rage of the combatants had nearly burnt itself out, besides which, the darkness bid fair to soon put an end to it altogether. It was a most fortunate circumstance for the Europeans, that the Sepoys had quarrelled amongst themselves; had it not been for this circumstance, they would no doubt have been ultimately overpowered. Major Forrester and his gallant companions managed to clear the bridge sufficiently to draw it back into its position, and he and his comrades were comparatively satisfied under the circumstances with the course events had taken for the present. It is quite certain the attack had been fairly repulsed, but they had to deplore the one gallant soldier of their party who had fallen covered with wounds in struggling with those few who had at one time succeeded in effecting an entrance into the fort.

Eternal praises upon the English soldier,

who, whether it be under the burning sun of India or in the frigid regions of Russia, marches manfully forward to fight his country's battles without a murmur. Badly paid, but too often badly fed, housed, or cared for in any way, he, nevertheless, under every disadvantage—in the most trying and adverse positions, which would make ordinary troops sink with despair, generally manages to hold his own to the last, and when he does fall—it is upon a bed of glory. It is asserted by continental nations, that England is not a military country. What other nation could have quelled the Indian revolt in the incredibly short space of time she has done? Indeed, what other nation could have held the large territory of India for the same number of years? There were no doubt many causes of complaints against their rule, which will be remedied, no doubt, as speedily as circumstances will permit; still the probability that India would never have been governed half so well by any other nation than the English.

When Major Forrester and his comrades came to make an inspection of the damage they had sustained, they found the dead body of poor Ensign Parker, with a heap of slain Sepoys near where their companion lay in his last sleep. There were in all eleven Sepoys lying slain inside the fort. They lost no time in stripping them of all the cartridges and ammunition they could find upon their persons, and were delighted at obtaining a tolerably good store. Having accomplished this, they proceeded to eject the bodies from their abode, and buried poor Parker were some of their other companions had found a last resting place.

"These are sad sights to witness," said Omelia, after Parker had been consigned to the earth, and a few short prayers had been said over his body. "Very sad! The loss of one faithful companion after another, is a contemplation too melancholy to dwell upon."

"It is, indeed," said Mrs. Forrester. "I have gone through fearful scenes, my dear girl, since the time you saved me from certain death."

"I suppose so; so, indeed, have most of us. You were, when I last left you, about to rejoin your husband; and I understood that you considered yourself out of danger when you once got safe to his quarters."

"So I did imagine! but oh! the remembrance even now distracts me. Major Forrester had the utmost confidence in the faithfulness of those native troops under his command, and so had he, against the advice of his fellow officers, neglected to disarm the Sepoy regiments, until one night—it is the old story—they set fire to our bungalow, and commenced an indiscriminate slaughter. Oh! the scene that then took place baffles all description. Major Forrester and some of the other officers flew to their horses, and mounting them, came up with a few of the English troops to the rescue; they charged the Sepoys, and the major and his brother officers shot down the ringleader, and for a short time they believed they had succeeded in quelling the revolt; but alas! it was a delusive hope: they renewed the attack, and I can hardly tell how it was accomplished; but I did succeed, under the convoy of a few of our faithful troops in making my escape with my children, my husband, and some of our friends—and oh! what scenes we have witnessed since then. Poor Miss Hilayard—she has lost her parent, and an only sister, a sweet little girl of about eleven years old. You may judge of her horrible situation on the occasion of the first outbreak of the Sepoys—who rushed into our bungalow, and commenced an indiscriminate slaughter as I before observed. They were, however, resisted nobly by three of our male companions, who were playing at chess on the ground floor. These gentlemen consisted of Doctor Elgood, Lieutenant Fitzmaurice, and a Mr. Osborne, a merchant, who was staying with us.

The first intimation they received of the affair was the door of the apartment being flung open, and poor Doctor Elgood, who was sitting with his back to it, intent upon his game, received a dreadful blow on the head with the butt-end of a musket which felled him to the earth. Fitzmaurice and Mr. Osborne sprang to their feet on the instant; the former instantly grappled with the villain who had wounded the doctor, and whilst wresting the musket from his grasp Mr. Osborne shot him dead with his revolver. Fitzmaurice now stood before the entrance and shot down three of the mutineers as they entered, and by this time those outside began to fire the building. Ah! what a dreadful scene then occurred. They overpowered the three Englishmen and rushed up to our apartment. I was a favourite with some few—of the men in particular—and one of them protected me and my children from their violence; but the rest—ah, mercy! I shall never forget the harrowing scene of that fearful night! I could hear the piercing screams going on in another apartment as the work of destruction went on. Poor Miss Hilayard was there, and crept under a sofa for concealment. Every individual in that apartment was ruthlessly slaughtered—men, women, and children. While Miss Hilayard lay concealed under the sofa what was her horror to find herself saturated with blood, which was dripping from the murdered victims lying above her. She involuntarily screamed out, and was dragged from her lurking-place by one of the men who had stayed behind his companions, and was now engaged in rifling the persons of all the valuables they had on, or were possessed of.

"Whether his thirst for bloodshed had been in some measure assuaged, or whether he was more tender-hearted than his companions, I do not know, but be this as it may, he thought proper to spare Miss Hilayard, and she succeeded in making her way to where I was situated, the only survivor out of all that apartment where this terrific slaughter took place; and, horrible to relate, we found in the court yard outside our bungalow, a pair of boots which we knew belonged to Miss Hilayard's little sister. They told a fearful tale—the feet were in them. Yes, the merciless wretches had actually cut off the poor child's feet while she was alive and playing about, quite unconscious of the dreadful fate which awaited her. We afterwards discovered that they hacked the poor dear child to pieces with their tulwars. Oh, Omelia, my heart bleeds when I reflect upon the fearful atrocities I have witnessed!"

"It seems almost incredible," said our heroine, that the wickedness of man should ever urge him to such frightful enormities." But how did you and your companions escape? I am deeply interested in all the particulars of the misfortunes that have befallen you since we last parted."

"I can hardly tell you how I escaped—by a miracle! The Major, myself and children, with several of our friends, managed to escape from our cantonment. We were fired at and pursued, but the gentlemen of our party offered a stout resistance, and they did not pursue us further. Well, we consequently managed to get fairly clear of those wretches who had already committed such dreadful butchery; but we were in an enemy's country, almost entirely at their mercy, and with little or no means of obtaining provisions. We did not know what place to make for, but marched on through that long night, heedless of our course as long as it took us far away from the scene of our late conflict. In the day time, we crept into jungles and hid ourselves when we saw any of the mutinous Sepoys coming along our way. Days were passed thus, and we were compelled to subsist upon what corn and grain we could pick up as we went along. Sometimes, indeed, we managed to get a meal furnished us by a stray cottager, but this was done always in great fear of being discovered, as they in-

variably said that if it were known by any of the revolted Sepoys, their house would be burnt over their heads, and perhaps they themselves slaughtered."

"Horrible! too horrible to conceive," exclaimed Omelia: "that an act of common humanity should be treated with such barbarity. But how did you eventually escape after all?"

"Ah, I should weary you if I were to give an account of all the many trials and adventures we went through, but we had with us a gentleman who had been sent out from England as a missionary; he had been very many years in India, and in his vocation, (that of a teacher of the gospel to the natives of India) was of course led into close communication with them. He had studied the Hindostanee language so well, and had become so familiarized with its accent, that it was hardly possible to detect him to be an Englishman. Well, an excellent thought occurred to one of our party, I forget from whom the suggestion came, but it was as this: the missionary clergyman was to represent a native of India, and be our spokesman on all occasions: so he was dressed up in the clothes of one of the natives, and coloring his face with some vegetable dyes, which he knew where to procure from the trees: he really looked exactly like a native, and passed as such on many occasions. I have always believed this was one of the main causes of escaping as we did."

"You interest me" said Omelia, "in an extraordinary degree. Did you soon succeed in finding a place of safety?"

"Indeed no, we had not as yet got through half our troubles, and we were so weary, with the long and painful marches we had undergone, that we were hardly capable of dragging one leg after the other. We used to march at night for concealment, and hide ourselves in the day: besides which, it was so intensely hot, that it was, in our exhausted state, almost impossible for us to bear the fatigue of a journey under the powerful rays of the meridian sun. One evening, however, we fell in with a strong body of native troops, who turned out to be belonging to the Nana's suite; the moment they caught sight of us, they set up a shout of vengeance, and marched forward to attack; we were near a river, which we were endeavouring to find some bridge to carry us over, as we had determined upon endeavouring to steer our way as well as we could to a small town my husband believed to be still in the hands of his countrymen. Upon our descrying the enemy, who threatened by their horrible menaces to destroy us, the major determined upon his plan of action. He told us, come what may, we must make up our minds to ford the river, while he and his comrades offered what resistance they could, should their opponents come up to prevent our escape. We rushed on to the river as fast as our legs could carry us, and shots were being exchanged by the few soldiers we had with us, and the advancing Sepoys. At length we succeeded in gaining the river's bank, and regardless of consequences, rushed in; each of the ladies were supported by a gentleman, who with his arm round her waist, encouraged by words of comfort, to bear up against the present misfortune; I was supported by the gallant McDarvish, the major being engaged in marshalling and ordering his men to resist any attack of the Nana's troop: and he managed to intimidate them by a show of defence, to allow us to nearly cross the river.

I thought at one time it was all over, as the water rose nearly to my chin. Poor Miss Hilayard was well nigh exhausted; she was supported by a noble young fellow, who now sleeps by the side of the brave. He has gone, my dear, where perhaps we may go shortly; but, be it when it may, let us die with honour to ourselves and country. We managed, after some short time had elapsed, to cross the river in safety, and ranging ourselves on the opposite bank, our soldiers prepared to give their enemies a warm reception, if they endeavoured to ford the river in pursuit of us. They seemed to think better of this, and contented themselves with a few shots, idle menaces, and fearful imprecations, and we again had to felicitate ourselves upon another narrow escape."

"You were fortunate to escape the Nana's troops, for it is not at all probable that you would have any mercy shown you from them. I have myself been in his power at one time, but luckily contrived, by the greatest good fortune, to escape. After then, I suppose you succeeded in arriving at some place of safety?"

"We did manage, thanks to the tact and address of our missionary gentleman to reach the town my husband was making for; but, upon our arrival there, it was in open revolt. The English troops, however, were sufficiently strong to offer a determined resistance, and held their enemies in check by force of arms. There was no telling how long this might last, for the Sepoys were receiving daily reinforcements, and only waited for a sufficient augmentation to their numbers to completely annihilate their late commanders. We succeeded, luckily, in joining our countrymen, however, and were not subjected to such frequent and imminent perils as we had been undergoing for some time previously."

"Then how came you in your present disastrous situation?" enquired our heroine.

"Oh! I should weary you with the details of our future disasters."

"Not at all; I am naturally interested in all that concerns you or any of your unfortunate countrymen."

We were compelled, or rather thought it advisable to evacuate the town, and cut our way through our opponents before they arrived in such numbers as would render it impracticable for our gallant soldiers to do so. Consequently our commanders gave orders for an immediate march, as they were about to endeavour to fall in with General Havelock's avenging band of troops, which were known to be scouring the country around.

We succeeded in cutting a passage through our opponents, and marched on for three days without meeting with Havelock's troops, and were exposed to continual attacks from the maurauding and predatory bands whom we fell in with on our march. Days passed over and we were not fortunate enough to meet with our anxiously looked for gallant countryman, when a new misfortune occurred to us, the details of which I shudder to reflect upon. The wretch, Tantia Topee, hearing of the position of our detachment, immediately hastened on towards us, and confronting our party, commanded us to surrender. A volley from our guns was the only answer he had for his temerity. He instantly answered our fire, and, oh, Omelia, a dreadful struggle then ensued. Every man of the English was determined never to surrender while he had life, and as Tantia Topee's troops were twelve times our number, you may judge of the sanguinary conflict that took place. The shot showered like hail upon our noble fellows, who fell thick and fast, not, however, without doing desperate execution among their enemies, but the immense superiority in numbers of Tantia's troops inspired them with a temporary courage, and, oh, it is agonizing to reflect upon the loss sustained by our unfortunate countrymen. After desperate efforts they succeeded in beating off for a time the opponents, who however followed them as they made good their retreat. Unfortunately our party got cut off from the main body, and Major Forrester, under cover of the night, managed to gain this fort, and here, as you know, we have been shut up without a possibility of extricating ourselves. Now you have had detailed a very brief and slender account of the trials we have undergone, and here I suppose we have arrived now at our last home."

"Let us hope not," said Major Forrester,

"whilst an Englishman has life, arms, and ammunition, he has no reason to despair."

"And provender," said his wife.

The major and his companions looked blank at the latter observation.

"We must see what can be done," said the major. "Let us be thankful that we have escaped the last affair so well as we have. At one time I thought we were doomed to certain and instant destruction. Who would have thought of the scoundrels having recourse to such a *ruse* to deceive us?"

It was now explained to Omelia the plan of attack which had been adopted by the Sepoys; and she became then, for the first time, aware that it was through faith in her integrity that had led to the Europeans being taken off their guard. She was

No. 90.

doubly inveterate against her countrymen when this information was conveyed to her.

"Major," said McDarvish, "I should c'enjistlikethatfield piece. They have pretty well all of them got a sickener of this day's business, and have, I believe, nearly all retired from the field. I should e'en like that bonnie piece."

"We have no ammunition for it, even supposing it were ours."

"I should like it," said the other, shaking his head gloomily.

"How is to be obtained? It would never do to run the risk of a *sortie* to seize it. Reflect, man, of the imprudence of such a step. Us men to abandon our strong position after such a fool-hardy enterprise as that."

"Perhaps so!—but—I should e'en like

the piece;" and he went away muttering sulkily to himself.

The major could not refrain from a smile at the Scotchman's brusk sententious manner. He, too, would have liked the piece, which with a tolerable amount of ammunition, would render their position almost impregnable. Supplied with food and ammunition, they might then withstand a siege for an almost indefinite period.

CHAPTER CCXIII.

THE BATTLE FIELD.—THE RAGE OF TAM-NEEGAL—THE BELEAGUERED PARTY.

As the golden sun rose on the following morning what a scene of frightful carnage did his rays light up. Heaps of stiffened corpses lay strewn around in various distorted attitudes, The form of man was disfigured and hacked into hideous pieces, shocking to behold. Some lay doubled up in their last agony, and others stretched upon the green sward, their faces turned upwards towards the sky, while the expression on their features in this their last hour was indicative of "hate and uncharitableness" towards their fellow men and brothers.

War! These are some of thy devastating works. The horrors that attend thy path, there is but one name for—legion. The fair form of man, and indeed sometimes woman, is shattered into a frightful mass, from which the sickening sense turns shudderingly away.

Talk of glory, look at the poor suffering mangled beings, who are offered up at the unholy shrine of this Moloch. Ask widowed women, childless mothers, and the many drooping forms and breaking hearts, who are doomed to carry about with them a silent sorrow, which brings them to a premature grave—ask these what potent power the empty name of glory has to assuage their grief, or to restore to them the irreparable loss they have sustained. Glory! springes to catch woodcocks."

Our heroine gazed upon the scene when lighted up by the morning's sun, and burst into tears. Viewed from that little fortress which had withstood so terrible a shock, the scene of slaughter presented a sickening sight. The very air was impregnated with the odour of the battle field; and the female companions of our heroine were melted to tears of anguish for the departed—a feeling that most generous minds entertain for a prostrate foe, however unworthy a one he may have been. As Omelia swept her eyes over the scene of the re-

cent conflict, she could nowhere discover the gun she had spiked on the previous evening, and a foreboding seized her that it had been removed by their enemies, to be used in another attack.

"Ah!" she exclaimed, "the gun! it has been carried off. I cannot see it anywhere."

"Na, na—y'yare not like to see it outside," said McDarvish.

"Indeed! where then?"

"I thought it might be useful, may be, in a time to come, sa I've e'en jist tuck him in."

It was true enough McDarvish had not been able to rest with such a heavy weight upon his mind as the gun in question; so, in the course of the night he had persuaded the ensign to join him in an endeavour to capture it. All was quiet on the field of battle, and the two providing themselves with a strong cord, harnessed themselves together, and managed to drag in the piece of ordnance, after which our friend Mc Darvish was able to sleep the "sleep of the just." He found the gun had been effectually spiked, but was not long in removing that impediment to its action. McDarvish had also, while he was outside the fort thought it best to avail himself of his temporary leave of absence to see what else he could pick up, and he gathered a perfect arsenal of ammunition from his prostrate foes, with the pithy remark, "that they would ne'er want them ag'in—puir fellows."

When Tamneegal determined upon abandoning the field, which, to say the truth, he may be said to have been the victor as far as the outside fighting was concerned—he searched every-where for her whom he chose to insist upon calling his daughter. They looked on all sides, and called her by name, but she was not to be found—he then began to fear she had been slain. Anathematizing himself and his companions for their imprudence in allowing her to accompany them, they instituted a vigorous search for her body; in which, of course, they were equally unsuccessful. He really began to think about grieving for our heroine. He was a wrong-minded man, this Tamneegal, and sunk into evil courses; mercenary, selfish, and at times unquestionably cruel, but he had some natural touch of affection lurking in that hardened breast of his—some little spring—choked up by weeds and dross; it may be still a little spring, that flowed sometimes with gentle affections from the endless font of the human heart. He had began to be pleased and proud of his adopted daughter, and it was in defence of her honor and word that he had been induced to undertake this desperate engagement.

He was not a man you would exactly

select to point out as a representative of the soul of honour, having, to speak the truth, but a low order of organisation, but nevertheless he could appreciate to some extent the superior character of others, at least he did so considerably in the case of Omelia. He had led but a lawless life, and I am sure it is not worth while gibbetting him here with all his manifold crimes. It is to be feared that he has enough to answer for, but as he seemed to evince some touch of sympathy for our heroine, we will spare the reader the recital of his transgressions. He did in this instance what is usual for men to have recourse to in most cases of loss or misfortune, that is, to turn round and blame their nearest friend. He darted an angry look at Goolooh, as he exclaimed savagely—

"Who is to know if not yourself? I gave her in your charge, and thought no one was better qualified to look after her, and nicely you have performed the task."

"I am much grieved as you are at her loss. It was no fault of mine, of that you may rest assured; but how, in the heat of battle, was it possible to keep an eye upon everything that passes around."

"Perdition! but this is the worst of all; she may be carried off prisoner by some of these designing rascals."

A man now stepped forward and informed Tamneegal that he had observed Omelia entering the fortress; this enraged him still more, and he was positively wild with fury.

"Oh," he exclaimed passionately, "this is worse than all;—fallen into the hands of the accursed Feringhee—lost!—lost!"

"Calm yourself," said Goolooh, "it may not be so bad as you anticipate; she has doubtless but sought a temporary protection from this dreadful scene around, or else was desirous of moving them to accept of our terms."

"Umph, perhaps so:" and Tamneegal appeared to be appeased in some measure by this reflection.

"I will myself see in the morning if such is the case, and let us hope at my appearance she will joyfully return."

"A pretty loss we have sustained by this night's business, all owing to some half-dozen of our worthless usurpers."

And in no very agreeable mood, the beligerents proceeded back to their secret haunt.

On the following morning, agreeable to his promise, Goolooh made for the fort. He took with him several followers, but, as he neared the building, he left them in the rear, and advanced alone. A shout from the major caused him to pause. "Fall back or I fire at once!" was the words that caught his ear.

"A moment, gentlemen, if you please; my intentions are friendly."

"Hold!" said our heroine, "it is one of my recent companions. I will hear what he has to say. I do not believe he means treachery. What do you want?" this was addressed to Goolooh.

"Thank heaven you are then safe; we had almost mourned you as dead. Let me conduct you back safely to your parent."

"I have none," was the answer, "and refuse to acknowledge he who assumes to be such, now and for ever.

"Oh, say not so, rash girl; hasten to me; everybody is anxious about you, and bears towards you the most friendly feelings. Do, I entreat, come back to those who take so deep an intrest in your welfare."

"No, never! you have my answer; I am with my friends, and those I intend to stand by till the last hour."

"At any rate grant me a few minutes' private audience. I have something to communicate which may be of the utmost importance. On my knees, as a last favour, I beseech—I implore you to take compassion on me, and grant this request."

Omelia's generous nature was touched by this appeal, and she would perhaps at once have promptly responded to the request, but was restrained by the other inmates of the garrison.

After some consultation, she answered: "Send back all your companions." This was promptly done; they moved several hundred yards away from the spot.

"Now," said Goolooh. "On my life I promise you not in any way to interfere with your wishes, or compel you to any act against your own will. You are free to return back, or go whither you please. If you trust me you shall see no cause to regret your generosity."

"I will make the trial," said Omelia to her companions, who had no faith in the man's promises. "This man, although leagued with a desperate set of companions, is, I believe, trustworthy; at least, I flatter myself he will be to me. Again, he may have communications to make which may prove of service to us all. Yes, I will risk it, and trust him thus far."

So saying, the bridge was lowered, and our heroine was soon by the side of Goolooh.

"Now," she said, "I place some trust in your honour, which is no common compliment; see that you do not betray it. What would you?"

Goolooh's countenance was radiant with pleasure at the approach of Omelia, and he said, in moving accents—

"I suppose you are lost to us. If you have made your election to follow the fortunes of our worst enemies, it is no persuasion of mine, I suppose, that will ever be able to alter your determination. I have not the gift of eloquence of yourself or the companions you appear to have always chosen for yourself; but still I tell you truth, when I say, that for years I have admired and loved you. I knew, when first this passion seized me: I knew at that time you had another who occupied your thoughts, and, therefore, I neither sought you or troubled you with my suit. Your father, Yunadar, knew well of my feelings towards you, but, from motives of delicacy, I begged of him not to urge my suit."

"Well," said our heroine, "you surely have not thought it worth while to seek this meeting to play the lover over so sanguinary a field as this;" and she looked shudderingly around.

"Hear me out, if you have patience. I know you have but little interest on this subject, but if it pains you I will desist. It is yours to command, and mine but to obey;" and he turned his head away with some emotion, which was evidently no simulated feeling.

"Go on," said Omelia, in more soothing accents, "I am here to listen, and have suffered, I am sure, quite enough myself to make me pity others."

"I was saying that I did not press my suit; indeed, I believe you never knew that you had inspired me with any tender feeling to you, until I first mentioned the subject on the occasion of my introduction to you by your foster father Tamneegal. I should not have pressed it then, but thought, as I told you, that your lover had treated you with neglect or unkindness, and——"

"Then you were mistaken, sir, in your supposition."

"So you informed me then, but you will surely pardon the mistake under which I was labouring. You know yourself what it is to be possessed with a strong passion, and see other arms clasping the form you fondly doat on."

Omelia changed colour at these observations, and a slight perceptible tremor shook her frame, which it was in vain for her to endeavour to conceal. Goolooh had fired off a random shot quite by chance, which went home to its mark before he was aware of it; he saw the effects of his observations, and now guessed, for the first time the cause of our heroine's estrangement from her lover. He endeavoured to repair the effect his observations appeared to have.

"At least, if you have not been a prey to the torturing pangs of envy for another's happiness, you know what it is to possess a mighty passion which mastered all others.

Have pity on me, then, for such I have borne silently for years—have pity on me who now sees, too surely, that it is a hopeless one."

There was a sincerity in the accents and words of Goolooh which impressed her with the truth of their meaning; they at once astonished and grieved her, but with the frank generosity which was one of her marked characteristics, she grasped the hand of Goolooh, and said—

"I believe, and I pity you: let us be friends; my love I can never give: this you already know: but oh, why herd with these savage men: your language denotes that you are possessed of better thoughts than they can appreciate, whose only course is rapine, plunder, and bloodshed."

Goolooh turned away with shame and mortification.

"Ask me not now," he said, hastily, "I have had good cause from the deep injuries I have received, to seek a just revenge; but enough of that, this is neither the time or place to enter into such particulars. You choose your own course, and I mine. Do you intend to follow the fortunes and fate, whatever it may be, of those people? and he pointed towards the fort, where he could descry its inmates anxiously watching the interview."

"Yes, that is my fixed—my unalterable determination."

"Your foster father will be grieved, as I know, violent, head-strong man as he is, that he bears for you the strongest affection."

"Tell him to alter the wicked course of life he is pursuing, and I may then learn to respect him."

"And these people," he continued, with a nod of the head towards the fort, "do they refuse any terms?"

"Yes. I cannot persuade them to put trust in your promises. You are surely not surprised at this after all that has occurred. They will die at their post."

"I would that it were otherwise, for all our sakes. See the dreadful consequences of their obstinacy." And he turned round with feelings of horror as he contemplated the slain which were strewed about.

"Ah, it is horrible!" said Omelia. "Your companions ought to give their comrades decent burial."

"They would do so willingly, if they could be assured of your friends not firing upon them."

"In their name I at once give a guarantee that they shall not be molested; they never take advantage of any act of humanity."

"It shall be done then with that understanding. And so you have made up your mind to perish behind those four walls, strange infatuation. They are hardly situated for food, I suppose.

Omelia turned away and made no reply.

"Ah, I suppose so. If you are obstinate and self willed, you have no right to starve. If you are determined, I will throw you over your rations, while you remain there. Mind they will only be for yourself, and now—I have detained you long enough. There is nothing to be done but the saddest of all—the parting; I had hoped"—here he broke off, and seemed overpowered with emotion. "No matter, my hopes are all vanished now truly—before I leave you, let me say that if you should ever meet a friend who will cheerfully lay down his body on burning embers, that you might pass with safety. Do not forget me."

Omelia was perfectly astonished at the strength of this man's attachment; and again taking his hand, she said:—

"My friend; I may call you by that designation, although you can never be to me anything else; you have taught me in the short time I have known you, to respect and admire the sentiments I believe to be sincerely expressed; still it is not in my power to reciprocate or return them: my heart has gone far beyond my own reach, and it is not in my power to ever call it back. It would therefore be the worst of deception, not to at once deal candidly, and avow a fact which is too painfully impressed upon me in every moment of my existence."

An expression of most poignant sorrow passed over the features of Goolooh, and raising the hand of Omelia to his lips, he respectfully saluted it, and hastily disappeared. Omelia gazed after him, and saw him rejoin his companions, and waved her hand as a farewell, and then retraced her steps back again to her English friends, who had begun to have misapprehensions respecting her safety, more than usually sorrowful upon her return to the fort, but her companions refrained from pressing upon her any obtrusive questions, imagining that the interview with Goolooh was of a private nature, connected only with her own affairs. Miss Hilayard, and indeed Mrs. Forrester, with the penetrating eye of women in most affairs of the heart, had even at that distance, observed sufficient in the demeanour of both of them, to imagine that their conversation was taking a tender turn. When after some little time had elapsed, Mrs. Forrester said:—

"Any good news—or is there another attack meditated?"

"No," was the reply, "I hope not: my interview with that young man was of a friendly nature, and I do believe he is so disposed to assist both myself and all in whom I take an interest to the utmost of his power; but he is only one out of some hundreds, and I regret he should be linked with such unfortunate associates, as I really believe he is worthy of a better fate."

Omelia, now with the natural ingeniousness of her character, explained to her female friends the nature of the interview, together with Goolooh's declaration which he had so ardently made to her. She also informed them that he had promised to victual her during her imprisonment in her present quarters. Later in the day substantial proofs were given of his sincerity in this respect, for behind the wall of the fortress there was discovered a large package addressed simply "For Omelia." This proved upon opening it, to be a plentiful supply of meat, rice, fruits, &c., which, to the half-starved garrison, was a luxury beyond description. Hungry people who had been chewing out the remains of a dead horse for their scanty sustenance, were charmed with the dainties now afforded them. There was a discussion amongst the English inhabitants about the propriety of their partaking of that which was given for our heroine's consumption alone; but although they coquetted with the provisions for some little time, nature's demands were of too imperative a nature to admit of the proffered boon, thus opportunely afforded being rejected.—"Accept the feast the gods provide you," is an old adage, but with starving people it is altered, to accept the feast anybody provides. The perhaps ungenerous thought crossed the mind of more than one, that this might only be another *ruse*, and the food might possibly be poisoned; but this thought was dismissed as an unworthy suspicion.

Goolooh appeared to have a very extensive notion of the digestive powers of his enslaver. Most heroines are supposed to live upon honey or the perfumes of flowers, or any sustenance rather than that which appeals to our grosser nature; but we believe this is quite fabulous, having known and had to do with a good many heroines in our time, and experience teaches us that the amount of provisions they are enabled to consume is something marvellous. The domestic heroine of our minor theatres for instance who are known by the initiated as *tearers*, are equally great at a feed as they are in harrowing up the feelings of their sensitive and discriminating audience.

The inmates of the fort not knowing how long this supply was to last, were moderate in their repast, wisely husbanding their resources. They had, however, no occasion for the precaution, for before the stock was exhausted another plentiful supply was again furnished them by their invisible and mysterious commisariat. The inhabitants of the fort were therefore able to pass their time day after day in comparative comfort, compared to what they had been previously enduring.

When Goolooh returned to the quarters of Tamneegal and informed him of Omelia's determination, the latter's rage knew no bounds, and this was still more increased when he was informed that his terms were distinctly refused by the garrison.

"Confusion!" he exclaimed, "why did you not forcibly bring her back here? You surely must have been worse than a madman to leave her to join our bitterest enemies—the accursed Feringhee! What is to be done now? We are foiled at every point; instead of having them in our power to make future terms with their countrymen, we have lost the chance of that—lost the treasure in the fort; and, worse than all, lost my daughter. But I will have revenge, a deep and terrible revenge; I will blow up the cursed fort, and utterly destroy its inhabitants!"

"How can you do so without destroying your daughter?" enquired Goolooh.

"How can I? Why of course I can't. What care I? She is no longer any daughter of mine, now twice she has made her own election, and thought proper to league with our enemies and forget her own kith and kin, why, let her blood be upon her own head. They must all fall victims to their own obstinacy." And he paced the apartment in a state of violent agitation, stung by the painful reflections which agitated and chafed his angry spirit. Goolooh waited till the first ebullition of rage had subsided before he deemed it advisable to address him, when he presently observed—

"I think myself under the present circumstances, that we had better let them be as they are, without further molestation. It is very certain they cannot escape from their present position, and by remaining passive for some short time, it will, perhaps, inspire them with confidence as to our sincerity, and ultimately that with the persuasions of your step daughter may induce them to surrender themselves into our hands. We shall no doubt obtain a large reward by giving them up as well as all that is concealed in the fortress, neither of which we should have if your course were to be adopted."

"Pshaw!" exclaimed Tamneegal, "your mind is warped by your enamerato. Do you imagine even if we were disposed to leave them unmolested that our opponents would remain quiet—not they a good booty is known or supposed to be concealed within the fortress,

and they hunger for its possession. More than this, they are actuated by the most vindictive feelings of revenge, made doubly violent since this last slaughter. If the fools had a grain of sense they would have long since given themselves up to the only party who are likely to spare their lives. Ten thousand curses that this obstinate hussey should thwart our schemes thus! What could induce you ever to let her return to her companions?"

"I had given my word."

"But why did you?"

"Because she would not emerge from her place of security, until I had done so."

"Obstinate, misguided girl! Well she must suffer for own rashness; why, she and her companions must starve in a few days."

Goolooh did not say that he thought that it was very unprobable they would die from inanition at present Neither did he deem it prudent to inform his irritable companion, that he had provided means for their support.

Goolooh's course of action was, what parliamentary gentlemen would call a middle or conciliatory course. He had borne, and did indeed have now a rooted hatred towards what he choose to term his English oppressors. He was goaded on by a series of wrongs, many imaginary, and some it must be admitted real grievances. It may appear extraordinary that, with these feelings, he should have offorded assistance to those who occupied the fort, but Goolooh tampered with his conscience, by solacing himself with the reflection, that it was but his enslaver he supplied, and if she choose to share her rations with the garrison, it was no fault of his.

He guessed shrewdly enough, that if he conveyed only enough provender for his enamerato's consumption, she would divide it with her friends, be it ever so small, consequently he thought it was his duty to provide a sufficiency for the purpose which he did without compromising his honour or principles. Do not blame him; other gentlemen, in a more enlightened and civilized country, have adopted a similar course of argument, to soothe their own consciences when it suited their purpose. When lovely women condescends to plead, who can resist her.

CHAPTER CCXIV.

TANTIA TOPEE'S SQUADRON.—TERRIBLE ASSAULT.—TOTAL DESTRUCTION OF THE FORTRESS.

THE unfortunate beleaguered English had for some days a respite from any further hostilities. Goolooh was permitted without molestation to bury those who had fallen in the late attack. Our friend McDarvish wished Goolooh would take it into his merciful consideration to supply him with a little ammunition for the field-piece he had so unceremoniously possessed himself of. Goolooh might have suspected when he went over the field that the piece had fallen into the hands of his enemies, but as to supplying ammunition for it to be employed against his own countrymen was an idea he would never consent to entertain. He, however, managed to persuade his comrade Tamneegal to abstain at present from further hostilities. The opposite party or rather parties of Sepoys had received so sound a dressing that they did not venture upon any other overt act beyond gathering at a respectful distance, and uttering threats and anathemas against the small band of warriors who had resisted them with such repeated acts of gallantry. A stag at bay is a dangerous foe, and the enemies had found to their cost that some half-dozen Englishmen, determined to sell their lives dearly in an intrenched position, were not to be assaulted with impunity.

A new disaster, however, now threatened the unfortunate garrison, and one which seemed as if it must end in their utter and complete destruction. Tantia Topee with a large squadron, accompanied with field-pieces of heavy calibre, and a plentiful supply of ammunition, was marching towards the neighbourhood of the fort. It is possible that Tantia might have passed it in his mind without imagining it contained any inhabitants, but it got whispered about amongst his troops as he neared the spot— and as it was an invariable rule with this miscreant to cut to pieces and destroy any of the enemy whom he thought were likely to fall easy victims for his troops to slaughter, he instantly determined to annihilate our unfortunate countrymen.

The first indications of his approach were conveyed to the ears of the beleaguered garrison by the sound of his band. They had English instruments, and were playing "God save the Queen." This band had formed a portion of one of the revolted Sepoy regiments, originally in the service of the Hon. East India Company, and it was therefore a cruel mockery for these wretches to be marching on to their work of destruction playing our national airs.

As the prolonged notes fell upon the ears of the garrison, joy beamed in every face; they thought very naturally that a detachment of British troops were marching towards them.

"Hark! Heaven," fervently exclaimed Mrs. Forrester, "saved at last! Oh, what rapture to hear those sounds, and that noble air, whose very note rings with the silver peal of hope and promise. Oh, joy, unutterable. Such an hour as this compensates us for all our painful sufferings," and she clasped Miss Hilayard, and shed tears of irrisistable joy. All the females formed a group, which, if they could have been then transferred to canvass would have immortalized a painter. The officers countenances, expressed a mingled feeling, they believed relief was at hand, but waited further assurances before they could feel confident of the certainty of the glad tidings which appeared too good to be true.

"Ye maun, wait a wee," said McDarvish, before ye gin way to such extravagant expressions, I'm nae sae sure they be our ain countrymen."

"Pray to Heaven they may be," said Major Forrester, "for if not them, then indeed they must be some of our worst foes, and our destruction is inevitable."

"Ah, yes," exclaimed Miss Hilayard, "Hear them now! that is an English band. We are saved! saved!" and she flung herself upon the neck of our heroine in a transport of joy. The officers rushed up to the top of the fort to catch a sight of the advancing party. With eager gaze they strained their eyes to see if they could discern the uniform of the British. The band still continued to play merrily, as though they were out upon a holiday festival. As they approached an involuntary groan of despair burst forth from the breast of each officer, which was answered by a scream of fright from the ladies below, who had been listening in breathless suspense to catch any expression from the companions above. They at once surmised that their hopes were without foundation the moment they heard the simultaneous groan from above. Miss Hilayard, whose nerves had been wound up to the highest degree of tenure, now fainted away and lay as one dead. Despair now set in the hearts of her companions, and it was only by a great effort that Mrs. Forrester could command herself to bear this new blow with anything like fortitude. Mrs. McDarvish and Omelia behaved with greater stoicism.

"The troops of Tantia Topee, by all that's horrible!" ejaculated Major Forrester, "and with them a number of the revolted scoundrels, and ah! they have several field pieces," and in spite of himself the gallant officer's countenance assumed an immovable expression as though he felt their last hour was now indeed come.

"Let us down with the flag," said the ensign, "It's just possible they may not know of our being here, and pass on without observing us."

"Nae, nae," said McDarvish, resolutely; "we winna strike England's flag to mon or fiend, while we have one drop of bluid left in our veins; nae, I have fought beneath these colours sin sick a time as when I was but a bairn, through mony and mony a long year, but never struck my country's colours, and if they are doomed now to be my ain winding-sheet, I'll die defending them."

"Retire below," said the major, "the scoundrels are preparing to open fire with their field pieces, and it is courting certain death to remain in this exposed situation."

The party instantly proceeded to the lower part of the fortress, and their countenances at once confirmed their female companions in their worst suspicions.

"I need not ask," said Mrs. Forrester; "we are lost: it is not our gallant countrymen that are approaching: tell me the worst at once; is it the Nana?"

Her husband shook his head.

"No, but I am sorry to say it is the villain Tantia Topee, who evidently meditates an attack. It is of no use, Beatrice, concealing or endeavouring to conceal the painful truth; our enemy is there, with the worst intentions, and we must fall as becomes the British soldier, at his post. Oh, that I had but one or two pieces, and ammunition."

But little time was allowed for reflection, for scarcely had these words fallen from the major, when crash—bang, and the first field piece opened fire: the shot came tearing along, and did no further mischief than carrying off one of the embrasures which surmounted the fort, close by where, a few seconds ago, the officers had been standing. It was evident that they had been observed by the troops of Tantia, and the gun had been directed against them. Another few minutes elapsed, and two pieces vomited forth their contents at the garrison; they chipped away small pieces of stone, and came against the walls of the building with such a fearful crash, that it seemed a wonder how stone walls could stand against so terrible a concussion.

"They have some heavy ordnance, sir," said the ensign.

The major shook his head.

"Yes," he said, "and the worst of it is that we are powerless to reply to the scoundrels."

While this conversation was occurring, the indefatigable McDarvish was gathering his materials together to see if he could reply to the bombardment. He had no cannon balls, but he had a few hollow shells, into which he had placed a number of cartridges, old keys, buckles, spurs, in fact, an heterogeneous mass of material he could in any way manage to collect together; having done this he asked his major's opinion.

"Ye'il see it would gie them a peppering e'en there, if they come to close quarters."

"Yes," said the major, "but it is of no use where they are, and would therefore be a useless waste of ammunition. It is a good reserve when they come closer. Our fort will resist them at their present range, and the probability is, that finding their fire unanswered, they will be led to surmise that we have no guns or ammunition, and therefore they will try a nearer range."

The Major's words were soon fulfilled, for Tantia, finding he could not make much impression upon the fort, advanced a party of his men, and commenced serving the guns at a shorter distance. The effect of this was soon visible, a portion of the building on the left side was carried away, and loud shouts of exultation arose from Tantia's troops. The cannonade now continued terrific, and a large body of men rushed forward to the guns to join their companions, in the highest state of exultation.

"Now," said the major to McDarvish, "you may, I think, try the efficacy of your gun." There was no need of a second bidding; the gun was already loaded and the muzzle well directed into the centre of the opposing party. Wuzz, crash, bang! and she belches forth her contents in the midst of the opposite gunners. The shot spread as though fired from a blunderbuss, and dealt death and destruction to the enemy, who was completely taken aback at this unexpected fire. They fell back in disorder; numbers were killed and wounded, as the shot had spread in all directions and punished the opposing gunners severely. After recovering their first surprise they proceeded again to work their guns, and sent forth continuous volleys, which, near as they were to the fort, seemed to threaten it with certain destruction. Pieces of stone were being carried away under the effects of their fire, and Major Forrester considered the ultimate doom of the fort was now certain. Nevertheless, McDarvish and his brave companions picked off the men of the opposing party, and laid heaps of slain around their guns; but Tantia urged them on to the contest, making sure of his ultimate success. Roar after roar of artillery continued, and eventually by a well-directed salvo, the whole of a bastion on the left side of the Fort fell with a terrific crash. The occupants were nearly blinded by the smother this occasioned, and believed the whole of the building was destroyed; but when, however, the dust

cleared away, they found it was the bastion in the inner walls which had fallen under the enemies fire.

"Not quite gone as yet," said the major; "but her fate is sealed, I fear."

"Nae matter," said McDarvish, "we'll work them to the last.

So saying, he again sent forth a murderous fire from his one solitary piece.

"They will come to the assault presently, I suppose," said the major, "and it will then be for us to rally round the standard of England, and die as becomes a soldier. We shall never master them, but let us stand to the last."

As he thus spoke, he proceeded with the ensign to reconnoitre about the spot where the bastion had fallen.

What was his surprise when he observed

No. 91.

a small gateway which evidently covered part of an arch upon which the bastion had been built, and which indeed formed its foundation.

He was more surprised when, after many violent efforts he was enabled to lift up the grating which swung upon hinges, and observed several stone steps, which were placed circularly, and formed, in fact, a well staircase to the vault below.

A dawn of hope beamed upon him as he made this discovery, and calling the attention of the ensign to it, the two proceeded at once down the well staircase to make a further inspection.

This led them into a subterranean vault, and they found themselves in all but utter darkness. The major procured a light, and was indeed astonished at the discovery he then made. In the vault were barrels of gunpowder, cannon-balls, shells, scrapnels, and a perfect arsenal. These were evidently stores laid in for a seige.

Upon examining still further, he discovered that this vault led to several others, upon which the building was erected; these were also full of arms, ammunition, and preserved meats and provinder. There were also bags of gold, and a large amount of treasure in precious stones and ingots of gold.

It was this then that had excited the cupidity of Tamneegal.

The major was breathless with astonishment, but lost no time in conveying whatever he and his companion could carry, in the way of ammunition, to supply McDarvish's gun.

The latter was indeed equally astonished when the major gave him the balls and shells to charge his piece with. It was hastily loaded with one of the latter, and sent in among their foes, and burst in the very midst of them,

It seemed by its fearful explosion to completely clear the guns of all the men who were around them, and struck a momentary panic amongst their companions.

"Now for it," said McDarvish, and he sent forth another upon its death-dealing mission

"Oh, that we should not have been aware of this before," bitterly ejaculated the major, "we might have held our own against all oposition. Here have we actually been put to the direst straits with ammunition, stores of provisions, and immense wealth lying uselessly under our feet: when, had we known this, it would have saved the lives of many of our brave companions. I fear the discovery is too late now; the fort is too battered to resist much longer, and we have but little time to arrange anything like an efficient fire. What had best be done?"

A hasty consultation took place, and an idea occurred to the major which he at once proceeded to adopt with a promptness which was his most remarkable characteristic in the hour of danger.

He conducted the ladies at once to the vaults below, as they were bomb-proof, and his female companions were out of danger of the shots of the enemy, which had been passing close to them, and threatened sooner or later their complete destruction.

Having done this, he conveyed several barrels of gunpowder into the fort; from these he laid a train of the same combustible material in such a manner that he could ignite it from the vaults below. Having made all these arrangements to his satisfaction he became more calm and satisfied in his mind.

His plan of operations were these. Foreseeing that it was quite impossible now to make an effectual stand against his opponents, who were armed with a large amount of ordnance, and were moreover in immense numbers, he determed upon a *coup de etat.*

McDarvish and his comrades were to work the gun, now amply supplied with admirable ammunition, as long as it was possible for them to serve it; but it was quite certain that the fortress would be eventually reduced and an assault made. As soon as indications were given of this being likely to take place, the whole of the party were to take refuge in the vaults beneath the building, and await the coming of their antagonists, upon whose arrival they would set light to the match and blow the whole fort up, and those of their opponents who were in it.

"And so they will find their own grave," said the major, "on the spot which has been the scene of all our sufferings."

"An excellent arrangement," said the ensign. "We must take our chance about blowing ourselves into the other world at the same time."

"We shall have a dreadful concussion to sustain," said the major, "but I think these walls will stand it. They are built bomb-proof, of course—they always are in fortresses of this description; any way it is the only alternative we have under the circumstances. The enemy have already made breaches that, if they were to attack us now, it would be impossible for us to resist with anything like effect, and a desperate case requires a desperate remedy."

"But it is impossible for us to annihilate them, and as soon as the explosion is over they will in all probability suspect we are concealed in the vaults beneath."

"Not necessarily so; they may imagine, indeed it is most probable they will, that we have blown ourselves up with our enemies rather than fall into their hands. We must conceal the gateway as well as we can; of course, enough space must be left for the admission of air, without which we should die from suffocation."

"It will be a terrible retribution to them."

"And one they deserve. Even in the event of their discovering us we shall be enabled to make another stand. We have the means of fastening down the grating, and can fire upon all who come near it."

"Yes, but the probability will be that they will stop it up, and endeavour to suffocate us."

"It is of no use anticipating troubles. This is the only course we can now possibly adopt. If we fall, we shall not be unavenged."

McDarvish and his companions worked at their gun with indomitable perseverence, and although they punished their assailants severely, an iron shower poured in against the brave little fort from an increased number of pieces, and gradually the walls were crumbling away.

It had originally been a rare piece of man's handiwork this little building, or it could never have withstood the attack so long; but it was evident it must soon succumb to the weight of metal brought to bear upon it.

Presently the smoke of the cannons cleared away, and McDarvish observed several of the sepoys belonging to the revolted regiments make towards the fort. They threw down their arms, and by their gesticulations seemed to indicate that there was a cessation of hostilities.

As they approached nearer McDarvish was about to treat them with the contents of his piece, when the major restrained him.

"Stay," he observed, "they are going to offer us terms, perhaps. Let us hear what they have to say."

As the men approached within hearing, they called out to the major to surrender, saying, that their commander, Tantia Topee, would grant them their lives, and treat them as honourable prisoners of war, if they surrendered without further hostilities.

"Never!" exclaimed the major; "we have had sufficient proof of his mercy to our countrymen already. Tell your master that we hold this fort in spite of him, and if he effects an entrance he will meet with certain death. We defy him, and make no terms with traitors."

A derisive jeer was given to this speech, and one of the men said—

"You know the impossibility of holding your position, and had better yield with a good grace."

"Never! Back to your companions, or we open fire upon you."

The men beat a hasty retreat, and upon their return a still more furious cannonade ensued.

The fortress fell piece by piece, and under cover of their guns McDarvish could see the enemy were forming a portion of their troops into an assaulting party. He watched till they had come within a reasonable distance, and then sent in the contents of his piece. This threw them into disorder, and they seemed to hesitate in making the attack, but just at this moment a fire from their comrades guns carried away the wall and embrasure which protected McDarvish and his companions, and left them completely exposed to their enemies guns.

There was no time to lose, so the English soldiers hastened to secure themselves in the vault, according to the arrangement made by the major.

On came the storming party, with another following them as a support, when finding themselves no longer under fire, they acquired new courage, and advanced with loud shouts of triumph.

Upon arriving at the fort, of course there was no opposition offered them, and they thought that perhaps the whole of the occupants had been put *hors de combat* by their guns. They were consequently perfectly elated with the easy capture, and the interior of the fortress was soon filled with sepoys eager for plunder and revenge.

They ran hither and thither in mad excitement to see what they could pick up and conceal on the sly, when all the while the match was slowly burning towards the train of powder which was to send them to certain and immediate destruction.

A breathless pause of anxious suspense held the occupants of the vaults below in a state of torture. They were in momentary expectation of hearing the explosion, and a foreboding seized them that perhaps the train, from some cause or other, would not ignite; if so, it was now too late to repair any evil or neglect in its management.

As they were awaiting this terribly expected event seconds seemed minutes, and minutes seemed hours. Short as the time was between the ignition of the match and the explosion of the powder barrels, it appeared an age of agonising suspense.

"Bang!—bang!—crash! a noise as if a dismemberment of a world, and the explosive instrument of death and destruction had performed its dreadful work.

The remains of the fort were thrown up as by the hands of a ruthless and desolating giant into a thousand pieces. Heads, legs, arms, and portions of human bodies were scattered around, many some hundred yards in distance from the spot upon which they had stood, with life and health, but a second or two before. Every man within and around the fated building was consigned to instant destruction, or else, what was worse, horribly mutilated and a lingering death.

Tantia Topee and his troops were completely panic stricken at the terrible climax which had now ended their attack. Many of those who had watched the onslaught at a considerable distance were struck by the scattered fragments of the building, and sudden fear fell upon his main body, which, for a time, completely paralised them.

When the first shock was over, and some time had elapsed, the clouds of dust and smoke cleared away and left nothing of the fort but a heap of ruins.

Tantia Topee, when sufficiently recovered from the surprise and fright occasioned by the terrible disaster which had befallen his men, advanced towards the ruins of the fort, and rescued from under the heap of rubbish those who gave any symptoms of life.

The grating, through which the Europeans had entered into their place of retreat, was so covered over with stones, rubbish, and dead bodies, that the occupants of the vaults were almost undergoing the horrors of suffocation. The concussion had been so tremendous that its report had nearly deafened and benumbed the senses of the occupants of the vaults, and an oppressive feeling, from want of a sufficiency of air, added to the terrors of their situation.

Tantia gave orders for his men to clear away as much rubbish as possible, and make a careful inspection.

He did this under the belief, in the first place, of finding perhaps some treasure, and in the next, to see if there were any remains discernible of the Europeans.

In both of these anticipations he was, however, disappointed; but in removing away a heap of ruins he discovered the small grating which formed the only entrance to the vaults.

His eyes dilated with surprise and curiosity at the sight of this, and suspecting that there were subterranean apartments, he gave hasty orders for the whole of the rubbish to be removed.

This was soon accomplished, and the unfortunate inhabitants were apprised of the fact by a stream of light and air making its way into their place of retreat, and the sound of voices being distintly heard. The major had fastened down the grating by a heavy chain, the end of which he had attached to a strong staple in the vault below. It was, therefore, a matter of some difficulty for any one from above to succeed in opening the grating; however, desperate attempts were being made to do so.

The inmates of the vaults heard them, and too surely divined their meaning; but the major insisted upon all maintaining the strictest silence.

"They will, I fear, never leave the spot," he said, "without endeavouring to effect an entrance; heaven only knows now what may be our ultimate fate. If they do so, we shall even then be able to offer an obstinate resistance."

The English party now heard the sounds of tremendous blows upon the iron-work. Tantia had ordered his men to break the bars of the grating by repeated strokes with a heavy hammer, and several of his men were engaged in this occupation; but their efforts were at present futile.

The grating was made of exceedingly strong wrought iron—so strong, that it bid fair to resist all their efforts.

A thought now entered the mind of Tantia that perhaps the English were concealed in the vaults below, and he gave orders to fire through the bars of the opening. Repeated volleys were discharged, but the Europeans took not the slightest notice. Finding himself so completely baulked, he determined not to abandon the spot without making an inspection, and after some time had elapsed, some files were procured, and several men were engaged in deliberately filing the bars sufficiently for them to yield to the blows of the hammer. This seemed likely to be a long job for the bars were exceedingly thick and hard in their temper.

There is no doubt, however, that eventually they would have succeeded in accomplishing their purpose had it not have been for more important considerations, which soon engaged their attention.

This was an advance of a detachment of Havelock's avenging column coming direct towards them. While Tantia's men were engaged in filing the grating, the whole of Tantia's army were taken by surprise by the contents of a howitzer falling among them, then crack!—ping!—bang! came close to them, then boom! almost splitting the drum of their ears, and a scrapnel-shell was discharged, and then burst from the muzzle of the gun a volume of smoke, and as it clears away—the startling noise rings around—a faint puff is seen, the report of the bursting shell is heard, the fragments of which fly whistling among Tantia's men, and causing them another immediate surprise. Havelock's gallant and heroic band are almost upon them.

They hastily form, and commence an immediate retreat. Away they start before the advancing foe, who follow them with rapid steps. They succeed in getting far away from the fort, and our poor concealed countrymen make no effort to discover themselves to Havelock's chasing squadron, as they were unconscious of their proximity.

After retreating for nearly half a mile, the sepoys belonging to Tantia take refuge in a dense jungle partly surrounded by a wood. Here they endeavour to make a stand; Havelock's troop throws out a number of skirmishers from his Rifle Brigade, and the sharp crack of their pieces is then heard in all quarters. The green-coated riflemen have to advance over some broken ground: they run quickly forward, and spring actively over the rugged hillocks and streams which cross their path, loading and firing as they go, and ever and anon completing with the bayonet the work which the bullet had but half finished. Having advanced thus, the troops of Tantia fly on all sides, and are fairly hidden from view, having taken either refuge in the jungle or wood.

The skirmishers are therefore checked in their advance, and the guns of the British are again brought to bear upon the enemy! bang! go half-a-dozen shells whistling and cracking through the trees and surrounding vegetation, and scouring the spots around most effectually. It is awkward work, fighting with a concealed enemy in his native wilds, and this was a precautionary measure to save unnecessary loss of life to the English troops who were then enabled again to push forward. "On to them now!" is the word of command given, and away dash the riflemen into the high jungle, followed by the rest of Havelock's gallant column—pop! bang! crack! with now and then the ping of a bullet, soon tells that the enemy are about, and the conflict proceeds in earnest. It is not possible, of course, in fighting in a jungle, for each man to tell what is going on around—friends or foes are equally lost to sight, Highlanders, riflemen, and a few Sikhs, were all engaged in the contest, and were lost to each others view, and could only form an idea as to each others whereabouts by the sharp and constant firing which was going on. Hush! there is a breaking and rustling of the leaves, and look! a Sepoy in full flight, he dashes across the path of an Englishman—but even as he goes the barrel of an Enfield is covering him, bang! a sharp report—a whistling of a bullet—and he is down, rolling a confused and bloody mass in the dust and dies—a few convulsive struggles—a little clutching at the grass which is beneath him, and which his blood as it swells forth is fast dyeing a dark red—a low moan or two and another victim is offered up at the dread shrine of war—while in hot and eager haste, breaking madly through the vegetation, follows an excited green-coated rifleman, his rifle smoking, his lips black with powder, biting another cartridge as he comes, and scarcely deigning to glance at the man whom he has just sent to his account. In all parts of the jungle these scenes or some such as these are being enacted—pop! bang! resounds from unerring riflemen, against whom even in their concealed position, the Sepoys are no match. The enemy are nowhere to be seen until one of Havelock's mounted officers, after some time had been consumed in this scrambling jungle fight, discerned a number of them behind the walls of a small village past the jungle. "Halt action!—shrapnel shell! look alive men!" boom goes the gun and more shells are sent into the body of Sepoys. Tantia's troops are completely disorganised by the contents of them bursting amongst them, and orders are given for the advance, "forward men! have at them! hurrah!" "now riflemen over with the scoundrels!" On rush Havelock's avenging columns—crack! bang!—bang! —bang!—in rapid succession, and almost

without intermission, and showers of bullets rattle in among the disorganised troops of Tantia, who now fly for their lives in all directions, some stop to exchange shots with their assailants, but only a few, the majority rush away with their utmost speed, and Tantia himself is far ahead of them surrounded by a few of his more faithful adherents. A desperate chase was given them in the hope of capturing Tantia, but he elluded the pursuit by taking to a route not known to the British, who were obliged therefore to content themselves with cutting down those of Tantia's troops who came within their reach, or else laying them prostrate by the formidable Enfield rifle.

After a fruitless search for Tantia, the English troops made for the village and took up their quarters for the night.

CHAPTER CCXV.

DESPAIR OF GOOLOOH.—RELIEF OF THE GARRISON.—MAJOR FORRESTER'S GREETING.

The few occupants of the besieged fort remained concealed in the vaults unconscious of the complete route which their enemies had sustained from the British troops. They were, however, aware that some power had forced the enemies from the field, and compelled them to beat a precipitate retreat. Stillness reigned around, broken only by the occasional groans of a few sufferers among the wounded. Towards evening Goolooh, Tamneegal, and a party of sepoys came to the spot which had been the scene of so many sanguinary and unequal conflicts. They swept their eyes over the rugged scene which had been the site of the late fortress, and shudderingly contemplated the debris of the recent conflict. Many of the dead and dying were strangers to Tamneegal, as they were mostly those who had belonged to Tantia's band. Tamneegal now beheld all his machinations at once, and for ever thwarted; he was under the full impression that the English inhabitants had perished in the explosions, and searched in vain for any traces of them amongst the mutilated remains which lay strewn around. A feeling of bitter remorse and grief took possession of him as he reflected upon the dreadful fate which his adopted daughter had met with, consequent upon her own disobedience and rashness—"her own disobedience," he muttered to himself, "has brought this melancholy catastrophe about." He itterated this several times as though it formed some excuse for his own persecutions of the unfortunate beleaguered English; but all was not well within. The heart of Tamneegal was borne down and oppressed with a deadening weight which he vainly tried to shake off. The loss of Omelia made a deeper impression upon him than he cared to evince to his companions, and now that he saw his hopes of agrandisement blown to the winds, he inwardly cursed himself for having been tempted to compass the death of the English from motives of cupidity. To do him justice, sordid man as he was, the life or safety of his step-daughter was valued far beyond any mercenary gain, and he took his way back to the cave with his companions moody and dejected.

Goolooh remained on the field of battle searching about for some traces of the remains of the only human being he worshipped with a species of idolatry. His grief was too mighty to admit of human companionship or consolation, and he hid himself from his companions and let them depart without him. As he saw them leave bearing off several of the wounded, he turned his eyes to the prostrate forms which lay around, and inwardly wished he was like them, in nature's last sleep. He looked at the ruins of that little fort which had contained all he had ever cared for on earth, that one being whom to have followed and tended on as an abject slave would have been superlative happiness to him to the latest day of his life. He knelt down, covered his face with his hands, and wept like a child.

"Oh, that I too, might have perished by her side," he bitterly exclaimed, "that I might never have lived to see this fatal hour or borne within me a coroding and consuming pasion for one who is now a spirit far beyond this world. Why should I be punished thus?" and he beat his breast in the impotance of his dispair. "Why was a fate so cruel ever reserved for one of the fairest of God's creatures? Idiot! dolt! that I was not to have devised some scheme for their escape; I can think of this now that it is too late. Oh, worse than idiot, to have let so terrible a consummation come to pass. Oh, cruel—cruel fate. If these mute walls could speak, they would say here is indeed a most unhappy man!" and he dashed his head against the broken ruins of the fort as though he would beat out his brains—then throwing himself full length on the stones, he moaned like one possessed or in great agony.

He continued thus for some time, when a new thought seemed to pass through his brain. "Oh!" he exclaimed, "it is here she perished, and on this spot will I also.—Never again—never again will I leave here with life—but near to where she perished will I too pass from a world which to me is now a dreary blank or desert."

He seemed comforted by this thought and was comparatively calm and resigned. The inmates of the vaults had heard the voice of Goolooh, but could not recognise the speaker by its tones, and were consequently not aware of the meaning of his mutterings. When he had subsided into silence they concluded that the speaker, whoever it might be, had taken his departure. Mc Darvish cautiously proceeded to the grating to clear it of its dead which encumbered the entrance, and prevented the passage of air to the vaults below.

With considerable caution the Scotchman loosed the chain and gently raised the grating. He quietly thrust his head through the opening and drank in a large draught of pure air—which was refreshing to the sense, compared to the mefetic atmosphere of the vault beneath. He then cautiously peered around—a scene of death and desolation met his gaze—and he observed Goolooh—at some little distance who was transfixed with surprise when he beheld Mc Darvish's features emerge as it appeared to him from the bowels of the earth. A superstitious fever seized the mind of the Hindoo, and he seemed rivetted to the spot incapable of motion or utterance. This alarm was increased when Mc Darvish silently retreated like a mole underneath the earth.

The poor Hindoo believed the vision was a purturbed spirit, roaming about the battlefield, seeking for a place of rest.

Mc Darvish acquainted his friends that he had seen a man who had been watching his proceedings, and naturally enough, thought it was a spy who had been placed there to keep watch. Mc Darvish was about to return to the opening, and discharge his piece at the intruder, when Omelia anticipating his intent, rushed up the circular stone steps, and opening the grating beheld Goolooh—who gazed at her with wondering eyes. She beckoned to him and he mechanically answered the summons, walking like one in a dream, when having arrived within a few yards of where she stood he knelt down as though worshiping a being of another sphere.

"Goolooh!" exclaimed our heroine, "it is me! Omelia, who although hemmed in by death on all sides is nevertheless still alive," then there came over the countenance of the Hindoo a radient smile of ineffable sweetness, and he looked up to heaven as though he would return his thanks for our heroine's preservation, and advancing, he grasped her hand and shed tears of joy as he saluted it with rapture. When looking into Omelia's face he seemed to ask for some solution to the mystery of her preservation, Omelia explained all to him how they had been attacked by Tantia Topee's troops, and eventually by a most fortuitous circumstance how they had discovered their present place of concealment.

"And now Goolooh, I believe I may trust you as a friend," said Omelia, "so therefore do not divulge to your companions our present situation, or that we are in existence at all."

Her companion gave her his assurance upon this head, and with that she escorted him into their retreat, without further ceremony.

The young Hindoo was introduced to Omelia's companions in misfortune, and she assured them that they need be under no apprehension respecting the faithfulness of her countryman. It was then for the first time that the occupants of the vaults were made acquainted with the fact, that the troops of Tantia had been scattered by the columns belonging to Havelock's regiment.

"What a sad reflection it is for us" said Major Forrester, "to think that our countrymen have passed over our heads and were unacquainted with our situation, and we should learn this fact when it is too late for succour."

"Not too late I hope" said Goolooh, "I understand they have halted at a village not far from hence, and be it my task to communicate with them. It would be impossible for you to venture to their encampment, as if you were met on the road by the disaffected native troops, you would of course be attacked."

"If you will, however, give me a letter to their commander, I will myself convey it to them at all risks."

"A thousand thanks, my excellent friend," exclaimed Mrs. Forrester, "sooner or later your generosity will be rewarded."

"I know not who is in command, or indeed what company they may belong to," said the major, "but it matters little. A few words will suffice to explain our situation," and he hastily wrote the following to the officer in command:—

"A few English officers and ladies who have stood a siege in the Redoga Fort, are now concealed near where it stood and sadly need assistance from their countrymen. The bearer of this—a faithful native—will conduct what troops can be spared to their assistance.

Signed,   "Major FORRESTER,
                        "Madras Engineers."

"Now my friend, you will be conferring an inestimable favour by conveying this to my countrymen," said the major, "that is if you can find out their whereabouts."

"I will not rest till I do, trust me," was the reply, and Goolooh at once emerged from the vaults and proceeded on his mission. He soon succeeded in ascertaining where the British troops were quartered, and upon arriving at his destination he was seized and taken prisoner by the picket on guard. He did not, of course, offer any resistance, indeed, he was not armed for any such purpose. He was brought before an ensign— a young man—who looked upon all who wore a dusky skin as traitors and scoundrels.

"So a spy, eh!" he exclaimed, "We will deal with him at once."

"I wish to see the officer in command," said Goolooh.

"Indeed! You can gratify yourself, my man, by looking at me."

"But I am no spy: I bring a letter from some of your countrymen who are in great distress and need your assistance."

The ensign stared at the speaker and thought it was a subterfuge to cover some other design.

"Oh! And who pray has thought fit to send so worthy a messenger?"

Goolooh produced the major's letter, and handed it to the speaker, who opened it, and perused the contents. He then reflected and became less hasty in his bearing.

"Major Forrester. Yes this is indeed his handwriting. I little deemed ever to see that again. Major Forrester, why he is returned dead on our list long ago. Did he give you this himself, my man?"

"Yes, sir."

"Oh, he did, eh! Well you must see the colonel. Wait here till I return," and he glanced at several of his men in a meaning manner, which told them that Goolooh was for the present a prisoner. In a few minutes he returned accompanied by a venerable looking gentleman with a soldier-like bearing, who, glancing at Goolooh, said as he held up the letter—

"You brought this from Major Forrester?"

"I did, sir."

"And where is he now?"

"He is with several others concealed in the vaults of a fort, where you attacked Tantia Topee's troops to-day."

"And could he not come himself?"

"It would be impossible. He and his unfortunate countrymen have been surrounded by enemies, and if he were to emerge from his concealment, he would be attacked by many of his vindictive foes."

"Well, what of that, he can defend himself with his troops, however small their number."

"He has no troops: one by one they have perished."

"Umph!" The colonel looked at the ensign and said—"Do you know aught of this man?"

The latter replied in the negative.

"It is singular, but there is no doubt that this is the handwriting of Major Forrester; but under what circumstances it has been written it is hard to say. He has been reported as dead long since; I forget now under what circumstances he was supposed to have perished. You must form a company, and follow this man's guidance as to where the major is concealed." This was addressed to the ensign, who left to obey the command.

"Look here, my man," said the colonel, "if there is any treachery in this affair, I have given orders for you to be cut down without mercy, so look to it."

Goolooh was marched off in the midst of a file of soldiers with fixed bayonets, and proceeded to where the English party lay concealed. Upon arriving near the spot, he pointed to the direction of the fort, or rather where the fort had been, and intimated to his escort that it was beneath the foundations of that building that they would find their countrymen. A suspicion crossed the mind of the ensign, that perhaps this had been mined, and he and his companions were only being drawn into ambush.

"Halt!" he said to his men.

"Now then" he observed to Goolooh, "where would you lead us?"

"You see yonder grating, sir, that is the opening to the vaults below, and after going down a flight of stone steps, you will discover Major Forester and his companions."

"Good! take this man" he said to two of his private soldiers, "to yonder grating, he is your prisoner till his story is proved true, so do not let him escape. It may be all right, but there is no telling where to have these gentlemen. If you have the least suspicion of treachery you know how to serve him."

"Goolooh was collared by the two soldiers and proceeded to the grating, shouting out the name of Omelia loudly as he did so, which was of course the most imprudent thing he could do. For had our heroine emerged from the opening, the English soldiers seeing a native of India would perhaps have suspected treachery, but Major Forrester hearing the voices of the English troops, at once opened the grating, and presented himself to view.

What a cheer greeted him upon his sudden appearance. Again and again was it repeated ringing through the still evening air in sonerous tones. Discipline was forgotten, for many of the men who were present had been under the major's command, and upon the impulse of the moment they rushed forward to greet him, they grounded their arms, sunk on one knee, and bowed their heads in respect to their beloved commander, who appeared to them as though just restored from the grave.

It was a trying time this for Major Forrester, his heart was too full for utterance and he could not find words to thank them.

He had borne bravely up for months past, and confronted with an indomitable resolution a series of trials, which let us hope seldom fall to the share of mortal man; but he was like to break down now and play the woman. The sudden alternations of hope and dispair had worked upon his nerves—strong as they undoubtedly were; but to be thus greeted upon emerging from his subterranean retreat by a few of his own faithful men, was almost more than he could bear without visible emotion. He looked very ill, the major—more like a ghost than a human being, and more than usual paleness was observable on his features, produced doubtless from the excitement of the moment, and many of his men fancied he faltered, so several lifted him up in their arms and placed him in the midst of them.

"Thanks, my worthy fellows, I am all right in health and strength, although I do present a haggard appearance. Oh! what would I have given to have had a dozen or two of you brave fellows in this confounded fort."

Another cheer was the reply to this brief speech, and more outpourings of sympathy were called forth upon the appearance of Mc Darvish and the other inmates of the vault. The soldiers would not be satisfied without carrying their several officers home, and a rude palanquin was formed for the conveyance of the ladies. Omelia, however, insisted upon marching by their side, and Goolooh took a hurried but tender farewell of our heroine, and returned to the cave of Tamneegal, his mind full of conflicting thoughts upon the scenes he had been just witnessing.

CHAPTER CCXVI.

STANLEY AND HIS FRIENDS.—THE INSIDIOUS FOE AGAIN.

We now return to take a peep at the quarters of Stanley and the worthy Colonel Bridport. The former had sought in vain to discover any traces of Omelia, or whither she had bent her course or had entered the services of the good Jahnsah, and Moorsha, shikaree, for this purpose, but all to no effect, and there appeared but a slender chance of her discovering the missing fugitive. Neither Jahnsah or Abdal had received a single line of communication from our heroine. There was good reason for this, as we shall presently see—Omelia had dispatched letters both to Jahnsah, and also to Abdal, but they did not reach their destination, having been intercepted by secret agency, employed by no other person

than the reader's acquaintance, the immaculate Mr. Natterly.

Stanley, although he had treated Clara with kindness, studiously avoided paying any attentions which might encourage her in the belief that it was possible for him ever to return her passion.

Recently Captain Robinson had paid her marked attention, and had been her constant companion, so much so, that it could not fail to be observed by most of the officers, and it became pretty generally whispered amongst them that Stanley must have observed the marked attentions of Captain Robinson.

So indeed he had, but it was with no feeling of jealousy that he noticed these unmistakeable demonstrations; on the contrary, he rather felicitated himself upon the circumstance. At the same time, however, he looked upon the affair as a mere harmless flirtation.

He was, however, undeceived upon this point when one day Captain Robinson, as they were alone together, at once sought his confidence thus—

"Lieutenant Stanley," observed Robinson, seriously, "a few words with you, if you please, upon a subject which deeply concerns one of us at least."

Stanley bowed expression of his undivided attention.

"You cannot fail to have noticed my marked attentions to Miss Clara, and I feel that the time has arrived to deal frankly with you, and I expect the same in return."

"Certainly; and from me you shall have perfect candour," said Stanley.

No. 92.

"I do not doubt it. You will, therefore, at once pardon my asking what may be considered perhaps under other circumstances an impertinent question. Of course I know Miss Clara, some time since, avowed a passion for you, which, I believe, you did not return. Let me ask, in common justice to yourself and me, are you under any engagement with her?"

"At once let me reply with perfect truth and frankness—certainly not," said Stanley. "You know, my dear Robinson, I am under an engagement with an unfortunate and wilful girl, whom, perhaps, I am never destined to see again. Nevertheless, it is of that nature which will not admit of my entertaining any thoughts of another."

"Enough," exclaimed Robinson, as he warmly grasped his friend's hand; "a thousand thanks for your candour. As an honourable man, I have now not the slightest impediment in offering myself to Clara. I have long wished to broach this subject to you, but hardly knew how to introduce it; however, the ice being broken, we can converse freely upon the subject."

And the two young men were engaged for a long time in communing with one another, when an interruption was put to their further converse by the entrance of a new actor upon the stage.

This was no less a personage than the indefatigable Mr. Natterly, who, whilst he was laying his meshes to entrap our heroine, actually had the audacity to affect a commiseration in her case, and waited upon Stanley to see what he could pick up in the way of information.

"Your servant, gentlemen," said Mr. Natterly, as he gracefully raised his hat with becoming courtesy. "Lieutenant Stanley, I believe?"

"At your service," was the reply.

"Ah, you were kind enough," he continued in oily accents, "to send the particulars of the existence of the daughter of an English lady, named Rose Harcourt, to the firm of Cottle, Leaf, and Cottle, at Calcutta."

"You are quite right—I did so."

"May I ask, if you have heard anything further about her."

"Not at present, but am in daily expectation of doing so."

Mr. Natterly drew a very serious expression to his countenance, and shook his head portentously, and then said, in slow and mournful tones—

"I am—afraid—not."

Stanley started and turned pale.

"How so?" he exclaimed, suddenly.

"Why, I am afraid the report which I have heard is but too true. I am given to understand that she perished in one of the recent conflicts."

A visible emotion passed through the frame of Stanley as he heard these words, for he implicitly believed in the integrity of the speaker.

"How have you learnt this?" he faintly inquired, when he had sufficiently recovered himself.

"From the report of one or two natives, who have waited upon Mr. Cottle"

This was a flagrant falsehood, as no one had vouchsafed any information to the firm in question.

"Still the news has not been confirmed, and, therefore, let us hope. This poor girl, who has such fair prospects before her, may be still alive, and is destined to enjoy the fruits of this lucky stroke of fortune. Let us hope and trust the report may turn out to be false," continued the sympathising Mr. Natterly. "I will make further inquiries upon the subject, for I really feel a deep interest in the affair."

"I shall deem it a personal favour, and one beyond recompense, if you will do your best to sift this matter to the bottom," exclaimed Stanley; and he took a hasty farewell of his visitor.

"So," muttered that individual, as he proceeded from the officers' quarters, "that's all well so far. He has heard nothing, and suspects nothing. I will set the inquiry on foot, of course, and by a seeming show of sympathy, wind myself into the good graces of this conceited puppy. I am then in the enemy's camp, and possessed of all his secrets. He has not heard, then Goryeboo has been so far faithful, and good to his word. I have not, though, the most perfect and implicit confidence in that scoundrel; but I have him under my thumb, and he is at my mercy, so must do my bidding. Nothing like having your thorough-faced villain with a halter round his neck. Ha, ha! the time will come yet when I shall hold the broad lands and princely wealth of the late bankrupt, Harcourt."

Musing thus, he struck into a bye path which led towards a neighbouring wood and jungle.

In a short time he was met by the thug, Goryeboo, who had been awaiting his coming.

"What news?" exclaimed Mr. Natterly.

"All goes on well; I have intercepted the letters, and have two, which at once tell us where to find her for whom we have been seeking."

He handed the documents in question to his companion, who instantly devoured their contents. They were letters from our heroine without doubt: one was addressed to the faithful Abdal, and the other to Jahnsah. They gave an account of her proceedings at the fort, and her present place of rendezvous.

"Admirably contrived," exclaimed Mr. Natterly.

"You bribed the letter carrier, I suppose."

"Yes; as you desired."

"And promised him a handsome reward for all future documents?"

"Certainly; upon the condition that they are to be delivered into my hands without reaching their destination.'

"Very good. Now you know where to seek your prey. Let it be done as quickly as possible, or even now she may escape you. What are your next proceedings?"

"I shall have considerable difficulty in my operations now that she is surrounded and protected by a large body of English troops."

"Oh, you will know how to manage that. Can you not by some pretext draw her away from them, and then—you know the rest."

A significant nod was the answer to this proposition.

"Now, my good Goryeboo, all seems to promise fair. Strike the blow at once as you think best, and your reward shall be princely I promise. Here is something as an earnest of my good intentions; I myself will be about this neighbourhood and lull suspicion. I have already seen this fellow Stanley, and have intimated to him that his beautiful *lura sposa* has already been food for powder, and I think he believes me. Finish your work, and I have but to tell him that the news is confirmed, and there will be an end of his hopes."

"He does not suspect you then?"

"Oh, no; on the contrary, he believes me to be highly interested in the behalf of his enslaver. So I am—ha, ha, ha! Now speed you at once on your journey, and success attend your efforts. I will be here upon your return, and shall be anxiously awaiting the issue."

"I am thinking how I shall draw her away from her companions without suspicion. The probability is that I shall be known perhaps to some of the English officers, and cannot, therefore, venture myself to their quarters. Could you not upon some pretext get a letter to her from this Stanley appointing a meeting close by?"

"I fear not. It would arouse his suspicions. I have it, though; I will write a letter in the name of Jahnsah, saying he desires an interview upon something that nearly concerns her. The probability is that she is not acquainted with his hand-writing, and therefore will at once proceed to the place appointed."

"Admirable thought. Do so at once, and I will get a stranger to deliver it, who will not know but what I am Jahnsah himself."

"Are you going alone upon the expedition."

"No, I shall be accompanied by a few of our band, although I shall not let them know the object of my journey. We shall see what we can fall in with in other ways."

"Ah, keep your own counsel as to your engagement with me, for the rest, of course, you can please yourself—it is no business of mine."

The letter, which was to deceive our heroine was written, and the despicable Goryeboo proceeded to carry out his fell purpose.

——

CHAPTER CCXVII.

FIRING FROM GUNS.—THE MARCH OF HAVE-LOCK'S TROOPS.—GORYEBOO'S MANŒUVRES.

Havelock's troops were not destined to remain in the spot where they had so futuitously rescued Major Forrester and his companions in misfortune and suffering.

The avenging column of this brave general, as is well known by the reports in our own journals, were continually on the march, dealing a just and retributive judgment upon the revolted native troops.

Major Forrester and his brave companions in arms were invalided—they were indeed too week and prostrated to be capable of very actual service. Our heroine was introduced to the officers in command, and the highest eulogiums were passed upon her for faithful and unflinching adherence to the English cause.

Mrs. Forrester and Miss Hilayard would insist upon her being with them never more to part, and a life of comfort and happiness appeared to be in store for them, compared to the one they had been lately doomed to. Omelia, now that the continual hourly excitement was over, began again to reflect upon him whom she treasured up still as her heart's idol, and she seemed cut off entirely from her old associations.

Her faithful friend Abdal had not replied to her letter—he might be dead; this thought was torture to her mind. Then the self-sacrificing love of Goolooh had made a deep impression upon her, and she ran over, with a retrospective glance, all the incidents of her early and chequered life, never very bright and sunny save in the presence of her beloved Stanley.

What would she give now if she possessed Fortunalus' cap to transport her invisible into the quarters of her lover, and to watch his actions, bearing, and demeanour? Her pride and self-respect would not admit her of entertaining the thought of again seeking him, but it cost her many pangs the resolution she had so rashly taken.

In a few more hours the English troops

had orders to march, but previous to this a trial took place of several sepoy prisoners, who were convicted of barbarously murdering their officers and their wives.

There was the clearest evidence given of their guilt, and they were condemned to be blown from guns

This was a scene which filled the minds of our heroine and female friends with dismay and horror, but there was no possibility of staying the stern decrees of military law.

It was an awfully imposing scene. All the troops, European and native, were drawn up on parade, forming three sides of a square, and drawn up so carefully that any attempt on the part of the disaffected to rescue the doomed prisoners would have been instantly checked.

Forming the fourth side of the square were drawn up the guns—nine pounders—ten in number, which were to be used for the execution.

The prisoners, under a strong European guard, were then marched into the square; their crimes and sentences were then read aloud to them, and at the head of each regiment; they were marched round the square up to the guns.

The first ten were picked out—their eyes bandaged, and they were bound to the guns, their backs leaning against the muzzle, and their arms fastened to the wheel—the port fires were lighted, and at a signal from the artillery major the guns were fired.

It was a horrid sight that then met the eye: a regular shower of human fragments, heads, arms, and legs appeared in the air through the smoke, and when this cleared away these fragments were lying on the ground in a heterogeneous mass of mangled human forms—fragments of Hindoos and Mussulmen, all mixed together—were all that remained of the ten mutineers.

Once more was this repeated, and so great was the disgust felt for the atrocities committed by the rebels, that there appeared no room in the hearts of the executioners for pity—perfect callousness was depicted on every European face—a look of grim satisfaction could even be observed in the countenances of the men serving the guns.

But far different was the effect on the villagers and native population, who were spectators of this horrible sight: their black faces grew ghastly pale as they gazed breathlessly at the awful spectacle,

It should be observed, that this is the only form of death that has any terrors for a native. If he is hung, or shot by musketry, he knows that his friends or relatives will be allowed to claim his body, and will give him the funeral rights required by his religion; if a Hindoo, his body will be burned with all due ceremonies—and a Mus-

sulman, his remains will be decently interred as directed by the Koran.

But if sentenced to death in this form, he knows that his body will be blown into a thousand pieces, and that it will be altogether impossible for his relatives, however devoted to him, to be sure of picking up all the fragments of his own particular body, and the thought that perhaps a limb of some one of a different religion to himself might possibly be buried or burned with the remainder of his own body is agony to him.

This dreadful ceremony having been performed, the troops proceeded on their march. They fell in shortly with a body of rebels, and a smart skirmish took place, when eventually the latter were routed with great loss.

Omelia was weary of these conflicts, and the many painful sights which they occasioned, and was too glad when the English again halted.

The character of the natives of India, whose conduct, as compared with our British standard, is the very antipodes of the moral world. Only by long experience can it be known. Viewed from many aspects they may appear gentle, respectful, temperate, quiet, orderly, confiding, kind, charitable, and sometimes susceptible of gratitude and fidelity. But, on the other hand, they have many opposite phases of character: they have been compared to the Indian tiger often so stealthy and retiring, but yet can spring as high. But the analogy will not entirely hold good, for they will spring not like the tiger upon the ranks of surrounding foes, but upon helpless and beaten victims. They may be rather likened to the tame ourang-outang, in Paris, who happened to escape from its keeper, seized a razor, and, madly thirsting for blood, slew several spectators. They are credulous in the extreme, and the more unreasonable the thing to be believed, the more implicit their faith. With blood heated by a scorching climate, they have a temperament subject to the most fitful impulses and to the strangest inconsistencies.

Their evil passions may often lie dormant, but when once awakened they are bitterly malignant.

Instances sometimes occur in which even converts to Christianity will, when disputing with one another, throw off their Christian habits for the nonce, and evince a truly native maliciousness.

It is useless to repeat what is known regarding their innate tendency to dissimulation; and with all their mildness they are in some respects cruel and even bloody. We have had instances enough of this to chronicle in this narrative; witness, also, many of their religious rites—witness the sacrifice of daughters to save the expense of dowry —the drowning or choking of aged or dying persons in the waters of the Ganges—the strangling of persons by the Thugs merely to rob them with more security—the habitual murder of children for the sake of their silver bracelets, and any other trinket upon their person.

They will generally " hit a man when he is down." In our Indian campaigns there are, after every battle, stories of the throats of our wounded soldiers being cut by the native enemy.

Whenever European officers have been killed, their dead bodies have been mutilated —as in the case of Macnoughton and Burnes at Cabul and Agnew, and Anderson at Mooltan. On the whole, persons thoroughly acquainted with the natives, would have anticipated that if by chance a general mutiny were to break out, it would be accompanied in many cases with barbarous insolence and wild atrocity.

Nor is the late revolt altogether without precedent in kind, though never equalled in degree.

There is much historical coincidence between the recent revolt and the mutiny of Vellore, in 1806. Then, as now, the sepoys believed it was intended, by breaking through their caste, to bring them ultimately to Christianity.

Then, as now, they designed to murder all Europeans, and to set up a Mahomedan pensioner of the British as king in their place. Then, as now, the officers, unable to believe in the treachery of their men, were startled by an outbreak threatening the stability of their power.

The only difference was this, that the authorities of that day insisted on trimming the beard and moustache, the obliteration of caste marks, and the new turban, despite the objections of the men. Whereas the Indian government of the present day withdrew the obnoxious cartridges as soon as objections were raised.

Notwithstanding the numerous communications from persons in India, which has been published, and the many essays from competent writers and judges, who were personal spectators, the mutiny still remains obscured in a haze of doubt and uncertainty.

Was it the result of a conspiracy long concerted and deeply planned? which had fixed upon Delhi as the place, and the king as the man, and the anniversary of the battle of Plecy as the time, and which got up the cartridge story as a sham pretext, and as a signal to warn the conspirators that the occasion was ripening?

Or is it that the affair really did begin with the greased cartridges, without any previous conspiracy? that the cartridges gave rise to stories rousing the suspicions of the army, and causing a seditious correspondence and combination, and that while mens' minds were in an inflamable state a spark was kindled at Meerut, which raised a flame that spread like wildfire to every station.

Now, at the present, it is not easy to give an answer to these questions, and most likely the entire truth will never be known.

After several days march, Havelock's troops reached the road leading from Jubbulpore and Saugor. There had been a mutiny of a serious character at both these places, and many disaffected troops were skirmishing about.

But a narrative of the movements of the British columns would exhaust our space to describe; we must proceed to recount the events more immediately connected with the characters of our tale.

Goryeboo, true to his agreement with his worthy employer, had hastily proceeded to the spot from where Omelia had dated her last letter. He arrived in time to hear the drums beating, and beheld his countrymen marched out on parade and lashed to the guns, and blown into the air.

This produced such a startling effect upon his nerves that he had serious thoughts of retracing his steps back to the place from whence he had come, but the execution over, he beheld the British army upon the march, and like a sneaking tiger at the tail of a troop of elephants, he followed at a respectful distance, determining to wait a favourable opportunity to put his project into practice.

This, however, did not occur so readily as he had hoped. Nevertheless, he was determined not to lose sight of Omelia, so when the English force halted he did so likewise, and hid himself in jungles and woods, sometimes, indeed, he procured accommodation from a neighbouring cottage.

He was accompanied by two or three of his most favoured companions. Both himself and his comrades were rather dashed in spirits as they witnessed the repeated conflicts and slaughter of their countrymen by Havelock's gallant troops, and they were able to form a shrewd guess as to their own probable fate if they were caught; they however stole along with a stealthiness peculiar to their vocation, and as the English halted for some time on the road leading between the towns of Jubbulpore and Saugor, the wily Goryeboo thought it an admirable opportunity for him to make a desperate effort to capture our heroine and ransom his son and earn the rupees.

———

CHAPTER CCXVIII.

TREACHERY SUCCESSFUL.—THE CAPTURE OF OMELIA.—MIRACULOUS AND UNEXPECTED RESCUE.

Goryeboo in vain endeavoured to persuade one of his associates to convey the letter written by Mr. Natterly to Omelia.

They distinctly declined the honour, having an instinctive horror of too close a proximity to the English force.

Threats and entreaties were alike useless. He declared upon his honour that it was a legitimate document, but his companions seemed rather dubious about his integrity. They had no confidence, these men, in each others sincerity, and this is hardly to be wondered at.

Goryeboo eventually succeeded in enlisting the services of a Hindoo youth about sixteen years of age, to convey the missive in question; telling him that he had an old friend who was with the English, and who was a great favourite with them, but, at the same time, she would be too glad to accompany him to the appointed place. He charged him to see our heroine alone, and give the letter into no other hands but her own.

The lad did not much like the task, but by repeated assurances from Goryeboo and his companions that it was unattended with the slightest danger, and that she expected to receive the document, he was ultimately induced, by the promise of a handsome reward, to undertake the somewhat onerous task.

Towards evening, therefore, the youth proceeded to the English camp, and having been challenged by the picket on duty, he explained the purport of his visit, and was ushered into the presence of Omelia and the English ladies then present.

He gave the letter to the former, who trembled with anxiety as she perused its contents, as she fully believed its authenticity, and surmised immediately that some harm had befallen Stanley.

"You will never be imprudent or rash enough to proceed alone to this interview?" said Mrs. Forrester, with some haste.

"I have the utmost confidence in this worthy man," replied our heroine. He is one of my best friends, and is, indeed the friend of us all. He has saved from perhaps worse than death numbers of your countrymen, and is incapable of harm to human creature."

"Take a small file of soldiers with you, at any rate, by way of precaution."

"No; I will not insult him by the appearance of any suspicion," was the calm reply, and she at once proceeded to accompany the youth to the appointed place.

As she went along she observed to him—

"Did my good friend Jahnsah give you this himself?"

"Yes, my lady. He charged me to deliver it into your own hands."

"Do you know him?"

"Yes."

This was said faintly, and Omelia looked furtively at the speaker. Her suspicions began to be aroused.

"What sort of a man is he?" was her next inquiry, as she somewhat slackened her speed.

The lad described as well as he could the appearance of the man who had given him the letter. It, of course, did not at all tally with that of Jahnsah. The circumstance looked suspicious, and she regretted her haste in refusing the advice offered by her friend Mrs. Forrester.

She paused and debated with herself the propriety of proceeding farther, and yet did not like to go back to her friends without some more positive grounds for doing so.

"Was the man who gave you this letter alone?" she inquired of the lad coming at the same time to a dead halt.

"No," was the prompt reply; "there were three others with him."

This decided her, and she said in hurried accents—

"Then I follow you no further. There is deception, and perhaps treachery here."

She was about to retrace her steps, when she was alarmed by a sudden and singular cry of surprise from the boy, who pointed with his hand to something moving in the adjoining foliage.

Omelia started with surprise, and sudden alarm seized her, as she beheld at some few yards distant the movements of something either brute or human in the neighbouring bushes.

It was Goryeboo, who had been watching at some distance the approach of his victim and her innocent companion, who was hurrying her on to a certain doom.

The miscreant seeing some hesitation and her eventual determination to return, judged that her suspicions were aroused, and he was therefore stealing along, under cover of the bushes, to spring out therefrom and effect a sudden and immediate capture.

A chilling foreboding passed through the mind of our heroine, as the boy directed her attention to the movements described, and a dark and fearful thought flashed across her as she remembered the caution respecting the Thug, on the occasion of her parting with the faithful Abdal. She was, luckily, provided with a revolver, with which weapon she might protect herself.

"Hold there!" she shouted, "approach one step further, and your life shall pay the forfeit."

But there was no reply to this, and although she strained her eyes to catch the most minute movement in the leaves of the bushes, she failed to detect the slightest motion.

Nevertheless, her wary foe was stealing along with stealthy and noiseless footsteps towards the spot, and watching her position with the eye of a rattle-snake, he made a circuitous course, and instantly sprang upon her from behind, and encircled her throat with a sash.

Omelia uttered a piercing scream, which was heard for some distance around, but her utterance was choked by the sash being tightly compressed around her throat. She struggled desperately, and fired behind at her assailant one barrel of her revolver, but without effect.

The youth, whose senses were benumbed for the moment by fear and surprise from the sudden attack, now somewhat recovered himself, and screamed out most vociferously.

Goryeboo called to his companions to silence the lad, upon which two of them darted forward and seized hold of him for this purpose.

A few more seconds and all would have been over with our heroine, and the Thug would have completed his hidious work; but while thus engaged with his intended victim he was suddenly set upon by a man, who rushed to the spot with breathless haste.

He literally sprang upon Goryeboo like a tiger, and securing him with both hands by the throat, bore him to the earth by the impetuosity of his assault.

Omelia was prostrated to the ground from the force of the attack, and although nearly powerless and deprived of her usual strength, she managed to unwind the instrument of death which compressed her throat.

A sharp, desperate, and determined struggle now ensued between Goryeboo and the new comer; so rapid were their movements, in their contortions to obtain the mastery, that our heroine could not distinguish one from the other.

The man who had sprang upon the Thug still held with an iron grip his antagonist, who appeared to be trying every feint to shake him off and set himself at liberty. His efforts, however, were unavailing, and Goryeboo shouted to his companions to come to his assistance. One rushed forward with a drawn sword, which he was about to bury in the body of Goryeboo's antagonist. Omelia divined his purpose—not a moment was to be lost to save the life of him who had risked his own so generously on her behalf.

As the Thug advanced with the drawn sword upon his foe, Omelia fired her revolver, and shattered his right arm above the elbow. It fell uselessly by his side, and with a howl

of rage and pain he rushed forward upon his assailant.

Omelia firmly pointed her pistol at his breast, and defied him to approach, upon pain of instant death: upon which he muttered several dreadful curses, and beat an immediate retreat.

The struggle continued between the two men; the Thug had unsheathed a dagger from his side, and would have buried it up to the hilt in the body of his antagonist, who foreseeing his intent, grasped his wrist firmly, and forced back his murderous arm.

After several more desperate struggles, Omelia saw the Thug raised in the air by his opponent and thrown several yards. From the sound, when he fell, she thought his skull was fractured, and was, therefore, quite astonished when she saw him immediately rise, and fly away at the utmost speed.

His antagonist was about to follow him when our heroine rushed forward and detained him, saying, hurriedly—

"Seek not to follow him, my noble preserver; he will but draw you into ambush, and set upon you with his worthless associates. You have risked already enough on my behalf.

The man turned to reply, and what was the astonishment of Omelia when she beheld the features of Goolooh turned upon her. He was very pale, and apparently exhausted with the contest, and fear for the safety of our heroine.

"Safe!" he exclaimed; "heaven be praised," and he fervently grasped the form of Omelia to assure himself of the fact.

"My excellent friend," said Omelia, "how much I owe you for all your kindness on this as on so many other occasions. By what marvellous chance was it that you arrived thus opportunely to save me again from a dreadful and certain death?"

Goolooh paused, and seemed either unable or unwilling to give a reply, when, after some further hesitation, he said—

"I did not deem you would have needed my humble services ever again. Still less did I think it possible that I should witness so terrible a scene as this."

"But how came you here—so many miles from—from your quarters?"

"You shall hear. It is true, as you say, I cannot be anything more to you than a friend. When you left with your English companions and General Havelock's troops, I followed them each day on their march, not from any offensive purpose, on the contrary; but it was some solace to me to be near where you were, to breathe the same air, to look towards the camp where I knew you to be in safety and comparative happiness. It was a foolish thought you will perhaps say, as I had no intention of obtruding myself upon your notice, or seeking your presence; but now how happy I am in the reflection that this foolish resolution should have led me to be near when you most needed assistance. That man, whom I would fain have given chase to, do you know who he is? He is a Thug."

"Yes," replied Omelia; "I too well know his purpose, and the hated class to which he belongs. Goolooh, he seeks my life with a pertinacity which appears surprising. What can be his motive I am totally at a loss to divine, but I know he has been seeking me out in all quarters where he thought it likely to find me, and he has, I believe, sworn to have my life sooner or later."

"Extraordinary! Do you know him?'

"No. I have never, to my knowledge, seen him before. Whether he is actuated by motives of revenge for some imaginary injury, I am at a loss to conjecture."

"Most likely in the employ of some more consummate scoundrel than himself," observed Goolooh. "I wish I had followed him, and given him his deserts."

During this conversation they had lost sight of and entirely forgotten the youth who had led our heroine to the spot. He now presented himself to their notice, and was very anxious to exculpate himself from any complicity with the Thug, and explained more fully the circumstances under which he was induced to undertake the mission. It appeared that the Thug who had detained and stopped him from raising an alarm by his cries, had flown off when he saw his companions leave, and the lad was therefore released from further molestation.

Omelia inquired if Tamneegal knew of her existence and escape from the fort?

"No," answered Goolooh; "agreeable to your expressed wish, I did not inform him of your preservation. He was under the full impression that the whole of the inhabitants of that ill-fated building had perished with its destruction. He takes it much to heart, and, although he says but little, I can observe many little signs which indicate how much the reflection distresses him. You do not, I think, give him credit for his attachment to you?"

"I would wish him to mend his present lawless course of life," was the reply; "however, do not let him trouble himself on the account of my supposed loss, therefore, I pray you, undeceive him, and say I am safe now with kind friends, who afford me shelter and protection. See you do this at your earliest convenience."

"It will afford me too much pleasure to do so."

"I must return now, Goolooh, my good and faithful friend—I know you to be this in

its widest and most enduring sense. If in earlier years we had met, and become associated with one another, matters might have been different—might, perhaps, have altered the current of our lives; but now what human hands can direct the course of the stream which bears us on to either fortune or destruction? Not our's, Goolooh. For myself I have, alas! drifted out upon troubled waters, and cannot discern a faint glimpse of a peaceful and happy shore."

Her companion made no reply, but proceeded to conduct her towards the English camp. When arriving close to it, Goolooh paused, he would not venture to accompany Omelia into the presence of those whom he still considered his enemies.

He was anxious to ascertain whether Havelock's troops were about to march, but this our heroine was unable to inform him.

Having arrived within sight of the British force, Goolooh took a farewell of her whom he had so generously saved, and Omelia joined her friends, who were astonished at her account of the attack made upon her, and her providential escape.

———

CHAPTER CCXIX.

CLARA AND HER LOVER.—FEARFUL ADVENTURE, AND MIRACULOUS ESCAPE.

Some few days after the conversation between Captain Robinson and Stanley, the former delared his sentiments towards Clara in impassioned terms.

She listened to the declaration of his passion not with any feelings of surprise, as his attentions had been sufficiently marked to lead to the supposition that his conduct was prompted by a tender feeling towards her; she felt flattered by the preference, and the honourable course he had pursued.

There could be no doubt respecting her feelings towards Stanley, but his general bearing had been such as to give her no encouragement; indeed he had owned to her with the utmost frankness that he could never under any circumstances abandon Omelia; true there did not appear much chance of his seeing her again at present, or finding out any clue to her whereabouts, nevertheless, he felt bound by the most sacred ties towards her, and recommended his friend Robinson most earnestly to the consideration of Clara, who had not, however, as yet accepted the latter in the character of a lover.

Matters were proceeding thus, when a circumstance occurred which, in some measure, tended to bring matters to an issue.

Colonel Bridport, his daughters, and a

numerous party were returning from a neighbouring town, whither they had marched upon military duty; towards evening they had halted for an hour or two's rest. Clara and the worthy Colonel's daughters were reclining on the grass in conversation; the former was near a large tree. Worn out with fatigue and the oppressing heat of the day, Clara had reclined against the trunk of the tree and fallen into a sound sleep. It is probable that none of the party had noticed this fact besides Captain Robinson, who frequently directed his glances towards his enslaver; he was panic-struck when he observed a large rattle-snake moving from side to side on Clara's chest. Upon the impulse of the moment, he was about incautiously to rush to her rescue, but upon a second reflection

No. 93.

he abstained from doing so, as perhaps any sudden movement would be only hastening the creature on to a sudden attack. In a hurried whisper he called Stanley to his side and directed his attention to the frightful situation of the sleeping and unconscious Clara.

"He may not perhaps mean any mischief after all," observed Hawkins, who had crept to Robinson's side.

"Make no noise, and it is very possible it will merely cross her body and go away."

In this, however, Hawkins was mistaken, for on reaching the sleeper's shoulder, the serpent deliberately coiled itself up, and although it made no immediate attack, it did not appear at all likely to leave the side of the sleeper.

"Leave it to me," said Robinson, as

Hawkins was about to approach, "I will rescue the dear girl from her perilous position. I know the habits of these creatures and how to treat them. Make no noise on your life, or all will be lost, but follow my directions."

His companions declared their willingness to obey his orders.

"Now," said Robinson, in a whisper, "you two advance in front to divert the attention of the snake, whilst I will approach noiselessly behind, and with a long stick remove the hideous reptile from her body. This is the only possible chance of saving her."

The two commenced their approach in front, agreeable to Robinson's instructions.

The snake upon observing the intruders in front of him, instantly raised his head and darted out his forked tongue, at the same time shaking his rattles; these were unmistakeable indications of anger.

Every one of the party was in a state of fearful suspense and agitation, for by this time all eyes were directed towards the proceedings, and became aware of the danger. There lay Clara like a beautiful statue, unmoved, sleeping the calm sleep of innocence. Robinson advanced stealthily behind, with a stick seven feet long, which he had procured for the purpose. In an instant, almost before the spectators had time to observe it, he succeeded in cautiously inserting one end of the stick under one of the reptile's coils, and flung the creature many yards from Clara's body. A wild and piercing scream of joy from the ladies present was the first indication Clara received of her danger and providential escape. In the meantime Robinson pursued the snake and killed it. It was three feet seven inches long, and eleven years old; this was ascertained by the number of rattles.

Robinson informed his companions that there was no danger attendant upon the destruction of the rattle snake, provided a person has a long pliant stick, and does not approach nearer than the reptile's length, for they cannot spring beyond it, and seldom act but upon the defensive. The party discovered, on searching about, a nest of these snakes near to where Clara had been lying, and after this incident they were a little more careful. Upon the impulse of the moment Clara threw herself into the arms of Robinson, and gave expression to her preserver of her warmest gratitude. This little incident was the turning point in Robinson's love course. It seemed to bind Clara towards him, and she listened to his harmonious voice as he breathed forth in melliferous accents his undying love and constancy. The fright having been got

over, Robinson was secretly rejoiced at the circumstance, and the Colonel could not resist a smile at the fortunate escape.

"It makes me shudder," he observed, "the sight of these reptiles, and the touch of them; ah! I would sooner meet with a dozen or two ferocious scoundrels rather than one of these. I remember a terrible encounter I had myself with a Cobra de Capella, when I was a young man, and the recollection, even at this distant period of time, is still vividly impressed upon my memory."

"Indeed," exclaimed several voices; "tell it us, Colonel."

"It was about the conclusion of the Monsoons of 1835," said the Colonel; "the quail was abundant, and after some hours of hard fagging through the dark and heavy grass, I felt inclined to rest, and an adjacent tamarind tree of noble growth yielded an inviting shelter from the sun. The few beaters that had accompanied me had set off to a neighbouring gaum to obtain some refreshment. From that state of pleasing indolence which sportsmen are apt to indulge in after severe fatigue, I was aroused by the barking of my dogs, on turning round I beheld a snake, of the Cobra de Capella species directing its course to a point that would approximate very close to my position, in an instant I was on my feet. The moment it became aware of my presence, in nautical phraseology, it brought to with expanded hood, eyes sparkling, and neck beautifully arched, the head raised nearly two feet from the ground and oscillating from side to side indicative of a resentful foe. I seized the nearest weapon, a short bamboo, and hurled it at my opponent's head, I was fortunate enough to hit him between the eyes. The reptile immediately ceased from its imposing attitude and lay apparently lifeless. Without a moment's reflection I seized it a little below the head, hauled it beneath the shelter of a tree, and very coolly sat down to examine the mouth for its poisonous fangs of which naturalists speak so much. While in the act of forcing open the throat with a stick, I felt the head sliding through my hand, and to my utter astonishment and terror I became aware that I had to contend against the most deadly of all reptiles in its full strength and vigour. Indeed I was in a moment convinced of this, for as I tightened my hold of the throat its body became wreathed round my neck and arm. My right arm, to enable me to exert my strength, was extended; I must, in such an attitude, have appeared horrified enough to represent a deity in the Hindoo Mythology, such as we often see rudely emblazoned on the portals of their native temples.

It now became a matter of self defence : to retain my hold, and prevent its head from escaping, required my utmost strength as my neck became a purchase for the animal to pull from. You are most of you aware of the universal dread in which the Cobra de Capella is held throughout India, and the almost instant death which inevitably follows its bite; you will in some degree be able to imagine what my feelings were at the moment; a shudder, a faint kind of disgusting sickness pervaded my whole frame, as I felt the cold clammy folds of the reptile's body tightening round my neck.

"Horrible!" exclaimed Clara, as the Colonels narrative called to mind her own situation. "How did you manage to obtain a mastery over the creature?"

"You shall hear. To attempt any delineation of my sensations at this time would be absurd and futile, let it suffice that they were most horrible. I had almost resolved to let go my hold; if I had done so I should never have been here telling this tale, as no doubt the head of the serpent would have been brought to the extreme circumlocution to inflict its deadly wound. Even in the agony of such a moment I could picture to myself the fierce glaring of the eyes and the intimidating expansion of its hood, ere it fastened its venomous and fatal hold upon my face and neck. To hold it much longer would be impossible. Immediately beneath my grasp there was an inward working and creeping of the skin, which seemed to be assisted by the very firmness with which I held it—my hand was gloved. Finding that in defiance of all my efforts my hand was forced each instant closer to my face, I was considering how to act in this horrible dilemma, when an idea struck me, that were it in my power to transfix the mouth with some sharp instrument, it would prevent the reptile using its fangs, should it escape my hold. My gun laid at my feet—the ramrod appeared to be the very thing required—which with some difficulty I succeeded in drawing out; having only one hand disengaged, my right arm was now trembling with over exertion, and my hold became less firm, when I happily succeeded in passing the rod through the lower jaw up to its centre. It was not without hesitation that I let go my hold of the throat, and suddenly seized the rod in both hands, at the same time by bringing them over my head with a sudden jerk I disengaged the fold from my neck, which had latterly become almost so tight as to produce strangulation. There was then but little difficulty in freeing my right arm, and ultimately to throw the reptile from me to the earth, where it continued to twist and writhe into a thousand contortions of rage and agony. To run to a neighbouring stream to have my neck, hands, and face washed in its cooling waters, was my first act after dispatching my formidable enemy. Thus we may see a moral even in this adventure. It proves that when a man is possessed of determination, coolness and energy, combined with reason, he will generally come off triumphant, and he may circumvent the subtlety of the snake or the ferocity of the tiger."

"And had it bitten you, father?" said Julia Bridport. "It would have——"

"Been certain death within the space of twenty minutes," replied the Colonel, "although the effects of the poison from the Cobra differs materially in its effect upon individuals; with some its action is much more rapid than with others, varying according to their constitution."

"But in most cases death supervenes, I suppose?" enquired Morley.

"Yes, I believe in all cases where a bite is inflicted. I have been at some trouble to enquire into the effects of the poison of serpents, and our good friend here has tried numerous experiments in conjunction with myself." It was Doctor Hamilton to whom the Colonel had alluded.

"It is a very remarkable circumstance," said the Doctor, "that the poison of serpents has most power over those whose blood is the warmest and the action of whose heart is most lively."

"In that case you would have been a certain sufferer," said Robinson to Clara, laughing.

"She can see no doubt about that," said the Doctor. "It is a fact beyond a question of doubt, that it is not a poison to the reptile itself, nor in general to cold-blooded animals; the reason appears to be that cold-blooded animals do not require a large quantity of oxygen to preserve their health; this is evident from the conformation of their respiratory organs. It does not however follow that no quantity of the venom would destroy them, for it is also evident from their possessing respiratory organs of any kind, that a certain quantity of oxygen is absolutely necessary, and hence we know that some of them, such as frogs, may be killed by the venom, although it always produces its effects more slowly upon them than upon animals with warm blood. I remember making some experiments upon the poison of serpents : one was with a large Cobra de Capella, which is perhaps the most venomous of the reptile tribe; this creature I made bite the hind leg of a dog, for which no medicine was used to counteract the effect of the bite. The dog upon being bit howled lamentably for a few minutes; he soon became paralysed, and in thirteen minutes he laid senseless and dead. Another dog was also bitten in the hind leg, and the wound was scarified and washed with luna caustic, and for two hours the dog continued lively and well, but he also died in the course of the day."

"No, I suppose nothing will withstand the venom of a Cobra," said the Colonel.

"The natives do profess to have some medicinal herb," said the Doctor, with which they say they can neutralize the effect of the poison, but I am very sceptical myself upon the matter. I witnessed, some years since, an agonizing scene with a Cobra. It occurred thus: several young officers at Madras had been to a large ball given in that town; the first of the English inhabitants were present, and altogether it was a grand affair, I can tell you. I had danced myself with one and another, until I was, like my companions, fairly worn out. The grounds were magnificently decorated with flags, marquees, tents, &c. And in these we had dined in an earlier part of the day. I had retired from the dancers with two or three officers into one of the tents, and we were enjoying the fragrant weed and some pleasant conversation, while a young man, a friend of mine, named Medhurst, was playing at chess with a brother officer. You must understand that the gentlemen were in full dress with flesh-coloured silk stockings and shoes. We had sat talking and joking some time, as Medhurst and his companion were intent upon their game, when one of the officers with whom I had been conversing, gently touched me on the shoulder and directed my attention towards Medhurst; judge of my horror when on glancing down to the spot he directed my attention to a Cobra de Capella winding himself round the leg of Medhurst. Poor fellow! he had evidently been quite unaware of the fact.

"Do not move on your life," said the officer who had called my attention to the horrible sight before us.

"Medhurst, my dear boy, you must remain perfectly calm and immovable."

"Well, I am so! What do you mean?"

He glanced round, and then I suppose feeling some tickling sensation, looked down towards his leg. I shall never forget his look of speechless horror when he beheld the serpent coiled round the calf. The creature had two coils already round his leg. One of his companions had procured some warm milk in a saucer, and had placed it within a short distance of the reptile, who regarded it for a moment or two, and then turned away from it. Another of the officers had procured some honey, which he had laid down in the hope of enticing the reptile from his present position. This seemed to be more efficacious, for the snake evidently smelt the honey, and was apparently well pleased with its perfume. Gradually he began to slowly unwind one of the coils round Medhurst's leg, and you may judge of the patient agony and suspense the latter was experiencing. Minute after minute elapsed, when we had the satisfaction to behold the reptile release itself from our friend and make towards the honey. No sooner was he once fairly detached, when one of the party flung him some yards away, by the aid of a long stick, in much the same way as our friend Robinson managed to rescue Miss Clara from her impending fate."

"And, Medhurst," said Morley, "he was all right, I suppose?"

"He was saved certainly," said the doctor, "but the shock to his system was so terrible that he never completely recovered it."

"Ah! I can readily understand that," observed the Colonel, "It is hardly possible to describe the horror of such a situation. The stress upon the nerves when the mind is kept in a state of harrowing suspense, cannot easily be imagined by those who have not been in a similar situation, small as is the Cobra compared to the boa constrictor, it is nevertheless one of the most deadly little reptiles this country furnishes, and it is not a few it can boast of."

"There is something very horrible in the idea of being crushed by a Boa Constrictor," observed the Doctor, "an old friend of mine, a naturalist named Captain Stedman, was bold enough to shoot one of these gigantic snakes, which measured twenty two feet seven inches, although the natives declared it to be a young one. As the account Captain Stedman gave me of the transaction may be interesting, I shall relate it in his own words:—'As he was resting on his hammock, while the vessel in which he was, floated down the river, the sentinel told him he had seen and challenged something black and moving in the brushwood on the head, which gave no answer, but from its size he concluded was a man. The Captain immediately manned the canoe which accompanied the vessel, and rowed on shore to ascertain what it was, when, to his great surprise, one of the negroes declared that it was no negro, but a large amphibious snake which he might shoot if he choose. However it seems Stedman had not the least inclination to do this, and therefore ordered them all to return on board. The negro then stepped forward and begged leave to shoot it himself, as he was quite certain it could not be far off, and assured his master that there could be no danger.

"This declaration," said Captain Stedman, "inspired me with so much pride and emulation, that I determined to take his first advice and kill it myself, provided he would point it out to me and be responsible for the hazard by standing at my side, from which I swore if he dared to move, I would level the piece at his head and blow out his brains. To this the negro cheerfully agreed, and having loaded my gun with ball cartridge we proceeded, David cutting a path with a bill-hook, and a marine following with three more loaded firelocks to keep in readiness. We had not gone more than twenty yards through mud and water, when the negro looking every way with an uncommon degree of vivacity and attention, and starting behind me he called out "me see snakee," and in fact there lay the animal rolled up under the fallen leaves and rubbish of the trees, and so well concealed was it that it was some time before I could distinctly see the head of the monster, distant from me not more than sixteen feet, moving its forked tongue, while its eyes, from their uncommon brightness, seemed to emit sparks of fire. I now rested my piece on a branch for the purpose of taking sure aim, and fired, and missed the the head, but the ball went through the body when the reptile struck round with such astonishing force as to cut away all the underwood around him with the facility of a scythe mowing grass, and by flouncing his tail, caused the mud and dust to fly over our heads to a considerable distance. Of this proceeding however, we were not torpid spectators, but took to our heels and crowded into the canoe. The negro now entreated me to renew the charge, assuring me that the snake would be quiet in a few minutes, and at any rate persisted in the assertion, that he was neither able or inclined to pursue us, which opinion he supported by walking before me till I was ready to fire; and thus I again undertook to make a trial, especially as he said that his first starting backwards was only to make room for me. I now found the snake a little removed from his former position, but very quiet, with his head as before, lying out among the fallen leaves, rotten bark, and old moss. I fired at it immediately, but with no better success than the other time; and now being but slightly wounded, he sent up such a cloud of dust and dirt as I never saw before but in a whirlwind, and made us once more suddenly retreat to our canoe; when, now, being heartily tired of the exploit, I gave orders to row towards the barge, but David still entreated me to allow him to kill the reptile. I was therefore induced to make a third and last attempt in company with him. Then, having once more discovered the snake, we discharged both our pieces at once, and this time with good effect, for he was shot through the head. Captain Stedman now secured the snake, by the aid of one of his servants, by passing a rope with a running noose on it over his head. This was effected with some difficulty, as the reptile, notwithstanding his being mortally wounded, still continued to writhe and twist about in such a manner as to render it dangerous for any person to approach him in this state. He was dragged to the shore, and still continued to swing about like an eel, until he arrived on board; where, upon due consideration it was agreed to convey the immense snake once more on shore, and have him skinned; it proved by measurement, as I before observed, to be twenty two feet seven inches long.

"I have seen them larger than that," observed the Colonel; "the natives of this country will sometimes attack and kill the boa, although it is at all times an enterprise of considerable peril. In some parts of India the skins of these creatures are used for ornamental clothes on account of their uncommon beauty, and as they are extremely rare, they are valued in proportion. Like the alligator, the boa is an object of great veneration, but this arises in all probability, more from the terror than from the love it inspires."

"It has never been my lot to see one," observed Stanley.

"You will be highly gratified," observed the doctor, "provided you are at a respectable distance."

After some further desultory conversation, the party were again on their march homewards; before they arrived, however, they were met and joined by Mr. Natterley, who had ingratiated himself into the good graces of Stanley by his pretended solicitude on behalf of Omelia. He had almost persuaded Stanley that our heroine was no more, and as no communication had been received by any of her friends, his assertion appeared to be corroborated. Stanley had daily become more moody and depressed in spirits. The melancholy circumstances attendant upon the estrangement of his heart's idol made a deep impression upon him, and the corroding influence of disappointment and grief, "which is beauties' canker," had somewhat thinned his features and paled his usually healthy colour. Soon after the incident of the snake, he was alone with Clara, when the latter turned her full gaze upon him, and said :—

"Stanley, you are daily becoming more and more dejected—more than you care to show."

"No," he observed, "not at all; it is but mere fancy on your part."

"The fancy is not confined to me, for all our friends and companions observe your altered demeanour as well as myself; I need not ask the cause, you are grieving for her whom you deem lost to you for ever, and I can readily sympathize with you in nursing a hopeless passion."

"Clara, do not misunderstand me, mine is not a hopeless passion. That girl and I have plighted our troth, and are bound by every human tie to be faithful to one another till death. I on my part shall never break my contract. And I am sure she will keep hers, but it would be vain for me to endeavour to conceal from you that I have serious apprehension as to her fate, so serious that they weigh heavily upon my mind, the more so as I am, or rather my imprudence is, the cause of her sudden departure. You remember that fearful day when she was aroused to a sudden and maddening jealousy. Since that time I have never seen or heard from her.—No, I am wrong though, I did receive one letter bidding me a last final farewell. What am I to think? My worst fears are aroused."

"And her friends! Have they heard nothing from her?"

"No! neither Abdal, Jahnsah, or any one that I can hear of have received any tidings. I am informed by this Mr. Natterley, who seems to take great interest in her welfare, that she has fallen a victim to some treachery in one of the recent outbreaks. He is not acquainted with the whole particulars. Oh, Clara! how agonizing is the thought, if such be really the case, I never will believe in so dreadful a termination to a love which was boundless and self-sacrificing on her part."

"Let us hope not," answered Clara. "To hear you talk, however, one would be disposed to believe there never was woman who loved with such sincerity as her. When in reality there are hundreds, nay, thousands such."

"That may be, but I have not met with them. Clara, we shall never agree upon this point. I fear your own jealous feelings will not admit of your being a dispassionate expositor upon the subject. You have a most worthy and excellent fellow sincerely attached to you, and ought therefore to be blest, and proud in his love, and feel also for my disappointment."

"So I do; I feel acutely for you in this respect; but as to my being blest in the love of Captain Robinson, that is my own affair, or rather as I view it. Need you be told that a woman's heart leaves her without will or volition of her own. She cannot control her fancies, or measure in an even scale the good and bad qualities of her suitors—it is not in her power to do so. In affairs of the heart, a woman is not guided by her reason. I can hardly tell you what she is guided by, or if she is so at all. I do not really believe she is. No, Stanley, it is hardly possibly to divine this secret influence which we mortals know by the name of love. Captain Robinson is a worthy, noble fellow, too noble for me to accept, when I can but give him a second hand—make-believe sort of love. Alas! I feel and know I can never give him my heart and affections as he deserves, and I would not deceive him by similating a passion. I did not feel,"

"Tush!" impatiently exclaimed Stanley. "You will feel it, you ought to feel it, you cannot possibly consider it discreet to reject a man whose whole thoughts are devoted to you, to pursue one whose heart is already engaged; and moreover tells you frankly that he can never return your passion. No, Clara, my dear girl, let us always be as we have been, the best, the sincerest of friends, and for the rest I have told Robinson my sentiments, and whether Omelia be still a denizen of this or another sphere is nothing to this purpose. I can never love another."

Clara grasped his hand, kissed it, and shed abundance of tears in silence.

"I cannot but admire your faithfulness to the object of your attachment. Oh! that it had been mine to have evoked such a noble and sincere passion," she presently exclaimed, and then sunk again into abstraction and silence.

Notwithstanding the pertinacity in her attachment for Stanley, she was beginning gradually to yield to her better reason. After frequent repetitions of such a scene as the one just described, the state of Stanley's real feelings gradually began to dawn upon her. It was certain that she entertained a passion for him, which perhaps no other man could call forth, and it is certain also that at one time the more he avoided and slighted her the more she seemed to persist in nursing an undying affection for him, and it had therefore cost Stanley no small amount of eloquence, backed by an unflinching determination to bring about a better and more healthy tone in her mind. It was therefore a most fortunate occurrence that Captain Robinson so opportunely stepped forward as a candidate for her hand and heart, as this circumstance, to say the least of it, served in a great measure to break her fall.

———

CHAPTER CCXX.

MR. NATTERLEY AND THE THUG—RAGE AND
DISAPPOINTMENT—REMARKABLE AND
UNEXPECTED DISCLOSURES.

WHEN Goryeboo made such a precipitate retreat from Goolooh, he fled on regardless of what had become of his companions, the old adage of "honor among thieves" did not form part of his category of morals. He was so bursting with rage, disappointment and revenge, that he was insensible to any other feeling, so he madly rushed on towards the locality of Mr Natterley. Fleet of foot as he unquestionably was, he had a considerable distance to traverse before he could see his worthy employer, and as he journeyed along, the thought came across him that it was not at all a pleasant task to communicate the unwelcome intelligence to Mr. Natterley, and he begun to question himself about the propriety of his telling him of the complete frustration to their designs, as perhaps that irrate individual might be tempted to take summary vengeance upon him through his son. "And even then I have but to—let me see, declare the fact—Ah!—It might serve me whether or no—it must serve me—if I could know who he is, myself—but that will never be—never!"

Thus reflecting and soliloquising, the Thug proceeded with a somewhat bolder heart towards the appointed spot where he could see or learn about his employer. The latter was felicitating himself upon the perfection of his schemes, by bribing the letter-carrier he had succeeded in keeping all communications from reaching the friends of Omelia. By unwearied attention joined to an oily tongue, he had managed to ingratiate himself into the good graces of Stanley and his brother officers, thus he was enabled to throw dust in the eyes of the latter, and by a well feigned commiseration for our heroine, make him believe he was actuated by the most sincere and philanthropic motives, who as an agent of Messrs. Cottle, Leaf and Cottle, was only too anxious to see Omelia come into her just rights. He had not said that he was the next of kin after our heroine, he had forgotten it perhaps. He was, however, a constant visitor at the officers' quarters, and for the present to enable him to visit them repeatedly and keep a watch on the proceedings of all parties, he had taken up his abode in a bungalow hard by. He was by this means close to all those whom he deemed dangerous to his schemes, viz.— Stanley, Jahnsha, and Abdal, and at the same time, he kept a sharp look out for the letter carrier. To all who made enquiries, Mr. Natterley was represented as an English merchant who was but pursuing his avocations.

Most anxiously had he been awaiting the return of Goryeboo, who was about to accomplish the last grand climax to his nefarious schemes.

Eventually his unworthy emissary arrived, by whose countenance he at once saw that he had failed to accomplish his purpose.

"How, now?" exclaimed Mr. Natterley, "hast thou performed the task successfully? Your looks answer no, speak at once! Have you been able to entrap the game?"

"Do not ask," said Goryeboo, "our scheme answered well enough, I got a messenger to convey your letter to the English camp, and upon her receiving it she at once proceeded to the appointed spot. She suspected treachery upon nearing it, and like a she-tigress as she is, pointed a revolver towards where I was creeping; this was behind some bushes out of which I was about to spring upon her and effect an immediate capture——"

"Well! you were not to be intimidated by a woman, I suppose?"

"I should hardly think so. I quietly stole along under cover of the bushes regardless of her empty threats, and succeeded in pouncing upon her, and passing the cord round her throat."

"Excellent! well!—did you succeed?"

"You shall hear. I had well nigh effected my purposes, when—curses on the meddling fool! I was sprung upon by some stranger who, it appeared had been attracted by the cries of the lad who had conveyed my letter. A desperate struggle ensued between us, and I was well nigh overpowering him, when he succeeded in flinging me from him; and, as I saw some English soldiers hastening to the spot, I could not venture to stop."

"And so you have come back here to tell me this lame story. Perdition!—ten thousand curses upon you for your bungling. I'll have no more of this; every time you come back with some such miserable excuse."

It would be impossible to describe the rage and chagrin evinced by Mr. Natterley, —a defeated prize fighter when the sponge is thrown up—a miser when he sees the hoard he has gathered together confiscated to the crown—a Captain when his vessel dashed against a coral reef—a council when his cause is lost by an unexpected witness appearing within a few minutes of the Judge summing up—a lover when he finds his mistress eloped with Captain Labertash the day before his wedding—a merchant whose insurance has run out a few hours before his worldly wealth is in flames, are but feeble types of what Mr. Natterley felt. He was perfectly wild with rage and disappointment—he paced up and down like a caged hyæna, and glared at his tool and instrument more like a wild animal than any human being.

"But I'll have no more of this!" he exclaimed, after he had indulged in a series of vituperations; this matter shall be brought to a close, and that speedily. It is evident you either care not or will not—which is much the same thing—do this trifling service for me. I believe you are playing fast and loose, and have not, and never had any intention of keeping faith with me, and so I shall hand your son over to the proper authorities at once, and yourself as well."

Goryeboo started back some paces, and drew his tulwar. Mr. Natterley was not taken by surprise; but, with an agility that astonished his companion, he unsheathed a sword which hung by his side, and presented it towards the chest of his companion, at the same time he put himself upon his guard.

"So!" he exclaimed, in a sarcastic tone, "you have at last thrown off the mask, and we are now avowed enemies!—Good!—so be it!—better that than a treacherous ally. I was quite prepared for this; and, indeed, fully expected it—sooner or later. One blast from this, and here he pulled from his breast pocket a small bugle, "and you will be surrounded by English troops, and eventually meet with your just desserts by being blown from a cannon's mouth."

Goryeboo turned ashy pale at these words, and trembled in every limb.

"It is very hard to be treated thus," he said, sulkily, "after I have done all in my power to accomplish what you desired; it is not my fault if I have not succeeded; I have thrice perilled my life, and am willing to do so again. I swear by the Great Spirit that I mean you fair."

"You are beginning to see it will best answer your purpose to speak me fair, but as to your promises—your protestations—your cringing servility—I despise them; I know you, my man, and I tell you that your son you will never see again in this world."

"What do you want of me? Tell me what you would have done, and all that man can do that will I."

"Pshaw!" you know what I want—have known it long enough. You and your scoundrel companions are not wont to make so much trouble in disposing of one life or a dozen for the matter of that, when it suits your purpose; but no more of this, our compact is broken."

"The Thug hesitated and seemed as though he would propitiate his employer by some assurance of his fidelity, which as far as the endeavour to do his behests was concerned there was really no reason to complain. Mr. Natterley took no notice but continued to chafe and pace backwards and forwards with angry strides. The Thug watched him for some moments in silence, when he said more mildly :—

"I think you deal hardly with me, master. If the chances have been against me as yet, there is no reason why they should always be so."

"Ah! you were beginning to show your teeth, my man, a few moments since, and now you would fawn upon me; now a bully and anon a sycophant."

"I mean fair," was Goryeboo's reply, now something more resolute. "To prove this, shall I tell you a secret?"

His companion started.

"That man whom you hold as a hostage of my good faith is not my son! No, nor any relation. More than than this—he is an Englishman!"

Had a thunderbolt fallen at the feet of his companion, or a chasm opened suddenly in the earth, he could not possibly have been more astonished. He regarded the thing with eyes of incredulity.

"An Englishman!" he exclaimed—"Bah! never; do you think I do not know my own countrymen?"

"What I tell you is true. He is indeed an Englishman. At any rate, he had one English parent."

"How came you to know this? and how came he to be brought up as your son? and assume your name?"

"If I were to tell you, it appears so little faith is placed in my word, that I should not be believed."

"Yes—yes you would—proceed, and prove what you say. I have, perhaps, after all been too hasty, and done you an injustice."

"Then, hear me. I am about to confide to you what I have never divulged to any human being, save those who of necessity became aware of the facts. You have imagined that your hostage is my son; but such, I have already told you is not the case. He is, however, without doubt, my adopted son, and I love him quite as much as if he were indeed mine own. If, therefore, you intend to give him up, I must tell you my course of action. It will be my duty, and one from which I shall not shrink in fulfilling, to present myself to the English authorities, and declare who and what he is. Whatever he may be charged with there will be no difficulty in his being exonerated from; for, in whatever outbreaks he has been engaged, they were entirely against his own will. I know it will cost me my life by appearing to save

aim, but that matters not. I have gone through much for him already, and, if it be necessary, will cheerfully lay down my life to save his."

Mr. Natterley looked at his companion in a state of perfect wonderment. He was quite unprepared for any human affection or feeling dwelling within the breast of him who was stained with a thousand crimes.

"I do not understand you, or the tie which binds you to this man," he observed. "He has the complexion and features of one born in your country."

"So he no doubt was born here, but let me tell you all the particulars concerning him. Many years ago I had a little boy of my own, an only son, whom cruel fate snatched from me. I was a happy man then, happy in a good, kind and gentle

wife, who has also passed from me. She died some five or six years before my son, but they both lay buried in one grave."

The Thug heaved a sigh, and paused for a few moments. Mr. Natterley was so unprepared for pathos being evinced by the unmitigated scoundrel before him, that he was perfectly speechless with surprise, and consequently let his companion have it all his own way, without interruption.

"My boy died when he was about seven years old; about a twelvemonth after his death I was journeying through the woods with my companions, and we had encamped for the night; I was a few hundred yards from them when I heard the cries of a child, shrieking and crying alternately. I rushed towards the spot from whence the cries proceeded, and to my infinite

surprise I beheld a full grown tiger stealing through the underwood with a little
boy in his jaws, which he appeared to hold
by his tunic. I was armed only with a
common gun, with an old fashioned lock
made of flint and steel. The piece could
never be relied upon to carry true, and the
chances are that had I fired from where I
stood, I should perhaps not have been able
to even wound the animal. He had evidently observed me, for I could see his
green eyes peering out of the foliage, and
heard a low suppressed growl. I approached nearer, and then saw that the boy
whom he was evidently about to convey to
his lair, to kill and enjoy at his leisure, was
about the same age as my own son whom I
had lost. This seemed to determine me to
make an effort to save his life, so I advanced with cautious steps nearer to where
the beast lay concealed. I covered him
with my piece as I advanced, well knowing
the habits of these animals, to make a
sudden spring upon their foes. The beast,
seeing my intention, let drop the child he
held in his mouth, and rushed out of the
bushes towards me. I let him come as far
as I dare with anything like safety, and
then discharged my gun full at him as he
advanced; the ball entered his chest, and
he rolled over with agony; believing he
was mortally wounded, I drew my tulwar
and advanced to give him a final stroke,
but he had still plenty of life, for he made
a sudden spring and was upon me, and I
was struck to the earth by the weight of
his body. Luckily for me, being so close
upon him, he sprang rather beyond his
mark, and upon my falling to the earth he
was a yard or two from me. It was his
hind quarters which had smote me upon
his making the spring; I had therefore
time to give him a deep gash with my
tulwar before he turned upon me. He
came on, however, notwithstanding this,
and punished me a little with his claws.
I however eventually succeeded in mas-
tering him."

"Upon my word," said Mr. Natterley, "I
should never have given you the credit of
so much heroism in the cause of mercy. I
do not doubt your story, but it seems a
species of knight-errantry, quite foreign to
your nature. What about the child? Did
you seek for it?"

"When I had fairly overcome the tiger,
my first thoughts were directed towards the
boy whom I had seen in the tiger's jaws.
I went towards the spot where I had first
seen the animal, and found the lad on the
ground where he had been let fall. He was a
little injured by the tiger's teeth in the back
and shoulders, but his wounds were but
superficial and where soon healed."

"Well," said Mr. Natterley, "what became of him, you adopted him I suppose."

"I did," answered the Thug. "You are
aware by the rules of our clan we apprentice
youths to our calling and teach them the
art and mysteries of thuggee. My companions were desirous that when the child
was old enough a similar course should be
adopted with him, I said nothing against
this, but the child had clung to me and so
fondled me that in a short time I became
attached to him. Indeed I was so from the
first, and I made up my mind to adopt him.
I have done so, and when he became old
enough I contrived to get off placing him at
the disposal of our gang, and he has never, I
am happy to say, followed our calling.
It has caused me much trouble, and many
serious quarrels with my companions, to
prevent this, but I managed to succeed by
taking him away to my own home and
putting him under the charge of my trusty
servant and housekeeper, whom you already
know."

"Do you mean to tell me that you have
brought up this man from childhood without recompense? Without making any
effort when he was first discovered, to find
out his parents?"

"Yes, every attempt was made, both by
myself and companions, as of course they
were anxious to have some reward for the
restoration of the child, but all our efforts
were unavailing. The child told us that
his father was an Englishman, and that he
had been brought up in a farmer's cottage
by an Indian family, but we could never
find out where this was situated or the
name of the farmer. It appeared, however,
that one day a tiger had entered the thatch
of the cottage and seized hold of the boy,
and bore him off for a long distance. He
lost all recollection of all that happened
and had but just recovered his senses when
he screamed out, and I rushed to his assistance."

"Umph, this story sounds like one conjured up by the agency of romance."

"It is strictly true in every particular,
exactly as I have described it."

"Be this as it may," observed Mr. Natterley, "it possesses but little interest for
me, and has nothing to do with our undertaking. You must devise some means to
carry out my wishes, or there must be an
end to our friendly understanding, and
then you know the consequences. I am
not a man to be thus trifled with."

"Give me a few days to reflect upon the
matter, and I promise to find out some
means of effecting our object. By inter-
cepting the letters we are acquainted with
all her proceedings, and it must go hard if
we cannot find another chance."

"Well," I will try you once more, and give you four days to make up your mind upon the future course of action, and if you fail a third time dread my just vengeance."

Gorzeboo promised to do all in his power, and with this assurance he left his employer, who upon his departure became sunk in deep reflection knitting his brows, he was quite absorbed in his own dark ruminations.

"So," he presently exclaimed, "this man then is an Englishman after all; I suspected as much long ago, and there is a mystery about him which yet remains to be developed. Ah, the greatest caution will be required, and under any circumstances I must and will retain possession of him. That tiger slayer, whom I have seen with Stanley—he spoke of a child being carried off by a tiger. Suppose this should be him? I must set enquiries on foot—but caution is the word, let me not be too precipitate—I have not been to my esteemed friends, Messrs. Cottle and Leaf, a complimentary visit would perhaps not be amiss now—a friendly call, from the great esteem I entertain for that respectable firm, Ah! Ah! I must see to that, egad, I have my hands full—Oh, if I could but remove that obnoxious Indian girl out of the way, and see her gathered to her fathers all would be well—Confusion!—to be thus thwarted—no matter, it must be accomplished This man speaks the truth about his supposed son—I think so—Oh, yes, there is an evidence of that in his manner, only that such an arrant scoundrel should coolly talk to me of his feelings. A blackguard, whose daily avocation is murder. Murder!—Ah! that word sounds harsh and discordant!—Murder! What a fearful signification does the utterance of it strike upon our senses? And yet thousands are being ruthlessly slain for some imaginary quarrel between two crowned mortals. Why should I hesitate upon sacrificing one for my own particular benefit? Pshaw! It is but a name. An advantage offered to me which I ought to have the courage to accept, and will! And then I shall be rich—amazingly rich—armed with the world's idol—wealth. Who is there to question how it is obtained? Who cares? Ah! no. I have toiled for years, prostrated all my best feelings before this sordid God, and it is too late now to turn saint. Indeed it does not suit me—no. I must at any cost possess the estates of the bankrupt Harcourt. He knew me when a boy—was kind to me, then although in after years he turned his back upon me. Well, who so fit to inherit his property? This Stanley, easy love sick fool, suspects nothing and is lulled by my frank open manner. Ah! Ah!"

After all there is more to laugh at in this world, to a man who has the wit to discover the humour, than there is to weep over; "to a man who has the wit to discover and appreciate its humour." Thus soliloquising, he was sowing his seeds in the hopes of reaping a golden harvest. Whether his seeds produced tares, briars, and brambles remains to be seen.

If indefatigable industry—unscrupulous principles—artful machinations—and guilty emissaries ensured success, then he most certainly seemed in a fair way of arriving at the height of his ambition. But man builds up habitations for others to inhabit; plants trees for others to fell; gathers wealth for others to spend.

CHAPTER CCXXI.

GRIEF OF ABDAL—HIS VISIT TO STANLEY.

DAY after day did Abdal watch, anxiously, to receive some tidings from his friend and relative, Omelia. He had considerably recovered his health and strength, and by the aid of the watchful Jungh, he was sufficiently restored to be able to get about, although still unable to boast of his wonted strength. He had interrogated the letter carrier respecting any epistles addressed to either himself or Tallee Sheboo. The reader will no doubt remember that upon Abdal's parting with our heroine, he had advised her to address her communications to this woman, to prevent the possibility of her enemy, the Thug, ascertaining Omelia's whereabouts. Had this advice have been followed, there is every probability that our heroine's letters would have reached their destination, and the machinations of Messrs. Natterley and Gorzeboo would have been, to a certain extent, thwarted. But, unfortunately, Omelia had either forgotten the injunctions of her faithful Abdal, or else had deemed herself sufficiently secure with her English companions, so that she disregarded the caution. The letters she had dispatched had been addressed to Abdal and Jahnsha, all of which had been intercepted. She had not sent any communication to Stanley, and even if she had, it would not have reached him, as the letter carrier was in the pay of Mr. Natterley, and would have delivered it to Gorzeboo.

The worst fears had taken possession of the mind of Abdal. He now began fully to give way to the belief in Omelia having fallen a victim to the silent, secret, and dreadful mode of death practised by the

748 THE SEPOY'S DAUGHTER.

Thugs. Poor Abdal, he had been a sufferer, both mentally and physically; his was a faithful heart; constant in his attention and solicitude for Omelia, whom he had followed through all her trials and misfortunes, with the fidelty of a watchful dog. The comparison may not be a very lofty or elegant one, but it conveys a deep meaning, nevertheless; for ah, my friend, man is often times more selfish than the obedient animal who attends him as a companion and protector.

Towards the close of the evening, Abdal was seated outside the door of his bungalow. The evening was calm and peaceful, and nature seemed to be gradually lulled to repose. The golden sun was sinking behind the Himalaya mountains, which appeared to spring from a purple gulf of haze. It was a lovely scene which lay before the open porch of Abdal's habitation: nature seemed to be here a prodigal: every kind of tropical, parisitical, and orchidious plant seemed teeming with vigorous vegetable life. Round the doorway of the bungalow Jungh had trained up immense beautiful creeping plants; and otherwise the habitation gave indications of care and attention.

Jungh was leaning against the open doorway while his master was seated in an easy chair formed of bamboo canes. He had placed aside the book he had been but lately reading and was contemplating the setting sun, whose spent shafts were now robbed of their meridian power and were being gathered up into a golden guinea. Abdal was leaning his chin upon his right hand while his elbow rested on the arm of his chair. He had been watching and reflecting thus for a long time, while his attendant who was observing him the while seemed tenacious of disturbing him in his reflections. After some time had elapsed Abdal turned his looks towards the habitation, and said:—

"Jungh, are you there?"

In a moment his attendant was by his side.

"My trusty companion," said Abdal, "without you, I should never be viewing so fine a sight as this which now lays before us, stretched out for miles and miles;" and he waved his hand towards the spot indicated.

"I wonder, Jungh, if the great spirit permits her to see our god go down in all his glory and effulgence, or whether she has passed away from us."

It should be mentioned, that when Abdal spoke of the sun as a god going to rest, that it is a common belief among many of the native inhabitants of India that the sun is veritably a god, and is worshipped accordingly. It is not surprising,

this, with their untutored minds. Indeed, it appears a natural sequence, considering their natural character. They see the sun, the great giver of light and life; beneath his rays seeds germinate, and the earth becomes clothed with verdure, and vegetation springs up with a rapidity that would appear almost incredible to our European ideas. What wonder then, that the poor superstitous, untutored Hindoos should worship the sun as a god whose bounty knows no bounds.

"I begin to give up all hopes of ever seeing her again," continued Abdal; "it is not all probable, if she were alive, that I should be left so long in ignorance of her proceedings, and so utterly neglected. No, Jungh," he said, as he heaved a deep sigh; "I do indeed now give up all hopes, and fear my worst suspicions have been realised. "Oh that I had gone with her when she departed hence."

"My good master, you could not!—you forget how weak you were at the time."

"True, true; but now, Jungh, I can stand this suspense no longer, and I have been thinking that I will set out to-morrow, and endeavour to find her."

His attendant looked at him with some surprise, and said:—

"But what clue have you?"

"I know not of any, or I should have been off long since, but I have been thinking that it is possible Lieutenant Stanley may have heard, and if he is still at the same quarters as when she departed, I shall be able to ascertain. I will journey there to-morrow, and gather all the information I can."

"Cannot I go?" enquired Jungh.

"No! he might think it a liberty; he knows me, and would, I am sure, be sufficiently aware that my enquiries were prompted by the best motives."

It was in vain that every effort and argument was used by Jungh to prevent his master departing upon this expedition. He represented to him that it was imprudent to leave his present abode, as Omelia was very likely to find her way back when perhaps they least expected it. Every argument was, however, futile; and, on the following morning Abdal, staff in hand and wallet on back proceeded on his journey. He was weak enough, poor man, but was borne up by an attendant—hope—who is the best to direct us mortals in this nether world during our weary pilgrimage.

In the due course of time he arrived at the cantonment of Colonel Bridport, when he was introduced to Stanley, who had not seen him for so long a period; he of course naturally thought that some tidings from his mistress was about to be conveyed through Abdal. He flushed with excitement, but what was his disappointment to find that Abdal, instead of bringing any news or message, had come himself to seek information.

"Lieutenant Stanley," began Abdal, "I am and have been for some time past, in the greatest state of anxiety respecting my friend and relation Omelia, and you will therefore excuse my waiting upon you to make inquiries. Have you heard from her?"

"Indeed no my good friend, I was in hopes that you had come to bring some tidings. I have heard nothing, neither has Jahnsha; but I am informed by my friend here," and he now directed Abdal's attention to Mr. Natterley, who was in the apartment. "I am informed by this gentlemen, that she whom I love beyond all else in the universe, has been snatched from us by the cruel and relentless hand of death."

Stanley paused and sank into a chair, overcome by his feelings.

Abdal was horror struck when he heard these words, and stared with surprise at the immaculate Mr. Natterley, who put on as rueful an expression to his countenance as it was possible for him to command on so short a notice.

"Then no doubt it is as I feared," sorrowfully exclaimed Abdal.

"Ah, what mean you?" enquired Stanley anxiously. "How did you last part with your friend? Alas, you know perhaps, that a fatal and unfortunate jealousy, as uncalled for on her part as it has proved to be ruinous to us all, caused an enstrangement between us. You know this, I suppose?"

"Indeed, yes, she informed me of such upon the occasion of our last interview. I was ill then or I would have followed her footsteps, had it been to the furthermost end of the world, but this was not to be, I knew she was surrounded by dangers which required the utmost watchfulness to surmount—dangers which my heart sinks within me, and my frame trembles with agitation as I reflect upon them. I knew at the time of her departure that she was being pursued by a Thug, who was bribed by some unprincipled, worthless scoundrel to accomplish her destruction."

It is impossible to convey the amount of surprise these words occasioned to those present. Mr. Natterley, in spite of his habitual control over his feelings was perfectly panic struck. In an instant it flashed across his mind that either Gorzeboo or some of his companions had proved treacherous and betrayed his secret machinations. He however with his usual caution made no sign of his feelings, although it could not fail to be observed by anyone present; Stanley of course attributed his emotion to commiseration for Omelia.

But the former was so prostrated at the words Abdal had just uttered, that he had hardly noticed anything around. He begged of Abdal to furnish him with every particular of his last parting with his enslaver, who immediately complied with his request, expressing his surprise at not having heard from Omelia agreeable to her last promise.

"I fear," sighed Mr. Natterley, "that there is now no hope of her ever communicating with any one again in this world. It is sad, very sad, to think that she should not have lived to inherit her just rights; but we are all creatures of circumstances, and at the disposal of a higher power than any human tribunal," and he uttered these observations in such a moralising tone as to impress upon his hearers the depth of his commiseration and sympathy.

"Who do you imagine this man was? This Thug, I think you call him? he must have been actuated I should suppose by some spirit of revenge."

"I fear he was prompted by a worse passion," answered Abdal. "From what I have heard, and but just now described, I fear he is a hired assassin, employed by even a more atrocious and worthless scoundrel than himself."

"It appears impossible there can be such an unprincipled person in existence," exclaimed Mr. Natterley, as he turned up his eyes in horror at the contemplation of such enormity. "No, I never can believe in such an amount of moral turpitude."

"Oh!" said Stanley, bitterly, "how disastrous has been the career of this unfortunate, noble-minded, self-sacrificing girl; a perfect environment of painful difficulties appear to have attended her path. The contemplation of them, and her probable untimely fate, weigh me down to the lowest depths of despair."

"I will know the worst," said Abdal, "I will search her out, and never rest till I ascertain the truth. I devote the remainder of my unhappy life for this purpose alone. If she has fallen, and I should be fortunate enough to discover her assassin, he shall meet with the direst vengeance."

Colonel Bridport came in at this point of the conversation, and Stanley made him acquainted with all that had occurred; he at the same time introduced to him Abdal, whom he mentioned to his senior officer as one of the most faithful and worthy subjects among the native population of India. The Colonel saw that Stanley was quite broken down in spirit; as, indeed, he had been for a considerable time past. The Colonel endeavoured to put a more cheerful face upon the matter; and said, in as confident a tone as he could assume:—

"Cheer up, Stanley. After all, I do not see any grounds for you to give way in this manner. After all, the whole affair is only surmise. You know her impetuous wilful nature; and she may be still safe under the protection of good friends. It is not the usual characteristic of Englishmen to despair for trifles. Wait with patience, and I will answer for it all will yet be well."

"I wish I could think so."

"Never fear, man—think the best. Let us not meet troubles half way. The time will come, let us hope, when we can afford to laugh at these idle fears. I have not lost confidence in all turning out well and satisfactory."

"I hope so," chimed in the sympathising Mr. Natterley. "I am going to the agents, Messrs. Cottle, Leaf, and Cottle, at Calcutta, perhaps they may have heard something that may throw some light upon this subject."

"You will be doing me a great service if you will kindly make all necessary enquiries," exclaimed Stanley. Mr. Natterley grasped his hand, pressed it, and nodded his head in silent eloquence, expressive of his deep anxiety, and affectionately took his departure.

"Ah," he exclaimed, when he had got some short distance from Colonel Bridport's cantonment, "so we have another dull-eyed, soft-tongued sympathetic fool to deal with, who evinces so much solicitude for this half bred hussey, as though she were some eastern princess or goddess. By the Lord, she seems to drive men crazy. The witch bears a charmed life, I do believe. I'faith, my curiosity is aroused to see her, to know what stuff she is made of, to thus charm all beholders. Perhaps she would cast a soft influence over me. Ah! I think I can chance that—yes, I think so. This sickly looking Hindoo, though, he has ascertained something about Gorzeboo, although, evidently, in quite a chance way. Not, as I had anticipated, through any treachery on his part. No, I believe the scoundrel means the thing that's right. If not, why he knows my determination. So now for my friends Messrs. Cottle and Co.

CHAPTER CCXXII.

THE OFFICE OF MESSRS. COTTLE, LEAF AND COTTLE—MR. NATTERLEY'S INTERVIEW.

FOR once, Mr. Natterley had spoken the truth, when he informed Stanley that he was about to proceed to the office of the Messrs. Cottle and Co. His anxiety to have his schemes matured kept him in a state of continual restlessness, and now that Gorzeboo had a short time allowed him to devise some new course of action, his master thought it a good opportunity to enliven up his mind by a visit to the agents of the deceased Mr. Harcourt.

He had neither heard or communicated with the firm in question, and began to be on the fidget and fume, in case anything might have oozed out respecting her who stood in the way of his inheriting such a large amount of worldly wealth. Indeed, it is a matter of surprise that the advertisements had not been observed by some of the English officers who were attached to Havelock's flying column, and it is more than probable that they were, and passed over without notice, as the name by which they knew our heroine was not mentioned in the advertisement, and consequently it was not probable they would guess it referred to her. Neither Major nor Mrs. Forester would have recognised their friend as the daughter of Rose Harcourt, so, as the reader already knows, she was in complete ignorance of the large fortune which only awaited her appearance to claim. If she had known of it, the probability is that it would have had but little weight with her. It was not worldly wealth she coveted, unless it was accompanied by the love of him upon whom she had set her heart.

When Mr. Natterley arrived at the office of Messrs. Cottle, Leaf, and Cottle, he found the partners too busily engaged to see him immediately. He was shown into the waiting room, and the head clerk came forward to know if he could attend to him. Was it—an account?—a consignment? or an ordinary transaction that he might in any way forward. He received short negatives in reply to these questions, and disappeared, leaving the gentleman to wait patiently the partner's leisure. I dare say you, reader, whose eye has wandered over this prolix tale have had the felicity of waiting in the outer chamber of a lawyer's office (happy many if you have not,) but if you have, you will agree with us that it is invested with little or no romance, and seldom with pleasurable sensations. The musty papers and parchments—the iron cases—the cobwebbed corners—the dingy windows—the remorseless clock which pertinaciously continues ticking—six—eight—six—eight—reminding you of that host of ills enumerated under the comprehensive title of costs!—all these tend to throw a damper upon the spirits which it is difficult to shake off. We know not if we are singular in the idea, but we think it almost impossible for a man to be facetious while waiting in the anti-chamber for Messrs. Clawem and Clutchem: of course we have a great respect for the law, but "'tis distance lends enchantment to the view." Mr. Natterley waited with exemplary patience; he examined every article of interest in the "hall of dazzing light" into which he had been so kindly shown. On one box he noticed the name of Lord Fiddlefaddle, in another the name of the Viscountess Jocelyn Squashtottle was inscribed in large letters—in "upper case," as the printers would say. Then an interesting umbrella-stand attracted his notice; next a bust of Lord Eldon. Lawyers always have that bigoted old chancellor in their office.

You never see the trenchant and combative features of Brougham adorning the offices of a solicitor,· his sweeping measures of reform having cruelly robbed them of all those enormous amount of costs which under the old regimen were the bulwark of justice and the corner-stone of our constitution. Having carefully scanned the expressive and playful features of the wise old Chancellor Eldon, who took so long a time to give a decision, that he let three generations die, before he could arrive at a just conclusion upon the legality of their claims. Mr. Natterley turned his eyes towards the desk upon which six pens were scratching paper with painful distinctness, these mighty weapons were wielded by six clerks, whose features were of course out of compliment to their employers of a parchment hue; Mr. Natterley scanned the different expressions on each of their countenances, and to beguile the time, made a running commentary to himself upon each—as to what were their feelings (if they had any), what their duties, pleasures, and their probable life, having summed this all up satisfactorily to himself, he looked around like "Alexander for new worlds to conquer," when he was aroused by the green baize door opening, and the head of Mr. Leaf emerged from the opening, as he said——

"Mr. Chisel—the papers connected with 'Jukes v. Squabbleright.'"

"Ah! Mr. Natterley, you will pardon us keeping you waiting," and he shook the gentleman by the hand and disappeared again behind the green baize door, which seemed to his visitor to have the appearance of a verdant coffin lid. Indeed, to speak the truth, the whole place had a tomb-like appearance; with its wills, post obit bonds, and leases of estates, granted to men whose own leases had long since run out, and who had paid the last debt we are most of us unwilling enough to pay, viz., the debt of nature. One of the musty boxes was ransacked by Mr. Chisel and an assistant clerk; and, eventually, after tossing over the last wishes of defunct men, he succeeded in finding the papers of Jukes v. Squabbleright. As the door opened Mr. Natterley caught the sound of a voice of a deep toned plethoric, who, with great volubility, was detailing to the partners how hardly he had been used. To have heard his injured tone, which he assumed, in the details of his woes, you would have imagined his care was the most harrowing it was possible for any one to conceive.

As the green baize door was left ajar, Mr. Natterley was enabled to catch a considerable portion of the conversation; from what he could make out, it appeared that the gentleman had bought an estate for a "mere song," as the saying is. He had given three thousand pounds for a noble estate in India, which, some few years after he had bought it, turned out, in consequence of the rail passing near it, and the neighbourhood becoming an important one, to be worth nearly ten times what he had originally given for it. This cause of grievance appeared to be with his next door neighbour, who occupied a farm immediately contiguous to his. Across a small piece of land which jutted out between the two estates there had been a right of way formed by custom for the farmer to drive his cattle home. The gentleman who had been explaining his injuries to the lawyers had disputed this right of way, and asserted the ground in question to be his entirely.

The farmer offered to forego and give up to him double the amount of land in another part rather than rush into litigation, but this was not enough. It was this identical piece of land the other insisted upon retaining. Its intrinsic value could not possibly amount to many shillings, nevertheless it was the cause of an expensive lawsuit. The gentleman finding it was a difficult point to ascertain even if the land were his at all, and a still more difficult question to contend was the right of way. In consequence of this, he caused it to be planted with rice, there being a great deal of that grain cultivated on his estate. The farmers' cattle had trodden down this said rice in their passage to and fro, and the present action was instituted to recover damages sustained to the crop. The loss was estimated to be three or four pounds of rice, value at the utmost one shilling and sixpence sterling. A surveyor had been employed to make a correct draft of the land in question, and an enormous amount of costs had been entailed over this paltry litigious action. To have heard the plaintiff indulge in a voluble category of his woes and injuries, the listener would have been led to imagine that the speaker had been the most injured of mortals. He detained Messrs. Cottle and Leaf so long a time that Mr. Natterley's patience was becoming quite exhausted. The surveyor's plan was canvassed over and over again, and there seemed to be no end to the intricacy of the question; but eventually Mr. Natterley had the pleasure of seeing the hot and irrate litigant emerge from the lawyer's office; but even after this he detained Mr. Leaf at the outer door in long consultation. At length, however, he fairly took his departure, when Mr. Natterley was conducted into the presence of the two partners. The elder Mr. Cottle received him politely, and handed him to one of the ponderous office chairs, and waited patiently his commands: like a cautious old lawyer he was not anxious to say too much.

"Well, observed his visitor; "I was passing through Calcutta once more, and thought it advisable to just give you a drop in to know if you have any news about the Harcourt affair. Any application from the supposed heir-at-law?"

"Not as yet, I believe," was the cautious answer.

"Ah, no, I should have been surprised if you had; indeed I believe it to be an impossibility. Since I left you last I have made the most searching enquiries in every quarter, and find that this Indian girl has been removed to another sphere; and is, therefore, not likely to put in an appearance here, to use a legal term. Ah! ah!"

"How have you obtained this information? Are you able to substantiate it upon evidence?"

"Not as yet, to use your own phrase; but there will be no doubt about my ultimately being able to do so. Her admirer and lover, Lieutenant Stanley is fully aware of her demise, and mourns her as dead. In fact, it is at his instigation that I have been induced to call upon you; for, to say the truth, although, of course, it would be ridiculous for me to say that I should not be glad to inherit the wealth left by Harcourt; still, at the same time, it would be very repugnant to my feelings as a man and a Christian to do so, to the prejudice of any just claimant, should there be such in existence."

Mr. Cottle gave the speaker a graceful nod at this fine sentiment, and no doubt gave him at the same time credit for about as much sincerity as is usual in such cases. Still it is necessary to keep up a number of fictions in all legal transactions; and, as far as the belief in the integrity of Mr. Natterley was concerned, it was a fiction of the wildest character.

"I may appear, and doubtless I do," continued the last speaker; "seem importunate respecting the settlement of this affair."

"Ah no, not at all, it is but natural your anxiety to bring it to an issue one way or another, If Lieutenant Stanley has any just reason to suppose that this party we were speaking of is deceased, I should suppose there can be no difficulty in furnishing us with all the particulars. No one would be so likely as himself to know the fate of his mistress, for I believe he and the party were betrothed to one another some long time since. I should place the utmost reliance upon the word and honour of Lieutenant Stanley, for he is an officer who does honour to the British Service, and his word is quite enough to satisfy us, still we must have legal evidence when so weighty a matter as this is concerned."

"Ah yes, of course I should wish you to have the most direct and indubitable proofs."

"Ye--s, and should we—are you sure Mr. Natterley, that you are right in your surmise respecting this young girl's death?" and here the speaker looked hard at his visitor as though he would read his very thoughts. Mr. Natterley winced under the fixed gaze of the lawyer, when somewhat recovering himself, he exclaimed suddenly and rather indignantly :—

"Right, of course! or I should not say so. You do not imagine that I am here with some trumped up idle tale?"

"I have never ventured to propound such a proposition," was the rejoinder, uttered in the mildest accents.

"You seemed by your manner to imply a doubt."

"My dear Sir, we always have a doubt until proof is obtained."

"This was the old doctrine of the blundering Eldon, who lived upon doubts and went on doubting for more than half a century, much to the edification of the suitors in the Chancery Court, many of whom made up their minds to trot off to another world, rather than wait here for his decision in the causes.

"My reason for asking you so pointedly whether you were quite certain as to the correctness of your information was this :— we suppose we have a clue————"

Mr Natterley turned ashy pale at these

words and fidgetted in his chair in a state of feverish excitement.

"Ah—indeed—you have, eh?"

"We think so," was the careless rejoinder.

"Pray what is it?"

Both Mr. Cottle and Mr. Leaf smiled blandley in unison, and gently shook their heads, as the former said, in soft and silvery accents—

"That we are not at present enabled to disclose."

Mr. Natterley assumed as careless an air as it was possible for him to command, and entered into some further desultory conversation, not immediately bearing upon the subject which lay nearest to his thoughts.

He was too well acquainted with the character of the two partners not to clearly understand that it would be impossible for him

to prevail upon them to enter into further particulars, and he, therefore, took as graceful a departure from the office as he could assume.

The announcement made by the partners that they were in possession of some clue to our heroine, kept him on tenter hooks.

He was at a perfect loss to imagine what it could be. Doubts and fears chafed his sordid spirit, and caused him to conjure up a host of imaginary and unsubstantial chimeras. Well nigh distracted with the thought that the prize he had so fondly hoped to obtain was about to be snatched from his rapacious grasp, he hastened on to put inquiries afoot in all quarters where he thought it at all likely for him to obtain information to solve the mystery.

In all Omelia's letters, which he had

opened and perused, not a word was mentioned about the property in question, and he was therefore led to suppose that at present she was in entire innocence upon the subject.

Still the words, brief as they were, which had fallen from Mr. Cottle were pregnant with a potent meaning, and fell upon his ear like a death knell to his hopes of aggrandisement.

CHAPTER CCXXIII.

A RETROSPECTIVE GLANCE.—ATTACK ON A CANTONMENT.—ESCAPE OF ENSIGN LIGHTFOOT.

It will be now necessary to go back to an earlier period of the Indian revolt, and leave for a short time the more immediate actions of our heroine, Lieutenant Stanley, Mr. Natterley, and all the other personages with whom the reader is well acquainted, and, let us hope, interested.

It is needful for the further understanding of the events which have to be recorded, as they follow thickly one after another, that this retrospective glance should be read with some attention, it being an important pendent upon the more direct course of our narrative.

The reader will no doubt remember in the description of the occupants of the beseiged fort that mention was made of Ensign Lightfoot being one of the party of Europeans. We have seen how at the eleventh hour this band of warriors were almost miraculously preserved. We must hasten to record a passage in the career of Ensign Lightfoot which occurred in the very earliest portion of the Indian outbreak.

At the time when Delhi was in the hands of the insurgents, and the native army of India appeared to have it all their own way, and threaten the entire extermination of the British, Ensign Lightfoot belonged to a cantonment a few miles from the fatal city of Delhi. The sepoys rose, and, as was usual in most, and indeed all cases where they gained the ascendancy, committed an indiscriminate and wholesale slaughter amongst their officers, and burnt their bungalows.

It was in vain for Ensign Lightfoot's superiors in command to endeavour to stem the torrent which was overwhelming them. A dreadful carnage ensued, too dreadful to expiate upon here.

Nevertheless, they endeavoured to sell their lives as dearly as possible. In the midst of the *emute* Ensign Lightfoot fought gallantly, surrounded by his enemies, who were fast overpowering him. One of his opponents struck the sword from his

hand, and was about to consign him to instant death, when the opposing tulmar was arrested in its progress by a young sepoy, who received the deadly weapon upon his own, thus warding off the blow. He, at the same time, spoke something to the insurgents which stayed their sanguinary proceedings.

He then hastily bid Lightfoot follow him, assuring the English officer that he was actuated by the most friendly motives. The two managed to escape the dense mob of savage miscreants who were at their work of destruction on all sides.

After they had emerged into a more unfrequented locality, the young man paused a moment, and then addressed the officer whom he had saved from death.

"Ensign Lightfoot," he exclaimed, "you are safe so far, but now what more I can do it is hard to say."

"You know me, then?" said the ensign. "You are not belonging to any of our companies?"

"No," was the laconic answer.

"Indeed; then whence this act of kindness and mercy?"

"No matter. Let it suffice that you are safe at present. You did me a service some long time ago, and do not say, or suppose, that an Hindoo is incapable of gratitude."

The ensign bowed his head, and stared at the speaker as though he would fain discover some recollection of his features, but the scrutinising glance with which he surveyed his companion failed to enlighten him upon the subject.

"I would wish to convey you to a place of safety," said the Hindoo, "but, alas, we are so surrounded by desperate and determined enemies, that I know not how to accomplish it. For myself, I live so far away that it would be worse than useless for us to endeavour to gain my habitation, and, indeed, even then I question if you would be safe, and, to say the truth, even my own life may be perilled by the attempt."

"Do not, I pray you, risk your own safety for my sake," said Lightfoot. "Leave me, my friend, with many heartfelt thanks for your timely succour and good intentions. Leave me to seek my own safety as best I can, and if I should escape, and meet you at a future period, believe me you shall not go unrewarded for your generous act of consideration towards me."

"If I abandon you now your fate is certain. You know not how invested the whole of your path is with the most malignant of foes. No, that will never do; your companions in arms have met with a dreadful fate, and yours will be one similar to them unless some place of refuge is found, where you may lay concealed till such time as you may find safe convoy to your fellow country-men. Even now I am afraid to stir, fearful lest we light upon some of your enemies.

The speaker paused irresolute, doubtful as to how he had best proceed. While debating with himself, he was startled from his reverie by the sudden appearance of a figure across his path, who called out in some surprise—

"Goolooh!"

It was, indeed, no other than Goolooh who had been instrumental in saving Light-foot's life, and whose acquaintance the reader has already made some few chapters back.

The man who had uttered his name, in some surprise was Tamneegal

"What is this?" said the latter as he ob-served Lightfoot with Goolooh. "Escorting one of our enemies."

"Yes; one whom I am desirous of saving from destruction. By our good fellowship, I conjure you to aid me in this object."

Tamneegal shook his head disapprovingly.

"I am not yours upon that subject," he said, sulkily; "It would be treason against my own clan."

Goolooh explained to him that he was de-termined to serve the European officer at all risks, and after a long and earnest appeal, he appeared to have overcome the scruples of his fellow countryman, and succeeded in wringing from him a reluctant consent to the proposition.

"If you are bent upon this object," said Tamneegal, "I see but one course to adopt. It is an alternative I am very unwilling to adopt, but it is the only one that we can have recourse to under the circumstances. This officer must trust to my honour, and lay concealed in an unoccupied portion of my bungalow. I think there he might do so for a long period, for it has the reputation of being haunted by bad spirits, and it is, there-fore, not at all probable that any of our com-panions would seek to discover him."

"Excellent thought," exclaimed Goolooh. "My good Tamneegal, will you for once serve me in this matter, without seeking to know further my motives?"

"It shall be done," was the reply.

Upon this understanding the three indi-viduals took their way along

Lightfoot felt of course that he was en-tirely at the mercy and disposal of the two companions whom he accompanied, and passively resigned himself to their guidance —indeed he had no other alternative.

They proceeded through a savage and un-frequented part of the country for many miles, occasionally dodging on one side, and laying concealed, when a party of mutinous sepoys crossed their path. When these had passed without observing them, they again proceeded on their journey.

After travelling several more weary miles, they at length came in sight of a ruinous and apparently untenanted bungalow. The greater portion of it seemed to have tumbled completely into decay; a wing of the build-ing appeared a perfect ruin, and was em-bowered in lichens and parasitical plants, which appeared to hold it together. The scenery around was of a savage character, in consonance with the building itself.

The shades of evening were beginning to descend, and Lightfoot, as he contemplated the place, was not surprised to find that it had the reputation of being haunted.

"Yonder apartment has been shut up for years," said Tamneegal, as he directed the attention of his two companions to the wing of the building, which jutted out at right angles from the house itself. "In that, sir, I think you may lay concealed with safety. It would not be advisable for you to ever enter the habitation itself, as it is the resort of many of my companions, who would treat you with little mercy if they should discover you."

"I am entirely at your disposal, and of course must be directed in all my move-ments and actions by your better discretion," said Lightfoot. Tamneegal gave a nod of acquiesence to this sentiment, and then pro-ceeded to observe, "I shall afford you such shelter as my friend here desires. You must effect an entrance into yonder apartment through the window. This can be easily accomplished, by climbing up the tree you see yonder in close proximity to it. Once there, you are safe for a time at all events, and must await future circumstances to de-termine your ulterior proceedings. In the present state of the country, your destruction would be inevitable, without this course were adopted, for however we might be disposed to you, our efforts would be entirely thwarted by more determined foes, against whose re-venge our two arms would be useless."

"I am bound to you for the succour thus kindly profferred," said the ensign. "It is too early to talk of rewarding your services in my behalf There will be time enough for that when I am safely delivered, but trust me, my friends, you will not be for-gotten."

"I am not acting in the expectation of receiving any reward," said Tamneegal, somewhat curtly, "your race are doomed to be for ever extinguished from our country before long. Nevertheless, as you have done my friend here a service, why we will try and save your life, till such time as you can with safety journey back to your own country."

This speech was uttered with intended dignity, which Lightfoot received with be-coming gravity. "Any port in a storm," is an old axiom, and it was not a time for Lightfoot to enter into any dispute which might compromise him in the opinion of his two companions.

Having arrived close to the wing of the habitation which Tamneegal had before directed their attention, he sent Goolooh to reconnoitre, to see if there was anybody in sight near the bungalow. The latter returned and informed them that the coast was clear, and Tamneegal proceeded to effect an entrance. Near to the window there grew a tree called the Indian Jack, the trunk of which afforded facilities for climbing. The branches of this tree sprang out sufficiently near to enable the climber to swing himself on to the sill of the window. Tamneegal mounted the tree in question with considerable celerity, and having alighted on the window sill, he sprang gently into the apartment, and then directed Lightfoot to follow his example, who lost no time in obeying his directions, which having accomplished, Goolooh followed. It was a ruinous looking apartment the two had so dexterously entered. The furniture in it seemed of a bye-gone age. It had evidently been costly, but had sunk into decay. The curtains which hung around the couch, were of the choicest fabric, interlaced with golden threads and silk of azure hue, but time had bereft them of more than half their original beauty, as he will some day or other serve you and I, my friend, if we but live long enough for time to carve crows feet and furrows in our faces. Tamneegal directed the attention of Lightfoot to the couch, and said—

"There you will be able to seek repose. This has been the resting place of one of our oldest princes in India, now long since gathered to his fathers—not however before he had been dispoiled of most of his possessions by your countrymen, which caused him to die of a broken heart."

"Peace be with him," said Lightfoot, "be he whomsoever he may. Has this been then a portion of an ancient palace?" he inquired, as his eyes wandered round the apartment, whose ceilings and walls were fretted with many rich and gorgeous devices.

"Yes," answered Tamneegal, "this is the ruins of an ancient palace, once occupied with sumptuous pomp by the good prince Laverah Doulah, whose race has for ever passed away from the earth. This building is only a small portion of the original palace occupied by the prince. The greater part of it has been destroyed, and this has remained unoccupied for many years, but there is enough left to afford you a shelter in the hour of need."

Lightfoot gazed with curious eyes upon the apartment, which had upon it the mouldering dust of ages. It struck him, as some-thing singular, that the original habitation of one of the dethroned princes of India, who had been dispoiled of his rights by the British, should afford him protection and shelter. The manner and bearing of Tamneegal was sufficiently friendly to give him assurance of his sincerity. Nevertheless, it appeared rather to be that of a man who had made up his mind to play a certain part from some cause or other, which was contrary to his natural instincts. He observed however, after Lightfoot had inspected the apartment, that he might rely upon being guarded with zealous care, so much so indeed, that he would be entirely alone.

"I shall myself," said Tamneegal, "bring you what meals you may require, until such time as you can safely leave, and when that takes place, I must beg of you never to mention the circumstance."

Ensign Lightfoot, of course promised to keep faith upon this subject, and his two companions took their departure through the window, and left him alone to his ruminations. A feeling of undefined dread took possession of the ensign shortly after they had gone. The appearance of the place was melancholy to the last degree; the sighing of the surrounding trees, the darkness of the coming night, and the silence and deserted appearance of the place, gave to it a sombre aspect; nevertheless, our ensign was brave, he had youth and strength, and was moreover armed, and he consoled himself, therefore, with the reflection that, come what might, he could protect himself in any emergency.

He examined the door—it was locked and bolted. The bolts were inside, and these he endeavoured to withdraw, but they were so rusty that he found it a difficult task; he, however, succeeded eventually in drawing them, back with some difficulty; he then tried the lock, this was firmly locked, and defied all attempts made to open it without a key.

"But why should I be so curious a fool?" he exclaimed, "doubtless this door leads to the other portion of the habitation, to enter which, would perhaps be certain destruction. My dusky friend informed me that this was cut off and isolated from the other part of the building. Let me be content with what he has provided for me. This place is curious enough, and the circumstances of my occupation of it, still more so." So saying, he sat down in an antique ivory chair, by the side of the couch, and reflected upon the terrible events which had taken place within the last few hours.

There are times when all of us commune with ourselves, and reflect upon the mutability of human affairs. When we have escaped from a situation of imminent peril.

and are shut up alone in a dreary habitation, such as the ensign occupied, I think most of us would be likely to take stock of our feelings, and examine the inner man. Lightfoot was fatigued enough, and, under ordinary circumstances, would have found no difficulty in courting the embraces of the "drowsy god;" but although the costly and richly ornate couch of Laverah Doulah was so kindly placed at his service, he did not seem at all disposed to seek repose; in fact, sleep appeared to be out of the question, so he drew the massive chair towards the window, and looked out upon the foliage which surrounded it, pursuing a train of reflections of no very agreeable character, he eventually fell off unconsciously to sleep. He knew not how long he had been so, but was awoke by a sensation of chilliness; the humid night air was streaming in through the open window, and wrapt his limbs in a cold embrace. He, at the same time, became aware that several men were in close proximity to the place, for he distinctly heard voices in earnest conversation, that, deeming it imprudent to present himself at the window, he closed the casement as gently as he could, and retired in the interior of the apartment, and without undressing, he covered himself over and sought repose upon the couch. An uneasy and feverish slumber at length overtook him, haunted as it was with a thousand wild and disjointed visions.

Soon after the morning sun had streamed into his apartment, he was aroused by the appearance of Tamneegal, who leaped through the window, without ceremony. Lightfoot started up in some alarm, at his appearance, not at the first moment recognizing him, and being naturally apprehensive that it was some less friendly visitor.

"It is lucky you had not fastened the window," observed Tamneegal; "or you had like to have had an unbroken fast to-day. The door has been too securely fastened, to admit of access to your apartment, but we must see to that;" upon which he proceeded to make a careful inspection of the door.

"Ah! you have drawn back the bolts, I see?"

"Yes, I did so last night."

"Ah! let us see if we can do the same by the lock;" and he pulled out a massive old-fashioned key, twisted into a most fantastic shape. Inserting it into the lock, he endeavoured to turn the catch, but all his efforts were futile. After many more unsuccessful efforts, he gave it up as a hopeless case, and proceeded with a screw driver, with which he was provided, to unscrew the fastenings and take the lock off. This was a difficult task, for the screws were rusted into the wood-work, and required no small amount of strength to turn. With the assistance of Lightfoot, he did however manage to accomplish his purpose. Then having the lock free, he proceeded to cleanse it from the rust, which had been eating its way into it for years. After which, he gave it a plentiful supply of oil, and fastened it again firmly on the door.

"Now sir," he said to Lightfoot, "I shall be able to supply you with your morning repast, and all your future wants without fear of detection or observation;" and so saying, he proceeded through the door and brought the ensign a plentiful supply of viands for his morning meal. Having placed them before him, he disappeared abruptly, closed the door, double locked it, and left his visitor alone.

"Umph!" exclaimed the ensign, "I appear to have tumbled into lively quarters; no other companions but some imaginary ghosts, with which this charming place is supposed to be haunted. I should be almost disposed to drop from the window and take my chance, did I not believe in the existence of some more substantial enemy outside, than my companions the ghosts. Well here goes to refresh the inner man;" and he proceeded to attack the food provided by Tamneegal with infinite relish.

The meal over, the ensign was left again to his reflections, and like a caged lion, the confinement chafed and fretted his active spirit. There was, too, a degree of depression occasioned by his solitary and isolated situation, which was considerably enhanced by the reflection of the incertitude of events.

CHAPTER CCXXIV

MORE OF LIGHTFOOT'S ADVENTURE.—A DARK EPISODE CONNECTED WITH THE FUTURE EVENTS OF OUR STORY.

Thus day after day passed in weary monotony and succession, Lightfoot saw not an individual, save Tamneegal, who himself waited upon him, bringing his meals, and then disappearing without indulging in any extraneous or unnecessary conversation. The ensign began to be fairly worn out with the tedium of his situation, and taciturnity of his uncommunicative host. When one day he was astonished to observe as the massive door swung back upon its hinges, a young female pause on the threshold for a moment, she held in her hand the provision for his required meal. Lightfoot sprang forward and took the tray from her hand. He was lost in wonderment, as he observed that she was surpassingly beautiful, and a deep carnation suffused her features as Lightfoot approached. He would have interrogated her, but before he had sufficiently recovered his first surprise, she suddenly disappeared, closing the door and locking it after her with the same caution and celerity as Tamneegal.

"By my faith!" exclaimed Lightfoot, "this is a much more pleasing hand-maiden than my gloomy friend, I wonder who she is?"

Her appearance had been so unexpected and her departure so sudden, that he had only time to notice that she was a young Hindoo maiden, possessed of great personal attractions, and appeared to be remarkably diffident and modest in her demeanour. Lightfoot was struck with her appearance. No wonder he should be. When a beautiful woman comes to tend upon man in his loneliness, she assumes the appearance of an angel, as the poet says—

Oh woman! in our hours of ease:
Uncertain, coy, and hard to please,
    And variable as the shade,
    By the quiver of the light aspen made.
But when pain and anguish wring the brow,
A ministering angel thou!

Lightfoot cordially responded to the sentiments expressed in these lines, and hoped that his lovely attendant would give him an opportunity of making a further acquaintance with her. In this he was not disappointed, as later in the day he heard the creaking of the lock as it was being turned by the key, and in a few seconds the door opened, and he beheld his female attendant. He hastened forward and taking her gently by the hand, would have led her into the apartment, but she did not seem disposed to enter.

"Fairest and kindest of beings," said the ensign, whose galantry had mounted to a fever heat; "vouchsafe to answer me a few questions ere you depart."

The female gently shook her head, and placed one of her fingers upon her lips, as if to enjoin silence, then laying her viands on an adjacent table, she again suddenly disappeared, and locked the door as dexterously as she had done on the first occasion of her presenting herself.

"Well!" exclaimed Lightfoot, "my attendants are both remarkably chary of their words; I suppose they intend to doom me to solitary confinement. It does one good however, to only look at her, and I suppose I must content myself with that."

When she next appeared, Lightfoot thought he would adopt a different course, and try stratagem, so when he heard the customary grating of the lock, which always preceeded the entrance of any one into his apartment, he stretched himself upon his couch and feigned to be asleep. When the female opened the door, she did not find her gallant

prisoner spring forward with his wonted eagerness. She paused, and her eyes wandered round the apartment in search of him, when resting on the couch she observed Lightfoot apparently fast asleep. She proceeded to place the viands upon the table, and then turned towards where the ensign lay, and contemplated him with some interest and curiosity. He was conscious that he was being scrutinized, and apparently arousing himself suddenly, he leaped from his couch, and falling upon one knee he caught hold of the hand of his attendant and exclaimed hurriedly—

"Stay, if only for one moment. You cannot, will not, surely leave me thus in silence day after day. What has become of my friend who brought me hither? And you yourself; in what light am I to look upon you? as a friend I am sure—I pray you speak, your sex is not wont to be so taciturn."

The young Hindoo smiled and said—

"Your friend has gone away for a time, and left you in my charge—but he will return shortly—and then"—she paused

"And then what? my fairest creature."

"Then whatever you wish to know or have to say, ask him."

"And yourself, are you his daughter?"

"No," and she laughed audibly at the question.

"His sister?"

"No!"

"His ——" Lightfoot paused.

"Yes, his wife!" said the female, divining the meaning of his unasked question.

"Oh!" said the ensign, rather dashed at the answer. "Then he is a man to be envied beyond all others."

She endeavoured to release herself upon hearing these words, but Lightfoot still retained hold of her hand, and seemed loath to let her depart.

"What more would you?" she exclaimed.

"Your company for a few minutes. You surely, gentle creature as you evidently are, would not grudge a poor forlorn captive a few minutes of human companionship"

"It may not be, I am charged to hold no converse with you, but to merely supply you with the necessaries you require, in silence. If I keep not my trust my husband would never forgive me."

"Oh, he would never be angry at your doing an act of common charity. I am shut up here, without a friend or soul to speak to, and it is the natural instinct of woman to comfort and cheer the afflicted. Tell me if there is any chance of my escaping from here with anything like safety, and if not now, do you see any probability of my eventually being enabled to do so?"

His female attendant became ashy pale as

he asked this question, and appeared to tremble at some imaginary evil.

Lightfoot instantly handed her a seat.

"Alas, sir," she exclaimed, with a greater warmth and earnestness of manner than she had hitherto assumed, "you and your race are the enemies of mine. Ask me not then what mercy you would have amidst your bitterest foes. Your only chance is lying concealed here. It is against the principles of my husband to succour you, but having passed his word you are safe in his sincerity. For myself, I shall keep your hiding-place secret till such time as he returns."

"Kindest and most noble-hearted friend, I do not for one moment doubt your good intentions, and to thank fate for having sent me such a guardian angel in my most urgent hour of need."

She again winced at these words, as she had hitherto done on every occasion when compliments had fallen from the lips of Lightfoot, and, at the same time, a deep blush suffused her handsome countenance.

She was very beautiful, this young wife of Tamneegal, so much so that it would hardly be possible for the most phlematic individual to be placed in the same position as Lightfoot, and remain insensible to her charms of person and manner.

The reader may perhaps feel surprised at the description of this female, when he remembers the account of Mugriah, some chapters since, who was introduced by Tamneegal to Omelia as his wife; and such indeed she was, but it must be remembered that we are now recording events which happened some considerable time previous. Mugriah was his second wife; of the fate of his first the reader will be able to discover as he peruses the following pages.

We are now for the reader's behoof separating the meshes and threads of a web which is soon too surely to wind round our unfortunate heroine, and close her in a dark and dreadful fate—but let us not anticipate.

Ensign Lightfoot, with that gallantry which is inherent in most military officers, sought frequent conversations with the wife of Tamneegal.

She had evidently throughout these endeavoured to conduct herself with a studied coldness, but gradually this had, to a considerable extent, worn off, and Lightfoot was more profuse in his compliments and expressions of gratitude and admiration than the circumstances of the case might warrant, or, at any rate, more than it was prudent for him to indulge in.

The situation of both was one of considerable peril; Tamneegal, from some cause or other, did not return, and his wife was of necessity the only companion and attendant upon a young and handsome Englishman, who as well as possessing a comely face and figure, united with it an eloquent tongue, gentlemanly bearing, and, it must be confessed, a heart which was made of combustible and inflamable materials.

There was no harm meant by Lightfoot, as, we suppose, there seldom is by any of us who first begin the soft whisperings to a beauteous woman, but there was, as will be presently shown, a vast amount of harm done, perhaps unwittingly.

His situation and bearing had made a more powerful impression upon his attendant than could possibly be imagined.

One day, when he had been more than than usually eloquent, his companion left him abruptly, and then, perhaps, discovered for the first time that she was on the brink of a precipice. We never discover these things, poor purblind mortals that we are until it is too late.

Upon her retiring from the ensign's apartment, she examined her own heart, and had recourse to woman's usual aid, and burst into a flood of tears.

It was then that she became aware, perhaps, for the first time, of the sentiments she felt towards the prisoner of war placed under her charge.

The next day it was late before Lightfoot received a visit from his fair attendant, and when she appeared, her manner and bearing was entirely changed.

Placing his meal upon the table, she turned towards the ensign a countenance of melancholy determination, and addressed him in these words, waving his advance back as he endeavoured to approach—

"Listen to me, sir, I pray you, for a few short minutes. Our intercourse must now for ever cease. Ater examining my heart, I feel that I should be doing myself an injustice to give ear to such speeches as you have lately been pleased to give utterance to. My duty to my husband, to whom I owe allegiance, will not admit of my holding any further converse with you. As an honourable gentleman, you will appreciate my resolution—one that is not lightly taken or determined upon without due reflection. You are here as our guest—nothing more; I had thought my husband would have returned long since to release me from a carge which I have some difficulty in performing."

"What is the meaning of this?" said the ensign. "Have I offended you?"

"No; but I feel and know that it would be best that our further acquaintance should now cease. When my husband, Tamneegal, left, he desired me to see to such comforts as you might require, but, at the same time, he charged me not to have any unnecessary converse with you; I have erred in disobeying his injunctions. Let me entreat of you not to endeavour to induce me to continue to do so. I shall continue to attend upon you on certain conditions only, and you must give me your sacred word to respect them."

"Anything you wish me to do you have only to intimate, and you shall be obeyed to the very letter," answered the ensign.

"Good! I believe you to be an honourable gentleman, who is incapable of taking a mean advantage of the situation of any woman, however lowly or humble her station. Listen then to my unalterable resolve. I enter this apartment, bringing your meals, and seeing to your comforts as well as I can upon this condition, sir: that you never address me, unless I first speak to you, and that, henceforth, you never let me see your face, but always lay concealed from my sight."

"Merciful powers! am I such a gorgon that there should be need of so rigid a restriction as this?"

"No matter, you have but just said that whatever I desired you would freely and cheerfully grant. I do most earnestly desire you to keep these conditions."

"I am almost afraid it will be impossible for me to keep such a promise, however disposed I might be to do so."

"Then, by the Great Spirit who sees and knows all hearts, I swear never to enter your presence again," ejaculated Lightfoot's attendant, with fervour.

"Oh, say not so," hastily answered the ensign, with some asperity; "your request is granted. I know not why you make it, and am entirely at a loss to comprehend your motives. It is enough for me that you wish me to pledge myself to these conditions. I do so at once; believe me you shall never have cause to upbraid me with endeavouring to violate your injunctions."

His companion regarded him with a look, the meaning of which he was at a loss to comprehend; a thought flashed across the mind of the officer that the lady was abberrative in the intellect, and the reflection was anything but a pleasing one.

After contemplating him for some time she extended her hand, which he grasped, and gently pressed to his lips.

"We are friends; still keep my conditions —farewell."

With these words she glided mysteriously from the apartment.

"Well," exclaimed the ensign, soon after she had departed, "this is the first time I have been considered such a hideous monster that it should be deemed necessary for me to hide myself from a woman's gaze. I dare say I am strangely altered; shut up in this cursed hole, I suppose I assume the appearance of a sort of Casper Hauser, or wild man of the woods. The lady is flattering, by Jove. Oh, she is clearly a little touched from some cause, and, egad! I believe I shall be so myself, if I remain here much longer, like a lost sheep in the wilderness, with no companion, and an attendant which dooms me to solitary confinement; I shall corrode away with rust from inactivity."

When next Lightfoot heard the signal of the grating lock, he threw himself upon his couch, and lay concealed under the covering. The young Hindoo woman entered the apartment, performed her mission, and as silently departed, without apparently noticing his presence.

He adopted a similar course on every occasion when she entered; having passed his word, he was determined, come what would, not to be the first to break through the compact.

Several days went on thus, with no change in the demeanour of either, when at length Lightfoot was surprised one evening by the appearance of Goolooh at the window of the apartment, through which he affected an entrance.

At first the ensign, by the obscure light, did not recognise him, and stood upon his guard, believing it to be an attack of some secret foe who had discovered his retreat; he was, however, soon reassured when he recognised the friendly tones of his saviour in the hour of peril.

"Hush!" said Goolooh, who appeared to be out of breath, and under some excitement. "You must have thought we had entirely deserted you, and left you to your fate. How fare you?"

"Well enough, for the matter of that, but most heartily weary of my solitary confinement. It is cheerful, my friend, to again have a human being to converse with, for, to say the truth, I began to think I should forget my own language."

Before the ensign had finished speaking, he beheld Tamneegal enter the apartment by the window with some difficulty.

He was very pale—was wounded, and seemed nearly exhausted from loss of blood. He uttered some brief observations in a husky voice to Goolooh, the meaning of which the ensign did not clearly understand, as he spoke to his companion in the Hindoostanee language, and his utterance was so rapid, and in such broken sentences, that Lightfoot did not succeed in catching the precise meaning of his words.

Tamneegal staggered to a chair, and beckoned the ensign to his side, who then observed that his body and limbs were bound up in several places with bandages.

"You are safe, then?" he said, as the ensign approached; "almost more than I had expected. You had better stay here no

longer, as your doing so would be fraught with danger to all of us."

"Do not let me in any way compromise you," said Lightfoot. "You have risked enough already on my account. I will proceed hence, and take my chance, by the aid of my good sword, in protecting myself as best I can."

"As you please," said Tamneegal, in painful and irritable tones; and then, turning to Goolooh, he seemed to make a mute appeal for him to explain his meaning more fully.

"Do not imagine that there is any intention to abandon you," said Goolooh. "A few miles from this spot there are some of your countrymen, and, perhaps, brother officers. If you will trust yourself to my guidance, I will endeavour to escort you to them; I

cannot answer for doing so with certainty, but will try my best."

"My excellent, disinterested friend, how can I ever repay you for all your solicitude in my behalf? I will follow you willingly, with a full assurance of your good intentions."

"And after this our compact is at an end, as far as this stranger is concerned," said Tamneegal, addressing himself to Goolooh, who bowed his head in acquiescence.

Ensign Lightfoot offered his hand to Tamneegal, as he gave expression to his sense of gratitude. The latter, however, did not seem disposed to accept it, but said, somewhat bluntly—

"No, saib; you and your countrymen are no friends of mine, and it would be ill in me to simulate a friendship I am far from feeling. I have done you what service was needed at the time to oblige a worthy and esteemed companion, but henceforth we are strangers to one another"

Ensign Lightfoot did not like the hasty and indifferent tone assumed by his host, and paused and hesitated how to act, when drawing himself up with some dignity, he said—

"Be it so, then As strangers let us meet in future, should we ever again cross each other's path: should a time ever come that you need assistance, remember the name of Ensign Lightfoot, and you shall never ask in vain."

Goolooh and the ensign now proceeded through the open casement, and dropping to the ground gently upon the tall grass by the aid of the tree before mentioned, they succeeded in alighting in safety, without being observed by any passing stranger.

CHAPTER CCXXV.

AN UNEXPECTED VISITANT.—PAINFUL REVELATION.—TERRIBLE EQUIVOQUE.

When the two had departed, Tamneegal continued seated in the chair, as though he felt quite unable to move.

He had been in a bloody skirmish with the very English whom he had started off Goolooh to seek for the ensign. His wounds were many, and the loss of blood had induced a faintness which nearly overpowered him from action.

After resting for a considerable period, and refreshing himself somewhat by a draught from his bottle, he essayed to open the door of the apartment. He had forgotten in the hurry of events that he had left the key in charge of his wife, and consequently found himself quite unable to effect an egress through the firmly locked door.

He felt himself too weak to attempt to drop from the window, and it would be useless his endeavouring to attract the attention of his wife, or any occupant of his domicile, for the apartment in which the ensign had been confined was too isolated and far removed from the other habited portion of the building for him to make himself heard by any of the inhabitants.

Worn out as he was, therefore, he gladly sought repose upon the couch which had, for many days past, been the resting place of Lightfoot. On this, therefore, he threw himself, while, at the same time, he wrapped his body over with the covering, for the evening began to be chilly.

It was not long before he sank into a deep sleep, made the more sound from the loss of blood he had sustained. His slumber lasted throughout the night without interruption, and when the morning sun found its way into his apartment he was still in a state of unconsciousness, so much so, that he did not hear his wife turning the lock preparatory to her entering as was her usual custom, with Lightfoot's morning meal.

She entered, and placed it on the table, and turned towards the couch; she was very pale, and seemed trembling with excitement, so that she was fain to seek the aid of the back of the chair for support.

"It has been all of no use," she began, ' my best resolution has proved futile—against a passion which has torn and consumed me daily. Why, young man, were you ever brought hither, to create a chasm which now, alas, can never be bridged over, I have wrestled and combatted with this fatal influence, God knows how obstinately—but all to no purpose. You can bear witness to my determination. At my request, you have kept yourself concealed from my sight, and have not let me hear the music of your voice, and well have you kept the promise so reluctantly given, but which, you nevertheless have respected with such firmness. Hear me now—I, who awhile bid you conceal yourself, now beg of you to rescind the compact, and let me again behold those features which have exercised such an overpowering influence over me."

The figure on the couch groaned deeply, and writhed apparently in torture.

"Ah!" she continued, "you may well shrink at the revelation. It is fatal perhaps to both of us. Despise me if you will, but let me again hear the sound of your voice, if be but to upbraid and curse me."

No reply was given to the speaker, and she continued more passionately—

"Young man, I love you! Do you hear those fatal words? Do you know, how day by day, I have endeavoured to stifle the guilty thoughts that have rushed unbidden tumultuously through the brain, and hurried me on to madness. Do you know what love is? Ah, perhaps you have never known this absorbing passion, and can therefore make no allowance for a poor erring creature who is borne on an eddying vortex, on which she is hastening to certain and dreadful destruction. What is this but fatality—have I not repulsed any slight advance you might have made?"

A prolonged sigh escaped from the recumbent figure on the couch, as she spoke these words.

"Have I not? You will not answer me—never again, perhaps—ah, I do not deserve it—why am I punished thus? Never more to know peace of mind, oh, its dreadful. Have pity on me—when I bid you be silent, you spoke in hurried and silvery accents, words which found their way into the inmost recesses of my heart, and now, when one syllable from your tongue would be ecstacy, you will not utter it, but remain mute and impassible You despise me—abhor the sight of her who has become abandoned and shameless, for your sake. Young man, your race is said to be the curse of our clime—Alas, I fear it will prove mine to the latest period of my existence. Hear me—hasten to me—have pity on me—I will consent to be your most abject slave, to follow your fortunes, be they whatsoever they may—to tend upon you with unremitting care—to be —anything to you—only to be allowed near your presence. I abandon home—friends and peace hereafter—all for your sake. Is this nothing to you? Or is there any other sacrifice you would need? Name it, and it shall be done."

A convulsive movement on the couch was her only answer.

"What, still silent! Will nothing move you? or are you turned to stone. Let me again see your face. If it be expressive of disgust for the wretched being who now addresses you. Let me once more behold it. Hast thou no pity? thou most unfeeling man. I shall be driven to desperation," and she tottered to the side of the couch, and under the influence of her mad infatuation tore the covering from Tamneegal. What pen can describe her horror, when she beheld the features of her husband, so distorted with passion, that they were hardly recognisable. His face was begrimmed with blood and dirt —his eyes bloodshot, and the expression of his features perfectly demoniacal. With a savage cry, more like the roar of a wild beast than a human being, he sprang up and grasped her by the throat with a supernatural strength, lent him, for the nonce, by the mighty passion which shook his frame.

"Abandoned wretch! shameless adultress! infidel!" he exclaimed fiercely, as soon as he could find utterance. Your last hour is come, thus will I stretch your worthless body upon the bed you have dishonoured," and he flung her with all his force upon the couch, while at the same time he drew his tulmar.

"Mercy! mercy!" shrieked his wife; "Spare me! I am not fit to die. Spare me for a short time, and then do with me as thou wilt."

She clung to his knees, embraced them, and looked beseechingly in his face. To any one, who was not under the influence of a demoniacal passion, her appeal would not have been in vain, but Tamneegal struck her brutally to the earth with his disengaged hand. He had waived over her head his tulmar, and she had arrested its progress by grasping his arm and clinging tenaciously to it with all her might, she fell prostrate to the earth, almost stunned by the force of the blow.

"Perfidious woman," he exclaimed, "whose guilty passion has severed every tie between us—lost for ever—to lift your eyes up to one of a race whose touch is pollution—shameless minion;" and uttering such broken sentences as these, he paced up and down the apartment, like some wild animal in its cage, while his wife lay stretched on the floor sobbing hysterically.

"I give you a few minutes to confess your sins, and then prepare to meet the fate your own crimes have brought upon your head."

"Mercy! mercy upon me. Ladroo. I have been a true and faithful wife to you, anticipating your very wishes, and tending on you as a loving companion—and a cheerful helpmate. Remember this, and say is it not hard to die so young—oh, very hard. It was not till I was sore tempted, beyond the power of resistance, that I ever gave you cause for suspicion."

"Art thou not a monster?" shrieked her husband, hoarsly.

"No! Heaven be my judge."

"Liar and perjurer! by your own confession, you are convicted of guilt of the very deepest dye."

"'Tis false! I am innocent!"

"Have I not but just now heard the full recital of your guilty passion, for one of that race who have been the direst curse of our clime. Oh!" he continued passionately, "fool that I was to nurture a viper, which was sure to sting me—without faith—without honour—without the commonest feelings of humanity to any of our people. Woman, are you prepared? for you must now die! and after then, be mine the task, to have a terrible and just revenge upon your seducer."

"Oh, say not so," screamed out his wife, in tones of fear and anguish." Say not so—do as you will with me, but spare him—in mercy spare him—he is innocent of any knowledge of my passion."

"Curses on you, abandoned hussey. Do you dare to plead for the miscreant to my very face. Curses, curses on you. Die in your own deceit and wickedness," and he rushed upon her with his drawn sword like a maniac. Her intercession for Lightfoot aroused his feelings of jealously to a fearful pitch.

It is probable, that had a more conciliatory course have been adopted by his wife, that he might not have turned a deaf ear to her proceedings; for to say the truth, Tamneegal had really loved his wife, as much as his savage nature was capable of He was, however, now worked up to the highest pitch of rage and frenzy. Springing forward upon his wife, he made a desperate and determined cut at her with his tulmar; she dexterously avoided the blow aimed at her, by seeking refuge behind the ivory chair, which she wheeled in front of her to intercept the further progress of her infuriated husband, whose descending weapon cut off a portion of the carved ivory-work at the back of the chair. Tamneegal, mad at being thus baulked in his onslaught, caught hold of the chair and flung it in his rage some yards from the spot; it overturned as it fell, and one of the ivory arms broke short off with the concussion. His wife flew to the next piece of furniture, with which she formed a breastwork to oppose her husband's progress. He followed her from place to place, like a tiger reeking for his prey.

It was a fearful scene which was now being enacted in the apartment so recently occupied by Ensign Lightfoot. As Tamneegal pursued his wife, she made most earnest and agonising appeals for mercy, which as they were now and then coupled with the name of Lightfoot, only added to his fury

At length he succeeded in catching hold of and detaining her. He struck furiously at her head with his tulmar, but she managed to ward of the blow with the arm of the ivory chair, which she had caught up in her progress. The sound of the descending blade was sharp against the hard ivory, but the next blow, which followed immediately, was almost noiseless, as it was received upon the unfortunate woman's arm, laying open a dreadful gash, and deluging her with blood. The enraged Tamneegal now sprang forward as his wife receded to deliver a *coup de grace*, but in doing so he stumbled over some articles of furniture, and tumbled to the ground like a felled tree, bereft of life and motion.

The excitement consequent upon the fearful scene, had been too much for him—weak as he was. He had held on under the influence of an absorbing passion of rage and jealously, but nature became exhausted—his wounds opened—blood poured down in streams from them—his sight failed—his head swam round, and he fainted. His wife was at a loss to understand her husband's sudden prostration. She was almost disposed to believe, that in the frenzy of the moment, he had committed self-destruction; with the natural kind and forgiving disposition, which is one of the most marked characteristics of the softer sex, she stooped down and examined her husband's condition. His wounds having opened afresh, and some of the bandages being displaced, he was covered with blood. His wife was not aware that he had been wounded, and now, for the first time, discovered it.

Taking a last look of her husband, she uttered a farewell, and binding up her own wound as well as she was able, left that night her house and home with a solemn vow never again to enter it alive. Gathering up a few things, she rushed onward like one bereft of reason, and as she proceeded, sobbed audibly. She had no definate notion as to whither she was journeying, but had not proceeded far when she was accosted by Goolooh, who was returning home, after having escorted Lightfoot in safety to his English companions. He was astonished at the unfortunate woman's distracted appearance; her hair was dishevelled—her dress stained with blood—and her face and appearance altogether so altered, that Goolooh could hardly believe that she was the same beauteous being whom he had known for so many years.

" Poutra! he exclaimed in some astonishment, "what is the meaning of this? whither are you going?"

The blush of shame rose upon the features of the unhappy woman he addressed; and she turned away in some trepidation.

"Ask me no questions," she exclaimed bitterly; "my husband has sought my life, and is now perhaps himself snatched by the hand of death—terrible retribution, terrible."

"You speak in enigmas. Pray be more explicit. Ah! you are wounded yourself. How is this?" said Goolooh in surprise.

"Oh, do not drive me mad," said Poutra, as she pressed her hands against her throbbing temples. "I am nearly so already, see to Tamneegal, he lays in that fatal apartment, without life or motion—see to him Goolooh—for my sake—my good friend—my dear companion from my earliest childhood. What will you think of her now, whose slender form you've borne across those hills with the swiftness of the roebuck, and whose merry laugh you used to say, cheered you in all your boyish sports. Do you remember those days? those happy hours, when our hearts knew no guile, before we were aware that sin and sorrow in this wicked world, is the heritage of us all."

"I remember—of course," answered her companion, not clearly understanding her drift.

"I remember you, Poutra, when you were a little child, as merry as the day was long—as light and graceful as the fawn—bounding over the hills like a deer, and defying me to catch you. Yes, I well remember all this, as though it were but yesterday."

"Then think of me as I was then," said Poutra, in a sort of half whisper, as she approached nearer to her companion; "forget me as I am now—or what I may be—n—what—"

Tears choked her utterance, and she ceased suddenly.

Goolooh stared at her in perfect bewilderment; he was quite at a loss to comprehend the sudden change in her appearance and demeanour.

He had known her from earliest infancy, and their families residing in the same locality, were on such intimate terms that they were almost more like brothers and sisters than friends.

Tamneegal, although many years older than Poutra, had made her a tolerably good husband, and treated her with kindness. His associates, and general habits of life, were perhaps of rather a questionable character, but with these Poutra had but little to do, and knew very little about.

She continued to weep passionately, and endeavoured to take an abrupt departure, but Goolooh detained her, that she might afford him some explanation for her poignant sorrow.

"I am pained beyond expression," he said, "to see you thus moved to tears. Let me, as an old friend—perhaps your oldest—know the cause; and, trust me, all shall be arranged to your satisfaction. Come, return with me."

"Never!" she exclaimed, with energy—"never! I return no more to my home, but bid a farewell to it for ever. The tie between myself and my husband is broken now, and henceforth I am alone in the world."

"Not alone, dearest Poutra—you have always found an earnest and devoted friend in me. Come, be frank, and let me know the meaning of this conduct—as your early companion and playmate I have a right to be in your confidence."

"Not now—some future time you will know all. Go at once to Tamneegal, and you will learn what it would break my heart to tell you. Kindest and best of friends, farewell—farewell. Leave me now, as a particular favour I ask you to return at once to the bungalow. You never refused me the most trivial request. Do not distract me by doing so now. Farewell—farewell."

And with these words she left her companion hastily, as though unwilling to protract the interview longer.

Goolooh acceded to her wishes, as he had always been accustomed to do, and hastened to the residence of Tamneegal.

When arriving at the habitation, he discovered the wretched man who had been a prey to his own violent passions prostrate on the floor, on the same spot where his wife had left him.

His appearance was so ghastly, that it naturally led to the inference that he was dead—and so, indeed, his companion at first imagined he was. But after placing him again on the couch, binding up his wounds, and administering restoratives, he comparatively revived

But his intellect began to wander, and an incipient fever began to seize hold of his frame, superinduced by loss of the fatal fluid, and the mental anguish he had undergone.

For many days he continued irrational, and raved incoherently about revenge—his wife, and the ensign. After he had a little recovered the equilibrium of his mind, Goolooh was made acquainted with the full particulars already detailed in the previous chapter."

———

CHAPTER CCXXVI.

THE RESOLVE OF POUTRA.—HER WANDER-INGS, AND INTERVIEW WITH ENSIGN LIGHT-FOOT.

When the ill-fated woman left the companion of her childhood so precipitately she proceeded on with rapid steps to get out of sight of the home she had disgraced. Her nature was sensitive and impulsive, her reasoning powers being small. She was too sensitive to ever admit any thought of returning to her husband's domicile.

She had ascertained that Lightfoot had been safely conveyed to his companions. This a relative of Goolooh had informed her. So infatuated was the unfortunate Poutra with the ensign, that she appeared to be directing her course towards where his regiment was quartered. Onwards—onwards, like a belated traveller, lured by a deceitful mirage, did Poutra pursue the phantom which had for ever destroyed her peace of mind and happiness.

She was not aware that the passing gallantry of a young English officer was but an evanescent affair, and believed, perhaps, that he was as hopelessly in love as herself. Remembering Tamneegal's threats respecting his destruction, she felt it her duty to explain the whole of the circumstances to him which had transpired since his departure, so that he might be upon his guard against any overt act contemplated by her husband.

It must occur to the mind of most persons, that the task she had imposed upon herself was a difficult and delicate one, and which perhaps in her calmer moments, she would have shrank from with horror; but she was yet fresh from the full burst of her declared love: she had made the revelation to a man, of all others, to whom it must have been the most painful, and the consequences of which could hardly fail to be the most disastrous, but she was yet strong in her determination to watch over and protect her lover. She payed a dear penalty for her folly, as most of us do, who let our passions bear away the sheet anchor—reason.

Ensign Lightfoot, when he rejoined his companions, had so long an account to give them of the fate of his comrades, and his own escape and adventures, that he had almost forgotten to mention the singular conduct of his female attendant.

It was with him but a passing pleasantry, which served for a mess-room anecdote for a future period, when the stock of raw mate rial for good stores was running short.

Lightfoot's spirits rebounded at being emancipated from his captivity. Never of a very taciturn disposition, the long period of silence which had been imposed upon him rendered his loquacious powers fresh and unimpaired in their pristine vigour. He kept his companions alive, therefore, with his narratives, which he told in his own dry and graphic manner.

Whilst indulging in the recital of various incidents, he was enabled to do justice to the wine, and the spirits of both himself and brother officers were elated therefrom. It was in the midst of this carousal that an Irish servant of the colonel's entered, and informed the ensign, "That a leddy would be afther suing his honour."

A roar of laughter from the officers succeeded this announcement.

"A lady," said one; "i'faith she's soon found out your quarters, Lightfoot. You haven't been here many hours, and, of course, the fond inquiry made for you is by a lady."

"What sort of a person?" inquired the ensign of the servant; "are you sure you are right?"

"Oh, a very proper sort of a kind of a person, your honour. She's as beautiful as a pacock; although, to spake the truth, she's a little bit travel-worn like, and seems rather lemoncholy."

"Of course," shouted his companions, "young ladies who are dying in love usually are so. Really, Lightfoot, you are positively incorrigible."

The ensign did not altogether see the force or wit of his companion's observations, but was at a loss to understand who it could be that had been inquiring for him. The last person in the world for him to have guessed would have been the infatuated Poutra.

He, however, followed the servant, and his astonishment may be imagined, when he beheld his late taciturn attendant, severely wounded—her hair and dress disordered—her features the very picture of grief and anguish, and her manner distracted.

The ensign gazed at her in mute astonishment for some moments, when she laid her hand upon his arm, and exclaimed—

"Safe! thank heaven!"

"Yes, thanks to your kind attentions. You are wounded, and have met with some disaster. Tell me how I can serve you?"

She paused for some minutes, apparently overcome by her feelings, when she at length said—

"I have come, young man, to throw myself upon your mercy."

"Mercy! Surely you do not need use such a term as applied to me."

"Indeed I do need mercy. You behold before you one of the most wretched creatures on earth. In an evil hour I have become lost and abandoned from my home. Young man, I love you!"

The ensign was staggered as she uttered these words with a determined energy. He was willing enough to have a passing flirtation with a pretty woman when not otherwise occupied in more important matters; but he did not appear at all anxious to bring his enamorato into the camp.

A vexed and troubled expression was observable on his features, and he was at a loss how to reply to this speech.

"You flatter me," he at length stammered out; "and I feel I do not deserve so great an honour."

He was unconsciously, perhaps, adopting a tone of irony, in the last observation.

"Hear me, sir," said Poutra; "for you I have given up house and home—husband—and every tie which ought to bind a woman. For your sake I have escaped my husband's vengeance, only by a miracle. For your sake I am willing to risk all—my hopes of peace here and hereafter. I have wrestled with this passion, and, as you know, interdicted you from speaking to me, or even presenting yourself before me—you remember this!"

"I—ye-es."

"Hear me out with my sad tale. You need me not to recal to your recollection all these particulars during your captivity. Actuated by a passion, which I had in vain endeavoured to combat with—overwhelmed by a love which incorporated itself with my very being, and was the ailment upon which I liv-d. I made up my mind, when I could endure the torture of silence no longer, to make you acquainted with my overpowering passion, believing you to be reclining upon the couch, which you had frequently so well concealed yourself from my sight. I explained my feelings towards you. I received no answer, but groans and sighs in reply. Judge my horror, when my husband started up in the most dreadful rage, and attacked me with his tulwar, swearing he would have my life."

"Merciful powers!" ejaculated the ensign, as he began to perceive the affair was assuming rather a serious aspect. "What an imprudent thing to do. To declare your love to a concealed man. It is dreadful."

"Dreadful indeed! I have left him for ever."

"Ah!" stammered the ensign. "In-deed, that seems to be rather a precipitate act."

"Yes, it is for your sake, you have inspired me with so deep and absorbing a passion, that I will abandon all in the world to follow your fortunes. Let me be your slave—your devoted attendant—anything, so that I be near you—hear the music of your voice, and hover around your path, till death. I have forsaken all else in the world My husband I shall never see again—my family—nor any of those friends or companions who knew me in my earlier days—I am devoted now to you alone."

Lightfoot looked possitively alarmed as she made the speech. "My dear young woman," he said, "let me entreat of you to return to your husband, who is your natural protector. You must be aware, that it is quite impossible for me to take charge of you, however much I might be disposed to do so. Come, your better reason will prompt you to repent of your rashness."

An expression of the most poignant anguish passed over the features of Poutra, as these words fell upon her ear. She gazed at the speaker, and burst into a flood of tears.

"Ah, you despise me then! Despise a poor wretch who has given up all for your sake Oh, why were you ever sent to poison the whole current of my life. I beseech you have pity on me—have pity—and let me conjure you to have a care for yourself. My husband has sworn to have a terrible revenge, and will never rest till he has your life."

"What for!" said the ensign, in some astonishment.

"For having ruined his peace of mind, and brought dishonour upon his name."

"I much regret that he should have become possessed with such an unfortunate chimera—for chimera it certainly is. As I owe him a deep obligation for his kindness towards me. Do my dear creature return and explain this matter to him, and all will be well again, I have no doubt. This is but a quarrel after all, under a mistaken feeling of jealously."

Poutra shook her head mournfully, and answered in a tone of the deepest despondency—as tears coursed down her cheeks. "You know not what you are saying, to talk thus: neither do you know his fierce and vindictive nature, when once aroused. But I see it all now, the mask is thrown aside. You fling back a love—the devotion of a life with scorn—and contempt. Was it well, think you, to wean from a poor weak, but too confiding woman, her fondest affections

—to separate her from her home and kindred—destroy her peace of mind for ever, and then, when that was done, to treat her with heartless indifference."

"My dear young woman, I have not, I hope, been guilty of such atrocity. It is not possible."

"You have! Witness your honied words—witness your looks of ardent admiration and love—witness your every action while an inmate of our abode. You have stolen from me my heart, and laugh—yes—laugh with derision—at the unfortunate wretch you have befooled and made a victim of your heartlessness. Farewell for ever the blissful scenes of youth; the dear friends who once loved me; and the happy home I once knew—gone—gone for ever. I am indeed a miserable outcast: a poor despised, broken-hearted woman;" and here her sobs choked her further utterance.

Lightfoot was pained beyond measure, to find that an imprudent flirtation had brought about such serious results, as were now presented for the first time to his understanding The manner and language of Poutra was too painful in its character, for him not to be fully impressed with the fact, that he had inspired in the heart of the young Indian wife, an attachment that was ready to brave all for his sake. It was equally clear, that circumstances had turned out so unfortunate, that she had become estranged from her home, and moreover, it did not seem at all probable, that any persuasion of his would be effectual in healing the breach. He was not guilty, the ensign, of anything but imprudence, but sometimes this venial fault is the cause of more mischief than actual crime. It was so in the present instance.

The ensign found himself hitched upon the horns of a very unfortunate dilemma, and so firmly hitched, that he saw no probability of extracting himself therefrom. To take charge of Tumneegal's wife was a duty he could not for a moment entertain, even a passing thought. To take her back to the husband, himself, was equally impossible, and to persuade her to go by herself, he found was also out of the question.

The ensign was troubled, perhaps, more than he ever was in his life; he had not calculated upon the hardened temperament of the daughters of India.

In this instance, he had most certainly, to use a nautical term, "missed his reckoning." He bitterly anathemised himself for having been so indiscreet, but it was too late now to repair the evil.

Instead of being pleased at the conquest he had made, poor Lightfoot beheld in it the presage of some dire misfortune, and would have given worlds to have recalled the events of the last few days. He had, at first tried to laugh it off, but found it impossible with the weeping victim before him, to view the matter in anything but a serious and melancholy light.

Ensign Lightfoot had youth, and abundance of animal spirits, and was what his messmates called a jovial companion; but all his wonted courage deserted him in the present instance, and he looked more like a man who had received orders for immediate execution than the merry young officer he was but half an hour previous to the present interview.

A weeping woman appeals directly to the hearts of most men, but when she is in grief for the love of one of us, he must indeed be hardened who witnesses her passion unmoved.

"What can I do to serve you?" he said kindly to Poutra, after there had been a pause for some minutes.

"Give me back the heart you have stolen from me," was the reply, " or let me follow you far away, and be your slave, to do with as you please."

" My dearest friend, you must see that this is impossible. My position in the service would not permit of my doing so."

" Then you never loved me, as you led me to suppose by your words and actions. Have I not tended on you with sisterly care—have I not risked all for your sake?"

"You have—most certainly; I do not deny it, and no man feels more grateful than myself for all your kindness. It is this gratitude expressed perhaps in too peculiar a manner which has led you to imagine I entertained a stronger and more tender passion."

" You never loved me, then?"

" I esteemed you, more than I can possibly tell—"

" Answer my question? You never loved me?"

" I should do wrong to love another man's wife."

She placed her hand upon his shoulder, and looked up into his face with a searching gaze full of deep and earnest passion.

"Answer my question," she said slowly and in measured tones.

Lightfoot quailed before the steady look of his companion, who seemed to read his inmost thoughts.

"Your answer," she again repeated, then, as he endeavoured to turn away from her, she added, " you love another."

He made no reply to this, but, after a short pause, said, seriously—

" I should be worse than villain to rob a man of his wife's affections, and that, too, when he was rendering me an infinite and gratuitous service."

" Ha, ha, ha !" she laughed hysterically, " much worse. Oh, what delicate scruples that villain then you most certainly are, and you know it as well as I do myself—you know that you have estranged my affections—warped my mind—destroyed my character—blasted my reputation—expatriated me from my house and home, and left me a wretched and despised outcast, drifting upon the waters of life to certain destruction. The veil has fallen from before my eyes—the mist is dispelled—the truth is disclosed in all its naked and hideous deformity. The rock upon which I leant for support has proved to be one of quicksand. Oh, young man, why did you ever come across my path to embitter my life—or why was I ever born at all? Farewell.'

So saying she rushed out of the presence of the ensign, like one whose mind was bordering on lunacy.

Her actions and alternate passions had been so rapid in their transient expression, that Lightfoot had been hardly able to cope with her, and had been at a loss how to receive her thrusts and parry them with anything like dexterity.

At one moment her language had breathed forth the most passionate love, and the next she indulged in a taunting satire, then she became broken down and sunk into the innermost depths of despair, on all, however, the ensign saw the indications of a loving and constant heart towards himself.

He would have followed her, but thought it best to let her pursue her own course for awhile, supposing that, in all probability, he should see her again in a few hours. He continued to look out upon the road, where he had seen her disappear, with the most melancholy and rueful expression upon his features it was possible to imagine, when he was aroused by the voices of three or four of his fellow officers and companions.

" What Lightfoot, my boy, are you moon-struck — love-sick — star-gazing or what? Why, man, you have the countenance of a condemned conspirator. Where is the lady?"

These questions and exclamations were spoken by one and the other of his brother officers in rapid succession.

" Hush," he said, " it is no joking matter."

" No, so it seems from your figure-head," said one of the party.

" Ha, ha! Come, a glass or two of wine, a jovial song, and a fig for all the sentimental girls in Christendom. Come, you have stood in the night air till you are actually shivering with cold."

The ensign suffered himself to be led in by his companions, and over the mess-table he explained fully the particulars of his interview, and every previous circumstance respecting his acquaintance with the unfortunate Poutra.

"Whew!" exclaimed one of his comrades, "the circumstance is an awkward one certainly; but let her alone. Nothing like letting a woman have her own way; she'll return, and make it up with her husband after a bit, and then you are all right; unless, of course, you like to—to—"

"But I don't like to take charge of her; I know what you would say."

"Well, then, it'sh wery cruel of you," said a young officer, who was supposed to be a mimic.

What with one joke and another they managed to rally the ensign out of his gloomy mood, and in a short time Poutra and her misplaced affection were forgotten for more pleasant topics; and Lightfoot consoled himself with the reflection that as he had offered her no encouragement, but,

No. 97.

on the contrary, had told her that it was impossible for him to respond to her absorbing passion, the probability was that she would see the folly of her course, and endeavour, sooner or later, to effect a reconciliation with her husband.

He was, however, again out in his reckoning, as will be presently seen.

CHAPTER CCXXVII.

UNREQUITED LOVE.—THE DESPERATION OF POUTRA.—HER TERRIBLE FATE.

What volumes might be written upon the subject of unrequited love—what hosts of ponderous tomes could be filled with a catalogue of the ills which have befallen the sons and daughters of Adam, through a misplaced passion, which never met with a return.

The subject would be inexhaustible to chronicle the heartaches, and wasting forms, which have nursed in their hearts a "silent sorrow," and "never told their love." We have had occasion in this, our narrative, to expatiate upon the theme more than once or twice, but, perhaps, no instance which we have had to record has been fraught with such sudden and disastrously fatal consequences, as this episode in our story, the more so, as it led up to after consequences which bore more directly upon our heroine. Not that she had aught to do with either Lightfoot or Poutra, and, in fact, she was not cognisant of either party until she saw the ensign with his companions in the fort. But in this chapter we have more especially to do with the ill-starred Poutra.

When she discovered that Lightfoot had no kind of attachment towards her—which she did not fail to divine from his manner—she felt like one whose whole current of life had been poisoned, to find that "there where she had garnered up her heart" was but a barren desert, and that the declaration of her attachment to Lightfoot was to him only as the hollow whistling of reeds on a sandy shore, which no one heeds or cares for. When she found this, and became fully assured of it, she gave herself up as lost for ever.

The severe wound which Tamneegal had inflicted upon her, would under ordinary circumstances, have caused her considerable pain and agony, but she was now quite heedless of it. The blood was mounting to her brain in hot and feverish currents—reason began to totter, whose light guides our footsteps from the cradle to the grave—a light which once quenched all else is void.

Alas, for poor Poutra! Imprudent, head-strong, guilty as may have been her attachment, she payed a fearful penalty for it.

When she left Lightfoot, she may be supposed to be no longer a rational being. She flew onwards with a savage impetuosity, as though she would fly from her own thoughts. She knew not whither she went—did not regard the road she was taking.

It was night, and, of course her path was beset with dangers, as animals of a savage nature were beginning to prowl about for their prey; but she was heedless of all around.

"Lost—lost!" she exclaimed, as she pursued her course; "for ever lost. Ah, what is that! the shining river! Kind heaven, to send me a friend in the hour of woe. See, its surface smiles a sparkling welcome. The river—in thy soft pellucid waters I can bury

all my sorrows and find a peaceful resting-place where sinful man shall never more obtrude himself upon me, then—what am I saying?—ah, my husband!—what of him?—Did I not leave him?—let me see—" and she paused, as if trying to catch her wandering intellect—" ah, my husband—was I not saying so—never again to meet—never. Come, prepare to meet your fate! Ah, what fate?—Peace—let me seek peace, at any price—peace—never to know it again. It is horrible the thought—"

The soft and mantling river lay before her; its waters rushed onwards like thoughts in a dream; the pale moonbeams were reflected in silver streaks by its ripples, and the air was cooled by exhalations from its waters.

It attracted the wandering gaze of the demented Poutra, and dreadful thoughts of suicide rushed through her brain She approached its emerald banks, and contemplated the dark and flowing stream with a fascinated gaze. What arm can stay her now in her fatal resolve? With an agonised cry she sprang from a neighbouring rock, and her beauteous form fell in the midst of the peaceful Ganges. Her dress buoyed her up upon its surface for a considerable period as she drifted down slowly with the tide; soon her clothes began to saturate with wet, and slowly the river sucked her down beneath the surface. A few eddying circles alone marked the spot where her body had disappeared; she rose and sank—rose and sank again—and then all was over with the ill-fated and unfortunate Poutra—" she slept well in death's last embrace."

When nature awoke, on the following morn, to light and life, and the birds carroled in the trees, and startled the echoing air with songs of melody, the silent waters of the Ganges bore on their surface the form of her who had, in life, "loved not wisely, but too well."

Peacefully she slumbered, and him for whom she had given up her life, little recked he of the sad fate which had befallen her.

* * * * *

Many days had passed since the scene we have described took place. Tamneegal had been seized, when we last left him, with a violent fever; upon recovering his reason, he began to remember the dark incidents which had taken place in his house and home.

He inquired of Goolooh about his wife Poutra. The former detailed the particulars of his last interview with her, and, also, their sudden parting.

When sufficiently recovered, Tamneegal, infuriate with Lightfoot, would have started forth to upbraid him with his conduct, and challenge him to mortal combat. He forgot, in the impulse of the moment, that the probability was that he would have been made a prisoner by the British officer in command, and consigned to an ignominious death. Goolooh pointed out to him the probability of this taking place, and it was agreed that the latter should wait upon the ensign, and appoint an interview for Tamneegal, at some distance from the English camp.

They found, however, upon inquiring, that the ensign and his companions in arms had marched away for some hundreds of miles, to a distant part of the country, and the probability was that they would never see them again.

A terrible blow awaited Tamneegal. The body of Poutra was discovered by a coolee, who was passing near the river's side, and the first intimation the husband received of his wife's fate, was the body being conveyed home to his residence.

When he beheld the dead body of his wife his sorrow knew no bounds, and his rage against Lightfoot was fearful to behold. "My bitterest curse cling to him for ever!" he exclaimed. "I swear by the God of my Fathers never to rest till I have had a bloody vengeance upon his murderous and traitorous head! Ungrateful monster! this is your barbarous work. Like a serpent you have found your way into my house, and your fangs have poisoned my existence. Vengeance!—vengeance! for this wronged and injured woman! By the heaven above I swear to devote myself to the task. If it be at the remotest corner of the earth you hide yourself, sooner or later I will find you out, and immolate you upon the shrine of outraged innocence. Oh, she was fair—exquisitely fair—kind—gentle, and loving—until her mind became poisoned and her reason dethroned by the wiles and machinations of a demon in human form. You trusted in this fiend, Goolooh; behold the consequences of your infatuation. They are all alike—one and all—and I swear to war with them to the death, until the whole of their accursed race are exterminated from our downtrodden country."

Goolooh, being fully impressed with the ingratitude and guilt of Lightfoot, reciprocated with Tamneegal in the sentiments he uttered.

"I swear to aid you in your just resolve," he said. "Vengeance against the Feringhee —a deep and lasting vengeance that may be complete and permanent, and exterminate their race from our oppressed country. At my instigation you saved this man's life; he had done me a good service, or I would not have asked you to shelter him; and now I bitterly regret it, as it has caused such disastrous results."

"I knew it—I felt that we were warming an adder into life when you first asked me to take charge of him; better to have let such a wretch be hacked to pieces than ever he should have been allowed an opportunity of practising his cursed arts upon this poor harmless woman, who could not injure a fellow-creature in thought or action. Oh, she was too credulous in man's sincerity— too good in her own character to be aware of the duplicity of others."

The painful circumstances surrounding the career of the unhappy Poutra tended in a great measure to fix and knit together both Goolooh and Tamneegal in a compact against the English residents and authorities in India.

It is not our purpose to enter into all the scenes and actions in which these two had played so conspicuous a part during the Indian outbreak. It is enough for the purposes of this tale that has been given to the reader in all its entirety, as it forms the key to events which are to follow. It must be borne in mind that the episode describing the love and ultimate fate of Poutra occurred almost on the eve of the outbreak in India. Tamneegal had since then married his second wife, Mugriah, to whom the reader has already been introduced.

He had never met with Ensign Lightfoot since the period of his departure from his house; he had, however, nursed up his revenge against him, never for a moment changing or faltering in his purpose of vengeance when the hour arrived for him to be enabled to satisfy it.

Had he been aware that his enemy formed one of the party shut up with Major Forrester and his companions in the fort, it is probable that the garrison would have perished. Indeed had Goolooh been aware of this fact, he would not have given the assistance which he did to the English residents.

Lightfoot himself had recognised Goolooh upon his first interview with our heroine, but thought it prudent to keep himself out of sight whenever the latter made his appearance, which, it will be remembered, he did on more than one occasion.

The fate of Poutra was unknown to Lightfoot, but he knew, even if she had returned to her husband's home, that he would be sure to entertain a feeling of revenge, and consequently he did not at all feel anxious to fall in with either Goolooh or Tamneegal to revive unpleasant associations and circumstances which he hoped time would bury in oblivion

It was lucky for his companions that prudence had directed him to adopt this course of conduct, for certainly had either Tamneegal or Goolooh been aware of the circumstance, affairs would have assumed a very different aspect to all parties.

Major Forrester, McDarvish, nor any of the ensign's fellow officers were not acquainted with the story of Poutra. Indeed Lightfoot himself had never evinced any anxiety to recur to the subject.

Omelia was also quite in the dark respecting the painful incidents recorded. Lightfoot, when he first saw Goolooh from the loopholes of the fort, had cautioned our heroine from mentioning his name to the latter, as he did not imagine he entertained any friendly feelings towards him, but he did not give the reason why he had such a supposition.

Tamneegal and Goolooh had formed two members of that band of conspirators who belonged to Yunadar's gang. They had inflicted terrible punishment on the English wherever they had an opportunity, but had been severely punished themselves, and considerably decreased in their number.

CHAPTER CCXXVIII.

MR. NATTERLEY'S RESIDENCE.—HIS PRISONER GORYEBOO'S SON.— THE ESCAPE. — MOORSHA THE SHIKAREE.

When Mr. Natterley had his last interview with Goryeboo the Thug, it will be remembered that the latter made the astounding announcement to his employer that the hostage he held for the fulfilment of his contract was not his son, but an Englishman's.

Such was really the case, but a long residence in the climate, and being brought up by the natives of India, and speaking their language, together with being clothed in their dress, would have led a superficial observer to come to the conclusion that he was really a native of their clime.

Mr. Natterley had a farm a few miles from Madrass. In his residence he held Goryeboo's supposed son in close confinement, and had instructed the resident manager of his estate to keep careful watch and ward over the prisoner during his absence.

The windows of the room in which he was confined were protected by strong iron bars, and every precaution had been taken to prevent his escape. Not that he had shown any disposition to do so; on the contrary, he worked in the fields on the estate during the day, and returned to his prison at night, otherwise he was treated with much kindness, and seemed well satisfied with his situation.

He had been repeatedly promised by Mr. Natterly to be restored to Goryeboo, whom he supposed to be his father, but "hope deferred maketh the heart sick," and he had had lately a yearning for liberty.

When once possessed of this feeling, he could not rest till he had made an attempt to regain it. Having by great stratagem procured a file, he set to work to see if it were possible to remove the iron bars.

This was a work of time, if it were ever accomplished at all. They were very thick and strong, and his tool was a very indifferent one with which he had to work. It was only at night that he was enabled to do this, and then with the greatest caution, fearful lest he should arouse any of the household; however, every night he performed a little of his labour, and each day he was in trembling and fear that his design might be discovered, in which case, he did not doubt but that he should be handed over to the English authorities, of whom he had a great dread.

The woman who attended to the household was cognisant of his design and favoured it, or rather connived at it.

At the present time, when we are about to direct the reader's attention to the residence of Mr. Natterley, our prisoner had succeeded in well nigh filing through the bars of the window which opposed his egress. They required, when this was sufficiently accomplished, some fearful blows to break each of them short off.

This was a difficult task to manage without discovery, as it would hardly fail to raise a great disturbance in the dead of the night, and after all had been ready for the final blow to be struck, the prisoner still hesitated to effect the accomplishment of his purpose, for even when he had succeeded in removing the bars, there were other serious impediments remaining to prevent his escape.

The window was so high, being on the top story of the house, that it was impossible to drop therefrom without considerable danger, besides which it was surrounded by a deep moat, beyond which there was a high wall, the top of which was surmounted by a high *cheveux de frieze*.

To drop from his apartment would be also a matter of no small difficulty, as the manager of the estate slept in the room immediately beneath the window, which commanded a view of the moat and surrounding wall.

All these circumstances, therefore, tended to cause the prisoner some hesitation in putting his scheme of escape in practice.

Whilst watching from his window night after night, and reflecting upon the probability of his ultimate success, the prisoner had observed a *shikaree* pursuing his occupations in a neighbouring jungle. He had watched and noted with interest his various adroit and skilful contrivances in entrapping and destroying various beasts of prey.

The *shikaree* had evidently noticed that his movements had been watched with a considerable amount of interest by the confined man, and he had more than once directed a curious and wistful glance towards the window of the prisoner, who at first had serious misgivings that his purpose had been divined by the tiger slayer, but from the expression of his countenance and general manner, he became assured that Moorsha entertained friendly feelings towards him.

One evening he became fully assured of this, for the tiger slayer came as near to the window as he possibly could, and by pantomimic motions seemed to express a wish to hold converse with the imprisoned man.

The distance, however, precluded the possibility of the two conversing with any degree of security, which the other, in reply to the motions of the tiger slayer, endeavoured to impress upon his understanding; he consequently took his departure that night in silence.

The next night the captive, when all had retired to rest, received through his open window what at first appeared to be a stone or some missile, which had evidently been thrown to him by the *shikaree*, for he observed him directing his attention to it by signs.

He hastened to pick it up, and then found it to be a stone, round which was wrapped a sheet of paper.

Hastily unfolding it he found it to be a letter which he immediately perused with interest.

It ran as follows—

"Young man,—I think I am not mistaken in surmising your intentions. You would escape from your present confinement. I have seen enough to be assured of this. If so, be candid with me; I am a friend upon whose discretion you may rely with implicit confidence. Make known your wishes, and if you need assistance command me Write an answer to this and throw it from your window towards where you see me stationed. Clear the wall and moat, or all may be lost if we are discovered. Yours,

"MOORSHA, the *shikaree*."

The captive was surprised to find a stranger evince so much consideration on his behalf, and volunteer his gratuitous assistance.

He hastily penned the following in reply, and having wrapped it round the stone, he tied it carefully with a silken cord, and threw it towards his newly discovered friend.

"To my unknown friend,—Accept my most heartfelt thanks for your consideration. I feel and know I may trust you. Although perfect strangers to each other, there is something within which tells me you are a friend. You are right in your supposition; I do wish to escape from captivity, which, of late, has become galling to me beyond endurance. I have succeeded in filing the iron bars which oppose my passage through the window of my prison, and it only wants a final blow to remove them entirely; but even then numerous difficulties surround me. I cannot drop from the window without falling into the moat, and, alas, I cannot swim, and should, therefore, be most likely drowned; besides which the room of the manager is immediately beneath mine. Can you aid me by any suggestion to overcome these impediments. Yours ever gratefully,

"TARAH."

The *shikaree* caught this missive from the hands of the captive, and having perused it, expressed, as well as he could by signs, that he would do his best to arrange some scheme, after which he took his departure.

The captive was now in better spirits, and awaited with considerable eagerness the next appearance of his unknown friend.

On the next night he was delighted to observe him at the old spot, where he had stationed himself on the two previous occasions.

He again threw his letter through the window. In it he informed Tarah that he had determined upon the plan of operations they were to adopt, and had made all the necessary arrangements.

He informed Tarah that he had come provided with a rope, the end of which he was about to throw towards the window, which he desired the captive to catch and tie firmly to something inside the apartment. The other end he proposed to fasten round the *cheveux de frieze*.

When this was completed he directed Tarah to alight by means of the rope, which might be done without noise, and unobserved from the window of the manager's room.

The next question was the removal of the bars; he conceived that it would be attended with too great a risk to break them by a blow, or rather by a series of blows, he had consequently come provided with an instrument which he had procured on purpose.

This was a sort of wrench of great power, which could be used in severing the bars now that they were sufficiently filed without making so great a noise as the blows given by a hammer. This wrench he proposed to convey by a rope to the prisoner.

When Terah fully understood these arrangements, he signalled his unqualified approval of them, and prepared to catch the rope, which, after two or three attempts he succeeded in laying hold of.

With this he hauled up the wrench, and again threw the end of it to his companion outside, that he might attach to a stronger one to be used for the purpose of his alighting.

Having obtained possession of the wrench, Tarah proceeded to test its power upon the bars of his window.

To his delight, the first yielded upon its application. Some of the others resisted all his efforts, and he had, therefore, occasion to again resort to his file, after which he managed to remove them, one by one, after a considerable time had been expended on his efforts.

Moorsha watched silently, and with intent eagerness all his movements, and gave an approving nod as he looked towards him whilst proceeding with his work of demolition.

Eventually he managed to break an aperture sufficiently large for the passage of his body, when he proceeded to fasten the rope firmly round the head of his couch, and then signalled for his assistant to adjust the other end.

He did so immediately, pulling the rope quite taut, as he wound it round the *cheveux de frieze*.

All this had been accomplished without any discovery on the part of any of the inmates of the domicile, and Tarah, with a beating heart, swung himself from the window, and slid down the rope with considerable agility.

Moorsha caught him round the shoulders and assisted him over the sharp spikes of the iron work, and he alighted on the ground in safety.

It is hardly possible to describe his first sensations of freedom. He would, on the impulse of the moment have shouted with delight, but prudence forbade him indulging in any such extravagant expressions of joy.

Moorsha did not allow him any time for reflection, but hastily dragged him from the spot, and the two proceeded at a pace which soon took them out of sight of the late scene of the prisoner's captivity.

The tiger slayer struck into a pathway known only to few besides himself, to prevent the possibility of pursuit.

When Moorsha deemed he was sufficiently far removed to feel assured of security from any attempt being made of a recapture, he, for the first time, addressed his companion.

"So," he exclaimed, "you are now safe, young man, from your enemies, be they who they may; and now the story of your captivity—its cause, and your own history. You have one, I suppose?"

Tarah at once proceeded to detail to his newly found friend what the reader already knows respecting Mr. Natterley.

He informed Moorsha that he and his father were both proscribed by the law, and that the latter was only saved at the eleventh hour by the instrumentality of his employer, who had retained him on his estate as a labourer, and had treated him with tolerable kindness. Altogether he did not speak ill of Mr. Natterley, being ignorant of the compact between that worthy and his parent.

"I understand," he said, in answer to Moorsha's inquiries, "that he has saved my father's life upon the condition that he is to do something for him in return, but what that is I am not able to inform you, but when this was accomplished I was to be restored to him, but I have been promised this so repeatedly that I had began to lose faith in the ultimate fulfilment of it, and I felt convinced that if my father failed to accomplish whatever he was required to do that I should be remorselessly handed over to the military authorities to be dealt with in a very summary manner."

"And do you know where to join your parent, now that we have safely effected your escape?" was Moorsha's next inquiry.

"Indeed, no, I have not at present any knowledge of his present abode. He is, I believe, under the surveillance of Mr. Natterley, and even if I did know where to light upon him, it would be imprudent for me to venture to his habitation, but I should fall in with my late master, who would, no doubt, in his first impulse of rage at my escape, hand me over to the military authorities."

"In that case, what do you purpose doing?"

"I must conceal myself somewhere till I can find out my parent, and devise some means of conveying to him the fact of my deliverance."

"I think I shall be able to direct your steps to some such haven of refuge. I am acquainted with a good priest, who, in any act of mercy, is ever willing to save and succour the oppressed His habitation is so remote and removed from all observation, that you may rest assured of its affording you a safe asylum, and you may, moreover, rely upon his discretion and good intention."

"You will be adding to the inestimable favours you have already conferred upon me, if you can recommend me to his good graces."

"It shall be done, and in the abode of the good Jahnsah you will be safe to find a happy home, as long as you require to partake of his hospitality and kindness. It is many miles hence, but to a fugitive who has just regained his liberty, it will be nothing."

Tarah joyfully accepted the kind offer and suggestion made by his friend, Moorsha, and the two hastened on with light hearts towards the dwelling of the worthy Jahnsah.

Each time that the escaped captive spoke, the *shikaree* observed him with curious eyes, and his voice and manner seemed to awaken to his recollection a thin thread of memory of byegone years, which he in vain endeavoured to account for and unravel.

The still landscape through which they were wending their way, was bathed in moonlight, that lit up wood, hill, and dale with a brightness which rendered all its various features as distinctly visible as in the day.

After they had journeyed some miles, the tedium of which had been relieved by occasional conversation, Moorsha paused on a grassy bank, upon which he reclined and rested awhile, motioning at the same time for his companion to follow his example. There lay before him, in the distance, a thatched hut, which was the residence of a native farmer, whose crops were gently waving as they were stirred by the slight breeze which was passing over them. Moorsha gazed at the scene before him with a more than usual intentness, and seemed lost in abstraction, which his companion did not like to disturb. Memory was busy with the past, and the *shikaree's* brain was filled with thoughts of his earlier and happier days of existence.

"There," he said musingly, " lays the once happy home which sheltered me in my early youth. It has passed into other hands now, and I am only permitted to see it therefore occasionally as I pass, and contemplate the spot upon which so many happy hours have been passed with those, who now alas, have vanished for ever from my sight."

"What is the name of the farm?" inquired his companion with some curiosity.

"It takes the name of the occupant whoever he may be. When my father owned it, by the neighbours around it was called his farm—but it is on the Kuley's estate."

"Ah, then, if I mistake not, I can sympathise with you, for if my memory serves me right, which it generally does, in the events of our boyhood, I too have been sheltered by that same thatched roof."

The *shikaree* gave a sudden and furtive glance at his companion, and appeared struck with some unaccountable momentary surprise. He was not, however, a man habitually given to any sudden demonstration of passion, being rather of a reserved and reflective temperament, and when he had looked inquiringly at his companion upon his making the last observation, he relapsed into his usual sedate demeanour, and said mildly—

"Sheltered you, my friend? I should hardly believe that possible, as I know the present owner, and all the occupants of the farm, and do not think it likely you could have ever been one of its inmates during his time."

"Perhaps not, it was most likely before he was in possession."

"Oh, no, impossible; why my father occupied it then, and he has been dead—ah, how many years?—long before you were born, I am thinking. No, you must be mistaken my friend. These houses and farms are so alike, in character and general appearance, that it is easy for you to be mistaken in their identity, and the probability is, that you are therefore misled in your present supposition."

"Well, it may be so, although I cling with some degree of tenacity to the memories of early youth, which seldom misdirect us. It was from that house—or some such—that I was carried away by a tiger, who having scratched a hole in the thatch, jumped through it, seized me in my jaws, and carried me, I know not wither, until my father rescued me inanimate from his jaws."

Amazement sat upon the features of Moorsha; unutterable amazement held him enchained, as these words were uttered. The current of his blood seemed to gather round his heart, and his limbs trembled with excitement. We have said just now, that he was not a man who usually indulged in the demonstration of either joy, sorrow, surprise, or any other passion which moved the human breast; but in the present instance, he seemed to be quite overpowered, and could not readily recover his usually possessed bearing and demeanour.

"Young man," he said slowly, "if this be indeed the case, the decrees of fate are wonderful. Tell me, I conjure you, all the particulars, that I may be assured of this fact. There has appeared to me, throughout our brief acquaintance, some invisible hand, which directed me to come to your succour and assistance. When my father occupied that farm, it was myself who was left in care of a child, who had been placed in our charge by the late Kerah Singh. During the absence of my parent, a tiger entered the thatched roof and bore off our charge before my eyes, and I was unable to render the slightest assistance to save him. This circumstance is indelibly impressed upon my memory, for the child was my constant companion, and I loved him as a brother, and have long since mourned him as dead. What a marvellous dispensation of fate it must be, if this same being should be still in existence! but ah, no, it must be impossible."

"It is surprising, and fills my mind with wonder," answered Tarah: "but I really believe that I am none other than he, and oh, if this be the case, what a dispensation of providence is it that has so miraculously brought us together. Tell me what age would the child have been, you have just mentioned?"

"Ah, a little removed from infancy, it

might be four years of age, as nearly as I can guess; for, to say the truth, I never exactly knew."

"What inmates were there of your father's abode, at the time you speak of?"

"My father, myself, and a younger sister."

"The same, I remember them all. Have I then to thank for my deliverence, the friend of my childhood; I am lost in amazement."

"Not more than I am myself," said Moorsha, in a voice of the utmost seriousness. "This child, when he was with us, had the second finger of his left hand broken, through an accident, and it had consequently grown crooked."

"Behold!" exclaimed his companion, "as he exhibited his left hand, with the distorted finger."

The *shikaree* gazed with eyes of curiosity upon the hand extended for his inspection.

"Humph!" he ejaculated; "there it is without doubt. When the boy was conveyed away by the savage beast, he was dressed in a green tunic, fastened with a belt, to which was attached a buckle set with torquois, in the centre of which was an agate."

"I have such at home."

"And round his neck there was suspended a small locket, containing the likenesses of two individuals, the one a male and the other a female."

"I have, or rather my father has them at home. He has carefully treasured them up for years, for what purpose I could never understand."

"He is *not* your father," said Moorsha, prophetically.

"He is not! then who is?"

The *shikaree* shook his head.

"I do not know any more than this, that he was an Englishman."

"An Englishman! impossible!"

"It is perfectly possible, and more than that, both probable and true, this much I can vouch for. It is likely enough you might be taken by many for a native of this clime, but upon a careful examination, there is every indication of your foreign blood. You were placed under the charge of my father, as I have before mentioned, by Kerah Singh, who at the time mentioned that you were the son of an English gentleman, an intimate and valued friend of his; and there cannot be the smallest doubt that such is the case, for Kerah Singh was a man of strict integrity, and his word was to be implicitly relied on."

"Does he still live?"

"No, he has been dead many many years."

"Then my birth and parentage must remain a mystery. "Do you know any other person who is likely to be in any way acquainted with my early history."

"Alas, no; so many years have passed away since that period, that children have become men—young men old—and a generation has passed away; but we have already had a manifestation of the wonderful decrees of fate. Let us not despair—who can tell what is contained in the hidden works of time?"

"Let me thank fate for having sent you to my assistance. Even now I think I can discern the features of my early playmate."

"Something struck me," said Moorsha, "that I was or had been connected with you when I first beheld your endeavours at the casement of your prison house, and I was instantly hurried on to learn something more. It was a wondrous instinct which prompted me to seek to know more about you and your intentions; in which we behold the finger of destiny."

It was long ere these two men thus thrown together in so remarkable a manner, could bring themselves to the determination of proceeding towards the abode of Jahnsah.

They had so many recollections of early youth to recount to each other, that time flew swiftly on, unheeded by them both, until Moorsha was awakened to the necessity of seeking a place of repose for his newly found friend and companion, and proceeded, therefore, for the purpose to the abode of the priest; upon arriving at which the two visitors were received with the usual kindness evinced on all occasions by Jahnsah to his brothers in misfortune.

"The ways of providence are inscrutible, my son," he said, when Moorsha had made him acquainted with the particulars of his recent discovery, "and beyond the ken of the most far-seeing or gifted mortal. It is but for us to humbly bow our heads to the decrees of the Most High without a murmur. It is His all wise directing hand who doubtless sent you to the assistance of a distressed brother, whom it will be my pleasing duty to shelter from his enemies."

"Thanks, worthy father," answered Moorsha; "I knew that he would find in you a friend who would cheerfully give him all the assistance which he needed."

And so saying he left the escaped prisoner to the care of the good Jahnsah, who rendered his guest all the comforts he desired.

———

CHAPTER CCXXIX.

DEPARTURE OF MAJOR FORRESTER.—OMELIA'S RESOLVE.—THE CONSPIRATORS AT WORK.

IT will be remembered by the reader that our heroine, after the attack made upon her by the Thug returned to her good friends Major and Mrs. Forrester and companions, and while with them she was safe from the machinations of her malignant enemies. Major Forrester's health had declined, and he appeared to be getting weaker every day, and his brother officers suggested to him the expedient of returning to England upon leave of absence; but this proposition appeared to be repugnant to his feelings.

No. 98.

Havelock's gallant band, when stationed near Jubbulpore, were joined by a portion of General Neil's division. The neighbouring provinces, were by this time, restored to peace and order, and the commander-in-chief—Lord Clyde, had directed the majority of the troops to withdraw, and join the main body, stationed near Cawnpore. He had ordered, however, a detachment to remain at Langor, to keep in check any of the fugitive rebels, who might be disposed to occasion annoyance. This detachment would have been placed under the command of Major Forrester, had that officer's health been sufficiently restored for him to take the command of a company; but the commander-in-chief, deemed very properly, that the Major had already endured too many hardships; and it was therefore intimated to him, that his general officer would be glad of his rejoining the main body of the troops,

The detachment, therefore, who were to invest Langor were placed under the command of an officer belonging to Neal's division, a Captain Midhurst, who was a strict disciplinarian and a man of inflexible resolution; under him were several other junior officers, amongst whom was our old acquaintance Ensign Lightfoot, with several of his quondam companions. It was to be in the society of these, and a natural yearning for active service which had induced the ensign to press his services to be accepted at Langor. Major and Mrs. Forester would have insisted upon Omelia's accompanying them to the head quarters of the Commander-in-Chief, but she seemed reluctant to consent to do so, saying that she should be an incumbrance to them, and might not be viewed with such favourable eyes by Lord Clyde as she had been by her attached friends and companions. It is probable, however, that these expectations would have been overruled had not Ensign Lightfoot offered his advice, by saying that it would be better for our heroine to be with the body of troops investing Langor, as she might be of infinite service to them, she being well acquainted with the country around, the habits of the inhabitants, as also their language. In consequence of the ensign's arguments, therefore, it was ultimately agreed that Omelia should remain under the protection of Ensign Lightfoot, who evinced an almost brotherly solicitude for her. And when Major Forester had joined the main body, had seen Lord Clyde, and a determination had been arrived at as to his future movements or destination, he insisted, as well as his wife, upon our heroine immediately joining them. So after many bitter tears at parting from the ladies, and heartfelt expressions of gratitude and friendship from the major and McDarvish, our heroine beheld her friends, with whom she had witnessed so many vicissitudes and hardships, take their departure with Havelock's and Neil's divisions. A sensation of deep despondency overcame her after they had left, and a foreboding of evil, in spite of all her efforts, seemed to take possession of her, which she in vain endeavoured to shake off. Ensign Lightfoot endeavoured to assuage her grief by unremitting attention; but nevertheless it was in vain for him to attempt to fill up the void occasioned by the absence of those to whom she had become sincerely attached.

They were comfortable quarters in which Captain Midhurst and his troops found themselves established at Langor, and but few disturbances occurred to occasion them any annoyance, and they maintained their position for some time in comparative tranquillity.

But dark clouds were gathering in the horizon, and a storm was soon destined to burst over their heads—of which they had not the slightest anticipation. The disastrous affair which we are about to relate commenced thus: in one of the foraging expeditions Ensign Lightfoot had command of a party of troops in the neighbourhood of his quarters, when he was observed by Tamneegal, who instantly recognised his supposed enemy. A dark and malignant expression lighted up his countenance when he beheld the ensign and party, but he concealed himself from the latter's notice, while the most violent feelings of revenge took possession of Tamneegal, which he at once determined to gratify. Following at some distance, he became acquainted with the knowledge of his whereabouts, and an unappeased feeling of vengeance remained as yet ungratified in his breast. This was the first link in the chain of events which followed one another in quick succession. It is easy to comprehend the occasion of Tamneegal's proximity to the ensign's quarters. Goolooh, who had hovered like a moth round a flame near to where Omelia was stationed, had brought with him his enslavers, foster parent, and hence the unfortunate rencounter with Lightfoot. Goolooh had not the slightest idea of the presence of Lightfoot, or he would have avoided the possibility of arousing the vindictive feelings of Tamneegal by a meeting with the former—who was, however, quite unconscious of having been observed by his malignant enemy.

Burning with rage—with all the most vindictive feelings aroused it was possible for the human breast to contain, Tamneegal, with a moody determination hastened to his home to brood over his wrongs, and devise a scheme for a speedy vengeance, to satiate which he brought all his most active imagination to bear upon the subject. With a stealthy caution respecting his fell purpose, he deemed it advisable not to consult Goolooh in the matter, as he entertained some doubts of his consenting to be in league against any friend of Omelia's. Tamneegal had recently formed a sort of alliance with Gorzeboo the thug, and to him, therefore, he confided the history of his wrongs, and the fact of his suddenly falling upon the unfortunate ensign. The thug had, of course, his own purposes to serve, and cared little about the injuries of Tamneegal; nevertheless he saw in the circumstance the probability there would be for him to work out his own schemes, in conjunction with the irritated and revengeful husband; and he lent, therefore, an attentive ear to the recital of all his woes and injuries. It is to the interview of these hopeful pair of scoundrels that we have now to introduce the reader.

"For so consummate a villain," said Gorzeboo, in a tone of sympathy, to his companion, after he had listened to the history of the fate of Poutra, "there is but one word, death!"

"I have waited anxiously for this hour to come," said the other, "and was assured sooner or later that I should have it; vengeance shall be mine—vengeance for her whose wrongs cry out beyond the grave; but now, my friends, a truce to idle threats and empty curses—this man must die! How is it to be accomplished?"

"We must manage by some means to draw him into ambush away from his companions in arms; this must be done by stratagem, and then—you know the rest."

"Can you suggest the means?"

"Yes, it must be accomplished through this step-daughter of yours. It is time you took her from the protection of this accursed race, make her instrumental in obtaining you the opportunity of gratifying a just revenge upon one of your most bitter enemies, and at the same time take possession of your daughter and restore her to the faith of her fathers."

"That would indeed be all I desire," answered Tamneegal; "but how shall we proceed in the accomplishment of this project?"

"It must and shall be managed," said Gorzeboo. "Insist upon regaining possession of your daughter, whom they have stolen from you, whose mind they have warped, and whose principles they have well nigh destroyed. You are her natural protector—and none other but you. Insist upon your right."

"It is of no use insisting in opposition to an overpowering force. The disobedient girl sides with our oppressors, and would therefore seek, as she has already done, their protection. No, that would be useless, and then we should be no nearer to the villian Lightfoot."

"Send, then, some messenger to Captain Midhurst, informing him that there are some of his countrymen who need his assistance, and that will occasion him to send out a few of his troops to release them. When they are sufficiently removed from Langor, you and your companions are sufficiently strong to attack them and cut them to pieces."

"Even then I should be as far as ever from obtaining possession of Lightfoot."

"Now, do you know, that he appears to be a young fellow who is always foremost on duties of this sort, and the probability is that he would be with them."

"He might, it is true; but there is no certainty of this. Well, some such scheme as this must be adopted."

"I will watch night and day," said Tamneegal, "but I will find an opportunity to sweep this miscreant from the face of the earth."

After many other propositions from Gorzeboo, the worthies parted with no definite settlement as to the plan of operations they intended to adopt. At present their schemes did not appear sufficiently promising to ensure a certain and immediate success. Eventually upon one or two more meetings they determined upon their plan of operations.

A circumstance occurred which favoured their designs, and of which they at once hastened to avail themselves. The other party of mutinous Sepoys, whom it will be remembered attacked the fort in which our English party were besieged, retained possession of several English prisoners whom they had captured in their flight from one district to another. They had not destroyed them, as they were anxious to retain them as hostages to propitiate the favour of Lord Clyde, and induce him to grant a pardon for their clemency. Tamneegal became aware of this fact, and knew moreover where they lay confined. This fact he made Gorzeboo acquainted with, who at once saw in it the means it afforded them of maturing their schemes of vengeance. Tamneegal, it will be remembered, was viewed by the party in question with feelings of mistrust, more particularly so after his desperate encounter with them outside the fort, but Gorzeboo was however on friendly terms with most of them, and he had therefore an opportunity afforded him of seeing the English prisoners frequently. They were civilians consisting of two merchants, their wives and families, and were stationed in a small village a few miles from Langor, and were in daily expectation of being destroyed by their persecutors. Gorzeboo affected to sympathise with them, and acted his part so well that they believed in his good intentions. He promised to endeavour to effect their escape, but this was an impossibility, as they were too well watched and guarded. Neither had he ever intended to do so even if an opportunity had occurred. After several interviews he informed them that he would answer for their being rescued by their own countrymen, if one would write a letter explanatory of their situation.

Now, a letter to Captain Midhurst was not what the Thug desired. He had always a great horror of the summary mode that English officers usually dealt with these matters, and his object was to attract our heroine from her place of security. He therefore informed the prisoners that a letter addressed to Omelia would be sure to have the effect desired. At the mention of our heroine's name one of the ladies gave a start of surprise, and upon further inquiry, it turned out that she had been intimately acquainted with our heroine in the early portion of the revolt, having been in fact a friend of the late Flora Melville—whom, no doubt, the reader well remember.

It was immediately determined therefore that this lady should write to Omelia, explaining their present situation, saying that the bearer of the letter would guide the footsteps of any detachment which might be sent to the rescue.

In the letter however it was stated, that ransom had been offered to the Sepoys by their prisoners, and they seemed disposed to accept of these terms, provided it was accompanied with a free pardon from the commander-in-chief. The writer therefore exhorted Omelia to endeavour to arrange the matter amicably, without resorting to violence. Having written the letter in question, and reminded our heroine of the writer's early acquaintance with her, it was entrusted to Gorzeboo to deliver—who of course had not the slightest intention of being himself the messenger for its conveyance. He therefore at once proceeded to Tamneegal, to consult with him and determine upon their future course of action. The latter suggested to the Thug the expedient of his delivering the letter himself, but this was immediately negatived by Gorzeboo, who proposed to his companion the propriety of employing Goolooh as an agent, at the same time as they did so, keeping him entirely in the dark as to their ulterior intentions.

"It would be the most certain course, without doubt," said Tamneegal, in reply; "but the fellow is so madly infatuated with my daughter-in-law, that it would break his heart if he did anything to cause her pain or trouble."

"Possibly so," answered the Thug, "but he need never know that he has been the cause of any misfortune to your daughter —of this miscreant Lightfoot—and indeed, to speak the truth, neither will he have been."

"He will have a shrewd guess."

"Let him; you have a right to obtain possession of your step-daughter upon any terms."

"True, it shall be done as you say, leave me the letter, and this very night I will propose the subject to our friend Goolooh.

Anything which takes him into the presence of his enslaver will be in itself a great fascination, and he will therefore be the more willing to seek her, for the purpose of doing an act of mercy."

The two rascals looked at each other and grinned sardonically, as these last words were uttered.

* * * * *

Langor, where Captain Midhurst was stationed, had remained tranquil, and but little had occurred to call into activity any of the British troops. Ensign Lightfoot, whose active temperament made him yearn to have, as he expressed it, "a brush with the rascals," regretted that no opportunity had occurred since the ensign's close confinement in the fort, he had had but little opportunity afforded him for active service. He was therefore both surprised and pleased when Omelia placed in his hands a packet which was addressed to her from some English prisoner some miles distant. The ensign read and re-read the document, and looking at our heroine, said enquiringly:—

"Who brought this?"

"A messenger upon whom I can rely!"

"Good, who is he? do I know him?"

"Yes, he is the same whose noble generosity provided us with provisions when in the Redouya fort."

"Oh, indeed, yes I remember perfectly well:" and the recollection of the fate of Poutra crossed his mind.

"You believe in his sincerity?"

"I cannot for a moment doubt it; he is a tried and valued friend."

"And who is to conduct a party to serve these prisoners?"

"I shall be enabled to do so myself," said Omelia; "this young man was to have done so, but in strict confidence he has made me fully acquainted with their position, and I shall therefore find no difficulty in lighting upon them, as I know every part of this country well."

"We must consult the captain," said Lightfoot; "this promises to turn out well. I will by your leave take this document to him at once."

"Do so, I should wish it."

The ensign proceeded therefore immediately into the presence of his superior officer. Captain Midhurst was a man whose stern countenance seemed an index of his own character and disposition; his beetling brows, overhung eyes, whose piercing glance bore some similarity to those of a hawk; a hard featured man was Captain Midhurst, with his falcon eyes, aquiline nose, and iron grey hair; nearly sixty summers had passed over his head, but he appeared to be in the full vigour of manhood. When the ensign handed the paper to his captain, the latter after he had ran his eye over the document, said, sharply:—

"Is there any truth in this statement?"

"I see no reason to doubt it. The man who brought it is well known, and would not lend himself to be the bearer of any false report or intelligence; he has already rendered us infinite service."

"Umph! where is this Indian girl? I would speak to her."

The ensign proceeded to Omelia, and brought her in the presence of Captain Midhurst. Our heroine had never entertained any particular feeling of partiality towards the captain since her short acquaintance. His manner was generally sharp and abrupt towards her, and she fancied moreover that he seemed to view her with some feeling of mistrust. When she entered, he glanced his eagle eyes towards her, and his countenance was expressive of suspicion, and altogether he assumed the appearance of a judge examining a criminal.

"This is from some friend of yours, I am informed," he said, in stern accents.

"It is from one whom I knew in the earlier portion of this unfortunate revolt, and who, it appears, now needs some succour from her countrymen."

"So it appears, from its contents. Who conveyed it hither?"

"One whom I have every reason to consider a friend, as he has proved himself such on many occasions."

"He is a countryman of yours, I suppose?"

"Yes."

"And you do not imagine this to be a trumped up tale to entice our men into ambush?"

"I will answer with my life for its truth."

"Ah! It may be so; but I have myself grave doubts upon the subject. However, we cannot let our countrymen perish without striking a blow to assist them."

"I should hope that would be hardly necessary; from the contents of that letter it appears that their enemies would in all probability consent to grant them freedom upon consideration of ransom and a free pardon from Lord Clyde."

"We do not feel disposed to make terms with traitors," said Captain Midhurst, haughtily.

"As you deem best, sir," answered Omelia. "It is not for me to suggest to your superior judgment, only when the object can be effected without bloodshed by a more conciliatory course, I should have

hoped you would have thought it well to adopt it."

The captain made no reply to this last observation, but considered the matter over for some minutes.

"There is no time," he said, turning to the ensign, "for us to communicate with Lord Clyde—even if such an uncertain affair as this warranted my doing so. What say you? do you think it advisable to send a detachment of men commanded by yourself, to enquire into this matter?"

"With your leave, sir, I would gladly undertake the task—my friend here would, perhaps, have no objection to accompany us."

This last observation, of course, referred to Omelia.

The captain bowed his acquiescence; then, turning to Omelia, he observed significantly:

"It is upon the faith of your word that I am induced to follow the advice of Ensign Lightfoot—upon your assurance alone! If we are deceived, therefore, it will be you who have been the cause of it—knowing these people better than any of us possibly can—we place the affair in your hands, to conduct our troops to the place you alone know. Ensign Lightfoot, we will at once call out a sufficient force to accompany you," and so saying, he left the apartment with his junior officer, to select a few tried soldiers for the duty.

CHAPTER CCXXX.

THE MARCH OF LIGHTFOOT'S DETACHMENT. THE SURPRISE AND AMBUSH.—DISASTROUS CONSEQUENCES.—DEATH OF LIGHTFOOT.

CAPTAIN MIDHURST proceeded to form a strong body of troops to accompany the ensign and our heroine upon their expedition. It was not without considerable misgivings that he did so, for the captain had but little faith in the word of any native of India, his prejudices being strong against them. He charged the ensign, therefore, to use the utmost caution, and march directly back to quarters if he had reason to suspect any treachery. Lightfoot, however, appeared to be in high spirits, and felt fully assured that his mission would turn out a successful one. He had the utmost confidence in Omelia's discretion and integrity, and did not fail to express himself with considerable warmth in laudatory encomiums upon her character to his superior officer, who received them with a certain degree of coldness. Forward!—march!—were the orders given, and the measured tread of the troops was heard in obedience to the word of command.

It was many miles from Langor that the ensign's company had to travel, before they could reach the spot mentioned in the letter addressed to Omelia, but she knew the road well, and had no difficulty in directing the course the ensign was to take, who felt elated at being again upon some active duty. The road through which they were journeying, was over an open plain—with here and there a few clumps of gigantic trees, surrounded by jungle. Hitherto there march had been uninterrupted by any incident, save a few straggling villagers, who gazed with feelings of awe at the compact body of men, who appeared to move like a solid wall. Upon arriving at the furthermost limits of the plain. they found its boundary to be several steep hills or mountains, which rose abruptly from the table land. To mount these would be a matter of no small difficulty, as their surface appeared to be very irregular, and to those unacquainted with their construction, the task was attended with some danger, and a considerable loss of time. Omelia directed the ensign's attention to a narrow defile or pass, formed through them, and this she pointed out as the direct route to the place of their destination. It was a deep cutting, sufficiently wide to admit three or four men abreast, and the rocks rose perpendicularly above—to a stupendous height. A thought crossed the mind of the ensign, that this was anything but a prepossessing passage, and he enquired of our heroine, if it would not be possible to force a passage over the mountains; but they were so steep and jagged, that it appeared almost an impossibility. Nevertheless Lightfoot did not seem disposed immediately to trust himself and troops in the narrow gorge—and he directed therefore a few of his men, to make an attempt to ascend one of the most favorable hills. They proceeded to act according to his directions, but after several attempts found it a matter of utter impossibility, without being provided with ropes and implements to assist them in securing a footing, and safe passage.

"Is there no other way besides this one?" he enquired of Omelia; and receiving a reply in the negative, he was compelled to adopt the only alternative which was left for his adoption. He therefore ordered his men to quick march through the pass in question. The road consisted of sand and chalk, and the rocks themselves through which this passage had been cut were composed of the latter material, intermixed with large pieces of lime stone, which increased in size as they neared the top. Lightfoot ran his eye through the defile and pronounced it an "ugly spot," and so indeed it was. In such an one the finest and most gallant troops in the world, find themselves at a discount and powerless against an aggressive foe. Lightfoot was brave, but his anxiety was of no common order, and he heartily wished to emerge from his present position. His alarm for the safe passage of the troops entrusted to his command, was considerably augmented, as he thought he discerned several dusky figures on the heights above. The poor ensign began to repent of his mission, as dreadful thoughts of treachery flashed across his mind, and the doubts of his superior officer were now felt in their full force.

"Would to heaven we were safe out of this suffocating passage," he exclaimed. "How far is it now?" this was addressed to Omelia.

"We are hardly half through it as yet," she replied.

"Humph! my patience is well nigh exhausted."

The clouds of dust which the soldiers threw up in their passage did not tend to improve their situation, as the day was intensely hot. After they had proceeded a short distance further they came to an insurmountable impediment to their onward progress. This consisted of a mass of dried wood, stones and rubbish, which completely choked up the narrow defile, and it appeared to run up as high as the rocks themselves. "Halt!" said the ensign, when he observed this impediment, and he turned with looks of surprise and horror towards our heroine. She darted upon him an agonised look in return, and began to be a prey to the most gloomy fears.

Lightfoot made a hasty inspection of the obstacles which impeded their progress, and found it to be so firmly wedged between the two rocks that it appeared hopeless to endeavour to remove it. He ordered, however, several of his sappers and miners to make the attempt; and they proceeded with their hatchets and other instruments to carry out his wishes. While the attempt was being made the unfortunate party of soldiers became aware of the dreadful situation into which they had been drawn. In the very midst of them there fell an immense piece of rock, which crushed several beneath it into a shapeless mass, and wounded as many others. They had not time to recover from this first surprise when another and another fell upon them with similar disastrous results. The whole affair flashed across the mind of Ensign Lightfoot. He saw, now that it was too late, the whole plan. The passage had been blocked up purposely; their course had been watched, and he did not for a moment doubt but that the letter and its contents was indeed, as his captain expressed it, a trumped affair. Lightfoot was nearly beside himself with rage, mortification, and despair. Cold drops of perspiration stood upon his forehead, and he was so appalled at the agony of his situation, and its complete hopelessness, that his senses seemed benumbed, and he was quite at a loss how to act. He was rendered perfectly furious as he beheld the stones continue to fall, and with them numbers of his gallant troops.

"It is too dreadful to contemplate," he exclaimed; "fire, men, fire up the ravine: see! cover the edges of the rocks ahead."

With this he formed his men singly in a line against that side of the rock which appeared to offer a little shelter, and directing their pieces to the edge of the opposite rock they awaited the appearance of any living object which presented itself to their sight. They had not long to watch, for they soon observed the forms of numbers of dusky figures approach the edge of the rock laden with heavy pieces of stone, which they were about to hurl down the chasm. In an instant orders were given to fire: a sharp volley rung through the air and was repeated by numerous echos, and two dead bodies came tumbling down almost at the soldiers' feet. Omelia recognised them instantly as belonging to part of her foster-father's gang, but she did not deem it advisable to make Lightfoot acquainted with this circumstance. The ensign marshalled his best marksmen (the rifle brigade), and directed them to pick off as many of their enemies as possible, as fast as they appeared on the summit of the rock above, at the same time he urged on his sappers and miners to remove as many of the bushes, felled trees and rubbish which choked up the passage. He did this not with any idea of cutting a passage through, for that was quite impossible, but his object was to obtain a place of shelter for a portion of his troops, from the terrible missiles which were falling so fast as to threaten their complete annihilation. The shouts and cheers of the attacking party were heard with fearful distinctness by the ill-fated British, but few however were visible on the opposite rock to where the rifle brigade were stationed. An immense mass of stones were however now showered down from the same side to where they stood, and numbers of the gallant fellows were prostrated therefrom, many dead and double the number wounded in a shocking manner.

It was impossible from their present situation to catch sight of their enemies, and their weapons were unavailing. Lightfoot's heart sank as he beheld the terrible urgency of the case, and he despaired of ever escaping with life from his present hopeless situation. He however gave orders for his troops to disperse themselves and retreat back to the opening they had just entered by. Litters were made for the wounded from the faggots which opposed their passage, and with heavy hearts the doomed soldiers proceeded on their disastrous march. In their passage along the defile numbers fell at every dozen yards. Their implacable enemy followed them step by step and discharged upon their devoted heads a continual shower of stones and broken rocks. Omelia had several narrow escapes from immediate death, which she disregarded; she would indeed have been thankful to have fallen a victim rather than have lived to witness this day's disaster and bloodshed. But Tamneegal, who was the chief of the aggressive party above, was careful in his directions for them to spare his daughter-in-law. It was Gorzeboo who had endeavoured to destroy her unobserved by his companions, and once or twice he had well nigh effected his object.

It was a horrible passage the troops were taking through this narrow defile, made more horrible from the fact of their being utterly unable to have the satisfaction of dying in fair fight, or give battle to their assailants in any way. Clouds of suffocating dust arose as each missile fell, and there seemed but a slender chance of any escaping with life. More than three-fourths of that devoted band of warriors had already found a warrior's grave, and disaffection and wild disorder took possession of the few remaining; Omelia had endeavoured to persuade Lightfoot to exhort his men to discipline, but the latter saw it was hopeless, it was nothing but a scrambling retreat, and it was useless to endeavour to form the troops into anything like order, indeed under the circumstances of their position it was an impossibility, never surely was there a more disastrous affair than this, if we except the Cabul Pass, to which, with the exception of the numbers, it was very similar.

When our unfortunate ensign came near to the spot where he had entered this passage of destruction, he endeavoured to form what few men remained. They did not number more than fifteen or sixteen out of one hundred and sixty. These few he addressed, and eventually succeeded in getting to form into line, to give battle to whatever enemies might be ready to oppose them upon their emerging from the fatal defile. Upon their arriving into the open plain, they were saluted with a volley of musketry from the Sepoys who were congregated in immense numbers. The British troops were infuriated beyond description, and rushed madly upon their numerous opponents, charged them, and committed an indiscriminate onslaught; but they fell slowly one by one, although they cut a passage through their opponents, who fell like corn before the sickle. Upon the ensign emerging from the defile, he was confronted by Tamneegal, Gorzeboo, and several of his companions. At the sight of the latter, so great was her horror of this man, and so terrible had been the scenes she had witnessed, that our heroine swooned away, and happily was lost to consciousness, when the last scene of this bloody tragedy occurred.

"Vengeance is mine!" exclaimed Tamneegal, as he confronted the ensign. "Vengeance for the wronged Poutra—man without heart or soul, your last hour is come." Lightfoot's cup of woe was quite full; the painful recollection of all the incidents connected with the unfortunate woman named by his opponent came to his memory in all their original distinctness.

It would be idle to endeavour to reason with a man whose lust of revenge had rendered a madman.

"Back!" he exclaimed, "blood-thirsty man; I never wronged you, as Heaven is my judge—I would not have my sword find a passage through the body of one who, in the hour of need did me a signal service—back, therefore, and let me pass."

"Never," roared out Tamneegal—"well, did you requite the favour you profess to have so keen a recollection of. Oh! how have I longed for this hour—I scorn and spit at you—the injuries to my injured wife can be washed out with your blood alone;" and he flew at Lightfoot with his utmost fury. The ensign parried his thrusts with skill and his accustomed address. He was an accomplished swordsman, and had several opportunities afforded him of destroying his opponent, but neglected to avail himself of them, and stood merely upon the defensive.

After a short and desperate conflict, the ensign succeeded in striking the sword from his opponents hand, and grasping him by the throat endeavoured to make him prisoner. Gorzeboo and another of his followers, seeing the critical situation of Tamneegal, rushed to his rescue, and simultaneously passed both their swords from behind through the body of the ill-fated ensign, who fell to the earth without a groan—dead.

Of the men who had attacked the Sepoys with such impetuosity, but few remained to tell the sad tale of this day's disasters. Some four or five, however, did succeed in reaching their quarters, to describe to Captain Midhurst the result of the unfortunate expedition.

Thus ended the career of poor Lightfoot, the victim of a false suspicion which had been aroused, perhaps by an act of imprudence, originally on his part, but which, as we have seen already, has been attended with the most fearful and disastrous results. The ensign was a smart, active, brave young officer, and gave promise of becoming a distinguished ornament to the service—but he was doomed to be cut off in the flower of his youth—and was sacrificed, as many men have been before and since, to the force of circumstances.

CHAPTER CCXXXI.

THE SITUATION OF OMELIA—THE REMOVAL BY TAMNEEGAL—MORE INCIDENTS—RAGE OF CAPTAIN MIDHURST.

WHEN Tamneegal was rescued so fortuitously by his two companions, his first thought, now that he had gratified his feelings of revenge, was for Omelia. He remembered to have observed her swoon away immediately upon her emerging from the defile, in which the British troops had met with such an untimely end. He hastened therefore at once to the spot where he had last observed his step-daughter. He found her prostrate where he had left her.

She was still unconscious; the terrible scenes she had witnessed, the disastrous termination to their expedition, and lastly, the sight of her enemy the Thug, entirely prostrated her. Tamneegal contemplated the beauteous being whom he would fain adopt as his own child. As she lay amidst the heaps of slain which surrounded her, she herself seemed to be in death's cold embrace, and lost to the painful contemplation of that scene which the wicked bad passions of man had rendered a pandemonium.

Gorzeboo was also contemplating the inanimate figure of our heroine with very different feelings to her foster-father. The latter knelt down and supported her head upon one knee, and chafed her hand. The action of rising her head and shoulders restored Omelia to consciousness. She opened her eyes, and beheld her father-in-

law bending over her, his looks indicative of much consideration and anxiety on her account.

She started to her feet, and sprang back in horror on finding the close proximity of Tamneegal; her fears were not in any way diminished when she beheld the Thug and several other evil-looking countenances in the back ground.

She passed her hand across her brow, as though she were desirous of shutting out from her sight the presence of these beings who stood so prominently before her vision.

Tamneegal knew it was impossible for her to effect an escape, he was not, therefore, so precipitate in his actions as, in a more urgent case, he otherwise would have been. He was desirous that she should recover from her first emotions of surprise and revulsion

No. 99.

before he addressed her. She turned round, and surveyed the *debris* of the late conflict, or rather slaughter, and in doing so lighted upon the prostrate and inanimate form of poor Lightfoot. Hastily stooping down, she examined his features, and found there unmistakeable evidence of death.

She was overwhelmed at this discovery—these last few drops in her bitter cup, which filled it to overflowing.

"Villains!" she shrieked, in bitter accent, "deep-dyed, remorseless, black, and heartless villains! This is your work! Behold!—gratify your sanguinary natures by the contemplation of your hateful work; but a time will come— aye, and that shortly, too—when you will be amply repaid for your fiendish and murderous acts. Was it for this you lured me and my companions by a specious, well varnished tale?—was it for this whole-sale butchery?"

"Peace, girl," said Tamneegal; "you know not what you are saying. This, as all other punishments, are brought on by their own crimes."

"Liar! wholesale murderer, it is false!—it is you who have stained your soul with a thousand crimes, which make me shudder to own that I am one of your race. It is you and your worthless associates who have brought disgrace upon the very name of humanity—you, whose path has been one of bloodshed, plunder, rapine;—hence!—be-gone!"

"Headstrong girl, you have been worked on and prejudiced by our natural enemies, and are, perhaps, more to be pitied than censured. Your mind has been poisoned, and you have become an alien from your race and creed; fate, which rules our destinies, has, you see, decreed that you should return to the true faith of your father's, and be again restored to your natural protectors. You are, therefore, henceforth known only as my daughter, following my instructions, and judged in all your actions by my supe-rior advice."

"Your daughter!—never! Sooner would I stretch myself a corpse over the body of this wronged and cruelly-used young man, than I would ever consent to herd with mur-derers. Never!—man of blood, I abhor the sight of you. Repent, ere it be too late—repent of your heinous crimes. What fiend-like and atrocious conspiracy was it that brought about this butchery? You and your associates, with specious, wicked, trumped-up falsehoods, have lured innocent beings into a certain and dreadful death. This innocent and noble-minded young man—"

"Not innocent!" roared Tamneegal, whose revengeful feelings towards Lightfoot were carried beyond the grave; "not innocent—he was guilty—guilty of a worse conspiracy than any we have had occasion to use. He stole, like a thief, into my house, in which I offered him an asylum and protection from his enemies, and robbed me of that which I held most dear—the affection and honour of my wife."

"He?" said Omelia, with unfeigned sur-prise. "Impossible! Ensign Lightfoot!—you must be dreaming."

"I am, and have been, too well assured of the fact," answered Tamneegal; "I have had most certain, most melancholy proofs offered me of the painful truth of which I have just stated. This man robbed me, I say, of the affections and honour of my wife—lured her away to follow his fortunes—he deserted her—laughed and scoffed at her—drove her to insensate madness, and—

'tis the old story—she committed suicide; and the first indication I had of the termi-nation of this sad drama was, her dead body being brought home by strangers."

"Ah, is this true?" said Omelia, seeing now the main spring which had set this plot in action. "But your wife still lives, I un-derstood," she said, as she remembered her own introduction to Mugriah.

"My wife Mugriah lives," said Tamneegal, "but it is not of her I speak. You remem-ber Poutra, when a child, I dare say."

"Poutra!" itterated Omelia in surprise. "Of course, I remember her well. What of her?"

"She died as I have described, through the arts of yon designing villain."

"I never will believe it. You are mis-taken. There are some circumstances which have been misunderstood; I never will be-lieve this young man was capable of such conduct—never!"

"You will never believe anything preju-dicial to the race who have estranged you from the home of your fathers. Ask Goo-looh if I do not speak the truth. He knows every minute circumstance—was present at all the occurrences; indeed, it was at his in-stigation that I was persuaded to harbour the viper which stung me."

Omelia was surprised beyond measure at this information: there was a truthfulness about the manner of her step-father which led her to opine that, at any rate, the story he had been telling of his supposed or real wrongs had in it some truth for its founda-tion.

Omelia remembered the unfortunate Pou-tra when a child, and had been considerably attached to her. She had, however missed sight of her for years, and had never been aware that she became the wife of Tamnee-gal, neither was she cognisant of her sad fate, or any of the circumstances which had led to it.

The reflection, therefore, that these details evoked, at once made her suspicious of the cause of the disastrous mission which she herself had prompted to rescue some sup-posed English prisoners; these she did not believe now to be in existence at all, and to go back herself to the iron-browed Captain Midhurst was a task she dreaded to under-take.

She took a rapid glance at the situation in which she found herself placed, and trem-bled at the terrible alternative of abandon-ing the protection of the English.

While she was reflecting, Tamneegal said, firmly—

"Your dream, I hope, is now past, silly, headstrong girl; hasten at once to accom-pany me who is now and henceforth your natural protector. You shall be treated with the greatest kindness," he said, as he slowly approached nearer to her; " no father, be he ever so fond, will cherish a beloved daughter with more zealous care than I will you. Come, fear not, no harm will befal you whilst under my watchful and anxious eyes. My good wife, Mugriah, already loves you as her own daughter, and will see to your comfort in everything. What, therefore, have you to fear? and wherefore do you hesitate, when every solicitude is evinced towards you?"

" I cannot herd with murderers," answered Omelia, " upon whose heads the foul stain of blood remains indelibly stamped."

" I have explained the cause which has led only to a just vengeance and retribution."

" Is this wholesale butchery just? or any such inhuman scenes as these justifiable to either God or man? Your wickedness has brought everlasting shame upon me as well as yourself and companions.

" It were idle to argue further with one so prejudiced as yourself," said Tamneegal, hastily. " You must remove from a scene which your gentle nature revolts at," and with these words he endeavoured to lead his step-daughter from the spot.

Omelia felt herself quite prostrate and unable to offer any resistance, indeed, to say the truth, she was at a loss how to act, being afraid to venture into the presence of Captain Midhurst, and render to him an account of the day's disasters. She therefore passively resigned herself to her foster father in moody silence.

It was a long journey to the latter's abode, which was the same into which she had been introduced previous to her escape into the Redowya fort.

When she reached the cave in company with Tamneegal, he again placed her in charge of his wife, Mugriah, who had always evinced a degree of kindness towards our heroine, who was glad, therefore, in her present position to have some opportunity offered her of endeavouring to recover from the shock consequent upon the disastrous engagement of which she had been a spectator.

The night wore wearily away with poor Omelia in her new abode, troubled and agonising thoughts kept her in a state of continual torture, and when she did snatch a short interval of repose its effect was neutralised by most frightful and hideous visions, which hurried on in a confused chaotic mass of incidents, each one being a succeeding horror more terrible than the last.

In one moment she beheld the unfortunate Lightfoot and herself start upon their ill-fated errand, and remembered the portentous words and expressions of doubt issue from the lips of the stern visaged Captain Midhurst. She saw again and again his looks

of mistrust directed towards herself, as he said, " It is at your instigation this mission is undertaken, and upon you, therefore, rests the responsibility."

What a responsibility now ! she tossed in agony at the thought of this. Then the wholesale slaughter of the troops in the ravine, and the dead body of the poor ensign rose up, like Banquo's ghost, in the direful tableaux of.

Such weir and spectre-like visions as these weighed her spirit down, and she was thankful when she awoke.

The night wore wearily on, "but upon weary night dawned wearier day," and our heroine was quite at a loss how to act or what course to pursue for the best in this her present difficulty.

Some little ray of sunlight did, however, find its way in the deep gloom which environed and enshrowded her, and this was the appearance of Goolooh, upon whose sincerity she still felt disposed to rely, notwithstanding the unfortunate termination of their mission.

Goolooh, habitually grave as he generally was, now bore more than usual solemnity in his demeanour. He had been so overcome when he learnt the news of the fatal issue of the encounter in the ravine, and the tool he had been made of by Tamneegal, that he gave way to the most extravagant expressions of rage.

He had not the slightest notion of Tamneegal's ulterior views when he consented to carry the message to Omelia from the English prisoners ; neither had he been aware of the presence of Lightfot in the English camp.

Tamneegal had mistrusted him too much to make him a confident upon the subject. It is true he had sworn to devote his life to find out the ensign, and avenge the death of the ill stared Poutra, but his partiality for Omelia, and the consideration he evinced to accede to her slightest wishes, induced his companion to entertain strong doubts about his consenting to become *particepe criminus* in the deed of atrocity which we have just chronicled.

Sure it is, that the natives of India have generally but little confidence in each other, hence the impracticability of their forming a permanent cohesion to carry out any particular object.

Goolooh had a much larger amount of good in his composition than his companion Tamneegal, who was headstrong in his resolves, and unscrupulous in carrying them out; and it is not at all probable that the former, notwithstanding his original oath of vengeance against Lightfoot, would have consented to become a participator or own any complicity in the late foul plot.

Tamneegal foreseeing the probability of this had, with the serpent's wile, used him as a blind instrument, and had kept his companion in the dark as to his motives.

When Goolooh discovered the part he had been made to play in the transaction, he upbraided Tamneegal in no measured terms, who, in reply to his vituperation, reminded him of the oath he had taken to avenge Poutra, and, moreover, remarked that an opportunity had occurred for him to recover possession of his foster child, of which he was determined to avail himself.

The fact of Omelia's detention did not appear objectionable to Goolooh, who, although he had received the most positive assurances from our heroine that she could never look upon him in the light of a lover, nevertheless was consoled by being allowed to hover about her and be indulged with occasional interviews.

When, therefore, he sought her in her apartment his countenance assumed a grave, melancholy, and troubled expression, and approaching her respectfully, he said, in a tone of tenderness, as he gently grasped her hand—

"You do not doubt your faithful and devoted servant, notwithstanding appearances are against him?"

"No," answered Omelia, sadly; "I should hope that you, at least, would never consent to be the prime mover in a heinous plot which disgraces our common nature. But why were you ever induced, young man, to be the tool of wicked and revengeful men?"

"I was as unconscious as yourself of this nefarious proceeding, believe me, upon my honour. And now, in what way can I serve you?"

"Alas, I know not. To return to Captain Midhurst is out of the question! he would never believe that I was innocent of the knowledge of my step father's intentions. The only course for me to adopt is to communicate with—with my friends, Major Forrester, but where to find them now I am at a loss to tell."

"Let me seek them out, I will never rest till I have endeavoured to make some reparation to you for the dreadful position into which I have, through my own want of prudence brought you. Ah, it is terrible to think that I who would cheerfully lay down my life for you should have been made the instrument of your destruction."

Omelia now inquired about Poutra, and all those circumstances with her and Lightfoot, with which the reader is already acquainted, the brief heads of which had been hinted to her by Tamneegal.

Goolooh corroborated all that the former had said, and recited the history of the transaction, adding that the death of the ensign was but a just retribution, but, at the same time, he did not approve of the means which had been employed to obtain this end.

A thought flashed across the now wavering mind of Omelia to endeavour to communicate with Stanley, but the reflection that all her letters had remained unanswered both from Jahusah and Abdal occasioned her to doubt if either they or Stanley were in the same locality; then again her pride interposed, she would not communicate with her lover now she was in difficulty. No, she would wait a little, and see and communicate with Major and Mrs. Forrester; meanwhile, Goolooh gave her repeated assurances of his faithful adherence and attachment towards her.

In the midst of the multitude of circumstances which had crowded upon her, she had forgotten to inquire about the appearance of the Thug amongst the companions and followers of her foster parent; as this occurred to her, she inquired of Goolooh the cause.

He was at a loss to account for it himself, being quite unaware that Tamneegal had been plotting with the miscreant she named. When, therefore, Omelia informed him that Goryeboo was with her foster father at the entrance of the ravine, and had fought by his side, at the sight of which she had swooned, her companion was more than ever astonished, he determined, therefore, to make inquiries of Tamneegal upon the subject.

So stealthy had been the movements of the dark emissary of the immaculate Mr. Natterley, that he had managed to render himself invisible whenever Goolooh was present; he knew well enough that Goolooh was the presiding genius, who watched over the safety of Omelia, and he had received sufficient proofs of this when he endeavoured to destroy her; consequently he had told Tamneegal that he courted obscurity, and in the presence of Goolooh he was not desirous of appearing.

He forgot to say, at the same time, the cause of his antipathy to be presented to the latter, but merely alluded to it as some old quarrel or grievance.

We must now return to those quarters where the ill-fated Lightfoot had started from full of hope, life, and spirit but a few hours previous.

The first intimation which Captain Midhurst received of the result of the expedition was from some four or five bleeding and wounded soldiers who had managed to cut their way through their opponents and reach their quarters alive.

When these came rushing in, breathless from their exertions, and presented themselves to their commander, it is hardly possible to convey to the reader the expression of surprise, and the numerous conflicting emotions which were observable upon the captain's features.

The thought that they had ignobly fled for a moment crossed his mind, or had been cut off from their companions by some unfortunate accident or mischance, but the supposition that all their comrades had met with their death never for a moment presented itself to his imagination.

"How now!" he exclaimed, impatiently; "where is your officer?"

A look of blank dismay was the only response to this question, the men hardly dared to enter into the harrowing particulars of the circumstances which had occurred.

"Where is your officer?—where is Lieutenant Lightfoot?" itterated the captain. "Have you lost the power of utterance or taken leave of your senses, that you are unable to answer my question? What have you done with your commander, that you thus return without either him or your companions?"

In reply to this, they informed Captain Midhurst of the whole affair: the loss of their comrades in the ravine, and the death of their officer.

It would be perfectly futile to endeavour to convey to the mind of the reader the captain's horror and rage at learning the result of the expedition and the fate of poor Lightfoot and his brave followers.

His rage knew no bounds; some of his choicest troops were completely destroyed, and he bitterly upbraided himself for consenting to the expedition, or having any faith in the word of Omelia.

He implicitly believed that she was the prime mover and instigator of the whole conspiracy, and that the destruction of his gallant troops had been compassed by her agency.

He was a man of that inflexible temperament, that, when once his mind became endowed with any fixed notion, it was almost impossible to alter its current.

He had, before this disastrous affair looked upon our heroine with eyes of considerable suspicion, but now he felt fully assured of her complicity of guilt with her more sanguinary companions, and he vowed not to rest till justice overtook them, and the death of Lightfoot was avenged.

Hastily mustering a considerable force, and taking the command himself, he proceeded at once to the spot where the terrible affray had taken place, and he became the mose incensed as he contemplated the *debris* of the late conflict.

He, however, met with but a few upon the field of battle upon whom he might revenge himself.

Those of the English troops who gave any signs of life were conveyed carefully back to their quarters, and the captain discovered some two or three wounded sepoys, whom he directed should be made prisoners.

Upon returning to his quarters he held an audience with these, and gave them to understand that he would guarantee their receiving a full pardon provided they would confess who were the ringleaders of the foul conspiracy. In the event of their refusing to make known to him those particulars, he threatened them with the most horrible tortures to wring it from them.

Was it Omelia who had devised the hellish scheme, he asked. They did not know. He was sure it was; what had become of her? They did not know—yes, one did: she had gone home with her father.

"Her father?—who is he?"

The sepoy explained the relative positions which Tamneegal and Omelia bore to one another.

"Ah, I see it all then," exclaimed the captain; "it is this perfidious wench and her criminal parent who have been the prime movers of the whole affair. May a complete and speedy justice overtake them for their foul treachery and the murder of my gallant fellows."

The captain now endeavoured to find out from his prisoners the abode of Tamneegal, but this they denied any knowledge of, declaring that he had no fixed residence, but was constantly on the move.

"Could they conduct his troops into the probable route he would be likely to take?" was the next inquiry.

"Probably so; they would try their best," was the reply.

The captain determined in any case to institute a vigorous search, and scour the country for miles around, but what he would endeavour to find out the originators of the transaction, and bring them to condign punishment.

He wrote a dispatch to Lord Clyde detailing the whole affair, and received in reply orders for him to endeavour to capture the mutineers, try them, and, if found guilty, make a terrible example of them.

Lord Clyde also informed the captain that Major Forrester and lady had left for Calcutta, the former having been invalided, and being about, as he understood, to return to England.

—

CHAPTER CCXXXII.

THE INSIDIOUS FOE AGAIN.—DREADFUL POSI-
TION OF OMELIA.—SHE IS DENOUNCED AS
A MURDERESS.—HER ARREST.—SCENE IN
THE CAVE.

Leaving Captain Midhurst to mature his
arrangements previous to his marching with
a flying column of troops, let us return to our
heroine.

Omelia found herself treated, in her present abode with a tolerable amount of kindness and consideration; Tamneegal observed
unmistakeable evidence from her manner
that his presence was not agreeable to his
step daughter, and he, therefore, with more
delicacy than we should have given him
credit for, abstained from forcing himself
upon her.

Mugriah, his wife, however, was our
heroine's constant companion, and Goolooh,
also paid her frequent visits. Omelia was
under no restriction, being at liberty to come
and go whithersoever she pleased.

She had dispatched a letter to Major Forrester explaining her present position, and
begging him to render what service he could
by his advice as to how she had better act.
This letter was addressed to the head quarters of the commander-in-chief; in fact, it
was enclosed under cover to Lord Clyde him-
himself.

To this she had, as yet, received no reply,
indeed, there had been no time for her to
have done so under the most favourable circumstances.

Matters thus stood previous to the enac-
tion of perhaps the most painful scene of
events which have sprung directly from
those connected with the fate of Poutra.

Hitherto the Thug, Goryeboo, had chosen
for his own particular purpose to remain in
strict incognito. It must not be supposed,
however, that he was idle, or had lost sight
of the main objects which had induced him
to so industriously ingratiate himself into
the good graces of Tamneegal by sympathising
with him in his revenge against the ensign.

Of course Goryeboo had but one object to
serve, and that was the destruction of
Omelia.

It would almost appear that some watchful spirit hovered around her, considering
the difficulties which sprung up to prevent
the Thug from accomplishing his fell purpose.

He thought himself now, however, quite
certain of his purpose. He knew where she
was located, had spies upon her actions, and
only awaited her appearance outside Tamneegal's abode to pounce upon her and accomplish his object.

For this he was laying in wait, and in the
daily expectation of; he could not do anything situated as she was, surrounded by so
many watchful companions.

He knew that Tamneegal, Goolooh, or
any of their followers would protect Omelia
from any harm, for she was too well liked
by most of them, so Goryeboo having his
prey in cover awaited the first opportunity
to effect a capture.

This soon occurred, Omelia had been informed by two of the Thug's spies that a
villager hard by had a son belonging to
Major Forrester's troop, who had just returned from the head quarters of the commander-in-chief, and this young man would
willingly afford her all the information she
desired regarding the movements and whereabouts of the major.

Anxious to be made acquainted with such
intelligence, our heroine started off one
morning alone to the villagers habitation.

She had not left the cave of Tamneegal
many minutes for this purpose when Goolooh came in, and inquired for her. He was
informed by Mugriah the course she had
taken and the object of the journey.

Goolooh suspected some mischief, and followed her footsteps hastily. It was lucky he
did so, for Omelia had hardly got half a
mile from the cave, when her old enemy
sprang upon her, and held both her arms in
an iron grasp. Omelia sent forth a series of
piercing screams, which were soon stifled by
a handkerchief being thrust into her throat,
and a companion of the Thug's fastened
around her throat the sash to complete his
hateful mission.

Goolooh, who had been following close at
her heels, heard the cries of our heroine,
and guided by them he rushed to her assistance.

"Mine at last," exclaimed Goryeboo;
"woman with a dozen lives, your race has
run."

He had scarcely uttered these words when
a pistol shot was heard, and the ball found a
home in the breast of his companion, who
sent forth an agonising cry, leaped a yard or
two in the air, and fell to the earth a corpse.

He had been shot through the heart by
Goolooh, who rushed forward, and, grasping
the muzzle of the discharged and still smoking pistol, struck the Thug a terrible blow
on the head with its butt-end. He reeled
some yards with the force of the well-directed
stroke, and was half stunned therefrom.

"Villain!" shouted Goolooh; "black-
hearted, remorseless villain! this time you
escape me not alive."

He was about to close with his antagonist,
when he found himself firmly held and
pinioned by unknown hands; another moment and he was surrounded by British

troops, and observed the Thug in charge of two soldiers, who were deliberately tying his arms behind him.

"So," exclaimed Captain Midhurst, when both prisoners were firmly secured, for it was his detachment which had come up at the time, attracted in the course of their march by the report of the pistol and the screams of Omelia; "a pretty pair of villains, forsooth, whose bodies are destined to grace the nearest gallows. Seize the girl, and secure her as you have done her companions; pinion her."

Omelia had unwound the Thug's scarf, which she held in one hand, and comparatively recovered her self-possession upon the urgency of the case.

"What means this indignity, Captain Midhurst?" she inquired, haughtily.

"Simply that you are charged with murder and rebellion, and must answer for the same to the proper authorities."

"It is false! I am innocent! and your own better judgment, in a calmer moment, will accuse you of treating a friend to your race with crulty and harshness. Hear my explanation of this sad affair."

"At another time you may give it, but not now. No English tribunal tries or condemns a prisoner without hearing all he or she may have to say in their defence."

"Tribunal! am I then a prisoner accused of—of—"

"Murder!" said the captain, sententiously.

"It is false!" exclaimed Goolooh, passionately, as he observed Omelia burst into tears which choked her utterance. "She is too good—too pure to injure by thought or deed any being in the world. I will answer with my life, ten times told, that she is innocent."

"You are eloquent," sneeringly replied the captain. "It is probable that you will have to answer with your life for your own crimes, let that suffice you. I would gladly temper justice with mercy, but in this case I see no extenuating features. The best thing for me to advise you to do is to make a full confession of your crimes, and offer what reparation you can by informing me who your accomplices are, and where they are to be found."

"Never!" shouted Goolooh. "I keep faith with my ill-used countrymen, and scorn to turn a traitor to them, or receive the price of their blood."

"Humph! a hero, I perceive, in your own peculiar way, no doubt; "and you, sir," he continued, as he turned to Goryeboo, "you are innocent, I suppose, like your comrade?"

"He is no comrade of mine," said Goryeboo, as he saw which way matters were turning, and made up his mind to act accordingly. "He is neither a comrade or companion of mine; on the contrary, my most bitter enemy. "I do not say that I have not been guilty of crimes against your government, but am willing to make a free confession, and do all in my power to assist you in pursuit of the offenders. I do not profess to have so much sympathy with men who have planned the wholesale slaughter of your gallant troops in the defile. It was against my wishes, and even but just now we were quarreling together upon this subject when you came up."

"Impudent liar!" exclaimed Goolooh; "it was your own murderous attack upon this innocent girl which caused my strife with you."

"Silence!" exclaimed the captain. "Speak in your proper turn, By heaven, if you dare interrupt my conversation with this man I will have you gagged instantly."

Goolooh was silent.

"Now, sir," said the captain to Goryeboo, "you may proceed."

"It is as I have stated. We were quarrelling about the late attack upon your troops. It was caused by motives of the most wicked and vindictive feelings of re-revenge which could possibly actuate the breast of any human being. I do not participate in them, I never have, I call heaven to witness."

"Oh, you unmitigated scoundrel," exclaimed Goolooh.

"Silence!" again thundered forth the captain. "Take that man off, and the girl, too. Corporal Shaw, take a file of men, and escort these prisoners to your quarters; see that they are put in close confinement, and mind, if any attempt is made at either escape or rescue, shoot them at once. Do you hear?"

"Yes, sir," answered the corporal, as he saluted his officer, and proceeded to carry out the orders he had received.

"You can say whatever you have to offer as an extenuation of your conduct; but mind, if I find you are indulging in a series of lies, it will be the worse for you. Do you know the originators of this fiendish plot which has ended in the loss of one of our most promising young officers, and I know not how many men."

"I do, sir, know the whole history of it."

"Well, I am ready to listen; go on, man."

"It originated with the girl's father."

"Ah, I thought so. Had she any hand in it?"

"Yes, sir, she was the chief mover of the whole conspiracy."

"Horrible! and with such an innocent bearing. Oh, the wile of woman. And this young man with whom you were quarrelling just now?"

"He was another of the chief conspirators."

"Humph! you must give me proof of all these assertions. Where is this father of hers?"

The Thug hesitated, and did not reply immediately to the question,

"Do you hear me man?" said the captain; "where is he? Speak; I'll not be triffled with."

"I can tell you," he replied, slowly, "but should hope you would not expect me to do all this without recompense. I shall receive a free pardon, I suppose?"

"I hardly know that I have a right to make promises to rebels, but your case shall receive the favourable consideration of the commander-in chief, provided you give such information as shall lead to the conviction of the murderers of Ensign Lightfoot."

The Thug now proceeded to detail all those circumstances with which the reader is already acquainted, respecting the deep animosity borne by Tamneegal towards the ill-fated ensign, the supposed seduction and ultimate death of Poutra; he then went on to inform the captain that when it became known that the ensign was amongst the troops stationed at Saugor, Tamneegal, Omelia, and Gooloh devised and put in practice the plot to draw the ensign into ambush.

He persisted in asserting that it was against his wish or arrangement. He did not deny but that he had had frequent interviews with the English prisoners, and had advised them to communicate with their countrymen at Saugor.

As a proof of this, he begged the captain to send to the prisoners in question.

"Then there are really, after all, some prisoners?" said the captain, in some surprise. "This part of the story was not a trumped up tale?"

"No, sir; there are really some prisoners who need your assistance; and to prove the truth of what I am saying, if you will allow me to accompany a detachment they can have ocular demonstration of the fact."

All this seemed very truthful, and the circumstances appeared to bear out the statement of the wily villain, who was beginning to have it all his own way.

"And now, to give an earnest of the truth of your statement, where is this girl's father? for it appears to me that he is the ringleader of the whole."

"I will conduct you at once to his place of retreat and concealment, which is about half a mile from this spot; he is, however, surrounded by desperate followers, and it will, perhaps, require a tolerably strong force to overcome them."

"We will risk that. Lead on at once."

Goryeboo was not anxious for the task, but saw no way of avoiding it so he was fain to make a virtue of necessity, and appeared to journey willingly in the direction of Tamneegal's cave, upon arriving at which he pointed out the entrance to Captain Midhurst, who proceeded at once with his troops and called out loudly for its inmates to surrender.

No answer was returned, and the demand was again repeated with no better success.

A volley of musketry was discharged into the cave, and several loud cries of pain from the wounded told that some of the shots had taken effect.

Another demand was made for its occupants to surrender, and threats were held out of the whole place being blowed up.

Captain Midhurst demanded the body of Tamneegal in the Queen's name, and a free pardon to any of those who might be disposed to place him in the hands of justice was offered.

Upon this a violent struggle ensued in the interior of the cave, and it appeared, from what confused sounds found their way to the ears of the British, that a general *melee* was taking place, which was in reality the case.

Again the captain shouted out loudly for the body of Tamneegal, and threatened another volley if no reply was given to his demand.

In a few minutes a second discharge of musketry was sent into the cave, and then came rushing out a number of wounded sepoys, who fell upon their knees and begged for mercy, at the same time, some of them expressed their willingness to give up the now truly wretched Tamneegal

The captain had no commiseration for the wounded miscreants, as he looked upon all as the murderers of his gallant troops, and their no less gallant officer, Ensign Lightfoot; while he was reflecting about his next proceeding, he was saluted with a volley in return, which did, however, but little damage, with the exception of two or three slight wounds, to his troops; however, this was enough to arouse his anger to more vigorous measures, and he sent in several severe discharges, and brought a field-piece to bear upon the opening of the cave—the effect of this was horrible to the last degree.

The occupants of the cave were packed closely together like rats in a hole, and the grape and canister shot which went into the very midst of them committed fearful slaughter.

It was cruel work without doubt, but such as perhaps many military men would justify in the exigency of the case, more especially as it was adopted by one who was smarting under the wholesale murder of his own men.

The discharge of the field piece created such a panic amongst the mutineers and rebels, that they felt disposed to dare anything rather than risk the chance of waiting to receive another discharge. Numbers therefore flew out in disorder, and were soon engaged with the British troops, from whom they received but little mercy. Another rush took place, of a larger and still more confused body of men, who as they emerged from the entrance, appeared to be fighting amongst themselves; several appeared to have hold of one in the very midst of them, who was fighting desperately to escape from their custody. This was Tamneegal, who had been seized by several of the disaffected, who were anxious to give him up. In this wish they were joined by many of their companions; whilst a large party on the contrary were for protecting him to the last. This it was that had caused the internal warfare, the noise of which had reached the ears of the British. They were fighting amongst themselves when Tamneegal and the confused mass of men which accompanied him emerged into the day light. Gorzeboo immediately pointed him out to Captain Midhurst, who instantly gave orders for his men to charge, which was obeyed with rapid impetuosity.

"Seize yon traitor," shouted out the captain as he put spurs to his horse. "Take him alive, men, if possible." They hastened to carry out his wishes, but in the confusion it was hardly possible to effect an immediate capture. Tamneegal was still fighting desperately with those who had turned out so faithless to him. He appeared to have a greater amount of animosity to them than he bore towards the British troops; he was wounded severely, but still held on. By a rapid movement of the British troops he became completely hemmed in, and they closed around his fast falling companions, and succeeded in effecting his capture. He struck at them madly with his tulwar as they did so, and wounded several. When finding himself firmly in their grasp, he endeavoured to commit suicide by passing the weapon through his own body, but his arm was arrested just in time to prevent his effecting his object. He ground his teeth with impotent rage, at thus being baulked in his purpose; and when a few minutes after, he beheld Gorzeboo, bound and evidently on a traitorous mission, his countenance assumed a still more diabolical expression. While he was being marched into the centre of the British troops, his wife Mugriah rushed from the cave and prostrated herself at the feet of Captain Midhurst, and in moving and imploring accents, begged the life of her husband. Her appearance was so sudden, her manner so distracted, and yet so full of energy, and her language and voice so plaintive, that the stern captain looked down with an expression of commiseration for her. In the rapid articulation in her own language it was impossible for him to understand all she said, but he knew she was appealing with a woman's eloquence for the life of her husband, and was endeavouring to convey to the mind of her listener that he had been wronged by the late ensign. Her husband, in a few brief sentences, told her that it was utterley hopeless for her to appeal to the British officer for mercy; he knew he should be condemned, but he had a great horror of being blown from a gun—which fate he fully expected to meet with from the hands of the English. Mugriah was taken away from the immediate presence of the captain by two of his guards; he told them not to use any unnecessary harshness towards her. As she proceeded along, she came nearer to where her husband was stationed, and catching sight of him, she sprang forward, and flung herself into his arms with every demonstration of love and tenderness towards him.

"Strange," muttered the captain to himself, "even such a blood-stained villian as that has a woman who appears to love him. Let them be," he said aloud to his soldiers, who were about to separate them; "it is their last parting." While Mugriah hung upon the form of her husband, he whispered some few words in her ear, which caused her to suddenly start and tremble. They were sad directions he was giving her, so

terrible, that let us hope it may never fall to the lot of woman to again listen to. It will be seen how well she obeyed them, for upon the troops of Captain Midhurst again resuming their march towards the camp, Mugriah followed in their rear, within a few yards of her husband. Upon arriving at a steep hill, Tamneegal placed his hand as near to his breast as he could, considering his arms were pinioned, and in an instant there was heard the sharp report of a pistol, and the wretched Tamneegal lay prostrate upon the earth, and a copious stream of blood flowed from a wound in his chest. A smile was observable upon his features in this his last hour, at the success of his *ruse*. A few more seconds and the wretched and guilty man had gone to another tribunal to answer for his crimes. So sudden had been the action of Mugriah, and so immediate the death which had followed it, that the captain had hardly observed what had occurred, when his ears were saluted with another report, and he rushed forward towards the spot, from whence the sounds proceeded, and beheld the unhappy Mugriah prostrate upon the earth—a corpse—with a bullet through her brain. The few words of dreadful import which Tamneegal had whispered to his less guilty and faithful companion, were to beg of her as a last request, to shoot him before he reached the English camp. The poor woman was panic struck, as well she might be, when this request was made, but he urged her to accede to the demand, as it would prevent him being blown from a gun, of which he had the greatest horror. Nerving herself up to the dreadful task, it has been seen how well she carried out his last wishes. The placing his hand near to his chest was the preconcerted signal for her to act upon, and at the same time it formed a guide for the direction of her aim. Having performed this last sad mission, the wretched woman saw the wreck of her future happiness before her, and determined therefore to fall by her own hand; she had reserved another bullet for herself. To add to other disastrous circumstances, it happened to be Omelia's revolver with which the two fatal deeds were accomplished.

The captain observed her name engraved on the stock, as one of his soldiers handed the weapon to him. Every circumstance seemed to tend in some way or other to the more direct implication of our heroine in a perfect labyrinth of suspicious facts, which seemed to point directly to her guilt.

"Ah!" ejaculated the captain, as he shook his head ominously—"her pistol. Did I understand you to say that this man who has been just sent to his account was this girl's father?"

This was addressed to Gorzeboo.

"He is her reputed father.",

"How mean you."

"I will explain, sir: this Tamneegal was brother to the girl's father, who dying, bequeathed her to him; consequently he is in reality her uncle and foster-father."

"Then what was the name of the real parent?"

"Yunader!"

"Ah! that villain, I knew the scoundrel well; he was her father. By my faith she seems to have come from a nice lot. Do you know who this pistol belongs to?"

"Yes, to Omelia herself; I ought to know it; it is the same one with which she threatened my life."

He then explained to the captain his conflict with Omelia, declaring that she was the aggressor, and that he himself was the injured party. The man's manner was so specious, and he seemed so anxious to tell the truth, by the promptness of his replies, that Captain Midhurst seemed disposed to believe all his statements, the more so as he was much pleased at having had the satisfaction of routing and cutting to pieces the greater portion, if not the whole of Tamneegal's band. "The fellow has earned his life, if it were only for this," said the captain to himself. As they were proceeding on their march back to quarters, he enquired of Gorzeboo respecting the English prisoners who had been the original cause of the ensign's detachment leaving their quarters upon their unfortunate expedition.

"I will readily guide you towards where they are confined, but should advise caution, as a too precipitate attack upon the natives would in all probability result in their immediate destruction. I have been in almost daily communication with these prisoners, and upon my advice they determined to apply to you for assistance: when I procured the letter from them, it was with the intention of delivering it myself, but in consequence of the cabal formed by the three individuals already named, I was thwarted in my object, and the young man with whom you saw me fighting was chosen instead."

"What was your object in interfering in the matter at all?"

"Because I expected, and had been promised, a good reward."

"How is it you did not convey the letter yourself, and say nothing about it to your companions."

"I was unable to do so, as they knew of my intentions with the English prisoners, and if I had flown in the face of their expressed wishes, the probability is that I should have been murdered before I reached your quarters. Besides this I do not conceal from you, sir, that I am proscribed by the law for being concerned in one of the early outbreaks."

"Humph! you deserve death, I have no doubt."

"Not if I make all the reparation in my power, which most certainly I am endeavouring to do."

"Perhaps not; to morrow you shall conduct me to these prisoners, and we will see what had best be done to secure them."

Upon the captain's return he found that Omelia and Goolooh had been conveyed to some vaults below. The head quarters of the captain consisted of a village church originally built by some of the earliest missionaries.

It was in the vaults of this building that Corporal Shaw thought proper to conduct his two prisoners.

CHAPTER CCXXXIII.

RELEASE OF THE ENGLISH PRISONERS.—DESPATCH TO LORD CLYDE.—THE COMMUNICATIONS TO MR. NATTERLEY.—HIS RESOLVE AND INTERVIEW WITH THE THUG.

ON the the following morning after the incidents described in the last chapter, Captain Midhurst prepared to muster a tolerable large force to accompany him to the village where the English prisoners were supposed to lay, With the vivid remembrance of the ravine and the fate of poor Lightfoot yet fresh in his recollection, he determined to act with considerable caution, and took care therefore not to proceed on his journey without being accompanied by one or two field pieces. He examined the Thug as to the way they were to take, who informed the captain that there was an easy mode of access across the mountains, and that there had not been the slightest occasion for Lightfoot to have ventured into the defile. All arrangements having been made satisfactory to Captain Midhurst, that officer proceeded on the same errand which had proved so fatal to the ill-starred ensign. It was broken and uneven ground through which his soldiers had to march, but where any doubt existed in the mind of their commander, he sent out a flying escort, and would not let his troops venture into any doubtful locality without being under cover of the guns, should it be found necessary to use them.

They were, however, unmolested during their march. Indeed those of the disaffected Sepoys who were left of Tamneegal's and the opposing bands took pretty good care to keep out of the way when the avenging column of men were on their march. When they arrived within sight of the village, the captain ordered his troops to halt; he then sent Gorzeboo in the midst of a file of soldiers who bore a flag of truce, and directed them and the Thug to offer terms and free pardon to all those who would cause to be given up those prisoners who were in their hands. Gorzeboo signalled to several natives whom he observed at some short distance from where he stood in the charge of the English soldiers; two of them came towards him, and he was enabled to explain to them the object of his present appearance in their neighbourhood. They informed him that the lady, who had sent the letter by Omelia had been ransomed by her husband, and had been escorted by several Hindoos to her home. There were, however, three or four other Europeans with children, and they entertained no doubt but their captors would freely give them up upon the assurance of a pardon, and some recompense for their trouble. Upon this the Thug returned to Captain Midhurst and informed him of what had passed. That officer directed him to inform them that their request should be immediately acceded to, and Gorzeboo once more, under strict escort, endeavoured to carry out the captain's instructions; the result of this was the production of the prisoners, who were at once placed under the care of the captain, who entered the names of those who had so promptly yielded to his demand. At the same time he informed them, that the terms which they had it appeared already arranged with the prisoners, should be sent them immediately upon the latter rejoining their friends. They were strangers to the captain, being civilians, who had escaped from one of the massacres, and had endured numerous hardships and vicissitudes. What unexpressible joy, therefore, did they once more feel at being again in the presence of their countrymen, which gave them unmistakeable assurance of their future safety. They expressed their gratitude in no measured terms, and expressed their willingness to handsomely reward those who had held them as hostages. It appeared that they had not been treated with any harshness beyond being retained prisoners, but at the same time they felt that it was impossible to tell how long this might have lasted, for events hurried on during the whole of the revolt in such a vortex, that it was more than probable they might have met with some foes, who would not feel disposed to treat them with the lenity observed by those in whose hands they had fallen.

When all these matters were satisfactorily arranged, Gorzeboo turned with an expression of triumph upon his sinister features, "I trust, sir," he said to the captain, respectfully, "you will feel now that I have done my best in this as well as in yesterday's transaction, and that I mean what is right? Had I have been allowed to act according to my own wishes, much unnecessary bloodshed would have been spared."

"You have done all that could be desired my man, certainly, and your conduct shall be duly reported at head-quarters—upon that you may rely. Are any of these people about here belonging to the clan of the late miscreant Tamneegal?"

"No, no! They were not on the most friendly terms with him, for when he had no better occupation he would make an incursion and rob them of whatever little property they possessed."

"Oh, then he did not confine his maurauding practices to the English alone, but levied black mail upon his own countrymen. He appears to have been the very prince of unscrupulous rascals."

"He was not particular with either friend or foe."

"This young man I hold in confinement, the one you were quarrelling with, is he a relation of Tamneegal's?

"No relative, sir, only a friend."

"Oh! Nor any of the girls?"

"He is an admirer, or lover of hers."

"I thought so by his eloquent appeal on her behalf; but she had an English officer who professed to be attached to her. Had she not?"

"Yes, sir, but that I believe is all over."

"Ah, so I should suppose."

"Ah, she has had numerous admirers, so I understand, but they did not last long."

Thus did this villain endeavour to hint at or throw a slight upon the character of our heroine. He had now fully succeeded in obtaining the ear of the captain, and acted his part with such well simulated candour and frankness, in which circumstances had so materially assisted him; he had completely ingratiated himself into the good graces of Midhurst, who did not doubt but he was or had been a consummate scoundrel, nevertheless, imagined him to be the lesser villain of the party. In this supposition, of course, the reader need not be informed our captain was quite mistaken. But Gorzeboo, when he liked, was no mean actor, and although nature had not endowed him with a prepossessing countenance, he contrived, somehow or other, when occasion required it, to call up a look and manner which impressed many with an idea that he possessed a sort of blunt frankness, and that the words he were uttering had in them some amount of truth. In the present instance, Captain Midhurst was disposed to give credence to all he said; his statements being, as they were, borne out by after circumstances. He had conducted the captain and troops to Tamneegal's cave, and had been the means of breaking up that infamous clan, and the next day he had been instrumental in rescuing several English prisoners; all appeared, therefore, fair to the eyes of the British officer, and he felt as thoroughly convinced of the fact that the recent diabolical plot had for its originators Tamneegal, Omelia, and Goolooh. Every circumstance seemed to bear out this hypothesis, and poor Omelia was enshrouded, and environed by a series of links in the chain of evidence through which there appeared no probability of her breaking.

Captain Midhurst marched back to his quarters, and shortly afterwards despatched an escort to accompany the prisoners towards their homes. He was about to send despatches to the Commander-in-chief, and he therefore placed the released prisoners under their charge. At the same time he gave a full account to Lord Clyde of the recent events which had taken place, and begged to know his wishes respecting the trial of Omelia and Goolooh. Gorzeboo, he recommended to mercy, saying, that he had fully earned a free pardon, and might be used in evidence against the others.

Having sent off his despatch, Captain Midhurst awaited the orders of his commander-in-chief, before he made any further movements respecting his prisoners.

When the Thug returned from his last expedition, he begged the favour of being allowed to write to his friends, who were of course unaware of his capture. The captain informed him that he saw no objection to his doing so, and at once granted him the desired permission. He instantly availed himself of this privilege to communicate with Mr. Natterley, and wrote the following :—

English Force, stationed at Langor.
"SIR,—I am here a prisoner; I believe I have earned my pardon however. There have been a series of plots, in all of which I have had but one object—the fulfilment of our contract. This Indian girl and her paramour are accused of murder and rebellion; I shall be the chief witness, and it will be my business to bring it home to them —this I do not doubt being able to accomplish. I have had a very narrow escape with my life from this girl's paramour, and have had a still narrower escape from being condemned. Come here to me, and give me your advice; you can of course see me by enquiry for the officer in command. The trial of Omelia will come on I expect in a few days. Yours, &c.,
"GORZEBOO."

This letter was addressed to Mr. Natterley's own residence, to be forwarded on to him immediately if he chanced to be away from home. When it arrived, however, he happened to be at his farm. In consequence of the escape of the Thug's supposed son, Mr. Natterley had been so incensed with his manager for allowing the young man to escape that he had threatened him with an immediate discharge, as a punishment for his want of care. He was in no very amiable mood when he last parted with Messrs Cottle and Co.; and his temper was doubly ruffled when he received his manager's letter informing him of the prisoner's escape. He hastened at once to his estate, and stormed and fumed to his heart's content; his manager, however, knew his man, and felt fully assured that he was in too many of his master's secrets for him to run the risk of his discharging him. This outburst of passion had hardly subsided when Mr. Natterley received the Thug's letter. Its contents were brief and sententious, from which he could augur but little beyond the fact that our heroine was accused of murder and rebellion. This was joyful intelligence for the wicked English merchant—farmer—schemer, and —villain!

The news lit up his face with a radiant smile of demoniacal joy. "Ah! ah!" he exclaimed. "Soho! This immaculate being has been plotting, has she, and is now accused of murder. Ah, murder! 'tis an ugly word. Well, if she is guilty, she must be punished, of course—severely punished. I hope they will manage the job without making much stir about the matter, or we shall have this love sick Stanley coming to beg her off, or something or other; not but what the fool thinks her dead. Who knows if this won't turn out for the best, after all; if she is condemned by the laws of the country, and dies the death of a felon and traitress, why, I think my friends, Messrs. Cottle & Co., must be satisfied then—eh! I should think so any way, it will take a heavy responsibility off my shoulders; and any exit she chooses to make into the other world would prove quite satisfactory to me—yes quite. I am not a particular man; as long as she takes her departure, I care not how it is accomplished. Ah! ah! I must hasten and see this Gorzeboo, and learn all the particulars. He has been industriously occupied, I know, and he assured me that his task would be completed shortly; but it appears the whole lot of them are prisoners; at least I suppose so. Ah, I must be off as speedily as possible."

And in obedience to this resolution, Mr. Natterly forthwith started for Langor, to see his unscrupulous tool and emissary. Upon his arrival, he at once boldly demanded to see the officer in command. He was introduced to Captain Midhurst, and immediately informed that officer that Gorzeboo had at one time been in his employ on his estate, and he had several questions to ask him respecting his business transactions. The captain cheerfully gave orders for him to be admitted to the prisoner's presence; for Mr. Natterley had the reputation of being a respectable merchant, and there could of course be no possible objection to grant so reasonable and natural a request.

"So," exclaimed Mr. Natterley, when he was left alone with the prisoner, "you are caged again it seems. How did it happen this time? You seem to be making terrible bungles."

"I do not deserve your reproaches, any way," answered his companion; "not if you hear the history."

"Let us hope not. Proceed with your account."

The other proceeded to inform his employer all those facts with which the reader is already acquainted, and he indulged his hearer with a very graphic account of the whole transaction, not forgetting to expatiate upon his own tact and address in throwing the whole weight of guilt upon Omelia and her companion in misery. He moreover plumed himself upon obtaining the good opinion of the captain, and doubted not the success of his manœuvres.

"Good!" said Mr. Natterley. "You have indeed my friend done the best it was possible under the circumstances. I see you have numerous difficulties to contend against, and I shall not fail to amply reward you for the trouble and danger you have had in this transaction. Now I believe we have indeed snared the she-fox. I will wait in this neighbourhood, and watch the future proceedings, and whatever may befall, you may rely upon coming off scathless. You will in all probability be the chief, if not the only witness against her, and you must stick to your tale without flinching upon a single point. I will see and get up whatever other circumstances in evidence it may be possible to bring against her. And understand, if a conviction is obtained, which I doubt not, I will not only give you the reward I have promised, your son back, or rather he whom you call your son, but I will make you a handsome allowance for the remainder of your life,

and the same shall continue to whomsoever you may choose to appoint your heir. Do you hear that?"

"Yes, and in reply, I have only to say that you may rely upon my doing my utmost to carry out our object."

"Who is this fellow that was taken along with her?"

"A sort of lover, or one that would wish to be so."

"Ah then, she is faithless to the milksop Stanley, eh?"

"No, I think not. Indeed I am sure not; she has offered this young man no encouragement, and, confound the wench, I do believe she neither has, or ever will look upon any other with kindly eyes but this Lieutenant Stanley. He must be kept in the dark about the affair until it is all over, and then it will be my satisfaction to enlighten him upon the subject." And the grin of the villain as he uttered these words were observable through the gloom of his dungeon.

"Good! we will see to all that when the affair is once over," said his employer; "I owe him a grudge myself as well as you. Now I'll be off. I have told the captain that you were in my employ, and that I have desired to see you to learn some information respecting a few trifling business transactions. Do they suspect you belong to the tribe of Thugs?"

"No, but that fellow will soon inform them, I have no doubt."

"What shall you say?"

"That I did belong to them once, but have become reformed. It's of no use denying it."

"I suppose not. Say that when you became reformed, you went into my employ and worked on my estate—no one can possibly know to the contrary; then call me to give you a character; my word will be taken immediately, and believed as gospel. I will back you up, and if it be necessary get a witness or two besides to speak to your good conduct. Indeed, if I see the captain as I go out, I will begin to sound your praises and deplore your present unhappy situation."

When Mr. Natterley left the prisoner, he met on his passage out, captain Midhurst, whom he immediately accosted.

"I have to thank you most sincerely captain, for your urbanity" he said in his blandest accents. "That fellow I understand has got himself into a sad scrape, so it seems."

"Yes, he is in custody with two others, but he has behaved in so straightforward a manner since his capture, and moreover been of such infinite service to us, that I can safely promise him a free pardon, I believe."

"Ah, I am glad to hear that. Do you know, I always thought him an honest creature, indeed I found him so whilst in my employ."

"Did you? well that is something in his favour, but he has been connected with a terrible set of scoundrels."

"Ye-es I sup-pose so—bad associations —bad associations—what mischief accrues therefrom; and then the majority of these fellows have no strength of mind to resist any such pernicious influence. What about the other two prisoners?"

"Ah," said the captain, shaking his head, "the weight of evidence is heavy against them—very heavy; one is a girl, who has certainly rendered several services to our countrymen, and who has received the strongest recommendations to all of us, from an officer in the Madras engineers— Major Forrester; but lor! it is impossible to tell if, while she was appearing to serve them, she did not act as a spy. The natives of India are so full of treachery and duplicity; and after all the major may have been entirely misled in his estimate of her character."

"Oh, ve-ry likely I should say—ve-ry likely."

"Of course his recommendation will be forwarded to Lord Clyde, but it cannot possibly do away with point blank, direct evidence. Why do you know sir, that through this girl's arts and persuasions, that I have had one of the smartest young officers in the British service, together with a whole company of men, ruthlessly murdered."

"Mercy on us! can this be possible?" and the start Mr. Natterley gave at this intelligence would have done honor to any of our dramatic authors.

"It is not only possible, but true—true. It makes my blood boil, when I reflect upon this melancholy affair. I have not seen this girl, or her companions in crime since they were made prisoners; for to tell you the truth, I cannot do so without revulsion, and the probability is that I should lose my temper, and, perhaps, castigate myself afterwards, for treating a woman with harshness. You must know she has been a resident in our camp, and petted by many here, which makes her case the worse."

"What is her name?" enquired Mr. Natterley with well feigned indifference.

"She is called Omelia."

"Ah, I have heard of her before; yes, she is, for a native of this clime, a very clever plausible girl? but treacherous— treacherous as a tigress."

"You think so? Well that was really my opinion, and to speak the truth, I never had much faith in her integrity."

"Ah, yes, sir, treacherous—treacherous."

"Ah!——"

"But don't let me prejudice the poor creature's case. God forbid I should aim a blow at a defenceless man, much less a woman."

"No, we would none of us do that I should hope, but facts—facts are stubborn things. I hope Lord Clyde will not place the affair at my disposal, for if he does——"

"You must do your duty, my dear Captain. Good night."

"Good night, Sir."

And Captain Midhurst retired to his own apartment, reflecting upon what his visitor had said, and felt still more convinced, if that were possible, of the guilt of our heroine. Poor Omelia, the darkest hour of your existence has come; that heart, which has held on bravely through so many trials, pulsates with many an agonized throe, and is filled well nigh to bursting.

CHAP. CCXXXIV.

THE COURT MARTIAL.—THE TRIAL.—THE CONDEMNATION.

In the course of a few days, Captain Midhurst received orders from the Commander-in-chief respecting the course to be adopted with the prisoners. A free pardon was sent for Gorzeboo, in consideration of his services, but he was not to be liberated at present until further orders were forwarded. Lord Clyde sent these instructions by a superior officer, a Colonel Maitland, who was empowered to try the prisoners, and sit as chief in the Court Martial. Accompanying this officer were several others, with a strong reinforcement of men, as it appeared a large body were ordered to leave Langor in a few days, for a different part of the country.

Hitherto, Captain Midhurst had not sought an interview with our herione, having studiously avoided doing so until he had received further orders. When Colonel Maitland arrived he made all the necessary enquires relative to the prisoners of the captain, and appointed a day for the sitting of the Court Martial. Omelia in this the heaviest hour of her affliction, had been attended upon by the wife of Corporal Shaw, who had shown her every womanly kindness it was possible under the circumstances. The corporal himself was a humane man enough, but obstinate withal, and was fully impressed with the guilt of both prisoners; and all the persuasions of his wife,

THE SEPOY'S DAUGHTER.

who declared that Omelia was as innocent as a blessed babe, could not convince him to the contrary. When Captain Midhurst found that a day was appointed for the trial, he desired Mrs. Shaw to see our heroine, and tell her of the fact, and at the same time say, that he, the Captain, would be glad to have an interview. Omelia heard this intelligence with apparent indifference; her senses since her confinement seemed to be benumbed.

"The sooner the better," she said faintly, when Mrs. Shaw had made her acquainted with the fact. "It will be more charitable to settle it all quickly; I am prepared and am quite indifferent about their determination. Would that it were all over."

"Dear child, cheer up," said the good natured Mrs. Shaw, encouragingly. "Who knows but this cloud may all blow over, and you may be again as happy——"

"As happy as what?" said Omelia as the other paused.

"As happy as you were before this horrible charge."

Omelia smiled faintly at these words; the amount of happiness she had experienced of late had not been the highest pinnacle of human bliss. Still she had never had her honour impugned, or even got herself so completely entangled in such a concatenation of suspicious circumstances; and dishonour to her was worse than death.

"You may tell the captain, if he wishes to see me, that I am at his service; he knows where I am, I am ready to receive him," said Omelia to Mrs. Shaw.

In a few minutes Captain Midhurst entered.

"Young woman," he said upon his entrance, "these scenes are always painful to the British soldier, made doubly so from the fact of your intimacy with us all here, but in the stern and rigorous duty which it behoves an English officer to fulfil, friendship and personal feelings must of necessity be sacrificed." This was a grand speech, and more conciliatory in its tone than those which usually fell from the captain.

"You must do your duty, Sir," was the calm reply, "or you would not deserve to hold a commission in an honourable service."

"Certainly not. Well, it is my duty to inform you, that your trial is fixed for next Thursday, and I cannot express to you how rejoiced I am that the responsibility is taken off me. You are to be tried by a venerable and distinguished officer, whom Lord Clyde has appointed. Now is there anything I can do to serve you, in collecting or causing to be collected any evidence which you may think likely to rebut that which will be brought against you?"

"No, I shall have none to offer."

"None! Not beyond your own statement I suppose. I am bound to tell you, young woman, that the evidence which will in all probability be brought against you is of a very serious character. I feel bound to tell you this, and in a question of life and death, it behoves you to make every preparation. Have you any friends to speak to your character beyond Major Forrester's attestation?"

"No."

"None? Have you not been acquainted with many other officers in the service besides the Major? which is but a recent one."

"None that I could or would call upon."

"Umph! I thought the Major told me you were acquainted with a Lieutenant Stanley."

Omelia blushed up crimson at the mention of her lover's name, and her frame trembled as the thought passed through her brain of his becoming acquainted with her present situation.

"Yes, Sir," she said sorrowfully, as she with difficulty restrained her tears. "It is true, I was acquainted with the officer you have just named, and if there is any favor I would wish to ask at your hands, it is, that he may remain in ignorance of my fate, be it whatever it may; I would request this as a particular favour from you."

"As you please—he shall not be informed by me or with my consent: upon that point you may be perfectly at ease."

"I thank you sir most sincerely for the promise. Believe me, a poor broken-hearted girl, does not want anything more to add to the bitterness of her sorrow. I thank you again and again, for this assurance."

"And if anything occurs to you in which I can be otherwise useful to you, I need hardly say that you may command me," said the captain, as he took his departure. As the door opened for his exit, Mrs. Shaw entered, and endeavoured to assuage the grief of the prisoner, with a woman's ministering kindness and sympathy.

The day soon arrived which was to decide the fate of poor Omelia. At the east end of a large room, which had been partitioned off for the particular use of the staff officers, sat Colonel Maitland and his brother officers, who formed the Court Martial, which had been summoned to try several prisoners, who had outraged the laws of government. Other cases had been disposed of on the previous day, with which we have nothing to do in the present history. Goolooh was already placed at the bar of the military tribunal, and Omelia was shortly ushered in, under the guard of a file of soldiers. Every eye was directed towards her upon her entrance, and a half

"Gentlemen," said Colonel Maitland, "we are about to try the prisoners present for conspiring with several others to lead into ambush the late, lamented officer, Ensign Lightfoot, in her majesty's service, and a company of the fourteenth regiment of foot. The prisoners having succeeded in effecting this object, by a false representation, the said Ensign Lightfoot and nearly the whole of his gallant soldiers were ruthlessly slaughtered by the comrades, companions or relatives of the two prisoners—consequently they are amenable to the law under the charges of conspiracy, rebellion, and murder. The names of the two prisoners before you are Goolooh and Omelia—at least, so they are set down in the indictment. Are there no other names, Captain Midhurst?" said the colonel, as he looked over the paper

No. 101.

he held in his hand; these strike me as being Christian names only."

"That is all they have given me," answered the captain. "If you do not deem it sufficient, we can ask them now their surnames."

"No; if they have been known usually under their present appellation it will suffice."

"My name is Goolooh Nusayree," said Goolooh.

"Oh, thank you; we will insert it in the indictment. And yours, young woman?"

No reply was given to this question.

"Your other name? Have you not any?" said Corporal Shaw, who stood by Omelia.

"Have you not another name besides Omelia?" said the colonel in a louder tone.

"No; I own no other," was the reply.

"Good; that is enough. Young woman you have heard me read over the charge? Do you plead guilty or not guilty?"

Omelia who knew no more about the forms of trial than she did about the planet Mars or Jupiter, made no reply to the question.

It was repeated again.

"You must plead, my dear," said the kind Mrs. Shaw, who was near her. "Say not guilty."

"I care not," said our heroine; "it matters little. Which you please, sir."

"Young woman, this is a serious matter; and is a question of life and death."

"Take my life in welcome. I have been long weary of it," she answered, sobbing bitterly.

"This is no answer," said the colonel, rather sharply. "You must say guilty or not guilty. If you say guilty, I am bound to say that your life will be forfeited. Cannot you understand? You surely know whether you are innocent of this charge or not?"

"I am innocent," she said, in a voice of so much energy, that it startled her hearers by its suddenness.

"Oh, that is enough," said the colonel.

"Yes, of course," said another officer; "she pleads not guilty; of course there can be no doubt of that, you might be sure she would."

"And you, young man, how say you? Guilty or not guilty?"

"If my life will satisfy you, gentlemen, take it in welcome: but oh, I charge you to spare this young woman, who is as innocent as a lamb. I will cheerfully, gladly plead guilty if my wretched life will suffice. For it has been through my own indiscretion that she has been brought into her present situation, and had I twenty lives, they should all be freely given to save her. She is innocent, I assure you—I solemnly swear she is perfectly innocent."

"This is no answer to my question," observed the colonel. "This is not the time for you to indulge in a melodramatic appeal on behalf of your companion in crime. You have only to answer for yourself. If she is innocent, the evidence will prove it; any appeal, therefore, you make in her behalf would be prejudicial; for, let me tell you, my man, you have been long known to be disaffected towards the present government, and have been in open rebellion. The very fact of this young girl being so dear to you, as from your language you would lead us to suppose, is one of the worst features in her case; consequently, if you have any consideration for her, which I doubt not, you will hold your peace, and let her answer for herself. Answer me, therefore, guilty, or not guilty?"

"Not guilty!"

"Of course," said the same voice which had spoken before, "he pleads not guilty. I knew he would—they always do, these fellows—always, of course—not guilty! they never are—never knew one guilty in all my life: it is the same story with them all."

"Gentlemen," again commenced Colonel Maitland, "it is now my duty as briefly as may be to state the circumstances of the case."

"You must pardon me, my dear colonel, "for interrupting you," said an officer on his left hand, "but you know I am a relative of poor Lightfoot's, and must of necessity bring something like a strong personal feeling with me in sifting this case. I think, therefore, that if you could place another officer in my place it is possible that justice might be more impartially administered. I was not aware, when sent upon this commission by Lord Clyde, that one of the cases would entail upon me the painful necessity of trying the murderers—or supposed murderers—of my poor nephew, Charles Lightfoot."

His voice trembled as he came to these words, and he sat down precipitately.

"My dear major," said the colonel, "I do not see that this fact in any way incapacitates you from forming a dispassionate and rational conclusion as to the guilt or innocence of these two individuals. The inquiry may be a painful one to your feelings, and I would spare them if I had any one else to appoint in your stead, but really we are thin enough already, and can ill spare one of our company. There really is no one else to appoint, unless Captain Midhurst would take your place. What say you, captain?"

"If it be absolutely necessary," replied the captain. "Of course, I cannot possibly refuse; but, upon my word, I would rather not for many reasons. You see, colonel, this female prisoner has received a strong recommendation to all of us at Saugot from Major Forrester. She has been a constant inmate in our quarters—was a supposed friend of the late unfortunate ensign, whom, I believed, imagined me prejudiced against her; besides this, there are many circumstances which render me, perhaps, unfit to sit upon this inquiry, and I feel and know this to be the case; therefore, I pray you to excuse me, if possible."

"Humph! what say you, major?"

"Oh, if that be the case, and you think it would be well for me to remain, so be it."

"I think so. Oh, yes; there cannot be the slightest objection. However painful this inquiry may be to your feelings, you will, I am sure, not shrink from doing your duty. Let me, therefore, endeavour to briefly state the case. Gentlemen, we are here assembled to inquire into the circumstances connected with the death of a much esteemed and deeply lamented officer, Ensign Lightfoot, and a detachment of her Majesty's troops of the Madrass Engineers. I will not prejudge the case against the prisoners before you, but will endeavour to put you in possession of those facts which occasioned this unfortunate expedition to be sent out. It appears that the young man—the prisoner Goolooh—brought a letter to the female prisoner, who was residing in this cantonment, and on intimate terms of friendship with the late unfortunate ensign. This letter purported to be written by an English lady who, with her companions, were held prisoners some miles distant by a portion of our disaffected troops. In it the writer begged assistance from her countrymen stationed here. In consequence of this statement, Captain Midhurst was induced to despatch a strong body of men, under tne command of the late Ensign Lightfoot. The female prisoner undertook to escort them to the place named in the letter, and in consequence of her asseverations that there was no premeditated treachery to be anticipated, Captain Midhurst was induced, however unwillingly, to sanction this disastrous expedition—disastrous indeed it turned out to be —for upon their arriving at a chain of hills which appeared impassable, the female prisoner advised the ensign to march through a narrow defile, and when about half way through the ensign and his troops were crushed to death by large pieces of rock and stones being thrown from the rocks above, and I believe I am not exaggerating when I say that out of that fine body of men there were but three or four who arrived here to tell the sad news of the day's disaster."

A murmur of indignation ran through the assembly as the colonel came to this part of his statement.

"It seems," he continued, "that after the destruction of the troops and officer in question, that the female prisoner, instead of finding her way back to Captain Midhurst, as one would suppose an innocent person would do, took herself off to, and resided with her foster father, who was one of the chief leaders, if not the chief leader of the aggressive party, and it was by chance only that Captain Midhurst fell in with her, which happened thus:—The captain had been reconnoitering near to where this disastrous affair took place, when he beheld these two persons quarrelling with one of their own party. This man, who is also still a prisoner, although in consideration of his services Lord Clyde has thought it advisable to grant him a free pardon, and he would, therefore, be enabled to give his evidence against the prisoners. I think these are all

the material facts which led up to this sad affair, but, in justice to the female prisoner, I ought to observe that she has hitherto borne an irreproachable character, was much esteemed by Major Forrester, whom we all of us here know, and, moreover, rendered that officer and his companions inestimable services when they were beseiged in the Redowya Fort, some time since. Indeed it is probable that without the assistance of her they would never have escaped with their lives. Captain Midhurst, we will, if you please, hear your statement," said the colonel.

The captain then proceeded to give a minute history of all those particulars with which the reader is already acquainted; the chief points of which were his own misgivings when the expedition started, and the protestations of our heroine to induce it to be undertaken.

Then came the damaging facts against Omelia, namely, her relationship to Tamneegal, her not returning to the English quarters after the affray, her pistol being in possession of Mugriah, the Thug directing the captain another road over the mountains instead of the narrow defile, the cause of Tamneegal's animosity to the late ensign, all these and many more facts were elicited, and dwelt upon with evident gravity.

Goryeboo was called as the next witness. Upon his making his appearance, Omelia uttered a suppressed shriek. Her horror of this man she was unable to conceal, and it was attributed by those present as an indication of dread on her part at what he was about to divulge.

He assumed a well acted appearance of humility and candour, and awaited, with downcast looks, the interrogatortes of the tribunal assembled.

"You know the two prisoners?" said the colonel.

"Yes, sir."

"And you were present at the slaughter of the British troops.

"Yes, sir."

"And assisted them?"

"I cannot deny but I did," he replied, after some slight hesitation.

"Do you know the cause of this wicked plot, and who were it's promoters?"

"I do, sir."

"Explain it, then."

"The original cause was a feeling of hatred aroused by the jealousy of Tamneegal towards Ensign Lightfoot. The former had sworn, as well as the prisoner Goolooh, to have the ensign's life, when upon their discovering him here, they, in conjunction with the prisoner Omelia, drew him into the defile and effected their object."

"How do you know this?"

"I had several interviews with the English prisoners, and one of them—a lady—gave me a note to the female prisoner to beg assistance. I should have delivered it myself, but knew her to be unfriendly towards me. Consequently I told Tamneegal of the circumstance, and he said he would undertake the management of it, and send his friend Goolooh to the English camp, and at the same time he offered me a handsome sum to give the letter up, which I did, and I afterwards found out what his object was in so doing."

"You did not know at the time his intentions then?"

"No, sir. I thought he was going to do what I had intended to have done myself, namely, convey the letter, get the prisoners safely ransomed, and obtain a good reward for so doing."

"You say that was your intention."

"It was, sir; I had no ill-feeling towards Ensign Lightfoot, and I hope I have proved my good intentions, for I have since conducted Captain Midhurst to the village where the English prisoners were confined, and have succeeded in rescuing them."

"How do you know the female prisoner was privy to this wicked scheme?"

"I have overheard her rejoicing with her foster father since the affair at the success of their sanguinary plot."

This was uttered with the greatest *sang froid* by the villain. Omelia sent forth a cry of horror, and Goolooh vociferated in his own tongue against the statement, at the same time anathematising the Thug in no measured term."

"Silence!" exclaimed the colonel.

"You positively swear that you know the female prisoner was privy to this plot."

"I do, sir. Her every act proves it. There was no necessity for her to have directed the troops through the defile, as I have proved there was another road; and she knew of the jealous feelings her father felt towards the ensign."

"Is the prisoner Goolooh related to her?"

"No, sir, he is a lover only."

"And he entertained feelings of hatred to Ensign Lightfoot."

"So much so that he took a solemn oath to have his life."

"What was the cause of his hatred?"

Goryeboo in reply entered into the whole particulars concerning the fate of the unfortunate Poutra, a portion of which was already known to some of the ensign's youthful companions. There was a pause of some minutes, which was filled up by mysterious whisperings among those who formed the court-martial. The colonel spoke again—

"This Omelia, the female prisoner, has borne an irreproachable character," he said solemnly; "and nothing but the clearest and positive evidence will convince me that she could consent to be a party to so diabolical a plot. Again I ask you, therefore, to consider what you are saying."

"I hope I am not here, sir, to give false evidence against one of my own countrywomen," said the Thug, with an air of injury at such a supposition. "I am here to speak the truth. I do not know much of her character, but am aware that long before this transaction she very nearly succeeded in destroying an English officer, named Lieutenant Stanley."

An expression of surprise escaped the court at the statement, and a faintness came over poor Omelia that she trembled and would perhaps have fallen, had not the kind Mrs. Shaw handed her to the seat which she had placed for her use.

"When and how did this occur?" said the colonel.

Goryeboo now entered into the particulars of our heroine enticing Stanley to the rock, over which he had fallen and narrowly escaped with his life, when he was afterwards taken to the abode of Jahnsah. This information seemed to make a most unfavourable impression on those present, and the colonel turned towards Omelia and said,

"You hear what this man has stated? Is it truth? You are at liberty to ask him any questions."

"I have nothing to say?" she answered, faintly.

"If this is untrue it can be disproved by applying to Lieutenant Stanley. Do you wish us to do so?"

"Oh, no, no," she ejaculated passionately.

The colonel evinced some surprise, and Captain Midhurst whispered a few words to him.

"Oh," said the latter, "we must assume the truth of the assertion then. How about this man, captain? Is his evidence borne out by after circumstances?"

"I am compelled to admit that it is," said the captain, and he described the whole conduct of the Thug since his capture.

"Humph! he has been, I dare say, an unmitigated rascal," said the colonel. "You have, I understand, my man, belonged to the accursed tribe of Thugs; is it not so?"

"I do not attempt to deny it, sir," was the reply, "but have long since seen the error of my ways, and have an English gentleman who will tell you that I was in his employ, and conducted myself with strict fidelity towards him."

"Is he present here to-day?"

"It's my intention to call him," said captain Midhurst. "Indeed he has kindly volunteered to give this man a character."

"Oh, indeed! Well that is something."

"But before doing so I have another witness, a follower of the scoundrel Tamneegal who perhaps may throw some light upon the matter."

"Let us hear him them."

"Have you done with the present witness?"

"Yes, for the present. We can call him again should it be requisite. We will proceed with the other evidence."

A stranger was now presented to the court to examine. He was unknown to either Omelia or Goolooh. He professed to have been a follower of Tamneegal, which in truth he was, having been captured on the occasion of the captain's attack on the cave.

"Your name?" said the colonel.

"Nulay Kerud," said the reply.

"Did you belong to the band of Tamneegal."

"I did, sir."

"Do you know the prisoners?"

"I do."

"Do you know if they were in any way connected with the late atrocious plot against the lives of our countrymen?"

"Yes, sir; I have overheard them concocting the arrangements for carrying out this plot with Tamneegal. At least I overheard the prisoner Goolooh converse with Tamneegal upon the subject."

"What did he say."

"He said he had seen the female prisoner and she had fully consented to aid them in drawing the English troops into ambush."

"You are sure of this."

"Yes, sir."

"Is that all you know of the transaction? Were you present at the slaughter of the troops?"

"No, sir."

"You are sure of this."

"Quite sure."

"Is this man to be tried or pardoned, or what?" inquired the colonel of Captain Midhurst.

"He has yet to be tried," observed the latter; "but there are, I believe, extenuating circumstances in his case, which will be produced in evidence."

"Good; he may retire. Any other witnesses?"

"You would perhaps like to hear the character of this man, Goryeboo, from his master?"

"Certainly—by all means. Is he within call?"

The captain left the apartment, and in a few minutes returned with the unprincipled Mr. Natterley, who entered with a vast deal of self-importance, tempered with a degree of dignified urbanity. Some of the officers knew him by sight, and returned his graceful salutations with prompt politeness.

"We understand Mr. Natterley," said the colonel, "that this man Goryeboo has been at one time in your employ, and are therefore, anxious to know what sort of a character he bore during that period."

"Of course—very natural," observed the individual addressed. All the information I can give you shall be promptly and cheerfully rendered."

While he was making these few observations he gazed with eyes of curiosity towards the female prisoner. It was the first time he had an opportunity afforded him of catching a glimpse of Omelia, and his curiosity had been piqued to see one who stood in his way of inheriting immense worldly wealth.

"What sort of conduct did the man evince during the time he was in your service?" inquired the colonel.

"I had no occasion to find fault with him in any way; I found him faithful, trustworthy and industrious. Indeed, from his general conduct, I was led to form a very good opinion of his character. When he came into my service I knew that he had been connected with dissolute companions, but he evinced a disposition to mend his ways and habits of life, provided he could obtain the means of earning an honest livelihood. He did so on my estate, and I considered him an excellent servant."

"He has given very direct evidence against the two prisoners," said a stout officer amongst the court martial. "Do you think his word can be taken?"

"Oh, yes—yes, certainly—I should say so —yes, I should be disposed to take it myself."

"Ah, that is sufficient. Do you know either of the prisoners?"

"No, I can't say I do," answered Mr. Natterley, as he directed his glance towards them; "no, I do not remember to have ever seen either of them before; the female of course I have heard enough about indirectly."

"Oh, indeed—how so?"

"Oh, from various quarters," and here he smiled significantly, "but as what I have heard is nothing to do with the present charge, why of course—of course—I should be sorry to prejudice your minds against either of the prisoners."

This speech was made with the intention of suggesting to the minds of those present that there was something known to the speaker which was injurious to the character of Omelia, and which from good motives he was anxious to suppress. There was a pause for a few minutes when Captain Midhurst who stood in the body of the room close to Mr. Natterley, said in a whisper—

"We have heard always the best account of the female prisoner previous to the present charge. I suppose you have also, eh?"

"Well—no—not exactly—not altogether

—but— It is immaterial to the present question."

"This man, who was in your employ has deposed that she at one time sought the life of Lieutenant Stanley. Do you know if that is true?"

"Quite true," whispered Mr. Natterley. "I had it from the lieutenant's own lips: indeed I am an intimate friend of his."

"Ah, that accounts for her horror when I proposed sending to him," thought Captain Midhurst. This information, although not given out loud, got buzzed about into every ear present, if we except the prisoners.

"This completes the case against the prisoners, I suppose," said Colonel Maitland to Captain Midhurst.

"I think there is nothing more to be added."

"Prisoners at the bar," said the colonel, "you have heard the evidence which has been given against you. What have you to say in reply to this dreadful charge of deliberate murder?"

"That the whole of that scoundrel's evidence is false!" exclaimed Goolooh, passionately. "I swear to you, on my soul, that this young woman is as innocent as any of you are yourselves of this foul charge."

"Answer for yourself," said the colonel. What have you to say in your own defence?"

Goolooh now entered into a rambling account of the whole transaction, declaring that he was in entire ignorance of Tamneegal's intentions, and that Goyeboo had told a tissue of falsehoods, that he had thrice attempted Omelia's life, and had himself been one of the chief actors in the sanguinary drama, all this and a great deal more he said, but the whole tendency of his observations were directed to exculpate Omelia; for himself he did not appear to care, as he felt quite certain, his life would be forfeited.

"Pray, sir," said one of the officers on the court martial, "will you answer me one question? Did you, or did you not swear to seek the life of the late unfortunate Ensign Lightfoot?"

Goolooh hesitated for a minute, and said—

"I cannot deny that when I found the companion of my childhood fall a victim to the ensign, that I did, in the anger of the moment, vow to have a speedy vengeance."

"Ah, I thought so."

"But I was in entire ignorance of the ensign's being here, and certainly had no hand in this fatal plot."

"Oh, of course not," said the same voice which had spoken at the commencement of the proceedings. "Of course not; I knew he would say that—I told you so. They never have any of these rascals—never knew any one of them ever to be connected with a plot against our countrymen. Oh, he is innocent—of course he is."

Were you not on intimate and friendly terms with the deceased Tamneegal?" inquired the first examiner.

"Most certainly I was—I don't deny it; but—" he appeared to break off suddenly— "It is not for my own life I am pleading— take it in welcome; I will acknowledge I deserve death, but it is for this poor injured woman I would plead, who, induced by her good faith in my word, has been led into one of the most dreadful situations it is possible to imagine. Oh, gentlemen, I swear to you that she is entirely innocent of this foul charge, which yon villain has sworn so falsely to. A time will come, sooner or later, when she will shine forth in all her purity, and her stainless character be seen in its true light. She esteemed and admired Ensign Lightfoot and was in utter ignorance of the late plot. I swear to you that she is innocent, and that this man, Goryeboo, is a villain who has attempted her life, and the whole of his statement is false."

"Have you anything to say in your defence?" said the colonel, turning to Omelia.

"No—nothing, only that I am innocent."

"Humph! that, is then, the whole of the case, gentleman," said the colonel. "It will be my duty to now review the whole of the evidence and direct your attention to the various circumstances which tell for or against the prisoners."

"I will beg to offer a few observations, which I feel I am bound to do by a sense of duty," said Captain Midhurst.

"Oh, very well, captain; we are all attention."

"In justice to this young woman," began the captain, "I feel it my bounden duty to inform you that she has held the highest character with all those officers with whom she has been acquainted; she has been of signal service to many on more than one occasion, and Major Forrester, Mrs. Forrester, our friend McDarvish, and the ensign himself esteemed her with that degree of affection more like a relative than an acquaintance. It does, therefore, seem an impossibility that one who appears to have deservedly won the good opinion of so many should be connected or partner in a plot of so foul a nature as the one in question. I know the evidence may, perhaps, appear overwhelming, still I would wish you to remember her previous high character."

We shall not fail to take all these matters into consideration," observed one of them.

"Gentlemen, it now remains for me to go over the evidence," said the colonel as he referred to his notes for this purpose. It appears to me that if we are to place reliance upon the witness, Goryeboo—and I know not how we are to ignore his testimony, backed as it is by the other witness—that the circumstances of the case present very strong points, which would point but in one direction, namely, the guilt of both the prisoners; however reluctant we may be to come to this conclusion with respect to the female before us, I do not see how we can do otherwise, if we assume that the two witnesses are reliable. I should be sorry not to give the benefit of a doubt where I could see one exist, and should be glad to do so in the present instance; for it does appear improbable as Captain Midhurst has justly observed, that a young woman of such irreproachable character should conspire with others to compass the death of one she seemed to entertain a friendly feeling towards. Still I know not how we can ignore the evidence, and if she be guilty I suppose it has been occasioned by the wicked influence used by the late miscreant Tamneegal."

The colonel recapitulated the evidence, and dwelt very carefully upon every minute particular. He seemed to think it singular that Omelia should not have offered some explanation of her conduct, or produced some witnesses for her defence. After the colonel had concluded, a long discussion arose amongst the officers, and Captain Midhurst was consulted about many particulars. At length a death-like silence ensued, the buzzing of several voices had ceased, and the colonel came forward with a grave and serious expression of countenance, which portended a grave conclusion.

"Prisoners at the bar," said the colonel; "you, Omalia, and you, Goolooh Nusayree, I have to inform you that, after a patient hearing of the evidence adduced against you, we are unable to come to any other conclusion than a conviction of your guilt, and we are bound therefore to return a verdict of guilty against both of you. The crime of which you stand charged is one of a most heinous description, and in justice to our poor countrymen we are necessitated to make an example of those who have been parties to their untimely death. I will not harrow up your feelings by dwelling upon the enormity of your crimes, but would advise you to seek pardon from a higher tribunal, and endeavour, by a sincere repentance, to make some atonement for your misdeeds. The sentence recorded against you is death—when, where, and how this is to be carried out must rest upon the determination of Lord Clyde to whom we shall furnish all the necessary particulars of this sad affair; at the same time I may observe that we shall not neglect to forward to our commander-in-chief the strong recommendations as to your previous good character."

This latter observation was, of course, addressed to Omelia, who seemed entirely prostrated and indifferent to what was going on.

A dead silence ensued after the colonel had made this address: in a few minutes afterwards there was heard a confused sound of voices in hasty and angry discussion at the entrance of the hall of justice. Captain Midhurst proceeded immediately to see the cause of this unexpected disturbance; before he had reached the doorway the whole assembly were surprised by the abrupt entrance of several figures. The first of these was Moorsha the shikaree, accompanied by Goryeboo's supposed son. Moorsha entered with an air of confidence, which rather surprised the officers assembled.

"Heaven be praised we are here in time," he said, as he took a survey of the company.

"What is the meaning of this?" angrily inquired the colonel.

"Fate!" said Moorsha.

The officers stared in some dismay, when a wild and piercing scream rung through the apartment, which was followed by several others, as Omelia sunk senseless in the arms of the kind Mrs. Shaw. The confusion was enhanced by the entrance of Stanley flushed with excitement. It was his appearance which caused the emotion of Omelia.

"The Thug! where is he?" said Stanley.

"He is in custody," said the captain.

"Good! and the Englishman?"

Every eye was turned in search of Natterley, but he was nowhere visible. Stanley's glance lighted upon Goryeboo; in an instant he was by his side, and grasping him by the throat, dragged him before the judgment seat.

"Villain!" he shouted, directing the point of his sword to his throat, "unsay your perjured calumnies against that innocent being, or your life's blood flows upon the spot."

"Order! Lieutenant Stanley what is the meaning of this?—Silence!—Close the doors —let no one escape," were the sentences which issued from a dozen lips. When calmness ensued Colonel Maitland said—

"Lieutenant Stanley, explain the meaning of all this."

"Fate!" said Moorsha.

"Unnatural, remorseless, perjured villain!" shouted Stanley; "unsay your foul calumnies against the spotless innocence of her whose life you have sought. Confess the foul part you have been playing, or unshriven I will send your soul to purgatory! Speak, wretched imposter," and he tightened his grasp of the Thug's throat that he was half suffocated his eye caught sight of his supposed son, and he trembled in every limb.

"Ah," shouted Stanley, "do you see the key to the mystery? Where is your employer? Come, we know all—confess, or, by heavens, I will dash your worthless brains out against yonder column!'

"What do you want me to do? I will tell the truth—indeed I will," gasped Goryeboo

"Answer me then. Have you not agreed to swear away the life of this innocent girl?"

Goryeboo writhed in the powerful grasp of his indignant enemy.

"Answer at once, or—"

"Ye es," stammered the Thug.

"This is not the way to extract evidence," observed Colonel Maitland.

"Pardon me, sir," said Stanley, "but with such a scoundrel, I fancy it is the only way. Have you not, in consideration of a reward, consented to swear away the life of this innocent girl? It is no use denying it; I hold the proofs of your guilt."

"I have, but it was at his instigation."

"You hear him, gentlemen? It is enough. Captain Midhurst, see to his safe custody. Gentlemen, we are only just in time it seems to expose a plot perhaps the most wicked that ever entered into the head of any human being. This scoundrel has, for months past, been seeking the life of this unhappy girl—not succeeding, he has—at the instigation of an Englishman I am sorry to say—been endeavouring this day to ensure her conviction by a series of false statements. This Natterly was here to-day, and gave his evidence before you. I much fear he has escaped. I bring with me proofs of the whole nefarious scheme. This girl's letters to her friends have been intercepted by bribery of the letter carrier, and her friends have consequently been kept in entire ignorance of her whereabouts. I hold documents which have passed between these scoundrels which place their guilt beyond a doubt. The details of the whole transaction will occupy you much longer in sifting and listening to than you can possibly find time for this day; but let it suffice that they entirely exculpate both the prisoners now before you. The verdict, which I understand has been given, must, therefore, be reversed."

"How have you obtained this information?"

"By various means, which I will explain hereafter. To meet the villain, I have been compelled to combat him with one of his own weapons; I, too, bribed the letter carrier, and have obtained from him the necessary documents to ensure the conviction of the worthless Natterley."

"What could possibly be his motive for seeking the life of an innocent girl?" inquired Colonel Maitland.

"He had the strongest motive. This poor injured girl is sole heiress to an immense sum of money which, were she dead, would fall into the possession of the villain Natterley. She has been quite unconscious of this fact, and Natterley has generally reported that she fell in one of the late outbreaks. In consequence of this he has employed this Goryeboo to destroy her. He has affected to commiserate with me upon her loss. I was fully persuaded that she had met with an untimely end, and so indeed she would, had I not discovered the whole scheme by the aid of this worthy man here," and Stanley pointed to Moorsha.

"Lieutenant Stanley," said the colonel, "you have relieved us all from a most painful duty, and no man in the assembly will feel more pleasure than myself at the turn this case has taken. It is too late to enter into the particulars of your statement now, but as they satisfy you, they will, no doubt, us. We had better adjourn, therefore, and listen to the details of this plot at our leisure."

"My inquiries have not ended here," said Stanley. "I have become acquainted with some facts which, if I mistake not, nearly and more immediately concern yourself, Colonel Maitland, and when the court rises I will explain to you more fully my meaning."

"Concern me?" said the colonel, with unfeigned surprise. "I am more astonished. In what way can I be connected with this affair?"

"It is not of this affair I would speak. But more of this when you are disengaged. For the present let me see to my own charge," so saying he went towards Omelia, who had, however, been removed from the court by Mrs. Shaw.

Stanley hastened to the apartment into which she had been removed, and oh, with what inexpressible joy did he again clasp in his arms the beloved form of her whose absence had cast a blight upon his path, and weighed his spirit down in the depths of despair.

"Look up, dearest Omelia,' he exclaimed passionately, as he pressed her fervently to his bosom. "We meet now to part no more on earth. Never again will I lose sight of your beloved form. Oh, if you knew the many anxious hours I have endured, and the anguish of mind your absence has occasioned me, you would have pity for your devoted Edward.

"To meet thus," said Omelia, with a sigh, and looking, with a melancholy expression into the countenance of her lover, "in dishonour and disgrace—arraigned as a murderess. Oh, Edward, it is indeed sad."

"Say not so, dearest; I bring proofs of your innocence, undisputable proofs. I have so much to tell you that I hardly know where to begin; but your innocence is established."

A smile of ineffable sweetness passed over the features of Omelia as she heard these reassuring words; and Mrs. Shaw, who had heard the last words uttered, shouted out in joyful accents—

"I knew it. I knew she would have her innocence proved. Hoo—rah!" And the little woman capered about like a frantic person, in her ebullition of joy. "The corporal—bah! he is an obstinate, thick-headed man, and self-willed too. I told him this dear creature was innocent; leave a woman alone for discernment in these matters. Ah, the coporal, he's obstinate," she said, confidentially, to the lieutenant. "Obstinate! and, Lord bless you, so easily imposed upon; but I knew I should be right—hoo-rah!" and off went Mrs. Shaw to lecture her husband upon his want of discernment.

The interview between the lovers was a long one. They had so much to tell each other of the circumstances that had happened since their last meeting, that Stanley

No. 102.

knew not how to part with his enslaver. He might well have said, in the words of the poet:

"Too long I've strayed, forgive the crime;
   How swiftly flew the hours;
How noiseless falls the foot of time
   Which only treads on flowers."

Colonel Maitland broke up the court upon Stanley's departure, and anxiously awaited the latter's presence to give some explanation respecting the supposed discovery he had made. Time flew rapidly enough with Stanley in the company of his beloved Omelia; but not so with Colonel Maitland, who counted the minutes off in weary anxious suspense, and hailed with some considerable degree of delight the appearance of Stanley.

"Pardon me, colonel," said the latter, on his entrance, "I fear me I have been rather tardy in seeking an interview, but——"

"Ah," rejoined the other, "when a lady is in the case—you know the old adage—" and he smiled pleasantly, and handed his junior officer to a seat.

"I cannot conceal from you," continued the Colonel, "that certainly my curiosity has been aroused by the words you uttered in the presence of the court marshal, and I have of course had a great wish to have a *tête-à-tête* with you. Events, my young friend, have hurried on with such extraordinary rapidity, that one feels almost prepared to hear anything. I assure you that I never was so pleased in the whole course of my life, at the turn affairs have taken. There was something so noble in the bearing of that young woman which completely belied the charge against her; still you must see that the evidence seemed perfectly overwhelming. How fortuitous was it therefore that you should arrive just in time to give us a key to the mystery."

"It will be my bounden duty," said Stanley, proudly, "to enter into the whole of the particulars and proofs which will exculpate this persecuted girl from any complicity in this heinous plot. I say, Colonel, this will be my duty, that her character may be understood and appreciated by yourself and brother officers who tried her. At present you have heard a tissue of falsehoods, such as man in his utmost wickedness, I believe never before devised. But enough of this for the present. When you and your brother officers find it convenient to meet for the purpose, I will lay my statement before you. What I am now about to enter into is one more nearly concerning yourself."

"Ah! indeed; yes—certainly," ejaculated the colonel, in evident anxiety and impatience. "Certainly, proceed, my friend; I am entirely at a loss to comprehend what your revelation may be, and am therefore most anxious. Proceed, pray."

"Well," said Stanley, "I hardly know where to begin, for it is, you see, rather an intricate affair, and I am afraid you will imagine I have been indulging in the unsubstantial creations of romance. Let me see—we have to go back half a life-time to begin."

"Bless me!" said his companion, in unfeigned surprise. "Why we shall never get through it in one night."

"Enough for our purpose, I hope," said Stanley. "Now, colonel, you must pardon my freedom, but I must begin by interrogating you."

"Good! I will reply to your questions as promptly as possible."

"Did you not know, in the earlier portion of your life, a native of India by name Kerah Bardah Singh?"

"Yes, certainly; of course I did most intimately. But how knew you this? He has been dead for years."

"I am aware of that. Do you know that this same Kerah Singh placed under the charge of a native farmer near to where he resided an English child to bring up and take care of?"

"Ye—s; my dear Stanley, what are you driving at? How came you acquainted with circumstances which occurred nearly thirty years ago? I never believed in second sight—but—really—you seem to have been having dealings with——"

"The evil one," said Stanley, smiling. "Well, so be it, colonel, if you will have it so. I have had a personal interest in these parties I am mentioning, for you must know that the wife of this said Kerah Singh was the mother of the persecuted girl you tried to-day."

"The wife of Kerah Singh, her mother! Lieutenant Stanley, you perfectly astonish me—why Kerah Singh, was one of my most intimate and esteemed friends. I do believe that this country never produced a better man."

"So I have always heard, but, Colonel, this strange history which I am about to relate, was connected with him, as well as yourself. I have said, that you placed a child under his care."

"I! What mean you?"

"As I suppose."

"You are speaking in enigmas."

"It may be so. It is possible that I am mistaken, but, I am, if you please, assuming that you did so. Am I right?"

"My young friend, I do not understand you. I understood that Kerah Singh had placed a child under the care of a farmer of his district. What has that to do with me? There can be no good attained by ripping open the past, and recurring to events which occurred nearly thirty years ago, some of which, indeed, are frought with anything but pleasurable sensations. This must be a strange life, indeed, which does not possess some incidents and transactions, upon which memory in its retrospective glance, finds it at times painful to dwell."

"That is true enough, as most of us know from experience, and, far be it from me to endeavour to disclose anything that may be painful for you to hear. Let it, therefore, be buried in the past," said Stanley, as he observed the Colonel was moved in no ordinary degree.

"No!" said the companion, "I would have it thus. You have broached the subject—continue therefore—put me in possession of all you know. I will not conceal from you, young man, although you have become acquainted, or in any way cognizant of the fact, I am at a loss to divine; but I will not, however, endeavour to conceal from you the fact, that I did place a child under the care of Kerah Singh. Yes, thirty years ago I confided one to his charge under circumstances that it would be needless for me now to dwell upon. Years have passed since then, and time, by his softening and mellowing influence, has well nigh worn away the painful recollections which the circumstance conjures up. That child, in an unhappy hour, was seized and destroyed by a tiger, and it is hardly worth while recurring to so painful an event."

"That child," said Stanley, firmly, "has grown up to a stalwart man, and now lives!"

A visible change came over the features of the colonel as these words were spoken. He became ashy pale and tottered to his seat, while at the same time he covered his face with his hands, and did not speak for some minutes.

"Lieutenant Stanley!" he said, solemnly, "Do you know what you are saying? Do not trifle with my feelings—that child was —was—my son!—this was my secret once —but now I will not deny it. What do you mean by stating that he is still alive?"

"Simply because such is the truth— Colonel Maitland, this young man, was rescued from the tiger's jaws by the very man who has perjured himself here to-day. This man Gorzeboo, has been for years his reputed father."

"Merciful powers! Can such things be," exclaimed the colonel.

"He was," continued Stanley, "held has a hostage by the scoundrel Natterley, to ensure the good faith of Gorzeboo. The man who entered with me your hall of justice, is the son of the farmer with whom he was placed, and by his aid he has contrived to make his escape."

"And where is he now?"

"He is here within—a few yards of us."

"Lieutenant Stanley, you are probing old wounds I had thought long since healed. Can it be possible that this young man lives?"

Stanley now entered into the full particulars of the history of Zarah's captivity, his escape from the same aided by Moorsha, and prior to that the account of his rescue from the tiger by Gorzeboo. He, moreover, informed the Colonel that it was by a most miraculous circumstance they had recently discovered the child had originally been left to the care of Kerah Singh, by an officer bearing the name of Maitland; and it was this which had caused them to imagine the Colonel was in some way connected with him.

"But you will learn more from his companion, Moorsha," he said, as the Colonel made further enquiries. "Have I your permission to introduce them?"

"Certainly; by all means."

Stanley retired, and soon returned leading by the hand Zarah, whom he introduced to the Colonel by that name. The look of surprise and utter bewilderment which the latter fixed upon his son as he entered, it would be difficult to describe. Zarah, in every respect resembled a native of India, and was dressed in their costume. The Colonel, as he looked upon his two visitors with eyes of wonder, enquired of Moorsha the particulars of the early history of Zarah, which the latter at once freely entered into.

"And how came you to know of the incarceration of this young man?" enquired the Colonel; "how were you directed to the residence of this Mr. Natterley?"

"By fate!" sententiously answered Moorsha.

"Humph!" muttered the Colonel, while at the same time he thought it was not a very satisfactory solution of the circumstance. He, however, promised to reward the faithful Shikarie for the services he had rendered to his son, whom he at once acknowledged. Indeed, the proofs were undeniable as to his identity. Stanley and Moorsha left the Colonel and Zarah to their own cogitations. The latter had the history of a life-time to detail to his parent, which is too prolix a narrative for us to record here, as we have to follow the footsteps of the defeated Mr. Natterley.

CHAPTER CCXXXV.

THE FLIGHT OF NATTERLEY.—HIS DESPAIR, THE MEETING WITH MESSRS. COTTLE AND LEAF.—THE CLOSING SCENE OF A BAD MAN'S LIFE.

WHEN that unprincipled, scheming, worthless man, Mr. Natterley, became aware, upon the entrance of Stanley, that his nefarious schemes had been discovered, and were about to be exposed in all their hideous deformity, like a coward as he was, he precipitately fled the field, leaving his tool Gorzeboo to his fate. From the little he had heard fall from Stanley, he did not doubt but he came armed with the full particulars of the whole plot, or rather series of plots against our heroine, and Natterley saw of course that in all probability his own life would be jeopardized therefrom, he therefore at once availed himself of the opportunity afforded him of free egress from the hall of justice and and hastened to make good his retreat. It would be a vain and idle task to endeavour to describe the agonizing and conflicting feelings which wrung this bad man's breast. The last game he had played so boldly for so large a stake he found himself a loser at the very moment of apparent victory. It was not remorse for past misdeeds which tortured the reckless trickster, but his feelings were more like a wild beast who, while he hungered for the blood of his victim, beheld it snatched from his grasp. The false god he had worshipped, mammon, at whose shrine he had prostrated his honour and self respect, left him in this, the hour of his affliction, a despised wretch, who was now in hourly expectation of being a convicted criminal and murderer.

A host of stormy and dark thoughts rushed through his brain. He did not doubt for one moment but that Gorzeboo would make a full and ample confession of all these transactions, and in this he would be borne out by his employers own letters —the testimony of the letter-carrier, and all those concurrent facts which it would be impossible to gainsay or deny. It would be therefore useless, to deny his complicity in the transactions. No, every circumstance pointed him out as the greater criminal of the two, and an ignominious and dreadful death stared him in the face—he trembled at the sight of an occasional passenger, fearing lest he might be an officer of justice, who had been sent off to take him prisoner before the assembled officers at Langor. With bent brows, and a trembling frame, Natterley hastily pursued his way towards his own estate. He had observed Zurah (the Thug's supposed son), enter with Moorsha, and not being aware of his escape, he hastened on towards his own home, to inquire of his manager the particulars. Fear, rage and despair, had so firm a hold on Natterley, that he was not aware of the near approach of a carriage coming along the road he was traversing, and he started like a guilty culprit, as he was, when he heard his own name shouted out—he trembled in every limb, and was so completely overpowered, that he had not the heart to reply to the speaker, whoever it might be; he made sure, however, that it was an officer of justice, and he would have taken to his heels, but his legs seemed to lose their power of volition, and locomotion was out of the question.

"What oh! — oh! Mr. Natterley! called out the same voice that had before spoken, and the individual addressed heard the sound of carriage wheels, and beheld the head of the elder Mr. Cottle protruding from the window of the vehicle, and ordering the driver to stop.

"Why what is the matter, my friend?" said Mr. Cottle, when the carriage had stopped, "you seem quite distraught, has any misfortune overtaken you?"

"Oh!—no—no, not exactly—no," stammered out the party addressed, while at the same time he was perfectly bewildered at the sudden and unexpected appearance of the two lawyers, for by this time he became aware that Mr. Leaf was also in the carriage.

"We are bound for Langor," said Mr. Cottle.

"Oh, indeed—ah—a pleasant journey, gentlemen," stammered out Natterley, endeavouring to be jocose by a desperate effort.

"Yes," said Mr. Leaf, "we are bound for Langor;" and at the same time he looked under his spectacles at the English merchant.

"Ah! indeed; upon business, I suppose?"

"Unquestionably," said Mr. Cottle, "lawyers, my friend, do not travel usually for the pleasure of the country, at least not without having an eye to business at the same time. But, my dear friend, this affair we have come about most deeply concerns you, for it relates to property of the merchant Harcourt, and what a singular circumstance it is that we should meet you, the very man of all others in the world who is perhaps the most interested in the affair. Why, my dear sir, you had better jump in and come along with us to Langor."

"Ah—no, I thank you, I had rather not;" and this reply was so prompt, and the speaker started back some paces at the bare suggestion of his accompanying the lawyer, that the latter looked at each other in some surprise at the altered demeanour of their client.

"Well, as you please," said Mr. Cottle in continuation. "I should have thought that you who have evinced such deep interest in the Harcourt estates—and, indeed, there is every reason that you should have done so —I say, that under these circumstances, I should have thought — yes, I should — have certainly thought—that—you would have been anxious to accompany us to see justice done — justice to all parties;" and the lawyer tapped the back of one of his hands as he slowly emphasised the last sentence.

"I have no time to spare," answered Natterley, tartly, "to see justice done to every one who may need it, or I should have enough to do, I'm thinking, I will leave it therefore to gentlemen of your profession; for myself, I am but a simple merchant, who has been used badly enough." He was beginning to recover his courage now, as he found there was no arrest contemplated.

"Very well, we have no wish to persuade you to any act against your wish," said the other, blandly, "only you know, my friend, that when you were at our office, you expressed a wish to be introduced to the Indian heiress which we had discovered. Well, now there is an opportunity for you to gratify your curiosity, for we are now journeying to Langor for no other purpose than being introduced to her; and you can, at the same time form her acquaintance."

"Pshaw!" exclaimed Natterley, "I do not desire to do so. How do I know, or you either, that she is the individual you are in search of. She's an imposter, sir! an imposter! You are on the wrong scent, and being befooled and cajoled by some deep designing knave. There—I know who you mean. You'll find out your mistake. By the Lord's truth you evince a monstrous fancy to find out this girl, to journey all the way from Calcutta for the purpose; however, it is nothing to me—I have no interest in the matter. I only tell you again you are misled."

"We think not," exclaimed both of the partners. "We think not. We come here at the urgent solicitation of Lieutenant Stanley, whom, it appears, has a host of facts to present to us, and desires our legal advice thereon."

"He's a liar! and a scoundrel!" yelled out Mr. Natterley. as his rage and fear began to be aroused. Rage against the lieutenant for his triumph over the guilty enemies of Omelia, and fear, lest the lawyers were cognisant of the position which he, Natterley, himself, stood respecting the affair. He did not wait for further parley, but rushed off, repeating to himself "Liar! and scoundrel!" The lawyers looked after him in some surprise, as he took his way along the road.

"Umph," said Mr. Leaf, "that man has been fairly baffled, and he cannot bear it with grace. If I mistake not he will have to answer something respecting the Harcourt affair, if not at Langor, it will be somewhere else."

"Yes," rejoined Mr. Cottle, "from the communications which we have received from Lieutenant Stanley, there can be no doubt but that he is amenable to the laws, but we were hardly justified as the case stands at present, in taking him in custody,

still, when the time arrives, there will not be much difficulty in finding him; so we will now go on to Langor:" and the carriage at once proceeded on its journey.

Mr. Natterley, after he had left the lawyers, went on with hurried strides towards his own residence, muttering curses the while against Messrs. Cottle, Stanley, and all connected with our heroine. When he arrived at his estate, his first anxious inquiry was for his manager. He was met by one of his labourers, who looked stupidly vacant at his master, and gave no reply to his questions.

"Speak, man!" said Mr. Natterley. "Where is Mr. Musgrave? Have you lost the power of speech, or taken leave of your senses? Answer me. Where is Mr. Musgrave?"

"He is not here, sir. He left with his family about ten days since."

"Left! for where?"

The man shook his head, and said "I do not know, sir."

"Not know! Did he not say?"

"No, sir."

"Where is Zarah?"

"He escaped, sir, before Mr. Musgrave left."

"How?"

"Through the window of his room. He filed the bars of the window, and passed a rope to an accomplice who is supposed to have been stationed at the wall which surrounds the moat; and by means of the rope he no doubt escaped."

"Perdition! You are a set of fools to allow this to take place—I will have justice upon you all," and muttering anathemas upon his whole household, he entered his residence, and learnt that his manager had decamped with a considerable amount of property, to where, no one knew.

Mr. Natterley fell into his chair, and covering his face with his hands, sobbed like a child.

"Oh, villain—villain! This is your requital for my kindness and confidence in your integrity," he exclaimed, bitterly, "after years of faithful servitude to be a plunderer and thief; at last everybody deserts me. Princely wealth was almost within my grasp, when I found myself foiled at the eleventh hour, and now—now I return to discover that I have been cruelly, ruthlessly robbed by one I deemed my most faithful steward. The tide has set in against me, let it drift me out to another shore—yes, another shore. I will leave this country for good and for all. I have not many that care about me in the old land—not many. No matter, to remain here is death—certain death. Yes, I will ship myself off as worthless, unsaleable goods--here it is impossible to stay. Let me see: where's my list? Ah! here, ah! The *Trincomalee* sails on the 10th inst.; I must go by that. I cannot realise on my estate before I go, but will empower Jukes to do so—yes, give him a power of attorney. Umph! very likely the villain will cheat me like the rest; but it can't be helped. Stay here, I cannot, to have the finger of scorn pointed at me—to be arraigned as a felon and murderer. Ah! the thought is dreadful. No, the game is up. I've played my last cards, and the chance has been against me. I must go—fly anywhere to avoid the meshes of the law."

For some hours Mr. Natterley was engaged in various arrangements previous to his departure for England. He saw Jukes, a neighbouring attorney, and informed him that business of an urgent nature called him suddenly away, and consequently he placed at his disposal all his property in India, that he might realise as much as possible, and forward him the produce thereof to his native country. Having satisfied himself thus far, Mr. Natterley returned to his domicile, and soon became lost in a series of miserable reflections. Seated in his arm chair, which overlooked the road which led to his house, he thought he observed by the moon's light several figures coming towards the spot. They were, or appeared to be, a long distance off; but a horrible misgiving seized upon the guilty man. What could they be coming for at this time of night? "the thief fears each bush an officer:" such was Mr. Natterley's case; he hastily got his pocket glass, and looked carefully at the coming party. Ah! they were English soldiers! There was nothing remarkable in this circumstance considering troops of men were accustomed to move about in all parts at any hour; but to Natterley's guilty mind they appeared to be after no one but him. Hastily calling his housekeeper, he informed her that it was probable some one would endeavour to arrest him about some law proceedings, and he begged her therefore to say he had gone out about two hours previously.

She was a faithful domestic enough, and promised to obey her master's instructions. Mr. Natterley now proceeded to lock up his house, and await the issue. From the apartment in which he stationed himself, there was a secret passage for him to effect an escape. By removing a panel in a large cupboard, a sufficient opening was obtained for the passage of a human being, and he felt comforted by the assurance that he should be enabled thereby to baffle his pursuers, should they turn out to be a party sent for his capture.

The few minutes that intervened, were anxious ones to the guilty man, and his heart beat audibly as he awaited the result.

He was soon aroused from his state of suspense, by a loud knocking at the door, and only waited to hear his own name pronounced by the officer in command, who demanded of his housekeeper to be admitted into his presence. As the wretched man sought flight through the panel, he heard an angry altercation at his door, and became aware that the party were armed with a warrant for his immediate apprehension. Fear lent him wings, and through a passage in the house, he gained the garden at the back, stooping down behind the low wall which surrounded it, he cautiously took his way along under its cover, when jumping over it at the farther end, he was felicitating himself upon his escape, when he became aware of the dreadful fact, that he was observed, for several voices cried out for him to surrender. They appeared to be at some distance off, judging from the sound, and he made no reply, but ran as fast as possible. Again, a demand was made for him to surrender, and the word "fire!" was given, and a volley of musketry was discharged at random after him, but he was out of reach of the shots.

He heard the dreadful order of "forward, men" given, and as the sound reached his ears, he hurried on at headlong speed. The wretched man now heard in the still night-air the tramp of many feet which he knew came from his pursuers, who were hunting him down like a wild beast. Dark and horrible thoughts flitted across the brain of the wretched man, and a confused mass of chaotic incidents of his early life, even in that brief space, were presenting themselves to his fevered imagination. Like a hare pursued by hounds, panting and palpitating, Natterley took his way, and with a speed it would have been impossible for him to have accomplished, he managed to completely distance his pursuers. He rushed now to the banks of the river Jumna, along a small path by its side. Having proceeded along this for more than a quarter of a mile, he arrived at a high bridge of three arches which ran across the river. He hastened on to this, and turned round panting and well nigh exhausted, to see if he could discern any traces of the party on his track. From his elevated position he had a command of the country around. All seemed quiet and undisturbed save the gentle rippling waters of the Jumna as it laved the banks or washed against the piers of the bridge. The scene was peaceful—the very reverse to the thoughts of him who contemplated it. Mr. Natterley leaned against the ballustrade of the bridge, and cooled his throbbing temples by laying them against the stonework. He was fairly exhausted, and felt incapable of further action.

Hush! Sounds meet his ear—sounds of feet—horrible! They are on his track! he hears the tread of troops. A shout is raised. A roar of musketry comes from—he knows not where. Why be hunted thus? He will surrender. Ah, no! Death! better to seek it now. Cheat them—aye, cheat them—excellent thought; ah, ah! In an instant he is on the parapet of the bridge; he casts one last glance upon the face of nature, now bathed in moonlight, and in another moment a loud splash in the water is heard, and the figure of the wretched man falls into its bosom, and in a few more minutes his earthly career is ended. The troops despatched by Captain Medhurst arrive at the bridge, and are at fault, as the man they are seeking is no longer visible. They had observed him leaning against the parapet, and had hastened on to effect a capture. Some few declared they heard a splash in the water, and the officer in command had his own suspicions of suicide, and he proceeded at once to a house, and borrowed, or rather took some rakes and ropes, with which he dragged the river, and, after a determined search, they succeeded in dragging on shore the body of the deceased Mr. Natterley, who had thus cheated the law of its due.

CHAPTER CCXXXVI.

THE COMPLETE EXCULPATION OF OMELIA.—THE ARRIVAL OF MESSRS. COTTLE AND LEAF.—DEATH OF GORZEBOO.

THE party of soldiers who had endeavoured to effect a capture of the criminal Natterley had been despatched off by Captain Medhurst immediately upon his discovery that he had beaten a retreat. The Captain took this step without consulting Colonel Maitland or his brother officers, who were in entire ignorance of the prompt measures he had adopted. Immediately after the departure of the company of men, Messrs. Cottle and Leaf arrived at Langor, and were of course introduced to Captain Medhurst, as the officer in command. They informed him of the communication they had received from Lieutenant Stanley, and desired him to introduce them to that officer; he was, however, at that time closeted with Colonel Maitland, and the lawyers had, therefore, to wait till his conference was over. Immediately upon his emerging from the colonel's room he sought the two legal gentlemen, and evinced much pleasure at their prompt attendance.

"Thanks, gentlemen," exclaimed Stanley, as he shook each warmly by the hand. "Many thanks for your immediate attendance to this matter. There will be no difficulty in proving the identity of Omelia as the daughter of Rose Harcourt, but previous to that I have to enlist your services in another suit. This poor persecuted girl has been charged with a heinous crime, and it must be my duty, assisted by yourselves, to entirely exonerate her from the foul charge."

"A heinous crime," they both exclaimed, in some astonishment, "Yes, conspiracy and murder. This vile charge has been got up at the instigation of no other person but the man who by her death would have inherited the property of the late Rose Harcourt."

"Mr. Natterley!" ejaculated the lawyer.

"The same; this Natterley has employed emissaries to carry out his wicked and nefarious schemes, and it has been only by a series of extraordinary circumstances that I have been enabled to get a clue to his proceedings, and only arrived just in time to save this unfortunate girl from, perhaps, an ignominious death, and what is more, loss of character."

"She is unfortunate no longer, my friend," said Mr. Cottle, "for she must be happy indeed in having so sincere a partisan in her cause as yourself, and happy also in being heiress to immense wealth. Can we see her?"

"At present it would hardly be worth while. No, we must arrange her full exculpation from the crime which she has recently been charged with."

"You act for her, I suppose?"

"Unquestionably; I will therefore at once put you in full possession of all the particulars."

Stanley then entered into all those circumstances with which he had become acquainted, and produced a mass of papers and evidence which showed the proceedings of Natterley and his myrmidon, Gorzeboo, in their true light. Upon this, the lawyer arranged all the necessary proofs in a businesslike order, and drew up a statement of the main facts to be laid before the court martial on the occasion of the next sitting; not that this was necessary, for the officers composing it, were sufficiently satisfied of Omelia's innocence already; but Stanley would not be content without being permitted to make a full statement before the assembled court, and receiving some expression of regret from them for the painful

THE SEPOY'S DAUGHTER.

situation in which his beloved Omelia had been placed. The wish in this respect was cheerfully responded to by Colonel Maitland, who appointed the court to sit on the following day, after Stanley had informed him that he was ready to open the case to them.

But before the Court sat another chief actor in this dark drama was removed from the scene of action. This was no less a personage than Gorzeboo. It will be remembered that when Stanley so suddenly interrupted the proceedings and seized upon the Thug with such determination and energy, he resigned the latter, after he had confessed his evidence to be a false perjury, to the care of Captain Medhurst. That officer saw him safely deposited in an upper apartment of the cantonment, to which place he was conducted by a file of soldiers. The Captain did not deem it necessary to handcuff the rascal, but contented himself with placing at his door a sentry, and two others well guarding the outside of the building at all times. The Captain thought, therefore, naturally enough, that sufficient precautions had been taken to secure the Thug, till such time as his brother-officers might want him. Now when Gorzeboo was locked up for the night, his reflections were of a most miserable nature. He saw nothing but certain death staring him in the face, and in all probability the death of all others he most dreaded, namely, being blown from a gun. So while dark and dreadful thoughts chased each other through his mind, the probability of effecting an escape suggested itself to his imagination. He looked at the window. Is was fastened, or rather it had never been made to open, being, in fact, one of the top windows which had originally been in the chapel. As he reflected, he did not doubt being able to effect a passage through it in the course of that night; but then its height from the ground was so great that it would be quite impossible for him to alight with safety. However, that he might continue, so urged on by the perspective view his imagination presented to him of his own beloved person being blown into a thousand pieces, he set to work with caution to effect an escape.

With great tact and address—for he was not deficient in either of these qualities—it is to be regretted he did not put them to a better use—he managed to remove two of the window-panes, and then he looked out upon the scene below. He saw one of the sentinels pacing his round with measured tread; he watched him turn the angle of the building, and calculated how long it took him to traverse the other end before he reappeared in sight; it appeared full five or six minutes. Now, thought Gorzeboo,

"if I can manage by some means or other, to drop down quietly while he is pacing the other end of the building, I shall be all right; taking a sash from his body which he wore round his waist, he measured its length and found it did not reach one-third down to the ground; to strip this into three was his next proceeding, and he then fastened the pieces together and rolling them round, a tolerably good rope was formed thereby. With this he purposed dropping on the earth. Having tied the end of his rope or sash firmly to the window frame, he watched the sentinel turn the corner, and emerging through the window he began to descend; he had not got half way down, when—oh! horror! the sentinel reappeared in sight, and he was joined by a companion; they both stopped, and Gorzeboo thought he was observed; he dare not breathe, cold drops of perspiration shot like needle points from his forehead, and he would if possible have stilled the beatings of his own heart; he looked intently; the two sentinels were conversing together, evidently unmindful of his presence; they did not seem likely to move from their present position, and Gorzeboo found himself becoming exhausted from the length of time he had been suspended in the air; he felt that his arms would fail him, and it would be impossible to retain his hold much longer if the sentinels did not proceed on their march. To relieve himself, therefore, he cautiously drew up the end of the rope, and tied it as well as he could into a noose above his head; into this he inserted his body, and was comforted by the relief it afforded to his arms. Presently he had the gratification of seeing the two sentinels separate, and each take to his own particular beat.

The moment he saw them turn the angle of the building, down he slid, to effect an immediate escape, but he was too precipitate, the rope had become so entangled, as he had swung about, that he was caught in his own trap; as he descended, the noose which he had made for his own relief, caught him round the head and right arm so firmly, that he could descend no farther. He made frantic efforts to release himself, by pulling his body up by his disengaged arm, and endeavouring to adjust the sash, but his efforts were futile; he seemed to be even more firmly fixed. From suspense, anxiety, and the efforts he had made, his strength was nearly gone, and besides this, he lost his presence of mind, and fought blindly with his left arm, until he nearly fainted from exhaustion; all this while, the sentinels were quite unconscious of the battle for life or death which was going on so silently a few yards above their heads.

When the morning's light came it disclosed to view a black and distorted corpse, hanging midway from the window to the ground.

The wretched man had undergone all the horrors of strangulation. Yes, he who had so remorselessly put to death numbers of innocent individuals, was himself doomed to fall by the same instrument—the Thug's sash.

When his body was discovered on the following morning, Captain Midhurst had no difficulty in divining the cause of his death.

On the following day, Stanley, assisted by Messrs. Cottle and Leaf, laid his statement before the assembled board of officers. He was listened to with profound attention, and an inward satisfaction was felt by many that

the two chief actors in the foul plot against our heroine had gone to their account.

When Stanley had ceased, Colonel Maitland rose, and addressed Omelia at some length; he begged to express his own deep regret, as well as that of his brother officers, that she should have been placed in so painful a position, but one which was attributable alone to the envy and wicked machinations of her enemies.

"I cannot express to you, my dear young lady," said the colonel, in continuation, "the pleasure it gives me to be here a witness this day of the triumph of virtue and innocence —a pleasure which is considerably enhanced by the fact of your coming into your just rights, and I am sure that pleasure will be, and is, no doubt, doubly enhanced from the fact that your esteemed friend and admirer,

Lieutenant Stanley has been mainly instrumental in bringing about this happy conclusion of events. From your uniform sympathy and kindness, at all times so cheerfully and promptly bestowed upon so very many of our distressed countrymen and countrywomen, we all feel and know that we owe you a debt of gratitude; and, for myself, I have only to say that any reparation I can make you for all the troubles you have undergone, I shall be glad to be enabled to do so. I should beg the favour, if you do not object, of introducing you to Lord Clyde, who will I am sure, be much pleased to see one who has rendered so many services during the whole of the late revolt. And now, is there any wish you have to express?"

"The prisoner Gooloob," said Captain Midhurst. "How are we to act respecting him?"

The colonel looked blank at this suggestion; the exculpation of Omelia, although it cleared Goolooh of any complicity in the late transaction did not entirely free him from misdemeanours.

"The prisoner Goolooh," said the colonel, in some embarrassment, as he turned and addressed his brother officers.

"Oh, I suppose we must enter into his case another time," said one of the officers. Let us not mar this day's proceedings by any unpleasant inquiry."

Omelia caught the meaning of the hurried whispers which were being passed from one to another, and she stepped forward upon the impromptu of the moment, and addressed herself to the colonel.

"Colonel Maitland," she said, proudly, "I have to thank you for the many kind expressions which have just fallen from your lips, and, believe me, they are received with their due weight and force by myself, for I am sure they come from the heart. You were about to ask me if there was any wish I had to express. May I take the liberty to say yes? I am about to become a pleader now myself—not for myself, that I should find impossible, but for another—a faithful friend who, although I am free to confess has perhaps been culpable—not through badness of disposition, but through the error of not understanding his real position. Gentlemen, it has been proved this day, that by the vilest stratagem which ever entered into the head of guilty man, that I myself, as well as this young man,"—and here she pointed to Goolooh—"have been the victims of a cruel plot. He is as innocent as myself, and I would, therefore, ask at your hands his prompt acquittal!"

There was a whispering among the officers when this demand was made, and some hesitation evinced, after which Colonel Maitland rose, and said—

"We entirely acquit him of any complicity in the death of Ensign Lightfoot, but "—and here the colonel stammered and hesitated—"but perhaps it would be advisable to wait further orders from Lord Clyde; there are other—other "—more hesitation.

"I know, Colonel Maitland," said Omelia, "that there are other overt acts with which he is, or may be, charged against the government, the which I will not attempt to deny; but he has had associates and advisers, and if he has done wrong through the ill advice of his companions, he has rendered your countrymen infinite service on many occasions. Major Forrester can testify to this, and he deserves, for such acts, condonation for past errors. The happy issue of this day's proceedings would be marred did I find one, whom I am proud to call friend, still under the ban of the law, and a proscribed man."

"You have said enough," replied the colonel. "Goolooh Nusayree, you have a full acquittal from all charges against you, and I have to compliment you upon your choice of an advocate; 'for when lovely woman," &c. &c. I am too old a man to indulge in the softer passion, but—but—there, I can't resist such a pleader. You are discharged, Goolooh, and make the best use of the clemency shown towards you."

Goolooh thanked the assembled officers for their kindness, and declared for the future he should remain a faithful and devoted ally of the English.

The other unfortunate miscreant, whom it will be remembered, gave his evidence against our heroine, in conjunction with Goryeboo was not brought forward upon the occasion, neither was his name mentioned during the day's proceedings.

The extravagant expressions of delight with which the worthy Mrs. Shaw thought proper to indulge in upon Omelia and Stanley emerging from the hall of justice it would be in vain to endeavour to describe. She was backed up in the manifestation of her feelings by three juvenile representatives of the Shaw geneological tree.

The clouds that have so long hung around the path of Omelia are now dispersing, and a bright flood of sunshine streams upon her and Stanley. The way that was of late so dark and dreary, now becomes a golden vista —of blossoms and flowers. Love lights the path—two hearts beat in responsive union with one another—distracting and torturing jealousy is no longer there, for Stanley has told his enslaver, amongst other scraps of news, that Clara is affianced to Captain Robinson.

This is welcome intelligence to Omelia, and any lurking, jealous fears she might have entertained are effectually dispelled.

"And now, dearest Omelia," said Stanley, "we meet to part no more on earth. I shall soon be able to claim you as my wife—a wilful one enough, I dare be sworn."

"No, Edward," she answered; "no longer wilful or headstrong. I have seen too much—have suffered prosecution and learnt mercy—and am too thankful after all my trials and vicissitudes for being safely restored to your arms, and doubly thankful as, by a turn of fortune, I am enabled to lay a handsome dowry at your feet.'

"Psha!" exclaimed Stanley, "it is no mercenary motive which actuates either of us."

"I know that, dearest Edward. "I have given instructions to Messrs. Leaf and Cottle to make out the lease of the estates and all the papers respecting the Harcourt property in your name."

"Omelia!" exclaimed Stanley, in utter astonishment.

"Silence, sir," she said, as she pressed her hand upon his lips. "Don't be rude. Hear me out. Ladies first, if you please."

"I am mute as a dumb waiter," said her companion.

"Very well; the papers are made out in your name. The property is yours—I will have none of it; and now, that matter being settled, it is for you to consider whether you won't lose caste by espousing a foreign girl like myself who is, at best, but half a heathen."

Stanley burst out in laughter at her piquant manner.

"Order, sir—order, if you please. What do you mean by laughing at so serious a subject. I say examine your own heart, and ask yourself the question seriously. Do you think you can, consistently with your own self-respect, degrade yourself—"

"Bah!"

"I say degrade yourself, by marrying one who comes of a race dissimilar to your own, and who is in every way inferior to yourself."

"In every way superior you mean."

"Inferior—by birth—habits—education—religion—everything. If you can, dearest Edward," she said, more seriously, "say that you have no fears for the future—no doubts that in after years, when the novelty has worn off—the toy become damaged—"

"Toy! Do you liken yourself to a toy, and me to a froward, fickle child?"

"Men are but children of a larger growth, and oftentimes, I fear, treat us poor women as toys; so my comparison is not out of place. Believe me, love, that the best of your sex, be his heart ever so tender, his love enduring beyond the average period of his fellows, he is still unable to cope with the self sacrificing, devoted spirit of woman."

"I know man is, by nature, more selfish—I acknowledge that."

"I am glad you confess thus much. Then only think what agony it must be when a woman discovers that he upon whom she has set her hope and trust no longer loves her—looks upon her as something that is in his way—a nuisance, that he is ashamed of ever having made so much fuss about, and is surprised how he could have thought it worth while to make so many sacrifices. Then comes neglect—some pouting—petulant words—a sharp retort—sulks—estrangement — angry words —recriminations — a quarrel, and—but why indulge in a catalogue of the descending passages in love's scale. The summit of bliss is supposed to be obtained for a short time, but how rapid the fall therefrom."

"My dearest Omelia," said Stanley, "what a melancholy and painful picture are you drawing, entirely from your own imagination."

"Oh, no, not from my imagination either. It is too often the truth, as women find out in after years. It is not when all things look colour-de-rose that they reflect upon these matters. You see, my dear Edward, I have been so knocked about in the world, that I don't take things exactly as they at first present themselves. I inquire a little further before I come to a conclusion; I have become quite a—what do you call it? —a—philosopher."

"So it seems," said her lover; "I am afraid that you are getting so extraordinarily clever, that it will be necessary for you to throw off a little of your waste steam in a three volume octavo. What say you? "The Life and Times of Omelia Harcourt" would be a taking title?"

"You are making a jest of the profound wisdom I have bought, dearly enough perhaps, by experience. This is no answer to my question, which is a serious one. Can you trust your heart and say sincerely that you will take me as your wedded wife without one regret hereafter?"

"I can and do say so most sincerely, and my only regret is that I am not more worthy of you."

In the midst of this playful conversation between the lovers, Corporal Shaw entered, and informed them that a person named Abdal desired to see our heroine.

She started up with delight, and hailed the appearance of her relative with unfeigned joy.

"Do I again behold you?" said Abdal; "it seems like a dream; how long and anxious have been my wanderings in search of you. I deemed you dead. Oh, why have you not written, according to your promise when we last parted?"

Stanley here explained the particulars respecting the interception of the letters through the instrumentality of the plotting Natterley.

"But you see, my good Abdal, she is now safely towed into port, never again to venture upon stormy and adverse seas. A peaceful calm awaits her in future. She will soon be sailing down the stream of life under convoy, and you, my friend, may for ever bid adieu to distracting cares or anxiety on her or your own account."

CHAPTER CCXXXVII.

PRESENTATION OF OUR HEROINE TO LORD CLYDE.—THE BRIDAL PARTY.—MARRIAGE OF OMELIA AND STANLEY, AS ALSO CLARA AND CAPTAIN ROBINSON.

Colonel Maitland, true to his promise presented our heroine to Lord Clyde, who received her with the utmost courtesy. He had heard of her unexampled character from Major and Mrs. Forrester, as also from McDarvish. Omelia found that the Major and his Lady had returned to England, but she had the gratification of receiving a warm greeting from Mr. and Mrs. McDarvish.

Having been lionised and feted for some short period, our heroine accompanied Stanley to Calcutta, where she intended to join her friends, Colonel Bridport and his amiable daughters, Doctor Hamilton, Morley, Robinson, and all those with whom she had been so intimately associated.

It was for the purpose of completing the arrangements for her wedding that our heroine was now bending her course to Calcutta.

She had for her attendant the kind Mrs. Shaw, who declared she would never leave her; and Lord Clyde had directed Colonel Maitland and a detachment of troops to escort her to the capital city of India.

Stanley had written off to Colonel Bridport, putting him in possession of all the particulars respecting our heroine, and intimating, at the same time, their forthcoming marriage.

The colonel read Stanley's letter to those officers present, and it was arranged between Clara and Captain Robinson that their marriage should, to use a sporting phrase, "come off" on the same day.

It would be useless to endeavour to describe the reception Omelia met with from her friends now stationed at Calcutta; there were so many inquiries to answer—so many incidents to relate—that her life was one round of excitement and unalloyed pleasure, and in a short time the day arrived which was fixed for the ceremony of her marriage to take place.

And here we must pause to take breath, and candidly confess that we feel quite unequal to the task of giving anything like an adequate description of this imposing ceremony—we feel our weakness and frankly own it. It *is* too lofty a subject to grapple with. We know what is expected by our female readers: of course a description of the bride's *trousseau*—her feelings upon the trying occasion—her gushing tears—the tears of affectionate sympathy shed by the bridesmaids—the deep feeling expressed by the venerable gentleman who personated the bride's papa, who, as he expatriated upon her manifold virtues, macadamised the hearts of his youthful hearers. Then there's the bells—the sonorous voice of the clergyman (clergymen have always sonorous voices in novels. We have known a few, however, who possess voices of such an irritating description, that a dry grindstone was music in comparison—but no matter, we will assume, for the nonce, that this gentleman had a sonorous voice). Then there are the garlands of flowers strewn in the bride's path—the cake—ah! we had well nigh forgot the cake—this, of course, was of leviathan dimensions—like Mount Etna, covered with perpetual snow, and like that mountain possessing richer and warmer material beneath its outward incrustation. Then there's the presents—oh, dear! a great deal must be left to the imagination of the intelligent reader.

It appeared that Colonel Maitland had expressed a wish to Stanley that he, the colonel, might be permitted to have the honour of giving away the bride; this was awkward, as Stanley had been arranging for Colonel Bridport to perform that office.

He was the elder friend of the two, and would, of course, expect to be asked. Still Stanley did not like to pass any slight upon Colonel Maitland, and was, therefore, rather hitched upon the horns of a dilemma—the two colonels forming the said horns. Now we have written the last sentence it looks ugly: the word horns, as applied to a bridegroom, is unpleasantly suggestive. No matter, we will let it stand.

Mentioning the subject to Omelia, she said, that she certainly considered Colonel Bridport ought to officiate, his daughters were to be her bridesmaids, and it would be a decided slight passed upon him to choose a comparative stranger.

This being her opinion, Stanley was fain to tell Colonel Maitland of the circumstances in which he found himself placed, and that officer, of course, at once resigned the task to his brother colonel; but as there were two brides to be given away, Captain Robinson begged of Colonel Maitland to stand as father to his beloved Clara, and thus an exchange was effected, and matters comfortably compromised.

The eventful day arrived. A hundred bells rang out their epithalamiums, as the principal streets of Calcutta are thronged with the carriages of rank and fashion; for there is to be a wedding to day of one of the richest heiresses in India—and wealth and beauty has its votaries, my friend.

When a bride—no matter how humble her station—is about to be led to the altar, it may be, by some rustic lover, she has many fervent prayers offered up by her parents and the friends of her childhood for her future happiness. She is venturing upon a new current in life, it may be a calm one, or she may be doomed to be tossed about on troubled waters; anxious thoughts go with her—the soft memories of early endearments—never, perhaps, forgotten in after life—but recurred to as the most pleasurable moments of existence. New troubles and cares await her, and, with them, new pleasures; they go hand in hand with most of us, but the green spots of our more sunny youth leave their impress more distinctly than any others in after life.

Omelia looked perfectly queen-like, or regal in her magnificent bridal costume. Her dress consisted of a boddice and skirt of white silk, around the bottom of which there was worked, with gold, silver, and azure threads, a beautiful arabesque running ornament studded with small flowers. She wore her long black hair plain, and around her head was a wreath of flowers. A magnificent veil of the finest and most costly lace completed her toilet, which was otherwise enriched with armlets, bracelets, and broaches studded with the rarest jewels the country afforded.

The regimental bands serenaded her early in the morning, and accompanied the wedding party to the church.

An elephant was caparisoned with a gorgeous covered howdah, the hammercloth of which was looped up with precious stones. This was destined to convey Omelia and her bridesmaids, who, when mounted upon the animal, were screened by curtains of silk lace, on which were worked many cunning and curious devices; on each side of the elephant there walked twelve virgins in white, strewing flowers on the path as she went along, and in front of the animal sat the *mahout*, or driver, who was no other than our friend Moorsha.

A native band, with drums, cymbals, and other instruments peculiar to the east, accompanied this part of the procession.

The Colonels Bridport and Maitland and Stanley were conveyed on horseback, and others of the party were in open or closed carriages. Several detachments of cavalry accompanied the procession, as also two of the British military bands.

The streets of Calcutta were hung with garlands and festoons of flowers, and various emblematical devices, and here and there a triumphal arch was thrown across the widest portions of the town.

The streets were thronged with a dense multitude, consisting of native as well as English residents, who cheered the party as they proceeded along, and white handkerchiefs were observed waving from the windows and house tops on either side.

When the procession arrived at the end of the principal street, they had to pass through a triumphal arch, after which they came in front of the parade ground.

They found on this space all the soldiers drawn out in lines, who saluted them by presenting arms, while, at the same time, salvos of guns were fired in honour of their passage.

This was quite unexpected by Colonel Bridport or any of the officers belonging to the wedding party, being, in fact, a little bit of performance got up by the officer in command.

Omelia's heart beat high at the honours shown her, and behind that curtain of silk gauze there were tears of joy falling thick and fast from more than one pair of eyes; but the great expounder of the power of fate, Moorsha, sat on the shoulder of the animal he so dexterously guided with his pronged stick imperturbable and unmoved, as though he were following his ordinary occupation and not forming one in a ceremony, the chief actors in which he had snatched from death some months previously.

Having arrived at the church, the party had to dismount and arrange themselves into something like order; this was a work which required considerable time to accomplish.

When Omelia dismounted, she was greeted by about a hundred-and-fifty of her own countrywomen, or rather girls, who chanted a native air in their own language, which was designed to express a benediction upon the bride. None would have imagined it to have been such, for, to say the truth, it was discordant enough, as is most of the music in India, but it was well meant, and received therefore in a good spirit.

In due time the two bridal parties took their station round the altar, and the ceremony was performed by the Bishop of Calcutta, assisted by several other clergymen. After which a short sermon was preached, prayers were offered up, peons sung, and the procession was again formed in due order to return to Colonel Bridport's quarters, in the gardens of which a magnificent repast awaited them, spread out under the cooling shade of gigantic tents and marques.

It is but justice to the tender heart of Mrs. Shaw for us to notice that the lady in question had shed abundance of tears in the fulness of her joy, in fact, she was a great actress in the way of these lachrymous demonstrations, in which she was ably assisted by several of the bridesmaids.

Upon the return of the wedding parties they received several other ovations, and more powder was expended in saluting them upon their emerging from the church.

It is an old saying "happy is the bride whom the sun shines upon," and if there be any truth in it, our two brides ought to be in the highest state of felicity, for there was enough sun that day to serve all the brides in Christendom: and, if the truth must be spoken, many of the party felt much more blessed when they found themselves under the shade of the tents, and within reach of champagne, claret, or hock.

A gay scene presented itself to their view when they arrived at the gardens of Colonel Bridport's cantonment. They were most tastefully decorated with garlands, ribbons, and rosettes of white satin.

An orchestra had been erected on the green, and a platform laid down for dancing in the evening. Variegated lamps and paper lanterns of different hues were hung around the various trees, to be illuminated as darkness appeared.

A very pretty device was painted as a transparency, with the initials O. & S. for Omelia and Stanley. This was placed at the back of the residence, overlooking the grounds, and could be seen from the road, and on the corresponding corner of the building was another with the letters C. & R. Clara and Robinson.

Besides these, there had been extensive preparations made for a grand display of fireworks, and, after the wedding feast, it was intended to admit a limited number to the hall and evening's amusements, for there were several other entertainments in the bill of fare.

A celebrated Indian juggler was to go through his performances, such as the pleasing feat of swallowing a sword, eating live coals, drinking boiling oil, dislocating his back by various amusing contortions. There was a snake charmer or two to be also there, and a sort of mask to be performed by puppets on a small stage erected for the purpose, so there was something to please all tastes.

As to describing the repast, even if such a thing were attempted, our readers would find it quite impossible to pronounce the names of many of the dishes provided, and

therefore we will spare them the infliction, as it will be enough to observe that every delicacy was there, and the feast was one of magnificence.

The chair and vice-chair were taken by the Colonels Bridport and Maitland, the former acting as chairman, and the latter facing him.

Dinner having been removed, the usual toast given was the Queen, the military bands, at the same time, struck up the national anthem. Then followed the next toast from Colonel Maitland, the army and navy, the bands playing Rule Britania, the Cambells are Coming, and Cheer Boys Cheer. Then Colonel Bridport rose to give *the* toast of the day.

"Ladies and gentlemen," said the colonel, "the pleasing duty devolves upon me to propose the next toast, which, I am sure, is one that will be responded to with enthusiasm by all of us here assembled on so auspicious a day. You have seen me as a fond and deeply affected parent give one of my beloved daughters in marriage this morning to our much respected friend and companion Lieutenant Stanley. I was not aware till a few days ago that I had such a lovely daughter to bestow upon that worthy officer (suppressed laughter); "but we live and learn," is an old adage, and if I journey to another quarter of the globe, I may perhaps find another dutiful child requiring my parental care and advice, but never—never, I am sure, shall I meet with one to exceed her whose surpassing loveliness I am permitted to behold this day. (Applause from the gentlemen). I am sure I need not tell you that she ought to inspire any man with eloquence to describe her various charms and virtues. Gentlemen, she has been bred in the stern school of adversity, and has come out scathless and refined therefrom. (Hear, hear). We are all of us the better for having a little of the "whips and scorns of the world,' which, as the bard of Avon beautifully expresses it, "patient merit from the unworthy take. I tell you, young men, and young ladies, too, that it is not well for it to be all smooth sailing with you through life—too much ease and comfort begets indifference to the cares of others. But the lady whose health I am about to propose has, I am sure, had her share of human suffering and woes; talk about walking upon red-hot ploughshares, treading with naked feet upon tares and brambless, or any other phrase expressive of a life of misery, why if I were to talk here till midnight I should be unable to describe a tithe of what she has gone through; aye, in all and every case she has, with true womanly instinct, lent to the side of mercy, and amidst overwhelming perplexities, with which she found herself surrounded on many occasions, she managed, ladies and gentlemen, to save—to her honour be it spoken—numbers of our countrymen and countrywomen from destruction. It is true she is allied to us by blood, being, in fact, by birth, more than half an Englishwoman, and, in spirit and kindness, she is wholly one, as well as a good Christian. (Hear, hear). It has been observed by the poet, "that the course of true love never did run smooth," and perhaps the truth of this observation was never more strikingly exemplified than in the instance before us; but what will not the devoted constancy of woman overcome? (Hear, hear). In the midst of the most tempestuous storms of life—in the hour of darkness—the bitterness of despair—the most agonising moment of peril, when dishonour, disgrace, and death threatened her, she kept her eye steadily upon the object of her heart's affection, and was comforted by the reflection that she had never done one act that would compromise her honour, and she could look into his face with a proud consciousness of her own innocence. Gentlemen, all the clouds are cleared away, and we are now enabled to see in all her effulgence, in all her radience and natural beauty, the "Star of the East" shine here upon us this day."

The colonel, as he said this, struck the celebrated tea-pot attitude: one arm a kimbo and the other stretched out towards Omelia, as he gracefully christened her for the first time by the euphoneous title just named. Vociferous cheering followed, after which the colonel continued—

"Yes, ladies and gentlemen, she is a star of no common order, the glances of her eyes brightens our board, and infuse light and life around; her bewitching smiles shine benignly upon us—and shine the more brightly as they come from one who possesses truth, honour, virtue, and all those higher attributes which adorn and shed an undying lustre upon the female character." (Hear, hear, bravo).

"Upon my word," whispered Morley to a brother officer, "the colonel is surpassing himself; he ought to be in parliament."

"I am not a young man," said the colonel in continuation.

"Yes, yes," said several voices.

"I say, no, no!" said the colonel, smilingly. It is no use endeavouring to conceal the advances of age—

'Believe me, my friends, ten years do not pass,
  And leave not some signs as they go;
For though they fly with the wings of the hawk, alas,
  They are marked with the feet of the crow.'"

And the colonel, in proof of the distich he had just quoted, pointed to his temples, where, it must be admitted, some wicked

bird appeared to have succeeded in leaving an impression of his feet.

"I say, and feel that I am not a young man, but, nevertheless, I am, I hope, not insensible to the charms of woman; who lightens our troubles through life—shares our sorrows—tends us in the hour of affliction, and is a companion and helpmate on all occasions. By the aid of her gentle influence the harsher and more rugged portions of our character become refined. It is love in its broadest and widest acceptance of the term which lights up our way through life from the cradle to the grave. A mother's kind and devoted ministering first guides our footsteps into the path of honour and rectitude; and most men of my age can testify to the influence of a loving wife. Let us hope that our friends here Lieutenant Stanley and Captain Robinson, will in after years be able to indorse the sentiment I am now expressing. Some of us here assembled are I am afraid getting almost worn out votaries of Hymen—myself for one—and others have as yet to make the sudden leap, whilst two swains have been this morning led with silken chains by two beloved partners. Peace be with them—long years of unalloyed happiness and wedded bliss attend them. Gentlemen, I will not trespass further upon your time, other toasts have to be given, I will, therefore, conclude by proposing that we drink the health, long life, and happiness of Omelia, the "Star of the East." To the bride!—may her life be one of unclouded sunshine, each day fulfilling the promises of yesterday still promising to-morrow!"

It is needless to observe that this was drank with enthusiasm by all present.

When the vociferous plaudits had become exhausted, Stanley rose to reply.

"Mr. Chairman and gentlemen," he said, "I am so overpowered by the eloquent and touching speech made by my esteemed friend Colonel Bridport, and the fervid manner in which you have responded, that I hardly know how to express myself in anything like words which may convey to your minds my deep sense of gratitude for the honour you have done to my wife. I am no orator, as our colonel is—(yes you are, and laughter) —I assure you I am not, being but a plain, blunt soldier. I cordially agree with the sentiment expressed by our esteemed chairman, when he says we are most of us the better for feeling a little of the "whips and scorns of the world;" this may look like egotism on my part, as most of you know that I have had my share of them, and I hope I am the better for it—but I am sure my wife is—(Oh, oh)—that is, if it were possible for her to be better. (Hear, hear). Gentlemen, I cannot express to you how proud I feel to-day at seeing so many kind friends and companions surrounding this board as witnesses of my happiness—many of whom I have known in boyhood. I feel fate has been kind to me after all, for you will agree with me that there have been stirring times of late, and while numbers of our brave companions sleep on the bed of honour, I may esteem myself more than usually blest to find so many of my early friends mustered here to-day. Gentlemen, on behalf of my wife, I beg to thank you most sincerely for the kindness you have evinced towards her, and the cordial manner in which you have drank her health. I am sure I may say for her that this will be one of the most pleasing recollections in her existence—a recollection to be recurred to in after years as an oasis in her path through life. I am quite sure that, if her life be prolonged to the very longest period allotted to mortality, the remembrance of this day, of your kindness, and the kindness of our respected and esteemed chairman will remain with her in all its pristine freshness and vigour. And, gentlemen, to you who have as yet not chosen a mate, let me hope that the time will come when you may be enabled to do so, and when that arrives let me express a sincere wish that your lives may be as long a round of happiness as I feel mine is likely to be. Gentlemen, let me again thank you for the honour you have done my wife—you are all kindness, and she, I am sure, is all gratitude."

Several lively pieces of music were played after Stanley's speech, and one or two of the ladies favoured the company with songs, accompanying themselves upon a grand piano which was placed beneath the chief tent.

After some lively conversation and repartee, in which our heroine joined, a tap on the table from the vice-chairman demanded order and silence, upon which Colonel Maitland rose, and began to address the company.

"Ladies and gentlemen, I believe, if I mistake not, that I have a lovely daughter here whom I have given away this morning to a young officer, while affectionate, sympathetic, paternal tears stood in my eyes, and I therefore wish to ease my anguished breast and riven heart by saying a few words expressive of the loss I have sustained. I have only known her a few days—(this was said *sotto voce*, and from the manner of the speaker it elicited roars of laughter,)—but it is astonishing with what rapid pace the feelings of a parent run. Now, gentlemen, I must make a clean breast, and tell you frankly without disguise that I find myself placed in rather a conflicting position. Of course, it is natural to suppose that I am, in the first place, overpowered with the recent loss of my—daughter; but that is not all.

(Murmurs of surprise). No, that is not all, I assure you. There has been in this matter some doubtful paternity. (Cries of oh, oh!) Let me explain to you. I am almost inclined to tell you that I find myself in a wrong position. I came hither in company with Lieutenant Stanley, and the beauteous lady whom my friend Colonel Bridport not inaptly names the "Star of the East;" as I came along, I need hardly tell you, being naturally of an inflamable and amorous temperament—(screams of laughter on all sides,)—I say, as my sensitive organisation makes me particularly sensibly of the soft influence of the charms of seductive woman I really began to ask myself one or two serious questions. (A perfect tumult ensued, as the speaker, with admirable mock gravity gave expression to the latter observation). You must perceive my friends that I am too old now to play the lover—(no, no; never too old). Well, I will do my best with any of the ladies present. (Laughter.) But, joking apart, I am too old, I say, to play the lover, and I therefore asked myself what part should I play in to-day's proceedings. Why the father, of course; and when I had made up my mind to this, you'd be astonished how parental I felt all at once towards the "Star of the East." Mind, I had not seen my other daughter at that time. Well, to show you how my feelings have been cruelly trifled with, it will be necessary to inform you that I acquainted Lieutenant Stanley with my parental feelings towards the "Star of the East," and that after serious consideration, I had felt myself justified in bestowing her upon him—(hear, hear,)—and how do you think my generosity was rewarded? You would never guess. Why, I was delicately informed that she had already a papa who had undertaken the onerous duty. I, of course, under these circumstances, considering that my feelings had been trifled with, retired and left her to more worthy hands. Still, you must admit that it was hard for a loving parent to bear. I was determined, however to be even with them, and have, therefore, had the supreme pleasure of presenting another of my daughters upon a worthy and gallant young officer, Captain Robinson, and I have now the pleasure of beholding Mrs. R. (Laughter). Gentlemen, I am not going to indulge in the ornate and seductive language of our chairman, when he uttered his eulogium upon the sex. We are none of us here insensible to their charms, I am sure—I'm not. Let me tell you, therefore, that I for one am happy to be present at the union of two young hearts. I am positive that Captain Robinson will find my daughter every way worthy of him. Cherish her, my young friend, she has been brought up in the school of

adversity and needs your tenderest care, the which, I do not doubt, you will cheerfully afford her. She has no longer an indulgent parent to look to. (Laughter.) She's as tame as a fawn, as graceful as a gazelle, and will, in future, own no thought but the wishes of her husband. You will forgive this feeling of a parent in parting with his only child, for in the language of the poet, I may with truth say—

'That to the fond parent who parts with his child
    A bridal is but a gilt and painted funeral.'

Gentlemen, I am sure you will respond to the toast I am about to propose, when I say it is to drink the health of one of the most graceful of Eve's daughters—the charming, modest, and beauteous Clara Robinson, the "Pearl beyond Price." To the bride! Clara!"

No. 104.

This was drank with customary honours, and more music followed, after which Captain Robinson rose to return thanks, which he did in a neat speech, brief but very much to the purpose.

The wine began to circulate freely, and the ladies made a movement to retire, but the chairman overruled it, as there were many more toasts to be given, and the gentlemen could not afford as yet to be deprived of their company.

Some glees and trios were performed by several of the company very credibly, and the utmost gaity reigned with all present.

The health of the unmarried ladies was proposed and drank, and our acquaintance, Doctor Hamilton was chosen to reply to this; which having done, he called the attention of the company to a graver theme, which, although perhaps ill chosen on the occasion of a marriage feast, sprang up impromptu, and the doctor was, perhaps, inadvertently led into it by the reflections evoked at the time; he concluded by saying—

"And now, gentlemen, having endeavoured to acquit myself of the charge of thanking you on behalf of the unmarried ladies, let me indulge in a few observations previous to my performing the next toast—observations which I hope may not be deemed inopportune. At the festive board, as well as on the battle-field, man is reminded of the mutability of human affairs. Lieutenant Stanley observed with much feeling that he had to thank fate for permitting so many of his early friends to be present in this happy hour of his existence. I share with him that feeling, and, like him, I too am thankful that I am able to meet so many old comrades, and as I gaze around upon the well remembered faces I cannot conceal from you that I am reminded, at the same time, of many who have passed from among us. You will, I am sure, pardon this melancholy reflection, but as it occurs to me, I think we will drink ' to the memory of the brave.'"

To the memory of the brave was drank in mournful silence, and some sober and grave reflections ensued after this toast, when to restore the equilibrium, Colonel Maitland rose, and said—

"I know, ladies, you are anxious to have leave of absence from our worthy chairman, but you really must listen to an old proser as he proposes one more toast. I promise then to grant you a furlough, and would do so now, but it is absolutely necessary that you should be present while I put in the pillory several individuals who richly deserve it. (Laughter.) When I look around me, and see the bright eyes, the dimpled cheeks, the alluring glances, of the galaxy of beauty before me, I sigh and wish I were a young man. When I see the choicest and rarest of my countrywomen, whose presence here fill the air with an indescribable and inexpressible delight, reminding us of the poet, ' that a thing of beauty is a joy for ever.' When I see all this my mind naturally recurs to several forlorn individuals—(laughter)—who are either insensible to the softer passion, or have not the courage to declare it. To such I say, 'Faint heart never won fair lady.' You see I am getting poetical. Young men, I have found out what you will do some day or other I have no doubt—that it is not for many years of our lives that youth is vouchsafed to us, therefore, I say, ' gather the rose-buds while you may.' Look at the boquet before you, —roses of every hue; pray do make haste and muster up courage. You do not want

it to storm a fortress, I'm sure, and how much more pleasant to carry one of those charming maidens by assault. The roses are before you, never let one of these say, in the words of the poet—I told you I was getting poetical; who would not become inspired by such a theme ?—

' She never told her love, but let concealment,
    Like a worm i' the bud, steal upon her damask
        cheek.'

There are damask cheeks enough for all of you. Come, take an old fool's advice and propose; and this last word reminds me of what I rose for, it was this, ladies, to propose the health of the unmarried gentlemen or bachelors, and may they soon propose to you in return. Ladies, the bachelors, and reformation to them !"

Amongst much tittering this toast was drunk by the ladies.

As it was one that most present were quite unprepared for, some confusion ensued about the proper party to answer it.

None of the bachelors seemed very willing to undertake the task, when eventually Morley, who was the eldest of the unmarried gentlemen, was pitched upon as the most fitting person, and shortly rose for that purpose.

"I am deputed, ladies," commenced Morley, amidst much merriment, " to return you, on behalf of myself and fellow sufferers, our thanks for your good wishes and consideration for such forlorn individuals as ourselves. I, for one, feel most acutely my isolated position in existence—never more strongly impressed upon me than on the present occasion. It has been my fate through life to see flowers springing up in my path—to watch the opening beauties of the rose—to see its damask petals expand, to breathe forth their grateful fragrance, and disclose their choicest beauties, and, when in the full pride of its youth and loveliness, it has been gathered by other hands, to bloom for other eyes, to glad the home of other hearts. Alas, no rose, as yet, has bloomed for me alone. A waif and stray upon the surface of society I have not been able to meet a kind, sympathising angel who would take compassion on me. It is hard, and perhaps humiliating to confess thus much, but I am not made in nature's mould sufficiently captivating. Others are formed, it seems, to ' please all hearts and charm all eyes,' but the very reverse appears to have been my case. Many of my companions in affliction tell me that they have found themselves in a similar position, and I sympathise with them most cordially; to use a sporting phrase, ' we find ourselves out of the betting,' nay more, we are almost returned as dead horses. This is not our fault, I assure you, but rather our misfortune. I've struggled hard against this state of things, and could, if it were deemed interesting, give you a long detail of my reverses in the pursuit of Venus. (Name, name, resounded on all sides.) I—a—hardly think it advisable to indulge in a recital of my own private woes; a man don't look in a very enviable position when he details to a committee of lovely females how he has been snubbed and jilted by their cruel sisters. No, I feel I must be silent upon this head. I was about to observe that I envied our friends Lieutenant Stanley and Captain Robinson, but as envy, I hope, does not form part of my constitual elements, it would be wrong to make use of such an expression. I may say, however, that I wish some gentle lady had taken compassion on me, and then how proud I should have been to be here a bridegroom to-day. Have you another daughter to bestow, Colonel Maitland?"

"If you are willing, I will see."

"Good; then I live in hopes. Ladies, I address myself more particularly to you, I am not so *very* ugly—(roars of laughter)—take compassion on me; and, if you discard me yourself, form yourselves into a committee, and hear my case at your earliest convenience; and then, perhaps, you may find me and my fellow sufferers some compassionate sisters who will look upon us with more favourable eyes. 'It is not wealth I covet.' No; love and a cottage is all I desire. I think I can find the cottage, but where the lady-love? Ah, ladies, a forlorn swain addresses you, or rather a flock of forlorn swains. I once thought of dressing myself up in shepherd's attire, with unexceptionable tights, a flap hat, a crook, and a mellow reed; that is the way I have seen captivating lovers depicted in pictures, and I thought perhaps it was the right thing. I can't write love verses, or I would try that. Now, I will tell you a secret—don't mention it again, as it would make me look ridiculous but I *once did* dress myself up as a trubador, and serenaded my enamorata; and what do you think was the result?—she called me a conceited fool for my pains; and so, without casting a sweeping censure upon your sex, I may venture to say that ladies are capricious. (No, no, and cries of shame.) I am afraid it is so. Why, I have a comrade here who is gifted with the rarest poetical talents and most insinuating manners, and he too has been snubbed in a most shameful manner. (Cries of order and name.) I will name, for I am not bound to secrecy—I will declare our woes to the world—it is Ensign Anslie, of whom I speak. (Cries of oh, oh; and every eye was directed to where that officer sat). Why will it be believed that the ensign actually wrote the words of a song to his lady-love, and having set them

to a touching melody, he sung them to her in a most ravishing style, and what was the consequence, think you? why, she anwered in a mocking buffo song, which sneered at his passion and turned his sentiment into ridicule."

"Impossible!" exclaimed the ladies.

"Ask him if it is not true," said Morley.

"It is quite correct," replied Anslie.

"The ballad—let's have the ballad," exclaimed several voices; and as there was no help for it, down sat Anslie at the piano, and sung the following, with much pathos—

Eh, dearest Jessie! listen now to me,
　This world would own no treasure—
　In life there'd be no pleasure,
Unless 'twere cheered by thee.
Through rugged tangled paths my footsteps then
　would fall,
And dark and gloomy thoughts my sinking heart
　appal;
No loving voice to cheer me along my lonesome
　way,
No tender bosom near me, with love's bewitching
　ray;
The earth would be a desert, for ever wrapt in
　night,
Till thy bright spirit turn'd the darkness into
　light,
　Eh, dearest Jessie! listen now to me,
　This voice, which spake in sadness,
　Now rings with jubelant gladness
As thy lovely form I see.
　My heart it leaps ecstatic—
　No longer am I erratic—
When again I'm cheered by thee.

"Touching in the extreme," said Colonel Maitland. "Oh, she never could resist that; she struck her colours at once, I suppose?"

"You shall hear," said the ensign; "this is the answer she sung in reply—

Fond youth, said the maiden, to her lover's deep
　sigh,
Give vent to your passion; you'll be better by-
　and-bye.
If your way is so dark, I'm thinking, my dear,
That a light I would buy, the darkness to clear;
And to all your fond strains, this is my only
　reply—
Look love! do you see anything green in my eye."

"Oh, cruel, cruel damsel!" exclaimed several voices, which were, however, nearly smothered in the burst of laughter which ensued.

After much more amusing conversation, in which good nature was blended with repartee, the company, who were to be admitted by tickets, arrived, and the sports of the evening commenced; a numerous party of dancers assembled on the platform, who, as the newspapers would say, " were determined votaries of terpsichore," and continued to foot it with light fantastic toe till nature was exhausted.

So merry a time was not remembered, as the newspapers would again say, " by the oldest inhabitant of the town."

Stanley had taken for a time, a magnificently furnished house in the vicinity of Calcutta, and proceeded thither, after the entertainment, with his bride.

They were saluted, upon their departure, with vociferous cheering, and the demonstrations of their friends were of the most flattering description ; but amidst all this hilarity there was one heart which beat heavily—one spirit which fretted and chafed —one eye which looked despondingly as though its owner had lost or missed something which would never again be restored to him.

Goolooh, although he was happy to think that Omelia had been treated as an eastern queen, could not see her snatched away by the hand of another without a pang. " Some natural tears he shed, the world was all before him where to choose," but she who was all the world to him had for ever disappeared from his sight.

He had followed the procession in the crowd, had seen her who was his heart's idolatry enter the church porch, and had returned to the gardens of Colonel Bridport's mansion ; but it was with a sorrowful mood that he paced these about, more like one who was attending a funeral than a marriage feast ; and so indeed it was to him, for he felt all his fondest affections were buried with the loss of her upon whom they had been placed.

Omelia observed him in the garden, and instantly sought an interview. She spoke words of comfort to him, cheered him as best she could under the circumstances, and introduced him to many of her friends.

He expressed his delight at her happiness —but she saw by his looks how ill they accorded with the words he was uttering.

Poor Goolooh, his was not a selfish spirit, nevertheless, it is hard to see a being upon whom the fond heart doats wedded to another.

There was a gentleness in the manner and language of Omelia towards him that perhaps softened the affliction, and in his quiet, unobtrusive way, he expressed himself again and again happy to be a witness of the day's proceedings ; but an inward monster whispered to him that he was compromising the truth in saying so.

Goolooh's was a nature which could not easily throw off an attachment when once formed.

———

CHAPTER CCXXXVIII.

THE HONEYMOON.—REUNION OF OLD FRIENDS. A FAMILY PARTY.

Omelia and Stanley travelled, immediately after their marriage, for some short time, revisiting many parts of India in which their associations were immediately connected.

The scenes in which they had endured many anxious hours were now dear to them from old recollections and associations, now viewed complacently enough in the more prosperous moments of their existence.

All our heroine's early friends were munificently rewarded, and there was not one who did not share her bounty. As a rich heiress now she distributed a portion of her wealth to all she thought deserving with no niggard hand.

Amongst others whom she visited was old Jahnsah ; she found him in his former habitation, removed from the world's strife, and meditating upon mundane affairs, and lifting up his thoughts to a higher being.

The old priest was delighted to see his former friends, and in spite of his usually passive bearing evinced strong demonstrations of joy at beholding them again.

A long history had to be detailed to him of all those startling incidents which occurred since Omelia had last visited him.

Omelia informed him with considerable delicacy that the lawyers, Messrs. Cottle, Leaf and Cottle, had instructions to pay him a yearly dividend for the remainder of his life.

This the old man was strongly against, but our heroine was inexorable, and would take no denial, saying that he might make use of it for her sake in doing good acts and assisting the unfortunate and deserving, upon which the old man agreed to become a recipient of the sum she had put apart for him.

In her suberb costume and other evidences of material wealth, the good Jahnsah could hardly recognise his quondam guest, but her language and manner soon made him at home with her as of yore.

" To your good and kind tutorage I owe more father than any other. I shall always consider it the turning point in my character, and had it not been for you I should not, in all probability have been in existence at all, to possess now so much happiness, and to have become the heiress to that wealth which it will be my duty to do as much good with as possible."

" Excellent principle, my daughter. We hold in this world wealth and power only in trust—only as stewards of the Lord, and I doubt not but you will be a trustworthy one."

"I hope so, father."

"It is to Him you have to offer up your thanks for a safe preservation from all perils which you have passed through, and they have been of no ordinary nature. To Him —not to me, who is at best but an humble and imperfect agent. Peace is now comparatively restored to our country, and let us hope a recurrence of such scenes as have been witnessed may never be again beheld. The few remaining sands of my life will run I hope in peace. Heaven bless you, my daughter, and you also my son, happiness attend your path; and I need not ask you to sometimes bestow a thought upon the 'Old Man of the Mountain.'"

With the blessing of old Jahnsah, the bride and bridegroom took their departure, and, after visiting many other places, they again returned to their mansion at Calcutta.

Upon their arrival Omelia made arrangements to have a family party of all those particular friends associated with herself; not fashionable acquaintances, but she wanted a reunion of those faithful hearts who had been true to her in the hour of adversity.

She had had a goodly gathering enough at her wedding feast—an heterogenous company—and she was almost pestered to death with the number of visitors who sought her acquaintance, and left their pasteboard in profusion, for Omelia and Stanley were now the lions of the day.

Wealth, rank, and power have always their parasites, who are ever ready to pay adulatory honour to those who have by their position become the "observed of all observers."

"It's a strange world, my masters," once obtain notoriety in the fashionable section of it, and you have abundance of blind devotees to the wonders of your genius.

The idol of one day is, perhaps the victim of the next. Omelia received such fashionables who sought her acquaintance with becoming courtesy, but her spirit yearned to those who were nearer her heart, and she had determined, therefore, to give an entertainment to those only, that she might enjoy their society uninterrupted by the superficial formalities of fashion.

She was the more anxious for this as it had been definitely settled between herself and husband that they were shortly to journey to England, there, for the future to take up their residence.

Family matters had rendered Stanley's return to his native land absolutely imperative; and Omelia had no other wish than that of her husband.

Consequently, very soon after her arrival at Calcutta, her favoured few were gathered around the hospitable board; these were not perhaps particularly fashionable, it is true, but some of them the reader will perhaps be interested in amongst her guests were Goolooh, Moorsha, Abdal, Tallee Sheboo, Lyrea (the boy who had endeavoured to save her from the Thug), Colonel Bridport and his daughters, Morley and several other officers under the colonel.

She would have invited Clara and Robinson, but they were travelling, and consequently too far removed.

As each of the guests arrived, Omelia received them with a sisterly kindness; there was no artificial semblance of a feeling which she did not possess in her demeanour towards them—no set phrases rolling off smoothly from the tongue—no meretricious affectation of sentiment.

Goolooh, whose unobtrusive nature caused him to shrink from becoming a guest at the entertainment, had at first refused the invitation, but his hostess would take no denial. Upon his arrival, Omelia ushered him into an apartment where she had an opportunity of conversing with him uninterrupted by intruders.

She had observed his desponding demeanour on the day of her wedding, and was anxious to conciliate him by demonstrating a marked preference in his favour.

He was dejected enough when he was introduced to her in her new abode. Motioning him to a seat, Omelia placed herself by his side.

"Goolooh," she said, in tender accents, "my good and worthy friend, you now behold me free from care; all our past troubles can be forgotten, or only remembered as a beacon and warning in times to come. Tell me, although I need not ask, you are happy in beholding me thus blessed?"

"Your happiness is also mine," answered the young Hindoo, mournfully.

"I feel assured of that."

There was a pause which Omelia hardly knew how to fill up; the appearance of the speaker ill accorded with the words he had been uttering.

"My happiness is also yours," continued Omelia, ruminating. "I know your self-sacrificing nature—have had sufficient proof of it—but, Goolooh, tell me, I think—at least you appear to have something which weighs down your spirits. If there is anything in the world that it is possible for me to do to serve you—anything that you may have on your mind in which perhaps I might be useful—I will never, no, never forgive you if you do not now make me your confident."

"I have nothing that troubles me," answered her companion.

"Then why this depression? unless—ah," a deep flush suffused the features of the speaker as she hesitated, "unless you are envious of my good fortune."

"Envious," exclaimed the other, reproachfully.

"No, no—I do not mean that—you cannot suppose I mean that?"—another pause—but, Goolooh, you mourn me as lost to you, perhaps, for ever. I am not lost to you, my ever valued and attached friend—I am not removed from you—but at the mention of your name my most tender thoughts will be evoked, and my finest sympathies aroused. Don't think that because I have an accession of wealth and am—am a wedded wife, that I shall forget those on whom memory will love to linger—from the very many proofs of their friendship it will brighten up. No, I am the same Omelia to you and all those who knew me in the more sorrowful part of my destiny. Kind, noble, generous-hearted Goolooh, cheer up, and think of her who now addresses you as your sister. Be frank with me—why this mournful silence?"

"We will speak no further upon this subject," said Goolooh. "A fond dream is over, and it would be out of place to discourse upon past events. You are happy, that is enough for me. If cruel and capricious fate had willed that I might have been your companion and sharer in all your joys, I should have been blest beyond all other mortals; but this was not to be. You ask me why I am moody and depressed. Alas, have I not beheld all those upon whom I fixed my affection taken from me — yes, taken from me, one by one, till I am left now with none to care for? This is sad you must admit—very sad."

"Do not say none to care for you. Have you not me?"

"Yes; but you are removed now beyond my sphere. I know your kind heart and generous nature, but you are far beyond me."

"In the world's wealth, perhaps, but in all else I am the same Omelia as of yore."

"I know it—I know it; ever kind," exclaimed Goolooh, as an expression of deep gratitude passed over his features.

"Well, then, let that suffice. Come—there, now you look more like yourself. Now we will proceed to the reception room—your arm—there, I am going to be escorted into the party by one of my most esteemed friends."

And so taking the arm of her cavalier, Omelia walked gracefully into the apartment set apart for her guests.

Stanley was doing the honours to a numerous assembly, to whom our heroine introduced Goolooh.

The whole formed an agreeable party, in which there was no restraint, and the stiff conventualities of society were ignored; indeed, Stanley and Omelia endeavoured to make every one at home, and they succeeded admirably.

Colonel Bridport, with his two charming daughters, and the officers who accompanied him, left early, to give Omelia an opportunity of having her own particular friends and countrymen to herself.

The colonel judged rightly when he conceived that she desired a *tete-a-tete* with them before her departure for England; and soon after his absence Omelia addressed those of her countrymen left behind.

"My most worthy and esteemed friends," she said, "I feel so much pleasure in having you around me, that my happiness is complete to-day. I have longed for an opportunity to have you here, as I am about to leave this country for England in a few weeks' time. Yes, I leave my native land to seek other climes; but those I leave behind will be never effaced from my memory. But this brings me to that which more particularly has induced me to mention the subject. I have no wish to leave any of you behind, consequently, those who will follow me have only to say so, and the matter shall be soon arranged. What say you, Goolooh? I have plenty of appointments to fill up—will you accept of one?"

"I'm going," said Mrs. Shaw, who formed one of the party; we must really beg her pardon for not mentioning her in due form.

"I thank you," said Goolooh; "from my heart I thank you, but I dare not leave my native country. I have been born and bred here, and although I should feel proud to follow so esteemed a friend as yourself, I fear I must decline your offer."

"Well, think it over," said Stanley, "there is no particular hurry. All I can say is that, if you like to accompany us, you shall be made as comfortable and happy as circumstances will admit."

"I do not doubt it, sir; I thank you for your kindness."

"Well, think it over, and let me know," repeated the Lieutenant.

But with all the thinking in the world Goolooh could not make up his mind to leave his native land. No—he was unselfish it is true, but he could not consume alone the daily grief of beholding Omelia possessed by another; besides this his native prejudices, although they had been very much softened, were still against the English, and his soul shrunk from going amongst them. No—to suffer in silence was his motto.

Omelia now turned to Moorsha, saying—

"Are you, too, so fond of your native country that you will not leave it?"

"Not if fate decrees it," said Moorsha.

"Ah," exclaimed Stanley, "then fate does decree it, or I do, which is the same thing. You will not have any tigers to entrap, or people to pick up who fall from rocks, or elephants to drive, unless it is the one in the Zoological Gardens or Astley's Theatre; but you will be made pretty comfortable, I have no doubt, at least it shall not be our fault if you are not. So I think you had better say no more upon the subject, and consider the matter settled.

"But Colonel Maitland wishes me to leave with him when he goes," said Moorsha.

"Oh, indeed—does he? Ah, I forgot his new found son was an old companion of yours."

"Yes."

"Ah, and perhaps you would prefer staying till he goes? As you please, only we should wish you to be with us. Have you promised the colonel?"

"No, sir—not at present."

"Oh, then you can promise me. You've known me the longest, and if we should be attacked by a tiger why we should feel more secure."

"Good," said Moorsha. "If you please, I go with you."

"Abdal," said Omelia, "you will of course follow us."

"I never intend to part from you of my own free will," replied her faithful kinsman.

After this arrangements were made to attach the boy Lyrea to their suite, and he cheerfully acquiesed to so pleasing a proposition.

Tallee Sheboo could not, of course, leave her family, so Omelia settled upon her a considerable sum of money before leaving.

As to Mrs. Shaw she did not require any solicitation, having made up her mind to become attached to our heroine's household, saying, in her own peculiar naive manner, that "if her mistress did not know when she had a good servant, she knew when she had a good mistress."

Matters having been thus satisfactorily arranged, Omelia and Stanley felt highly satisfied in retaining in their suite some few *souveniers* of the old country, which would serve to remind them of those scenes which they had passed through.

It is true our heroine viewed the evident despondency of Goolooh with some misgivings, but after all, she reflected, that perhaps it was but natural that he should evince a repugnance to accompany them, as the fact of his presence would only daily remind him of his hopeless passion.

Poor Goolooh—she pitied him, and, without his knowledge, she gave instructions to Messrs. Leaf and Cottle to give him a handsome allowance, at the same time, she directed these lawyers not to let him know from whom it proceeded, as it was more than probable, she thought, that he might not feel disposed to accept it; and so, these and all other friends cared for, the newly married couple prepared to start for England.

CHAPTER CCXXXIX.

THE SCENE SHIFTS TO ENGLAND. — PRESENTATION AT COURT OF SIR EDWARD AND LADY STANLEY.

The Indian rebellion is over—the last smouldering remains of the late terrible struggle are stamped out under the heels of Lord Clyde's victorious columns. The arms of the British are again invincible, and their Queen is declared ruler of India.

The few characters who have played so conspicuous a part in this prolix tale are soon to retire from the stage on which they have appeared in so many diversified scenes and make their final bow to the audience.

It is our duty now to follow across the ocean the noble vessel which conveyed our heroine, husband and suite across the surging waters.

It is not our purpose to describe a sea voyage. It is, to those who have experienced it, monotonous enough, and to those who have not description would be useless.

No—the pen of the novelist flys faster than steam or sail, and we are therefore enabled to take a glance at Omelia and Stanley without undergoing the annoyances attendant upon a sea voyage for some thousands of miles.

Our heroine and her husband accompanied by Moorsha, Abdal, and Lyrea—and not forgetting Mrs. Shaw, we beg her pardon for neglecting to name her first—arrived safely in England.

Stanley succeeded to a baronetcy soon after his return, and was promoted to a colonelcy for his services in the late Indian war.

In a palatial mansion contiguous to Belgrave Square the young couple took up their abode. The house itself was furnished with sumptuous magnificence. Let us take a glance at them.

Omelia—now Lady Stanley—and her husband, Sir Edward Stanley, Bart., are arrayed in full court costume; there is a drawing-room to day, and Sir Edward and his lady are about to be presented at court—yes, our Indian beauty is to have the honour of an introduction to the Queen of these proud realms. No less a personage than the Duke of Cambridge is to present them in due form.

If you doubt it look to the papers of—we

forget the date, but turn over the journals for the last few months and you will find their names carefully recorded.

And now hundreds of carriages of stately proportion and decoration, emblazoned with the crests of their owners, are to be seen wending their way down Piccadilly and St. James's Street, and all the chief west-end thoroughfares. Shoulder-knotted puppies with unexceptionable calves are swinging behind, two and three abreast: fierce-looking officers, bearded like pards, are observed nursing their swords in the interior of their carriages, with a self-satisfied complacency —old men with tottering steps, with silver air rugose visages are tricked out in gold and scarlet to kneel at the feet of their sovereign. Fat dowagers are chaperoneing a bevy of youth and beauty who are "coming out," as the phrase goes, and are therefore, as a patent of gentility about to salute the hand of a good little woman whom we suspect is heartily weary of the ceremony: but the patrician and parvenue are both there, for, somehow or other the latter do manage to creep in the select circle

It is a brilliant and gay scene. If there were nothing else to admire in it, it is worth seeing to note the beautiful horses and an occasional glance at some fair daughter of the aristocracy would repay the spectator for the trouble and fatigue attendant upon such scenes as these.

In the midst of all this galaxy of wealth, beauty, and aristocracy, the carriage of Sir Edward and Lady Stanley takes a prominent position. The rich heiress, with all her attendant antecedents has become a person of mark, and the romantic incidents of her chequered life have been "noised abroad," losing nothing in their narration from the many lips which have conveyed the whole particulars amongst the fashionable world.

Omelia has cast aside her oriental attire, and is apparelled as becomes an English lady of rank in full court costume; her hair was worn plain, as on the day of her marriage, being looped up with pearls and various other precious stones, and various other costly jewels adorned her arms and bust, and altogether she looked surpassingly lovely.

Her clear soft skin assumes a fairer hue since her sojourn in England, and a heightened colour from excitement gives a yet brighter hue to her lustrous eye.

We are most of us familiar with the vestibule and state apartments of St. James's Palace, and enough has been said in our public journals of the crush of visitors on the days appointed for drawing-rooms. It is on these occasions that our patrician dames and damoiselles elbow and jostle one another much after the fashion of the plebeian crowd entering the pit of an overcrowded theatre.

Wonderful is the attraction of royalty—to salute the digets of one who wears a crown is a patent card, gentility and exclusiveness, and every class, from the locktaw Indian to our English peeress, have their own conventional rules to guide them.

When Sir Edward Stanley's carriage set down its occupants at the entrance to St. James's Palace, our heroine was not much struck with the palatial grandeur of the building compared to those occupied by the rajahs of her own country; neither did the crowding and crushing she experienced on her passage up the staircase give her very elaborate notions of comfort.

Our old acquaintance Moorsha followed in her suite, and heard the remarks made upon her by many of the company present.

"Awh, who is that party?" drawled out a young gentleman, in full uniform, with moustachois about as big as a small sized skipping-rope. The dark lady in the white tulle dress. Egad, a fine woman, by Jove."

"Oh, that is Lady Stanley," answered a fat dowager; a rich Indian heiress. She is wife of Sir Edward Stanley, Baronet, and has played a very conspicuous part in many scenes of the late Indian revolt, and being highly recommended by Lord Clyde to the notice of her majesty, his Royal Highness the Duke of Cambridge is about to present her and her gallant husband."

"Awh—indeed! Is she of noble blood?"

There was a graceful shrug of the shoulders at this question.

"Noble blood! I can hardly tell you— but I should say not. She may be esteemed so in her own country, but with us you know—"

"Awh—ye-es—the case is very different."

"Sir Edward Stanley, her husband, comes from a respectable family enough."

"Awh! and he has married her for money, I suppose?"

Another shrug.

"Love, they say."

"Love!—bah!"

"So I am told. He was madly and desperately fond of her.

A look of incredulity was observed on the features of the officer with the skipping-rope moustachois as the lady made the last remark

"You never believe. Earnest," said a young and beauteous belle by the side of the last speaker; "no, never believe in man's sincere attachment to the opposite sex."

"Who—I?—awh, oh, yes—I'm told there are such things as love matches. There must be, I suppose, but—awh—I—awh— have not—at least it has not been my lot to

witness them," drawled the young man, with an affected lisp.

"Ah, Earnest, you are a cold creature," and here the speaker's eyes flashed brighter rays than the jewels she wore.

"Well, I suppose I am; "we are not all born with the same warm temperaments. Lady Stanley has some eastern blood in her veins?"

"Yes; and has been devoted to her lover and saved his life on more than one occasion. Pray tell me Earnest, if any one had been so truthful to you, as they say Lady Stanley has been, would not your own sense of gratitude beget a fondness for her?"

"Gratitude! Oh—awh—possibly."

"Possibly!—Certainly, I should have said."

"You forget, my dear, that I have never

experienced such devotion evinced towards me, and, therefore, am unable to speak of the sensations it might occasion. We none of know the effects of these things till they are tried upon us. Who can tell how he will be effected by galvanism, mesmerism, a cold shower-bath, or by—by inhaling ether or chloriform, until he has tried and tested their effect upon his constitution by an application."

"Oh, Earnest, you are really incorigible to compare the divine passion to ether or a shower-bath. It's shameful."

"My dear, it's only as a comparison."

"Well, choose some better simile—it has no analogy to the subject in question."

"Oh—awh—hasn't it? I thought it very appropriate, but I suppose I am mistaken."

"What is my charming Lady Arabella

Clementina Beechcroft pouting at?" said a portly nobleman, as he sidled up to the party addressed, and playfully touched her fair cheek with his hand.

"Ah, Lord Fogle," she exclaimed, with evident pleasure.

The nobleman's spring time of youth had passed away, nevertheless he was a gallant old boy, and whispered soft nothings in the ear of beauty occasionally.

"Oh, I am glad you have come," continued the fair belle addressed. "What a crowd, I feel positively oppressed with the heat."

"Can I be of any service to conduct you hence!" said Lord Fogle. "I should be proud to assist you. Need I say, my dear Lady Arabella, that in me you behold a most devoted slave."

"Ah, ah,—thank you, I know that. Your lordship is ever ready to rescue—"

"Beauty," said Lord Fogle, bowing low, and finishing her sentence at the same time with a flourish.

She smiled at the compliment.

"Thank you—no," she observed, "I am waiting with my friend here to effect an entrance into the throne-room, that is, if the crowd ever intends to clear away."

"Ah, I have just come from there," said Lord Fogle.

"Gallant man, to effect so dangerous a passage. It is quite full, I suppose? Tell me, my lord, who is there now?"

"Oh, too many notabilities to notice within the limits of this bill, as we say in common parlance. When I effected a safe retreat, Sir Edward Stanley, and his beauteous eastern wife were being presented to her majesty."

"Ah, the very parties we were talking about when you came up. She is a beautiful woman. Do you not think so? We females are not allowed to be a judge of each other's personal attractions, but she is, to my thinking a perfect beauty. What says your lordship—you were always a judge in these matters?"

"Oh, certainly—certainly. For the matter of that she is a fine woman enough, and would doubtless draw murmurs of admiration from all around were there not a star of still brighter magnitude here to-day."

And the old nobleman, as he uttered these words, pressed his embroidered hat against his chest to still the beatings of his too sensitive heart, and bowing low at the same time focussed his eyes upon the lady in a manner which might lead her to infer that he was still writhing in torture and agony, completely transfixed by love's dart.

To an indifferent spectator his manner would no doubt have appeared irresistibly comic, as indeed it unquestionably was.

"Psha! My lord, you were always a flatterer," said the lady, as she playfully tapped him with her fan.

"Is speaking the truth to be considered flattery? unjust Lady Arabella. But what was your ladyship pouting at when I first caught sight of you? Is our friend here as incorrigible as ever?"

This was said in allusion to him of the skipping rope moustachois.

"Oh, positively and most completely incorrigible. I ventured to assert that Sir Edward Stanley married for love, and he laughs at the idea of any man being so foolish."

"Oh, monstrous! Love is the very soul of our existence—a beacon in the hour of distress—a music to the soldier's march—a staff in the traveller's hand; 'love rules the court, the camp, the grove,' as the poet says."

"Awh, I'm not a poet," drawled out the young officer.

"No; but you are a man and a warrior, and Venus and Mars, you know, have ever been coupled together. I can see, Captain Squasher, how it is you are sneering at the master passion—merely to tease your fair cousin."

"Who is that party with a clerical appearance, having on his arm a lady with a bird of paradise in her head?" inquired a voice immediately behind Lord Fogle.

His lordship turned round, and recognised a friend.

"Ah!—what, Sir Cuthbert, there you are," and he shook hands with the last speaker. "Who do you mean? the short gentleman in black, with black silk stockings and buckles in his shoes?"

"Yes—the very same."

"Oh, he's a nobody, I believe. He comes from some remote northern district in England, and rejoices in the euphoneous patronymic Sproggles.

"What on earth brought him here, then? Why did he not keep to his own native wilds?"

"He desires an introduction to her majesty. The fellow has been the founder of some new system of education to elevate the minds of the masses."

"Bah—rubbish!"

"Well, sir, it forms part of the cant of the present day, and an eminent political economist has undertaken the office of presenting him. We live in an age of progress, Sir Cuthbert."

"We shall soon live in a country governed by democracy if we go on in this way. Progress, indeed—humbug, sir—all humbug. We don't want to elevate the masses. Keep them down, sir—keep them down in their proper sphere."

"Well, Sir Cuthbert, I have not introduced our friend Sproggles. Don't look so hard at me, pray."

"I didn't say you have; but is it not monstrous so many of our fair country-women should be kept waiting to their great inconvenience while that square-toed plebeian takes precedence of them?"

"Talent must be encouraged, you know," said Lord Fogle, with a lurking sneer upon his features.

"Talent!'

"Yes, he is the inventor of the Sprogglo-tonian system of national class education; by the aid of his invaluable plan he undertakes to convey knowledge into the juvenile mind with a rapidity hitherto unattainable. The teacher is in a sort of rostrum, with a long wand in his hand, and with this he directs the attention of his pupils to the lessons on the wall. He undertakes to teach as many as a hundred, or even a hundred and fifty at the same time. I do not know the whole particulars, but they say it has proved eminently successful in its operation."

"And who is this coming down the grand staircase now?"

"Oh, don't you know him? That's the Marquis of Galloghen. Got one of the finest studs of horses in the kingdom. He owns the favourite for the Derby this year."

"Does he though?—he's worth knowing. I should like amazingly to be introduced to him. Oh, that is Galloghen, is it? Egad! a knowing card I'm told. Strange I have never tumbled over him on the course. Umph!—yes, he owns 'Dragon Fly,' the first in the betting: a rare horse, sir—all bone and muscle."

"Ah, Lord Fogle, better luck to you this year," said the Marquis of Galloghen, as he shook the proffered hand of the party addressed.

"Thanks for your good wishes," returned the other. "I shall lay heavy on 'Dragon Fly.' What is he going to do?"

"Going in to win."

"Good! then I'm on, and if I lose, shall know whom to blame."

"Oh, don't take my word—judge for yourself. In sporting matters, every man for himself, and no favours."

"Allow me to introduce your lordship to Sir Cuthbert Stockstill, well known on the turf."

"Happy to have the opportunity of making Sir Cuthbert's acquaintance, I am sure, and shall be more particularly so when I have an opportunity afforded me of showing him my stud of horses. I think they are worth looking at."

"I am delighted to meet your lordship," said Sir Cuthbert, highly elated.

"Lady Arabella Clementina Beechcroft," said Lord Fogle, "and her amiable mamma, the Viscountess Beechcroft, of Sloshington Hall, Shropshire."

The ladies curtsied, and the gentleman bowed.

The throne-room of St. James's palace was crowded to excess upon Sir Edward and Lady Stanley entering its sacred precincts.

Omelia's heart beat high as she found herself surrounded by the nobility of England. The situation in which she found herself placed was one so entirely new to her that it seemed hardly to be real, and the figures floated by like a beautiful vision.

She observed her majesty at the further end of the room, seated beneath the canopy in her chair of state; she could, however, but catch, every now and then, as the crowd moved, but an imperfect view of the Queen of England, but even in these fitful glances she was impressed at once with the amiability of her countenance, and the affability of her demeanour.

Omelia's situation was the more trying from the fact of her attracting the notice of nearly all the company present. She was painfully conscious that she was the most observed person in the room, at least, such was her impression.

Many noble personages were introduced to her by Sir Edward who received her with much courtesy.

In the due course of time it became her turn for presentation, she became aware of this as she gradually neared the throne. His Royal Highness, the Duke of Cambridge escorted her to the throne, followed by Stanley, and Omelia was introduced in due form. Falling on one knee, she kissed the hand of her majesty, who said a few kind words to her, the precise nature of which Omelia was too excited to accurately remember; then some few further observations to Stanley and the ceremony was over.

The Duke again escorted her to the head of the staircase, when, bowing gracefully, he left her to the care of her husband, and, fluttering with excitement, our heroine found herself in the ante-room close to the party who had been conversing about her, and behind whom was Moorsha and many other of her attendants.

She heard the buz of admiration and the suppressed whispers of the company as she proceeded down the staircase, and was glad to escape from the gaze of so many eyes.

"Ah, Sir Edward Stanley," said Lord Fogle, "allow me to congratulate you," and he gave a meaning glance towards Omelia.

Stanley looked at the speaker, bowed, but could not call to his recollection any previous knowledge of him.

"You do not recollect me, I dare say,"

said Lord Fogle; "but I dare say you remember my nephew, the Hon. Vincent Soft-
ansour. He was in your regiment, the 14th,
some years ago. I dined several times at
your mess, if you remember."

"Oh, ah—I remember," said Stanley; "it
is Lord Fogle, I have the honour of addressing. Allow me to introduce to your lordship
Lady Stanley."

"I am enchanted to make your ladyship's
acquaintance," said his lordship. "I have
several relatives in your country, and my
nephew found his last home there, poor fellow, as Sir Edward well knows."

And the speaker endeavoured to look pathetic, but we are afraid it was a failure.

He was a harum-scarum young scion of
the nobility, who was about as much fit to
command a regiment as General Tom
Thumb. He was a nuisance to his fellow
officers, and did certainly fall in India—not,
it is true, leading on his gallant troops to
victory, covered with wounds and glory, but
he fell a victim to his bacchanalian propensities.

"I am sure, if all the daughters of the
east are as fair as yourself," said Lord Fogle,
addressing Omelia, "our ladies must enrol
themselves into a society to obtain some re-
strictive measure from parliament to prevent
their importation into our country."

Omelia smiled.

"Your lordship is complimentary," she
observed, "but unjust to your own countrywomen, than whom there is not a more
beautiful race in the world."

"Lady Stanley is as generous as beautiful," said his lordship, turning triumphantly
to those immediately around.

"She is just," said the Marquis of Galloghen. "I am afraid Lord Fogle scatters
compliments indiscriminately around."

"Not at all."

"He was but just now," said the officer,
with the skipping-rope moustachois, "saying
that my cousin here was the most beautiful
lady present."

"Oh, Earnest, how can you say so?" said
the Lady Arabella, as all eyes were directed
towards her.

"It's a fact, 'pon honour."

"Ah," said Lord Fogle, "I am really very
remiss. Allow me to introduce you to the
Lady Arabella Clementina Beechcroft, and
the Vicountess Beechcroft, of Sloshington
Hall. There now we have two perfect beauties, one a blonde and the other a brunette,
both perfect in their style of beauty. I propose we call them night and morning. Ha,
ha! quite a poetical simile."

The Lady Arabella, who was really an
amiable and charming person, at once entered into conversation with Omelia, in a
frank and natural manner that at once won
the respect and the good opinion of our heroine.

"Sir Edward Stanley," said Lord Fogle,
"allow me to express a hope that this accidental meeting may be a precursor of a more
intimate acquaintance. I need not tell you
how delighted I shall be to enjoy the society
of a comrade and fellow officer of my late
lamented nephew,"—he was trying to look
sentimental again with the same amount of
success as heretofore. "These wars, my
friend, rob us of our nearest and dearest
relatives."

It was not the war, thought Stanley, but
Bacchus; nevertheless, he told his lordship
he should be much pleased to meet him at
all times; he could not forget, however, that
some years previously the same nobleman,
who appeared so solicitous of his acquaintance was wont to pass him without any recognition.

"I admire your taste," said Lord Fogle.
"You have imported a perfect eastern
beauty."

"She is like myself, my lord," said Stanley, "not used to compliments and honied
words, being indeed herself quite unsophis-
ticated."

'Ah, the more charming."

"Sir Edward Stanley used to be a judge
of horses,' said the Marquis of Galloghan.
"I should be pleased if he would do me the
honour of paying me a visit when his other
engagements will permit," and at the same
time he handed his card to Stanley.

"Thank you, my lord," said Stanley.

"You must pardon me for not at first recognising you. The Marquis of Galloghen
I believe."

The nobleman bowed.

"I remember—a friend of my fathers," he
said, as he turned to Lord Fogle.

"Yes, your father and myself used to do
a little together in the betting line, and if I
can be of any service to you in putting you
on the right thing you may command me,
Sir Edward—command me."

"I thank your lordship," said Stanley.

"You must excuse me now," said the
Marquis of Galloghen, or I shall be too late
for Tattersall's. Adieu, gentlemen! Sir
Edward, I shall have the pleasure of seeing
you shortly let me hope, when we shall be
both more at leisure."

And so saying, after a graceful obeisance
to the ladies, the marquis took his departure.

The announcement that Sir Edward
Stanley's carriage stopped the way, caused
its owner and Omelia to also retire from the
scene. The latter had given a pressing invitation to Lady Arabella Beechcroft, for her
ladyship and mother to pay her an early
visit, and the two last named ladies threaded

their way towards the throne-room as Omelia and Stanley were being conveyed towards Belgrave Square.

CHAPTER CCXL.

COLONEL MAITLAND AND HIS SON.—DOUBTS AND FEARS.—THE PREVAILING EPIDEMIC.

Our scene shifts again to India, that we may be enabled to take a glance at those few characters who have played their respective parts in the present tale.

Colonel Maitland, who had been so jocose on the occasion of our heroine's wedding, wore now a somewhat graver aspect. Indeed, his demeanour might have been characterised as melancholy.

The reader will remember his miraculous discovery of his missing son, since which period he had clothed him in European costume, and placed him under the guidance and instruction of an English tutor.

It was somewhat late in the day for the man's habits of life to be altered or his character changed, and the colonel could not fail to observe that his sympathies and feelings appeared in direct antagonism to the course.

There was a degree of depression about the young man, and an estrangement from his parent—so much so, that he appeared to have some difficulty in realising his present situation.

The death of Goryeboo—villain as he unquestionably was—seemed to have made a deep impression upon Tarah. Strange the latter appeared fond of his foster parent, and his terrible death caused him to evince a grief which both surprised and annoyed the colonel to a considerable extent.

Then the loss of his old companion Moorsha, the death of Natterley, the mystery of his birth, all these things appeared to weigh heavy upon his mind.

It is true he had found a parent—an officer in a high position, of considerable wealth, and highly respected, but notwithstanding this, the young man did not appear to take to his father as might have been expected, and viewed him more in the light of a master or a superior, who was too far above him to ever become his companion or elicit implicit confidence.

The colonel who was naturally a kind man, and indeed his winning bland manners it might have been imagined would of themselves set aside any restraint, did not, however, appear to have such an effect in the present instance.

He saw this, and was therefore inexpressibly annoyed at the reflection that evidently,

although he did not say so, his son more deeply regretted the loss of the scoundrel Goryeboo, than was elated in finding a new parent.

This thought of itself was humiliating enough to the colonel, and jealousy would perhaps be hardly a proper word to express his sensations, as they were more of a mixed character, still jealousy formed certainly an integral part.

Oh, who can root out the impressions and attachments of early youth? "As the tree is bent so it grows," is an old adage, the truth of which was made fully apparent in the present instance.

Tarah's mind was full of prejudice—he had, unfortunately, been brought up in a school which had caused him to imbibe deep-rooted prejudices which it might be found impossible by the most rigid teaching ever to eradicate.

It is, of all things, the most apparent that the character of man is for and not by himself.

Colonel Maitland was anxious to have his newly discovered son accept a commission in her majesty's service, but to this he did not seem inclined. One day the colonel urged the point rather strongly, but could not overcome his son's objections.

"You must remember," said the colonel, "that all the Maitlands have been soldiers, and many have done credit to the country which gave them birth."

"But it is in this country I was born," observed Tarah.

"Ah—yes," said the colonel, rather taken aback by this reflection. "Yes, certainly; but you are an Englishman, nevertheless, and ought to be proud of the appellation."

"And my mother—was she an English-woman?"

The colonel was embarrassed at the home question. There were circumstances connected with the young man's mother which were painful to dwell upon.

"Ah—hem—a—no, she was not a native of our country certainly; hem—no, she was by birth a Hindoo."

"Is she alive?" inquired the other, with a furtive glance.

"Alive! God bless me, no!" exclaimed the colonel, with much surprise. "Poor soul, she has been dead for more than five-and-twenty years."

"Umph!—ah!" and the young man seemed lost in reflection. "Then how do you feel certain that I am the same person, or do you know me to be your son?" he inquired.

"Because, as I have before told you, I placed a child, which was no other than yourself, under the care of Bardah Singh, whom, it appears, consigned it to the charge of Moorsha's father. You know the rest of your history, how you were carried off by a tiger—how you were rescued by Goryeboo, and how eventually Moorsha enabled you to escape from the estate of your employer."

"Ah," said Tarah, "all of whom are now dead."

"No, not all. Moorsha still lives and is happy. When we return to England, you will be able to see your old friend and companion."

"Yes, I suppose so."

"And now, my dear son," said the colonel, affectionately, "I have had some difficulty it appears in making you understand that you are my son—your happiness is my chief consideration. If you do not like the military profession, I will not press it upon you. There is no absolute necessity for you to follow it, for in any case I am sure to be content as long as you are satisfied. Come, deal frankly with me, you have something which appears to weigh heavily upon your mind. Tell me what it is?"

"Nothing—I have lost several friends."

"True; and found several new ones."

"Yes."

"Well, make a debit and credit account of the matter, and you are a gainer.

"Yes; I know I ought to be thankful for my altered position, and know and feel that I have not evinced sufficient gratitude towards you for all your kindness; but I have been depressed. I am free to confess there are circumstances—or rather, have been—some which have caused me some pain."

"What were they? Nothing but what I know of, I suppose?"

"No; Goryeboo's dreadful death is not pleasant to reflect upon."

"Certainly not; but, my dear boy, you must know as well as I do that he was a man saturated with the deepest and most sanguinary crimes."

"True; but he was good to me."

The colonel actually started back with evident chagrin, as he still observed the attachment which his son bore towards his foster parent.

"Good to you—yes. We do not dispute that, and I would, in consideration of this circumstance, have used my influence in endeavouring to save his life, although it would certainly be against my own conscience, my sense of justice, or the duty I owe to my country to have done so. Nevertheless, for your sake I should have sunk all these weighty considerations; but he brought his own fate upon himself, as you know."

"True. I know, my dear father, that your conduct and actions are actuated by the kindest and gentlest of motives, and I have to thank you for your evident consideration for one whom I am sure you must and

ought to look upon as unworthy of your consideration."

The colonel could not help admiring his son's feeling of gratitude towards his foster parent, and regretted that the object of his solicitude had not been a deserving object of sympathy.

Doctor Hamilton being announced Tarah took his departure.

"There appears to be something which depresses that young man," said the colonel to his visitor, "which I am unable to fathom."

"Umph!" said the doctor, and he looked prodigiously mysterious.

The colonel was at a loss to interpret his meaning.

"Have you not observed a certain unaccountable air of dejection about him?" he inquired of the doctor.

"That I most certainly have."

"Can you assign its cause?"

"Perhaps—at least, I can make a shrewd guess."

"You can? My esteemed friend, if you understand the diagnosis of his disease, with your skill you may be able to apply a remedy."

"Perhaps," was the brief reply.

The colonel looked again at his visitor, whose features wore a quiet smile, half satirical and half humourous.

"What is it, doctor?"

"He is afflicted with the prevailing epidemic."

"Good gracious! why did you not make me acquainted with this before? For mercy's sake, do explain your meaning? Is he in a very bad state of health?"

"Corporeally no."

"Then his disease is of the mind. Why that is worse. Doctor, you possitively alarm me. I love this boy. Spare no expense. What is to be done? From what is he suffering?"

"The prevailing epidemic—love!"

"Love! You astonish me."

"It is true nevertheless. You must know, colonel, that this passion seizes the human species in various ways, the symptoms baffle the most skilful. With a phlegmatic constitution its course is not so rapid, but with the more sanguine or active temperament its fires are as consuming as the action of a volcano. It is at times erratic and tangental in its course, nearest at times when it appears at a distance. Men are creatures of imitation. When once the epidemic—for I can call it by no other name—makes its appearance, it seldom ceases till it has attacked the weakest or most susceptible vessels and decimated the population. This last one commenced with Lieutenant Stanley and Omelia; then it attacked Clara and our friend Robinson. They have taken some matrimonial pills, and will soon be in a fair way of recovery—let us hope. Since then, many other officers have been attacked, and now your son. This case is, I fear, at present a bad one, for it assumes the character of unrequited love, which is the very worst form of the disease, the most malignant in its character, and consequently the most difficult to combat with."

"You are perfectly incomprehensible," said the colonel.

"I endeavour to explain as clearly as my insufficient powers will allow."

"Who is the lady? I suppose there is a lady in the case."

"Oh, certainly, there always is, where mischief is concerned," said the doctor with a smile.

"Oh, no doubt, who is she then?" asked the colonel.

"Oh, she is a worthy object enough. But perhaps I am not justified in betraying the young people's secrets."

"Psha! hang your scruples. You have already half done so. You do not think I shall rest till I find out the particulars of this affair."

"I suppose not, so I will be candid with you, and state all I know of the affair. You must know, that for some time past, that your son has given unmistakable indications of being smitten with Colonel Bridport's daughter, Julia."

"Indeed! I never observed it."

"Very likely, but others have, and have not failed to remark it."

"Ah, I should be disposed to think this is only idle gossip."

"You may think what you like, but first hear me. Some few evenings ago, I was walking in the colonel's grounds, reading intently a medical work upon diseases of the heart, when all of a sudden from an adjacent alcove, I heard several deep sighs, after which I heard the low murmurs of a masculine voice, who seemed to be pleading some cause, in what appeared to me from the little I could catch, in an elegant and pathetic manner. Ah, ah, thought I, here is evidently some unfortunate mortal afflicted with the old disease, which came in with our first parents, and bids fair to last as long as the world or man does, at any rate. I paused in my walk, of course, not wishing to interrupt the gentleman whoever he might be. Perhaps it was agreeable to the lady, and my gallantry to the sex forbid my intruding upon so delicate a situation. I walked in another direction, when to my astonishment I beheld your son on his knees at the feet of Julia Bridport, and instead of taking the matter seriously, I observed her laughing immoderately. I did not wait to hear any

more, but at once beat a hasty and precipitate retreat."

"Julia Bridport! There is no wonder then, he was unsuccessful in his suit," said the colonel.

"At present, I should suppose he was. Of course these things will get talked about, as you well know, and the *on dit* of the mess room is the affair."

"I am sorry for this," said his companion seriously. "Sorry that the young man's feelings should have been unnecessarily wounded, because of course he will naturally attribute his rejection to the circumstances of his birth and education."

"I fear so, and he is of a temperament very likely to take it to heart. I regret the circumstance as well as yourself, and made up my mind to put you in possession of all the facts which have come to my knowledge. It would be as well, perhaps, to mention the subject to her father, Colonel Bridport, and advise with him thereon."

"Certainly, if I have your permission, I will make a point of doing so."

"Oh, do as you please, I beg, the matter is no secret, of that I am quite certain."

"Perhaps Julia Bridport is already engaged or about to be."

"I have not heard of any other candidate for her hand, but of course it is impossible to tell. Girls are so remarkably mysterious in these affairs. She may have some attachment; but still, as I have already observed, I have never heard of any.

"It is evident enough to me now, how this has weighed upon my son's mind, as he interrogated me just now somewhat closely, as to whom his mother was. It is the fear of his being half caste, which no doubt troubles him, and to this fact he no doubt attributes his refusal. Ah, doctor, we pay dearly enough, sooner or later, for the indiscretions of our youth. This young man's mother was as fair and beauteous a Hindoo maiden as ever was seen. I saw her fade away in the very flower of her youth. I did all in my power to save her, but 'twas useless. She pined daily, and sank eventually into an early grave. Ah, these were mournful circumstances connected with the affair from first to last. It is no use opening old wounds: at another time, perhaps, I will enter into the particulars of her history, but do not feel sufficiently nerved to do so at present."

The colonel paused suddenly, and paced the apartment in evident agitation, when in a short time afterwards the doctor took his departure.

"So," exclaimed Colonel Maitland, to him, after his visitor had left. "I suppose the fair Julia Bridport does not deem a half caste worthy of her notice, and sneers at the proposition as an insult perhaps. Oh, very likely, the prejudice of girls run strong enough when once aroused. Then the circumstances of his birth—his illigitimacy—Bridport knows enough of this, and perhaps has hinted it to his daughters. I do not know that I can blame him—most likely should have done the same myself. Well, I will see the colonel, he is as frank and open-hearted a man as I ever met with in the whole service."

CHAPTER CCXLI.

GOOLOOH'S DESPONDENCY AND WANDERINGS.—TAMNEEGAL'S GRAVE.—THE DEATH OF JAHNSAH.

After the departure of Omelia and Stanley for England, poor Goolooh wandered about in silence perfectly inconsolable.

The sun which had lighted up his path in life was for ever gone from his gaze—for him the world had no charms—the breadth of boundless oceans lay between him and her who was his life and light.

Bereft of all his early associates and friends, he had no one to fill up the void and chasm made by the loss of Omelia.

He roamed about indifferent to whither he was going—he revisited the spot made memorable to him by the Redowya Fort, where the goddess of his idolatry had been shut up with Major and Mrs. Forrester. He then proceeded to the haunt of Tamneegal; some few of his followers were still in existence, and they hailed him as an old friend whom they had hardly expected to see again.

It appeared, so they told him, that the bodies of Tamneegal and his wife, Mugriah, had been taken to a neighbouring church, or rather cemetary with a primitive chapel attached thereto, and there buried.

It afforded him some consolation to visit this spot, and towards the evening of the day on which he was made acquainted with this intelligence, he visited the grave of his deceased friend and companion—for he garnered up any recollection of those who had known him in his earlier years.

Upon his arrival at the cemetary he discovered in a remote corner a smalll headstone with the names of Tamneegal and his wife engraved thereon.

He contemplated it in silent sorrow—the slanting rays of the declining sun lit up the scene with an expiring glory.

Memory was busy with the recollections of all those painful details connected with the death of two beings who now slept so peaceably beneath the green hillock which marked the place of their last abode.

The uncertainty of human life was painfully impressed upon the beholder.

He lingered on the spot as though loth to leave it. Tamneegal, with all his faults, had been his early friend, and the silent grave buries all animosity. Turning away, he left the cemetary with sad and dreary reflections.

After staying a short time with the few companions left out of Tamneegal's band, he bade them a sorrowful farewell, and pursued his wanderings.

He bent his steps towards the place where Colonel Bridport had originally been stationed: here he made a short stay, and then proceeded to the quiet retreat of the good Jahnsah, who had, upon the occasion of his last interview, extracted a promise from Goolooh to pay him a visit.

Upon arriving at the old priest's abode he received no answer to his knock. He called him by name, when a feeble voice returned an answer.

Goolooh entered. No one appeared in the first apartment, and the place seemed to be deserted. From the hollow tones which had saluted his ear, a superstitious fear seized upon the mind of Goolooh that they proceeded from the grave.

He paused irresolutely, when again the well known voice of the old priest was heard, although weak and faint in its utterance.

The traveller proceeded into the inner apartment, when he was pained to behold the good priest stretched upon the couch, evidently in great suffering, and prostrated from excessive weakness.

He held out his thin and emaciated hand to his visitor, and a smile of ineffable sweetness passed over his pale and attenuated features.

"Goolooh, my friend, this is kind; you have not forgotten your promise."

"Merciful heavens! you are—"

"Passing away," said the prostrate man.

"Can it be possible?"

"Passing away in peace," said the other, solemnly.

"But you must have advice—must seek efficient remedies"

"No, Goolooh, it is heaven's will; I am beyond the reach of mortal aid."

"Gracious powers! but it is dreadful to be left thus alone to die, perhaps, unattended."

He hastened to the side of the sick man, and administered what comforts were necessary. Jahnsah revived slightly, and sat up on his couch.

"You are better now, and may, by good attention yet be well."

The old man gently shook his head.

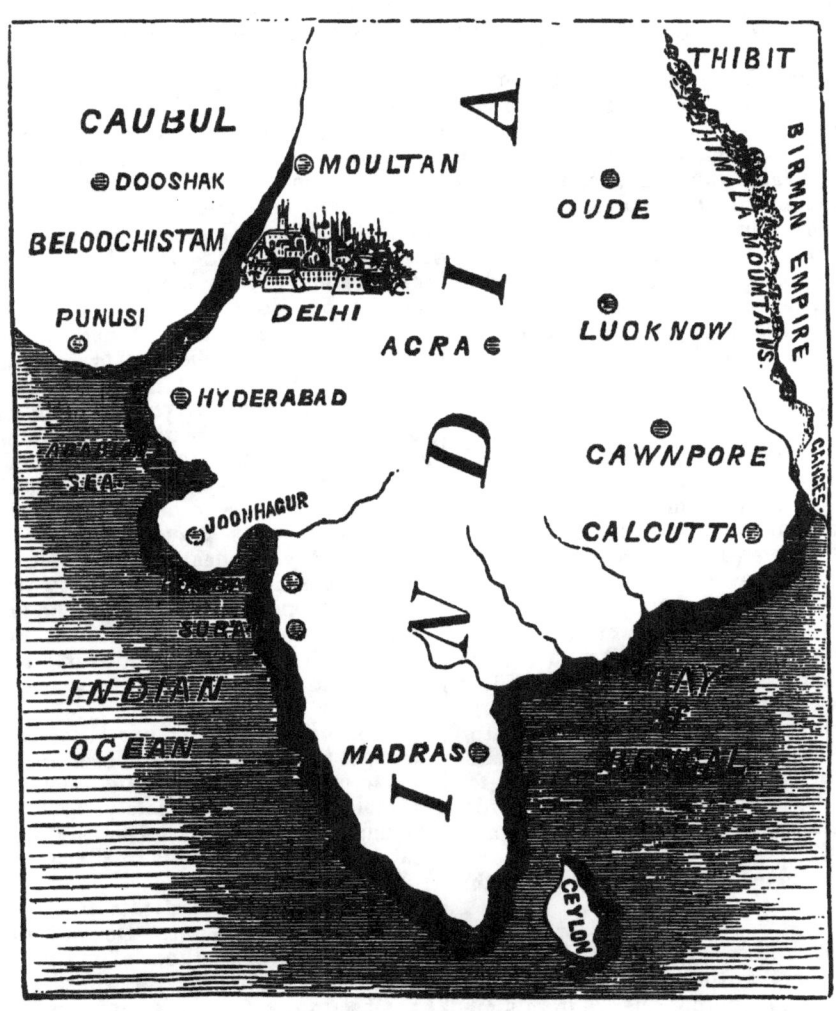

[MAP OF INDIA, SHOWING THE DISTRICT INCIDENTAL TO THE TALE.]

"The lamp of life flickers in its socket," he said, slowly; "a little while its expiring rays may be visible, and then—the rest is silence."

"Oh, say not so," said Goolooh, in a tone of undisguised anguish. "All my friends, one by one, are snatched from me."

His rising tears prevented him from proceeding further.

"It is the fate of man that it should be so," said Jahnsah; "then why repine at that which is inevitable. It is our common lot—the heritage of us all—our irrevocable destiny. The bonds which bind us to this earth are severed one by one. The progress of time is marked in our passage. Slowly and surely the fetters which confine our spirit unto sinful clay are gently released until the soul is permitted to soar freed from

No. 106.

its shackles. It is the wise decree of a beneficent creator that it should be so, then murmur not."

"Peace be with you!" said Goolooh.

"What have I to repine at?" said the old priest; "I have already lived as long or longer, perhaps, than the term usually allotted to mortality, and have seen in my time the young prematurely cut off; for you. my friend, Goolooh, there are, let me hope and trust, many long years of happiness in store."

"Happiness!" exclaimed his companion, bitterly.

"Yes, I hope so. Why not?—You have youth, strength, and the means and taste to enjoy existence. It is not at your time of life that existence has been robbed of half its charms. Use your time wisely, keep honour in view, and in your old age you will have pleasant recollections to dwell upon—for half the happiness of age consists in a retrospect of an honourable and virtuous youth."

Goolooh sighed to think how superior the philosophy of a weak sinking old man was to his own.

"Father," he said, after a pause, "you must let me take you hence, and see if, by change of scene and good advice, I am not able to restore you."

"I do not desire it, my son. It is here that life's expiring ray must be permitted to burn out in peace. Why torment a dying sinner; you are young, and I would not have you pained by staying in this gloomy place."

"I will never leave you," said Goolooh, vehemently.

The old priest gently clasped his hand, and pressed it fervently.

"Have you heard from your friends, Omelia or Lieutenant Stanley?" he said.

Goolooh answered in the negative.

"Indeed! I have."

"What—since their departure?"

"No. I received a letter on the eve of embarkation. Would you like to see it? Put your hand in the drawer of yonder desk—touch the spring—ah, that's it. Now turn out the papers; you know her handwriting—there, you have her letter in your hand Open and read its contents; read aloud, for I should like to hear again her last words, and my eyes are getting too dim to read myself. Now."

Goolooh did as he desired, and read the following—

"Calcutta, Sept. 1858.

"Dearest Father,—I cannot leave the country without writing a few brief lines. I know you do not require thanks from a fellow mortal for any favours you have conferred, and those you have bestowed upon me have been of too inestimable a nature for me ever to requite. To you I not only owe my life, but what is more, the wisest of mental counsel and instruction, which has, I hope, quite regenerated my mind and sentiments. I must beg of you to reconsider my proposition respecting your taking up your abode with my kind friend Colonel Bridport, who would be much pleased if you would consent to such a course. You are alone and unattended in your present retreat, and the thought of this is painful to me. Even if you would not consent to be with the colonel, you might fix your quarters in Calcutta near to him and many of those who hold you in so much esteem. I pray you to consider this proposition seriously. I leave here the day after to-morrow, as our ship sails then. Upon my arrival in England I shall write again to you, directing my future

letters to the care of my solicitors, Messrs. Cottle and Leaf. Should you desire to communicate with me, anything you may send to them will be immediately forwarded on. Now, my dear father, see if you cannot accede to my proposal. I enclose you a letter for Goolooh; he was very despondent when we parted, and I was pained to observe it. I do hope he will consider the unalterable friendship I bear him; tell him this and say everything that is kind to him: I need not tell you this though—tell him to write to me. I would not trouble you with this letter for him but do not know where to address him with any certainty. I have given instructions to my solicitors to honour any drafts you or Goolooh may wish to make on them. If either of you should desire to come to England they will make the necessary arrangements to enable you to do so. Tell Goolooh this—perhaps he would like to come some time or other, and now, dearest father, with many prayers for your happiness, I bid you once more farewell. Your ever grateful daughter, "OMELIA."

Goolooh once trembled when he came to those passages which referred to himself, and he with difficulty proceeded in his articulation, and the old priest was also much affected.

"You will find the other letter, my son, amongst the papers. I have been most anxious to convey it to you," said Jahnsah.

Goolooh's eye immediately lighted upon the superscription, and he hastily opened it and devoured its contents in silence.

It ran as follows—

"Calcutta, Sept. 1858.

"Dearest of Friends,—Do not imagine me unmindful in the hour of my prosperity of the few faithful hearts whose sincerity have been proved in darker and more troublesome days. I know your worth Goolooh, and the sincere esteem of one honest guileless heart is dearer to me than the flatteries of the parasites that cling round the rich and great and poison their ears by fulsome flattery. I shall never forget the scenes we have gone through together. Do not smile—I say never. They will be cherished in the succeeding years of my existence.

"I know you have lost many of your most intimate associates; and perhaps you would like to come over to England. If at any time you could make up your mind to such a course, I have given instructions to my solicitors, Messrs. Cottle and Leaf, of Calcutta, to arrange for your passage. Your name is well known to them, and I should wish you to call there at your earliest opportunity. You will not fail also to call upon our good friend Jahnsah, occasionally I hope, by this time, you are not quite so desponding as when I last saw you. In two days I sail from India, but were there the breadth of fifty oceans between us, they would not wash out the memory of absent friends. I shall write again soon, and let me hear from you. I shall be much pained if you neglect to do so. And so, my ever dear friend, farewell at present. Yours faithfully, "OMELIA."

"To Goolooh Nusayree."

Having perused this letter to himself, Goolooh read it to Jahnsah. The young Hindoo would not leave the couch of the sick man, but took up his quarters in the abode of Jahnsah, and attended upon him with unremitting care. He was assisted in these kind offices by Tallee Sheboo, whom it appeared had been daily in the habit of visiting the sick priest. A few more days passed over, and Jahnsah gave visible signs of a diminution of bodily strength, although in mind he was passive, and resigned to the will of providence. When one day as Goolooh was busy in an adjoining apartment, his attention was arrested by the voice of Tallee Sheboo, calling him by name, in a tone of suppressed alarm; he hastened to the sick chamber, and observed the old priest supported by his female attendant; an evident change had come over him, and his last hour was at hand. He smiled faintly as Goolooh entered, he had, evidently by signs, been endeavouring to make known his wishes, but had lost the power of articulation. Goolooh hastened to his side and half supported him in his arms, when after the administration of a cordial, which the priest prescribed for himself—for he was greatly skilled in surgery—he appeared somewhat better, and was able to speak again.

"So—that is well," he said faintly.

"You are better now," said Goolooh.

"Yes—a little—for a short time only. You will find, Goolooh, in the desk, a paper expressing my last wishes, when I am gone open it. I need not tell you to obey its injunctions; ah," and he was now in evident pain. "Nearly run out—a little while longer," and he offered his hand to Tallee Sheboo, who grasped it and bedewed it with her tears. "Bless you—an old man's blessing rest on your head," he said solemnly. Tallee wept so bitterly, that to hide her emotion she receded towards the further end of the apartment.

"Bless you, Goolooh!" said Jahnsah, placing his thin hand upon the young man's head. "Keep a good heart under all misfortunes. Do not give way to despair. I pass in peace—as I wished—thanks—thanks;" and he uttered to himself a long prayer. Goolooh watched him attentively, his lips ceased to move; an expression of calm serenity was visible on his features, and his attendants thought he slept—so he did

—the long and dreamless sleep which knows no waking.

CHAPTER CCXLII.

THE PREVAILING EPIDEMIC AGAIN.—ITS MALIGNANT ATTACK ON THE DOCTOR.—MRS. FITZFIRKIN AND HER SUITORS.—THE DUEL.

Our old acquaintance, Doctor Hamilton, who had been so remarkably demonstrative to Colonel Maitland, upon the effects produced upon man by the softer passion, was not, it appeared, doomed to come off scathless himself.

The doctor had always the reputation of being what is called a "ladies man," although, certainly, the spring time of his more verdant youth may have been said to have long since passed away; nevertheless, he was a comely man enough, with a gentlemanly bearing, a soft voice, agreeable manners, and had, moreover, in his general demeanour, that which could not fail to impress most persons with an integrity of purpose, and a gentleness of disposition. He was remarkably good natured withal, kind hearted, and particularly fond of children—I would not give a dump for a man who was not—so that he was what is termed a general favourite.

It is hardly possible to define the exact qualifications necessary to win universal approval, as the late Mr. George Robins used to observe of his eligible estates, "they must be seen to be appreciated." Well, it so happened, that the doctor was seen, by a very numerous and select circle of acquaintances; for although since we have had anything to do with him, he has, been attached to the British army; it must be understood, that his being so was a voluntary action on his part. He had, previous to the Indian revolt, carried on an extensive practice as a surgeon at Calcutta, but when the mutiny broke out, conceiving his services would be of more service as an army surgeon, he became attached to Colonel Bridport's staff. He did this the more willingly, as the colonel was one of his oldest and valued of friends.

While engaged in this capacity, his Calcutta practice was attended to by his nephew and an assistant; but more recently, upon his return to that city, he had resumed his old practice. Amongst his patients was one lady, a Mrs. Fitzfirkin, by name; she was the widow of a deceased drysalter, very rich—very affable—and rather *en bon point*, but was nevertheless, what the world calls a fine woman. She had a delicate clear complexion, a bright hazel eye, the sunniest of smiles, displaying a white and regular set of teeth, and had a suavity in her manner which rendered everybody at ease and comfortable in her presence.

It was rumoured that her first dip into the matrimonial lucky-bag had not been altogether so fortunate as could have been desired; her husband was supposed to be what was called *short* in his temper, which, we suppose, means being short of good temper; he was, moreover, said to be of a jealous temperament, but all this might have been scandal.

It is certain, however, that Mrs. Fitzfirkin at the time we are about to make her acquaintance was a very charming woman, she was still what is called fresh, although in the summer of her existence, with the prospect of a bright and glowing autumn. It is true that there was an indication of another chin making its appearance beneath the one with which nature had favoured her, and that her hair, although bright and shining still and untinted by grey, was, nevertheless, not quite so abundant as when Mr. Fitzfirkin led her, a young and blushing bride to the altar; but for all these slight drawbacks there was an inexpressible charm about her, and numerous suitors "sighed like a furnace" when they thought of the handsome and fascinating widow; for she did not, like the veiled ladies of the east keep her charms concealed from the vulgar gaze of man—on the contrary, she delighted in indulging in balls, parties, soirees, conversationes, and occasional pic-nics. With ample means, she liked to enjoy herself and see others do so likewise.

The doctor was a great favourite with her he listened to her complaints, most of them imaginary ones, prescribed for her, attended to all her little fads, gave her advice upon her worldly affairs, and made himself very agreeable to her on all occasions. She never gave any party without sending cards of invitation to Dr. Hamilton, that is, when he was in Calcutta.

Since the doctor's absence, however, there had appeared on the stage another gentleman who had been remarkably and perseveringly attentive to her. This was a Mr. Scollops, an agent for bottled ale and stout in Calcutta. During the doctor's absence from that city he had been a frequent guest at the widow's, escorting her about shopping and driving her out in the neighbourhood.

Scollops had an eye to the main chance, he liked the widow well enough, but he liked her money-bags a great deal more, and had always considered that the doctor stood in his way, as the fair lady evinced a marked preference for the man of drugs.

When, therefore, he took his departure from Calcutta Scollops was amazingly pleased at the circumstance, and had it, of course, all his own way.

Whether he confessed the ardour of that love which was daily consuming him our chronicles do not say—perhaps he was only merging towards a proposal; be this as it may, the fair widow smiled as blandly upon the doctor as of yore; perhaps she was a flirt—a coquette!—we hope not."

The widow's cards of invitation for her forthcoming party were plentifully distributed round the *salons* of the *elite* in Calcutta. She was a lady of excellent taste, and liked things to be done a little out of the common way.

Her card of invitation was novel and *recherche* in the extreme. It consisted actually of a real rose-leaf, upon which were written, in letters of gold, "Mrs. Fitzfirkin's *soiree* Tuesday, Sept. The favour of your company is respectfully requested."

Of course Colonel Bridport, Morley, and all the officers already known to the reader were invited.

"You will go to my friend Mrs. Fitzfirkin's *soiree*, I suppose?" said Doctor Hamilton to Colonel Bridport, as the latter turned over the tasteful card of invitation.

The colonel smiled, saying—

"Well, doctor, I am afraid it is hardly adapted for a quiet old card like me."

"Oh, nonsense; she is the most charming creature imaginable. You must go."

"Oh, certainly, papa, you must," said Julia Bridport, "we shall be dreadfully disappointed if you refuse, as we can neither of us go without you."

"Oh, nonsense, my child; the doctor can escort you and your sister."

"Yes, I can," said the doctor, "but I should like you to go as well."

"Very good, then, so be it. What is it— a ball, or what?"

"No, not a ball. There will be dancing in one of the rooms, music, cards for those who like them, and, of course, conversation."

"Ah, a sort of mixed entertainment."

"Yes, precisely."

"Oh, how nice," said several young ladies present. "I shall go to the dancing-room. Yes—and I."

The evening of the party arrived, the widow was radiant and perfectly dazzling in her white satin and pearls: even the doctor, who had seen her in most of her phases, found his breath completely taken away when he first saw her upon this eventful night. He was really unprepared for such sincillating splendour. The whole suite of apartments were completely metamorphosed, they were decorated with leaves, tendrils, creeping-plants, and flowers, and represented a sylvan retreat, or bower of bliss. From dense masses of tastefully arranged foliage sprang out lustres, held by carved figures of nymphs and rustic groups. Refreshments of every description were distributed in various nitches in the foliage, and a series of surprises were expressed by the guests as they discovered some choice dainty in a remote nook or crevice. Fruit of every description were intermingled with the foliage, and only awaited the gathering to be eaten. At the end of one of the rooms, there was a magnificently carved-oak fire place. It had often been the admiration of many of the widow's guests, but they hardly knew it now, round the oak there was placed real ivy, not the leaves only but thick stems of the plant, as though it were growing from the floor of the apartment, indeed it was impossible to imagine otherwise, so perfect was the allusion. It wound its stems round the oak and seemed to have grown there for ages; this was entwined with several other creeping plants, which were interlaced and mixed together, forming, from the fire-place to the ceiling, one dense mass of foliage.

In the midst of this there were several rustic seats or arbours, where whispering lovers might sigh and make eyes at each other to their heart's content. Talk about a ball-room, why, the widow's suite of rooms looked more like the wood of Arden, enriched by the produce of Flora, Pomona, and Cornucopia. Within the foliage which surrounded the old oak fire-place, the visitor would find every conceivable want supplied; little quaint figures of faries and satyrs held in their hands tiny baskets of cigars, pipelights, sweetmeats, custards, ices, bonbons, &c., &c. You went to help yourself to one of these, perhaps, and were surprised that in your doing so some fresh discovery awaited you, for on turning the leaves there became disclosed several taps concealed beneath, from these every visitor could help themselves. The name of each liquor was written on a wreath which surrounded them. Wines of every description, liqueurs, iced drinks, sherbet, and an endless variety of refreshing beverages were there in profusion.

Ah, it was a great affair, was Mrs. Fitzfirkin's party! It is impossible to describe one quarter of its many and pleasing charms.

In the course of the evening, after the dancers, singers, and players were getting exhausted, they were woke up by a new and still more marvellous surprise. The centre room of the apartments had somehow or other, become either wholly or nearly deserted; the guests had been judiciously drawn off by one and another, either for cards, music, or dancing, as the centre-room was used as a sort of lounging place or saloon.

Those who had some amusement to follow, had betaken themselves to the apartment more particularly designed for such species of pleasure as they chose. If it were dancing,

there was a room for the purpose of enjoying the pleasures of the lively polka, or graceful waltz. If it were music, there was a room with a grand piano, harp, guitar, and a table laden with songs and duets. Then there was one for general conversation and promiscuous amusements, and one also for cards, chess, draughts, &c., &c. There were five rooms in all—the centre being the largest.

When the guests began to give indications of fatigue, their hostess announced that whenever they were disposed, supper should be served. No satisfactory answer could be obtained to this, so, as Mrs. Fitzfirkin observed, "silence gives consent," she gave her orders accordingly. What was the surprise of the guests, when they observed, as if by magic, a table laden with costly dishes, rise up from the floor of the centre apartment. It rose noiselessly, and was lighted by beautiful lustres; its appointments in the purest taste, and in harmony with the decorations of the apartments themselves. The plates were in the form of leaves, of various hues, from a verdant green to sombre or russet. The company were, of course, perfectly astonished; as to Doctor Hamilton and party, they were completely taken off their legs, as the saying is. Talking of the doctor, reminds us that we have to return to our starting point, for in the description of the widow's arrangements, we have missed sight of our characters.

When the eventful evening arrived, Doctor Hamilton started with Flora Bridport under his charge, while the colonel took his other daughter. A large party of both sexs, accompanied them. Upon arriving at the widow's abode, the lady received them with her accustomed grace and courtesy. The *salons* were already half full, and two individuals—we beg pardon, gentlemen—were standing by the fire-place, in the reception-room. They seemed fixtures, and did not appear disposed to move from the widow's side. One of these gentlemen was a tall thin featured man, with long yellow hair, a hook nose, sallow complexion, a tuft of hair coming down to a point beneath his chin: he dressed rather loud, had gigantic buttons to his garments, stripes to his trousers, and spots to his handkerchief or neck tie. He was an American, Rushworth by name.

The other gentleman was the renowned Mr. Scollops, he was a full-faced man, with protruding eyes, puffy eye-lids, long hair, with a pair of mustachois that absolutely persisted in sticking up and pointing to the corner of his eyelids like a sign-post, as though they would direct the strangers attention to the staring eyes of their owner.

Mrs Fitzfirkin introduced the doctor and party to these two gentlemen. Scollops bowed stiffly, looked down his nose, and twirled his moustache.

More guests arrived, and more introductions; the widow was getting excited and flushed with her exertion—it is an anxious time with the best of us to do the honours of a large party. The host or hostess generally comes off worsted in the conflict.

Doctor Hamilton, as an old friend, offered to relieve her of her duties, and, eventually, she took his arm, under the pretext of showing him round the rooms.

"Now, my dear doctor, what do you think of my arrangements? There is, I hope, something to please everybody."

"Oh, they are charming, my dear madam —almost as charming as yourself."

"Oh, you men, what flatterers you are," said the widow, endeavouring to put on a reproving look, although evidently well pleased the while. "As long as I can please a gentleman possessed of the refined taste of Doctor Hamilton I am content."

"You always please me," was the reply, "but now I am enchanted and bewildered."

"Where are you bound for?" said Colonel Bridport, who was immediately behind the hostess.

"Whithersoever you please, colonel; I was about to ask my kind friend here if I might have the honour of leading her to the dancing-room."

"With pleasure," answered the lady, "but it must be by-and-bye, you know."

"Very well, we will adjour to the concert-room, and wile away a little time. What say you, ladies?"

"Oh, yes," was the reply, and the motion was carried *nem con.*

By the time they arrived there, they found a foreign gentleman, a professor, the widow informed them, had sat down to the piano, and was singing a romance of his own.

"I have not had an opportunity offered me of introducing him," said the hostess, "but he is the celebrated Baron Luftentooff who composes for the Theatre Royal—ah, I forget the name now—oh, the Theatre Royal La Squala. Listen! he has a magnificent barytone."

After a prelude upon the piano that would have led any rational person to imagine that the instrument was in fits, the professor began, and as the words of the song were in German, and consequently impossible for us to translate, the reader must remain in ignorance of the libretto of the baron's song. Whatever the subject might be, it seemed to excite the expressive powers of the singer to the utmost, for he rolled his eyes, and pulled such a lachrymous visage, that it is to be inferred therefrom that it was descriptive of some person in great pain or agony.

Great applause ensued when he had com-

pleted his task; people generally think everything sublime that they do not understand, that is, provided it comes from a foreigner.

"Charming, isn't it?" said one.

"Magnificent!" exclaimed another.

"Sublime!" ejaculated a third.

By this time Mr. Scollops and Rushworth had found their way into the apartment.

The former looked glum as he beheld the doctor enjoying a cozy *tete-a-tete* with Mrs. Fitzfirkin.

"Pardon me," he said, hesitatingly, "you are engaged?"

"Oh, no, Mr. Scollops—not at all. I've time for all my friends."

"I was going to ask the honour of having you as a partner for the next dance."

"I am sorry I cannot do myself the pleasure," said the widow, "for I am already engaged to my friend here," and she pointed to the doctor.

A dark shade came over the features of the ale and stout man, and the demon of jealousy began to grasp him in his invisible hands.

"Engaged!——ah—I thought—that is, I didn't know."

"Well, I guess you'd be a pretty considerable smart sort of chap, if you did," said Rushworth.

"But you know, my dear Mr. Scollops," said the widow, in her blandest accents, "you can wait, and I can dance with you afterwards—you know."

"Ah—yes—thank you—certainly;" and he walked away with Rushworth.

"Confound old pill-box," said Scollops. "I didn't know the old buffer was a dancing man."

"It seems you were mistaken," said his companion, stuffing his tongue in his cheek, in lieu of his accustomed quid, and, giving with his lips, a short whistle, as though he were blowing off the steam.

"Pill-box is the favourite horse, I'm thinking," said the American.

"What do you mean?" asked the other.

"Wall, just this—that he is likely to come in first, if he runs for the Fitzfirkin stakes."

"Bah! what do I care, if he does," said the other, pettishly, "why, you ain't riled—aire you? There's many as good a man as you, get the mitten before now—make a jealous man, that's the way to work her. Come, let us go to the dancing room," and he took his companion by the arm. There was not a bit of pride about Rushworth—not a bit, I assure you.

"There's a fine woman, by Jove!" said the American. "What a bust! what shoulders! You can't see such a thing in our country, all as flat as a muffin cap. Make up to her—see—they have just finished," and so saying, he dragged his companion towards an ottoman, where the lady was fanning herself, after the fatigue consequent upon a gallopade.

She was a beautiful woman, certainly, or rather, what might be termed showy; that is, she was magnificently dressed, made a plentiful display of arms and shoulders, which were as white as ivory. She had dark-brown hair—it looked black in the ball room by the gas light—blue eyes, and a pleasant smile. The American, who was a go-a-head character, and had as much impudence as would have served half-a-dozen at least, was the first to address the lady.

"Warm, ain't it," said the Yankee.

"Very."

"Can I help you to some refreshment?"

"I thank you, sir, I have a friend who has—endeavouring to procure me something to drink."

"We'll do better than that," said Rushworth. "Allow me," and offering his arm to the lady, he led her to the oak fire-place, where, as we have already observed, every species of fluid was procurable, from thin seltzer water to ripe port and cognac. She had some sherbet, and the gentlemen filled a couple of glasses for themselves, of—no—perhaps it was not sherbet. While tossing off his glass, the American winked at Scollops, and in a suppressed whisper, said, "strike up to her." Scollops made a graceful bow, and asked if she were engaged for the next quadrille.

"No, she was not."

"Might he solicit the honour."

A seraphic smile—and a low "yes with pleasure," was the reply. The lady took his arm and returned to the ball-room. They were taking their places—yes—the widow and Doctor Hamilton were to be the *vis-a-vis* of Scollops and his partner. The dance proceeded—bow to partners—change places—the old thing over and over again. Scollops was watching the motions of the doctor and Mrs. Fitzfirkin; then he paid fulsome attention to the lady by his side, to see if he could arouse the widow to jealousy. His efforts were in vain, however, for she seemed to be too much taken up with her companion. More dancing—more fanning—more flirtation. Rushworth was in for a polka, with a pretty little dark-eyed damsel; he passed Scollops as he went round, and whispered into his ear—

"Keep it up, my boy, don't ask her to dance more, you are better engaged—do you understand?"

A nod was the reply, as he saw the Yankee disappear like a dissolving view. There was a pause after this, and the Yankee, who made it a rule never to waste much time upon a woman, sidled up to Scollops, and said—"How are you getting on?"

"Oh, charmingly," said Miss Puffpowder,

this was the name of Mr. Scollops's fair partner.

"Charmingly. It's quite delightful. Do you not think so?"

"Ye—as," said Rushworth, as he sat himself down by the side of his friend Scollops.

"I'm going to ask old pill-box to have a game of billiards, as I want some exercise for my arms—legs are getting tired. What say you, will you make one in four."

"Yes, presently. I will join you in the billiard-room," said the ale and stout man.

"Good!" and off went the American to the farther end of the room, where sat the doctor and Mrs. Fitzfirkin.

"Ah, Mr. Rushworth, so you have come to take compassion upon us forlorn individuals," said the widow, as she made room for him on the settee.

"I've come to bask in the eyes of beauty," said Rushworth; "and, after then, I shall want the doctor."

"Want the doctor!" said the widow, in evident surprise. "Dear me, that is very singular."

"I mean, I was going to ask the doctor to join me in a game of billiards."

"Ah—I see."

"I shall feel much pleasure," said the doctor; "but mind, I am no player."

"Nor more am I."

"Then, if you will excuse me, I will leave you, gentlemen, to your game," said Mrs. Fitzfirkin, as she rose to depart. The doctor and Rushworth proceeded to the ball-room.

"We must make up four," said the former.

"Ah, no fear about that, Scollops will make one."

By the time they had got in the room, they found the individual in question, already there. The fourth player was a Mr. Defast, Secretary to the Archæological Society. He was a gentleman who appeared to have been born with spectacles, in a musty trunk of the middle ages.

"Toss for partners," said Rushworth. "Ah! it's you and I Scollops, against the doctor and Defast." The game proceeded—Defast made some splendid strikes. It was soon seen by those around, that the American and his companion had but little chance against the other two practical players. One—two—three rubs were lost, and the losers were evidently chagrined.

"We're queered," said Rushworth, throwing down his cue. "Other gentlemen want to play. What say you to a hand at whist; there's a table unoccupied."

"I'm ready," said Defast.

"And I," said the doctor.

"Shall we cut for partners?"

"No," answered Rushworth. "My friend and myself will play against you two."

"Good—so be it."

They cut. It is the American's deal. The first game is played—the Yankee wins. The next—the doctor. The next, the doctor gets in the nine hole. A dispute arises between the doctor and Scollops, who is now fairly out of temper. He declares that Defast has revoked. The cards are appealed to. The doctor, in his own mild way, endeavours to show Scollops that he is mistaken. The American, who is himself a bit riled, takes side with Scollops.

"You had a heart in your hand, sir, when you trumped my king—sir," said Scollops, addressing himself to Defast.

"You are mistaken, Monsieur Dollops," says Defast: "as I shall prove to you."

"Stuff—nonsense, you cannot prove it. You know you had a heart."

"I do know dat I have von heart here," said the other, laying his hand upon his breast, and bowing to the speaker.

"Ah, ah," laughed several of the spectators, who had been attracted to the spot, by the noise of the dispute. This rendered the disputants more irrate.

"Give de trick to de gentlemon," said Defast.

"Certainly not," said the doctor. "If we are right, which we unquestionably are, I do not see that we have any right to be intimidated to acknowledge ourselves in the wrong. You have not revoked, and I play the game as it stands, or not at all."

"Now, look here, strainger, I ain't a going to be cornered by you, or any man," said Rushworth. "You are tarnation bad upon my friend, and have been so the whole evening."

"I do not see it," said the doctor.

"But I do, sir," exclaimed Scollops, as the points of his moustachois pointed more determinedly towards the corner of his eyes. "I do sir," he repeated with still greater energy.

"Hollo!" said one of the young officers present; "Scollops is getting up."

"It's more than is beer is," said another, in a whisper, but loud enough to be heard by all.

"Mistare Dollops! said Defast.

"Scollops, sir," exclaimed the other.

"Vell, Mistare Scollops, you are not polite, de gentlemon here has explained to you that de heart was in your partner's hand. I have no heart but de von dat I have here. You must see dat you are wrong. De doctor is a gentlemon, who would scorn to tell a falsehood; bah! for a paltry game of cards. It is von pity dat peoples vill not lose with good temper."

"Come, come," said Anslie, who by this time had entered the room. "*Bottle up* your indignation, Scollops."

"You are very witty, sir, but that is no reason I should submit to be cheated quietly."

"Cheated!" said the doctor. You are a low-bred fellow, to make use of such an expression in the company of gentlemen."

"And you are a cheat and a liar," said Scollops, as he flung the cards at the head of the doctor, and tore from his seat in indignation.

"You are an impertinent scoundrel," said the doctor, as he proceeded to leave the apartment; and but for the consideration of the lady, in whose house we are in, I would inflict personal chastisement upon you, as it is, sir, you will have to answer for your insults another time," and the doctor strode majestically from the apartment.

Scollops wanted to fall on him, but was seized by Morley, who detained him.

"What are you thinking about," said Morley; "to insult the worthy Doctor Hamilton. Why, man, you'll have to fight the whole of our regiment."

"Who will be *bottle*-holder then." said Anslie, who would have his joke under any circumstances.

"Horrible thought, that Scollops should prematurely come to his *bier*," said another.

"Never mind, Scollops, keep a *stout* heart, and you'll be all right," said Anslie.

"What is the matter?" said Miss Puffpowder, who with several other ladies, now entered the apartment, attracted by the angry voices of the disputants.

"De gentlemons have been disputing about my having a heart," said Defast.

"Oh, dear," said Miss Puffpowder; "I hope you have."

"I do hope I have one sensitive and susceptible one," said Defast, as he leered most comically through his spectacles.

"Who is the aggressor?" inquired a strong-minded woman of the party.

"The dealer in drugs," said the American.

"That must be Scollops, then," exclaimed Anslie.

"Don't hamper the man," said another, and the offence was thus laughed off for the present.

"Come," said Miss Puffpowder to Scollops, "I shall pass sentence on you."

"Enclose him in one of his own casks," shouted out several voices.

"I'm not to be made a butt of, gentlemen," said Scollops, endeavouring to retort upon his tormentors.

"Why do you bring your hogshead here, then," said Anslie, who was down upon him in a moment.

"Gentlemen, silence, if you please," said Miss Puffpowder; "I sentence Mr. Scollops to dance the next dances with—whomsoever he likes."

"I willingly submit," said the man of ale and stout.

"Yes," said Anslie, "you are used to *hops*."

"He's as light as a cork," said Morley.

"And is famous in giving large *kicks* to his bottles," chimed in Anslie.

"Really, gentlemen, you are too sharp," observed the strong-minded woman.

"More than some people's beer is," said Anslie, who was determined to keep the ball in play, "that's flat enough."

"Do not ferment a quarrel, mine goot friends," said Defast.

"No, give balm to the wounded and bruised spirit," chimed Morley.

Scollops was conveyed away under convoy to the ball-room, where he commenced dancing off his annoyance as best he could

No. 107.

beneath the radiating smiles of Miss Puff-powder.

The doctor, when he observed him enter, retired with Mrs. Fitzfirkin into the music-room.

He did not choose to risk another rencontre, and explained to his hostess the particulars of the dispute in the card-room.

She made a pretty shrewd guess of the original cause of all this disturbance, but as they were observed, she led him into a green-house filled with exotics at the further end of one of the rooms. Here they could converse together without being overheard.

"It is a silly dispute, make the best of it," said the widow, as she seated herself beneath some acacias in the conservatory.

"Yes, but not in any way my seeking," said the doctor. "In consideration of my kind hostess, I have submitted to an insult and indignity which is, of course, hard to bear; but a truce to so unpleasant a subject. While I have so much sweetness by my side it compensates me for any trivial annoyance."

The widow looked bewitching.

"Oh, Mrs. Fitzfirkin, if I could only think—" here he paused; he had hold of the widow's hand at the time.

"I hope you can think, doctor—indeed, I am sure you can."

"Ye—es. You misinterpret my meaning; what I was about to say was this,—if I could only bring myself to think that I was—ah—eh—not repugnant to you—"

"Repugnant!" exclaimed the lady, deprecatingly. "My dear Mr. Hamilton, you surely do not imagine—"

"Oh, no—not for a moment; but I mean if—that is—Mrs. Fitzfirkin, I love you!"

And the doctor fell on his knees before her.

It was really a splendid scene—quite pastoral, with the lady beneath the acacias, and the gentleman with some cactuses in full bloom by his side.

Mrs. Fitzfirkin turned away her head, placed her disengaged hand on her side as if to still the beatings of her too susceptible heart.

"My dearest lady, it is not that you are beautiful only, but your many and varied graces, which adorn the character of woman—your kindness of disposition—your ever ready smile of gentleness. It is not one or all of these that hold my soul in fascination and enchantment, for oh, Mrs. Fitzfirkin, I love you more than words can tell; and if I thought—if—"

Here the doctor came to another pause.

"If what, Mr. Hamilton?" feebly inquired the widow.

"Why, if I thought that I was distasteful to you—that I should be rejected, I—"

"Oh, don't—pray don't," said Mrs. Fitzfirkin, in some alarm.

"If I thought that Scollops—"

"Don't mention him, the odious monster," said the widow.

"I breathe again!" gasped out the doctor—for love-making in a conservatory is hard work.

"May I hope?"

The widow squeezed his hand, and looked down shyly upon him.

He rose up, folded her in his arms, and saluted her—well, we won't say how many times. Then he poured into her ear the growth of his passion, recalling every little incident, which he need not have troubled himself to have done, for the lady remembered them without a prompter; but he took a delight in dwelling upon the first

dawn of love. It's very charming we must most of us admit, but 'tis a pity it does not last.

They made so long a stay in the conservatory that the guests began to wonder what had become of them. Colonel Bridport sought everywhere for his friend but in vain, eventually a little girl who had been dancing informed him that she saw Mr. Hamilton and Mrs. Fitzfirkin enter the conservatory. The colonel hastened thither, and as he neared it, the doctor observed him.

"Here's the colonel," he said; "let us go and meet him; most probably he is seeking us."

"He is coming this way," said the widow, "take no notice, he will find us I doubt not. See here, have you observed these camelias? are they not beautiful?" and she gathered one and gave it to the doctor.

"Oh, you truants," said Colonel Bridport, as he approached the door of the conservatory. "What a pair of runaways."

"Come into our bower, colonel; the doctor was admiring the flowers. Take one," and she presented the colonel with a camelia.

It was gracefully done with an air of negligence, but did not deceive the acute officer, upon whose features a scarcely perceptible smile was visible.

The heightened colour of the two occupants of the conservatory, and the hesitating shy manner of the doctor, at once put his friend upon the right track, and as they all three proceeded to join the guests, the colonel slyly asked the doctor if he thought the heat of the weather was likely to have any influence upon the the prevailing epidemic.

The man of drugs looked foolish, and the widow saw there was some meaning in the inquiry, but could not, of course, guess what it meant.

Supper was served in the way we have already described. The doctor was placed as far away as possible from the odious Scollops, who was doing the gallant to the fair Miss Puffpowder, whom, it seems, had been jealous of some other lady present, the consequence of this was, that a very lively repartee was carried on at their end of the table.

Poor Scollops! what with love, jealousy, the exertion of dancing, and, it must be admitted, sundry potations, was beginning to be elevated, and was what is vulgarly termed beginning to make a fool of himself, and he got himself most unmercifully chaffed by the young officers present.

Defast, too, had been dancing with Miss Puffpowder, but did not deign to exchange a word with Scollops.

It is almost impossible to notice all the movements of a large party, but we should have observed that amongst those present was Tarah, Colonel Maitland's son.

He did muster up courage enough to dance with the Miss Bridports, and made a more favourable impression on them perhaps. There was, however, even in this large assembly of gay persons, a degree of melancholy about the young man which was observed by many present.

The mystery of his birth seemed to still weigh heavily upon his mind, otherwise he was wonderfully improved in appearance and manners. The supper over, and a few more dances, the guests began to slowly depart. As Doctor Hamilton proceeded down the staircase, they heard an angry altercation proceeding from some disputants in the hall.

"You aire un berr——igand, un monstré. on vepaire—Mistaire Yankee man," said a voice which they knew to belong to Defast; "and I will not let you go sare without knowing who you are. Your card, sir, your card."

What's the matter?" inquired Colonel Bridport, as he arrived at the scene of action.

Mistare Yankee man! va-ry insulting— Bah, vary!" said Defast, when, upon suddenly catching sight of the Miss Bridports, who were immediately behind the gentlemen, he took off his hat with a grace that would have done credit to a Brummell, and making a bow, he said :—

"Pardon, Mademoiselles."

The ladies smiled, of course.

"Here Parlez vous," said Rushworth, as he thrust a card in the hand of Defaust, "and look here, stranger, I'll just trouble you for your own bit of pasteboard." Cards were exchanged, and away walked the American.

"Doctor Hamilton's carriage stops the way," said the link, man, and our doctor with Miss Julia Bridport on his arm proceeded towards his chariot, but on looking for his carriage he found some confusion. Scollops, when he saw the doctor's chariot make for the entrance endeavoured to take precedence of it, and he cut in between the pavement and the vehicle in question; the consequence was that he locked his fore wheel in the hind one of the doctor's, and nearly overturned himself in the bargain. Then he began swearing at the doctor's coachman, for by this time he was quite "tight." Of course the coachman retorted, in which he was assisted by other knights of the whip, and a pretty altercation took place. Doctor Hamilton saw how the case stood, and said to his man :—

"Withdraw your wheel, James, as quietly as you can from the gentleman's carriage."

As soon as the man endeavoured to do so, Scollops lashed his horse, drove off, and prevented him. The doctor then very quietly laid hold of the horse's head, and backing him relieved the vehicle. Down jumped Scollops, and said to the doctor, as he stood in a menacing attitude :—

"You'll leave my horse alone, you old humbug. or I'll punch your head." He then made a blow at the doctor, who guarded it off; when, securing him by the collar, he struck him twice across the shoulders with the cane he carried. He then threw the ale and stout man from him. Scollops was about to rush madly at the doctor, when Rushworth restrained him by main force. He knew the state his friend was in, and said, as he held him firmly :—

"Keep quiet, my boy now; this is not a time for cowhiding; wait till the morning, when we will both have satisfaction."

"Leave me alone," screamed out Scollops; who observed the doctor hand the ladies into the carriage, jump in himself, and drive off, without deigning to take further notice of them.

"Mr. Scollops' carriage stops the way," shouted the man, and by main force Rushworth dragged his friend to his vehicle and succeeded in making him drive off.

"Take preshe—dence of me, indeed," grumbled Scollops, as he went along. "Take preshe—dence of me, indeed, I'll stick to him like a leech—like a leech."

"That's it, my boy," said Rushworth; "make him swallow some of his own medicines. Wal—I calkilate I'm right; Pill box will come in furst for the Fitzúrkin stakes, and I am afraid Scollops is out of the betting. Well, there's the Puffpowder cup to be run for.

"Puffpowder be——" said Scollops, and he lashed his horse most unmercifully.

———

CHAPTER CCXLIII.

THE DUEL.

Scollops awoke in the morning after the widows' party with a racking headache; he felt remarkably seedy; and, to use an old phrase, his evening's proceedings did not bear the morning's reflections. Fortifying himself with a drain of brandy, he proceeded to this wharf. A large stock of ale and stout had arrived that morning, and his men were busy in landing them from the vessel which had brought them from England.

Scollops watched them for some time, the breeze from the water cooling his throbbing temples, he reflected upon the turn affairs had taken with him since Doctor Hamilton's return; just as he had thought to make it all right with the widow he was entirely baulked, It was very mortifying—vexatious in the extreme. He sauntered towards the counting-house; when, upon his arriving there he was surprised to see Captain Morley awaiting his presence. He bowed stiffly to the captain, and offered him a chair.

"An unpleasant duty devolves upon me, Mr. Scollops," said Morley, with well-assumed gravity; "a very unpleasant duty. Nevertheless it is one I cannot possibly shrink from performing. My old friend Doctor Hamilton has been insulted—most unwarrantably so, and has therefore commissioned me to wait upon you and demand that satisfaction which is due from one gentleman to another."

"What do you mean?" said Scollops, whose courage was at low water mark.

"Simply that we must manage a meeting, I suppose. You'll excuse me, you don't object to smoke, I presume?" said Morley, as he struck a fusee and lighted a cigar; having done which he pulled out of his pocket a paper addressed to Mr. Scollops, which he handed to that gentleman, who opened it and ran his eye over its contents, which were as follows :—

Sept. 1858.
Sir,
As you have entirely forgotten the line of conduct which is usually adopted by gentlemen, and made use of last night language of a grossly insulting nature towards myself. I have deputed my friend Captain Morley to arrange the time and place of a meeting.

Yours,
LEIGH HAMILTON.

Scollops turned towards Morley in some surprise.

"What does he expect me to do?" said the boer merchant to his visitor.

"Fight him," was the laconic answer.

"Ah, I never fired a pistol in my life."

"It's time you learnt, then, if you go about insulting people."

"I think, Mr. Morley, that I am the insulted party."

"Ah, that's a matter of opinion."

"Well, you know more about these things than I do. What is to be done in this matter?" asked the beer man.

"Why, fight, of course, unless you wish to be called a poltroon and coward."

"Oh, indeed! but I am not a military man."

"What of that? you are a gentleman, I suppose, or would wish to be considered one. You are rivals, are you not? I mean rival suitors to a fair widow."

"Oh, I don't know about that."

"Don't you—then who does? you know whether you are one of her suitors."

"Yes, I know that, of course," said the ale and stout man.

"Then I know the doctor is another."

"Oh, you do," said Scollops, the demon of jealousy beginning to clutch him again in his invisible arms; "you know he's a lover of the widow's."

"Why, of course, man, and so does everybody else."

"Ah, oh, I'll fight him," said Scollops.

"That's well said, and the survivor have the lady."

"Survivor, oh!"

"Yes, of course. Let us hope that you're not both doomed to fall."

Scollops looked very uncomfortable at the prospect of such a catastrophe, but said, with an assumed courage—

"I accept the challenge, and leave the arrangements to you."

"Yes, leave it to me and your second. Who do you appoint?"

"I have not thought of it. I suppose Mr. Rushworth would not mind officiating on the occasion."

"You know best—but I rather think that gentleman has an affair of his own on hand."

"Indeed! With whom?"

"With Mr. Defast, I believe."

"Then I suppose it must be put off."

"That will look bad. Couldn't you manage with Anslie."

"If you think he'd have no objection."

"Oh, I'll answer for that."

"Very well."

"Now your time and place. What do you say to to-morrow morning at six? The sooner these affairs are over the better?"

"As you please."

"So be it then. Now write a few words to the doctor; accept his challenge. As you are the challenged party, you are entitled to chose your own weapons, and if pistols are determined on, you will have the first fire."

"But I have no pistols."

"Never mind that, I will provide them. I have a first rate pair, rifle barrels and hair triggers.

"Oh, th—ank you," stammered out Scollops, whose courage was entirely deserting him.

"Well, then, I believe that is all arranged satisfactorily. Now, the letter?"

"Ah—yes," said the other, who did not know what to write.

With a desperate effort, however, he sat down to his desk and penned the following—

Magnum Bonum Wharf, Calcutta.
Sept. 1858.
Sir,
I beg to acknowledge the receipt of your letter, per Captain Morley, who has undertaken to arrange a meeting for to-morrow morning.

I am yours,
THEODOSIUS SCOLLOPS.

"Short and sweet, like a donkey's gallop. That will do," said Morley, as he quietly transferred the epistle to his pocket book. "Now, Anslie will wait upon you, when we have settled upon the place for this little affair to come off. Good morning, Mr. Scollops;" and the officer raised his hat and retired from the merchant's counting house.

Scollops was in a state of trepidation the whole of the day. He was an arrant coward at the best of times, and the idea of a duel drove him to desperation. To strengthen his nerves he had recourse to several doses (not homœopathic ones) of brandy, and left the office earlier than usual for his lodgings in the High Street. In the evening Anslie was announced, and shown into the merchant's rooms.

"So it seems," said the former, "that I am to be your second."

"Ye-es," faintly replied Scollops. "Have you chosen the ground?"

"Yes, at the back of Fungdoors Palace. I have been trying to effect an amicable arrangement; but regret to say that I have not been able to succeed; but keep up your spirits, old boy, you'll be able to wing your man, I dare say.

"I can't hit a hay stack," said the beer purveyor.

"How do you know till you try? you must do as I tell—stand firm and erect, hold your pistol thus;" here Anslie held out a pistol in his right hand; "fix your eye upon the third button of the doctor's coat, that is if he wears it buttoned; if not, you must carry you eye to the second button up his waistcoat, then when the word is given, fire."

"Oh! oh!" said Scollops, "it would be murder."

"Pshaw! I thought you said you couldn't hit a hay stack. Oh, you are a dead shot, I see."

"I tell you I never fought a duel. Hadn't I better make my will?"

"It would be as well perhaps," said Anslie, stroking his chin in a reflective manner.

"You think it would?"

"Certainly!"

"And about the morning, will you come round for me? but, law, I don't think it worth while to go to bed."

"Nonsense, man; consider your nerves; get a few hours' sleep, by all means, or you will shake like an aspen leaf."

"You've fought a duel, I suppose?"

"Ah, ah, I should rather think I have."

Anslie was delighted with the sport this affair promised to occasion all the spectators. He was an old customer of Scollops, and had already extracted a fund of amusement by teasing him; but the idea of getting him into a duel, it was perfectly enchanting.

On the following morning at six o'clock, or rather a quarter before, the Doctor, Morley, and Colonel Bridport were on the ground. The colonel had endeavoured to dissuade his friend from the meeting; but the latter was inexorable. He was a remarkably quiet, mild man, the doctor as we have already observed; but, like many or most quiet persons when once roused, he was not easily diverted from his purpose.

"Here they come," said Morley, as he observed in the distance Anslie and Scollops. It was a misty grey morning, a heavy dew having fallen in the night, and the air was by no means warm. Presently the two figures arrived on the spot, Anslie had got up his man splendidly; he was enveloped in a large Spanish cloak, the end of which was thrown over the left shoulder. He looked really brigand-like; and he was smoking a cigar too as well as Anslie, with an unusual air of *nonchalance*. The seconds and Colonel Bridport shook hands, when the former proceeded to measure the ground.

"Stay," said Anslie, "I will consult my friend;" and walking to Scollops, he said, "how about distance; shall we say twenty or thirty paces?"

"Th—ir—ty," faltered out the importer of stout.

"Thirty let it be," said Anslie, winking at Morley; "my friend is best at a long shot."

"Cannot this matter be arranged, sir?" said Colonel Bridport to Scollops, as he walked towards him.

"I—do—not—know; it is arranged, isn't it?"

"I mean amicably," said the colonel; "you must be aware that you conducted yourself very rudely towards my friend, Doctor Hamilton, last night; and surely you, as a gentleman, would hardly object to apologise."

"No," said Scollops, eagerly catching at the chance; "I have no objection to apologise, and express regret for what I said in the heat of the moment."

"Anslie!" shouted the colonel, as he beckoned that officer towards him, who was immediately by his side; "it seems," said the colonel, "that your friend here has no objection to offer an apology, and surely that is all that can possibly be required—consult with Morley."

"I do not see, sir," said Anslie, "that my friend can consistently do so now: if after the first shot——"

"Oh, yes, I will—I'll apologise now," said Scollops, eagerly.

"You cannot," said Anslie. The colonel walked towards Morley.

"Are you mad?" said Anslie, as he

shook the importer of stout by the shoulder, "do you wish to be eternally branded as a coward?"

"Oh! Oh! I don't care.

Anslie walked towards Colonel Bridport, Morley, and the Doctor, who were consulting together.

"It seems the man of battles wants to back out," said Morley, as the other second came up with the party.

"Oh, no; it is impossible now," said Anslie, who was determined to see the fun out; "quite impossible."

"So I should say," rejoined Morley. "Place your man, if you please."

"Certainly," said Anslie, with eagerness, as he returned to Scollops, and led him to the spot, who was, however, very loth to follow his second.

"Does he refuse an apology?" stammered out Scollops, his knees almost knocking together with fright.

"You cannot consistently make one now, I tell you," said Anslie, savagely, in an under whisper; then, speaking in loud tones, he shouted out—

"Place your man, Captain Morley. We are ready!"

Doctor Hamilton took up his position.

"Give me your cloak," said Anslie. "Ah! that's it. Now mind, the third button!" and he gave his man the pistol.

Scollops was positively blue with fright.

"Now, you must understand, when we say, 'one, two, three—fire.' You walk forward till we say 'fire!' then discharge your pistol."

"Now, gentlemen, are you ready?"

"Yes."

One, two, three. Bang! went Scollops' pistol. It was pointed down; he found it impossible to hold it out. The ball lodged in the earth, about three yards from where he stood.

The Doctor fired in the air.

"Now let there be an end to it," said the colonel. "You apologize, of course, Mr. Scollops?"

"Y-e-s, y-e-s," said that individual, "I am very sorry for what has occurred, and beg to offer the Doctor every apology that is possible for my unseemly conduct."

The parties shook hands, and left the field.

"Don't think much of your man," said Morley to Anslie, as they left.

"I should think not, was the reply."

While this affair of honour was taking place, another had come off a few fields distant. This was a meeting between Defast and Rushworth. They had exchanged cards the night before, as will no doubt be remembered. In the morning the American had sent the injured Defast a challenge, desiring him to appoint a time and place, and choose his weapons. Defast agreed to meet the Yankee on the following morning, and chose swords, rapiers—and a meeting ensued some half-hour earlier than the one we have just described.

After the few first passes, the American found that he had more than his match. He had underrated the prowess of the musty-looking Defast, who, from long practice in the use of the rapier, both in France and Germany, was really a most accomplished swordsman. He moreover surprised his antagonist with his surprising agility; and Rushworth had quite as much as he could do to defend himself on the first onslaught. Presently he received a wound in the sword-arm, from which the blood flowed copiously.

"Ah! Monsieur Yankeeman, are you satisfied wid de affair thus far."

"No Mounsur, I ain't *cornered* yet," answered Rushworth, as he bgan to submit his arm to his second to bind up. "No, stranger, I'll on to you again," and he placed himself in position.

"You will not blame me if I take your life," said Defast. "I call you gentlemons to vitness dat I do not want to seek dis man's life, dat I might have had before now if I had deserved it."

"You be darned for a boasting fool," said Rushworth, as he pressed hotly on his antagonist, who defended himself with matchless skill and address, and parried the thrusts with the utmost coolness. Still Rushworth persevered in his attack, believing that Defast was incapable of doing ought else but defend himself. The American became hot and excited, and tried every move to throw his enemy off his guard. It was in vain. In a minute or two more Defast's sword passed through Rushworth's body, between the shoulder and chest—he fell to the earth with a deep groan. It was at this juncture that the doctor's party, who were returning home, arrived at the spot. They found Defast bending over the prostrate body of the American, staunching his wound and evincing the utmost anxiety on his behalf. Doctor Hamilton instantly rushed to render what services he could to the sufferer. He examined his wounds and pronounced it not to be mortal, and instantly proceeded to bind it up with his accustomed skill.

"I will de-clare dat I have not sought dis. No man can be more sorry dan my-self for this unfortunate occurrence. I did tell dis infortunate gehentlemon that I did not wish to continue the contest; but I could have passed my sword through his body a dozen times, at least, but he would not believe me—one foolish headstrong man.

Ah! I am, so ve-ry, ve-ry sorry," said the kind-hearted Defast, with almost tears in his eyes. "I am ve-ry, ve-ry sorry—ve-ry!"

"How does your patient, doctor, now?" said Colonel Bridport.

"I think he will do; the hemorrhage has been considerable, and we must find some means of conveying him home, with as little disturbance as possible. The sword has passed beneath the cluvacle, and come out at the edge of the scapulu. No fatal organ has been touched, but of course it must of necessity be some time before he can hope to be fairly recovered."

"Dear me, what a silly dispute this has been," observed the colonel, "over a paltry game of cards."

"It is my own fault," said Rushworth, "I was fool-hardy; the Frenchman is not to blame: I am deservedly punished. How has Scollops and your friend got on?"

"Exchanged shots and apologised," said the doctor.

"The wisest course," said the American. "We were both in the wrong."

"I am glad to hear you say so; it is creditable to a man to acknowledge himself in error when he knows it to have been the case."

A litter was formed, and the wounded man conveyed carefully to his lodgings. Scollops looking the while more like a ghost than a living being; the sight of his bleeding friend had quite unnerved him.

Upon Colonel Bridport and his party returning to their quarters, they found Mrs. Fitzfirkin there in a state of terror and alarm, for her darling Doctor Hamilton. The duel had got wind, and the widow had rushed down in the hope of being in time to prevent a hostile meeting; but it was with unfeigned joy that she greeted the doctor upon his return. Scollops, happily for himself perhaps, was not witness of her expressions. He had accompanied his wounded friend Rushworth home to his lodgings. He was by this time in a perfectly demented state, having endured enough, poor man, to almost dethrone his reason with his own duel, but to wind up with so distracting a sight as his wounded and bleeding friend presented, was more than his shattered nerves could well bear. When our doctor had soothed the fluttered feelings of his enamorato, he, after having accompanied her home, directed his steps towards Rushworth's abode, and administered the best his medical skill devised in the case. He found Defast already there, attending with brotherly care upon the injured man. As to Scollops, he could not possibly be of any use, only in the way; and at the suggestion of the doctor, he gladly availed himself of his advice, to make the best of his way home. Thus far ended the tragical sequent to the fair widow's party.

—

CHAPTER CCXLIV.

THE TWO COLONELS.—THE INTERVIEW.— THE EXPLANATION.

WHILE the events were occurring described in our two last chapters, Colonel Maitland, after Doctor Hamilton's intimation respecting his son's attachment, had questioned the young man upon the subject, and elicited from him the truth of the Doctor's allegation. He at once made up his mind the course of action he should pursue; indeed, he had already done this, before his son's corroboration of the circumstance.

On the following evening after the two duels, the two colonels met to talk over the events which had occurred from the party of the renowned Mrs. Fitzfirkin, for renowned she certainly had become now, since her charms had occasioned a hostile meeting between two of her most ardent admirers. The matter of course found material for some playful gossip between the two Indian warriors. Colonel Bridport had the "Calcutta Express" in his hand when his brother officer arrived at his quarters. He was perusing a paragraph in the paper, which ran as follows:—

"We understand that a fair widow, whose gay *salons* are the resort of many of the *élite* of this city, has inspired by her many charms a distinguished disciple of Esculapius with the tender passion. At her last *réunion* the latter met a gentleman, a resident of our city, who was also a suitor for the fair and fascinating widow. A quarrel ensued, and a hostile meeting on the following morning was the consequence, happily without fatal results to either party in this instance; not so, however, with two other gentlemen, who were, it seems, friends of the rival candidates for the widow's hand, for it appears that some words ensued between the friends, and they had a meeting on the same morning as the others. After a sharp and well-fought contest with rapiers, we regret to announce the fact that one fell, severely, if not mortally, wounded. This gentleman was a Mr. Rushworth, an American merchant, staying here upon business. He received his wound from a gentleman well known in the scientific circles, and whom many of our readers will no doubt know by repute when we state that it was no less a person than Mr. Defast, L.C.C., S.A., and Secretary to the Archæological Society."

Colonel Bridport handed the paper to

his brother officer to peruse, and explained to him those particulars of the transaction with which the reader is already acquainted.

The latter smiled. It afforded him a good opportunity of broaching the subject upon which he was most anxious to speak. "Love!" said Colonel Maitland, "what troubles you have occasioned sinful man for centuries past."

"But the wounded man had nothing to do with the affair," rejoined his companion. "His was a piece of gratuitous bragadocio, for the love of fighting, I suppose."

"Ah! that is a species of knight errantry which I can see no amusement in myself; but I suppose every gentleman has a right to choose that pastime which best pleases him."

"And now, Bridport," continued the speaker, more seriously, "I have been anxious to see you upon a matter which concerns myself, or rather one who is near and dear to me."

The colonel was all attention.

"You see I have, as you know, but recently found the young man whom I call my son."

"Yes, I know, on the occasion of that trial about poor Lightfoot's death."

"Yes, precisely. Well, I find the young man, or at least I have found, that he was very much depressed in spirits; estranged from me, I thought. Of course I attributed it to the circumstances attending his previous life."

"Of course, a very natural supposition."

"So it was; but you must know that more recently I have discovered that there has been another cause."

"Of that I also make no doubt."

"Oh! you do not; then perhaps you know what it is?"

"I think so. He is in love. The old story, Maitland," said his companion, smiling.

"And you know who with, perhaps."

"I am told with my daughter Julia."

"Ah! It is quite true. He is madly and desperately in love."

"Well, I do not see, colonel, how it is possible for us to help these things. They have taken place before we were born, and will do, I suppose, while the world lasts."

"Oh! no doubt; but I have been anxious to talk the matter over with you, as my son is placed in a position which renders him particularly susceptible of any slight; and he is, moreover, of a very sensitive nature. I know he has many disadvantages in the way of—of birth, perhaps, and education also; that, however, I am endeavouring to repair."

"Birth! I do not endorse that observation. He is your son; that is enough."

"Ye-es; but you know, colonel, his mother was, not an Englishwoman."

"Possibly not."

"Well, that, in the young lady's opinion, is no doubt an insurmountable barrier against her ever condescending to look at him."

"I have not heard her say so."

"Oh; but she rejects him."

"She has not accepted him, certainly."

"No; nor ever will, I suppose."

"Well, that I do not say. He was too premature and hot-headed. Why, she has not known him long enough to know whether she likes him or not. I do not think myself that he is repugnant to her; at least, I think not."

"I thank you for your candour thus far, Bridport," said the other, taking his hand, "and in return let me be equally so. You must know that this young man is my only son and heir, and his interest and happiness is my chief care. I need not tell you how, in very early life I lost my first wife in England long before I ever saw the country. I need not tell you also, how many campaigns I had been through before I commenced my long sojourn here. Soon after I arrived, for I had not been in India for a year or so, I became acquainted with a beautiful young female daughter of the Rajah Nerya—we met frequently—her fascinating manners—her gentle, child-like nature and shrinking modesty won upon me, and, in short, I loved her, and the passion was mutual—I waited upon the Rajah to beg his daughter's hand, and he treated me with scorn, and said he would rather see her dead body floating in the Ganges than she should ever marry an Englishman. I was incensed at his manner, lost my temper, upbraided him, and, of course, by that means made matters worse. He forbid her ever seeing or speaking to me again, and for months I was disconsolate; when I met her by chance at one of our hunting excursions, and I renewed my suit to her with greater ardour—she eventually consented to fly with me, for it appeared her parent treated her with great harshness and cruelty; so I arranged all the necessary preliminaries, carried her off and wedded her at Madras. Some time afterwards I waited, at her instigation, upon her father, taking her with me to ask his forgiveness. His rage knew no bounds, he cursed her, accused her of murdering her mother, whom, it appeared had died since her absence. I led her away perfectly senseless—she had fainted. From that hour she never held up her head—she was a delicate, fragile flower, incapable of bearing the rougher usage of the world, and, above all, so dreadful a ban passed upon her by her parent. A few months passed, and

she gave birth to a child—this young man. After then she gradually sank; she lingered about ten months longer, and then—died in these arms." The old colonel could proceed no more in his narrative, and he paused, overcome by emotion.

"There, you have the whole history of that painful episode in my life, which I cannot recal to my recollection, Bridport, without being unmanned. I placed the child out under the care of Kurah Sing, and you know the rest of the history—for more than five and twenty years I have been in ignorance of his existence—believed him to be dead—in fact it is a long gap in a life-time—a long blank. Well, no matter—I have found him—but oh, if I had been allowed by cruel fate to have brought him up his sympathies would have been with me more than they

are, but it is useless to repine now for the past."

"Your story," my dear Maitland, "is indeed a melancholy one. I had heard something of it, it's true, but never liked to mention it to you, in consideration of your feelings."

"I can see," said his companion, "that this boy inherits a good deal of the disposition of his mother: he is kind, gentle, and impressive in his character; and I need not tell you that now I have found him, that I do not want to see him fade before my eyes, as his unhappy parent did."

"Heaven forbid!"

"Well, then, that is the main object I have in mentioning this subject to you. He will, of course, inherit all I have. He will, I am sure, be soon improved under his present tutorage; and if you thought him a worthy husband for Julia, need I say how happy I should be to see them united. I do not say at present: let them wait till they are better acquainted—time will do much. If she is not already engaged, she may learn to look more kindly on him. Does this meet with your approval, Bridport?"

"Most decidedly; you know, my dear Maitland, I cannot possibly have any objection, as long as they are pleased with one another, that is all to be desired. If I had a dozen daughters, I should always let them have the man of their choice, provided he was anything near the mark. No, I should never endeavour to control my daughters; I should, of course, express my opinion if asked, on that as any other subject; but beyond that I should not endeavour to go."

"Then I can understand, Bridport, that you would offer no objection?"

"Certainly not, quite the contrary."

"It gives me joy to hear you say so; for I am free to confess that I entertained very serious doubts upon the subject, when Dr. Hamilton first mentioned it to me."

"Oh! the Doctor first made you acquainted with it, did he? How was it that he became lovers' messenger, I wonder?"

Colonel Maitland here explained the particulars of the scene in the gardens of the Cantonment, which the Doctor had so graphically described. This was news for Colonel Bridport, and he laughed most immoderately at the recital.

"Hamilton has become quite a gallant, gay man himself all of a sudden," said Colonel Bridport; "it is positively dangerous, ha, ha!"—and the two colonels laughed outright.

"I am glad I have mentioned the subject to you, and that we understand each other so well," said Colonel Maitland, as he shook his companion warmly by the hand as he departed. "Let us hope that time will soften all asperities, and that events will turn out as we desire; farewell, my friend—adieu;" and the colonels parted, well pleased with each other.

CHAPTER CCXLV.

JAHUSHA'S WILL. GOOLOOH'S INTERVIEW WITH MR. COTTLE. HIS ENGAGEMENT WITH DEFAST.

WE left Goolooh by the bedside of the dying priest. When he discovered that the good old man had departed, his sorrow knew no bounds. One by one had Goolooh beheld his friends depart and leave him alone in the world. A vast gathering of Jahusha's followers came to pay their last respects to the dead, and they went through numerous rights according to the custom of their country and creed. After the ceremony of interment was over, Goolooh opened the paper containing the last instructions of Jahusha. He found by its contents that the priest was worth a considerable sum of money, a portion of which he left to be distributed amongst various poor, but worthy natives, who had long been recipients of his bounty. The bulk of the money he wished to go towards paying for the endowment of a chapel and schools attached thereto, where a more liberal education should be afforded to the poor natives of India, and free from those religious prejudices which were indigenous to the country. In short, although Jahusha did not subscribe exactly to christianise his countrymen, his scheme went half way towards it, and separated the idolatry of the various religions professed by the natives of India. In his will he directed Goolooh to express his wishes to Omelia, and beg her co-operation in his scheme. He proposed it should be called the Stanley endowed schools. When Goolooh saw the contents of the paper, and the expressed wish therein contained, he at once made up his mind as to the course of action he should pursue, which was one that, unless pressed by circumstances of a sense of duty, he would have found repugnant to his feelings, perhaps. This was to wait upon Messrs. Cottle and Leaf, and explain to them the particulars of the old priest's will. Goolooh therefore hastened to the lawyer's office at Calcutta. Mr. Cottle received him with the utmost courtesy, and informed him that his client, Lady Stanley, had left instructions for him to act in the same spirit towards all her friends as she should have done herself.

"And now, young man," said Mr. Cottle, "the best thing I can advise you to do is to allow me to make arrangements for your journey to England, where you will be able to explain to your beloved friend all those circumstances which you have detailed to me. Lady Stanley will then in all probability communicate with our firm to have the wishes of the deceased man carried into effect. What say you to the course?"

"It would, without doubt," said Goolooh, "afford me infinite pleasure to be with one whom I so deeply respect, but I have been too long associated with my own country to ever think of leaving it."

"How so, seeing that in it you have lost so many of your most esteemed companions?"

"It may not be."

"Why not? What is your objection?"

The Hindoo shook his head very mournfully.

"Come, let me persuade you to think better of this matter. However you must pardon my freedom, but you are evidently in a desponding state, you are reminded while here of those whom you have lost, an additional reason why you should seek another clime, where from a change of scene, melancholy reflection would in all probability be for ever dispelled. There now, take my advice, the more so as I know it is the most particular wish of Lady Stanley that you should do so. Indeed she expressed herself very warmly upon the subject before leaving both to myself and Mr. Leaf."

"I thank you, sir, for your kind intentions as well as her for whom you are acting," said Goolooh, "but I must really decline, not out of any disrespect, I am sure, but there are reasons, there are—in fact I would rather not leave my own country. Perhaps you will be good enough to write all the particulars to Lady Stanley, and when her wishes are made known, I will see you again."

"You are certainly very obstinate, I must say," observed Mr. Cottle, who was rather piqued that his endeavours had not met with the success he had desired—"yes very obstinate."

"You would not wish me, sir, to do that which is against my own wishes or judgment."

"Certainly not; far from it. I have of course only your own welfare in view, when I propose to you to adopt this course, as I feel convinced you will see cause to congratulate yourself if you adopt my advice."

The worthy lawyer used his utmost endeavours to persuade his visitor, but with no better success, and eventually Goolooh left with an understanding that he would call at a future day, to see what the wishes of Lady Stanley were.

He then directed his steps towards the residence of Colonel Bridport; Goolooh was naturally shy, and would not have sought an interview with the colonel under other circumstances perhaps; but he felt it his duty to wait upon him and acquaint him with the death of Jahusha. Upon his arrival there, he was greeted with the warmest expression of friendship by the kind hearted colonel, whom Omelia had begged, previous to her departure, to show what attention were possible to the desponding Hindoo.

"You are a queer fish, Master Goolooh," said Colonel Bridport, after he had heard his story; "you never come to see any of us, but take yourself off to the Lord knows where. Now you have come, I shall insist upon you stopping."

Goolooh started back in some surprise.

"Ah, but I shall, though; you do not leave here for awhile, I can tell you; if you will not go over to England, you must and shall stay with those who care about you."

"I—I—" Goolooh was beginning to stammer out something, when the speaker stopped him with a deprecating gesture.

"Now, I know what you are going to say: you have other business to attend to, now I happen to know you have not, and even if you have, that is no reason why you cannot spare a short time with us; you must—nay you shall, I tell you."

"Is this the friend of Lady Stanley whom I heard so very often spoken of?" said Defast, who was present at the above conversation.

"It is," said the colonel, "and he refuses to share our hospitality."

"I do not say that," said Goolooh, now reassured by the colonel's warmth of manner. "If I shall not be in the way——"

"Tut, man! Do you think we ask people to be in our way? What we say we mean?"

The Hindoo gave a grave smile.

"I would feel ve-ry mooch obliged," said Defast, who saw how the case stood, "if de gentleman vood favor de colonel by staying one short time; and I would be still more obliged if he vood consent to occompany me on one journey through de provences of India."

"What say you to that, Goolooh?" said the colonel.

"Of what service could I be?" he asked.

"Let me explain to the gentleman," said Defast. "I have to go one long ways; all over de countray. Ah, me! ve-ry long ways. I have to make some grand researches connected wid our Archeological Society; but I have not been able to go. No, for I have note met vid one garçon upon whom I can rely as a guide, a conducteur. Entendez vous?"

"Do you comprehend?" said the colonel to Goolooh.

"Yes, sir, I understand the gentleman's meaning," he replied.

"Vell, I cannot express to you vat a great service you would be doing me if you would consent to accompany me upon researches, as I should have confidence in one friend of Lady Stanley. I should know dat he vas one man of honour, to be relied on. And considare, mon ami, how much you vood be benefiting science."

At the latter observation Defast so threw himself back, that Goolooh thought he must have dislocated his spine; and he gazed through his spectacles at the Hindoo as though he expected him to leap with delight at the suggestion.

"Possibly he may not have the same amount of reverence for science that you have," said the colonel, smiling.

"Perhaps not; but when he is told dat I am engaged by de Hociatic Society—de Archeological Society—to collect mat-erials for one of de garentest vorks de world ever saw, and dat his name will, of course, appear in it as my guide and companion—ven he is told dat his vork is thirty-eight volumes quarto, and that his name will be handed down on one of its pages to posterity, I tink dat he vil see dat he is fulfilling a high mission, sa."

"You must understand," said the Colonel, in explanation to Goolooh, who had evidently not understood all Defast had been saying, "that this gentleman is at the head of a very learned and important society; indeed, he is connected with other learned societies, and he is over in this country to collect materials for a large work, to be published in England as well as on the continent—"

"And Ame-rica," said Defast.

"Yes, and America. Well, he wants a conscientious man like yourself as a guide. You know many or most parts of India, would be invaluable as a guide and companion to him, and would certainly be rendering both him and science a great service by consenting to accompany him. Now, do you understand?"

"Yes, sir," said Goolooh. "If my services can be of any use for the purpose, I shall be well pleased to do my best."

"Well spoken," said the colonel; "and we may consider the matter settled. You stay with me until such time as Mr. Defast is ready to start; then take your tour with him, and return and let me know the wonders you have inspected. Eh, Defast?"

"Dat is eexactly as I should veesh."

The colonel foresaw the excellence of this arrangement. It would keep Goolooh from brooding over his sorrows. Nothing like employment for a chafed spirit. Again, it would familiarise him with European company; and Defast, although eccentric enough, was nevertheless a kind, simple-hearted man; crochetty and wrapt up in his own theories, it is true, but still of a gentle nature withal. By accompanying him through the districts of India, Goolooh would have his mind continually occupied, and the colonel hoped upon his return that Goolooh might then be persuaded to go to England, perhaps. After staying with the colonel for some weeks, the party of scientific gentlemen—for there were others besides Defast—started upon their wanderings, and if the reader has the patience to turn over the Asiatic transactions in the reading-room of the British, Museum he will find himself much edified thereby in noting our friend Defast's quota to the work in question.

CHAPTER CCXLVI.

BEING A SHORT CHAPTER, IN WHICH A GENERAL GLANCE IS TAKEN OF THE CHARACTERS.

WE think of opening a matrimonial agency office, for we have been enabled to bring to a successful issue so many matches, that we really feel quite up to the mark in this line. We do not know if the same success would attend our efforts here as has crowned them in a tropical clime; but still we are rather sweet upon the idea; for, after all, who would be single if they knew the joys of wedded life. Bashful bachelors and neglected maidens send the particulars of your woes to the publisher of this work, and we will see what can be done. You see how comfortably Omelia is married (a baronet, too); well we have now to record the nuptials of Dr. Hamilton and the fair widow, Mrs. Fitzfirken. Soon after the departure of Goolooh, Defast, and party upon their exploring expedition, this affair came off, and a mighty big wedding it was, as our trans-Atlantic brethren would say. It would be "gilding refined gold" to enter into the whole of the details. To describe the company, carriages, decorations, dresses, bouquets, &c., &c., would exhaust the descriptive powers of the reporter for the "Morning Post."

The bride, young and blushing was given away by Colonel Bridport. His daughter, with several other young ladies were bridesmaids, amongst whom was Miss Puffpowder. After a magnificent entertainment the happy pair took a wedding tour to the most agreeable spots in the country. Scollops saw the procession pass through the high street, rushed into his office, and it is reported drank two bottles of his own stout, but Anslie, who related the circumstance to his brother officers said that it was a species of lunacy, which appeared to him to be incredible; it is certain, however, that he knocked his errand boy down for coming in grinning and saying that the wedding party had just gone into the church; he had the gratification of going round to the residence of Miss Puffpowder, and hearing her version of the ceremony, she did not fail to pull a good deal of it to pieces, as she knew it would please the wounded feelings of Scollops.

Some months after the widow's wedding,

Scollops managed to uncork his pent-up feelings, and lay the state of his affections bare before his admirer, Miss Puffpowder. That lady, with the amiability of her disposition sympathised with him, took compassion on him, and said, in a weak, faint voice, whilst rising blushes suffused her handsome features.

"I am your's, Scollops; your's till death."

The party addressed clasped her to his arms with rapture.

"When would she name the happy day?"

There was a good deal of coquetting at this home question.

"Oh, it must not be at present."

"Why not?"

There was a pause, and some hesitation.

"Oh! many reasons."

However, by perseverance Scollops did at last manage to get her to fix the time when he was to be made a happy man.

His friend Rushworth had comparatively recovered from his wound, although he still felt its effects. To him was given the onerous duty of standing father on the occasion of Scollops's marriage, and a very troublesome job he had, for when it came to the point the bride was very nearly doing a faint over the affair—she was so very nervous. So was Scollops—so were the bridesmaids, and so——no! Rushworth was as firm as a rock. Anslie, who certainly was of a mischievous turn declared that the clerks and porters in the beer merchant's establishment speak of their master's marriage to this day—the reason he assigns for their vivid remembrance of the circumstance is this—he asserts, but, of course we all know what he is, that Scollops gave the poor fellows a holiday, sent for a vehicle for them to go into the country and have a pic-nic, at the same time providing them with viands, and an unlimited quantity of bottled ale and stout, the latter of which two articles was unsaleable, having turned sour. Anslie says that in their hilarity they took an enormous quantity of the beer, enough to float a four-oared cutter, he understood, and the consequences may be imagined; the pains they suffered for the next day or two were something fearful. Anslie said that by this means Scollops impressed the recollection of the happy day upon his servants; for, said Anslie, "if you want to call a dog's attention more particularly to any subject, pinch his tail," and he moreover declared, did this Anslie, that it was a constant wish amongst the men in the docks that the bride wouldn't turn out as sour as master's ale, but, of course, as we said before, we do not give any credence to this statement. It is certain, however, that Anslie was at the ceremony, and sang a song afterwards, descriptive of the bride's beauty, &c. We warned the reader that we were getting in a matrimonial trim, and so we may as well record here the issue of Farah's suit, he was re-christened Edmund now, after his father. He persevered in his attentions to Julia Bridport, till his gentle unassuming manners won upon her by degrees, and eventually consented to be at once his, to the great joy of her suitor, and an equal joy to Colonel Maitland. They were married with great pomp and ceremony, and it might be really termed a military wedding, as both fathers were colonels of distinction in the British service.

Captain Robinson and our old friend Clara were present at this ceremony. They had returned from their wedding tour to Calcutta some time before it took place, and were much grieved to learn that Omelia and Stanley had gone to England without seeing them before their departure.

Edmund Maitland, as we must call him now, was a devoted and attentive husband to Julia. We are sure our female readers will be glad to learn this, as such beings are generally considered rare. In the due course of time, the happy couple proceeded to England, accompanied by Colonel Maitland, who had made up his mind to retire from active service, and settle down to spend the remainder of his days in his mother country. Our tale cannot be considered entirely a record of births, deaths, and marriages, although they form an integral part; so without any fear of coming under such a charge, we may as well, perhaps, inform our more curious readers, that there was a birth, with the Maitlands, then another, and another. Old Colonel Maitland lived to see a numerous progeny of grandchildren around him; and even as advancing years came upon him, (as they will upon you and I, my friend, if we live long enough) he was merry and cheerful to the last.

Our friend Morley we must give up as incorrigible, he would and did persist in remaining a bachelor. He asserts that he cannot succeed in inspiring any woman with a sufficient amount of affection for him to warrant him in making her his wife. He reasons like some grave old philosopher upon the subject, and with an obstinacy that is really unpardonable for a man of his intelligence and veracity, that it is not his own fault: it is a poor excuse this, not to be believed; however, Morley remains obstinate; there is always one black sheep amongst a flock. Hear what he says for himself, in answer to the taunts of his companions. We are in the mess-room now, and several officers are lounging about on various seats, in picturesque attitudes. Morley is smoking a cigar, as indeed are most present. Anslie, who we know to be a teaze, in his own peculiar way, says to his companion, Morley—

"What are you ruminating about, old boy? You are as silent as a sentry on duty."

"The mutability of human affairs," was the answer.

"I suppose you are going to change your condition, Jack," said Anslie, with a cunning smile. "By Heavens, I believe you are in love."

"Not that I know of."

"Well, then, you ought to be by this time. Really, Jack, you should get married. Upon my word you ought. It's not creditable to the service. Ought he not to get married?" continued Anslie, as he turned to several present.

"Most undoubtedly," was the general response to this question.

"Why don't you, Jack?" inquired Anslie, with a mock serious and reproving look.

"Why don't you?"

"Ah, I am young and foolish."

"That's the very reason why you should."

"Well, but do now, there's a good fellow," continued his tormentor.

"Here's a lot of fellows waiting for you. They don't like to take precedence of their senior officer."

"They may wait, then, in welcome, Mr. Harry" he continued more seriously. "I've marched in single file for many years, now, and the chance is that I shall, when my time comes, march off so to the other world. I'm too old a soldier to dance at a woman's heels. I've had enough of that, my lad."

"Ah, jilted! I suppose, eh?"

"What do you mean?" said Morley, somewhat sharply; then, as if apparently angry with himself for the ebullition, he laughed at his companion, and said more pleasantly—

"No, not exactly that, Harry; but you see my habits are now fixed, and I am not so easily moulded to please the whim of a woman, for after all they act more from caprice and whim than aught else. You know I commenced life a poor man. When I came into the service, I had to fight my way up in the world. I've not fought my way into a very high position now, you'll say, which is true enough. Well, you see, during these years marriage was out of the question; and—and—I might at one time——"

"Ah, you have then——"

"Yes, Harry; I have loved, you were going to say, I suppose?"

"Precisely."

"Well, that's a hard question to answer. I thought I loved. It was one above my station in worldly wealth. Bah! she was a mercenary huzzy; and I could not bid enough for her; and so she married an old curmudgeon, who broke her heart. I didn't wish that, with all her faults; but so it was. She married for money and position, and had them; but that is all. And worldly minded as she was, they did not suffice. Ah! you cannot reason with a woman, Harry; and so you'll find out, if you have not done so at present."

"I do not attempt to reason with them," said Anslie.

"So much the better for you. I did, and have found it a failure."

"But surely," said another officer, "you would not stigmatize the whole sex because you have met with one heartless woman."

"I have not said she was heartless," said Morley, sharply.

"Well, mercenary, then."

"No, I do not do so, I hope; but you see the hey-day of my time is past."

"Pshaw! you are young enough for any woman."

"That may be; but not young enough to have the fresh and ardent passion, as I might some dozen or fifteen years ago. No, love is a pure stream at first with us, the very reflex of the human heart. In the spring time of our youth it bears us calmly on with a compassion pleasantly enough; but pass a certain period of life, and the stream becomes broken up. It is turbid, abounds in shoals and shallows."

"What a melancholy picture you are drawing, old boy," said Anslie. "I hope I have not passed the time you speak of."

"Get along with you. When you come to my age you'll know what I mean."

"Why, you are a most determined bachelor."

"Situated as I have been, yes," said Morley. "If I had met with some more humble maiden, who would have loved me for myself alone, the case might have been different. Or if I could find such now it might still be so. But law, that's an idle thought."

"Oh, then, you are still open to competition?" said Anslie.

Morley laughed. "Yes," he said; "what a number of bidders."

"Why, look at our Doctor," said Anslie. "He has managed to bring down his lady."

"It may be so; he's a more fortunate man than me, I suppose. I was not born under a lucky star, as far as women are concerned, at any rate, and I am sure I shall not give myself much trouble now to repair my fortune. What says one of our most original writers?"

"What?"

"It's a song," said Morley, "and more

in your line than mine. I'm no singer, you know."

"Well, repeat it."

"LOVE AT TWO-SCORE.

"Ah! pretty page, with dimpled chin,
    That never has known the barber's shears,
All your aim is woman to win.
This is the way that boys begin.
    Wait till you've come to forty years.

"Curly locks cover foolish brains;
    Billing and cooing is all your cheer;
Sighing and singing of midnight strains,
Under Bonnybell's window-panes.
    Wait till you've come to forty year.

"Forty times over let Michaelmas pass,
    Grizzling hair the brain doth clear;
Then you know a boy is an ass,
Then you know the worth of a lass,
    Once you have come to forty year.

"Pledge me round, I bid ye declare,
    All good fellows whose beards are grey,
Did not the fairest of the fair
Common grow, and wearisome, ere
    Ever a month was past away?

"The reddest lips that ever have kissed,
    The brightest eyes that ever have shone,
May pray and whisper, and we not list,
Or look away, and never be missed,
    Ere yet ever a month was gone.

"Gillian's dead, Heaven rest her bier,
    How I loved her twenty years syne!
Marian's married, but I sit here,
Alive and merry at forty year,
    Dipping my nose in Gascon wine."

"There," said Morley, when he had finished, "that's what our accomplished and gifted author, Mr. Thackeray, says upon the subject."

"Ah, now you quote celebrated authors, I have done," said Anslie.

CHAPTER CCXLVII.

ANOTHER GLANCE AT OUR HEROINE.— MEETING WITH OLD FRIENDS.

"But what of your heroine?" exclaims some impatient reader whose eye has wandered over the descriptive passages incidental upon our friend Mr. Fitzfirkin's soirée. Be content, she is not forgotten, we promise you. The pen that has described the many and varied chaotic incidents of her chequered and eventful life will not be laid down without taking one more glance at her who, with all her errors of education and impetuosity of temperament, nevertheless, from the warmness of her heart and generosity of her disposition awake our warmest sympathies. We left Omelia, we mean Lady Stanley, in the vestibule of St. James' Palace, whither she had been for presentation to her Majesty. Let us take another glance at her.

In one of the most magnificent streets lying to the right of Belgrave Square, Sir Edward and Lady Stanley are located. We dare not give a nearer or more particular description of their whereabouts, as, of course, half London would besiege her doors, anxious to obtain a glimpse of their darling heroine. No one must temper kindness with discretion, and, however we may feel anxious to satisfy the curiosity of an eager and anxious public, we must not dare to obtrude upon the sanctity of private life, but if the reader has so large an amount of curiosity respecting her that his rest at night becomes disturbed, we would suggest the following sedative. Let him go up Piccadilly until he comes to Apsley House, then turn down St. George's Place, just round by that frightful statue of the Iron Duke; having proceeded a little way down he will find a turning which will lead him to Belgrave Square. Make half the circuit of the square, and he will then see a turning on the opposite side which faces the one he has entered by, he is close to our heroine's residence then, we dare not say more, but if he be a patient man, and chooses a summer's evening for his ramble, say between six and seven o'clock, he will, by a little careful watching, be able to catch a transitory glance of Lady Stanley through one of the French windows of the first floor. For his behoof, however, we are about to take a last parting glimpse of her ourselves.

It is evening; lights blaze from every window of the palatinal mansion of Sir Edward Stanley, carriages emblazoned with heraldic devices throng the avenues of Belgrave Square.

There is a party at Sir Edward Stanley's to-night, as may be seen by the throng of gentlemen in yellow plush, green crimson, and plush of every other variety of hue who throng round the doors of Sir Edward's mansion. We are not going to exhaust the whole of the Court Guide in enumerating the parties who were there, having only to do with those which more particularly concern us. See, we are in the hall now: what a blaze of light. How beautifully they fit up these modern houses—look at the staircase—there's a specimen of light iron casting. Who is that above, on the marble steps at the top? It is Lady Stanley—how beautiful she looks—how bright her eyes—how seraphic her smile. Ah, there is something which lights up her features with a more than vaunted pleasure to-night. What can it be? Oh, she is locked in the fervant embrace of a loving friend. It is Mrs. Forrester—now another, it is Mrs. Mc Darvish. Now she is greeted warmly by the major and the children, and now by the stoical Mc Darvish himself, yes, this is her first meeting with her old friends since her last parting with them in India. She takes them to a private apartment where they can converse alone, and leaves Sir Edward to do the honours of the assembled guests.

"Dearest, kindest, and best of friends," said Mrs. Forrester, as she again embraced our heroine, "how can I express my joy at beholding you again under such favourable circumstances. No Redouga fort now. Eh, Omelia! I beg pardon, Lady Stanley."

"Inded not," said Omelia, "I should wish you always to call me by the former name. What is more dulcet to the ears of all of us than to be called by the same name our mother called us, and the friends of our earliest infancy. Never call me otherwise, I hope. Lady Stanley, indeed! it sounds cold, formal, and unfriendly."

"The same Omelia as of old," said Mrs. Forrester, turning to her husband, "not a bit altered, I declare. No pride with all her accession of wealth and title."

"Why should there be?" said Lady Stanley, laughing.

"Whew; but there very often is," said Mc Darvish.

"And your friend," said Mrs. Forrester, "the young man who so kindly provided us with the means of living in the Redouga Fort? What has become of him?"

"Ah, he was melancholy enough when I last parted with him. I wished to persuade him to come over to England, but my efforts were in vain. Ah! he is a gentle, simple-hearted creature, and I learn from a communication received from my solicitors, Messrs. Cottle, that the good priest whom you have heard me speak of, the kind Jahusha, has passed from this world to, let us hope, a happier sphere. Thus we lose in our passage through life the few hearts that love us," said Omelia, sadly. "He died in peace with all mankind."

"You have passed through affliction enough yourself, my child," said Mrs. Forrester.

"I had a still more severe trial after you left," observed our heroine, and she then proceeded to detail all the particulars of the death of poor Lightfoot and her own trial. Both Major and Mrs. Forrester expressed their surprise and horror at her narrative.

"You have been tested by the corrosive acid of deep affliction," said the major, "and have been found current gold."

"Thank you for the compliment, major; to have you and all my friends around me at the present time—" At this period of their conversation the Lady Arabella Clementina Beechcroft entered, apologizing for her intrusion, when she observed the company present.

"Pardon me," said her ladyship; "I am intruding. I thought you were alone, or I should not have taken the liberty."

"It is a pleasure," said Omelia, courteously. "I am glad of the opportunity it affords me of introducing you to some of my nearest and dearest friends," and she then introduced her ladyship, who had become an especial favorite with her, to those present.

"These are some of the few," continued Omelia to her companion, "that have known me before the sun of prosperity deigned to smile upon so unworthy an individual as myself."

"And such that I am sure you are not likely ever to forget," replied her ladyship.

"I hope not."

"And I am sure not," responded Mc Darvish.

Lady Stanley now made a movement to rejoin the company, introducing her friends to most of those present, amongst whom was our recent acquaintance Lord Teagle.

"Why does the fair Lady Stanley hide her charms from her hundreds of admirers?" said the gallant nobleman, as Omelia entered, "these *salons* are like a sun without a world during her absence."

"Flattery as usual," said the Lady Arabella, smiling.

"I writhe in agony at the absence of two such queens of beauty—so peerless in their loveliness," continued the old courtier.

"Your lordship basks in the sunny favour of the Court," answered Lady Beechcroft, "and have caught much of its sweetest honey, I am thinking."

"I would rob the Hybla bees of all they possessed did I think it would obtain one smile from, or win the favour of, Lady Beechcroft," continued Lord Teagle in his most winning tones.

"We rough soldiers, my lord," said Major Forrester, "are not used to tune our voices to indulge in adulatory encomiums, which flow so glibly from your lordship."

"Major Forrester does us sufficient honor by his presence here this evening," continued Lord Teagle; "his eloquence lies at the point of his sword, and he owns a brighter renown than us poor civilians."

"His lordship is weel oup in smoothed-tongued des-course," whispered McDarvish to Omelia.

The latter nodded her assent to the latter observation.

"Hence you heard," said Lady Beechcroft, to our heroine, "that my cousin, Colonel Maitland has arrived in England and shortly intends paying you a visit."

"Your cousin! Is Colonel Maitland related to you?" said Omelia, in some surprise.

"Oh yes, did you not learn that he arrived last week with his son, who has married one of Colonel Bridports daughters?"

"Indeed, you astonish me; Colonel Bridport is one of my oldest friends. Which daughter did the Colonel's son marry?"

"Julia Bridport."

"I am delighted to hear it—A most charming girl I assure you."

"So I have understood."

"Oh yes, one of my choicest companions."

"You will soon be surrounded by all whom you hold dear."

"It is a happiness more than I deserve."

"Nay, not more than you deserve—more than you expected perhaps?"

"Indeed, yes."

In such pleasing intercourse did the evening pass away with our heroine, made the more so from the presence of her old friends. The lights are extinguished—the company gone, and then in the silence of her deserted halls did Omelia give her thoughts and mind up to those few, who, far away on the other side of the hemisphere, still dwelt vividly in her mind.

A round of uninterrupted bliss is now the share of Lady Stanley;—we have followed her through many perils and many a lonely hour, when the past was all grief and the future all fears, but the sun of prosperity shines upon her faith—surrounded by all the evidences of material wealth—rich in the possession of a devoted and attached husband—the idol of the circle in which she moved—what more earthly joy does she need but a contented mind? and this she happily possessed; and many years of happiness, let us hope, are in store for her; and in this long narrative of her earlier life and sufferings some moral may be adduced of keeping a true and honest heart under all trials and affections, if so the perusal of this story will not have been lost upon the reader.

The contingences of a world often place the best and bravest of us in situations in which the heart shrinks from contemplating. It has been truly said by an old writer—"If we knew how much we had to go through in our probation on earth we should never be able to survive it." But a wise providence keeps from the eyes of mortal man his future destiny—it is well it does so. Man is of a ductile nature, and woman more so, and they neither of them know what they are capable of withstanding. The world is full

of changes.—The endless wheel of fortune is ever revolving; hug not to yourself, therefore, sinful man that you are beyond the reach of trouble and sorrow, it may be your turn to-morrow to feel grief's sharpest pang; yes, even you, my friend who have been nurtured in luxury and all the soft appliances of wealth and fortune; for sorrow will find its way behind silken curtains, eat its corrosive way into the heart of the millionaire, bow down the stalwart limbs of youth with premature age, furrow his cheek with wrinkles, and take the brightness from the eye of beauty—such things have been before and will be under the sun while the world lasts; look, therefore, with a kindly eye upon an erring brother or sister, and remember him who said, "Let the wretched come unto me."

We think there are many noble battles fought against the poor and ignorant in the strife for existence than the world ever dreams of. If some fall into paths of dishonour, remember how many thousands have been sorely tried, tempest-tossed, and fretted by the ceaseless waves of misfortune; these stormy passages on life's sea are never entered in the log-book of those who sail so smoothly with balmy breezes, and placid waters, wafted on by the sou'-west gales of future.

In the records of that inner life of suffering man, his aspirations, disappointments, and despair, there is much to awaken our finest sympathies, but they are seldom outspoken.

The theme is not a pleasing one to the multitude, and men care not when they have climbed up the world's ladder themselves to look down upon those beneath them with any other feeling but contempt; it is this complete estrangement or separation of one class of society from another, that is the cause of incalculable mischief in our own country. The aristocratic circle look upon merchants and tradesmen as entirely different to themselves in character and disposition. The tradesmen look upon the working-man as a being inferior to themselves, and so on down to the lowest grade in the social scale, forgetting the while that the Deity as oftentimes enclosed the most humble artisan with the rarest talents and sublimest gifts it is possible for the intellect of man to imagine. We do not come into the world coronetted and titled. Nature is a mother kind alike to all, and the "toe of the peasant is often close to the heel of the courtier."

It has been shown in the late Indian war, and more particularly in the Crimean campaign, that the men who rose from the body of the people were the only efficient soldiers, and aristocratic influence was the curse and bane of the service. A time must and will come when these things will be re-formed entirely.

CHAPTER CCXLVIII.

THE SCIENTIFIC PARTY.—THEIR WANDER-INGS.—A LAST GLANCE AT GOOLOOH.—THE MEDAL OF MERIT.

If Mrs. Fitzfirkins' party had led to two affairs of honour, as by courtesy they are termed, it was the cause of one very fortunate circumstance, as far as Goolooh was concerned. It resulted in his having an introduction to Defast, who, by affording him active occupation, diverted his thoughts from the one absorbing topic which had been preying upon his mind.

By degrees Goolooh became used to the quaint manners and the many peculiarities of the archæological secretary, and he gradually became aware of the fact that there was an undercurrent of genuine good feeling and an enlarged humanity flowing beneath the upper structure of his employer's character; besides this, there were many pleasant gentlemen travelling in the scientific exploring party; Goolooh got familiar with their ways, and a vast change came over him thereby.

It is not our purpose to follow the footsteps of the travellers through the various districts of India. Their wanderings are already recorded in books devoted to the purpose, but we have found it necessary to briefly mention them as the future career of Goolooh was materially influenced by his connection with them.

Their tour extended over a period of eighteen months, and Defast found his guide so faithful, and gentle in his manners —so devoted to the interests of all, that he was loth to part with him at the expiration of their journey.

Goolooh, on his part, had become greatly attached to Defast, and consequently he agreed to accompany him upon another expedition, be it in whatever part of the world it might.

The consequence of this was, that Goolooh had to follow his master into the centre of Africa, and, after then, Asia; he had previous to these expeditions, become enrolled a member of the society, of which he had become so useful and indefatigable an agent.

We should mention, also, that prior to his departure from his native country, he had another interview with Messrs. Cottle and Leaf, and that they had received instructions from Lady Stanley, to build the schools and chapel agreeable to the last expressed wishes of Jahnsah. This was done, and Goolooh had the satisfaction before he left India of beholding a very handsome building finished from the design of an eminent English architect, under the title of "The Priest's Blessing," with a motto over the facia as follows—"Let little children come unto me for they are mine."

After Goolooh's protracted stay in Asia and Africa, we now take a last glance at him.

*　　*　　*　　*　　*

Beneath the porch of a cottage, situated in a small village near Cologne, in Germany, is seated the figure of a man passively enjoying the fragrant weed, inhaled through a deeply-coloured meerschaum. The cottage itself is in a charming position. A few yards in its front flows a beautiful river. Its back is skirted by a plantation of vines, and tendrils and creepers embrace its facade in graceful profusion.

Whilst the man is smoking and reading several papers which he holds in his disengaged hand, a female appears on the scene. She is stout but of good proportions, and her merry, good-humoured features, are an index of her character. She is certainly not beautiful, in the common acceptation of the term, yet her countenance is pleasing and agreeable. She addresses her husband and points to a chateau in the distance, which is observable on an eminence some leagues off.

These two figures are Goolooh and his wife. Yes, the Hindoo is settled comfortably enough, having married a German wife who is almost as brown in complexion as himself.

The chateau in the distance is the residence of Defast, who has made his old servant and companion, Goolooh, a present of the cottage, which was built on his own estate.

Goolooh is reading a long letter from Omelia, for our heroine has not forgotten to correspond with him.

While the two are conversing, another figure appears upon the scene. It is Defast himself; he converses freely, and appears to be in high glee. He informs his friend, Goolooh, that there is to be a distribution of prizes on the following day to be awarded to the meritorious members of their society. A German nobleman, distinguished by his learning, is to give them away. It is with a considerable degree of pleasure that he informs his companion that the society have awarded him a gold medal of the first order, for his indefatigable efforts in the furtherance of the cause of science.

Goolooh's heart swells with exultation as he is informed of the honour awaiting him.

On the following day, the chief members of the society are assembled in the large hall in the ancient city of Cologne. There is a grand meeting of notabilities, from various surrounding towns. The very learned Baron Hoffmann is seated in an elevated position in the centre of the building—he presides over the day's proceedings. Defast is more than usually busy; he has been preparing a statement of his own doings, as well as those of the society in question, which he has to read aloud to those present. In the course of this narrative, he expatiates upon the very many services rendered by Goolooh, who, in the course of the day, receives from the president, a gold medal, expressive of the society's gratitude. The medal, with the gold chain to which it is attached, is hung round the neck of Goolooh, by the learned Baron himself, amidst the plaudits of the whole assembly. This is a proud moment for Goolooh, as he bows on one knee to receive the high honour conferred upon him. Defast appears to be even more delighted than his protegee. But upon the termination of the day's proceedings, what can describe the joy of both, when they find upon their return home to Defast's chateau, that Mr. and Mrs. Hamilton (late Mrs. Fitzfirkin), are there. They have been making a continental tour, and dropped in upon Defast on their journey home. The secretary was nearly beside himself with joy. He jumped about with the activity of a boy, till Mrs. Hamilton fairly roared with laughter. "I thought we should take you by surprise," said the doctor, good humouredly.

"Surprise! I am overpowered with joy," said Defast. "Mon goot friend, dis has been von day of excitement. Mon goot companion and attendant has received von high honour—von very grand honour. He has von gold medal, of de first ordare, of merit, for de services he has rendered to de cause of science."

"I am indeed most delighted to hear it," said the doctor, " as I am sure he well merits the distinction."

The medal was shown, and all parties expressed their approval of its beauty, and the compliment it conveyed.

"Vell, and now about all our acquaintances in India," said Defast.

"Ah, we've a lot to tell you," said the doctor.

"How is Mistare Dollops," said Defast, with a twinkle of the eye through his spectacles.

"Ah! Scollops has married—that you know."

"Yes. I did no doubt—before I left," said Defast.

"Well, report says the lady's a bit of a shrew."

"Ah!" exclaimed Mrs. Hamilton " you men—what traducers you are."

"No my dear, I hope not—I am only saying what report says."

"Ah, that is goot," said Defast. "Mistare Dollops vill do very vell vith one screw. And Mistare Rushworth, what of him ?"

"We managed to put him all straight, as he himself expressed it. He recovered, and has returned to his own country. He said in parting with me—'Look here strainger, you aire one of the right sort, I doo guess, and if you should ever come to 'Merica, hang up your hat with J. Rushworth, and we'll keep a light burning while you stay, and no mistake. Remember me to old barnacles—he knows how to handle his toasting-fork, and can let daylight into a man, as quick as a flash o' lightning, but he's not a bad un, although he is a rum un to look at."

"Ah, ah, ah!" laughed Defast. "Ah! he said that, did he ? I'm glad he vos so merry, I did not vant to injure de man, and vos very sorry; but he vould bothare me vith his stupede game—bah! Vell, and Colonel Bridporte ?"

"Oh, the colonel has returned to England. His daughter, Julia, married Colonel Maitland's son, and his other daughter has more recently been married—so I learn from the newspapers—to a son of the Earl of Beechcroft."

"Ah, dat is goot—very goot; and de gentlemon vat used to joke ?"

"Yes, Anslie you mean, I suppose ?"

"Oui, Mistare Anslie."

"He has married a rich heiress in Calcutta, the niece and ward of a clergyman."

"Clergyman! dat is out of Monsieur Anslie's line ?"

"No he makes her an excellent husband, and is very much liked by her guardian."

"Had the schools opened before you left, sir?" said Goolooh, to the doctor.

"Yes; I attended the first half-yearly meeting, and distributed several prizes to the pupils. Lady Stanley wrote from England desiring me to do so as a particular favour."

"Lady Stanley was well, I hope?" said Goolooh.

"Perfectly well and happy, the last time I heard."

"Now, Madame Hamilton, as you have condescended to visit a poor student of science, I hope you will make a long stay with me," said Defast.

"I shall be too much pleased," replied Mrs. Hamilton, "to be with a gentleman so distinguished for his learning, but am fearful that we shall be intruding upon his valuable time; besides which, myself and husband only had time to give you a passing call."

"But you must stay, and see our beauteeful Rhine—de river of rivares—You must not go for one—two—weeks."

"Thank you," said the doctor; "you are very good, but we did not intend to stay more than to night, but as we are in such excellent society, I think we can stretch it to two or three days."

"Oh, dat is bettare," exclaimed the secretary. "Do you know, I cannot tell you how it cheers up mon heart to see one friend dat I have seen in one foreign countray; dat is goot for de-de-di-gestion."

"And for the spirits," said the doctor.

"Ah, de spirits—vell thought of. I have some real schiedam, fourteen years' old. Will you have a tumbler, or will you have de bordeaux?"

"Thank you," not at present."

"Now *Mon Amie*, but you must, we are all so vary tirsty in Germany. You must, to warm your heart."

"My heart is warm enough, I hope,' laughed the doctor. "Pray don't let us quarrel about hearts again."

"Ah, I did forget," said Defast. "No but vo do not—vat you English say—ve do not keel von grunting animal every day."

"Ah," laughed the doctor. "We do not kill a pig every day you mean, It is a common saying in England."

"Ah, yees—dat vat I mean, *tres bein*."

"Well, you are surely not going to kill me with your schiedam."

"Ah, non Monsier, non; it is de liquor vat cures not kills. No, as mild as—as Mrs. Dollops," and the secretary burst off in a fit of laughter, as though he had lighted upon a most witty simile; and he gave instructions for his housekeeper to bring in materials for brewing potations from his favourite liquor, under the influence of which, the spirits of the party rose, and a lively conversation ensued, and a pleasant evening was past.

"I vill drink to de health of Madame Hamilton," said Defast, as he waived a bumper of good old schiedam; "and, as I do so, de recollection of the vary many pleasant hours dat I have spent in her charming society, rushes through my brain. It is one grande ting, to be beside dose friends dat you esteem for dere great worth."

"Thank you, my friend," said the doctor. "I am truly glad to see you, and should have castigated myself not a little, if we had gone away without giving you a call."

"Gone, by, without having a look at de old secretary. Ah, bah. You nevare could be so cruel."

"In this beautiful place of yours you want but one thing to make it perfection," said Mrs. Hamilton.

"And dat is your presence, which renders it a paradise," answered the polite Frenchman.

"Thank you. I did not mean that. I thought to complete your happiness you wanted a wife."

"Oh, oh! Oui! Madame Dollops."

"No, but a nice domesticated quiet wife to make your home happy and comfortable."

"Ah," said the secretary, seriously, "I am wedded to science. What would a woman do with a musty old bachelor like me? Bah! laugh at me, perhaps."

"I should hope not."

"I do think it very likely. Even if I could get one to consent to have me at all. Is Mistare Morley married? he said suddenly to the doctor.

"Not that I have heard of," was the reply. "No, I am afraid Morley is a confirmed old bachelor. It's a pity, for he is really a good-hearted, worthy fellow, and it often surprised me that he did not strike up to one of the colonel's daughters. I don't believe he would have found their father make any objection; but the fact is, Morley's a bit proud—it is not that he is so well off in the world, perhaps, but he has too much pride to marry a woman in a better position than himself."

"Oh, dat is foolish—very foolish."

"Yes, it may be so, and probably is, but you cannot alter the disposion of men, and so I begin to think that Morley is doomed to single blessedness."

"Ah, he is proud, and I am timid, there's the difference," said Defast.

On the following morning Mr. and Mrs. Hamilton, accompanied by Goolooh, took a short tour up the Rhine, whose many and varied beauties well repaid them for the trouble. The secretary threw aside his scientific pursuits, and devoted his time to his friends, and he had hardly ever been known to have been in such spirits as on the occasion of the doctor's visit.

Goolooh, too, in his own quiet way, evinced a more than wonted pleasure in their society; but to speak the truth, Mrs. Hamilton was herself so cheering a woman that it was impossible to be dull in her company.

After a stay of four days, the doctor and his wife bade their hospitable friends a reluctant farewell, and as they were about to return to England, Goolooh gave them many long messages to deliver to our heroine. A sadness came over him when she became the topic of conversation—a sadness which he could not subdue.

CONCLUSION.

We have missed sight of Clara and Captain Robinson for some time past. They returned from their wedding tour, and were present at the nuptials of Julia Bridport and Edmund Maitland.

Most of our old acquaintances have by this time taken their departure from India, which formed the wide and diversified scene of action. In Captain Robinson Clara found a loving and devoted husband. The duty of the service, in which he was not an undistinguished member, required his sojourn in the east, and up to such time as we have anything to do with him, we find his amiable partner and himself still located in the Indian territory.

The last account we heard of the happy pair was from Lady Stanley, who, with her accustomed courtesy, placed in our hands a letter from her friends, which, for the readers behoof, we are at liberty to transcribe in these pages. It was as follows—

"Madras, 1859.

"My dear Lady Stanley,—I am sure you do not need me to express to you my unfeigned joy at your present happiness and accession of fortune, but I am afraid you must have thought me very neglectful in not writing to you before this, but really, my dear friend, there have been so many things to distract my attention that I am sure you will excuse the neglect. You will be delighted to know that I find Alfred the kindest and most considerate of creatures. We often laugh together at our double marriage, and the scenes on that eventful day. Who that was there can ever forget it? I have great pleasure in informing you that I have given birth to a fine boy (did any one ever hear of anything else but a fine child on these occasions?) He is now two months old, and is the very picture of Alfred. We have had him christened after his father, and Morley stood Godfather on the occasion. We wanted him to be christened after him, but the obstinate fellow would not have it, saying that the first one ought to be named after his parent, and there would be plenty of opportunity with the others—just as if we were going to have a dozen. We had, after I left you, a most delightful tour through many parts of India. I never enjoyed myself so much in my life, I do believe, but find myself now comparatively deserted by all my late friends. In fact, we are left almost solitary here, as most of our old companions, as I suppose you already know, have left the country. Goolooh, too, poor fellow, he has become attached to a Mr. Defast, a foreign gentleman, and has gone to Asia with him; and you know, also, that

Dr. Hamilton has married a most delightful widow. He has gone; in fact, there are very few left but Morley and Anslie, the latter of whom has made a first rate match. I do not, however, repine at my lot—I have, I am sure, no reason to do so. I should certainly like to see again old England, and must live in hopes of doing so some day or other, but for the present it is out of the question. Alfred is compelled to stay here for some time, in any case, but I do not despair, my dear friend, of again having the pleasure of seeing you. How delighted I was with the paper containing the account of your presentation at court. What an honour! but no more than you deserve, I am sure, for all you have gone through and suffered. Some few weeks since, myself and Alfred paid a visit to the schools under the name of the "Priest's Blessing," and a blessing indeed they are to the surrounding neighbourhood. Poor Jahnsah! his was a gentle nature—a noble, self-sacrificing man. Peace to his memory. When we visited the schools, we called upon Tallee Sheboo, who gave us a very long account of Jahnsah; poor soul, she seemed to almost deify him. It appeared that he had been very good to her for many years previous, to his death. Ah, Omelia! (you must excuse me calling you that name now,) no one knew the many acts of kindness that man did in secret. In his own humble way he was a pattern, I am thinking, to many of our fine people in England with all their education and boasted Christianity. I hope you will not fail to give my kind remembrance to Sir Edward, but, perhaps, he is too great a man now to care about such an humble individual as myself—I say, perhaps, but I think not, and therefore, send my regards, as, also, to my parent, who was certainly a most excellent one, viz, Colonel Maitland; tell him I hope to be in England, some time or other, to receive his blessing. I suppose you know that the lady whom Dr. Hamilton married gave a grand party, at which some dispute arose, and the doctor fought a duel with Mr. Scollops, an ale stout merchant, of Magnum Bonum wharf, Calcutta Oh, that party! it was the talk of the town for the months afterwards. I wish you had been here at the time. I was not, however, present myself, but have heard enough about it. This Mr. Scollops has married a Miss Puffpowder, and they say she leads him a terrible life, poor fellow. I suppose you never intend to come to India again?—you are too much petted where you are, and I should imagine you to be too good a judge to leave so comfortable a home and position. We have to fight our way in the world, at least Alfred has; he will be made a colonel of in time, I hope, at any rate I know he deserves to be one. Alfred desires me to say that if you have any commissions—I do not mean any commissions in the army—but anything you require seeing to here, write to me, and we will do whatever you may require. I know you have your lawyers, Messrs. Cottle and Leaf, but still there may be many little things you may desire seeing to that would be out of their province. Now, do not fail to let me know if there should be any such. I shall not consider it friendly if you make strangers of us, or stand upon any unnecessary ceremony. You see I am the same blunt creature as when you first knew me— I shall never alter I suppose now. Alfred don't wish me, he says—there's a compliment, it is not often, so it is said, that you get one from a husband after the honeymoon.

What an excellent match the elder Miss Bridport has made—at least, so I hear. Is it true that she has married the son of the Earl of Beechcroft? You are acquainted with the family, I understand. Do write and let me know the whole particulars, and also what other news you have to tell about friends in England. You cannot conceive, my dearest friend, what pleasure it affords us to receive a communication from you, and how eagerly the contents of your letters are devoured by us both over and over again. What news is so welcome to the wanderers in distant climes as that which tells of home and those connected with it? Although the breadth of boundless oceans lay between it, the spirit turns to that spot which nurtured its infancy; and although I saw trouble enough in my native land still my thoughts recur to it with pleasurable sensations, and I long again to tread the soil my footsteps pressed in my early years With kindest love, believe me your ever attached friend,
            "CLARA ROBINSON."

Our story is ended, but as it may be of interest to some of our more curious readers we extract the following from the *Morning Post*, which appeared some months after the last glance at our heroine :—

"There was a very numerous and fashionable attendance, consisting of several leading members of the aristocracy, at St. George's church, Hanover Square, upon the occasion of the christening of Sir Edward Stanley's first-born child. The Earl and Countess of Beechcroft stood as sponsers. The ceremony took place on Friday last, and a vast concourse assembled, many, no doubt, of whom went for the purpose of catching a glance at the renowned and beauteous Lady Stanley, whose many charms and virtues have won for her the appellation of " the Star of the East."

FINIS.

R. BEARD, PRINTER, BRUNSWICK PLACE, CITY ROAD.